AS TIME GOES BY

Carter Lane, an ordinary backstreet in Bermondsey, is home to Dolly and Mick Flynn and their five grown-up children. At the onset of World War II Dolly's boys volunteer and her daughter Sadie seems determined to throw her life away on a married man. Dolly's neighbour, Liz Kenny, is there to offer a shoulder to cry on and Charity and Cynthia Lockwood, two elderly sisters, are always willing to offer a helping hand. As the Blitz takes its toll the inhabitants of Carter Lane take comfort in the knowledge that their wounds will heal—as time goes by.

To Doctor Frank Rugman, consultant haematologist, Royal Preston Hospital, with gratitude and with the realization that, without his dedication and professionalism, this book may never have been written. And to his wife, Elizabeth, and their children, Edward and Peter.

AS TIME GOES BY

by

Harry Bowling

Magna Large Print Books
Long Preston, North Yorkshire,
England.

British Library Cataloguing in Publication Data.

Bowling, Harry
  As time goes by.

  A catalogue record for this book is
  available from the British Library

  ISBN 0-7505-1435-3

First published in Great Britain by Headline Book Publishing, 1998

Copyright © 1997 by Harry Bowling

Cover illustration © Nigel Chamberlain by arrangement with Headline Book Publishing Ltd.

Published in Large Print 2000 by arrangement with Headline Book Publishing Ltd.

Magna Large Print is an imprint of
Library Magna Books Ltd.
Printed and bound in Great Britain by
T.J. International Ltd., Cornwall, PL28 8RW.

PROLOGUE

September 4th 1939

Albert Levy opened up his wireless shop at the stroke of nine on Monday morning and went straight into the back room, which served as a workshop, to put the kettle on. It was a ritual he had carried out almost without thinking for the past six years and he had always been eager to get another day of trading under way. Today however a dark shadow lay over him; his mind was troubled and his insides were churning. Less than twenty-four hours ago he had sat on the sofa in his living room along with his wife Gerda while the Prime Minister spoke to the nation over the radio. He had taken the news calmly but Gerda had broken down and sobbed quietly into her handkerchief. 'This will kill Abel. I know it will,' she had gulped. 'He's talked of nothing else for weeks now.'

Albert had tried to reassure her but he too feared for his old friend. Abel had said it many times and he was utterly convinced of it: if war was declared the country would be overrun within weeks.

As he poured the boiling water into the chipped china teapot and covered it with a cosy, Albert glanced up at the clock on the wall. It was nearly ten minutes past the hour and Abel had still not made an appearance. Lately business had been brisk and there were at least half-a-dozen wirelesses awaiting repair and several accumulators to be put on charge, which Abel was well aware of. Normally he would have been standing outside the shop chafing at the bit but, as Albert hardly needed to remind himself, today was no ordinary workday.

At nine thirty Albert Levy put the closed sign on the door and walked out into the bustling Old Kent Road. His old friend and employee lived ten minutes away, in Carter Lane, a small, insignificant backstreet in the riverside borough of Bermondsey, and as he hurried along Albert could not suppress the tension inside him. It was in the air, everywhere, and it showed on people's faces as they passed by.

The international events of the past few days had been shocking, but had succeeded in drawing together two countries as unlikely allies, and the shopkeeper took comfort in knowing that the country of his birth and England, his adopted country, had become united in their opposition to the Nazis. Albert Levy was Polish and had moved with his family to Germany at two years old when his father, a minor official in the Polish Diplomatic Corps, was posted to Frankfurt. He had been happy growing up in Germany and remained there with his mother in a small Jewish community in Wiesenbad after his father died in office. Proud of their roots the family decided to retain their Polish nationality, and Albert prospered in business, opening his first shop in Wiesenbad while still in his twenties.

As he made his way into Carter Lane to seek out his old friend and employee, the shopkeeper thought how different it would have been for him and Gerda now, had his mother decided to become a German citizen all those years ago.

Abel lodged with Daisy and Bill Harris at number 12. He was a frail, private man in his mid-fifties, in the habit of keeping a discreet distance from his neighbours, not out of cussedness, but rather from a natural shyness and an inability to comprehend the language properly. The locals knew him as Mr Abel the Jew and that was about it. His full name was Abel Finkelstein and he had a six-digit number tattooed on the inside of his right forearm. Once a skilled technician at a large radio firm in Wiesenbad, Germany, Abel had enjoyed a good life until the Brownshirts began their campaign of terror. Arrested and convicted on trumped-up charges by a vindictive gauleiter during the early days of the persecution, he was convicted and sent to a concentration camp in eastern Germany.

Albert Levy had been Abel's childhood friend and had left Germany for England with his wife Gerda at the first serious signs of German racial purification, before it became obvious that a mad canker was consuming a nation's soul. He had built up his wireless business and had managed to save enough to secure the release of his old friend with a large bribe before the loophole was finally closed.

Abel Finkelstein arrived to begin a new life in England in '37 as a refugee sponsored by Albert, but the scars of his internment remained with him, and when he listened to the Prime Minister's broadcast on Sunday morning he knew without a doubt that the nightmare was about to start again. It was just a matter of time.

'Good morning, Mrs Harris,' Albert said, doffing his trilby. 'I'm calling to see if Abel's well. He hasn't come in this morning.'

Daisy Harris knew Albert Levy from his weekly visits to Abel, when the two men enjoyed a game of chess and a few glasses of wine, but today she looked troubled. 'I 'aven't 'eard 'im about this mornin' ter tell yer the trufe,' she replied. 'P'raps yer'd better go up. 'E was worried sick last night over the war startin'.'

Albert climbed the steep flight of stairs and knocked on Abel's bedroom door. Getting no answer he went in and saw his old friend lying on his back in the bed with his hands clasped at his throat. His eyes were closed tight and a film of froth had dried around his blue lips. On the chair at his bedside was a tablet bottle with the lid lying beside it, next to a half-empty bottle of brandy. Albert turned to Daisy as she stood behind him speechless, and he shook his head sadly. 'We'd better get the police,' he said. 'It looks like he's left us.'

The declaration of war had had an immediate impact on two of Carter Lane's residents.

One was now past caring about anything this Monday morning, but the other was slowly and painfully coming to life in a police station cell. His head felt as if it would explode at any minute and he groaned in agony.

'Yer better pull yerself tergevver, Joe,' the duty policeman said grinning as he handed him a plate of streaky bacon, an over-fried egg and a slice of burnt toast on a tray. 'The beak'll chuck the book at yer if 'e sees yer like this.'

Joe Buckley eased his legs over the hard bed and sat forward, supporting his pulsing head in his huge hands. It was slowly coming back to him now and he winced. 'Is the dingo pressing charges?' he asked.

'I dunno, I've only just come on duty,' the officer told him.

Joe ate the food with some difficulty, but after using the toilet he began to feel a bit better. 'I hope I didn't give you any strife, mate,' he said to the policeman who came to escort him.

'Nah, yer came in like a good 'un,' the officer said with a smile. 'Mind you, yer language wasn't all that clever, considerin' we 'ad Farvver Feeney 'ere at the time.'

'What's he been up to?' Joe asked.

' 'E was visitin' a prisoner,' the policeman replied.

Joe noticed from the wall clock that it was ten o'clock as he was escorted up from the cells and taken along to the court, where he sat pensively on a hard bench alongside the officer and waited to be called.

9

'Joseph L Buckley, you have been charged with drunk and disorderly conduct, assault, and damage to property at The Sun public house in Dockhead. How do you plead?'

Joe looked up at the elderly magistrate and gave him a sheepish grin. 'Guilty, your worshipful. Guilty as hell.'

Mr Durrant looked over his spectacles at the huge character before him and smothered a smile. 'Sir will do, and we can dispense with the expletives,' he said in a reedy voice.

Joe nodded dutifully. 'Guilty, sport. I mean guilty, sir.'

Durrant had the case file in front of him and he studied it for a few moments. 'I see here that you are Australian.'

Joe nodded with a brief smile.

'I understand that the aggrieved has decided not to press charges and the publican has waived the claim for damages,' Durrant continued. 'I would say that you are a very fortunate man. You could have been in much more trouble than you are, but nevertheless the charge of being drunk and disorderly still stands. Throwing someone over a pub counter because they disagree with your point of view is not a proper way to carry on, and taking up police time by refusing to move from the pavement is deplorable. Do you realise you had to be carried into the police van?'

'I was dead beat, sport—sir,' Joe said quickly. 'I was stretched out ready to sleep when the blue boys came along.'

'Do you consider that sufficient justification

10

to have said, according to Constable Perkins' report ...' The magistrate turned the papers in front of him and frowned. ' "Chew on your boot, you Pommy shirtlifter. May your ears turn into arseholes and crap on your shoulders, Mate." ' He looked up and fixed the accused with an intent stare. 'Do you have anything to add to that before I pass sentence?'

Joe scowled inwardly. The bloody poofter didn't have to write that down, he fumed. Next time I'll just save my breath and conk him. 'If you don't mind, sir, there is something I'd like to say,' he replied, standing up straight and throwing his shoulders back.

'Go on, and be brief,' Durrant said peremptorily.

'I shouldn't be here in the first place,' he began, 'but things got a bit smelly back home, so I decided to move on.'

'So you chose England.'

'No, I went up to Queensland where I earned some good money as a jackaroo on a sheep station. It was fair yakka really, but I got the ants in me shoes again an' off I went.'

'To England?'

'No, Padang.'

'Padang?'

'Yeah. It's in Sumatra.'

Mr Durrant sighed in exasperation. 'I asked you to be brief, Mr Buckley,' he said in a tired voice.

'I will be, sir,' Joe answered, 'I just wanted to give you the drum, so to speak. You see I'm a marine engine mechanic by trade an' I thought if I went to Sumatra I could make a fresh start. A good mate o' mine was in the marine diesel business there, but when I arrived I found out that the bastard 'ad crocked it.'

'Watch your language, please, Mr Buckley.'

'Sorry, your worship. "Died", I meant to say.'

The magistrate pinched his temples and slowly drew in a deep breath. 'Go on, Mr Buckley,' he sighed.

'I suddenly got this idea o' seeing the old country,' Joe continued. 'I knew that things were starting to go down the pan over here, what with Adolf digging in dirtier than a shithouse rat, and I thought the Royal Navy could do with a good marine mechanic if the worst came to the worst, so I worked me passage on a ship bound for Southampton. I wanted to get in on this war but I wasn't too keen on going back to Oz and waiting to be drafted into the infantry.'

'So here you are,' Durrant said summarily. 'In the country five minutes and already you've caused criminal damage and assaulted a customer at a public house.'

'I couldn't stand by and listen to the crap this dill was coming out with,' Joe replied with conviction. 'He said we should've signed a pact with Hitler and let Poland get on with it. I told him he was talking cobblers and he chucked a punch at me. I just grabbed him, to restrain him, like.'

'And somehow he ends up being "restrained" over the bar counter,' Durrant said sarcastically.

'I was spitting blood, your worship,' Joe went

on. 'Our two countries are mates, after all. We fought together in one world war and it looks like we're together in this one too, so I let him know the best way I could that you don't kowtow to the likes of Adolf Hitler.'

'Your sentiments are admirable,' the magistrate said, moving his spectacles up onto the bridge of his nose, 'but your methods leave a lot to be desired, and I have to treat your unruly behaviour with the due means at my disposal. Tell me, are you still intending to join the armed forces?'

'Soon as ever I can, judge,' Joe told him firmly, 'I'll be off like a bride's nightie.'

Durrant cleared his throat and looked very serious. 'Taking your patriotism into consideration, I fine you forty shillings or fourteen days,' he declared.

'That's a pity,' Joe said sighing. 'I'm pretty well cleaned out at the moment. I'll have to take the fourteen days.'

An hour later Aussie Joe Buckley was back at his lodgings in Carter Lane. His landlady Liz Kenny had been in court that morning and she had paid the fine. She also had a few words of advice for her erring lodger. 'Yer'd better control that temper o' yours in future, Joe,' she said sternly. 'You was lucky this time.'

The big Australian looked up at her as he sat at the parlour table, his wide blue eyes full of remorse. 'Yeah, you're right, I'll pay you back as soon as I can, Liz,' he said. 'I hope your Bert doesn't lose 'is dummy over this.'

'You let me worry about Bert,' she told him.

13

'Now get cleaned up an' I'll fix yer somefing to eat.'

'You haven't got a drop o' the old grog handy by any chance, have you?' he asked.

Liz held back a smile as she nodded toward the sideboard. 'I dunno why I bovver,' she sighed.

Joe poured himself a tot of whisky. 'I hope Sadie Flynn doesn't get to hear about me little barney,' he said anxiously.

'Don't make me laugh,' Liz chuckled, slipping her hands into the arms of her clean apron. 'It'll be all round the street in no time.'

'Yeah, that's what I thought,' Joe replied with a pained look on his wide handsome face.

CHAPTER 1

Carter Lane was a small backstreet of two-up, two-down houses that faced each other, with a corner shop and a public house called The Sun at the Old Kent Road end and a small factory at the other end. The turning linked Defoe Street with Munday Road, which ran alongside the railway. The factory was owned by the Solomon family and had been there as long as anyone could remember, producing leather goods and providing employment for some of the Carter Lane folk. The corner grocery shop was owned by Tom Jackman and his wife Sara, a genial couple in their late fifties.

At number 11 Carter Lane, Dolly Flynn was chopping vegetables into a large stew-pot on the scullery table. She was a buxom woman with grey hair which she had fixed hurriedly on the top of her head that morning. She was nearing her fiftieth birthday and was still attractive, with a wide, open face and piercing blue eyes which were watering as she sliced a large Spanish onion. Dolly felt like crying anyway, without the onion's pungent fumes. Her boys had been full of the war last night and she knew it wouldn't be long before they were in uniform. The eldest Frank had been going on about getting into the navy and Jim was set on the air force. Pat, the baby of the family, was an independent cuss and he had announced that if his brothers were for the air force and navy then he had no choice other than to go in the army.

'Surely they won't take all three of yer,' Dolly had said. 'They didn't in the last war.'

'Oh yes they did,' Mick had told her. 'The Sullivans 'ad four in uniform at one time.'

Dolly recalled how she had rounded on her husband and sons. 'You treat it like a Sunday-school outin', an' you should know better, Mick. You saw enough fightin' in the last one. This'll be a bloody sight worse, you mark my words.'

Mick had realised how upset she was and tried to make light of it, but even he could not hide the concern and worry in his grey eyes. The girls had had their pieces to say too, just for good measure. Sadie reckoned that all single women would be called up for war-work, and young Jennie had said she was going to see about joining the ARP.

A knock on the front door jerked Dolly back to the present and she smiled when she saw Liz Kenny standing on her doorstep. They were old friends and Liz could always be relied upon to cheer her up when she was feeling down. 'Come in, luv,' she urged her, 'I was just doin' the veg fer ternight.'

'Don't let me stop yer,' Liz replied. 'Carry on what yer doin' an' I'll make the tea.'

'Nah, you sit yerself down,' Dolly told her. 'I've almost finished anyway.'

Liz Kenny walked into the parlour and sat down in the armchair with a deep sigh. Slightly built with dark hair and brown eyes, she presented a distinct contrast to her old friend, but they shared much, not least a lively sense of humour. Today though there was little gaiety in either woman's voice. 'Gawd knows what's gonna 'appen to us all now,' Dolly sighed when she came into the room. 'I still can't get it inter me 'ead that we've gone ter war.'

'Nor can I,' Liz said heavily. 'An' ter crown it all I bin up the court this mornin'.' She saw the enquiring look in her friend's eyes and smiled wryly. 'Big Joe got in some trouble last night at The Sun.'

'Yeah, Mick told me about it,' Dolly replied. 'From what 'e said, Cafferty got what 'e deserved. 'E's a loud-mouth git at the best o' times. Mick can't stand 'im.'

' 'E seems to 'ave done a runner anyway,' Liz went on. ' 'E didn't press charges an' Charlie Anson didn't ask fer damages. But it still don't

16

alter the fact that Joe was out of order doin' what 'e did.'

'Ter be fair, Liz, Big Joe ain't one ter take liberties,' Dolly remarked. 'Mick told me Cafferty punched 'im first, an' 'e ain't no light-weight.'

Liz shrugged her shoulders. 'Anyway, Joe got fined forty shillin's. 'E didn't 'ave a pot ter piss in an' they was gonna give 'im fourteen days, till I told 'em I'd pay the fine. Mind you 'e'll pay me back as soon as 'e can. 'E was upset about it but I fink 'e was more concerned about your Sadie findin' out. Joe finks the world of 'er.'

'It's a pity she don't feel the same way about 'im,' Dolly replied. 'She could do a lot worse. I just can't understand 'er at times.'

'Is she still seein' that feller?' Liz asked.

'Yeah, but it's an on-an'-off fing,' Dolly told her. 'If you ask me the bloke's tryin' ter patch it up wiv 'is wife, from listenin' ter Sadie. Why she ever got in tow wiv 'im I'll never know. Gawd almighty, there's enough single fellers about. A gel don't need ter get 'iked up wiv a married man.'

Liz rubbed her aching calf muscle and settled back in the armchair while Dolly went out to see to the tea. 'What about young Jennie? Is she still keen on that feller at work?' she called out.

Dolly grinned despite herself. 'Nah, it's all off,' she answered.

A few minutes later she came back into the room with two mugs of tea. 'I don't fink I'll ever live ter see all my crowd married off,' she sighed. 'The boys are the same. They spend

17

most o' their time up The Sun. Young Pat'll be the first one ter get spliced. 'Im an' that Ross gel seem ter be 'ittin' it off, so I s'pose I gotta be fankful fer small mercies.'

A knock at the door interrupted their conversation, and when Dolly finally came back into the parlour she looked shocked. 'That was Mrs Bromilow. Did you 'ear what she was sayin'?'

Liz shook her head. 'No, I never.'

'Apparently they took a body away from number 12 this mornin'. Mrs Bromilow finks it's their lodger.'

'Mr Abel?'

'Yeah.'

'Good Gawd. I didn't know 'e was ill,' Liz said quickly. 'Then again, p'raps 'e wasn't. It could 'ave bin an 'eart attack or a stroke.'

' 'E always looked a sick man ter me,' Dolly remarked. 'A very nice man though. 'E always nodded an' gave me a smile.' She sipped her tea. 'Did you know 'e was in prison in Germany?'

Liz shook her head. 'No, I never did.'

'Mrs 'Arris told me,' Dolly went on. 'Apparently 'e 'ad a number tattooed on 'is arm. Abel's guv'nor paid ter get 'im out an' bring 'im over 'ere by all accounts. Cost 'im quite a bit too.'

' 'E must be a good guv'nor,' Liz chuckled.

'It's that feller who owns the wireless shop in the Old Kent Road,' Dolly explained. 'That one next ter the greengrocer's by the Dun Cow.'

'Yeah, I know it,' Liz replied, 'though I've never bin in the shop.'

The two women sipped their tea in silence and then Dolly put her mug down on the table. 'Will your Bert 'ave ter go on war-work?' she asked.

'I shouldn't fink so,' Liz told her. ' 'E's gonna be needed 'ere if the air raids start. Bert knows the buildin' game inside out. 'E can do plasterin' an' joinery an' everyfing else. Besides, 'e's talkin' about goin' in the rescue squad. They're callin' fer volunteers ter do trainin'.'

'It's the same wiv Mick, 'im workin' fer the Council on the roads,' Dolly said. ' 'E's gonna be needed too.'

Liz put her cup down next to Dolly's. 'Well, I'd better be off. I gotta sort me washin' out.'

Dolly saw her to the door and then went back into the quiet room. Normally she enjoyed the lull in her busy day, but this morning it was different. The quietness set her thinking too much and she slipped on her coat to go out for some air.

Big Joe Buckley had recovered sufficiently from his drunken exploits at The Sun to visit the recruiting office in the Old Kent Road. When he arrived he found a crowd milling around the entrance and there seemed to be some heated discussions going on.

'It's a bloody disgrace,' one slim young man was saying. 'There's a bloody war started an' you can't sort fings out.'

'We can and will, if you'll just be patient,' the recruiting sergeant replied with a sigh. 'They're sending me some help and in the meantime

19

I'll take your particulars, if you'll just form an orderly line.'

As Joe reached the unruly mob a man who looked to be in his fifties turned to him. 'Short staffed, would you believe?' he growled. 'In the last war they come round the street wiv the brass band an' we all marched off be'ind 'em. I was in France before I 'ad time ter spit. Four years I did. Saw it all frew. Lucky Bob they called me. I got trench foot an' dysentery though. Bloody painful that trench foot.'

'I should fink you've done your bit already, mate,' the slim man remarked to him.

'Yeah, an' I'm ready fer anuvver basinful,' the older man replied enthusiastically.

Joe smiled. 'I'm after goin' in the navy.'

'You sound like an Aussie,' the older man remarked.

'S'right. Joe Buckley's the name. Anything's me game.'

'Yer'll 'ave ter go ter the navy office in East Street then.'

'East Street? Where's that, digger?'

'See that pie shop over there across the road?' the man said pointing.

'Yeah, I got it.'

'Well it's down the side o' there.'

Joe thanked him and set off, only to discover when he arrived that things were no more organised over there. The place was full of volunteers and a long disorderly queue curved round the room.

'Over an hour I've bin standin' 'ere an' the

20

bloody queue ain't moved,' the man in front of him complained.

Joe stood patiently for a while and then decided to come back the next day. By then things might be more organised, he thought. He walked off, his mouth grown dry and his head still aching from the hectic night before. His pockets were empty and he desperately felt the need for a drink. He couldn't ask Liz Kenny for a sub. She had already paid his fine and it wouldn't be right. Maybe he should go into The Sun and apologise for the upset he'd caused last night. Charlie Anson might feel disposed to giving him a drink on the house. Then again he might show him the door and tell him he wasn't welcome anymore.

As he was about to turn into the backstreets Joe got an idea.

One of the very few possessions he had of any value was the fob-watch nestling in the breast pocket of his shirt. There was no chain with it but the watch itself had cost him quite a bit back in Sydney when he had money to spare. He might be able to get a few pounds on it and he could redeem it when things looked brighter.

The pawnbroker screwed his eye up round the lens and grunted. 'Yes, it's a nice piece but it's only gold-plated. I couldn't let you have more than two pounds, what with the war and all.'

'Can't you make it fifty shillings, mate?' Joe asked.

The pawnbroker took the glass from his eye and looked at the fresh-faced young man across the counter. 'All right. I'll give you a ticket.'

Joe walked out of the shop feeling as though he'd parted with an old friend. The watch had gone everywhere with him and now he had two pounds ten shillings in his pocket that would soon evaporate.

He made his way back to Carter Lane and gingerly pushed open the door of the public bar.

'Cor blimey! Look who's shown up,' Danny Crossley said grinning.

Joe smiled sheepishly at Charlie Anson as he walked to the counter. 'Watch'er, sport. Am I still welcome?'

Charlie looked at him severely. 'You cost me a nice few bob last night,' he growled. 'It's a good job the mirror wasn't smashed. It's a figured antique.'

'I'm very sorry, Chas, but you saw what happened,' Joe said holding out his hands. 'That one-pot screamer was out of his stroller, going on like that.'

The landlord looked a little confused. 'Well, that's as it may be, but yer can't go chuckin' customers over me counter every time yer fall out wiv 'em,' he said firmly. ' 'Ow d'yer get on in court?'

'Forty shillings,' Joe told him with a shudder.

'You should fink yerself lucky,' Charlie replied. 'They could 'ave sent yer down.'

'It won't happen again, mate,' Joe assured him. 'Now let me shout you a drink.'

The elderly Danny Crossley ambled over and gave the Australian a toothless grin. 'I gotta tell yer,' he said with a wink, 'me an' the regulars were pleased yer sorted that Cafferty geezer out. 'E caused trouble 'ere the ovver night wiv 'is poxy rebel songs. Shorty Beaumont was gonna give 'im what for an' I 'ad ter stop 'im. Yer know what Shorty's like when 'is dander's up.'

Joe smiled as he laid a ten-shilling note down on the counter. Danny Crossley's friend was seventy if he was a day and he coughed noisily every time he lit up his Nosegay-packed clay pipe. 'Yeah, I know,' he said, and turned to Charlie Anson. 'Give Danny a drink too, Chas.'

The Sun at lunchtime was usually busy, but today it seemed as though very few people were in the mood for drinking and Danny remarked on how quiet it was. 'The bloody place feels like a morgue. I should fink they've all gone ter join up. I only wish I was a few years younger. I'd be there.'

'I've just tried to sign up,' Joe told him. 'I've gotta go back tomorrow.'

'What yer put down for, son?' Danny asked.

'The Royal Navy.'

'Good fer you. Yer'll look the part in that uniform,' the old man chuckled. 'Yer'll 'ave all the young women after yer. I just wish I was young enough ter go.'

The door opened and Shorty Beaumont walked purposefully in. 'Bloody 'ell!' he said, holding on to the bar as he fought to get his breath back. 'I was sayin' ter me ole dutch last night, you reminded me o' the Iron Duke the way yer bounced that no-good git over the counter.'

'The Iron Duke?' Joe queried.

'Yeah, the wrestler. The Iron Duke's the British 'eavy-weight champion,' Shorty informed him. ' 'E chucks 'em out the ring every time.'

The landlord leaned on the counter. 'I understand there's a few schools round 'ere sendin' the kids away ter the country,' he said, apropos of nothing. 'Just as well too. They should evacuate all the kids before it gets really nasty—an' it will, mark my words. We'll be in fer a right ole pastin' before long. Yer've only gotta look at what's 'appened in Spain wiv the German airforce. Besides, they'll be after sortin' out the docks an' wharves, an' the factories round 'ere'll be on their list too, yer can bet yer life.'

' 'Ere, that reminds me,' Shorty piped in. 'I just come past that shelter in Munday Road an' I saw a couple o' geezers stickin' up a wooden stand outside. I stood there watchin' 'em fer a while an' then I 'ad to ask 'em what they was doin'. Apparently they was puttin' up a poison gas warnin'. There's a flat board wiv paint on it an' when it comes inter contact wiv gas it changes colour. So that's 'ow yer know.'

'That's bloody stupid,' Danny Crossley remarked scornfully. 'I was in the trenches in the last lot when they dropped gas shells on us. I can just picture our ole sergeant major sniffin' the air an' sayin', "It smells like gas. 'Ang on lads, I'll just take a look at the board ter check." '

Their merriment died abruptly when another elderly customer walked in and announced that the German navy had sunk a freighter in the North Atlantic. 'It come over the wireless just as I was comin' out,' he said wide-eyed.

Joe finished his drink and refused the landlord's offer of one on the house. Somehow he felt that he couldn't stomach it and he made his excuses to leave. The two pounds nestling in his pocket would repay Liz Kenny and then it was the navy or bust.

On the first full day of the war the Flynn family gathered round the table for their evening meal of beef stew laced with dumplings. Dolly sat at one end and glanced lovingly from one to another as they chatted together. Mick her husband sat at the head of the table facing her, his shirtsleeves folded back over his brawny arms and his thick dark hair combed back from his forehead. To his left Frank sat mopping up gravy with a thick hunk of dry bread. At twenty-six he was the eldest of the brood, dark, stocky and broad-shouldered like his father, with brown eyes and a physique kept well toned by his job as a drayman at the local brewery. To Frank's left was Sadie who was a year younger. She had fair hair that was cut short and set in soft waves around her ears, and her pale blue eyes seemed preoccupied as she cut into a dumpling. Jennie, who sat the other side of Frank, was a pretty redhead with large hazel eyes, a small nose and expressive lips. Facing her was Jim who was eating like a starving man, and Dolly had to smile to herself. Food was a passion with him and her beef stew was his favourite. Jim was dark like Mick and Frank, though he had deep blue eyes which sometimes looked almost violet. He too worked at the brewery as a drayman, and was as muscular and broad-shouldered as his brother. Patrick, coming up to nineteen and the youngest of the clan, sat at the corner of the table wedged between Dolly and Jennie. He was sandy-haired with grey eyes like his mother, of a slighter build than his two older brothers, and he was a carpenter by trade.

'There's some more stew left if anyone wants any,' Dolly told them.

Everyone shook their head contentedly, with the exception of Jim, who gave his mother a crafty smile. 'I fink I could just about manage some more,' he said, looking round for a reaction.

'I dunno where 'e puts it,' Mick remarked shaking his head.

Jim smiled. 'I'm tryin' ter put a bit o' weight on,' he replied.

Dolly ladled the steaming stew onto Jim's plate and added a dumpling. 'I fink I'll let you do the washin' up,' she joked.

'Yeah, I'll do it,' the young man answered, reaching out for another slice of bread. 'I ain't above 'ouse'old chores like those two,' he said grinning at his brothers.

Dolly sat down again and tried to appear relaxed, but it was not easy. Here before her was her family, the ones she loved more than life itself, and hanging over their heads was the war. Soon there would be spaces at the table with the boys away, fighting for their country.

They seemed eager to go and Dolly had to concede that their sentiments were noble, if foolhardy. But she knew that sooner or later they would all be called up anyway and there was nothing she could do about it.

'That was a bit special,' Jim said, sighing as he rubbed his midriff.

Sadie pushed her chair back. 'You put yer feet up, Mum. Me an' Jennie'll wash up.'

Mick stood up and belched loudly. 'I'll put the news on,' he said.

Dolly watched while her two daughters cleared the table, then ignoring their suggestion that she relax she went out into the backyard. The sky above was clear and tinged with orange as the sun sank slowly into the west. This night, with the whole family sitting round the table together, was something she wanted desperately to imprint on her mind. A moment in time she would be able to call up in the uncertain days ahead. What the future held for them all was something Dolly tried not to think about, but the thoughts came regardless, and her heart was breaking.

CHAPTER 2

By Wednesday Joe Buckley had managed to volunteer for the Royal Navy and he went back to his lodgings around midday feeling pleased with himself. He had also managed to waylay the works foreman at the site where he had done some casual trench-digging work and he had finally got his money. At that moment he was free of debt, and if his call-up came soon he would stay that way.

'You look like the cat that's ate the canary,' Liz remarked as he sat down at the scullery table.

'Yeah, I just got meself all fixed up, Liz,' he told her with a wide smile.

'You signed on?'

'Too true I did.'

'I'm gonna miss yer, Joe,' she said. 'Bert will too.'

'I'll be lobbing in when I get some leave, don't worry about that,' he replied.

Liz Kenny sat down at the table facing him and clasped her hands on the well-scrubbed surface. 'What time d'yer make it?' she asked, her eyes narrowing slightly.

Joe glanced over at the battered alarm clock on the dresser. 'Is that bloody contraption jiggered again?' he replied. 'It's about ten after twelve.'

Liz stood up and reached for the clock. 'I fergot ter wind it last night,' she told him, moving the hands round the dial. 'Give us the exact time, could yer,' she said, staring at him.

The big man tapped the breast pocket of his grey cotton shirt and grinned evasively. 'Strewth, I ain't got me watch.'

'You pawned it, didn't yer?' Liz said knowingly.

Joe shrugged. 'I needed the money, girl,' he replied.

28

'There was no need ter pay me back so soon,' she chided him. 'I told yer I could wait.'

'Aw it's no hardship,' he assured her. 'I got paid up for the work at the site so I've got a few quid, and I'm gonna ask Sadie Flynn out for a drink as soon as I see her.'

'I fink yer wastin' yer time, Joe,' she warned him. 'Yer know she's seein' a bloke. Apparently 'e's married, so Dolly Flynn told me.'

'Well, I'm not chucking the towel in yet,' Joe said firmly.

'I wish yer luck,' Liz sighed.

Frank and Jim Flynn had finished early that afternoon and they sat together in the brewery canteen discussing their plans.

'I've bin givin' it some thought,' Frank said sipping his mug of tea. 'I've decided it's gonna be the army fer me.'

'You've changed yer mind quick,' Jim said frowning. 'Why's that?'

'I wanna get in soon, Jim,' his brother told him. 'Vic Moseley was tellin' me 'e volunteered fer the navy two weeks ago an' 'e's still waitin'. 'E was tellin' me they're pickin' men wiv trades that's suitable, like engineers an' electricians.'

Jim put down his empty mug. 'Are yer goin' down the recruitin' office terday?'

'Yeah.'

'Come on then, let's go.'

Frank gave his younger brother a questioning look. 'You're goin' in the RAF ain't yer?'

Jim grinned at him. 'Nah, I've changed me mind. We'll join up tergevver. Yer gonna need

29

somebody ter look after yer, yer dozy big git.'

'You saucy little sod,' Frank said slapping his brother round the head playfully. 'You show a bit o' respect. Well come on then, let's get goin'.'

Albert Levy walked into the small workshop and sat down heavily on the high stool, staring down sadly at the tiny solder balls and bits of coloured wire that were strewn over the wooden worktop. A wireless chassis stood apart from its Bakelite casing ready for inspection, and to one side was a box of assorted valves. Abel was gone for ever and Albert found it very hard to come to terms with the fact that he was dead.

'Why, old friend?' he mumbled aloud. 'You were safe here in London. The Nazis'll never reach here. You should have known that. Didn't I tell you? Every time we spoke about those things I tried to reassure you. Was I talking to myself? It seems I must have been. And what about me? Did you give me a thought when you poured that brandy down your throat and swallowed those tablets? Who do I play chess with now? Gerda can't play, as well you knew. You were good, Abel. Very good. I was getting your measure though. Soon I would have beaten you. I nearly did the last time we played. It's all right, I collected the chess box and board as you instructed. But you left me feeling guilty, old friend. I should have listened more than I did, not given up till I was sure that I'd put your mind at rest. I should have insisted you stayed with me and Gerda, instead of letting you go into lodgings, even though I knew it was what you wanted. At least I'll always be thankful I was able to get you out of that camp. It was the one thing I took real pleasure in being able to do. Well anyway, you're at peace now and I know that wherever you are you'll think of me kindly. We'll talk some more, old friend. Now I've got to see the young man who's going to take your place. According to his references, he seems skilled enough, but he won't come up to your standard. You were the best, Abel.'

Albert Levy walked out of the room and glanced round at the smart wirelesses and the two new press-button sets that were on display. Abel had mastery of them all and it wouldn't have taken him long to get the measure of those push-button ones too, he thought. Later he would have to go through his old friend's personal effects that were still in the workroom cupboard. Abel had been a hoarder and it was going to be a painful experience.

The leather-goods factory on the corner of Carter Lane seemed to have been there for ever and the older locals thought that it hadn't changed much since old Abraham Solomon drove up every morning in his horse-drawn trap. Now the firm was run by Abraham's two grandsons Martin and Joseph, and on Wednesday morning the two of them assembled the workforce in the main workshop to give them the news.

'I reckon we're goin' on war-work,' one of the stitchers remarked.

'I reckon it's about that shelter they were finkin' o' puttin' in down the basement,' her workmate said.

Sadie Flynn worked in the accounts office, and as she hurried down from the first floor to join the rest of the workers she feared the worst. Rumours had been flying round, and when she saw Joseph Solomon standing at the side of the room talking to Leonard Parker the works manager she knew it was a serious matter.

'Good afternoon, everyone,' Joseph began his address. 'I have some important news to give you. From next week we will be working solely on Government contracts. Our luxury range of leather goods will be suspended for the duration of the war, and as from next month we will be producing leather flying suits and gloves, as well as various other items of equipment for military, naval and airforce use. Now obviously you will be unfamiliar with the new methods of manufacture, so I want you to know that ample training and guidance will be available, which brings me to the most important point of all. As you will be aware, this area of London is vulnerable to air attack, given its position with regard to the docks and wharves, so in the light of that, and because of our important contribution to the war effort, it has been decided to move our operations to Bedfordshire.'

A mumble of voices grew in volume and Joseph Solomon raised his hands. 'It is unfortunate that this step has to be taken, but rest assured that all of you who decide to move with us will be found accommodation locally, with the advantage of being near enough to London to come home for the weekends. Now the company does understand that for some of you this move will be out of the question, for family reasons, so we will be talking to every one of you personally in the next few days. We have to move fast on this because of the training programme which will begin in two weeks' time. At the end of next week those wishing to leave may do so with two weeks' wages in lieu. Our factory in Bedford is being prepared and we hope to make the move by the end of the month. Now if there are any questions Mr Parker will be able to deal with them, which only leaves me to say good luck to you all whatever you decide to do.'

Sadie went back to the office and sat down to think. She had been happy at the firm and she had made some good friends, but the thought of being away from her family during the week did not appeal to her. It wouldn't be so bad at the moment, but what if air raids started? She would be worried sick if she were not around. Then there was Len Regan to think of. She would only be able to see him at weekends and he wouldn't be too pleased about that, to say the least.

'What are you gonna do, Sadie?' one of the girls asked her.

'I really don't know,' she said frowning.

'I'm gonna move wiv the firm,' the girl told her. 'My bloke'll be goin' in the forces soon an' I'll be alone 'ere anyway. I might just as well get away from London in case the bombin' does start.'

A few minutes later Audrey Smith the office manager walked into the room and sat down heavily at her desk. 'I've just left a sorry sight,' she said, sighing sadly. 'Some of the girls are crying and poor old Mrs Chambers is inconsolable. She's been here for donkey's years.'

Sadie tried to concentrate on her work but found it almost impossible. She was meeting Len Regan at lunchtime, the first time for a whole week after his extended business trip to Brighton, and she was looking forward to seeing him again.

'I've heard that Martin Solomon's going in the army soon,' Audrey told her colleagues. 'I always felt he was more approachable than Joseph.'

'Yeah, he's very nice,' one of the girls remarked. 'He could take me out anytime.'

'If we stay in London we'll end up being recruited for war-work,' another girl groaned. 'There's been a lot in the papers and on the wireless about recruiting single girls for essential work. We could be sent anywhere.'

Midday could not come quickly enough for Sadie, and when she finally stepped out into the warm sunshine excitement was rising inside her. Len had arranged to meet her at Giuseppi's Restaurant in the Old Kent Road, one of his usual haunts, and Mario Giuseppi would have made sure Len's regular table was available.

As expected she saw him sitting by the

window and he looked immaculate in his light-grey suit and pale-blue shirt. His thick dark wavy hair was brushed back from his forehead and partly covered his ears, his slim silver tie was knotted tightly and the peaks of his shirt collar were held together with a thin gold tie-pin. He smiled at her, showing his even white teeth, and Sadie felt a familiar thrill as she slipped into the seat facing him. A few of the customers were looking at them together. Len was well known in the area and his position as business manager and right-hand man to Johnnie Macaulay gave him respect. Mario tended to fawn over him and there were always nods of recognition wherever he went, but he rode the attention calmly and with good humour.

'You look good, Sadie,' he said smiling. 'Are you eating?'

Mario was there at her side with his notebook, pencil poised. 'Would the lady like something to drink first?' he asked.

Sadie shook her head. 'Er, just water, please,' she replied.

Mario was soon back with a jug of iced water and he filled the two tumblers. 'I can recommend the meat pie and veg,' he said encouragingly. 'Or maybe an Italian dish. The spaghetti's very ...'

'I'll 'ave the meat pie,' Sadie decided.

'That'll suit me fine too,' Len said smiling at the owner, and as Mario hurried off he leaned forward over the table. 'The poor geezer's worried sick. Apparently there's bin some threats made against 'im. Someone dropped a letter

35

frew the door this mornin' sayin' the place was gonna be torched. It's all this talk about Italy comin' inter the war. It's a shame. Mario was born over 'ere. 'E's as English as you or me.'

'Is there anyfing you can do about it?' Sadie asked as she sipped her cold water.

Len shrugged his broad shoulders. 'The word'll go out that if this restaurant gets done a few known troublemakers'll answer for it,' he told her. 'That'll ensure that the small mobs keep their 'ot-'eads in order. At least it should work that way, but yer never know. It could be someone independent, someone wiv a grudge, or a nutter. Anyway, let's not get too tied up wiv Mario's problems right now.'

'Tell me about Brighton,' Sadie said brightly.

'It went off very well,' Len replied. 'We've got control o' the Blue Max night club an' Johnnie's bid fer the big 'ouse facin' the promenade was accepted.'

'What's 'e want that for?' Sadie enquired innocently.

'You shouldn't ask,' Len said with a sly smile.

'Let me guess. It'll be turned into a brothel.'

'A top-notch one, not some seedy establishment.'

'I shouldn't be knowin' these fings,' Sadie said, her face suddenly becoming serious. 'You won't be involved in settin' it up, will yer, Len?'

'Nah, of course not,' he chuckled. 'Chance'd be a fine fing. No, I'll get a suitable person ter recruit the right gels an' run the place, an' I'll organise a bit o' back-up in case o' trouble, an' that's me finished.'

'I've missed yer, Len,' she said in a low voice as Mario came over carrying a laden tray.

'I've missed you too, kid,' he replied with a saucy wink.

They tucked into a delicious meal, chatting casually, and Sadie told him of her firm's plans to move away from London. 'Obviously I won't be goin' wiv 'em,' she said, 'but I'll need ter get a job locally that's involved in war-work, or I might end up in some munitions factory 'undreds o' miles away.'

Len pushed his plate back and sighed contentedly. 'Mario was right. That pie was first rate,' he remarked, then reached for his cigarette case. 'I shouldn't worry about lookin' fer anuvver job just yet. I might be able ter come up wiv somefing.'

'There's no way I'm gonna work in that Brighton establishment,' she said wide-eyed and smiling.

'No seriously, leave it ter me,' he told her. 'I'll see what I can do.'

'Len Regan can fix it,' she mocked. ' 'E can fix anyfing.'

'That's what Johnnie Macaulay pays me for,' he grinned.

' 'Ow did yer get involved in the first place?' she asked. 'You were gonna tell me, remember?'

'Not 'ere,' he said quietly. 'Let's get some air.'

They walked out into the bright daylight and

37

the tension was evident everywhere. Serious-faced people passed by, many already carrying their gas masks over their shoulders. Sandbags were being placed outside the Council rent office and in every building windows were being strengthened with brown paper strips. The tops of red pillar-boxes were now all painted in a yellowish gas-detector paint and high above in the clear blue sky silver barrage balloons floated like huge toy elephants.

'Johnnie an' me grew up round 'ere,' Len said as they walked into a small Council park in Defoe Street. 'We were good pals. We did Borstal tergevver an' then Johnnie got two years fer ware'ouse breakin'. I was able ter take care o' fings for 'im while 'e was away an' 'e never fergot.'

They sat down on a wooden bench facing a row of swings where children were playing noisily and Len smiled. 'Me an' Johnnie used ter play on them, would yer believe. It seems a lifetime ago now, an' I s'pose it is. We went our own ways after we grew up, as usually 'appens, an' Johnnie got involved as a minder wiv the Logans. 'E built up a reputation an' went from strength ter strength. People were beginnin' ter sit up an' take notice.'

'An' what about you?' Sadie asked.

'I went inter business cartin' machinery up an' down the country an' fings were lookin' good,' Len remarked, his face becoming more serious. 'I 'ad three lorries an' plenty o' work, an' then it fell apart. It was soon after I got married when the trouble started. Ann was very ambitious an' she encouraged me ter go in wiv 'er farvver who 'ad a transport company workin' out of Essex. They 'ad a big contract fer movin' sand an' gravel an' fer a while fings got better an' better. I sold my lorries an' the machinery contract an' bought four tipper lorries. The money I 'ad left I sank inter the gravel business. We 'ad plans ter make the company the biggest around, but it wasn't ter be.'

'What went wrong?' Sadie asked, intrigued.

'Ann's farvver was a compulsive gambler,' Len said contemptuously. 'Unknown ter me an' the rest o' the directors 'e started filchin' money from the company. That was the beginnin'. Then Ann started 'avin' an affair. I s'pose it was partly my fault. I was obsessed wiv buildin' up the business an' I left 'er alone fer too long. Anyway one night I came 'ome an' caught 'em tergevver. I went over the top an' beat the geezer up pretty badly. I was sent down fer two years an' it would 'ave bin fer longer if I 'adn't 'ad a good barrister. It cost me a fortune but after all, two years was better than seven, an' that's what I was starin' at. When I got out the business was failin' fast. Ann's farvver did a runner wiv a lot o' cash an' there were creditors under every stone. So that was it. I cut my losses an' pulled out, wiv less than two 'undred smackers.'

'Let me guess,' Sadie cut in. 'It was then that yer met up wiv Johnnie Macaulay again.'

'Yeah, but not in the way yer fink,' he told her. 'I moved back ter Bermon'sey an' went inter business wiv an ole pal o' mine, Joey Spain. We rented one o' those arches

39

in Druid Street an' got a contract ter make wooden crates fer the local brewery. We was doin' very nicely, but what we didn't know was, we were steppin' on Johnnie Macaulay's toes. We were undercuttin' one of 'is concerns an' 'e came round mob-'anded ter put us out o' business. When 'e saw it was me 'e couldn't get over it. Mind yer 'e still closed us down pronto, but me an' Joey got work wiv 'im. It was small stuff ter begin wiv, but 'e must 'ave seen that I 'ad somefing about me an' I started gettin' important jobs ter do. It just went from big ter bigger.'

'An' now you're the top man.'

'Yeah, yer could put it like that.'

'An' what about Joey Spain?' Sadie asked.

'Joey's still around,' Len said with a smile. ' 'E's one o' Johnnie's minders.'

'Do you ever see your wife?'

Len shook his head. 'I told yer she was a Catholic, didn't I?' Sadie nodded and he stared down at his hands. 'I can never get me freedom, an' frankly I don't care a toss. Marriage an' me don't work.'

Sadie looked sad. 'It would 'ave done, if yer'd met the right person.'

'If I'd met you first it could 'ave bin different,' he said quietly, 'but it's all water under the bridge now. We got it tergevver, kid, an' let's enjoy it. Life's too short ter go makin' too many plans.'

They left the park and walked back to the factory, and Sadie stretched up on tiptoe to kiss him on the lips as he clasped her shoulders.

'When can I see yer, Len?' she asked.

'I've got some business wiv Johnnie this evenin',' he replied, 'but I'll be free on Friday night. See yer at the same place?'

'Same place, same time,' Sadie said smiling. 'Take care, Len.'

CHAPTER 3

The Lockwood sisters shared the house at number 20 Carter Lane. They had lived together ever since the winter of '29 when Cynthia's husband Aaron Priestley went missing. Charity Lockwood had called in to offer her younger sister her support and comfort and never left.

Cynthia Priestley was not really in need of much comfort and support. In fact she was glad to see the back of her uncouth, lazy and lecherous husband. Aaron had had many bad habits, as Cynthia soon discovered, but being the dutiful wife she had devoted herself to his comfort and well-being and suffered him in silence for twenty-five years.

When Aaron went missing Cynthia was sporting a black eye, which she explained away by telling her neighbours that the wind had slammed the backyard door in her face. The neighbours nodded their heads in sympathy and concurred that Cynthia Priestley was a poor liar. They knew of Aaron's violent temper and his drunken habits, and they were all glad to

41

see the back of him. Had Cynthia been a more robust woman, with perhaps a more volatile temper, they might even have suspected that the good woman had had something to do with his disappearance. As it was, they all knew that Cynthia was too meek and mild even to step on an insect.

Charity Lockwood was a little less meek, though she too was very mild-mannered and retiring. She had never married, and when she realised that her younger sister would be alone in the house at night, in a rough area such as Bermondsey, she rallied to her aid. There were things to be done and Charity took charge. She forced Cynthia to report her husband's disappearance to the police, and between the two of them they furnished the attending officer with a fine description. Charity told the police that Aaron Priestley was an ugly, lecherous pig and when Cynthia added that her husband was not too particular about changing his underclothes on a regular basis, the constable had to remind the sisters that this was not exactly the information he needed. A facial description, height and build, colouring and distinguishing marks on the body were the kind of details he required from them, and they duly obliged.

Aaron was never found, though there were a few reported sightings, to which the sisters reacted unequivocally when they got to hear.

'As long as the old goat doesn't come back here,' Cynthia would say to her neighbours.

'If he does you must send him packing with

a flea in his ear,' Charity would remind her in front of them.

Now in their late sixties, the sisters were seen as sweet, quaint and eccentric by everyone in the street. They spoke very properly, dressed neatly and tidily, with their grey hair carefully waved and set, and they always went out together, be it to the market or to church on Sundays or the local park on warm balmy evenings to feed the ducks and pigeons.

With the coming of the war Cynthia wanted to go and live in the country but Charity decided otherwise. 'We have our friends and neighbours here,' she pointed out. 'In the country we wouldn't know anybody and when it snows we could be cut off from civilisation.'

Cynthia felt that they were hardly likely to be cut off in Clacton, and she said as much, but as usual Charity came back with an answer. 'Yes, but do you realise that Clacton is on the east coast? The Germans could come that way. We'd be in the front line, and at our time of life. We could be raped and pillaged.'

'We might get raped, though I doubt it at our age,' Cynthia remarked, 'but we certainly won't get pillaged. Property and belongings get pillaged.'

'Well all right, but I still don't think that Clacton is a good idea, especially at this stage of the proceedings,' Charity persisted.

With the decision made the sisters decided to visit the saloon bar of The Sun to drink to it, and as always they ordered sweet sherries.

Cynthia looked troubled as they waited for the

drinks to be poured. 'Would you say you were as alert as me, Charity?' she asked. 'I mean, do you notice things, little things, things that don't look important but are?'

'Whatever are you getting at?' Charity said sighing, as Charlie Anson put the drinks down on the counter.

'On our way to the market this morning I noticed something about that pillar-box in Munday Road.'

'What about it?'

'A man was painting the top of it.'

'Well?'

'I was going to mention it to you,' Cynthia went on, 'but you started talking about poor old Mr Abel.'

'Cynthia, pillar-boxes do get painted occasionally,' Charity told her with a patronising note in her voice.

'Yes, red, not yellow.'

'Yellow?'

'Yes, yellow—well the top of the pillar-box anyway.'

'I didn't notice,' Charity said.

'No, you were too busy talking, but I noticed it,' Cynthia replied smugly. 'Postboxes are Government property and it's a criminal offence to interfere with a pillar-box.'

'Quite right too,' Charlie cut in. 'Pillar-boxes are Crown property ter be exact.'

'Then who gave that man the right to paint a pillar-box yellow I'd like to know,' Cynthia said indignantly. 'Pillar-boxes should be red. That's where the name comes from, pillar-box red.'

44

'P'raps 'e's a fifth-columnist an' 'e's tryin' ter disrupt fings,' Charlie remarked, trying his best to keep a straight face.

Charity Lockwood sipped her sherry. 'Come now, Mr Anson,' she said stiffly. 'You don't think things would be disrupted by someone painting the top of a pillar-box yellow, do you?'

'Ah but 'e might 'ave just started,' Charlie replied with due seriousness. 'P'raps 'e was gonna paint the 'ole of it yellow, then people wouldn't be too sure whether they could still post letters there or not.'

Cynthia nodded. 'Quite right too,' she said with a smile playing on her small lined face. 'Charity, I think we should report this to the police, just to be on the safe side.'

Charlie Anson did not have the heart to spoil their day by frightening them about the gas-detector paint, feeling that perhaps this was a classic case of ignorance being bliss. 'Good fer you,' he said, walking along the bar to serve a customer who had just come in.

Chief Inspector Rubin McConnell had been at Munday Road police station for more than twenty years now and there wasn't much he didn't know about the area and its denizens. The Lockwood sisters were well known to him and the large file he had devoted to them proved it. The pair had come in to report some pretty outrageous goings-on over the years and Rubin had learned to open his file and take their report down without comment, a ploy that got the two quaint women out of his hair as soon as possible.

On that Wednesday afternoon, according to protocol, the Lockwoods walked into Munday Road police station and demanded to see Chief Inspector Rubin McConnell. 'It's no disrespect to you, young man,' Charity told the duty officer, 'but this is very important and only for the inspector's ears. Besides, he always sees us.'

Hiding a smile the young policeman spoke to his sergeant, who pulled a face and went to let the inspector know that trouble had arrived in the guise of the batty sisters.

'Come in, ladies, and take a seat,' Rubin bid them. 'Now let me get my file out so we can get things moving.' Then putting on his glasses he took his pen and looked up at their intent expressions. 'Right, I'm ready,' he said with a resolute smile.

Cynthia knew the drill off by heart and she did the talking, encouraged by occasional nods from her older sister. 'This morning about nine fifteen exactly ...'

'Just a moment,' the inspector stopped her, keen to show he was taking the report seriously. 'Was it about nine fifteen or nine fifteen exactly?'

'About,' Cynthia replied with a smile. 'About nine fifteen my sister and I were on our way to the market at East Street when we chanced to pass a pillar-box that is situated in Munday Road, a few yards away from this police station.'

46

'Yes, I know it,' the inspector said helpfully.

'My sister and I noticed that there was a workman, well he looked like a workman, painting the top of the pillar-box yellow.'

Charity smiled at being credited with the same powers of observation as her sister and she folded her hands in her lap contentedly.

'At first we took no notice, but then while we were having a morning sherry we got to thinking,' Cynthia went on. 'Pillar-boxes are Crown property and are always painted red. Why then should this man be in the process of changing the colour? Was it to confuse the public, and if so, why, we asked ourselves?'

Rubin McConnell was writing furiously, praying that he wouldn't start laughing. 'Why indeed?' he said quickly.

'The only answer we could come up with was that the man doing the painting was a fifth-columnist,' Cynthia continued. 'If he'd been from the IRA he would have more likely blown the box up.'

'Quite so,' Rubin replied. 'Right then, ladies, I have your report word for word and rest assured I will act on it forthwith.'

Cynthia and Charity looked pleased with themselves as they went out of the police station, leaving in their wake a relieved detective who was thankful to have got off lightly. 'Honestly, Johnson,' he told his subordinate, 'I couldn't bring myself to spoil their day. Besides, it would only put the fear of God into the poor old things if they knew the Germans might be thinking of using poison gas.'

'But surely they would have heard about all the emergency precautions taking place,' the detective sergeant replied.

'Not those two,' the inspector assured him. 'They have the knack of closing their ears and their minds to everything they don't want to know. But nevertheless, they are public-spirited. You'd be surprised if you saw some of the reports in that file. Two months ago they came in to report that they'd seen a man who looked very much like the Hoxton Creeper, would you believe?'

'The Hoxton Creeper?' Johnson said grinning widely. 'He was a product of Edgar Wallace's imagination, surely?'

'Be that as it may, the sisters came in to report that a man who resembled the Creeper was working on the cat's-meat stall in East Street Market.'

'Do they ever come back to see what progress we're making?' Johnson asked.

'Never,' McConnell told him. 'Once they report an incident they forget it, or at least I hope they do, otherwise we'll be looking at the largest backlog of police work in England.'

The Wednesday evening meal at the Flynns was eaten quietly and with little conversation. Dolly and Mick had been told by their lads that they had volunteered for the armed forces, and Mick drew comfort from the fact that Frank and Jim had put in a request to serve together. He felt pleased too that Pat was going in the airforce, until the young man told him that he was

48

volunteering for aircrew as soon as he could. There was no stopping them and Mick knew that it was useless trying to get Patrick to change his mind. Dolly had very mixed emotions. She felt a sense of pride in the gesture her sons were making but she was terribly fearful about what might befall them. She was also furious with them for treating the war like some adventure. They would soon learn otherwise, she thought fretfully.

'What about you, Sadie?' Pat asked after the meal was over. 'Are yer gonna go ter Bedford wiv the firm?'

She shook her head. 'No, I'm gonna stay round 'ere, if I can.'

'If yer can?' Dolly queried.

'I'm single, Mum. Me an' Jennie'll get called up fer war-work before long.'

'Well, you should both try an' get a war-work job local before they're filled up,' Dolly told them.

Jennie ran her fingers through her red hair and stretched. 'Well, I'm certainly not gonna stay at Jones and Whatleys fer the duration,' she said firmly. 'I might apply fer the services too. I fink I'd look good in a Wren's uniform.'

'Oh no you don't, young woman,' Dolly said sharply. 'It'll be bad enough wiv the boys away, wivout you joinin' up.'

Sadie pushed her chair back and gathered up the dirty crockery and Dolly followed her out into the scullery. 'Try ter talk Jennie out o' doin' somefing silly, Sadie,' she said sighing. 'I couldn't stand 'er bein' away too.'

'I'll try, Mum,' the young woman told her with a warm smile. 'But you know 'ow 'eadstrong Jennie is. Anyway it's early days yet. Anyfing might happen.'

'Yeah, all bad fings,' Dolly replied. 'It makes yer blood go cold when yer listen ter that wireless. This mornin' they was on about the amount o' shippin' that's bein' sunk by U-Boats.'

Sadie poured the boiling water from the kettle into the stone sink. 'Go an' put yer feet up, Mum,' she said. 'Jennie'll 'elp me wiv the dryin' up.'

'Ain't you goin' out ternight?' Dolly asked.

'No, Len's just got back from some business in Brighton an' 'e's got too much on.'

'Won't 'e be gettin' called up in the forces?' Dolly remarked.

Sadie chuckled. 'Len, in the army? I don't fink so.'

Dolly sighed sadly. 'I know I must sound like a broken record but I do wish you'd seriously consider all the pitfalls in goin' out wiv someone like Len Regan.'

'Look, Mum, I know yer mean well, but I love 'im,' Sadie said quietly. 'I never came between 'im an' Ann. The marriage was over long before I came on the scene. Len was straight right from the start. 'E spelled it all out. She'll never give 'im 'is freedom an' there's no point 'im worryin' about it. The both of us are enjoyin' our lives. I couldn't be 'appier, Mum, believe me.'

'I wanted ter see you all 'appily married before I snuffed it,' Dolly replied defeatedly.

Sadie reached out and put her arms around her. 'You're the bestest Mum, an' we all love yer. Don't get gettin' all sad an' miserable. Not now, please.'

Dolly brushed back a tear as her daughter released her. 'The boys'll be all right, won't they?' she said fearfully.

'Course they will,' Sadie assured her, 'especially now that Frank an' Jim are goin' in the same regiment. Those two 'ave always taken care of each ovver. Remember when that bully set about Jim at school? Frank nearly killed 'im.'

'What about young Pat though?' Dolly fretted. 'I wish we could talk 'im out o' volunteering for those aircrews.'

'It's no good, Ma,' Sadie replied. 'Pat can be the most cantankerous sod at times. We'll just 'ave to 'ope 'e changes 'is mind.'

Jennie came bounding into the scullery. 'Sadie, is there any chance o' borrowin' that nice black dress o' yours? I'd be grateful fer ever an' ever.'

Dolly left them to bargain and stepped outside into the backyard. The evening was balmy with a few stars showing between the gathering clouds. She saw the rusted tricycle that Pat used to ride as a kid and which she had never been able to get rid of, and she felt the tears coming again. There was the carving on the lavatory door and the old tin bath that all her brood had climbed into in front of the fire on Friday nights. Little things, ancient things, and things that would forever remind her of them all. She turned to go back into the house

51

and Mick was there, standing in the doorway watching her.

'I was gonna offer a penny fer yer thoughts but I didn't dare,' he said with a warm smile on his large weatherbeaten face.

'I was just rememberin',' she said simply.

He stepped out into the yard and slipped his arm around her waist. 'Look, I know it's bin a terrible few days, but we're not alone, gel,' he said in a quiet voice. 'All over the country young men are preparin' ter go off an' fight. In almost every family 'ouse in the land there'll be spaces round the table an' bedrooms not bein' slept in. There's nuffink me, you, nor anybody else can do ter change it. It's up ter the politicians an' the warmongers ter realise that whatever 'appens, 'owever bitter the fightin', there'll come a time when they'll 'ave ter get tergevver round the table an' talk. All we can do is pray that it comes sooner rather than later.'

The stars had all gone in and the heavy clouds were full of rain. The sound of brass-band music drifted out from next door and a dog barked in the distance.

'Come on, gel, let's listen ter the news,' Mick said.

'Mick?'

'Yeah?'

'It doesn't matter.'

'Now come on, out wiv it.'

'Mick, do you still feel the same as yer did when we were young?'

'About you yer mean?'

'Who else d'yer fink I meant?'

52

'The answer's no.'

'What?'

Mick squeezed her waist and chuckled. 'I love yer fifteen bob more than I did then,' he told her.

'Well, that's all right then,' Dolly said sternly. 'Come on let's go in, I'll make a mug of cocoa.'

CHAPTER 4

The early days of the war were warm and sunny, with a frenzy of activity going on everywhere in an atmosphere that seemed unreal. Brick surface shelters were hurriedly erected in streets where children played, and in the parks people had picnics beside anti-tank trenches and concrete barriers. Railway stations became staging points for the services, and military uniforms mingled with the crowds of everyday commuters and families on weekend trips. Everyone learned the art of queuing and had to practise getting in line. Ration books and petrol coupons were issued and scientists and doctors worked out a basic diet guaranteed to sustain good health, while in the West End of London prime steak and lamb cutlets, pork chops and lavish cuts of beef were still on the menu at all the hotels and restaurants. Pubs saw a rise in trade as well and people danced to the big bands in the top night-spots of London.

The war at sea was raging and the toll of shipping sunk grew daily, but for the people at home it was a time of waiting and worrying, as their young folk left for the armed services. Constant reminders of the unseen dangers and patriotic exhortations were posted up at every vantage point. It was a time to 'Dig for Victory', and to remember that 'Careless Talk Costs Lives'. Collections were made in backstreets and everyone was urged to bring out their old pots and pans and any other metal scrap that they might have in their gardens and backyards. More signs encouraged folk to 'Beat that Squander Bug' and 'Save for Victory'. Iron railings and metal gates were removed for the war effort, and even the children's playgrounds were stripped of everything metal.

The strictness with which the blackout was enforced was an ominous suggestion of things to come, and often a careless moment would be met with the cry, 'Put that light out!' Torches could be carried to light the way home, provided the beam was dimmed with a double layer of tissue-paper. Vehicles' headlights were restricted by the use of slitted metal caps and the road accident toll grew alarmingly. Directional signs were removed and premises were taken over for air-raid wardens' posts. In every area civil defence command posts were installed and cars were commandeered for stretcher-carrying. And while all the preparations and conversions, innovations and transformations went on, so did the waiting ...

Frank and Jim Flynn passed their army medicals and were waiting eagerly for their call-up papers, and Patrick Flynn had no trouble being accepted for the RAF. His trade as a carpenter would help him become an air-frame fitter, so the recruiting officer informed him, and the young man nodded compliantly. First things first, he told himself. Like his two brothers he sailed through the medical, and along with them he waited for an official letter to drop onto the mat.

Big Joe Buckley was called up into the navy and the night before he left he sat talking to Bert Kenny in the parlour. 'I've really enjoyed lodging here, mate,' he said with a smile. 'I'm gonna miss the both of you. I couldn't have got better tucker anywhere and you two have made me feel like one o' the family.'

Bert smiled self-consciously. 'Me an' Liz look on you as one of our own,' he replied.

Joe shifted his position in the armchair. 'By the way, I'm sorry if I disturbed you both last night. I was with a few o' the berko buggers from the building site. We were on a bit of an elbow-bender.'

'So yer won't be goin' out ternight then?' Bert said grinning.

'Aw yeah. Tonight I'm gonna drown me troubles in a tubful o' Bermondsey brainrot,' Joe replied enthusiastically. 'But in a civilised sort o' way, and I'd be delighted to buy you and Liz a drink if you don't mind stickin' your heads in The Sun.'

'Liz 'as gone fer a chat wiv Dolly Flynn,'

55

Bert told him. 'I'll see if she's game when she comes back. Anyway, what troubles 'ave you got? A young man like you wiv no ties can please 'imself where 'e goes an' what 'e does. You wait till yer get spliced. Yer'll see the difference then.'

'That's probably right, Bert, but I'd willingly give up all the old cobblers for Sadie Flynn. Now there's a beaut, if ever I saw one. I've been after asking her out for a drink but I ain't seen anything of her lately.'

' 'Ave you ever really spoke to 'er?' Bert asked.

'Nah, not really. Not a single bloody word, now I think of it.'

'I was gonna say why don't yer go an' knock at 'er door,' Bert said, 'but I s'pose yer can't unless yer on speakin' terms.'

'Nah, it'd be a bit ocker,' Joe agreed. 'Anyway as soon as I get some leave I'll put that right. I'll get to know her and see what a nice new uniform does for her. Like the old song says, all the nice girls love a sailor.'

'Well, I wish yer luck, but don't get yer 'opes up too much, Joe,' Bert warned him. 'Yer know she's goin' out wiv Len Regan.'

'Yeah, so I've heard,' Joe replied. 'He's a big man around here, according to the ole bush telegraph.'

' 'E's more of a front man really,' Bert remarked. 'It's common knowledge that Len Regan runs Johnnie Macaulay's affairs but Macaulay's the big fish. 'E owns pubs an' clubs, an' they say 'e controls all the mobs

56

this side o' the river. You name it—'e's into it. Gamblin', prostitution, protection, an' Gawd knows what else.'

Joe shook his head slowly. 'The Flynns seem a nice family. Why would Sadie Flynn wanna get involved with the likes of him?' he asked. 'The way I see it there's only bad times on the trolley for that sort. The bigger they are the harder they fall at the end o' the day.'

Bert shrugged his shoulders. 'It could be the excitement that attracted 'er in the first place. You know the sort o' fings, night-clubs, racin' meetin's, shows an' the like. A lot o' gels' 'eads are turned by that sort o' fing. But that's only one way o' lookin' at it. Yer gotta consider too much that she might really love the geezer. I understand from what Liz told me that 'e's quite a bit older than 'er. Some gels are attracted to older men, not that I'm an expert on that sort o' fing.'

Joe laughed aloud. 'You could've fooled me, Bert,' he replied. 'Anyway I'm going for a shave. The rubbity-dub'll soon be open to all chunderers.'

While the big man was getting ready to go out Liz returned. 'Poor Dolly,' she said as she sat down in the armchair facing Bert. 'She's just 'ad a few tears. Those lads of 'ers are gonna be off very soon. It's bad enough one goin', let alone three.'

Bert nodded sadly, then his face brightened up. ' 'Ere, luv. Why don't we get Dolly an' Mick ter come up The Sun fer a drink wiv us? Joe wants ter buy us a drink anyway. It'll make a change, an' it might cheer the poor sods up fer a bit.'

Liz thought for a few moments, then she nodded. 'Sadie ain't out ternight, p'raps she might come up there as well. Joe's bin tryin' ter get ter know 'er. It'll be a chance fer 'im ter chat the gel up. By the way, if you wanna come too get yerself a shave. Yer look like Burglar Bill.'

Friday nights were music nights at The Sun public house and Blind Bob was already at the piano tinkling on the keys, a pint of beer within his reach. Joe was standing at the counter surrounded by the friends he had made in the short time he had lived in Carter Lane.

'We're gonna miss that ugly mug o' yours round 'ere,' the elderly Danny Crossley remarked.

'Yeah, me, too,' Shorty Beaumont added.

'I know somebody who's gonna be glad ter see the back o' you, though,' Alf Coates piped up.

'So do I,' Danny chuckled into his beer. 'Since that night I don't fink anybody's seen 'ide nor 'air o' Sid Cafferty.'

'I 'ave,' one of the street's dockers said. 'Cafferty's usin' The Bull now.'

' 'E wants ter be careful in there,' another of the group remarked. 'There's a right crowd gets in there. They won't stand fer any nonsense.'

'Nor do we, come ter that,' Danny said rolling his bony shoulders.

The pub was gradually filling up and wreaths of cigarette smoke hung in the air as Blind Bob got into his stride on the ivories.

' 'Ere, Bob. What about, "All the nice gels love a sailor"?' Lofty Knowles called out.

'What about it?' Bob called back, cocking his ear in the direction of the counter.

'Play it, yer daft git,' Lofty growled at him.

Everyone in the saloon bar joined in the ditty and Joe stood in the middle of the group feeling embarrassed as they sang to him with gusto. It was then that the Kennys and the Flynns walked in and Big Joe immediately noticed Sadie. She stood talking to her sister Jennie while Bert and Mick ordered the drinks and she glanced over at him and gave him a brief smile of recognition. Joe swallowed quickly and tried to pick up on the inane chatter passing back and forth around him but it was all going over his head. 'Excuse me, mates,' he said, moving away from the counter.

'Don't look now but Big Joe Buckley's lookin' over,' Jennie said, giving her sister a sly smile.

'I 'ope 'e don't come over,' Sadie hissed.

'Why? Don't yer like 'im?'

'It's not that,' Sadie replied. ' 'E just makes me feel uneasy.'

Jennie pulled a face. 'Sadie Flynn, Len Regan's gelfriend, an' a bloke like Big Joe makes yer feel uneasy. You've gotta be kiddin' me.'

Sadie glanced furtively toward the counter. 'Joe's a decent sort o' bloke, I s'pose, but I've never actually spoke to 'im. I dunno what it is about 'im. It might be 'is size, or the way 'e looks at me when we pass in the street. Anyway don't keep lookin' over there.'

Jennie was not to be put off. 'I like 'em big

59

an' 'andsome. Big Joe could chat me up for any day o' the week.'

Dolly Flynn and Liz Kenny were gossiping together round a small iron table and Bert was standing to one side with Mick, discussing football. Sadie went uncharacteristically quiet and Jennie began to feel a little bored as she sat sipping her port and lemon. 'As we were sayin'. It's nice in 'ere, ain't it?' she said with heavy sarcasm.

'Sorry, Jen, I was miles away,' Sadie said weakly.

'Len trouble?'

'Not really, but 'e's 'ere, there an' everywhere lately,' Sadie replied. 'It's that Brighton business I was tellin' yer about. I 'ardly see 'im. 'E's bin back an' forwards at least four times this week.'

'Look, there's Ken Bennett over at the counter,' Jennie said nudging her. 'Let's go an' stand up there, 'e might notice me.'

'You're a pushy little bitch,' Sadie laughed, smiling fondly at her. 'C'mon then.'

As they got up and made their way over to the end of the counter where it was less crowded Joe Buckley walked up. 'Er, excuse me,' he said, hesitantly, addressing Jennie. 'I'd like to buy your party a drink. Can you tell me what they're having?'

Jennie smiled up at him. 'That's very nice of yer, ain't it, Sadie? Now let me see, Mr an' Mrs Kenny are ...'

'Yeah, I know what they're drinking,' Joe said quickly. 'I mean you an' your mum and dad.'

60

'I'll find out,' Jennie said, walking back to the table.

'What would you and your sister like?' Joe asked, giving Sadie a disarming smile.

'It's all right, I've still got this one,' Sadie said holding up her drink.

'Let me refill it for you. It's the last chance I'll get to buy my good neighbours a drink,' Joe told her as he leant one arm on the counter. 'I'm off tomorrow.'

' 'Ave yer bin called up?' Sadie asked.

'Yeah, I'm going in the Royal Navy,' Joe said proudly. 'I've gotta report to Chatham or I'll get shot.'

Jennie had memorised the order but delayed going back to the counter when she saw Joe and Sadie talking together.

'I wish yer luck,' Sadie said, averting her eyes self-consciously.

'I'm gonna miss this area,' he said sighing.

' 'Ow long 'ave yer bin 'ere now?' Sadie asked.

'Three months, but it seems much longer,' Joe replied.

The barman was looking at him expectantly. 'What'll it be, Joe?'

'What the lady's having and I'll have the usual overpriced rubbish,' the big man told him. 'The rest of the order seems to have got held up.'

'Mine's a port an' lemon, same as Jennie,' Sadie said.

'Do your worst, and one for yourself,' Joe said, laying a pound note on the counter.

Sadie drained her glass and set it down to be

61

replenished. 'It must seem strange fer you,' she remarked, 'livin' in a small community I mean, after livin' in Australia.'

'As a matter o' fact I grew up in a little community back home,' Joe replied. 'It was in the suburbs o' Sydney.'

'But it's such a big country,' Sadie said.

'Yeah, but you don't really think much about that, till you grow up a bit,' Joe told her. 'It was only when I left home and travelled, went walkabout as we say, that I started to realise just how big it is.'

'What made yer come over 'ere in the first place?' Sadie asked, beginning to feel intrigued.

Joe shrugged his shoulders, giving her a wide smile. 'Now that's a big question. I suppose I had itchy feet by then, and I got to find out that my folk originally came from England. Things weren't going all that well in Oz and I was at a loose end, so I signed on as an engineer on a liner and worked me passage to the old country, as we call it.'

'What about yer family?'

'I never knew them,' Joe replied. 'I was brought up in an orphanage.'

'I'm sorry,' Sadie said, catching a fleeting look of sadness in his wide blue eyes. 'It can't 'ave bin the ideal way ter start out.'

Joe shrugged his shoulders again. 'Such is life. At least it taught me to look after meself. I left the orphanage when I was fourteen and they fixed me up at a marine engineering firm, where I got the chance to do an apprenticeship. There's not much I don't know about marine

62

engines, which is a good thing really, 'cos I know bugger all about anything else. That's how I managed to get in the navy so quickly.'

The barman put two port and lemons down on the counter along with a frothing pint of beer and Sadie chuckled. 'It seems Jennie's got somefing else on 'er mind,' she said, nodding over to where her sister was chatting away intently to a young man.

'That's my good luck,' Joe said, giving her a shy smile. Then he struggled with himself for a moment or two. 'Would you mind if I told you something?'

'It depends what it is,' Sadie replied, beginning to feel relaxed.

'Ever since I've lived in Carter Lane I've been wanting to talk to you, but I could never find the spunk to do it,' he confessed. 'You seemed different to all the other girls in the street. You have that proud walk and a sort of air about you that scared me off. Does that sound stupid?'

'Not really,' Sadie said smiling. 'You 'ad that effect on me.'

'Did I?' Joe replied, looking surprised. 'Ripper!'

Sadie sipped her drink. 'Anyway yer'll be gettin' some leave, won't yer, an' then we can 'ave a chat when we meet up wivout us feelin' scared of each ovver.'

'That'll be something to look forward to,' Joe said in a serious voice. 'This area's become like home for me and the Kennys feel like me own. Your mother and father are dinkum too and I've enjoyed a few true blue nights in here with your

63

brothers. I know that you're going steady but it'll be nice if I can count on you as a friend as well.'

The drinks and the unexpected conversation had made Sadie feel a little light-headed and she held out her hand. ' 'Ello, friend.'

Joe took her hand in his much larger one. 'Pleased to meet you, friend,' he said smiling broadly.

Jennie finally walked over. 'Sorry to interrupt,' she said, giving Joe a big grin. 'I've got the order.'

'This is my friend,' Sadie said with a dignified expression. 'Jennie, meet Joe.'

The night was wearing on and Joe was pulled away for a toast, then Charlie Anson came round the counter to say a few words as Blind Bob took a breather. 'Joe, we're all sorry ter see yer go,' he began, 'but we know it won't be the last o' that ugly face round 'ere. Liz Kenny told me that 'er an' Bert are keepin' yer room for yer an' there's always a space at the bar fer you while me an' Kath are runnin' the gaff. This is a small backwater in a small country, but the people round 'ere 'ave got great big 'earts an' they've all taken ter yer. So 'ere's ter you, an' may whoever's bin smilin' down on yer keep doin' so. Gawd bless yer, son.'

Liz Kenny came up and gave the big man a hug and Bert shook his hand vigorously. People were slapping his back and Sadie suddenly noticed the tears forming in his large blue eyes as the demonstrations of affection overwhelmed him.

'Joe's a smashin' feller,' Liz said, wiping her eyes.

'One o' the best,' Bert agreed, swallowing hard.

' 'E's lovely,' Jennie sighed to her older sister.

'Yeah, 'e's nice,' Sadie said calmly, but she felt like kissing him.

CHAPTER 5

Albert Levy sat down on the stool behind the counter and opened his packet of sandwiches. When Abel was working at the shop Albert had been free to take a short break for lunch at the nearby cafe or the pub opposite, knowing that his old friend could cope with any customers who might come into the shop. Now though it was different. Bernard Shanks, the young man he had employed, was skilled enough in his trade but was not familiar with selling and lacked confidence, so Albert spent the whole day behind the counter and ate his make-do lunch when it was quiet.

Apart from the radios on show, Levy's Radio Store sold light bulbs and torch bulbs, as well as batteries, accumulators and electrical bits and pieces. Radio accumulators were charged in the shed out the back and in the two rooms upstairs Albert kept his stock. At first he and Gerda had lived in the cramped quarters over the shop but as the business developed he was able to get a mortgage for a Victorian terraced house in New Cross. It was only a short tram ride away and it suited him.

When he had finished the fish-paste sandwiches and eaten the rosy apple Gerda had put in his bag, Albert went into the workroom to make a cup of tea. He had finally got around to clearing Abel's personal things from the back of the cupboard and there was nothing there that he felt he wanted to keep. A few old receipts and radio magazines, along with some technical manuals which he had passed over to Bernard, was the sum total and it saddened Albert. 'There wasn't a lot to remember you by, was there?' he said, thumbing through a manual on valves and transformers. 'Still I've got the chess set and that's nice. I can see you now, Abel, when you looked up with that apologetic smile as you checkmated me. I'm sure you would have preferred me to win sometimes, but I know how your mind worked. You felt it might upset me if you treated me like some incompetent youth and pretended to make a little mistake or two. Like I said before, Abel, I was getting your measure. By the way, it's Gerda's birthday tomorrow. We're going over to Whitechapel to be with her family. They're doing something special for her fiftieth.'

Albert looked towards the front door of the shop, suddenly feeling a little self-conscious about talking aloud. If anyone walked in, he thought, they would probably assume he was going off his head. He turned back to stare at the paraphernalia on the bench and saw in his mind his old friend sitting hunched over a dismantled wireless with a soldering iron in his hand and a look of extreme concentration on his thin face. That was the time to avoid talking to him. A word or question would be met with a tut-tut and a nervous cough, and Abel would be in a bad mood for the rest of the day. Such was his dedication to his trade and his single-minded proficiency.

'The new technician seems quite all right, Abel, though he's a strange lad,' Albert continued. 'Not very fit by the look of him. I'm sure he's undernourished. I was thinking earlier, if you can hear me you'll know how things are going with the war, but I'll keep you up to date with my assessment anyway. Do you know what I think? I think there'll be a stalemate now that the Nazis have got Czechoslovakia and overrun Poland. I think they'll be after settling for that. It's all quiet on the Western Front and they'll have their work cut out breaking through the Maginot Line. I shouldn't be too surprised to see things moving towards an armistice before long, certainly early in the New Year. We'll talk some more later, old friend. Bernard will be back from lunch in a few minutes.'

Daisy Harris had been putting off the task of cleaning Abel's rooms, but on Saturday morning she finally faced up to doing it. She had given all his clothes to the Salvation Army and Mr Levy had gone through the cardboard box containing his personal effects. The rooms

67

needed scrubbing out and a good airing before she could consider taking in a new lodger. The doors and cupboards needed some fresh paint and the cracked oil-cloth would have to be replaced too.

Bill Harris did the painting, which took him well into the afternoon, and then Daisy pulled up the oil-cloth which she folded into manageable pieces for Bill to tie up and leave by the dustbin. The last piece of floor-covering that Daisy pulled up was around the fireplace, and on the lefthand side there was a small piece that had already been cut into an oblong shape, presumably by Abel. Beneath it a flap of wood was loose and Daisy prised it up with curiosity. In the recess she could see a brown paper parcel and, loath to touch it, she called out for Bill.

'It could be anyfing,' she said, stroking her chin.

'Well, there's only one way ter find out,' he said going down on his knees.

'You be careful,' she said fearfully.

Bill gave her a disdainful look and removed the small bundle. The wrapping was not tied and as he unfolded the paper he saw the diary. It was bound in leather with gold-leaf figuring on the front cover. Quickly he flipped through the pages and perused the tiny scribblings and figures. 'I can't make 'ead or tail o' this—it's in some foreign language,' he said, looking up at Daisy.

'You shouldn't be lookin' at it anyway,' she admonished him. 'That's Mr Abel's personal diary. I'd better let Mr Levy know about it.'

'Why should 'e wanna stick it away like that?' Bill wondered, scratching his head.

' 'Cos it's personal,' Daisy said pointedly.

'Yeah, so yer keep sayin',' Bill growled.

'I'll pop it in ter Mr Levy's shop before 'e shuts,' Daisy decided. 'I gotta go next door ter the shoemender's anyway.'

Jennie Flynn had grown more and more disenchanted with the idea of being a saleswoman, especially a saleswoman for the venerable company of Jones and Whatleys. Travelling to and from the West End every day was bad enough, without having to work on Saturdays. Then there was the system at the old Royally chartered establishment. The senior staff were all long-term employees who felt privileged just to be part of such a fine company, judging by the way they spoke and acted, and whenever any of the owners or directors appeared in the store they would grovel and bow and scrape in a way that left Jennie and some of the newer girls feeling disgusted at it all.

At first Jennie was pleased to be taken on, as she was led to believe that promotion would soon be awarded to staff showing the right initiative and motivation. 'The sky's the limit with Jones and Whatleys,' the personnel manager had informed her during her initial interview. Well it wasn't, unless the hopeful young sales assistant quickly learned the art of fawning and kowtowing. Now, with four years under her belt, Jennie was ready to seek pastures new.

'I should think it over very carefully,' Mrs Collins told her during the morning break as they sat together in the staff room. 'You could do a lot worse. The conditions here are not at all bad and there are openings for the right people. Take me—I've only been a senior saleswoman for two years and at the present moment I'm on the shortlist to take over a floor.'

'Well, I've bin 'ere fer four years now an' there's as much chance o' me gettin' a senior saleswoman's post as goin' ter the moon,' Jennie said dismissively.

Mrs Collins smiled. 'It's all about attitude and presentation,' she remarked smugly. 'Either you've got it or you haven't.'

'Yer mean I don't come over as a good saleswoman?' Jennie retorted quickly. 'I speak proper when I'm be'ind the counter an' I always try ter be all smiley an' 'appy.'

'Yes and you do very well,' the older woman replied. 'No one would question you on that score. But it goes much deeper than that, you see. This company is an old establishment with a Royal charter. Those at the very senior level have worked very hard to get where they are and they expect to be treated accordingly. You take Mr Forbes as an example. He likes to be called sir by the staff, and whenever he makes an appearance on the floors he expects the staff to recognise and respect his position. He spent fifteen years on menswear and another five years in furnishings before he went upstairs as junior buyer. Now he's a senior buyer and whenever he requests anything he expects the staff to jump.'

'Well, you can say what you like about Mr Forbes, but ter me 'e's just a lecherous ole goat who could do wiv a little more soap an' water,' Jennie said with disgust. ' 'E reeks o' sweat, an' if 'e expects me ter call 'im sir, 'e can whistle.'

Mrs Collins secretly admired the young woman's pluck, but she dared not let her know. As it was, Jennie was right about her prospects for promotion. Mr Forbes had her pegged as a troublemaker and malcontent and he had been instrumental in ensuring that she would remain a junior saleswoman for as long as she worked at Jones and Whatleys.

'Well, if you won't bend a little and show a little more respect where it matters you can't expect to move upwards,' Mrs Collins said sighing.

Jennie picked up her bag from the chair beside her. 'It could all be up in the air anyway,' she said as she stood up to go back to the handbag and accessories counter.

'Up in the air?' Mrs Collins queried.

'Well, if this new law comes inter force single women are gonna be recruited fer war-work,' Jennie replied. 'If that's the case then 'alf o' Jones an' Whatleys' staff are gonna be leavin', an' who knows, they might even call up that ole goat Forbes.'

Mrs Collins shook her head slowly as the young redhead walked off. Jennie Flynn was incorrigible, but with a figure like that and her pretty face she needn't be tied to the likes of Jones and Whatleys.

On the fourth floor at the accessories section there was a minor crisis blowing up and Jennie walked right into it.

'Ah, Miss Flynn, just in time,' the effeminate salesman said, looking a little ruffled. 'The lady here wanted a grey crocodile-skin handbag and I'm afraid we're out of them at the moment.'

Jennie looked at the large woman dressed in green tweeds and immediately sensed trouble. She was a classic example of 'the predator', as the junior staff had named the breed of shopper who looked upon them as fair game. The woman was holding a grey crocodile-skin handbag under her arm and eyeing the young man with hostility.

'It's all right, Leon. I'll deal with it,' Jennie told him.

'Madam wants to change the bag for another of the same you see,' Leon went on.

'Yes all right, leave it to me,' Jennie said calmly.

'This handbag is defective,' the woman declared in a booming voice as she banged the item down on the glass counter.

'Let me take a look,' the young woman said, smiling as she pulled at the stitching.

'Inside. Look inside.'

When she opened the bag Jennie saw the split satin lining and noticed that it was stained.

'Could I ask what you have been carrying in this, madam?' she asked.

'Nothing. It was like that when I bought it,' the woman retorted in a louder voice.

'Madam, we always remove the paper packing

72

from each handbag that we sell to check that the lining is in perfect condition,' Jennie told her.

'Are you calling me a liar, young woman?' the predator boomed out.

Jennie realised that she would have to change her tack. 'Could I see the receipt for the bag, please?' she asked.

'I haven't got it, but what if I had? You seem to be out of this type,' the woman said haughtily.

'If you have your receipt, then we can refund your money or order you a replacement.'

'Young woman, are you calling me a liar?'

'Certainly not, madam.'

'You seem to be implying so.'

'I'm sorry, but it's company policy,' Jennie tried to explain. 'Without a receipt showing that the bag was purchased here there's nothing I can do.'

'Now you listen to me,' the woman said menacingly. 'I've been shopping at Jones and Whatleys for many years and I've never encountered anything like this before. Go and fetch your superior at once. Do you hear me?'

Jennie took a deep breath to control her temper as it started to rise dangerously. Her job did not seem very important at that particular moment, and as for the old adage driven home daily to the staff that the customers were always right, it was all a load of hot air. 'Madam, it looks to me like you've been carrying a couple of housebricks in that bag by the state of the lining,' Jennie said in a measured tone of voice, 'but as you wish, I'll fetch the floor manager.'

The predator's eyes were bulging with disbelief at what had just been said to her and for a moment she was rendered speechless. Leon had been listening from behind a rack of scarves and, feeling sorry for Jennie, he had already hurried off to get the manager. On the way he bumped into the venerable Mr Forbes who was on one of his forays and decided to let him know what was taking place at the handbag counter.

'All right, Miss eh, Miss Flynn, I'll deal with this,' the senior buyer said in his superior manner. 'Would madam like to sit down first? Flynn, fetch madam a chair.'

'And where am I gonna get a chair from?' Jennie asked acidly, dropping her saleswoman's voice. 'If you fink I'm goin' all the way up ter the rest room yer've got anuvver fink comin'.'

'Miss Flynn,' Forbes almost screamed out. 'Do as you're told.'

'Get somebody else,' Jennie said spiritedly.

The awkward customer was beginning to attract the attention of other shoppers as she glared at the buyer. 'Look at this handbag. I purchased it here in this store, at this counter, only yesterday. The lining's damaged and stained.'

'I just told 'er she must 'ave bin carryin' bricks in it,' Jennie butted in.

'Go away, Miss Flynn,' Forbes told her, beginning to sweat profusely.

'I want that young woman sacked immediately. Do you hear me?' the virago snarled.

'You just leave that to me,' Forbes said, eyeing Jennie with venom. 'Now let us see.

74

Have you the receipt?'

'I'm afraid I've mislaid it,' the woman told him.

'She's tryin' ter pull the oldest trick in the book an' you, yer silly git, are fallin' for it,' Jennie remarked, beginning to enjoy the confrontation now that she was certain to be sacked on the spot.

'Trick? What do you mean by trick?' the woman shouted.

'They buy imitation gear dead cheap at the markets an' then try ter say they bought the item at a West End store,' Jennie explained to Forbes. 'She 'ands in a bag werf four an' a tanner an' gets a three guinea bag as a replacement, if she's lucky, which she ain't this time. Shall I fetch the police?'

'Go away! Leave us!' the senior buyer screamed out.

'I'll fetch the police anyway,' Jennie said, giving the woman a piercing look.

Shoppers were standing around listening and many had smiles on their faces. The staff too had become aware of what was happening and they were watching the proceedings from vantage points throughout the fourth floor. A young soldier with his forage-cap shoved through his epaulette grinned at Jennie as she hurried by. 'Well done, luv,' he told her. 'You're a diamond.'

Once out of Forbes' view Jennie made a detour and worked her way round to the lift. The restroom was situated in the basement and when the young woman walked in still puffing from her exertions she was greeted with handclaps.

'What a gel,' the doorman said grinning.

'Well, if yer gotta go that's the way ter do it, out wiv yer 'ead up 'igh,' one of the elderly cleaners remarked.

Jennie had hardly sat down to catch her breath when Leon came hurrying in. 'Jennie, I thought I'd die when you stood up to that nasty woman,' he told her with feeling. 'I said to myself, Leon, she's just talked herself out of a job. I was trembling all over. I still can't stop shaking now. Look at me, I'm like a Hartley's jelly.'

Mrs Collins came in and sat down facing Jennie with a smile on her face. 'Well, you've finally done it, but I know it doesn't worry you. You'll make out, and perhaps that little episode, if you can call it that, might help blow some fresh air through the musty corridors of Jones and Whatleys.'

Mr Forbes had gone to lie down, fortified with a couple of Aspros, and the dire deed was left to the floor manager, who was strangely supportive when he came over to inform Jennie of her fate. At four o'clock that evening she left the store with her cards and a week's wages. The sun was still hot and the sky a clear blue, dotted with the silver barrage elephants. Khaki, navy-blue and airforce-blue uniforms contrasted with city suits and rolled umbrellas as Jennie strolled along Regent Street among the crowds. She felt elated, her step light and bouncy, and in a moment of euphoria she decided to go into Lyon's Corner House at Piccadilly Circus for a coffee. She had never been in the establishment before, and little did she know then that it was a decision she would look back on fondly for the rest of her life.

CHAPTER 6

On Saturday afternoon Daisy Harris collected her shoes from the menders and then called next door. Albert was serving a customer who seemed unsure about the torch bulb he was buying. 'It's a bit bright,' he remarked as Albert tested it on a battery.

'It's the one you'll want,' the shopowner told him. 'It'll be all right as long as you put tissue-paper over it.'

While Daisy waited she glanced around at the new wirelesses. Her old set was run from a large battery and grid bias and she had been getting on to Bill for ages now to fork out for one of those push-button sets. There was one on the top shelf which looked very smart.

'Afternoon, Mr Levy,' she said as the satisfied customer left the shop.

'Afternoon, Mrs Harris,' Albert said smiling. 'Not after a new wireless, are you?'

'As a matter o' fact I was lookin' at that push-button one yer got up there, but first fings first,' she replied. 'Me an' Bill 'ave bin cleanin' Abel's rooms out an' we found this.' She took the brown paper bundle from her large handbag.

'It was under the oil-cloth, well actually, under a loose floorboard. We're changin' the oil-cloth yer see or we'd never 'ave found it.'

Albert took the small bundle from her and unwrapped it. 'A diary. Abel's diary,' he said excitedly, his dark eyes widening. 'That's very interesting.'

'Me an' Bill thought you should 'ave it, you bein' very close ter the poor man,' Daisy told him.

'I'm grateful to you for thinking of me,' Albert replied, flipping quickly through the pages. 'Abel wrote in Yiddish, as you probably noticed.'

'We never looked inside, Mr Levy,' Daisy said quickly. 'It wouldn't 'ave bin right. Diaries are very personal fings, as I told Bill. No, we wrapped it up again straight away.'

Albert laid it down reverently on the shelf behind him and turned back to Mrs Harris. 'I don't think Abel would mind very much if I read his notes, do you?'

'I'm sure 'e wouldn't,' Daisy replied.

'Now, Mrs Harris, about a new wireless. Let me show you this one. It's the latest Phillips model and I could do you a reasonable discount.'

Daisy watched while Albert took the radio down from the top shelf and placed it in front of her. 'The case is made of strong Bakelite which wears very well,' he informed her as he quickly ran a duster over it. 'It's a mains set. You have got electricity in the house?'

Daisy nodded. 'Yeah, it was put in about five years ago.'

'Well then, this set also has a magic eye.'

'A magic eye?' Daisy echoed, looking confused.

'Let me show you,' Albert said, plugging the set into a power-point. 'There we are. Now when you find a station you watch that green light and when the two lights go into one that means that it's fine-tuned. In other words the reception will be nice and clear. There we are, can you see?'

'That's very clever,' Daisy remarked, stroking her chin.

'Now here's another feature,' Albert went on. 'These push buttons here. You get certain stations by just pressing them in, like so.'

'Well, I never did,' Daisy said, by now sold on the new radio.

'This new model is priced at twenty-two guineas, but I can knock two guineas off for you. How does that sound?'

'Do you do it on the book?' Daisy asked.

Albert nodded and made a few quick calculations. 'Let me see,' he said. 'If you can pay one pound seventeen and six down it'll work out at eighteen and a tanner per month over two years, that's with the interest as well. If you decide to buy the set on instalments your husband would need to sign the agreement.'

Daisy left the shop promising to fetch Bill straight away, and although he was alone once more Albert resisted the temptation to look inside Abel's diary. It would be better to wait until later, he told himself. It was something better broached in the quiet of evening with a large brandy at hand.

When Jennie walked into the Lyon's Corner House she saw it was fairly packed, but she managed to find a small table near the window and sat down to wait for the waitress to take her order. It had been a crazy day all in all, she thought, but the feeling of freedom, of having to plan what to do next was exciting and she smiled to herself. Suddenly she realised that a young soldier sitting alone a few tables away was eyeing her with amusement. She gave him a cold look and turned away to stare out of the window. After a moment or two she sensed someone next to her and turned to see him standing by her table. 'I'm sorry to disturb yer,' he said quickly, 'but I 'ad to admire the way yer dealt wiv that ugly ole witch this afternoon. I thought you 'andled it really well.'

'You were there?' Jennie asked in surprise.

'Yeah, I saw yer storm off an' I called out well done, or words ter that effect,' the soldier said grinning.

She grinned back at him. 'That's right, I remember catchin' a glimpse of yer.'

'I was in Jones an' Whatleys ter buy a present but I never got it,' he told her. 'By the way, I don't wanna interrupt yer if yer meetin' anyone.'

Jennie shook her head. 'No, I'm takin' a break before I catch the bus 'ome,' she replied. 'Sit down if yer like, unless you're meetin' someone.'

80

He shook his head as he sat down facing her. 'Fanks. I was beginnin' ter feel conspicuous on me own.'

'Yeah, I don't like comin' in these sort o' places on me own eivver,' Jennie agreed.

He smiled showing strong white teeth, and his eyes were laughing. 'I 'ope they didn't give yer the sack.'

'Jones an' Whatleys couldn't do anyfing else,' she replied mockingly, 'but I consider meself well out of it.'

'Well, I'm glad I didn't get that present there now,' he remarked. 'By the way, I'm Con, Con Williams, currently Private Williams of the Rifle Brigade.'

'Jennie Flynn, currently unemployed,' she responded with a smile.

'Really it's Conrad, but everybody calls me Con,' the young soldier told her. 'Gawd knows 'ow I ever got 'iked up wiv that moniker. Me dad must 'ave bin drunk at the time.'

'It's an unusual name but a nice one, though I prefer Con,' Jennie replied.

A tired-looking waitress came over and stood staring at them, and Con looked enquiringly at Jennie. 'I just wanted a coffee,' he said.

'Yeah me, too,' she answered.

'Two coffees it is then.'

As Con watched the waitress hurrying away Jennie looked at him. He couldn't be much more than twenty-two or three, she guessed. He had a smooth face with no sign of stubble and his fair hair was cut short. His nose was small and straight and he had a strong, square chin. His eyes were his most striking feature though, Jennie thought. They were a very pale blue, almost grey, and they shone kindly.

'Who were you buyin' the present for?' she asked as he turned to face her again.

Con's face grew sad. 'As a matter o' fact I was after gettin' a silk scarf fer me Gran. I live wiv 'er or I did, till I got mobilised.'

'Mobilised?'

'Yeah, I was in the territorials, an' as soon as the war started they called us inter the colours,' he explained. 'Most of my lot 'ave gone ter France already but I got delayed 'cos I 'ad ter take compassionate leave when me gran got ill wiv pleurisy. She's over it now but she's very miserable. I was gonna get 'er a scarf. It might 'elp cheer 'er up a bit.'

Jennie felt a sudden warmth towards the young man and she nodded in agreement. 'Your gran's a lucky woman to 'ave someone like you ter take care of 'er.'

Con looked out of the window for a few moments and when their eyes met again she could see that he was still upset by it. 'They've looked after me since I was knee-'igh to a grass'opper,' he said quietly. 'My mum died when I was five an' me dad was in the merchant navy. I 'ardly knew 'im. 'E married again apparently an' last I 'eard 'e was livin' in Glasgow.'

' 'Ave yer got any bruvvers or sisters?' Jennie asked.

'There was a bruvver two years younger than

82

me but 'e died o' diphtheria when 'e was two,'
Con replied.

The waitress came over with a laden tray and
Con quickly picked up the bill and slipped it
into his tunic pocket. 'Wanna be mum?' he said
grinning.

Jennie filled the two cups from the squat
coffee pot and passed one across the table.
'Where d'yer live, Con?' she asked.

'Dock'ead.'

'I live in Bermon'sey,' she told him. 'Carter
Lane, off the Old Kent Road.'

'That's not far from me, is it?' he replied.

'Only a stone's throw.'

' 'Ave you got a family?'

'Three bruvvers, one sister.'

'That's nice.'

'Me mum an' dad are really worried,' Jennie
went on as she poured milk into the hot coffee.
'Me bruvs are all waitin' ter go in. They all
volunteered soon as the war started.'

'The army?'

'Frank an' Jim the eldest two are goin' in
the army but Patrick, the baby o' the family,
signed on fer the RAF. 'E's dead set on bein'
aircrew.'

'I'd sooner 'im than me,' Con replied as he
ladled two large spoonfuls of sugar into his cup.

'So yer still gotta buy a present,' Jennie said
sipping her coffee.

'I dunno if a scarf's the right fing ter get,
now I come ter fink of it,' he said sighing.
'What can yer buy fer an ole lady who never
'ardly goes out?'

83

'Does she take snuff?' Jennie said helpfully but Con shook his head. 'What about slippers? Carpet slippers?'

'I don't know 'er size,' the young soldier replied.

'Well, what about a nice shawl? A bright colour might 'elp ter cheer 'er up a bit.'

Con's eyes lit up. 'Of course. A shawl. She wears a shawl all the time an' it's really tatty.'

'Don't get it over 'ere though, yer'd pay frew the nose,' Jennie advised him. 'There's some good ones at the markets. East Lane's the best, on Sundays.'

'I'd 'ave time,' Con said nodding. ' 'Er birfday's not till next Tuesday an' I don't go back until Monday mornin'.'

Jennie finished her coffee and glanced up at the clock. 'Well, I'd better be goin' or me mum's gonna be worried where I've got to,' she told him reluctantly.

Con nodded. 'Yeah me too, or Gran's gonna get all worried. There's me a fightin' soldier an' she's worried in case I get knocked down or somefing, would yer believe?'

Jennie laughed. 'It's bin really nice talkin' to yer,' she remarked.

'Yeah, it's bin really good,' he said. 'I 'ope yer boyfriend doesn't get to hear about it.'

She shook her head. 'No, I'm not courtin' at the moment.'

'Could I ...' Con hesitated for a second or two. 'Could I ask yer somefing?'

'Yeah, sure.'

84

'Would yer like ter come fer a drink termorrer night?'

'Yes, I'd like that very much,' she told him with a smile.

His eyes flashed happily. 'Where shall we meet?'

'You could call round if yer like.'

'Yeah, I'd like to.'

'Number eleven Carter Lane.'

'Is eight o'clock okay?'

'That'll be fine,' she replied.

Con counted out some silver and put the coins on the small silver tray at his elbow, adding a shilling tip, and then as they stood up he chuckled. 'I fink we're goin' the same way 'ome, ain't we?'

Jennie nodded and gave him a quick shy smile as they walked out into the busy street. 'I usually get a fifty-three bus ter the Old Kent Road,' she told him.

'Yeah, I could do that an' change at the Bricklayers Arms,' he replied.

A large queue had formed at the bus stop but two buses came along together and they managed to get on the second one. They found a seat on the upper deck at the rear and chatted casually as the vehicle crawled through the heavy rush-hour traffic. All too soon it seemed the bus pulled up at the Bricklayers Arms, and as Con slipped out of his seat he laid his hand on her arm. 'I promise not ter be late,' he said with a grin, then he was gone.

Much later that evening Albert Levy took

advantage of Gerda's trip to the women's meeting at the local synagogue by pouring himself a very large brandy. Gerda would have been horrified, he thought with a smile. She felt that brandy speeded up the heart rate too much and preferred him to confine his intake to a tiny glass with coffee after an evening meal. But this one he sorely needed. The diary was lying on the small table beside the divan as though mocking him, daring him to open it and peer into the very soul of his old friend Abel Finkelstein. Taking a deep breath, Albert settled himself and picked it up, certain that his heart was not beating faster because of the brandy.

At ten o'clock Gerda came home and sighed sadly as she sat down alongside Albert on the large divan. 'It was very depressing and it's left me with a splitting headache,' she told him. 'We were discussing the possibility of forming a group to try to help the Jewish people in the occupied countries and Germany itself, but it seems there's very little we can do except try to work with the Red Cross.'

Albert grunted a reply and Gerda kicked off her shoes. 'I need something for this headache,' she said, preparing to get up.

Albert grunted again and Gerda gave him a hard look. 'Normally you get me some tablets,' she complained.

'I'm sorry, dear, I was miles away,' he said quickly as he stood up. 'I'll get them for you, you just relax and put your feet up.'

When he came back with the medication Gerda noticed the worried look on his face. 'Is there anything wrong?' she asked. 'You don't look yourself.'

Albert sat down heavily and waited until his wife had swallowed the tablets. 'How long were Abel and I friends?' he asked her. 'Ten years? Fifteen years? No, we were friends from the first day at school, when we held each other's hand, friends until the day Abel took his life. A lifetime of friendship, true and steadfast throughout all the persecution, a friendship that would last beyond the grave, or so I believed.'

'Albert. What is it?' Gerda asked, beginning to feel frightened.

'It's all there. There in the diary that Abel left behind,' he replied. 'I just can't believe it. After all I did to obtain his release from that concentration camp, and the problems I faced in getting him over here, and to find out after his death that it counted for nothing.'

'Albert, please. Whatever's wrong?'

'Wrong? I'll tell you what's wrong,' Albert replied with his eyes flaring and his breath coming fast. 'My good, old friend of a lifetime, Abel Finkelstein, has been unburdening himself in his diary.'

Gerda slumped down in the divan. 'The diary?'

'The diary,' he repeated. 'It's all there, plain and simple. Abel has betrayed our friendship.'

'Where is it?' Gerda asked.

'It's in my desk drawer.'

'I want to see it.'

'Not tonight,' he said firmly. 'Tomorrow we'll look at it together and you'll see. Then it will be time for a decision. Do we go ahead with the memorial plaque? I don't see how we can. It would be sacrilege.'

'What was so terrible to make you talk like this?' she asked him. 'What has he said?'

'It's what he has done,' Albert said bitterly. 'Abel has been robbing me. Systematically robbing me. For years!'

CHAPTER 7

Sara and Tom Jackman were a genial couple who worked long hours in their grocery shop on the corner of Carter Lane. Tom had taken over the business from his father more than fifteen years before when it got too much for the old man to manage. He was forty years old then and still single, but six months later he married a widow Sara Viney, the daughter of a local market trader, and people immediately started to talk. Many felt that Sara was marrying Tom for his money and believed the shop would fail with her working behind the counter of the old family concern. What they didn't know was that the shop was failing anyway and that Tom had inherited a lot of debt.

Sara proved everybody wrong and it was largely due to her shrewd management that the shop was finally transformed into a little goldmine. She worked very hard to win over the locals and from grudging admiration they came to genuinely like her.

Now in their mid-fifties the Jackmans were working harder than ever, what with food rationing and customer registration. Almost everyone in Carter Lane and the adjoining Brady Street and Munday Road registered at the corner shop and there was hardly a time when there wasn't a queue waiting to get served. It was only natural for people to chat while they queued, and it was at the corner store that the locals picked up all the latest gossip. Tom Jackman shut his ears to most of the chatter but Sara was inclined to store the juicy titbits in her head and pass them on to a select few whenever she could. There was no malice intended on her part, only a sense of being neighbourly and communicative towards her loyal customers.

Bill Harris knew all that was going on in the immediate area from listening to Daisy and he had dubbed the store 'The Ministry of Information'. He was always prepared for some bit of news whenever his wife came in with the groceries and normally it went in one ear and out the other. He ignored his wife's lengthy account of Mrs Bromilow's heartbreak at being forced to leave the leather factory and he didn't even raise his eyes from the paper when he heard about Alice Smithson's daughter leaving home, but he did show some interest when Daisy told him about the Conroys' boy. Ted Conroy was a drinking pal and many a time Bill had lent a supportive ear to his family problems, which mostly concerned Ted's son Alec.

'Rene Conroy's worried out of 'er life,' Daisy began. 'She said Alec's told 'er an' Ted that 'e's definitely not goin' in the forces an' if they want 'im they'll 'ave ter come an' get 'im.'

'That's exactly what they will do, make no mistake,' Bill told her.

'Rene said Alec's goin' on twenty-four an' 'e'll be in the first batch ter get called up,' Daisy went on. 'It's a bloody shame what 'er an' Ted 'ave ter put up wiv. Alec's never bin any good. 'E was in Borstal at twelve years old an' then 'e got two years fer that trouble over in Dock'ead. Sara said they might not take 'im, what wiv 'is prison record an' all.'

'They'll take 'im right enough, don't you worry about that,' Bill said firmly. 'If 'e refuses ter go they'll send a military escort, an' if 'e don't knuckle down to it they'll stick 'im in an army detention centre, an' then 'e'll know all about it. They're not as soft as civvy prisons, not by a long chalk.'

'Sara was sayin' about the shame Alec was bringin' down on Rene an' Ted,' Daisy continued. 'Rene said she wouldn't be able to 'old 'er 'ead up in the street, what wiv everyone else's sons goin' in the forces.'

'Well, it ain't 'er an' Ted's fault, not the way I see it,' Bill commented. 'They've tried ter do their best fer the boy but 'e's just a bad apple.'

Daisy had some more intriguing snippets for Bill but he'd heard enough for one day and he gave her one of his special looks which told her it was time to shut up and put the kettle on.

90

Albert Levy sat alongside Gerda in their comfortable living room and shook his head slowly as she read out the entry for the second of January in Abel's diary.

'An encouraging start to the year. Fifteen shillings is not much, but trade has been very slack since the Christmas break so I have to be careful. It's best that I carry on the way I left off last year.'

'Look at the end of January,' Albert told her. 'No, turn over again. Just there, look.'

'One pound seven and sixpence this week. Things are beginning to look up. Must still be on my guard though.'

Gerda glanced up and saw the sad look in her husband's dark eyes. 'It seems hard to believe,' she sighed. 'After all you did for the man.'

Albert took the diary from her and flipped the pages. 'Every week without fail,' he said. 'Look at this entry here. March the fifth.'

'It was a little distressing to hear Albert talk about that new automatic till on the market. If he does get one of them it'll make things very difficult. Apparently every transaction is recorded. He'll know his daily takings to the last penny.'

'I should have got one of those new tills,'

Albert growled. 'That would have stopped his little game.'

Gerda took the diary back from Albert and turned some more pages. 'I'm not so sure about that, if you read this bit,' she pointed out.

'Albert's been going on again about the new till. Still never mind, there's more than one way to skin a cat, as they say. Customers don't always notice what's being rung up and if they did query the price it could always be put right. Have to be careful of the stocks though. Albert knows his stock. Very rarely runs out of anything.'

'According to that he's been filching my stocks too,' Albert groaned. 'But I've never noticed any unaccountable shortages in the shop.'

'Well, I'm sure I don't know,' Gerda replied. 'I just find it so hard to believe.'

'It's all there in black and white,' Albert told her. 'I've totalled it all up until the last entry at the end of August. It comes to almost forty pounds. Then there's the previous years, or at least one year that he referred to. God knows how much he's taken me for.'

Gerda got up and went over to the sideboard where she poured her distraught husband a large brandy. Normally it would have been a very small tot, but tonight he looked like he needed more.

Jennie Flynn sat on the edge of Sadie's bed while her elder sister rummaged through her wardrobe. 'What's the name o' the club?' she asked her.

'The Black Cat,' Sadie replied. 'It's a big do ternight an' Len wants me ter look me best.'

'Oh 'e does, does 'e,' Jennie said scornfully. 'Is that what 'e said? Well, I fink 'e's got a bloody cheek. You always look yer best when yer go out.'

' 'E didn't mean nuffink by it,' Sadie was quick to point out. 'There's a lot of important people comin' ternight an' Len wants me ter circulate around. You know the fing, keep 'em topped up wiv drinks an' make small talk.'

'Who are these important people?' Jennie asked her.

Sadie hung the black dress she had picked out on the door of the wardrobe and sat down on the dressing-table stool. 'They're mainly business people wiv money ter burn,' she explained. 'Some are down 'ere from Glasgow an' Liverpool an' it's all about puttin' money in the venture.'

'The Black Cat?' Jennie queried.

'Yeah. Johnnie Macaulay's turnin' it into a gamblin' club,' Sadie went on. 'Trouble is 'e can't get a gamblin' licence so it's all cloak an' dagger stuff.'

' 'Ow excitin',' Jennie said with sarcasm.

'You don't like Len Regan, do yer?' Sadie remarked, her eyes narrowing slightly.

Jennie shrugged her shoulders. 'I've only seen 'im a couple o' times when 'e's called round, but I worry fer you,' she said earnestly. 'It all seems like the roarin' twenties films ter me. Gamblin', nightclubs, an' Regan doin' the biddin' of the big man Macaulay who seems ter be runnin' everyfing round 'ere. The impression I get is that Macaulay's nuffink more than a gangster an' you're bein' drawn inter that way o' life by 'is messenger boy Len Regan.'

'Len's not a messenger boy, 'e's Johnnie Macaulay's manager, an' 'e's got respect round 'ere,' Sadie replied defensively.

Jennie stood up and went over to her elder sister. 'We've always bin close, Sadie, an' I'm concerned for yer,' she said, resting her hand on her shoulder. 'I don't want ter see yer get 'urt.'

Sadie stood up and gave her a quick squeeze. 'Don't worry, sis, I can look after meself. I'm a Flynn don't ferget.'

Jennie smiled and turned to view herself in the full-length mirror on the wardrobe door. 'D'yer fink I'm puttin' on weight?' she asked.

Sadie chuckled as she appraised her sister's trim figure and small firm breasts. She was at least half a stone heavier with large breasts and a more round figure. 'I wished I looked like you,' she remarked.

'Funny, I always wish I looked like you,' Jennie told her. 'Me breasts are too small. You've got nice curves an' yer legs look really shapely, 'specially in yer 'igh 'eels.'

'So do yours.'

'D'yer really fink so?'

'I wouldn't tell yer if it wasn't true.'

'D'yer like the way I've done me 'air?' Jennie asked.

Sadie nodded. 'I like it short, 'specially the way yer got it set round yer ears. Redheads can get away wiv short 'air.'

'Yours looks very nice too,' Jennie replied, admiring the black dress as she stroked the fabric.

'I'm lettin' it grow a bit,' Sadie told her. 'I want it shoulder-length, then I'm gonna get one o' those wavy perms.'

'Yer'll really be a roarin' twenties gel then,' Jennie said grinning. 'I 'ope you can do the Charleston.'

Sadie smiled and went over to the wardrobe again. 'I dunno about this dress. D'yer fink this one looks better fer a special occasion?'

Jennie pinched her lip as she looked at the silver-grey dress Sadie was holding up. 'Yeah, I like that one better,' she remarked. 'I like the way it's cut at the front.'

'Right then, I'll wear it,' Sadie decided. 'You can borrer the black one ternight if yer like. It'll fit yer. I 'ave ter squeeze into it anyway.'

Jennie shook her head. 'I'm only goin' ter the pub fer a drink,' she replied. 'I don't wanna shock 'im wiv that low front.'

Sadie sat down at the dressing table and picked up a nail file. 'What's this Con Williams like? Is 'e good-lookin'?'

Jennie nodded. 'I fink so. 'E's a bit taller than me an' 'e's stocky like our Frank. 'E's got a nice smile an' 'e's ever so friendly. Yer'll be able ter take a gander when 'e calls, that's if yer still 'ere.'

'What time's 'e callin' for yer?' Sadie asked.

'Eight o'clock.'

'That's all right. Len's pickin' me up at nine.'

'An' no oglin' 'im,' Jennie warned with a smile.

'As if I would,' Sadie replied with a sly look.

Jennie sat on the edge of the bed for a while, watching Sadie manicure her fingernails, and then she got up to look down into the quiet evening street below. 'It seems 'ard ter realise there's a war on,' she remarked.

Sadie nodded. 'I feel the same way when I'm out wiv Len. The places we go to are full o' people gettin' drunk an' chuckin' their money about. There's not a uniform in sight an' no one ever mentions the war.'

'It's all gonna blow up soon, I feel certain,' Jennie said quietly. 'People are gonna 'ave ter take notice then.'

'D'yer reckon we'll get bombed?' Sadie asked.

'I'm sure of it,' Jennie replied.

'Yeah, I fink so too,' Sadie said, studying her nails.

'By the way, 'as Len said any more about that job 'e was gonna try an' get yer?'

Sadie shook her head. ' 'E's bin so busy lately, but 'e won't ferget.'

'Long as it's not workin' in one o' those clubs of Macaulay's,' Jennie said. 'Still that wouldn't be classed as essential war-work, would it? Or would it? Comforts fer the troops.'

'Officers more like,' Sadie corrected her.

Jennie looked out again through the crisp net

96

curtaining. 'There's Alec Conroy goin' past,' she said. 'Did you 'ear what Mum was sayin' about 'im?'

Sadie nodded. 'Not many round 'ere 'ave anyfing good ter say about 'im but I don't fink 'e's as bad as 'e's painted out ter be. All right, I know 'e's bin ter Borstal an' done time in prison, but 'e's kept out o' trouble fer some time now an' 'e's got a regular job.'

'The trouble is 'e ain't gonna endear 'imself ter people if 'e refuses call-up,' Jennie remarked.

'I s'pose there'll be a few white feavvers bein' sent frew the post before long,' Sadie said. 'Dad was tellin' me it was common in the First World War. They even sent 'em to people who weren't fit ter go in the army. If it 'appens again, I expect Len'll get one.'

'Will 'e be liable for call-up?' Jennie asked.

'Well 'e's firty-five so 'e's got a bit o' time yet,' Sadie replied. 'I fink it all depends on 'ow long the war lasts. If all 'ell breaks loose an' there's a lot o' casualties then they'll call up older men.'

'All this talk's beginnin' ter get me depressed,' Jennie groaned. 'Tell me somefing nice.'

Sadie chuckled at her childish expression. 'Get out of 'ere an' let me finish gettin' ready,' she said, pointing to the door.

Jennie was loath to move. 'Why? Yer've got till nine.'

'Shouldn't you be gettin' ready?' Sadie pressed.

'It's only twenty past seven,' her younger

97

sister replied. 'I've only gotta slip inter somefing allurin'.'

' 'Ere, you watch yerself,' Sadie said, getting up from her stool. 'Now leave me alone an' go an' worry yer bruvs.'

As soon as she was alone Sadie sat down again at the dressing table and stared at her image in the mirror. There was no chance of ever getting married as long as she was with Len, and lately it seemed to be hard work keeping his attention when they were socialising. He always had things to do, people to take care of and negotiations to be undertaken. Len's life wasn't his own, he was at the beck and call of Johnnie Macaulay twenty-four hours a day. At the moment everything was going well, but it could all change and the loyalty and dedication shown by Len would count for nothing if a scapegoat was needed. Donna Walsh had said as much when they were talking together not so long ago. Donna had been close to Len at one time and it was rumoured that they had been lovers. It mattered very little to Sadie. It was before her time and now Donna Walsh was bloated with drink and pushing forty. She worked as a barmaid in one of Macaulay's pubs, the Royal George in Rotherhithe, and whenever Len took Sadie there Donna made a point of waylaying her for a chat. Donna truly felt that Johnnie Macaulay was overstretching himself and the day would come when it would all blow up in his face.

Much as she wanted to discount Donna's

predictions Sadie felt obliged to listen at least. Donna had the ear of many of the local villains and in her view it was not all sweetness and light within the Macaulay empire.

CHAPTER 8

Con Williams felt a little awkward, fiddling with the knot of his striped tie while he waited on the doorstep of number 11, and when Dolly answered his knock he gave her a shy smile. 'I er, I ...'

'You must be Con,' Dolly said cheerily. 'Jennie'll be down in a minute. Won't yer come in?'

The young man followed her into the parlour. 'It's a warm evenin',' he said as he returned Mick's nod.

'Take a pew, son,' the older man bade him as Dolly went to the foot of the stairs and called up to Jennie. 'Yer in the army then?'

'Yeah, the Rifle Brigade.'

Mick nodded. 'That's an old East End regiment. Are you from over the water?'

'No, I was in the territorials at the Dock'ead depot an' they mobilised us inter the Rifle Brigade,' Con told him.

Mick nodded. 'Jennie tells me yer goin' back termorrer an' you expect ter go off ter France very soon.'

'It's pretty certain,' the young man replied.

'We're gonna be part o' the British Expeditionary Force.'

'Well good luck ter yer, son,' Mick said as Jennie came bounding into the parlour.

'I 'ope yer've not bin grilled about the army,' she said smiling.

'It's a good job our lads are out or 'e would 'ave bin,' Mick said, turning back to Con. 'Me sons are waitin' fer their call-up, did she tell yer?'

'Yes, I did,' Jennie remarked. 'I'm ready, Con, shall we go?'

'Don't be too late,' Mick called out as she led the way out into the passage.

Jennie raised her eyes in mock horror. 'Don't they make yer sick,' she groaned. 'It's the weekend, fer God's sake.'

They walked out of the turning in the balmy evening and Con smiled at her. 'I was finkin' we could try The Boatman down by the river,' he said. 'It's pretty lively at weekends.'

'Why not?' Jennie replied lightly.

As they walked over the railway bridge towards Jamaica Road the young man turned to her. 'It's a bit of a walk. We could get a bus.'

'No, let's walk, it's a lovely evenin',' she replied. 'Can I take yer arm?'

Con's face lit up. 'Yeah, course. I wanted yer to.'

After a short distance she asked, 'Did yer manage ter get that shawl fer yer gran?'

He pulled a face. 'I fink I got the wrong colour,' he told her. 'She always wears black fings so I decided to get 'er a nice bright one

100

fer a change. Anyway I saw this green shawl on a stall at East Lane so I took a chance. When I got 'ome I wrapped it up in some fancy paper ter put by 'er bed before I leave termorrer, but then I got finkin'—s'posin' she doesn't like the colour—so I gave it to 'er straight away.'

'An' did she say she liked it?'

'Oh yeah, but the look on 'er face gave 'er away.'

'She'll get used to it, I'm sure,' Jennie said, taken by the young man's thoughtfulness.

They crossed Jamaica Road and ambled on towards the river, breathing in the sour smell of mud and the pungent tang of spice and pepper seeping from the creaky old warehouses in Shad Thames.

' 'Ave yer decided what yer gonna do next?' Con asked.

Jennie shook her head. 'I might get some shop work fer the time bein',' she told him. 'There's a job goin' in the local baker's.'

They could hear piano music coming from the pub up ahead and Con smiled. 'They've started early by the sound of it.'

As they walked into the saloon bar Jennie looked around at the pewter pots and pans hanging from the tarred rafters and saw the old prints arranged along the walls. 'This is nice,' she remarked.

Con nodded towards the elderly woman pianist as they reached the counter. 'That's Sal Terry,' he said quietly. 'She used ter be on the stage.'

He ordered a pint of bitter for himself but

Jennie only wanted a shandy, and after they had been served their drinks by a disinterested barman they found a vacant table in a dimly lit alcove. Old men sat around on the long padded bench by the wall, one or two with clay pipes hanging from their mouths, and younger customers lounged at the counter or sat in the other alcoves by windows.

'I like these old riverside pubs,' Jennie grinned.

Con looked at her, his eyes appraising her pretty face and shining red hair. 'Do you really?' he replied. 'I was wonderin' if it might be too scruffy for yer.'

She laughed, her white teeth flashing in the low light of the alcove. 'I always reckon it's not where you are but who you're wiv that counts,' she said with emphasis.

'I wish I 'ad more time ter get ter know yer,' he said, running the tip of his forefinger round the rim of his glass. 'I loved the way yer dealt wiv that woman in the store an' I wanted ter tell yer there an' then, but when yer marched off I thought, well Con, yer missed yer chance there, didn't yer? Seein' you again in that Lyon's corner 'ouse was like fate. It gave me anuvver chance ter make yer acquaintance, an' I wasn't gonna pass it up.'

'I'm glad yer didn't,' Jennie said quietly.

'Can I ask yer somefing?'

'Yeah, course.'

' 'Ave yer got any photos of yerself?'

'One or two, but not wiv me,' she replied.

He thought for a moment. 'Would it be askin'

102

too much fer you ter give me a photo?'

She chuckled. 'You really want a picture o' me?'

'I really do.'

'I could send one on, I s'pose.'

He smiled happily. 'If you address it ter Rifleman C Williams, Second Battalion, Rifle Brigade, BEF France it'll reach me. By the way, yer'll need me army number. I don't s'pose yer've got a pen, 'ave yer?'

She shook her head, then fished into her small handbag. 'Right, pay packet, lipstick,' she said triumphantly. 'Tell me your army number.'

Con rattled it off, shaking his head at her improvisation. 'You amaze me,' he said.

'Why?'

'Yer just do.'

Jennie was pleased with the compliment and she relaxed a little in her seat. He was nice to be with, and unlike some of the other young men she had dated he appeared to be more interested in her than in himself. ' 'Ave yer dated many girls?' she asked suddenly.

The question caused him to flush up a little and he shook his head. 'Not many,' he admitted. 'I seem to 'ave spent more time in men's company this last two years.'

'What made yer join the territorials?' she enquired.

Con studied his clasped hands for a few moments as he thought about how to explain properly. 'I'm not sure,' he began, 'an' I'm not avoidin' the question, but it's difficult ter put into words. Every night when I came 'ome

103

from work the 'ouse was quiet. The ole lady was usually noddin' in the armchair an' the place seemed dark an' gloomy. There was little or no conversation, an' I gradually felt like I was losin' somefing. It wasn't like a family 'ouse where there's noise an' laughter, an' bruvvers an' sisters ter chat wiv. I used ter make us a meal an' clear the place up a bit, then I'd sit wiv 'er, listenin' while she talked about when she was a young woman an' all about the 'ard life she 'ad, an' slowly I got more an' more depressed. I was beginnin' ter feel like an ole man meself. Can you understand?'

She nodded. 'I fink I can.'

'A pal at work told me 'e'd joined the terriers,' Con went on. ' 'E told me all about the good time 'e was 'avin' an' I thought, that's fer me. So I signed on. I went ter the drill 'all two nights a week an' then there was the odd weekend camp. I was wiv ovver people my age an' it lifted me more than I can tell yer. It wasn't as though I was neglectin' me gran. I still took care of 'er an' there was the woman next door who I paid ter look after 'er personal needs. Course I didn't realise at the time that I'd be mobilised, well not at first, but I guessed it'd come, if fings did deteriorate. Now I'm in the regular army, but nuffink's changed. The woman next door still looks after me gran an' there's the welfare people who come ter see 'er every so often.'

Jennie had been staring into his pale blue eyes all the time he was talking and she was suddenly assailed by a strange sadness that seemed to flow through her. There was something there in the

104

young man's eyes that burned like a beacon and it melted her heart. She heard the singer, the tinkling piano and the clatter of glasses but it seemed far away, a vague cacophony of sounds muted behind glass. It felt as if time was standing still, and she shivered to break the spell. 'Yer gran'll be all right,' she said, but the words sounded flat and cold, and she quickly added, 'I'm sure it was the right move back then, even though yer've bin mobilised. If you 'adn't joined the terriers you'd 'ave bin called up anyway sooner or later.'

He nodded, and suddenly he reached out his hand and gently touched hers. 'I'll be finkin' about yer all the time I'm away,' he said in a quiet voice. 'Will yer give me a thought now an' then?'

'Yes, I will,' Jennie replied with a smile.

The young man collected the two glasses and walked over to the counter and Jennie quickly straightened her dress before searching her handbag for her powder compact. The evening was going well, better than she had expected and there were so many more questions she wanted to ask him.

When he returned to the alcove and set the drinks down on the polished table he smiled at her. 'This one's on the 'ouse. Sammy the landlord knows I'm goin' back off leave termorrer.'

'That's nice of 'im,' she replied.

Con nodded. 'This is where I bring me gran sometimes, when she's feelin' able. She likes a milk stout. Ses it bucks 'er up.'

Jennie could see him now, holding on to the old lady, fussing over her and getting her comfortable in a seat and she smiled back at him. 'I fink your gran's very lucky to 'ave you look after 'er needs,' she told him.

'It's no more than she deserves,' he replied. 'She looked after me when I was a kid, when there was no one else. If it wasn't fer 'er I'd 'ave ended up in some children's 'ome.'

'You're a nice man, Con,' she said.

He flushed slightly, two spots showing on his pale cheeks and he averted his eyes for a few moments. 'I fink you're very nice too,' he said.

Sal Terry had been suitably fortified with her usual concoction and she pounded the keys with determination. People were singing loudly, and when Sal struck up with 'Knees up Mother Brown', two elderly ladies decided to demonstrate their dancing skills. Jennie and Con were forced to raise their voices over the din as they chatted happily, and in no time at all the bell sounded for last orders.

'I've really enjoyed this evenin',' Jennie said as they left the little riverside pub.

'I can't remember a better one,' Con replied.

'Can we go an' look at the river fer a while?' she asked.

A full moon hung in the velvet sky like an everlasting lantern and stars glimmered at the periphery of its pale glow. The dark river was at low tide, still and calm before its cold, muddy waters flowed back in again. From their vantage point at the river wall the young people could see Tower Bridge framed against the blacked-out City of London, and downriver a brace of barges rocked gently on their moorings in midstream, before the darkness deepened towards Galleon's Reach. The two held hands as they gazed out at the scene, sensing the fragility of this moment in time for their hometown, their homeland, and with a subtle movement Con turned to face her. Like gentle magnets their bodies slowly joined together and their lips met in the tenderest of kisses. Her sweet breath excited him and he pulled her closer and tighter, and feeling the controlled strength of his arms and the flat pressure of his hands on her back she let the hungry embrace possess her.

Con glanced up at the moon for a brief second or two as they moved apart and his handsome face was smiling. 'It was 'is fault,' he said. 'Just look at 'im grinnin'.'

As Jennie looked up into the night sky she saw the dusty cloud moving across the white face like a stage curtain at the end of a scene. 'Who d'yer blame on moonless nights?' she said smiling.

'The first star.'

'Can we do it again?' she asked, surprised at her own daring.

He pulled her gently to him and very slowly touched her lips with his. He could feel her warmth and the sweet taste of her, and he encircled her waist with his arms as the kiss grew in passion. He relished the sensation of her hands on his neck, her body pressed unashamedly to him and he knew then that he was holding the woman of his dreams.

As heavy cloud moved in, the blackness of a capital at war deepened around them, and now only the sour smell of river mud told them where they were. They finally set off, along the cobbled lane that led into Dockland, and neither spoke as they enjoyed a silent reverie of their moonlight embrace.

Carter Lane was empty and quiet, and the two young people lingered for some time at Jennie's front door.

'Will you write to me?' he asked.

'Every day,' she said.

'Will you send me that photo?'

'The best one I can find.'

'Will yer fink of me some times?'

'All the time.'

It was time to say goodnight and they embraced, a soft, gentle kiss tingling with an electric emotion, then Con stepped back to look at her, to brand the image of her into his mind, and he took her by the hands. 'Do you believe in God?' he asked.

'I say my prayers every night,' she told him.

'Pray fer me, Jennie, an' I'll pray fer us,' he said.

They kissed again, briefly, then she waited at the door until his footsteps faded in the blackness, and that night, as she lay sleepless in her bed, Jennie marvelled at the way the evening had gone. She hardly knew him. It was a first date that she would have expected to end with a nervous peck that had to suffice for a goodnight kiss. But they had kissed as lovers, talked together intimately and discovered a bond that would span the distance between them, binding them together until the day when they could once again walk hand in hand by the river and challenge the mocking moon.

CHAPTER 9

Early on Thursday morning the postman pushed two letters through the letterbox of number 11, and as Dolly Flynn picked them up her heart sank. The letters OHMS told her the worst and she put them on the parlour table. The kettle was singing loudly and the toast had started to char by the time she pulled herself together. It had to happen soon, she thought as she spooned tea leaves into the large enamel teapot.

'Was that the postman, Ma?' Frank asked a few minutes later as he came into the parlour yawning widely.

Dolly nodded towards the table. 'There's one fer you an' one fer Jim,' she said, trying to appear casual.

Frank tore his open. 'It's the Rifle Brigade,' he said. 'I gotta report ter Winchester next Thursday.'

Jim came into the parlour and looked at his older brother. 'Rifle Brigade, did yer say?'

'Yeah. There's one fer you there.'

Jim quickly tore the envelope open. 'Well, at least we'll be goin' tergevver,' he said grinning.

'I told the geezer at the recruitin' office I'd need ter keep me eye on yer.'

Dolly went out of the room brushing back a tear, and returned with the teapot, cups and saucers and toast on a large tray. 'We're out o' marmalade but there's some strawberry jam left,' she told them, disappearing again before they saw her watery eyes.

Mick Flynn came into the room, closely followed by Patrick, who looked somewhat the worse for wear. They sat down at the table and helped themselves to the tea.

'Muvver ses yer got yer papers,' Mick said, glancing up as he stirred his cup. 'Rifle Brigade. That's the regiment Con's in.'

'Con?' Frank said frowning.

'Yeah, the young man who called fer Jennie last night.'

'Ain't there no papers come fer me?' Pat asked, rubbing his forehead tenderly.

'It doesn't look like it, does it?' Frank said, smiling at Jim as he lifted his plate. 'They ain't under yours, are they?' he joked.

'Now don't piss-ball about,' Pat growled. 'I ain't in the mood fer frivolity this mornin'.'

'No, I shouldn't fink so, the way you come in last night,' Mick remarked with a shake of his head. 'You literally fell up them stairs. Gawd knows what young Brenda must fink of yer.'

'Frankly I couldn't care less,' Pat told him. 'We 'ad a ruck last night over me volunteerin' an' she stormed off. She thought I was gonna go chasin' after 'er but I got drunk instead.'

'That's charmin',' Mick replied.

110

Pat slurped his tea and reached for the last piece of toast. 'I tried ter reason wiv 'er but she wouldn't listen,' he said gruffly. 'I told 'er if I didn't volunteer I'd be called up soon anyway, an' the waitin' would only put a strain on both of us.'

'Well at least yer won't need ter buy 'er the engagement ring now,' Frank remarked with a smile.

'She'll come round,' Jim said supportively. 'Yer wasn't plannin' on gettin' engaged till next month anyway. There's plenty o' time yet.'

'It's the ole battleaxe who's stirred the poison,' Pat gulped as he washed down the toast with hot tea. 'She's always stickin' 'er oar in. Trouble is Brenda's scared of 'er. I've told 'er I ain't bendin' over backwards ter please 'er muvver. Bloody ole cow.'

Frank looked at Jim for support. 'They say that women become like their muvvers as they get older,' he said with a grin playing in the corner of his mouth. 'What d'you fink, Jim?'

'So they say,' he replied. 'What's Brenda's muvver look like, Pat? Is she ugly?'

Mick tried to catch Frank's eye but his son ignored him and glanced over at Patrick. 'If Brenda don't change 'er mind you could always work yer ticket, I s'pose.'

'Work me ticket?' Pat echoed in disgust.

'Yeah, you could act the queer, or balls everyfing up they tell yer ter do.'

'That's a good idea,' Jim remarked. 'They'd soon chuck you out if they thought yer was bent.'

111

Pat gave both his brothers a hard look in turn as he got up from the table. 'I ain't got time ter listen ter you pair o' dopey gits,' he growled. 'I'm off ter work.'

'Don't go fallin' off no ladders,' Frank called out after him.

Pat shouted an unintelligible reply and the front door slammed shut.

'You two do go on at 'im sometime,' Mick said, trying to look stern.

'Pat's all right, 'e knows we're only jokin',' Jim told him.

Dolly came into the parlour as Mick and the boys prepared to leave for work. 'Yer better take yer big coats, it looks like rain,' she said.

When Frank and Jim had hurried off, Dolly turned to Mick. 'I'm really gonna miss those boys,' she said tearfully. 'I'm worried sick about 'em.'

Mick slipped his arm around her shoulders and pecked her on her cheek. 'They'll be fine, Ma, an' yer gotta be fankful they're goin' in the same regiment. They'll watch out fer each ovver, they always 'ave.'

'What about our Pat?' she went on. 'Who's gonna watch out fer 'im? Fancy 'im wantin' ter go in the aircrew. What's 'e finkin' about, puttin' that worry on me shoulders?'

'Our shoulders, gel.'

'Yeah well, 'e shouldn't be so Jack-the-lad.'

' 'Im an' Brenda's split up, did yer know?'

Dolly shook her head. 'When was this, last night?'

Mick nodded. 'That's why 'e got pissed.'

112

'I s'pose it was over 'im volunteerin',' Dolly replied. 'I can see 'er point o' view, what wiv 'em plannin' ter get engaged next month.'

Mick shrugged his shoulders. 'Well I can't stop, gel,' he said quickly. 'It's a quarter ter bloody eight.'

Carter Lane was coming to life and at number 20 the elderly sisters were making plans. 'I think it's a very good idea,' Charity remarked. 'Mind you, we'll need to sound everyone out.'

'I suppose we could invite people here to find out their feelings,' Cynthia replied. 'We could use our best china and I can make a few rock cakes.'

Charity held back on a sharp reply. Cynthia's rock cakes usually came in a condition befitting their name, and she recalled the last time her sister was moved to do some baking. She had nearly choked on an iron-hard rock cake, and the jam tarts had been little better. 'We don't need to go to all that trouble,' she said diplomatically. 'We could buy a dozen or so jam tarts at the cake shop, and maybe a nice apple pie to cut up.'

Cynthia nodded. 'We could call our idea "Carter Lane Women's comfort for the Troops Club".'

'It sounds a little long-winded,' Charity said, stroking her chin. 'I know—why don't we call it the "Knitting for Victory Group"?'

'What a good idea. You are clever, Charity.'

'You're the clever one,' her sister told her. 'It was you who thought up the idea.'

113

'Yes, I did, didn't I?'

Charity put her empty teacup down on the table and felt her neatly permed hair with the palm of her hand. 'I think we should get the chores done early and then do some canvassing, don't you?' she suggested.

Cynthia's face lit up. 'Isn't it exciting?' she said breathlessly.

Lunchtime in The Sun saw the return of Sid Cafferty, and his entry was met with a scowl from the elderly Danny Crossley. 'What's that no-good git doin' back in 'ere?' he growled.

Alf Coates took his clay pipe out of his mouth and tapped it on the heel of his boot. 'They must 'ave got fed up wiv 'im at the ovver pub,' he remarked.

' 'E wouldn't 'ave the nerve ter show 'is face in 'ere if Big Joe was still around,' Danny said with passion.

'No, yer bloody right.'

'Just look at the big flash git.'

'I 'ope that bloody pint chokes 'im.'

Danny leaned back in his chair and stared over at the counter. 'What's the matter wiv Charlie Anson? Why don't 'e tell 'im ter piss orf out?'

'Don't ask me,' Alf growled. 'I fink 'e's bloody frightened of 'im.'

The lumbering malcontent leaned on the counter as he talked to the landlord. 'I was in the wrong, Charlie, an' I'm the first to 'old me 'ands up,' he declared. 'Don't you worry though. I won't give yer no grief. I'm just

114

gonna 'ave me pint or two an' keep meself ter meself.'

'As long as yer do, Sid,' the landlord warned him. 'That last turn cost me enough.'

'Well, I appreciate yer kindness, Charlie,' Sid said. 'Give us anuvver pint, an' one fer yerself.'

Danny Crossley shook his head sadly. 'All the boys are goin' off ter war an' there's that ugly great git enjoyin' 'imself,' he said disgustedly. ' 'E ain't too old ter go in.'

' 'E ain't too old, but they won't take 'im,' Alf replied. ' 'E's got gastric trouble.'

' 'E'll 'ave more than gastric trouble if Big Joe comes 'ome on leave an' sees 'im in 'ere,' Danny remarked as he refilled his pipe.

The public bar of the corner pub was filling up as usual at that time of the day and soon a group of building workers came in and spread themselves along the bar. Alec Conroy was amongst them and after he was served he detached himself from the rest and sat in a corner reading the *Daily Mirror*.

'What's the matter wiv 'im?' one of the newer members of the group asked the worker next to him.

'Take no notice of 'im,' he was told, ' 'e's just a miserable git.'

'Conroy lives in this street. I don't fink 'e wants the locals ter know 'e works wiv us crowd,' another worker cut in.

'Why?' the young man asked.

' 'Cos we're a rough tough mob who work 'ard an' drink 'ard.'

115

The answer pleased the new recruit to the building site and he stuck out his chest and tried to look as tough as the rest. 'Sod 'im then,' he remarked.

Alec Conroy was unaware that he was being talked about, but had he known it would not have troubled him unduly. He was a loner who preferred his own company, except when he was able to see Ada Monahan who lived a few streets away. Ada was married to a merchant seaman, and the long days and nights she was forced to spend apart from her husband were made bearable by her association with the young loner. With him she could talk about her fears and worries, her hopes and aspirations, something she could never do with her husband, on the odd occasions when he was around. With all his faults Alec Conroy was a good listener, and with her he was able to relax and be himself, something he found difficult with others.

Sid Cafferty had downed three pints by the time the building workers arrived, and spotting the young man sitting alone he ambled over with the fourth pint in his large hand. 'I made me peace wiv Charlie,' he said in a slightly slurred voice as he sat down at the table.

Alec looked up and nodded. 'That's okay then,' he replied.

'Mind you though, the big Aussie git was out of order that night,' Sid went on. 'All I was sayin' was, we should let ovver countries fight their own battles.'

'Yeah, that's right,' Alec replied, without taking his eyes from the paper.

'So you won't be volunteerin'?'

'Nope.'

'Yer'll just wait till they call yer up then?'

'Yup.'

'What's yer preference? Army? Navy?'

'None.'

'Yer gotta 'ave a preference.'

'Why?'

'Yer just 'ave to.'

Alec folded the paper and put it down on the empty chair beside him. 'Look, millions o' men died in the last war,' he said with emphasis, 'an' countless more frew the effects o' mustard gas. That was the war to end all wars, so they said. Now we're at it again. We don't make the wars. Politicians make the wars, but it's the ordinary people who 'ave ter fight 'em. Well, I ain't gonna be cannon fodder, not fer no bloody politician.'

'Gettin' involved in ovver people's wars is one fing,' Cafferty growled, 'but I'm sodded if I'd stand by an' let the Germans walk in 'ere an' take over our country.'

'Let me tell you somefing,' Alec replied sharply. 'If every ordinary man in whatever country said 'e was gonna refuse ter fight, what'd 'appen then?'

'They'd be put up against the wall an' shot in Germany,' Cafferty told him.

'That's a load o' balls,' the younger man growled. ' 'Ow many could they shoot? Ten, fifteen, twenty million?'

'So what 'appens when they comes for yer?' Cafferty asked.

117

'I'll disappear.'

'They'll catch up wiv yer.'

'Well, we'll 'ave ter wait an' see, won't we?'

All the malice in Cafferty's resentful heart came rumbling to the surface as he eyed the thin, pale-faced young man. 'Yer know what I fink?' he sneered. 'I fink you're a yeller-livered, no-good bastard who'd let 'is mates do the fightin' an' dyin' for 'im. That's what I fink.'

'Well, you can fink what yer like,' Alec Conroy said as he got up, picked up his newspaper and walked smartly out of the pub.

Charlie Anson had been kept busy serving pints, but he caught the last of the exchanges between the two and he turned to his wife Tess. 'I was a bloody fool ter listen to 'im,' he growled. 'I should 'ave barred 'im fer good.'

'You still ain't lost yer chance,' she replied acidly.

In the relative quiet of the saloon bar Cynthia and Charity Lockwood sat sipping their sherry.

'Well, it wasn't too bad, was it?' Charity remarked.

'No, I was quite pleased really,' her sister replied, looking at the list of names written down in the small notebook lying on the table. 'We've got Mrs Harris, Mrs Flynn, Mrs Bromilow and Mrs Arrowsmith. Then there are some maybes: Mrs Jones, Mrs Wilson and that woman from number fifteen. I can never remember her name.'

'Wickstead,' Charity reminded her.

118

'That's right, Mrs Wickstead,' Cynthia said smiling.

'We'll need to do some more door-knocking,' Charity said with enthusiasm. 'If we get twenty people we can get the wool and needles at cut price. It said so on the wireless. The lady on the programme said it was mainly socks and scarves the troops needed, especially with the winter coming on.'

'We could send little notes to the troops inside the parcels,' Cynthia suggested. 'You know the sort of thing "Keep your pecker up, we're all thinking of you".'

'What a nice thought,' Charity replied. 'You do get some bright ideas, Cynthia.'

The younger sister smiled happily at the compliment and reached into her handbag. 'I know this is being very daring, but I think the situation calls for it. I'm going to have another sherry. Would you like another?'

Some time later the two elderly sisters walked back along Carter Lane arm-in-arm and smiling to all and sundry.

'I feel positively tiddly,' Cynthia sighed.

'I feel like I'm walking on air,' Charity remarked.

'Don't let me go, will you?'

'And you hold on to me too.'

'Charity?'

'Yes?'

'Can you knit socks?'

'I've never tried.'

'Nor have I.'

'All I know is you have to use four needles.'

'Charity?'

'Yes?'

'I can see two of everything.'

'That's funny, so can I.'

'Aren't we awful?'

'No, just a little tipsy,' Charity replied with a lop-sided smile, 'but doesn't it feel good?'

CHAPTER 10

The weather had suddenly turned cold, with a chill wind threatening a severe winter, and in Carter Lane chimneys belched smoke as people hurried about their business, eager to get back indoors. A few wore sad and worried expressions. Dolly Flynn had seen two of her sons go off to war and Mrs Jones, Mrs Wickstead and Mrs Bromilow had each said goodbye to a son during the same week. Mrs Wilson's boy Dennis had joined the navy the previous week and her daughter Claire had gone off to work in the Land Army.

The Sun public house on the corner of Carter Lane had become a kind of bastion for the local families and it was there in the cosy public bar that the locals took heart and gained support from each other.

'I'm not worried too much about my Dennis,' Mrs Wilson lied to Mrs Jones. ' 'E's always bin able ter look after 'imself. 'E makes friends easily an' 'e's a good swimmer. 'E got a certificate fer swimmin' a mile when 'e was at school.'

'I wish I didn't worry about my Jerry,' Ivy Jones replied as she picked up her Guinness. ' 'E's always bin such a little daredevil. D'yer remember that time 'e fell in the water down by Tower Pier? Tryin' ter climb inter one o' those barges, 'e was.'

'Yeah, I remember that time, Ivy,' Mrs Bromilow cut in. 'My Freddie came runnin' 'ome ter tell me that your boy was drowned.'

'The little cow-son nearly was,' Ivy went on. 'They fished 'im out the water down by Chamber's Wharf. 'E'd floated right down under Tower Bridge an' the lighterman who pulled 'im out said it was a miracle 'e never drowned, what wiv the currents an' all.'

That Sunday lunchtime Danny Crossley and his old drinking partner Alf Coates were sitting nearby, listening in on the conversation.

'The boys'll be all right,' Danny said, giving the woman a smile of encouragement. 'Anyway, the war might not last long. Old 'Itler knows we ain't no pushover fer 'im or anybody else. 'E'll be suin' fer peace next year, you wait an' see.'

'Yeah, an' I'm a Dutchman,' Alf growled under his breath. 'This is goin' on fer a long while yet, you mark my words.'

'I feel the same,' Danny told him, 'but yer can't say that ter them now, can yer? Poor ole Dolly Flynn's just seen two of 'er boys go off an' young Pat's waitin' ter go any day now.'

Alf nodded and tapped his clay pipe against the leg of the table. 'Did you 'ear Cafferty goin' on at young Alec Conroy the ovver day?' he asked.

Danny shook his head. 'Nah, I'd left 'ere before it started, but I did 'ear from Lofty that Cafferty was right out of order.'

'Too bloody right 'e was,' Alf went on. 'All right the 'ole street knows the boy's feelin's about goin' in the forces, but that don't give that loudmouth git the right ter go shoutin' 'is mouth off. I tell yer somefing, I'd never 'ave let 'im talk ter me like that, old as I am. I'd 'ave crowned 'im wiv a quart bottle.'

'Yeah, me too,' Danny agreed.

Alf filled his pipe thoughtfully. 'Cafferty's bin strongin' it wiv the booze lately,' he remarked. ' 'E's staggered out of 'ere pissed out of 'is brains the last few nights. I just 'ope 'e don't run inter Big Joe. Yer'd see the sparks fly then.'

' 'Old up, talk o' the devil,' Danny Crossley said quickly.

The old friends sat watching as Sid Cafferty walked unsteadily towards the counter, and Charlie Anson puffed irritably as he faced him across the polished surface. 'Sid, I ain't gonna serve yer,' he said boldly. 'You've 'ad enough. Why don't yer go 'ome an' sleep it off. Come back ternight when yer more steady on yer feet.'

'Yer mean yer barrin' me?' Sid growled, his bleary eyes trying to focus on the landlord.

'No, I ain't barrin' yer,' Charlie replied. 'I've just said yer'll be welcome 'ere ternight, but not now, not in that state.'

'I can 'old me beer,' Sid slurred. 'I won't be

a nuisance to anybody.'

'Look, pal, yer got stroppy the ovver day when you was pissed an' I was gettin' ready ter bar yer then. I would 'ave done too if young Alec Conroy 'adn't 'ad the sense ter get out of 'ere before it went too far.'

' 'E's a yeller-livered coward an' I told 'im so,' Cafferty snarled as he slouched over the counter. 'You should be barrin' the likes of 'im, not me.'

'I ain't barrin' yer, Sid,' Charlie sighed, 'but I ain't servin' yer now, not while yer in that state.'

'If that's the case I'll take me custom elsewhere,' the big man scowled as he turned on his heel.

'Yeah, you do that, Sid,' the irate landlord told him.

Bernard Shanks checked the soldered connection with the meter contacts and then eased the metal chassis back into the casing. It was nearly five o'clock and he had been working for the last two hours on the difficult repair. 'It's fixed, Mr Levy,' he announced as he put his head round the door. 'It needed a new diode.'

'Well done, lad,' the shopowner told him. 'Mrs Fredricks'll be lookin' in again first thing Monday morning. You might as well go now. I'll be closing in half an hour.'

After Bernard had left Albert Levy counted the day's takings and put them into a large brown envelope which he then folded and slipped into his coat pocket. He turned the open sign on the front door round to closed and went into the workroom to gather up his overcoat and Homburg. All that week he had deliberately not sat down at the bench, for if he had he would have felt bound to deliver a few home truths to Abel. Tonight though he knew that he could not face another weekend with the knowledge of his old friend's deceit eating into him. Things had to be said and now was the time.

'Abel, I don't know if you'll turn away from me tonight, but I hope you won't,' he began. 'God knows, you and I have been lifelong friends and that has to count for something. Why? Why I ask myself? Was it something bad that compelled you to rob me? Gambling, women? That I could understand, but not you. I knew you too well to believe it could be something like that. What then, I've asked myself a thousand times? I paid you good wages and I always looked out for you. My house was always open, as far as you were concerned, and how many times has Gerda wanted you to call round for a meal? It's driving me mad, Abel. You of all people to rob the hand that fed you. Did I ever harp on the time I saved you from that death camp? Did I ever mention how much money it cost to buy your freedom? No never, and you know it. What could have turned one old friend against the other?'

Albert sat down wearily and leaned his head in his hands on the wooden bench. 'If only you could give me a sign, let me know and put me out of the misery I face every day now.

It's destroying me, Abel. Can't you see, or are you gloating from wherever you are? Listen to me, my old friend. Three weeks ago I spoke to Rabbi Bloomfield. I told him I would like to have a plaque put up in the synagogue in your memory and he agreed it would be a fitting epitaph to a friendship that spanned the many years we shared. I'm to see him again soon to go over the details, but how can I go ahead with it now? It would be a sacrilege. Why, Abel? Why did you see fit to rob me in such a way, and then to mention the sordid details in your diary? Was I meant to see it? No, I'm sure I wasn't. The diary was well concealed, and only discovered by chance. But then that was typical of you, wasn't it? Secretive to a fault. Even when you took your life you never left me a letter of farewell. Nothing, Abel. You left me nothing, nothing that would explain the reasons for the terrible and tragic decision you took. All right, I knew how you felt about war coming, we'd discussed it so many times, but to leave no goodbye, no farewell old friend, only the terrible thing you did to me that has now come to light.'

Albert got up slowly, buttoned up his heavy overcoat and reached for his hat. 'I'm tired, Abel,' he sighed. 'I'm tired and dispirited beyond your understanding, because I'm still living. Maybe one day the truth will out. Maybe you'll send a sign, and show me why you did this to me. Maybe never. Maybe I'm destined to carry the burden of this mystery to my grave. Good night to you, Abel, and sleep the long sleep. I'll talk to you again, when my heart is not so heavy.'

Rene Conroy cut thick slices from the crusty loaf and coated them liberally with salted margarine. The hunk of cheese was going mouldy at the edges and she carefully pared it before cutting slices and laying them on the bread. Cheese or brawn sandwiches with pickles was the regular supper in the Conroy household and Alec would be in from the pub soon.

Rene worried over her only son, and lately she had had good reason to. He had openly told her and Ted that under no circumstances was he going to put on a uniform. Ted had tried to get to the bottom of it but failed. Alec was not one to open up and have a lengthy discussion of the whys and wherefores, and to say merely that the war was wrong and people shouldn't be made to fight was not enough to satisfy her or Ted. Alec had shrugged his shoulders and clammed up when they tried to delve, and his true reasons for the stance he was taking remained locked in his head.

The kettle was coming to the boil when the young man came in the house and Rene glanced up at the clock. He was earlier than usual and she gave him a searching look as he slipped off his coat and hung it behind the scullery door.

'I left a bit early,' he said. 'It was gettin' a bit silly.'

' 'Ere take yer sandwich in the parlour an' I'll bring yer tea in soon as it's brewed,' she told him.

Ted Conroy was sitting by the fire reading the evening paper and he looked up as his son walked into the room. 'You're early,' he remarked. 'They ain't run out o' beer, 'ave they?'

Alec ignored the joke. 'What's the news?' he asked. 'I 'aven't seen the paper this evenin'.'

Ted passed it over without comment and Alec settled himself into the armchair facing him.

Rene heard it first as she poured the boiling water into the teapot, and she went into the passage to listen. The shouting got louder and it carried into the parlour.

'It's Sid Cafferty, take no notice,' Alec said quickly, putting his supper plate down on the table.

'Alec Conroy. You're a coward,' the voice called out. 'Come out an' let us all see yer.'

Ted got up quickly but Rene took him by the arm. 'Don't you dare go outside,' she said anxiously.

'Can you 'ear me, Conroy? I know yer in there. Come out an' let us all see what a yeller-livered coward looks like.'

'I'm not gonna put up wiv this,' Ted growled as he tried to break Rene's grip on his arm.

Alec got out of his chair with a deep sigh. 'Leave it, Dad,' he said calmly. 'It's me 'e wants, not you.'

'You stay right where you are,' Rene told him. 'I'll see ter this.'

'No yer can't, Mum,' Alec said shaking his head. 'Sid Cafferty's bin lookin' fer a confrontation so I might as well face 'im.'

127

'You're no match fer that ugly great git,' she shouted at him.

'It's not a question o' matchin' 'im, it's about facin' 'im,' Alec told her. 'Just leave me ter sort this out in me own way.'

People were coming to their front doors to find out what was going on and in the light of the moon they could see the large figure of Sid Cafferty standing in the middle of the cobbled roadway with legs splayed apart and hands hitched into his belt.

'Just look at that drunken git,' Bert Kenny remarked to his wife Liz. ' 'E looks like someone out o' one o' those western pictures.'

'Well 'e certainly ain't no Billy the Kid,' Liz growled.

Cafferty ambled further along the turning. 'Can you 'ear me, Conroy?' he bawled.

Both Cynthia and Charity Lockwood had been curious to see what the rumpus was about and they looked a little frightened as they stood by their front door with coats over their flowered dressing gowns.

'Come out an' face me, Conroy,' Cafferty bellowed. 'Let's see what yer made of.'

The sisters saw that their neighbours were at their front doors and Charity was moved to respond to the taunting. 'Why don't you go home, you silly man,' she called out.

'Charity, do be careful,' her sister warned. 'The man's drunk.'

'I know very well that he's drunk, Cynthia,' she replied. 'All the more reason he should go home and let us get some sleep.'

'I don't know if I could sleep now,' Cynthia said shivering.

'Why don't you piss orf an' go ter bed,' Bert Kenny shouted out.

'Keep out o' this,' Cafferty snarled back. 'This is between Conroy an' me.'

Suddenly the harangued young man stepped out from his house into the cobbled roadway and walked very slowly towards the bigger man. 'I don't know what yer beef is,' he told him, 'but you're out of order. Why don't yer go 'ome an' sleep it off.'

'Leave it, Alec,' Bert Kenny called out to him. 'Get back indoors.'

Alec was only a few feet away from his tormentor when Cafferty lunged at him. The first blow grazed the young man's cheek but the next one landed full in the face, dropping him to his knees. A trickle of blood ran down from his nose onto his chin and Alec shook his head as he staggered to his feet. Cafferty grabbed him in a bear hug, his head going backwards as Conroy tried to press his fingers into the bigger man's eyes. The attacker was roaring like a bull and Alec felt the life being slowly squeezed out of him. With his remaining strength he brought his knee up sharply and caught Cafferty full in the groin. He was free as the big man gasped and fell down on one knee.

'Go 'ome, Cafferty,' he gulped.

'I'm gonna tear you apart, yer little rat,' the drunkard snarled as he climbed painfully to his feet.

Bert Kenny had pulled away from Liz's

restraining grip and he hurried over to the combatants. 'Right, that's enough,' he bawled as he got between the two of them.

Cafferty swung round and caught Bert with a quick blow to the chin and the older man staggered back into the kerb. Alec Conroy immediately went for the bully and rained blows on him, most of which were parried. People were screaming out for an end to it and suddenly Mick Flynn ran over and grabbed the young man by the waist, lifting him off his feet and swinging him away from the bigger man. Women ran out to remonstrate and Dolly held a rolling-pin menacingly in her hand.

'It's over,' she said. 'Now go off 'ome, Cafferty, or as sure as Gawd made little apples I'll open yer 'ead wiv this.'

Cafferty looked at the rolling-pin held up in front of him and he backed off. 'This ain't over, Conroy,' he called out as the young man was led away. 'I'll finish yer next time.'

Dolly raised the rolling-pin over her head and moved forward, only to be grabbed by Mick. 'Come on, luv, it's all over,' he urged her as Cafferty turned on his heel and walked unsteadily out of the little turning.

A dazed Bert Kenny was led into his house by Liz who sat him down in a chair and gently pressed her fingers around his chin. 'You was lucky,' she told him. 'That ugly great slummock could 'ave busted yer jaw.'

'That would 'ave kept me quiet fer a while, wouldn't it?' Bert said, grinning painfully.

'Just you wait till Big Joe comes 'ome on leave

130

an' I tell 'im what's 'appened. 'E'll go bloody bananas.'

'You just keep your mouth shut, d'you 'ear me?' Bert said sharply. 'I don't want 'im in any more trouble.'

'Big Joe finks the world o' you, Bert,' she told him. ' 'E'll slaughter that ugly big git when 'e does find out, an' believe me 'e will. All right, I won't say anyfing to 'im but yer gotta remember there were plenty o' people who saw what 'appened ter yer ternight, an' someone'll tell 'im, make no mistake about that.'

Bert nodded slowly. He knew only too well that in a small community like Carter Lane it would be impossible for Big Joe not to find out, and knowing the Australian's temper he feared the outcome.

CHAPTER 11

Life went on for the families at war as the bad weather closed in, and in Carter Lane the prospect of the young servicemen coming home on leave was one of the main subjects of conversation. Like many of their neighbours, the Flynn family were eagerly awaiting the homecoming of their three sons. Patrick Flynn had finally gone off to join the RAF and like his two brothers in the army his basic training was coming to an end.

Jennie Flynn had found herself a job at a

bakery in the Old Kent Road and her sister Sadie was still hopeful of getting some war-work in the area. She had despaired of Len Regan coming up with anything, although he tried to convince her that there was time yet. He had been increasingly pre-occupied during the last two months with the establishment in Brighton, and now that it was up and running successfully, Sadie hoped that he would have a little more free time. Jennie however was a little concerned about her elder sister and she was quick to voice her opinion when the two were together in the scullery on Saturday morning.

'You should be out enjoyin' yerself on Saturday nights,' she remarked, 'but you 'ardly ever go out lately.'

'I'm seein' Len ternight,' Sadie told her. 'An' you're a fine one ter talk.'

'It's different wiv me,' Jennie responded. 'Con's over in France an' I'm not interested in playin' around while he's away.'

'Yeah, but you 'ardly knew 'im before 'e left,' Sadie went on. 'Surely it don't 'urt goin' out wiv ovver lads, as long as it don't get too strong. There's plenty round 'ere who'd be only too glad ter take you out.'

'I'm just not interested,' Jennie said. 'Con writes ter me all the time an' we're gettin' ter know each ovver pretty well from the letters. Besides, most o' the presentable young men are away in the forces now.'

Sadie shrugged her shoulders as she got up to check the cake baking in the oven. 'Well it's up ter you, it's your life,' she sighed.

132

Jennie took out the small photo of Con from her handbag and studied it. 'Don't yer fink 'e's a bit like our Pat in looks?' she asked.

Sadie leaned over her sister's shoulder. 'Yeah, I can see a likeness, around the eyes.'

' 'E's got lovely eyes,' Jennie drooled. 'They make me go all soppy when 'e looks at me.'

Sadie picked up a tea towel and went over to the oven. 'I'd better take this out before it gets burnt,' she said, moving back as the heat billowed out. 'There we are, perfect.'

Jennie picked a roasted almond from the top of the fruit cake and nibbled it. 'There's no end to your talents, is there?' she joked. 'When yer gonna cut it?'

'This is goin' away till the boys come 'ome on leave next week,' Sadie replied quickly. 'Mum's found me a tin ter keep it in, so keep yer 'ooks off.'

Gerda Levy had become increasingly worried about her husband and she took it on herself to visit Carter Lane.

'I'm sorry to trouble you, but I'm Albert Levy's wife,' she told Daisy timidly when the Harrises' front door was opened to her. 'I wonder if I could have a few words with you?'

'Of course yer can. Come on in,' Daisy said pleasantly.

Gerda walked into the tidy parlour and stood by the table. 'It's about my husband really,' she began.

'Look, you take a seat an' I'll get us some tea,' Daisy told her. 'I've got some brewin'.'

133

She was soon back and she gave her visitor an encouraging smile as she handed over her tea. 'I always find a cup o' Rosy Lee goes down well in the afternoon.'

Gerda took a small sip and looked up at Daisy. 'You remember the diary you found under the floorboards in Abel's room?' she said without wasting time. 'Well, it contained something which has upset my husband very much. In fact it revealed that Abel was robbing the till at my husband's shop. He actually made notes about it. There were dates, amounts and certain remarks written down which upset Albert terribly, and it's got to the stage where I'm beginning to fear for his sanity.'

'Good Gawd!' Daisy said quickly. ' 'Ow shockin'.'

'I don't know if you're aware that Abel was in a concentration camp in Germany before the war,' Gerda remarked.

'Yes, I did know that as a matter o' fact,' Daisy replied. 'I only found out when I saw the number printed on Abel's arm. 'E told me that your 'usband managed ter pay fer 'is release.'

'That's true, which makes this business all the more terrible,' Gerda said sadly. 'Never once did my husband ever remind Abel about what he did. They were childhood friends and he felt it was only his duty to save him from the camp. It was almost impossible to get out of one of those camps, and Abel was one of the lucky ones, thanks to Albert.'

Daisy shook her head slowly. 'Your 'usband's a very nice man. 'E was always pleasant when

134

'e called ter play chess wiv Abel an' we often joked about different fings. Abel seemed ter worship 'im. It seems so out o' character that 'e should end up robbin' 'im, after all that was done fer 'im.'

'This was going on for some time by the look of it,' Gerda told her. 'Although there was only one diary Abel did make references to the previous year and he even had a total that he carried over.'

'Now yer've told me this, I wish I'd never discovered the diary,' Daisy said with sadness etched in her voice. 'I did take a look inside ter tell yer the truth but it was written in a foreign language an' I felt that your 'usband should 'ave it, considerin' 'ow close they were.'

'I don't put any blame on you, Mrs Harris,' Gerda was quick to remark. 'You did the right thing. But Albert's suffering over what he discovered. The knowledge has been eating into him and he's taken to talking to himself. He doesn't sleep either. Many a night I've woken up and found him sitting in the lounge mumbling to himself. He's on tablets that his doctor prescribed but they don't seem to help much.'

'I'm so sorry,' Daisy said with compassion. 'I wish there was somefing I could do.'

'As a matter of fact there is,' Gerda told her. 'Can you search your memory and think of anything Abel might have told you concerning his life or anything he might have mentioned about Albert? Any little thing, however trivial it may seem, might hold the key.'

Daisy thought for some time then she shook her head again slowly. 'Abel was a very private person, an' we respected 'is privacy,' she replied. ' 'E never spoke much about 'imself nor your 'usband, apart from mentioning when 'e'd call round ter play chess.'

Gerda finished her tea and put the cup and saucer down on the table. 'If anything does come to mind I'd appreciate it greatly if you would contact me. There's my address. Maybe your husband might recall something.'

'I'll certainly speak to 'im,' Daisy said, glancing down at the slip of paper Gerda had handed her, 'an' if eivver of us remembers anyfing I'll definitely get in touch.'

'You are very kind and I do appreciate it,' Gerda said as she got up.

Daisy saw her visitor to the door, and she was still shaking her head and frowning as she went back into the parlour. It beggared belief that Abel would do such a thing, she told herself. Such a nice, quiet, inoffensive man who would jump at the slightest sound. He hadn't the nerve nor the inclination to resort to robbing his friend. That she was sure of.

Len Regan was looking a little harassed when Sadie arrived at The Swan off the Walworth Road. 'Look, I'm up against it ternight, kid,' he told her as he took their drinks to a secluded table in the saloon bar. 'There's a party down from Glasgow an' we've got anuvver team from Kent who are interested in puttin' some dough in a project Johnnie's got lined up. I gotta get

136

down ter The Black Cat later, but I'm s'posed ter meet the Glasgow boys first. We've gotta look after 'em while they're in London.'

'So bang goes our quiet evenin' tergevver,' Sadie said with irritation in her voice.

'I'm sorry, kid, I really am,' he said.

'It's not good enough, Len,' she told him. 'Our time tergevver seems ter be gettin' less an' less.'

'I know, an' I'm gonna make it up ter yer very soon,' he replied. 'In the meantime I wanna ask yer a big favour. Yer can say no if yer like, but it would be a great 'elp if yer'll do it for me.'

'What is it?' Sadie asked sighing.

'If I get Nosher ter run yer down ter Kent can yer act as 'ostess ter the Kent mob till I get there?'

' 'Ow long are yer gonna be?' she asked. 'I can't be expected ter nursemaid 'em all night. I don't know 'em anyway.'

'I should get down there by eleven or thereabouts,' he estimated. 'All yer gotta do is introduce yerself as Len's assistant an' make sure they get all the booze they want. Tell 'em I'm due soon an' just make small talk. I know yer can do it. The barman's already bin primed up an' 'e'll give yer all the drinks yer need. There's a table reserved as well. Say yer'll do it.'

'An' what if I say no?' Sadie replied.

'Well it's fer you ter decide, kid, an' I wouldn't dream of askin' yer if I thought yer wasn't up to it. Yer've 'eld the fort before remember.'

' 'Ow's many comin'?' Sadie asked.

137

'Four.'

'An' yer promise me yer won't leave me roastin'?'

'I promise.'

'All right then, just this once,' she sighed.

'Yer a diamond an' I love yer, Sadie.'

'Yer could 'ave fooled me,' she told him with a grudging smile.

Frank and Iris Ross had lived in Carter Lane ever since their wedding back in nineteen eighteen when Frank came back from the war. Two years later their daughter was born, and due to complications at the birth when Iris almost died the couple decided that Brenda would be their only child. They doted on their precious gift and spoiled her in the process. Neighbours remarked that Brenda was the best-dressed child in the street and at Christmas and on her birthdays she would always have the most expensive toys. Iris and Frank always sought the very best for her and when she won a scholarship to St Olave's Grammar School for Girls they were delighted. They saw a good future for her and hoped and prayed that one day she would marry a wealthy businessman who would worship her and give her everything her heart desired.

To Brenda's credit she did not take advantage of the privileged position she was in. In fact she was sometimes embarrassed to witness the struggles of the families around her, especially during the years of the depression as she was growing up. Her family seemed to manage quite well in contrast and her father's job as chief clerk in the Council wages office was never in jeopardy. Her mother worked too as a welfare officer and all in all things were prosperous for them throughout the bad years.

Brenda grew into a beautiful young woman, dark-haired and with large hazel eyes, and the boys soon came calling. Her parents watched her progress with due concern and they kept a tight rein on her activities, often warning a young buck off or vetting a prospective boyfriend until Brenda began to rebel. The young men who came calling or tried to chat her up did not turn her head or make her pulse race overmuch, for Brenda had already lost her heart, to the one young man in the street who did not seem to realize that she was now a very desirable young woman.

As children Brenda Ross and Patrick Flynn had played together. They were often seen hand in hand going off on some big adventure or sitting together at the kerbside chatting away, as Pat showed her his new penknife or instructed her in the art of woollen rein-making on a cotton reel with four nails punched into one end. Brenda would in turn teach him the words of the latest songs and show him how to play four-stones, which the lad found hard to master. A childhood full of fun and happiness, while the world about them was moving ever closer to conflagration.

Frank and Iris Ross saw no harm in the childhood friendship. Patrick Flynn was a fine lad from a good hard-working family, but a few years later they became worried when their teenage daughter started to make her feelings felt. It was obvious to them that Brenda was very fond of her childhood friend and as far as she was concerned their association had taken on another dimension.

'It's only natural for Brenda ter like the lad,' Frank remarked. 'After all, they grew up tergevver in the street.'

'Yes, but it's obvious 'e don't feel the same way about 'er,' Iris replied. 'Patrick's bin out wiv quite a few gels lately.'

'Only one or two,' Frank said.

'Well all I'm sayin' is, Brenda's gotta realise that there's plenty o' fish in the sea,' Iris answered irritably, 'an' she shouldn't be wastin' 'er time pinin' over the likes o' Patrick Flynn.'

On the day when the Prime Minister Neville Chamberlain returned from Munich waving a piece of paper to declare that it was peace in our time, Brenda Ross went to a dance at the local palais and met Patrick there. He had been stood up and he had decided to drown his sorrows at the bar. From where he stood looking down on the dance area on the floor below he could see the beautiful young woman he had grown up alongside moving with gossamer grace to the big-band music and he forgot his drink. Men were cutting in to dance with her and she seemed to be in constant demand. Not being a very confident dancer himself he was loath to approach her, but he thought of their childhood together and knew that she would

140

be nice enough not to criticise him for his shortcomings.

Brenda and Patrick danced all evening to the exclusion of the other young hopefuls and then they walked home together, deep in conversation. Brenda's heart was light and pumping excitedly while Patrick cursed his stupidity at not noticing how beautiful Brenda had become until that evening. They slipped furtively into the dark doorway of a warehouse in Brady Street and kissed goodnight, a young, innocent kiss that lasted until they were breathless, and they arranged to meet again. Their new-found love soon became obvious to everyone, and even Iris and Frank had to agree that Patrick Flynn was the man their daughter would one day marry.

It was a time for love, for planning, for looking at rings and wedding gowns, but it all paled in the shadow of an army on the march. When the Germans moved into Poland it was clear to everyone that war was imminent, and Brenda and Patrick's plans were thrown into disarray.

'I've gotta join up,' Patrick told her as they sat by the river on a balmy night a few days after war was declared.

'You can't, Pat,' she said. 'I won't let yer go.'

'I can't not go,' he persisted. 'Look, darlin', I'll be called up soon anyway an' I won't 'ave much choice then. It'll be the army more than likely.'

'I thought I meant somefing to yer,' she said with a break in her voice.

'You mean everyfing ter me, but I just can't sit back while all the ovver young blokes are signin' on.'

'You men are all the same,' Brenda rounded on him. 'You fink this is a game. "Look at me, mate. Look at all the medals I've got".'

'Don't trivialise it, Brenda,' he said quietly. 'It's not a game an' you know it. If we don't fight the Germans'll overrun the country, an' where would we all be then? In slavery—that's where.'

'Well, if that's the way yer feel then at least wait till they call yer up, please,' Brenda pleaded.

'I can't. I gotta do it now, luv,' he said sighing. 'The sooner we all get into it the sooner it'll be over.'

'An' the sooner yer'll get yerself killed.'

'Don't fight me on this, darlin'.'

'I will an' I'll keep on till yer see sense.'

'It won't matter 'ow long yer go on about it, Brenda, me mind's made up,' Pat said firmly.

'Well, in that case yer better make the choice,' she told him with tears of anger filling her eyes. 'If you volunteer then me an' you are finished.'

A few days later Patrick Flynn joined the Royal Air Force, and Brenda Ross put his photograph face down in her dressing-table drawer.

CHAPTER 12

Nosher Smith had said very little during the journey down to The Black Cat nightclub which was situated on the outskirts of Maidstone. He was an ex-fighter who had never reached the heights, but rather been the one all the rising young pro boxers were expected to get past on their way to fame and fortune. Now employed as a chauffeur, minder and general handyman to Johnnie Macaulay, the ageing ex-pugilist did as he was told and found it a good policy to keep his thoughts to himself.

'You are waitin' around, Nosher, aren't yer?' Sadie queried as the car swung off the road into a long, curving drive lit only by the light of the full moon.

'Yus, miss,' he grunted in reply. 'Mr Regan told me someone else'll be bringin' 'im down later.'

Sadie gathered up her calf-long dress as she got out of the Daimler and pushed open the door of the darkened nightclub. Inside the air was tainted with tobacco smoke and she could see in the low lights a crowd assembled round the long bar. The stocky-looking barman smiled at her as she walked up to him and nodded toward the far end of the counter. 'The party's arrived, Sadie,' he told her. 'The table's reserved, the one by the stage.'

As the young woman walked over to the group of well-dressed men she noted that one looked far younger than the other three and he seemed to be doing the talking. Two of the others were grey-haired and wore spectacles, while the third was completely bald, the dome of his skull shining as though it had been polished.

'Ah, this must be Sadie Flynn, if I'm not mistaken,' the young man said cheerily as she reached them.

'In person,' Sadie said in her best voice, smiling at each of them in turn. 'I hope you're all being looked after.'

The young man held up his drink. 'Yes thank you, and we're looking forward to the show. I understand there's a good singer here tonight.'

'Yes, Alma Deane sings with the big bands and she's just done some cabaret work with Debroy Summers,' Sadie told him.

'Very good,' the bald man cut in. 'And what about you? Are you in the entertainments business?'

'Of sorts,' Sadie said smiling. 'I'm Len Regan's assistant and I look after his clients while he's on other business.'

'And very well too, I'm sure,' the man replied with a leer that Sadie found repulsive.

'I understand Mr Regan's coming down later tonight,' the young man said.

'Yes, he'll be down as soon as he can,' Sadie told him.

'Well, I think I'd better do the introductions,' he said. 'I'm George Barton, and this is James Carrington and Jowett Howland of Howland

144

Enterprises. And this is Warren Tate who has business interests along the south coast from Brighton to Portsmouth.'

The handshakes from the two grey-haired men were quite perfunctory but when the bald Warren Tate grasped her hand his flesh felt cold and clammy, and reminded Sadie of holding a slippery fish. The contact was slightly longer than it should have been and the look in the man's dark puffy eyes made her skin creep. She guessed that he was in his mid-forties, his build turning to fat around his jowls and midriff. His face was flat and there was no sign of stubble. In fact his features seemed to be as smooth as his large head, glistening with sweat.

'We have a table reserved for you,' Sadie told them. 'Are you ready or would you prefer another drink at the bar? There's time yet, the show doesn't start until eleven.'

George Barton looked around for guidance. 'I think we might as well take the weight off our feet,' he concluded.

Sadie led the way to a round table set out with cutlery and wine glasses sprouting red table napkins which had been expertly folded. The waiter took the drinks order and then Warren Tate took out a flat gold case from his coat pocket and extracted a coloured cigarette with a gold tip. 'This is certainly very nice,' he remarked, looking around. Then turning to George he added, 'Macaulay seems to have done well here.'

The drinks were served and the men chatted amongst themselves, occasionally turning to

Sadie so as not to seem impolite.

'There's a gaming room here, I understand,' Carrington remarked to her.

'Yes, it's to the right, by the palm,' she told him with a smile.

Warren Tate constantly glanced in her direction and Sadie found herself wishing that Len Regan would hurry down and take the sorry bunch off her hands.

The waiter came back to take the food order and Sadie suddenly noticed George Barton acknowledging a very suggestive smile from a young man sitting with an elderly group of jewel-bedecked women and tired-looking old men. The young man stood out in the group and his manner left little to the imagination. He was openly flirting with Barton, who appeared to be enjoying it.

The soup was followed by fish and vegetables which were presented in large silver tureens, and as the party tucked into the delicious meal the cabaret got under way. Scantily clad dancing girls kicked their way through an exerting routine, and as they side-stepped off the club manager climbed up onto the stage to introduce the main artiste. Loud applause greeted her appearance and Alma Deane did not disappoint. Her repertoire contained both new and old songs, and while her voice mellifluously soared as purely as a nightingale Warren Tate sat staring like an alley cat eager for its prey. His mouth hung open and his dark brooding eyes never left the singer. The cigarette in his hand was forgotten till it seared his flesh and even then he stubbed it out on the plate without removing his gaze from the stage. Loud, lengthy applause rang out at the end of the performance and Alma Deane obliged with two more songs before she made her final exit.

Sadie looked round as the waiter came over to take the dessert order and saw that George Barton was missing from the table. She had not noticed him get up and she turned to Jowett Howland. 'I didn't see George leave,' she remarked.

'He's otherwise engaged, my dear,' the elderly man replied, giving his colleague a knowing glance. 'It seems he's found a friend and they've moved to the gaming room.'

'Yes, and I think I'll try my luck there too,' Carrington declared.

With the meal over and the band pianist playing a medley of bland melodies Carrington got up. 'Are you going to join me, Jowett?' he asked. 'And what about you, Warren?'

'I think I'll stay here for a while,' the bald man replied, much to Sadie's distaste. There were two hostesses available in the gaming room to assist any novice and encourage the more daring player and she would not be expected to follow the men into the salon, but she felt obliged to sit with Warren Tate as long as he stayed at the table.

'The same again?' Tate asked as he motioned to an attendant waiter.

'No, just some water, thank you,' Sadie replied.

'Nonsense. Have another gin and lemon,' he said firmly.

'All right then, but just a small one,' she told the waiter pointedly.

Warren Tate fixed her with an intent stare as he spoke at length about his early days and his rise to becoming a very successful businessman, then suddenly his manner changed. He started to delve and pry into the lives of Johnnie Macaulay and Len Regan, and some of his questions shocked the young girl. 'Are you his woman?' he asked brazenly.

'I'm his girlfriend as well as his assistant,' Sadie replied, trying to maintain a smile.

'Do you like the water?' he asked, and seeing her puzzled frown added, 'Sailing?'

'I've never tried it,' she answered.

'I've got a powered sailing sloop moored at Hayling Island,' he announced. 'You should come down some weekend and I could take you out on it. I have a crew to man it, and I'm sure you'd enjoy yourself. Len Regan too, though I'd prefer it if you came alone. I understand from talking to Mr Regan that he's a landlubber. His words, mind.'

I bet you would, Sadie thought, giving him a noncommittal smile.

The barman was making signs and Sadie excused herself to go over to him. 'What is it, Sam?' she asked.

'Mr Regan's just been on the phone,' he told her. 'Something's come up and he can't make it tonight. Can you pass on his apologies to the guests and make sure they're looked after while

148

they're at the club? Oh and will you see to it that Nosher drives them to the Manor Hotel when they're ready.'

Sadie cursed her luck as she nodded to the barman. Warren Tate was doing a good job of making her skin crawl and she had been praying for Len to come and take him and his cronies off her hands. Now it seemed that she was stuck with them for the next few hours.

Before going back to the table she went into the gaming room and sought out her charges. Carrington was standing beside Jowett Howland who seemed to be on a winning streak and she passed on the message.

'Never fear, my dear, I'm on a roll,' Jowett told her.

'Have you seen Mr Barton?' she asked him.

'He left some time ago,' Jowett said winking.

I wish Tate would, she thought as she went back to join him.

The bald man was keen to learn more about her and his questions became more personal as the late night drifted on into the early hours. He had consumed a large amount of whisky but he still appeared to be alert and no less searching in his manner.

A few minutes after two o'clock Carrington and Howland came out from the gaming room and walked over to the table. 'We've had a very nice evening,' Howland told her, patting his breast pocket. 'We're ready to leave now, my dear. Are you coming, Warren?'

'No, I think I'll stay on a while,' Tate said, glancing over to where couples were dancing together to the dreamy music. 'I might even be able to coax the young lady into dancing with me,' he added, smiling and showing his small tobacco-stained teeth.

Sadie excused herself while she saw the elderly men out to the courtyard where Nosher was sleeping behind the wheel of the large grey Daimler. 'Don't ferget ter come back fer me, Nosher, whatever yer do,' she whispered to him as the men climbed into the back seats. 'I can't wait ter get out of 'ere. I'm still lumbered wiv that bald-'eaded lecher. Just wait till I see Len Regan.'

Nosher smiled and drove off, and Sadie took a deep breath of cold night air before she went back inside, desperately wishing the time away.

For the next hour she was subjected to Warren Tate's objectionable chatter which was growing more and more suggestive. The whisky had given him the courage to pursue his objective, which Sadie knew only too well was to get her into his bed.

'I think it's time we left,' she finally told him. 'People are going home now.'

Tate had a fixed grin on his face as he stood up. 'By the way, I've something important for Mr Macaulay,' he slurred. 'Can you see that he gets it?'

'Yes, of course.'

'It's a folder and it's back at my hotel.'

White mist was rising from the fields and crows cawed from the coppice beside the frosty driveway as they walked out into the cold fresh air, Tate holding her arm whilst warning bells

150

sounded furiously in Sadie's head. The reliable Nosher was sitting huddled behind the wheel and he gave the young woman a questioning glance as she climbed into the car. Tate got in after her and sat down heavily, his bulk pressed against her as Nosher eased the car out on to the deserted highway. The journey was short, and Tate drummed his fingers on his leg nervously as the Manor Hotel loomed up out of the thickening mist.

'Wait for me, Nosher,' Sadie said as she climbed out on to the gravel driveway. Tate leaned back into the car and said something to the ex-boxer, and as he turned to Sadie the car drove off.

'What are you doing?' Sadie asked him sharply. 'I need that car.'

'It's all right, I couldn't expect you to make the journey back to London at this time of the morning,' he replied. 'I told the chauffeur to come back around ten o'clock. It'll give you time for a few hours' sleep and a freshen-up. Don't worry, you can have the bed, I'll sleep on the divan.'

'But I want to get back to London,' Sadie persisted irritably. 'This isn't what I'd planned.'

'Nonsense,' Tate said dismissively as he took her arm and shepherded her into the warm interior of the hotel. 'You've been taking care of us all night and now it's my turn to look after you.'

Sadie saw the knowing look on the night porter's face as he handed Warren Tate the key to his room and she gripped her hands

151

into tight fists as they entered the lift. Unless she was very much mistaken Warren Tate had designs on her, and from the impression she had got he was not a man who took no for an answer.

He led her into the room and she saw him put the 'Do not disturb' notice on the outside doorknob. 'A livener to take away the chill,' he said as he hunched his shoulders over the drinks cabinet.

Sadie put her handbag down on the chair by the door and pretended to look down into the courtyard below, all the time watching his movements closely. She had heard stories from Len Regan about clients spiking drinks and she felt sure Tate was up to something of the sort.

'There we are,' he said as he handed her a very large gin and tonic. 'This'll take care of any worries and fears you might have.'

'I beg your pardon?' Sadie said quickly.

'Come now, Sadie, you are a little wary of me, aren't you?'

'Not at all,' she replied with a frown. 'I just want to get home right away.'

'It's nice and warm in here and I can make you glad that you accepted my offer of a bed,' he said, moving towards her and taking her by the forearm. 'Go on, drink it down.'

Sadie put the glass to her lips and immediately detected a faint acrid tang. She was right. He had spiked her drink. 'Look, I'd better go,' she told him as she backed away. 'Give me the folder an' I'll phone for a cab.'

'At this time in the morning?' Tate said incredulously. 'All the way to London?'

'Len Regan can pay,' Sadie answered with spirit. 'It's 'is fault I'm 'ere anyway.'

'You disappoint me, Sadie,' Tate said, coming towards her again. 'Regan told me that you were a woman of the world. Hostesses usually are. I expected more from you.'

'Like takin' me ter bed?' she charged him angrily.

'It would be very nice, and I'm sure you'd enjoy the experience,' he said leering.

'That's it,' Sadie declared quickly as she grabbed her handbag from the chair. 'I'm leavin'. You give Regan the folder.'

'Oh no you don't, you little tramp,' Tate snarled as he made a grab for her. 'You knew the score when you came up here with me. Was the drink not to your liking? I only added a little something to heighten your natural desires. You would have enjoyed the feeling it produced.'

'Let me go,' she shouted as he slipped his arms around her waist.

'Relax and just let it happen,' he gasped as his wet blubbery lips sought out her neck.

With a supreme effort she pressed his chest backwards and at the same time brought her knee up sharply. Tate screamed and doubled up, his eyes bulging as he gasped for breath. 'I'll kill you, you ungrateful bitch,' he spat out hoarsely.

Sadie did not stop to watch him recover. She left the room as fast as she could and dashed down the stairs, to the surprise of the night

153

porter who watched open-mouthed as she ran out into the mist clutching her handbag to her bosom.

As she hurried headlong down the path she heard the crunch of tyres on the gravel behind her. 'Nosher! I thought yer'd gone back ter London,' she gasped as he pulled up beside her.

'I take orders from Len Regan, nobody else,' he replied with a dignified air.

'Nosher, you're a diamond,' she said with feeling as she slipped into the seat beside him. 'That bald-'eaded ole coot told me 'e 'ad some information fer Johnnie Macaulay in 'is room an' I'm afraid I fell fer it. 'E tried it on but I managed ter get out before any 'arm was done, ter me at least.'

Nosher pulled the car up sharply at the end of the drive. 'Maybe I should go an' 'ave a quiet word wiv the geezer,' he said, clenching his large fist suggestively.

'No, leave it,' Sadie said quickly. ' 'E didn't feel too well when I left, an' anyway Len Regan can sort this mess out.'

Nosher drove back to London carefully with diffused headlights, through a thick mist which seemed like a solid wall in front of them. Sadie leaned her head back against the seat and tried not to let herself get too angry. Len had gone too far this time though, she told herself. He had used her as a plaything for his unsavoury clients while he swanned about back in London. She betted that he had had no intention of coming down to the nightclub and had left her holding the candle. Well he wasn't going to get away with it, she vowed. And she wasn't going chasing after him either. If he wanted to know how things had gone he would have to contact her.

As Nosher drove into the outskirts of London Sadie reached into her handbag and took out the little notebook she always carried with her. Slipping the tin pencil from the binding coil she scribbled a few words down and tore out the page. 'Nosher, can you go past Len Regan's place?' she asked. 'I wanna slip this frew 'is letterbox.'

'Sure,' he replied.

Soon they were carefully negotiating familiar backstreets to emerge into the New Kent Road, and Nosher swung the car into a side turning and pulled up outside a row of large Victorian houses. 'Stay there, I'll put it frew,' he told her.

As he walked up the flight of steps to the front door Sadie leaned across to his side of the car and glanced up in the breaking dawn at Len's bedroom window. She saw the curtains move slightly, sending out a shaft of light, then they closed again. Len had seen the car.

'Right then, let's get you 'ome,' Nosher grunted as he slipped back behind the steering wheel.

When the Daimler finally pulled up in Carter Lane Sadie turned sideways and kissed the ex-pugilist on his stubbled cheek. 'Fanks, Nosher,' she said affectionately. 'I wish everybody was as reliable as you.'

155

He smiled, embarrassed at her show of gratitude. 'No sweat, Sadie,' he replied. 'That's what I get paid for.'

The young woman let herself into the house and crept carefully up the stairs to her bedroom where she quickly undressed and slipped between the cold sheets. Sleep would not come, after everything that had happened that night. In her troubled mind she pictured over and over again the way the curtains had moved, and she could not get the feeling out of her head that Len Regan had not been alone in that bedroom.

CHAPTER 13

Another week of war had passed and Carter Lane seemed full of khaki and navy blue. Frank and Jim Flynn were home on leave from training and their younger brother Pat was due home the following week, while Mrs Wilson's son Dennis was home from the navy, looking the part in his tight-fitting top and bell-bottoms. His younger sister Claire had managed to get home from her job in the Land Army to see her brother before he went back to Chatham and Mrs Jones' son Jerry was home too. Mrs Bromilow was very proud of her son Freddie, who looked every inch a Grenadier Guardsman. Mrs Wickstead too was feeling very proud of her boy Chris who was in the Royal Fusiliers. He carried the uniform well, with the distinctive feathered plume on the front of his beret.

The Sun public house did a roaring trade that week and Charlie Anson lost no time in telling everyone who was interested that he had finally barred Sid Cafferty for good.

'Well, ter be fair 'e couldn't do much else, could 'e?' Danny Crossley remarked to Alf Coates. 'Big Joe's due 'ome any day now an' when 'e gets ter know about Cafferty smackin' ole Bert Kenny 'e's gonna wipe the floor wiv 'im.'

'Yeah, an' there'll be more than a few glasses broke this time if Joe catches Cafferty in 'ere,' Alf agreed.

'I bin finkin' about what 'appened last week,' Danny went on. 'If Alec Conroy's the coward Cafferty makes 'im out ter be, why did 'e stand up to 'im? I mean ter say, the ugly git must be four stone 'eavier at least.'

'Search me,' Alf replied.

' 'E'll 'ave ter go in the end, or they'll lock 'im up,' Danny said.

'P'raps 'e'll register as a conshie.'

'Yeah, 'e might do.'

' 'Ere, I know what I was gonna ask yer,' Alf remarked suddenly. ' 'As your ole woman joined that knittin' fer victory fing?'

'Yeah, she 'as,' Danny told him. 'Mind you, she ain't much of a knitter. Yer wanna see the navy scarf she's makin'. It's about six foot long an' she ain't finished it yet.'

'My ole woman wanted ter join but she can't knit,' Alf said shaking his head. 'Those Lockwood sisters said they'd teach 'er, but I

157

fink they're wastin' their time. Anyfing like that an' she's all fingers an' fumbs. I tell yer somefing. The ovver day me braces' buttons come orf me strides so the ole gel sorts frew the ornaments where she keeps all the bits an' pieces an' she finds these two buttons. Grey they were. Anyway, she sews 'em on, after a fashion, an' when I come ter put me braces on I can't button 'em up. Know what she done?'

'No.'

'She'd sewed two poxy overcoat buttons on me trousers. They must 'ave bin two bloody inches wide. They looked like a couple o' dustbin lids stuck on. I ses to 'er, " 'ere, Flo, 'ow the bloody 'ell am I expected ter button these up?" Went orf alarmin' she did. Told me I was never satisfied. Then she finds me a poxy safety pin. I told 'er I could 'ave done that in the first place. Bloody useless where sewin's concerned she is.'

Despite a few negative responses the Lockwood sisters had succeeded in recruiting enough of their neighbours to form a fair-sized knitting group and they applied for wool and knitting needles from the WVS and other agencies. The idea had been for the women to meet up at the Lockwood home and work together over cups of tea and rock cakes, but it never quite worked out like that. Mrs Bromilow, who was an expert knitter, declined to become that sociable. 'I'll knit scarves an' socks, no problem,' she said to her friend Ivy Jones, 'but I couldn't sit there all the time. Yer gotta watch yerself in their gaff. When I drop a stitch I'm inclined to eff an' blind an' yer can't do that wiv them around, they go all funny. Besides, 'ave you ever tasted their tea? It's like cat's piss. An' those rock cakes they make! Gawd Almighty, I 'ave enough trouble wiv me choppers as it is, wivout tryin' ter bite frew them bleedin' fings. Rock's the word. I fink they must 'ave got the bakin' powder mixed up wiv cement.'

Dolly Flynn knitted for the group whenever she found the time, and Daisy Harris became the street's fastest sock knitter. Mrs Wickstead went to the Lockwood house on a couple of occasions but found it hard work trying to knit while the sisters chatted about their early lives and Cynthia's brute of a husband, who had mercifully disappeared from the scene some ten years ago.

Mrs Bromilow found the ideal solution. She took her knitting bag to The Sun at lunchtimes and sat knitting over a glass or two of milk stout. Ivy Jones soon realised that Amy Bromilow had the right idea and she joined her. At first the clicking of needles irked Charlie Anson, but he soon got used to it, and when his wife Tess decided she would have a go at making socks he could only shake his head in resignation.

Frank and Jim Flynn were due to catch the late train back to Winchester that Sunday evening and Dolly wanted the dinner to be just right. Frank liked his Yorkshire pudding crusty while Jim liked plenty of roast potatoes on his plate, but they both revered her meat stock gravy, and as she stirred in the beef cube Dolly dipped her finger in the thick mixture to sample it. She had chopped the cabbage and shelled the peas, mixed the Yorkshire and made the mustard for Mick, and she felt pleased that it was all under control and on time. Normally the girls would help her get the Sunday meal ready, but today everything had to be perfect and she did not want them getting under her feet.

Up in Sadie's bedroom the two girls were taking advantage of their release from scullery duty by chatting about one or two things that their parents were not privy to.

'So yer've not seen 'im since?' Jennie queried.

'Nope.'

'Yer mean 'e didn't reply ter yer note?'

'Nope.'

'So what yer gonna do then?'

'I dunno, but one fing's certain,' Sadie replied with gusto. 'I ain't gonna go runnin' after 'im.'

'I should bloody well fink not.'

'I wouldn't 'ave minded, but it was as though 'e was usin' me as some ole prosser,' Sadie went on.

'You should've let Nosher give that geezer a goin'-over,' Jennie said.

'I couldn't very well,' Sadie replied. ' 'E was one o' Johnnie Macaulay's clients after all. It would've only got Nosher inter trouble an' 'e's a really nice bloke.'

'Anyway I reckon Regan'll come callin' before long,' Jennie remarked. ' 'E's done it before when yer've given 'im the elbow.'

160

'Well, 'e can please 'imself,' Sadie said sharply. 'I might not answer the door to 'im. I might let you do it, an' you can tell 'im I'm out.'

'Good fer you,' Jennie told her, bouncing up on the edge of the bed. ' 'Ere, s'posin' yer bump inter Big Joe while 'e's 'ome on leave an' 'e asks yer out. Would yer go?'

'I might,' Sadie said, shrugging her shoulders.

'You like 'im, don't yer?'

' 'E's all right. 'E's a nice enough feller.'

'I could tell 'e finks a lot o' you.'

'I 'ardly know 'im.'

'What difference does that make?' Jennie pressed. 'I 'ardly know Con but I fink 'e's a dream.'

'All your fellers are dreams,' Sadie scoffed.

'Not the way Con is,' Jennie said sighing as she cuddled the pillow. 'As a matter o' fact I fink I'm in love wiv 'im. Do you believe in love at first sight?'

'It can 'appen, I s'pose, but it's never 'appened ter me yet.'

'You told me yer loved Len.'

'Yeah, but it sort o' grew on me.'

'D'yer still love 'im?'

'I dunno. I dunno what I feel at the moment.'

'After the war I'm gonna marry Con an' 'ave 'is babies,' Jennie drooled on. 'We'll get a nice place in the country an' the kids can grow up in the fresh air wiv fields ter play in.'

'It sounds lovely, but it can only be a dream while this war goes on,' Sadie reminded her.

They heard their mother's voice calling them down to Sunday dinner and Jennie sighed deeply

161

as she slid from the bed. 'I say me prayers every night,' she confided quietly, 'an' they say that if yer pray 'ard enough dreams do come true.'

'Yeah, course they will,' Sadie replied, giving her a warm smile.

Another week and the khaki and navy blue had gone from the lane, where a sprinkling of snow now lay on the cobblestones. An icy wind promised more and it cut through the young airman's greatcoat as he hurried along the turning. He had written a letter to her saying when he would be home on leave, asking her to meet him at midday on Saturday. The little tea bar in the Old Kent Road was the place where they had often sat chatting together in happier days, but as he strode on the young man was prepared for the worst. Brenda was a beautiful woman with a passion that sometimes surprised him, and he had spent many lonely hours back in camp wondering about her. Not all the local young men were in uniform yet and there were a few who wouldn't be slow to come calling, given the opportunity.

The cafe was warm and welcoming and the smell of bacon frying drifted out from the kitchen. Pat carried a large mug of tea over to a window seat and loosened his greatcoat as he made himself comfortable. Brenda was never one for punctuality and while he waited patiently for her to put in an appearance he watched the passers-by and the fairly heavy traffic through a circular space he cleared on the steamy window. It had been a long six weeks and he wondered how the parting had affected her. At least she would have had time to think clearly, though knowing Brenda she might have pushed it all into the background and decided to have a good time.

He suddenly saw her pass the window, and as she came into the cafe Pat was on his feet. ' 'Ow yer doin', Brenda?' he asked as casually as he could.

'Fine. An' you?'

'Yeah, fine.'

'Yer look like yer lost weight, Pat.'

He smiled awkwardly as he led her over to his seat. 'Can I get yer a cuppa?'

'I'd like a coffee please. Milky.'

They sat facing each other, hardly knowing what to say, and it was Brenda who finally made a start. 'You never wrote ter me while you were away, before askin' if we could meet terday,' she said, flicking her eyes up at his.

'I wanted to,' he sighed, 'but I thought we'd said everyfing before I left ter join up.'

'You could 'ave let me know 'ow you were gettin' on, told me about the trainin',' she remarked.

He shrugged his shoulders. 'If I 'ad done would you 'ave bovvered ter reply?'

'I dunno,' she said, staring down into her cup. 'Yer made it quite clear you were gonna volunteer an' I could like it or lump it.'

'I didn't say it like that,' he replied defensively.

'Not in as many words, but that's what yer meant,' Brenda told him. 'It was as though it

163

was a big adventure an' what I wanted fer us didn't matter.'

'But it does,' Pat said quietly. 'The fing was, I wanted ter get it over wiv, joinin' up I mean. Frank an' Jim decided ter volunteer instead o' waitin' ter be called up an' we talked about it. I agreed wiv 'em. It made no sense to 'ang around scratchin' ourselves.'

'Yeah, but it's all right fer them,' Brenda retorted. 'Neivver of 'em's got a steady girlfriend. Wiv you it was different. We were talkin' about gettin' engaged. We could 'ave done it before yer got called up, but no, you couldn't wait. I was so mad. It seemed ter me I didn't count fer anyfing. You just made yer mind up wivout talkin' it over. Surely I 'ad the right ter be told of yer feelin's before yer made the decision.'

'Maybe yer right,' Pat conceded. 'But please don't fink I treat this as some schoolboy adventure. I know what war means from listenin' ter me dad an' people of 'is age. It's terrifyin' an' bloody, but we're in a war an' that's that.'

Brenda looked up into his eyes. 'I was 'opin' yer wouldn't 'ave ter go,' she said quietly. 'There's plenty o' people in reserved occupations. I wanted you 'ere wiv me, not in the firin' line.'

He smiled. 'I'm not exactly in the firin' line, Brenda. At the moment I've passed out o' basic trainin' an' I'm gonna be trained up as an aircraft frame fitter.'

'You told me you was gonna volunteer fer aircrew,' Brenda reminded him.

164

'So I am, but there's no guarantee I'll be accepted.'

'But why?' she pressed him. 'I just can't understand. Surely you're doing yer bit bein' a fitter or whatever, wivout volunteerin' fer a dangerous job like that.'

He sighed deeply, struggling for an explanation which he could put into words. 'Don't ask me fer reasons, Brenda,' he replied helplessly.

She pushed her empty cup away from her, her eyes flaring angrily as she stood up and leaned across the table towards him. 'No, course not,' she said coldly. 'You put yer name down fer one o' the most dangerous jobs yer can find an' yer don't know the reason? Well, I know the reason. It's that manly fing. "Look at me, everybody? Ain't I big, ain't I smart, ain't I brave?" You men are born wiv it. You 'ave it as kids an' it never leaves yer. You be big, Pat. You be smart an' brave too, but don't expect me ter sit at 'ome prayin' fer yer next letter an' worryin' meself sick every time a plane goes missin'. I've got a life too, an' I wanted it wiv you. I wanna be seen in a white weddin' dress, not mournin' black.'

Pat saw the tears welling up in her eyes as she turned away from him and stormed out of the cafe. People were looking over and he felt his face grow hot. He got up quickly, and as he hurried towards the door an old lady sitting alone at a table grabbed his arm. 'She'll come round in time, luv,' she said quietly. 'It ain't easy fer anybody these days.'

165

It snowed again that week and a general feeling of depression settled over Carter Lane. The servicemen had all returned from leave, Claire Wilson had gone back to Wiltshire and Mrs Jones' daughter Alma had left to join the WAAF. Even the corner shop couple, Sara and Tom Jackman, seemed to have lost some of their cheeriness. The queues grew longer and food supplies became short as the toll of shipping sunk mounted daily, and while the Jackmans refused to engage in what had now become known as the black market, certain foodstuffs were available 'under the counter' at many shops. If a customer could afford the price and knew where to go they could buy almost anything. Silk stockings were almost impossible to get hold of unless a person had the right contacts, and thereby a much-used epithet entered the English language. The 'spiv' always seemed able to lay hands on even the most scarce of commodities, and if the money was forthcoming so were the goods.

It was a bitterly cold morning when Big Joe Buckley finally walked back into the turning and knocked on the Kennys' front door.

'Oh my good Gawd, it's you!' Liz gasped.

'It was, the last time I copped a squiz at meself in the mirror, Liz,' Joe said grinning widely. 'Well, are you gonna let me in or what?'

'Come in, son,' she said, hugging him as he stepped into the passage. 'Bert, it's Big Joe.'

Liz's husband hurried down the stairs and

166

grabbed the Australian by the hand. 'Blimey, you look well,' he remarked. 'We thought yer'd fergot about us.'

'Not a chance, mate,' Joe replied as he walked into the parlour.

'Sit down by the fire, son,' Liz said quickly. 'Bert, give 'im that cushion. Cup o' tea, Joe? Blimey, it is good ter see yer. Yer look smart in that uniform. Doesn't 'e look smart, Bert?'

' 'E certainly does,' Bert replied.

Joe smiled. 'You are now looking at Leading Seaman Joseph L Buckley, no bloody less,' he declared drolly, pointing to the red anchor sewn into the arm of his uniform.

Liz fussed and Bert had many questions, and the big Australian settled back in the armchair with a huge mug of sweet, steaming hot tea.

'I've bin out wiv the flu,' Bert told him. 'I'm goin' back on Monday though. I'm glad I was 'ome when yer knocked. Bloody 'ell it's good ter see yer, mate.'

'And it's good to see you two,' Joe said, his smile growing even broader.

' 'Ave you 'ad anyfing to eat this mornin'?' Liz asked him.

'Yeah, I had some breckie before I left the barracks.'

'Don't tell me yer couldn't manage egg an' bacon,' Liz persisted.

Bert got up from his armchair. 'I won't be long, son, I'm just gonna go fer the mornin' paper,' he said.

'You stay where you are,' Joe told him. 'It's

167

colder than a polar bear's arse out there. I'll get it.'

'She likes the *Daily Sketch*,' Bert reminded him. 'She only gets it fer the bloody 'oroscope.'

In a small community such as Carter Lane it would not have taken long, and fifteen minutes later Big Joe came back with the paper under his arm and a look of thunder on his handsome face. 'I want a word with you two,' he said sternly.

CHAPTER 14

The cold weather was not likely to prevent the likes of Danny Crossley and Alf Coates from making their usual trip to the corner pub, and at ten minutes past eleven on Tuesday morning they stepped into the public bar to announce that it was cold enough to freeze the balls off a brass monkey.

Charlie Anson had got the fire going and the intrepid two took their pints over to a nearby table and stood for a few minutes by the hearth warming themselves.

'By the way, Big Joe's 'ome on leave,' the landlord called over as he poured Mrs Bromilow's milk stout. 'My missus saw 'im at the paper shop this mornin'. 'E told 'er 'e'd got 'ome yesterday.'

'That's nice to 'ear,' Danny replied. ' 'Ere, 'e ain't on the wagon, is 'e?'

'I shouldn't fink so. Why d'yer ask?'

'Well, I would 'ave thought 'e'd 'ave looked in 'ere last night.'

'No sweat, 'e told Tess 'e was gonna pop in this lunchtime.'

The two elderly gents made themselves comfortable at the table and sat watching Amy Bromilow unravelling a skein of thick navy-blue wool as she sat a little way away.

Alf took out his stained clay pipe from his top pocket and examined it before getting out his penknife to scrape the bowl into the hearth. 'Better than a briar,' he remarked to Amy. 'When yer burn 'em in they taste as sweet as a nut.'

'You could 'ave fooled me,' Amy said sarcastically. 'That stuff you smoke in that pipe smells like 'orseshit.'

'Nah, it's dark shag,' Alf told her. 'It don't burn away as quickly as that light stuff.'

Amy was struggling with the wool. ' 'Ere, Danny, give us an 'and will yer?' she asked him. 'Come an' 'old this while I wind it.'

The elderly man reluctantly went over and sat facing her while she slipped the skein over his outstretched hands and proceeded to make a ball. 'Now keep yer 'ands still,' she said, 'an' don't let it slip off or I'll be all day unravellin' it.'

Just then Big Joe made his appearance wearing his uniform, and he stood inside the door taking in the scene. 'Now that's what I call a nice picture,' he said grinning. 'I wish I had a camera. The folk back in Oz

169

wouldn't believe it.'

Danny grinned sheepishly and Alf got up to pat the young man on the back. 'Nice ter see yer, son,' he said. 'Come on, let me buy you a pint.'

Big Joe put his arm around the old man's shoulders. 'I wouldn't bloody dream of it,' he replied. 'I'm gonna buy you one, digger.'

Charlie Anson shook the big man's hand vigorously. 'Yer look very well, Joe,' he said. ' 'Ow long you 'ome for?'

'Seven days,' Joe told him.

'It ain't long.'

'It's enough to sort a few things out,' the Australian said as he watched the landlord pour the drinks.

Charlie glanced up quickly at the tone of his voice and saw the steel glint in Joe's deep-blue eyes. 'You just take it easy, son. Yer 'ome ter rest, remember.'

Joe insisted on buying Charlie a drink as well as Amy and the two pub fixtures, and when he had settled himself at the table beside them he took a long draught. 'I got to hear about the barney with the Conroy boy and that boofhead Cafferty,' he remarked, glancing at each of the old gents in turn.

' 'E was well out of order,' Alf said quickly. 'Whatever the rights an' wrongs there's no call fer the bloody ox ter go pokin' 'is nose in ovver people's business.'

'I s'pose you 'eard about Bert Kenny gettin' clocked?' Danny queried.

'Yeah, I did,' Big Joe growled, 'and Cafferty's

170

gonna 'ave to see me about that. That dingo's gonna be as scarce as rockin'-horse shit round here when I've finished with him.'

'You can't afford ter get involved, Joe,' Alf warned him. 'If yer come up in front o' that beak again 'e'll chuck the book at yer.'

'Don't you worry about me,' Joe replied. 'I'll flush that nong down the dunny before the blue boys get here.'

'You just be careful,' Danny added. 'Bert Kenny finks the world o' you an' 'e wouldn't want yer gettin' inter trouble on 'is account.'

Joe took another gulp from his glass. 'I understand the Flynn boys were home on leave a couple o' weeks ago,' he said, changing the subject.

'Yeah, but it was a pity Frank an' Jim missed young Pat,' Alf replied. 'As they went back so Pat comes 'ome. 'E went back last Sunday. 'E was in 'ere on Saturday night wiv some of 'is pals an' 'e ended up gettin' as pissed as an 'andcart.'

'How's the Flynn girls?' Joe asked casually.

'Young Jennie's got a job at the baker's in the Old Kent Road,' Amy cut in, 'an' Sadie's started work at the gasworks offices up on Canal Bridge. Oh an' as you can see I've joined the Lockwood sisters' sewin' club.'

'Good fer you, Amy,' Joe said grinning. 'Is that a scarf you're knitting?'

'Looks more like a bed blanket,' Alf chuckled.

'None o' your cheek neivver,' Amy growled at him. 'This is fer a sailor, an' those navy boys need long scarves ter keep 'em warm while they're at sea.'

'Our Amy's a good ole knitter,' Danny remarked. 'Yer should've seen the pair o' socks she's just finished. The bloody size of 'em. I ses to 'er, ain't those socks s'posed ter be worn under their Wellin'ton boots. I thought I was gonna end up wearin' 'er glass o' stout.'

'I wouldn't waste it on the likes o' you,' Amy said disdainfully.

Joe studied his near-empty glass for a few moments and then he leaned over the table. 'Have either of you seen anything o' Cafferty lately?' he asked quietly.

Alf shook his head slowly as he filled his pipe. 'I expect Bert Kenny told yer that Charlie barred 'im from 'ere, and I've 'eard 'e's usin' The Dun Cow now. Apparently Cafferty's the yard foreman in the Council buildin' depot just round the corner in Lynton Road.'

'Yeah, one o' the buildin' lads was tellin' us,' Danny cut in. ' 'E said Cafferty's there every lunchtime shootin' 'is mouth off about one fing or anuvver. The guv'nor at The Dun Cow won't stand too much o' that, mark my words.'

Joe looked from one to the other, a smile forming on his broad features. 'Do you still go on those little walkabouts?' he enquired.

'Yeah as long as it's dry,' Alf told him. 'The cold don't worry us, does it Danny?'

'Nah, long as we're well wrapped up.'

'Apart from Cafferty are you two known at the Dun Cow?'

'Nah, we never go in there,' Alf replied.

'How would you like to do me a big favour?'

'You name it, son,' Alf told him.

'Right then, here's the plan, but first let's get some more drinks in,' Joe said, smiling slyly.

At five o'clock Sadie walked out of the gasworks office and waved goodnight to her workfriends, pulling her coat collar up around her ears as she turned into Lynton Road. After a few yards she felt a hand on her arm and turned quickly to see Joe Buckley smiling at her. 'Hello, Sadie,' he said cheerfully.

'Well I'll be ...' Sadie said in surprise. 'What are you doin' up 'ere?'

'Time was on me hands and I suddenly got this idea that maybe you might be a bit bored walking home with no one to talk to,' Joe said smiling.

'Well, it's very nice, but 'ow did yer know where I worked?' she asked.

'How do you keep a secret in a place like Carter Lane?' he replied.

Sadie smiled back. 'An' I s'pose yer've caught up wiv all the ovver news?'

He nodded nonchalantly. 'Yeah, this and that,' he said.

'Well, I 'ope yer not gonna get yerself inter trouble over that set-to in the turnin',' she remarked.

Joe was still holding on to her arm as they walked up the rise that led over the railway lines, feeling the chill wind on their faces. 'Nah, I've gotta be a bit careful after last time,' he said with a sigh. 'Still, I'm sure that big bully'll get his comeuppance one day soon.'

'Yeah, 'e will, that's a dead cert,' Sadie replied. 'So you just let it rest. Bert's fergot about it I'm sure.'

'Yep, sure thing, Sadie,' Joe said blithely.

She looked into his eyes, a smile playing on her lips. 'Try not ter ferget yerself when yer've got a few pints inside yer, won't yer?' she told him. 'Just mind what yer doin'. Liz Kenny won't take kindly ter bailin' yer out again.'

He winced noticeably. 'Yeah, best behaviour,' he said with a sheepish smile.

'I wasn't gettin' at yer, Joe,' she said quickly. 'It's just that people in Carter Lane like yer an' they wouldn't wanna see yer gettin' into any more trouble.'

'Does that include you too?' he asked.

'Yeah, me too.'

'Sadie, are you still with that feller?'

'Well, if yer must know it's bin an off-an'-on fing lately, but I'm still seein' 'im occasionally.'

Joe looked pleased with her answer. 'Look, is there any chance of coming out for a drink with me?' he asked. 'Tonight maybe?'

'Well, I was gonna wash me 'air an' do some ironin',' she told him.

'Aw, your hair's not dirty yet,' he replied. 'And ironin' ain't very exciting.'

'An' comin' out fer a drink wiv you would be?' she teased.

Joe pulled a face. 'I'm not very good at this sort of thing,' he said solemnly. 'But if you decide to come out for a drink I'd be honoured.'

His serious expression looked very comical and her heart bounded. 'You're on,' she said smiling.

Joe's face lit up. 'Ripper,' he said, punching the air.

They turned left into Munday Road and left again into Carter Lane whereupon Joe let go of her arm. 'Is eight o'clock okay?' he asked as they reached her front door.

'Yeah, fine. See yer then,' Sadie said, giving him a smile as she let herself into the house.

On Wednesday morning Alf Coates and Danny Crossley wrapped themselves up against the inclement weather and took a stroll along the Old Kent Road to The Dun Cow. 'I understand Sid Cafferty drinks in 'ere,' Alf said to the barman as he waited for his glass to be filled.

'Yeah, that's right,' the barman said, eyeing the elderly man curiously. 'Why d'yer ask?'

'It's just that we don't like ter see trouble where it can be avoided, do we, Alf?' Danny cut in.

'Trouble?'

'Yeah, it seems that Sid Cafferty's card's bin marked.'

' 'Ow d'yer mean?'

'Well, me an' my mate 'ere was 'avin' a livener in The Sun public 'ouse down in Carter Lane yesterday,' Danny went on, 'an' we 'eard the geezer called Alec Conroy shootin' 'is mouth off. 'E was sayin' that Sid Cafferty was a no-good git an' a yeller-livered coward

175

ter boot, an' if 'e ever showed 'is face around Carter Lane again 'e was gonna get sorted out good an' proper. This Conroy bloke said that it was only the neighbours interferin' that saved 'im last time but the next time round they wouldn't get the chance. 'E went on ter say that Cafferty 'ad better keep ter The Dun Cow or 'e'd do 'im over bad.'

'Yeah, that's right,' Alf said. 'We're on our way ter Peckham ter see me daughter so we decided it might be a good idea ter pop in 'ere while we was in the area an' warn Cafferty off from goin' anywhere near Carter Lane. I can't stand ter see people bashin' each ovver up. It's bad enough wiv the bleedin' war.'

' 'E'll be in around twelve,' the barman told them. 'Why don't yer 'ang about.'

'Nah, I'm afraid we ain't got time,' Alf replied. 'Me daughter 'as ter go out at twelve. P'raps you could warn 'im. We wouldn't like ter see the bloke get duffed up, would we, mate?'

Danny shook his head as he put on his most stern expression. 'This Conroy bloke seems like 'e means it. 'E was slaggin' Cafferty off unmercifully. Best if yer warn 'im ter keep well away from The Sun.'

As the two old friends walked back to Carter Lane they could not help looking a little pleased with themselves.

'You know somefing, Alf,' Danny said grinning. 'I make you out ter be one lyin' ole git.'

'You ain't so bad yerself,' Alf replied.

176

Big Joe Buckley was wearing his civilian clothes as he sat alone at a table in The Sun waiting for the two to arrive back. Last night had been a very nice evening, he thought dreamily—a few drinks in The Anchor, an old timbered pub by the river, sitting by a log fire and chatting away non-stop about almost everything. He had told Sadie more about his life back in Australia and she had spoken about her childhood days in the street. They had laughed and joked together, and she had told him a little bit about her relationship with Len Regan. She had been light-hearted about it but he had sensed an undertow of discontent. He had gained the impression that Regan wasn't taking things serious enough and she needed more from their relationship. He also got the message that Sadie had no intention of cheating on him. To her the evening was nothing more than a friendly chat between two neighbours and he should read nothing into it. Okay fair go, he thought, but as far as he could work out, the door had been left ajar, and it was up to him to make his mark, let her see that he was truly pretty mad about her, despite Len Regan. How he was expected to achieve anything though, what with the war and being away most of the time, was beyond him and the problem left him feeling a little frustrated.

The look on both Alf and Danny's faces as they walked into the pub told Joe that things had gone according to plan and his heart pounded with anticipation.

' 'E'll get the message,' Alf said grinning.

'Cafferty's gonna be fired up like a mad bull,' Danny added. 'You'd better be careful, Joe.'

Come lunchtime, the pub was filling up, which suited Joe very nicely. If Cafferty did take the bait and come calling he would be on his opponent's ground and be unlikely to have a cohort nearby to back him up, should things not go his way. It was also important to the big Australian that Cafferty should be shamed away from the area once and for all.

Time moved on. Twenty past the hour, twenty to two, and still no sign of Sid Cafferty. Joe was beginning to feel that his plan had failed and he considered getting another drink, but at fifteen minutes to two a young workman came into the bar looking a little agitated. 'Is Alec Conroy in 'ere?' he asked the elderly man sitting just inside the door.

Joe heard the remark. 'Who wants him?' he asked.

'A big geezer across the street,' the workman said timidly.

Joe looked through a clear gap in the figured glass of the door to see Sid Cafferty leaning against the wall opposite. He was wearing a duffle coat with a scarf loosely tied around his bull neck. Suddenly he straightened up and cupped his hand to his mouth. 'Come out, yer mouthy git, I know yer in there,' he bellowed out.

Joe took a deep breath, threw out his chest and stepped out into the street. 'You never learn, do you, Cafferty,' he called back.

The bully's face grew dark. 'I should 'ave

suspected somefing like this,' he growled as he stepped into the roadway. 'Keep out o' this, Buckley. I got no beef wiv you. I'm lookin' fer Conroy.'

'He's not been in the pub for a couple o' weeks,' Joe told him calmly.

'Yeah, that figures,' Cafferty said, gritting his teeth. 'Yer set me up, didn't yer?'

'Well, it wasn't hard,' Joe told him with a laugh. 'You ain't got enough brains to give yerself a headache. An' now you're gonna answer to me for Bert Kenny.'

'Bert Kenny? Who's 'e?'

'The man you conked when he tried to stop you beating the Conroy lad up,' Joe replied. 'Bert's a good mate o' mine, so when I've finished with you you won't work in an iron lung.'

Cafferty realised there was no way out of the straits he found himself in and he got ready by slipping out of his heavy coat and unravelling the scarf from around his neck as Joe moved closer to him. Still holding the scarf he suddenly lunged forward, attempting to get it round Joe's throat but the Australian was too quick for him. A short right in the midriff made Cafferty gasp but he swung round smartly and planted a left hook on the side of his opponent's head. For a moment Joe saw flashing lights and he realised that Cafferty was not going to be a pushover. He turned, his fists held up in front of his face, and when the bully darted forward he was ready. The first blow smacked full into Cafferty's face and the looping left hit him behind the ear. The

179

hulking bruiser spat blood from his split lips as he staggered back, then with a roar he rushed forward and grabbed Joe round the waist. With his hands pinned to his sides and the breath slowly being pressed out of him Joe butted Cafferty in the face, at the same time bringing his knee up sharply into his groin.

They moved back from each other, circling like dogs looking for an opening, oblivious to the cries of people watching the fight.

'For goodness sake stop them somebody,' Charity Lockwood called out.

'Let 'em fight,' Alf Coates called back, dancing from one foot to the other with excitement.

'Why don't somebody do somefing?' Mrs Wickstead shouted.

'What d'yer suggest, gel?' another chuckled. 'A bucket o' water?'

Fists smashed out with sickening thuds and both men were beginning to spill blood. Cafferty's nose was broken and his eyebrow cut, and Joe had a gaping gash on his cheekbone. They circled once more, breath coming in rasping gasps and then as Cafferty rushed forward in a last desperate effort a swinging right with all Joe's force behind it slammed home and it was all over. Cafferty went down as though he had been poleaxed and lay prone on the cobblestones, dead to the world.

Joe made his way painfully back to the pub, and as he glanced back he saw Bill Harris in the process of dowsing Cafferty with a bucket of cold water.

'I don't fink we'll see 'im round 'ere any more,' Alf Coates remarked to Danny.

'Good riddance, I say,' his friend replied.

Later that evening as soon as Alec Conroy got home from work Rene told him about the fight. 'Joe slaughtered the ugly git,' she said with passion. 'Me an' yer dad was sayin', we've never seen a fight like it.'

Alec slumped down in the armchair and kicked off his shoes. 'Yeah,' he said flatly.

'I thought yer would 'ave bin well pleased,' Ted remarked.

Alec looked up at his mother and father in turn. 'What did it solve?' he asked them. 'Tell me what it solved.'

'It put a bully in 'is place, that's what,' Ted said sharply. 'It's what this war's all about. About standin' up against the bully. You stood up ter Cafferty, so why won't yer stand up ter the biggest one of all?'

'Well, if it makes yer feel better, I volunteered fer the army this mornin',' Alec told them.

CHAPTER 15

1940

The first Christmas of the war had been a very quiet affair for the people of Carter Lane. With so many empty spaces around the festive tables it had been almost wished away as people looked forward hopefully to a New Year that would bring peace. A freezing January and snow in February gave way to seasonal March winds, and with them a general realisation that the war was not going to end that soon after all. With news coming through of naval activity off the coast of Norway and the massing of the German army in the Baltic ports it seemed to almost everyone that it was only just beginning to hot up.

Riflemen Frank and Jim Flynn were now serving in France with the British Expeditionary Force along with Con Williams, and so too was Chris Wickstead of the Royal Fusiliers. Amy Bromilow's son Freddie was sent to France in January with his battalion of Grenadier Guards and Ivy Jones' son Jerry was serving with a Royal Marine brigade which was making ready to land in Norway. Big Joe Buckley had used his special knowledge of marine diesels to get selected for a secret and elite force, and in the early new year he was training at a remote base somewhere in Scotland.

Early in April the German army swept into Denmark and Norway and within twenty-four hours Denmark was in German hands. Its ports and inlets were now available for an assault on Norway, and as the depressing news filtered through, Ivy and Ben Jones had good reason to worry when they heard that the Royal Marines were amongst the British forces which had landed in Narvik. Ben Jones kept a map of Norway and he was able to follow the military movements as the German army swept down from the north of the country. Reports were coming through of heavy casualties, and when the army was evacuated from Norway on the third of April Ivy and Ben said a special prayer that their son Jerry would be amongst the survivors.

As the weather changed for the better at the end of April people felt that maybe the summer would bring some good news for a change, but their hopes turned to nightmare when in early May the German army swept through the Low Countries and attacked France through the Ardennes. Their units pushed back towards the coastline, the sons of Carter Street were now fighting for their lives.

Sadie Flynn dried the last of the plates and hung the wet tea towel over the line above the gas stove. For some time now there had been a strained atmosphere between her and her parents and when she complained to Jennie she had got little support.

'It's understandable when yer stop ter fink,' Jennie reminded her as they sat together in Sadie's bedroom. 'Frank an' Jim are fightin' in France and Pat's away, an' there's you swannin' it wiv that wide-boy Regan.'

'What am I s'posed ter do, pack 'im in, just 'cos 'e's not out there fightin' as well?'

'I'm not sayin' that,' Jennie replied, 'but it don't 'elp when yer told muvver the ovver night about that party at the nightclub. I mean, champagne an' all the best food, while people round 'ere are 'avin' ter pay frew the nose fer under-the-counter stuff. It ain't on, is it?'

Sadie sighed sadly. 'I can understand 'ow people must feel, but as I tried to explain ter Mum, not everyone can just put on a uniform. Life 'as ter go on at 'ome. Lots o' young men are in reserved jobs an' they're doin' their best, even though people tend ter slag 'em off fer dodgin' call-up.'

'I fink it's all right fer people in reserved occupations,' Jennie went on, 'but it's people like that Johnnie Macaulay an' your feller who are takin' advantage by dealin' in the black market. 'Ow d'yer fink our bruvvers'd feel if they were riskin' their lives on those convoys bringin' food in an' then they 'eard about all this dodgy business that's makin' certain people rich.'

'I don't fink Macaulay's in the black market,' Sadie said defensively. 'All right, so they buy stuff under the counter like a lot of ovver people but as fer dealin' in it, I don't believe they do.'

Jennie shook her head slowly. 'What you're really sayin' is yer don't wanna believe it,' she corrected her. 'Face up to it, Sadie. Johnnie Macaulay an' Len Regan run this area, an' from yer own admission they control almost all the goin's-on. They just use ordinary people, an' if yer want my opinion I fink they're usin' you. Look at yerself. Last year there was this fing you got about Len playin' fast an' loose. You felt sure that 'e 'ad someone else, an' what 'appened? Soon as 'e contacted yer you came runnin'. 'E's a sweet talker an' you're lettin'

184

yerself be swayed by it. What future can you 'ave wiv a bloke like 'im? There's no chance o' you ever gettin' married, yer said so yerself. Are you always gonna be at Regan's beck an' call? What 'appens when you're older, inter middle age? There's all yer friends married an' wiv their kids growin' up, an' there's you, still single an' lookin' over yer shoulder at every young sort who comes on the scene in case she turns 'is 'ead.'

'There's a war on and I'm not lookin' that far ahead,' Sadie replied, her sister's words of wisdom weighing more heavily than she cared to admit. 'We could all be dead before the war's over.'

'Well, if that's all yer can say then I feel sorry for yer,' Jennie said with irritation.

'You don't 'ave ter feel sorry fer me,' Sadie answered quickly as she swung round on the dressing-table stool and snatched up her hairbrush.

Jennie sighed deeply, thinking that she had perhaps gone too far. 'Look, Sadie, I'm yer sister, the only one yer've got, an' we've always bin close, able ter tell our secrets to each ovver, talk to each ovver about the lads we went out wiv, an' that's the way it should be. Lately though yer've become very defensive, sharp if yer like, an' that's why there's an atmosphere in the 'ome. Well, it's part of it anyway. You seem ter jump lately when anyfing's said about where yer goin', what yer doin'. I don't fink you're 'appy, the way fings are wiv Len Regan. In fact I'm sure you're not.'

185

The remarks hit home and Sadie gulped back a tear as she turned again to face her younger sister. 'Last year, when I suspected Len o' seein' somebody else,' she said quietly, 'I decided to 'old fire instead of accusin' 'im outright. After all, I didn't 'ave any proof that anyfing was goin' on. It was just a lot o' little fings that began ter trouble me. Anyway I decided ter pull meself tergevver an' act as though I didn't 'ave a clue. So after a few days I came runnin', as you described it. I thought that if anyfing was goin' on I'd find out fer sure sooner or later, but d'you know, from then on fings got much better between us. Len got really attentive an' I was gettin' involved in more an' more of 'is business. I even done some work on the firm's books. Then last month Len 'ad ter go down ter Brighton, ter that place they set up.'

'The brothel,' Jennie said helpfully.

'Yeah, the brothel,' Sadie continued smiling. 'It's a posh set-up wiv a lot o' senior officers an' professional people amongst its clients. Len was gone fer a whole week an' when 'e came back 'e seemed different. I can't describe it, but I could feel it. Fings started ter slip back ter the way they were before an' now when we get tergevver we find it 'ard ter relax wiv each ovver. D'you understand what I'm sayin'? We both seem ter be on a short fuse an' I don't like it. I'm pretty certain now that Len 'as got someone else.'

' 'Ave yer fronted 'im about it?' Jennie asked quickly.

'Yeah I did, an' 'e denied it of course,' Sadie told her.

'But yer still don't know fer sure?'

'I can tell. I can tell when we make love,' Sadie said, picking away at the brush hair. 'It used ter be good, really good, but now it's as if 'e's preoccupied all the time, an' ter be honest 'e's not that keen any more, not like 'e was.'

'It could be the pressure of the job 'e's doin', or 'e might not be 'undred-per-cent fit,' Jennie suggested.

Sadie shook her head. 'I'd know if it was that.'

' 'Ow?'

'I just would.'

'So what yer gonna do?'

'I'm gonna play it cagey an' wait fer 'im ter make a mistake. They do, they always do.'

'Come back, Big Joe,' Jennie said, raising her hands to the ceiling. 'Come 'ome on leave an' sweep my big sister off 'er feet.'

'Yeah, it'd be nice ter see 'im again,' Sadie agreed, smiling at Jennie's pose. 'But don't get any wrong ideas. Me an' Joe are just good friends.'

'Do just good friends write lots o' letters?' Jennie asked with raised eyebrows. 'Don't worry—I ain't bin rootin' frew yer drawers. I've got ter recognise the 'andwritin' on those letters ter you that keep droppin' on the mat. Big Joe must be writin' to yer four times a week at least. God, what can one good friend keep on writin' about to anuvver good friend?'

'Jennie, yer've just outlived yer welcome,' Sadie said, making a threatening gesture towards her.

'All right, all right, I'm leavin',' Jennie giggled as she got up from the edge of the bed. 'I bet 'e's writin' poetry an' sayin' lovely fings, ain't 'e? Can I see one o' those letters?'

'Get out,' Sadie growled as she threw the hairbrush at her fleeing sister.

Down in the parlour Dolly leaned back in her armchair and screwed her face up against the tiredness inside her. The wireless had been left on and soft music drifted through the room, lulling her to sleep, but it was suddenly interrupted when Mick came home from the pub. 'Good news, gel,' he said loudly. 'The Joneses 'ave 'eard from young Jerry. 'E's safe. 'Is unit landed in Iceland an' 'e's managed ter send 'em a letter.'

'Fank Gawd fer that,' Dolly said with feeling as she straightened herself in the chair. 'Turn the wireless up a bit, luv, the news'll be on soon.'

Across the narrow strip of water that had thwarted many an army and at least one armada, an army was massing at the coast around Dunkirk, tired, disorganised and fighting for its life. Moving in to crush the remaining resistance were the well-trained and disciplined German divisions, and in reserve a Panzer regiment and the dreaded S.S Corps waited to perform the coup-de-grace.

The Rifle Brigade had taken heavy casualties as it fought to keep the road to Dunkirk open, and now the remnants were being rallied for a last-ditch stand. The battalion commander had been killed and the adjutant severely wounded, leaving the senior officer Captain Morgan in charge. His first duty was to send a runner to summon the B company commander, and amid the din of battle with shells flying overhead and machine-gun emplacements picking off anyone who showed themselves above the redoubt, Second Lieutenant Garry Baker slid down into the trench to be told that B company was to fight a rearguard action until their ammunition ran out, in an effort to allow the rest of the battalion to get to Dunkirk. There was no time for an explanation as to why B company had been chosen, and Lieutenant Baker did not dream of asking for one. The truth was, his company had taken less casualties than the other companies and they would be able to provide the best cover available.

'Sergeant Brody, take your squad up to the rise. Corporal Williams, take your squad over to the farm. Hold your fire as long as possible,' Baker told them. 'Make every round count. When you have to fall back make for the road and then it's a question of fighting our way down to the sands. Good luck.'

Frank Flynn looked around the dust-covered members of C company as they slithered down into the redoubt and to his immense relief he saw his brother Jim who raised his hand in greeting. Frank slid over to him, careful to keep his head down and Jim grinned, his white teeth standing out against his blackened face.

'Okay, bruv?'

'Yeah. You?'

'B company's makin' a stand at the farm by all accounts.'

'Poor bastards.'

' 'Ave yer got a fag?'

'Right out,' Frank told him. 'If yer wait a minute I'll pop up ter The Sun an' get a packet.'

'What wouldn't I give ter be sittin' in there right now,' Jim said sighing.

The noise of battle increased and the men of C company knew that their pals in B company were locked in battle, giving them the chance to make the dash to the sands of Dunkirk.

'Fall in, you beautiful shower,' Sergeant Stanford bawled out. 'Let's go, an' keep those stupid 'eads down.'

A firm favourite with the company and a veteran of the First World War, Stanford was believed to be immortal and the men would have followed him right into hell if he had led the way. But hell was already gaping all around them, here in this once green and serene landscape, a charnel-house of corpses, both human and animal, where bullet and shell, machine gun and grenade, had turned the flatlands into a bloody, battle-scarred, dust-caked nightland which defied belief.

The men trudged on, weary beyond caring. Hungry, thirsty men who less than a year ago were practising their trades, dating young women, swilling pints and tucking children into bed. They could see the town of Dunkirk ahead with its church spire still intact, and they knew that there on the beaches was the rendezvous point, where they would be fed and watered and then taken off by luggers and ships' boats to the vessels anchored in deep water. What they didn't know yet, although they heard the din and roar, was that Stuka dive bombers were strafing the beaches and sinking ships, turning the beaches into another hell-hole, another place to die, cut to ribbons by the planes' machine guns as they made their runs, flying low above the dunes.

As night fell and the enemy aircraft left to rearm and refuel, C company were herded together and Sergeant Stanford spelt it out. 'We're to assemble by the upturned wreck,' he told them. 'We've been allocated one large ship's boat and a few dinghies. Some of you will have to go in the water and be towed out, but I don't want any panic, understood? Too many in the boat and it'll capsize. Take orders from the matelots and don't over-fill those dinghies neither. You know your capabilities. The strongest swimmers will give up their places and the wounded get first priority in the boat, which goes without saying. Right then, my merry little men. Let's go.'

Dawn was breaking as the empty boat returned to the prearranged spot, and as the men waded out up to their waists and were hauled aboard, the Luftwaffe returned. Those in the water had no chance and puddles of blood spread in the sea as the cannon and machine-gun fire sprayed down amongst them. The two matelots were cut down and the boat reduced to splinters as it took a direct hit from a plane's cannon. Men who had survived swam out towards the ships, towing their wounded comrades, while those still on the beach ran headlong into the dunes.

Jim Flynn felt the wetness on his arm and realised that a bullet had ripped through his tunic and cut a deep furrow in his upper arm. Frank was next to him and looked unscathed.

'What did I always tell yer,' Jim said as his older brother quickly ripped the top of his tunic and applied a field dressing to the wound. 'Did I or did I not tell yer it was important yer learnt ter swim well.'

'Shut up, kid, yer sound like me,' Frank replied grinning.

'It's nuffink ter laugh at,' Jim went on. 'I told yer I'd 'ave ter take care of yer. You just stay close ter me when we go in the water. If yer get tired just relax an' let me tow yer, all right?'

'I can make it on me own,' Frank insisted.

'It's a bloody mile ter those ships,' Jim growled. 'All you could ever do was a width at the baths, an' yer splashed an' struggled like some beached whale.'

'Fanks fer the vote o' confidence, bruv,' Frank replied as the roar of aircraft grew louder.

Bullets cut into the sand as dive bombers screamed like a tribe of banshees, then just as quickly it grew quiet again.

'Come on, it's now or never,' Frank shouted.

The brothers dashed to the sea and dived into the surf, struggling to get into deeper water. They realised that the planes were concentrating on the men still trapped in the dunes and they said a silent prayer. Suddenly Jim saw a figure rise up out of the surf and fall back onto the sand. 'It's Stanford,' he shouted. 'You go on, I'll catch you up, an' swim easy, don't tire yerself too quickly.'

As he waded back Jim saw that Stanford had taken a bullet in his left shoulder and his arm was hanging useless at his side. 'Come on, Sarge. Put yer good arm round me an' let me do the work,' he told him firmly.

'Don't you go orderin' me about, young Flynn,' the sergeant roared. 'I'll 'ave you on a charge before you can blink.'

'Shut yer stupid row up,' Jim growled as he pulled the wounded sergeant into the sea.

The water was very cold and Stanford was losing consciousness as Jim turned him on to his back and towed him by his shirt collar into deeper water. Up ahead the nearest ship seemed miles away, and the distance impossible to close as the survivors desperately swam on. Frank was further out by now and seemed to be swimming well enough, though hampered by his thick uniform. Bombs hit the beach and the screams of wounded and dying men reached hauntingly across the sea as the captain of the Thames paddle steamer searched the water through his binoculars.

'There, two points to starboard. Men in the water,' he bawled out. 'Loosen the painter.'

Frank and Jim were finally pulled aboard the ship's boat, along with the unconscious company sergeant and a few other troops swimming alongside.

An elderly man with white hair and a handlebar moustache stood in the prow wearing a fawn duffle coat, sea boots and a rollneck jumper. 'Keep your heads down, lads, the Boche are coming back,' he shouted in a cultured voice as his younger companion turned the boat back towards the paddle steamer. 'Any more for the *Skylark?* Two and sixpence for a one-way trip to jolly old Blighty.' Then, to everyone's amazement, he began to sing with gusto.

'Comrades, comrades, ever since we were boys.
Cheering each other's sorrow,
Sharing each other's joys.
Comrade's a man to be born with,
Faithful what 'ere may befall.
And when I'm in danger my daring old comrade
Is there by my side.'

Stanford had regained consciousness and he groaned with pain as he tried to move.

'Lie still, it won't be long now before we're aboard ship,' Jim told him.

The company sergeant looked up at Jim Flynn and narrowed his eyes. 'If I remember rightly you gave me some lip, son,' he growled.

'It must 'ave bin the pain, Sarge,' Jim said smiling.

Stanford smiled back. 'It must 'ave bin. You wouldn't 'ave dared bawl me out,' he said through chattering teeth. 'I'd 'ave 'ad yer guts fer garters.'

At eleven o'clock that morning the *S.S Medway Queen* docked at Newhaven with her human cargo, bedraggled remnants of

194

the British Expeditionary Force, and Jim and Frank Flynn gratefully tucked into plates of sausage and mash, washed down with mugs of hot sweet tea.

CHAPTER 16

Through the last days of May and into June as the exhausted British and French troops were being lifted off the beaches of Dunkirk, continuous wireless broadcasts kept the Carter Lane folk huddled by their sets, their faces white and gaunt with the anxiety and fear. Was my son amongst those taken off? Will he make it back, or is he one of those already fallen, left alone in the dirt beneath a foreign sky?

Throughout the whole country news of survivors was patchy, and the people of Bermondsey suffered the same uncertainty as everyone else. Hurried letters were sent to loved ones as soon as possible after debarkation and police stations, libraries, corner shops and businesses took phone calls and relayed the good-news messages. 'Your son is safe.' 'See you soon, Ma.' 'Back in Blighty.' And for some, no message came.

The Flynn household got their news from Sara Jackman at teatime. The shopkeeper had taken the call from Frank herself and she came running, her face flushed with excitement. 'The boys are safe, Dolly,' she gasped. 'Your Frank phoned just now. 'E said ter tell yer Jim's bin a pain in the arse but they're fit an' well. They don't know if Con got away.'

Dolly cried and Mick strolled out to the backyard to hide his overflowing emotion. Jennie and Sadie hugged each other, and then when the first flush of happiness and relief subsided a little Dolly put her arm around Jennie. ' 'E'll be all right, you'll see,' she said encouragingly.

' 'Is gran'muvver might 'ave 'eard somefing,' Jennie replied.

'D'yer know 'er address?'

'Only that she lives in Dock'ead.'

'Keep yer pecker up, luv. Con's gonna be all right,' Dolly told her.

'I wonder if Amy or Ivy's 'eard anyfing yet,' Sadie remarked.

'They'd 'ave come over ter tell us,' Mick replied.

'I must go an' tell 'em the good news,' Dolly said, slipping into her coat.

As she hurried across the cobblestones she saw Amy Bromilow standing in her doorway sobbing, with Ivy Jones holding on to her hand.

'A policeman's just bin,' Ivy told Dolly as she came up to them. ' 'Er Freddie's safe.'

'I can't stop cryin',' Amy gulped. 'I'm so 'appy.'

The good news travelled fast, but there were those who still had to wait, and for many the waiting was ended by an official communication, a telegram or a War Office letter to say that their son or husband had been killed in action.

Later that evening Jennie sat alone in her tiny bedroom on the bend of the stairs going through the letters she had received from Con. Where was he now, she wondered, her stomach churning as she recalled the news broadcast earlier that evening. Had he been taken as a prisoner of war, or was he at this very moment just lying there, dead on the beach? Perhaps he was badly wounded and could not write a letter or use the phone. There were still many soldiers on the beaches and they were being lifted off nonstop. That was it. He would be one of the last ones to leave. That was Con sure enough.

'Are you all right, Jen?' Sadie asked as she put her head round the door.

'I was just sittin' 'ere finkin',' Jennie replied.

Sadie came into the room and sat down on the edge of the bed. 'That's all there is fer us to do,' she sighed. 'Just sit an' wait, an' fink.'

Jennie quickly gathered her letters together and re-tied them with their silk cord. 'I know it sounds silly, but when I read those letters I can imagine it's Con talkin' ter me,' she said smiling. 'I can 'ear 'is voice an' see the expression in 'is eyes. I take comfort from it.'

'It's not silly at all,' Sadie said kindly, weighing the bundle of letters in her hand. ' 'Ere, I've got a bundle like that.'

'Do yer reply to 'em?' Jennie asked.

'I 'ave a couple but I find it difficult.'

'Why?'

'I dunno,' Sadie said shrugging. 'It's funny really. I work in an office an' I'm quite used ter puttin' letters tergevver when customers' bills are overdue or when I 'ave ter send out some information, but when it comes ter writin' personal letters I find it very difficult.'

'Take anuvver look at Big Joe's letters an' answer in the same vein,' Jennie suggested.

'It's not as easy as that,' Sadie replied. 'Joe makes everyfing so interestin', like when 'e describes what it was like fer 'im as a young lad, I feel as if I know the places 'e writes about. I couldn't write fings down like 'e does.'

'Yeah, but yer don't 'ave to,' Jennie persisted. 'Fer instance, just sit down quietly like I do an' fink about 'ow the day went, what the weavver was like, who yer met, what yer did. There's no end to it.'

'Oh, 'e wouldn't be interested in all that chit-chat,' Sadie said dismissively.

'That's where yer wrong,' Jennie told her. 'This is Joe's new 'ome. 'E's missin' it, an' if yer write about all the little fings around yer it'll keep 'im in touch, 'elp 'im ter remember everyfing back 'ere.'

'I s'pose I could do that,' Sadie replied, rubbing her chin, 'but I gotta be careful. I don't wanna give 'im any wrong ideas, like lettin' 'im fink I wanna get serious.'

'That wouldn't be such a bad fing,' Jennie said. 'Yer'd get a lot more attention an' lovin' from 'im than Len Regan.'

'Don't go on about that,' Sadie pleaded. 'I'm all mixed up as it is. I fink about Len, an' I go over in me mind what I'm gonna say next time I see 'im, an' then when we do meet it's like it's all sweetness an' light. Then there's times when one o' Joe's letters drops frew the letterbox. I get excited as I open it, an' I ask meself why. Christ, Jennie, I've only bin out wiv 'im once an' 'e never forced 'imself on me or anyfing like that. We just talked.'

'But didn't yer feel anyfing when you was tergevver?' Jennie asked.

'I felt comfortable an' sort o' cosy. Joe's easy ter talk to an' 'e was interested in what I was talkin' about too, I could tell.'

'I know just what yer mean,' Jennie remarked. 'When I first saw Con in the cafe an' 'e came over ter my table an' got talkin' I found meself studyin' 'im, watchin' 'is eyes an' the way 'e 'as of grinnin' out the corner of 'is mouth. It was little fings I noticed, an' I felt comfortable too. There was no bells ringin', no earth-shakin' moment when me life changed, just a nice cosy feelin' inside, an' I could 'ave sat there all day just talkin' to 'im.'

'An' now?'

Jennie sighed. 'A bundle o' letters later an' I take 'im ter bed wiv me at night. I cuddle the piller an' make out it's 'im. Does that sound terrible?'

Sadie laughed aloud. 'Nah, that sounds like true love.'

'I do love 'im, Sadie. I love 'im more each day.'

' 'Ow d'yer cope?'

'What d'yer mean?'

'Well, yer've always bin like a flitterin' butterfly,' Sadie explained. 'At least that's what Mum used ter say about yer. You was always flyin' from one lad to anuvver an' never in the 'ouse fer five minutes. It was eivver dancin' or the flicks, or trips up West. Now you never go out. Ter be honest, if someone 'ad told me a year ago you'd be quite 'appy ter sit in a corner wiv a book or magazine I'd 'ave said they were mad. Since yer've met Con yer've changed so much.'

'Contentment, Sadie, that's what it is,' Jennie told her. 'War changes everybody an' I'm no exception. I'm not interested in ovver fellers. I want Con, an' I know 'e feels the same way about me. The war's parted us, but in some strange way it's brought us closer tergevver, an' as time goes by I know that the feelin's we 'ave fer each ovver can only get stronger. Can you understand?'

'D'yer know somefing,' Sadie said, 'I envy you. I was always lookin' fer the glamorous life, goin' places, seein' fings, 'avin' a smart 'ome, wiv good clothes ter wear an' money in the bank. I wanted out o' this place, I wanted ter get away from Bermon'sey an' its factories, wharves an' smells, an' 'ard-up people livin' in run-down 'ouses an' damp, ramshackle buildin's. I told meself there 'ad ter be somefing else, somefing better.'

'Don't you fink we all feel like that?' Jennie said quickly. 'I'd like to 'ave lots o' nice fings an' plenty o' money, but yer gotta look at the ovver side o' the coin. Take the people, fer instance—yer won't find better anywhere yer go. An' yer talk about the smells, but I love 'em. I love ter walk along Tower Bridge Road when 'Artley's are boilin' the Seville oranges an' I love the smell of leavver tannin' an' the lovely aromas from the spice ware'ouses down Shad Thames. An' there's the sharp tang of 'ops from the brewery an' sour vinegar as yer pass by Sarson's, not fergettin' the river o' course. I love the smell o' the river an' the grey mud down below when I walk along the embankments. That's Bermon'sey, an' that's what makes it so different from anywhere else yer could name. All right, it might all disappear. If the bombin' starts a lot o' factories'll move out o' London or be destroyed, an' the old buildin's an' little 'ouses won't last fer ever. It'll all change, but while fings are as they are you can keep anywhere else, Bermon'sey suits me just fine.'

'Jennie, you amaze me, you really do,' Sadie declared with feeling. 'The way you just described it makes Bermon'sey sound like paradise. I'd never 'ave guessed you felt so passionate about it.'

'Well, there you are,' Jennie said smiling. 'An' that's the sort o' stuff you could put in that letter ter Big Joe.'

'I'm gonna write to 'im,' Sadie said enthusiastically. 'I'm gonna write to 'im ternight.'

'Good fer you.'

Sadie got up from the bed and went to the door. 'By the way,' she said, turning back on her heel. 'Fanks fer the chat, an' fanks fer makin' me feel shallow an' selfish.'

'Sadie, I'm sorry. I didn't intend ter make yer feel bad,' Jennie replied, looking concerned.

'Don't apologise, sis. It was just what I needed. It was better than a kick up the backside,' Sadie told her, grinning broadly.

Across the Channel the last of the British forces were fighting a rearguard action, back through hedgerows and fields, through muddy lanes and country roads to the beaches. Remnants of the Royal Fusiliers and Rifle Brigade were amongst the exhausted troops who finally reached the sands as night fell, and in the failing light they came upon the carnage. Most of the large ships had left but some small boats of various description were struggling against the tide to reach the shore. Men clambered aboard and others swam alongside, hoping to be picked up once they were out at sea. The bodies of their dead comrades had to be left on the sands along with the badly wounded, but those who could still walk were helped down to the water and into the small overflowing craft.

Fusilier Christopher Wickstead had taken a bullet in his chest and was left for dead in a dune. Fortunately two privates from the decimated Northamptonshire Regiment sheltering nearby heard him groaning and they managed to drag him to the water and into a small launch.

Corporal Conrad Williams and his depleted squad had held out at the farm until they were almost out of ammunition and they withdrew under heavy fire to the road. The four survivors only covered a short distance before they came under more fire from both sides. Two men died instantly and Con dived into a ditch alongside the only other survivor, Rifleman Cohen from Bethnal Green. They could hear heavy footsteps running and shouted commands in German, then it went quiet. For a while they remained where they were, and finally Abe Cohen eased himself across to Con. 'I'm out of ammo, Corp,' he said.

'I've got a few rounds left,' Con told him. 'I fink we'd better make a move before we're overrun.'

The rifleman grabbed Con's arm. 'Save the last one fer me, Corp,' he said matter-of-factly.

'What you on about?' Con said irritably.

'If we're captured put yer last bullet in me, an' make sure yer do a good job,' Cohen told him.

'Don't piss-ball about,' Con growled. 'Let's go, an' keep close.'

'I'm bein' serious,' Cohen hissed. 'If we're captured they'll take our army books fer identification, you know that.'

'So?'

'What chance d'yer fink I'll 'ave wiv a name like Abraham Cohen? They'll shoot me on the spot. I'd sooner you do it.'

Con grabbed Abe Cohen by his shoulder webbing and shook him. 'Now you listen ter me,' he muttered. 'You an' me are goin' up on the road an' we're gonna make it ter the beach, understood? Now c'mon, let's go.'

The dark country lane seemed deserted as the two soldiers hurried along with their heads held low, and at a curve of the track they nearly stumbled over a dead soldier lying twisted on the ground, his rifle still at his side. Con checked the weapon and released the magazine to find that there were still some rounds left in it. ' 'Ere,

203

take this,' he said, throwing it to Abe Cohen.

'This feels better,' Abe said, slipping the safety catch of his rifle.

Ahead the town of Dunkirk was lit up with flames and smoke was rising high up into the night sky. The two soldiers followed the lane round as it veered sharply and suddenly they found themselves looking down gun barrels.

'You two left it a bit late, didn't yer?'

Con saw it was Sergeant Brody and his blackened face relaxed into a wide grin. 'Yer made it then, Sarge.'

'Yeah, four of us,' Brody said bitterly.

'We're all that's left of our squad,' Con told him as he shouldered his rifle.

'It's not a pretty sight on that beach,' Brody puffed, 'but there's no option. If we're not away ternight it'll be a prison camp fer the rest o' the war.'

The remnants of B company moved down into the port, passing the burning buildings and installations on their way to the dunes.

' 'E wasn't jokin', was 'e?' Cohen remarked as they saw the results of the constant strafing.

Bodies were everywhere, broken and lifeless, and back from the water the badly wounded had been laid together and covered with greatcoats, their heads resting on army packs. There was no moon, but the burning port lit up the dunes and cast a hellish red reflection on the sea for some distance, till the blackness swallowed it up.

'The boats 'ave bin comin' in waves,' Sergeant Brody told his men. 'They've bin usin' megaphones to announce their arrival.

204

Flares would only alert the German gunners up above the town.'

'What about those poor sods over there, Sarge?' Abe Cohen asked, pointing to the wounded.

'There's nuffink more we can do,' Brody sighed. 'We've just gotta 'ope the Germans'll look after 'em.'

'I just 'ope the S.S units don't get 'ere first,' Cohen mumbled to Con.

That night under cover of darkness the last of the fighting rearguard put to sea in a small river launch, piloted by an elderly man who like hundreds of other pleasure-craft owners had answered the call for boats. An off-shore wind had made the operation difficult, but with considerable skill and detailed knowledge of his particular boat the skipper of *Lady Luck* had managed admirably.

' 'Ere, Corp, if we'd bin captured would you 'ave done what I asked?' Abe Cohen wanted to know.

Con shrugged his shoulders, beginning to feel queasy as the small boat bobbed up and down like a cork in the heavy swell. 'I dunno, I might 'a' done.'

'Sergeant, can you take the wheel while I rustle up some soup?' the skipper asked. 'Just keep it on this course.'

As the smell of tomato soup rose up from the tiny cabin below deck Con felt his stomach turn over. Abe Cohen was sitting next to him and he smiled. 'Not feelin' too good, Corp?' he asked casually.

'Leave me alone,' Con growled.

'I'll 'ave your soup if yer don't want it,' Cohen said grinning.

'If you don't shut yer trap I'm gonna put that last bullet in yer 'ead right now,' Con scowled.

'Promises, promises,' the irrepressible young soldier said as he wedged his feet against the bulwarks to counter the roll and pitch.

As the dawn light filtered into the sky the *Lady Luck* docked at Newhaven and a party of very sick landlubbers came ashore. They were given huge mugs of steaming tea and dry clothes, and then taken to a makeshift canteen where they were served with the inevitable sausage and mash.

'What, no roll-mops?' Abe Cohen remarked.

'What the bloody 'ell's roll-mops?' the soldier next to him in the queue asked.

'Soused 'errin's,' Cohen told him.

Con was standing behind the soldier and felt his stomach move again. 'Will someone loan me a rifle, now?' he growled. 'An' make sure it's loaded.'

CHAPTER 17

On a bright June morning a letter arrived at number 11 and Dolly Flynn's face lit up as she picked it up off the doormat. 'Mick, it's a letter from our Frank,' she shouted up the

206

stairs. 'I can tell it's 'is 'andwritin'.'

'Well, go on then, open the bloody fing,' Mick growled as he hurried down.

Dolly read it and tears welled up in her eyes as she passed it to him. 'The boys are comin' 'ome on leave soon,' she told him.

Mick read the letter and then looked up. 'Con's company 'ad ter stay be'ind 'em, accordin' ter Frank,' he said sadly. 'Young Jennie's gonna be upset. Still we mustn't look on the black side, 'e could be a prisoner o' war.'

Dolly took the letter from her husband and studied the postmark. 'This letter's three days old,' she said. 'Frank must 'ave wrote it the same time as 'e phoned. Jennie's young man might 'ave got back after the letter was sent. It said on the wireless that soldiers were still bein' picked up from Dunkirk.'

'It's quite possible,' Mick said encouragingly, though he knew what a rearguard action meant. In his time it was a case of sacrificing a few to save many and it wouldn't be any different now.

When Sadie came in with the shopping and read the letter she was overjoyed, but her heart went out to Jennie. On the surface her sister was being calm and contained, but she was not fooling anyone. Inside they knew she must be in turmoil. 'I wonder if Con did get back an' phoned 'ome,' Sadie said.

' 'E might well 'ave done,' Dolly replied. 'Trouble is there's only 'is ole gran, accordin' ter Jennie, an' she couldn't be expected ter let us know. She don't even know where we live

207

fer a start. An' it's quite possible that Con ain't even told 'er about Jennie.'

'There's only one answer,' Sadie said quickly. 'We've gotta find out where the ole lady lives.'

'An' 'ow yer gonna do that?' Dolly asked.

'Jennie said she lives in Dock'ead, an' let's face it Dock'ead ain't that big,' Sadie remarked.

Early that evening when Jennie got home from her job at the baker's shop and read the letter from Frank she broke down in tears. Sadie put her arm round her and Dolly hurried out to the scullery and came back with a cup of tea. 'Now drink this, an' try not ter worry too much,' she told her kindly. 'We was only sayin' this mornin' that Con could 'ave got back since that letter was sent.'

As Jennie sipped her tea in the armchair Sadie knelt down beside her. 'Do yer know if Con told 'is gran'muvver about you?' she asked.

'I don't know,' Jennie replied. ' 'E never said.'

'Right then, we're gonna find the ole lady.'

' 'Ow we gonna do that?'

'When you an' Con went fer that drink where did yer go?'

'A little pub down by the riverside,' Jennie told her.

'In Dock'ead?'

Jennie looked up smiling and sniffed back her tears. 'Of course,' she said quickly. 'Con takes 'is gran there sometimes. People in the pub would know where they live, wouldn't they?'

'Yeah, I'm sure they would,' Sadie replied.

208

'Right then, my gel, after tea me an' you are goin' fer a stroll.'

'But you're goin' out ternight wiv Len.'

'Not anymore.'

Rabbi Friedman leaned back in his armchair and joined the tips of his fingers together in contemplation. He was a diminutive individual with thick grey hair, well known for his sometimes acid-sharp tongue as well as his wicked sense of humour. He was held in high esteem by Bermondsey's Jewish community, who felt that he was a man who would listen and sympathise with their problems and generally administer sound advice. On Saturday evening though, Rabbi Friedman was feeling slightly irked by Albert Levy's change of mind. 'Only a few weeks ago you came to me and asked me to consider your request for a bronze plaque to be installed in the synagogue to the memory of Abel Finkelstein,' he reminded him, 'and now it seems you don't care to remember him. Tell me, Albert, has he come back to haunt you or something?'

The shopkeeper cringed in his armchair facing the rabbi. 'Many a true word is spoken in jest,' he replied. 'Actually, the simple truth is I can't bring myself to honour his name, and Gerda agrees with me.'

'I'm sure she does,' Friedman said sarcastically. 'But then your devoted wife Gerda knows more about this than I do. Maybe I'll agree too, once you have explained yourself fully.'

Albert Levy shifted uncomfortably in his seat. 'Rabbi, do you believe we can communicate with the dead?'

Friedman smiled. 'I have to, at some of my services. There are times when I feel that half my congregation are dead, or well on the way out, judging by the expressionless look on their faces. But to be serious, no I don't believe in communication with the dead.'

'I've been speaking to Abel for some time now,' Albert told him. 'At quiet moments I go to the back of my shop, to the workroom where Abel used to mend the wireless sets, and I speak to him, or I used to, until recently.'

'I think we all tend to speak our thoughts when we're troubled,' the rabbi replied. 'But it's not communicating as such, it's more of an exercise in getting things off our chest. Things left unsaid. Angry thoughts, and questions that need answering. It's a part of bereavement. Do you understand what I'm saying?'

'It's finished now though,' Albert Levy said sadly. 'My old friend bit the hand that fed him. He betrayed me, the man who loved him like a brother, and I told him so, the last time I spoke to him.'

Friedman raised his hands in front of him in puzzlement. 'Now, let's get this straight,' he said. 'You found this out after Abel died?'

The shopkeeper took Abel's diary from his coat pocket and passed it over to Friedman. 'It's all in there,' he told him. 'See for yourself and then tell me, if you can, what could have possessed Abel to do such a thing.'

As he thumbed through the pages the rabbi's face creased in a smile and he looked up at his visitor. 'Quite a bit of money,' he said, raising his eyebrows. 'Have you been able to put a figure on it?'

Levy nodded. 'Taking the carry-over figure from last year at the front of the diary and totalling up the entries, I made it almost one hundred and twenty-seven pounds, give or take a few shillings. To rob an old friend of all that money! Why, rabbi? Why?'

Rabbi Friedman held Albert in his deep gaze for a moment or two. 'When Abel first came to talk to me about his plan I was a little unsure of how to advise him,' he said finally, the smile still lingering in his eyes. 'You of all people know that Abel Finkelstein was a very meticulous man. Unfortunately for him he could not be completely exact in this instance, which troubled him. It had to be guesswork. You see there was no rate of exchange available for the old German Mark against the pound because of the roaring inflation in Germany during that time. It could only be calculated by the cost of comparable items in both countries at that period, but even that was very difficult. As you know, even the price of a loaf of bread changed daily in the worst times. I could only surmise, and I felt that the figure should be around two hundred pounds, which Abel concurred with.'

Albert Levy sat with his mouth hanging open, his eyes popping like organ stops. 'You mean to tell me you were in on this?' he gasped. 'You advised him? You set a figure?

I don't believe it. I'm dreaming. Tell me I'm dreaming.'

Rabbi Friedman felt a wave of pity for the shopkeeper and he raised his hands in front of him again. 'Now listen to me, Albert,' he began. 'The figure Abel Finkelstein and I agreed upon was the amount we estimated you would have paid in pounds for his release from that prison camp. Now you've done your sums and come up with the figure of one hundred and twenty-seven pounds, which leaves a shortfall of seventy-three pounds.'

'A shortfall of seventy-three pounds!' Albert exploded. 'The shortfall is one hundred and twenty-seven pounds, the total Abel took from my till.'

The rabbi smiled indulgently. 'What I'm saying is, if Abel had lived the shortfall would have been rectified in time.'

'Am I hearing this right, or am I going stark raving mad?' Albert said in consternation. 'You're telling me that if Abel had not taken his life the figure would have reached two hundred pounds. And what then?'

'That would have been the end of it,' Friedman replied.

'I am going mad,' Albert Levy wailed. 'You, a respected rabbi, in league to systematically rob one of your own.'

'No, not rob,' Friedman said calmly. 'Re-imburse is the word you're looking for. All those figures in Abel's diary refer to the money he slipped into the till when he could. He was paying you back, Albert, paying you back what he hoped would be every penny of the money you spent to obtain his release. It was the only way. He knew that you would refuse to take it if he offered it to you. That's why he came to me with the plan. To get my approval, which I was happy to give him.'

Albert Levy lowered his head and his shoulders heaved. 'I loved him, rabbi,' he sobbed. 'I loved him like a brother, and I ended up cursing his memory.'

'Many a harsh word is spoken in anger and in haste,' Friedman said rising from his chair. 'You were not to know the truth of it and the wording in the diary led you to believe the worst.' He laid his hand on Albert's hunched shoulders. 'Let's talk some more of the memorial plaque, shall we?'

Sadie led the way into the busy little riverside pub, ignoring the curious glances from the locals, who were not used to seeing unaccompanied young women enter the bar.

'Yes, ladies?' the landlord asked. 'What can I get yer?'

'I'm sorry ter take up yer time while you're busy,' Sadie began nervously, 'but d'yer know a Mrs Williams who comes in 'ere sometimes wiv 'er gran'son Con, who's in the army? We're tryin' ter contact 'er. It's very important.'

The landlord looked from one to the other and then he walked along the bar and put his head through some bead curtains. 'Got a minute, Vi?'

A buxom blonde wearing heavy make-up came through from the saloon bar, and after the landlord mumbled a few words in her ear she came up to the two young women and gave them a quick smile. 'Could you come frew?' she said as she lifted the counter flap.

Sadie and Jennie looked at each other in surprise as they followed her through the curtains and into a small back room that led off the saloon bar. It was sparsely furnished with a table and four chairs and some shelves around the walls.

'Sit yerselves down,' the woman told them, pulling up a chair facing them. 'I know yer can't be related ter the ole lady or yer'd know 'er name wasn't Williams. It was Franklin, Ida Franklin. I say was, because I'm afraid they found 'er dead in 'er chair yesterday mornin'.'

'Oh my God!' Jennie gasped. 'Poor Con.'

'I remember yer face now,' the woman said. 'I saw you in 'ere wiv young Conrad once.'

'Con's my boyfriend an' 'e's in Dunkirk, yer see,' Jennie said anxiously. 'That's why we were tryin' ter locate the old lady. We thought she might 'ave 'eard somefing.'

The buxom woman smiled sympathetically, showing a row of large white teeth. 'I never ferget a face. I remember sayin' ter my bloke what a nice couple yer made. Anyway, I fink yer'd better speak ter Mrs Crosier. She did the cleanin' an' ran a few errands fer the ole gel. She may know somefing. She was the

214

one who found 'er. Must 'ave bin a terrible shock; after all, Mrs Crosier ain't no chicken 'erself. She lives in St Saviour's Buildin's by the way, by Shad Thames. D'yer know the place?'

'We'll find it,' Sadie said. 'D'yer know Mrs Crosier's number?'

'Nah, I don't, but she lives on the ground floor facin' the street, next ter the rubbish chute,' the blonde told her.

'We're very grateful, an' sorry to 'ave taken up yer time,' Sadie said smiling as she and Jennie stood up to leave.

'It was no trouble,' the woman replied. 'I do 'ope you 'ear some good news. Con's a very nice lad. 'E'll be upset when 'e finds out about the poor ole gel.'

The two sisters linked arms as they walked through the river mist towards Shad Thames, an ancient riverside byway noted for its pepper and spice warehouses. The ramshackle tenement block loomed up ahead and Sadie shivered. 'It gives me the creeps round 'ere.'

'This must be the flat,' Jennie said, lifting the doorknocker.

'What yer want?' a scratchy voice called out from within.

'My name's Jennie Flynn. I'm Con's gel-friend,' Jennie called back through the letterbox. 'Can I talk ter you fer a minute?'

Bolts were slid back and the door opened slowly to reveal a tiny woman in an apron with a black shawl over her shoulders. Her feet were clad in carpet slippers and she was wearing

215

metal-framed spectacles. 'Are yer sisters?' she asked.

'Yeah, we are,' Jennie told her. 'I'm Jennie an' this is Sadie.'

'Yer look very much alike,' the woman said, screwing her eyes up behind her glasses. 'Yer'd better come in. It's too late ter stand gassin' at the street door.'

They followed her into a small front room lit by a gas lamp and warmed by a low fire.

'It's nice an' cosy in 'ere,' Sadie remarked as she looked around.

'I need a fire,' the woman replied. 'It gets damp an' chilly at night, bein' so near the river. Can I get yer a cuppa?'

'No, it's all right,' Jennie said quickly. 'We were told in the pub that Con's gran'muvver 'ad died an' you was the one who found 'er. I'm really sorry. The landlady told us you was the lady who did 'er cleanin' an' run errands for 'er, so we took a chance an' called round. I'm worried about Con. I wondered if yer'd 'eard any news yet.'

Mrs Crosier shook her head. 'No, I 'aven't, but as soon as Con gets back 'ome 'e'll phone The Boatman, I feel sure. They knew Ida Franklin very well in there. Look yer might as well make yerselves comfortable by the fire an' 'ave a cuppa, it's no trouble.'

Sadie and Jennie exchanged glances and Sadie nodded to the old lady. 'All right then. Fank you.'

'I can't 'ave the fire too 'igh, not till I get that chimney swept,' Mrs Crosier told them.

216

'Trouble is I've just not 'ad the chance. It's a bloody day's work clearin' up after our ole chimney-sweep.'

'It must 'ave bin a terrible shock findin' the ole lady,' Jennie remarked.

Mrs Crosier nodded her head slowly. 'She looked very peaceful though, an' she 'ad that new shawl round 'er shoulders, the one young Con bought 'er. There was a Bible restin' in 'er lap, open at the twenty-third Psalm it was. "The Lord is my Shepherd." The wireless was on as well. She must 'a' bin listenin' ter the news an' no doubt sayin' a few prayers. She was a God-fearin' woman was Ida.'

' "Yea, though I walk through the valley of the shadow of death, I will fear no evil",' Jennie quoted. 'I remember that Psalm at school. We all learned it off by 'eart. Mrs Crosier, d'yer fink Con will phone the pub?'

'I'm sure 'e will, an' soon as 'e does I'll try an' let yer know,' the old lady replied, 'if yer'll give me yer address.'

'We live in Carter Lane off the Old Kent Road,' Jennie told her. 'It's a bit of a way from 'ere. We'll go back ter the pub an' leave 'em the phone number of our corner shop. I'm sure they won't mind phonin' if they 'ear anyfing from Con.'

'There's no need fer you two ter go runnin' back there this time o' night,' the old lady said. 'I'll take the phone number there meself termorrer mornin'. I usually go in fer me bottle o' Guinness at openin' time.'

217

'That's very nice of yer,' Jennie said smiling.

Mrs Crosier put her empty cup and saucer down on the table. 'Ida Franklin wasn't Con's real gran'muvver,' she remarked, 'although 'e always called 'er gran. She was only a neighbour, but when the boy was left on 'is own she took 'im in ter save 'im goin' in one o' those children's 'omes. Poor as Lazarus she was, an' wiv no ole man neivver, but she managed ter make a nice 'ome fer the boy. That's the sort o' woman she was. Con loved 'er like 'is own, an' she took great comfort in that.'

Sadie and Jennie thanked the old lady for her hospitality and hurried back home through the dark empty streets.

'There's nuffink else we can do now except wait,' Jennie said sighing.

'I honestly don't fink yer'll be waitin' very long,' Sadie told her comfortingly. 'I bet yer'll get some good news termorrer or Monday.'

When they arrived home their mother had some other news for them. 'Mrs Wickstead knocked while you two were out,' she said excitedly. ' 'Er boy Chris is safe. A copper come ter tell 'er. 'E was wounded but 'e's sent a message 'ome from the military 'ospital ter say not ter worry 'e's doin' well. An' Freddie Bromilow's back 'ome wivout a scratch.'

'Fank God fer that,' Sadie replied.

Jennie bit on her bottom lip to control her emotions. The men of Carter Lane were gradually returning home. Would her prayers be answered too?

CHAPTER 18

Jennie turned over on to her back and opened her eyes to bright sunlight streaming through the window. For a moment she lay there gathering her thoughts, and then she sighed thankfully when she realised it was Sunday morning. Before the war started the church bells would have been pealing but now they were silenced, to be rung only in the event of an invasion. Some things had not changed though, she thought. The smell of bacon frying for one, and the noise her father made in the backyard where he dubbined his workboots and polished his Sunday best. The distant sound of a passing train was familiar and comforting and the young woman turned over for a few more minutes, until she heard knocking and excited voices.

'Jennie. Are you awake?'

'Yeah, I'm just gettin' up.'

'It's Con. 'E's safe,' Dolly shouted from the foot of the stairs. 'That was Sara Jackman. A pub in Dock'ead just phoned 'er. Con phoned the pub late last night.'

Jennie's face glowed with happiness as she hurried down the stairs to hug her mother. ' 'E must 'ave phoned just after we left,' she said. 'A bit earlier an' we'd 'ave bin there. What exactly did Mrs Jackman say?'

'All she said was the pub got a phone call from Con ter say 'e was safe an' well an' comin' 'ome terday on a seventy-two hour pass.'

'Terday!'

'That's what she said.'

'I wanna meet 'im,' Jennie said quickly as she followed her mother into the scullery and saw her father framed in the backyard doorway with a big smile on his wide face.

' 'Ow yer gonna find out about the trains?' Dolly asked her.

'Frank phoned from New'aven,' Jennie recalled. 'That's where they're landin' all the soldiers I should fink. Now let me see. That's the Brighton line. 'E'll be comin' in at London Bridge. Maybe Frank an' Jim too.'

'They didn't say anyfing about that in the letter,' Dolly reminded her.

'Yeah, but it was only a rushed letter,' Mick cut in. 'They most likely didn't know when they were gettin' leave.'

'Mick, I gotta get prepared, just in case,' Dolly said quickly. 'I'll need ter put anuvver tray o' spuds in the oven an' one Yorkshire won't be enough.'

'Don't build yer 'opes up too much,' Mick warned her. 'Our two might not get leave till later, maybe next week.'

'Nah, they'll be 'ome terday along wi' Con,' Dolly said confidently. 'I can feel it in me water.'

'I can't let Con go straight 'ome,' Jennie fretted. 'The people at the pub might not 'ave 'ad the chance ter tell 'im about 'is gran'muvver.

220

It was more than likely a rushed call anyway. At least I can break it to 'im gently.'

'Before yer fink o' goin' up the station yer'd better get this down yer,' Dolly said as she ladled a fried egg onto a plate with rashers of crisp streaky bacon.

Albert Levy went to his shop on Sunday morning, something he had never done before. Today though he felt a compelling need to go. Only there could he be really close to Abel, in the little workroom where his old friend had sat day after day, humming tunelessly when things were going well, cursing when they were not. Only in that little backroom, which was now orderly and tidy, could he say the things he needed to say.

'It's been a while, old friend, but you know the reason,' Albert said as he sat down at the bench. 'The last time I spoke to you was an occasion I deeply regret, but I take comfort in knowing that what I said didn't hurt you nor trouble you in any way. Pain and anger can't touch you now and I know you suffered my angry outburst because you understand the weaknesses and frailty of us mortals. I deeply regret that I misconstrued your actions but fortunately for me I was able to talk to Rabbi Friedman, and although he let me roast for a while, it was no more than I deserved. In hindsight I should have put the diary into the fire and refused to believe that you could ever have taken it on yourself to deceive me. You couldn't, and I should have known that, but as

221

I said, I am mortal and suffer all the frailties of mortality. Don't think ill of me, old friend. You still are my friend, and that could never change. I know you would never forsake me, not in your world, where the grass is always green and where the roses hold their scent forever. .

'I'm going to say goodbye for now, old friend, but before I go I must tell you that everything's underway with regard to the bronze plaque. I know it'll make you smile, but I've decided to have one made like the Rosenblum plaque that's just inside the entrance to the synagogue. You know the one I mean. It will cost a good few shillings more but I feel that the original round plaque wouldn't do you justice. You'll be pleased with this one and the extra cost will be my penance for having doubted you. Farewell, Abel. Gerda sends her love as always.'

Albert Levy locked up his shop with a light heart. He was happy to have gone some way to restoring the bond. It would be even stronger from now on, he thought as he crossed the main thoroughfare.

The tram was gathering speed and there was no way the driver could have prevented the accident. People gathered round the figure lying prone in the gutter and one young man bent down to feel for a pulse.

'I saw it 'appen,' a man said in a shocked voice. ' 'E just walked straight inter the tram. It wasn't the driver's fault.'

'Yeah, I saw it as well,' another remarked. ' 'E was sent flyin' an' 'e whacked 'is 'ead against the kerb. It sounded fer all the world like the crack of a whip.'

'Is 'e dead?' asked an old woman fearfully.

A policeman pushed his way through the crowd. 'Don't move 'im,' he ordered. 'I'll phone fer an ambulance.'

Jennie was determined to go to the train station at once, ignoring any objections. 'They could be arrivin' any time, Mum,' she said quickly. 'I've got to be there.'

With her heart beating excitedly she hurried out into the Old Kent Road and caught a number 21 bus, which would take her directly into the station forecourt. The short journey seemed to last forever and she closed her eyes and said a silent prayer that she wouldn't be too late.

London Bridge Station was busy on that sabbath morning, with servicemen and women milling around or standing waiting by mounds of suitcases and equipment. Military police patrolled the concourse in pairs, strutting officiously with their hands clasped behind their backs and their eyes obscured and inscrutable beneath the stiff peaked caps they wore. Porters pushed luggage on large two-wheeled barrows and children ran excitedly from one empty chocolate machine to another while steam hissed from huge tenders and bored-looking train drivers and firemen leaned on the footplates idly watching the feverish activity.

'Er, excuse me, but 'as the troop train come in yet?' Jennie asked a passing porter.

The man eyed her with some amusement. 'Which one would you be referrin' to, miss?' he enquired.

'The one from New'aven,' she said quickly.

'Well, we've 'ad one in—no, come ter fink of it, it was two this mornin', countin' the milk train,' he told her. 'They stuck a couple o' Red Cross carriages on the milk train yer see. Stretchered wounded.'

'Is there any more due in terday?' she asked anxiously.

'Yer know I shouldn't be givin' yer that sort of information,' the porter said, trying to look serious. 'I mean ter say, you could be a fifth columnist fer all I know.'

'My bruvvers were at Dunkirk,' Jennie replied puffing, 'an' me boyfriend too. They're comin' 'ome terday. That's why I'm askin'.'

The porter smiled and took her arm. 'Let's see now,' he said as he steered her away from an approaching truck full of baggage. 'See that RTO office over there? They'll be able ter give yer some information. Actually there is a troop train due in very shortly from New'aven, that I can tell yer. It's comin' in on platform four. I should get yerself a platform ticket. If yer loved ones aren't on that train go over an' make some enquiries at the office. An' good luck, miss.'

Jennie thanked him and hurried to get a ticket from a machine, her heart beating even faster as the minute hand on the large clock above the concourse climbed towards the hour. Other people were waiting, looking anxiously up at the clock and down the empty track to where the rails arced away out of sight. Beyond the ticket gate more people were standing around, and when the first puff of steam was seen in the distance everyone moved impulsively a little closer to the edge of the platform. It was coming in now, the large locomotive belching steam, its fireman resting his arm on the brass rail of the footplate while the burly driver wrestled with the levers.

As the train ground to a halt at the buffers the carriage doors sprang open. Servicemen jumped down looking haggard and unkempt. Some wore their berets at a rakish angle, others had their tunics undone and cuffs turned back. Normally the military police would be ready to pounce at such flagrant disregard of prescribed military dress code, but this was a train carrying men straight back from hell and no one was going to demand any strict applications of the regulations at such a time.

Jennie saw Jim first, and then Frank. They were chatting together and when they spotted her they rushed up to lift her off her feet. 'It's great ter be back 'ome,' Frank sighed.

'Yeah, great,' Jim echoed. 'Con's in the end carriage.'

She saw him now, walking beside another soldier who had a bandage covering one eye. Jennie squealed out and Con's face lit up as he spotted her.

Frank caught Jim's eye and turned to Jennie. 'We'll wait for yer by the clock,' he said.

Con came up and threw his arms around her, gazing eagerly at her as if at a vision. 'You're even prettier than the picture I've carried round inside me 'ead,' he laughed.

'I thought I'd never see yer again,' Jennie croaked as she hugged him tightly. 'Especially when Frank told us you were in the rearguard.'

'Did yer pray for me every night?' he asked with a smile.

'Of course. An' you?'

'Every night.'

'I'm so 'appy,' Jennie said, almost choking.

Con released her and moved back a pace. 'By the way, 'ow did yer know I was comin' in this mornin'?'

'Me an' Sadie went ter The Boatman an' they agreed ter phone our corner shop as soon as they 'eard anyfing,' she told him.

He smiled. 'I see. You wanted ter be in on the kill, did yer?'

Jennie's face suddenly became serious. 'Con. There's somefing I gotta tell yer,' she began. 'You obviously 'aven't 'eard.'

'It's me gran, isn't it?'

'Yeah I'm afraid so.'

'She died?'

'Yeah. I'm terribly sorry.'

He nodded his head slowly and saw the questioning look on Jennie's face. 'I 'ad a bad dream last night,' he said quietly. 'All I could see was these miserable faces comin' right up ter me. There was wailin' an' groanin' an' I tried ter move away but I was fixed ter the spot. I could see me gran but I couldn't reach 'er. She was callin' fer me wiv 'er arms 'eld out, an' then I woke up in a pool o' sweat. I knew then that

226

somefing 'ad 'appened to 'er.'

As they walked slowly from the platform Jennie told him what Mrs Crosier had said, and she chanced to remark upon the old lady not being his real grandmother.

'She was as good as a granny ter me,' Con replied with a sigh. 'She loved me callin' 'er gran. It was a game we played an' she loved it. So did I, come ter fink.'

'I wish I'd 'ave got ter know 'er,' Jennie said sadly. 'Me mum wants yer ter come 'ome fer Sunday dinner terday. Yer will, won't yer?'

'Yeah, I'd be delighted,' he told her, his face brightening.

Frank and Jim were standing together sharing a cigarette, and when Jennie told them about the old lady they each put an arm on Con's shoulders. 'Yer better come 'ome wiv us fer a while,' Frank said.

'I've already asked 'im,' Jennie said quickly.

'She's a pushy little cow, Con,' Jim warned him. 'Still I expect yer know the way ter deal wiv that sort.'

Jennie gave him a sisterly look. 'Watch it, Jimbo, or I'll tell Con a few of your secrets.'

'I didn't fink I 'ad any,' Jim countered.

'An' what about the teddy bear you ...'

'All right, all right, I'll be'ave,' Jim replied quickly, grinning at Con.

Gerda Levy sat by Albert's bedside at Guy's Hospital, her eyes never leaving the ashen face of her husband. The doctors had informed her that he had a fractured skull and was in a coma

227

which could last indefinitely.

'I know you can hear me, Albert,' she said softly. 'I've told the rabbi, and do you know what he said? He told me that it was preoccupation that caused your accident. How many times have you told me to look both ways before I cross the road? You treat me like a child, but I don't mind. That's your way of showing that you care for me, but you should have practised what you preached. I know it was to talk to Abel that you went, but you could have talked to him at home. He can hear you wherever you are.

'I've spoken to the doctor, Albert. He said there's no knowing how long you'll be in the coma. Open your eyes and talk to me soon, dearest. When I was talking to Rabbi Friedman about your condition he smiled and said that I shouldn't worry. What a sense of humour! He said I must talk a lot, worry you into waking up, it was the only way. He said that I should remind you about the shop. He said if I did you'd most likely spring up in bed and ask for your clothes.'

Just then Albert's mouth seemed to twitch and Gerda reached out and took his hand. Suddenly she felt a slight movement in one of his fingers.

'It's a very encouraging sign,' the doctor said when he looked in on his rounds. 'It's much too early to say yet, but it does indicate that he may be moving towards consciousness. Just keep talking to him.'

In the late afternoon, as the sun dipped down

and a fresh breeze sprang up, the two young people walked hand in hand through the cobbled lane that led toward the river.

'It seems like I've known you ferever,' Jennie said quietly.

Con tightened his grip on her hand. 'That's exactly the way I feel. Those letters you sent me told me everyfing I wanted ter know. It was almost as if I'd known you as a child. I got ter know yer likes an' dislikes, I understood a little bit about 'ow you saw fings, an' best of all I knew you cared fer me. Did my letters tell yer what you wanted ter know?'

She nodded and smiled at him. 'I always put the latest letter under me piller when I went ter bed,' she told him. 'I 'eld it in me 'and when I said me prayers.'

He turned towards her, gazing at her pretty face, her impish smile and her hazel eyes glowing with life. He saw how she carried herself, the way her red hair danced on her shoulders and the natural sway of her hips and he sighed deeply. 'I gotta tell yer, Jennie, you're a very lovely woman.'

'Well fank you, kind sir,' she said smiling broadly.

They stopped in the deserted lane and he took her in his arms. The kiss was gentle and sweet and he could feel the warmth of her young body against his. This was a moment to savour, to remember, come what may.

Strolling along to where the ancient stone steps led down to the water's edge, they stood for a few moments, watching the turning tide and the swirling eddies.

'They'll be reformin' the brigade,' Con told her. 'I'm gonna be made up ter sergeant so they told me.'

'What does that mean?' she asked.

'Well I'll be involved in trainin' the new intake,' he replied. 'Then when the battalion's ready we'll ship out.'

'To where?' Jennie asked anxiously.

'It's all a big secret at the moment an' I'm not sure if it's bin settled yet,' Con answered, 'but the whisper is it's the Middle East. Don't go repeatin' this though, will yer, Jennie?'

'Of course not.'

'Anuvver battalion's standin' by in this country in case of an invasion,' he went on. 'I could be wiv that one. It's all in the lap o' the gods.'

They found a secluded place by the river wall and held each other close, watching the rise and fall of the moored barges midstream. They saw the gulls dipping and soaring, the still cranes and the shuttered wharves and Jennie fretted. 'I'll never get used ter sayin' goodbye,' she sighed. 'I'll always choke on the words.'

He smiled and squeezed her to him. 'War will always be about goodbyes,' he replied. 'But we'll cope, 'cos there's nuffink none of us can do about it. We 'ave ter be strong, an' I'm sure each of us'll gain strength an' win frew, as time goes by.'

CHAPTER 19

The summer streets of Bermondsey were quiet now after the few hectic days that followed Dunkirk and the homecomings of the servicemen. In Carter Lane women chatted on their doorsteps much as they had before, but they were often sad-faced and serious.

'Poor Mrs Dunkley's out of 'er mind,' Amy Bromilow told Ivy Jones. 'She got a telegram two days ago.'

'So did Mrs Bentley from Brady Street,' Ivy replied. 'Tommy was 'er only son.'

'At least Chris Wickstead's doin' well,' Amy went on. 'Ada told me 'e looked more 'is ole self last weekend when 'er and Jacko went ter see 'im. Apparently they're gonna send 'im down ter Wales ter recuperate. It must 'ave bin terrible fer those poor lads. My Freddie didn't say too much about it all, but I could see 'ow it must 'ave affected 'im. One night 'e woke up screamin'. Frightened the life out o' me it did. I wondered what the bloody 'ell it was. In a pool o' sweat 'e was.'

Ivy shook her head slowly. 'Gawd knows what lastin' effect it's gonna 'ave on those boys,' she sighed.

Dolly and Mick Flynn had deliberately refrained from asking too many questions when their two sons came home, but Dolly could not fail to notice the bandage on Jim's upper arm while he was washing at the scullery sink. He passed it off as a scratch that had got a little infected and was now healing nicely, though it still made his arm a bit stiff. Frank was non-committal when she asked him about his brother's wound, but he stressed that it was really nothing to make a fuss about, considering the injuries some of the lads had suffered. The usual banter between the two that had become second nature over their years as brewery draymen was still in evidence but both Dolly and Mick realised that it was now a little contrived, as if put on for their benefit. They felt that of the two Frank seemed the more affected, and at times when he had that faraway look in his eyes Dolly wanted to hug him in the way she had when he was a child. She knew that the scars of war were already indelibly there, seared into both her sons' minds, as they were for all the other sons and husbands who had fought their way back from the maw of death across the narrow Channel, and aware of her inadequacy she suffered in silence.

The wartime summer was warm and balmy, but now the clear August skies over Southern England were criss-crossed with tracer streaks, cannon fire and duelling aircraft darting and diving as the Battle of Britain raged. Airfields and coastal installations were targeted in the fight for supremacy between the Royal Air Force and the German Luftwaffe, and all the time an armada was being prepared across the

Channel. An invasion date had been set by the German High Command and ill-prepared and undertrained battalions of British troops were rushed to the coastline to join up with a fully mobilised Home Guard, as ready as they would ever be to defend the country against an imminent landing. Everything hinged on the fate of Fighter Command. The skies above the landing points had to be made safe first, but the Spitfire and Hurricane pilots were proving to be more than a thorn in the side of the German forces. Losses on both sides were high, and on every placard outside every newsagent and paperstand battle scores and losses were printed in bold lettering. People rushed to buy the newspapers, reading the accounts and noting the scores as they might those of a cricket match in more peaceful times but this game was deadly serious. Everyone knew that their whole future existence was in the hands of a few brave and exhausted pilots, who were slowly whittling down the might of the Luftwaffe and winning the battle of the skies.

It was some time before anyone on this side of the Channel realised that, due to their huge losses, the German war machine had decided the invasion of England would have to be postponed. However, a new and terrible plan was slowly taking shape. England had to be forced into submission one way or another, and where once the airfields in Northern Germany and occupied France had been full of fighter aircraft, they now became bases for the heavy bombers.

Saturday the 7th of September 1940 was to be a day that no one in London would ever forget as long as they lived, but on the eve of the cataclysm people went about their business and got on with their lives as they had always done. The women queued for food and prepared meals, holidaying children played in the warm streets and people came home from work looking forward to a restful weekend.

In the Flynn household it was a normal Friday evening, and with the meal over Sadie hurried up to her bedroom to get ready to go out. As usual Jennie looked in and sat chatting with her, curious to find out why Sadie had suddenly changed her plans. 'I fink Len Regan can twist you right round 'is little finger,' she said, pulling no punches. 'Only this afternoon you was goin' on about not bein' put upon an' then 'e shows up in that flashy car an' you start jumpin' frew the 'oop.'

Sadie sighed indulgently as she brushed out her fair hair. She felt very close to Jennie and generally tended to put up with her forthright remarks, knowing that they were said out of love and concern rather than malice, but this evening she took the bait. 'You just don't understand, Jen, so don't start goin' on. This is important business. Len's got some problems an' it's only right 'e should ask me fer some 'elp.'

'It must be serious if 'e couldn't say what 'e 'ad ter say in the 'ouse instead o' draggin' you out ter the car,' Jennie answered regardless. 'What must people fink?'

234

'Frankly I'm not interested in what the neighbours fink,' Sadie said quickly. 'Sod 'em, that's what you always tell me.'

Jennie shrugged her shoulders. 'Is this a big secret, or are yer gonna let me in on it?' she asked, her face assuming a saucy smile.

Sadie swivelled round to face her younger sister. 'It's this Brighton business,' she began. 'Apparently there's bin some disagreement wiv the people Johnnie Macaulay was cultivatin' an' it looks like the big deal's gonna fall frew. It seems that the people from Glasgow 'ave pulled out as well, an' that was where most of the backin' was comin' from.'

'It's all above my 'ead,' Jennie sighed.

'It's a question o' raisin' enough money ter buy inter the gamblin' set-up on the south coast,' Sadie explained. 'Macaulay's invested 'eavily in that Brighton business an' now 'e's lookin' ter raise some money by gettin' some new backers.'

Jennie's irritation was obvious as she pulled a face. 'So 'ow does all this concern you, apart from bein' involved wiv Regan?' she asked.

'There's a big meetin' ternight at Brighton an' some important business people are invited,' Sadie went on. 'Len wants me to 'elp 'im take care of 'em.'

'An' you're gonna stand fer that?' Jennie said incredulously. ' 'Ave you fergotten what 'appened at that club down in Kent? Yer gotta be mad.'

'It's nuffink like that,' Sadie told her. 'Len's

235

gonna be there all the time an' 'e won't let no one take liberties.'

'I thought yer said yer wouldn't be seen dead in that place,' Jennie remarked. 'Yer said yerself it's nuffink more than a brothel.'

'I was angry at the time an' I went over the top when I told yer that,' Sadie replied. 'Actually it's a smart 'otel that doubles as a dinin' an' gamblin' club. There's some 'ostesses employed there an' they encourage the customers ter drink an' gamble. It's their job an' they get commission. If they fancy a customer an' the customer fancies them, so what? If there wasn't any bedrooms there they'd book in somewhere else anyway.'

'Oh I see,' Jennie said sarcastically.

Sadie picked up her hairbrush once more. 'I don't fink yer do,' she sighed. 'Anyway I've agreed to 'elp out ternight so that's that.'

'Just as long as yer not expected ter play the 'ostess game,' Jennie persisted.

'What d'you take me for?' Sadie said angrily.

'I'm just concerned for yer, that's all,' Jennie told her in a sincere voice.

Sadie smiled. 'I know you are, but stop worryin'. I know what I'm doin'.'

'By the way, 'ave yer replied ter Big Joe's latest letter yet?' Jennie asked.

Sadie shook her head. 'I was gonna do it ternight. I'll do it termorrer fer sure.'

'Yer wouldn't want Joe ter fink out o' sight means out o' mind, would yer?' Jennie pressed.

'I said I'd do it, didn't I?'

'Yeah all right, touchy Lill.'

'Well you do go on at times.'

'Sorry fer breavvin'.'

Sadie put down the brush and let her shoulders slump. 'If yer must know I'm findin' it a bit difficult answerin' Joe's latest letter,' she said. 'It wasn't a problem replyin' ter the ovver ones, after me an' you 'ad that little chat. I just told 'im about what it was like growin' up round 'ere, like you suggested, an' I told 'im all the little chit-chat from the street, an' 'is replies were in the same vein, but this last letter from 'im seems different.'

'Different? 'Ow d'yer mean?'

'I dunno really. 'E just seems more serious.'

' 'As 'e asked yer ter be 'is gelfriend?'

'No, it's just the general tone o' the letter.'

'Well unless I read it I can't offer any opinion,' Jennie said with a wry smile. 'But don't fink I'm pressin' fer you ter show me it. I know it's private.'

'You're welcome ter read it,' Sadie replied, opening the dressing-table drawer and taking it out. 'There's nuffink soppy in it.'

Jennie read the two pages carefully and then handed them back to her sister. 'I must admit it does sound a bit serious,' she remarked. 'That bit about you bein' special to 'im an' 'opin' that you feel the same way, and the bit about rememberin' 'im wiv love if fings go wrong. It seems as though 'e expects somefing to 'appen.'

'That's what I thought,' Sadie agreed. 'The problem is, 'ow do I reply wivout committin' meself? Big Joe knows the score wiv me an'

237

Len. I just can't tell 'im I love 'im.'

Jennie looked thoughtful as she studied her sister's anxious face. 'I don't fink 'e used the word love in that way,' she said quietly. 'Just fink about it. Joe's trainin' up in some remote part of Scotland, an' the location suggests ter me that this is all preparation fer a dangerous job. If that's true, then 'e most likely feels 'e might well end up gettin' killed when it goes off. That could be why 'e's askin' you ter remember 'im wiv love. Someone to 'old on to, someone special who'd keep 'is memory alive, that's what 'e's sayin', Sadie, I'm certain of it.'

'You could well be right,' Sadie replied. 'After all, Joe's thousands o' miles away from the country where 'e was born and raised. Back 'ome people'd mourn 'is passin' an' 'ave their own special memories of 'im, but over 'ere 'e prob'ly still feels like an outsider ter most people.'

'I fink yer'll write that letter now,' Jennie said smiling. 'What's more, I'll be willin' ter bet that even wivout committin' yerself yer'll make 'im a very 'appy man.'

Albert Levy opened his eyes and stared fixedly for a few moments at the shadowy figure by his bedside. Slowly, as his vision cleared, he saw Gerda smiling down at him. 'Where's Abel gone?' he croaked.

Gerda felt her heart sink. His brain's damaged, she thought. He can't remember. 'Abel went some time ago,' she faltered.

Albert smiled wearily and slid his hand across

the crisp white bedsheet. 'Abel was standing there,' he replied. 'I saw him at the foot of the bed and he told me I'd been very careless. Is it true I was knocked down?'

Gerda nodded as the tears came. 'Abel wouldn't lie,' she gulped.

'No, of course not.'

'Close your eyes now and rest,' she told him. 'I'll be back soon.'

'Abel was there all the time,' Albert said, his voice hoarse with emotion. 'He listened to all my ravings and he understood. I asked his forgiveness for ever doubting him and he said there was nothing to forgive. He came to tell me, Gerda. He gave me the sign. At last I can be in peace.'

'Close your eyes, dearest. Sleep deeply and when you wake up I'll be at your side,' she whispered.

'Of course, my dear,' Albert answered. 'You always are.'

The doctor smiled as he patted Gerda's hand. 'He'll be fine now,' he said.

Liz Kenny made her usual call on Dolly Flynn and the two sat sipping their tea while they filled each other in on the street's developments.

'Big Joe sent us a nice long letter,' Liz said. ' 'E's such a carin' young man. 'E was concerned about my Bert. You remember Bert wasn't very well when Joe was 'ome on leave.'

'Our Sadie's 'ad a few letters from 'im too,' Dolly told her.

'I'm so glad,' Liz remarked. 'Wouldn't it be

nice if those two got tergevver.'

'Yeah, it would,' Dolly replied. 'I don't like 'er bein' wiv that wide-boy Regan. 'E's nuffink but trouble if you ask me.'

'Does your Sadie answer the letters?' Liz asked.

'Yeah, I'm sure she does.'

'That's nice. Big Joe finks the world of 'er, yer know.'

'Yes, I know.'

' 'Ere, while I fink of it,' Liz said suddenly, 'I bumped inter Rene Conroy down the market this mornin'. 'Er Alec's due 'ome on leave very soon. Apparently 'e's in the Royal Engineers. Who'd 'ave thought it?'

'Yeah, it was strange 'ow 'e just went an' signed on, after all 'e'd told 'is muvver,' Dolly replied. 'The poor cow was goin' out of 'er mind over 'im. She said she wouldn't be able ter stand the shame of the police comin' fer 'im.'

Liz Kenny put her empty cup and saucer down on the table. ' 'Ave yer done any more knittin' lately?' she asked.

Dolly shook her head. 'Nah, I ain't 'ad the time, what wiv the boys bein' 'ome an' all. I'll get back ter doin' it again though. Those Lockwood sisters don't let up, do they?'

Liz grinned. 'What a strange couple they are.'

'Yer tellin' me,' Dolly agreed. 'Mind you though, yer gotta feel sorry for 'em. Poor Cynthia got knocked from piller ter post by that ugly git of an ole man, then 'e pisses orf an' leaves 'er wiv debts up to 'er eyeballs.'

'Strange about the way 'e disappeared,' Liz went on. 'Everyone was very surprised. 'E led a life o' Riley wiv Cynthia. She used ter do everyfing fer 'im. 'E even 'ad 'er puttin' 'is bets on, the lazy bastard.'

'Mind you, she's 'appy wiv Charity bein' there wiv 'er,' Dolly remarked. 'They're very close an' she does fuss over 'er. It makes a change fer someone ter fuss over the poor cow.'

'Didn't she ever marry?' Liz asked.

'Nah, it was the ole story,' Dolly explained. 'Someone told me once that she looked after 'er sick muvver until the ole gel was in 'er nineties, an' by then it was too late.'

'Bloody shame.'

'Yeah, what people 'ave ter put up wiv.'

'Well I s'pose I'd better get back or Bert'll fink I've left 'ome.'

'Anuvver cuppa 'fore yer go?'

'All right then. 'E'll be snorin' 'is 'ead off anyway.'

apper Alexander Conroy wiped the sweat from his brow and blinked quickly. The loose earth had been cleared from around the bomb and its grey wet surface glistened in the light of the portable lamp.

'So what now?' the voice crackled over the wireless set.

'I'm about ter remove the detonator,' Alec answered in a whisper through the mouthpiece.

'Don't jerk the spanner, ease it. Message understood?'

'Loud an' clear,' Alec replied.

The evening felt chill as the last of the light faded and the young sapper shivered as he picked up the large spanner and slipped the end onto the protruding nut. Slowly he applied pressure, lightly at first, then with more force when the nut resisted movement. It was turning, coming out easier now and Alec paused for breath. The rest could be done with his fingers and he slowly turned the nut until it came away from the casing.

'Report,' the command crackled down the line.

'Detonator removed. Goin' fer the wires.'

'Check the wiring first.'

Alec shone the torch into the recess and saw that the red wire was connected to a small metal case and the blue wire ran into the darkness of the bomb casing. 'Cuttin' the blue wire,' he said, his throat suddenly dry.

'Why the blue?'

'Red wire booby-trapped.'

'Proceed.'

Alec gingerly eased the blue wire up until he managed to get a proper grip on it with the snippers, then with a silent prayer he cut the wire clean through. The ugly buzzing made him jump back in fright against the wall of the crater, and he looked up fearfully to see the sergeant approaching.

'You bloody fool. You just killed yourself, Conroy,' he bawled.

'I saw that the red wire was attached ter the condenser,' Alec said taking a deep breath. 'That's why I cut the blue.'

242

'Without checking where the blue ended up,' the instructor growled. 'If that'd been a real unexploded bomb you would have blown yourself and your assistant to kingdom come. In future don't take anything for granted. You can't afford to in bomb disposal. The red wire attached to the condenser was a decoy and you fell for it. The blue was booby-trapped.'

Alec rubbed his grimy hand across his sweaty forehead and the sergeant gave him a sympathetic smile. 'Come on, Conroy, let's get back to the truck. I don't think you'll make that mistake again.'

CHAPTER 20

Simm's bakery in the Old Kent Road ran out of bread as usual around midday on Saturday and the last bake was snatched up as soon as it came out of the ovens, which pleased George Simm as he had a wedding function to attend that evening. He chased around cleaning the mixer equipment, while his wife Addie scrubbed the wooden worktops in the back of the shop. Jennie took her cue from the rush and dash around her and cleaned the shelves, tidied up in general and counted out the till.

'I fink we broke the record terday,' Addie smiled as she wiped the sweat from her forehead with the back of her hand.

'Four o'clock, that's not bad,' George remarked. 'We can close up early. You might as well get off, luv,' he told Jennie. ' 'Ave a nice early night fer a change.'

Jennie needed no persuasion and she hurried out into the sunlit thoroughfare, looking forward to another letter from Con. She normally received one on Saturday morning but the postman invariably came after she had left for work, and her mother would put it on the mantelshelf in front of the chimer for her to find as soon as she got home.

As she turned into Carter Lane she saw Liz Kenny standing on her doorstep and the woman beckoned to her. 'Got a minute, luv?' she asked.

'Yeah, course.'

'We got a letter from Big Joe this mornin' an' it seems 'e won't be able ter write fer a while,' she said as she led the way into her parlour.

'Did 'e say why?'

'No, but I don't s'pose 'e could very well,' Liz remarked. 'I fink it's somefing very secret if you ask me. The last couple o' letters 'ave bin a bit different, like 'e was tryin' ter tell us somefing. Well, that's what my Bert seems ter fink.'

'It's funny you should say that,' Jennie replied. 'Sadie gets letters from Joe, as yer know, an' she said the same fing.'

'Yeah, well I wanted ter catch yer comin' 'ome from work ter let yer know so you could pass it on ter Sadie,' Liz explained. 'I wouldn't want the gel ter fink that Joe wasn't bovverin' ter write. 'E finks the world of 'er. 'E's always

244

askin' after 'er in 'is letters.'

'Sadie finks a lot of 'im too, but she's not sure of 'erself at the moment,' Jennie told her. 'That Len Regan's a pain in the arse as far as I'm concerned. 'E seems ter be able ter twist 'er round 'is little finger, an' I told 'er too. I wish she'd give 'im the elbow.'

'She'll learn the 'ard way,' Liz sighed. 'I know yer mum worries over 'er. We were only talkin' about 'er an' 'im the ovver day. Regan's a right spiv. 'E seems to 'ave 'is fingers in everyfing.'

Jennie nodded. 'Regan's s'posed ter be Johnnie Macaulay's right-'and man but from what Sadie tells me it seems that Regan's the one who's runnin' the show.'

'D'yer want a cuppa while yer 'ere?' Liz asked.

Jennie looked up at the clock and saw it was twenty-five minutes past four. 'No, I'd better get off, fanks all the same,' she replied. 'Claire Wilson's 'ome fer the weekend an' me an' 'er are goin' ter the pictures ternight. I got me 'air ter wash an' some ironin' ter do.'

When Jennie let herself into the house Dolly pulled a face and jerked her head toward the stairs. 'Sadie's in 'er room but be careful what yer say to 'er,' she warned. 'She's in a violent temper. Nearly bit my 'ead off when she walked in. All I said was that she looked a bit peaky.'

Jennie climbed the stairs and knocked gently on Sadie's bedroom. 'Are yer takin' visitors?' she said quietly.

'Don't be funny, come in,' Sadie growled.

'Man trouble?' Jennie said with a disarming

245

smile as she took her usual place on the edge of the bed.

'If yer call him a bloody man,' Sadie replied.

'Phew. 'E didn't leave yer ter ...'

'Don't ask,' Sadie said, gritting her teeth with temper.

' 'E never.'

'Tell me, Jennie, do yer really fink I'm shallow an' stupid?'

'Course I don't,' the younger sister said quickly. 'Yer not still broodin' over that little chat we 'ad the ovver day, are yer?'

'I've decided,' Sadie declared with a serious look on her face, 'I'm gonna go inter nursin'.'

'You, nursin'?' Jennie said in surprise.

'Yeah, me. Don't yer fink I'm up to it?'

'I fink yer'd make a very good nurse,' Jennie replied quickly. 'But why the sudden decision? Is it anyfing ter do wiv what 'appened last night?'

'Ter be honest I've bin toyin' wiv the idea fer some time,' Sadie told her. 'I can't sit back an' do nuffink till the powers that be decide I should be in war-work. I thought about nursin' after I saw the boys back 'ome an' sittin' round the dinner table. I knew then that I 'ad ter do somefing, but last night really made me mind up once an' fer all. I'm gonna try an' get in the Queen Alexandra's Nursin' Service.'

'They're army nurses, ain't they?'

'That's right.'

'Well, good fer you, sis,' Jennie said getting up and putting her arm around Sadie's shoulders. 'Yer'll make a crackin' nurse.'

246

'D'yer really fink so?'

'I know so.'

Sadie swivelled round on her stool at the dressing table and clasped her hands together as Jennie resumed her place on the bed. 'Me an' Len are finished,' she announced, as if to put the seal on it.

'So what 'appened?' Jennie asked.

'The evenin' started off very well, funnily enough,' Sadie began. 'Len was all charm when we were goin' down ter Brighton. Nosher drove us an' me an' Len chatted away in the back, all nicey nicey, then when we got ter the 'otel 'e introduced me ter those clients of 'is. They were the usual sort yer'd expect. Smart suits an' gold watches an' rings, wiv money comin' out o' their ears. Len seemed ter be gettin' on famously wiv 'em an' then after a while 'e left 'em talkin' ter Johnnie Macaulay, an' me an' 'im went inter the gamblin' room. I was surprised ter see a few uniforms there. Army officers they were. One of 'em was just a young lad really, couldn't 'ave bin no more than twenty-two, twenty-three, an' 'e 'ad the shakes, literally. One o' the 'ostesses was 'angin' on to 'is arm an' encouragin' 'im ter place bets. All over 'im she was. Len told me that the feller was the son of a local businessman an' the family were stone rich. Anyway, I watched the goin's-on while Len placed a few small bets. Didn't win anyfing, but 'e was on form, chattin' away to everyone. Then we went ter the bar fer a drink an' we stood talkin'. Apparently this young officer 'ad bin at Dunkirk, an' Len said 'e'd just come out

247

of a military 'ospital. 'E was sufferin' from shell shock. Honestly, Jen, it was pitiful ter see. The lad 'ad a bulgin' wallet an' this tart was actually takin' the notes from it ter buy more chips. The poor sod didn't know what day it was. I'm sure she pocketed some of 'is money, but when I mentioned it ter Len 'e just laughed. " 'E won't miss it," 'e said. I felt sick ter me stomach. I could see our Frank an' Jim in me mind an' I thought, this could be them. This could 'appen ter them, given the same circumstances.'

' 'Ow 'orrible,' Jennie said, shaking her head sadly.

Sadie stared down at her hands for a few moments. 'Len was drinkin' double whiskies an' 'e began ter get very sarcastic as the drink took effect. 'E told me that the war could be a godsend if yer knew yer way around the obstacles an' 'e said 'e wanted some o' the action. Course I made the mistake o' tellin' 'im that if it was action 'e wanted why didn't 'e join up like me bruvvers. Blew 'is top 'e did. I felt so embarrassed. People could 'ear 'im goin' on an' I'm sure they were laughin' at me. 'E started ter tell me about the money bein' made on the black market an' all about the goin's-on at Brighton. What done it fer me was when 'e told me they were settin' up a club fer servicemen near this big army camp somewhere on the south coast. It's gonna be a cheaper version of the 'otel, fer ordinary soldiers wiv less money who wanna apply fer membership. I just lost me temper completely an' I told 'im that all 'im an' Macaulay were doin' was takin' advantage of

248

young men who were away from their loved ones an' feelin' lonely. "Too bad," 'e said. "An' who are you ter criticise? Are you turnin' inter some Bible-thumpin' campaigner?" '

'So yer told 'im straight you was finished wiv 'im?'

'No, not then,' Sadie went on. 'This young officer was at the roulette table an' 'is number came up. 'E started ter get very excited an' this 'orrible tart who was wiv 'im persuaded 'im ter let it ride. You know, stay on the same number. Now the chances o' that givin' yer a result are one in a million, but the young man didn't seem ter know where 'e was, let alone what 'e was doin', an' 'is face was all distorted. It was so sad ter see. Then the people round the table started ter laugh at 'im. I just saw red. I walked over an' in a loud voice I told 'em all that they should be bloody well ashamed o' themselves. This tart told me ter piss off an' the next fing I remember was grabbin' an 'andful of 'air an' tuggin' on it. She started ter scream an' Len came over an' yanked me away.'

'Wow!' Jennie exclaimed. 'I wish I'd 'ave bin there ter see it!'

'It wasn't very pretty,' Sadie said with distaste. 'Anyway, Len marched me outside an' started ter lay the law down an' I told 'im a few 'ome trufes. I told 'im 'e could go back ter whoever 'e was knockin' off an' 'e nearly exploded.'

' 'E didn't touch yer, did 'e?' Jennie asked quickly.

'Nah, 'e never actually slapped me, but 'e did shake me. I just kicked 'im in the shin

249

an' stormed off. Nosher brought me back, an' me an' 'im 'ad a very good chat on the way 'ome. Apparently there's a lot o' trouble brewin' between Macaulay an' those businessmen I 'ad to entertain at the club that time, an' Nosher reckons I'm well out of it an' should stay well clear of the lot of 'em.'

'It must be serious if Nosher warned yer,' Jennie remarked. ' 'E's bin drivin' fer that crowd fer years, so you said.'

'Yeah, that's right,' Sadie replied, 'but me an' old Nosher get on very well, an' 'e treats me sort o' like 'is own daughter. 'E knows 'e can trust me not ter repeat anyfing 'e tells me, an' I've decided I'm gonna take 'is advice.'

'Good fer you, sis.'

'I mean it, Jen.'

'I know yer do,' Jennie said smiling. 'It just wanted somefing like this to 'appen ter bring yer ter yer senses. By the way, Liz Kenny stopped me on the way 'ome from work. She got a letter from Big Joe this mornin'. Apparently 'e can't write any more fer a while. Liz said 'e didn't explain why but it follows on from what we were sayin' about 'is last letter bein' a bit different. After listenin' ter Liz I reckon Joe's goin' on somefing very dangerous.'

Sadie nodded thoughtfully. 'I'm gonna write 'im a letter ternight,' she declared suddenly. 'I'm gonna tell 'im I'll be finkin' of 'im an' I'll say a prayer fer 'im every night.'

'That's lovely,' Jennie said, sighing extravagantly.

'I'm not committin' meself, mind,' Sadie said quickly, 'but it will 'elp give 'im somefing to 'ang on to if 'e is goin' on some dangerous mission.'

'Will yer tell 'im yer ditched Regan?'

'I might.'

'Course yer will.'

Sadie turned to face the mirror once more, feeling her cheeks flushing slightly, and then suddenly the air-raid siren wailed out. The young women looked at each other and Jennie smiled as she fought to stay calm. 'It's probably just one o' those try-outs,' she said dismissively.

They soon began to hear the drone and distant thumping and they jumped up at the window and peered out. A few people were standing at their front doors and pointing skyward.

'Somefing's 'appenin',' Jennie said, hurrying out of the bedroom.

Sadie followed her down the stairs and they found their parents already standing on the pavement outside.

'What is it?' Jennie asked.

The azure sky was full of aircraft, flying high in formation. Shells were bursting amongst them and Mick Flynn let out a sudden yell. 'Get inside! It's an air raid!'

Dolly and the two girls ignored him, all three rooted to the spot as they gazed up at a sky dark with planes. Explosions could be heard now and the drone became deafening. Large palls of smoke and flames rose high above the rooftops and the din of engines and destruction grew so loud it almost drowned out the whine of the air-raid siren.

'It's the docks!' Bill Harris screamed out from across the street. 'They're bombin' the Surrey Docks!'

'Oh my good Gawd!' Dolly gasped, her hand held up to her face.

A man carrying a service gas mask over his shoulder and wearing a steel helmet marked ARP dashed into Carter Lane. 'Get inside! Take cover!' he yelled, blowing on a whistle.

'Don't you shout at me like that,' Charity Lockwood told him sharply as he dashed past her front door.

'I thought it was very strange a little while ago,' Cynthia remarked to her sister. 'The wireless went dead and I knew it wasn't the accumulator. I only changed it yesterday.'

'I didn't know,' Charity replied.

'No, you were having a snooze and I didn't want to disturb you.'

'Look at those flames and all that smoke,' Charity almost shouted.

'It's the Surrey Docks,' Ted Conroy told them. 'The place is crammed full o' timber. Gawd 'elp the poor sods who live Downtown.'

Downtown Rotherhithe was an island, formed by the natural loop of the River Thames. The one main road around the island followed the bank of the river and led over bridges which spanned the canals and creeks that linked the chain of docks. The rising and swivelling bridges were the only land access to what had become known many years ago as 'Downtown' by the residents, mainly dockers and factory workers who lived in old tenement blocks and two-up, two-down houses and prided themselves on their isolation, and the area was cut off when the bridges were operating and a freighter was passing into or out of the dock system in the centre of the island. The dockyards were always stacked full of timber brought from Russia, Finland and Scandinavia, and in the local pubs in Downtown Rotherhithe weird and wonderful concoctions of drinks could be had and a dozen different languages heard. Around the perimeter of the island riverside factories and small warehouses abounded, storing or processing supplies and produce dropped off in barges and small freighters. It was a vibrant and busy area, and an obvious target for the raiding Luftwaffe which visited a hellish punishment upon it that balmy Saturday afternoon.

It didn't take long for the fire chief to assess the situation and he quite simply called for as many fire tenders as possible. Appliances were brought across the river and rushed up from Kent and Sussex and still they could not cope. A sea of resin melted the firemen's boots and the iron sheds were twisted into grotesque shapes by the heat. The people who lived Downtown were trapped on their prized little island. Bridges had been blasted and those still in place were burning fiercely, making it almost impossible for the fire crews to get to many of the blazing yards. It was growing hotter by the minute as the oxygen was sucked out of the air, and as more fire tenders arrived exhausted firemen took a short breather before going back to tackle the conflagration once more.

As the evening wore on the light from the raging inferno could be seen as far north as Hertfordshire and from the Kent Sussex borders. It also acted as a beacon, lighting up the heartland of London, and most people realised only too well that the Luftwaffe would be certain to make good use of it before the night was out.

In Carter Lane, as in other Bermondsey backstreets, people had to make a decision. If, as seemed likely, there was another raid that night, should they use the public shelters, or should they sleep under the stairs or in the downstairs rooms?

'I couldn't possibly go in one of those public places,' Cynthia groaned.

'No, nor could I,' Charity agreed. 'There's no privacy and what about our bodily needs?'

Amy Bromilow put it more crudely. 'I couldn't piss in one o' those buckets,' she said firmly. 'Besides, everyone can 'ear yer.'

'What about the tube?' Ivy suggested. 'They say it's safe down there.'

'Yeah, unless yer go sleep-walkin',' Amy replied.

'Ada Wickstead said that the jam factory was bein' used as a shelter. Mind yer, that's a bit of a trek every night.'

Amy was adamant. 'I'm gonna take me

254

chances under the stairs an' if it's the Lord's will that I go, then it don't matter what shelter I use, does it?'

Dolly and Mick Flynn had made up their minds to stay in the house for the time being, but should the raids get worse then it would have to be a public shelter.

Liz Kenny and Daisy Harris stood talking to Dolly beneath a blood-red sky as the all-clear sounded, speaking quietly as though fearful of reawakening the devils of destruction.

'I was wonderin' what the workmen were doin' ter that empty 'ouse next ter the factory,' Liz said. 'It turns out it's gonna be a command post fer the ARP. That's what Mrs Jones told me.'

'Did yer notice they've started sandbaggin' it?' Daisy cut in.

'I looked in this mornin' on me way back from the market,' Dolly said. 'The men were puttin' big wooden posts up ter support the ceilin'. Now that's the place ter shelter.'

As it grew late the sky still threw back the orange glow of the fires, making the streets as bright as day, and fretful children puzzled by it all found it hard to sleep. Families sat together round their wireless sets, and as the Grimethorpe Colliery Band struck up with 'It's a Long Way to Tipperary' hundreds of aircraft at airfields in France and Northern Germany were roaring into life and moving onto the runways. Soon they would be back, flying over the Kentish fields and up the Thames estuary towards London, carrying in their bellies a metal cargo of death and destruction. The first night of the London Blitz was about to begin, and it would be seventy-six consecutive nights before any respite came.

CHAPTER 21

Very few people were surprised when the air-raid siren blared out on Saturday night. Danny Crossley and Alf Coates refused to leave the public bar of The Sun until they had finished their drinks and Charlie Anson decided to let the pub stay open for a while to see how things went. Many people had already gone to the public shelters to make sure of getting a place, but most of the Carter Lane folk had decided to stay at home, at least for the time being.

Soon the roar of the anti-aircraft guns in the local parks and open spaces became deafening and then came the dreaded sound of falling bombs. Explosions shook the very foundations of buildings and ceiling dust and plaster fell like snow. Never before had there been anything like it. Dogs howled and cats scurried under beds, children wailed and adults prayed as the din increased and explosions got louder. Windows cracked, but for the most part stayed in their frames due to the protective strips of brown paper that had been stuck on them. Ornaments toppled from shelves as houses shuddered, and shouts and running footsteps could be heard as the ARP services went into action.

For what seemed an eternity the deafening noise of bombs and guns reverberated, then there was a brief lull before the second wave of bombers flew over the burning capital. Fires were raging everywhere, and as the onslaught continued relentlessly families moved out of their parlours to shelter under the stairs. All night long it went on, until four-thirty the following morning, when people gradually emerged from their homes to inspect the carnage. The pre-dawn sky was lit up with an orange and red glow and a strong, acrid smell of cordite and charred wood filled the air. The factory at the end of Carter Lane was burning fiercely, defying the efforts of the exhausted firemen. Shattered roof slates and glass splinters lay on the cobbles, and from the reinforced house next door to the stricken factory two ARP personnel with blackened faces emerged to take a well-earned rest.

'That was a close one, Miss Watson,' the male controller remarked to his female colleague.

'I thought it was our lot, to tell you the truth, Mr Bayley,' she replied.

Nigel Bayley jutted out his square chin and took stock. By day he was employed on the London Underground, where his organising skills helped to keep the vital service running on time, and at night he was the controller responsible for linking the local ARP resources. 'I think we'd better have a general clear-up and then catch some shut-eye. What say you, Miss Watson?'

Karen Watson was in charge of a large City typing pool by day and like Nigel she gave up her nights to supervise the volunteer ARP runners, whose job it was to carry messages to and fro when the lines were down. Shapely, attractive, and with wide grey eyes, Karen took her work seriously. To all intents and purposes she was the ultimate professional, maintaining a formal rapport with her superior officer yet friendly and outgoing to those working under her. 'Right-o, Mr Bayley,' she replied. 'Shall we get started?'

As they went back inside, Ted Conroy emerged from his house with a large jug of tea, accompanied by Rene who had scrounged some large mugs from her neighbour Amy Bromilow, and the firemen received the refreshment with much gratitude.

When the last of the volunteers had gone and the reinforced control room was looking a little more clean and efficient, Karen turned to Nigel. 'At last, darling.'

'I think we did well, dearest.'

'Hold me, Nigel.'

'There there, don't let this get to you.'

'I feel that nothing can harm me when I'm in your arms, Nigel darling.'

'You were very brave, Karen.'

'Was I?'

'Umm. I was very proud of you.'

'And I of you.'

'We make a good team, don't we, darling?'

'We certainly do.'

At six o'clock that Sunday morning the

controller and his assistant emerged from the control post and locked the front door.

'Good day to you, Miss Watson.'

'Good day to you, Mr Bayley.'

As they walked off in opposite directions the Sunday morning dawn light rose in the ragged orange sky and the people of Carter Lane took to their beds for a very welcome, if all too brief, slumber.

Vehicles from the Royal Engineers bomb-disposal squad drove into Southwark Park early on Sunday morning and the sappers began to set up a base inside a fenced-off area which contained hurriedly constructed huts. Later that morning the commanding officer introduced himself to the soldiers assembled outside the mess hut. 'I'm Captain Joseph Fairburn, officer commanding Baker Company, which is what this squad will be known as from now on,' he began. 'Our area of control will be the Bermondsey and Rotherhithe district, but we are to be flexible, should the need arise. Now you men are all fully trained for the hazardous operations you will be required to perform and the situations you will encounter in bomb disposal, but for my money the term of reference does not fully do credit to the service you will be providing. Disposal of unexploded bombs and devices is the easy part. Before that comes the little task of rendering them impotent.'

The men gathered before him smiled and nodded in agreement, and a young Bermondsey lad was already feeling a little more confident that his commanding officer was not going to be a complete and utter bastard.

'Now we are lucky, inasmuch as we have two sappers amongst us who know the area very well. Sergeant Kilbride and Sapper Conroy will be able to get us to the job in hand without too much map work, saving valuable minutes. Conversely, I have to tell you that we have drawn the short straw to some extent, being based in what is considered to be the eye of the storm. As you will all be aware, this area is a prime target for the Jerries, and as such it is currently looking forward to a considerable pounding. I don't need to tell you that the Surrey Docks is still burning out of control as I speak, and when stock is finally taken we will be set to work there, make no mistake. It will be your blooding, and I want nothing less than a one-hundred-per-cent commitment from you all and no six-foot boxes ending up down the post office. Remember my words. Promotion comes quickly in the bomb-disposal section of the Royal Engineers, and so does death. Kingdom come is at our elbow all the time, and only your expertise and know-how can prevent an early and rather energetic shuffling off of mortal coils. A brutal and callous assessment you might say, but then I am a brutal and callous man. So bear with me and remember, never take the Jerries for fools. Never underestimate them, nor their specialists, who will constantly pit their wits against yours. Good luck, men, and may your particular gods go with you always.'

Enthusiastic applause broke out and the

captain gave a salute of acknowledgement before climbing into a waiting car.

'Well, 'e couldn't 'ave put it more plainly,' Sergeant Kilbride remarked.

Alec Conroy smiled as he glanced over to the bandstand and the gun emplacement further on. 'This used ter be a nice park at one time,' he said. 'It's gone ter the bloody dogs now.'

Kilbride put his hands on his hips as he looked around the encampment. 'Come on, lads, let's get workin',' he yelled. 'We're expected ter be operational by this time termorrer.'

Sunday dinner at the Flynns was eaten with very little talking. Mick had been to The Sun for a pint and learnt that one of his workmates and his wife had been killed by a blast which had brought the front of their house down. He had also found out that one of his drinking pals, Vic Slater, had lost his son when his ship was torpedoed in the North Atlantic. Dolly was quiet and thoughtful, having been told by Sadie that morning of her intention to join the army nursing service. True to form Jennie had also sprung a surprise.

'There's no way I'm gonna sit in some shelter while ovver women do their bit, Mum,' she had said firmly. 'I'm gonna see about joinin' the ARP.'

Dolly knew better than to argue with her youngest daughter when her mind was made up and she worried in silence. Mick had already told her that the men in the street were planning on getting themselves organised into a fire-watching team and that didn't exactly detract from her worries. 'I can see I'll be talkin' ter me bloody self wiv all you lot doin' yer bit,' she had said.

Dolly was feeling decidedly better now though. Liz Kenny had called in with her own little plan that afternoon and cheered her up.

'I was talkin' ter Mrs Spencer this mornin',' Liz began. 'Yer know 'er ole man's a fireman, well, she said they want women volunteers ter back up the fire crews. I'm finkin' of givin' it a go.'

'Yer don't mean 'elp 'em fight the fires, do yer?' Dolly asked incredulously.

'Course not, yer silly mare,' Liz said grinning. 'When the firemen are at a big blaze an' they can't leave it, canteen vans go round wiv tea and food. That way the blokes can take a short break in turns wivout leavin' the fire.'

'Sounds a good idea,' Dolly remarked.

'Yeah an' I'm gonna volunteer,' Liz said proudly.

'What does Bert fink about it?' Dolly asked her.

' 'E wasn't too keen at first,' Liz replied, 'but like I told 'im, while 'e's out fire-watchin' I ain't stayin' in the 'ouse on me own. Besides, as I said to 'im, lightning don't strike the same place twice. If a place 'as bin bombed I'll be safer there than cowerin' under the bloody stairs in our 'ouse. Let's face it, Dolly, a bleedin' good shove would knock our 'ouses over, let alone a bomb!'

'When yer gonna volunteer?' Dolly enquired.

'Termorrer mornin'.'

'Where?'

'At the fire station in the Old Kent Road.'

'Give us a knock an' I'll come wiv yer.'

'That'll be nice,' Liz said excitedly. 'Me an' you'll make a bloody good team.'

' 'Ere, who's gonna drive the canteen van?' Dolly asked.

'They've got drivers already,' Liz told her. 'It's servers they're short of.'

'Don't rush inter this, Mum,' Sadie implored her when she found out what her mother intended to do.

'Now listen 'ere,' Dolly said resolutely. 'It's all right you lot decidin' ter do yer bit an' then springin' it on me, but I'm s'posed ter stay 'ere on me own wiv the bombs fallin' all round. Well, you can bloody go an' whistle. I'm gonna do my bit an' that's that.'

'It could be dangerous, luv,' Mick remarked. 'A lot o' firemen get killed on the job. Walls fall on 'em an' floors give way.'

'Be sensible, Mick, fer Gawd sake,' Dolly said sighing with impatience. 'They won't park canteen vans under dangerous walls, now will they?'

'You'd be safer in a shelter, Mum,' Jennie told her.

'I see,' Dolly growled. 'Yer want me ter sit twiddlin' me thumbs all night worryin' about all o' you an' 'avin' ter listen ter the likes o' the Lockwood sisters goin' on about their aches an' pains. No fear! What's good fer the goose is good fer the gander, so that's the end of it.'

Mick and the girls were worried but they had to admit defeat, and they glowed with pride inside when they envisaged Dolly in a steel helmet, braving the air raids while serving tea and buns to hardy firemen.

The Sunderland flying boat took off from the remote base in Scotland and flew due south, hugging the coastline. At first light on Sunday morning it landed near the submarine base in Portland and four Royal Navy personnel, as well as supplies and equipment, were transferred to the submarine *Porbeagle*. At midday the submarine left port and sailed in a south-westerly direction, staying on the surface to conserve power. Once past the Scilly Isles it dived to ten fathoms and steered a more southerly course, still keeping well clear of French waters. A storm was brewing in the Bay of Biscay, but after coming up to periscope depth and scanning the area, the captain decided to surface and the four men who had joined the crew were able to go up on deck briefly.

'Bloody nectar,' Big Joe remarked as he drew in deep gulps of air.

Petty Officer Stone nodded as he quickly filled his pipe. 'All being well, we'll be in Gib by tomorrow night,' he said.

The other two passengers, Petty Officer Chivers and Leading Seaman Preston, stood a few feet away on the slippery deck chatting together, but any chance of further relaxation was abruptly curtailed when the lookout suddenly shouted out, 'Clear the decks!'

The last man down the Jacob's ladder spun the wheel of the hatch and the submarine dived steeply.

'The aircraft might have been friendly but we couldn't afford to wait and find out,' the executive officer told the startled team as the vessel levelled off below the surface.

Leading Seaman Joe Buckley sat down in the cramped mess, sipping a mug of disgusting coffee while he re-read Sadie's letter. He closed his eyes, trying to evoke a vivid image of her in his mind but it eluded him. He put the letter back into his breast pocket and tapped it meaningfully as he made his way along the companionway and climbed up into his bunk. There was little to do except rest and he took advantage of the free time by sleeping as much as he could do while the submarine was in transit to Gibraltar.

The last two days had been very hectic, with the dress rehearsal on Saturday afternoon which went on late into the night, then a de-briefing before sleep, which was cut short by the arrival of the flying boat. Joe had had no access to a wireless and was unaware that London had been bombed, until he heard two ratings discussing it.

'There were lots of people killed, according to the reports on the news broadcasts,' one said. 'I'm glad my folk don't live in London.'

'They say the place took a fair old bashing,' his mate added.

'When was this?' Joe interrupted him.

'Saturday afternoon,' the sailor replied. 'The

265

Surrey Docks in London were destroyed and there were hundreds of casualties.'

The rest of the journey to Gibraltar was a nightmare for the young Australian. Was Sadie all right? And what about the Kennys? Would they all have been caught up in the bombardment?

A whole day in Gibraltar was needed before confirmation came through that the mission was on, and during that time the four men on special service spent their time looking around the Rock and visiting the busy bars where they sat in the sun sipping ice-cold beers. At the appointed hour they returned to the dockside and were immediately summoned to the submarine's wardroom.

'Right, men, we've got the go-ahead,' Captain Fellows told them. 'We set sail at twenty-one hundred hours and our destination is Oran on the Algerian coast. Your target is the German surface raider *Kaiser Wilhelm*, which intelligence informs us has just arrived there.'

The four looked at each other excitedly. All the training, all the preparation was over and done with. Now it was the real thing and very soon they would be slipping into the night waters of the Mediterranean and setting off into the unknown.

'Our roundabout route will bring us ten miles off the Algerian coast by tomorrow evening and we'll stay submerged until darkness,' the captain went on, 'then we'll surface and move in closer. You will then set off at twenty-two hundred hours. Assuming that all goes well, and I'm sure it will, you will make your way in an easterly direction, following the coastline to this point, about a mile from the port.'

The men leaned forward over the table as the captain stabbed his forefinger down on the chart. 'It's a deserted spot with a small cove that's inaccessible by land but easily recognised by two large rocks here and here. The locals call them the Sentinels. You will wait there until 04.30 hours when you should see our signal. There'll be two flashes at ten-second intervals and you'll reply with two flashes. Our acknowledgement will be three flashes and you will then take to the water. Okay so far?'

The men nodded quickly and the captain looked from one to another. 'Now if for some reason we don't get your acknowledging signal we will wait for one hour. Here are the maps for you to study before you leave. You'll see that there's another rendezvous point marked further along the coast. Failing contact at the initial rendezvous, we'll be waiting off this point the following night between twenty and twenty-three hundred hours. I hope this back-up point will not be needed but study the map and digest the information very carefully—your survival depends on it. Good luck, men. I'll be seeing you again at your departure time.'

Joe Buckley wrote two letters that night as the submarine made its way beneath the dark waters towards a hostile coast, and after arranging with the ship's bosun to have them forwarded should anything go wrong the big Australian settled down to sleep.

CHAPTER 22

During the first few days of the Blitz people walked around as if dazed, hardly believing what they saw. Buildings, factories and homes that had been an intrinsic part of their lives were now piles of rubble. They rushed home from work to eat their evening meal and get prepared before night fell, gathering up bundled blankets and flasks of tea for the nightly trek to the local shelters. Whether it was the London Underground system, factory shelters or public shelters of the backstreets which they hurried to, it made no difference. The idea was to get there early for a place before dark and to pray for rain and cloudy skies, for a blanked-out moon and for providence to spare them and their homes.

Many families who had previously ignored the call for children to be evacuated now sought to get their young ones out of London as soon as possible, while others still resisted the urge, taking the fatalistic view that if a bomb had their name on it then they would all go together. Some people, distressed by tales of bad treatment meted out to evacuees, decided that they did not want to subject their own children to such a risk, and tired nervous children joined their parents on the nightly trek.

Not everyone was happy about using the shelters, feeling that they were unhygienic, and that it was a risk in itself being crowded into a restricted place which could receive a direct hit. Under the stairs or in the cellar of their own or their neighbours' home was the choice of many at first, but as the fury of the Blitz increased and more and more homes were hit by the blast from nearby bombs so public shelters became the only sensible choice. At least there, people could feel less exposed to the dangers of blast and injury from flying glass and debris.

During the first week of the Blitz the folk of Carter Lane reluctantly accepted that the shelter in the adjacent Brady Street offered the best protection and they booked their nightly places with the warden in charge, who was coming under increasing pressure to limit the number of people using the place for safety reasons.

'You can see fer yerself,' he said to Amy Bromilow and Ivy Jones when they approached him one evening outside the entrance. 'The shelter's split inter two arches an' each one can't take no more than one 'undred people. At the moment there's only wooden benches but soon they're gonna put bunks in. If I allowed more than that number o' people ter shelter 'ere, what's gonna 'appen when the bunks arrive? Some would 'ave ter be turned out.'

'Ain't yer got no room fer us two then?' Amy asked.

'Yeah, there's still a few spaces left,' he replied, 'but don't go tellin' all yer neighbours there's room for all o' them when there ain't, that's all I'm sayin'.'

Amy and Ivy booked their places, as did Mr

269

and Mrs Wickstead and the Harrises. Liz Kenny and Dolly Flynn had never considered the shelter as an option, expecting to be otherwise engaged with the fire service, and as for the Lockwood sisters their philosophy was that it would be better to be buried under a few timbers and roof slates rather than tons of reinforced concrete.

'But yer'd be safer there than under yer stairs,' Mrs Wilson told them. 'These old 'ouses ain't very strong. A bomb in the street could bring 'em all down.'

Charity and Cynthia had already discussed their options in detail and they were adamant. 'That's as it may be but we're prepared to take a chance,' Charity said for both of them. 'We fit in nicely under the stairs and we've got our palliasse and a couple of warm blankets. We'll manage quite nicely, thank you very much.'

On Friday of that first week Sadie Flynn went to the local Labour Exchange and made enquiries about becoming an army nurse, while Jennie called in to the Town Hall and was enrolled as a trainee ARP warden.

'They gave me a tin 'elmet, a gas mask an' an armband, oh an' a whistle too,' she told her sister that night. 'I gotta report every evenin'.'

'I've got this big form ter fill in,' Sadie said, pulling a face. 'I 'ope this ain't gonna be all drawn out. I'm impatient ter get started.'

'I don't fink it'll take long,' Jennie replied. 'I should imagine they'll be cryin' out fer nurses.'

'Well, nobody can say this family's not doin'

their bit,' Dolly reminded them all. 'Even yer farvver's joined the fire watchers.'

'We're worried about you though, Mum,' Sadie remarked. 'Are you sure you're doin' the right fing?'

'Don't you go worryin' about me, my gel,' Dolly said indignantly. 'I ain't exactly confined to a rockin' chair wiv a rug roun' me yet awhile. I can do me bit. Me an' Liz Kenny'll be reportin' fer duty on Monday night.'

'What we gonna do, still stay under the stairs?' Jennie asked.

'Yeah, I fink it's as good as anywhere,' Dolly told her. 'Besides, Amy Bromilow said we'd 'ave ter book places in the shelter an' we won't be needin' 'em, will we?'

'I'm still a bit concerned about you though, Mum,' Jennie persisted. 'You could ...'

'Fer Christ sake, don't keep goin' on about it,' Dolly cut her off quickly. 'What's done's done an' I don't wanna 'ear any more on the subject, is that clear?'

Jennie nodded. When her mother adopted that tone of voice there was no use arguing with her.

Late on Friday night, with the Blitz at its height, a high explosive bomb fell in the yard of Gleeson's leather factory in Munday Road, just round the corner from Carter Lane, causing a large crater which uncovered a grisly relic. It was discovered by the fire crew who had just shut off the water pouring from the exposed fractured pipes.

271

'What the bloody 'ell's that?' a fireman said to his colleague, pointing into the moonlit crater.

'What? Where?'

'Look, there, just below the pipes.'

The two scrambled down into the hole to take a closer look.

'It must 'ave bin there fer some years,' the fireman said as he shone his torch on the skeletal remains of a human hand.

' 'As it got a body attached to it, I wonder?' his colleague remarked.

'We'd better not go pokin' about,' the first fireman replied.

'The bomb could 'ave uncovered an ole burial ground,' the second fireman went on.

'I'll go an' let the chief know.'

' 'Ang on, I'm comin' wiv yer. This place is givin' me the willies.'

On Saturday morning a police team, under the local pathologist's supervision, removed a complete skeleton from the crater.

'It's early yet,' the pathologist told the police sergeant, 'but from a preliminary examination I'd say that the body has been in the ground about ten, twelve years.'

The *Porbeagle*'s captain scanned the sea above him through the periscope and then issued the order to surface. The night was clear, with a waxing moon casting a silverish sheen on the calm waters of the Mediterranean, but the two small black rubber dinghies and their crew in wet suits and masks blended in with the surface as they paddled steadily away in a

272

south-westerly direction, the leading one some ten yards in front.

All the advice and well wishing had been expended and now there was an ominous silence, broken only by the sound of the paddles and the soft slap of water against the flimsy rubber craft. Ahead was the Vichy-controlled port of Oran with its flotilla of French navy ships and the visiting surface raider, the *Kaiser Wilhelm.*

The four men paddled steadily, conserving their strength for whatever might befall them, and every fifteen minutes they took a short rest while Petty Officer Chivers in the leading dinghy checked the position with his compass. After two hours the dark shape of the raider loomed up dead ahead and Chivers raised his arm, steering the craft portside of the target. At a certain point the leading crew stopped paddling and the rear dinghy drew alongside. A loop was attached to keep the craft together and a killick anchor dropped overboard. Chivers made a downward movement with his thumb, donned his breathing apparatus then picked up two small metal discs from the well of the dinghy before slipping backwards into the water. The others followed suit and together they swam beneath the surface until they saw the dim outline of the raider's hull directly in front of them.

The operation had been rehearsed many times and without having to think the teams set to work. Chivers and Preston dived under the hull and placed their magnetic charges on the starboard side while Big Joe and Petty Officer

273

Stone placed theirs on the port side. The operation took barely a couple of minutes and then keeping close together the four underwater saboteurs swam away from the raider. Suddenly Preston found it difficult to breathe, and he motioned to Chivers to check his tank. There was nothing for it but to surface. The leak in the breathing tube leading from the oxygen tank was sending a stream of bubbles towards the surface and very soon the air would be gone.

The underwater conversation was conducted in swift hand signals and clearly understood. Preston and Chivers would continue up above while Stone and Buckley carried on submerged. By the time the first pair reached the surface Preston had swallowed mouthfuls of sea water and was choking into his mask as Chivers tore it off his face, supporting him while he coughed and spluttered and glancing anxiously behind them.

The dinghies were finally reached and the distressed saboteur was helped aboard. As they slipped the joining attachment and cut the anchor rope the beam of a strong searchlight sliced through the dark night and arced towards them. The crews fought desperately to put some distance between themselves and the doomed raider but Chivers was at a disadvantage. His partner Preston was hanging over the side choking up water. Stone and Buckley paddled in unison, making quick progress, and seeing the problem Joe threw Chivers a rope so that he could tow the dinghy away faster. Chivers would have none of it and bravely battled on alone, like a Red Indian in a war canoe, using the paddle on both sides of the craft to keep a straight course.

Joe looked back again and saw to his horror that the following dinghy was bathed in light, and then the sound of gunfire split the silence. Bullets sprayed along the water and Chivers suddenly fell backwards overboard. Preston seemed to be moving about in frantic confusion and Joe saw him start to paddle furiously before he too was cut down. There was nothing to be done—nothing could be done—and Joe gritted his teeth as he threw all his energy into paddling away.

The searchlight was probing in an arc some distance behind and any second it could rise and pinpoint them. Stone nudged Joe and pointed to the water. He was right, it was their only hope. Still towing the dinghy they swam below the surface, with Stone checking their progress on his sub-aqua wristwatch. Experience told him how much distance they could cover in a specific time, and when he signalled Joe to surface he was spot on. There, looming up from the sea and leaning slightly shorewards, were the two Sentinels. The sound they had heard underwater came more faintly through the air but it was growing closer, and they guessed it to be the powerful engine of an E-boat hunting them. Stone led the way ashore and the two men hauled the dinghy after them on to the smooth wet sand.

'The charges should be going off any second now,' Stone gasped as he threw himself down some way from the water's edge.

'They'll find the two bodies,' Joe remarked, aware that the air inside the wet suits would keep them afloat.

Petty Officer Stone nodded. 'If they figure there was only one dinghy we've got a better chance,' he replied. 'If not they'll be searching the coastline. Come on we'd better get this boat out o' sight.'

Together they dragged the dinghy up to the sheer cliff and covered it with broken branches and leaves from withered vines that dotted the high rock-face. Suddenly the night sky was lit up and a split second later a loud explosion rent the air, followed immediately by two more. There in the cove the two men could not witness their handiwork but the explosions and light in the sky told them all they needed to know. They punched the air and hugged each other exultantly for a few moments, then Stone turned to gaze out to sea. 'Well done, lads,' he said sadly.

'Yeah, good on you, shipmates,' Joe said quietly.

They finished camouflaging the dinghy and then Stone unzipped the top of his rubber suit and took out a bar of Fry's chocolate. 'This is all we'll get for supper, I'm afraid,' he said grinning.

The noise of the hunting powerboat had faded away but now it grew louder again, getting nearer this time.

'If it comes too close we'll need to be out of here or we'll get picked off,' Stone growled.

'How?' Joe said looking puzzled. 'We can't take to the water.'

Stone glanced up at the cliff face. 'It'll have to be the water,' he replied. 'We can't scale that without ropes and climbing gear.'

The noise of the E-boat was still getting louder and the two men looked anxiously at each other. They could see it now some way westwards, its powerful searchlight scanning the coastline.

'Come on, let's go,' Stone said, dashing down to the water's edge.

They swam on the surface to conserve their dwindling air supply and a few hundred yards to the east they paused to see the E-boat settle down in the water outside the cove. In the light of the moon they could clearly see a small boat being launched and armed men piling into it.

'That's our dinghy gone for a burton,' Stone said, cursing aloud.

Joe took the lead and the two continued swimming along the coast towards their back-up rendezvous. Midway between the two points they waded ashore into a rocky inlet. 'This'll be as good as anywhere to hole up for a while,' Stone remarked.

Joe started to smile and then his smile turned to a low chuckle.

'What's so funny?' Stone asked him.

'It all looks so neat and tidy on paper, doesn't it?' Joe replied. 'If the first rendezvous is out use the second and see you the following night—and now here we are stuck between the two, a couple of shark's biscuits with an E-boat hunting us down.'

Stone nodded slowly. 'The question is, now what do we do?'

Joe looked out to sea. 'I reckon it all depends on those buggers,' he replied.

'Yeah, if they leave we can go back to the cove,' Stone went on, 'but if not we're caught between the monster and the clashing rocks, to paraphrase the ancient Greeks.'

Suddenly they saw another light further out to sea and then heard the familiar roar of powerful engines.

'They've sent another boat out,' Stone growled. 'It seems to be searching further along the coast.'

'Yeah, right by our second bloody rendezvous,' Joe puffed.

Stone settled down with his back against a hard rock and Joe eased himself down beside him. Water lapped around their feet and above them the moon smiled down mockingly.

'D'you ever question yourself and your motives?' Stone asked after a period of silence.

'Yeah,' Joe replied with a laugh. 'I've just been asking myself the question I reckon you've been asking yourself. Why the hell did I volunteer for this?'

'What answers did you come up with?'

'Nothing as useful as tits on a bull.'

'That's okay then,' Stone grinned. 'At least I don't owe you a sensible answer, if you're as crackers as me.'

Joe leaned his head back against the rock

and smiled. 'Yep. Two mad bastards in the moonlight. Ship? What bloody ship? I reckon it'd make a good song.'

The sound of the searching boat got gradually louder and the two hunted men looked at each other, their hearts sinking. The E-boat was dropping anchor directly off shore. If it stayed there until the rendezvous time of 04.30 the submarine would abort the pick-up, which meant another twenty-four hours dodging the enemy.

'What do we do now?' Joe hissed.

Stone shook his head. 'Outside of praying, nothing I guess.'

CHAPTER 23

The factory in Carter Lane was now a tangled mass of charred timbers, blackened iron girders and brick rubble. Next door the ARP post had survived, but only just. The wall adjacent to the factory had cracked from the heat and blast and the ceilings were missing plaster, showing the bare ribs of wooden laths in places. The Sun public house had fared much better, which one or two elderly locals at least uttered a prayer of thanks for. Charlie Anson had already boarded up the large plate-glass windows, leaving a smaller square for light which he covered after closing time. The Jackmans' grocery shop was left in a sorry

279

state, however, with glass from the two broken windows scattered amongst the tins of food and packets of tea and sugar that the blast had swept from the shelves.

'This'll take us a week ter clean up,' Sara groaned.

'We ain't got a week,' Tom reminded her firmly. 'It don't make no difference ter the customers what state we're in, they'll still expect ter get served.'

The Jackmans set to work clearing up the shop, with the help of Alf Coates, who had little else to do until the pub opened.

'I should've knocked at Danny's,' the elderly man remarked to Sara. ' 'E'd be only too glad ter give us a bit of 'elp.'

'We can manage between us, Alf,' Sara told him quickly, realising from experience that once the two pub fixtures got together nothing would get done.

The gruesome discovery in Munday Street was reported to the local press and everyone was talking about it.

'It could be one o' those victims o' the plague,' Danny Crossley remarked to Alf Coates over a beer.

'Could be,' Alf replied. 'They say there's fousands o' plague victims buried in Bermon'sey.'

'I shouldn't fink so,' Charlie Anson cut in. 'Yer talkin' about four 'undred years ago. There'd be nuffink left of 'em by now.'

'It's a bit creepy though,' Danny said. 'If that

bomb 'adn't landed there the bones would never 'ave come ter light.'

'It just shows yer,' Alf remarked, studying his pint. 'Yer never know what yer walkin' over.'

'You never know what you're walkin' frew,' Danny said grinning. 'If there's any dog shit on the pavement you'd step in it.'

Alf was not to be sidetracked. 'They'll soon find out who it was,' he went on. 'They've got ways an' means.'

'Yeah, it's bloody clever the way they work fings out,' Charlie agreed.

Very soon the findings of the pathologist were on the chief inspector's desk, and they made interesting reading. Tests revealed that the body had been that of a male, five feet seven in height and aged around fifty at the time of death. The jaw contained a full set of large teeth, less the two front ones, and there was some wear on the hip joint. A square hole in the right side of the skull indicated that the man had been dealt a heavy blow, with possibly a lath hammer, which although a roofer's tool could be found in most households. Lath hammers had a square head with a sharp, flat blade for levering up tiles, and were used domestically for chopping wood. They also had a groove at the side for levering out nails. One other interesting discovery was that the two joints were missing from the skeleton's left ring finger.

The first task confronting Chief Inspector Rubin McConnell was to check back through the missing persons files, and again the results proved interesting. In nineteen twenty-nine

Aaron Priestley had been reported missing by his wife Cynthia. Her description was very precise. He was five feet seven, stockily built, and missing two front teeth due to a fight some years earlier. Aaron was reported as having a permanent limp, which Cynthia put down to arthritis, and she had been able to produce a photograph of her husband standing beside her as she sat in a chair, with his left hand resting on her shoulder, and what was more a large ring could clearly be seen on his third finger. The inspector was pleased with the progress so far, but now came the task of finding out just how the victim had come to be buried below a series of water pipes in a factory yard.

Working on the assumption that the body had been placed there during the time the pipes were installed, the inspector assigned his detective sergeant to make the necessary enquiries. A visit to the Town Hall planning department revealed that the leather factory in Munday Road was erected at the turn of the century, which disproved the initial theory. The next stop was the Metropolitan Water Board, which was quick to point out that their records for repairs to water pipes going back more than five years were stored at the local office at Rotherhithe, but they had all been destroyed in a fire on the first night of the Blitz.

Feeling disheartened by the lack of progress Sergeant Johnson stood up to leave, and then the chief clerk made a suggestion. 'Look, it might not lead anywhere, but you could have a word with Albert Banks. He's been with us for over thirty years and he used to be on maintenance gangs. You'll find him in the yard, or I could send for him.'

'No, it's all right, I'll have a word with him on my way out,' the sergeant said, smiling his thanks.

The elderly man was sweeping the yard when the sergeant approached him.

'Yeah, I'm Albert Banks, son. What can I do yer for?'

'Can you recall ever doing any work on the water pipes in Gleeson's leather factory, Munday Road?' the sergeant asked him.

Albert rested his broom against the wall. 'Funny you should ask that,' he replied as he led the way over to a stack of thick wooden shorings. 'Firty years I've worked 'ere an' I've lost count of 'ow many repair jobs I've done. Most of 'em I can't even remember, but I can remember that one. That one was different.'

'Different? In what way?'

Albert sat down on the shorings and proceeded to fill his pipe. 'It was back in the winter o' twenty-nine. I'd just bin made ganger an' that was me first job in charge. What's more I was pissed as an 'andcart the night before. My eldest daughter 'ad presented me wiv me first gran'child an' I was out celebratin'. Anyway the next mornin' me an' the lads 'ad ter fill the 'ole in an' tidy up like. It'd bin pissin' down 'eaven's 'ard all night an' yer can imagine what it was like. I was still feelin' the effects an' the pile of earth was all clay an' stuck ter the shovels fer a start, then the bloody' ole

283

was full o' water up ter the bottom o' the new pipes. Anyway we set about fillin' it in, an' yer gotta remember that when there's water in an 'ole an' it gets filled up wiv earth there's always a bit of subsidence as the water drains away. Now when it's dry yer just use the road roller ter flatten it but we 'ad ter wait till the next day fer it ter dry out before we could finish the bloody job, an' there's me the new ganger all keen ter show 'ow quick me an' me boys could work. Mind you they couldn't very well blame us fer it pissin' down wiv rain, could they?'

'That's really helpful, Albert,' the sergeant told him. 'Now can you give me the exact day?'

Albert studied his filled pipe for a few moments. 'My Betty's lad's goin' on eleven. 'Is birfday's the twenty-fourth o' November. As I say I remember it well. It was a Sunday, so we must 'ave filled the 'ole in on Monday the twenty-fifth o' November.'

The sergeant shook the helpful old Water Board man by the hand and made his way back to the station. Things were starting to fall into place. The victim would most likely have been thrown into the hole on Sunday and ended up submerged in the mud and silt at the bottom. The next step was to find out the exact date Aaron Priestley was reported missing.

'That's good work, sergeant,' the inspector said, thumbing through the file. 'There we are. Priestley was reported missing on Monday the ninth of December, two weeks later. It all ties in nicely.'

'So we're working on the theory that he was murdered,' the sergeant remarked.

'The shape of the wound backs it up,' the inspector replied. 'If he'd gone into the yard to relieve himself, for instance, and had accidentally fallen into the hole and cracked his head on the pipes there would have been a compressed fracture of the skull, not a square, clean hole. As for the motive, it might well have been robbery, considering the two missing joints, but that could have been an afterthought on the part of the attacker. The record says Mrs Priestley stated that her husband didn't have any enemies, as far as she knew, but he didn't have many friends either. Anyway, we can close the missing person file on Aaron Priestley and open a murder file, but I'm of the opinion that the new file's going to collect just as much dust. Let's face it, the murder took place more than ten years ago and now there's a war on. People are getting killed every night and a lot of locals have been evacuated. We're going to need nothing short of a miracle to solve this one, I'm afraid.'

The night was black to the east but westwards the fire-glow from the stricken German cruiser lit the sky. On the dusty roads above the shoreline troop carriers spilled out their human cargo and lit up the rocky terrain with powerful searchlights, and the hunt began.

'We've got to think of something,' Stone said after a while. 'Come first light that E-boat's going to resume the search.'

'Well, we can't go back to the original rendezvous,' Joe replied.

Stone eased his back against the hard rock. 'There's no time now anyway. It's turned four. The sub'll spot that E-boat through the periscope soon and abort the surfacing.'

'We'll never last out for another twenty-four hours,' Joe said quietly, 'even if we did manage to make the second pick-up point.'

'I think we should wait until after four thirty and then take to the water,' Stone suggested. 'We'll swim as far westwards as we can and then try to get away overland.'

Joe nodded. 'The next time I get the silly idea to volunteer for anything I'll bite me bloody tongue off instead,' he growled.

'You'll be there, just like me,' Stone replied. 'It's in our blood.'

'Are you married, Sam?' Joe asked, realising that it was the first time he had used Stone's christian name.

'I was, but she took off with a sub lieutenant about a year ago,' Stone told him. 'What about you?'

'I got a girl back home, well sort of,' Joe said smiling to himself.

'That doesn't sound very positive,' Stone said.

'We write letters to each other and we've been out for a drink together,' Joe explained. 'Trouble is she's going out with the local wide

286

boy, as they call them, and I'm hoping I don't turn out to be the spare dick at a wedding.'

'Doesn't it figure,' Stone said bitterly. 'While we're away fighting, the spivs and shysters are coining it. Not only that, they can't keep their dirty little hands off our women.'

'Sadie's not exactly my woman,' Joe said. 'Not yet anyway, but give the ole Buckley charm a bit more time.'

Stone grunted as he moved his cramped legs. 'While I was on destroyers I got pally with a chap called Peter Simmons. Crazy over this woman he was. Had her photo pinned up in his locker and her name tattooed on his forearm. He used to write a letter to her every night and posted the lot together soon as we docked anywhere. Never seen anything like it. Anyway we pulled in to Chatham one night for repairs and they gave us all a forty-eight hour pass. Simmons came back in a terrible state. Apparently his girlfriend had taken up with one of the wide boys and she was pregnant by the bloke. There was nothing any of us could do or say that would help poor old Peter. The second night out he went missing. He'd obviously gone overboard. It turned out that he'd clobbered the spiv to death and strangled his girlfriend and he just couldn't live with it.'

Joe shook his head. 'Everyone's got their breaking point, Sam,' he said quietly.

Captain Fellows had seen the stricken raider

287

through the periscope lying low in the water and burning out of control, and now he checked the chart and gave the order for the sub to come up to periscope depth again. Stooping he gripped the cross handles and carefully scanned the moonlit surface of the water, then with a grunt of annoyance he straightened up. 'Take her down.'

The executive officer stood by the chart table waiting as the captain turned to him. 'There's an E-boat anchored offshore by the pick-up point,' he growled. 'It's a damned nuisance but at least it suggests that the men have eluded capture.'

'Let's hope so, Cap'n.'

The captain stroked his beard. 'The boat will have scoured the coastline and will no doubt resume the search at dawn. The Jerries will know that the cruiser was safe from attack by torpedo behind the anti-submarine nets and they'll be looking for frogmen. They have to decide whether or not the attack originated from land or sea. Did the frogmen set off from shore or were they dropped from a sub? It's my opinion that a sub chaser will be arriving on the scene before long and if we hang around here for another twenty-four hours we'll certainly be picked up on their sonar.'

'It's a tricky situation right enough,' the executive replied.

'What would you suggest, James?' the captain asked.

'I'd be reluctant to use torpedoes on such a small target at this distance, Cap'n, and if we move closer we'll be picked up on their instruments.'

'Go on, James.'

'I'd surface as arranged at 04.30 and bank on the element of surprise,' the executive officer continued. 'I'd use the guns, going in head-on and if need be run the boat down.'

Captain Fellows nodded. 'We'd quite possibly sustain damage for'ard and have to rely on our stern tubes.'

'Considering there's four ratings depending on us I'd deem it worth the risk.'

The captain smiled. 'That's the way I see it too,' he said, turning toward the intercom. 'Gun crews forward.'

Sam Stone glanced at his wristwatch. 'It's almost time,' he said, looking out into the darkness.

At that moment the alarm sounded on the E-boat and all hell broke loose. The two stranded men saw the tracer bullets rip into the boat as the submarine bore down on them. Engines roared as the E-boat tried to take evasive action then suddenly the night was lit up as a loud explosion violently blew it apart.

'They hit the magazine!' Joe shouted out. 'It's a bullseye.'

Stone was already signalling with his torch and answering flashes came from the sub's conning tower. 'They've seen us!' Stone shouted. 'C'mon, Joe, let's go!'

The submarine swung broadside on, perilously close to the shallows as the two men swam towards it, Stone still using his torch when he could to signal their position. A rope ladder was thrown over the side and as the men clambered up it Stone grabbed a helping hand. 'The other two didn't make it,' he gasped.

'E-boat approaching!' the lookout shouted.

Bullets sprayed the sub's hull as the second boat came in fast, and the answering fire from the gun crew deafened the two saboteurs as they clambered down through the hatch. Joe laid eyes on the captain and his face broke into a grin. 'Ya blood's worth bottling mate!' he exclaimed.

The E-boat swung round to make another run and the gun crew scurried down the hatch and slammed it shut. 'Dive! Dive!' the command rang out.

A steady 'ping' on the radar sounded loudly at first but then diminished as the submarine put distance between itself and its adversary, and the captain smiled at his executive officer. 'It went well, James,' he said.

Down in the mess two exhausted men sat with blankets round their shoulders, sipping hot cocoa. They did not speak for some time, both dwelling on their two comrades who had not made it back, and when his trembling subsided somewhat Stone glanced up at Big Joe, struggling for something, anything to say. 'We should be in for some leave after this,' he said finally. 'I suppose you'll be seeing this girlfriend of yours.'

'Bet your boots on it,' Joe replied positively.

CHAPTER 24

There was no let-up. Every night the air-raid sirens wailed and the bombers came. People huddled together in the shelters or under their stairs, all convinced that their neighbourhood and indeed all of London was slowly and systematically being pounded to rubble. Every night they endured the endless explosions, emerging tired and fearful in the dusty morning light to witness the results. Rest centres were opened for homeless people and non-serious casualties were bedded down in hospital corridors, exhausted ARP volunteers took a well-earned breather before going off to their place of work, if the office, shop or factory still existed, and firemen stayed until the fires were finally extinguished.

One night the spice warehouse in Shad Thames was hit by an oil bomb, and as the firemen staggered away to take a short respite the canteen van was ready and waiting.

'Come on, lads, get this down yer,' Dolly said smiling encouragingly as she handed out mugs of steaming hot tea, her steel helmet pushed back on her head.

Liz Kenny worked alongside sploshing tea in mugs and slapping down hot meat pies on the counter, and she seized upon the chance to exercise her wit. 'There yer go, son, that'll

291

put some lead in yer pencil,' she said grinning as she handed a steak and kidney pie to a young fireman. The driver of the canteen, Ben Chadwick, was an ex-firefighter himself and he had come out of retirement to drive the vehicle. ' 'Ow's the water goin', gels?' he asked.

'It's gettin' low,' Liz told him.

Ben came back with a brimming bucketful which he poured into the propane gas boiler. 'That should do it, gels. Five more minutes an' we've gotta be off ter Long Lane. There's a big 'un there.'

With Liz and Dolly sitting beside him Ben hurled the canteen van through the rubble-strewn streets to the next fire.

'Oi! Take it easy, Ben,' Dolly shouted at him. 'You ain't drivin' a bloody fire tender now yer know.'

'Yeah, my arse is bleedin' sore bouncin' up an' down,' Liz complained.

Ben grinned. 'Never mind, gels, you can 'ave yer feet up in a couple of hours.'

'Yeah, I should fink so,' Dolly growled. 'I got ironin', washin' an' my bloody shoppin' ter do.'

'Yeah, me too,' Liz added. 'You men fink we've got it easy, but you ain't got a clue. 'Ow's the boys, Doll?' she asked between bumps.

'We've 'eard from 'em all,' Dolly told her. 'Frank an' Jim are back at Winchester an' our Pat's goin' fer trainin' soon.'

'Aircrew yer said, didn't yer?'

'S'right.'

'I bet you're worried sick.'

292

'Not 'alf. I don't know why 'e couldn't stay where 'e is. It's a bloody sight safer on the ground.'

' 'E'll be all right, Doll.'

'Yeah, course 'e will.'

Another fire, another exhausted crew to take care of, and as the general public made its way to work through the battered streets, two tired but satisfied women hung up their gas masks and steel helmets and brushed out their hair before leaving the fire station to manage their families.

Jennie Flynn had spent her first night as an ARP runner at the command post in Carter Lane and it had been one she would never forget.

'Good evening, Miss Flynn. I'm Nigel Bayley, the controller, and this is my assistant, Miss Karen Watson.'

Jennie smiled. 'Pleased ter meet yer.'

'Can you ride a bicycle, Miss Flynn?' the controller asked her.

'I used to 'ave one as a kid,' she told him. 'I s'pose I still can.'

'Righty'o. Now this is Miss Peggy Freen and this is Mrs Irene Copley. They're runners too. I'm sure you'll all get on like a house on fire.'

'Mr Bayley,' Karen said, speaking with some amusement as a teacher might to a naughty child.

'Sorry about that,' the controller said, grinning sheepishly. 'It was probably a little too apt, wasn't it? Never mind, to the job in hand. Throughout the air raids we need to have a clear picture of what's going on in the area, as you no doubt are aware from your initial training. The runner's job is to carry messages to other posts that we can't reach by phone and to report unattended fires and bombed ruins where people might be trapped. A lot of your work is going to be dangerous and not very nice to say the least. However, you'll acquit yourself very well, I feel sure, as Miss Freen and Mrs Copley invariably do. Now I suggest you get to know your co-runners and we'll talk some more once I've a few minutes to spare.'

Irene Copley smiled as the controller walked out of the side room. She was a thick-set woman in her forties with a ruddy complexion and pale blue eyes. 'I'm widowed and on my own,' she explained, 'so I thought why not? I find this better than spending my nights in some horrible shelter.'

'My boyfriend's in the navy,' Peggy said proudly.

'Mine's in the army,' Jennie replied. ' 'E was at Dunkirk.'

Peggy smiled. She had a small elfin face and longish fair hair tied at the neck with a ribbon, and looked rather childlike.

Nigel Bayley came back into the room. 'We've received the standby message,' he said, his square chin jutting out. 'We should be getting a red alert shortly, ladies, so prepare yourselves.'

Five minutes later he was back again. 'It's a red alert, team,' he announced.

Jennie followed the other two runners into the control room and saw Karen sitting by a small telephone switchboard. On the large table a map was spread out and dotted with coloured pins.

Nigel beckoned for the runners to gather round the table. 'Now as you can see, the places marked with the yellow pins are business properties,' he began, 'but here and here the blue pins indicate residential areas. The red pins show where properties have already been bombed. Thus, should we get a report through of a bomb in this street marked red then we call it low grade priority, whereas a bomb in a blue grade has to be top priority for fire and heavy rescue services. This will all be very familiar to you, Peggy and Irene, but we have to introduce the set-up to Jennie, so bear with me. Now when you come across a house or a block of buildings that's taken a direct hit you must first try to establish with the local ARP teams or street wardens whether there are any people buried, then you must relay to us the location and situation by whatever means at your disposal. A phone call using our special number is the ideal way but not often very feasible. On most occasions it's all about cycle power, as I like to describe it. You will be exposed to shrapnel as well as all the other obvious dangers, so it is vital to wear your steel helmets at all times.'

'Don't forget about the gas masks, Mr Bayley,' Karen piped in.

He gave her a quick look. 'Oh yes, the gas masks. Now when you cycle through streets that have just been bombed there may be fractured gas-pipes so it makes good sense to carry your gas masks at all times while on duty. They will offer you some protection and they do not mist over as quickly as the civilian type.'

Jennie had visions of pedalling like mad through backstreets wearing her gas mask and frightening the life out of everyone, and she looked at her two runner colleagues and saw that they were both smiling demurely. She was to learn later that Irene Copley carried her make-up and sandwiches in her gas mask case. Peggy Freen also confessed to a pretty cavalier attitude to her gas mask, saying that she would sooner die than be forced to wear one.

The air-raid siren began to wail about the usual time that night and soon the anti-aircraft guns opened up. A loud explosion suddenly rocked the command post and ceiling dust fell down onto the large map. Karen seemed unperturbed as she sought to establish contact with the local fire station and Nigel Bayley calmly checked the position of the coloured pins. A policeman looked in, his face streaked with soot, to say that Sumner Buildings had taken a direct hit and been reduced to a pile of rubble. 'This is one for you, Jennie,' the controller said quickly. 'Take care now.'

Feeling that at last she was doing something important the young woman pedalled off as fast as she could, wincing every time a gun fired, and soon she arrived in Sumner Road to see the damage wrought. The street was full of brick dust and the strong, acrid smell of cordite hung in the night air. Fires were flaring nearby and the buildings themselves were unrecognisable, as though a giant and malevolent force had stamped them into the ground with its foot. An old man was being helped along by a warden and Jennie cycled up to them. 'Will there be many trapped under that lot?' she asked urgently.

The warden shook his head. 'This was the only one. The cantankerous ole git wouldn't do as 'e was told an' go ter the shelter like all the ovvers. No, 'e decided ter stay where 'e was an' lucky fer 'im 'e was blown out inter the street. Good job 'e lived on the ground floor or 'e wouldn't 'ave survived.'

The old man looked dazed and disorientated. 'I 'ad all me comforts in the flat yer see, miss. I got bad legs an' they give me what for if I 'ave ter sit up all night.'

'Well, yer goin' down the shelter now, Sharkey, like it or lump it,' the warden told him.

Jennie cycled off towards a fire that was raging in nearby Crawford Street. It was a factory that had been reinforced with sandbags at ground level and as she drew closer she could see that the fire was confined to the top two floors. The building faced a railway line and stood apart from a row of houses, separated on one side by a bomb ruin and on the other by a Council builder's yard. She looked around in vain for a telephone box and decided to pedal back with the report but just as she was about to remount her heart missed a beat. There over the sandbags she saw the shelter sign with its arrow pointing towards the end of the factory. She hurried along, pushing her cycle, then a loud rumbling sound seemed to shake the ground under her feet. Part of the roof and top level crashed down in front of her, showering her with brick dust and sparks. She felt a sharp stinging pain in her cheek and brushed at it as she picked herself up. A giant mound of bricks and burning timbers covered the shelter entrance at the far end of the burning factory and Jennie guessed that this would be the one occupied by the tenants of the nearby Sumner Buildings.

She pedalled as fast as she could and arrived back at the command post a few minutes later, gasping for air. She staggered through the door and fell into the arms of Nigel Bayley. 'Sumner Buildin's are gone! All the tenants are trapped in the shelter under the burnin' factory in Crawford Street!' she gasped as a red mist started to swim before her eyes.

Karen sent the message through and then helped Nigel lift the young woman on to a wooden bench. 'Here, drink this,' she urged her.

The strong spirit burned Jennie's throat and made her cough and she opened her eyes. 'That was a silly fing fer me ter do,' she said when she gathered her thoughts.

'No, it wasn't,' Karen told her. 'In fact you did very well. I should think you'll have earned a vote of thanks from the people of Sumner Buildings come morning. Here, use this.'

Jennie took the handkerchief Karen held out to her and wiped her forehead. 'Is there a mirrer 'andy?' she asked.

Nigel grinned and was about to say something but Karen cut him short with a stern look. 'Just a moment, I've one in my handbag,' she replied.

Jennie studied her face and saw the nick on her cheek. 'I fink I'll survive,' she said smiling as she dabbed at it.

'I think you'll do very well as an ARP runner. Welcome aboard,' Nigel remarked with a grin.

Another dawn, another day to recover, and the day for Chief Inspector McConnell to break the news to Cynthia Lockwood about her missing husband.

'Why, if it isn't the nice inspector,' Charity said smiling. 'Do come in.'

McConnell walked into the tidy parlour and saw Cynthia sitting by the fire working on a piece of embroidery.

'Good morning, Miss Lockwood,' he said, knowing that she preferred to be addressed as such. 'Bad one last night, wasn't it? Actually, I've called about quite an important matter.'

Cynthia put down her embroidery and Charity motioned him into an armchair by the fire. 'Can I get you some tea?' she asked.

'No, I'm fine, thank you very much,' he replied, and looked from one to the other. 'I suppose you've seen the report in the papers about the find in Munday Road.'

'The skeletal remains,' Cynthia said. 'Yes we have, inspector.'

McConnell looked down at his clasped hands for a few moments. 'We have reason to believe that it's most certainly the remains of your husband.'

'Oh my God!' Cynthia gasped, bringing her hand up to her face. 'How awful.'

'Deary me,' Charity added. 'After all this time. You are sure it is Aaron?'

'Without doubt,' McConnell replied.

'My goodness, you people are so clever,' Cynthia remarked, still with her hand up at her face. 'It's remarkable.'

'I don't wish to distress you, ladies,' the policeman went on, 'but the evidence seems incontrovertible. The jaw contained large teeth, minus the two front ones. There were signs of damage to the left hip, possibly some bone disease, and the pathologist was able to establish that the remains were those of a man about five feet seven tall and around fifty when he died, some ten to fifteen years ago. So you see it all matches the very thorough description of Aaron which you supplied us with.'

Cynthia took out a small lace handkerchief from her dress sleeve and dabbed at her eyes. 'I know it was a long time ago that Aaron went missing,' she sighed, 'but you coming here today brings it all back, you see.'

'I'm very sorry but I am obliged to follow these things up,' McConnell explained.

'We understand implicitly, inspector,' Charity cut in. 'As a matter of fact Cynthia's not feeling too bright today and your news has come as a shock. It's all this bombing. We hardly get any sleep and my sister's feeling utterly exhausted.'

'I appreciate that, Miss Lockwood,' he replied. 'Look, I'll leave you now. Maybe you might both like to call in the station when your sister's feeling better. There are a few loose ends to tie up.'

'We certainly will,' Charity said. 'And thank you for being so understanding. I'll see you to the door.'

McConnell bade goodbye with a pleasant smile as he stepped out into the street and Charity suddenly took him by the arm. 'Do you suspect he was murdered?' she asked in a low voice.

'It appears that he was dealt a fatal blow to the head,' the policeman replied.

'My goodness, that's terrible,' Charity remarked, covering her mouth with the tips of her long fingers.

'We'll talk some more when you call in,' the inspector said.

Back in the house Cynthia was pacing the room. 'I'm all of a quiver,' she said painfully.

'Now look, there's no need to distress yourself,' her sister told her sternly. 'You sit yourself down and I'll make us a nice strong cup of tea. I believe we still have some of that Lyons strong brew left.'

'You are a comfort to me,' Cynthia said sniffing.

'Nonsense. You're very brave,' Charity replied encouragingly. 'And remember dear, we stand or fall together.'

301

CHAPTER 25

The air raids were getting worse each night and more and more people started to use the shelters, many after experiencing terrifying hours huddled under the stairs while their little homes were blasted and shaken. In Carter Lane, windows replaced during the day were blasted out again at night and on some of the roofs tarpaulin now covered the missing slates. The strain was showing on everyone's faces and the lack of proper rest and sleep was becoming a real problem. Homeward-bound workers often fell asleep on buses, trams and trains and found themselves two or three stops down the line. People fell asleep at their place of work and many began to develop the technique of 'cat-napping'. Ten minutes at mid-morning break and a half-hour sleep at lunchtime got them through the day, and in the shelters people developed the knack of sleeping soundly while sitting upright on uncomfortable benches.

Sadie Flynn had had the house to herself for a few nights, with her father fire-watching, her mother working on the canteen van and Jennie at the ARP command post, but the need to be with someone during the bombing led her to take up Daisy Harris's suggestion that she stay with her and Bill during the raids. Daisy was an enthusiastic member of the Carter Lane knitting circle and she put her expertise to good use by instructing her young neighbour, who was a self-confessed muddle of fingers and thumbs where knitting was concerned. One week saw a marked improvement, with Sadie managing to progress from plain and purl to cable stitch, but any further honing of her new skill was cut short when the letter came from the Woolwich Military Hospital instructing her to report for initial training.

The young woman took up residence at the nurses' quarters and began her new career with a single-minded determination that was severely put to the test during the traumatic experience of training on wards full of badly wounded servicemen.

For the Lockwood sisters the shelters were still out of the question, and they both decided to remain in what they had come to see as their impregnable position under the rickety stairs. Charity was as ever the prop for Cynthia, whose nervousness and timidity had not been helped by the visit from the police inspector bearing the news of the discovery of her missing husband's body. Still facing her was the ordeal of going over it all at the station and she baulked at it as long as she could.

'Look, I know it must be terrible for you, dear,' Charity said kindly, 'but it has to be faced sooner or later. Why don't we get it over with. You'll feel much better once you've been to see the nice inspector.'

Cynthia had to agree, and on a bitterly cold

morning she and Charity presented themselves at the police station.

'We'll not try to keep you too long,' McConnell told them with a smile. 'There's just one or two questions I need to ask. Now I know it was a long time ago, but I want you to think back to round about the time your husband went missing. Did he act any differently? Did he seem worried or concerned about anything?'

'No, nothing,' Cynthia said, shaking her head slowly. 'He was being very nasty to me though about that time.'

'Was he violent towards you?' McConnell asked.

'He most certainly was,' Charity cut in. 'Cynthia doesn't like to paint too bad a picture of him, she's still too loyal, but I can tell you that he was physically abusive to her.'

'I see,' the policeman said, scribbling into a notepad. 'Was he a betting man?'

'Yes, he liked a bet, on the greyhounds as well as the horses,' Cynthia told him.

'Did it come as a shock when your husband went missing?' the inspector probed. 'What I mean is, did you suspect there was someone else in his life, another woman?'

Cynthia shook her head. 'I don't think so, inspector,' she replied.

'Another woman wouldn't have had him,' Charity said forcibly. 'He was a pig of a man. Do you know that a couple of days before he went missing he ...'

'Please, Charity, the inspector doesn't want to know ...'

304

'Well, I'm going to tell him anyway,' the older sister said firmly. 'Every bit of information might prove helpful, wouldn't you say, inspector?'

'Yes, anything might help.'

'It was a Sunday evening,' Charity went on, 'and I called round to see if Cynthia wanted to join me for the evening service at St Margaret's. Aaron was out, but I could see that my sister was in a terrible state. Her wrists were bruised and her eye was almost closed where he had punched her.'

'Charity, please.'

'No, it has to be said. Aaron had tied Cynthia in a chair, inspector.'

'Look, can I get you some tea?' the policeman offered.

'That would be very nice,' Charity replied.

McConnell left the room for a few moments to order the tea, and to pull himself together. This looked like it was going to take some time, but overworked as he was he felt sympathy for Cynthia Lockwood, wondering what had made her fall for such a brute in the first place.

Sitting comfortably in the warm office with cups of sweet tea, the Lockwoods listened attentively as the inspector resumed his questions.

'Do you happen to know if your husband was in the habit of taking a lot of money out with him?' he asked.

'The only time he had much money was when the horses or dogs came up,' Cynthia replied.

McConnell stroked his chin thoughtfully. 'You see, we're working on the theory that your husband was robbed, Miss Lockwood, after which he was thrown into the hole that the Water Board men had dug in the factory yard.'

'But surely his body would have been discovered by the workmen the next day?' Cynthia queried.

'It happened to be pouring with rain all night and we have to assume that the body was immersed in water and mud.'

The sisters exchanged quick glances and Charity put down her empty cup and saucer and rested her hands on top of the handbag in her lap. 'Tell me, inspector, is there any doubt in your mind that the remains were those of Aaron?' she asked.

'None whatsoever.'

'Well, I'm not saddened by it. I think he got his just deserts.'

'To be fair, Charity, he wasn't always a brutal man,' Cynthia said quickly.

'Not at the very beginning, granted, but it didn't take him long to show his true colours, dear.'

McConnell looked from one to the other, and although he wanted to mention the missing finger joints he thought better of it. Both women looked very upset as it was, without having to hear more gruesome details, and besides, the photograph of Aaron Priestley wearing a large jewelled ring already answered his question. 'I think that will suffice for now, ladies, and thanks very much for calling in,' he told them. 'Should there be any developments I'll certainly keep you informed.'

Back in their home Charity made a pot of tea and fussed over Cynthia, who was feeling the effects of all the strain. 'Now, you drink this and try to get some sleep before the raids start,' she encouraged her.

'I've tried so hard to forget everything,' Cynthia said tearfully, 'but today brought it all back. Was it me that made Aaron into the monster he became? Was I lacking in something? Was I that bad a wife?'

'I won't listen to that sort of talk, Cynthia,' her sister said firmly. 'No one could have been a better wife than you, and well you know it. Now finish that tea and close your eyes for a while.'

The house was quiet, with only the low sounds of light music coming from the wireless and the rattle of the wind on the window frames, and as Charity sat sewing she felt very uneasy. Cynthia was showing signs of cracking, she realised, and the effects would be far reaching, for both of them.

Sadie slipped a few toiletries and clothing into a small case and took her first leave of the nurses' quarters for a weekend at home. The first week of practical patient care, of learning to take temperatures, blood pressures and pulses, perfect the noble art of regimental bed-making and change dressings on terrible wounds, as well as all the classroom work, left her feeling exhausted but filled with a deep sense of fulfilment. At last she had found her vocation. Intrigue, villainry and the seedy side of life were now a world away, and so was the

307

boring, soul-destroying nine-till-five existence of totalling figures, answering telephones and office small talk. Now at last she could hold her head up high and face a new day without any self-recrimination, and it felt good.

She sat on the upper deck of the number 38 tram as it rattled through Woolwich, Greenwich and past New Cross into the Old Kent Road. Bomb-blasted shops, ruined homes and piles of rubble swept back from the pavement could be seen all along the route but her fellow passengers seemed not to notice, and she marvelled at their indifference. She noticed how they sat, erect in their seats, heads inclined as they read a newspaper or else stared dispassionately at nothing, at the void that had opened up around them. Maybe if she had to make a regular journey through once-familiar streets that had been blown to pieces she would do the same, she thought. Pretend that nothing's changed. Ignore the destruction, the shop that was there yesterday, the gap in the tall building. Think on good thoughts, thoughts of years ago when the son or daughter in uniform was the child who whipped tops, jumped in and out of twirling skipping-ropes, or chased coloured marbles along the gutters.

Sadie Flynn stepped down from the tram and made her way home through the war-torn backstreets. Just one short week away and how different it all looked. As she turned from Defoe Street into Carter Lane her heart rose. It was still there, battered, scarred but sweeter in its rawness, more than ever a part of herself.

' 'Ello, gel, nice ter see yer back,' Amy Bromilow said cheerily.

'There she is, our little Miss Nightingale,' Ivy Jones remarked smiling warmly.

As she stepped into the house Sadie was grabbed by Dolly and Jennie who hugged her in turn, while her father stood back with an amused smile on his face. ' 'Ere, give us a chance,' he grinned as he too hugged her.

'Guess who's 'ere,' Dolly said when she had regained her breath. 'Oi, Pat, come down an' see our little nurse.'

The young man bounded down the stairs and hugged his sister. 'Yer lookin' good, sis,' he said grinning.

'Yer look good yerself, bruv,' she replied, holding him round the waist.

'Guess what else,' Dolly said, motioning with her eyes to the two letters resting side by side on the mantelshelf. 'That's from Frank: the boys are comin' 'ome on embarkation leave termorrer. An' that's one from Big Joe.'

Sadie flopped down in the armchair and tore the letter open. 'Joe too,' she said happily. 'Some time next week.'

Mick rubbed his hands together and licked his lips. 'I fink I'd better warn Charlie Anson ter get some extras in,' he joked. ' 'E's likely ter run dry when the lads get 'ome.'

Dolly's head was swimming with all the excitement. ' 'Ere, I'd better get down the market before all the best o' the stuff goes,' she announced.

'Sit down an' catch yer breath, Mum,' Jennie

told her. 'I'll make us all a cuppa then me an' Sadie'll come down the market wiv yer, all right, sis?'

As Jennie left the parlour there was a knock at the door and she answered it to a flustered Liz Kenny who grabbed her arm and dragged her back to the others.

' 'As anyone seen the papers this mornin'?' she asked, her face flushed with excitement.

Mick shook his head. 'Only the racin' page,' he told her.

'Read that,' Liz said, taking the *Daily Sketch* from under her arm and pointing to a prominent article. Mick proceeded to read it aloud.

'It can now be confirmed that the German surface raider *Kaiser Wilhelm* was sunk by limpet mines and not torpedoes as at first reported.

The limpet mines were attached to the hull of the cruiser by a pair of two-man teams of Royal Navy divers. Unfortunately two of the divers failed to return from the mission and they can now be named as Petty Officer Peter Chivers of King's Lynn and Leading Seaman David Preston of Luton.

The surviving team of Petty Officer Samuel Stone and Leading Seaman Joseph Buckley spent the night evading patrols before being picked up by a submarine whilst under heavy fire.

The First Sea Lord added his congratulations at yesterday's War Cabinet meeting, saying that this heroic action was in the highest tradition of the Royal Navy.'

'I just got this letter from 'im,' Sadie said excitedly, 'an 'e never mentioned a fing about it.'

' 'E wouldn't be allowed to, not till the story got released,' Mick told her.

'I'm all of a twitter,' Dolly said, dabbing at her eyes.

'Me too,' Liz Kenny replied. 'I nearly fainted when I saw it in the paper. I knew from Joe's last letter that somefing was in the wind.'

Sadie stared down at the neat handwriting of Joe's letter and felt a warm glow inside, then, worried that her feelings might show, she folded it away and stood up. 'I fink you should let me an' Jennie get yer shoppin' this mornin', Mum,' she said.

'Nah, I'll be all right,' Dolly told her. 'Me an' Liz are frontliners now, ain't we, gel? We can take it.'

'Too bloody true,' Liz said with spirit. 'Ole Jerry can't get us down.'

Mother and daughters trudged through the damaged backstreets to the East Lane market, where the sarsaparilla man told everyone that his potions were guaranteed to sweep away the shelter blues and ward off bombs; a shopkeeper hung a sign over his damaged store that read, 'Get your rubble here. Bricks going at half price'; and a stallholder announced in a sing-song voice that 'Yes, we have no bananas, we have no bananas today.' Further along a trader stood on an upturned crate telling passers-by

311

that his restorative was good for bile, piles and stomach ulcers, as well as for growing girls and undernourished children and other afflictions. It prevented the common cold, flu and lumbago, and in short was now recognised to be the greatest medical breakthrough this century, the only sure alternative to the restorative on sale at the other end of the market.

The few potential customers stood listening suspiciously to the rhetoric, and a small dog spoke for most of them by cocking his leg against the crate before briskly trotting off.

The day was cold, and ahead a night filled with danger, death and destruction awaited, but for the present moment life went on as it always had, and stalls were beginning to display their wartime Christmas decorations. Nathaniel Bone had given up though. For years he had walked through the market with his banner stating that 'The End Is Nigh'. Now, cursing the Germans for upstaging him, he had resigned himself to handing out a few tracts on Saturday mornings, before using the rest of the day to get steadily drunk.

CHAPTER 26

Jennie Flynn had not been too worried about not receiving a letter from Con on Saturday, believing that as he was now a sergeant instructor at the Winchester depot he would not be sent abroad on active duty, but she was wrong. On Monday morning his letter dropped on the mat and Jennie felt a cold shiver run down her back as she read it.

'Where d'yer fink they'll be sent?' Dolly asked her husband that evening.

'Gawd knows,' Mick said shrugging his shoulders. 'There's bin fings said on the wireless lately about sendin' more troops ter the Middle East, but yer never know. We got troops stationed all over the place. Africa, the Far East.'

'I dunno, it's one load o' worry, what wiv one an' anuvver of 'em,' Dolly said sighing. 'There's our Pat an' all. 'E'll be finishin' 'is trainin' soon an' goin' on them bombin' raids. I dunno about goin' grey. I'll end up bloody white before long.'

'What's 'appenin' about 'im an' young Brenda?' Mick asked.

'I fink it's all off,' Dolly told him. 'I saw Iris Ross down the market the ovver mornin' an' she said that the two of 'em 'ad a row last time Pat was 'ome. From what I gavvered from Iris it was over Pat volunteerin'. Brenda felt 'e should 'ave applied fer exemption frew 'is firm. I can understand 'er point o' view. They were plannin' on gettin' married next year, wasn't they?'

'Yeah, but yer never know fer sure wiv Pat,' Mick replied. ' 'E's never bin one ter let yer know much. 'E keeps 'is cards very close to 'is chest, does that one.'

'Pat prob'ly finks Iris Ross was be'ind it all,' Dolly went on. ' 'E don't go a lot on 'er, yer

313

know, 'e let as much slip. 'E reckons she's a very dominant woman an' Brenda takes too much notice of 'er. It's a sad business when yer come ter fink of it. They seemed made fer each ovver, them two. Even as kids they were never apart. It's the bloody war. It's ruined so many people's lives.'

'Fings'll work out fer 'im, given time,' Mick said supportively.

'They won't if they're not seein' each ovver, will they?' Dolly retorted. 'Pat ain't got much time before 'e goes back an' I don't s'pose Brenda's gonna sit at 'ome pinin' fer 'im. She's a very pretty gel an' she can take 'er pick o' the fellers.'

Both Dolly and Mick would have been heartened had they been privy to a particular conversation at the Ross household a few days previously.

'Ter be honest, Brenda, I'm gettin' a bit tired o' you mopin' around the 'ouse,' Iris told her sternly. 'You've said yer piece an' made yer decision. No one forced yer ter split up wiv Pat.'

'No, that's right,' Brenda replied quickly. 'No one forced me, but you never offered any advice or gave me your opinion. In fact I fink you were secretly pleased. You an' Pat don't exactly see eye to eye, yer never 'ave done.'

'That's not true,' Iris said sharply. 'We've always made 'im welcome.'

'Yeah, but you would 'ave preferred me ter get involved wiv someone wiv a good job an' plenty o' money,' Brenda replied. 'You told me that yerself when me an' Pat started ter get serious.'

'P'raps I did, but me an' yer dad were only tryin' to advise yer o' the pitfalls,' Iris went on. 'What future is there fer carpenters? All right, it's a trade an' there'll always be work around, but when yer married an' children come along there's lots of extras needed. I could just see you wiv a tribe o' kids, spendin' the best years o' yer life scrimpin' an' scrapin' like everyone else round 'ere. Me and yer farvver felt you deserved better, that's all.'

'I couldn't get better than Pat Flynn,' Brenda responded. 'Anyway, money's not everyfing. I'd sooner be poor an' 'appy than rich an' miserable.'

'Well, it's your life,' Iris said sighing. 'Me an' yer farvver never stood in yer way. We understood that if it was Pat yer wanted, then so be it. But yer gotta get yerself sorted out. Eivver get back wiv 'im or accept it's over once an' fer all. The way fings are you're just wastin' yer life sittin' in every night mopin' around. You could always 'ave a night out wiv that Barry at work. You said yerself 'e's keen on yer.'

Brenda shrugged her shoulders, appearing noncommittal, but deep down inside her she knew what had to be done. She had been selfish, thinking only of herself and not trying to understand why Pat would want to jeopardise their future by volunteering to go off and serve his country, but it was different now. The Blitz had helped her see things in a new perspective, made her realise that there would be no future for her, Pat, or anyone else, until the war was won, and that seemed a long way off. Pat had done what he thought was best and she should really have given him the chance to explain himself instead of flying off the handle and getting angry with him.

'Don't worry, Mum, I'll sort fings out,' she sighed, not knowing just how she was going to begin.

The week wore on with nothing changing: days full of dread and nights of mayhem from the skies. The moon was full and lit the way—a bomber's moon they called it—and the carnage grew nightly. On Monday night there were no survivors when a block of buildings in New Kent Road took a direct hit, and as more backstreets were reduced to rubble many more people never saw the dawn.

On Tuesday night the synagogue off the Old Kent Road was destroyed and Albert Levy despaired. At lunchtime the following day, when his mechanic was taking his break, he sauntered out into the workroom. 'Hello, old friend,' he said. 'First time I've had the chance of a chat since coming back to work.' He sat down at the bench with a tired sigh. 'Of course you know the synagogue's gone. A nice square plaque just inside the entrance, that's what I had in mind for you, but it won't happen now, not till we can rebuild the place, and we will one day. Anyway, you know that the bronze wouldn't have gone up right away, not while the war's on. They would have reserved the space and entered it in the book. Rabbi Friedman will be heartbroken. The synagogue was his life, and I must go to see him this evening to offer my support and help. Poor Friedman, I really feel for him. By the way, Gerda often speaks of you and I know she would send her love if she knew I talked to you, but I can't very well tell her, can I? She'd put it down to that knock on the head I got.'

Albert drew breath as he eased himself on to the high stool. 'It was nice of you to be with me at that time, old friend. I took great comfort in seeing you standing there at the foot of the bed. Mind you, I was a bit scared at first. I thought they'd sent you to collect me. Times are very bad now, Abel: the bombing seems never ending and it's getting worse. The news is very bad from the Continent too. More and more of our people are being rounded up and taken off to the camps. We're getting reports from our friends in the occupied countries that the Nazis are building many more of these places. God only knows what terrible things go on there. I feel so sad and angry about it all. I'm tired and depressed, and untroubled sleep is something I can only remember enjoying when I was a young man with big ideas. You too will remember those days of yore. How we planned and schemed. Now it seems that everything is dark and gloomy. But enough of that. I have to carry on like everyone else. After the war there will be so much to do, so much rebuilding and making good. We will rise again as a people and we elders will need to be at the forefront, should

317

we live as long, God willing. Wish me luck, old friend, and keep me in your thoughts.'

The control post at Carter Lane was working as efficiently as the situation permitted. Land lines were constantly down and the three women runners were stretched to the limit. Karen Watson manned the switchboard without a break throughout the nightly raids and Nigel Bayley tried desperately to keep abreast of the ever-changing situation in the area, poring over the large map that was now covered with coloured pins. Not a square inch was left bare and he knew only too well that a square inch represented just a few backstreets or a mere factory or two. It was getting out of control. The whole borough seemed to be collapsing beneath the tons and tons of high explosive and incendiary bombs.

Occasionally there were short lulls during the air raids and on Wednesday night just before midnight it became quiet. Karen took off her headset and swivelled round in her chair to catch sight of Nigel sitting at the map table with his head resting in his hands. Irene Copley was sitting in the far corner fast asleep, snoring gently with her head against the wall.

'Nigel, are you asleep?' Karen said quietly.

He looked up, his eyes red-rimmed with fatigue and he gave her a tired smile. 'Almost,' he sighed.

'Let's get some air,' Karen said getting up.

They walked out into the night and stood by the wall of sandbags, gazing at the glow in the

318

eastern sky. 'That'll be the Stepney area,' Nigel remarked. 'They've certainly been getting their share.'

Karen reached out and clasped Nigel's hand in hers. 'You look all in, darling,' she said.

He nodded. 'I feel so inadequate,' he sighed.

'Inadequate, never,' Karen replied with spirit.

'I am,' he said. 'The whole borough's slowly turning into a giant ruin and there's me plotting the progress with those ridiculous coloured pins. I feel like some kind of ghoul looking down on the world, watching it grinding itself to dust.'

'You'll feel better after a rest, darling,' she told him kindly. 'We all will.'

'How do you do it, Karen?' he asked as he took her by the shoulders. 'You never lose that cool calmness, even at the height of the bombing. I look at you and see a very attractive young woman, unperturbed and unafraid. I listen to your voice on the switchboard and there's never a quiver. You're amazing.'

She smiled. 'A woman can take great comfort from the company she keeps. With you around I feel safe and secure. Nothing can harm me, nothing can touch me, as long as you're near.'

'Darling,' he said, pulling her to him in a tight embrace.

Their lips met and she slipped her arm around his neck, and there in the empty street, lit by a bomber's moon, time stood still.

'I want to make love to you,' he whispered.

'I want you to, but you know I can't,' she told him. 'Even though nothing would make me happier.'

319

'Yes, I know,' he sighed. 'We can have our dreams though.'

'And we can share these precious moments,' Karen added. 'Let it be our staff, our strength, and let these all too short moments serve to remind us that there is another time, a time for us.'

'I live for that,' he smiled.

'It fills my waking hours,' she said.

They heard the drone of aircraft and saw Peggy Freen pedalling furiously into the lane.

'Come on, Miss Watson, we have work to do,' he said stoutly.

Jennie Flynn had taken a message to the fire chief at nearby Lynton Road and was pleased to see her mother and Liz Kenny there, busily serving tea and hot pies to the exhausted fire crew who had been tackling a blazing warehouse.

'You should be wearin' that tin 'at,' Dolly reprimanded her.

'It's all quiet at the moment,' Jennie replied.

' 'Ere, grab this,' Liz said quickly, handing her a large mug of steaming hot tea.

The young woman gulped it down gratefully. 'I've gotta check on the command post at the Borough,' she said. 'We can't raise it on the phone.'

'That's a bit of a way,' Dolly remarked. 'Yer'd better get goin' then while it's quiet.'

Jennie set off, pedalling energetically through the rubble-strewn streets, fearing that the command post at Lindsey Street had taken a direct hit. On the way she heard the ominous drone and winced as the anti-aircraft guns opened up once more. When she steered her bicycle into Lindsey Street she was relieved to see that the post was still intact. The controller, an elderly man with grey hair and a ruddy complexion, smiled at her concern. 'It's only the lines, luvvy,' he told her. 'We're tryin' ter link in to anuvver line. When we do we'll give you a call. Give my regards ter Nigel.'

Jennie started back, and as she turned the corner by the Children's Hospital there was a deafening crash and dust rose in a billowing cloud from the adjacent bomb ruin. At first she thought it was a wall that had collapsed but then she saw the hole. Something had fallen into the basement of the ruin and the young woman got off her bicycle to take a closer look. Down in the gloom of the debris she could see moonlight glimmering dully on the cone-shaped metal object and her heart missed a beat. There, only yards away from the hospital, was a very large unexploded bomb.

The large tea urn was kept constantly hot in the Royal Engineers' mess hut at the Southwark Park camp and as Sapper Conroy refilled his mug he saw Sergeant Kilbride coming towards him. The man's face was lined with strain and tiredness and he seemed to have aged years in the last two weeks.

'Conroy, we've got a bad one. Sergeant Fletcher'll be your NCO. 'E's outside briefin' the back-up. Five minutes, okay?'

Alec nodded. Already that night he and Kilbride had steamed out an unexploded bomb at Dockhead and he had been looking forward to a few hours' sleep, but when Kilbride said it was a bad one all thoughts of sleep vanished. The sergeant was not one to exaggerate. If he said it was bad, then it was bad.

Sergeant Fletcher stood over six feet four in his socks, with a build to match. A regular soldier and one of the best in the bomb disposal business, he had a cool head and the ability to transmit his unflappability to his assistants. Conroy was happy to be teamed up with him, especially when he learned of the task ahead.

'Jump in the truck, Conroy,' Fletcher told him quickly. 'I'll brief you on the way there.'

The fifteen hundredweight Bedford swung out of the park and along the Jamaica Road, swerving now and then to dodge the rubble lying in the roadway.

'Sergeant Kilbride said this was a bad one,' Alec remarked as he hung on to a tarpaulin strap in the back of the truck.

'Yeah, it is,' Fletcher told him. 'The bomb was found by an ARP runner who reported its whereabouts immediately. Apparently it's lying in the cellar of a bomb ruin. There are no residential properties in the immediate vicinity but here's the rub: next to the bomb ruin is the St Stephen's Children's Hospital.'

'Lindsey Street,' Alec replied.

Fletcher nodded. 'The runner warned the hospital and there's an evacuation taking place at this moment. That's the good news.' Conroy

322

gave him a questioning glance as he drew breath. 'The bad news is they've got an emergency there. A five-year-old with a burst appendix. The surgeon said if he delayed the operation the child would surely die. He'll be washing up now and while we're playing with another of Jerry's toys he'll be doing his best for the lad. He's a brave man, son. He knows that if we make a mistake the blast will bring down half the hospital. Apparently the only functional operating theatre's located at the end of the building nearest the ruin. So now yer know.'

Alec Conroy felt the familiar trembling in his hands and the pain at the pit of his stomach but he did not dwell on it. It had always been that way, from his first assignment to the present one, and this would be his thirteenth.

Sapper Pete Swift stopped the Bedford at the end of Lindsey Street and Sapper Steve Fowler ran a phone line to the bomb ruin. Fletcher and Conroy walked across the bombsite and the sergeant shone his powerful torch down into the cellar. 'It's an ugly-looking bastard. A thousand-pounder by the look of it. If we get this one wrong that hospital's going to end up much the same as this place.'

The two set to work, occasionally reporting their progress to the back-up team, and Fletcher soon had his plan ready. 'Now look, we can't fiddle around using securing chains on this one,' he said matter-of-factly. 'For a start it's jammed tight between the foundation timbers, and secondly it ain't going nowhere. Right now we'll prop this torch up like so, and you can pass me the large wrench as soon as I squeeze round to the bastard's nose cone.'

Slowly and carefully the securing nuts on the mechanism housing cover were loosened, but as Fletcher was about to reposition himself a bomb fell in the roadway midway between the truck and the ruin, knocking the two back-ups out cold with the blast. The cellar shuddered and the unexploded bomb moved with a loud grating noise.

'My arm!' Fletcher shouted. 'I'm pinned! I can't move!'

Conroy cursed as he eased himself round to see the extent of the sergeant's injury. The man's forearm was crushed between the bomb casing and a supporting wall. 'I'll get some 'elp,' he said quickly.

'There's no time. You're on yer own, son,' Fletcher told him between clenched teeth. 'Just remember that kid in the operating theatre and you'll do okay.'

Alec Conroy picked up the phone to report the situation but found that the line was dead. He said a silent prayer and set to work, removing the nuts one by one. With a sweating hand he reached for a long screwdriver and used the tip to prise off the housing plate, and as it came away a steady tick started deep down in the dark heart of the bomb.

Fletcher cursed aloud. 'That's all we want,' he growled. 'This is one of their latest delayed-action bombs and we don't know a lot about them. Bugger all, in fact.'

Alec shone the torch into the hole and saw the

three wires, two red and one blue. A red and a blue wire snaked down into the darkness and the remaining red led off to the left and disappeared into a small black box. Without taking his eyes from the bomb's insides he relayed his findings to the sergeant, and when he heard a groan he glanced sideways and shone his torch across to see a trickle of blood running out from under the metal. Fletcher must have fainted from the loss of blood, he thought, suddenly feeling utterly exposed and alone. The back-up team must have been caught up in the blast too or they would have come onto the site when they realised the phone link was down.

There was no time to speculate, and as he picked up the snippers Alec remembered the training session. 'You've just killed yourself, Conroy,' the sergeant had said. It was different now. One wrong move and there would be a few more people joining him in the hereafter. 'Think, man, and for God's sake don't get it wrong,' he mumbled aloud. The red lead to the small box would act as an earth lead, he reasoned. Ignore it and concentrate on the two longer leads. Which one first? The blue. No, the red. God, don't let me get this wrong. How long was there? The ticking seemed to have been going on for ever. A minute before the detonator activated? Thirty seconds? Don't delay. Make the cut.

The snippers shook as he fought to control himself and then with a sudden flash of inspiration he moved to the red lead that stretched to the box and quickly applied pressure. The lead was severed but still the ticking went on. It was now a two-to-one chance. A wrong guess and it would be over for all of them. His hand moved to the red lead, then over to the blue one. He was about to make the cut when something warned him to stop. He reached his fingers into the hole and gently pulled on the blue lead. It was long and looped round, and about two feet along its length it forked, with a spur leading back to the concealed side of the black box. A classic Dubrovny short-circuit. 'So you're the decoy, you little bastard,' Alec growled as he quickly snipped the red lead. The ticking stopped, and he turned away and vomited on the dusty floor.

It took the heavy rescue team over an hour to free Fletcher, and as he was being stretchered from the bombsite he gave Sapper Conroy a weak grin. 'You did well, son,' he said.

The back-up team were recovering at the roadside and Alec sat beside them to have a cigarette, but he found that he could not pull one from the packet for the shaking of his hands.

'Here, let me do that for you,' a tall man said, bending down over him.

'Fanks, pal,' Alec said with a dry throat.

'I think the thanks are owed to you,' the man said. 'Mind if I join you?'

'Take a pew,' Alec told him. ' 'Ave a fag.'

The man took one out of the packet and lit it from the glowing tip of the cigarette held in Alec's shaking hand. 'It was touch and go tonight, but it turned out well in the end,' he said.

'Yeah, sometimes important decisions 'ave ter be made on the quick,' Alec remarked.

'That's very true,' the man replied. 'I couldn't delay or the child would have died, but I knew we were in good hands.'

Alec looked up at the man with a glint in his eye. 'I'm sure that lad was in good hands too,' he replied.

'That lad's doing very nicely as it happens,' Sir Roger Carmody told him.

CHAPTER 27

It was not until Saturday afternoon that Brenda Ross heard Pat Flynn was home on leave, and then it was only through a chance meeting at the market between her mother and Dolly Flynn. The letter she had written to Pat would not be needed now, thankfully. It had been hard enough as it was to put her true feelings down on paper, and even then the words did not fully convey what she felt inside. She had intended nevertheless to slip it through the Flynns' letterbox with an attached note asking Dolly to forward it on, but now there was the chance to meet face to face.

Brenda started to write another letter, a brief note asking Pat to call round at six o'clock and saying that she would be ready and on the doorstep, realising how he felt towards her mother and not giving him the excuse to avoid her for that reason. She sealed it up and suddenly threw it on the fire. This was stupid, she told herself. She would have to go round to Carter Lane to deliver it anyway. Better to swallow her pride and knock at the door instead. After all, he could only say no.

When she arrived at the Flynns' front door Brenda took a deep breath before knocking, and with her heart pounding she raised the knocker and let it fall lightly, as though fearful of what might happen.

Pat himself answered the knock and her spirits leapt as she caught his reaction.

'Brenda. You're the last person I expected,' he said with a nervous smile.

'Was you expectin' someone else?' she replied.

'No, I wasn't expectin' anybody,' he said quickly. 'Come in.'

'Is it a good idea?' she responded. 'I mean ...'

'It's all right, there's no one in. Well, only Jennie an' she's takin' a nap,' Pat told her. 'Mum an' Sadie are out shoppin' an' me dad's gone ter the football match.'

Brenda walked into the warm parlour and loosened her heavy winter coat. 'I wrote you a letter, Pat,' she said, 'but I tore it up. It's better fer us ter talk.'

'I thought we'd exhausted the talkin',' he replied quickly, then bit his tongue. 'Anyway let me take yer coat. Sit down by the fire. Can I get yer a drink? Tea, coffee?'

'No, I'm all right,' she replied as she took a seat.

Pat sat down facing her, leaning forward in the armchair with his hands clasped. 'You look very well,' he remarked.

'So do you, except I fink yer've lost a bit o' weight.'

He sighed. 'An' there's me finkin' I'd put some on.'

'Is yer trainin' over?' she asked.

'Almost.'

'Then yer'll be ...'

'Joinin' a bomber squadron as a tail gunner.'

'That's a dangerous job, isn't it?'

He shrugged his shoulders. 'Not really—well, no more dangerous than any ovver flyin' job.'

'When's yer leave up?'

'Termorrer.'

'I only found out you were on leave this afternoon,' Brenda said. 'I wish I'd known sooner.'

'I've bin finkin' about yer,' he said shyly.

' 'Ave yer?'

'Yeah, quite a lot.'

'Me too. Pat, I've bin so stupid,' she said with a break in her voice.

'Yeah, me too.'

'No, you did what you 'ad ter do an' I wasn't big enough to accept it.'

'Why should yer?' he replied. 'It must 'ave seemed like a selfish fing ter do an' you 'ad the right ter do yer nut, I s'pose, the way I told yer about it.'

'It was just that I could see all our dreams

329

an' plans goin' up in smoke,' she said sadly. 'I thought that if yer waited till you was called up we might 'ave 'ad the time ter get married.'

'I know,' he sighed. 'I thought about that too, but can't yer see 'ow it would 'ave bin. We'd just be gettin' settled in a place an' then I'd 'ave ter leave yer all alone. At least now you're livin' wiv yer family.'

'I could 'ave gone back to 'em while you was away,' she replied.

'No, yer wouldn't. Yer'd 'ave made the place nice an' cosy an' spent yer time alone, waitin' fer the odd letter an' fer me ter get some leave.'

'Fousands o' newly married couples are doin' just that,' she reminded him.

'Yeah, I know,' he replied.

Brenda looked down at her clasped hands and squeezed them until the knuckles showed white. 'Tell me the trufe, Pat,' she asked him. 'Do you still feel the same way about me? I mean, is it different now that we've bin apart?'

'I feel more for yer than I've ever done, an' that's the God's honest trufe,' he said quietly. 'In fact I wrote you a letter too.'

' 'Ave yer still got it?'

'No, I tore it up.'

'Why?'

'Fer the same reason that you tore your letter up, I s'pose,' he told her. 'I just couldn't put me feelin's inter words.'

'It's so difficult,' she sighed.

'I was gonna send you a poem too,' he went on. 'There's a bloke in our billet who reads a lot o' poetry an' we've got friendly. As a matter o' fact, I was talkin' to 'im about you, about 'ow close we were an' 'ow the war caused us ter split up, an' 'e showed me a poem. It's a bit deep but it some'ow ses what I wanted ter say but couldn't.'

'An' yer tore that up too, I s'pose,' Brenda said.

'No, I've still got it.'

'Can I see it?'

He hesitated and then reached into his back pocket. 'Look, I'd prefer it if yer wait till yer get back 'ome before yer read it,' he remarked. 'I'd feel embarrassed.'

'Whatever for?' she smiled. 'D'yer fink it's bein' sissy ter like poetry?'

'No, it's just that I ... sort of ...'

'Patrick Flynn, 'ow could I ever fink that you're a sissy,' she said, smiling broadly as she took the folded sheet of paper. 'All right, I won't read it now.'

'I'd like ter see you again before I go back termorrer mornin' but Frank an' Jim 'ave just come 'ome on embarkation leave,' he explained. 'I've promised to 'ave a drink wiv 'em ternight. There won't be anuvver chance an' I may not see 'em both fer some time.'

'I understand,' she replied. 'You should spend some time wiv 'em. Maybe I could come ter the station ter see yer off.'

'I'd like that,' he said.

'Look, I'd better go,' she said quickly. 'I'd feel a bit embarrassed if I'm still 'ere when yer family come in.'

'It's all right,' he assured her.

331

'No, I'd better go,' she insisted. 'What time termorrer?'

'I was gonna leave 'ere about 'alf ten,' he replied. 'I'm catchin' the eleven forty-five from Liverpool Street.' He saw her hesitate. 'You could meet me on the corner o' Defoe Street at ten if yer like. It'd give us a bit o' time ter talk.'

'That'll be fine,' she said as she stood up to leave.

Pat got up and took her gently by the shoulders. 'I know this must 'ave bin a bit difficult for yer, Bren, but I'm very grateful yer did call round.'

'I just 'ad ter see yer, Pat.'

'I've missed yer so much,' he told her quietly.

She stood on tiptoe and planted a soft kiss on his lips, feeling him squeeze her arms. 'Termorrer at ten o'clock. Corner o' Defoe Street.'

He stood at the front door until Brenda turned the corner, then went inside feeling elated. Tonight at The Sun was going to be a night to remember, he thought.

At number 20 Carter Lane an intense conversation was in progress, and Charity Lockwood expressed her shock in no uncertain terms. 'I just don't understand you, Cynthia, really I don't,' she said sharply. 'What purpose will it serve? After all this time too. Goodness gracious me, I've never heard such a feeble, senseless reason. No, I can't let you do it. I won't let you.'

'I'm sorry, Charity, but my mind's made up,'

Cynthia told her. 'You may think it's feeble but to me it's not. Sometimes we are given a sign from heaven. Last night was a sign.'

'Don't be so ridiculous,' Charity retorted smartly. 'That shell cone that fell in the backyard didn't come from heaven, it came from the sky, from the anti-aircraft shell, and well you know it. Go out in the street after an air raid and you'll see lots of pieces of shrapnel lying around; yes and shell cones too. It was just that last night one happened to fall in our backyard.'

'Yes, but it was just as I was coming in,' Cynthia reminded her. 'I could have been killed. In fact I nearly was. It just missed my head.'

'So you feel it's a sign, do you?' Charity said mockingly. 'It's been more than ten years now and you feel that God finally got round to giving you a sign. Deary me, Cynthia, don't you think the good Lord's got enough to do with all the problems of the war, without suddenly remembering to give you a sign. It's pathetic.'

'Maybe, but there's something I haven't told you,' the younger sister went on. 'I prayed for a sign. I've been praying for a sign for a while now, and at last it's come.'

'I suppose you did consider my feelings and my future when you decided on your course of action,' Charity remarked. 'Maybe not. No, she's the strong one, she can survive. She doesn't need me to wipe her nose or powder her bottom.'

'Don't be cruel, Charity,' Cynthia replied. 'You know I always think of you in every decision I make, which isn't many. Usually it's you who decides for us, and I'm not complaining. I'm happy for you to show your caring side and your compassion, but there comes a time when I have to do the thing I know is right.'

'Then you must understand that sometimes I too have to do what I feel is right, despite what others might think.'

Cynthia looked up at her sister and saw the determined look in her eyes. 'I don't quite know what you're trying to tell me, Charity,' she said, 'but please don't think there's anything you can do that will dissuade me from doing what I have to. I've made my decision and I'm sticking to it.'

Charity sat down with a deep sigh and shook her head slowly as she reached for the paper. 'We shall see,' she said craftily.

All day Saturday it had been damp and cold, with a light fog that would normally have prompted most people to remain by their fireside rather than visit the public house. On this particular Saturday night, however, it was different. It was a time for families to gather together while they could, despite the threat of the bombing. Normally in winter people would yearn for the balmy days of summer and the cool bright evenings, but again it was different now. Everyone prayed for a thick fog on Saturday night, and it appeared early on in the evening that their prayers were being answered.

'It looks like it might be a quiet night

ternight,' Danny Crossley remarked as he took possession of his first pint of the evening.

'Gawd willin',' Alf replied. 'As long as the rain don't come.'

Another customer came in to announce that the fog was thickening and Danny ordered another pint for him and Alf. 'We'd better drink ter that,' he said grinning.

By eight o'clock the visibility was down to a few yards and Tess Anson began to feel that providence had intervened. 'They won't be over ternight,' she told Charlie confidently.

'I do believe you're right,' he replied.

'I 'ope yer got enough booze in,' she said.

'Plenty,' he assured her.

The customers and the landlord and landlady of The Sun public house had never known a night like it. Both bars were packed from early on in the evening and in the saloon bar it was difficult to reach the counter. Pints flowed endlessly from the taps and the pianist was kept busy from the moment he showed his face in the bar. The whole of the Flynn family joined with Bert and Daisy Harris and the Kennys in drinking to the health and good fortune of the young men of Carter Lane who would soon be going off to war again.

Ivy Jones' son Jerry looked resplendent in the Royal Marines uniform as he stood talking with Grenadier Freddie Bromilow, who had managed to get a forty-eight-hour pass so that he wouldn't miss the going-away party for his childhood friends.

'So are you on a forty-eight-hour pass too

then, Jerry?' Freddie asked.

Jerry nodded. 'I'll be 'ome again soon on embarkation leave,' he replied. 'We're paintin' all the unit vehicles a shitty yellow an' we're due ter be kitted out next week wiv tropical gear. A lot o' the lads fink we're bound fer Egypt, or at least somewhere in the Middle East.'

'Well good luck, pal,' Freddie said clinking glasses.

Everyone was determined to relax and enjoy the evening while they could, knowing full well that when the weather broke the raiders would be back in force.

Sadie was home for the whole weekend and she was feeling excited as she chatted to Jennie. 'It's very 'ard an' they don't give yer much time ter get acclimatised,' she was saying. 'In the first week I 'ad to assist in changin' dressin's on amputees an' then I 'ad ter learn 'ow ter give injections.'

Jennie shuddered. 'Sooner you than me, Sadie, but everyone's proud o' yer. Who'd 'a thought it? Our Sadie a nurse.'

'It's what I wanna do, Jen. I'm really 'appy at the 'ospital. I like the practical stuff better than the classroom work.'

'An' yer got no regrets about givin' Len Regan the elbow?'

'No, none whatever,' Sadie said positively. 'I'm sure 'e was two-timin' me, though I could never prove anyfing. The woman works in one o' Macaulay's pubs in Rovverhithe. She's a piss artist, ter tell yer the trufe, an' she looks every bit 'er age, but she was a good looker before the drink got to 'er. Len was dead keen on 'er but they fell out before I come on the scene.'

'An' yer fink 'e's back wiv 'er?'

'Yeah, I'm pretty sure.'

Jennie took a sip from her glass. 'Anyway, let's ferget that crowd. Joe's gonna be comin' in soon an' yer gotta look pink an' lovely.'

'Does me 'air look all right?'

'Yeah, course it does.'

'What about me make-up?'

'Just perfect.'

'An' this dress ...?'

'Sadie, will yer shut up an' relax? I'm goin' over ter rescue Con from our bruvs.'

Bert Kenny had slipped back to the house and on his return he made his way over to Charlie Anson. ' 'E's out the tub an' dressed,' he reported. ' 'E'll be 'ere any minute now.'

Everyone who needed to had replenished their glasses and when Big Joe finally walked into the crowded pub wearing his freshly pressed uniform he was greeted with a big cheer. The pianist started up with 'For He's a Jolly Good Fellow' and the customers almost brought the roof down.

'Aw, you shouldn't have made a fuss,' Joe said, his face flushed with embarrassment.

'Shut yer noise, Joe,' Jerry called out. 'Charlie wants ter say a few words.'

The landlord made his way round the counter and held his hands up for attention. 'Now this is a special night fer all of us,' he began. 'We all know about Big Joe's little adventure not so long ago, an' I say little adventure because 'e'd be the last ter make a big fing of it. Nevertheless, it's blokes like 'im who make it certain that the Jerries will never beat us.'

' 'Ear, 'ear,' voices called out.

'This country stands alone now an' we're gettin' a right ole pastin' every night,' Charlie went on, 'but we can take it, because we 'ave to. It's not in our nature to 'old up our 'ands an' surrender. We'll take it all, every last bomb they drop on us, an' then our turn'll come. We'll give it back tenfold, an' one day in the not-too-distant future the Jerries'll be the one ter put their 'ands up. In the meantime we can feel safe, safe an' proud that our freedom an' a future fer our kids are in the 'ands o' people like Big Joe, the Flynn boys, Freddie Bromilow an' Jerry Jones, Alec Conroy, Chris Wickstead an' Dennis Wilson.'

'Good ole Chris.'

'Cheers, Denny.'

'Gawd bless all of 'em, I say,' an elderly woman remarked, raising her glass of stout.

Charlie Anson held his hands up for silence. 'A lot of us remember these lads kickin' a tin can in the turnin' or cheekin' the market traders, an' I would imagine Big Joe was doin' the same down under, but now they've got a job ter do—kick the Jerries right back where they came from—an' they'll do it. So I ask you all ter raise yer glasses to our lads in uniform, an' may the good Lord go wiv 'em.'

The pub suddenly erupted and in the din and hubbub of the moment Joe sought out Sadie. The Flynn boys and Con were in a huddle when Jennie went over to them. 'Will yer just take a look at our Sadie,' she said happily.

The brothers looked across the bar and saw their sister laughing aloud as Joe made motions with his hands.

'It's nice ter know she's given Regan the elbow,' Frank remarked.

'I'd like ter fink so, but 'e can be a persuasive bastard,' Jim replied.

'I don't fink even Regan would relish tanglin' wiv Big Joe,' Pat told them. 'Come on, let's join 'em.'

'Oh no yer don't,' Jennie said sternly. 'Give 'em a chance ter get ter know each ovver.'

A pretty young woman with blonde hair winked over at Jim Flynn and got a response, and for a few minutes the two flirted with their eyes.

'I'll see you lads in a minute,' he said mysteriously.

Con slipped his arm round Jennie's waist. 'It's a good night,' he remarked with a twinkle in his eye.

'It is now,' she said, snuggling up to him.

Tucked away in the far corner, Sadie and Big Joe were chatting happily together.

'I really like what I do, Joe,' she told him. 'It gets a bit scary at times an' I don't like goin' on theatre duty, but I know that nursin's fer me.'

'I'm glad for you, Sadie,' he replied. 'That's the way I feel about the navy, but like you say, it ain't all bonzer.'

'No, I don't s'pose it is,' she said, giving him a knowing look. 'You try an' keep out o' trouble.

I don't wanna see you in one o' those 'ospital beds.'

'They don't take matelots at your place, do they?' he asked.

'Look at those lot gettin' all lovey-dovey,' Alf Coates remarked from his usual vantage point.

'Yer only young once, Alf,' Danny said philosophically.

'Lookin' at them kids canoodlin' takes me back,' Alf chuckled. 'We're bloody past it now though, ole mate.'

'You speak fer yer bloody self,' Danny told him indignantly.

'You ain't on anuvver promise wiv Widder Winkless, are yer?'

'You mind yer business.'

'It's nuffink ter do wiv me, but once yer done the deed don't sit there complainin' that yer back's gorn again,' Alf replied.

Danny looked up to see Big Joe squeezing past him on his way to the toilet. 'Watch'er, mate,' he remarked. 'You ain't off yet while, are yer? We ain't seen anyfing of yer yet.'

'No, I've just gotta drain the dragon,' Joe replied. 'I'm busier than a one-armed Sydney taxi driver with the crabs in here tonight. How are you keeping?'

'Well, can't complain,' Alf said, and a wicked grin appeared on his face. 'By the way, we ain't seen anyfing o' your mate.'

'My mate?' Joe queried, then he caught the old man's drift. 'Aw, let me guess. Ugly as a hatful of arseholes, and never shuts his bunghole long enough to think. Last seen kissing the road.

Nah, we fell out. He never bought a round.'

'Talkin' o' which,' Danny said with a wink and a winning smile, glancing diplomatically at his glass.

The evening wore on, the damp and fogbound darkness outside providing a blessed relief, and in that wartime interlude, while the skies were quiet, a few long-lasting alliances were tightly bonded.

CHAPTER 28

Carter Lane was very quiet on that bitterly cold and gloomy Sunday morning. For most of the folk it was the first taste they had had for what seemed like ages of sleeping in their own beds without fear of being disturbed by an air raid, and on awakening they took the opportunity of a lie-in. Frank and Iris Ross were no exception, but their daughter Brenda was up early, and after lighting the fire and making herself some tea and toast she sat by the hearth wrapped in her thick corded dressing-gown. In the breast pocket was the poem Pat had given her and she had read it over and over again before going to sleep last night. She took it out again, wanting to memorise the last two lines so that she could recite them to Pat, and make him aware that she understood it all now.

'To Lucasta, Going to the Wars'

Tell me not, Sweet, I am unkind
That from the nunnery
Of thy chaste breast, and quiet mind,
To war and arms I fly.

True; a new mistress now I chase,
The first foe in the field;
And with a stronger faith embrace
A sword, a horse, a shield.

Yet this inconstancy is such
As you too shall adore;
I could not love thee, Dear, so much,
Lov'd I not honour more.

Richard Lovelace.

The words had made her cry, and now her eyes
began to mist again. The sad pride of the poem
had served to purge her mind of all her doubts
and selfish anger. The two of them had been
inseparable once, and she remembered taking
his sticky hand in hers and going to the corner
shop for Golly bars and bags of hundreds and
thousands. How clearly she remembered the
times they sat at the kerbside rubbing shoulders
as she taught him how to make a cat's cradle
from a length of string she worked between her
fingers.

Brenda stared into the flaring coals and saw
the tall lean lad who had now begun to treat
her with a new respect, and she smiled to herself

as she recalled how she had thrown back her shoulders to let him see that she too was growing into a woman. The innocent kisses came later, stolen in the darkness of the wharf doorways and on the muddy foreshore as the tide ebbed and the summer sun dipped down in the sky to leave its orange and purple afterglow. Halcyon days, they seemed now, when the growing pains were hard to bear and the strange feelings in her loins made her shake and tremble with a desire that she did not fully understand. Her childhood fondness, natural and unaware, was now a full-blooded love for him, a yearning for him to come to her in the dead of night, to share her bed and enter her aching body. But how could she open her heart to him, how could she unlock the feelings and desires that beat inside her and let them take wing?

As she prepared to leave the house Brenda was under no illusions. They were grown-ups now, and grown-ups often had to make choices. She no longer cared to walk to the altar pure and chaste, to deny the temptations of love out of respect for the proper order of things. The war had made her see life in a different light. The world was not rose-coloured anymore, just cold and grey, and life had to be lived to the full, while it was still there to be savoured. Marriage could wait, love could not, lest the war took him from her forever, as it had already taken so many others.

She saw him on the corner, his greatcoat pulled up around his ears and his face red with the wind. He smiled, the easy smile that she knew so well, and she felt a warm glow deep down inside. He took her arm and kissed her cheek before they set off along the quiet street.

'I cried last night when I read that poem,' she told him.

He smiled. 'I think it said it all, all that I wanted ter say but couldn't find the words for.'

'Will yer come back ter me soon, Pat?' she asked.

'Soon as ever I can.'

'In a few weeks?'

'The trainin' finishes in two weeks,' he replied. 'I should be able ter manage a forty-eight-hour pass.'

'I'll want you all ter meself, darlin',' she grinned.

'Every wakin' minute of every hour.'

The train was about to leave and Pat took her in her arms. He could feel her body pressed to his and he kissed her full lips with all the passion within him, then he climbed aboard, turning to look out of the door. 'I love you, Brenda.'

'I love you too, Pat.'

The guard raised his flag and the young woman reached out and touched him. 'The last two lines o' the poem. Say them ter me.'

'I can't remember 'em.'

'I can,' she said smiling. ' "I could not love thee, dear, so much, loved I not honour more." '

The train moved away from the platform and he blew her a kiss. She waved until the carriage disappeared round the bend out of sight, then she turned away, tears welling up in her eyes. 'Damn this war,' she cursed aloud, hurrying from the platform out into the winter gloom.

The fog was back with a vengeance that evening and the Luftwaffe would stay away for the second night running. At the Flynn household it was a quiet time with Frank and Jim recovering from their lunchtime sortie to The Sun, undertaken solely for medicinal purposes according to Jim. Dolly and Mick relaxed in the fireside chairs, warmed by the coke fire as they listened to the wireless, and upstairs Sadie and Jennie chatted together while they waited for Con and Big Joe to call.

'If the picture's over in time we could call in The Sun fer a nightcap,' Jennie suggested.

'Good idea,' Sadie replied. 'I expect Frank an' Jim'll drag themselves up there.'

'Will they mind, you goin' back termorrer instead o' ternight?' Jennie asked.

'Nah, long as I'm there for nine o'clock,' Sadie told her. 'That's when us trainees usually start.'

'You an' Joe looked a very nice twosome last night,' Jennie remarked.

'We talked an' talked,' Sadie replied. 'I told 'im there was no way back fer me an' Len Regan an' 'e asked me if I'd be 'is gel.'

'Ah, that's nice,' Jennie sighed. ' 'E is a sweety, so old-fashioned.'

' 'E's not that old-fashioned,' Sadie said indignantly.

'You know what I mean,' Jennie replied. 'Big Joe reminds me o' those fellers in the ole films, all manly an' charmin'.'

'The perfect gentleman, 'cept fer some fruity sayin's 'e's got.'

'Yeah. 'Ere, I 'ope 'e wasn't too pissy ter kiss yer goodnight.'

'Course 'e wasn't,' Sadie said quickly.

'What was it like? Did it make yer toes curl up?'

'Jennie, don't be so nosy.'

'When Con kisses me I'm all of a tremble.'

Sadie shook her head slowly. 'Look, are you all ready?'

'All but me stockin's,' Jennie told her. 'I'm leavin' 'em till the last minute in case I ladder 'em.'

'Well, will yer go an' make a cuppa while I finish gettin' ready?'

'Yeah, okay,' Jennie said without attempting to move from the edge of the bed. 'I'm so glad Pat an' Brenda got back tergevver again.'

'We don't know fer sure, do we?' Sadie replied.

'I do,' Jennie said. 'You could see the look in Pat's eyes when 'e said Brenda was gonna see 'im off this mornin'.'

'It's a shame Pat 'ad so little time wiv Frank an' Jim,' Sadie remarked thoughtfully. 'Still it was a really good night, wasn't it?'

'Not 'alf,' Jennie said with passion. 'Con enjoyed 'imself too. I'm gonna see as much of 'im as I can while 'e's 'ere. God knows 'ow long it'll be before 'im an' the boys get 'ome again.'

346

There was a knock at the front door and Sadie jumped up quickly. 'Bloody 'ell, they're early. Quick, get yer stockin's on.'

As the night wore on the fog thickened, but by morning it had gone, giving way to a bright and bitterly cold day, and people went off to work knowing that the respite from the bombing was over. In the Lockwood household the discussion of the previous day continued, but try as she might Charity could not persuade her sister to change her mind. 'All right then, if you insist, but I'm coming with you,' she said adamantly.

'I'd like that,' Cynthia told her. 'It'll make it easier for me if you're there.'

They left the house, with Cynthia holding on to Charity's arm and walking upright and proud, the collars of their heavy coats turned up against the elements. They made their way into Munday Road and up the steps of the police station and Cynthia took a deep breath as they walked through the doors. 'I'd like to see Chief Inspector McConnell if you please,' she said.

The desk sergeant knew the sisters well enough not to ask questions. 'If you'll just give me a minute I'll see if he's free.'

As they were escorted along the corridor Rubin McConnell came out of his office to greet them. 'Good mornin', ladies. What can I do for you?' he asked.

'I've come to report a murder,' Cynthia told him.

The inspector looked shocked. 'You'd better come in the office,' he said, pulling up two chairs in front of the desk.

While the sisters made themselves comfortable McConnell phoned for Detective Sergeant Johnson to join him and the detective sat at the back of the room with a notepad in his hand.

Cynthia cleared her throat. 'As I said I want to report a murder, namely the murder of Aaron Priestley.'

'But we already have that information,' the policeman said quickly.

'If I'm not mistaken you are assuming my husband was murdered, but you don't know for sure.'

'I think we can be sure, Miss Lockwood. The wound tells us as much.'

'Well, I can tell you for sure, because I know the identity of the person who killed him,' Cynthia went on.

'You know the person responsible?'

'Yes, I do.'

'You saw the murder?'

'I was there.'

'Good Lord! And you've only just thought of telling me. Who was it?'

'Me.'

'You!'

'Yes, me.'

McConnell swallowed hard. 'Are you trying to make a fool of me, Miss Lockwood?' he asked sternly.

'Heaven forbid,' Cynthia replied with equal seriousness.

'You're telling me that you killed your husband?'

348

'Yes. I killed him with a single blow to the head with a hammer, then I put him in the bassinet that I used for the bagwash and wheeled him round to the hole the workmen had dug in the factory yard in Munday Road and tipped him in it.'

The policeman reached into the desk drawer and took out a folder. 'This is what I call the Lockwood file,' he said in a long-suffering voice. 'Over the years you've both come in here with snippets of information to report to me. The last, let me remind you, was the case of the pillar-box. Now you turn up first thing on a Monday morning, expecting me to believe that you actually killed your husband and then tipped him in the hole.'

'Of course I expect you to believe me,' Cynthia said quickly. 'It's the truth.'

'And you're prepared to make a statement to that effect?'

'Yes.'

McConnell leaned back in his chair and wiped a shaky hand over his face. 'Why did you kill him?'

'Because I could not stand any more of his bullying, his physical and mental abuse, that's why.'

The policeman picked up a plain sheet of paper and laid it down on the blotting-pad in front of him. 'Right then, let's ...'

'Just a moment,' Charity cut in. 'You'll be wasting your time taking a statement from Cynthia. She didn't kill Aaron. I did.'

'No, she didn't.'

'Oh yes, I did.'

McConnell held up his hands. 'Now just a minute. Both of you couldn't have killed him.'

'I did it,' Cynthia said calmly. 'I've lived with the secret for over ten years, and now the body's been found I feel bound to confess. I prayed for guidance and the Lord has answered me. I killed Aaron Priestley.'

'No, she didn't. I did it,' Charity declared. 'And you know full well, inspector, that you can't charge both of us, considering the evidence you have.'

'Oh I see,' McConnell replied with sarcasm. 'Well, in that case let me make you a little proposition. Perhaps Cynthia could give me her version first and then you can give me yours. On the basis of what you say I'll make the decision as to which one of you I formally charge. If that's to your liking.'

'That's fair of you, inspector,' Cynthia said. 'Well to begin with, Aaron had been beating me unmercifully that evening, and then he went out to the pub. Later he came home very drunk and started to hit me again. I grabbed a hammer that was lying on the sideboard and struck him with all the force I could muster. I knew he was dead because his eyes opened wide and then went all glassy. So I got the old bassinet and put it by the bed. It wasn't very difficult to roll him into it and then I took him to the hole. It was raining very hard and it was also very late. There wasn't a soul about. When I tipped him into the hole I saw him slither down to the bottom and there was a sort of muddy puddle there. He just disappeared.'

McConnell opened the folder and studied it for a few moments. 'Tell me, Miss Lockwood, did you tamper with the body once you had done the deed?'

'In what way?' Cynthia asked with a puzzled look.

'Well, did you remove any of his clothing, take off any rings or a wristwatch maybe?'

'Certainly not.'

'And I suppose if I asked you to give me your version it would be similar to your sister's,' the policeman said, eyeing Charity closely.

'Exactly.'

'Now let me tell you both something,' he continued. 'When we removed the remains from the hole the pathologist did a thorough check and he found that there were two joints missing from the ring finger of the left hand. We know from the photograph you supplied us with that Aaron Priestley wore a large ruby ring on that finger. So it follows that whoever killed him tried to take the ring off and when they found it was too tight to remove they chopped the finger off. It wasn't either of you. You said that you didn't tamper with the body after death.'

'Someone could have seen the body in the hole and decided to help themselves to the ring,' Cynthia replied.

'The evidence we have doesn't support that theory,' McConnell told her. 'The remains were lying face up with the arms at the side. Besides, you said the body disappeared under the water and mud.'

The two women looked at each other in confusion. 'Well, if you're sure I suppose we'll have to go along with it,' Charity said. 'Come along, Cynthia, let's not waste any more of the nice policeman's time.'

As soon as the two had left the office McConnell reached into his desk drawer for a bottle of whisky and two glasses. 'Can you imagine either of those two hammering anyone to death?' he sighed.

Johnson smiled as he accepted the tot of whisky. 'What possesses them?' he asked with a slow shake of his head.

McConnell tapped the folder with his fore-finger. 'When you've time you should go through this,' he replied. 'They've been coming in here for years with all sorts of information and requests. I think they're just seeking attention, though I could be over-simplifying it. Whatever it is, those two women have plagued me for years.'

Johnson sipped his drink. 'Well, we know the Lockwoods couldn't have killed Priestley, but someone did, though I don't think we're ever going to find out who it was.' He emptied the glass and stood up, a smile suddenly lighting up his face.

'What is it?' the inspector asked.

'I was just picturing the old biddy pushing that pram through the streets with a pair of legs sticking out,' Johnson told him.

'I just had a thought too,' McConnell remarked. 'I've just had my first whisky and it's only ten thirty. Those two will be the death of me.'

CHAPTER 29

Time hung heavily on Con Williams while Jennie was working during the day and he spent the time sorting through his adopted grandmother's belongings at the flat in Dockhead. The rent was paid up until the end of the month but things had to be disposed of and arrangements made for the furniture to be cleared. Mrs Crosier was very helpful in getting everything moving and it was she who arranged for the Salvation Army to collect the bits of furniture and clothing that might still do someone a turn. The crockery was all cracked and chipped and the few pots and pans only fit for the dustbin.

'Ida didn't 'ave much, did she?' Con remarked to the elderly lady.

'A lifetime o' struggle, that's all she 'ad,' Mrs Crosier replied sadly. 'Never mind, Con, she did right by you an' I'm sure she'll be favoured up there.'

The papers and documents in the flat were of no importance, mainly receipts and old letters from relatives and friends, and Con could find no insurance policy that would serve to reimburse the local church for their kindness in arranging a dignified funeral for the old lady. 'I'm a bit surprised,' he remarked. 'She was always tellin' me that she'd put a few bob aside fer 'er funeral.'

'Yeah, she used ter put a few coppers in that jug every week,' Mrs Crosier told him, 'but then one day when I was doin' a bit o' cleanin' for 'er she asked me ter pass the jug down to 'er. She was sufferin' wiv that phlebitis at the time an' she couldn't move out o' the armchair. I watched 'er count the coppers an' then she gave me one o' those saucy smiles she was good at. "This wouldn't even bury our ole tomcat," she said, "an' I don't fink I'm gonna last enough ter fill the jug up. 'Ere, take it an' bring me back a nice little bottle o' tiddly." What could I do? It was 'er wish, so I fetched 'er a small bottle o' gin. I was worried though, what wiv 'er complaint. I don't fink the gin would 'elp 'er. Anyway I looked in on 'er that night an' there she was 'appy as Larry goin' frew all 'er ole photos. I left 'er sleepin' in the armchair and she told me later that was the best night's sleep she'd 'ad in ages.'

Con thanked Mrs Crosier for all her help and then closed up the flat, leaving her with the key for when the Salvation Army people called. It was as if the door had closed on a large part of himself and he felt alone and empty inside. His leave was up tomorrow and tonight he would stay at the working men's hostel in Dockhead, which he felt was preferable to staying another night in the grimy, lonely flat with all those childhood memories crowding in on him.

Following their visit to the police station the Lockwood sisters felt drained, but as always Charity was a rock. 'Now listen to me, Cynthia,' she said resolutely. 'I know it came as a shock to hear about the missing finger. It's a complete mystery, but we'll never know the rights of it, so it's not worth dwelling on it. It's all in the past now and I think we should agree never to talk about the matter again.'

'I think you're right,' Cynthia said.

'We must stop pestering that nice inspector too,' Charity added. 'He has enough to do without us troubling him.'

'Yes, you're right,' Cynthia replied. 'But it doesn't mean we should walk around with our eyes shut.'

'No, of course not,' Charity said. 'If we do see anything untoward happening it's our duty to report it and I'm sure that the inspector would be grateful, but let's not get carried away.'

'I couldn't agree more,' Cynthia replied.

This was to be the last family meal before the boys went back from leave and Dolly had asked Jennie to bring Con along. 'The poor sod's all on 'is own an' I can't let 'im go to a cafe or a bloody fish shop fer 'is tea,' she said. 'I've managed ter get a nice joint o' beef an' there'll be plenty ter go round. 'E might as well stay 'ere ternight too. 'E can sleep in our Sadie's bed.'

That evening Con arrived in uniform, carrying his kitbag and a small case ready for the journey back to camp the following morning, and Dolly spared no effort. She used her best white linen tablecloth with the green china dinner set, the meat was tender, the vegetables were done to perfection and her special meat stock gravy was relished hungrily by Frank and Jim in particular, who loved to soak their bread in it.

Watching them wipe their plates with thick slices and seeing Con follow suit, timidly at first, made her want to hug them all. She was reminded of peaceful times when her children were all growing up, when a grazed knee or a bump on the head was something she could deal with. Now the young men were going off to war, and what good could she be, standing by with the medicine chest?

When the meal was finally over Dolly had to get ready for her nightly spell on the mobile canteen and Mick left for his fire-watching duty at the nearby fire post on the roof of the Defoe Street bacon factory. Frank and Jim, sensing that they were going to be in the way, decided to go to The Sun for a game of darts. Jennie was grateful for the opportunity to be alone with Con but she made light of it. 'We'll pop in the pub later, once I've tidied up,' she remarked.

It was quiet in the house now and Con sat in the armchair staring thoughtfully into the fire while Jennie busied herself in the scullery, but she soon came into the parlour and immediately slipped onto his lap. 'We've 'ad so little time alone,' she said regretfully.

He smiled. 'Never mind, it's bin very nice, just ter be wiv yer.'

She put her arms around his neck and kissed him. 'We're alone now,' she sighed.

He pulled her across him and kissed her open lips, feeling the warmth of her shapely slim body. 'I would 'ave liked to 'ave taken yer ter the flat, but I couldn't, Jennie,' he said with a heavy breath. 'It's dingy an' depressin' an' I just couldn't ask yer. I couldn't 'ave relaxed there an' I don't fink you could 'ave neivver.'

'It's all right, Con, you don't 'ave ter feel guilty,' she said, and her face broke into a saucy smile. 'I know yer a little bit frightened o' me.'

He smiled as he held her close. 'So yer've sussed me out.'

'I was only joking,' she told him. 'I bet yer've bin wiv lots o' gels.'

'I've 'ad a few dates, but I've never bin serious wiv anyone before,' he replied quietly.

'Are we serious?' she asked.

'I thought so,' he grinned.

'Well then, stop talkin' so much an' kiss me,' she said huskily.

Their lips met and Jennie could no longer hold herself in check. Tonight was the last night they would spend together for a long time and she was determined to make him love her fully. She ran her fingers through his hair and then slowly undid the buttons of his shirt, slipping her hands onto his chest. He was aroused, cupping her small firm breasts in his hands and she encouraged him, undoing the buttons of her blouse and unclipping her bra. The feel of his large hand on her bare skin made her shudder with pleasure. 'I want you, Con,' she whispered. 'I've dreamed of this. Let's go upstairs.'

As she slipped from his lap she caught the uncertain look in his eyes. 'What's wrong?' she asked.

'I've ... I've not got any ...'

'Who needs 'em?' she said smiling at him. 'It's not the week for me ter get pregnant anyway.'

They climbed the stairs and Jennie took his hand in hers as she led him into her bedroom. Her arms went round his neck and she arched her body into his, daringly and provocatively, moving sensuously against his rising ardour. They kissed hungrily and she undid the buttons of his trousers, making him gasp as she held his stiff erection. Manoeuvring round she fell back on the bed, pulling him down on top of her. He had trouble getting out of his thick uniform trousers and she helped him urgently, panting with the passion swelling inside her. Their naked bodies touched, pressed together and he gritted his teeth as she guided him into her, unable to wait any longer, and Con's inexperience was matched by Jennie's almost bursting desire for him. She groaned as she felt his first thrust deep inside her and his movements became frantic as they hastened to a frenzied and delicious climax.

Big Joe stepped down from the bus outside the Woolwich Military Hospital and made his way into the gravel forecourt. He was wearing his uniform and greatcoat, with his naval cap at a saucy tilt. Sadie had told him that she was confined to the nurses' quarters during the week but some of the women trainees engaged in clandestine meetings with their boyfriends. She had said it in a matter-of-fact way while they were chatting at the pub and he knew that Sadie was not hinting for him to come and see her, but here he was, and he felt almost as nervous as he had when he slipped into the dinghy that night in the Mediterranean.

The night sky was clear, lit by the waning moon, and the large main building loomed up in front of Joe as he assessed the strategy of his self-appointed mission. He guessed that the nurses' quarters would be to the rear of the building but he did not want to be mistaken for some voyeur or pervert, so he decided to tackle the problem with a frontal assault and use diplomacy, falling back on high explosive as a last resort. Walking boldly through the main doors he sauntered up to the reception area and smiled. 'Good evening, sister,' he said to the young nurse on duty. 'I phoned earlier about an appointment with ...'

'Yes, we have the message,' the nurse told him, smiling at being called sister. 'If you'll just take a seat I'll get someone to attend to you.'

Big Joe nearly fell over with surprise, and before he could respond the nurse picked up the phone and said simply, 'The seaman's arrived.'

Joe was still wondering if Sadie had somehow anticipated his visit when a large stern-looking sister approached and whispered a few words in the nurse's ear. She nodded and hurried off, following the martinet and leaving Joe scratching his head. Someone was coming towards him, a male nurse walking quickly. 'If you'll follow me,' he said.

Joe shrugged his shoulders and did as he was bid.

'In there,' the nurse told him. 'Slip your bottoms off and put the gown on. You'll find it on the bed.'

Once again Joe made to protest but the man was already hurrying off.

'Is this a military hospital or a bloody looney bin?' the Australian mumbled to himself.

'Haven't you made yourself ready yet?' a voice said, and Joe span round to see a Medical Corps captain glaring at him.

'I think there's been a few wires crossed, sir,' Joe remarked.

'A few wires crossed? Is that how you describe catching the pox?' the medic said sharply. 'You phoned the hospital for an emergency check for VD, didn't you?'

'No, I bloody didn't,' Joe said quickly. 'I've been too busy to catch me breath, apart from anything else. I'm here with a message for one of the nurses and it's all gone a bit arse-up.'

The officer sat down heavily in the chair and laughed. 'My God. You almost got the umbrella up your pride and joy.'

'I'm very sorry, sir, but I didn't get a chance to give 'em the drum,' Joe explained.

The captain narrowed his eyes for effect. 'That's an Aussie accent if I'm not mistaken?' he said.

'Sydney, to be precise.'

'Well now, you're a long way from home.'

'Bermondsey's been my home for a couple of years now,' Joe told him.

The captain looked at him closely. 'You say you have a message for one of the nurses?'

'Trainee nurses, to be exact,' Joe replied.

'Name?'

'Miss Sadie Flynn.'

'I know her. Good prospects. Very good prospects in fact,' the captain remarked. 'The message. Nothing bad I hope?'

'No, sir. Her two brothers have lobbed, sorry, come home unexpectedly on embarkation leave and they wanted to let her know. They tried to phone but all the lines are down in Bermondsey.'

'Right then,' the medic said officiously. 'Proceed in an orderly fashion to the nurses' quarters and if that barbarian matron there gives you any problems tell her I gave you permission.'

'That's very kind of you, sir,' Joe said saluting smartly.

The barbarian matron turned out to be a sweetie in Joe's estimation, and when a very surprised Sadie appeared in the reception area the elderly woman allowed the two to use her office and even sent a nurse for some tea.

'I had to see you, Sadie,' Joe told her. 'I'm going back off leave tomorrow.'

'I know,' Sadie replied, stroking the back of his hand. 'Everyone seems ter be goin' back termorrer. The boys, Con, and now you too. I'm gonna miss yer, Joe.'

'I'm gonna miss you too, Sadie,' he replied. 'I know we've already said our goodbyes but I couldn't get the picture of you out of me head. I needed to see you once more, just to look at you so I can keep it fresh in me mind.'

361

'You took a chance o' gettin' court-martialled just ter take anuvver look at me?' Sadie said shaking her head slowly. 'I should feel gratified, but I'm not, I'm angry. You're incorrigible.'

'Is that contagious?' he asked, smiling easily.

Her composure slipped and she gave him a big grin and leapt into his arms. 'Take this back off leave with yer,' she said, kissing him passionately on the lips.

The matron peered into the room and Sadie quickly straightened her dress. 'He's just leaving, matron,' she announced.

Joe strolled out of the hospital whistling happily, smiling at the nurses and a nervous-looking sailor in reception. With a bit of luck his next tour of duty would be in the North Atlantic, which meant he would be home again before too many months, providing his ship steered clear of the marauding U-Boats.

CHAPTER 30

It was a very quiet Christmas for the Carter Lane folk. The Luftwaffe stayed away but with the shadow still hanging over their lives the Yuletide was celebrated in a reserved and thoughtful way. For many families it was a time to drink to their absent sons and reflect hopefully on what the new year would bring. Con Williams and the Flynn boys had now reached the Middle East, as had Chris Wickstead with his battalion of Royal

Fusiliers. Ivy Jones' son Jerry had been posted to Scotland with his Royal Marine squadron and throughout the festive season they were engaged in training for a special mission behind enemy lines. Freddie Bromilow the Grenadier joined his battalion just before Christmas to learn that they were bound for India and Dennis Wilson was serving on a destroyer somewhere in the North Atlantic. As for Big Joe Buckley, he was surprised to learn that he and Petty Officer Stone had been awarded the Distinguished Service Medal, also awarded posthumously to Petty Officer Chivers and Leading Seaman Preston. He also learned that he was being sent to Plymouth for further underwater training.

With Christmas over the raids began again, but after the severe bombardment of December the twenty-ninth, when the Thames was at its lowest ebb and the City of London burned all night, the raids became more spasmodic. It was during this time that the work done by the Royal Engineer bomb-disposal squad was properly assessed, and for his part in saving the children's hospital Sapper Alec Conroy was awarded the Military Medal. People now began to sleep more in their own beds, though they were often roused by the wailing of the air-raid siren in the dead of night, and it was time too for the ARP personnel in the command post in Carter Lane to wind down their operations. Both Karen Watson and Nigel Bayley immersed themselves in their daily jobs, and any pleasure in getting back to normality was overshadowed by their sadness at seeing less of each other.

As the bitterly cold winter gave way to a mild spring, people felt as if they were slowly emerging from a long dark tunnel. Light nights were ahead and sunny days, but the menace was still there, and it was brutally brought home by a sudden and savage air attack in early May. The Luftwaffe flew over in strength, once again picking the night when the Thames was at its lowest for the year. The raid started at six thirty in the evening and wave after wave of bombers flew over the capital leaving devastation in their wake. Their prime targets were the docks and the East End and during the eight-hour raid seven hundred tons of high explosive and one hundred thousand incendiary bombs were dropped. Almost fifteen hundred people died that night and eighteen hundred more were injured.

Dolly Flynn and Liz Kenny worked around the clock with their canteen van and Mick Flynn, Bill Harris and Bert Kenny felt utterly exhausted as they fought ceaselessly with the rest of the fire watchers to put out the incendiaries. Jennie and Peggy Freen pedalled to and fro carrying messages and during one sortie Irene Copley was knocked off her bicycle by blast and badly shaken up.

The morning came as a blessed relief and people went to work still in shock, dreading what the coming nights had in store for them, but they were not to know at the time that the terrible night they had just experienced was indeed the end of the Blitz. The Germans had now turned their attention eastwards and Russia was suddenly invaded. More bombs were to fall on the capital at various times but in comparison the damage and casualties were light.

Summer days were arriving and operations to repair the battered capital were quickly getting under way. Dolly and Liz were now made redundant and the firemen at the Old Kent Road station presented them both with signed illuminated certificates of merit. Jennie Flynn took her leave of the command post, and Karen and Nigel spent some time together tidying up the converted house that held so many memories of warm caresses in stolen moments and secret kisses. Now it was time to move on, and Karen felt particularly sad as she made her weekly trip to the nursing home tucked away in the pretty countryside of Buckinghamshire.

Life had been sweet and kind to her in the years before the war. She had met Douglas Price, a fellow student, at a college dance and they immediately fell in love. Two years later they were married and Douglas followed his father into the family's engineering business. The young couple lived in a nice house in Buckinghamshire and enjoyed all the trappings of wealth, travelling abroad and partying on a lavish scale. Then tragedy struck. Douglas was riding his powerful motorcycle through a country lane one dark night when he was hit head-on by a speeding car. For almost a month the young man lay in a coma with massive head injuries, and when he finally regained consciousness the doctors realised that he had suffered irreversible brain damage. Douglas was now imprisoned in a broken body, dependent on others for his every need.

As she sat in the train, watching the colours of summer flash past the window, Karen relived those terrible early days after the accident. The trauma of the constant vigil at his bedside and the horror and devastation she felt when the doctors spoke with her and Douglas's father had never fully left her, and only the compassion and unselfish love shown by Nigel Bayley had helped to comfort her and give her some relief, albeit brief and occasional.

The room was sunlit and quiet, tastefully decorated, and they were left alone, with a call button at hand should Karen need assistance. Douglas sat slumped in the wheelchair, his body at an awkward angle, his head tilted unnaturally as he mumbled unintelligible words, his tongue hanging out of his mouth and dribbling on to a pad fixed to his front. He was frail and his condition was getting worse, but Karen smiled bravely as she tried to communicate with him. She spoke of mundane things, of flowers in bloom, of the pink roses that Douglas had once cultivated to arch over their front door and along the wall of the house. She persevered, but it was like trying to draw water from a dry well. He had left her for ever, that bright spirit of his trapped in a limbo, his eyes rolling and his hands twisting in spidery gestures.

He closed his eyes in sleep and Karen sat staring at him, angry at the arbitrary, meaningless blow fate had dealt them. A young man with everything to live for, now lost to the world in a wheelchair, his life irrevocably snapped. And every time she thought it would be better for him to die she felt horribly guilty for wishing his life away. He still breathed and moved, and inside that damaged brain his feelings and intelligence might still somehow be intact, like a prisoner in dead flesh. She could sense a presence in his manner, in his rolling eyes. Was he trying to tell her of his suffering, or remembering the time they had together? She would never know, but she must never desert him or forsake him, not while the tiniest spark of life remained. God would never forgive her. Forsaking all others, in sickness and in health, till death us do part. Thank goodness for Nigel. He understood fully, and made her existence bearable.

Karen sat deep in thought as she travelled back to war-scarred London. The doctors had told her that Douglas was losing his fight and at most he would only survive for a few more months. She almost shut her ears and her mind to the news, lest she wish the time away. Better too that she did not tell Nigel the news. Better to carry on as though nothing had changed, enjoy the brief, incomplete moments with him and remain at some kind of peace with herself.

Through the long summer months of 1941 the women of Carter Lane stuck together in a common bond of support and encouragement. They still knitted woollens for the forces and met together on Friday evenings in the saloon bar of The Sun to chat and exchange news. A letter received from a serving son was proudly brought along and read out to the rest without any inhibitions. Maps of the war situation published in the newspapers were studied and particular attention was paid to the war in the Libyan desert where the Eighth Army were fighting.

The younger women were drawing closer too and Brenda Ross made a point of calling round to the Flynn home whenever she got a letter from Pat. He was now based in East Anglia and flying on bombing missions to the heart of Germany. Jennie had never really got to know Brenda very well, but now with both their boyfriends on active service the two women grew closer.

'D'you know what, Brenda, I fink you an' me should 'ave a night out,' Jennie said to her one evening.

'We could go ter the pictures,' Brenda suggested.

'I was finkin' more of goin' dancin',' Jennie told her.

'I used ter like dancin' but I dunno,' Brenda said hesitantly. 'It could get a bit tricky.'

' 'Ow d'yer mean?'

'Well, when it gets ter the last dance.'

'Yeah, there's always some flash feller fancyin' 'is chances,' Jennie agreed, 'but we don't 'ave ter wait till the last dance.'

'I dunno, it could be awkward tryin' ter get away, especially if some feller's got 'is eye on yer.'

'You're prob'ly right,' Jennie conceded. 'We'll go ter the flicks instead then.'

'When?'

'This Saturday night?'

'Okay, you're on.'

Pat Flynn was now a flight sergeant and tail gunner on a Wellington Bomber, and he shared his billet with another flight sergeant by the name of Tom Darcy with whom he had become very friendly. Tom loved poetry and spent a lot of his free time reading the works of the greats, Chaucer, Spenser and Dryden, as well as Tennyson and the earthy verse of Kipling. 'All life is there in the works of those poets,' Tom remarked to Pat as they lounged on the grass outside their billet one hot September day.

'Well, I 'ave ter say that one about goin' off ter the wars certainly touched Brenda,' Pat replied. 'It said all I wanted ter say.'

'I suppose in fifty years' time there'll be poems taught in schools about this war and the effect it had on people's lives,' Tom said thoughtfully.

' 'Ow come you got interested in poetry?' Pat asked him.

'I dunno really,' Tom reflected. 'Maybe it was escapism, trying to find beauty where it didn't exist.'

'In the land of dark satanic mills,' Pat said smiling.

'Yeah, sort of,' Tom said, shifting his position on the grass. 'I was born in the Midlands and we moved around a lot as a family, but my lasting memories of that time are belching chimneys and damp foggy days spent in the sloping cobble-stoned streets of little industrial towns. I was very young when we lived there, then when I was about ten or eleven we settled in Derbyshire. Christ, what a difference. There on our doorstep were the peaks, and I used to spend hours just tramping up those slopes to the top. The views were like nothing I could describe, with shades of colours and shifting textures stretching as far as the eye could see. Poetry can describe such a landscape though. Tennyson can.'

'It's far removed from the business we're in though,' Pat replied soberly. 'When we're goin' out I look down over the countryside an' marvel at the sheer beauty of it, an' then we cross the Channel wiv our load o' bombs, our bomb-aimer presses the button an' whoosh.'

'That's war,' Tom sighed. 'They come over and try to turn our cities into burning ruins and we do the same to them, only the difference is, they'll get it tenfold, twentyfold. The rumour is we'll be getting four-engine bombers next year. The Lancaster, I believe it's called. The bomb-load will be greater and the destruction more widely spread. But we have to remember that the London Blitz didn't bomb the people into submission and I don't honestly think that we can bomb the German people into submission either.'

'I s'pose not,' Pat agreed, 'but if we succeed in destroyin' their war industry it'll certainly shorten the war.'

Tom Darcy nodded. 'Keep that conviction

370

at the front of your mind, Pat, and you'll stay sane,' he said smiling.

'And you keep readin' that poetry book of yours,' Pat replied.

Tom got up and brushed the loose grass cuttings from his uniform. 'We'd better get ready for the briefing,' he remarked, then when Pat had straightened his jacket he said, 'By the way. If I cop it before you I want you to have this book. I've already said so inside the cover, look.'

Pat read the words. ' "To Patrick Flynn, my good pal, with best wishes for a safe and successful tour of ops." Fanks, Tom. I dunno what ter say.'

'There's nothing to say,' Tom said with a carefree smile. 'Come on, let's go.'

Inside the briefing hut a hubbub of voices was suddenly stilled as the station commander and his executive officer stepped on to the rostrum. 'Our target for tonight is Essen,' he announced. 'Visibility status is expected to be light cloud and a full moon.'

The subsequent murmur of voices stopped when the commander held up his hand. 'We have information that a squadron of German night fighters has moved into the Utrecht area of Holland, so be on your guard. That's all. Will pilots and navigators please remain.'

Once outside the hut Tom put his arm round Pat's shoulders. 'I hope I didn't get to you,' he said, 'talking about bequests.'

'Of course not,' Pat told him. 'This time termorrer we'll be sunnin' ourselves as usual.'

As they strolled over to the mess hut Tom suddenly smiled. 'I'm writing a piece of poetry.'

'Is that a fact,' Pat said grinning back. 'Can I take a look?'

'I'd prefer it if you waited till it's finished,' Tom confessed.

'I'll look forward to it, Tom.'

The evening grew dark and the roar of engines shattered the countryside quiet and bent the long grass. Laden Wellingtons taxied out to the runway, roaring off into the night sky one after the other, moving into formation as they climbed to operational height. Soon they were passing over the moonlit North Sea towards the coast of Holland and Pat heard his pilot give the order to test the guns. The short burst was repeated by other planes, and then there was only the steady drone of the engines as the formation flew on towards their allotted target in the heart of the Ruhr.

CHAPTER 31

With the Nazi war machine directed towards Russia and the threat of invasion diminishing, people began to change their way of thinking. There was a difference of tone in the papers and in broadcasts on the wireless, an apparently concerted effort to get the populace to change from their siege mentality to a more positive outlook. Metal collections were redoubled and people were encouraged to hand in all their old pots and pans and any scrap metal they had to aid the war effort. Competitions were held throughout the country for slogans urging folk to buy savings certificates, producing such gems as 'Lend your money to defend, freedom is the dividend', and in Carter Lane the knitting circle was encouraged by the Lockwood sisters to keep up their efforts.

More and more young men were being called up and single women were now required to register for war-work. Incoming convoys were suffering terrible losses at the hands of the U-Boats and certain foods became scarce in the shops. Life at home continued to wear a wartime cloak, but cinemas and dance halls were still open for business and football matches and greyhound racing meetings took place as usual. Another year was drawing to its end and maps took up more space in the newspapers as the fighting in the Middle East intensified. Every day there were accounts in the papers and on the wireless of the RAF bombing missions into the heart of Germany, and the inevitable postscript: 'Some of our planes failed to return.'

At an RAF bomber base somewhere in Lincolnshire there was a general feeling of relief when news came through that bombing raids were to be suspended for three weeks after that coming night's operation, allowing the air crews to train on the new type of aircraft coming off the production lines. There was talk too that maybe some leave would be available. The squadron had taken a terrible pounding during the last few months and the number of crew replacements had now overtaken the original number of personnel present when the base first became operational.

'There's going to be a change of tactics when we get the Lancaster,' Tom Darcy remarked to Pat. 'With four-engined bombers we'll be going right into Eastern Germany and the Balkans.'

'Don't remind me,' Pat replied. 'Essen's far enough.'

Tom ran a hand over his face and leaned back on his bed. 'Terry Tomlinson and his crew have just completed their tour of ops,' he said.

Pat shook his head. 'They're well due for their rest. God, I've only done seven.'

'I've got nine,' Tom told him. 'To be honest I thought the Essen raid was going to be my last. Fensome did a marvellous job coaxing the old crate back home.'

Pat studied his friend. The strain was telling on him and he wondered if Tom got the same impression about him. 'If we get any leave I'm gonna spend mine sleepin' an' gettin' drunk, in that order.'

Tom grinned. 'No, you won't. You'll be awake early, tossing and turning and trying to get back to sleep again, and then you'll be kicking your heels for most of the day. In the evenings you'll take that girlfriend of yours to the flicks or dancing, then when it all gets too much you'll be glad to get back here.'

'You've gotta be jossin' me,' Pat laughed. 'There's no way I'll be lookin' forward ter comin' back ter this camp, ter this God-forsaken part o' the country.'

Tom grinned. 'All right, you just wait and see,' he replied. 'When I got that shell splinter in my shoulder on my second trip and they patched me up I got a seven-day pass. It was lovely for the first couple of days, but then I got restless. My girlfriend got me looking at engagement rings at every opportunity and she was constantly making plans for us after the war was over. How could I tell her that every time we go on a bombing mission the odds shorten and we'll be bloody lucky to live to see the end of the year, let alone the war.'

'We'll see it out,' Pat said encouragingly. 'You an' me both.'

'I like your style,' Tom Darcy replied. 'Ever the optimist.'

'What else is there?'

'Acceptance.'

'Of what? Not reaching the magical twenty ops?'

Tom leaned forward on the bed, clasping his hands. 'Yeah, that's about it,' he said quietly. 'I've accepted that sooner or later I'm going to cop it, and I've told myself that it doesn't matter whether it's on the next trip or the nineteenth. That way I don't worry so much. All right, I say a silent prayer every time we lift off, but then after that I try not to think about it. I think about the poetry I've read that day, and I look around at the planes flying in formation and wonder what torments the crews are suffering as we approach the target. It makes me feel detached, complacent in a way, though not about my job on that mission. I realise that I'm there in that tail bubble to help protect the aircraft and crew, but I tell myself that everyone on the flight's tempting fate, the hunter with a giant hand that can reach out and pluck any of us out of the sky in a moment. Sometimes when we turn for home and my spirits surge I start to think about a piece of poetry that's impressed me and try to add my own verses to it. That's my acceptance, Pat my friend.'

Pat Flynn was quiet for a while, absorbing what Tom had said, then he swung his legs over the edge of the bed and sat facing him. 'It's said that we should all be aware of our mortality, Tom, but I couldn't function if I 'ad ter dwell on that advice,' he replied. 'I look forward to a bright future in a peaceful world, wiv a wife an' kids, a nice 'ome ter live in an' a good job ter go to. I dream about my kids growin' up wivout the fear of war, an' eventually bringin' their kids round ter see us. That's what I cling to. That's what keeps me from crackin' up.'

'You hang on to that, Pat,' his friend said smiling. 'Dream hard enough and it'll see you through.'

On Saturday night Brenda and Jennie walked arm in arm to the Trocadero cinema at the Elephant and Castle and sat through a dreary pre-war melodrama, in which the heroine finally died of consumption and the hero sought comfort in the arms of the heroine's younger sister. Jennie wiped the occasional tear away

376

while Brenda was still trying unsuccessfully to get involved in the story. Her thoughts were elsewhere, prompted by the letter from Pat that she carried in her handbag, and as the film drew to its close she had finalised her own script. She would be the heroine and Pat the hero, but their story would have a happy ending. Daring, shocking, and one to keep the people talking.

'Stupid film,' Jennie said sniffing, as they walked out into the moonlit night.

'Yeah, it was a bit morbid, wasn't it?' Brenda agreed as they set off home along the New Kent Road.

'Never mind, it'll be great ter see Pat next weekend,' Jennie reminded her.

'I can't wait,' Brenda sighed. 'I'm takin' the followin' week off. I wanna spend as much time as I can wiv 'im. I've only seen 'im twice this year an' I'm missin' 'im terrible.'

Jennie smiled sympathetically. 'Those forty-eight-hour passes don't give yer much time tergevver, do they?'

Brenda shook her head. 'When I got the letter this mornin' I answered it straight away,' she said. 'Pat should get it early next week. I told 'im I was takin' the week off an' I said ...'

'It's all right, luv, yer don't need ter tell me,' Jennie said, sensing her friend's sudden embarrassment.

'Jennie, would yer mind me askin' you a very personal question?' Brenda ventured.

'Nah, course not,' Jennie replied with a smile. 'We are good friends.'

' 'Ave you ... I mean, are you an' Con ...'

'Lovers?'

'Yeah, that's what I was tryin' ter say.'

'We made love the night before 'e went back off leave,' Jennie said matter-of-factly. 'It was the first time fer us an' I wanted ter give Con somefing ter remember while 'e's away. I'm pretty certain 'e'd never made love wiv a gel before an' it made what we did seem right an' good. What must it be like fer a young man ter go off an' fight a war wivout ever experiencin' love.'

'Me an' Pat 'ave never done it,' Brenda said bravely, encouraged by Jennie's forthrightness.

'No, I didn't fink you 'ad,' Jennie remarked.

'Does it show wiv us?'

'No, it's just circumstances that make me say that,' Jennie replied. 'You an' Pat were like two little peas in a pod when you were kids. Love didn't come along an' kick you right where it 'urts, it was always there, an' I imagine it grew wiv yer both. I've always thought that you two would find it difficult ter suddenly become lovers in the full sense o' the word. You know what they say, chaste down the aisle an' chased into bed.'

'You're very perceptive,' Brenda told her, 'an' you're dead right. We agreed ter wait till after we were married, but fings 'ave changed now. Like you just said, 'ow terrible fer a young man ter die wivout knowin' what love was all about. 'Ow terrible fer the gel that's left wiv nuffink for 'er to 'ang on to.'

They held arms tightly as they turned into

378

the Old Kent Road, sensing a new closeness between them.

'I'm scared, Jennie,' Brenda said suddenly. 'I'm scared that one day Pat won't return from a bombin' mission an' I'll be left alone. I can't let that 'appen.'

'It won't, luv,' Jennie said kindly. 'You an' Pat were made fer each ovver an' you'll get married one day when all this is over. I'm sure God's lookin' out fer the two of yer.'

'I was gonna tell yer about that letter I sent to 'im,' Brenda remarked. 'I told 'im just 'ow I felt an' I said I wanted us ter become lovers. Does that sound awful?'

Jennie laughed aloud. 'I fink it sounds wonderful.'

'I want us ter go away fer a week, somewhere nice an' quiet in the country,' Brenda went on.

They turned into the backstreets, walking through Defoe Street into Carter Lane, and Brenda turned to face her confidante as they reached her front door. 'Fanks fer lettin' me bend yer ear,' she said smiling.

'An' fank you fer lettin' me in on yer plans,' Jennie replied, returning her friend's smile. 'Yer secret's safe wiv me. You two should grab every bit of 'appiness yer can. Me an' Con did, an' it'll sustain us both while we're apart.'

Brenda smiled shyly as she reached into her handbag for her front-door key. 'It won't be much of a secret when both our families find out we intend ter spend a week away tergevver,' she remarked.

'Don't let it worry yer, Brenda. You can 'andle it, I'm sure,' Jennie replied with a saucy wink.

Pat Flynn's mind dwelt on the coming leave as he fitted himself into the cramped gun turret. 'Please God get me through this night,' he mouthed aloud as the engines roared into life.

The Wellington Bomber lifted up into the night sky, banking to join the gathering air armada that was bound for Cologne. The planes flew in tactical formation out towards Holland, above a sea that looked calm and empty. Ahead there were gauntlets of gunfire to run, and maybe night fighters to contend with, but for the moment there was just the noise of the calibrated engines. As they neared the target, flak began to burst around them and they could see fires raging from incendiaries dropped by the pathfinders. Over the target the calm voice of the bomb-aimer could be heard on the intercom. 'Left, left, steady now. Bombs away!'

Bursting cannon shells splintered fuselages and peppered wings, and Pat saw a Wellington going down in flames. 'Did anyone get out?' the pilot shouted into the intercom.

'No one.'

Another Wellington lost a wing and it spiralled down, and yet another spurted flame from one of its engines.

'All right, chaps, let's get this kite back to Blighty. Christ! We're losing oil from the port engine.'

Another bomber lost its tail section and turned over before dropping down in a large arc. Pat saw three parachutes billowing out below and gritted his teeth. If the three were lucky they'd spend the rest of the war in a prison camp, but stories were emerging of flyers being killed summarily by Gestapo units. Gunfire increased and the pilot made a quick manoeuvre to dodge the searchlights, then came the race for the coast. The port engine was faltering but they managed to maintain their height and Pat experienced a glorious feeling of release as the enemy coast slipped away below them.

The remainder of the journey home was accomplished with crossed fingers as the port engine threatened to pack up altogether and it spluttered and faded as the airfield came into view. The pilot made a perfect touchdown, and as the plane taxied to the side apron the jeeps were ready. The tired, shaky crew were transported to the debriefing hut where other crews were already giving their accounts of the mission.

'I saw number seven go down in flames.'

'I can confirm that.'

'Did anyone get out?'

'No one.'

'There was no time.'

Tom and his crew had not returned and Pat sat on the step of the billet waiting for any stragglers to fly in, but as the dawn light filtered into the sky he realised with sickness in his stomach that the names of Tom Darcy and his crew would join the ever-growing list of flyers killed in action.

The lonely billet was hard to face now. All that remained were a few possessions in the locker, and the book of poems lying there on the bottom of Tom's crumpled bed. 'What does it matter,' he had said. 'The ninth or the nineteenth.' He was gone now, for ever, his spirit lost to earth among the heavens.

The book was dog-eared from constant use, the cover grubby and stained, but Pat clutched it to his chest with delicate reverence, the most valuable book he would ever hold. The days ahead would never be the same now and he slumped down on Tom's unmade bed, his tears falling as he cried in the painful solitude of the quiet billet.

CHAPTER 32

Brenda Ross was employed as a secretary in an old-established firm of solicitors in the City and her elderly boss was very sympathetic to her request for a week off outside the holiday season. She had been truthful in explaining that her future husband was coming home on leave and she wished to spend some time with him. Simon Whatley was aware that Brenda's young man was a flyer, and with a son of his own flying Spitfires he knew just how she felt.

'Yes, of course we'll manage, Brenda,' he said

kindly. 'Miss Fredericks can stand in for you and it'll give her some good experience. You just enjoy your time together.'

Frank and Iris Ross were not so accommodating however, and they reacted with alarm and dismay that their daughter could be so brazen as to go away for a whole week with Pat Flynn before they were married.

'It's not right,' Iris told her. 'Me an' yer farvver 'ave always tried ter bring yer up right an' you end up lettin' us both down. I'm really shocked.'

Brenda shrugged her shoulders. 'I'm sorry, Mum, but you 'ave to understand the way fings are,' she replied. 'Me an' Pat are gonna get married anyway when the war's over an' if we could we'd get married sooner.'

'That's not the point,' Iris went on. 'A young gel should go ter the altar pure. The ovver business should wait.'

Brenda looked at her mother with disgust. 'Ovver business? Is that what you call it?' she stormed. 'I'd prefer ter call it love.'

'Well, I'd call it lust,' Iris said sharply. 'You young gels don't seem to 'ave any morals at all. I tell you somefing, I wouldn't 'ave dared go ter my muvver wiv the news that I was gonna spend a week away wiv a young man. Me an' yer farvver did fings right an' we expect you ter do the same.'

'Yeah, but you've gotta remember it was peacetime when you an' Dad got married,' Brenda puffed. 'The war's changed fings, changed people's way of lookin' at fings.'

'Oh yeah, blame the war,' Iris growled. 'I s'pose yer'll blame the war if yer go an' get yerself pregnant.'

Brenda felt tears of anger rising and she swallowed hard. 'Turn that wireless on any mornin' an' listen ter the news,' she said furiously. 'Yer'll 'ear about last night's bombin' raid over Germany. Listen ter the end of it, the bit about the number o' planes that failed to return. I listen to it, an' every time I 'ear those words I go ice cold. I fink of Pat an' I wonder if the Flynns are gonna be one o' the families who get a telegram ter say their son's amongst the crews shot down. The way I see it, Pat's livin' on borrered time an' me an' 'im are gonna grab what 'appiness we can while we can, an' if God willin' 'e survives the war I'll be quite 'appy ter walk down the aisle wivout wearin' white.'

Iris realised that she was never going to make her daughter see reason and she sighed in resignation. 'I can't stop yer doin' what yer've planned but fer goodness sake be careful,' she warned. 'I couldn't 'old me 'ead up round 'ere if yer got yerself pregnant.'

On the cold autumn weekend that Brenda and Pat were reunited, Sadie came home to hear that Joe had managed to get a forty-eight-hour pass.

'Joe called in an' we've 'ad a nice chat,' Dolly told her. 'I said to 'im yer'd give 'im a knock soon as yer got 'ome.'

'I must look a right mess,' Sadie fussed as

she studied herself in the parlour wall mirror.

'Yer look just fine, luv,' Dolly remarked, 'but before yer go there's somefing in terday's paper I wanna show yer. It's about that Macaulay bloke. 'E's bin shot dead.'

'Shot dead? I can't believe it!' Sadie gasped as she grabbed the newspaper.

'Bermondsey Businessman Murdered.

The body of Johnnie Macaulay was discovered late last night on the steps of a Brighton hotel. He had been shot twice in the chest and was pronounced dead on arrival at the hospital.

Macaulay was a successful Bermondsey businessman and entrepreneur whose interests included boxing and greyhound racing. He was recently involved in a business deal with a South Coast consortium and the Brighton police have declined to make any comment other than that they are treating his death as murder.'

'You did the right fing givin' Len Regan the elbow,' Dolly told her. 'Whoever killed Macaulay could be after Regan too.'

'I've gone all cold,' Sadie said in a shocked voice. 'I met some o' these people once an' they scared me ter death.'

'Well, it's not your worry now,' Dolly said positively.

Sadie hurried along to the Kennys' house and Big Joe met her at the front door with a big hug. 'You look very nice,' he said smiling broadly.

385

'I've just got 'ome,' Sadie replied. 'My 'air looks a real mess.'

'How about me taking you out for something to eat,' Joe suggested.

'Now?'

'Why not?'

'Where can we go?'

'What about your old Saturday usual?'

'Pie an' mash?'

'If you like.'

'I'd love it,' Sadie said enthusiastically.

'I'll just go and get me cap,' Joe said. 'I don't wanna get caught improperly dressed, though there's not much chance of running into a shore patrol in the Old Kent Road.'

They strolled out of Carter Lane chatting busily, with Sadie holding his arm and leaning close against him. 'This is a lovely surprise,' she remarked as they walked out into the Old Kent Road.

'I'm being posted abroad very soon,' he told her. 'I don't know where yet but the old bush telegraph has it as Gibraltar.'

'Will you get embarkation leave, Joe?' she asked.

He shook his head and sighed. 'It's all very hush-hush. We could be off like a bucket o' prawns in the sun.'

They walked into the pie shop and joined the queue, watching as the shop assistant served up steaming-hot meat pies and large scoops of mashed potato, topped with a liberal amount of parsley liquor, as well as stewed or jellied eels in thick china bowls.

'Do you know something,' Joe said. 'When I first arrived in London I couldn't abide this sort of food, but now I love it. Just watching it being served up makes me mouth water.'

'Yeah, me too,' Sadie replied. 'When we were kids I used ter take our tribe down ter Manzies' pie shop in Tower Bridge Road fer our Saturday dinner. I was in charge o' the money.'

'Do you wanna double up?' Joe asked her.

'Double up?'

'Yeah, have a double portion.'

'No, I couldn't manage that much, but you double up,' she told him smiling.

They were finally served and they found a bench seat at the back of the crowded establishment, chatting together between mouthfuls of food, and later as they strolled along the wide thoroughfare looking at the shops Joe slipped his arm around her waist and steered her to a vacant wooden bench beneath a tall spreading plane tree. 'Let's sit down for a second, I've got something to show you,' he said mysteriously.

Sadie waited intrigued as Joe took a tiny cloth-covered box from his greatcoat pocket. 'I want you to have this,' he said, opening the box with care.

Sadie saw the ring with its single diamond and gasped. 'You mean this is fer me?'

Joe nodded. 'It's been sewn into the side of a grubby old bag o' mine for years, an' even when I was living on the bones of me arse without a brass razoo I never dreamt of selling it. It was left in trust for me when I was a kid and I could never find out who it was from. It's been like a big silent mystery in me life, and it made me think that sometimes something happens to you that's too mysterious and too big for you to understand. I felt like I wanted to give it to you.'

Sadie stared down at it and blinked hard before she looked up into his deep blue eyes. 'What a lovely thought,' she said with feeling.

Joe looked embarrassed as he took the ring from the box. 'Let me see if it fits your finger,' he said.

'It's perfect,' she sighed.

Joe smiled and was taken by surprise as Sadie kissed him on the lips. 'I'm glad you like it,' he said.

'Like it? I love it,' she whispered. 'It's so beautiful.'

They set off back to Carter Lane with Sadie chatting eagerly about her nursing job, trying to calm the excitement fluttering inside her, and as they turned into Defoe Street a large car pulled up beside them. Sadie turned and saw Nosher beckoning to her and she leant down to the open window.

'I was just comin' round ter see yer, Sadie,' he told her urgently. 'It's all gone boss-eyed. Macaulay's bin done in an' Len Regan's 'idin' out.'

'I read about Macaulay,' Sadie replied. 'It was in terday's paper.'

'Len wants to see yer,' Nosher said. 'There ain't much time.'

Sadie looked at Big Joe anxiously and he

nodded. 'It's all right, I'll come with you,' he said.

'I dunno about that,' Nosher replied quickly.

Big Joe fixed the older man with a hard look. 'She goes nowhere without me, mate,' he growled.

'All right then, I ain't got time to argue wiv yer,' Nosher said impatiently. 'Get in.'

They climbed into the back of the large saloon car and Nosher put his foot down, swinging it back into the Old Kent Road. 'Regan's 'idin' out in Lambeth,' he said. ' 'E's wiv Donna Walsh. You remember 'er?'

'Yeah, I remember 'er,' Sadie replied.

Joe looked bemused by the situation and he glanced at Sadie. 'This Macaulay joker. Wasn't he the gang boss you were telling me about?'

'Yeah,' Nosher piped in. 'I run Macaulay down ter Brighton two days ago an' then yesterday Len Regan told me ter stand by ter take 'im down there too. The next fing I know is the Walsh gel's bangin' on me front door last night. Two geezers came in the George pub askin' fer Len, an' when 'e fronted 'em one o' the bastards knifed 'im.'

'Oh my God!' Sadie gasped. ' 'Ow terrible. Is 'e 'urt bad?'

' 'E got it in the stomach but they fetched a doctor ter patch 'im up. 'E'll be all right so the quack said but 'e's very weak from loss o' blood. It's that bastard Brighton mob what done it, excuse me language.'

'What does 'e want wiv me?' Sadie asked him.

Nosher shrugged his shoulders. 'Donna Walsh 'as cracked up an' Len's fast run out o' friends. We're all 'e's got left.'

They reached the Elephant and Castle and crossed the wide thoroughfare into Lambeth Road. 'I'll need ter drop yer off short,' Nosher told them. 'There may be someone on the lookout an' they'll recognise the car. I'll wait where I drop you off till I 'ear from yer. It's number nineteen Fensome Lane, 'alfway down Lambeth Walk. Be careful 'ow yer go.'

Sadie and Joe walked along the main road and turned into the little backstreet trying to look as unobtrusive as possible, but they were observed by two bulky men wearing dark overcoats who were standing across the street. As they reached the front door of number 19 the two men had come up behind them. 'Visitin' Mr Regan, are we?' one asked.

Joe turned round casually. 'I don't know about you two, but we've come to see Mrs Brown,' he said calmly.

'On yer way, sailor boy, an' take yer bit o' skirt wiv yer,' the man growled. 'This 'ouse is out o' bounds.'

'Shut your bunghole and choof off, drongo,' Joe growled back at him as he raised his hand to the doorknocker.

One of the men grabbed Joe by the lapels of his coat while the other one quickly pulled out a switchblade but the big Australian butted the first one across the bridge of his nose and swung him round toward the knifeman. Sadie had moved away out of reach and she watched in awe as Joe threw the bloodied villain at his compatriot and smartly planted a size eleven shoe in a tender spot. The man screamed out as he doubled up and Joe punched the knifeman in the throat and grabbed his wrist. The switchblade went spinning into the gutter and the few onlookers who had stopped to watch stood wide-eyed as the assailant did a cartwheel on to the pavement. A broken nose, a dislocated shoulder and a painful groin were enough to send the two villains scampering off in panic and Joe smiled. 'That navy training is the bloody business,' he remarked. 'Are you okay?'

Sadie nodded, still trying to control her shaking. 'I've never bin so frightened in all me life,' she gasped.

Donna Walsh looked pale and gaunt as she led the two into the dark passage and up the bare staircase to the first floor. ' 'E's in 'ere,' she said, pushing open the door and standing to one side.

Sadie and Joe walked into the dingy room and saw Len Regan sitting back in an armchair with his hand pressed to his side. He was unshaven and dressed in bloodstained trousers and a heavy sweater. 'I'm sorry, Sadie, but I 'ad ter try an' contact yer,' he said in a tired voice. 'Yer've 'eard about Johnnie?'

'Yeah, it was in the papers.'

The villain looked up at Joe. 'Are you ...?'

'My boyfriend,' Sadie cut in. 'An' yer've got 'im ter fank fer sortin' out those two 'orrible gits outside.'

'You sorted 'em out?' Len replied with a surprised look.

'Yeah, they weren't very friendly,' Joe said sarcastically.

'I'm sorry, Sadie, but I thought yer'd come alone an' I was 'opin' they'd fink you was visitin' the people upstairs.'

'Well, it's a good job I didn't come alone,' she countered.

Len winced at the pain in his side. 'I really didn't want you dragged inter this,' he puffed, 'but Donna's crackin' up an' she can't 'andle it. Those two goons outside were just watchin' in case I tried ter get away. The big man 'imself's due any time now an' I'm trapped 'ere.'

'Who's the big man?' Sadie asked.

'It doesn't matter, you wouldn't know 'im anyway, but 'e's out ter get me the same way 'e got Johnnie.'

'But why?' Sadie asked in confusion.

'It's too long a story an' too complicated,' Len replied, 'but if I tell yer Johnnie Macaulay was rippin' the consortium off yer'll understand.'

'Skimming the profits?' Joe remarked.

Len nodded. 'That an' more. I warned Johnnie but 'e wouldn't listen. 'E underestimated 'em. Country bumpkins 'e called 'em. Some bumpkins.'

'We gotta get you out of 'ere before those two get some 'elp,' Sadie said anxiously. 'Joe, 'elp 'im up an' I'll get Donna.'

They stepped out into the afternoon sunlight with Sadie holding on to the distraught Donna's arm and Joe following, holding up Regan.

Two streets away they saw the car and it quickly drove across to them. Len Regan was manoeuvred into the front seat of the saloon then Sadie, Donna and Joe climbed into the back, and Nosher breathed a huge sigh of relief as he accelerated away from the kerb. 'I wasn't sure if you was gonna make it,' he said, glancing quickly round at Sadie.

'Fanks a lot,' she replied with some humour, then she leaned forward and touched Len on the shoulder. ' 'Ave you got somewhere ter go?' she asked him.

'Yeah, I got a pal up North,' he told her. ' 'E'll let me an' Nosher stay there till fings quieten down.'

'An' then?'

'I've got some money stashed away,' Len replied. 'I'll start again. Me an' Nosher tergevver.'

Sadie looked at the woman sitting beside her, her bloated face wet with tears. 'An' Donna?'

'Yeah, Donna too,' Len said. 'She needs the country air more than I do.'

Joe and Sadie stepped out of the saloon on the corner of Lynton Road and set off to walk the short distance to Carter Lane.

'Joe, I'm sorry. I wouldn't 'ave wished this on yer for the world,' she said humbly.

He grinned a little lopsidedly, the grin that Sadie had come to love. 'No sweat, kid,' he replied.

'You were wonderful the way you 'andled those two men,' she told him.

'It was no trouble,' he said grinning even

393

wider. 'That character Popeye does it on spinach; Big Joe does it on pie an' mash. I just hope it's not all been in vain.'

' 'E'll make it,' Sadie remarked. 'I've learnt the 'ard way that Len Regan's a no-good, liberty-takin' git, but 'e's one o' those who'll fall over in shit an' come up smellin' o' roses. Besides 'e's got Nosher, an' Donna, God 'elp 'im.'

CHAPTER 33

Brenda had found the Gloucestershire country hotel in a Tatler magazine that was lying around in the waiting room at her office and it seemed perfect. There were nice colour photographs of the grounds, and the prices did not seem too expensive. It was advertised as being open all year round and ideal for a quiet retreat from wartime city life. With fingers crossed she phoned the hotel from the office during her lunchtime and was able to make a reservation for a week in a double room under the name of Mr and Mrs Parkes, her mother's maiden name. She then slipped out of the office and did something which she prayed she would be forgiven for. She went into a jeweller's shop and bought a cheap imitation gold band, the sort women wore when they had secretly pawned their wedding ring.

Brenda had always considered herself to be

394

a Christian, although she was not a regular churchgoer, and what she had done troubled her that afternoon. Maybe it would be taking the Lord's name in vain slipping on the ring without the blessing and vows, but in her heart she felt that God understood. She was doing this out of love, and if her plan worked out fully she would know that God had really colluded.

On Monday morning Brenda and Pat set off from Paddington Station, relaxing in a comfortable carriage along with two elderly ladies dressed in tweeds with hats pulled down over their coiffured grey hair. When the train pulled in at Swindon two soldiers got into the carriage and sat chatting quietly together. The ladies talked occasionally, mainly in monosyllables and nods, but everyone seemed to keep to themselves and Brenda was content. One slip of the tongue, one unthinking word might serve to ruin the pretence, and for a whole week they wanted to masquerade as Mr and Mrs Parkes.

It was mid-afternoon when the train pulled into Cirencester and soon the two young people were speeding through the country lanes in an ancient taxi. Pat was wearing his uniform with a brevet over the left breast pocket, a single wing and the letters AG enclosed. Brenda wore a heavy fawn winter coat and high-heeled shoes, with a silver scarf wrapped loosely around her neck. Her fair hair was cropped short and waved around her ears and she carried a brown leather handbag.

'There we are, sir,' the driver said as he

steered the car into the gravel drive of the Firscroft Hotel. 'I hope you'll enjoy your stay.'

Pat tipped the driver and Brenda suppressed a giggle as the man touched his forehead in a salute before driving off.

'Come on, Mrs Parkes,' Pat said with a grin as he picked up the large suitcase.

The proprietress smiled as she pushed the register towards Pat. 'We're usually pretty quiet at this time of year but we do have a few guests who stay here regularly,' she remarked. 'If you'll bear with me I'll see if I can find Norman. I'm Mrs Withers by the way. Actually I'm holding the fort for my husband. He's in the navy.'

Brenda took Pat's hand in hers and gave it an encouraging squeeze as the woman went out. She soon returned followed by an elderly man who shuffled along behind her with stooped shoulders.

'Show our guests to room sixteen, Norman,' Mrs Withers told him. 'Oh by the way, dinner's served from seven thirty till ten and breakfast is at seven till nine thirty. If there's anything you need, do come and see me.'

Norman led the way along a corridor grunting with the weight of the case and Pat wished he had offered to carry it. The florin brought a warm smile to the old man's face though and he shuffled off to make himself scarce.

Once they were alone Pat took Brenda in his arms and kissed her. 'Just fink of it,' he said sighing contentedly. 'One 'ole glorious week wiv just you an' me.'

She hugged him tightly. 'This'll be our

unofficial 'oneymoon an' I want it ter be perfect, Pat,' she said with feeling.

'It will be, darlin',' he told her. 'Let's unpack an' take a look round before dinner.'

The Firscroft was set amid rolling hills and was fairly isolated, with just a hamlet called Oakley about half a mile westwards. The two young people walked hand in hand along the winding lane towards the small village through a crisp carpet of fallen leaves. Overhead the sky was leaden, a winter dusk that brought a chill and Brenda shivered.

'You're cold, let's get back,' Pat said quickly.

'It's all right, I just 'ad a bad moment,' Brenda replied.

'A bad moment?'

'Yeah, I was just finkin' of us tergevver an' 'ow fragile it all is.'

'Not us. Not our feelin's,' Pat remarked with a supportive squeeze of her hand.

'No, not us, the situation we're in,' Brenda said sighing. 'I couldn't 'elp finkin' 'ow the war could so easily take it all away from us. All our plans, all the love we share. If anyfing 'appened ter you I could never share a love wiv anybody else.'

Pat was about to reply but the drone of an aircraft in the evening sky grew very loud as it passed overhead above the sodden clouds. Brenda was right, how fragile it all was. Fate was the hunter and life itself was made of fleeing moments, of happiness taken greedily and unashamedly, of filling one's cup to the full, and an acceptance of it all. 'Believe me, darlin', we'll grow old tergevver,' he said with conviction. 'You'll come ter feel it too, as time goes by.'

They had their evening meal in the tastefully decorated dining room and took the opportunity of discreetly studying the other guests. There was an elderly couple who hardly spoke, the heavy-set woman idly glancing around while her husband read a folded evening paper as he ate. Another couple were sitting nearby, younger and obviously in love. The man was paying a lot of attention to his vivacious partner and she responded with demure smiles. Another guest sat alone at a table, a bulky middle-aged man in a tweed suit and brown bow tie over a cream shirt. He ate the meal with relish and beckoned with a mouthful of dessert to the frail-looking waitress for some coffee. The one other diner was an old lady who picked at her food, her eyes darting around like a bird wary of capture.

The vegetable soup and the main dish of plaice were delicious and the sweet of raspberry trifle and coffee served in tiny cups rounded the meal off to perfection. Later, as the cold winter night cloaked the countryside, Pat sat trying to read the evening paper while he waited for Brenda to finish in the bathroom. After a while he folded the paper up and leaned back in the settee, staring up at the ceiling and its ornate cornices lit by the bedlamp, and he began to feel increasingly nervous. Both he and Brenda were inexperienced in the art of love and he desperately wanted to please her. She was a virgin and his total knowledge of physical love amounted to a youthful fumbling with a more worldly wise girl which had been little short of a disaster, at a time before he and Brenda had started going out together seriously. He would have to be careful too not to get her pregnant. She obviously trusted him and he dared not betray that trust.

'It's all yours,' she said as she emerged from the bathroom and Pat swallowed hard. She was wearing a long black diaphanous nightdress which clung to her shapely figure and complemented her fair hair, which she had fluffed up around her ears and over her forehead. She looked lovely and he struggled for words as she swayed towards him.

'Do yer like it?' she said with a shy smile.

'God, you look ... you look gorgeous,' he fumbled.

She went over to the bed and pulled the covers back and Pat turned away from her to go into the bathroom, hardly daring to dally. He showered, shaved with care and dabbed on a sprinkling of lotion, then combed his short sandy hair back from his forehead. Last of all he cleaned his teeth, brushing furiously and hoping that the meal had not made his breath smell. He was feeling as nervous as a kitten as he donned his pyjama bottoms and stood looking at himself in the mirror. This was stupid, he told himself after another splash of spirit to his flushed face. This was supposed to be what men bragged about.

'Pat? Are you all right?' Brenda called out.

'Yeah, just finished.'

'Pat?'

'Yeah?'

'What are these fings under the piller?'

'Oh Christ!' he hissed under his breath. 'She wasn't s'posed ter find them.'

He walked into the bedroom looking at her sheepishly and saw the amused smile on her face. 'I gotta be careful, Brenda. We've both gotta be careful,' he said quickly. 'What 'appens if you get pregnant? I'd be well out of it, but you'd 'ave ter face the neighbours every day. Then there's yer muvver. God, she'd go mad. Yer dad too. What would 'e say?'

'Who ses I'm gonna get pregnant anyway?' Brenda replied. ' 'Ow'd yer know it's the week? Gels can't get pregnant any time. It's all ter do wiv the monthly cycle.'

'Yeah, I've read about that,' Pat said, 'but I 'appen ter know it's not certain. I read that some women fall fer kids any time.'

'Oh, so you're an expert on such matters, are yer?' she replied smiling.

'Don't wind me up, Brenda,' he pleaded. 'I'm scared.'

'Come 'ere, you big daft sod,' she said kindly, and then she pulled him to her and hugged him. 'Listen ter me an' get this inter that fick skull of yours. I'm not gonna let you use anyfing. I want this week ter be somefing I'll never ferget. I also want ter make a baby, our baby.'

'You can't be serious, Brenda,' he replied in a shocked voice. 'I've just spelled out the problems.'

'They won't be our problems,' she told him

400

firmly. 'If my muvver an' dad are shocked then it's their problem. I want our baby an' if God ferbid somefing 'appens ter you there'd still be a part of you wiv me fer ever. Can't you see?'

'I can see what yer mean, but I don't fink you've thought it frew,' Pat said anxiously. ' 'Ow could you support the child? You'd 'ave ter pack up work. And fink of the stigma.'

'Sod the stigma an' sod the consequences,' she growled. 'Pat, I want your child an' I've never bin so sure of anyfing in my 'ole life. Now will you reach over an' turn that bleedin' lamp out, or shall we leave it on?'

He sighed in resignation, switching off the light and lying down in her arms, suddenly realising that he was calm, deeply calm, and he could sense that she was too. She caressed him as he stroked her soft skin through the satin nightdress, feeling the delicious roundness of her young body. 'God, you're beautiful,' he gasped.

She eased herself up, allowing him to slip her nightdress off her, and as she slipped it over her head he kicked his pyjama bottoms off. They lay side by side, their warm skin touching, and his hands gently moved down from her stomach, feeling the small bulge and the softness of her pubic mound. She was wet and ready and he let her take control, easing him into her. He arched his body and pressed, and she stiffened as he broke her maidenhead, then she found his lips and he responded, kissing her with all the passion he could no longer contain while he hardly moved inside her. He was on the verge and so was she, and with a cry of excitement she moved quickly on him and he suddenly exploded.

They lay locked together, he recovering his breath and she purring with satisfaction. 'It was very quick, but it was complete, darlin',' she told him.

'I couldn't wait any longer,' he said as he moved and raised himself up on one arm. 'I was so scared of spoilin' it for yer.'

'Let me 'old yer,' she sighed. 'Sleep, darlin'. Sleep sweetly.'

Outside the barren trees moved like dervishes in the rising wind and the heavy cloud began to scud across the dark sky, revealing brief glimpses of a waxing moon. A night creature screamed and the window frames rattled, but nothing troubled the young lovers. Pat breathed shallowly in Brenda's arms as she lay awake beneath the warm blankets, utterly contented and feeling more than a little wicked. Poor Pat. He had looked so shocked. He moved and mumbled her name and she squeezed him to her. What the future held for them both was in the lap of the gods, she knew, but nothing and no one could take away the memories they would both carry away with them when the week was over.

Snow fell and settled, and the countryside was a pure white blanket as the train rattled on towards London. Two young people sat in the corner of the crowded compartment, their bodies touching, their hands clasped. Neither spoke for a long time, each wrapped up in dreams and the warmth of a fulfilled love. Soon he would be flying again, and she would wait, every morning dreading the words 'Some of our aircraft are missing.' Waiting and hoping, praying and wondering, and at the same time, please God, eager for the first signs to let her know that the Almighty had smiled down sympathetically on their liaison, that she was carrying Pat's child.

CHAPTER 34

The Carter Lane folk celebrated the Christmas of '41 with a new-found optimism. America had now come into the war and there had been some military successes in the Middle East, while in Europe Russian troops had managed to hold up the German advances and were now counter-attacking on a wide front. At home the weather was very cold and the food shortages were becoming more severe, but the general feeling was that in the coming year things were going to get much better.

Early in January Brenda Ross went to the hospital, where it was confirmed that she was pregnant. Now she faced the task of breaking the news to her parents and she was determined to make them see that it was what she had hoped and prayed for. She knew how much they both loved her and was sure that after the initial shock they would be sure to rally round her. What she was not prepared for, however, was her mother's first reaction.

'I knew it,' Iris said calmly. 'Muvvers can sense these fings an' I could see it in yer face.'

'In me face?'

'Yeah, yer look like yer face 'as filled out a bit an' yer eyes are bright.'

Brenda took a deep breath. 'Look, Mum, this wasn't an accident,' she began. 'I wanted Pat's child an' I 'ad ter talk 'im into it. It wasn't easy.'

'No, an' I'd 'ope not,' Iris said indignantly. 'As a rule men don't seem ter realise that it's the woman who 'as ter bear the brunt of 'avin' children, not them.'

'I expected a different reaction, ter tell yer the trufe,' Brenda said. 'I thought yer'd go off alarmin'.'

'Don't you worry, yer dad will when 'e finds out,' Iris replied. 'I knew what you was up to though, but what could I say ter dissuade yer? You're not stupid, you know the implications. There's the neighbours fer a start. They'll be givin' you a right name. Then there's the money ter fink of. Yer'll lose yer job an' babies 'ave ter be fed.'

'Don't worry, I've got some money put away,' Brenda said. 'It's not a lot but it'll tide me over fer a while. Pat'll make me an allowance as well. I'll get by.'

'We'll get by,' Iris told her in a firm voice.

Brenda hugged her tightly. 'I'm very lucky to

404

'ave a mum like you,' she said affectionately. 'Some gels would 'ave bin turned out on ter the street.'

'I can understand why yer've done this,' Iris remarked, 'but it's a big step, a big decision, an' yer gotta be sure that yer can face up to it. If anyfing 'appens ter Pat, God ferbid, it's gonna be very 'ard for yer, an' me an' yer dad won't always be around to 'elp yer out.'

'Don't worry, Mum, I've thought all this frew very carefully,' Brenda said quietly. 'I want Pat's child more than I've ever wanted anyfing in me 'ole life. We do love each ovver.'

'I should bloody well 'ope so,' Iris replied with passion. 'Yer'll 'ave ter get married as soon as yer can now.'

Brenda nodded. 'I'm gonna write ter Pat ternight,' she said. 'Wiv a bit o' luck they'll give 'im some leave. In the meantime I'll go an' see the vicar at St James's Church an' get the banns put up.'

'Yer'll need Pat wiv yer, I would 'ave thought,' Iris told her.

'I dunno, but I'll see the vicar anyway,' Brenda replied, then she smiled. 'I just 'ope Dad's as understandin' as you about it.'

'Yer'd better let me break it to 'im,' Iris suggested. 'When 'e comes in you make yerself scarce, till the dust settles.'

'Promise me somefing, Mum,' Brenda said. 'If anyfing 'appens ter stop me an' Pat gettin' married quickly don't let the neighbours get ter yer. There'll be a lot o' talk once I start ter show, it's only ter be expected, but decent

405

people will understand. They won't all be callin' me a loose woman.'

'Well, at least we'll 'ave one family on our side,' Iris remarked.

Early in January '42 a secret high-level meeting was held at the War Office in Whitehall, and gathered together with the chiefs of staff of the armed forces and top Government ministers was a tall, studious-looking individual who went by the code name 'Moonbeam'. He held the floor for fifteen minutes, and when he finished speaking anxiety and concern was etched on everyone's face.

'We sent out two agents,' Moonbeam began. 'They were successful in making contact with the appropriate French resistance workers and able to confirm that highly skilled aeronautical engineers have been dispatched to Germany along with Albert Deschard, the French scientist, who's known to be top in his field, the development of rocket fuel. What's more, Deschard was reportedly seen recently at Peenemünde on the Baltic. Reconnaissance photos of the area tell us that there's a large building programme going on there. It's early days yet, but all the signs point to the site being made ready for the construction and deployment of revolutionary weapons that would have a far-reaching and devastating effect on long-range targets. We have no choice but to destroy the works before they become operational. Any delay could well change the whole course of the war.'

Air Chief Marshal James stroked his chin thoughtfully. 'It would be a long distance mission, the losses could be catastrophic,' he pointed out.

Moonbeam nodded. 'Unfortunately I don't see that we have any alternative,' he replied. 'Our information tells us that the buildings under construction are very well guarded, as well as being isolated. Sabotage would not achieve the necessary results, even if our agents could penetrate the complex. The building programme is far too extensive.'

Air Chief Marshal James met later with the war minister and top ranking officers of Bomber Command, and the decision was taken to send a heavy force of Lancasters to Peenemünde on the night of the next full moon.

Mick Flynn found himself outnumbered on Saturday evening, and without much encouragement from Dolly he decided to go to The Sun for a few drinks with Bert Kenny, whose wife Liz had been invited to the get-together at the Flynns' home.

'Yer can't talk wiv men around,' Dolly said. 'They're eivver puttin' their spoke in or tryin' ter organise everyfing.'

'You're jokin', ain't yer?' Liz grinned. 'My Bert couldn't organise a piss-up in a brewery.'

Dolly smiled as she poured the tea into her best china cups. 'The reason I asked yer ter call in this evenin', Liz, is ter do wiv Brenda an' our Pat,' she remarked. 'I wanted you ter be the first ter know. They've decided ter get married.'

'Well, it's about time,' Liz replied. 'If any two kids are made fer each ovver it's those two. When's it ter be?'

'The first Saturday in March,' Dolly told her. 'It was touch an' go but they've allowed Pat a forty-eight-hour pass.'

'It's a bloody shame,' Liz remarked. 'They won't 'ave much time tergevver, will they?'

Jennie and Sadie had been sitting listening and they smiled at each other.

'They'll make it count,' Jennie said with a saucy smile.

Dolly ignored her. 'Brenda an' 'er muvver are comin' round soon, but I want you ter stay, Liz,' she said. 'We're gonna get fings organised in plenty o' time an' you can put yer two penn'orth in.'

'Are yer sure?' Liz asked.

'Course,' Dolly said quickly. 'You've always got on well wiv Iris Ross, an' after all, we're all neighbours tergevver. I'm gonna suggest we talk ter the vicar about 'irin' that big room be'ind the vestry, the one the scouts an' cubs use.'

'That'll be nice,' Liz replied. 'There's a joanna there an' my Bert's fick wiv the pianist at The Sun. 'E might be able ter persuade 'im ter play at the reception, unless yer know anybody else.'

Dolly shook her head. 'No, I'll leave that ter you, luv, soon as we can sort the room out.'

'I reckon the Jackmans'll chip in wiv an extra few rations,' Sadie said between sips of her tea. 'They're pretty good like that.'

'Will Brenda be in white d'yer know?' Liz asked.

'I dunno, I expect so,' Dolly replied.

Jennie and Sadie exchanged quick glances. Both had been taken into Brenda's confidence and from what they had gathered from their friend, her mother was vehemently against her going down the aisle in white.

'It doesn't 'ave ter be white, does it?' Jennie queried. 'I'd be quite 'appy ter get married in blue or pink.'

'You would,' Dolly said, giving her a quick glance. 'Anyfing ter be different.'

Sadie smiled at her sister's comic expression. 'As long as yer take the vows an' it's all done wiv decorum what difference does it make what colour yer wear on the day?'

'It's all about purity, that's what,' Dolly told her. 'It's tradition.'

'Sod tradition,' Jennie growled under her breath.

At that point Brenda and her mother arrived, and after being given a cup of tea and made comfortable the conversation continued.

'Yer don't mind Liz bein' 'ere while we talk, do yer?' Dolly asked.

Iris Ross smiled. 'Of course not. The more the merrier. I'm 'opin' it'll be a big turn-out at the church too.'

Brenda sat by Jennie and Sadie at the table and Jennie secretly squeezed her hand in support as Iris began to lay out the plans for the day. 'I've bin lookin' at some rose-pink taffeta at that shop in Tower Bridge Road,' she remarked.

'You know the one, that does all the weddin' dresses.'

'So yer 'avin' pink then?' Dolly said.

Iris nodded as casually as she could. 'Yeah, it'll make up lovely, an' we've decided to 'ave my sister's two daughters as bridesmaids. Louisa's seven an' Betsy's goin' on nine. They're both beautiful kids wiv fair curly 'air. They're a right couple o' Shirley Temples.'

'I dunno who Pat's gonna 'ave as best man,' Dolly said, pinching her chin thoughtfully.

' 'E's tryin' ter get one of 'is mates at the camp ter do it,' Brenda cut in, 'but it all depends if they'll give 'im leave or not. It's very dicey at the moment, what wiv all the nightly raids goin' on.'

Dolly refilled the empty teacups and then made herself comfortable in the armchair. 'Now this is what I 'ad in mind ...'

Pat Flynn reclined on the hard bed and stared up at the dusty rafters of the billet. The letter resting in his breast pocket had confirmed what he already knew in his heart, but try as he would he could not dispel the nagging fear deep down inside him that he might well never live long enough to see his son. It would be a son, he felt sure; fair-haired and bonny, and with his mother's looks. Seventeen missions under his belt and ten more still to go before his tour of ops was completed was not something he wanted to dwell on, but it was impossible to put it out of his mind in the way Tom Darcy had. Tom had been resigned to the fact that he

410

would not survive his allotted missions but Pat now prayed harder than ever to be spared.

'Briefing in ten minutes,' the orderly sergeant called into the billet and Pat sat up quickly. There had been a lot of activity at the base lately, he recalled, with a couple of visits from the bomber group commander, and everyone seemed to sense that the next bombing mission was to be an important one involving the whole six-hundred-strong force of number five bomber group.

'The target for tonight is Peenemünde,' the camp commander said bluntly. 'We'll have a full moon and we'll be attacking in full strength.'

'Christ Almighty!' a navigator sitting next to Pat exclaimed in the sudden hubbub of voices. 'That's in the Baltic, if I'm not mistaken.'

'You don't need me to remind you that you'll be flying over enemy territory for more than nine hours in all,' the commander continued, stabbing the large wall map with his pointer stick, 'so operational procedures and tactics will have to be strictly adhered to. This target is by far the most important one we've attacked yet and it's imperative that it's taken out. The full moon will assist you in precision bombing and I'm confident that you'll all give an excellent account of yourselves and the mission will be a totally successful one.'

While the pilots and navigators stayed behind for further briefing the rest of the crews left the hut looking very serious. The Berlin bombing raid had been bad enough but this was something else, and Pat went back to the quietness of his billet to write a letter to Brenda. When he had finished it he took out a folded slip of paper from inside the back cover of the poetry book Tom Darcy had given him and put it in with the letter. There was one more letter to write, to his family, and then he did something he had never done before. He went to the camp chapel.

CHAPTER 35

The people of Carter Lane were proud of the contribution they had made to the war effort. Their sons and brothers had gone off to fight and they themselves had done their bit. Most of the men had been fire watchers or ARP wardens during the Blitz and Sadie Flynn was an army nurse. Her sister Jennie had been an ARP runner and Dolly Flynn, along with her old friend Liz Kenny, had been in the front line serving refreshments from a mobile canteen. The Wilsons' girl Claire was serving in the Land Army and the Lockwood sisters were running a very efficient scheme knitting comforts for the armed forces, and as if that was not enough, Big Joe Buckley the Aussie and Alec Conroy had both been decorated for gallantry.

'It makes yer proud,' Danny Crossley remarked to his old pal Alf Coates. 'A little backstreet like this, wiv people just out ter mind their own business an' get on wiv their lives, an' then the war comes an' it brings out fings in people yer'd never 'a' guessed. Take that Conroy boy fer a start. 'E wasn't gonna wear a uniform, d'yer remember?'

'Too right I do,' Alf replied. 'I remember that nasty git Cafferty goadin' 'im, till Big Joe sorted 'im out.'

'No one can say this little street ain't done its bit,' Danny said sticking his chest out as he picked up his pint.

The old men's assessment of Carter Lane's war effort was true but premature, for the full story had not yet been written. On Monday morning a major in the Royal Engineers called on Mr and Mrs Conroy to tell them that their son Alec had been killed while seeking to defuse an unexploded bomb which had been found in the Surrey Docks. Londoners read the account in the evening papers of how Sergeant Fletcher and Sapper Conroy had been working on what was thought to be a routine job when the bomb exploded, but everyone in Carter Lane already knew and they were quick to rally round the distraught Ted and Rene Conroy.

Death in the line of duty was the terrible consequence of armed conflict and it had been borne by the older generation, who were still haunted by the First World War and the terrible losses it had engendered. Now the younger generation were experiencing it as well, and Carter Lane went into mourning, not only for Sapper Conroy, but for Freddie Bromilow too.

'It's 'ere in the Star,' a tearful Dolly Flynn pointed out to Mick.

'Bermondsey Guardsman Wins Posthumous V.C

Corporal Frederick Bromilow of the Grenadier Guards rallied the survivors of his squad and led a charge against a Japanese machine-gun post in Malaya. Though wounded he charged a second post single-handed and succeeded in silencing it before he fell. Corporal Bromilow died of his injuries, and for his bravery he was awarded the Victoria Cross.'

Once again the neighbours rallied to comfort Amy Bromilow, who held her head high and walked proud, despite the desolation in her heart.

'It makes yer wonder what's next,' Mrs Wilson remarked sadly to Ivy Jones. 'This street's more than paid its dues.'

The women were soon to find out. On Tuesday morning they heard over the wireless that a large bomber force had successfully attacked strategic targets in Eastern Germany, but that some of the bombers had failed to return.

Brenda Ross heard the news too, and as always she prayed that Pat had returned safely. That evening Mick Flynn opened his front door to a telegram boy and with shaking hands and his heart thumping he tore open the small fawn envelope and read that Flight Sergeant Patrick Flynn's aircraft had been shot down over Germany and he was missing, presumed killed.

The sudden and tragic loss of three brave sons out of one small Bermondsey backwater was chronicled in the local newspaper, but other streets too had suffered losses and everyone knew only too well that the toll would rise as long as the war lasted. In many homes now little mementoes of childhood were jealously guarded and photos of smiling young men shrouded in black velvet stood on mantelshelves, sideboards and in bedrooms, and a dark depression descended upon everyone.

Brenda Ross learned about Pat from Jennie, who had bravely volunteered to go to her, and for a long time the two sat together in the dimly lit parlour, sharing their grief over a lost brother and lover. Words of comfort and a shoulder to cry on were all Jennie could offer initially, but she realised she had to find something to say, even though her own heart was breaking, some few words of hope that her friend could cling on to. 'Look, I know it's only a slight chance, Brenda, but Pat could 'ave baled out,' she said. ' 'E could be a prisoner o' war, please God.'

'I 'ope an' pray ter God 'e is,' Brenda replied tearfully, 'but I gotta face it. There's bin bits in the papers about our airmen bein' killed by the Germans when they bale out over there. Even if 'e is alive 'e could be badly injured, burnt even. Oh God, Jennie, what am I gonna do?'

'Do as I'm gonna do, Brenda. Pray fer 'is survival,' Jennie told her with passion. 'That's all any of us can do.'

It was dark when Jennie returned to her

grieving family and tried to comfort her distraught parents. Eventually she went to her room, wanting to be alone with her thoughts. Pat had to be alive, she told herself. They would hear soon that he had been taken prisoner. He had to live, for Brenda and the baby she was carrying inside her. What else was there to do but cling on to the tiniest hope that somehow he was still alive. Yes, he was alive and one day soon he would be reunited with them all. Con and the boys, Frank and Jim would come home safely too and people would learn how to smile again. Life would be good once more.

The short days and the long lonely nights of winter seemed never-ending, but very slowly the weather became less severe and gentle April showers burst the buds and drew forth leaves on the bare branches. Plane trees were now full of chattering starlings and a warm sun shone down from a less threatening sky.

In the High Church of St James's the vicar preached a sermon about loss, in which he described the passing of a loved one as merely a passage to another room, a room which awaited us all and where we would all be together again one day. Brenda tried to believe as she sat between her mother and father in the lofty church and gently felt the growing life move inside her. She had to be grateful, she told herself. Pat would live on in their child, and the glorious memories of that last week they had spent together would never fade.

Alf Coates was a very perceptive old man, a thinker who drew on his life experiences and deployed them effectively in his arguments and discussions with Danny Crossley, an old friend of many a long year, and on Sunday morning he wore a serious expression on his face as he sat with Danny in the public bar of The Sun. 'I saw Amy Bromilow yesterday when I was standin' at me front door,' he began. 'I watched 'er dab at 'er eyes as she came out o' the 'ouse an' then she frew 'er shoulders back an' walked up the turnin' as if ter say, I'm copin' all right. She knocked at the Conroy 'ouse an' Rene came out, then the two of 'em walked over ter Dolly Flynn's front door arm in arm. Dolly comes out an' I saw the three of 'em march off out the turnin'. They didn't 'ave any shoppin'-bags wiv 'em so they wasn't goin' down the market.'

'Just off fer a stroll, I expect,' Danny replied.

'Well, it was a nice bright day yesterday,' Alf went on, 'so I decided ter take a stroll meself down Lynton Road an' over the bridge ter the church gardens. They're well tended, an' the place 'as got that lovely quiet an' peaceful feel about it. The sort o' place yer can sit an' ponder. Anyway, as I walked in the gate I saw the three of 'em sittin' on a bench. They never saw me 'cos I dodged round the ovver pathway. It wouldn't 'ave bin right to intrude on 'em. I realised then that that's where they go ter share their grief. I felt very emotional ter tell yer the trufe.'

'It's bloody sad,' Danny sighed as he picked up his pint. 'Still, they most likely get some sort o' comfort there.'

'I s'pose so,' Alf agreed. 'Who was it said, yer nearer ter God in a garden than anywhere else on earth.'

On Sunday afternoon Karen Watson laid a sprig of flowers against the marble headstone, and after a few moments alone with her thoughts she hurried out of the cemetery. The sun was shining and a few feathery clouds rode high in the azure sky. Nigel was waiting by the gates and she slipped her arm through his.

'Are you all right, Miss Watson?' he asked.

'Yes, Mr Bayley,' she replied with a faint smile.

They set off along the quiet tree-lined avenue to the main thoroughfare and caught a bus back to Bermondsey. Neither said anything for some time, then Karen turned to him. 'Thank you for being so understanding,' she said. 'I needed to do it alone. The last goodbye.'

He smiled. 'You've been very brave, darling,' he told her.

'Life has to move on,' she said, 'and I take great comfort in knowing that Douglas is at peace now. He doesn't have to suffer any more.'

Nigel nodded, then he studied his clasped hands for a few moments. 'Are you still sure about Canada?' he asked.

'Yes, I've no doubts whatever, dearest,' she replied. 'My father was Canadian and it'll almost be like going home, for me at least.'

'It'll be a wonderful experience for me too,'

he said with enthusiasm. 'I could apply to join the Mounties, or maybe I could become a lumberjack.'

'Oh no you won't,' Karen told him firmly. 'There'll be plenty of openings for someone with your qualifications.'

'By the way, Miss Watson, if you look out of the window you'll observe that we're now approaching the Elephant and Castle.'

'So?'

'Well, I thought it might be as nice a place as any to do my duty.'

'You're not intending to kiss me on this bus, are you?' Karen replied in mock horror.

'No, certainly not,' Nigel said grinning, 'but I would like to take this opportunity to formally propose to you. Would you do me the honour of becoming my wife, Miss Watson?'

'I'd be delighted, Mr Bayley.'

He sighed contentedly, and then as the bus slowed down at the Bricklayers Arms he nudged her. 'We'll get off here,' he said. 'There's a jeweller's shop in Tower Bridge Road and I've seen an engagement ring in the window that we should be able to acquire with a stout housebrick, if you feel up to a quick dash afterwards.'

On Monday morning Bernard Shanks busied himself re-wiring a new transformer into a battered old wireless set, and when he had finished he went into the front of the shop. 'Er excuse me, Mr Levy, could I slip out fer a while?' he asked.

'Yes, of course.'

'I won't be long.'

'Take your time.'

Bernard hurried from the shop and made his way to the Labour Exchange in Peckham Road. 'I'm lookin' fer a post as wireless mechanic,' he said to the elderly bespectacled clerk.

'Are you unemployed at the moment?' the official asked.

'No, I'm in employment but I wanna leave.'

The clerk looked at him over his glasses. 'Any special reason?'

'Yes, as a matter o' fact there is,' Bernard told him. 'I've good reason ter believe my employer's goin' off 'is 'ead.'

'Goodness me,' the clerk replied. 'Who is your current employer?'

'Mr Albert Levy. Levy's Wireless Shop, Old Kent Road,' Bernard said quickly.

The clerk took his glasses off and proceeded to polish them on a large handkerchief. 'As you know, your job comes under the reserved occupation category,' he remarked, 'and you'll need our authority to change jobs. We can fix you up in another post under the circumstances, I feel sure, but you'll need a green card and on it you have to state your reasons for leaving your present job, so I suggest you let me have the details.'

' 'E talks ter cupboards, well one cupboard in particular,' Bernard replied. ' 'E finks there's somebody in there called Abel.'

'Abel?'

'Yeah, Abel.'

'And where exactly is this cupboard?'

'In the workroom where I do the repairs.'

'Have you confronted him about this?'

'No fear,' Bernard said quickly. ' 'E gives me the creeps.'

'And he talks to this Abel while you're present?'

'No, 'e waits till I go ter lunch, then 'e talks to 'im.'

'So how do you know this?'

' 'Cos I came back unexpectedly one day an' 'eard 'im.'

'What exactly was he saying?'

'It was somefing about payin' 'is dues,' Bernard went on. 'Mr Levy was tellin' Abel that when the new synagogue went up there was a place reserved for 'im on the wall.'

'Good Lord!'

'It was scary,' Bernard said with a shiver. 'I went in the workroom expectin' someone ter be there but Mr Levy was on 'is own an' 'e was lookin' right at this cupboard while 'e was talkin'.'

'And what was his response when he saw you standing there?'

' 'E didn't see me. I crept out again an' made a noise as though I'd just come in the shop,' Bernard explained.

'Umm, this is very strange,' the clerk replied.

'I'll say it is,' Bernard declared smartly. 'It's put the fear up me. I even looked inside the cupboard a few times. I can't stay there much longer.'

'All right, we'll see what we can do, but you

must work your notice,' the clerk impressed on him. 'Come and see me again once you've left Mr Levy's employment.'

Bernard Shanks walked out of the Labour Exchange feeling a lot better, but back in the workroom he could not help glancing up at the cupboard occasionally, half expecting a Yiddish ghost to jump out on him.

On Monday evening Jennie came home from work to find her mother sitting in the armchair sobbing into a handkerchief with Mick standing over her, his arm round her shoulders. 'Oh my God no!' she cried. 'Con? The boys?'

Mick shook his head quickly and smiled at her. 'No, luv, it's our Pat,' he said, his voice breaking. 'The Red Cross 'ave been in touch. They've confirmed that Pat's alive. 'E's a prisoner o' war.'

CHAPTER 36

1944

On Tuesday morning the 6th of June listeners to the wireless were told to stand by for an important announcement, and a few minutes later the newsreader came on the air to say that Allied armies had landed on the coast of France. The invasion had begun and the streets suddenly filled with excited people who listened to every newscast with bated breath. This was the beginning of the end, everyone felt. The war would be over by Christmas and serving sons, husbands and brothers would all be coming home.

A few days later the truth began to dawn. Fighting was heavy and the Allied armies were making slow progress against a fanatical enemy. There was still a long way to go, and with that realisation came another sobering development. Six days after the invasion a new weapon was aimed at London, and once again the dreaded air-raid siren rang out at all times of the day and night as the flying bombs made their appearance.

The rocket-propelled weapon flew low in the sky and looked like a cigar-shaped firework as it came over spurting flames and roaring like a badly tuned motorcycle, then abruptly it spluttered and there was silence. The bomb suddenly dived and reduced another street to rubble, another factory or tenement block to a heap of smouldering ruins. It could often be seen during the day, and people tended to watch the flying bomb's progress and then throw themselves to the ground as it fell, getting up again to dust themselves down and gaze at the large pall of black smoke appearing from somewhere beyond the rooftops. The bombs soon became known as 'doodle-bugs' or 'buzz-bombs' and once again London was in the front line. The invading Allied forces were now hell-bent on overrunning the launching sites in Northern France before the Nazis could use the more nightmarish weapons they were rumoured to be readying.

Cynthia Lockwood was a rather efficient person who kept a list of special dates and memos in her little notebook, and every now and then she consulted it to keep check. 'Goodness me, how time flies,' she said aloud to herself as she saw that in a few days' time it would be Charity's seventieth birthday. 'I must get her something really nice.'

A few months earlier, during a stroll through the East Street market and out into the busy Walworth Road, Charity had chanced to remark on a silver pendant in a jeweller's window. It was priced at four pounds seventeen and sixpence, and Cynthia had tried to persuade her sister to buy it. Charity would not hear of it however. 'Much as I'd love it, it would be sinful to be so extravagant at a time like this,' she said firmly. 'Those sort of things are for birthdays and special occasions.'

Cynthia had made up her mind that she would buy the pendant, but therein lay the problem. Charity always insisted that they went out together. On this occasion Cynthia was unwontedly adamant. 'Look, Charity, I'm only going to get you a birthday card,' she sighed. 'I don't want you looking over my shoulder to see which one I pick. Goodness gracious me, I am capable of going to the Old Kent Road on my own.'

'But supposing one of those doodle-bugs comes over?'

'Then I'll do what everyone does in the circumstances, I'll throw myself down on the pavement.'

'How undignified,' Charity snorted.

'It's better than catching the full blast,' Cynthia reminded her.

'Well, for goodness sake be careful and try not to be gone too long,' Charity bade her sister.

Cynthia set off feeling quite excited. The East Street market was bustling and the sun felt warm on her face. She made her way to the end of East Lane, and just as she waited to cross Walworth Road she heard the dreaded roar. The flying bomb came over from the direction of New Cross and started to splutter. Cynthia had turned back from the kerbside and was seeking the shelter of a brick wall when someone crashed into her, sending her spinning. There was a blinding light and an explosion in her head as it cracked against a kerbstone, and a trickle of blood began to drip down into the gutter.

Back in Carter Lane Charity got on with the chores and then she made herself a refreshing cup of tea. Two hours later Cynthia had still not returned and she felt that something must have happened to her. The air-raid siren had sounded about an hour after she had left the house but it hadn't lasted long and no flying bombs had landed locally. 'That sister of mine'll be the death of me,' she said aloud as she slipped on her coat and hat.

The landlord of The Sun shook his head. 'No, luv, she 'asn't been in 'ere terday,' he

425

said sympathetically.

Charity was not surprised, though she had had to make sure. Cynthia had her faults but she wasn't a secret drinker. The Jackmans had not seen her either and as Charity walked round the block then back up to the Old Kent Road she was beside herself. There was only one thing to do, and she turned on her heel and went to see Chief Inspector Rubin McConnell.

'You say your sister's gone missing?' the policeman said as he pulled up a chair for her. 'When?'

'She's been gone for over three hours,' Charity told him.

McConnell stifled a sigh. 'Look, I think maybe you're being a bit hasty,' he remarked. 'She could have gone to see a friend and stayed for a while.'

Charity shook her head. 'We never go out separately,' she informed him. 'The only reason she's gone out alone this time is because she wanted to buy me a birthday present. I'm seventy on Friday.'

'Well, you certainly don't look it,' the policeman said smiling.

'Right now I feel every bit my age,' Charity grumbled. 'Something must have happened to her.'

The inspector picked up the phone and rang the two local hospitals. 'There's no report of a Miss Lockwood being admitted to either,' he said finally.

Charity dabbed at her eyes with a lace handkerchief she took from her sleeve. 'I'm so worried,' she said tearfully.

'Look, I'll put someone on the case,' McConnell told her. 'In the meantime you go home and try not to worry. I'll be in touch soon as ever I find out anything.'

While Cynthia was being checked over at St Giles' Hospital in Peckham she regained consciousness but was not able to give the attending police constable any details about herself.

'This does happen occasionally when a person has suffered a severe knock on the head,' the casualty doctor told the officer. 'Her memory should return within a day or two. At least there's no fracture to the skull, but she needs rest.'

The policeman nodded. 'I'll need to find out who she is for my report,' he replied. 'Her next of kin will have to be informed.'

'Nurse, will you show the officer where the lady's things are,' the doctor asked.

The nurse led the way to a side room. 'Apart from her clothes she was only carrying this purse,' she said.

The policeman opened it and counted five one-pound notes, one half-crown and a few coppers. In the side pocket he found a folded slip of papers with a few words on it and he frowned. 'Any idea what this might be?' he asked the nurse.

She glanced at the piece of paper and smiled. 'They're brand names of wool,' she told him.

'Ah, this looks promising,' the policeman said

as he took out a receipt. 'It's a pawn ticket. King's Jeweller's and Pawnbrokers', Old Kent Road.'

Peckham police station was hard-pressed that afternoon dealing with the aftermath of the flying bomb attack, which had left a small backstreet in ruins and caused a lot of disruption to local services, and the desk sergeant shook his head when the police constable filed his report. 'We can't spare anyone to follow this up,' he said irritably, then as an afterthought added, 'Maybe we can pass it on. The Old Kent Road comes under C division.'

At six o'clock that evening Inspector McConnell knocked on the Lockwoods' front door after making a detour to speak with the pawnbroker. 'We may have a lead,' he told Charity as she showed him into her parlour. 'A woman answering to your sister's description was admitted to St Giles' hospital in Peckham early this afternoon with head injuries.'

'Oh my God!' Charity gasped.

'It's all right, the injuries were only superficial,' McConnell was quick to explain. 'The woman has a loss of memory, which is not uncommon in such cases, but the doctor feels sure that it's only temporary. As a matter of fact a police constable accompanied her to the hospital, and although he could find no identification there were two clues, a pawn ticket issued from a pawnbroker's by the name of King in Old Kent Road, and a slip of paper with some brand names of wool written on it.'

Charity looked a little puzzled. 'Cynthia would

428

have no reason to use a pawnbroker's,' she said with emphasis, 'but she might have jotted down some brands of wool for reference. As you know we run a forces' comforts scheme. I just wish Cynthia had had her identity card on her. I always carry mine with me wherever I go.'

'Yes, it would have expedited matters, and it is supposed to be carried at all times,' McConnell replied. 'I'll take you to St Giles now if you like.'

Charity found her sister propped up in bed with her head swathed in bandages, looking very pale and drawn, but she now had full recollection of the accident.

'The doctor told me it wasn't loss of memory, more like confusion,' Cynthia explained.

'Inspector McConnell brought me here,' Charity told her. 'Wasn't that nice of him.'

'Yes, he's a very nice man.'

'He's waiting outside and he'd like a few words with you for the report he has to write,' Charity said.

Cynthia looked suddenly sad. 'I never got that present for you,' she said regretfully.

'I'm not worried about the present, as long as you're all right, dearest,' Charity replied with a sweet smile. 'I'm going now so that the inspector can have a chat with you, then you must get some rest.'

McConnell took Charity's place at the bedside and leaned forward with one hand resting on the spotless quilt. 'How are you feeling?' he asked.

'A little shaky,' Cynthia told him. 'It was very nice of you to bring Charity in your car.'

429

The policeman smiled. 'I wanted to have a word or two,' he replied.

'Charity said you would,' Cynthia remarked, patting his hand.

'When you were brought in you were unable to give the doctor any information about yourself,' McConnell told her, 'and the policeman who came in the ambulance with you had to search through your purse to see if there was any name or address inside. He found a pawn ticket.'

Cynthia closed her eyes tightly and the inspector looked at her with concern. 'Are you all right?' he asked anxiously.

She opened her eyes and bit on her lip. 'Yes, I'm all right,' she sighed. 'I take it you went to see the pawnbroker.'

He nodded. 'The ticket number indicated that it was issued back in 1929. As a matter of fact, the pawnbroker had to go down to the cellar and search through some old receipt books.'

'Did he tell you what it was issued for?'

'Yes, he did.'

'So you know enough now to bring charges?'

'Not really, but I would like you to tell me everything,' the inspector said with an arched eyebrow. 'If you feel up to it, of course.'

'I'm ready,' Cynthia sighed. 'This has become a burden that I sometimes found hard to bear, but I did manage to bear it, not for my sake but for Charity's. She never knew the full truth, and when I explain everything you'll understand.'

'I'm listening,' he said quietly.

Cynthia took a deep breath. 'The night before Aaron died I was subjected to the most vile form

430

of brutality from him, which I won't dwell on, but suffice it to say that I felt I was going to die by his hand. When he came home the next night and started to hit me again, I grabbed the hammer from the sideboard and killed him with a single blow to his head. Charity was staying with me that night in the spare room, and I woke her up after I realised I had killed Aaron. We talked for some time and came to the conclusion that Aaron was too wicked a man for me to swing for, and decided we should get the body out of the house.'

'And the ring?' the inspector queried.

'His hand was resting on the top of the blanket and I saw the ruby ring shining in the light,' Cynthia continued. 'Why leave it on him, I thought. It was a very valuable ring and I remember thinking it would be the only nice thing I ever got from him. All right it might sound calculating, but you never knew the man, and that night I was capable of anything, God forgive me. Anyway, I took up his hand and I remember how cold and clammy it felt. I tried to remove it but I couldn't get it over the knuckle. Then Charity told me to leave it. "It'll only bring you bad luck to remove it," she told me. I said I would, but when she went out in the yard to fetch the old bassinet I took the hammer and used the back part to chop Aaron's finger. I hid the ring and Charity never knew.'

'Was that why you never mentioned the finger when we spoke at the station?' the inspector asked.

Cynthia nodded. 'For a while after I killed Aaron I experienced a lot of misfortune. Small things that all seemed to add up and I began to feel that Charity was right. The ring was bringing me bad luck, so I pawned it. Strangely enough my luck seemed to improve within a very short time and Charity and I started to enjoy life once more. Aaron's body was not discovered and it seemed that the Almighty had forgiven me, so we lived the lie. As far as anyone knew my husband had deserted me.'

'Then after all those years the mystery of Aaron's disappearance was resolved by that bomb in the factory yard,' McConnell remarked.

'You'll probably laugh at this,' Cynthia replied, 'but I felt I had angered God in some way and he was punishing me by letting Aaron's remains be found. I felt that the only way I could atone was to make a clean breast of it, but then when the time came to confess I found I couldn't bear to let Charity know I'd deceived her and lied to her about the ring, so I kept quiet. I told you about my bad luck, but Charity had her share too. She fell in love with a very nice widower and he died suddenly of pneumonia. Nineteen thirty-two it was. They were engaged to be married, as a matter of fact.'

'That's very sad,' the inspector frowned.

'Will Charity have to know about me deceiving her?' Cynthia asked anxiously.

'I can't say what the outcome will be,' McConnell told her. 'Look, I need a cigarette. I'll send your sister in and then I'll come back and we'll continue our chat.'

Fifteen minutes later he came into the ward again and smiled at Charity as she got up to leave. 'I promise I won't be more than a few minutes,' he said.

'When I come out of here will I be taken to the cells and have my fingerprints taken?' Cynthia asked fearfully.

The policeman smiled and shook his head. 'You were telling me earlier that maybe God was punishing you for something you'd done,' he reminded her. 'Well, I believe in God, although I have to say I'm not a churchgoer. Nevertheless I'm convinced that the Lord does work in mysterious ways. Just now I walked out into the hospital grounds and I took a cigarette out to light it, but lo and behold I'd no matches. Then I spotted some men pulling down the ruined building across the street and they had a fire going. I walked over and took a piece of paper out of my pocket, reached into the fire for a light and started to smoke my cigarette. I'd been puffing away merrily when it suddenly dawned on me. I'd lit the cigarette with that pawn ticket, the only piece of evidence I had to connect you with the crime. No evidence, no case to answer. If I was you, Cynthia, I'd try to get some rest. No one need never know our little secret, not even Charity.'

'Certainly not Charity,' Cynthia replied with a smile. 'Take care, inspector, you really are a very nice man.'

'You take care too, Cynthia.'

CHAPTER 37

Albert Levy opened up his shop on Monday morning and went into the workroom to make himself a cup of tea. Bernard Shanks had terminated his employment the previous Friday evening and he had left everything neat and tidy. There were no outstanding jobs of work and it was now a question of getting someone in quickly, he thought. Until then it did not make sense to accept repairs but he could manage to do the accumulator-charging himself for the time being.

'Where did I go wrong, Abel?' he asked his old friend as he sat sipping his first mug of tea for the day. 'The lad seemed quite happy here, and I never pushed him, even though there were some times when I felt he was slacking. It seemed a weak excuse he made for leaving, if you ask me. Most of us have to travel to work and this new job he's got in Peckham isn't all that much nearer where he lives. He still needs to catch a bus.'

The sound of the air-raid siren startled Albert and he sighed in resignation as he put his steaming mug down on the workbench. 'It's a bit early this morning, Abel,' he remarked. 'Never mind, I can make another cup of tea before I open up. I don't expect any customers before the all-clear sounds.'

Just then there was a loud report from the direction of the shed out back and Albert jumped again. 'I bet that lad forgot to press the carboy stopper right in and the gases have made it pop,' he said as he got up from the stool. 'It wouldn't have happened in your time, old friend.'

Everything seemed in order when Albert walked out to the shed. The two carboys of acid were fully sealed and the electricity control panel was switched off. What could it have been? he wondered, scratching his head. Suddenly he became aware of a throaty roar that grew louder and louder, and he crouched down in the shed as he heard the engine splutter. There was a loud swishing noise and then an explosion that sent him reeling backwards against the wall. Dust and smoke filled the air and Albert staggered out to find that the front of his shop had been blown out. More frightening was the sight of the fallen girder that had crushed the workbench and splintered the stool he had been sitting on only a couple of minutes ago. The wall cupboard was still in place but its door was lying on the floor. He had always kept that cupboard locked. Inside were a few mementoes of Abel, and a photograph of him in a cheap iron frame. It was facing Albert now, and Abel's smile seemed to be wider than usual.

'That bang was your doing, wasn't it?' the shopkeeper said, shaking his head slowly. 'You wanted me out of the room, you sly old fox.'

The flying bomb had landed on a furniture

shop a few doors away and when Albert saw the carnage he was physically sick. Casualties were being moved and attended to, and there were people sitting at the kerbside in shock. Two policemen were carrying a body out from the butcher's shop and a pair of young women with their heads covered in blood were being comforted by some shopworkers from down the road.

'Bloody 'ell, Albert, we've bin searchin' frew the debris fer you.'

The shopkeeper turned to see Bill Walker the greengrocer staring at him in disbelief. 'I was out the back checking the accumulators when the bomb landed,' he told him.

'Fink yerself lucky,' Bill remarked. 'You'd 'ave bin killed stone dead otherwise. All I can say is there must be someone up there lookin' after yer.'

'You could be right, Bill,' Albert said reverently.

Jennie Flynn arrived home that evening feeling very fortunate to have survived the bomb. The baker's was less than fifty yards away from the furniture shop and it was only the protective paper stripping which had saved the front window from shattering. As it was the ceiling plaster had showered down and the morning batch of bread and rolls had been ruined.

'I managed ter save these fer the baby,' Jennie said taking two jam tarts from a paper bag. 'I'm gonna go over an' see Brenda ternight.'

'She 'ad the baby out in the pram this

436

mornin'', Dolly told her. 'We sat in the church gardens chattin' fer a while. That little mite's gettin' on fine. Jabberin' away 'e was, good as good. 'E's really got our Pat's looks.'

'Poor little sod,' Jennie joked.

'There was more on the wireless this mornin' about some prisoner o' war camps bein' overrun,' Dolly said. 'I 'ope an' pray one of 'em's where our Pat is.'

'Wouldn't it be lovely,' Jennie replied excitedly. ' 'E'd be 'ome fer Christmas.'

'I s'pose they'd let us know by telegram,' Dolly said. 'Trouble is, every time the telegram boy cycles in the turnin' yer fear the worst.'

'Don't you worry, Mum,' Jennie told her with an encouraging smile. 'We're survivors. It'll all be good from now on, you'll see.'

Brenda reached out and extracted Patrick from the high chair. 'Come on, you little monster,' she said smiling. 'Let's get you ready fer bed. I want you lookin' all pink an' shiny when Aunt Jennie arrives.'

Frank Ross chuckled as the baby protested at having the remains of his evening meal wiped away from his cheeks with a wet flannel and Iris pulled a face. 'What's that naughty mummy doin' ter my little chubby-chops then?' she cooed.

Frank watched with pleasure as Iris followed her daughter and the baby into the scullery. When Patrick was born his wife had seemed to take on a new lease of life, he thought. She had bathed, changed and fed the baby whenever she could, as well as taking up with her knitting once more. It felt as though the house had really come to life again and Frank was happy. It hadn't been too bad really, he considered. There had been a bit of talk, which was only to be expected, but on the whole the street folk had been supportive and understanding. Pat would be released soon, please God, and then there would be a wedding to look forward to, and a reception where he would most likely get completely plastered. And he wouldn't be at all surprised if Iris did too.

The Christmas of '44, the coldest for more than fifty years, was celebrated quietly, but the new year was seen in with much enthusiasm. This would surely be the year when peace returned once more, when families were reunited and life could begin anew.

On the twenty-second of January a Russian patrol came upon a country road and saw the barbed-wire fencing up ahead. When they peered through the wire they saw scenes which turned even their battle-hardened stomachs. A pile of frozen bodies lay in the snow and people moved amongst them, living, breathing skeletons. The Russian troops would soon discover that the huts they saw were full of starving inmates, many dying of typhus and diphtheria, and beyond the camp was a deep trench full of bodies shot by the SS before they left. The patrol realised they needed to summon help at all speed, and very soon the whole world was to know the name of Auschwitz.

That same day the advancing Soviet forces overran Stalag 27, a prison camp for airforce personnel.

The long and roundabout journey home from the camp in Poland had taken its toll, but Pat Flynn now felt excitement pulsing through him as the train drew into Waterloo Station. Flags decorated the platform and a military band was playing as the train squealed to a halt and the carriage doors swung open. He could see her now. Yes, it was her, holding a baby, his baby. His legs felt like jelly and he swallowed hard as he shouldered his kitbag and hurried along to her. She shouted his name almost hysterically and they hugged, gently for fear of harming the baby between them, then she handed him his son Patrick.

Back home in Carter Lane there would have been a more public homecoming but too much tragedy had touched the street for flags and bunting, Dolly reasoned, though the Conroys and Amy Bromilow were there to welcome Pat home. Mick brushed away a tear and blew hard into his handkerchief, while Dolly, Sadie and Jennie fussed and pandered to Pat's every need.

'Look, Mum, I might look tired but I'm okay, really,' Pat protested. 'I can move ter get the paper, an' I can undo me shoelaces. Just sit an' relax, an' let me catch me breath.'

Brenda sat on the hearth rug at his feet, with her head resting against him as he stroked her hair. Patrick was sleeping on the settee covered with a blanket and the house was quiet. Dolly, Mick and their daughters had gone to The Sun, along with Frank and Iris Ross, and Jennie had promised to come home to mind the baby later so that Pat and Brenda could join the families for a celebration drink.

'You don't need ter talk about it now, Pat,' Brenda said quietly.

'It's all right, it was a long while ago an' it doesn't bovver me anymore,' he replied. 'I saw a few of our planes go down in flames an' I knew we'd got some flak damage ter the port wing but the pilot told us we'd manage it back okay, wiv a bit o' luck. It wasn't ter be though. Our luck 'ad just run out. We were caught in the belly an' the starboard engine an' we tipped over. The plane was goin' down an' the pilot gave the order ter bale out. We all managed ter clear, except the bomb-aimer. 'E'd took the full force o' the blast. We landed in a field near a large wood an' after we buried our chutes we set off. God knows what we were tryin' ter do, apart from evadin' the Germans. We were 'undreds o' miles inside Germany at the time we baled out. Anyway, as we got near the wood we were suddenly confronted by a German patrol. They must 'ave bin out lookin' for us. There was nuffink we could do. They roughed us up a bit an' dragged us into a lorry. As it 'appened the German officer who grilled us wasn't too bad. 'E spoke good English an' gave us cigarettes. 'E told us that we were lucky 'is men found us before the SS unit operatin' in the area got there, or we'd 'ave bin shot out of 'and.'

'Don't tell me any more, darlin',' Brenda said quickly.

'That's about it anyway,' Pat replied. 'They stuck us on a train an' we ended up in Poland.'

Brenda reached out and took up the handbag that was lying at her feet. 'I've kept your letter wiv me all the time,' she told him, taking it out of the zip pocket. 'The poem made me cry.'

Pat smiled wistfully. 'As I said in the letter Tom never got round ter finishin' it, so I did it for 'im. I fink 'e would 'ave wanted me to.'

Brenda opened the letter and read the poem aloud while Pat stared distantly into the glowing fire.

'The Mission

The engines roar, we lift and climb,
Aiming for the moon.
Down below the fields, the Downs,
Behind us all too soon.

Now it's a calm and silver sea below,
But we must sail the sky.
Though full of hopes and aspirations,
Some of us must die.

The bombs away, we'll bank for home,
The fires burn below.
We remember it was London burning,
Not that long ago.

With the starboard engine feathered,

We set out for the coast.
Beyond, the sea, our sceptred isle,
And then we'll drink our toast.

We'll raise our glasses, spare a thought,
For those who had to die.
We know they've cast their earthly bodies,
And their spirits soar the sky.

Their names will be on monuments,
They will not feel aggrieved.
As long as we remember,
Once they walked, and talked, and breathed.

Tom Darcy'

She saw that his eyes were misty and she reached out to him. 'I love you, Pat Flynn,' she whispered.

'I love you too, Brenda Ross,' he said intensely. 'More than honour. More than life itself.'

EPILOGUE

Pat Flynn and Brenda Ross were married during the spring of 1945, and later that year, soon after the Rifle Brigade returned from the Middle East, Con Williams and Jennie Flynn got wed.

Frank and Jim Flynn returned to work at the brewery looking lean and tanned, and they soon found themselves being pursued by the Gordon twins, Denise and Diana, who worked in the accounts office. The Flynn boys were adamant though: marriage was not for them, not yet awhile, there was too much catching up to do.

Big Joe Buckley had been sent to the Far East and when he returned after the Japanese surrender he had a chat with Sadie about the future. 'I've always considered meself a rover,' he remarked, 'but now I'm a petty officer in the King's navy I kinda like it, Sadie. It fits me like a bum in a bucket, so I've decided to sign on for another five years.'

'If that's what yer wanna do, Joe,' she replied. 'It's that way wiv me an' nursin'. It's what I really wanna do.'

'We can make it work though, kid, the two of us together.'

'Are you talkin' about marriage, Joe?'

'Too bloody true.'

'Is that a firm proposal?'

'You bet.'

'Then there's only one fing I can say ter you.'

'Go on, kid, I can take it.'

'The answer's yes, you great oaf.'

Rabbi Friedman was pleased with the way his restoration fund for the synagogue was coming on and he was looking forward to work starting that year. 'Don't misunderstand me,' he said to Albert Levy one afternoon over coffee. 'It's laudable that you should want to remember

Abel Finkelstein with a large bronze plaque in the entrance hall, and it's very generous of you to make that donation to the fund, but you're a businessman and I'm sure you'll appreciate what I'm going to say.'

'Which is?'

'A slightly smaller bronze plaque and a slightly larger donation might make better sense,' the rabbi replied. 'Have a word with Abel if you're not sure.'

Albert Levy arched his eyebrow as he took out his cheque book. 'What's the use of discussing it with Abel,' he growled. 'He's on your side anyway.'

Karen Watson and Nigel Bayley sailed for Canada early in 1946, and after due consideration Nigel decided against joining the Royal Canadian Mounted Police. Instead they prospered in the retail business, selling electrical appliances.

Carter Lane survived until well into the sixties, when the area came under a redevelopment programme. Smart houses now stand where once there were two-up, two-down homes, but interested visitors might still chance to wander into Carter Walk and maybe catch a glimpse of what has passed, and what was lost.

444

POSTSCRIPT

Very few areas of Britain escaped the German bombing and all the major cities suffered heavy damage and loss of life. The cathedral cities of Bath, Exeter, York and Canterbury were badly damaged in what were known as the Baedeker Raids, and the terrible daylight raid on Coventry led to the word 'Conventration' entering the English language.

In London alone there were seventy-one major air raids between 7th September 1940 and 16th May 1941, during which nearly 19,000 tons of bombs were dropped. A total of 43,000 civilians lost their lives during that period, more than half of them in London. 86,000 were severely injured, and a further 150,000 were slightly injured. Over 2,000,000 homes were destroyed or damaged, sixty per cent of them in London.

At the end of the Blitz the Heavy Rescue Services in Bermondsey were asked by the Government to nominate a few of their men for bravery awards. Their reply went as follows: 'Medals? We don't want no f ... medals. Everybody in Bermondsey should get a f ... medal.'

Lest we forget ... as time goes by.

The publishers hope that this book has given you enjoyable reading. Large Print Books are especially designed to be as easy to see and hold as possible. If you wish a complete list of our books, please ask at your local library or write directly to: Magna Large Print Books, Long Preston, North Yorkshire, BD23 4ND, England.

This Large Print Book for the Partially sighted, who cannot read normal print, is published under the auspices of

THE ULVERSCROFT FOUNDATION

First published in Great Britain 1978 by
The Macmillan Press Ltd

Published in the U.S.A. by
Halsted Press, a Division of
John Wiley & Sons, Inc.
New York

Printed in Hong Kong

Library of Congress Cataloging in Publication Data

Morgan, Brian.
    Monetarists and Keynesians, their contribution to monetary theory.

    "A Halsted Press book."
    1. Money. 2. Keynesian economics. 3. Chicago school of
economics. 4. Neoclassical school of economics. I. Title.
HG220.A2M59 1977   332.4'01   77–10905
ISBN 0 470–99305–7

To the memory of my father
E. J. MORGAN

Contents

Preface and Introduction

This book developed from a course of lectures, given first at Middlesex Polytechnic and more recently at The Polytechnic of Central London, which attempted to introduce undergraduates to monetary theory in the light of the continuing debate over the meaning of the Keynesian revolution.

The message underlying this book is that Keynes, in *The General Theory of Employment, Interest and Money*, revolutionised economic theory and developed a realistic theory of accumulation in a modern, money-using capitalist economy. Keynes's theory focused on the problems of uncertainty, expectations, wealth, interest and money in *disequilibrium* situations and it is argued that this theoretical approach is far better equipped for solving current economic problems than that offered by either modern-day Keynesians or Monetarists. In fact, the debate between Monetarists and Keynesians is a difficult one to resolve, precisely because both approaches are firmly based on *equilibrium* theory. Specifically their theoretical foundations are those of the Walrasian general equilibrium system and it is this system that underlies the *IS/LM* model within which the analysis of both schools is formulated. However, the *IS/LM* model is inappropriate for illustrating Keynes's theoretical innovations because it largely assumes away the problems of uncertainty and expectations which bedevil capitalist systems and with which Keynes was grappling.

It will be obvious to the reader that this interpretation of Keynes owes much to the writings of Axel Leijonhufvud and in fact one of my aims in writing this book has been to place students in a better position to read and understand both Keynes's original work (now published in full by the Royal Economic Society) and Leijonhufvud's now classic doctoral thesis *On Keynesian Economics and the Economics of Keynes* (described by Harry Johnson as a 'monumentally scholarly study').

However, this book probably would not have been written without the valuable insights into monetary theory provided by my former

teacher at the London School of Economics, Mr Laurence Harris. I would also like to acknowledge my debt to Professor David W. Pearce for being infinitely patient with an awkward author, to my students who have read and criticised the manuscript through numerous revisions and to Christine Morgan for some valuable advice in the preparation of the final chapters. Responsibility for errors of omission and commission of course remain with the author.

June 1977   BRIAN MORGAN

1
An Overview

During the last half-century most Western capitalist countries have experienced dramatic changes in economic conditions. The mass unemployment of the 1930s gave way to near full employment with creeping inflation during the 1950s and early 1960s and more recently we have experienced the sad combination of creeping inflation (with a higher rate of 'creep') together with less than full employment. Now to some extent it may be argued that the purpose of economic theory is to explain and (it is hoped) predict changes in economic conditions but, over the same period, the failure of economic theory to achieve a high degree of either explanatory or predictive power has resulted in changes in the underlying theory of equal magnitude to the changes in economic conditions. In this context no area of economics has undergone as much change as has the subject-matter of monetary theory.

At the beginning of the period the accepted framework within which (classical) monetary theorists analysed the economy was the quantity theory of money. As we will see in Chapter 2 this was largely a theory of the price level and it paid little attention to the determination of the other important economic magnitudes in which economists are now interested, namely the levels of employment and output. It was generally accepted that various forces associated with a competitive market system, such as flexible wages and prices, would automatically ensure that the levels of output and employment would be at a level consistent with the full employment of the economy's resources. Any departure from this optimum solution was regarded as transitional and as occurring only while the economy was adjusting towards a new equilibrium.

The persistent unemployment of the late 1920s and early 1930s was then *explained* in the classical theory by pointing to the rigidities that existed within the economic system (especially wage rigidity and the

immobility of labour) and it was *predicted* that the removal of these rigidities would ensure the automatic functioning of the system at full employment. However, in addition to explanation and prediction, economic theory should ideally be prescriptive, i.e. it should prescribe economic policies for the authorities to undertake in order to counteract the malfunctioning of the economic system. The problem faced by classical monetary theorists during this period was that of making policy recommendations about the distressing subjects of wage rigidity and labour immobility (subjects which in any case did not really fall within the confines of monetary theory). The result was that by 1930 there existed a monetary theory which was of dubious relevance to the problems of the day, in that it was concerned more with the price level than the level of employment and it was largely impotent in regard to policy recommendations (The reader is not meant to infer from this paragraph that economists at this time were actually advocating wage cuts as the *only* way out of the depression. In fact, many economists (and particularly Pigou) were strongly in favour of public works programmes to reduce unemployment. The contention is simply, that (*a*) classical theory predicted that *if* money wages could be reduced *then* unemployment would fall, and that (*b*) prescriptions for policy other than reductions in wages could not be derived either consistently or convincingly from existing monetary theory.)

The emphasis by monetary theorists on the price level to the exclusion of output and employment was then gradually reversed by the writings of John Maynard Keynes, who insisted that, in the first place, inherited theory was incapable of adequately *explaining* the phenomena of mass unemployment. A watershed in monetary theory came in 1930 with the publication of his *Treatise on Money* [44] (in reference to which Keynes wrote later: 'When I had finished it I had made some progress towards pushing monetary theory back to becoming a theory of output as a whole.') and the transition from price-level analysis to a more general monetary approach to employment and output was completed with the publication in 1936 of *The General Theory of Employment, Interest and Money* (hereafter referred to as *The General Theory* [46].

In these two works Keynes offered an alternative *explanation* of persistent unemployment that proceeded by identifying some of the peculiar characteristics of a monetary economy that would prevent the automatic attainment of full employment even when wages and

2

prices were completely flexible. He stressed in particular the role of uncertainty and expectations in such an economy and the consequent information problems to which they gave rise.

In this way Keynes was attempting to build a theory of output and employment that would be capable of 'analysing the economic behaviour of the present under the influence of changing ideas about the future' ([46] p. vii). Money played an important role in such a theory because it was 'a subtle device for linking the present to the future' ([46] p. 294). Keynes insisted that in a monetary economy in disequilibrium it is possible for pessimistic transactors to behave as if they cannot afford to buy the output which the economy is capable of producing and no amount of price and wage flexibility can alter this behaviour, i.e. wage cuts, even if they could be implemented, would not achieve full employment. Thus, he *predicted* that, in a situation such as that which characterised the United Kingdom in the 1930s, only an external stimulus to demand, sufficient to counteract the self-defeating expectations engendered by the depression, was capable of alleviating the mass unemployment. His *prescription* for policy therefore favoured increased government expenditure to raise the level of effective demand to a level consistent with full employment.

Therefore, through Keynes's writings, monetary theory was transformed from a theory of the price level to an expectational theory of output and employment as a whole, and it was in describing this transformation that the term 'the Keynesian Revolution' was initially coined. Ironically, the new avenues for monetary theory opened up by Keynes's writings turned out, in retrospect, to closely resemble culs-de-sac and the Keynesian Revolution, in fact, signalled the opening of a period during which monetary analysis stagnated. This was, in part, probably due to the fact that when Keynes's theory was put to the test and increased expenditure on war resulted in a return to full employment his theory came through the test so convincingly, i.e. its explanatory, predictive and prescriptive power was recognised as being so much greater than its predecessors', that the control of aggregate demand through government expenditure came to be regarded not merely as the main pillar but, in some cases, the only pillar of the 'revolution'. Keynes's analysis of uncertainty and expectations, and their relationship to and importance in a specifically monetary economy was overlooked and largely ignored in the post-war scramble to estimate consumption functions and later

3

build static, short-period, simultaneous-equation models of the economy.

However, despite the divergence of views which soon emerged between Keynes's analysis and that of his followers, within a decade of the publication of *The General Theory* Keynesian economics had become the ruling paradigm. Once established as the new orthodoxy the Keynesian system came increasingly to be represented (by Patinkin and others – see [63] chs 9–11) as a special type of aggregate general-equilibrium system with four markets – goods, money, labour and bonds – and with the emphasis being placed on the real, as opposed to the monetary, variables of the system. This representation of Keynesian economics in the form of a simultaneous-equation model was the result of the consensus of opinion that gradually emerged in the debate between the supporters and critics of the Keynesian Revolution. This consensus involved compromising, to some extent, the revolutionary character of Keynesian economics and it has since become known as the 'neoclassical synthesis'.

In this synthesis some of Keynes's most important contributions are rejected, including, especially, his claim to have produced a more general theory than the classics. For example, those that subscribe to this synthesis accept that Keynes introduced some useful concepts into macroeconomics but they contend that in terms of pure theory his approach simply amounted to the addition of a few (albeit realistic) assumptions to the existing theoretical structure. Although it is true that these assumptions give us greater insight into the problems of the real world, it is concluded that they cannot really be regarded as the hallmarks of a *general* theory. In contrast, the neoclassical synthesis claims to have produced a macro model of complete generality in the sense that, given a certain set of assumptions, it can be used to prove the macroeconomic propositions of classical economists *and*, given a *different* set of assumptions, it can be used to validate Keynes's conclusions. Thus the two approaches are accepted as being essentially similar, differing only in the set of assumptions adopted. However, in this context it is emphasised that not only were Keynes's assumptions *different* from the classics, it is claimed they were also more *restrictive*, i.e. less general, so the conclusion of the synthesis is that his analysis can be regarded as a special case of the more general classical theory.

Another problem associated with this general model is that once the model had been accepted as the foundation of the Keynesian

system the only worth-while task remaining in which Keynesian economists could become involved was the refinement of the basic tools of analysis. Research was concentrated, therefore, on developing more sophisticated approaches to (say) consumption-function theory, a development which in one sense simply amounted to the filling in of the 'empty boxes' that existed within the accepted framework but it did not involve an over-all critique of the system itself.

Now from the viewpoint of *monetary* theory these developments weakened the Keynesian system in two respects. In the first place the general-equilibrium model adopted by the neoclassical synthesis achieves equilibrium simultaneously in all markets through relative price adjustments, but equilibrium situations, because they abstract from real-world problems such as uncertainty, also succeed in completely ignoring the essential properties of money. Indeed, in the general-equilibrium system it is often difficult to distinguish money from any other good in the system. Second, for the Keynesian monetary theorist, the alternative to working within the general model was to fill in one of the 'empty boxes'. Because of this monetary theory was forced to develop as a very narrow discipline and those who chose to work in the monetary field became specialist researchers into (say) the supply or demand functions for money in the same way that other orthodox economists became specialists on the consumption or investment functions. These developments meant that the influence of money on the rest of the economic system received insufficient attention within the new orthodoxy, so that in both respects, not only was monetary theory weakened but it became far removed from Keynes's broad conception of the subject.

During this period, when Keynesians were intent on refining the underlying functions of the system, it is not surprising that those economists actively engaged in the study of monetary processes from a wider perspective did not appear to have much in common with the economics of the ruling paradigm. Indeed when monetary economics again became a growth area in the late 1950s and 1960s, the impetus to research was basically anti-Keynesian in nature and the movement was labelled the 'neoclassical resurgence'. Therefore, although Keynesian economics soon succeeded in becoming the new orthodoxy, reservations concerning it persisted and in addition a number of problems arose which ensured that these reservations gradually became more outspoken.

In the first place, the authorities soon experienced difficulties in

5

trying to implement the type of fiscal policy suggested by the 'revolution'. It was soon discovered that sole reliance on fiscal instruments for the purpose of stabilisation involved considerable problems of 'fine tuning', i.e. the problem of knowing *when* to inflate or deflate the economy and by *how much*. And these problems were not easily overcome, with the result that the conclusion of the major policy study of the period was that fiscal policy in the United Kingdom had been a *destabilising* factor in the economy (see Dow [17]). Furthermore, the policy tools favoured by Keynesian economics were found insufficient to deal with the continuous balance-of-payments problems and creeping inflation that most countries were experiencing and this further weakened the support pillars of the ruling structure.

The difficulties experienced in attempting to find a solution to these policy problems, together with the objections raised against the rigid theoretical structure of the new orthodoxy, contributed to the emergence in the 1950s of an alternative school of thought which offered a different *explanation* of the economic conditions that were being experienced.

This school's alternative explanation was framed in terms of the money supply and its rate of change, in the sense that they regarded changes in the money supply as being the major cause of fluctuations in money income. Such an explanation of current conditions obviously lends itself quite easily both to prediction and to the formulation of policy prescriptions to deal with economic disturbances. In fact, the money supply played a central role in both the theoretical and applied studies of this group and it is not surprising, therefore, that their approach was subsequently named the Monetarist School. The fact that this school emerged as a viable alternative to Keynesian economics is due largely to the intellectual leadership of Professor Milton Friedman, who in the 1950s laid the foundations of this approach with his reinterpretation of the classical quantity theory of money and his subsequent empirical work in this area (see [20] and [22]).

The applied aspects of this school's work soon received the greater part of their attention and this concentration on empirical work, together with their emphasis on only one of the variables of the economic system, was in line with the methodology that underlay the whole of their research. This was the idea that the test of a good theory is 'its ability to predict much from little', and in developing this

approach they constructed a considerable edifice of statistical evidence to support their case. However, their empirical findings alone were insufficient to convert those on the Keynesian side of the fence, and the reason for this can be traced in part to the failure of the Monetarists to offer a consistent account of the adjustment process through which changes in the money supply were supposed to affect other economic variables. Keynesian theorists, on the other hand, claimed superiority in this respect in that their framework allegedly provided such an account of the adjustment process. During the 1960s, therefore, there developed two alternative schools of thought, one Monetarist and the other Keynesian, with the former increasing in importance along with the number of unsolved problems but with the latter remaining the established orthodoxy.

Ironically, at the same time as the Monetarist attack on Keynesian orthodoxy was being countered on theoretical grounds the theoretical foundations of the ruling paradigm itself came in for serious criticism from a new faction which claimed no allegiance to either school of thought (but whose aim appeared to be the improvement of the Keynesian approach). These criticisms slowly initiated a reappraisal of the Keynesian system and the credit for this can be traced in part to the work of Professor R. W. Clower [12] and [13]. He has shown that the basic theoretical differences between Keynes and the classics were not adequately brought out in the long debate of the 1950s (a debate which culminated in the so-called 'neoclassical synthesis') and that the differences were of a far more fundamental, even revolutionary, nature than had so far been appreciated. Clower was, in fact, among the first to challenge the accepted Keynesian framework from the viewpoint of internal consistency rather than empirical validity and he was particularly critical of the general-equilibrium model within which the ideas of Keynes were now being expounded.

These criticisms were then debated and to some extent digested with the result that the emphasis within Keynesian economics gradually began to move closer to the original ideas of Keynes. It can be regarded as a move back to Keynes in the sense that a broader conception of monetary theory began to evolve and research began again to be concentrated on the dynamics of monetary change and the consequent problems of expectations and uncertainty. A related development in this field was the emergence in the latter half of the 1960s of the 'new microeconomics' of employment and inflation

7

theory which concentrated on the dynamics of wage-setting and employment decisions under conditions of uncertainty.

Finally, in concluding this overview it is necessary to point out that although we have traced out a development that in a sense goes full circle and eventually comes back to the original ideas of Keynes, some of the early Keynesians never in fact strayed very far from the line of thought that Keynes was pursuing. Traditional Keynesians, like Professor Joan Robinson and Professor G. L. S. Shackle, remained detached from either of the main schools of thought during this period and continued to develop Keynes's ideas independently. Mrs Robinson, for example, has extended Keynes's analysis in the area of capital theory and Shackle has done much to clarify the problems of uncertainty with which Keynes was struggling. It is not simply that the modern critics of Keynesian orthodoxy can claim these traditional Keynesians as their allies; it is rather that the recent critics are in many respects merely elaborating upon the much older criticisms that these original proponents of the Keynesian Revolution had always levelled against the orthodox interpretation of Keynes.

It is the purpose of this book to outline critically the twists and turns that have occurred in monetary theory since the Keynesian Revolution and to guide the reader through the main contentions involved in these developments. Our approach will be a comparative one and, to the extent that any survey has to be selective, we will tend to concentrate on those aspects of the debate which are relevant to our understanding of the present state of the subject. This comparative approach will be revealed in the contents of the following chapters, which may be summarised as follows: in the next chapter a classical and Keynesian model will be developed and compared to bring out the main differences between the two approaches; in Chapter 3, the subsequent Keynes–classics debate, leading to the Neo-Classical Synthesis, will be outlined; in Chapter 4 the Monetarist approach will be adumbrated and contrasted with the Keynesian position; in the following chapter we will analyse the current debate and the recent reinterpretation of Keynes's position will then be compared with both the Monetarist and Keynesian approaches; finally, by way of a conclusion, we will analyse in Chapter 6 this movement 'back to Keynes' in the light of recent developments in related fields such as inflation and capital theory.

2
Classical and Keynesian Models

A CLASSICAL MODEL

Commenting on the title of his book in chapter 1 of *The General Theory* Keynes writes 'The object of such a title is to contrast the character of my arguments and conclusions with those of the Classical theory of the subject. . . . I shall argue that the postulates of the Classical Theory are applicable to a special case only and not to the general case.' However, at the time Keynes was writing, no comprehensive or authoritative account existed of the classical theory, but in the course of the debate since the publication of *The General Theory* a recognisable classical model has emerged and we will proceed to construct such a model for the purpose of comparing it with the familiar Keynesian model that has now become the standard textbook representation of Keynes's theory. We pointed out in Chapter 1 that Keynes attempted to identify those forces within the economy that would prevent the system adjusting automatically to full employment and, subsequently, Keynesian models have emphasised the need for discretionary government policy to ensure the full employment of resources. The distinguishing feature of classical economics, on the other hand, is that it presents a model of full employment.

The Goods and Labour Markets

In the classical theory the equilibrium level of output is determined basically by two functions – the production function and the supply curve of labour. The production function $Y = Y(N, \overline{K})$ relates the level of output Y to the level of employment N on the assumption that

9

the capital stock K is fixed in the short run (which is indicated by the bar over the K in the production function). With K fixed the production function will exhibit decreasing returns to labour and it can be represented graphically by a function concave to the employment axis as in Figure 2.1 (a).

The concavity of the production function means that the marginal physical product of labour MPP_L, i.e. the increase in output resulting from the employment of one more unit of labour, will be diminishing as more labour is employed and this is shown in Figure 2.1 (b) by the downward-sloping MPP_L curve. The latter is important because it forms the basis of the classical theory of the demand for labour.

The demand for labour by a profit-maximising firm operating under conditions of perfect competition will be derived from the level of output at which the firm's marginal cost is equal to the price of its product (where the latter is exogenously determined and is regarded as fixed from the point of view of the firm). However, in the case where labour is the only variable factor, the marginal cost, defined as the additional cost per unit of output, is simply the ratio W/MPP_L because W, the money wage, is the increase in cost and MPP_L, the addition to output. Therefore, the profit-maximising condition, $MC = P$, can be rewritten: $W/MPP_L = P$, or alternatively $W/P = MPP_L$, i.e. the level of employment consistent with profit maximisation is determined where the real wage W/P is equated to the marginal physical product of labour. Furthermore, since the latter diminishes as more labour is hired the demand for labour will be an inverse function of the real wage. This relationship is represented graphically in Figure 2.2 and it illustrates that in classical theory the demand curve for labour coincides with the marginal physical product curve.

The equilibrium levels of N and W/P are determined in the classical system in a competitive labour market by the demand for and supply of labour. The former has been shown to be an inverse function of W/P and the classics assumed that the supply of labour also depended on W/P. They postulated a familiar upward-sloping supply schedule for labour based simply on the proposition that a larger real reward was necessary to induce an increased supply of labour. Equilibrium is then achieved when the demand for labour is equal to the amount supplied.

In disequilibrium situations, e.g. if the market was characterised by excess supply, then it was assumed that those unable to obtain work

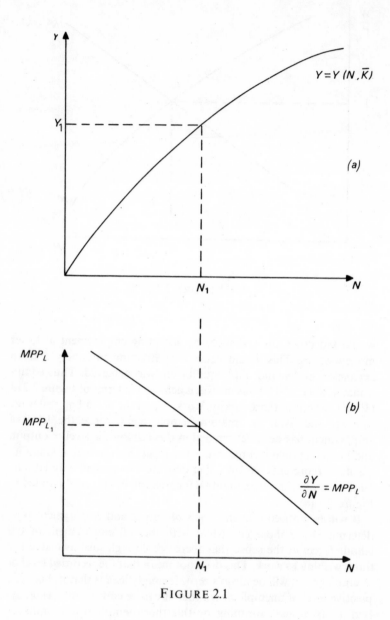

FIGURE 2.1

11

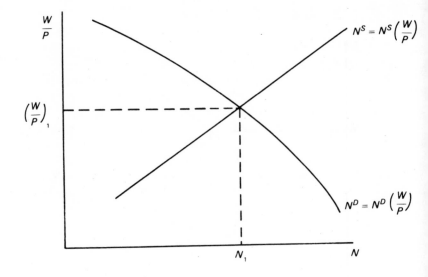

FIGURE 2.2

would bid down the real wage by accepting employment at lower
money wages. This would cause a contraction in supply and an
expansion in demand until equilibrium was achieved. Thus equilibrium in a classical labour market is achieved in terms of Figure 2.2 at
$(W/P)_1$ where all those seeking work, N_1, at the prevailing real wage
rate are successful in obtaining employment. Once the level of
employment has been determined in this fashion the level of output,
and hence national income, is derived from the production function,
e.g. if N_1 represents *the level* of employment consistent with labour-
market equilibrium then national income will by Y_1, as illustrated in
Figure 2.1 (*a*).

It will be noticed that the levels of output and employment thus
determined are those consistent with the full employment of the
labour force, in the sense that there are enough jobs available for
those wishing to work. This does not mean that the recorded level of
unemployment will be always zero. It simply means that if there is a
positive level of unemployment then it can be conveniently categor-
ised as 'frictional', meaning by this those temporary amounts of
unemployment which arise after some unforeseen disturbance and

12

persist only as long as it takes the industry or sector involved to adjust to the new situation.

The classics therefore readily accepted the existence of a transitory type of unemployment but a *persistent* excess supply of labour over and above the amount demanded was precluded from their system as long as money wages were flexible, i.e. 'involuntary' unemployment in the sense of workers seeking work but not finding jobs anywhere in the economy, either at the going real wage rate or at lower real wage levels, simply did not exist in the classical model. They assumed that a disequilibrium of this nature could be avoided in a competitive labour market by the unemployed workers accepting lower money wages; and it was assumed that this would, by reducing costs, increase the demand for labour and also cause some contraction on the supply side until those seeking employment were successful in obtaining it. If this adjustment mechanism was prevented by (say) trade unions insisting on maintaining money wages at too high a level then the consequent unemployment must be regarded as the result of labour pricing itself out of the market and to this extent may justifiably be termed 'voluntary' unemployment.

Thus in the classical system flexible money wages assure the full employment of labour and this amount of labour applied to the existing stock of capital then determines the full-employment level of output. The determination of national income therefore seems to depend almost exclusively on technological factors with no part at all being played by the level of aggregate demand in the economy. The classics in fact ruled out any deficiency of aggregate demand by a variation on the theme of Say's Law of Markets. Say's Law is usually summed up by the maxim 'supply creates its own demand', and what it amounts to is a denial of the possibility of there existing a general glut of commodities, i.e. overproduction. It is usually supported by the observation that people work only in order to buy goods and services with their remuneration and that an increase in the supply of labour services or any other factor of production must be matched by a corresponding increase in the demand for commodities otherwise the original decision to supply more labour would not have been made. This observation is, in general, false but in a barter economy it would be true because then wages would be paid in the form of the commodities produced so that it would be impossible to sell a commodity or service (say labour) without simultaneously buying or accepting another commodity or service in exchange.

Stated in terms relating solely to a barter economy Say's Law becomes a simple truism and is known as Say's Identity. However, the classics felt that this identity could be restated in terms of a monetary economy on the supposedly reasonable assumption that people had no demand for money as such, since money is simply a medium of exchange, but only a demand for the things that money could buy. Thus there could be no demand for 'idle' money balances in their system and it was assumed that any excess of income over expenditure would therefore be loaned out, at a profitable rate of interest, to those people whose planned expenditure exceeded their current income. It was this extension to a monetary economy which led the classics to reject the naive version of Say's Law, i.e. Say's Identity, in which aggregate demand and supply are identically equal, in favour of a more refined version in which this equality between planned expenditure (aggregate demand) and expected income (aggregate supply) is ensured only in equilibrium via the effect of the interest rate on the levels of investment and consumption.

The basis of the classical argument can be brought out clearly in terms of the Figure 2.3 and in this form it can be more easily compared with the Keynesian approach – which will be developed in the second half of this chapter. In Figure 2.3 (a) both consumption C and savings S enter as horizontal lines because the classics did not postulate any relationship between consumption and income. The level of S is determined in Figure 2.3 (b) along with the level of investment I, where both are shown to be functions of the interest rate r, the latter negatively and the former positively related to r, representing demand and supply curves for loanable funds respectively (note that the axes have been reversed from their normal usage). Once S is determined in Figure 2.3 (b) the level of consumption at each level of income is easily found since $C = Y - S$. The level of aggregate demand is then calculated in Figure 2.3 (a) by adding together the levels of consumption expenditure and investment expenditure.

Assume that the economy is initially in equilibrium producing the full-employment level of output Y_1, (determined by the production function and supply curve of labour) and that expenditure is at a level sufficient to absorb this output level, i.e. with an interest rate of r_1 and the saving schedule S' the amount saved will be S_1 and the amount consumed C_1, investment will be at the level I_1 and therefore aggregate demand will be E_1. Assume now that consumers become increasingly uncertain about the future and decide to increase their

14

Expenditure

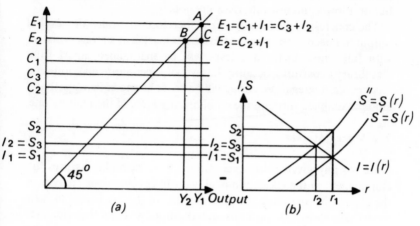

$$E_1 = C_1 + I_1 = C_3 + I_2$$
$$E_2 = C_2 + I_1$$

$$I_1 = S_1$$

45°

$Y_2 \, Y_1$ Output

(a)

I, S

$S'' = S(r)$
$S' = S(r)$

$I = I(r)$

$r_2 \ r_1$

r

(b)

FIGURE 2.3

level of savings as a precautionary move; the saving schedule therefore shifts to S'' in Figure 2.3 (b) and at an unchanged rate of interest the level of savings rises to S_2, which means that consumption falls to C_2. The level of expenditure is now only E_2, which is insufficient to absorb the full-employment level of output Y_1, and therefore creates an excess supply of goods, $Y_1 - Y_2$. There is now no obvious position of equilibrium in the diagram with the choice having to be made from points A, B and C. However, the latter point is obviously not a position of equilibrium since it is off the 45° line along which expenditure and income are equal. The classics also claimed that point B was not an equilibrium position because the excess planned supply of goods which exists at B would involve an undesired accumulation of stocks on the part of firms and on their assumptions this would have repercussions on the interest rate. Specifically, the undesired accumulation of stocks, i.e. unintended investment, would imply an excess of planned saving over planned investment, but since both planned investment and savings are functions of the interest rate such an excess would lead to a fall in the interest rate from r_1 to r_2, which would raise investment to I_2 and lower savings to S_3, i.e. increase consumption to C_3 and thereby raise the level of aggregate demand in the economy back to E_1. Thus the only true position of equilibrium is

15

point A, where the full-employment level of output is being purchased but at a lower interest rate than previously.

The conclusion of this analysis is therefore that once the level of output has been determined in the labour market at a level consistent with full employment, this level will be maintained, apart from temporary departures, because the level of expenditure on goods and services, i.e. aggregate demand, will be brought into equality with the amount supplied through the equilibrating force of the interest rate.

The Money Market

Since for any given price level, money-wage flexibility assures full employment in the classical model, we will conclude our analysis of the classics by analysing the determinants of the price level in their model. The classical hypothesis, stated simply, was that the price level was determined by the amount of money made available by the monetary authorities. This hypothesis is referred to as the Quantity Theory of Money, and it is usually written in one of the following forms, which are variants of the famous 'equation of exchange':

$$MV = PT \qquad (2.1)$$

$$MV = PY \qquad (2.2)$$

$$M = kPY \qquad (2.3)$$

In equation (2.1) MV stands for the stock of money multiplied by its average velocity of circulation and represents monetary expenditure over a certain time period (say one year). PT stands for the volume of transactions multiplied by the average price of each transaction and represents the value of monetary transactions within the same time period. Equation (2.1) is a simple truism in that it states that the total money spent during a year equals the total value of goods and services bought in the year.

The difference between equation (2.1) and equation (2.2), which are both examples of the 'transactions version' of the Quantity Theory, centres on the definition of the term T. In (2.1) it includes all monetary transactions while in (2.2) it excludes the purchase and sale of existing assets and includes only the volume of current output purchased during the period; it is therefore distinguished by using the symbol Y. The definitions of P and V then have to be modified slightly to fit in

16

with this narrower (but more meaningful) definition of T. Thus in equation (2.2) P is defined as the average price level of current output so that PY is simply national income measured at current prices and V is defined as the income velocity of money.

However, both (2.1) and (2.2) are simply accounting identities in the sense that they provide a convenient framework within which to analyse the variables involved in monetary change, but they become a theory of the price level when certain restrictions are placed on the values of V and T or Y, e.g. in respect of equation (2.2) it was assumed that V was determined by the customs and payments habits of society so that V would be greater if people were paid each week than if they were paid monthly, i.e. money turns over faster under a weekly payments system. However, since these factors change only slowly it was felt legitimate to take V as an institutionally determined constant in the short run. Similarly, as we have seen above, the volume of output Y was taken as fixed in the short run at the full-employment level by technological factors. Thus with both V and Y assumed constant and M regarded as exogenously determined by the monetary authorities the price level becomes the dependent variable of the equation. It follows that changes in M must cause proportionate changes in P and therefore this version of the Quantity Theory concludes that P will simply depend upon the amount of money in circulation.

Equation (2.3) is an interesting variant of the Quantity Theory and is known as the 'cash-balance version'. It is not simply an accounting identity and is better regarded as a condition of equilibrium in the monetary sector. The right-hand side of the equation can be taken to represent the demand for money while M, as before, represents the money supply. In this version, the price level adjusts to bring the demand for money into equality with the fixed supply. The demand is taken to be some fraction k of the value of national income and with k assumed to be constant in the short run and the volume of output fixed at full employment the price level is again seen to be proportional to the money supply.

However, this approach to the Quantity Theory is more interesting for our purposes than is the transactions version because it gives us some insight into the adjustment process through which changes in M cause proportional changes in P. For example, assume that there is initially equilibrium in the monetary sector where the demand for money kPY is equal to the existing money supply, but that the

17

equilibrium is now disturbed by a doubling of the money supply. The community then finds itself holding a greater quantity of money than it either desires or needs to support its present level of transactions, and it will attempt to re-establish equilibrium by spending more money on goods and services. In other words, there will be an excess supply of the means of payment and since money earns no interest it was assumed that the community would not desire to hold its wealth in this barren form. Of course the additional expenditure which results from this excess supply of money will not lead to a reduction in the nominal amount of money in circulation, but with Y fixed at the full employment level and k assumed constant, it will succeed in forcing up the price level, and in this way the community is able to determine the *real* value of the money supply that it is willingly prepared to hold. Thus when M is doubled, with k and Y constant, equilibrium, in the sense that the existing stock of money is willingly held, will only be re-established when prices have doubled, thus causing the demand for money to double, with the result that the real value of the money supply will return to its previous level, i.e. $M/P = 2M/2P$.

Thus the essence of the cash-balance version of the Quantity Theory is that with a stable demand for real-money balances any increase in the nominal amount of money in circulation will simply lead to an increase in prices sufficient to restore the level of real-money balances to their original level and thereby re-establish equilibrium in the monetary sector. It will be noted, however, that a crucial assumption in this adjustment process is that money functions solely as a medium of exchange and thus people do not wish to hold idle money balances but simply wish to hold some constant fraction of their income in the form of money sufficient to cover their transactions needs. It will be recalled that a very similar assumption was involved in applying Say's Law to a monetary economy, i.e. it was assumed that money was not held for its own sake but only for its use in facilitating transactions. The point is, of course, that money is not simply a means of payment or a medium of exchange in that it enables us to avoid the awkwardness of barter, it is also a store of value, i.e. it enables us to set aside some of our present income for future consumption. The classics, while recognising that money had other uses thought that its store of value function could be safely ignored because of the presence, in a modern economy, of interest-bearing alternatives to the holding of wealth in the form of non-income-yielding cash. (However,

18

Keynes was later to demonstrate that things are not quite this simple, and that the interest rate is an additional determinant of the demand for money.)

In summary, the classical theory can be represented by the following four equations:

$$D\left(\frac{W}{P}\right) = S\left(\frac{W}{P}\right) \text{ (labour market)} \qquad (2.4)$$

$$Y = Y(N, \overline{K}) \text{ (production function)} \qquad (2.5)$$

$$I(r) = S(r)$$

or

$$-I(r) = Y - C(r) \text{ (goods market)} \qquad (2.6)$$

$$M = kPY \text{ (money market)} \qquad (2.7)$$

The real wage and the level of employment are determined by *labour-market* equilibrium. With N known the level of output or aggregate supply is determined by the *production function*. The rate of interest is determined by the real forces of productivity and thrift via equilibrium in the *goods market*, and when the goods market is not in equilibrium the interest rate varies so as to bring savings and investment into balance, i.e. to bring the level of aggregate demand ($C + I$) into equality with aggregate supply. With all the real variables thus determined the sole function of the *money market* is to determine the price level. This independence of the real and monetary sectors is referred to as the 'classical dichotomy'.

A KEYNESIAN MODEL

So far in this chapter we have analysed the individual working of and to some extent the interaction between the labour, goods and money markets in a typical classical model. We will now proceed to develop a Keynesian model which will be similar in that it will also contain markets for labour, goods and money, but it will be dissimilar as regards the workings of each market and the interaction between them. In this respect we can be at least as brief as in our development

of the classical model because although the Keynesian model is the more complex of the two it is so well covered in modern macro textbooks that only an outline of most of the basic functions will be presented here. However, those aspects of the Keynesian system which are at the centre of the current debate will be given broader coverage; these include the concept of the marginal efficiency of investment, the speculative demand for money and the role of money wages.

In the Keynesian model the goods and money markets are more closely linked together than they are in classical theory and they are usually represented together in the familiar *IS/LM* diagram. We will discuss these two markets first and then proceed to a discussion of the labour market.

The Goods Market

In the goods market one of the major Keynesian innovations is the substitution of the consumption function for the classical hypothesis that consumption and savings are simply related to the interest rate. The consumption function relates expenditure specifically to the level of *current* income and it postulates that consumption will increase as income rises, but not by as much as the rise in income. This statement is merely a paraphrase of the famous 'psychological law' that Keynes used to deduce the shape of the consumption function and it gives rise to a function of the following type:

$$C = a + bY$$

Here consumption is taken to be a simple linear function of income, where the marginal propensity to consume b lies in the range $0 < b < 1$ and where the average propensity to consume declines as income rises. However, the important thing to note about this consumption function is that it emphasises the level of current income as the effective constraint on consumer expenditure.

This type of consumption function is an important component of any Keynesian model but it is no longer based upon an *adhoc* psychological law. In the first place many theories of consumer behaviour have since been advanced which to some extent support this law but which have the advantage of being derived theoretically from basic economic propositions (e.g. see [21]). Second, these new theories have the added advantage of being able to reconcile the short-

20

run *non*-proportional relationship between C and Y with their long-run proportionality, i.e. the average propensity to consume, when measured over the business cycle, *declines* as income rises, but it remains *constant* in the long run. This reconciliation has been achieved in the modern versions by developing a consumption—wealth relation in addition to the short-run consumption—income relation, which causes the latter to shift over time. The important thing to note about these modern theories of the consumption function is that they attach *less* significance to the level of current income as a determinant of consumer expenditure and emphasise instead longer-run concepts of income or wealth.

The other major Keynesian innovation in the goods market is the introduction of the marginal efficiency of capital schedule, m.e.c., as a determinant of investment demand. The m.e.c. is defined by Keynes as 'that rate of discount which would make the present value of the . . . returns expected from the capital good . . . just equal to its supply price' ([46] p. 135). If we let the supply price or present cost of the capital good be given by q, then the discount rate d, i.e. the m.e.c., can be solved from the following equation, in which R_i are the returns expected over n years of the asset's life:

$$q = \sum_{i=1}^{n} \cdot \frac{R_i}{(1+d)^i}. \tag{2.8}$$

The m.e.c. of an investment project is therefore that value of d which equates the right and left-hand sides of this equation. This approach to investment decision-making is known as the *internal rate of return method* and it pronounces an investment project profitable if the internal rate of return d, i.e. the m.e.c., is greater than the market rate of interest r. On the assumption of diminishing returns d will decline as capital is increased relative to other factors of production, and therefore once the capital stock has been expanded to the point where $d = r$ any further expansion will require a fall in r relative to d. Thus the demand for capital goods will be inversely related to r.

A similar but more direct approach to determining an investment project's profitability was also suggested by Keynes. This is known as the *present-value method* and our reasons for analysing it in addition to the internal rate of return method will become clear below. This method involves determining the present value of a project's expected

21

returns by discounting them at the current market rate of interest r. The present value (PV) of the expected returns is then given by:

$$PV = \sum_{i=1}^{n} \frac{R_i}{(1+r)^i} \qquad (2.9)$$

This present value can be interpreted as a *demand price* for the capital asset under consideration, in the sense that it represents what one would be prepared to pay in order to obtain the asset. The demand price can then be compared directly with the asset's supply price in order to determine its profitability – if the demand price exceeds the supply price it is worth while acquiring the asset. However, equation (2.9) illustrates that a *fall* in the current market rate of interest will *raise* the demand price for capital goods, and therefore the present-value method, like the internal rate of return method, also postulates an inverse relationship between the demand for capital goods and the interest rate.

It will be noted that so far we have been analysing the investment decision at the *micro* level, and at this level the present-value method has been shown to be superior to the internal rate of return method for reasons which do not directly concern us here (see [1]). However, the present-value method also has some advantage over the internal rate of return method when we analyse investment at the *macro* level. We require a macro rather than a micro approach because we are not interested in the demand for capital goods as such but in the amount of investment actually undertaken each time period, and the present-value method is useful in indicating how we get from the demand for capital to the *rate of investment*. For example, if the demand price for capital assets *DP* exceeds the supply price *SP*, then the micro approach tells us that the capital stock could be profitably expanded, but the amount of new investment actually undertaken will be indeterminate unless some mechanism exists whereby *DP* and *SP* are again brought into equality. The question is then what brings about the equality between these two prices and hence determines the rate of investment. Does *DP* fall as more investment is undertaken or does *SP* rise?

DP can be expected to fall as more capital is produced because the marginal physical product of capital will diminish as capital increases relative to other factors of production (this is a straight forward application of the law of diminishing returns). However, we are

22

interested in the *short run* when by definition the change in the capital stock is small relative to the size of the existing capital stock, and will therefore be insufficient to depress its marginal physical product. Therefore, equilibrium between DP and SP, and thus a determinate level of investment, can only be achieved in the short run by a *rise in* SP. This is where the micro/macro distinction becomes important: although the individual firm can legitimately take SP as fixed, at the macro level when all firms choose to expand their stock of capital, SP is likely to rise because the capital-goods industry, like any other industry, will be facing increasing short-run marginal costs.

At the macro level, then, investments in new projects earn lower returns i.e. their marginal efficiencies diminish, not because the marginal efficiency of the capital stock diminishes as more investment is undertaken, but because the cost of additional capital goods increases in the short run. This inverse relationship between the rate of investment and the return to investment is summed up in the marginal efficiency of investment schedule, m.e.i., which is illustrated below in Figure 2.4 (*b*) (note that the axes have been have been reversed from their normal usage). It illustrates that in the short run new investments will be undertaken only up to the point where the returns from investment are brought into equality with the market rate of interest via rising supply prices. However, the important point to note about this aggregate investment schedule is that it is a function of both demand and supply conditions, i.e. it depends on the m.e.c. schedule and the cost curves of the capital-goods industry.

The Keynesian approach therefore specifies an aggregate investment function which depicts a negative relationship between investment and the interest rate. However, the same negative relationship was assumed in classical theory, so why did we describe this relationship as a Keynesian innovation? In the classical analysis the downward-sloping investment schedule is taken to be a demand for loanable funds and there is a corresponding supply schedule of savings; these schedules, taken together, determine the market rate of interest. The novelty of the Keynesian approach is twofold. On the one hand the relationship between I and r is more clearly specified by using either the internal rate of return or present-value method, and is shown to be the result of the interaction, at the macro level, of demand and supply conditions in the capital-goods industry. On the other hand, the whole role of the interest rate is reversed, e. g. the Keynesian analysis takes the market interest rate as given and either (*a*) compares

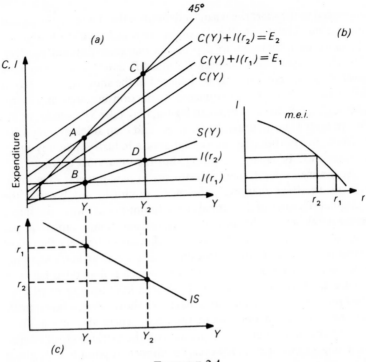

FIGURE 2.4

the internal rate of return of each investment project with this given interest rate, or (b) uses the market rate of interest to discount the expected returns from the capital asset to determine its present value or demand price. Thus the interest rate must first be ascertained from some other source *before* the investment decision-making process can begin. In other words, in the Keynesian analysis the interest rate is not determined in the goods market by the interaction between the investment and savings schedules but is in fact taken to be largely independent of these schedules.

The basic Keynesian propositions in respect of the goods market are then obtained by combining these two innovations of Keynes, i.e. the consumption function and the m.e.i. schedule to obtain the equilibrium condition for the goods market. This is written:

$$Y = C(Y) + I(r) \qquad (2.10)$$

or

$$S(Y) = I(r) \qquad (2.11)$$

24

Equilibrium is achieved when the level of aggregate demand, i.e. the sum of consumption expenditure, which is a function of income, and investment expenditure, which is a function of the interest rate, is just sufficient to purchase the existing level of output. However, since the interest rate is taken as given in the Keynesian analysis, the interaction between these two components of the goods market cannot determine the equilibrium level of the rate of interest but instead determine the equilibrium level of national income. The process by which equilibrium is achieved in the goods market is illustrated in Figure 2.4.

In Figure 2.4(b) an m.e.i. schedule is drawn indicating a diminishing marginal efficiency of investment and illustrating that new investment is undertaken only up to the point where the m.e.i. is reduced to the level of the current market rate of interest. The amount of investment spending is therefore determined in Figure 2.4 (b) and this amount is then transposed on to Figure 2.4(a), where the other element of aggregate demand, consumer expenditure, is determined via the consumption function $C(Y)$.

The inverse relationship between I and r is illustrated in Figure 2.4 (a) by upward shifts in the investment schedule when the interest rate falls. Given the consumption function the 45° line also enables us to derive a savings function $S(Y)$ and the determination of the equilibrium level of national income can then be illustrated either with reference to equation (2.10) or equation (2.11), e.g. (2.10) is satisfied when the level of aggregate demand $C + I$ is equal to the current level of output Y. A graphical representation of this solution is given by point A when the interest rate is r_1, so that the level of expenditure is E_1 and therefore the equilibrium level of income is Y_1, and by point C at the lower interest rate r_2 where the level of aggregate demand is E_2 and the equilibrium level of income is at the higher level Y_2. In terms of equation (2.11) the corresponding points of equilibrium are B and D respectively. These latter points indicate that in contrast to the classical theory a disequilibrium between savings and investment has an effect upon the level of income rather than the interest rate.

Figure 2.4 (a) and (b) illustrate that for every level of the interest rate there will be a different equilibrium level of income, and those combinations of r and Y that result in equilibrium in the goods market are plotted in Figure 2.4 (c) to form the negatively sloped IS relation. The slope of the IS curve is determined by the slopes of the consumption or savings functions and that of the marginal efficiency of investment schedule. Thus the steeper the savings function and the

more interest inelastic the m.e.i. schedule the steeper will be the *IS* function. The position of the *IS* curve in turn is determined by the position of the expenditure functions in Figure 2.4(*a*), e.g. the *IS* curve will shift to the right if these expenditure functions shift upwards independently of changes in the interest rate.[1]

However, it will be noted that the curve derived in Figure 2.4(*c*) is a *locus* of equilibrium points between *r* and *Y* but it does not determine the actual equilibrium level of either. This is because our analysis has proceeded by assuming a particular rate of interest and then finding the corresponding level of income. But this implies that the goods market is underdetermined, i.e. we have only *one* equation, (2.10) or (2.11), to determine the *two* variables *Y* and *r*, and in order to overcome this problem we need to introduce into the analysis the Keynesian theory of the money market.

The Money Market

The major innovation in the money market is the introduction of the interest rate as an important equilibrating force in addition to the level of money income. It will be recalled that in the classical analysis money income PY was the main equilibrating force in the sense that the price level P fluctuated to maintain equilibrium between the demand for and supply of money, on the assumption that the level of real income Y and the velocity of circulation V were constant. As a result the classical Quantity Theory of Money became a theory of the determination of the price level. The Keynesian theory of money on the other hand is a theory of the determination of the interest rate and it is based on Keynes's pathbreaking analysis of the demand for money.

Keynes formulated his theory in terms of the motives for holding money and he classified these into the transactions demand, the precautionary demand and the speculative demand. These three motives taken together determine the individual's demand for money, or his 'liquidity preference', and the novelty of the Keynesian approach is brought out clearly in the algebraic formulation of this demand function which is written:

$$M^D = kPY + L(r). \tag{2.12}$$

The demand for money is thus split into two parts. The first is taken to

26

be proportional to the level of money income PY and is held in order to satisfy both the *transactions demand*, i.e. 'to bridge the interval between the receipt of income and its disbursement' and the *precautionary demand*, i.e. 'to provide for contingencies requiring sudden expenditure'. Both these demands arise from the need to hold the medium of exchange, i.e. the need to have available the accepted means of payment when entering into a transaction. Thus the rationale for the first part is similar to that underlying the cash-balance version of the quantity Theory in that people are assumed to hold some fraction k of their income in the form of money to facilitate transactions, and since these balances are held only with the intention of being spent on goods and services they are referred to as *active* balances.

The second part of the demand for money function is taken to be an inverse function of the interest rate r and these balances are held in order to satisfy the *speculative demand*, i.e. 'the object of securing profit from knowing better than the market what the future will bring forth' ([46] pp. 170, 196). The market referred to in this quotation is the bond market and the statement therefore implies that money balances are held because they act as a useful substitute for other financial assets, i.e. they act as an alternative store of value, and since these money balances are *not* held with the intention of being spent in the near future on goods and services they are referred to as *idle* balances.

Equilibrium in the monetary sector is established when the amount of money demanded for both 'active' and 'idle' purposes is equal to that supplied. However, it is the adjustment process through which equilibrium is approached that is the important factor in the analysis because this will determine how monetary impulses are transmitted through the economy. For example, in the cash-balance version of the Quantity Theory people adjust their actual money holdings to those desired by spending excess money balances on goods and services, and this approach therefore assumes that the effects of a change in the quantity of money are transmitted through the economy via the medium of exchange function of money, i.e. through transactions or 'active' balances. However, the Keynesian view of the adjustment process and consequently of the transmission mechanism is entirely different. For example, the process by which people adjust their actual to desired holdings of money is complicated in the Keynesian analysis by the presence of the interest rate as a determinant of desired money

27

holdings, i.e. by the existence of the speculative motive. Keynes in fact gave great prominence in his model to this motive 'because it is particularly important in transmitting the effects of a *change* in the quantity of money' ([45] p. 196). Therefore in Keynes's view monetary impulses were transmitted through the economy via the store of value function of money, i.e. through speculative or 'idle' balances, and in view of the great importance attached to the speculative demand in Keynes's model we shall find it useful to analyse further the rationale that underlies this motive for holding money.

Keynes's basic assumption regarding the speculative motive was that in attempting to secure a profit in the bond market speculators held *inelastic expectations* about the future course of the interest rate, i.e. if the current rate fell it was assumed that bondholders would not expect the future rate to fall by as much as the fall in the current rate. This stickiness of interest-rate expectations was based on the notion that each bondholder, when faced with the intractable problem of uncertainty about the future, was forced to have recourse to a convention which Keynes labelled the *normal rate of interest*. By this he meant the rate to which a bondholder expects the current rate to return. Thus, if the current market rate of interest is higher than the rate regarded as 'normal', a bondholder will expect the current rate to fall because of the inverse relationship between interest rates and bond prices he will expect bond prices to rise in the future, thus earning a capital gain on his bondholdings.[2] Such an individual will therefore prefer to hold his wealth in the form of bonds and his demand for speculative balances will be zero. Similarly, if the current market rate of interest is below the normal rate then a capital loss will be expected on bondholdings and therefore all wealth will be held in the form of money.

If the opinion of bondholders were unanimous concerning the normal rate then the demand for money for speculative purposes would be a discontinuous function showing only money held when current rates were below the normal rate and only bonds held when current rates were above it. However, such unanimity is unlikely to occur because the normal rate is subjectively determined in the mind of each investor and a continuous downward-sloping relationship between the speculative demand and the interest rate will exist as long as investors differ in their opinions of the 'normal rate', i.e. as long as there exists 'a variety of opinion about what is uncertain' ([46] p. 172).

There are therefore two important considerations to be borne in mind when the negative relationship between the demand for money and the interest rate is based on Keynes's speculative motive. In the first place the negative relationship is seen to be the result of investors being forced to make rational decisions in the face of an uncertain future, i.e. they attempt to overcome the problem of uncertainty by adopting the convention of a normal rate. On this basis the sole intelligible reason for demanding money as a store of value is the existence of uncertainty. Second, although uncertainty is a necessary and sufficient condition for the existence of a speculative demand for money it is not sufficient to ensure a downward-sloping demand function for money. The latter requires the existence of a 'variety of opinion' and if such a variety does not exist then the demand for money function will be discontinuous, e.g. if at some low rate of interest investors are unanimous that the rate is going to rise then the function becomes horizontal, i.e. liquidity preference becomes absolute. It is this situation which is referred to as the 'liquidity trap'.

The basic Keynesian propositions in respect of the money market are then obtained by confronting the money demanded to satisfy all three motives with the available supply of money. The equilibrium condition for the money market can be written:

$$\overline{M} = kPY + L(r). \tag{2.13}$$

Equilibrium is achieved when the demand for money to satisfy the transactions and precautionary demand kPY plus the demand for speculative balances $L(r)$ is just sufficient to absorb the existing money supply $\overline{M}$. If we take the level of money income as given then the interaction between the demand for and the supply of money will determine the equilibrium rate of interest. The process by which equilibrium is achieved in the money market is illustrated in Figure 2.5.

In Figure 2.5 (a) two demand curves for money M_1^D and M_2^D, are drawn representing different levels of money income. The former is drawn up for money income level PY_1 and the latter for the higher level of money income PY_2, illustrating that the demand for money schedule shifts to the right when money income increases.[3] This is because the demand for transactions balances increases proportionately with the rise in income, and the greater is the value of k the further will the demand schedule shift to the right. Thus the position of these schedules is determined by the transactions motive. The

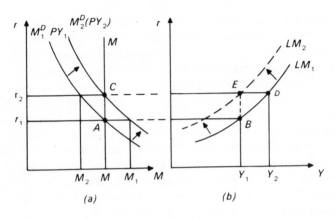

FIGURE 2.5

slope of these schedules is determined by the speculative motive, and its importance in the adjustment process, through which desired and actual money holdings are brought into equality, can be illustrated as follows. Assume that the level of money income is initially PY_1 and the money supply is fixed at $\overline{M}$. If the market rate of interest was r_2 then this would result in an excess supply of money equal to $\overline{M} - M_2$. The implication of this excess is that bondholders expect the current rate to fall, i.e. r_2 is *above* what they regard as the normal rate and therefore they expect a capital gain on their bondholdings. Hence they will have an excess demand for bonds corresponding to the excess supply of money, and in attempting to increase the proportion of bonds in their portfolio they will bid up bond prices, or in other words bid down the rate of interest, until equilibrium is achieved at point A, where the interest rate has fallen to r_1. At this *lower* interest rate the initial excess supply of money will be absorbed into speculative balances.

Similarly, if the money market were initially in equilibrium at point A but the level of money income was to rise to PY_2, causing the demand for money to shift to $M_2{}^D$, then at interest rate $r_1^{\cdot}$ there would exist an excess demand for money equal to $M_1 - \overline{M}$. In an attempt to satisfy this excess demand for money, bondholders will sell bonds with the result that bond prices will be bid down and the interest rate bid up until equilibrium is achieved at point C, where the interest rate has risen to r_2. At this *higher* interest rate the speculative demand will be lower and thus equilibrium is re-established when the initial excess

demand for transactions balances has been met via a decline in the holdings of speculative balances.

Figure 2.5 (a) illustrates that for every level of money income there will be a different equilibrium level of the interest rate and those combinations of Y and r that result in equilibrium in the money market are plotted in Figure 2.5 (b) to form the positively sloped LM curve. The *slope* of the LM curve is determined by two factors: (a) the slope of the demand for money function; and (b) the value of k, which determines the shift in the demand curve in response to a change in money income. Thus the steeper the demand curve and the greater the value of k, the steeper will be the LM function. The *position* of the LM curve is determined by the stock of real money balances, i.e. the real value of the money supply, $\overline{M}/P$. For example, if the shift in the demand for money schedule from $M_1{}^D$ and $M_2{}^D$ had been caused by a rise in prices rather than real income, as previously postulated, then the money market would be in equilibrium at a *higher* interest rate r_2 but the *same* level of real income Y_1, causing the LM curve to shift leftwards to pass through point E. A similar shift would be occasioned by a reduction in the money supply from M to M_2. Thus a fall in real balances brought about either by a reduction in the nominal amount of money in circulation or a rise in the price level will cause the LM curve to shift to the left.

However, the LM curve, like the IS curve, represents a *locus* of equilibrium points between r and Y but does not determine the actual equilibrium level of either. The equilibrium value of r is only found after assuming a particular level of money income. There is therefore a certain circularity of reasoning involved in the separate analysis of the goods and money markets in the Keynesian model because in order to determine the equilibrium level of income in the goods market the interest rate must first be known, but in order to determine the interest rate in the money market the level of income must first be known. Thus a simultaneous approach is required whereby the levels of r and Y are jointly determined such as to be compatible with equilibrium in both markets, i.e. the equilibrium values of r and Y must lie on both the LM and IS curves, and this is only possible at point E in Figure 2.6. A combination of r and Y other than that given by the intersection of the IS and LM curves would mean that either the goods market was in disequilibrium, which would be the case at point A, or the money market, point B, or both, point C.[4]

31

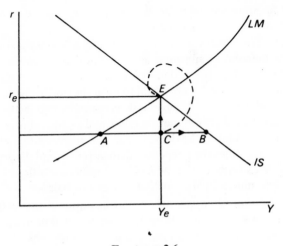

FIGURE 2.6

The Labour Market

We complete our outline of Keynesian economics by introducing the labour market into the model and it will be seen that this market remains broadly similar to that of the classical analysis.

The similarity is made evident by the factors underlying the demand and supply schedules of labour. The demand for labour again depends on a comparison between the marginal product of labour, derived from the production function, and the real wage. The analysis underlying this comparison has already been outlined (see above, pp. 9–13) and the conclusion was that the demand for labour will be an inverse function of the real wage. The supply of labour, however, leads a sort of schizophrenic existence in the Keynesian model. Sometimes the money wage is assumed rigid, in which case the supply of labour is viewed as being a function of the fixed money wage, while at other times money wages are assumed flexible, in which case the supply of labour is taken to be a function of the real wage. We will analyse both these cases separately because in the Keynesian literature they are viewed strictly as alternatives.

When the labour supply is taken to be a function of the money wage there is the obvious connotation that the labour force 'suffers' from *money illusion,* i.e. labour is assumed not to respond to a change in real income but only to changes in money income. This analysis can be

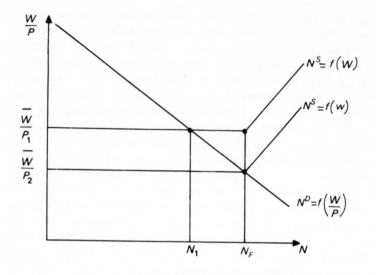

FIGURE 2.7

illustrated diagrammatically (see Figure 2.7). At the fixed money wage $\overline{W}$, although the whole of the existing labour force N_F is willing to accept employment there is *involuntary unemployment* of $N_F - N_1$ at the current price level P_1 because the real wage is such that only N_1 is demanded.[5] In this model full employment can only be achieved by a rise in the price level to P_2 which would cause the real wage to fall and therefore the labour-supply schedule to shift down until the excess supply, or involuntary unemployment, is eliminated. When full employment is achieved, i.e. when all those wishing to work at $\overline{W}$ are employed, a further increase in the amount of labour demanded can only be satisfied by bidding up the money wage, thereby encouraging more people to enter the labour market and causing an upward kink in the supply schedule.

The upshot of this is that in the absence of a rise in the price level the assumption of a downwardly rigid money wage enables the labour market in the Keynesian model to be in equilibrium at less than full employment. However, is the Keynesian analysis materially different from that of the classics? For example, it was pointed out that in the classical analysis full employment was ensured as long as money wages were flexible. Thus the difference between the two approaches

on this point is purely *semantic* because whereas the Keynesians would describe the unemployment resulting from rigid money wages as 'involuntary', the classics would simply have called it 'voluntary' unemployment, since in their view the labour force, for whatever reason, had chosen not to accept lower money wages. However, the Keynesians went further than the classics in one respect, and attempted to rationalise the money illusion implicit in the labour-supply schedule by pointing to such real world phenomena as minimum wage laws and powerful trade unions, but despite these rationalisations it is obvious that the *assumption* of a rigid money wage cannot in any way be regarded as a Keynesian innovation.

As if anticipating this conclusion, an alternative formulation was proposed where money wages were assumed flexible and the labour supply was taken to be a function of the real wage but where the labour market remained in disequilibrium. The possibility of there still existing large amounts of involuntary unemployment despite money-wage flexibility was then supported by an analysis of the way in which the labour market adjusts to equilibrium. Since this analysis is the one part of Keynesian labour-market theory which is based upon Keynes's original discussion of the subject, we will find it useful to go into the analysis in some detail. Therefore, starting from a situation of equilibrium in the goods market, where planned invest-ment and saving are equal but where there exists involuntary unemployment in the labour market, we will proceed to analyse the role of money-wage flexibility in restoring full employment.

When unemployment exists and the money wage is bid down by unemployed workers competing for the existing jobs, the classics would predict an expansion in employment because the lower money wages would reduce costs of production and thereby increase the demand for labour. The argument is therefore that as wages fall marginal costs fall and output and employment expand. However, Keynes went one step further and enquired whether the extra production would be consumed. His analysis of this problem can best be illustrated by reference to Figure 2.8.

In Figure 2.8(a) the level of aggregate demand $C + I$ is such that the equilibrium level of income Y_1 is less than the full-employment level Y_F with the result that money wages will be bid down. This is illustrated in Figure 2.8(b) where the demand and supply curves for labour are drawn as functions of the real wage. At the initial real wage (W_0/P_0) there is an excess supply of labour which bids down the

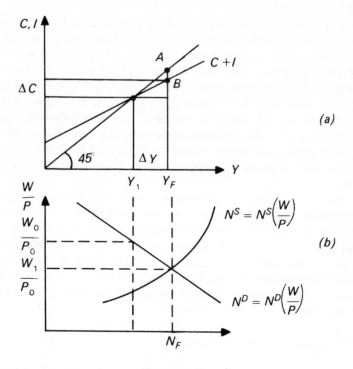

FIGURE 2.8

money wage to W_1, thus causing the real wage to fall to (W_1/P_0). If this fall in costs is sufficiently large then it will induce producers to expand employment and production to N_F and Y_F respectively so that full employment is achieved in the labour market. However, with a marginal propensity to consume of less than one $(\Delta C/\Delta Y < 1)$ only a fraction of this increase in output will be consumed and the remainder AB will take the form of an accumulation of stocks. Therefore, Y_F is not an equilibrium situation and prices will be reduced and output contracted until the excess stocks are eliminated, which will only be the case when output has fallen to Y_1. But if output contracts to its initial level then labour input will also be reduced to N_1.

Thus, if we look at the labour market in isolation, we obtain a distorted view of the adjustment process because the increase in employment which results from a fall in money wages is purely transitory, and when we delve deeper into the process and look at the goods and labour markets together, we see that cuts in money wages

35

will not succeed in returning us to full employment. Indeed, if the system returns to the initial levels of income Y_1 and employment N_1 and since N_1 workers are only employed when the real wage is W_0/P_0, it follows that the price level must eventually fall in proportion to the fall in money wages. In other words, the real wage returns to its initial level and with no change in the real wage the labour-market adjustment mechanism is therefore prevented from functioning. Therefore, Figure 2.8 illustrates that money-wage flexibility does not ensure a return to full employment in the Keynesian model when its effects on the labour and goods markets are analysed jointly.

The above analysis of the labour market can be summed up as follows: the Keynesian model either assumes that money wages are rigid, in which case involuntary unemployment can exist but only on the same grounds as in the classical model, or it assumes that even when money wages are flexible and are bid down in the face of involuntary unemployment, these reductions fail to *directly* equilibrate the labour market because prices fall proportionately, thus preventing a reduction in the *real* wage.

The Complete Keynesian Model

As a conclusion to this chapter, we will draw together our separate analyses of the goods, money and labour markets into a complete Keynesian model and then compare it directly with the classical model. The Keynesian model can in fact be represented in one diagram, and this is useful because the interrelationships between the various markets are so important in the Keynesian analysis that it is pointless trying to analyse any one market in isolation.

In Figure 2.9 (a) the level of aggregate demand in the economy is represented in terms of the IS/LM framework, and it indicates that if the conditions in the goods and money markets are represented by IS_1 and LM_1 then equilibrium will be achieved at r_1 and Y_1. In Figure 2.9 (b) a production function is drawn which is identical to that in classical theory. From this production function is derived the marginal product or demand curve for labour and this is illustrated in Figure 2.9 (c) as an inverse function of the real wage. Also, in Figure 2.9 (c) is drawn a positively sloping supply curve of labour with respect to the real wage which implies no money illusion on the part of the work-force.

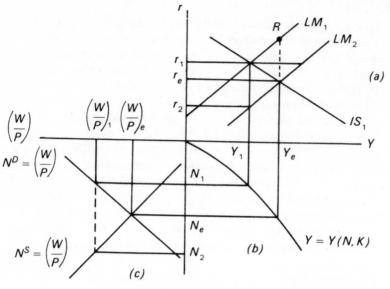

FIGURE 2.9

The demand for and supply of labour together determine the level of full employment N_e and the equilibrium real wage $(W/P)_e$. The production function then indicates the level of output Y_e necessary to ensure the full employment of labour.

Figure 2.9 (b) and (c) therefore represent the technical aspects of production, and the analysis underlying them is very similar to that of the classics. Thus, given the state of technology and the current real wage, Figure 2.9 (b) and (c) indicate what firms plan to supply, e.g. if the real wage is $(W/P)_e$, then output level Y_e can be regarded as the *planned* supply of goods. However, in the Keynesian model there is no obvious reason why this level of output should actually be produced because, from our analysis of part (a), there is no reason why the IS and LM curves should intersect at the level of output corresponding to full employment. In fact, with the goods market in equilibrium along IS_1 and the money market in equilibrium along LM_1, the level of aggregate demand in the economy is such that the equilibrium level of output will be Y_1.

The level of output corresponding to the point of intersection of the IS and LM curves can be regarded as the *actual* supply of goods, and this will then determine the actual level of employment. Thus when the actual supply of goods is below the planned supply the amount of

37

labour demanded will be below the level of full employment, e.g. when equilibrium in the goods and money markets is achieved at Y_1 the actual level of employment will be N_1 and there will be involuntary unemployment equal to $N_2 - N_1$. However, if conditions in the money market had been represented by LM_2 rather than LM_1 (or if the IS curve had been further to the right so as to pass through point R), then the actual and planned supplies of goods would coincide and the actual level of employment would be at the level of full employment N_e. The complete Keynesian model therefore apparently points to a number of possible equilibrium positions, and unless the LM and IS curves happen to intersect at $[Y_e, r_e]$ the level of employment will not in general be 'full' employment. However, as long as money wages and prices are assumed to be flexible, it can be demonstrated that the complete model will, over time, tend towards a single position of equilibrium and that this position will be one of full employment.

The Keynes Effect

To illustrate this tendency to move towards full employment assume that in Figure 2.9 above the goods and money markets are initially in equilibrium along IS_1 and LM_1, so that the interest rate is r_1 and the level of income is Y_1; the corresponding level of employment will then be N_1 and the real wage will be, $(W/P)_1$. The goods and money markets are therefore in equilibrium but the labour market is in disequilibrium, with involuntary unemployment equal to $N_2 - N_1$. If we assume that money wages and prices are flexible, then the pressure of excess supply in the labour market will bid down money wages. However, Keynesian labour-market analysis predicts that the fall in money wages will eventually lead to a proportionate fall in the price level which will leave the real wage unchanged at $(W/P)_1$. Thus the labour market will apparently remain in disequilibrium. However, we pointed out above that changes in the price level affect the *position* of the LM curve and a *fall* in the price level will cause the LM curve to shift downwards to the *right*. This occurs because a fall in prices will lower the demand for active balances, causing the demand for money function shown in Figure 2.5 to shift downwards, thus creating an excess supply of money at the prevailing rate of interest. This will result in a corresponding excess demand for bonds, and bond prices will be bid up, thus causing the interest rate to fall until the initial excess supply of money is absorbed into speculative or idle balances.

38

However, since the interest rate is a determinant of investment expenditure, the lower rate of interest will encourage more investment, i.e. it will lead to a movement along the *IS* curve, and since investment is an important element in aggregate demand the latter will increase. But it is the level of aggregate demand in the Keynesian model that determines the actual supply of goods. Therefore the levels of output and employment will also expand.

This indirect mechanism by which reductions in wages and prices initially reduce the demand for money (increase the demand for bonds) and then, via reductions in the interest rate, increase the level of aggregate demand will eventually eliminate the involuntary unemployment in the labour market because as long as there exists an excess supply of labour, wages and prices will continue to be bid down and the *LM* function will continue to shift to the right until full employment is achieved. In our previous example, which took account of the goods and labour markets only, money-wage cuts failed to equilibrate the labour market because, with a marginal propensity to consume of less than one and no increase in planned investment, the level of output returned to its initial level. However, in the complete model planned investment *does increase* because falling wages and prices succeed in eventually reducing the interest rate. Therefore the complete Keynesian system does have an automatic tendency to move towards full employment.

The effect of falling wages and prices on the interest rate has become known as the *Keynes effect* because Keynes was the first to examine the mechanism by which reductions in money wages eventually succeed in restoring full employment. There are two things to note about the 'Keynes effect':

(*a*) It postulates a relationship between the price level and the level of aggregate demand in the economy, i.e. a price-level fall lowers the interest rate and induces a greater demand for investment goods; and

(*b*) It is based on a *wealth effect* in the bond market. By wealth effect we mean the relationship between a stock of wealth and an expenditure flow. Thus a price-level fall raises the real value of the *stock* of money balances and causes a rise in the *flow* demand for bonds which in turn lowers the interest rate and induces a higher *flow* of expenditure on investment.

The 'Keynes effect' therefore refers to the wealth effect by which

39

reductions in money wages and prices eventually succeed in stimulating demand, and it illustrates that the way in which full employment is 'automatically' achieved in a Keynesian model with flexible wages and prices is through a bond-market wealth effect. However, it must be emphasised that having elaborated this mechanism Keynes then posed the question of whether a policy of wage cuts was the *best* policy to achieve full employment, i.e. if the only favourable effect of wage cuts was to reduce the interest rate, and since the authorities could reduce the rate of interest more directly via monetary policy, it seemed illogical to advocate reductions in money wages as a cure for unemployment. In fact if such a policy was advocated, then according to Keynes, 'we should, in effect, have monetary management by the Trade Unions, aimed at full employment, instead of by the banking system' ([46] p. 267).

In summary the Keynesian theory can be represented by the following four equations:

$$I(r) = S(Y) \tag{2.14}$$

or $\quad\quad I(r) = Y - C(Y) \quad\quad$ (goods market)

$$\overline{M} = kPY + L(r) \quad\quad \text{(money market)} \tag{2.15}$$

$$Y = Y(N, K) \quad\quad \text{(production function)} \tag{2.16}$$

$$N^D\!\left(\frac{W}{P}\right) = N^S\!\left(\frac{W}{P}\right) \quad\quad \text{(labour market)} \tag{2.17}$$

The levels of income, consumption, investment, saving and the interest rate are determined simultaneously by equilibrium in the *goods* and *money* markets. With the level of income known and the capital stock fixed the *production function* determines the level of employment. We are then left with two variables, W, the money wage, and P, the price level and only one equation to determine both. However, if equilibrium in the *labour market* determines the real wage then taking the historically given money wage as a constant enables us to determine the price level. Therefore the solution to the Keynesian system presupposes knowledge of the money-wage level.

A PRELIMINARY COMPARISON

Having thus outlined the Keynesian approach, we are now in a position to make a preliminary comparison between the Keynesian view of the working of the economic system and that of the classics. In comparing the two models we will draw attention to some of the crucial differences between them but a more detailed comparison will not be attempted until Chapter 5.

One general point of difference is that whereas markets are interlinked in the Keynesian system, such interrelationships between markets are almost non-existent in the classical model. The classical system is in fact made up of three independent sub-systems: equations (2.4) and (2.5) above determine the levels of N, Y and (W/P), equation (2.6) determines separately the level of I, S and r, and equation (2.7) determines the price level. In the Keynesian system all three sections are linked together by the fact that Y is determined jointly in the goods and money markets and this level of output then determines the actual volume of employment. Consequently, although the models appear similar in that they both tend to an equilibrium at full employment when money wages are flexible, they remain quite distinct because the mechanism which ensures full employment in the Keynesian system differs from that of the classics.

More specifically, the most important link in the Keynesian chain of inter-market relations is the money market but in the classical model the money market plays no part in determining output or employment – it simply determines the price level. The money market is very important in the Keynesian model because it determines the interest rate; its crucial role in determining equilibrium in the labour and goods markets can be illustrated in the following two examples.

In respect of the labour market we can take disequilibrium to entail the existence of involuntary unemployment and we pointed out that in the classical analysis full employment is approached through forces operating in the labour market alone, i.e. with the price level fixed in the money market, reductions in money wages lead directly to reductions in the real wage which succeed in equilibrating the labour market. However, in the Keynesian model the price level is not tied to the quantity of money and is instead linked to costs of production. This means that reductions in money wages lead to reductions in costs and, eventually, prices, with the result that the real wage is not reduced sufficiently to *directly* equilibrate the labour market, and equilibrium

then has to await the indirect effect of the fall in prices on the demand for money, i.e. the Keynes wealth effect. Therefore the money market is crucial to the determination of equilibrium in the labour market.

In respect of the goods market we can take disequilibrium to entail a deficiency in aggregate demand, i.e. current expenditure less than current output, and such a deficiency can be remedied in both the classical and Keynesian models by a reduction in the interest rate. This remedy is easily achieved in the classical model because both investment and saving are functions of the interest rate and therefore an excess of saving over investment will exert direct downward pressure on the rate of interest, which will stimulate investment and discourage saving, i.e. encourage consumption until the deficiency in demand is eliminated. Thus the goods market, like the labour market, reaches equilibrium without reference to any other part of the model. However, in the Keynesian system the matter is complicated by the fact that the interest rate is not determined in the goods market but in the money market and in order for there to be a reduction in the interest rate there must be a revision of interest-rate expectations on the part of speculative holders of money. Thus the liquidity preference of potential bondholders puts a check on the adjustment mechanism and prevents an accommodating change in the interest rate which would otherwise correct the imbalance between savings and investment. Thus the money market is also crucial to the determination of equilibrium in the goods market.

However, while equilibrium in the goods market is awaiting the gradual revision of expectations in the money market, there is a far more direct mechanism restoring equilibrium in the short run in the Keynesian model. This is of course the level of output. The deficiency of aggregate demand, i.e. the excess of saving over investment, will be resolved more by a reduction in output and income than a reduction in the interest rate until saving out of current income is equal to the (low) level of investment. Thus when expenditure is less than output it is a reduction in the latter rather than an expansion of the former which restores 'equilibrium' in the Keynesian model. The classics on the other hand would have reversed this conclusion.

In the opening paragraphs of this book we pointed out that economic theory should fulfil three functions: it should have explanatory power; it should be able to predict changes in economic conditions; and it should be able to prescribe economic remedies when things go wrong. We are now in a position to contrast the

classical and Keynesian theories in term of their ability to satisfy these criteria.

If we assume an initial situation in which there is a large amount of unemployment, the classical model would *explain* this phenomena in terms of the labour market alone. It would *predict* that a reduction in money wages would be a sufficient condition for the restoration of full employment and, if the level of aggregate demand was insufficient to purchase the output level produced by a fully employed labour force, it then made the *further prediction* that the interest rate would be bid down until the level of aggregate demand was raised to the level of aggregate supply. Therefore its policy *prescription* in the face of unemployment is to induce firms to supply more by reducing costs of production through cuts in money wages.

The Keynesian model on the other hand *explains* the unemployment in the labour market in terms of the insufficiency of aggregate demand in the goods and money markets, i.e. the *IS* and *LM* curves intersect at an output level below full employment. It *predicts* that reductions in money wages will not restore full employment unless they succeed in increasing aggregate demand via the Keynes effect, and therefore its basic prediction is that the unemployment will be eliminated if, and only if, the level of aggregate demand can be increased. Its policy *prescription* therefore is for the government to induce households and firms to increase their planned demand for goods. Although it is true that money wage cuts may be successful in this respect they succeed only indirectly through their effects on the interest rate and there is therefore a much more direct policy tool available to the government in the form of open-market operations, which can *directly* reduce the interest rate. Furthermore, since the aim is to increase aggregate demand and since the rate of interest affects only the investment component of expenditure, the government could have an even more direct impact on the problem by reducing taxes and thereby inducing greater household expenditure or simply by increasing its own expenditure.[6]

Thus the mass unemployment of the 1930s which persisted despite reductions in money wages could not be adequately *explained* by the classical model and, indeed, because of the certainty of full employment in their model, the classics had paid little attention to the possible emergence of such a chronic disequilibrium. A failure to even explain a problem naturally precludes an ability to make informed predictions or policy prescriptions. Fortunately full employment was

43

not guaranteed with certainty in the Keynesian model and it was therefore at least better suited to providing an answer to the problem of chronic disequilibrium. The Keynesian explanation in terms of a deficiency of demand was credible enough and the policy recommendation that the government should attempt to increase the level of aggregate demand rather than planned supply eventually formed the basis of short-run macroeconomic policy in most Western countries.

However, the fact remains that the Keynesian theoretical model, in the absence of wage and price rigidities, has an automatic tendency to move towards an equilibrium at full employment. Therefore, the Keynesians, too, are faced with the problem of *explaining* how the economic system goes 'wrong' and why it does not succeed in *righting* itself *despite* flexible wages and prices. In Chapter 3 we will analyse how the Keynesians answered this question and in Chapter 5 we will examine the explanation offered by Keynes. Thus the problem facing both the Keynesians and Keynes was to explain how unemployment became so widespread *without resorting to the classical explanation which 'blamed' labour-market imperfections.*

3
A Consensus?

'It is usually considered as one of the most important achievements of the Keynesian theory that it explains the consistency of economic equilibrium with the presence of involuntary unemployment' (Modigliani [60]). This quotation illustrates quite effectively that the debate which followed the publication of Keynes's *General Theory* centred on the conditions under which the Keynesian system could settle at a position of unemployment equilibrium. It will be recalled that the classical system could remain at such a position only if money wages were rigid and therefore the question raised by the debate was whether the Keynesian system could remain at less than full employment *despite* flexibility of money wages. However, we illustrated in Chapter 2 that even when the *IS* and *LM* curves intersect at less than full employment, flexible wages and prices would, via the Keynes wealth effect, ensure a return to full employment. Therefore, if conclusions different from the classical analysis were to be arrived at, Keynesians needed to expound the conditions under which the Keynes effect would not succeed in generating a return to full employment.

Keynesians did in fact point to two obstacles which had to be surmounted before wage and price flexibility would succeed in automatically ensuring the full employment of resources. These obstacles to full employment were the possible existence of either an interest inelastic m.e.i. schedule in the goods market or an infinitely elastic liquidity-preference function in the money market. It was argued that the existence of either of these situations would prevent the Keynes effect from bringing about a return to full employment. We will now examine these two possibilities in some detail.

INELASTIC INVESTMENT FUNCTION

In our discussion of the goods market in the Keynesian model we pointed out that the more interest inelastic the m.e.i. schedule, the steeper will be the *IS* function. In the limit when the investment schedule becomes perfectly inelastic, the *IS* function becomes vertical. If we were to draw such an *IS* curve in Figure 2.9 then at the initial equilibrium levels of income and interest rate the curve IS_1 would become a vertical line through Y_1 in Figure 2.9 (a) intersecting LM_1 at interest rate r_1.

However, at this income level there exists involuntary unemployment in the labour market which will result in a bidding down of the money wage and this in turn will cause a proportionate fall in prices. The Keynes effect, which is the effect of the fall in prices on the real value of the money supply, will cause the *LM* curve to shift to LM_2, but this is no longer sufficient to bring about a return to full employment because the reduction in the interest rate has no effect on investment expenditure (investment demand is completely inelastic) and therefore there is no effect on the level of income. Even a reduction in the interest rate below r_e (i.e. that previously required for full employment) is incapable of generating an increase in aggregate demand and hence in the level of income. Moreover, a completely vertical *IS* curve is a stricter condition than we actually require to prevent the Keynes effect returning the system to full employment because as long as the *IS* curve is very steep and intersects the horizontal axis to the left of Y_e then there exists no positive interest rate at which investment expenditure will be sufficient to ensure the full employment of resources. Therefore the Keynes effect is prevented from operating despite the fact that it succeeds in reducing the interest rate because the level of aggregate demand does not respond to the fall in the rate of interest.

INFINITELY ELASTIC LIQUIDITY PREFERENCE FUNCTION

In our discussion of the money market in the Keynesian model it was pointed out that at some low rate of interest bondholders could become unanimous in their expectations that the interest rate would

rise in the future and their fear of incurring a capital loss on bonds would cause the liquidity-preference function to become infinitely elastic at the current rate of interest, i.e. there would exist a 'liquidity trap' implying that any increase in the money supply would be willingly absorbed into idle balances. However, we also noted that the flatter the liquidity-preference schedule, the flatter the LM function, and in the limit when liquidity preference becomes absolute the LM curve becomes horizontal.

In order to incorporate such an LM schedule into Figure 2.9 we could postulate that at interest rate r_1 bondholders are unanimous that the rate is going to rise and under these conditions the LM curve would become a horizontal line through r_1. Therefore r_1 can be regarded as a minimum interest rate in the sense that current expectations are such that a lower rate cannot be achieved.

If we begin the analysis again at income level Y_1, where there exists involuntary unemployment, the reduction in money wages and prices will increase the real value of the money supply, but in a situation of absolute liquidity preference this will have no effect on the interest rate, i.e. the real value increase in the money supply will be willingly held in the form of idle balances and no attempt will be made to exchange these balances for bonds because of the unanimous fear that a capital loss will be incurred on bond holdings. Thus bond prices will not be bid up and although the LM curve will shift rightwards it will remain horizontal at r_1. Thus the Keynes effect is again prevented from operating, not because aggregate demand does not respond to a fall in the interest rate, but because there is no reduction in the interest rate.

Thus the Keynesian position can be summarised as follows. Full employment is ensured in the Keynesian model by an indirect mechanism known as the Keynes effect. This is a movement along the IS curve brought about by a shift in the LM curve which in turn has been induced by reductions in money wages and prices. However, Keynesians insist that there is no guarantee that the system will be returned to full employment via this mechanism because the movements along the IS curve may be either insufficient (because the function is very steep) or prevented (because of the liquidity trap). Thus Keynesians conclude that the assumption of rigid wages is not a necessary condition for the persistence of unemployment.[1]

These then were the support pillars that underlay the Keynesian claim to have provided a theoretical explanation for the coexistence

of involuntary unemployment and flexible wages and prices (see above the opening statement of this chapter). However, the argument appeared only fairly respectable at the theoretical level because in order to generate conclusions different from the classics, the Keynesian model had to make the special assumptions of either a steep *IS* curve or a horizontal *LM* curve, but Keynesians were quick to point out that these assumptions were in fact well grounded empirically and were therefore of a more general nature than appeared at first sight.

For example, empirical investigations such as the Oxford surveys in the late 1930s failed to find any substantial correlation between the spending decisions of borrowers, particularly business firms, and the interest rate [61]. This was taken as evidence that the *IS* function was, in fact, very steep. Second, the stickiness of the yield on long-term government securities, which never fell below 3 per cent during the 1930s despite attempts to expand the money supply and reduce interest rates, was taken as evidence that the *LM* function was in fact horizontal at low interest rates. Also, early evidence by Tobin [78] supported a 'trap'. Therefore, since the assumptions appeared to conform to reality it was claimed that it would be a misnomer to refer to them as 'special'.

THE 'PIGOU EFFECT'

Thus the Keynesian model appeared to have provided an alternative theoretical system which produced different conclusions from the classical analysis in the sense that it was able to account for the *persistence* of unemployment through time. However, the claim to have provided such a system was soon challenged by Pigou and others who claimed that Keynesian analysis of the effects of deflation did not go far enough. According to the Keynesians a deflation of money wages and prices leads to a *shift* in the *LM* curve and a *movement along* the *IS* curve. Pigou, however, claimed that falling prices would also affect the *position* of the *IS* curve, e.g. 'As wealth increases, the amount that he so desires to save out of any assigned real income diminishes and ultimately vanishes' [65].

In order to understand the reasoning behind this claim it is necessary to recall our analysis of the goods market in the Keynesian model. As illustrated in Figure 2.4 above, the Keynesian goods market is represented by the *IS* function, and the position of this

function is determined by the level of expenditure on consumption and investment goods. Pigou's basic argument was that the level of consumption expenditure would rise in response to a deflation of prices. To illustrate this Pigou assumed that individuals saved in order to obtain some target level of wealth and he insisted that this assumption was particularly apposite in the Keynesian model where the level of saving is determined by current income. Thus saving can be positive even when the rate of interest is zero. But, asked Pigou, why should anyone save when there is no income to be earned from saving unless it is in order to achieve a certain target level of wealth? Therefore Pigou insisted that his assumption was implied by the Keynesian model.

Moreover, the appropriate measure of wealth in Pigou's analysis was its real value so that the level of wealth varied inversely with the price level. Thus if prices fell and the real value of wealth increased, individuals would save less in order to reach their target because their previously accumulated savings would have increased in value. Pigou was therefore postulating an inverse relationship between the real value of wealth and the proportion of income which is saved, in other words a *direct* relationship between real wealth and consumption, i.e. as wealth in real terms increases, consumer expenditure will also rise. It is this relationship which has become known as the Pigou effect. (Note that, like the Keynes effect, it postulates a relationship between the price level and the level of aggregate demand, i.e. it is based on a wealth effect in one sector of the model. However, in Pigou's analysis it is the consumption sector which reacts to changes in the real value of its wealth and therefore the Pigou effect implies the existence of a wealth effect in the goods market. It will be recalled that the Keynes effect was based on a wealth effect in the bond market.)

Pigou therefore insisted that an additional wealth effect was implied by the Keynesian model and it should therefore be explicitly taken into account. Below we incorporate the Pigou effect into the model and analyse the implications of this extension in terms of the Keynesian conclusion that the economic system can settle at a position of unemployment equilibrium.

The Pigou effect can be included in the model by expanding our analysis of the demand side of the goods market. Instead of writing planned expenditure as a function of income and the rate of interest only, i.e.

$$E = C(Y) + I(r),$$

49

the consumption function is expanded to include the level of real wealth:

$$E = C\left(Y, \frac{W}{P}\right) + I(r), \qquad \frac{dE}{d\left(\dfrac{W}{P}\right)} > 0.$$

A change in the price level will cause the consumption and expenditure functions to shift and this will induce a shift in the *IS* curve; in particular a *fall* in prices will cause the *IS* curve to shift to the *right*.

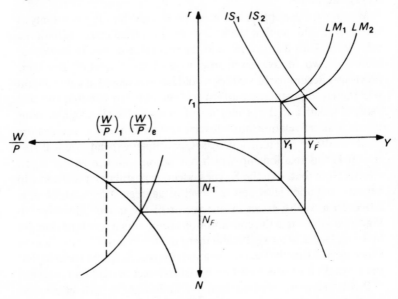

FIGURE 3.1

The implications of this rightward shift in the *IS* curve are explored in Figure 3.1. Suppose that initially the economy is at $[Y_1, r_1, N_1]$ and that money wages and prices fall because of the excess supply of labour. If the fall in wages and prices is proportional then it will leave the real wage unchanged and will have no equilibrating effect on the labour market, but the fall in prices will eventually stimulate aggregate demand and shift both the *IS* and *LM* curves to the right

50

(because of the Pigou and Keynes wealth effects respectively). The rise in the demand for goods will check the rate of fall in prices and the real wage will begin to fall because money wages will be falling faster than prices and therefore the excess supply in the labour market will gradually diminish. Furthermore, since wages and prices will continue to decline as long as there is unemployment, the IS and LM curves will not remain in a stable position until full employment is reached, i.e. they will shift to the right until they intersect at income level Y_F. Thus as long as prices are flexible there is an automatic tendency to full employment.

Furthermore, note that it is the Pigou effect rather than the Keynes effect which ensures full employment in the above analysis because the slope of the LM curve in the diagram implies the existence of a liquidity trap and the slope of the IS curve implies an inelastic investment function – two conditions which would prevent the attainment of full employment in the absence of shifts in the IS curve. Thus if we explicitly include the Pigou effect in the Keynesian model we obtain a rather non-Keynesian result – the economy will always have a tendency towards full-employment equilibrium unless wages and prices are inflexible downwards.

However, Keynesians attempted to refute this result and the debate continued at both the theoretical and empirical level. In terms of pure theory the debate centred on the four-equation model of the Keynesian system with one extension – the level of real wealth was included in the consumption function. This extended-equation system in fact forms the basis of Patinkin's work on the 'real-balance effect', where the latter is Patinkin's terminological choice for the Pigou effect (see [63]). Patinkin formalised the debate and demonstrated that in a static equation system which incorporates the real-wealth/consumption relation the only possible equilibrium position for the system is that of full employment. This is illustrated in the appendix to this chapter.

Hicks, in a review article of Patinkin's book, attempted to refute Patinkin's argument but the attempt failed and in terms of pure theory it became (grudgingly) accepted that equilibrium at less than full employment in the static Keynesian model was the result of rigid wages, e.g. 'In my opinion . . . the Pigou Effect finally disposes of the Keynesian contention that under-employment equilibrium does not depend on wage rigidity. It does. . . . [Thus] it turns out that Keynes' theory is a special case of the Classical' (H. G. Johnson [39]).

THEORETICAL OBJECTIONS TO THE PIGOU EFFECT

Defenders of Keynes who claimed to have produced a more general theory than the classics were then forced to delve deeper into the mechanism by which the Pigou effect was supposed to stimulate expenditure. This enquiry led to a number of quasi-theoretical objections being raised:

(1) In the first place it was objected that not all assets were eligible for inclusion in the wealth component upon which the Pigou effect was based. In particular it was claimed that assets issued by the private sector should not be included because the increase in real value, viewed from the creditor's side, would be offset by the adverse effects on the debtor. The only debtor not influenced by increases in the real value of its debt is the government. Thus it was felt that the only part of private net worth which could possibly be relevant to the operation of the Pigou effect was the net liabilities of the government to the private sector. This element of net worth is known as 'outside' debt (see Kalecki's reply to Pigou [65] and [39] for a summary).

However even this overstates the case because the interest cost of government debt will rise in real terms as prices fall and this will have to be financed by taxing the private sector. Thus the relevant wealth variable should be written as:

$$W = \frac{M_0 + \lambda B/r}{P},$$

where M_0 represents notes and coins, B government bonds, r the interest rate on bonds, and λ measures the extent to which consumers treat as net private wealth the value of government debt. If $\lambda = 0$ then wealth reduces simply to the real value of the notes and coins issued by the government, M_0/P, i.e. the real value of outside money. Thus in the limit all other forms of government debt are excluded, along with that part of the money supply which is backed by private debt, i.e. demand deposits at commercial banks, referred to as 'inside' money.

However, the number of monetary assets eligible for inclusion in the Pigou effect has recently been expanded following the work of Pesek and Saving [64]. This book raised a number of important issues in relation to wealth effects but we shall discuss just one of them, namely their rejection of the standard accounting framework as an

adequate basis upon which to assess the net worth of financial intermediaries (for a comprehensive discussion of the whole issue, see Johnson [40]). Pesek and Saving argue that the present-value technique should be used to assess the liabilities of banks, and some probability distribution used to determine the extent to which deposits are likely to be withdrawn (the instant 'repurchase clause'). The fact, then, that the accounting balance sheet sums to zero (i.e. bank's assets are matched by liabilities) should *not* be taken to read that the banking sector's contribution to the public's wealth position is zero. Some 'inside money' must be included in the public's wealth because the present value of banks' liabilities will be *less* than the present value of their assets (assuming that the probability of realisations of the 'repurchase clause' is not unity). And the point is, of course, that banks typically do not act as if the value of their liabilities are equal to their assets.

Thus the inside/outside money debate did not satisfactorily refute the theoretical basis of the Pigou effect.

(2) It was also claimed that there were 'distribution effects' which could make the Pigou effect inoperative, e.g. typically it is the richer members of society that benefit from the increase in the real value of monetary assets but their marginal propensity to consume is likely to be smaller than that of other sections of society whose wealth position is *adversely* affected (debtors, etc.). Therefore the net effect on expenditure may be negative if the losers *decrease* their consumption by more than the gainers *increase* theirs. Further weight can be given to this argument if we extend our analysis to take account of the effects of falling prices on the investment expenditure of firms. If it is the case that firms are on balance debtors then a persistent price decline may cause some firms to go bankrupt, in which case it is very unlikely that the effects on debtors and creditors will cancel each other out. The monetary value of a debtor's assets will be drastically reduced by bankruptcy. Therefore a price decline may not result in a positive net effect on total expenditure [62].

(3) In extending the analysis to include the effects of falling prices on a firm's demand for goods we have ignored the supply side of the analysis. However, it has been pointed out by Bailey that changes in real wealth also affect the supply of goods [4]. His argument is based on the fact that cash balances are a factor of production. In a modern economy goods are produced by a combination of labour and capital but this combination in the industrial process can only come about

through the use of money as a medium of exchange to facilitate transactions. The existence of money balances therefore contributes to real output and it is possible that real output will be greater, the greater are real cash balances. This can be reflected by including real balances in the production function of the macroeconomic model. The production function then becomes:

$$Y = Y\left(N, \frac{M}{P}, \overline{K}\right).$$

Similarly, the demand function for labour will also include real balances because the marginal productivity of labour depends on the other factors of production, M/P and K. Specifically, an increase in real balances will shift the demand curve for labour outwards and thus the full-employment equilibrium level is increased. However, if the full-employment level increases as real balances rise, then the effectiveness of the Pigou effect in restoring full employment is weakened, e.g. a fall in wages and prices in the face of unemployment will induce wealth effects in both the goods and money markets and thus cause the demand for goods to rise but the increase in the real value of money balances will also induce an increase in the planned supply of goods (the full-employment level increases). Therefore the original excess supply of goods may remain unchanged or even increase depending on whether supply is stimulated to the same extent as demand or to a greater extent.

(4) A final objection at the theoretical level was based on the role of expectations. It was suggested that expectations concerning future price levels will weaken the Pigou effect if a fall in the present price level leads to an expectation of further falls because under these conditions present consumption would be postponed to take advantage of lower future prices.

This argument was very appealing, especially to those Keynesians who were trying to defend Keynes's theoretical position, because it approached the issue from a dynamic viewpoint rather than adopting the static simultaneous-equation approach. It was felt that a dynamic analysis was required because of Keynes's emphasis in many sections of his work on the important role of expectations. However, it was soon pointed out that the assumption concerning expectations in this context, and used as an argument against the Pigou effect, was at variance with the analysis of expectations in other parts of Keynes's

work, e.g. if it is assumed that a fall in the present price level leads to expectations of further falls then one is assuming that people hold *elastic* or extrapolative expectations about price-level changes. However, it was pointed out in Chapter 2, in our analysis of the Keynesian money market, that the basis of Keynes's theory of interest was that bondholders have *inelastic* expectations about bond prices. Therefore, for Keynes's theory to be consistent and 'general', it seemed to require a symmetrical treatment of transactions in different markets. It was argued that the asymmetry apparent in this treatment of the goods and money markets could not be supported in an argument purporting to provide a *general* theory.

In addition to this criticism of the asymmetric role of expectations in the two markets, there was the theoretical possibility that despite expectations of further price falls, consumption in this period may rise if individuals have positive rates of time preference, i.e. if the marginal utility of present consumption is higher than that of future consumption this can be illustrated in an indifference-curve diagram by the indifference curves between present and future consumption being such as to produce a result similar to the negative income effect in ordinary consumer analysis. Thus even if consumers have elastic price expectations, the Pigou effect could still stimulate aggregate demand.

Thus, on balance, the theoretical arguments did not decisively rebut the claim of the proponents of the Pigou effect that unemployment equilibrium depended on the assumption of rigid wages.

EMPIRICAL OBJECTIONS

The debate, however, continued and it became centred increasingly on empirical criteria. Basically it was argued that since the Pigou effect was based on a relatively insignificant section of total wealth, i.e. outside money, some fraction (λ) of outside bonds and some fraction of inside money (following Pesek and Saving), the Pigou effect would be empirically weak. Thus, although there might be a positive correlation between the real value of wealth and consumer expenditure, the coefficient might be so small that reliance on the effect would involve long periods of unemployment.

This statement can be illustrated by a rough calculation of the size of the Pigou effect in the United Kingdom in 1930. At that time the quantity of outside money was £320m., the quantity of inside money

was £1750m. and the stock of government bonds in the hands of the public was £3000m. Thus the level of wealth felt to be relevant to the operation of the Pigou effect can be calculated from the formula:

$$W = \frac{M_0 + \gamma M_i + \lambda B/r}{P},$$

where the variables are as above with the addition that M_i represents inside money and γ represents the proportion of inside money which is regarded as wealth by the public, including the banks.

The magnitude of the Pigou effect on the real value of wealth can be estimated as follows: assume that γ and λ are roughly equal to 0.4 and that the interest rate is 4 per cent, if the price level was to fall by 50 per cent then the increase in wealth from the point of view of the public would have been:

$$\Delta W = \frac{320 + 0.4(1750) + 0.4(3000/4)}{2} = 660.$$

If we further assume that the price fall was an unexpected, once and for all change and the public expected prices to remain at the lower level, then all of the £660m. can be regarded as an increase in net wealth. The question we then have to ask is: what effect will this have on consumers' expenditure?

The best way to approach this question is via Friedman's permanent-income theory [23]. The increase in wealth outlined above corresponds to Friedman's concept of a 'windfall' – an unanticipated favourable change in circumstances. However, only that part of it which increases permanent income will result in an increase in consumption, and in order to estimate the effect on permanent income Friedman introduces the concept of the 'horizon'. If we follow Friedman and assume that the typical horizon is three years, so that only 33 per cent of any change in wealth affects *current* income expectations, and therefore *current* consumption, then with a marginal propensity to consume of 0.8 the effect on consumption will be:

$$£(0.8) (0.33) (660) = £165m.$$

The level of consumers' expenditure in 1930 was £4000m. Therefore the effect of a *50 per cent* fall in the price level would be to raise consumption by approximately 4 per cent. Such an increase would have been too small to have brought about a return to full employment in the 1930s.

Furthermore, the assumed fall in the price level was greater than that which actually took place. Between 1930 and 1933 prices fell by only 20 per cent. Incorporating this change into the above estimation would have led to the prediction that consumer expenditure should have increased by roughly 1 per cent. For the record, consumption actually *fell* by 6 per cent between 1930 and 1933 and GDE by 10 per cent. This perverse effect was undoubtedly due to the fact that the conditions necessary for the Pigou effect to work – a once and for all change with no adverse effects on price expectations and business confidence – were not present in the 1930s, i.e. prices fell slowly over a period of years giving rise to expectations of further falls and creating pessimism amongst the business community.

A CONSENSUS

Thus the empirical evidence pointed to a fairly insignificant real wealth effect on consumption even at the theoretical level while in practice the dynamics of price-level changes resulted in a non-existent or even perverse effect on consumers' expenditure. Also, it implied that even in theory the time lags involved in an adjustment process based solely on the Pigou effect would be so long that business confidence would necessarily be adversely affected. Therefore, no reliance could be placed on the Pigou effect as an equilibrating factor.

The empirical weakness of the Pigou effect was further emphasised by the acceptance of both sides of the debate that wages and prices were in fact relatively inflexible in the real world, leading to the conclusion that the Pigou effect was a theoretical concept with little practical application. This was acknowledged in fact by Pigou, who insisted that his analysis of wealth effects 'are academic exercises, of some slight use perhaps for clarifying thought, but with very little chance of ever being posed on the chequer board of actual life',[66].

Thus despite the apparent theoretical weakness of the basic Keynesian model it was argued that its main conclusions were unaffected by the debate over the Pigou effect. For example, the debaters had found common ground in accepting that a policy of wage flexibility to counter unemployment was impractical because of lags, adverse expectations, etc. Also, it was generally accepted that wages and prices are in fact fairly sticky in a downwards direction. From this consensus of opinion it was only a short step to the conclusion of Samuelson and others that if only Keynes had simply

57

stated that he was assuming that wages and prices were rigid downwards, then 'most of his insights would have remained just as valid' [73]; or, 'Keynes' theory started from an empirically relevant special assumption, derived some important meaningful results from it and provided a useful approach . . . to a wide range of problems' [39].

What were these insights, these meaningful results? If they were simply that unemployment equilibrium could be caused by rigid wages then they were not very different from those of the classics. In fact it was not at the theoretical level that the results were lauded. It was insisted that the greatest achievement of Keynesian economics was that its theoretical analyses could be easily applied to operational policy-making and the importance attached to the Keynesian Revolution therefore came to be based on its policy prescriptions.

POLICY IMPLICATIONS

The policy recommendations of the Keynesian model are based on an analysis of the two special cases outlined at the beginning of this chapter. It will be recalled that the implication of these two cases is that, in the absence of the Pigou effect, wage flexibility will not succeed in restoring the economy to full employment – basically because shifts in the LM curve are frustrated either by an inelastic investment schedule or the liquidity trap. But if shifts in the LM curve are negated for either of these reasons then not only is a flexible wage policy ineffective, but *monetary policy is also ineffective*, and the LM curve can be moved to the right either by a fall in the price level or an expansion of the money supply. If a shift due to a fall in the price level has no effect on the level of income then a shift due to an increase in the money supply will also be ineffective. The conclusion of Keynesian theory therefore is that under certain conditions monetary policy is impotent.

It is worth concentrating at this point on the reasons for the impotency of monetary policy. In the Keynesian model an increase in the money supply will result in an excess supply of money and it is predicted that this excess of money balances will be channelled into the bond market because bonds (i.e. financial assets) are assumed to be the main substitute for money. The inflow of money into the bond market will bid up the price of bonds – bid down the interest rate –

and this will stimulate investment expenditure. In these circumstances monetary policy is said to be effective. However:

(1) if there exists a liquidity trap in the money market so that speculators are unanimous that the interest rate is already below its normal level, i.e. bond prices are expected to fall in the future, then the excess money will not be channelled into the bond market and interest rates will not be bid down – monetary policy is therefore ineffective; and

(2) in the absence of a liquidity trap the interest rate will fall, but if it fails to induce a greater level of investment expenditure – because (say) businessmen are very pessimistic about the future – then monetary policy is again ineffective.

Under these special conditions monetary policy is therefore impotent. Note that Keynesians believed that the circumstances giving rise to these special cases were not uncommon, i.e. they believed that the *IS* schedule was very steep and that the *LM* curve could become horizontal. Therefore monetary policy came to be regarded as generally ineffective in stimulating expenditure and various metaphors were introduced into economic analysis to emphasise this point, e.g. 'you can't push on a string', or 'you can lead a horse to water but you can't make him drink', etc.

Having demonstrated the unreliability of both a flexible wage policy and monetary policy as a means of guaranteeing a return to full employment in a depressed economy, Keynesians come to the conclusion that the only effective policy tool was that of fiscal policy. To illustrate this point consider Figure 3.2. In the circumstances depicted in the diagram monetary policy is completely ineffective because both special cases prevail, e.g. an increase in money supply shifts the *LM* curve from *LM*$_1$ to *LM*$_2$ but this has no effect on the interest rate and hence no effect on investment. Furthermore, even if the interest rate was reduced this would not be sufficient to achieve full employment because investment expenditure is not sufficiently responsive to interest-rate changes. However, the government has the power to alter not only the *LM* schedule but also the position of the *IS* curve via the use of its budget, e.g. an increase in government expenditure or a reduction in taxes will shift the *IS* curve to the right. Therefore, even in conditions such as those underlying Figure 3.2 the government can directly stimulate aggregate demand and restore the

economy to full employment by altering its expenditure and taxation policies so as to shift the *IS* curve to IS_2.

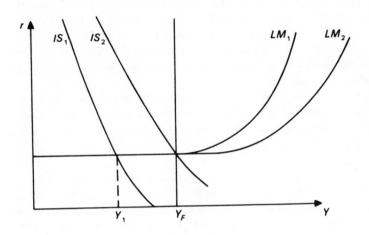

FIGURE 3.2

In the light of this analysis the conclusions of Chapter 2 regarding policy prescriptions can be amended to take into account these Keynesian positions. Under certain circumstances money wages cuts will be unsuccessful in restoring full employment. Under the *same* circumstances one of the more direct policy tools available to the government, i.e. open-market purchases intended to increase the money supply will *also* be ineffective as a means of restoring full employment. When these circumstances prevail the only effective policy tool that can with certainty restore full employment is fiscal policy. Thus fiscal policy is completely general in that it is successful under all circumstances while the efficiency of monetary policy is more restricted; and for many Keynesians this general effectiveness of fiscal policy was interpreted as a correct restatement of what Keynes actually meant by entitling his book *The General Theory*.[2]

However, the purpose of introducing the Pigou effect in this chapter was to point out that from the point of view of pure theory the Keynesian analysis becomes a special case of the classical. The question is, therefore, does the Pigou effect also have implications for the generality of the *policy* conclusions of the Keynesian model?

According to the theory underlying the Pigou effect consumer expenditure can be stimulated by a rise in real value of the community's wealth and the real value of the money supply is an important element in real wealth. However, the real value of money can be increased either by a fall in the price level or by a rise in the nominal amount of money in circulation. Therefore, even in the special conditions outlined above, monetary policy can still be effective in restoring full employment because it can directly increase wealth by expanding the nominal money supply. Therefore the Keynesian emphasis on fiscal policy to the exclusion of monetary policy seems unfounded.

Thus the Pigou effect rehabilitates and provides an effective role for monetary policy even in the presence of inelastic investment demand and the liquidity trap. But is this rehabilitation really necessary, i.e. are the Keynesian special cases likely to materialise? At first Keynesians believed that they were feasible but the consensus of opinion eventually changed when later research indicated that they were unlikely to occur, for example:

(1) As regards inelastic investment demand, it was argued that if interest rates fell to zero then many long-lived capital projects yielding low rates of return would become profitable. An example of this would be extracting oil from shale or land reclamation and, as Bailey has observed, 'Even if expectations were so bad that gross investment of the current type fell to zero . . . there would be some positive rate of interest low enough to make these investments worthwhile given their durability' [4]. Also, capital projects are not the only thing sensitive to the interest rate – consumer expenditures on durables and housing are also likely to be stimulated by very low interest rates. Therefore a vertical *IS* curve is very unlikely.

(2) Regarding the trap, initial research by Tobin indicated that such a phenomena did exist at low interest rates but more sophisticated studies found fault with Tobin's statistical techniques and produced no evidence of a liquidity trap, e.g. Bronfenbrenner and Mayer found no tendency for the interest elasticity of the demand for money to increase as the rate of interest fell [8].

If neither of the special cases are likely to exist then there is scope for an effective role for monetary policy even in the absence of the Pigou wealth effect on consumption. Thus, in theory, monetary policy can claim at least as much influence as fiscal policy and under certain

circumstances it can claim to be even more effective, i.e. the money multiplier may not only be greater than zero but it may also be greater than the fiscal multiplier. This, in one form or another, is the basic claim of the Monetarists and we shall be investigating their position in the next chapter.

THE NEOCLASSICAL SYNTHESIS

Finally, to conclude this chapter we will look at the type of model that emerged from the debate over the Pigou effect. A general macroeconomic model resulted which can be represented by the following equation system:

$$I(r) = S(r, Y, W) \quad \text{(goods market)} \quad (3.1)$$

$$\frac{\overline{M}}{P} = L(r, Y) \quad \text{(money market)} \quad (3.2)$$

$$Y = Y(N, \overline{K}) \quad \text{(production function)} \quad (3.3)$$

$$D\left(\frac{W}{P}\right) = S\left(\frac{W}{P}\right) \quad \text{(labour market)} \quad (3.4)$$

It is this simultaneous-equation model that has become known as the 'neoclassical synthesis' and the main differences between this and the Keynesian model are the inclusion of the interest rate and real wealth as determinants of consumption and the more general form of the money demand function making the demand for real money balances a function of the interest rate and the level of G.N.P.

This system has an automatic tendency to full employment on the following assumptions:

(a) all prices are flexible;
(b) price expectations are unit elastic (expected future prices change in the same proportion as current prices); and
(c) there is no 'money illusion' (transactors respond to real, not money values).

Basically these assumptions assure that neither of the Keynesian special cases apply and accordingly the model grinds out classical results in the sense that price flexibility ensures a return to full-employment equilibrium. In order to produce Keynesian results – in

particular involuntary unemployment – one or more of these assumptions must be dropped, e.g. if the second assumption is dropped then this allows inelastic expectations in the money market to produce a liquidity-trap situation.

The neoclassical synthesis therefore aspires to a high degree of generality in that given differing sets of assumptions both schools of thought can be incorporated into it. But note that within this framework it is the Keynesian School rather than the classics that appears the *least* general of the two, in that its results are achieved only by making special behavioural assumptions. The synthesis therefore seems to view Keynes's theoretical contribution in fairly poor light. However, its conclusion that Keynes's theory is simply a special case of the classics can stand some re-examination and by way of an introduction to recent developments in this area let us question whether the neoclassical synthesis is as general as it appears at first sight.

In the first place note that the model is entirely *static*, i.e. it takes no account of time in the process of economic change and is concerned solely with equilibrium states. For example, when using the model to analyse certain events the analysis typically begins in an initial equilibrium position, assumes some change such as a decrease in investment expenditure and compares the resulting equilibrium with the original position. This type of analysis, known as *comparative statics*, simply involves comparing different equilibrium positions without regard either to the time involved in getting from one position to another or even the process of change itself, i.e. comparative statics do not *explain* the movement from the initial equilibrium to the final position but merely *assume* that the final equilibrium is eventually reached.

But is the return to equilibrium so inevitable? This assumed inevitability which is so crucial to the neoclassical synthesis is derived from the works of the early general-equilibrium theorists, i.e. Walras and Edgeworth. They were the first to grapple with the problem of how a perfectly competitive system returns to equilibrium following a disturbance, and although they succeeded in demonstrating the conditions necessary for stability they were forced to adopt very restrictive and artificial assumptions. The neoclassical synthesis not only accepts the assumptions of Walrasian general-equilibrium theory but the prominence of the synthesis in economic theory is largely due to its claim to have integrated Keynesian monetary theory

63

into the existing general-equilibrium model. But the point is that Keynes specifically rejected the assumptions underlying existing theory, e.g. in the Preface to *The General Theory* he writes: 'if orthodox economics is at fault, the error is to be found not in the superstructure, which has been erected with great care for logical consistency, but in the lack of clearness and of generality in the premises. Thus . . . my object [is to] persuade economists to re-examine critically certain of their basic assumptions' [([46] p. v.]).

Thus the static neoclassical model may not be the best viewpoint from which to assess Keynes's work and it would appear that a different frame of reference is needed. Thus we may need to appraise Keynes from a more dynamic standpoint in order to do justice to his theoretical contributions. This will be our approach in Chapter 5 where we will re-examine the foundations upon which the neoclassical synthesis has been built and analyse Keynes's views on the subject.

APPENDIX

In this appendix we present a simultaneous-equation model of the economy in which wealth effects are included in both the goods and money markets. The analysis is outlined in terms of a specific example because more formal treatments are available elsewhere (e.g. [64] mathematical appendix). The analysis below illustrates that with Pigou and Keynes wealth effects included in the model, it always tends towards the full-employment level of output as long as money wages and prices are flexible, i.e. neither a liquidity trap nor a vertical *IS* curve are sufficient to prevent the economic system automatically restoring full employment. Thus any persistent unemployment must result from *rigidities* in the system and (without actually blaming the unemployed themselves) the conclusion follows that such unemployment is essentially *voluntary*. The following example illustrates the main points involved.

Assume a two-sector model, (no government or foreign trade) and assume that the following variables are determined exogenously:

$$\text{Money supply, } M = 150 \qquad (3.5)$$
$$\text{Price level, } \quad P = 1 \qquad (3.6)$$
$$\text{Money wage, } \quad W = 1 \qquad (3.7)$$

The underlying behavioural relationships are:

Consumption function, $\quad C = 150 + 0.5Y \quad\quad$ (3.8)

Investment function, $\quad\quad I = 200 - 25r \quad\quad$ (3.9)

Demand for real money balances $\quad \dfrac{M}{P} = 0.5Y - 25r \quad\quad$ (3.10)

Production function $\quad Y = 40N^{\frac{1}{2}}$ (K assumed constant) $\quad$ (3.11)

Given the production function, the marginal product of labour can be derived and set equal to the real wage to determine the demand for labour:

$$\frac{dY}{dN} = \tfrac{1}{2}(40\ N^{-\frac{1}{2}})$$

$$= \frac{20}{N^{\frac{1}{2}}}.$$

Setting this equal to the real wage ($W/P = 1$) (and assuming that labour supply is completely elastic) gives:

$$\frac{20}{N^{\frac{1}{2}}} = 1, \text{ or } N = 400,$$

implying that the full-employment level of output:

$$Y_F = 40\sqrt{400} = 800.$$

The *actual* levels of income and employment can be obtained by solving the *IS/LM* model implied by the above exogenous and endogenous relationships. An *IS* relation is obtained from:

$$C = 150 + 5Y$$
$$I = 200 - 25r,$$

giving $Y = 700 - 50r$ as the equation for IS_1. An *LM* relation is obtained from:

$$\frac{M}{P} = 0.5Y - 25r,$$

where $M/P = 200$, giving $Y = 300 + 50r$ as the equation for LM_1. Setting $IS = LM$ gives

$$700 - 50r = 300 + 50r$$
$$r = 4 \text{ per cent}$$

65

$$Y = 500, \text{ or } N = \left(\frac{500}{40}\right)^2 = 156.$$

Thus the equilibrium level of income is about 40 per cent below full employment and the consequent unemployment in the labour market will put downward pressure on money wages and prices. However, if we introduce into the model the two Keynesian special cases then full employment will not be restored and the above position will correspond to *unemployment equilibrium*, e.g. in terms of Figure 3.3 if wages and prices are bid down, the *LM* curve shifts to the right but the most that can happen is that output expands to the point at which IS_1 cuts the axis (inelastic *IS*). Also if we postulate that 4 per cent is the minimum rate acceptable to bondholders, then the *LM* curve becomes horizontal at this 'trapped' interest rate. The economy then remains at output level 500 as values of the *LM* relation of less than 4 per cent are not obtainable (indicated by the dotted lines).

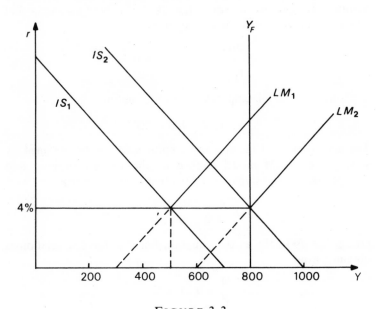

FIGURE 3.3

However, according to Pigou, this analysis omits the influence of *wealth* on consumers' expenditure. To take this into account, wealth

with the problem of finding an acceptable measure of wealth to include in the demand for money function.

To overcome this problem Friedman made use of a basic principle of capital theory, i.e. that wealth is simply the capitalised value of income. Basing his analysis on capital-theory concepts, Friedman then rejected the use of current income as a proxy for wealth because in the short run current income is subject to erratic fluctuations. Instead Friedman introduced into monetary analysis a longer-run concept of income – one which he had developed in his work on the consumption function – i.e. *permanent* income [21]. This is an average of past, present and future incomes and conforms closely to an individual's expected or normal income. In this way Friedman refined the income concept until it approached a wealth concept and he then included *permanent income* in the demand for money function as a *proxy* for *wealth*.

Wealth, however, is important not only in providing the relevant budget constraint but it also has important effects on the demand for money through the various forms in which wealth can be held. In this respect the alternative ways of holding wealth, specifically in human or non-human form, pinpoint the other two general determinants of the demand for money:

(1) Since some forms of wealth are more liquid than others it is necessary to take into account the ratio, H, of human wealth to non-human wealth. This is necessary because human wealth is very illiquid, e.g. it is sometimes difficult to turn human wealth into income when there is little demand for labour (unemployment). Therefore the greater is the proportion of human wealth in total wealth, the greater will be the demand for money in order to be prepared for those times when the marketability of human wealth is low.

(2) The decision regarding the diversification of one's holdings of *non*-human wealth will be based on the available rates of return. Therefore the bond rate r_b, the return on equities, r_e, and the expected rate of inflation (the return on money), $(1/P)\,(dP/dT)$, are also included in the demand function for money.

The Monetarists' Demand for Money

Bearing these points in mind, Friedman arrives at the following

explicit form for the determinants of the demand for real money balances:

$$\frac{M}{P} = f\left[(r_b, r_e, \left(\frac{1}{P}\right)\left(\frac{dP}{dt}\right), H) \; Y \right],$$

or, grouping together the determinants in the small brackets and representing them by the symbol k, we have:

$$\frac{M}{P} = kY, \text{ or } M = kPY, \text{ or } MV = PY,$$

where $V = 1/k$. Written in this form the reformulation of the new Quantity Theory looks remarkably similar to the *Old* Quantity Theory but there are two vitally important differences:

(1) V (or k) is no longer taken as an institutionally determined constant. Instead, velocity is regarded as a *stable* function of a *limited* number of observable magnitudes (interest rates, expected inflation, etc.);

(2). The symbol Y in Friedman's equation stands for *permanent* income and is included not as a proxy for the current level of transactions, as in the old version, but as a proxy for the current level of *wealth*: 'this emphasis on income as a surrogate for wealth . . . is conceptually perhaps the basic difference between the reformulation and the earlier versions of the quantity theory' [26].

However, although the modern Quantity Theory *is* substantially different from the old version, is it very different from the generalised Keynesian money demand function, i.e. $M/P = L(r, Y)$? If r is taken to represent the rates of return on various forms of wealth, the only real difference is the more explicit account taken by the Monetarists of wealth. However, this difference is important and it is not simply a matter of the more elaborate theoretical foundations which underpin the Monetarist approach, i.e. their application of capital-theory concepts to money demand. The emphasis on wealth has important consequences for the importance that each school attaches to the various arguments of the demand for money function and it highlights the main difference between Monetarists and Keynesians.

Income versus Substitution Effects

The main distinction between the two schools is that Keynesians

76

emphasise the *substitution* effects of money as an alternative to other financial assets, while the Monetarists emphasise *income* or *wealth* effects. In other words, Keynesians see money as a close substitute for other *financial* assets because these assets serve as a store of value in a similar manner to money balances. Therefore an excess demand for money will be eliminated in their system by individuals selling such assets and an excess supply will be followed by individuals purchasing such assets. In this respect a *high* degree of substitutability in the financial sphere leads to the assumption of a *high* interest elasticity of money demand in the Keynesian system.

On the other hand, the Monetarists do not regard money as a close substitute for a narrow range of financial assets. They regard money as an asset with certain unique characteristics which cause it to be a substitute for *all assets*, both real and financial. Friedman, for example, insists that 'the most fruitful approach is to regard money as one of a sequence of assets, on a par with bonds, equities, houses, consumer durables etc.' [20]. To the Monetarists an excess demand for money will be eliminated by individuals selling a wide range of assets such as equities and consumer durables and an excess supply will be followed by individuals purchasing a similar range of assets. They therefore predict a *low* degree of substitutability in the financial sphere and this leads to the assumption of a *low* interest elasticity of money demand in the Monetarist approach.

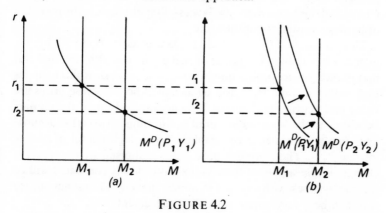

FIGURE 4.2

The importance of this distinction is illustrated in Figure 4.2. Figure 4.2(a) represents the Keynesian analysis of how individuals react to changes in the money supply, e.g. if the government increases

the money supply from M_1 to M_2 then Keynesians would predict that individuals would buy financial assets with the excess money, and this would bid up the price of such assets and lower interest rates until equilibrium is re-established. The point is, however, that if the demand for money is as interest elastic as that in Figure 4.2(a) then only relatively small variations in the interest rate are necessary to restore equilibrium between the demand for, and supply of, money following an exogenous change in the latter. But the smaller is the effect of a given change in the money supply on interest rates, the smaller will be the eventual effect on investment expenditure, and hence on goods and services, i.e. on money income. The money supply therefore will not then be a very important policy instrument.

Figure 4.2(b) illustrates the Monetarist approach. If the government increases the money supply from M_1 to M_2 then the Monetarists would predict that in an attempt to reduce their holdings of excess money balances individuals are just as likely to adjust to their equilibrium positions by increasing their planned expenditure on goods and services as by purchasing financial assets. The demand for money will therefore be unresponsive to interest-rate changes and if money demand is as interest inelastic as that in Figure 4.2(b) then there is *no* possibility of re-establishing equilibrium in the money market simply by variations in the interest rate. Substitution between financial assets will not therefore eliminate the excess supply of money and the excess money balances will spill over into the purchase of houses, consumer durables, etc.

Thus in addition to the prices of financial assets being bid up, i.e. interest rates falling, the prices of real goods will also rise, and this may induce greater production of goods and services. If this happens then money income $P_1 Y_1$ will be increased both because prices are rising and because real output is increasing and this will continue, according to the Monetarists, until equilibrium between the demand and supply of money is re-established at a higher level of money income $P_2 Y_2$. Therefore the more widely disbursed are the effects of changes in the supply of money, the more closely correlated will be the money stock with changes in money income. The money supply will then be a very important policy instrument.

Thus an important element in the Monetarist challenge involves providing proof of a close link between the supply of money and nominal income and they attempt to do this by denying the existence of a significant substitution effect between money and other financial

assets. Then, if income effects can be shown to be dominant, the money supply becomes an important policy tool. However, before taking the step from the first money demand function in Figure 4.2(*b*) to the second demand function, the Monetarists must postulate some transmission mechanism whereby increases in the money supply *cause* increases in money income.

But even without an adequate account of the transmission mechanism, if the monetarists can illustrate the superiority of income effects over substitution effects then they have made considerable progress towards establishing a close link between the money supply and money income.

Income Effects – the Evidence

Monetarists have attempted to show that income effects are dominant in a number of ways, e.g. the earliest attempt was by Friedman, who produced figures to show that secular changes in the real stock of money are highly correlated with secular changes in real income [22]. A 1 per cent increase in real income was shown to be associated with a 1.8 per cent increase in real cash balances, i.e. a 0.8 per cent *decrease* in income velocity. Income effects therefore appear dominant in the long run. However, prior to Friedman's 1959 article most studies of the demand for money had shown that velocity and income move in the *same* direction over business cycles and the main determinant of the observed cyclical change in velocity in these studies had been the interest rate (e.g. Latané [55]). This implied that the rise in income forced up interest rates and this reduced the demand for money and increased velocity, i.e. substitution effects were felt to be dominant in the short run. However, Friedman [22] challenged this accepted explanation of the cyclical change in V and offered an alternative explanation based on his permanent-income hypothesis. He justified the introduction of permanent income into the analysis by claiming that 'holders of cash balances determine the amount to hold in light of their longer-term income position rather than their momentary receipts'.

Permanent income, like current income, will fluctuate over the course of a business cycle but because permanent income is an average measure of current income it will rise less than the latter during expansions and fall less during contractions. Normally income velocity is calculated as the ratio of *current* income to the

money supply but Friedman insists that if velocity is computed in terms of *permanent* income then it is possible for velocity to fall during the expansionary phase, i.e. the demand for money to rise and vice versa during contractions. This type of cyclical movement of velocity conforms with the idea that income effects dominate the demand for money. The point that Friedman is making is that if the demand for money is insensitive to current income (because cash-holders respond to 'their longer-term income position'), then the *real* demand for money is underestimated in expansionary phases and overestimated during contractions.

Therefore Friedman reconciles the apparent contradiction between the secular and cyclical evidence on velocity by pointing out that in the long run, when income fluctuations average out, current income is a good proxy for permanent income. Therefore it gives a *good* estimate of money demand; but in the short run current income overestimates fluctuations in permanent income and therefore leads to *false* predictions about the real demand for money. However, the main point of the analysis is that if changes in velocity can be adequately accounted for by changes in permanent income then there remains very little variation to be explained by changes in interest rates. Thus Friedman concludes that after explaining movements of velocity in terms of permanent income, 'The remaining movement in velocity is much too small to reflect any very sensitive adjustment of cash balances to interest rates' [22]. Furthermore, if the demand for money is determined by permanent income rather than interest rates then in order for equilibrium to be achieved between the money supply and money demand, permanent income must be the equilibrating factor.

Friedman's analysis can therefore be summed up as follows. The demand for money is dominated by income effects where the relevant concept of income is not current measured income but a longer-term concept of expected income. Any discrepancy between the demand for, and supply of, money can be reconciled only by variations in permanent income and not by interest-rate changes. However, since permanent income fluctuates less than current income, changes in the money supply must produce magnified changes in current income in order for equilibrium in the money market to be re-established, i.e. changes in the money supply cause *large* changes in income. Therefore, by introducing permanent income into monetary analysis, Friedman succeeded in doing two things:

(1) explaining why velocity varies pro-cyclically without relying on interest-rate changes;

(2) explaining why the short-run monetary multiplier ($\Delta Y / \Delta M$) is so large.

The implications of this analysis are that *the income velocity of money is the key relationship in macroeconomics and the money supply is the crucial policy variable.*

To test the significance of these findings Friedman and others have embarked on various research programmes to evaluate the predictability of monetarist relationships and to ascertain the direction of causality between changes in the money supply and changes in money income.

In this respect an important study was that of Friedman and Meiselman [29] in which they attempted to assess the relative importance of the income velocity of money and the simple Keynesian multiplier as determinants of money income. Thus they tested whether the Keynesian multiplier relationship:[2]

$$\Delta PY = \frac{1}{1-b}\Delta A,$$

where PY is money income, b is the marginal propensity to consume and A is autonomous expenditure (i.e. $I + G + X - M$), gave better predictions of money income than the Monetarist relationship:

$$\Delta PY = V\Delta M,$$

where M is the money supply and V the income velocity of money (which can also be interpreted here as the monetary multiplier). They found that for the period 1897 to 1958, and various sub-periods, that money had the higher correlation with money income, that the monetary relationship was the more stable, and gave better predictions of variations in money income than the Keynesian model. Thus on the basis of this evidence they concluded that the income velocity of money was the *key macroeconomic relationship.*

More recently, Andersen and Jordan [3] tested a single-equation model of the U.S. economy to ascertain the relative importance of fiscal and monetary policy in explaining post-war fluctuations of money income. They found that changes in the money stock had a large, almost immediate effect on money income – about 25 per cent of

the impact effect of ΔM on ΔY took place in the first quarter – while fiscal policy actions took more time to be effective and were less predictable in their effect on money income. On this evidence they concluded that the *short-run monetary multiplier was large and the money supply the crucial policy variable.*

Other evidence, favourable to the Monetarist case, was obtained by analysing certain interesting aspects of monetary history, e.g. in a study with Schwartz [31] Friedman challenged the accepted view that the Great Depression of the 1930s illustrated the impotency of monetary policy. Thus they point out that between 1929 and 1933 the Federal Reserve engineered a considerable monetary contraction and passively acquiesced in the consequent banking collapse. This added to the severity and length of the depression but they insist that had the Federal Reserve instead undertaken an expansionist policy and increased the money supply then the depression would have been short-lived. Friedman and Schwartz therefore see the severity of the contraction as evidence in favour of the effectiveness of (bad) monetary policy.

However, although much of this evidence was convincing and the correlation between past changes in M and past changes in Y impressive, there still remained the problem of *causality*. Thus some of the examples cited by the Monetarists concerning the effects of changes in the money supply were not entirely independent of concurrent changes in money income and under these conditions a high correlation between M and Y can just as easily be interpreted as a link from Y to M as from M to Y. To avoid this interpretation the Monetarists produced considerable evidence on the *timing* of economic relationships and in particular they investigated the leads and lags between time series of the money supply and money income at business cycle turning-points.

For example, in another study with Schwartz [30] Friedman found that peaks in the *rate of change* of the money supply preceded peaks in money income by sixteen months and the turning-points in the money stock itself also preceded turning-points in money income, but with a shorter lead. This evidence is very significant because, as Goodhart and Crockett [32] have pointed out, 'in the absence of evidence to the contrary a consistent lead is prima facie evidence of causation'.

Thus the Monetarists, via their work on the velocity function and through their evidence on timing, etc., have demonstrated a close link

between the money supply and money income. However, to legitimately take the step from the first demand schedule in figure 4.2(*b*) above to the second schedule, associated with a higher level of money income, the Monetarists must postulate a *transmission mechanism* whereby the effects of changes in the money supply interact with real phenomena to produce changes in G.N.P. and/or the price level. Before looking at the Monetarist view of the transmission mechanism we will investigate the Keynesian analysis of how money permeates the economy. We will find that the Monetarist approach is in many respects an expanded version of the Keynesian view.

The Keynesian Transmission Mechanism

It was emphasised above that Keynesians regard money as a close substitute for financial assets. The starting-point in their analysis is therefore the asset portfolios chosen by households and the impact of monetary policy is then traced via its effects on these portfolios. Thus if the central bank decides to increase the money supply it typically buys bonds and this results in an excess of cash in households' portfolios, i.e. portfolio imbalance. The adjustment to portfolio balance proceeds via the purchase of financial assets, and this drives up the price of these assets and reduces market rates of interest. Thus the impact of the money-supply increase on households is simply to induce them to alter their portfolio of financial assets; monetary policy, therefore, is assumed to have little direct impact on households' planned expenditure on goods and services.

However, this financial effect eventually has repercussions on the real sector of the economy because the rise in the price of financial assets encourages firms to issue new assets and the proceeds from these new issues will be used to purchase capital goods. This view of the mechanism by which monetary impulses are transmitted to the real sector has been elaborated succinctly by Tobin [80]. For Tobin, the crucial variable in this transmission mechanism is the supply price of capital goods, e.g. after firms have acquired external finance by selling new financial assets and have used these funds to increase their demand for capital goods, the effect will be to bid up the price of newly produced capital equipment (supply price of capital). Therefore the initial impact of monetary policy on G.N.P. is assumed to occur in the capital-goods sector and the increase in the supply price of capital then acts as an indicator as to whether or not a monetary

expansion has been successful. Once the monetary authorities have succeeded in raising the supply price of capital, the consequent increase in capital-goods production (investment) will cause aggregate demand to rise further via the 'multiplier' effect on consumer spending.

Portfolio balance is then re-established as follows: the central Bank has increased the supply of money by purchasing bonds; this has both increased the price of bonds and reduced their supply; because bonds are now relatively expensive households will be attracted into holding more private debt (equities) and less bonds but in so doing they bid up the price of equities; in response to the rise in the price of equities and the general fall in market rates of interest, firms will sell more financial assets and use the proceeds to purchase capital equipment; capital-goods production will therefore expand, and since the firms producing capital goods face rising marginal costs in the short run, the supply price of capital will be bid up; the price of capital goods will rise until the demand for, and supply of, capital are brought into line with each other; finally, the expansion in the capital-goods sector will increase the level of money income via the investment multiplier.

The excess money supply, the original cause of the portfolio imbalance, is then eliminated in two ways:

(1) The increase in income will make households and firms more willing to hold the increased money stock because the *transactions demand* for money will rise along with the rise in money income; and

(2) The *speculative demand* for money will have risen along with the fall in interest rates – in this way the increased stock of money is eventually absorbed into asset portfolios.

The Keynesian view of the transmission mechanism is therefore based on a portfolio-adjustment process whereby portfolio imbalance, following an increase in the money supply, has repercussions throughout a range of financial assets, eventually affecting the level of aggregate real expenditure. However, the initial *real* effect is on investment spending with expenditure on consumption goods increasing only when incomes are affected. (Note that it is this analysis that underlies movements from one equilibrium position to another in the *IS/LM* model, e.g. an increase in the money supply shifts the *LM* curve to the right, and this lowers interest rates (i.e. raises asset prices) and induces a movement along the *IS* curve via, initially,

84

increased investment spending and, second, multiplier effects on consumer expenditure.)

The Monetarist Transmission Mechanism

On the whole the Monetarists are in agreement with the view that monetary impulses are channelled through portfolio adjustments and only then are they transmitted to other economic variables. However, they object to the Keynesian concentration on a narrow range of financial assets and capital goods and they insist that portfolio adjustments have effects 'on a much broader range of capital assets and correspondingly broader range of associated expenditures' [29] than those suggested by Tobin.

Specifically, the Monetarists insist that every durable good owned by either households or firms should be treated as a capital asset because these goods are not consumed immediately after purchase but instead produce a flow of services through time. The present value of these services can be obtained by discounting them by an appropriate interest rate, and households and firms will be satisfied with their current asset portfolios only when the present value of each asset, both physical and financial, is equal to its supply price.

As in the Keynesian approach, monetary-policy impulses, via their effects on interest rates, change an initial equilibrium position into one of portfolio imbalance. However, in the Monetarist analysis, both households and firms are now assumed to make adjustments to their stock of assets, both real (houses, factories, consumer durables, etc.), and financial (bonds, equities, etc.), in an attempt to return to portfolio balance, and in so doing they directly affect the level of expenditure. The main difference between this and the Keynesian approach is that consumer expenditure is stimulated directly along with expenditure on capital goods instead of being induced indirectly via the multiplier effects of investment spending.

However, portfolio balance is re-established through channels similar to the Keynesian approach, i.e. following an expansion of the money supply, bond and equity prices are assumed to be bid up (interest rates fall) with the familiar effects on firms' planned expenditure on capital goods, but now there will also be an effect on the present value of the services yielded by consumer durables so that households' planned expenditure on goods and services are also affected. Therefore, along with the supply price of capital, the supply

85

prices of consumer goods will be bid up, leading to an expansion of durable-goods production and hence a rise in the level of output and incomes. The excess supply of money, which originally threw portfolios out of balance, is then absorbed into asset portfolios primarily through the effect that this rise in money income has on inducing a higher level of money demand.

The Unreliability of Interest Rates

If the Monetarist transmission mechanism is based on a portfolio-adjustment process in which lower interest rates play a significant role in inducing higher expenditure, it may appear odd that they should attach such importance to the stock of money *per se*. However, according to Friedman this concentration on one asset within a spectrum of assets is justified because changes in the stock of money are the best available measure of monetary-policy impulses. This is because some of the assets included in the Monetarist analysis are not quoted on financial markets and therefore have *no observable rates of return*. Those market rates of interest which are observable are only useful in making predictions about the narrow range of assets highlighted by the Keynesians but for the Monetarists the total portfolio adjustments of both households and firms cannot be accurately predicted by observable market interest rates. Therefore they take the rate of change of the money supply as a 'second-best' indicator of monetary-policy changes.

Furthermore, interest rates are also regarded with suspicion by the Monetarists because of the need in their eyes to distinguish between the initial impact effect of monetary policy on rates of interest and the final effect, e.g. Friedman insists that an expansionary monetary policy may lower interest rates only temporarily and that when the increased money supply filters through into increased spending, and hence increased money income, the initial fall in interest rates may begin to be reversed [24]. However, not only will rates begin to rise as production and prices are affected, but they may even rise above their original level if inflationary price expectations are given a boost, e.g. if people come to expect prices to continue rising then borrowers will be willing to pay higher nominal interest rates and lenders will demand higher nominal rates. The combined effect of increased prices and inflationary expectations could then force up interest rates quite sharply. Nominal rates of interest will then be high despite the

monetary expansion, although real rates (i.e. nominal rates adjusted for inflation) need not rise.

According to the Monetarists this distinction between real and nominal interest rates explains why the cheap-money policies of the late 1940s were both disastrous and doomed to failure, For example, in the United Kingdom Chancellor Dalton attempted to keep interest rates low and expanded the money supply to achieve this objective. Although Dalton was successful in this policy from 1945 to 1948 he was continually forced into larger and larger open-market purchases. The effects of these purchases on prices and price expectations finally forced the abandonment of this policy and after 1948 interest rates rose and by 1954 they had doubled. Thus, from an historical standpoint, high and rising rates are associated in the Monetarist analysis with rapid *increases* in the money supply and, therefore, to them, high rates are a sign that monetary policy *has been* easy. Thus Friedman concludes: 'interest rates are a misleading indicator of whether monetary policy is tight or easy. For that it is far better to look at the rate of change of the quantity of money'[24].

The Role of Monetary Policy

To the Monetarists, therefore, the rate of change of the money supply is the best available indicator of monetary policy. Furthermore, knowledge of this rate of change is also important from another standpoint – it enables predictions to be made about future changes in money income. In this respect Monetarist research into the timing of economic relationships is important and it will be recalled that, according to Friedman and Schwartz [30], peaks in the rate of change of *M* are followed, with a lag on average of sixteen months, by peaks in the rate of change of money income. However, the lag between changes in the money stock and changes in money income is acknowledged by the Monetarists to be both long and variable so that, although money and money income are closely correlated in the long run, over short periods the same relationship is very difficult to predict. Because of the inability to predict accurately this relationship the Monetarists insist that monetary policy *cannot* be used for 'fine tuning' the economy, i.e. it cannot be used with any precision to offset short-run fluctuations in economic activity. Indeed, since changes in the money supply have their effects on money income only after a long time lag, attempts to use monetary policy as an instrument of

stabilisation are liable to make the economy *less* rather than more stable.

Thus the Monetarists' prescription for monetary policy is that the monetary authorities should simply avoid sharp policy changes and they insist that the best way to achieve this objective would be for the authorities to adopt publicly the policy of attaining a steady rate of growth in the stock of money equal to the rate of growth of G.N.P. They base this somewhat pessimistic conclusion on their interpretation of previous business cycles in which they identify many periods during which fluctuations in economic activity have been *caused* by erratic or erroneous government policies. Therefore their policy prescription is for a steady growth in the money stock in the hope that the central bank can at least prevent changes in the monetary system from being *themselves* a major source of economic disturbances.

However, the Monetarists are quick to point out that this negative conclusion in respect of monetary policy is just as valid, if not more valid, for fiscal policy, because this also operates with a long and variable lag. Moreover, they also regard fiscal policy as a relatively *ineffective* instrument for influencing the level of output. Their position is summarised in Figure 4.1 above. Expansionary fiscal actions which shift the *IS* locus to the right by an amount *AB* have only a small effect on the level of income. The Monetarists explain this result as follows. The horizontal shift *AB* is a measure of the simple government expenditure multiplier of Keynesian theory, that is:

$$AB = \frac{1}{1-b}\Delta G.$$

This, however, overstates the effectiveness of fiscal policy because the increased government expenditure will force up interest rates. Expenditures which are responsive to interest rates, including the purchase of consumer durables and houses, and even local-authority expenditure, will then be reduced. Thus if public spending 'crowds out' a significant amount of other expenditure, the original expansionary effect may be offset, leaving only the small net increase in income illustrated in Figure 4.1.

Thus discretionary fiscal policy is disqualified on the grounds that not only does it operate with unpredictable lags but its 'crowding-out'

effects on other forms of expenditure make it an ineffective policy tool. Monetary policy, on the other hand, has a significant effect on the level of income but it too is disqualified as a discretionary instrument of stabilisation because of our lack of knowledge of the lags involved. Therefore, instead of being used with discretion, monetary and fiscal policies should simply aim at providing a stable environment within which a private-enterprise economy can flourish and attain a high level of economic growth.

The Major Monetarist Propositions

In summary the Monetarist position can be outlined as follows:

(1) The demand for money is a *stable* function of a limited number of observable variables of which permanent income is the most important. Interest rates are not regarded as important determinants of money demand.

(2) The money supply is *exogenously* determined by the monetary authorities. Therefore, in order for the existing stock of money to be willingly held, the demand for money must change whenever the money supply is altered by the authorities.

(3) However, because substitution effects between money and other financial assets are small, i.e. the interest elasticity of money demand is low, it is the level of income which must change in order to bring the demand for money into line with the altered money supply: 'The *key insight* of the quantity-theory approach is that such a discrepancy (between the demand for and supply of money) will be manifested primarily in attempted spending thence in the rate of change in nominal income' [25].

(4) Furthermore, since holders of money respond to *permanent income* and since current income has only a fractional weight in permanent income, there must be large changes in income in the short run in order for equilibrium to be re-established in the money market. The emphasis on permanent income is important for two reasons: (*a*) it implies that the effect of the money supply on current income (the money multiplier) will be large; and (*b*) it explains the pro-cyclical movement of velocity and implies a stable, predictable velocity function when measured in terms of *permanent* income.

(5) *The evidence* accumulated by Friedman [22] on the demand for money, by Friedman and Meiselman [29] on the stability of velocity

and by Andersen and Jordan [3] on the money multiplier largely support the above propositions. In addition, to preclude the Keynesian interpretation of the evidence as merely implying an *endogenous* money stock which responds to past changes in income, the Monetarists have assembled some convincing evidence on the leads and lags of income and money-supply series at business-cycle turning-points. Specifically, changes in the money supply were found to precede changes in money income by some sixteen months [30].

(6) However, Friedman himself acknowledges that this evidence is by no means decisive and accepts that some *transmission mechanism* must be outlined whereby monetary impulses are first channelled through the financial and real-goods sectors before affecting the level of money income. The Monetarist transmission process is based on the adjustments which households and firms make to their asset portfolios in response to a change in the money supply. Interest rates play an important role in this process, not only the narrow range of recorded rates which feature prominently in Keynesian analysis, but also included are the unobservable rates of discount which consumers use to value the services yielded by durable goods. However, despite the important role played by rates of interest in transmitting monetary impulses, attention is still focused exclusively on the stock of money (and its rate of change) because of the *unreliability of interest rates* as indicators of monetary policy. In the first place not all of the relevant interest rates are observable and, second, rates respond both to price changes and to price expectations so that high and rising rates may be a consequence of *expansionary* monetary policies. Thus there is a need to distinguish between *real* and *nominal* rates of interest.

(7) The money supply is therefore both the crucial policy variable and the best policy indicator, but although changes in the money supply have important effects on money income there is a long and variable lag between cause and effect, making short-run predictions difficult. Therefore discretionary monetary policy cannot be used effectively as a stabilising influence in the short run. Indeed, lags and uncertainties will make discretionary economic policies of any kind more likely to be destabilising than stabilising. The best solution, therefore, is for the government to maintain a steady growth of the money supply in line with the growth in money income and to avoid sharp swings in those policy instruments over which it does have

90

control. Discretionary fiscal policy in particular should be avoided because of its 'crowding-out' effect on private expenditure.

This pessimistic conclusion regarding discretionary monetary and fiscal policies is not viewed with dismay by the Monetarists because they insist that the underlying dynamics of the private sector is in fact basically stable and would not give rise to large, prolonged fluctuations in economic activity in the absence of over-reaction on the part of the authorities.

In recent years the Monetarist position as outlined above has become relatively influential and policy-makers throughout the world now appear to be guided by it. However, the relevance and accuracy of the theories and evidence underlying the Monetarist case are still controversial and it continues to occupy the centre of serious critical debate. To conclude this chapter, therefore, it seems appropriate to look at some of the criticisms that have been levelled against it.

Monetarist Discrepancies

If we analyse further the above seven major propositions of Monetarism a number of discrepancies can be indentified:

(1) Although most studies agree that the demand for money bears a stable relationship to its determinants, few studies agree with Friedman that interest rates are unimportant: 'there is an overwhelming body of evidence in favour of the proposition that the demand for money is stably and negatively related to the interest rate' (Laidler [51]).

(2) Many studies point to the money supply as being partly *endogenous*, e.g. Teigen [77] finds that the money supply responds positively to interest-rate changes. Thus the monetary system may respond to the 'needs of trade' so that as (say) investment prospects improve and the demand for finance increases, banks may expand the money supply. This supply response often occurs with the help of the monetary authorities, who for debt-management reasons do not want the rise in demand to lead to a sharp rise in interest rates.

(3) Therefore the demand for, and supply of, money may not be strictly independent and Friedman's 'key insight' into how a discrepancy between demand and supply manifests itself in changes in

nominal income may be erroneous. In particular, if the money supply is endogenous then an alternative interpretation of monetary time-series date is possible. For example, assume that an increase in investment expenditure leads to a rise in the level of income and hence an increase in the demand for money. To prevent this forcing up interest rates the monetary authorities allow or encourage the money supply to increase, and if the demand for money is responsive to interest rates then only a small increase in the money supply may be necessary to hold interest rates steady. However, historical interpretation of the data could then associate relatively large changes in income with small changes in the money supply, i.e. a large money multiplier, but, in fact, our example implies the reverse causation.

(4) Thus Friedman's introduction of the permanent-income hypothesis into monetary analysis in an attempt to 'explain' the apparent large money multiplier may be superfluous. The large multiplier may be the result of a spurious correlation between M and Y as outlined in the above paragraph. Furthermore, the alleged long-run stability of velocity and its short-run pro-cyclical movements can also be explained in terms of an endogenous money-supply response and without reference to permanent income, e.g. a stable velocity ratio between money income and the money stock will be observed in the long run if the authorities continually adjust the money stock to prior changes in money income. In the short run, the pro-cyclical movement of this ratio can be accounted for by the fact that during an expansion money income rises first, interest rates are then bid up and the velocity ratio increases as the demand for money falls; the money supply is increased only after some lag.

(5) It was to forestall this endogenous interpretation of monetary time-series data that the Monetarists put forward their evidence on timing. However, Tobin [80] has demonstrated that in addition to being inconclusive the timing evidence actually highlights some inconsistencies in the Monetarist approach, e.g. Tobin investigated the timing implications of an economic model in which the money supply was *entirely endogenous*, and found that it implied cyclical timing patterns between money and money income identical to those found by Friedman and Schwartz [30]. He thus demonstrated conclusively that timing evidence alone provided no support for the Monetarist thesis.

(6) In addition, in order to highlight some of the inconsistencies in the Monetarist case, Tobin related the evidence on timing to two

separate Monetarist themes: (a) the permanent-income theory of the demand for money; and (b) the Monetarist version of the transmission mechanism.

As pointed out above, the permanent-income hypothesis is important because it 'explains' both the large money multiplier and the pro-cyclical movement of velocity (though an endogenous money-supply response can just as easily 'explain' these phenomena). However, a large short-run money multiplier implies a *rapid* response of current income to changes in the money supply and this is borne out by Andersen and Jordan's results [3]. But this rapid response is not consistent with the timing implications of Friedman and Schwartz's results because their evidence points to a *lag* of some sixteen months [30].

As regards the Monetarist transmission mechanism, this does not imply that excess money balances are immediately absorbed by rapid increases in money income but rather that such excess balances are gradually absorbed through changes in interest rates and the prices of financial and physical assets. This analysis is consistent with a sixteen-month time lag, but it cannot explain either the pro-cyclical movements in velocity or the large multiplier effect that changes in the money supply apparently have on current income. Thus the permanent-income hypothesis, the evidence on the money multiplier and the evidence on timing are at variance with each other.

(7) As regards the inadequacy of discretionary economic policies, it must be pointed out that the advocacy of automatic policy rules is not the prerogative of the Monetarists. For example, many Keynesians in fact are sceptical of using fiscal policy for 'fine tuning' and advocate reliance on automatic stabilisers, such as progressive income taxes. Also, the Radcliffe Report came out strongly again using monetary policy as an instrument of stabilisation in the short run. Thus it is difficult to comprehend the correlation between a belief in Monetarism and a distrust of discretionary policies.

Therefore Keynesians conclude from this analysis that the various propositions of Monetarism neither fit together consistently nor follow logically from one another. Indeed, Keynesians are not surprised by this conclusion because until recently there existed no coherent statement of the *theory* underlying either Monetarist research or their policy prescriptions. This gap, however, was partially filled in 1970–1[3] when Friedman produced a theoretical model for

the determination of national income and the price level and contrasted it with the Keynesian position [26]. Next we analyse the extent to which this new Monetarist framework differs from the accepted Keynesian paradigm.

Is there a Monetarist Theory?

Friedman [26] points out that the Keynesian IS/LM model is underdetermined, i.e. there are three variables, r, Y and P, and only two equations. According to Friedman, Keynesians solve the problem of the 'missing equation' by assuming that P is fixed so that the model then determines r and Y. By contrast Friedman outlines the Monetarist position as one in which the level of real income is determined exogenously by the Walrasian system of general-equilibrium equations. Then, given Y, the Monetarist version of IS/LM determines r and P.

This seems a direct-enough contrast but the problem is that Friedman's interpretation of the Keynesian position is incorrect; although the IS/LM model does require some extension if it is to determine the price level, the Keynesian extension is not the assumption implied by Friedman, i.e. a constant price level; instead, in the Keynesian model P is determined by the interaction of the labour and product markets.

For example, the complete Keynesian system, outlined in Chapter 2 above, incorporates a production function and a labour market, and this extended system links together the price level and the level of output in two ways:

(1) As outlined in Chapter 2, the Keynes effect, which relates price changes to the interest rate, implies an aggregate *demand* function whereby lower prices are associated, via shifts in the LM locus, with higher output levels.

(2) Also implied in the complete model, but not specified previously, is an aggregate *supply* function through which lower prices are associated with *lower* levels of output, e.g. if money wages are sticky lower prices will increase real wages and this will result in a lower demand for labour. The lower utilisation of labour will then, via the production function, lead to a reduction in the total volume of goods produced. Thus an upward-sloping aggregate supply curve is also included in the Keynesian model.

The price level is then *endogenously* determined by the complex

interrelations between real wages, employment and output. In the complete Keynesian system, therefore, there is no 'missing equation' and, therefore, no need for an exogenous price level. Furthermore, the endogeneity of P has always been a feature of Keynesian empirical studies, e.g. the 1955 Klein–Goldberger econometric model and its successors included labour-market-adjustment equations for the purpose of determining the absolute level of wages and prices.[4]

Thus if P is already endogenously determined within the Keynesian system, what advantages are to be gained by adopting Friedman's version of the IS/LM? With Y fixed independently of IS/LM via the general-equilibrium system of equations and with wages and prices assumed flexible the implications of Friedman's analysis are that all *real* factors are determined exogenously. The complex interactions between real wages, employment and output that are an important feature of the Keynesian model have no role to play in Friedman's theoretical framework.[5]

However, if changes in money wages and prices cannot affect the level of employment, neither can monetary or fiscal policies, because although they are capable of shifting the LM and IS curves, they only affect the price level and interest rates because output and employment are determined independently of IS/LM. Therefore in the Monetarist model nominal interest rates and the price level are determined endogenously while the levels of employment and output and all other real magnitudes are determined exogenously.[6]

Which Model is Best?

If we assume that both models are internally consistent then it is very difficult to answer this question because, since both are based on the IS/LM model, it follows that it must be the assumptions underlying the theoretical structure, rather than the structure itself, that differentiates the two schools. But the validity of assumptions is not a question of logic and the only progress that can be made involves asking rhetorical questions like: which model's assumptions are the most relevant for solving real-world problems, or which are the most realistic? We might then conclude that the Monetarist model, in which the full-employment level of output is determined exogenously and over which monetary and fiscal policies have no influence, is less relevant than the Keynesian model, in which persistent unemployment may be present and both monetary and fiscal policies can

95

influence its level. However, questions concerning the relevance of assumptions are notoriously inconclusive.

Therefore, since the debate over assumptions is unlikely to resolve the dispute only one course remains – an appeal to the facts. This conclusion, in fact is in complete conformity with the methodology of the Chicago School – a theory should be tested by analysing its *predictions* and not by investigating its assumptions. Friedman has always emphasised the importance of empirical evidence and insists that the test of a good theory is whether it can 'predict much from little'. This is also the position of Brunner, Andersen–Jordan and other Monetarists. Therefore we conclude this Chapter with a brief analysis of the extent to which the available empirical evidence is likely to resolve this dispute.

The Evidence

The monetarists claim that the accumulated evidence largely validates their propositions; the Keynesians, of course, dispute this. To get at the heart of the current debate we will concentrate on two Monetarist propositions – that *velocity* is stable and the short-run *money multiplier* is large.

Although recent evidence overwhelmingly rejects a completely interest-inelastic demand for money function (velocity therefore varies with interest rates), is it possible to conclude that velocity is 'relatively' or 'almost' constant? Friedman's study with Meiselman [29] is important in this respect because it was used as evidence both in favour of a stable velocity function and as evidence against a significant Keynesian multiplier relationship.

Friedman and Meiselman compared correlations between money income and the level of autonomous expenditures on the one hand and the money supply on the other for the period 1897–1958 and found that the monetary relationship had the higher R^2 (correlation coefficient). They concluded that velocity was more stable than the consumption function and also a better predictor of money income.

This evidence, however, has been challenged on a number of fronts. In the first place it was pointed out that the results crucially depended on the precise definition of the variables included in the regression equation, and the definitions used by Friedman and Meiselman were biased against the Keynesian equation. Second, and more importantly, it was pointed out that a high R^2 is *not* a measure of stability. Stability requires constancy in the regression coefficients and constant

96

terms through time and the Friedman–Meiselman results did no satisfy this condition (thus the relative stability of velocity is still very much in dispute). Third, the whole methodology of the approach was suspect because both a stable velocity function *and* a stable consumption function are important ingredients of the *IS/LM* model which underlies both the Keynesian and Monetarist models. Therefore such a test cannot differentiate between the two schools.

In fact the main conclusion that emerged from the debate over the Friedman–Meiselman results was that the important questions that divide the two schools were not likely to be settled by a comparison of the R^2s of *single-equation models* which were not only too naïve to adequately represent either theory but, in the Friedman–Meiselman paper, were in fact consistent with both schools of thought. Therefore, Keynesians argue, that in order to successfully differentiate between the two theories, *large-scale structural models* are required within which each theory can be adequately specified. However, the Monetarists specifically reject the need for large-scale econometric models and they insist that detailed knowledge of the various sectors of the economy is of secondary importance and can be ignored in analysing policy changes at the macro level.

Thus the question of whether or not there is a need for structural models to analyse aggregate relationships has been elevated to a major point of contention between the two schools. This is due partly to the controversy surrounding the Friedman–Meiselman results, and its implication for a stable velocity function, and more recently to the controversial results of Andersen and Jordan [3] which presented evidence on the other Monetarist proposition in which we are currently interested – the short-run money multiplier. Andersen and Jordan also preferred the single-equation approach for analysing aggregate economic relationships, which in their case involved a test of the relative significance of the effects of monetary and fiscal policies on national income. Thus they set up the equation:

$$Y_t = \overline{a} + b\Delta G_t + C\Delta I_t + d\Delta M_t + e_t,$$

where Y is income, G is government expenditure, T is tax, M is monetary policy, e is a stochastic error term, t is time and $\overline{a}$ stands for 'all other forces that influence spending'. Running this equation on quarterly data they found that the total effects of G and T on Y were not only negligible but had the wrong sign. On the other hand the

effects of M on Y were significantly large with the correct signs. Thus they concluded that fiscal policy is impotent while monetary policy is very important, i.e. the money multiplier is large and exceeds the fiscal multiplier.

However, this evidence has again been challenged on a number of fronts. Like the Friedman–Meiselman results the findings appear to depend critically on the definitions of the variables involved but two more important criticisms emerged which were closely related to the Monetarist preference for small, single-equation models.

In the first place is has been pointed out that the inclusion of 'all other factors that influence spending' in the constant term $\bar{a}$ involves a mis-specification of the equation, because the error term e_t and the constant term $\bar{a}$ will not be independent of each other [7]. Statistical techniques such as those used by Andersen and Jordan will then give *biased* results (thus the relative size of the monetary multiplier is still very much in dispute). This mis-specification is a fault of the single-equation approach in general because, being restricted to one equation, Andersen and Jordan were forced to omit 'all other forces' except fiscal and monetary policy from their model.

Second, Andersen and Jordan treat monetary and fiscal policy as *independent* of changes in the level of income. However, in general both policies will have been set so as to influence income changes, i.e. the government, via its budget, may have attempted to *offset* changes in income. But if the government reacts to anticipated changes in Y, then ΔG and ΔT will *not be independent* of ΔY. This interdependence has important implications for the interpretation of Andersen and Jordan's results. For example, assume that in the past the government had been entirely successful in following a counter-cyclical fiscal policy so that budget manipulations had entirely eliminated fluctuations in income. The evidence would then point to the level of income as being constant through time while government expenditure and taxes would be dominated by fluctuations. Simple regression analysis would then indicate a zero correlation between fiscal policy and observed changes in income. Thus, paradoxically, the more *successful* is fiscal policy in stabilising the level of income, the more *insignificant* it will appear as a determinant of observed income changes in simple regression analysis.

Single-equation tests are therefore unlikely to settle the debate because, first, they are forced to omit too many factors from the equation, which increases the danger of *mis-specification,* and second,

if the factors included are policy instruments then it is *unlikely* that they will be truly *independent* variables.[7]

CONCLUSION

Thus we conclude that in order to effectively distinguish between the two schools of thought (either at the theoretical or empirical level) a structural *Monetarist* model is an essential prerequisite. This is necessary at the *theoretical* level because the small models favoured by the Monetarists cannot be differentiated from the Keynesian analysis except on the basis of their assumptions. Furthermore, the debate over the Friedman–Meiselman and Andersen–Jordan results illustrates that small models also make *empirical* differentiation difficult. (Because of these difficulties the contrast between Keynesians and Monetarists is not as sharp as that between Keynes and the classics.) However, some differentiation must be attempted because the two schools offer different policy prescriptions.

The recent policy debates between the Monetarists and Keynesians seem to revolve around the question of how much does money matter. Does it matter very little compared to fiscal policy or does it matter very much? If the *LM* locus is very flat and the *IS* curve very steep, then it follows that fiscal policy is superior, while if these slope coefficients are reversed, then monetary policy is superior and money matters very much. However, the empirical evidence (summarised in the appendix to this chapter) shows that the interest elasticity of money demand lies in the range -0.1 to -1.0, too low for the *LM* locus to be horizontal and too high for it to be vertical. The evidence on the interest elasticity of the money *supply* also goes against an extreme slope for the *LM* locus; it points to the money supply as being partly, but not completely, endogenous. As regards the slope of the *IS* curve, the interest elasticity of investment appears to be low but significantly different from zero. This suggests that neither extreme has been discovered in practice and that an eclectic position midway between the two extremes is closer to the truth.

Therefore the Monetarists have not proved that money is *all* that matters. However, they have succeeded in generating a certain amount of scepticism about Keynesian policy proposals. Thus where the Pigou effect cast doubt on the *theoretical* innovations of Keynesian economics, Monetarism has cast further doubts on its

99

policy superiority, and these doubts have been given a certain amount of credence lately following the apparent failure of recent U.S. fiscal actions to contain inflation, e.g. according to the Monetarists the 1968 tax surcharge was essentially a failure because prices rose faster in the period following the tax than in the preceding period. This they claim illustrates the impotency of fiscal policy. Furthermore, since monetary policy was expansionary in the period 1967–9 it also demonstrates the relative effectiveness of monetary policy.

Keynesians, of course, are quick to reject this view and point to factors other than the expansion in the money supply to account for the ineffectiveness of the surcharge,[8] but despite their attempted refutations the picture that emerges is of the Keynesian school under attack from all sides and of the prestige of the ruling paradigm slowly but steadily declining.

However, before we conclude from this that the Keynesian Revolution in economic theory is largely discredited, a number of points must be borne in mind. First, it must be emphasised that since both schools can be incorporated into the *IS/LM*, framework the theoretical differences between the Monetarists and Keynesians are *minimal*. Second, it must be remembered that the *IS/LM* model underlies the neoclassical synthesis and that this synthesis is based on *general-equilibrium theory*. Third, the general-equilibrium model always assumes that, following some disturbance, an initial equilibrium is quickly superseded by a new equilibrium position and the Monetarists have never questioned this part of the analysis. (In fact, Friedman's 'theoretical framework' is specifically based on the general-equilibrium model.)

The implication of this theoretical similarity is that for both models equilibrium is quickly re-established, and cumulative movements away from equilibrium are therefore necessarily excluded from the analysis (this emphasis on equilibrating tendencies is criticised below, pp. 125ff.). However, there are occasions when deviations from equilibrium are accentuated and periods of mass unemployment or hyperinflation result. Theoretical models should be able to account for such cumulative changes in output or prices away from equilibrium. According to the Monetarists, the private sector of the economy is inherently stable and therefore destabilising movements are attributed to *monetary mismanagement by the central bank*; therefore, adopt the right monetary rule and cumulative movements will disappear. Similarly, in the Keynesian analysis cumulative move-

100

ments can be caused only by *persistent shifts* in the investment function or other autonomous disturbances in which case discretionary stabilisation policies will be required.

Thus both models rely on continuous *exogenous* shocks to create accentuated deviations from equilibrium but nothing *within* either model could account for such phenomena – they are essentially static, equilibrium models. Such models preclude the emergence of long and persistent phases of economic stagnation or other disequilibrium phenomena. However, if such phenomena are not uncommon then it would appear that in respect of both models there is more than just a 'missing-equation' problem to be solved – the whole structure underlying both schools may well be misconceived.

Is it possible then that the Monetarist versus Keynesian debate is essentially sterile, concerned with the underlying details of a theoretical structure which is itself obsolete? In fact, recent developments tend to undermine the theoretical foundations of *both* schools of thought, and in the next chapter we will outline an alternative approach in which considerable emphasis is placed on destabilising, cumulative changes in output and where money plays a crucial role in causing the instability. The analysis underlying this approach is, according to some recent contributions, essentially what Keynes was striving to establish. Recall that at the end of Chapter 3 we questioned the relevance of the Pigou effect and the subsequent neoclassical synthesis in the light of Keynes's stated intentions in *The General Theory*. In a similar way we will end this chapter with a quotation which casts doubt on the relevance of the Monetarist challenge but which highlights the importance of the alternative approach. In the Preface to *The General Theory* Keynes sees the main tasks facing him as:

(1) analysing 'the *effects of changes* in the level of output'; and
(2) explaining how 'money enters into the economic scheme in an essential and peculiar manner'.

In subsequent chapters these two problems are shown to be intimately connected. However, in the general-equilibrium approach, favoured by both the Monetarists and Keynesians, the *effects* of changes in output, i.e. the paths leading from one equilibrium to another, are not even considered. Furthermore, money plays no essential or peculiar role except when it is mismanaged by the monetary authorities. Therefore an alternative approach which

101

highlights disequilibrium behaviour and which also emphasises the role played by money in such situations deserves serious attention. This will be the purpose of Chapter 5.

APPENDIX: A SAMPLE OF THE EMPIRICAL EVIDENCE

Interest Elasticity of Money Demand ·

Study	Data	Definition of money	Interest rate	Interest elasticity
Courchene and	Annual U.S.	Narrow	Long	−1.00
Shapiro [15]	Annual U.S.	Broad	Long	−0.58
Teigen [77]	Annual U.S.	Narrow	Long	−0.2
	Quarterly U.S.	Narrow	Long	−0.07
Laidler [51]	Annual U.S.	Narrow	Long	−0.72
	Annual U.S.	Narrow	Short	−0.21
Brunner and	Annual U.S.	Narrow	Long	−1.09
Meltzer [9]	Annual U.S.	Broad	Long	−0.73
Laidler and	Quarterly U.K.	Broad	Short	−0.26
Parkin [54]				
Goodhart and	Quarterly U.K.	Narrow	Long	−0.08
Crockett [32]	Quarterly U.K.	Broad	Short	−0.09

Thus the interest elasticity depends on the data. In general, if annual data, a narrow definition of money and the long-run interest rate are used, the elasticity tends to be higher than otherwise.

Interest Elasticity of the Money Supply

Study	Data	Definition of money	Interest rate	Interest elasticity
Teigen [77]	Quarterly U.S.	Narrow	Short	0.2
Brunner and	Annual	Broad	Short	0.72
Meltzer [9]	Annual	Narrow	Short	0.66
Rasche [68]	Quarterly	Narrow	Short	0.24

The type of data is again seen to be significant. Annual data and a broad definition of money give the highest elasticity.

Interest Elasticity of Investment

Industry	Interest elasticity
Food	−0.33
Textiles	−0.71
Petroleum	−0.78
Motor-cars	−1.77

Source: Evans [18].

These results suggest that the more durable is the capital stock and the more important it is as a factor of production the greater the elasticity. In general, Evans concludes that a change of one percentage point in the long-term rate of interest will change investment by between 5 and 10 per cent over a period of two years.

5
A Reappraisal

In *The General Theory* Keynes attempted to prove the possible coexistence of macroeconomic equilibrium with involuntary unemployment. However, with the introduction of the Pigou effect, the neoclassical synthesis concluded that in terms of theory Keynes failed to prove his case and the Monetarists appear to be in agreement with this conclusion, e.g. Friedman [26] accepts the theoretical impossibility of unemployment equilibrium and states that 'Keynes's error consisted in neglecting the role of wealth in the consumption function'.[1] However, the implications of the Pigou effect are that price flexibility is sufficient to ensure full employment and therefore Keynesians and Monetarists accept that price rigidities must be the root cause of unemployment, e.g. Friedman's explanation of the existence of unemployment is entirely consistent with the conclusion of the neoclassical synthesis: 'All sorts of frictions and rigidities may interfere with the attainment of a hypothetical long run equilibrium position at full employment . . . but there is no fundamental "flaw in the price system" that makes unemployment the natural outcome of a fully operative market mechanism' [26].

Thus both schools accept that the price mechanism *can* efficiently allocate resources in such a way as to ensure that all productive resources are fully employed. This implies that, to them, perfect price flexibility is a sufficient condition for the attainment of equilibrium in all markets, including the labour market. Such a situation is known as a position of general competitive equilibrium and it depends on a set of equilibrium market prices being established at which the excess demands for all goods are zero. Both schools in fact assume the logical existence of such a set of equilibrium prices and they accept that in the absence of various rigidities the economic system would be stable and full employment the norm.

The difference between Keynesians and Monetarists is then seen as

largely an empirical matter – are the rigidities in the system so great that they prevent the economic system from adapting with sufficient speed to outside disturbances, thus requiring discretionary fiscal and monetary policies to ensure full employment (Keynesian position), or is the system sufficiently flexible so that a monetary rule is all that is required for stability and full employment (Monetarist position)? Thus Friedman is justified to some extent in concluding that 'the basic differences among economists are empirical, not theoretical' [26].

However, is this theoretical consensus justified, i.e. did Keynes produce results different from the classics only by incorporating various price rigidities into his system? According to recent contributions (e.g. Clower [12] and Leijonhufvud [56]) Keynes was intent on demonstrating that even in the absence of price rigidities the economic system will not gravitate towards a general-equilibrium situation at full employment, i.e. equilibrium prices will not be established even if prices are perfectly flexible. In order to appreciate this reinterpretation of Keynes's work it is useful first of all to outline the artificial process via which the market system is assumed to establish equilibrium prices.

THE WALRASIAN SYSTEM

The pioneering work in this area was undertaken by Leon Walras [83]. He observed that in order to prove the existence of a set of equilibrium prices it was necessary to determine all prices *simultaneously*. This is because the equilibrium price of (say) cars will depend on the price of oil, etc., and therefore since demand and supply functions will depend on other prices it is not legitimate to solve for one price separately from all the others. Walras then formalised the conditions necessary for an equilibrium set of prices to be determined simultaneously.

For example, assume an exchange economy in which there are n goods which are fixed in supply. Let $S_i(i = 1, \ldots, n)$ represent the supply of the ith good, P_i the price of the ith good, and $D_i = D_i(P_1, \ldots, P_n)$ represent the total demand for the ith good, where demand is assumed to be a function of all prices. We can then state the problem formally as follows. Does there exist an equilibrium set of prices (P^e) such that $D_i(P^e) = S_i$ for all values of i? Thus to Walras the problem was one of solving a set of simultaneous

equations in which there are n prices and n demand and supply functions to determine them.

Walras made two important observations about this set of equations. First, if labour is included as one of the n goods (and therefore one of the price variables is the wage rate) then it can be assumed that the demand functions are homogeneous of degree zero, i.e. if all prices, including the wage rate, are multiplied by some constant, then the quantity demanded of every good will remain unchanged. This is known as the *homogeneity postulate*. However, if each price is multiplied by the constant $1/P_1$, (the reciprocal of the first good's price), then the first price becomes unity and all other prices become *relative* prices in terms of this *numéraire*. The number of unknowns is then reduced to $n-1$ because the first price will then be determined, but there are still n demand and supply functions. Therefore it must be the case that one of these equations is redundant.

This led to Walras's *second* observation. According to Walras, the equations are, in fact, not entirely independent of each other and are related by the following budget constraint:

$$\sum P_i D_i \equiv \sum P_i S_i$$

This constraint is known as *Walras's Law*; it states that the total value of demands must always equal that of supplies at any set of prices, not just equilibrium prices. This identity holds true because of the budget constraint facing each individual and it states that for each economic unit there cannot be an excess demand for, or supply of, all goods taken together, *including money*, e.g. the planned inflow of goods and money must equal the planned outflow of goods (including labour services) and money. Thus an excess demand for goods must involve an excess supply of money and an excess supply of goods must imply an excess demand for money. The budget restriction merely states therefore that an individual's plans are assumed to be consistent and that there cannot be a net excess demand for, or supply of, all goods in general, including money. Then, summing over all individuals, the excess demands in the economy as a whole must sum to zero:

$$\sum P_i D_i - \sum P_i S_i = 0.$$

Essentially this is all that Walras's Law amounts to but it will be shown below to have important implication for the current debate.

106

However, for our present purposes it suffices to note that the implications of Walras's Law are that the n demand and supply conditions are not independent because if $n-1$ markets are in equilibrium, the remaining one must be in equilibrium also in order for Walras's Law to be satisfied. Thus one equation is redundant. However, with only $n-1$ independent equations we can only determine $n-1$ prices, i.e. the homogeneity postulate and Walras's Law together indicate that only *relative* prices are determined within this model and it does not permit the determination of the absolute price level. Thus multiplying all prices by some constant does not affect the equilibrium position.[2]

However, if we ignore the absolute price level it appears that an equilibrium set of relative prices does exist because there are $n-1$ unknown relative prices and $n-1$ independent equations to determine them. But, as Walras realised, counting variables and equations gives no guarantee of the existence of a solution and he was forced to develop a proof. This involved approaching equilibrium via a series of successive approximations which he called the *tâtonnement process* and it was supposed to represent the way in which the market mechanism actually allocates resources on the basis of demand and supply relationships.

According to the *tâtonnement* process the market 'feels' or 'gropes' its way to equilibrium by trial and error. The basic assumption is that there is an *auctioneer* who cries out prices for the goods to be traded, first at random, and then compares the demand and supply offers at these prices. If, as is likely, the quantitites demanded differ from those supplied then he calls out another set of prices, but this time *not* at random. He *raises* those prices for which there was an excess demand at the first auction and *lowers* prices for those goods for which there was an excess supply. This is the basic equilibrating mechanism in the Walrasian system but it leads to an equilibrium set of prices only if it is further assumed that all transactors, apart from the auctioneer, make no attempt to fix prices and that they do not enter into any trade until equilibrium prices are established. This last assumption implies an ability to *recontract*. i. e. the intermediary offers which help establish equilibrium prices are not actually carried out and all offers can be renegotiated when the final equilibrium set of prices is known.

Thus, in essence, the Walrasian general-equilibrium model assumes that all transactors except the autioneer are price-takers, contracts are not binding and no trade takes place until the market-

clearing list of prices is announced by the auctioneer – in Hicks's terminology, there is no 'false trading', i.e. no trading at disequilibrium prices.

The whole point of these artificial assumptions is to ensure that market transactions take place under conditions of *complete certainty*. However, since economic activity is undertaken through time the auctioner must announce both present and future prices. Therefore Walras had to assume that transactors were provided with perfect information about *all* prices, e.g. 'if we suppose the prices of goods and services and also the dates of their purchase and sale to be known for the whole period, there will be no occasion for uncertainty' [83]. However, as Jaffé has pointed out, these conditions involve a complete 'abandonment of reality' and are simply a means of 'contriving market models to elucidate mathematical systems instead of developing mathematical models to elucidate market systems' [83]: 'It is indeed an astonishing intellectual achievement to be able to utilise a framework which assumes a "groping" process to obtain equilibrium and simultaneously assumes perfect knowledge about all future markets' [16]. Thus the Walrasian system is essentially timeless.

However, under these very restrictive assumptions it has been demonstrated that a *tâtonnement* process with recontracting can lead to the establishment of a set of equilibrium prices,[3] i.e. a solution to the general-equilibrium system of equations does exist, but the implications of this solution are not very realistic and in fact the analysis is riddled with anomalies. For example, if the actual exchange of commodities always takes place at equilibrium prices then demand will equal supply in all markets, *including the labour market*, implying that there will always be full employment. Thus the Walrasian system simply assumes away *unemployment*.

Another anomaly is that although money is assumed to exist and forms part of the budget constraint (Walras's Law), there is no significant role for money to play in a general-equilibrium model, e.g. since all traders are provided with perfect information, the exchange of goods and services can be organised by the auctioneer. Goods can be allocated amongst transactors in accordance with the equilibrium solution and this leaves no role for money to act as the *medium of exchange*. Also, in a world of certainty in which everyone knows just how much of every commodity to give up in exchange for some other commodity, the hoarding of a *store of value* such as money becomes

unnecessary and there is no need for anyone to hold stocks of sterile cash balances. Therefore the Walrasian system cannot adequately account for the existence of money and in this sense it resembles a barter economy.

Uncertainty

Since the *tâtonnement* process leads to the assumption of full employment in an economic system in which money plays no role, it is obviously deficient as a description of the operation of a market economy. Therefore, if it is to throw any light on real-world situations, the Walrasian system requires restructuring. In this respect its major deficiency appears to be its assumption of complete certainty, i.e. in reality there is no auctioneer and perfect knowledge of equilibrium prices is not available to all transactors. Thus transactors are uncertain about present and (especially) future prices.

If we relinquish the assumption of perfect certainty and accept that in the absence of the auctioneer trade often takes place at disequilibrium prices, then it is possible to account for some of the anomalies of the general-equilibrium system. In particular it can be shown that the existence of uncertainty is sufficient to explain both the emergence of unemployed resources and the existence of money.

Unsold Goods and Services

With *perfect* information of present and future prices individuals who are currently unemployed are faced with the choice of accepting employment at the best available wage rate or remaining unemployed. However, with only imperfect information of job opportunities unemployed workers face two problems – they do not know the best available wage rate, and they are uncertain as to whether they can supply all the labour services they have available at this rate. In the face of uncertainty about wage rates and employment prospects unemployed workers will have to search for work and this will involve them in costs. However, they will probably continue searching i.e. remain unemployed, until they believe they have found the best job offer (in the sense that the benefits from further search are unlikely to cover the costs involved).

From the point of view of the individual worker it can be assumed that eventually he will accept employment – unemployment will be temporary or frictional – but the point is that the labour market does

109

not operate in isolation and the main function of the price system is to co-ordinate activities between various markets. Thus, if the labour market takes time to adjust because of imperfect information, this will have spillover effects on other markets which are also faced with imperfect knowledge of equilibrium prices, e.g. firms do not know market-clearing prices either. Thus limited information of equilibrium prices may lead firms to produce more than can be sold at current prices (especially if there is unemployment in the labour market), and in the absence of the auctioneer this will lead to an unintended accumulation of inventories. However, rather than react to this by lowering prices, lack of knowledge about market-clearing prices may lead firms to stockpile and eventually produce less, which will worsen the unemployment situation and create greater uncertainty in the labour market. Thus imperfect information and the resulting uncertainty can account for the emergence of unemployment and unsold stocks of goods in general (this idea is elaborated below, pp. 130–4).[4]

Money

Limited information about equilibrium prices and the quantities that can be sold at these prices will mean that transactors will enter into exchange only if offered an acceptable store of value in return. In a decentralised economy the risks involved in buying and selling will ensure that an article is only exchanged in return for something which has intrinsic value. The exchange process could be based on barter but this solves the problem only at considerable cost, e.g. in order to exchange good A for good Z and to avoid the double coincidence of wants it may be necessary first to exchange A for B, then B for C, etc. and only eventually obtain Z. This means, however, that one must acquire considerable information about the saleability of goods B, C, etc. or accept considerable risks. If, then, a good existed which was generally acceptable in exchange for all other goods, it would reduce the number of transactions required to exchange A for Z and also reduce the risks involved in each transaction. Thus, in the absence of perfect information, money in its role as a medium of exchange performs a valuable function in co-ordinating activity and minimising the transaction costs involved.

Money's other major role, that of a store of value, can also be understood once we break out of the straitjacket of perfect infor-

mation, e.g. the uncertainty attached to the sale of labour services and goods in general will mean that households and firms will have an incentive to hold a stock of assets which are generally accepted as a means of payment in order to be prepared for those times when goods and services cannot be easily sold.

Thus in the uncertain world in which we live the existence of an asset that acts as a medium of exchange and serves as a store of value is not difficult to understand. Therefore, although the existence of unemployment, unsold goods and money is difficult to account for within the Walrasian model they are important ingredients of the real world.

KEYNES'S INTENTIONS

To make any progress towards understanding the monetary economy in which we happen to live, the Walrasian assumption of perfect certainty must be abandoned. In fact, this is the distinguishing feature of Keynes's theory and he concentrated his attention on analysing a modern, capitalist economy in which wealth, assets and debts were accumulated over time and where this process of accumulation was based on flimsy expectations about an uncertain future. However, although Keynes explicitly abandoned the assumption of perfect certainty it would be wrong to assume that the classical economists had held rigidly to it. The classical system, for example, assumed the existence of both unemployment and money and did not in general assume complete certainty, but according to Keynes the classics had not fully appreciated the significance of this departure from the rigid Walrasian assumptions and they included uncertainty and money in their system in a very mechanical fashion. This led them to believe that the conclusions of the Walrasian system could be easily adapted to the real world. This is where Keynes and the classics actually parted company.

According to the classics, in order for Walrasian theory to be made applicable to the real world it was sufficient to tinker with the structure of the model. That is, although it was never intended as a description of actual behaviour, the classics believed that the Walrasian model was *non-categorical,* in the sense that new behavioural relations could be introduced into the model without reconstructing it entirely. However, Keynes believed that the model

was *categorical*, in the sense that it was closed to extension in precisely those areas in which he was interested, i.e. involuntary unemployment, etc. Thus Keynes insisted that the whole Walrasian analysis had to be abandoned, e.g. in an article written in 1933 [45] Keynes states that the belief that it is easy to adapt the conclusions of the Walrasian system 'to the real world of Monetary Economics is a mistake. It is extraordinarily difficult to make the adaptation.' This is because the rigid assumptions of that system 'are precisely the same as those which will ensure that crises do not occur'. And, in a letter to Hicks dated 9 December 1934, Keynes wrote: 'I shall hope to convince you some day that Walras' theory and all the others along those lines are little better than nonsense!'[5]

Thus, according to recent contributors, the task Keynes set himself was precisely that of rejecting Walras's law and the Walrasian system in general and of developing instead a monetary theory of output and employment in which uncertainty played a crucial role. Supporters of Keynes in this respect would include Robinson, Shackle, Davidson, Clower and Leijonhufvud, and they can be contrasted with the two dominant schools of thought: Keynesianism and Monetarism – that is, the two groups described as follows:

(1) With those Keynesians such as Patinkin, Tobin, Samuelson, etc. whose refinements of macroeconomics have led to it becoming largely a highly specialised form of general-equilibrium theory in which the decision-makers are consumers, investors and the government $(C + I + G)$. But because of the absence of an auctioneer, G has to be used to offset fluctuations in C and I; and

(2) With the Monetarists for whom the Walrasian system determines the long-run trend (natural rate) around which the real world fluctuates and who regard the factors omitted from the Walrasian system as random disturbances that largely average out over time without destabilising effects. Therefore, although there is no auctioneer, compensatory changes in G are unnecessary.

Thus in the extreme we can view Keynes, Robinson, Shackle *et al.* the 'true' Keynesians, as being opposed not only to the classics but also to modern Keynesians and Monetarists because much of classical analysis is still incorporated in the former and it underlies much of the latter. As a means of summarising the analysis of these 'true' Keynesians we will now develop a view of macroeconomics which closely accords with that of Keynes.

112

THE ECONOMICS OF KEYNES

In an article written in 1937 [47] Keynes restated 'the comparatively simple fundamental ideas which underlie my theory' and produced an explanation of unemployment in terms of uncertainty, money, interest, wealth, expectations and their combined effects on the level of investment. (In the following summary most of the quotations are from this article.)

To Keynes the great problem facing rational men was uncertainty. Thus 'the price of copper and the rate of interest twenty years hence . . . [is something about which] we simply do not know'. However, despite our imperfect knowledge, decisions about the future have to be made, and to overcome this problem we fall back on various conventions – we make predictions for the future based entirely on the present, we conform to the behaviour of the majority and accept conventional judgement – in other words we *pretend* to have knowledge: 'Now a practical theory of the future based on . . . so flimsy a foundation is subject to sudden and violent changes.' Economic theory should be capable of accounting for this instability, but according to Keynes the classics preferred to ignore it.

Keynes, however, acknowledged that the classics were justified to some extent in ignoring uncertainty because they were largely concerned with 'a world in which economic goods were necessarily consumed within a short interval of being produced', i.e. classical economics was based primarily on the merchant or farmer buying and selling goods on the market. Keynes on the other hand was concerned to analyse a modern, capitalist economy in which the accumulation of capital over time was one of the main objects of economic activity. However, by its very nature decisions about capital accumulation are concerned with the future 'but our knowledge of the future is fluctuating, vague and uncertain'. Therefore classical economics, which ignores the whole process of decision-making under uncertainty, 'requires considerable amendment if it is to be applied to a world in which the accumulation of wealth for an indefinitely postponed future is an important factor.' Thus 'I accuse the Classical economic theory of [trying] to deal with the present by abstracting from the fact that we know very little about the future . . . . This is particularly the case in their treatment of money and interest.' Keynes, in developing his own theory of investment

113

decision-making under uncertainty, then attempts to bring out the interrelationships that exist between money, interest, wealth and expectations. He proceeds as follows:

Stage 1. Since money is barren, 'why should anyone outside a lunatic asylum wish to use money as a store of wealth? . . . our desire to hold money as a store of wealth is a barometer of the degree of our distrust of our own calculations and conventions concerning the future. The possession of actual money lulls our disquietude; and the premium [the interest rate] which we require to make us part with money is the measure of the degree of our disquietude.'

Stage 2. 'The owner of wealth who has been induced not to hold his wealth in the shape of hoarded money still has two alternatives between which to choose' – bonds or physical capital. 'He can lend his money at the current rate of interest [buy a bond] or he can purchase some kind of capital asset.' Thus the price of capital assets will move relative to the interest rate (price of bonds) to offer equal advantages between bonds and physical capital at the margin. The rate of interest is therefore one important determinant of the price of capital assets. The other determinant is the expected returns on the capital good which 'are themselves subject to sharp fluctuations'.

Stage 3. However, 'Capital assets are capable in general of being newly produced', and as long as the demand price of capital assets (determined as in Stage 2) exceeds their costs of production, the amount produced will increase, i.e. the volume of current investment will rise. But even with stable cost levels the volume of investment may fluctuate widely, 'For it depends on two sets of uncertain judgements – the propensity to hoard [i.e. liquidity preference which affects the interest rate] and on opinions of the future yield of capital assets', which taken together determine the demand price. 'Nor will fluctuations in one of these factors tend to offset the fluctuations in the other. . . . *For the same circumstances which lead to pessimistic views about future yields are apt to increase the propensity to hoard.*'

To state Keynes's argument in more familiar terms, the m.e.c. schedule (which embodies views about future yields) is intimately bound up with the liquidity-preference schedule (the propensity to hoard).

114

Thus to Keynes the real and monetary sectors are *not independent* of each other. Furthermore, in the type of economy in which Keynes was interested, i.e. a modern capitalist system, the reason for this interdependence is not difficult to appreciate because the ownership of the existing stock of real assets as well as the production of new capital assets requires funds to be made available by the monetary or financial sector. Thus in an economy with well-organised financial markets, uncertainty about the future can rapidly influence the availability and cost of funds and hence the production of real assets, i.e. current investment.

In this respect it is possible to discern two themes underlying Keynes's work. In the first place he seeks to emphasise that fluctuations in employment and output are caused by fluctuations in investment but, secondly, that fluctuations in investment are in turn the result of instability in the monetary sector because the inter-relationships between money, interest, wealth and expectations determine the demand price for capital assets and are traced out on financial markets. Thus although fluctuations in investment create fluctuations in output and employment, the root cause of the instability is to be found in the financial institutions of a sophisti-cated, capitalist economy. In such an economy, therefore, Keynes concludes that the scale of investment will fluctuate for reasons quite distinct from the technical factors of production or the propensity to save, i.e. under conditions of uncertainty investment may have little to do with the 'productivity and thrift' of the classics. However, Keynes accepted that 'If on the other hand our knowledge of the future was calculable and not subject to sudden changes . . . [then] the whole of the available resources would normally be employed; and the conditions required by the orthodox theory would be satisfied.'

To Keynes, therefore, the methods used to overcome the problem of uncertainty within a modern financial system are of crucial importance in understanding unemployment. Uncertainty about the future plays such a crucial role because there are very few market institutions linking together the present production of goods and services with future production. In a capitalist economy future production requires the *prior* production of new capital assets but there are few market signals upon which producers can base their production plans, i.e. because there are practically no forward markets in goods it is difficult to co-ordinate production and

115

consumption plans through time. As noted earlier in this chapter, without an auctioneer the limited market information available to transactors complicates the problem of co-ordinating production and consumption plans even in the present but it makes the intertemporal problem of resource allocation through time a particularly difficult one for a market economy to solve.

Keynes was particularly sceptical about those financial markets, such as the Stock Exchange, that do perform an intertemporal function, claiming that they tended to be dominated by speculative activity. To the extent that they are so dominated they do not offer an efficient link between the present and the unknown future from the point of view of the production of capital assets, and 'when the capital development of a country becomes the by-product of the activities of a casino, the job is likely to be ill-done'. This is the crux of the problem – the real and financial sectors should have a stabilising influence on each other in order to create the right climate for capital investment to be undertaken, but, unfortunately, this seldom happens.

However, without an efficient market mechanism the information made available to market participants will be insufficient to enable them to co-ordinate their activities and a break-down in the system then becomes a distinct possibility, e.g. an increase in saving may depress current production without stimulating future production because an act of saving 'does *not* necessitate a decision to consume any specified thing at any specified date'; thus no market signals are transmitted and therefore no information is made available to prospective investors about which production processes to expand. 'There is [no] nexus which unites decisions to abstain from present consumption with decisions to provide for future consumption; the motives which determine the latter are not linked in any simple way with the motives which determine the former' [46]. Moreover, such a communications' failure is possible in any market, not just those concerned with future production, if the information required by transactors is unavailable. According to Shackle, Leijonhufvud and others this is the central theme underlying Keynes's work; in a decentralised capitalist economy with no auctioneer the information needed to co-ordinate the activities of individual firms and households through time is often not available, either because of the lack of organised markets in certain crucial areas (such as capital accumulation), or because of the difficulty of obtaining information in

116

certain decentralised markets (such as the labour market). We will now analyse in some detail this radical reinterpretation of Keynes.

DEPRESSION ECONOMICS

Starting from a position of full employment Keynes was concerned to analyse the type of disturbance which would cause the economy to slide into a depression from which, unaided, the economic system would find it increasingly difficult to escape. (This led to Hicks's comment that 'the General Theory of Employment is the Economics of Depression' [35]). Typically, Keynes's analysis involved either a decline in the marginal efficiency of capital or an increase in the propensity to save – both connected with the uncertain future. Assume therefore that entrepreneurs become more pessimistic about the future and that this leads to an inward shift in the m.e.i. schedule and a considerable cut-back in entrepreneurs' planned expenditure on capital goods. Let us trace out the likely consequences of this changed view of the future.

Prior to the increased pessimism entrepreneurs had planned to purchase capital assets, which implied that they were willing to hold wealth in an illiquid form, i.e. a new capital asset designed for a specific purpose is essentially a non-marketable asset in the sense that once purchased it is very difficult to resell. Ownership of such an asset drastically reduces one's choice of action in the future, so that increased pessimism is likely to lead entrepreneurs to acquire a more marketable asset, i.e. one which is more liquid and allows the firm greater flexibility of action. The great advantage of holding liquid assets is that they allow decision-making to be postponed until future developments are more apparent. This idea was central to Keynes's analysis of decision-making under uncertainty – as more evidence is accumulated through time the confidence with which future events are predicted can increase rapidly.[6]

However, what type of asset ensures the flexibility sought by entrepreneurs at times of uncertainty? Ideally they would prefer an asset which is easily marketable at a fairly stable price. This latter condition would seem to preclude the purchase of bonds and similar assets because of their price instability and leaves only liquid assets such as short-term bills, bank deposits, etc., to satisfy the demand for flexibility. In *The General Theory* there are only two

117

financial assets – bonds and money – and the latter stands for all marketable assets which are 'realisable at short notice and without loss' (Keynes's definition of liquidity' [44]). It is to these liquid assets that Keynes's liquidity-preference function applies, and therefore when entrepreneurs postpone their purchase of fixed capital assets and decide instead to hold their wealth in a more liquid form, Keynes's liquidity-preference function shifts to the right.

Even if entrepreneurs are themselves content to hold illiquid bonds (because they are at least more liquid than fixed capital) liquidity preference still has a vital part to play. For example, if they decide to buy bonds, the price of bonds will be bid up and interest rates will begin to fall, but at unchanged levels of income this will cause (bear) speculators with *inelastic expectations* about bond prices to increase their demand for speculative money balances. Therefore the initial fall in interest rates will create an excess demand for money by speculators which will then prevent the interest rate from falling any further.

Thus the monetary implications of a cut-back in investment expenditure can take two forms: (a) the one emphasised by Keynes in which shifts in the m.e.i. schedule cause shifts in the liquidity-preference schedule (see Stage 3 of Keynes's theory above), but this, perhaps, places too much emphasis on a special case in which changes in investment expenditure are exactly matched by changes in the demand for idle balances – however, at times of increased uncertainty, when we are concerned with large displacements from full-employment equilibrium (as Keynes was), this special case might well apply; (b) the one in which the liquidity-preference schedule does not shift and increased pessimism leads to a purchase of bonds – even in this case the implications are essentially the same because if entrepreneurs decide to buy financial assets this will induce a movement along the liquidity-preference schedule and because the demand for money is interest elastic any change in interest rates will result automatically in changes in idle balances. Thus the move away from illiquid capital assets either by entrepreneurs moving directly into liquid assets, or indirectly via the bond market, will create an excess demand for idle money and it is this excess demand for money that is the root cause of unemployment. The main thrust of the argument can be shown diagrammatically as in Figure 5.1.

Increased pessimism reduces the expected return on capital and causes the m.e.i. schedule in Figure 5.1 (a) to shift to the left. At an

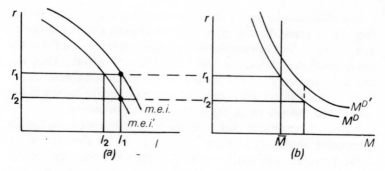

FIGURE 5.1

unchanged interest rate, r_1, this would result in a large fall in the demand price of capital assets, and investment expenditure would be reduced from I_1 to I_2. However, the fall in investment expenditure could be prevented if the interest rate were to fall to r_2 because then the demand price could be kept high despite the reduction in expected returns, i.e. the pessimistic views about future yields embodied in m.e.i.' discounted at the *lower interest rate, r_2,* would determine the same demand price for capital assets as before. However, the move by entrepreneurs to the more liquid end of the asset spectrum may cause the liquidity-preference schedule in Figure 5.1 (*b*) to shift to the right, which would create an excess demand for money even at the original interest rate r_1. On the other hand, if entrepreneurs decide to buy financial assets this will bid up bond prices and create an excess demand for money on the part of bear speculators. For either reason, then, the excess demand for money will prevent the interest rate falling to the level required to maintain investment at its original level. Thus liquidity preference prevents the rate of interest from being sufficiently flexible to offset fluctuations in investment and switches the burden of adjustment from the money market to other sectors of the economy.

In terms of the dichotomy between active and idle balances the process can be explained as follows: entrepreneurs originally demanded money to purchase capital goods, i.e. they had a demand for active money or money as a medium of exchange but because of increased pessimism they now demand money to hold – they demand money as a store of value. However, because money is the medium of exchange the excess demand for idle money can be satisfied merely by entrepreneurs and others curtailing their spending relative to their

119

inflow of income, i.e. by reducing the amount of active balances that they plan to spend. In this way an excess demand for money shows up as a general lack of demand for other goods and services but this will cause the flows of income and expenditure to shrink. Thus the increased demand for idle balances by pessimistic entrepreneurs (or by bear speculators) will reduce the amount of active money in the system and this will cause the level of income to contract.

Increased pessimism therefore sparks off a process by which speculative and precautionary hoards increase at the expense of active balances, and this prevents the required adjustment in the interest rate from taking place. Thus expenditure has to be curtailed relative to income in order for the excess demand for money to be satisfied. However, equilibrium in the money market is then achieved only at the cost of reduced flows of income, expenditure and, eventually, output. Liquidity preference therefore plays a central part in Keynes's theory because it forces the burden of adjustment on to the supply of goods and services and away from the rate of interest.

Moreover, this is not the only way in which liquidity preference complicates the adjustment process because in a developed financial system there is a need to distinguish between borrower's risk and lender's risk. The analysis above has concentrated on the liquidity preference of the investor (borrower) at times of uncertainty but similar reasoning applies to the lender. Increased uncertainty makes lenders less willing to part with their money and leads to higher loan rates and a preference on the part of lenders for shorter-term loans – instead of interest rates falling to the required level they might well be forced higher. Thus the availability and cost of funds can be adversely affected by the preference for liquidity on the part of *lenders*, and such financial repercussions will *reinforce* the fall in the demand price of capital.

If the liquidity preference of either borrowers or lenders prevents the interest rate from falling then the production of new capital assets will contract and the *investment multiplier* will ensure a reduction in the level of national income. However, as the level of income falls, the demand for transactions balances will contract and the liquidity-preference function will begin to shift inwards so that, eventually, the excess demand for money will be eliminated at a lower level of income. However, there is no reason why the interest rate should fall much below its original level, i.e. starting from the schedule $M^{D'}$ in Figure 5.1(b) the reduced demand for transactions balances will take

time to reduce the liquidity-preference schedule below M^D. However, even if the liquidity-preference schedule had not shifted outwards in the first place, and entrepreneurs had switched instead into bonds, this would have reduced the interest rate but bear speculation would prevent it falling far. A substantial fall in the interest rate requires the concurrence of speculators who would only concur if they expected interest rates to remain lower in the future than they had been until recently. Such a revision of expectations would require some time to take effect. Also, at times of increased uncertainty it is unlikely that the cost of borrowed funds would fall because of the effect on lender's risk. This in fact accords with experience – funds for investment are not cheaper and easier to obtain as the economy slides into a depression. All this reinforces Keynes's analysis: the long-run interest rate is very inflexible and does not fall fast enough to maintain the demand price of capital assets at a high-enough level when the future looks bleak.

In summary, increased pessimism in a modern capitalist economy with a developed financial system can have far-reaching effects. An initial postponement of investment demand filters through into the financial sector and increases the demand for liquidity. At the initial income level the desire for liquid assets by both borrowers and lenders leads to an excess demand for money and this prevents the interest rate from facilitating an easy adjustment. The excess demand for money leads to curtailment of spending and results in reduced flows of output and employment. Thus the onset of a depression, during which the level of aggregate effective demand falls below that of the total supply of goods, is seen as a specifically monetary problem involving an excess demand for (idle) money. Perhaps we are now in a position to appreciate the following comment: 'A monetary economy we shall find is essentially one in which changing views about the future are capable of influencing the quantity of employment' ([46]) p. vii). (See [37] for an elaboration.). Thus, to Keynes, multiplier contradictions in output and employment were essentially *monetary* phenomena.

THE STANDARD MODEL

As illustrated above, for Keynes the level of output depended upon the complex interaction of the real and monetary sectors. However, instead of pursuing the ideas developed by Keynes in *The General*

Theory and in his 1937 summary of that book [47], Keynesian economics in fact set off in a different direction and developed and refined Hicks's 1937 summary of *The General Theory*, i.e. the article 'Mr Keynes and the "Classics"' [35]. In this article Hicks originally formulated his *IS/LM* apparatus and this became the established framework within which Keynesian economics developed (see [35, 60, 63]). Therefore at this stage it will be useful to compare Keynes's analysis with the standard interpretation of his work in terms of the *IS/LM* model.

The analysis underlying the *IS/LM* model is quite different from that envisaged by Keynes, e.g. uncertainty is not an important feature of the model and the real sector (*IS*) and monetary sector (*LM*) are taken to be independent of each other. However, the *IS/LM* model is often portrayed as a general model within which classical, Keynesian, Monetarist (and other) theories can be incorporated – all that is required is that the two curves be drawn with the relevant slopes. Therefore, to what extent does the model's description of (say) the monetary implications of a fall in investment expenditure differ from that of Keynes?

In Figure 5.2 (*a*), where the slopes of *IS* and *LM* curves indicate that 'money matters' in the model, assume that initially they intersect at Y_F, the full employment level of output. Assume now that entrepreneurs become increasingly pessimistic about the future profitability of their prospective investment projects and that the m.e.i. schedule shifts inwards. If this leads to a large cut-back in investment expenditure then in the absence of compensatory fiscal or monetary actions it would be reasonable to assume that such a

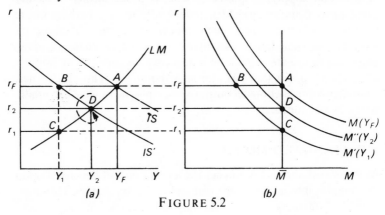

FIGURE 5.2

disturbance would lead to the onset of a depression, but in fact this is ruled out except under very special circumstances.

For example, the decline in investment expenditure will shift the *IS* curve horizontally to the left, and (ignoring the effects on the money market) this would, via the multiplier, lead to a large fall in income from Y_F to Y_1. However, the fall in income has monetary repercussions; in particular it will cause a reduction in the demand for transactions balances, e.g. as income falls towards Y_1 the demand for money in Figure 5.2(*b*) will shift downwards towards $M'(Y_1)$ and this will create an excess supply of money at r_F *which will induce a fall in the interest rate towards* r_1. The fall in the interest rate, however, will stimulate those expenditures which are interest elastic (i.e. investment, house purchase, etc.) so that the contraction in income will be halted before it reaches Y_1 and equilibrium in the goods and money markets will be re-established at a point such as $[r_2 y_2]$ with the demand for money at $M''(Y_2)$, i.e. we could assume an adjustment path going from A to D along the dashed line.

Thus with the *IS* schedule relatively elastic and the *LM* curve relatively inelastic, i.e. when 'money matters' in the model, it is impossible for cumulative processes to develop because the large decline in investment expenditure will cause only a relatively small reduction in income and hence employment. However, we know that depressions do occur. Therefore in order for the *IS/LM* model to describe reality, i.e. explain the onset of a depression, one or more of the following propositions must be assumed to hold:

(1) the *IS* function is very steep;

(2) the *LM* function is nearly horizontal ((1) and (2) are Keynesian special cases);

(3) the monetary authorities are mistakenly contracting the money supply so that the *LM* curve is continually shifting to the left (Friedman's explanation of the Great Depression).

However, these propositions imply that monetary factors are important only when the money supply is mismanaged. In fact it can be shown that these arbitrary restrictions are necessary only because of the erroneous way in which the *IS/LM* model seeks to resemble the real world.

IS/LM *Interdependence*

Underlying the model's analysis of the monetary implications of a

cut-back in investment expenditure is the assumption that the fall in income creates an excess supply of money and that this leads to a reduction in the interest rate. In this analysis the level of income apparently contracts *independently* of the amount of money being spent, i.e. income falls first (via the multiplier) and this reduces the demand for active money. But this sequence of events must be wrong because *money is the medium of exchange*, i.e. the level of income can fall only *by* less money being spent. Thus in our previous analysis (cf. the section on depression economics above) it was correctly pointed out that the fall in income is in fact caused by an excess *demand* for money, i.e. the move along the liquidity spectrum by pessimistic entrepreneurs induces an excess demand for money (as a store of value) and this reduces the amount of active money in the system which in turn causes a contraction in expenditure and income. Thus the fall in the amount of transactions balances is not a consequence of the fall in income but rather its *cause*. Moreover, the level of income will continue to contract until the excess demand for money is eliminated, i.e. multiplier contractions have *monetary* causes.

It should be clear, therefore, that there is no excess supply of money generated in the system and indeed to assume an excess supply of money *and* an excess supply of (investment) goods is surely erroneous. In this respect the *IS/LM* analysis appears to be in error because it fails to account for the interdependence in a capitalist system of the real and monetary sectors, i.e. the *IS* and *LM* curves are not independent of each other. Thus shifts to the left in the *IS* curve because of a fall in investment prospects may have the effect of inducing a shift to the left in the *LM* schedule because of increased liquidity preference.

Moreover, this is not the only conceivable link between the two schedules, e.g. in a series of articles [48] defending the monetary analysis of *The General Theory* Keynes analysed an additional motive for holding money – the finance motive. He postulated that an increase in planned investment may require money to be obtained before the investment can take place: 'if decisions to invest are [e.g.] increasing, the extra finance involved will constitute an additional demand for money'. Thus changes in investment plans will react on the money market making the 'finance motive' another factor linking together the real and monetary sectors and shifts in the *IS* schedule will be correlated with shifts in the *LM* schedule.

Other examples of interdependence could be enumerated but

enough has been said to indicate that it is often illegitimate to undertake comparative statics with the *IS/LM* model because the two functions are not independent. 'It is a great fault of symbolic pseudo-mathematical methods . . . that they expressly assume strict independence between the factors involved and lose their cogency and authority if this is disallowed' [46]. But this interdependency is particularly prominent when large displacements from full-employment equilibrium are being considered because the movement out of real assets and into monetary assets or vice versa are likely to be more pronounced and under such conditions the model gives no clear prediction of the final outcome.

However, it can be argued that for minor disturbances such interdependence will be less marked and that the model may then be useful for comparative statics. But even under these conditions it is open to criticism because it gives very little insight into the adjustment process by which new equilibria are established, i.e. it ignores the underlying dynamics.

Importance of Dynamics

In this respect the major deficiency of the standard macro-model is that it is too mechanical and portrays economics as pseudo-mathematics. However, this is hardly surprising in view of the fact that its originator (Hicks) was a leading contributor to Walrasian general-equilibrium theory, and in fact the *IS/LM* framework can be seen as a special case of the Walrasian system, e.g. typically there are assumed to be four markets – goods, money, labour and bonds – but by application of Walras's Law the analysis is concentrated on the first three. The model then consists of four equations: one equation for each market and an aggregate production function relating the goods and money markets (demand side) to the labour market (supply side). In order for comparative statics to be carried out, each market is assumed to be stable by appealing to either the Walrasian or Marshallian equilibrating mechanisms. However, a digression into dynamics will indicate that such an assumption is unwarranted.

For example, stated in Walrasian terms the quantity demanded and supplied of any good is assumed (*ceteris paribus*) to be a function of the prevailing price. The price is set each period but it changes from one period to the next in response to excess demand or

125

supply, i.e. increasing towards the equilibrium value if there is excess demand and vice versa. When discrepancies are reduced in this way the system is said to be deviation-counteracting, or to operate with *negative feedback*, and as long as demand and supply curves have the correct slopes the *Walrasian* adjustment process ensures that the market is stable and converges towards equilibrium. Similarly, the *Marshallian* process, with negative feedback, also ensures stability, e.g. here the supply and demand prices are assumed to be functions of the amount traded on the market. The quantity available is fixed per period but it changes from one period to the next in responce to an excess or shortfall of supply price over demand price, i.e. quantity falls towards the equilibrium value when supply price exceeds demand price and vice versa.

However, although both processes lead the system towards the equilibrium position as long as demand curves slope downwards and supply curves upwards, if *both slope downwards* then either process can be destabilising, e.g. in relation to Figure 5.3 the Walrasian process leads to an equilibrium solution only if, as we move in a *vertical* direction, the supply curve cuts the demand curve from below, while the Marshallian process leads to an equilibrium solution only if, as we move in a *horizontal* direction, the supply curve cuts the demand curve from below.

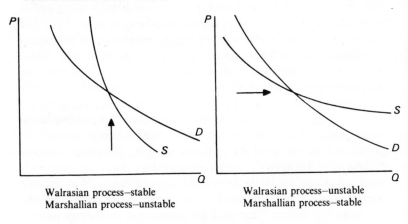

Walrasian process—stable
Marshallian process—unstable

Walrasian process—unstable
Marshallian process—stable

F IGURE 5.3

Therefore the first thing to note is that even when analysing each market in isolation, the stability of equilibrium depends upon the

126

type of dynamic adjustment process assumed and hence we can appreciate the importance of Samuelson's statement that 'One interested only in fruitful statics must study dynamics' [72]. Further, even if each adjustment process taken in isolation converges towards equilibrium, it follows that when prices (assumed fixed each period by Walras) and quantities (assumed fixed each period by Marshall) are *both* changing so that the two equilibrating mechanisms are operating and interacting *together*, they may *not* produce a process that will lead to equilibrium, e.g. if P over-reacts to changes in Q and vice versa, or P reacts to lagged changes in Q, then the system might well explode as in the 'cobweb' model. Thus, in general, whether or not an adjustment process in a single market converges to equilibrium depends not only on the slopes of the curves but also upon the underlying reaction functions and lag structure.

Despite this the *IS/LM* model simply assumes that each market *taken in isolation* is stable, but it then goes one step further and assumes that equilibrium positions are always reached even in a system of *interrelated* markets where each market reacts on the other. This extension from single-market equilibrium to the equilibrium of the system as a whole is achieved by the application of Walras's Law – according to which an excess supply of one commodity must be matched by an excess demand somewhere else in the system. Thus as long as these excess demands and supplies initiate deviation-counteracting effects, each market will tend towards equilibrium and therefore the system will be stable, e.g. corresponding to an excess supply of goods there must be an excess demand for something else, say, bonds. Negative feedback will then ensure that goods prices are bid down and bond prices are bid up, reducing the demand for bonds and increasing the demand for goods, and thus facilitating a move back to equilibrium in all markets. Therefore the assumed stability of each market and the application of Walras's Law guarantees the stability of the whole system. However, Keynes remained unconvinced by these equilibrating assumptions and in particular he questioned the authenticity of Walras's Law. Subsequent research has highlighted two reasons why Walras's Law does not hold in the type of economy in which Keynes was interested, i.e. a modern, money-using, capitalist system. The first is due to Shackle [74] and the second, equally devastating, to Clower [12, 13].

127

In a system in which there exists a durable capital stock, the present value of any long-lived asset will depend on expectations as to its future value. But expectations are liable to fluctuate and therefore, since:

> Values of assets of 'lasting' type can thus be created and destroyed in a moment . . . Walras' Law applied to any interval of finite length however short must be abandoned, for between its beginning and end a man's total wealth can increase, not by productive effort or saving, but 'out of nothing'; and can likewise dissolve. [Therefore] the conception of economics as hydraulics and the view of it even as accountancy, in the sense that validates Walras' Law, must go by the board [74].

Thus it is illegitimate to concentrate the analysis on (say) three markets and assume that the fourth will merely (or always) reflect changes in the other three. A monetary economy does not therefore function in such a neat, hydraulic manner and, following a disturbance, the attainment of a new equilibrium is not so automatic. (For a synthesis of Shackle's view; see [75].) This brings us to Clower's criticism of Walras's Law.

Clower

According to Clower there is a need in a modern, monetary economy to distinguish between *notional* demands and *effective* demands and he insists that Walras's Law can be applied correctly only to the former. The term 'notional' refers to the demand functions which are obtained when it is assumed that transactors can buy and sell all the goods and services they wish at prevailing prices. However, such an assumption is true only when all markets are in equilibrium, i.e. when prevailing prices are also market-clearing prices, because if unsold goods exist in any market this will mean that suppliers of these goods will have difficulty financing their proposed purchases in other markets.

Notional demand functions are therefore based on the assumption that planned sales are always achieved, thus ensuring that planned

purchases can always be carried out. The term 'effective', on the other hand, explicitly takes account of the fact that plans can be disappointed. Thus if the actual demand in any market falls short of planned supply, sellers will be faced with unsold goods or labour services which will force them to curtail their demand for other goods and perhaps cause excess supplies to emerge in other markets. *Effective* demand is therefore based on the idea that the income received from the current sale of goods and services will place some kind of constraint on current expenditure, i.e. effective demand is demand backed by an ability to pay.[7]

Notional and effective demands will be identical only where all markets are cleared, i.e. in full or general equilibrium, but in all other cases 'planned consumption as expressed in effective market offers to buy will necessarily be less than desired consumption as given by the demand functions of orthodox analysis' [12]. In such situations Walras's Law will not apply: 'although valid as usual with reference to notional market excess demands, it is in general irrelevant to any but full employment situations'[12]. This is because underlying Walras's Law is the assumption that every household expects to be able to buy or sell any quantity of every commodity at prevailing market prices but if at current prices transactors cannot sell all they want to then it can be shown that Walras's Law is irrelevant. (For a formal treatment see the appendix to this chapter.)

For example, when unemployed workers fail to sell their labour services, there is no way of determining what they would have purchased had they been successful in gaining employment, i.e. notional demands are not transmitted to suppliers. However, faced with an excess supply of labour services, the unemployed are forced to reduce their demand for other goods, i.e. effective demands (or the lack of them) are transmitted to suppliers and in fact these will provide the relevant market signals. But this means that the excess supply of labour is not matched by an *effective* excess demand for anything else: 'Contrary to the findings of traditional theory, excess demand may fail to appear anywhere in the economy under conditions of less than full employment,' [12].

Clower's analysis therefore points to the overriding problem as one of communication – the unemployed have a demand for work and also have a *potential* demand for goods but they are unable to communicate these demands to employers, i.e. they are unable to make their demands effective. However, because of the in-

129

terrelationships between the various components of the economic system, a disturbance in one market will be transmitted to other markets, thus causing further excess supplies to emerge. Now, both Walras and Keynes appreciated that the various markets in the economy are not independent. However, Keynes based his analysis on *effective* demands and concluded that this interdependence made the system inherently unstable, while Walras, concerned only with *notional* demands, believed that these interrelationships were a stabilising factor. We should conclude therefore by asking why is Keynes's model inherently unstable while the Walrasian world is characterised by stability?

KEYNES VERSUS WALRAS

Following Clower and Leijonhufvud,we can identify *two* fundamental differences of approach – both concerned with the amount of information that is transmitted through the market system. For example analysing the transmission of information in terms of effective demands highlights certain communications' failures that are entirely absent when the analysis is conducted in terms of notional demands. The first communications' failure explains the *emergence* of unemployment in Keynes's system, the second explains its *persistence*. We shall now examine these in turn.

Emergence of Unemployment

Unemployed resources emerge in Keynes's model because price adjustments are not instantaneous, e.g. when increased pessimism results in a fall in investment expenditure and causes an excess supply of capital goods to emerge, the prices of capital goods do not *immediately* fall to restore equilibrium. Similarly, in other sectors of the economy where the excess supply of capital goods is matched by an excess demand for (say) bonds, prices also tend to be sticky and do not respond sufficiently to restore equilibrium. In the Walrasian model, however, the auctioneer would simply reduce the price of capital goods and raise the price of bonds sufficiently to clear all markets. But, in the absence of the auctioneer, are price adjustments likely to be of sufficient magnitude to restore equilibrium – i.e. will the required information be communicated?

130

Firstly, take the market for capital goods. Without an auctioneer, firms will be supplied with only limited information about the new market demand for their products. Specifically, since they do not know market-clearing prices they will not know to what level price should be reduced and therefore they will be reluctant to change price. Furthermore, this reluctance is perfectly rational because for a firm to accept immediately a lower price for its output implies that it is indifferent to large fluctuations in the present value of its future sales, i.e. its wealth. In fact, rather than reduce price to the level that would ensure the sale of all current output, a more rational response would be for a firm to utilise the knowledge it has acquired from recent market experience to estimate a *reservation price* for its output, i.e. a price below which it would be reluctant to sell its product until more information on the market situation was available. In the short run, therefore, imperfect, information may induce firms to adopt reservation prices for their products and to absorb the reduced demand by allowing unsold goods to accumulate. However, eventually, as their wealth becomes tied up in illiquid inventories, they will be forced to reduce output. Thus in conditions of uncertainty a rational response to a fall in demand may be an adjustment in quantity rather than instantaneous price changes.

Therefore Keynes's scepticism about the likelihood of instantaneous price adjustments can be justified as an attempt to bring greater realism into economic theory. To illustrate that there is nothing arbitrary about the assumption that prices will *not* be perfectly flexible, let us turn now to the *bond market*.

Keynes insisted that the mechanics of the bond market were also more complicated than allowed for in the Walrasian system, e.g. again there is no auctioneer to raise price (lower interest rates) so that bondholders will also be supplied with imperfect information about market-clearing prices. Thus they will be uncertain about the future course of bond prices (interest rates) and are forced to have recourse to a convention – Keynes's 'normal rate of interest'. This, however, is nothing other than the inverse of the reservation price of bonds – a price below which speculators will be reluctant to sell but above which they will be quite happy to sell. Therefore, as bond prices rise above some normal level, speculators will sell bonds in the expectation that they can be later repurchased at lower prices. Speculators engaged in this type of activity are said to have *inelastic expectations* of bond prices and if a majority of bondholders react in this way bond prices

will be prevented from rising much above their initial level. (This is simply another way of stating Keynes's liquidity-preference theory of the rate of interest – see above, p. 28.)

Bond prices will therefore tend to be inflexible. However, to illustrate the normality, as opposed to the arbitrariness, of this inflexibility, note the essential similarity between the reluctance of producers to immediately accept lower prices and the speculative activity of bondholders. Both have to estimate reservation prices for their assets and do so by referring to recent experiences. Where behaviour is influenced in this way by recent experience, transactors are described as having *inelastic expectations* – they believe that prices are only temporarily high or low and will soon (it is hoped) return to their previous levels. However, in the meantime they are uneasy about accepting large fluctuations in their wealth (i.e. the present value of bondholdings for speculators and of future sales for producers) and respond to fluctuations in demand by quantity adjustments (selling bonds or reducing output) rather than accepting price fluctuations.

Thus the emergence of unemployment can be traced to the failure of bond prices and capital-goods prices to respond fast enough to changed conditions of demand – liquidity preference and reservation prices prevent the necessary price adjustments. However, note that at this stage price adjustments *would be effective* in preventing a contraction in output and employment, e.g. if increased pessimism results in an inward shift in the m.e.i. schedule (see Figure 5.1), price adjustments could prevent investment falling below its current level if: (a) interest rates fall sufficiently to induce a movement along the lower m.e.i. schedule, or (b) capital-goods prices fell sufficiently to shift the m.e.i. schedule back to its original position. Stated in another way, increased pessimism has resulted in the *demand* price for capital goods falling below the *supply* price; in order for quantity to remain unaffected, either the demand price must be increased (by interest rates falling), or the supply price must be reduced (by capital-goods producers offering their products at lower prices). There is therefore a maladjustment between what entrepreneurs are willing to pay for capital goods and the current cost of these goods. The difference between Keynes and Walras regarding the *emergence* of unemployment is simply that in the Walrasian system instantaneous price adjustments would eradicate this maladjustment, while for Keynes imperfect information and inelastic expectations would result in these initial price adjustments being postponed and instead the

132

system may well respond via quantity adjustments (however, see p. 156 below for a more realistic analysis which takes *stocks* of goods into account).

However, quantity adjustments in the capital-goods sector eventually lead to reductions in output and employment, which will reduce effective demands in other markets, thus amplifying the original contraction and causing more unemployment. A cumulative contraction may then set in which has two interesting aspects. First, when firms become convinced that the fall in demand is not temporary, they may decide to reduce price but the requisite price adjustments then become even more difficult to gauge because the multiplier repercussions will mean that prices will need to fall eventually by more than the amount required to offset the original disturbance. Also, each firm will face the difficult task of obtaining a greater share of a falling market, i.e. as aggregate demand contracts the substitution possibilities of price cuts will be limited. Thus the dynamics of the situation will be such that even when firms are prepared to reduce price, they are still no clearer about what price to charge. Second, as the system contracts the excess supply of capital goods will be eliminated by a reduction in output; this will cause a general contraction in incomes and employment which will also eliminate any remaining excess demand for bonds or money. However, the system does not return to *general* equilibrium because there will still exist an excess supply of labour – Keynes's 'unemployment equilibrium'.[8]

Once the economy has contracted into this state Keynes insisted that price adjustments are even less feasible but in any case are no longer sufficient to restore full employment; it is at this stage that unemployment becomes *persistent*.

Persistence of Unemployment

When the economy has contracted into a situation of unemployment equilibrium (or disequilibrium) the two approaches still diverge because for Keynes *Walras's Law no longer holds* – the excess supply of labour is not matched by an excess demand for anything else in the system. Thus, although it may be said that the unemployed are unable to purchase all the commodities they desire, this is simply a potential demand and it does not represent an effective demand for goods because it is not backed by an ability to pay. The sum of effective

excess demands is not zero.

In the Walrasian system, on the other hand, where notional demands are taken into account, since the unemployed have a (notional) excess demand for goods the system is assumed to be stable as long as real wages (W/P) fall. This can be achieved either by money wages falling, or by the price of commodities rising, either of which could easily be accomplished by the auctioneer. But in the absence of this *deus ex machina*, will anything happen? 'According to the Walrasian way of looking at things the pressure of excess demand for commodities should be stronger the higher is unemployment' [57]. But the notional demands of the unemployed are not transmitted in the type of economy in which Keynes was interested because the unemployed first have to obtain *money* before they can effectively demand commodities.

In a *monetary* economy, as opposed to a *barter* economy, there is no direct link between an excess supply of labour and an excess demand for commodities. For example, in a barter economy workers are paid in the form of the goods that they produce so that the offer of labour services is directly connected with the demand for additional output. However, in a monetary economy the unemployed demand *money wages* and their offer of labour services is not interpreted by employers as an increased demand for *goods*. 'Their notional demand for commodities is *not communicated* to producers; not being able to perceive this potential demand for their products, producers will not be willing to absorb the excess supply of labour [even] at a wage corresponding to the real wage that would "solve" the Walrasian problem' [56]. That is, in a situation of unemployment equilibrium even if the money wage demanded by the unemployed is less than the value of their marginal product, employers may not be willing to accept the offer of labour services because the demand for labour is a *derived demand*, i.e. the marginal conditions of Walrasian analysis are only relevant on the assumption that the extra output can be sold at current prices, but in a situation of low demand and widespread unemployment firms would be unlikely to make such an assumption. Thus even if the money wage is no greater than that which would obtain in full-employment equilibrium, firms still have no incentive to hire the unemployed.

To emphasise the above point Keynes pointed out that since wages are set in the monetary unit of account it may not be possible for workers as a group to affect real wages by accepting variations in money wages, and he insisted that the classics (Pigou in particular) had never grasped this vital point: although workers bargain for *money* wages 'traditional theory maintains that the wage bargains between the entrepreneurs and the workers determine the real wage'. However, 'in assuming that the wage bargain determines the real wage the classical school have slipped in an illicit assumption. . . . There may exist no expedient by which labour as a whole can reduce its *real* wage to a given figure by making revised *money* bargains with the entrepreneurs' ([46] p. 13).

The point is that cuts in money wages reduce real wages only if the price of goods does not fall along with money wages, i.e. only if the increased output can be sold at current prices. 'Thus [in a monetary economy] the fact that there exists a potential barter bargain of goods for labour services that would be mutually agreeable to producers as a group and labour as a group is irrelevant to the motion of the system'[58]. Because of this neither employers nor prospective employees are capable of avoiding the resulting unemployment, and this explains why Keynes chose to describe it as *involuntary unemployment*, i.e. workers want to work, employers want to expand production and make full use of expensive capital equipment; however, because the unemployed are unable to *effectively* demand the goods they desire, this lack of effective demands (involuntary underconsumption on the part of the unemployed) prevents producers from offering employment (involuntary underproduction on the part of employers). 'The resulting miseries are nvoluntary all round.' In this respect Keynes's definition of involuntary unemployment is illuminating:

Men are involuntarily unemployed if, in the event of a small rise in the price of wage-goods relatively to the money-wage, both the aggregate supply of labour willing to work for the current money-wage and the aggregate demand for it at that wage would be greater than the existing volume of employment ([46] p. 15).

Thus for Keynes, if workers are prepared to accept employment at

lower real wages resulting from an *increase in prices*, then part of the existing level of unemployment must be involuntary. Note that Keynes is not concerned here with that part of unemployment which the classics chose to call 'voluntary' unemployment, i.e. frictional and structural unemployment, or even that part of unemployment due to unions, or minimum-wage laws setting money wages at too high a level, because these types of unemployment would exist *even if commodity prices rose*. Thus Keynes sought to identify a separate type of unemployment which required for its reduction a rise in the price of commodities relative to money wages. However, a bidding up of commodity prices requires an increase in the aggregate demand for goods, and therefore involuntary unemployment can be viewed as that type of unemployment that can be reduced by an expansion of aggregate demand (hence it is often referred to as deficient-demand unemployment). [9]

Thus the important factor in reducing involuntary unemployment is the change in commodity prices, and as long as these *rise* the money wage can either fall or remain constant, i.e. it is of *secondary importance*. Because the behaviour of money wages is not crucial to the analysis, it is convenient to assume them stable, but this has led to the general belief that the whole of Keynes's theory of involuntary unemployment is based on the assumption of rigid money wages. This is not in fact true; for example, in developing his argument in *The General Theory* Keynes assumes that money wages are constant, 'But this simplification with which we shall dispense later, is introduced solely to facilitate the exposition' ([46] p. 27). Consequently in the latter half of the book this assumption is dropped and chapter 19 is entitled 'Changes in Money-Wages'.

However, it is still instructive to enquire why Keynes chose to analyse the problem of involuntary unemployment largely in terms of commodity prices rising rather than reductions in money wages. In fact it can be shown that he adopted this approach basically because a rise in prices conveys *different information* than a fall in wages and is, in general, the only effective way to reduce unemployment.

For example, there are a number of reasons why workers may react differently to cuts in money wages than to a rise in prices. One is that they 'suffer from money illusion' but Keynes did not offer this explanation. Instead he pointed to the following *information problem*: if wages are cut across the board and if employees know that money wages everywhere are lower, then they will not quit jobs to search for

employment elsewhere. The problem is of course that employees will think that only their wages have been reduced and they will not be prepared to accept such a reduction. 'Since there is, as a rule, no means of securing a simultaneous and equal reduction of money wages in all industries, it is in the interest of all workers to resist a reduction in their own particular case.' [46]. Thus, according to Keynes, workers are particularly concerned with *relative real wages*, and, as Tobin has pointed out, in a decentralised labour market with no auctioneer 'A general rise in price is a neutral and universal method of reducing real wages.' Thus 'rigidities in the path of money wage rates can be explained by workers' preoccupation with relative wages and the absence of any central economy-wide mechanism for altering all money wages together' (Tobin [82]).

The Labour-Market-Adjustment process

In the face of this group concern with relative money wages, two developments are then possible as aggregate demand falls: either money wages are cut despite this resistance, or the resistance is so strong that employers announce redundancies. In either case individual workers are faced with the problem of deciding how to adjust to the changed situation:

(1) In the face of money wage cuts, do they passively accept them or do they quit and search for a job with a money wage equivalent to their previous one?

(2) Finding themselves redundant, are they prepared to accept a sufficiently low wage in another industry to ensure immediate re-employment or, again, are they more likely to search for an equivalently paid job?

Not having full knowledge of employment prospects but with past experience indicating to them that they could reasonably expect to find a job at the old wage level, they would probably prefer to sample the job opportunities available before accepting a lower wage. Moreover, this response is perfectly rational, and for the same reasons as those outlined above for capital-goods producers and bondholders (pp. 130–3), e.g. if workers passively accepted wage cuts or accepted the first wage offer once unemployed this would imply that they regarded large fluctuations in the present value of their

137

labour services, i.e. their human capital, as normal. If, as seems probable, workers attach some importance to past experience, they are more likely to place a *reservation price* on their labour services, i.e. a price below which they would be reluctant to sell their labour unless all money wages fell uniformly. Thus they will act individually as if they held *inelastic expectations* of future wage rates.

However, this concern with relative wages on the part of labour as a group and inelastic expectations on the part of individuals will make it probable that a *quantity adjustment* occurs in the labour market as aggregate demand falls, and since there is no auctioneer to cut money wages uniformly across the board, unemployment will develop. Of course, in time as money wages generally begin to fall the unemployed will realise that their reservation prices will need to be adjusted downwards, but, even as they begin to make these adjustments, the multiplier repercussions of the initial rise in unemployment will induce second-round reductions in aggregate demand and complicate the adjustment process.

The point is that the type of adjustment process postulated by Keynes, whereby quantities adjust quickly relative to prices, results in a magnification of the initial disturbance. The multiplier, which is based on quantity adjustments, is a 'deviation-amplifying mechanism' and is destabilising. However, as aggregate demand falls and transactors are supplied with imperfect information about market opportunities, a quantity adjustment rather than perfect price flexibility is seen to be the *rational* response of transactors in all decentralised markets (such as the goods, bond and labour markets). Also, since the assumption of imperfect price flexibility is applied uniformly in all markets and in each case is based on reservation prices and inelastic expectations, it can hardly be called an arbitrary assumption.[10]

However, in relation to the labour market Keynes was not content simply to rationalise the resistance to wage cuts but went further and insisted that it was *preferable* that money wages were inflexible and did not respond rapidly to fluctuations in demand because this gave an element of stability to the economic system. For example, having explained why the labour market is one of the most difficult in which to achieve price flexibility, Keynes went on to ask what would be gained by greater flexibility.

In chapter 19 of *The General Theory* Keynes analyses the most important practical repercussions of money wage cuts, and notes that to have any lasting effect on the level of employment reductions in money wages must affect either the consumption function, the investment schedule or the interest rate – otherwise an increase in output will simply lead to an excess supply of goods because aggregate demand will not rise at the same rate as output (the m.p.c. is less than unity, see p. 35 above). However, since money wage cuts are unlikely to favourably influence consumer expenditure, 'it follows that we must base any hopes of favourable results to employment from a reduction in money wages mainly on an improvement in investment due either to an increased marginal efficiency of capital or a decreased rate of interest.' As regards the m.e.c. this will increase only if wages fell *once and for all* and reduced costs right across the board, but a situation 'in which money wages are slowly sagging downwards . . . serves to diminish confidence'. However, since 'there is no means of securing uniform wage reductions for every class of labour . . . it would be much better that wages should be rigidly fixed . . . than that depressions should be accompanied by a gradual downward tendency of money wages' ([46] pp. 264–7).

Thus the only favourable effects of money wage reductions on employment are likely to be those that decrease the rate of interest: 'if the quantity of money is virtually fixed it is evident that its quantity (in real terms) can be indefinitely increased by a sufficient reduction in money wages' (i.e. the Keynes effect outlined above on p. 38).

> We can produce precisely the same effects on the rate of interest by reducing wages . . . that we can produce by increasing the quantity of money. . . . [However] having regard to human nature and our institutions, it can only be a foolish person who would prefer a flexible wage policy to a flexible money policy ([46] pp. 267, 268).

Therefore, since greater flexibility achieves very little and in particular achieves nothing more than an expansionary monetary policy which is also easier to implement, it follows that it is a good thing that money wages are set for finite periods and are not subject to large fluctuations because at least they have a stabilising influence on monetary values. Indeed 'the chief result of [flexible wages] would be

139

to cause a great instability of prices, so violent perhaps as to make business calculations futile'. This point has been well summed up by Patinkin: 'From Chapter 19 it is quite clear that wage rigidities are *not* an *assumption* of Keynes' analysis but rather a policy conclusion that follows from his investigation of the probable effects of *wage flexibility*' [63].

Furthermore, if we regress a little and reiterate the initial cause of the contraction, it can then be seen that money wage cuts are *socially unjust*. For example, Keynes's analysis of involuntary unemployment typically begins with a fall in the demand for new capital goods. As the demand price for capital (determined by interest rates and expected returns) falls below the supply price (determined in the short run by marginal costs – largely wages) production is reduced and unemployment develops as workers are made redundant. However, it is very naïve to assume that the cause of the disequilibrium is to be found in that market experiencing the most dramatic excess supply, i.e. the labour market. If the problem is too low a demand price for capital then it would be unjust to force the labour market to bear the whole burden of adjustment.

Therefore, since high money wages are not the cause of unemployment and since reductions in money wages will have little effect in reducing unemployment (except via the Keynes effect), there is no justification for wage cuts. Thus, although wage (and price) flexibility may be useful in preventing the *emergence* of unemployment, money wage cuts, even if they could be implemented, are useless as a policy for curtailing the *persistence* of unemployment. What then is required?

Wrong Relative Values: (1) *Background Material*

In order to appreciate Keynes's analysis of the problem it is important to make a distinction between what was *new* in The *'General Theory'* and what had been carried over from the earlier *Treatise* (noting that to Keynes the two books represent 'in my own mind . . a natural evolution in a line of thought which I have been pursuing for several years'). The innovations of the later book largely corrected the faults of the earlier work: 'the outstanding fault of the [*Treatise* was] that I failed to deal thoroughly with the effects of *changes* in the level of output', and to overcome this error The *General Theory* emphasised the consumption function, investment multiplier

and quantity adjustments in general, as discussed above. However, there was another (older) part to Keynes's theory which was not given as much attention in *The General Theory* – having already been covered in the *Treatise* – namely, the linking together of monetary theory (concerned with the determination of the aggregate price level and output) and value theory (concerned with relative prices).

In the *Treatise* Keynes broke away from the traditional distinction between these two branches of the subject and brought them together in an attempt to explain how disequilibrium situations (initiated, say, by monetary-policy actions) produce changes in money incomes and prices. In order to trace out these developments the *Treatise* disaggregated total output into *consumer goods* and *capital goods* and analysed changes in money incomes in terms of changes in the relative prices of these *two* commodities. The analysis was carried over into *The General Theory*: 'One of the objects of the foregoing chapters has been to bring the theory of prices as a whole back to close contact with the theory of value' ([46] p. 293). Consequently, Keynes in *The General Theory* also distinguishes between wage goods (consumer goods) and capital goods. Indeed this distinction is crucial to Keynes's analysis of unemployment and of how the real and monetary sectors are linked together.

For example, drawing together monetary and value theory Keynes's analysis proceeds as follows. A depression is characterised by wrong relative values, where despite excess capacity demand prices lie below supply prices, i.e. the price transactors are prepared to pay for goods is less than their costs of production. Assuming that wages are the major element in short-run costs, what is required is a rise in commodity prices relative to money wages. For the reasons analysed earlier in this chapter, Keynes chose to analyse the problem on the assumption that the money wage was 'correct', i.e. it was at a level consistent with full employment and was not a barrier to expanding production. Thus his analysis was based on the assumption that demand prices were too low rather than supply prices too high.

It is at this stage that the distinction made in the *Treatise* between consumer and capital goods becomes important, e.g. in order for there to be an expansion of total output and hence employment in a two-commodity model the demand price for at least one component of output must exceed its supply price. However, the demand price for consumer goods is itself largely a function of current output $(C = f(Y))$; therefore there is unlikely to be much stimulus to

production from this direction. The demand price for capital goods on the other hand is not simply a function of current output but is a function of the future income that a capital asset will generate, i.e. it 'depends on the anticipated price-level of the utilities which these investments will yield up at some future date and on the rate of interest at which these future utilities are discounted for the purpose of fixing their present capital value' [44]. The demand price of capital goods is therefore an *independent* factor in the analysis, whereas the price of consumer goods is *dependent* on current income.

This emphasis by Keynes on two commodities and two prices was an important departure from the classical Quantity Theory analysis, where only 'the' price level was taken into account and where relative prices were ignored. However, it also highlights a further difference between Keynes and the *IS/LM* model, the importance of which will now be illustrated.

Keynes's macro model, like the *IS/LM* model, consists of *five* aggregates – consumer goods, capital goods, labour services, money and bonds – but only *three* relative prices – the interest rate, the money wage and the price level. Therefore the value of one aggregate would be indeterminate unless it was linked closely to the value of one of the other aggregates. To overcome this problem Keynes treated bonds and capital goods as close substitutes and assimilated them together in sense that bonds became the representative long-term asset. However, because bonds and capital goods are treated as indistinguishable, Keynes's liquidity-preference theory needs to be interpreted more broadly than is usually the case as it represents the choice between liquid assets (money) and all other illiquid assets (bonds and capital goods). But this means that the long-term interest rate also requires reinterpretation as representing the demand price of all illiquid assets (assuming expectations are given). Thus the prices of bonds and capital goods rise and fall together and this explains why in Keynes's model such importance is attached to the interest rate – given the state of entrepreneurial expectations the interest rate determines the demand price of an important component of total output. A low-enough interest rate can therefore act as a stimulus to production by raising the demand price of capital above its supply price.

How does Keynes's method of aggregation compare with the *IS/LM* model? There, the problem of too many aggregates is solved by assimilating consumer and capital goods by means of an aggregate

production function into one commodity called 'output'. The price level then represents both consumer and capital goods. The upshot of this is that the interest rate is divorced from the price of capital goods and is not an important variable in the determination of investment – it merely represents the borrowing cost of money and has no direct impact on the demand price of capital.

Which method of aggregation is superior? The conclusion of one contributor is quite illuminating on this point:

> It has been argued by Keynes that it is the rising marginal costs of the capital goods industries which limits the rate of capital accumulation. As the demand for capital rises the costs and prices of these goods rise in relation to the prices of all other goods. . . . In any *single* commodity model, however, the price of capital cannot rise in relation to the price of the consumer good. . . . For this reason the rate of investment cannot be determined analytically within the confines of a single commodity macroeconomic model . . . a two commodity model is needed at the very least ([85]; on the theory underlying this quotation see the analysis above, pp. 21–23).

Thus the *IS/LM* method of aggregation differs from Keynes's in two respects: (*a*) it denies the significance of the interest rate as an important, direct determinant of investment; and (*b*) within the confines of the one-commodity, *IS/LM* model, the rate of investment is itself indeterminate.

Wrong Relative Values: (2) *The Issue*

We are now in a position to appreciate the importance of the relative price problem for which Keynes was seeking a solution and to deduce its implications for the Keynes/classics debate.

Keynes's analysis of the causes of fluctuations in income centred on the demand for new capital goods, i.e. on whether investment demand was sufficient to provide a stimulus to the production of new capital assets. Since such production would require more labour input there exists some volume of investment that would ensure full employment at the current level of money wages – all that is required is a high-enough demand price of capital. However, if the relationship between this demand price and the money wage is too low to induce investment then involuntary unemployment will persist and a de-

flation of money wages and commodity prices will follow. Then, in order for the economic system to return to full employment *automatically*, a deflation must raise the demand price of capital or consumer goods above their respective supply prices; the only way Keynes could envisage such a deflation 'righting' itself was via its effects on reducing the demand for liquid assets, thereby reducing the long-term rate of interest (the Keynes effect).

Such a reduction has two effects: first, it increases the demand price for illiquid assets – bonds and capital goods – thereby stimulating investment expenditure; second, the increase in asset prices has a 'windfall' effect on consumer expenditure, for example:

> The consumption of the wealth-owning class may be extremely susceptible to unforeseen changes in the money value of its wealth. . . . Perhaps the most important influence, operating through changes in the rate of interest, on the readiness to spend out of a given income, depends on the effect of these changes on . . the price of securities and other assets ([46] pp. 93–4).

Thus relative prices are very important to Keynes: the 'price-relative' between capital goods and money wages is an important determinant of investment expenditure and the 'price-relative' between capital goods and consumer goods is an important determinant of consumption expenditure. If the price level of long-run assets is allowed to fall then these crucial 'price-relatives' may become too low to generate full employment.

However, in the face of widespread unemployment a *general* deflation of *all* money prices would be particularly unhelpful because it would not solve the basic problem, which is one of wrong relative values. In order for a deflation to succeed in returning the economy to full employment it must become unbalanced in the sense of creating a relatively greater proportionate fall in money wages and consumer-goods prices than in the price of capital goods. For Keynes, this is likely to occur only, if the deflation engineers a reduction in the long-run interest rate: 'But the most stable and the least easily shifted element in our contemporary economy has been . . . the minimum rate of interest acceptable to the generality of wealth owners' ([46]p. 309). Thus even an unbalanced deflation may not be self-correcting and what is then required is decisive action by the monetary

authorities via open-market operations (at the long end of the market) to raise the value of capital assets.

However, Keynes derided the weak attempts by central banks to prevent capital-asset prices from initially falling and he was also sceptical of their ability to raise asset prices once they had fallen to a low level because, once low asset prices and general unemployment had been allowed to develop, entrepreneurial expectations may then become too pessimistic 'to be offset by any practicable changes in the rate of interest'. At this stage it would be necessary for direct government expenditure on public works to 'pump-prime' the economy and revise business expectations upwards. Such a policy would bring into production previously unemployed workers whose demand, once made effective, would give a further boost to producers' sales expectations. To some extent this will offset the pervading pessimism and give a much needed stimulus to capital-asset values. Thus to Keynes a depression was unlikely to be either self-correcting or amenable to correction by the monetary authorities once entrepreneurial expectations had been allowed to decline too far; *then* the only solution to 'unemployment equilibrium' would be a 'pump-priming' fiscal action.

Although Keynes's belief in the self-adjusting properties of the economic system was strictly limited, his analysis at least concentrated on the crucial maladjustment of relative values which underlay the problem. The classics on the other hand tended to ignore relative prices at the macro level, i.e. although they were greatly concerned with the determination of relative prices at the *micro* level their analysis concentrated on *absolute* prices at the macro level. There the classics relied on the Quantity Theory of Money, which took account of only one price – the aggregate price level of output (or transactions). Similarly, in the neoclassical synthesis, a depression results in a general decline in all money prices and this ensures a return to full employment via the *Pigou effect*. We will conclude this chapter by reexamining this claim.

'The Pigou Effect is an effect *on* real consumption expenditures. It is due to an increase in real balances which, in turn, has been brought about by a proportional fall in all money prices (except bonds)' ([56] p. 324). In terms of the *IS/LM* model this means that the price level of 'output' falls, the money wage falls, but bond prices (the interest rate) remain constant.

However, if the price level of 'output' falls, i.e. if both consumer and

145

capital goods fall in price, what incentive have producers to increase their output? They will in fact increase production only if the price of at least one commodity falls less than money wages (costs). Thus the Pigou effect will be effective in increasing output and employment only if the deflation becomes unbalanced and the fall in commodity prices is halted, i.e. the Pigou effect must also work through a movement in relative prices.

Once this is accepted it can be shown that the Pigou effect and the Keynes effect are very similar. In the first place, since the Pigou effect stipulates that bond prices remain constant while other prices fall, it depends to some extent on a relative rise in the price of *illiquid* assets. In this respect it is similar to the Keynes effect – that too depends on a relative rise in long-term asset prices, but to Keynes the rise was brought about by falling interest rates, which not only raised bond prices but also increased the price of capital assets. Thus although similar, the Keynes effect has a broader impact. In the second place, both effects attach great importance to the rise in the real value of money balances during a deflation. However, to Keynes the increase in real balances would reduce interest rates and increase asset values. Investment expenditure will increase but in order for *consumer* expenditure to increase this would require that the rise in 'the price of securities and other assets' creates a 'windfall effect' on consumption. He regarded the *direct* affect of the increase in real balances on consumer expenditure (*à la* Pigou) as of *secondary* importance at a time of falling incomes. Thus the main difference between Keynes and Pigou was that the former felt that a deflation would be more likely to become unbalanced in the direction of capital-goods prices and he felt that consumer expenditure would rise only via the 'windfall effect' of higher capital values.[11]

To sum up, the only real hope of recovery from a depression (in the absence of government intervention) focuses on an unbalanced deflation, i.e. we have to depend on a relatively greater proportionate fall in wages than in the demand price for some component of output. Demand prices can be raised relatively to wages by the (wealth) effect of falling commodity prices on asset values. However, the Pigou wealth effect has a much weaker impact on relative values than does the wealth effect proposed by Keynes (even so, Keynes did not advocate reliance on it). For example, the Pigou effect is concerned solely with financial (basically monetary) wealth, while the Keynes effect takes into account changes in the value of durable capital assets

146

and hence incorporates a much broader conception of wealth. (However, this does *not* imply that 'money does not matter' in Keynes's model – indeed, this broader conception of wealth is essential for analysing money's important role: 'For the importance of money essentially flows from its being a link between the present and the future . . . [and] 'It is by reason of the existence of durable equipment that the economic future is linked to the present.')

Therefore for a deflation to succeed in bringing the economy back to full employment, it must reduce money wages in greater proportion than the demand price of capital goods. In other words we have to rely on an interest-rate effect. Keynes's contribution to economic theory can then be seen as an attempt to overcome the defects of the classical theory – which was incapable of explaining the mass unemployment of resources – by unifying monetary and value theory and thereby developing a theory of interest in which changes in the long-term rate of interest formed the basis of a relative price mechanism by which the economy might return to full employment. Thus the following claim seems largely vindicated:

> But our method of analysing the economic behaviour of the present under the influence of changing ideas about the future is one which depends on the interaction of supply and demand and is in this way linked up with our fundamental theory of value. We are thus led to a more general theory ([46] 'Preface').

APPENDIX

According to Clower, the *classics* failed to distinguish between notional and effective demands because they assumed (erroneously) that household decisions on how much to sell or buy are always made simultaneously – in Clower's terminology they adopted a *unified-decision* hypothesis [12, 13]. However, *Keynes*, on the other hand, had always been careful to distinguish between buyers and sellers, between borrowers and lenders, between investors and savers, etc., and, according to Clower, this distinction is fundamental whenever actual sales fall short of planned sales because decisions on how much to buy or save will then need to be revised. Therefore, where plans are capable of disappointment we need what Clower terms a *dual-decision* hypothesis, i.e. although transactors may attempt *initially* to

147

maximise their utility subject to the constraint of their notional or potential income, they are forced *eventually* to maximise their utility subject to the constraint of their *realised* income. Therefore the dual-decision hypothesis recognises 'that current income flows may impose an independent restriction on effective demand, separate from those already imposed by prevailing market prices'.

However, underlying the *classical* analysis is the implicit assumption that demand and supply functions depend solely on relative market prices (homogeneity postulate). The implications of this analysis and its contrast with that of Keynes are illustrated in the following maximisation models.

A. *Households* can be viewed as attempting to maximise utility subject to an income constraint. Formally, this can be written:

$$\max U = U(X^D, N^S) - \lambda(PX^D - WN^S),$$

i.e. utility is a function of the demand for goods (X^D) and the supply of labour (N^S), where the consumer attempts to maximise the former and minimise the latter subject to the constraint that total expenditure (PX^D) has to be financed out of wage income (WN^S).

Mathematically, we then have the following conditions for a maximum:

$$\frac{dU}{dX^D} - \lambda P = 0 \quad \text{(marginal utility equals price)}$$

$$\frac{dU}{dN^S} + \lambda W = 0 \quad \text{(marginal disutility of work equals the wage)}$$

$$PX^D - WN^S = 0 \quad \text{(budget constraint is met)}$$

This gives three equations in X^D, N^S and λ which can then be solved, giving:

$$X^D = X^D\left(\frac{P}{W}\right), \ N^S = N^S\left(\frac{P}{W}\right),$$

so that the demand for goods and the supply of labour are simply functions of relative prices (homogeneity postulate).

However, suppose that households are unable to sell all the labour services they desire at the current real wage, i.e. $\bar{N}^S$, the *actual* or *effective* supply of labour is less than the desired or notional supply,

148

N^S, then the maximisation process must be repeated under this *new* constraint. Thus households now have to:

$$\max U = U(X^D, \overline{N}^S) - \lambda(PX^D - W\overline{N}^S).$$

for a maximum:

$$\frac{dU}{dX^D} - \lambda P = 0 \text{ (as before)}$$

maximisation with respect to $\overline{N}^S$ no longer possible

$$PX^D - W\overline{N}^S = 0 \text{ (new budget constraint)}$$

This gives:

$$X^D = \frac{W}{P}\overline{N}^S.$$

The effective demand for goods X^D is not simply a function of relative prices but depends on the effective supply of labour, and hence on the level of wage income. (The other side of involuntary unemployment is involuntary underconsumption.) This dependence on wage income is inconsistent with the classical theory because, in that, wage income itself is taken to be a choice variable.

B. *Firms* can be viewed as maximising profits subject to a revenue constraint and a production relation:

$$\max \pi = PX^S - WN^D - \mu[X^S - \phi(N^D)],$$

i.e. profits depend on the revenue received from supplying goods (PX^S) and the costs of producing goods (WN^D) (labour is taken to be the only variable factor), where firms attempt to maximise the former and minimise the latter subject to the constraint imposed by the production function ($\phi[N^D]$) via which inputs (N^D) are transposed into outputs (X^S).

For a maximum we require:

$$-W + \mu \frac{d\phi}{dN^D} = 0 \quad \text{(real wage equals marginal product)}$$

$$P - \mu = 0 \quad \text{(marginal revenue equals marginal cost)}$$

$$X^S - \phi(N^D) = 0 \quad \text{(production constraint is met)}$$

149

This gives three equations in X^S, N^D and μ which can be solved, giving:

$$X^S = X^S\left(\frac{W}{P}\right), \; N^D = N^D\left(\frac{W}{P}\right),$$

so that the supply of goods and the demand for labour are simply functions of relative prices (homogeneity postulate).

However, suppose that firms cannot sell all the output that they produce at current prices, i.e. $\overline{X}^S$, the actual supply of goods, is less than the notional supply X^S, then profit maximisation simply requires the use of the minimum N necessary to produce $\overline{X}^S$. Thus firms now have to:

$$\max \pi = P\overline{X}^S - WN^D - \mu[\; \overline{X}^S - \phi(N^D)].$$

For a maximum:

maximisation with respect to $\overline{X}^S$ no longer possible

$$-W + \mu\frac{d\phi}{dN^D} \text{ (as before)}$$

$$\overline{X}^S - \phi(N^D) = 0 \text{ (new production constraint)}$$

The effective demand for labour, N^D, is not simply a function of relative prices but depends on the effective supply of goods, $\overline{X}^S$, i.e. on the amount of output that can be sold. (The other side of involuntary unemployment is involuntary underproduction.) This dependence of the demand for labour on the level of output is inconsistent with the classical theory because, in that, the level of output is itself a choice variable.

What the above analysis indicates is that 'Keynesian economics brings current transactions into price theory, whereas traditional analysis explicitly leaves them out. Alternatively, we may say that Keynesian economics is price theory without Walras' Law.'

This type of analysis (initiated by Patinkin [63], Clower [12], and extended by Baro and Grossman [5]) yields the following relationships:

$$X^D = X^D\left(\frac{W}{P}, \overline{N}^S\right)$$

and

$$\overline{X}^S = \phi(N^D), \text{ or } N^D = \phi^{-1}(\overline{X}^S),$$

which are similar to those given in *The General Theory*. For example, in chapter 3 Keynes defines:

$$D = f(N) \qquad \text{(the aggregate demand function)}$$

and $Z = \phi(N)$ (the aggregate supply function)

which is redefined in chapter 20 as:

$$N = \phi^{-1}(Z) \qquad \text{(the employment function)}$$

However, although this analysis appears consistent with that of Keynes, he did not assume that prices and wages were as inflexible as they appear in the above example. In fact, he accepted the need to analyse relative prices but from a broader perspective than the classics. Specifically, it was not simply the relation between wages and *the* price level that was important to Keynes but between wages and the price of different *components* of total output, in particular the price of capital assets in a two-commodity model.

6
Concluding Notes: Is It Relevant?

LIQUIDITY PREFERENCE AND THE MARGINAL EFFICIENCY OF CAPITAL

In the preceding chapter we have tried to show that Keynes's *monetary* theory was intimately bound up with his theory of *capital* and that *together* they form the basis of an analysis of the causes of fluctuations in output and employment. It is interesting to note that in a recent book [36] Hicks – the founder of IS/LM analysis – comes round to the same conclusion.

> I pass to consider the other main parts of the Keynes theory – the *marginal efficiency of capital* and the *theory of money*. I shall take them *together*, for I think I can show that they belong together . . . [and in a footnote Hicks continues] In my 'Mr Keynes and the Classics' Econometrica, 1937, I similarly reduced Keynes' three relations to two,[1] taking the multiplier with the marginal efficiency of capital to form the SI curve. I have come to feel that the alternative grouping, which I am following here, is more revealing' ([36] p. 31).

However, in spite of this it seems only fair to conclude with a few remarks on the relevance of the preceding excursion into depression economics to *current economic problems*.

INFLATION

In relation to inflation and unemployment the main points have been

152

well summed up by Tobin in the article referred to on page 137 above:

> The world economy today is vastly different from the 1930's. . . .
> Economics is very different to . . . But there are some notable
> constants . . . *economists* [*still*] *debate how much unemployment is*
> *voluntary, how much involuntary* [and in this respect] Keynes'
> treatment of labour market equilibrium and disequilibrium . . . is
> remarkably relevant today. [Indeed] the issues are remarkably
> similar . . . [e.g.] *Phillips curve doctrine* is in an important sense the
> post-war analogue of Keynesian wage and unemployment theory,
> while *natural rate doctrine* is the contemporary version of the
> Classical position Keynes was opposing' [82].

Tobin goes on to outline some of the limitations of the natural-rate
hypothesis compared with the analysis underlying the Phillips curve
but the whole debate has been well documented by Fleming [19],
making a detailed discussion redundant here. Suffice it to say that the
'new' microeconomics of job search and inflation builds on many of
the ideas introduced in the 'reappraisal of Keynes' (Chapter 5 above).
For example: (1) much of the debate is concerned with the problems
of imperfect information in the labour market and the cost of
acquiring information in a non-Walrasian world; (2) in the 'new
microeconomics' a significant role is reserved for *price expectations*
and this is rationalised in terms of the institutional fact that although
workers are interested in relative *real* wages they can only bargain for
money wages – however, since the latter are set for fixed periods of
time, it is price expectations that perform the important function of
linking together real and money wages during the period of the wage
bargain; (3) it has been pointed out by Brunner and Meltzer [10] that
the Phillips curve versus the natural-rate debate turns on whether
buyers or sellers adjust faster to inflation, e.g. 'Producers' anticipations and purchasers' anticipations form separately and at
different speeds in the presence of costs of information . . . a constant
short-run *Phillips* curve requires that producers always adjust more
slowly than purchasers. If producers adjust more quickly than
purchasers, a Phillips curve estimated from the data will show
unemployment *rising* as prices rise.' Similarly a vertical Phillips curve
follows if producers' anticipations equal those of purchasers (in
addition to Fleming and Brunner and Meltzer, see Friedman and
Laidler [28] and Alchian [2]. Alchian in fact originally introduced

153

the problems of information costs and inelastic/elastic anticipations into the analysis and thereby drew attention to many of the concepts subsequently developed by Leijonhufvud.

However, although the debate has been conducted along lines consistent with the Keynesian reappraisal, the new microeconomics has yet to formulate an acceptable dynamic theory of inflation and employment in the Keynesian tradition, e.g. it has been criticised by Tobin for implying that natural rates of unemployment arise from 'voluntary' job search and are somehow socially optimal. Thus despite the development of the new microeconomics the involuntary/voluntary question remains unanswered.

INVOLUNTARY AND VOLUNTARY UNEMPLOYMENT AND FISCAL POLICY

An illustration that the distinction between involuntary and voluntary unemployment still perplexes economists is provided in the recent publication of a collection of papers devoted entirely to this topic: *The Concept and Measurement of Involuntary Unemployment* [86]. The paper by Kahn presents an illuminating picture of Keynes's own interpretation of involuntary unemployment and suggests that Keynes's policy prescription for dealing with it would have differed widely from those adopted in his name, e.g. Kahn quotes from a series of articles written in 1937 by Keynes entitled 'How to Avoid a Slump' [49] in which Keynes argues *against* a further general stimulus to aggregate demand (even though unemployment was still around 10 per cent) because the 'economic structure is unfortunately rigid . . . [thus the] later stages of recovery require a different technique'.

Kahn points out that here Keynes was relying not on the distinction between involuntary and voluntary unemployment but on the concept of regional unemployment, e.g. to quote Keynes again, 'We are in more need today of a rightly distributed demand than a greater aggregate demand.' The upshot of this is that Keynes was not a 'fiscalist' and indeed argued against reliance on aggregate demand management once the economy approached unemployment levels of less than 10 per cent.[2] In fact he was prepared to advocate public works only as a 'pump-priming' exercise and not as a counter-cyclical stabilisation weapon at full employment. 'Thus public works even of doubtful utility may pay for themselves over and over again at a time

154

of severe unemployment. . . . But they may become a more doubtful proposition as a state of full employment is approached' ([46] p. 127). Thus the 'blame' for the *over*-reliance on aggregate demand management as a panacea for our economic problems in the post-war period cannot be attributed to Keynes. Indeed, in his view once the sheer waste of large-scale involuntary unemployment had been overcome it was legitimate to advocate only those policies which utilised resources efficiently and productively: 'To dig holes in the ground (or build pyramids) paid for out of savings will increase not only employment but the real national dividend of useful goods and services. It is not reasonable, however, that a sensible community should be content to remain dependent on such fortuitous and often wasteful mitigations' ([46] p. 220).

As Joan Robinson has pointed out [69]: 'Nowadays . . . building weapons . . . has turned out far better than pyramids ever did to keep up profit without adding to wealth.' No doubt other 'fortuitous' examples could be constructed but because of this 'Full employment has become·a right-wing slogan [in that] any product is as good as any other.' The relevant question to ask, however, is what the employment should be for? More consumption or more investment? More public consumption or more private consumption? And so on. However, Keynes's remarks on the need for efficiency in investment and the need to correctly distribute demand amongst the different sectors of the economy rather than simply increase it, together with his questioning of the relevance of public works near full employment, suggest that he was, at least, aware of the dangerous situation that might evolve when full employment becomes an orthodox objective of policy (and its success is ensured by the absorption of an ever-increasing number of people into the public sector – the consequences of which are all too painfully obvious in the United Kingdom at the present time). (See also Hicks's conclusion in [36] p. 84.)

STOCKS AND FLOWS AND FISCAL POLICY

In this context a recent paper by Leijonhufvud provides some theoretical support for the argument that fiscal policy should be used only in chronic disequilibrium [58]. His basic premise is that the economic system reacts differently to large than small displacements

from equilibrium. The argument runs as follows.

In contrasting Keynes's analysis with that of Walras's (i.e. effective *versus* notional demands), an exaggerated view of the underlying disequilibrium tendencies can be obtained if the analysis is carried out entirely in terms of *current flows* of income and output, e.g. if the current flow of income from employment is the only constraint on demand then as soon as employment falls, consumers' expenditure must fall, and a cumulative contraction will set in. To be more realistic, however, we should take into account the current situation in regard to *stocks*, i.e. the real world is a stock–flow world and the existence of stocks has important implications for the analysis of disequilibrium situations.

For example, traders and producers carry large physical stocks of goods together with financial stocks of liquid assets, and any discrepancy between flow demands and flow supplies is reflected in stock changes. Thus if the flow demand for goods exceeds flow supply, physical stocks will be run down, and because current receipts will then exceed current expenditure, financial stocks will increase. Alternatively, if supply exceeds demand, financial stocks will contract and traders and producers will see their wealth becoming tied up in illiquid inventories. Some flexibility is then possible in regard to production runs as long as producers and traders are prepared to absorb temporary fluctuations in flow demands or supplies via stock adjustments; the degree of flexibility, however, will depend on their expectations of the future and the extent to which current fluctuations are seen to be transitory.

As long as fluctuations are absorbed by stock adjustments, market-equilibrating forces will predominate and disequilibrating cut-backs in output and employment will be avoided. However, if producers are subjected (say) to a fall in sales which is larger and of longer duration than expected, then physical stocks will build up to unacceptable levels and liquid financial stocks may become exhausted. At this stage current flows will have to be altered and output and employment will contract. Thus as long as exogenous shocks do not impinge too heavily on existing stocks, they will be absorbed by the economic system and deviation-counteracting tendencies will return the system towards its equilibrium path. However, if stocks become exhausted during the process (or become too large) then current flow supplies will be affected, which may produce deviation-*amplifying* tendencies and move the system further away from its equilibrium path.

To highlight the different adjustment processes involved, Leijonhufvud describes the region within which equilibrating forces are strong as 'the corridor', and as long as fluctuations do not succeed in moving the system outside this region then income-constrained processes will be largely absent and multiplier repercussions will be small; cumulative contractions will then not be generated. On the other hand, disequilibrium tendencies, which bring into effect income-constrained processes and multiplier contractions, only occur when shocks displace the system outside 'the corridor'; it is then that effective-demand failures become the overriding problem. Thus inside the corridor buffer stocks are relatively large while outside they are no longer sufficient to absorb fluctuations; thus current flows are affected.

Using this basic stock–flow approach it is then possible to put into perspective some of the current controversies in economics, e.g. the 'modern' theories of the consumption function are anti-Keynesian in that they deny that current income imposes an effective constraint on consumers' expenditure and suggest instead a longer-term concept of expected income (which acts as a surrogate for wealth). Thus according to the 'permanent-income hypothesis' the marginal propensity to consume out of current income is low so that multiplier effects are also likely to be low and fiscal policy ineffective. The reasoning behind this is that consumption will be largely maintained when current income falls as long as wealth (or permanent income) is not seriously diminished. However, two questions need to be asked: how is consumption to be financed in the meantime and for how long is it likely to remain unaffected? In fact these questions are related – consumption will be financed out of liquid assets and the length of time it remains unaffected will depend on the *size* of consumers' buffer stocks of liquid assets.

However, once these assets have been exhausted, consumption can be maintained only by selling other assets and/or borrowing, but both of these alternative sources of finance will impinge on expected future income and may reduce wealth '*by more than is avoidable* by simply cutting current consumption until income starts to flow at its "permanent" rate' [58]. Thus, outside the corridor, when buffer stocks become exhausted, permanent-income expectations are revised downwards and it is at this stage that multiplier contractions and income-constrained[3] processes come into effect and tend to make the system unstable. Note that instability requires two things: (*a*) an unanticipatedly large displacement from equilibrium which

157

exhausts liquid buffer stocks; and (b) a revision of expectations. However, if expectations are revised downwards at a time when output and employment are already contracting then such revisions will be destabilising (or 'dysfunctional'). The multiplier therefore emerges from this analysis as an 'illiquidity phenomenon' and takes hold only after a revision of permanent-income expectations.

The analysis underlying the emergence and persistence of unemployment in Chapter 5 can be restated: the inelasticity of expectations on the part of unemployed workers, producers, etc. was emphasised as a causal factor in the emergence of widespread unemployment. However these expectations are not in themselves destabilising as long as sufficient buffer stocks exist, i.e. as long as the unemployed maintain consumption by running down liquid buffer stocks and as long as producers are encouraged to maintain production by either themselves or traders building up physical stocks, then market-equilibrating mechanisms will come into operation and produce movements back to equilibrium. It is only in the absence of such stocks that quantity adjustments and deviation-*amplifying* mechanisms dominate and move the system away from equilibrium.

This analysis can also be extended to throw some light on the fiscal-policy versus monetary-policy debate. In particular, in a situation of near full employment (inside the corridor) fiscal measures are unlikely to have a magnified impact on aggregate demand because buffer stocks are likely to be sufficient to absorb 'expected' fluctuations. Multiplier effects are likely to be weak, and in order for fiscal policy to have much effect, *unanticipatedly* large fiscal measures must be introduced. The larger these measures, however, the more likely it is that fiscal policy itself will be destablising – e.g. because of adjustment lags, stop–go cycles, effects on confidence, etc. On the other hand, outside the corridor, when the system has been 'squeezed dry of liquidity', fiscal measures have important effects on output because current income then becomes the operative constraint and private-sector demand is largely 'ineffective'. At this stage multiplier effects are potentially large.

Alternatively, monetary policy is likely to be *ineffective* in a depression because, though it can increase the stock of liquid assets, it is unable to put these into the hands of those transactors whose current demand is ineffective, i.e. transactors must either sell illiquid assets or borrow from banks in order to acquire the liquid assets being made available by the central bank, but such forms of finance

reduce expected future income streams. (Also, banks may be reluctant to lend money to 'risky' individuals whose current stock of liquid assets is zero.) Thus, though their *potential* marginal propensity to consume is high, monetary policy is able to provide them with finance only on terms that impinge too heavily on permanent-income expectations. On the other hand, *inside* the corridor monetary policy is likely to be effective because the existence of large buffer stocks enable central bank injections of liquid assets to be channelled through financial markets to those transactors wanting to spend money, thus enabling them to obey the price incentives transmitted by monetary policy (i.e. lower interest rates). Thus, within the corridor, as long as the central bank acts decisively to prevent a contraction, it will be largely successful. In fact its policies should aim at achieving the 'right' level of interest rates (asset prices) so as to encourage investment and also make available enough liquidity to enable consumption and production plans to be maintained; it will then avoid a downturn. [4]

This dichotomy between states of the world in which fiscal policy is effective and others in which monetary policy is effective was central to Keynes's analysis of the U.K. economy in the interwar period, e.g. he advocated reliance on monetary policy as long as entrepreneurial expectations were favourable and in particular favoured low interest rates to ensure that the market rate was kept in line with the 'natural' rate. However, because of the inflexibility of long-term interest rates, this required decisive central bank action in the long end of the market (in contrast to the 'Bills-only' policy favoured by the Bank of England). Failure to pursue the correct monetary policy would result in liquidity drying up, cash-constrained processes taking effect, etc. and the economy contracting into a slump at which stage entrepreneurial expectations would become unfavourable, (permanent) income expectations of consumers would be revised downwards and only a 'pump-priming' fiscal action such as 'public works' would suffice to correct the situation. However, although fiscal policy is effective, even imperative in a slump, its efficacy should not be overestimated because 'if our assumption is correct that the marginal propensity to consume falls off steadily as we approach full employment, it follows that it will become more and more troublesome to secure a further given increase of employment by further increasing investment [in public works]' ([46] p. 127).

In fact Keynes's position in this respect remained unchanged

throughout the interwar period: 'I believe you have first of all to do something to restore profits [public works, etc.] and then rely on private enterprise to carry the thing along.' In other words public works may 'break the vicious circle' but they should not be regarded as a substitute for industrial production. Of course private enterprise may fail to produce the goods, particularly if 'the activities of a casino' (i.e. the Stock Market) proceed to hamper industrial investment. In this case 'a somewhat comprehensive socialisation of investment will prove the only means of securing an approximation to full employment' ([46] p. 378).

VALID DICHOTOMIES

The above discussion has indicated that it is often necessary in economic analysis to distinguish between different states of the world, e.g. there is a need to distinguish between situations in which expectations are inelastic and those in which they become revised downwards, between situations when stock adjustments are equilibrating and those in which they amplify disturbances, etc. In this context we can identify Keynes's theoretical position with an attempt to discover *valid dichotomies* in economic analysis and in *The General Theory* Keynes formalised a theory which attempted to differentiate between normal and slump situations, between equilibrium and disequilibrium situations, between situations in which expectations are fulfilled and those in which they are disappointed, between different types of goods – capital goods and consumer goods – and between different types of transactors – buyers and sellers, savers and investors, etc. These are the hallmarks of Keynes's theory and they can be contrasted with general-equilibrium theory in which none of these distinctions are made. Thus the latter is not 'general' in the sense that it is applicable to different states of the world. Furthermore, this lack of generality permeates *current* economic theory to an extent that is not normally appreciated and it is in this area that the Keynesian Revolution has yet to be carried to its logical conclusion. Two further examples from the writings of Kaldor and Robinson serve to illustrate the relevance of the 'reappraisal' to current controversies in economic theory.

In a recent critique of general-equilibrium theory Kaldor has extended the above analysis on stocks and flows and highlighted a major shortcoming of the equilibrium approach to economic problems, e.g. Kaldor begins by differentiating between *stock* demands and *flow* demands but insists that although stocks exist (and are ignored in general-equilibrium theory), the main upshot of the analysis is not simply that stocks perform an equilibrating function and allow markets to absorb temporary fluctuations — the point is that stocks (and the behaviour of stockholders) allow industries operating under increasing returns to expand production and at the same time experience a growing demand for their product; these two things together are indispensable ingredients of economic growth.

For example, one of the basic axioms of general-equilibrium theory is that technology is convex, i.e. there are no increasing returns, despite the fact that 'nobody doubts that . . . in industry increasing returns dominate the picture . . . an increase in size is bound to bring further cost reductions since capacity is bound to increase faster than construction cost' [42].

However, 'an increase in the production of a commodity may involve the generation of additional incomes which in turn generates additional demand for other commodities' [42]. It is in allowing this chain sequence to develop and continue that stocks are important, e.g. as long as stocks are absorbed, a growth in production will lead to a growth in incomes and thus in *effective* demand. (This suggests a dynamic version of Say's Law, where supply, at least potentially, creates its own demand.) However, under what conditions will stocks be absorbed? Traders will absorb stocks in the event of an excess supply as long as their expectations of future prices are *inelastic*, i.e. they will be prepared to increase the value of their stocks when current prices sag as long as prices are expected to return to normal. On the other hand producers will absorb stocks due to excess supply as long as their expectations of the future volume of sales are *elastic*.

Thus as long as expectations are favourable increasing returns can be interpreted as a form of investment expenditure and will lead to an increased demand for goods (However, this also requires that the banking system makes available enough liquid buffer stocks to finance such investments.) An excess of flow supply over flow demand

161

is then no problem as long as stocks are absorbed and finance is made available because incomes will be generated and eventually the stocks can be sold. However, an excess of flow supply becomes a problem at times of increased uncertainty when the temporary nature of disturbances is doubted and both traders and producers go instead for liquidity – less risks involved and lower carrying costs, etc. There is then no increase in effective demand.

This analysis highlights the irrelevance of the general-equilibrium assumptions in a growing economy, e.g. the assumption that prices are perfectly flexible and move rapidly to ensure equilibrium between flow demands and flow supplies, together with the convexity assumption, effectively rule out economic growth. However, in conditions of increasing returns a certain stickiness in prices is seen to be a precondition for a growth in output, for only then will it be matched by a growth in effective demand. Kaldor's analysis therefore quite neatly draws together in a dynamic context a number of the criticisms of the general-equilibrium approach mentioned above, i.e. its emphasis on notional demands, infinite price velocities, and the complete absence of uncertainty and increasing returns – all vital ingredients of the real world.

Joan Robinson

At the centre of Kaldor's criticism is the assumption of decreasing returns, an assumption that lies at the heart of general equilibrium theory and finds its embodiment at the macro level in the neoclassical concepts of the aggregate production function and the marginal productivity theory of distribution. To conclude this chapter we will look at Joan Robinson's criticism of these concepts and other anti-Keynesian developments in the area of capital theory.

According to Robinson [69, 70, 71] Keynes's great contribution was that he brought back *time* into economic theory:

In [neoclassical] models it is explicitly assumed that there is and has always been correct foresight or else 'capital' is malleable so that the past can be undone (without cost) and brought into equilibrium with the future; in short they abolish time. But this is not enough to ensure full employment. They have also to assume that the wage bargain is made in terms of product; the real wage rate finds the

level at which the stock of 'capital' is squeezed up or spread out to employ the available labour force [71].

Joan Robinson's main quarrel is with this definition of capital as 'putty' and the consequent marginal productivity theory of wages and profits that follow from it. For example, in neoclassical theory all the man-made factors of production (capital) 'are boiled into one, which we may call *leets* . . . [which] is endowed with the capacity to embody various techniques of production. There is a well-behaved production function [no increasing returns] in leets and labour for each kind of output . . . [and] to simplify still further, output is also taken to be made of leets; the whole Walrasian system is reduced to a "one-commodity world"' [70]. The upshot of this is that if 'leets' can be squeezed up or pressed out to accommodate less or more workers, capital goods will always be fully employed. It is then possible to hold this stock of 'leets' constant and measure the marginal product of labour. If the wage bargain is also made in terms of product ('leets') we need only add the assumption of perfect competition to demonstrate that the real wage will be equal to the marginal product of labour.
However:

> capital equipment *actually* consists of a variety of hard objects which cannot be squeezed up or pressed out without cost [in which case it is impossible to define the marginal product of labour, let alone prove that the real wage is equal to it. So what? Is it relevant? In fact it *is* relevant because the neoclassical conception of the world] blocks off economic theory from any discussion of practical questions. When equipment is made of leets there is no distinction between long and short-period problems . . . . There is no such thing as a degree of utilisation of given equipment rising or falling with the level of effective demand . . . . There is no room for imperfect competition. There is no possibility of disappointed expectations – indeed, there is no difference between the past and the future . . . . There is no problem of unemployment . . . . Unemployed workers would bid down wages and the pre-existing quantity of leets would be spread out to accommodate them [70].

But these ideas were the hallmarks of the orthodox theory which Keynes was opposing, and the point is that they have been smuggled

back into current neoclassical models. This is what the debate about the meaning of 'capital' is all about.

Thus, in order to achieve a Keynesian Revolution it is not sufficient simply to tinker with existing one-commodity equilibrium models, e.g. Patinkin [63] and Barro and Grossman [5] have included Keynesian ideas into standard models by defining 'points off' labour demand and supply curves, but this is illegitimate. The labour demand curve specified is the marginal product of labour and the point is, of course, that this is a mis-specification. In fact, it is impossible to be *off* a properly specified demand curve (see [84] and [16] for further analysis, and for a more accurate derivation of the aggregate demand curve for labour, see [59]).

What we need, therefore, instead of further elaboration of equilibrium models, is the development of *historical* models – models which can analyse movements in the real world:

> A model applicable to actual history has to be capable of getting out of equilibrium; indeed it must normally not be in it. To construct such a model we specify the technical conditions obtaining in the economy . . . the state of expectations of the characters concerned (whether based on past experience or on traditional beliefs). The system may be going to work itself out so as to fulfil or so as to disappoint them [69].

However, equilibrium models simply cannot handle disappointment. (For attempts to build historical models in the Keynesian tradition see [16], which also contains an excellent fusion of the ideas of Keynes with the recent work of the 'true' Keynesians: Robinson, Kaldor, Shackle, Clower, etc.)

THE CURRENT STATE OF ECONOMICS

In Chapter 5 it was pointed out that Keynes's claim to have produced a more general theory rested on his integration of monetary theory (macro) and value theory (micro). Forty years later these two branches of economics are still very distinct, e.g. irrespective of what is happening to the economy as a whole, the maximising behaviour of individuals and firms is assumed to go on regardless. But the behaviour of firms and households, and the flow of information

through the economic system, depend to a great extent on the state of the economy – on the type and magnitude of any disequilibrium. Thus, when disequilibrating forces are absent there will be a willingness to absorb stocks at the micro level and this in turn will have repercussions at the macro level by allowing incomes and effective demand to rise along with increases in supply. However, the co-ordination of the planned activities of households and firms in decentralised economic systems (with an irrevocable past and an uncertain future) is a very difficult task, and co-ordination failures are a distinct possibility – particularly in situations involving future consumption where prior capital accumulation is required. In such situations asset prices may fail to adjust or convey the wrong information and exacerbate any underlying disequilibrating tendencies. Stock adjustments may then be insufficient to avoid cumulative contractions and micro reactions will reinforce macro disturbances.

A proper integration of macro economics and microeconomics which can account for these different states of the world is obviously a long way off, but the economics underlying the 'reappraisal of Keynes' at least offers some hope for the future. For example, according to many recent contributors, a valid integration is still missing because economic analysis is still based on the axioms and assumptions of the orthodox neoclassical school. If we can finally break away from these assumptions, a more dynamic (historical) approach to aggregate economic problems is possible, based on (and better integrated with) a more relevant microeconomics. The present position has been admirably summed up by Stiglitz [76]:

Conventional economic theory has been constructed on the basis of a set of assumptions and related concepts which fit together neatly . . . for instance the assumptions of perfect competition, perfect information and convexity of technology and the concept of equilibrium. . . . And out of these assumptions, a certain world-view of how the economy operates has developed. We think of the economy as being at least approximately in equilibrium at each moment. . . . There are of course numerous attempts to extend the model, to make it more realistic. . . . Usually they take the form of altering one assumption at a time. What our analysis has shown is that the introduction of a little bit of 'imperfect information' alters the analysis in fundamental ways; the theory does not appear to be

sufficiently robust to withstand modifications of a kind which any acceptable theory ought to be able to withstand. . . . An alternative theory would focus on imperfect information, non-convexities and imperfect competition not as minor footnotes to the normal case but as essential to understanding the workings of the economy.

Stiglitz concludes by attempting to communicate to the reader 'the excitement that I feel as at last we begin to explore systematically an area, the potential importance of which has long been felt but whose full implications we are only now beginning to grasp.'

It is of interest to compare this conclusion of Stiglitz with that of Keynes: 'The composition of this book has been for the author a long struggle to escape. . . . The difficulty lies, not in the new ideas, but in escaping from the old ones' ([46] p. viii).

It is ironic that although this was written over forty years ago economists, it seems, are still struggling to escape. Obviously the analysis underlying this book is not meant to imply that Keynes knew all the answers but it does suggest that he at least posed the relevant questions. However, these are not the questions that have featured prominently in the Monetarist versus Keynesian debate.

Notes and References

Chapter 2

1. An important cause of shifts in the expenditure function are changes in business expectations; another cause would be increases in government expenditure (fiscal policy). Note that shifts in these functions are assumed to cause magnified changes in income and output, e.g. as investment increases from $I(r_1)$ to $I(r_2)$ in Figure 2.4 (*a*), the level of income rises from Y_1 to Y_2. However, the change in income (ΔY) is greater than the change in investment (ΔI) and can be calculated from the familiar Keynesian multiplier equation $\Delta Y = \dfrac{1}{1-b} \Delta I$. Since b, the marginal propensity to consume, is less than one it follows that $\Delta Y > \Delta I$. This is known as the investment multiplier and in more realistic models other multipliers can be derived such as the government's fiscal multiplier.

2. The price of a bond is simply the present value of the stream of income offered by it. Thus equation (2.9) can be used to calculate this price where R_i represent the annual interest payments on the bond. Thus bond prices vary inversely with the interest rate for the same reason that the demand price for a capital good varies inversely with r. Because of this Keynes treated bonds and capital goods as close substitutes (see Chapter 5).

3. The increase in income is here assumed to be caused by a rise in *real* income from Y_1 to Y_2, and it traces out a *movement along* the curve LM_1 in Figure 2.5(*b*). However, if the increase in money income had been caused by a rise in *prices*, the *LM* curve would have shifted towards LM_2.

4. The arrows and dotted line in Figure 2.6 can be explained as follows. At point *C* there exists excess demand in both the goods and money markets. However, the excess demand for money will put upward pressure on interest rates (vertical arrow) and the excess demand for goods will put expansionary pressure on output (horizontal arrow). The two forces together are then likely to produce a move towards the equilibrium position *E* via the dotted line. On this point, however, see Chapter 5, pp. 122–5.

5. Involuntary unemployment is a term that we shall associate with Keynes's analysis in *The General Theory* and we shall interpret it to mean 'deficient-demand unemployment'. However, the term itself has a longer history than is usually appreciated – see the article by R. F. Kahn in [86]. Our analysis of involuntary unemployment will be expanded in Chapter 5.

6. The classics would have opposed this prescription by arguing that the amount of resources available for investment was fixed. Thus, if the

government attempted to expand its own expenditure, it could only do so by bidding resources away from the private sector and this would not expand the economy as a whole. This is the so-called 'Treasury view'. However, although it can easily be shown to have been *incorrect* during the 1930s when vast quantities of productive resources were simply lying idle, two points need to be stressed: (*a*) the Treasury view was *not* the view expressed by most of Keynes's contemporaries (Pigou, Robertson, *et al.*) who in fact all supported Keynes in his call for a programme of public works; and (*b*) although the Treasury view was easily refuted in the 1930s it does not mean that it is necessarily fallacious in all circumstances, e.g. the *present* debate over the 'crowding-out effect' of government expenditure is not so easily controverted (see Chapter 4).

Chapter 3

1. However, rigid wages do appear to be a necessary condition for the existence of unemployment *equilibrium*, i.e. wages and prices will continue to fall in the face of unemployed resources. Therefore there is a tacit assumption that money wages do not fall continuously but the point is that even if further reductions could be achieved they would have no effect on the level of unemployment. The labour market therefore exhibits a tendency to remain in chronic *disequilibrium* and this phenomenon will be examined in more detail in Chapter 5.

2. Where fiscal policy has significant effects on income and employment it is said that the 'fiscal multiplier' is large. Similarly where monetary policy does not effect income and employment it is said that the 'money multiplier' is zero.

Chapter 4

1. When a large increase in government expenditure results in only a small increase in output, the size of the *public* sector increases at the expense of the *private* sector. In this situation the government expenditure is said to 'crowd out' private investment expenditure and this reduces the size of the fiscal multiplier.

2. Friedman and Meiselman actually used 'induced expenditures' as a proxy for PY in their regression equations to avoid spurious statistical correlations between PY and A.

3. However, the gap still remains quite wide, e.g. Frank Hahn writes in a recent article: 'I shall only make occasional references to Monetarists . . . partly due to the difficulties I have had in discovering a precise statement of this theory and partly due to the fact that monetarists seem to base themselves on empirical induction rather than theoretical proposition' (F. H. Hahn, 'Money and General Equilibrium', *Indian Economic Journal* (Dec 1975)).

4. Subsequently the Phillips Curve literature expanded this analysis to

take account of the *rate of change* of both prices and wages as determinants of the levels of employment and output.

5. Friedman's framework implies a vertical aggregate supply function drawn through the exogeneously determined level of output, i.e. the output level determined by the Walrasian general-equilibrium system of equations which in turn determines the 'natural rate' of unemployment.

6. It is not without significance that this conclusion closely resembles the classical dichotomy between the real and monetary sectors (see above, p. 19).

7. However, the latter point is not just a criticism of single-equation models; it is a criticism of all models that do not specify macro policy goals before testing and interpreting statistical data. In other words, the authorities' 'reaction function' to *expected* changes in G.N.P. must be specified before meaningful causal relationships can be inferred from simple regression models. However, recent work [7] suggests that the biases due to the neglect of reaction functions are much more problematic in single-equation models than in structural models.

8. For example, Keynesians argue that the 1968 tax surcharge was explicitly temporary and if consumers respond only to *permanent* income changes then a temporary tax is unlikely to greatly affect consumers' expenditure. Also, government expenditure actually increased between 1968 and 1969, thus offsetting the deflationary impact of the tax.

Chapter 5

1. See Friedman's permanent-income hypothesis [21] for an attempt to empirically verify the importance of wealth as a determinant of consumption.

2. According to Patinkin [63] this indeterminacy of the absolute price level is the result of a basic error in the classical system. In fact he claims that relative prices cannot be the sole determinants of demand and he insists that the 'real balance effect' needs to be included into the analysis in order to make the various strands of classical theory consistent. In particular, he claims that the classical dichotomy is invalid.

3. See, for example, the proof developed in J. Quirk and R. Saposnik, *Introduction to General Equilibrium and Welfare Economics* (New York: McGraw-Hill, 1968), based on the original work of Arrow and Debreu.

4. It cannot be overemphasised that since the *tâtonnement* process ensures equilibrium situations, it has nothing to say about unsold stocks of goods. But the point is that unsold stocks of goods, including labour services, are unlikely to be evenly distributed throughout the economy and instead are likely to be concentrated amongst certain firms and individuals with the effect that *their* demand for goods and services may be restricted. This is one of the major criticisms of general-equilibrium theory developed by J. Kornai in *Anti Equilibrium* (Amsterdam: North-Holland, 1972). Its relevance to modern monetary, macro theory is discussed below (pp. 128–34) and the important role played by stocks is emphasised in Chapter 6 (pp. 155–60).

5. Reproduced by R. Clower, 'Reflections on the Keynesian Perplex', in *Zeitschrift für Nationalökonomie* (1975) pp. 4–5. However, in spite of this

Hicks and others continued to refine their analysis of the Walrasian system, *but* by the end of the 1960s many general-equilibrium theorists were found to be in close agreement with Keynes's original position of 1933–4, e.g. 'It must now I fear be admitted that the study of the Walrasian *tâtonnement* process has not been very fruitful. . . . The Walrasian economy is essentially one of barter.' (Hahn [34]). 'The Arrow–Debreu model describes a world in which none of the problems which interested Keynes can occur' (F. H. Hahn, 'Money and General Equilibrium', *Indian Economic Journal* (Dec 1975)).

6. This had been a central theme in Keynes's *Treatise on Probability* [43]. There the probability attached to a future event is viewed as essentially subjective and conditional upon the available evidence because 'accession of new evidence increases the weight of an argument'.

7. Note that Clower's distinction between effective and notional demands involves a rigorous derivation of, and rationale for, Keyenes's consumption function where consumers' demand for current output is effectively constrained by current income: $C_t = f(Y_t)$. However, this constraint could be more loosely interpreted as a *cash-constraint* on consumer spending and interpreted in this way it emphasises the *monetary* nature of Keynes's multiplier analysis. See below, pp. 156–9.

8. Involuntary unemployment obviously implies that the labour market is not in equilibrium so that here 'equilibrium' should be taken to imply 'no tendency to change'. Keynes was not therefore talking about a static equilibrium in the sense that all markets are cleared but rather the tendency of some markets to remain persistently in *dis*equilibrium.

9. According to Keynes, an expansion in demand would raise prices relative to money wages, and hence reduce *real* wages, but this is not crucial. The rise in demand may bid up both prices and money wages. Moreover, if unemployment can be reduced *without* a fall in real wages, there is even more justification for describing it as 'involuntary'.

10. Stated in these terms the multiplier emerges as a much more important and complicated process than it does in the *IS/LM* model. For example, instead of being analysed in static terms and defined in terms of $\left(\dfrac{1}{1-b}\right)$, etc., the multiplier should be interpreted as a dynamic process during which multiplier contractions develop as a consequence of inelastic expectations about money wages and prices. During this process an excess demand for money emerges which leads to income-constrained (or cash-constrained) quantity adjustments and this leads to an amplification of the original disturbance. Stated in this way the monetary nature of the multiplier process then becomes apparent. (See also the discussion below on pp. 155–6).

11. Also, if the deflation did become unbalanced in the direction of *capital* goods, it would have a greater impact on employment and aggregate demand because consumer goods have 'a relatively low elasticity of employment', compared to capital goods ([46] p. 287).

1. Keynes's three relations are of course the consumption function, the investment function and liquidity-preference function.

2. This conclusion of Keynes is similar to the conclusion reached by Laidler in [28] pp. 45–7:

> 'Keynesian economics tells us how we may attain *any* level of unemployment we think desirable simply by manipulating monetary and fiscal policy. . . . [But] the implication of the natural unemployment rate hypothesis is that, if higher employment levels than are consistent with a vertical long-run Phillips curve are desired, *the way to achieve them is to operate with policies directed towards the structure of the labour market and not with demand management policies. . . .* [thus] *it is the tools of high employment policy, rather than its goals, which must be changed.'* (italic in original).

3. In view of the importance attached to *finance*, Leijonhufvud suggests that a more meaningful terminology would be *cash-constrained* [58].

4. This suggests that a proper integration of stocks and flows into macroeconomic analysis is required before the Monetarist versus Keynesian debate on the relative effectiveness of monetary and fiscal policies can be adequately evaluated.

Bibliography

[1] A. A. Alchian, 'The Rate of Interest: Fisher's Rate of Return Over Cost and Keynes's Internal Rate of Return', *American Economic Review* (Dec 1955) (see also Dec 1956 issue for comment by Robinson).

[2] A. A. Alchian, 'Information Costs, Pricing and Resource Unemployment', *Western Economic Journal* (June 1969).

[3] L. C. Andersen and J. L. Jordan, 'Monetary and Fiscal Actions: A Test of their Relative Importance in Economic Stabilization' *Federal Reserve Bank of St Louis Review* (Nov 1968) (see also Apr 1969 issue for comments).

[4] M. J. Bailey, National Income and the Price Level, 2nd ed (New York: McGraw-Hill, 1971).

[5] R. Barro and H. I. Grossman, 'A General Disequilibrium Model of Income and Employment', *American Economic Review* (Mar 1971).

[6] W. J. Baumol, 'The Transactions Demand for Cash: An Inventory Theoretic Approach', *Quarterly Journal of Economics* (Nov 1952).

[7] A. S. Blinder and R. M. Solow, 'Analytical Foundations of Fiscal Policy', in *The Economics of Public Finance* (Brookings Institution, 1974).

[8] M. Bronfenbrenner and T. Mayer, 'Liquidity Functions in the American Economy', *Econometrica* (Oct 1960) (see also July 1963 issue for comments).

[9] K. Brunner and A. H. Meltzer, 'Some Further Investigations of the Demand and Supply Functions for Money', *Journal of Finance* (May 1964).

[10] K. Brunner and A. H. Meltzer, *The Phillips Curve and Labour Markets*, Carnegie – Rochester Conferences on Public Policy, vol. 1 (Amsterdam, North-Holland, 1976).

[11] G. Clayton, J. Gilbert and R. Sedgwick (eds), *Monetary Theory and Monetary Policy in the 1970's* (Oxford University Press, 1971).

[12] R. W. Clower, 'The Keynesian Counterrevolution: A Theoretical Appraisal', in *The Theory of Interest Rates*, eds. F. H. Hahn and R. P. R. Brechling (London: Institute of Economic Affairs, 1965) (also in [14]).

[13] R. W. Clower, 'A Reconsideration of the Micro-foundations of Monetary Theory', *Western Economic Journal* (1967).

[14] R. W. Clower (ed.), *Monetary Theory* (Harmondsworth: Penguin, 1969).

[15] T. J. Courchene and H. T. Shapiro, 'The Demand for Money: A Note from the Time Series', *Journal of Political Economy* (Oct 1964).

[16] P. Davidson, *Money in the Real World* (London: Macmillan, 1972).

[17] J. C. R. Dow, *The Management of the British Economy 1945–60* (National Institute of Economic and Social Research/Cambridge University Press, 1964).

[18] M. Evans, *Macro-economic Activity: Theory, Forecasting and Control* (New York: Harper & Row, 1969).

[19] J. F. Fleming, *Inflation* (Oxford University Press, 1976).

[20] M. Friedman, 'The Quantity Theory of Money: A Restatement', in *Studies in the Quantity Theory* (Chicago University Press, 1956).

[21] M. Friedman, *A Theory of the Consumption Function (Princeton University Press, 1957)*.

[22] M. Friedman, 'The Demand for Money: Some Theoretical and Empirical Results', *Journal of Political Economy* (Aug 1959).

[23] M. Friedman, 'Windfalls, the Horizon and Related Concepts in the Permanent-Income Hypothesis', in *Measurement in Economics*, ed. C. Christ (Stanford University Press, 1963).

[24] M. Friedman, 'The Role of Monetary Policy', *American Economic Review* (Mar 1968).

[25] M. Friedman, *The Counter-Revolution in Monetary Theory* (London: Institute of Economic Affairs, 1970).

[26] M. Friedman, 'A Theoretical Framework for Monetary Analysis', *Journal of Political Economy* (Mar – Apr 1970).

[27] M. Friedman, 'A Monetary Theory of Nominal Income', in [11].

[28] M. Friedman, and D. E. W. Laidler, *Unemployment versus Inflation* (London: Institute of Economic Affairs, 1975).

[29] M. Friedman and D. Meiselman, 'The Relative Stability of Monetary Velocity and Investment Multiplier in the U.S. 1897–1958', in *Stabilization Policies* (Washington, D.C.: Commission on Money and Credit, 1963).

[30] M. Friedman and A. Schwartz, 'Money and Business Cycles', *Review of Economics and Statistics* (Feb 1963).

[31] M. Friedman and A. Schwartz, *A Monetary History of the United States 1867–1960* (New York: National Bureau of Economic Research, 1963).

[32] C. A. E. Goodhart and A. D. Crockett, 'The Importance of Money', *Bank of England Quarterly Bulletin* (June 1970) (reprinted in [41]).

[33] F. H. Hahn, 'On Some Problems of Proving the Existence of an Equilibrium in a Monetary Economy', in *The Theory of Interest Rates*, ed. F. H. Hahn and F. Brechling (London: Institute of Economic Affairs, 1965) (also in [14]).

[34] F. H. Hahn, 'Some Adjustment Problems', *Econometrica* (1970).

[35] J. R. Hicks, 'Mr. Keynes and the "Classics": A Suggested Interpretation', *Econometrica* (Apr 1937).

[36] J. R. Hicks, *The Crisis in Keynesian Economics* (Oxford: Blackwell, 1974).

[37] G. Horwich, *Money, Capital and Prices* (Purdue University, 1964).

[38] H. G. Johnson, 'Monetary Theory and Policy', *American Economic Review* (1961) (also in *Essays in Monetary Economics* (London: Allen & Unwin, 1967).

[39] H. G. Johnson, 'Monetary Theory and Keynesian Economics', in *Money Trade and Economic Growth* (London: Allen & Unwin, 1962) (also in [14]).

[40] H. G. Johnson, 'Inside Money, Outside Money, Income, Wealth and Welfare in Monetary Theory', *Journal of Money, Credit and Banking* (Feb 1969).

[41] H. G. Johnson (ed.), *Readings in British Monetary Economics* (Oxford University Press, 1972).

[42] N. Kaldor, 'The Irrelevance of Equilibrium Economics', *Economic Journal* (Dec 1972).

[43] J. M. Keynes, *A Treatise on Probability* (London: Macmillan, 1921).

[44] J. M. Keynes, *Treatise on Money*, vols I and II (London:

The minor pleasures of Cotswold

Edith Brill and Peter Turner

The minor pleasures of Cotswold

J M Dent & Sons Limited London

Made in Great Britain at the
Aldine Press Letchworth Hertfordshire
for J M Dent & Sons Limited
Aldine House Bedford Street London

ISBN 0 460 03985 7

Contents

Illustrations

Cotswold

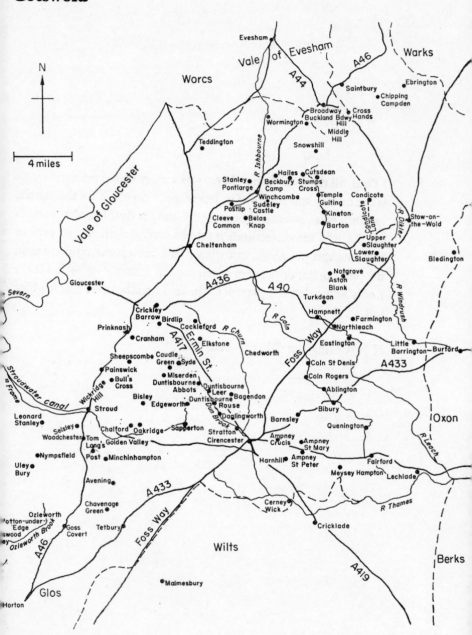

'Thus, all things in Cotswold possess a unity whose primary source is the quality and nature of its limestone. So much for the matrix, but into what essence of beauty this unity is distilled, that escapes me. Partly I can disintegrate it into its several elements, its various rhythms and phrasings, but what it is I can answer no more than the philosopher or the man of science can answer, "What is life?". I only know that it is present in the air I breathe upon that madder soil. . . .'

H J Massingham *Wold Without End*

A note on the illustrations, by Peter Turner

Although the camera is essentially a recording instrument and can see nothing other than what is presented to its lens, the mind and eye behind it can produce more than a simple record, however detailed and exact. It is here that the photographer will begin to feel the need for more elaborate equipment, and also to process his own work: for the creation of pictures, as distinct from snapshots, is achieved in the dark room as much as on site. A good photograph is the result of contemplation first of the subject, and then of the negative. It is an attempt to re-create a personal experience; to show the essence rather than a likeness.

The key to understanding is contemplation, and that demands silence, leisure and concentration. My advice to one on pilgrimage to Cotswold is to go there in the winter. Then the tourists are few; even streets can be seen relatively uncluttered. With the fall of the leaves views are opened and the bones of the land laid bare. Sunshine can throw its long shadows and reveal new tones in the stone, with paler washed colours over the landscape. On such a day the road through Selsley to Nympsfield takes one through a world still inhabited by those who built Uley Bury; one can stand on the escarpment and forget the atomic power-station and the Gloucester haze. For me true Cotswold is the world of the flint axe, and later of the shepherd.

Having all my life wandered on Cotswold and sought to discover the inner nature of its appeal, I have tried to communicate visually the wonder and delight of the beloved hills.

Introduction

The history of Cotswold has been told many times; the rise and fall of its wool and clothing trades, the part it played in the Wars of the Roses and the Civil War, its decline into a rural backwater in the nineteenth century and its resurgence today as a first-class farming and tourist area. And a great number of books have been written about the Cotswold landscape and architecture by authors unable to resist the elusive quality of Cotswold stone and the way it has fashioned the region throughout the ages.

We make no apology for another Cotswold book; there is always something left unsaid. Our intention – and our delight in making it – has been to emphasize the grace-notes on the principal themes, to present the whole through the details and so portray a more intimate picture. Often the most revealing and evocative experience of a place comes from a small part of it seen in a moment of vision. A carved stone hoary with lichen or a beech clump on an open hill-top can illuminate the wider pattern and continuity of the whole, bringing nearer to our understanding the way the Cotswold scene was shaped and the piety, humour, stubbornness and native good taste of the people who helped to make it what it is.

1 Cotswold stone

Plate 1

Oolitic limestone or roe-stone takes its name from the egg-like granules of crystalline calcite of which it is composed. It was formed in geological times by the movement of the sea, grain by grain, layer by layer settling into the solidity of underwater plains, and then when the waters had receded the throes which racked the earth bent them into the curving undulations we know as limestone wolds.

A great belt of oolite stretches across England from Dorset into Lincolnshire, but whereas outside Cotswold local stone was replaced by alien materials for building as the need for cheap housing rose sharply with the Industrial Revolution, on Cotswold the population decreased and its heart remained unchanged.

It is seldom necessary to blast stone from a Cotswold quarry, a crowbar is all that is needed to split it into movable blocks. When blasting takes place today it is to provide crushed stone for the artificial stone bricks that too often take the place of the natural stone. Fresh from the quarry it is easily shaped, but it hardens with exposure and so withstands weather and hard wear, gaining not only in durability but taking the play of light upon its surface to reciprocate the moods of morning, noon and evening. It can appear intangible as mist under lowering skies and in sunshine shafts of the original colour still glow through the silver and purplish bloom of age.

It comes in all tones of cream, yellow, buff, orange and silver

1

grey according to the quarry and the district. Around Painswick, for example, it is more silver than yellow while nearer the Oxfordshire border the colour deepens to orange-buff. It has been used for building on Cotswold for at least 4,000 years, for the men who raised the long barrows on the hills made the inner chambers and walls of stone before covering them with a mound of earth.

2 Drystone walling

Plates 2 – 4

The many miles of drystone walling enclosing the fields are a comparatively modern addition to the Cotswold landscape. As W. E. Tate says in *The Village Community and the Enclosure Movement*, 'the hedge, the fence and the wall are the makers of modern rural England'. The first Gloucestershire Enclosure Acts were for Horton in 1664 and Farmington in 1713, but there were enclosures before then, land-grabbing being one of the traits of the human race. But after 1760 the number of Enclosure Acts increased rapidly until the wolds took on the pattern we see today. One can distinguish lengths of walling belonging to those days – though they have probably been repaired many times since – the stones are thinner and fit into each other more exactly and, weathered to an antique grey and covered with centuries of dead and living growths of lichen, have become as much a part of the natural scene as the herbage about their feet.

During the farming depressions of the early 1900s stretches of field walls fell into ruin, but it is heartening to see the walls being renewed and repaired wherever one goes on Cotswold now that the traditional aspects of the region are recognized as assets and not as old-fashioned encumbrances standing in the way of progress. Newcomers to the region are punctilious in preserving old walls, the utility of the past having become the pride of the present.

Although practically every Cotsaller can handle stone there are some who specialize in drystone walling. The procedure is simple

but it must be understood if the wall is to stand up. Nor can the work be done quickly for each stone has to be scrutinized. This makes for much deliberation and develops a contemplative attitude exasperating to anyone not understanding the nature of the work. It would be absurd to say that one poor stone could ruin a wall but careful choice of the stones to be used is essential.

After a few inches of soil have been dug to make a bed a foundation of large blocks is laid. Then comes the gradual building up as each stone is roughly shaped with a heavy boat-shaped hammer – a tool made specially for the job – and then fitted into place, with larger stones at intervals to assist the locking-in process which keeps the wall together. The stone should be quarried in the right season and then laid on the wall in the same way as it was laid down in the quarry, otherwise it will flake and crumble after frost, as many an amateur building terrace walls for his garden has discovered.

Different districts show variations in the pattern of their walls and the walls around gardens of big houses are sometimes dressed more neatly and laid in even courses. The traditional finish is by toppers, that is large stones laid on edge, often slanting a little, but sometimes dressed stones would be laid flat, though this requires more time in selecting and handling, and is seldom used for field walls. Where a wall comes to a gate the stones have to be chosen and shaped so as to fit tightly into each other to give extra stability and a neat finish that will leave no gaps between wall and gate-post.

The modern finish is a rounded coping of mortar along the top or the toppers inserted in a bed of cement to prevent vandals pushing the stones out of place. In the old days this kind of useless destruction was rarely seen.

The craft of drystone walling has a long history. The horned false entrance of Belas Knap was sealed originally with drystone walling of thin stone flakes. When the barrow was taken over as an ancient monument and restored by the Office of Works in 1931

4

they were able to find men to rebuild the entrance in the same skilled manner, using many of the ancient layers of stone left after various excavations and supplementing the old with new stone slates less than an inch thick fitted together so accurately that it would be difficult to insert a knife blade between them.

One of the pleasures of a good piece of drystone walling is the way the grey stone makes a background for the wayside wild flowers that flourish in a limestone root-hold.

3 Long stone

Plate 5

In most instances the solitary standing stones of Cotswold are the remains of prehistoric burial mounds after their rape by early tomb robbers in search of treasure, by antiquarians of the eighteenth and nineteenth centuries looking for pots or other grave goods, and the subsequent use of the denuded mound as a quarry where stone could be easily obtained for road-making or other domestic uses. To the casual eye these standing stones appear as rough and unworked blocks crumbling into decay, their pitted surfaces a refuge for minute plants and cushions of moss, but a touch is sufficient to discover that they have toughened into a core of adamantine hardness against which no stone-breaker's hammer could prevail. Not that any stone-breaker would be rash enough to try; although nobody will admit it the folk memory of ancient magic still clings to these stones long after the tales of their potential for good or evil have been forgotten.

All traces of tooling, if any ever existed, have disappeared but their forms do suggest some kind of rough shaping, especially those which narrow upwards from a wide base. One finds the same shape amongst the stones of Avebury and Rollright, and it may, or may not, have had some special prehistoric significance.

4 The Saxon Cross at Wormington

Plate 6

About two miles south-west of Broadway a minor road leads west from the A46 and in about two miles goes through the small parish of Wormington before joining the B4078 on its way to Winchcombe. This is a countryside belonging more to the Worcestershire borderland than Cotswold but the hills are only a few miles away with the ridge holding Burhill and Shenbarrow Hill just east of the main road and solitary Dumbleton standing out on the plain to the west.

Wormington is a quiet place, its small fields bounded by tall hedges watered by the Ishbourne and its many brooks. Worcestershire's influence can be seen in the timbered walls of some of its buildings, and from Cotswold have come roofs of mossy stone tiles and one of the most appealing and strangely beautiful pieces of Saxon sculpture to be found in Gloucestershire. This is a crucifix of local stone, about two feet high, now fixed to the wall of the south aisle in the little church of St Catherine's. The crucifix is believed to date from the tenth century and was found buried in the garden of Wormington Grange. It could have come from Hailes Abbey; before the Dissolution, the Grange belonged to Hailes.

There is infinite pathos in the drooping head, the curves of the outstretched arms, the long thin body and large nailed feet. The man who carved it must have felt the story of the Crucifixion with the full force of his being, for the intensity of his awareness per-

meates the work. It was no pretty vision: his tool cut deeply into the stone as he shaped with unfaltering lines a body heavy in death, and as in all religious Saxon sculpture the corrosion of time and the crude simplicity of the workmanship heighten the emotional impact.

5 Norman doorways and tympana

Plates 7 – 10

Cotswold churches are renowned for their Norman work. In nearly every village church Norman doorways and chancel arches are to be found, often with a tympanum carved in a simple repetitive design or illustrating a religious story. The church of St Swithin at Quenington, in the wooded valley of the Coln a little more than two miles north of Fairford, has north and south doorways adorned with ornate mouldings and sculptured tympana. Practically the whole range of Norman patterns, including billet, chevron, cable, star, beakheads, can be seen on the mouldings, and despite centuries of weathering the original boldness of the axe strokes is still apparent. The Norman mason's chief tools were a two-bladed axe and a hammer axe. Gervaise of Canterbury, writing about the building of Canterbury Choir at the end of the twelfth century, says that the new capitals and arcades were carved with the chisel whereas the older work had been carved with the axe, so one can assume that the chisel was then coming into general use and its superiority for more delicate work recognized.

It is the stark impact of the individual strokes, each one differing by a minute fraction of an inch, the fact that the spaces between were calculated with the eye and not by instrument, as well as the varying vigour of the strokes, which give life to the ornament. This can be clearly seen if one compares original work with the poorer restoration of the last century.

9

Pattern worked by mechanical aid loses its vitality and becomes monotonous.

These decorations give us a glimpse into the Norman attitude to religion, their determination to impress it forcibly upon the population. Mildness was not one of their characteristics. Their God was a jealous god and hell more important than the gentleness of heaven. Their angels were more likely to wield flaming swords than to spread comforting wings around the sinner.

The sculptured tympana, however, are another story. Here are no harsh deep-cut strokes hacked with a virility that implies the conqueror, but a less brutal conception, the figures crude but their arrangement far more subtle. It is likely that native masons were used, for the Normans could not have built so many new churches without them, and it is likely also that among the natives employed were professional sculptors, for the fragments of Saxon work remaining today are evidence of this.

The tympanum above Quenington's south doorway showing the Coronation of the Virgin has a pattern of figures in straight and curving lines fitting perfectly into the semicircle below the bold rows of chevrons, the folding wings of the angel breaking the regularity and giving the whole an authentic touch of artistry not usually associated with Norman work. The north doorway portrays the Harrowing of Hell. On the right of the figure of Christ piercing the bound Satan at his feet with the Cross is a rayed sun, a symbol rarely found in religious carvings. It might not be too fanciful to see a local emblem in the ram's head above the figures, Cotswold even at so early a date being renowned for its wool.

HARNHILL TYMPANUM

Within a triangle of Cotswold borderland that lies between Ermin Street and a line slightly to the north of the Cirencester – Fairford main road, taking Cirencester as the apex and closing the triangle with the minor road from Meysey Hampton to Cerney Wick,

there is a cluster of villages whose churches hold a wealth of early stone carvings.

Ampney Crucis has a churchyard cross whose original gabled top, with figures of the Madonna, St Lawrence with his grid, Longinus with his sword, was found concealed in the roodloft stairway and restored in 1860. Ampney St Mary has a sculptured tympanum showing what seems to be a lion striding over two coiled creatures, possibly representing the forces of evil; Ampney St Peter has part of a nude female figure said to be of Saxon date. All these churches show signs of Saxon masonry.

Harnhill, less than two miles south-east of Cirencester and the smallest of the villages, contains the most striking piece of sculpture of them all, the tympanum over the south doorway of the little church of St Michael. It shows St Michael slaying a dragon, a beast with a horse's head and forelegs and a narrowing body ending in a tail that curls full circle under the heavy wings rising from its shoulders. St Michael is wielding a stout sword and protects himself with a shield. Only the essential lines are carved and these in deep relief. The simplicity of the conception and the curving outlines of a pattern full of movement remind one of the carving of the Saxon Cross at Wormington. Saxon influence if not a Saxon sculptor seems likely, for the dragon is large and fearsome without being grotesque in the usual Norman style; one accepts it as a monster but not as a freak of bizarre imagination. And it must be remembered that this countryside of brooks and twisting lanes was in the line of the Saxon advance up the Thames Valley and homesteads were established here in the earlier years of the Saxon invasions and settlements.

The beast's rising anger is felt in the up-rearing neck and chest and by the advancing forelegs with their lion-like claws. St Michael is shown not as a figure of might and glory but clad in a short simple tunic, his thin arms and legs without armour, protected only by his shield, so that the courage of his fight with the evil one gains emphasis by the contrast. The downward sweep

11

of the wings from his shoulder to the bottom left-hand corner complement the lifting of the dragon's wings on the opposite side. The man who carved the tympanum was not only skilled in his art but one who saw the battle between St Michael and the dragon not as a religious fable but as a reality.

6 Hampnett birds

Plates 11 and 12

A few yards beyond the Northleach junction of the Foss Way with the A40 Cheltenham to Oxford road a byway leads westward to a constellation of villages, Hampnett, Turkdean, Aston Blank and Notgrove, enfolded in wide upland landscapes and wider skies. Here when the hills were open sheepwalks the Midwinters and other wool-factors came to buy wool and fleeces, and it was wealth from these which helped to build the splendid church at Northleach.

But the churches of these small villages are not wool churches; the upstanding glories of the Perpendicular passed them by. Though they have suffered drastic nineteenth-century restoration, the impression still remains of the close-knit intimacy of the times when the villages were ruled by the lords of the manor whose memorial monuments still have pride of place within the church walls.

Hampnett is the first village one comes to along the minor road as it takes a rising shallow curve into the hills when, in a little more than half a mile, a cluster of farm buildings and its church tower come into view. Opposite the church is a noble stone barn with high cart porches. Other massive farm buildings equally pleasing to the eye, with their stone-slated roofs and stout grey walls, stand near by. The church is lifted above the road un-dwarfed by their amplitude, a point of rest in a perfect entity.

Inside there is a late Norman chancel with bold-ribbed vaulting,

and two archways of the original central Norman tower whose upper part was pulled down in the thirteenth century, when a tower of three stages was added at the west end. There is also a north doorway with a diapered tympanum. Other Cotswold churches have similar Norman features but Hampnett possesses some Norman carvings of considerable charm on the capitals of the west archway leading to the chancel. One does not associate charm with Norman work, but here the more natural decorative forms that developed later into the Early English style had already begun to take the place of the fierce grotesqueries of Elkstone and other Cotswold churches.

The two carvings, one on each side of the archway, each represent a pair of large-beaked, swan-necked birds, one pair feeding from a bowl, the other pair preening themselves, the curve of their bodies and spread of wings a simple repetition of half-circles flowing around and through them. Deeply cut and without angularity, they stand out boldly; the strong lines indicating wing and tail feathers, the large round eyes and the beaks are reduced to the minimum, so that nothing interrupts the satisfying completeness of the rounded shapes. The vigour of the carving adds its own vitality.

7 Roofs
Plates 13 and 14

Whatever its size or importance the correct finish to a building in the Cotswold vernacular is a roof of stone slates. Although in other parts of the country stone slates may have followed wood shingles as a more permanent roofing material this has never been the case on Cotswold, where slates have been used from Roman times onward.

The characteristic steep pitch is necessary because the stone is porous; the intensity of the rainstorms which sweep over the wolds need a good slope to enable the water to run away quickly. The slates being heavy, a roof must have strong supporting timbers. As the stone is practically indestructible the timbers beneath are usually the first to deteriorate, which explains the curving dipping roofs one sometimes sees on old neglected buildings. There are many references in old church accounts of money paid for 'pack moss' and 'moseying'. Moss, hay or straw was once used as bedding material under the slates for extra warmth and to keep out snow and rain.

The slatter's tools were simple and home-made and, as the trade usually ran in families, handed down from generation to generation. A list from Randle Holme's *Academy of Armoury* of 1688 gives Hatchet, Trowel, Hewing Knife, Pick to Hole, Pinning Iron to widen the Holes, Hewing Block, Lathing Measure and Stone Measure. The hatchet, hewing block and hewing knife would be used to shape the oak pins, one for each tile that went

through the hole in the stone and held it in place. The stone measure may be the wooden rule about two feet long with grooves and notches for measuring inches and half-inches, with a nail or screw at the head to agree with the hole in the slate. Iron nails, more expensive than oak pins in those days, were for the more important buildings and many have been found at excavations of Cotswold Roman villas.

The slates are arranged with the largest at the eaves and growing smaller as they come to the roof ridge. The ridge, resembling a miniature roof, was then finished off with lengths of sawn stone placed on edge. Finials, a ball or some other simple shape on a small stand, might be added for decoration, an exclamation mark of pleasure at the end of a job well done.

Holme gives contemporary names for the slates and these differed in different parts of the region according to local wit and explicitness. Bachlers and Wivetts are still known today, and most of them have a prefix, 'long' or 'short'. The largest for the eaves were called 'heavers'. The oldest slates, including those found at Roman villas, were mainly hexagonal, but later the tail was squared and the head shaped in a rough oval. Barns and lesser buildings seldom received this extra refinement.

The season for quarrying is from April to October. The stone is then left exposed for the frost to expand the film of clay and water between the layers of stone, thus making easy and natural cleavage the following year. Freshly dug stone is tinged with all shades of grey, brown and yellow, as pleasing to the eye as when the roofs have weathered to a dark grey. The irregular surface encourages traceries of lichen and tiny mosses and this subtle variety of texture and colour changes with the amount of light in the sky. When the sun shines the darkest roofs show glints of the original colour, on a misty day they can recede into the landscape and become as much a part of it as the hills and dark woods.

In the 1920s a great number of stone tiles were taken from old Cotswold buildings during an American building boom and sent

across the Atlantic to fetch high prices. New slates today are a costly luxury, old ones bring even higher prices, a tribute to their aesthetic value as well as being a status symbol for their owner. The traditional way of hanging them has been modified and improved and they are no longer bedded in moss or hay, but modern techniques are used to give better protection from wind-driven rain and snow.

Farmington, a hill village east of Northleach, stands so remote and secluded in its encircling trees that it is hard to believe the roar and bustle of Midland industrial traffic on the Foss Way is only a mile away. The heart of the village is grouped about a green knoll girt about with tall trees, one an ancient sycamore with a massive bole, its centre piece an octagonal shelter that once covered the village pump, and played an important part in the daily life of the villagers before water was laid on to the cottages. The original roof of the shelter was thatch, but now the roof with its eight miniature gables is covered with stone slates fitting as snugly as scales on a fish from the eaves to the cupola, topped with a ball finial. It is an excellent example of modern stone-tile roofing, and shows how the modern tiler has arranged the slates of the swept valleys, always the most difficult part of the roof to cover adequately.

8 Sir William de Postlip

Plate 16

Postlip, a mile west of Winchcombe, consists today of a paper mill situated in the valley of the Ishbourne and, just below the crest of the hill reached by a long private drive, a gabled Elizabethan mansion, Postlip Hall, a small chapel with a Norman doorway and chancel arch, and a medieval tithe barn built by Sir William de Postlip in the first half of the twelfth century.

Erect on a finial of small gables high at the end of the barn roof stands the worn and battered effigy of Sir William, and having been exposed for centuries to the wind and weather of that high place the figure is now reduced to a basic shape of two remarkably stout legs, a rectangular body in a short tunic and a head on a thick neck, its rounded top suggesting a good crop of hair cut off at ear level. The features and any distinguishing marks of clothing or rank have worn away; the figure looks so ancient and battered it could be a primitive idol.

I have sometimes wondered if it originally represented not Sir William but a figure that was old when he built his barn, and was given his name by local people long after he was dead, for in the days when stories were transmitted orally country people had a way of telescoping history and legend. Whoever it represents, saint, the lord of the manor or local god, it has taken on at least one attribute of prehistory. The story told of many an ancient standing stone is also told about the figure: it is said that when he hears the clock strike midnight he gets down from his high place to drink at

18

1 Cotswold or roe-stone: oolitic limestone, magnified to show the egglike granules of its composition.

2 Drystone walling. Making a field wall of new stone.

3 A new wall but using an old stone post.

4 Wall at The Wells, Bisley, showing thin layers of dressed stone so skilfully laid that mortar was unnecessary.

5 Long Stone, Woeful Dane, near Minchinhampton. There are many such Standing Stones on Cotswold with surfaces pitted and gnawed by centuries of exposure to wind and weather.

6 Saxon Cross, Wormington, believed to have come from the ruins of Hailes Abbey.

7 Norman doorway at Stanley Pontlarge, showing large billet pattern on hood-mould and band of large stars around the tympanum.
8 Harnhill tympanum, with sculpture depicting St Michael and the dragon.

9 Quenington north doorway with its elaborately ornamented jambs of many Norman designs and a sculptured tympanum.

10 Lintel at Ampney St Mary of an irregular semi-octagonal shape enclosing a carving of symbolic animals.

11 and 12 The western Norman arch in Hampnett Church shows jamb shafts whose carved capitals represent a pair of doves.

13 Old stone-tiled roof at Chalford. A typical example of slates laid
with the largest at the eaves and growing smaller as they come
to the roof ridge.

14 Barn at Ablington, typical of many on Cotswold, with massive cart
porches and steep-pitched roof.

15 Effigy of Sir William de Postlip on the end of the roof of the fourteenth-century tithe barn at Postlip.

16 One of the two carvings of shears on a buttress of the tower of Cranham Church signifying that a sheep-shearer or cloth-cutter helped to build it.

17 Gargoyle, Coates. The scouring effect of wind and weather has added to the original grotesquerie.

18 Medieval glass roundel from Ebrington Parish Church, probably
one of the series that represented the months or seasons.
19 A madonna with outstretched hands from the fragments of fifteenth-
century glass put together in a memorial window in Bagendon
Parish Church.

20 Merchant's mark of John Taylour, woolman, from his memorial brass in Northleach Church.
21 Merchant's mark of John Fortey, woolman, restorer of roads and churches, from his memorial brass in Northleach Church.

22 The little church of Ampney St Mary stands alone in a meadow almost hidden by trees.

23 Syde's tiny church enclosed on three sides by the walls of great stone barns.

24 St Nicholas's Church at Condicote, a remote village high on the
Wolds.

25 Cottage at Ablington showing gables and dormers.
26 Cottage at Caudle Green in the Cotswold vernacular sitting snugly into rising ground.

the wishing well near by, once probably a holy well and earlier a drinking place for prehistoric travellers on the old track along the ridge. The story is more than a rustic riddle to amuse the children but has its origin deep in the labyrinth of folk-lore.

Postlip itself is in the midst of prehistoric Cotswold. Not far over the hill lies Belas Knap, the famous chambered long barrow with the horned entrance, and a mile or so away Beckbury Camp overlooks the valley where Hailes Abbey once stood.

9 Shears on Cranham church tower

Plate 16

Cranham, a small parish between Cheltenham and Stroud, is noted chiefly for its beech woods, part of a great natural beech forest which once covered many hundreds of acres. The church of St James, practically rebuilt in 1894–5, has a fourteenth-century tower, a Tudor chancel and a Perpendicular oak screen carved in a tracery of roses and vines as a record of its earlier foundation.

A pair of shears carved in the stone of one of the buttresses of the tower is a reminder of the days of the great wool merchants, one of whom probably gave money towards an earlier restoration of the building and had the shears carved as a symbol of his calling. The carving has no aesthetic value apart from the satisfaction to be found in the shape of any useful implement or tool and the magic wrought by age and weathering. One imagines the craftsman was concerned only with making a large representation of a pair of shears that would be easily recognizable from below, and it is the simple act of recognition which gives us pleasure today, emphasized by the knowledge that centuries ago someone because of a quirk of the imagination or for a more significant reason had them portrayed on the tower.

One finds this device in several churches in the wool country of Wiltshire and Gloucestershire. In Northleach church it can be seen as a memorial to William Scors, incorporated in the memorial brass of Thomas Fortey, William Scors being the first husband of Agnes, Thomas Fortey's wife.

10 Gargoyles
Plate 17

The function of a gargoyle is to carry away rainwater from the roof. Who first hit upon the idea of decorating the head of a water-spout in this way we shall never know: a master mason, perhaps, seeing an opportunity to use his creative talent by the literal translation of a head into human or animal form. But, the idea accepted, it became common practice. By far the most popular of all water-spout figures is a grotesque human head allied to a bird or animal body, and one seldom finds two gargoyles alike even on the same building.

To keep the rainwater from pouring down the walls the gargoyles had to protrude from the building, and this could have supplied the motive of the winged body clinging to the masonry as if about to take off. It was necessary to provide a large hole for the water to run through, and in a head the obvious place for this was a mouth, so that one gets the lolling tongues, the evil grins, the expressions of agonized terror or despair a wide-open mouth can express. From this point it was easy to let the spirit of grotesquerie have its head, so to speak, to add large ears, great hollow eyes, overhanging brows, noses hawklike or bulbous according to the fancy of the carver. The form invited crude humour or wry comment on pain or infirmities, like the man with the toothache or a squint.

It could be an opportunity for paying off old scores, for caricature. Tradition tells that the gargoyles on Winchcombe parish church

were carved to resemble some of the monks of Winchcombe Abbey, there being much ill-will between the parish church and the Abbey authorities. The quarrels were even referred to the Pope, for a Bull of 1399 orders 'that no bell of the Parish Church ring after curfew on the Monastery Bell until Morning Prime'. The Vicar, it seemed, had been annoying the monks by ringing the bells at night and during Abbey services. According to Eleanor Adlard in *Winchcombe Cavalcade* an actual person, Ralph Boteler of Sudeley, who helped pay for the rebuilding of the church, is said to be represented by the fierce mustachioed gargoyle on the south leads. During the 1914–1918 war, however, it was renamed Kaiser Bill.

The variations on the theme are endless. A head suggests headgear, and one can find many forms of caps, hats and hair-styles, and nature often provides an adornment for them with a fern, a plume of coarse grass, a ragged wallflower or other tough plant whose seed found a damp crack in which to germinate. In their exposed position scouring winds and rain can also accent the ferocity of their aspect, or give the distorted countenances that look of blank dismay one sees on the faces of clowns, a look meant to make us laugh by features pulled awry. And that is what the men who carved the gargoyles seem to be doing, pulling faces not in the clown's medium of muscles, flesh and skin but in stone.

11 Medieval glass
Plates 18 and 19

Cotswold is noted for its painted and engraved medieval church glass. In many a village church one can find remnants of glazing once rich in colour and story. The Madonna, tiny figures of saints whose powers of healing and supplication were an intrinsic part of religious faith, fragments of a simple piety that can never be regained, portrayed with a freshness of concept and jewelled delicacy clear as the waters of a Cotswold spring.

The most famous and most complete can be seen in St Mary's church at Fairford, a church built at the end of the fifteenth century by the rich cloth merchants, John Tame and his son Edmund. It has twenty-eight painted glass windows believed to be the work of Barnard Flower, who was famous for windows in Henry VIII's Chapel at Westminster and King's College, Cambridge. A host of stories have grown up about the Fairford glass and the manner of its survival during the religious troubles of the sixteenth century when so much precious glass was destroyed, and later during the Civil War when it was secretly removed and hidden to save it from Cromwell's soldiers. In our own time it had to be protected against Hitler's bombs. Now once again St Mary's is glorified by its rich glowing colours, its vivid representation of heaven and hell and the felicities of its gentler details such as glimpses of river landscape one would like to identify with the Coln.

Bledington, a few miles south-east of Stow-on-the-Wold, has

an enchanting collection, particularly in the clerestory windows, including a Madonna in a white cloak and golden crown, Mary Magdalene in blue, St George on horseback. At Buckland, near Broadway, three panels of the east window – part of a series given by the rector, William Grafton, in 1480 representing the Seven Sacraments – so impressed William Morris by their beauty and craftsmanship that he paid for their re-leading.

A delightful and unusual roundel can be seen in Ebrington's parish church of St Aedburgha's near Chipping Campden, enchanting not only for its delicate colour and skilful drawing but because it is one of the few pieces to give the impression of an almost nonchalant lightheartedness, not a quality one associates with the religious temper of the period. Could the man who made it have known the Elizabethan poet's 'with innocence goes jocound merriment', I wonder?

It illustrates the parable of the sower and must have been one of a set showing the seasons or months of the year, for the word OTTOBRI appears on a wide floating scroll within an outer square. An elegant figure this sower, in a Tudor cap, with long shapely legs and slender long-pointed shoes. He resembles a page rather than a peasant, for those dainty shoes and hose seem most unsuitable wear in a field newly prepared for sowing in October. That he did not find it heavy going is apparent in a pose suggesting a dance rather than field work. Two birds follow him, one hovering on outstretched wings almost touching his wallet, the other picking the seed as it falls, but he goes on quite unconcerned as with outstretched hand he scatters the grain. Movement is achieved by the few lines of the figure and the curving strokes of the scroll with its upcurled ends. The window is as fresh as an Elizabethan madrigal.

In St Margaret's church at Bagendon, a tiny village near the site of the old town of the Dobunni some three miles north-west of Cirencester, there are some fascinating fragments of fifteenth-century window-glass in the south chancel windows. Among

saints and coats-of-arms there is a Madonna strong in its appeal with hands outstretched in an all-embracing compassion. The same haunting quality emanates from it as from some of the religious stone sculptures of pre-Roman origin. The vision of the craftsman who created it, the emphasis on great hands with their palms upward, the large sombre eyes, have produced an effect at once archaic and modern. The message gets through and is the more forceful because of the restrictions of the artist's technique and the medium he worked in.

12 Merchants' marks

Plates 20 and 21

The merchant's mark of John Taylour inscribed on his memorial brass dated 1490 in the Lady Chapel of Northleach church shows two shepherds' crooks in the form of a cross upon a woolpack below a fine upstanding sheep. We find sheep in plenty on woolmen's brasses but recognition of the men who tended the sheep is rare.

A cross or other religious symbol is generally incorporated into the device as a protection against the hazards of travel. There were hazards at sea as well as on land, not only for the merchandise but for the merchants who, after collecting wool and fleeces from the various Cotswold centres, often took them in their own ships to the staple towns of the Low Countries.

The effigies on woolmen's brasses have their feet resting on a woolpack. The unknown merchant's brass in Northleach church, taken from the old Norman church when later wool merchants replaced it with the splendid Perpendicular building we know today, shows the typical woolpack with its tied corners. The memorial of John Fortey (*obiit* 1458), who rebuilt the nave and clerestory, presents him with one foot on a woolsack, the other on a sheep, and his mark, the initials J. F. between a banner and a cross inside a wreath, can be seen at the end of his girdle and repeated many times around the border.

Thomas Bushe, who died in 1525, made it very plain to the world he left behind that he had been a woolman. His effigy with

26

that of his wife lies under a double canopy, their feet resting on a woolpack and a horned sheep, while other horned sheep under a large bush with the arms of the staple of Calais further emphasize his calling. His mark was a cross springing from a monogram. The later the date of the memorial the more richly decorated it became, illustrating the pomp of earthly life, whereas in the earlier brasses the austerity of death was the main theme.

William Grevel's brass in Chipping Campden church, dating about 1400, is an exception, perhaps because he was one of the most influential merchants on Cotswold whose family had risen in the social scale thanks to successful business ventures and advantageous marriages. We know he was acquainted with the court and lent money to Richard II, and it is stated on his tomb that he was a 'citizen of London'. But he asked to be buried in Chipping Campden whose church he helped to restore, and he is remembered there not only by his highly ornamented brass but by the beautiful old house in the High Street which bears his name. His mark, a cross on a globe with streamers attached to the shaft, can be seen on the pediments of the double canopy over his effigy and the effigy of his first wife; the globe is to indicate his world-wide activities.

At a time when the greater part of the population could not read, a merchant's mark was his signature and his bond and was recognized as such. He was proud to have it inscribed on his tomb.

13 Smaller churches

Plates 22-24

As well as the handsome Perpendicular churches built by the woolmen, such as Chipping Campden, Northleach and Fairford, whose towers dominate the landscape for miles around, there are many smaller churches not so easily seen by travellers passing through the region. They are reached by minor roads, often little more than metalled lanes, which branch off the main roads to go winding and undulating into the quiet countryside. And though the village may not be more than a mile or two away from a main road one gets the impression that the distance is much greater in time as well as mileage.

One rarely finds the smaller churches rising above the general level of the scene and even when they are perched on a bluff the trees about the churchyard keep them hidden. Mostly they fit snugly into a shelf or hollow with no more aspiring upward than a saddlebacked tower and a gable crowned with a cross. The basic shape is the same as for the barns and farm buildings around them and their walls of roughly hewn stone could have been built by the same masons. Remains of Saxon work may not mean that a church is a pre-Conquest building but that Saxon masons were employed in the early Norman period.

St Andrew's church at Coln Rogers in the Coln valley is the richest in Saxon masonry with a pilaster strip on the south of the nave, long and short quoins at the nave's south-east angle and two more Saxon pilasters on the north side of the chancel.

St Michael's of Duntisbourne Rouse has herringbone masonry on its west wall, and long and short work at the angles. Situated on an open slope above the stream and just below the narrow road which winds up and down through the Dun valley, its hoary walls could easily be mistaken at casual glance for those of an ancient farm building. A closer look, however, reveals one of the most interesting churches on Cotswold, for not only did it escape the restorers of the nineteenth century but it has the unique feature of a crypt under the chancel, the builders making use of the steep slope of the churchyard instead of being defeated by it. St Michael's also has a Norman chancel arch, but this is not rare on Cotswold where nearly every church shows Norman work. Some of the best preserved arches and doorways are to be found in the churches of remote villages.

The interiors often contrast with their homely exteriors, particularly those adjacent to a manor house and approached by the same driveway, so that the church seems to belong more to the big house than to the village. They are sometimes filled with the altar tombs and other memorials to the families who once held the manor, going through the generations in progression from the freestone effigy of a crusader in chain mail to elaborate marble and other wall monuments carrying, above long Latin pronouncements of the virtues and honours of the dead, classical urns, weeping willows, clinging but chaste female figures, and busts of bewigged gentlemen. After the end of the eighteenth century the memorials become less ornate and less revealing to the social historian.

Some three and a half miles before Ermin Street comes to the top of the hill at Birdlip a byway leading to the hamlet of Syde branches off west through gateposts, thus giving the first intimation of its secluded position. Though only a mile from Ermin Street's main-road traffic it might as well be twenty in its isolation under the hill.

Syde consists of a complex of manor house, massive farm build-

29

ings and a tiny church shut in on three sides by the walls of great stone barns. The church stands on a shallow terrace just below the road and is reached by descending worn shallow stone steps. The saddleback west tower, the cross at the east end on the apex of the roof and a huddle of headstones and a few plain box tombs in the tiny churchyard reveal its function. Dark grey walls and a darker moss-encrusted stone-tiled roof are evidence of Cotswold's swirling rain-storms and mists rather than of its happier aspect of sun and wind. The interior is more cosy, the diminutive size suggesting the intimacy of family worship. There are box pews and a medieval font carved with roses, and the tiny nave has kept its ancient roof timbers. A chancel arch takes the church's foundation back to the Norman period.

14 Cotswold cottages

Plates 25 and 26

Old Cotswold cottages have no architectural pretensions. Most of them were erected by the cottagers themselves with the help of a village mason. Often the only dressed stones were the quoins and window-mouldings, the remainder of the fabric being a mixture of blocks whose angles had been roughly scabbled with an axe and a natural coursing where the stone came out of the quarry in thin layers. The general practice was to build solid to the roof timbers, the walls, from eighteen inches to two feet thick, being filled internally with rubble. When enlargement became necessary further bays or right-angled projections were added.

The Elizabethan style continued on Cotswold long after the Elizabethan period because it adapted so well to local conditions and materials, and within the convention of steep-pitched, stone-slated roofs, dormers and gables, and mullioned windows surmounted by drip-mouldings the builders found considerable scope for design. The siting, as well as the way each cottage differs from its neighbour by some slight variation, has its own fortuitous charm. Even when the cottages line a village street there is no monotonous uniformity, while garden plots are rarely confined within neat rectangles but seem to have been laid out by rule of thumb, and a gnarled twisted thumb at that.

The eye is continually delighted by what seems a happy accident of grouping, particularly where there is only a narrow strip of level ground so that the cottages had to be perched on different

31

levels and fitted snugly in any available flat ground. Because stone from local quarries was used throughout the village for barns, sheds, gate-posts, pigsties and stiles as well as for the dwellings and the church the result was in harmony with its surroundings and with itself.

When these cottages were built England was predominantly rural, its crafts and industries carried on with a large proportion of the working population still holding a stake in the land. In Cotswold the best period was between the late sixteenth to the end of the eighteenth century when the wool and clothing trades flourished. The Enclosures and then the decline of the clothing trade reduced the farm workers, the weavers and spinners to less than subsistence level and their pride of proprietorship in the land lapsed during the hard years of poverty and disillusionment of the nineteenth century. There was no surplus to spend on keeping their homes in repair and thousands fell into decay or were crudely patched up.

Today an old cottage is valued for its picturesque qualities. It has acquired value as an antique with a status for its owner that an antique bestows, but it has a more genuine significance. It reflects the working conditions, aptitudes and skills of the English character and gives substance to one aspect, at least, of the sentimentalists' 'good old days'.

15 Cotswold waters

Plates 27 – 31

Cotswold has a number of small rivers and numerous streams which feed them, each one having a distinct personality and its own kind of river landscape yet all belonging unmistakably to the region. They are clean, bright and sparkling, the water coming from the hills cleansed by its passage through the limestone and by flowing over it. In many cases the name of the river is part of the name of the village it serves, as in the string of Coln and Leach villages. Between the villages they wind through a pastoral countryside of green water-meadows, fields and woodland, and all have sloping hillsides reaching to the unfolding hills.

The contrast between the bare exposed light-toned hills and the dark trees and richer vegetation of the valleys is one of the charms of the Cotswold scene. In earlier times when life was impossible without natural resources of water in the vicinity the contrast must have been more compelling. The people who worked and lived on the Chedworth Roman villa estate laid out an altar in a water shrine as part of the establishment, and higher up the wooded slope behind the villa is a tumulus made by men who knew the river Coln long before the Roman invasion and who worshipped their own gods of the life-giving waters. There must have been many shrines and temples dedicated to the nymphs and gods of streams and brooks that have disappeared, and not all the Holy Wells of the Middle Ages originated with the saints whose names they bore, but were taken over from pagan gods.

Another charm of Cotswold rivers, especially those in the north, is that they are small enough to know intimately and so inspire affection. The Windrush, one of the longest, has only thirty miles or so to travel from its birth as a bubbling of bright drops out of a tiny green hollow above Cutsdean to where it enters the Thames near Newbridge in Oxfordshire. Fed by brooks and springs, in less than three miles it goes through Temple Guiting, Kineton and Barton as a sizable stream. In Domesday Book Temple Guiting is called Getinge, or the valley of the torrent, but today the ancient name would not apply, for the large springs that once gushed from the hillside with amazing force are now piped by a water company.

We know that all the little rivers worked mills, and most riverside villages have a Mill Lane to remind us. These mills began as corn mills but in the south Cotswolds they were taken over for fulling and cloth making, some as early as the twelfth century but the majority in the seventeenth and eighteenth centuries. A few continued to play a dual role as at Grindstone Mill on the Ozleworth brook, let to a clothier as 'one grindstone mill and one fulling mill' when it belonged to Kingswood Abbey near Wotton-under-Edge.

The waters of North Cotswold were never harnessed to the clothing trade in the same way as the Little Avon and the Stroudwater in the south, and so did not share in the prosperity or the later catastrophic decline, but kept their sylvan quietude untouched.

Two of the earliest fulling mills on Cotswold, however, were at Barton, on the estate of the Knights Templars who gave their name to Temple Guiting. Fosbrooke in his *History of Gloucestershire* says that the Templars made them before 1175, and they were still working in 1327 when the Bishop of Hereford, who then had custody of the manor, rendered account of his stewardship to the new king Edward III. The amount of rent paid for the mills shows that Barton must have been an important centre of wool manufacture and that the mills played a large part in the economy of the Templars' estate.

34

The fulling mills have disappeared but a low footbridge spanning the Windrush at Kineton may belong to those days, though it has probably been rebuilt several times since then. Its three great slabs of stone raised on stout piers of rough uncut stones and worn smooth by water, weather and the tread of feet stand by the ford in a green hollow at the bottom of a steep sunken lane leading from the village above, an idyllic spot to linger on a summer's day when the clear shallow water sparkles in the dappled shade of trees and untrimmed bushes and where one can still catch a glimpse of a kingfisher darting through the narrow tunnel of greenery beyond the bridge.

After passing through the ford the lane immediately begins its twisting way to higher ground, the slopes of the hillside beyond the tangled hedges too steep to plough and bright with wild flowers, the meadow cranesbill whose petals take on a deeper blue on a limestone soil, rock-roses, small scabious, milkwort and others that revel in a limestone roothold.

Although the oolitic limestone has first place in the making of Cotswold, the abundant waters of the region play a great part in the appeal of its landscape and together they make some of the most enchanting Cotswold pictures.

Less than two miles north-west of Cirencester a minor road leaves Ermin Street at Stratton and wanders north-west along a narrowing valley into the hills. A stream shares the valley with a few farms, three villages and the road serving them until its source at Duntisbourne Abbots where the valley comes to an end. Daglingworth, the first village after leaving Stratton on Ermin Street, straggles in haphazard fashion on varying heights above the stream with the church and a big house perched on a knoll at its highest point. Duntisbourne Rouse is more secretive with cottages and farms half hidden in orchards and farmyards and reached by short steep byways leading to the brook, while at the hamlet of Duntisbourne Leer where the valley is much narrower the course of the stream is only a few yards from the cottage doors. People living

there must have its soft murmurings perpetually in their ears and from their windows can watch the water-wagtails prinking in the shallow water and the other birds who come to drink and bathe in its gentle ripples.

When one comes to Duntisbourne Abbots from the valley road a few cottages on the banks of the stream have a backcloth of lush greenery and tall trees, but the main part of the village is dotted about the rim of an upslanted green bank. At the bottom of the bank a spring which is the chief source of the Dun brook falls into a large semicircular stone trough, once the village water-supply and dipping place. The trough, waterworn and darkened by age, is a simple piece of masonry edged with mosses and water-loving plants and made out of a solid piece of stone to trap the waters for domestic use. Long before there was a village here the men who travelled the ancient trackway on the ridge between the Duntisbourne valley and the uppermost part of the Golden Valley must have known of this spring and stopped to drink its refreshing waters.

The trough no longer serves as a focal point and gossip centre for the village and the water no longer tumbles into it with the same abandon as in the old days before the spring was tapped, but it is still a pleasant spot at which to spend idle moments musing on the life of a Cotswold village before modern amenities and the less peaceful aspects of modern life intruded upon its rural peace.

Bisley, perched on a hillside in the south Cotswolds and reached by narrow winding roads that were once packhorse trails, is renowned for its waters, exceeding all other villages in the copious springs gushing from the rocks in a never-failing supply. The numerous prehistoric and Roman remains in the neighbourhood show that earlier inhabitants appreciated this abundance. When cloth-making was the district's main occupation many of the cottages dotted about the banks housed weavers and spinners who had settled there because the yarn could be washed at the springs

on their doorsteps. The subsequent loss of the clothing trade, the misery of the Bisley weavers, who were reduced to near-starvation, and the decline of Bisley from a populous village to a bleak poverty-stricken hamlet must have made mockery of those sparkling waters.

16 Green roads

Plates 32–35

An important line of communication along the wolds in pre-historic times was the Cotswold Ridgeway, part of a throughway that ran across England from the Bristol Avon to the Humber. On each side as it traversed the hills, winding out of course and then back again to avoid ravines and difficult ground, are hill-forts, earthworks, tumuli and other prehistoric remains, evidence of activity in the region from the time of the long barrows onward.

From Bath the Ridgeway follows the watershed between the Bristol Avon and the Severn and then the watershed between the Severn and the Upper Thames basin. Until it enters Worcester-shire at Broadway only three miles of its line is not represented by roads and tracks today.

As far as Goss Covert much of it roughly coincides with today's main road from Bath to Stroud. It then leaves the main road to turn north-east to Chavenage Green, where the Romans, accord-ing to the Ordnance Survey Map of Roman Britain, cut off the corner. It continues below Avening to between Sapperton and Sapperton Park, joining Ermin Street near Birdlip. Ermin Street descends to the vale of Gloucester but the trackway follows the escarpment, first south of Cheltenham where it may have crossed the infant Churn, possibly near Cockleford. It then goes east of Cheltenham to Cleeve Common. It continues to wind eastward, past Belas Knap to Roel Gate, a meeting place of trackways, then north to Sudeley and north-east to Stumps Cross. From there it

keeps south of Snowshill, over Middle Hill and past the tower to come to the main road from Stow to Broadway. Here it leaves the Cotswolds.

Offshoots branch off. For instance, from Sapperton a trackway leading up the valley of the Frome passes Edgeworth, Miserden and Cranham and descends the scarp at Prinknash, passing over the once swampy ground of the vale by a low ridge, the Portway, to a point where the Severn could be crossed and the traveller continue into Wales.

In the days when Cotswold was open country saltways followed the course of prehistoric and romanized trackways, climbing up from Worcestershire and spreading into Gloucestershire as a network of minor tracks across the wolds, with deviations to the manors and monasteries who owned salt pits and springs in Droitwich. They left the high country to come to Lechlade and from there the journey would be continued by water.

The ridgeways, the Roman roads and Saxon droves and the meandering medieval ways linking villages to small towns have long been incorporated into the modern road system, but there remain here and there, often when the original line has been diverted, a few stretches of unmetalled track kept in use as foot-paths or because they provide access to fields, and on these quiet reaches a traveller can still find a sense of kinship with those earlier men who walked the old green roads, and enjoy in solitude the wide skies and spreading prospects of Cotswold.

CONDICOTE LANE

If one could imagine Condicote village taken out of its frame of high encircling wolds and wider skies the fascination it holds for lovers of the Cotswold scene would surely disappear. Its few grey cottages and larger barns are homely, sturdy and without decoration, their siting haphazard. Most Cotswold buildings, however humble look as if they had been set down in just the right place to blend into the landscape, but at

Condicote this is not so evident. On a bleak day one wonders why the original settlers chose such a remote desolate spot, and even in the sunniest weather it has few charms for the tourist in search of the picturesque; an elaborate late Norman doorway in its tiny church, a fourteenth-century Wayside Cross with its original steps but without its head, are its recognizable graces. The situation is all, for it is a place haunted by the long-forgotten past. Spend but an hour there and the isolation of its position works upon the imagination.

In the vicinity are two prehistoric earthworks, numerous tumuli, the meeting place of two ancient trackways. Condicote Lane, the more important of the two, coming from the crossing of the Dikler some half a mile east of Lower Slaughter and going across the wolds into Worcestershire, continued in use until drovers ceased to drive their cattle along its lonely reaches at the end of the last century.

The Cross is on the old road beside a spring, once the watering place for the village, and a powerful attraction on those high waterless wolds. One wonders how many wayfarers in the past journeying along the trackway stopped to drink there, and perhaps in medieval times stopped to rest on the steps, perhaps to pray for a safe journey's end. For those were the days when Condicote Lane was busier and more important than it is today.

17 Signposts

Plates 36 – 38

To the true traveller a signpost is more than a means of directing him to a certain place. It can be as romantic as a love story, as evocative as a smell, as nostalgic as an old song. It can symbolize the beginning of a new way of life or the coming to the end of an old one, and of all the objects man has invented to help him extend his knowledge of other places it has the most poetic content.

The earlier signposts were the handing-posts of the eighteenth century erected by private benefactors. The ends of the arms were shaped like hands, the fingers pointing the way adding a dramatic emphasis. Before then the stranger had to depend on human guides, though in the Campden district from 1612 until Sir Baptist Hickes's fine mansion was destroyed by the Royalists some thirty years later the lantern in the great dome served as a guide and comfort to benighted travellers lost on the unenclosed sheepwalks above the town.

Two of these old handing-posts survive in north Cotswolds. One, at a spot called Cross Hands, stands on a meeting place of four roads just before one comes to the crest of Broadway Hill, stretching out four gaunt iron hands with outstretched fingers on which are written: The Way to Warwick, the Way to Oxford, the Way to Gloster, the Way to Woster, the distances on them accurate within a mile or two. It was erected by one of the Izods of Campden in 1669 and local tradition says that the iron spike at the top was used to impale sheep-stealers and other robbers.

Its gaunt and rather sinister appearance may be the reason for this horrid tale. Algernon Gissing's little book on Broadway written at the beginning of the century describes it thus: 'Flung upon the skyline between the trees, to the ancient traveller its suggestion must have been one of warning, even of terror . . . pointing in affright over the desolate wolds their action, belying their innocent words, says, "Fly! Fly! Anywhere but here – speed!"'

The other old handing-post is Teddington Hands, where the road from Evesham meets the A438. The direction hands come out of a stone pillar and once pointed towards six roads, as the pillar proclaims:

> Edward Attwood of the Vine Tree
> At the first time erected me
> And freely he did this bestow
> Strange travellers the way to show.

Today Teddington Hands looks forlorn and curiously ineffective in the midst of roads it no longer serves, roads filled with the rattle and roar of great lorries and fast main road traffic, but in its day many a lost traveller must have blessed the man who put it up.

Some twenty years or so ago before the upland cross-roads were staggered to make the crossings safer for motorists there was a modern signpost on one of the oldest signposts of all, Crickley Barrow, where six lonely hill roads met at an ancient six-went way, two from the Foss Way, one from Coln St Denis, Eastington and Northleach. Crickley Barrow is now a low collection of shapeless heaps but in its original crouching form it must have been a prehistoric meeting place when the trackway coming to it from the north was one of the through ways across the wolds, and later in medieval times part of a Saltway coming from Droitwich to the Thames at Lechlade.

There are several signposts on Cotswold which point routes that were once part of a network of prehistoric and Roman roads.

One of these is at Bull's Cross, where the B4070 from Stroud to Cheltenham meets the line of the Cotswold Ridgeway coming from Wickridge Hill and then goes with it, ascending all the time to reach Birdlip and 975 feet at the top of the escarpment. There is also a milestone at this road junction, made out of an old mounting block, another example of the Cotsaller's habit of adapting discarded material to a new use.

Two minor roads branch at Bull's Cross, one to Painswick, the other to the little village of Sheepscombe, both important centres of the woollen industry that flourished in South Cotswold from the seventeenth century to the late nineteenth century. Today the roads are mostly concerned with local and tourist traffic but in those days they carried wool, yarn and cloth to and from the clothing mills on the streams running through the Painswick valley, and the big Wight's Mill at Sheepscombe on its own brook. Now these mills are names only, some of the buildings have disappeared altogether, others have been turned into farmhouses and other dwellings so peaceful and secluded in their picturesque setting of woods, streams and hillsides that it is hard to imagine the days when hundreds of workers were employed there.

Tom Long's Post, another signpost around which stories have gathered, stands at a high, lonely cross-roads on Minchinhampton Common, a point where six roads open to the green plateau come together. It is an unbenign spot when the hill mists thicken over the vast spread of the Common and wrap it in brooding silence or when the chill winds of evening empty it of wayfarers, picnic parties and lovers as the distant hill-tops fade out in the dusk. It is then one remembers the ancient people who raised the earthworks on the Common, and the highwaymen who, tradition says, were buried there and whose restless spirits haunt its wide expanse.

18 Churchyards

Plates 39–41

One does not usually associate the Cotswold scene with romantic ruins; at the Dissolution Henry VIII's hatchet man Thomas Cromwell did his work of destroying the great religious houses of Gloucestershire too well. Winchcombe Abbey has entirely vanished and the few fragments of Hailes, now National Trust under the guardianship of the Ministry of Public Building and Works, are too well kept, shadow being more important than light, 'for the beams of lightsome day, gild but to flout the ruins grey'. A certain unruliness of vegetation helps to create the right atmosphere of mystery, but this is a quality which quickly disappears under the eye of officialdom however enlightened.

There are a few deserted churches in solitary places, the result of a village moving to a new site after the Plague or when it was depopulated by the making of sheep-walks, but in the last few years these churches have been partially restored for safety reasons, their interiors kept garnished by a few loving hands. They are sad places, without the titillation of romance.

But there is one place which still maintains this intangible and outmoded fantasy, a place rich in ancient story and ancient memories where one feels the ghosts of the past must surely mingle. This is the old churchyard at Woodchester, less than two miles south of Stroud, where the scattered fragments of a Norman church long since fallen into ruin can be seen among a collection of eighteenth-century tombs in a luxuriant woodland setting. No land-

owner, in the days when the practice was common, wishing to add a look of sentimental antiquity to his pleasure gardens by the erection of mock ruins, could have improved upon the crumbling wall, the empty window, the creeper-clad Gothic arch and the Norman doorway with its band of carved ornament above the pillars, ornament obviously cut with a chisel and not hewn out with an axe. Jane Austen's heroine who revelled in Northanger Abbey would have enjoyed these ancient stones, and Victorian young ladies and their drawing masters in search of the picturesque would have found them an ideal subject.

Beneath the churchyard lies part of the foundations of an important Roman villa whose tessellated pavement is occasionally laid bare from its protective covering of sand. The original builders of the church were unaware of what lay below their chosen site, but the existence of the mosaics was known in 1693 according to Bishop Gibson's edition of Camden's *Britannia*, though it was not until about a hundred years later, in 1789, that Samuel Lysons began his excavations, after the digging of a vault for an interment had laid open part of the pavement. Before this time, however, grave-diggers had complained of the difficulty of deep digging when their spades were obstructed by the hard Roman cement.

Some of the tombs placed above the burials are fine examples of the monumental mason's craft. They were made when the clothing trade of the district was flourishing and a new middle and upper class had emerged. The raising of an ornate tomb had become not only fashionable but an expression of the family's importance, taking the place of the brasses of the medieval woolmen, the effigies and memorial monuments of the old lords of the manor.

The tombs have several basic shapes, rectangular, six-sided, pepper-pot, and combinations of all three. Some are lidded with plain heavy stone slabs, others have moulded courses decreasing to a rounded top, there are domes finished with a ball on a small plinth, and bolster-like covers which may be a formalized representation of a corded wool-bale and which take on a darker hue

because the slanting lines deeply scored into the stone trap the damp and encourage moisture stains. The sides are ornamented with carved symbols of opulence, cornucopias, swelling fruit, swags of fruit and leaves, fat-cheeked cherubs, cockleshells, scrolls and curling acanthus, with an occasional skull to remind the living of man's mortality, but mostly the decoration suggests exuberance and not decline. The richness and variations in shape and adornment make one marvel at the skill of the masons who rang the changes of every pattern in the book, for one rarely finds two alike.

How bright they must have looked in the pristine glory of newly quarried stone and crisply cut decoration when first carried from the stone-mason's yard! They are more suitably clad in mourning today now that the people they commemorate have been long forgotten, for the wind and rain, the sun and mist of the past two centuries have muted the stone to a melancholy grey, rounded the sharp edges of the mouldings and over-run the decoration with traceries of lichen.

Nearly every Cotswold churchyard holds a few fine eighteenth-century table tombs, particularly in the south of the region where the cloth trade flourished. The largest and most distinguished collection must be at Painswick whose many wealthy clothiers were fortunate in having a famous monumental mason, John Bryan, living in the town. There is a less widely known example at Ozleworth, a remote village near Wotton-under-Edge, and in Quenington churchyard the tomb of Elinor Thomas, who died in 1697, finished with heavy moulding, plain panels and a carved shell at each end could serve to illustrate the more austere decoration of the seventeenth century before the heavy swags, the plump cherubs, the skulls and hourglasses and all the other obscure symbols of mortality from the Book of Emblems, used by the eighteenth-century monumental masons, became the fashion.

Elinor Thomas's tomb was renovated in 1957 by George Swinford and Albert Cass, and is proof that the old skill still survives and is used today.

19 The English Renaissance

Plates 42–44

Cotswold had its share in the wave of building influenced by the renaissance of classical learning and art which swept the country in the seventeenth and eighteenth centuries, for it came at a time when cloth manufacture, despite political, foreign and domestic troubles, brought considerable prosperity to the region: clothiers were going up in the social scale and in many instances had taken over the old manor houses from their former owners.

It is not the purpose of this book to discuss Palladian mansions such as Barnsley Park near Cirencester, though it might be mentioned that Sir Christopher Wren's greatest achievement, St Paul's, was built with the aid of several master masons from the Burford area of Cotswold including the Kempster families and the Strongs. We confine ourselves to the smaller architectural pleasures of the period.

As well as churches and new mansions designed entirely in the new style, scores of handsome porches and doorways were added to existing houses. In the south it was mainly the rich clothiers who brought their dwellings within the prevailing fashion, men familiar with the new ideas because their business took them to London and Bristol, both centres of the classical revival; and their womenfolk, already enjoying the silks, porcelain and other exotic furnishings brought home by the East India Company found the new persuasions irresistible.

The alterations were aimed at changing the façade and consisted

47

of classical-type porches, balustrades, sash windows and shell-headed doorways. Surprisingly, they fitted well into the old idiom, the nature of the stone subduing the severity of the lines and providing a medium in which they could exist together without discord.

The earlier work, when the new style was only just beginning to be accepted and grace and proportion were more important than weight and pompousness, gives the impression that the masons found fresh inspiration and skill in the English Renaissance, and doubtless those who studied the new patterns were those who prospered.

The two-storied Jacobean porch on the Elizabethan manor house at the southern end of Upper Slaughter is a good example of how gracefully the two styles can blend into each other. The perfection of the proportions of each part to the whole, the discretion of the mouldings and pilasters, the austerity of the ornament show a delicate perception of the classic spirit. Fine workmanship and well-chosen stone enhance these qualities. The house, with its twelve gables and roofed with ancient slates, is in the best Cotswold tradition; the porch adds a note of elegance to its quiet dignity and charm.

A shell-headed doorway became a much favoured addition to the Cotswold vernacular as the classical revival spread to the smaller town houses. At the time there were probably those who saw it as an upstart fashion ousting traditional design but today it harmonizes perfectly with its surroundings, giving the building a focal point the eye rests upon with pleasure. Whether one gets the low rambling kind of structure with added bays as the need for more accommodation arose, as one sees at the Swan Inn at Bibury, or the more compact and typical façade of St Mary's Mill House at Chalford, it looks equally fitting.

A humble example is the little lock-up at Bisley, built to accommodate two prisoners. One feels the builder was concerned with appearance as well as utility and, aware of the laws of proportion

governing the style, employed them to make a presentable façade. Two elegant curves lead up to a ball finial and above each narrow barred doorway is a semicircular window filled with an iron grille. A neat oval plaque gives the date, 1824. Only those on the outside, however, could appreciate these things, the interior being dark, dank and unwholesome.

20 Bread oven

Plate 45

An example of the countryman's instinct for using whatever came to hand can be seen in the tiling over the bread oven in the picture and in the economical arrangement of tiles over the little window and on each side of it to keep the rain from running down the plastered sides of the oven and the wall outside it.

This kind of oven, where bundles of brushwood were placed inside the cooking space, the ashes removed when it was burnt and the bread then left to bake in the heated cavity, was not confined to the Cotswolds but was common all over the country until the early 1900s, but here we see the oven given a distinctive Cotswold touch. In the same way a cottager who did not aspire to a porch would place a row of stone tiles above his cottage door to give a little protection from the weather, and so add a piquant finish to an otherwise plain front.

Utility was the chief reason for this and many another minor embellishment; charm crept in fortuitously, an afterthought, a little flourish like a curlicue at the end of a signature. The humbler cottages of the later nineteenth century and after seldom delight us in this way, for by this time canals, railroads and better transport generally meant that mass-produced materials from outside the area could be obtained more cheaply. The capacity for contrivance remained but the temper of the times was alien to the kind of homespun felicitous touches we admire today.

27 The river Coln at Ablington.

28 Low footbridge of three great slabs of worn stone over the
    Windrush at Kineton.
29 The Dun at Duntisbourne Leer almost laps the doorstep of a
    cottage.

30 Dipping place at Duntisbourne Abbots.

31 Seven Wells, Bisley, where springs gush out from spouts and gabled recesses in a stone wall, restored in 1863 in memory of Thomas Keble.

32 A romanized track near Condicote.

33 The way to Condicote.

34 A stretch of old road known
   as Condicote Lane.

35 Condicote Cross,
   a fourteenth-century wayfarers'
   cross standing by springs, a great
   meeting place in earlier times.

36 Tom Long's Post on the lonely cross-roads on Minchinhampton Common.

37 Milestone on an upping-block, Bull's Cross.

38 Izod's handing post erected in 1669 at Cross Hands above Chipping
Campden.

39 Ruins of old church at Woodchester, showing the late Norman archway.

40 Eighteenth-century tomb at Ozleworth.

41 Tomb at Ozleworth with domed cover.

42 Shell-headed porch, the Swan Inn, Bibury.

43 Two-storied porch of the old Manor House, Upper Slaughter, added in the seventeenth century to the original sixteenth-century house.

44 Lock-up of two cells at Bisley, dated 1824.

45 Bread oven, Caudle Green. A characteristic Cotswold finish is the use of stone slate to deflect the rain.

46 Scraper set in a cottage wall, Duntisbourne Abbots. An example of a local craftsman's ingenious use of an outdated stone structure.

47 A well at Oakridge, with the original bucket, still usable.

48 Saintbury Cross, with medieval shaft and steps.
49 Plain blocked-up Norman doorway at St Nicholas's Church, Saintbury.

50 The ancient sundial in low relief above the south doorway.

51 The 1914–1918 War Memorial, a water fountain, at Ablington, no longer in use.

52 Window of an outhouse in Winchcombe which may have come from the ruins of the old church replaced in 1465 by St Peter's.

53 Oval window at Chalford.

54 A fourteenth-century window in a barn at Leonard Stanley, once part of a complex of buildings belonging to the lost priory.

21 The scraper

Plate 46

Anyone who walks or works in the Cotswold countryside soon becomes aware of the remarkably adhesive quality of its soil in wet weather. Men and children, particularly, know that a clean kitchen floor soiled by muddy boots can provoke domestic discord, though gumboots have helped to lessen the problem in recent years. Before they came into common use, however, a scraper at the door was a necessary piece of domestic equipment. One does not usually connect it with Cotswold stone but the picture shows how this homely article was put together with a few blocks and the aid of a blacksmith to make yet another instance of the old saying that a true Cotsaller can do anything with stone except eat it.

Originally the stones could have been part of a structure over a springhead or dipping place in the days before water was piped to the village. At one time derelict buildings and even the foundations of Roman roads were regarded by local people as free quarries where stone could be taken for patching walls, gateposts or any other small building job. Nowadays worked stones have become valuable to the restorers of old cottages and no longer lie around for the taking.

The scraper is in a garden wall near the gate leading to a cottage door in Duntisbourne Abbots, and is yet another illustration of the way an object of utility can be pleasing to look at because it was evolved out of native wit and local material.

The same cottage has a porch with a miniature steep-pitched

roof in the Cotswold vernacular. The masons who built the old cottages would always ring the changes in porch design to give each cottage its own singularity. It is rarely one finds two of the same pattern side by side; individuality will out, however humble the dwelling. They are personal touches without ostentation, and while adding variety fit perfectly into the overall picture.

The cottages of Little Barrington, three miles west of Burford, grouped round part of the rim of a bowl-shaped green show this plainly. A diversity of porch and doorway gives each cottage, even those in a short terrace, a character of its own, yet all are at one with the ancient pollarded elms that share with them the half-circle of the outer edge of the green, and with the distant prospects of the wolds seen from the open road on the opposite side as it dips and rises on its way to other Windrush villages.

22 Well at Oakridge

Plate 47

In the old days lack of water was seldom a problem on Cotswold. Most of the villages came into being in the valleys whose little streams and brooks were fed by innumerable springs gushing from the hillsides. The settlements on the high wolds, however, often had to rely upon wells whose water, deliciously cold and fresh after coming through the cleansing limestone, is sometimes recalled nostalgically by older natives on a hot day when they turn on their taps. But although there was never any lack of water this did not mean it was always easily obtained for domestic use. Larger houses and farms had their own wells, but smaller cottages often had to share with neighbours some distance away. A central watering-place, possibly on the village green, was occasionally provided by the local squire interested in the improvement of his territory; an additional benefit to the women being that it supplied a natural meeting place where village gossip could be exchanged.

This well at Oakridge is still usable and keeps its original bucket. It is interesting also for the stonework of the shaft, a fine example of circular drystone walling. When one remembers the confined space in which the waller had to work, the airlessness and poor light, this would be considered a considerable feat of craftsmanship today; to the man who made the well it was probably a job to be done like any other which came his way, the satisfaction he must have felt in using his skill a secret bonus he paid himself.

23 **Saintbury**

Plates 48–50

The tiny village of Saintbury has a special place in the hearts of those who love the Cotswolds because of its association with Algernon Gissing who wrote about it with such grace and understanding in *The Footpath-way in Gloucestershire*. His book was published in 1924, but the picture he paints so lovingly is of life in a remote hamlet at the turn of the century when differences between country and town were far greater, in spirit as well as substance. In the last few years most of the cottages have become residences with the more picturesque embellishments of rural England imposed upon them. For example when the villages planted cherry trees in the old days the beauty of their flowering was a by-product and fruit the main concern; the new villagers plant ornamental cherries to keep alive the tradition of Cherry Wake Sunday.

Saintbury has the best of both worlds with its feet in the Vale and its head in the hills. It begins around the ancient Cross that stands on the low road from Stratford to Broadway where a steep lane deeply sunken between tall tree-shaded banks branches from the main road to serve the church, the few farms and dwellings half hidden by great elms and orchard trees that make up the rest of the village. The lane leads to the top of the escarpment overlooking the Vale of Evesham with tremendous views across the vale to Bredon, the Malverns and the far blue shadows that are the Welsh mountains.

Domesday records one mill, but later when the manor belonged to Evesham Abbey there were two. Sir Robert Atkyns, in his *History of Gloucestershire* published in 1712, gives the number of houses as fifty-four, the population about 200. Some fifty years later Samuel Rudder in his *New History of Gloucestershire* records only thirty-one houses and 138 inhabitants, suggesting that Enclosure could be the reason for the decline. The decline continued, and on the War Memorial outside the church only one name from the Second World War is inscribed.

The steps and shaft of the Cross go back to the early fifteenth century; the original head was probably destroyed by Cromwell's soldiers, its position on a main road making it an easy target. Since then it has had several different heads, a painted pineapple in the eighteenth century, and a Maltese Cross. It now bears a sundial with a plain cross on the apex. Until recently there were local people who remembered its serving as a resting place for funerals on the way to the little church on the hillside, and very welcome the rest must have been before the cortège made its way up the winding rutted track.

The way to the church goes off almost secretly from the lane as if to a private drive; there is yet another short climb up a grassy bank to the churchyard gate and a stiffish lift of worn steps brings one to the church revealed against a background of tall trees and the continuing slope of the hillside. It is one of the few Cotswold churches with a tower and a spire, and the best view of it is not from the hill but from the vale. Despite its small size it shines out from the hillside with startling clarity, the distance seeming to have no diminishing effect; on a dull day it still points the way to the Cotswolds for travellers on the low road as it has done for the past six hundred years.

On the exterior south wall above a filled-in Norman doorway with a lozenge-patterned tympanum is an ancient sundial in a remarkably good state of preservation, reputed to date from Saxon times. The outer circle has a low raised edge and within it carved

in relief instead of the usual incised lines are three radii each with a cross at the end indicating the times of the services of Mass, Sext and Compline. There are two other ancient carved stones: one above the Norman doorway within the porch shows a hideous face; the other, in the splay of the window of the south wall, is a small crudely cut figure of a man with stumps for legs and a square body resembling a primitive idol which could have come from the original Saxon church.

24 Stone steps at Ablington
Plate 51

Ablington on the Coln near Bibury has several attractive features. There are the manor house, the home of Arthur Gibbs, scholar, foxhunter and fisherman, who wrote *A Cotswold Village* as an expression of his deep pleasure in the life of a Cotswold squire; a splendid barn buttressed like a cathedral; and a road leading out of the valley to the Saltway and the more austere landscape and invigorating winds of the uplands. And, of course, the river with wooded steeps falling to the water's edge, a stone bridge where trout lurk in the shadows of its arches and silvery willows are reflected in the shallow shimmering river; the picturesqueness of the whole, I imagine, was not so discreet and well-groomed when Arthur Gibbs lived there at the end of the last century.

There is also a memorial to the men of Ablington who died in the 1914-1918 war, a water-tap in a rectangular recess in the wall below the road, a place where the thirsty could drink, though the metal cup on a chain has now disappeared. The tap is reached by a low flight of semicircular stone steps, plain and unassuming yet satisfying to the eye. It is true that steps of any kind contain the elements of drama, as designers of stage sets know well, and that their function has become impregnated with abstract interpretations, but in this case they have little dramatic value. Age also has not added its patina of sentiment, like the old worn steps of churches hollowed with the wear of centuries.

Those who remember the dead of the 1914-1918 war grow

fewer with each passing year and soon they will have passed into history. We are left with four names and a simple inscription on a bronze tablet, and four graduated steps widening to a full half-circle by the water-tap. Whether we look at them with this awareness or regard them as a convenient way of stepping down from the road it cannot be denied that the stone and the mason who shaped the stones worked together in the traditional Cotswold harmony of man and his material. The eye does not always have to rest on masterpieces to find content.

25 Cotswold windows

Plates 52–54

The typical window-openings of the Cotswold vernacular have drip mouldings with the lights separated by stone mullions, but in several villages one can find on farm buildings and dwellings carved and decorated windows that have come from an old church or religious house and been inserted as decoration, to preserve an ancient piece of stone-work, or because it was cheaper and easier to use stone already shaped.

Before the fashion of renovating old cottages gave old worked stone a high value, derelict buildings were often used as a free quarry by local inhabitants looking for material for make-do-and-mend or do-it-yourself jobs, and as any true Cotsaller naturally preferred stone to any other material one can find numerous homely examples of the ingenious use of discarded workable and carved stones. The drastic restorers of churches in the nineteenth century threw out many such fragments.

Antiquarians of the last century occasionally exchanged interesting bits amongst themselves, such as a Norman window from Daglingworth said to have been given to Barnsley church by a local clergyman. This can befuddle the local historian and provide fascinating problems for investigation.

The window in the little building in Winchcombe, now used as a lavatory, perhaps most of the building itself, may have come from Winchcombe Abbey after the Dissolution, or from the old parish church of St Peter's rebuilt by Abbot William of Winch-

combe in the fifteenth century. To quote from the Rev. David Boyce's notes in his translation of *The Landboc*, volume 1, this was 'where stood the old church of St Peter, then in decay, at the west end of the Abbey Church'.

The traceried window in the barn by the church at Leonard Stanley could have come from the old Priory whose conventual buildings were mainly destroyed except for parts treated as farm buildings, and later attached to a Priory House erected in 1740: the splendour and dignity of tithe barns are in their size and proportion, and they were rarely decorated with traceried windows.

The oval window at Chalford has the look of antiquity, and would appear to be a local fashion in ornament, for I have not seen the pattern elsewhere on Cotswold.

Index

RUSSIA, SLAVDOM
AND THE WESTERN WORLD

Some books by the same author

DOSTOEVSKY

IBSEN

NIETZSCHE

TOLSTOY

PUSHKIN AND RUSSIAN LITERATURE

STUDIES IN EUROPEAN LITERATURE

ASPECTS OF MODERNISM

RUSSIAN AUTHORS (N.Y.)

AN INTRODUCTION TO THE RUSSIAN NOVEL

FROM PUSHKIN TO MAYAKOVSKY

GOGOL

GONCHAROV

LERMONTOV

etc.

RUSSIA, SLAVDOM AND THE WESTERN WORLD

by

JANKO LAVRIN

PUBLISHED BY

GEOFFREY BLES
LONDON

© JANKO LAVRIN, 1969

SBN: 7138 0254 5

Printed in Great Britain
by Cox & Wyman Ltd, Fakenham

Published by
GEOFFREY BLES LTD
52 Doughty Street, London, W.C.1
36–38 Clarence Street, Sydney
353 Elizabeth Street, Melbourne
246 Queen Street, Brisbane
CML Building, King William Street, Adelaide
Lake Road, Northcote, Auckland
100 Lesmill Road, Don Mills, Ontario
P.O. Box 8879, Johannesburg
P.O. Box 834, Cape Town
P.O. Box 2800, Salisbury, Rhodesia

Contents

The substance of several of these chapters has previously appeared in The Russian Review (Stanton University) to the Editors of which my thanks are due.

CHAPTER ONE

The Two Worlds

I

Any serious discussion of Russia and the Russians invariably tempts one to compare them with Europe or with the Western world in general. Needless to say, such comparisons are often but guesswork consisting of plausible half-truths which can always be modified according to one's prejudices and predilections. Still, the fact that Russia has played and is playing such an important part in contemporary history makes the effort to understand her better almost obligatory for anyone who is anxious to get familiar with some of the more hidden recesses of present-day discords and tensions. For the "iron curtain", separating Russia from the West, is not only a matter of political and social ideology, but also of psychology – with all its elusive imponderables, its conscious or unconscious antagonisms. These may be of long standing and more complex, even more deeply rooted, than one would like to think, but they may not be irrelevant, where a genuine rapprochement between Russia and Europe is concerned. After all it is not without significance that the political and cultural annexation of Russia to Europe, which took place at the beginning of the eighteenth century, had met at the outset with strong opposition to the reforms of Peter the Great among the Russians themselves. Moreover, towards the middle of the nineteenth century, when the process of Europeanisation had already a number of vital achievements to its credit, the dilemma of Russia and Europe kept cropping up again and again, notably in the disputes between the Russian Westerners on the one hand and their Slavophile opponents on the other.

The real cause of those disputes was, of course, provided by the two entirely different approaches to Europe herself. Whereas the

9

liberal-minded Westerners considered Russia a backward part of Europe and therefore advocated (quite in the spirit of Peter I) a thorough Europeanisation of her vast territory, the Slavophiles – or at least the majority of them – regarded Peter's reforms as a mistake. They insisted that Russia not only had a mentality but also a culture and a historical destiny of her own the essence of which was different from, or – in its basic trend – even "superior" to, that of Europe. During the controversy between the two factions the Slavophiles were doing their utmost to point out those specific Russian characteristics which might have served as illustrations of such "superiority". They idealised the pre-Petrine past of their country in a manner designed to prove that they were right. Yet their claims were bound to be inadequate for the very reason that they were conditioned not only by frequent historical inaccuracies, but by all sorts of romantic blinkers whenever the differences – whether psychological or otherwise – between Russia and Europe, between East and West, were in question.

It stands to reason that the basic features of the so-called *homo sapiens* are more or less the same throughout the human kind. In what they differ, though, is the proportion between them, their stage of development, as well as those peculiarities which result from the environment, the climate and the vagaries of the terrain a nation or a race has to cope with. Thus the endless plains of Russia and her erratic climate with its extremes of hot and cold were bound to affect her inhabitants accordingly. Love of extremes and an aversion to pettiness and pedantry are among the very first features an outsider cannot miss when watching the average Russians. And so is their peculiar passivity and frequent careless-ness. Unpredictable and not exactly reliable or disciplined in ordinary walks of life, they are yet unsurpassed in endurance which, in their case, is often tinged with fatalism, or even with a resigned cult of suffering hardly thinkable in Western Europeans, let alone Americans. It is this trait in particular that enables them to put up with the most difficult conditions and to wait until the worst is over. This patient resignation, on the other hand, makes the Russians store up their energies in order to meet all sorts of

perilous historical emergencies, no matter how great the ordeals and sacrifices incurred. This was how Russia survived the Tartar yoke, the chaotic "troubled period" at the beginning of the seventeenth century, not to mention her triumph over Napoleon's invasion in 1812, or Hitler's invasion in 1941. Another feature which can hardly escape the attention of a foreigner is the spontaneous emotionality of the Russians as well as their warmhearted gregariousness. In a small, hard-working and thickly populated country one is almost instinctively inclined to see in a newcomer a potential rival or even enemy, whereas in a vast realm such as Russia he is more likely to be welcomed as a guest whose company may enliven the tedium of a monotonous existence. On the other hand, a certain lack of self-assertive egotism in the Western sense makes the Russians all the more receptive, eager to imitate and to be influenced from outside. Yet once they have been stimulated in this way they frequently overtake or even outstrip those whose examples they follow.

This need of incentive and stimulation from outside may have been one of the reasons why some observers are prone to regard, whether rightly or wrongly, the Russians as a "feminine" race. Bismarck himself once referred to them as the "feminine half of humanity" (*die weibliche Haelfte der Menschheit*). The well-known existentialist philosopher Nicholas Berdyayev, too, insists in one of his works on the femininity of the Russian character, while Alexander Herzen uses the same label in his brilliant book of memoirs, *My Past and Thoughts*.* But he adds several other features (both positive and negative) to substantiate his own judgement. "The essentially receptive character of the Slavs [in this case the Russians]," Herzen says, "their femininity, their lack of initiative, and their great capacity for assimilation and adaptation, make them pre-eminently a people that stands in need of the other peoples; they are not fully self-sufficing. Left to themselves the Slavs readily lull themselves to sleep with their own songs, as a Byzantine chronicler observed. Awakened by others they go to

---

* Translated by Constance Garnett (Chatto & Windus). Quotation is taken from this work.

farthest consequences; there is no people which could more deeply and completely absorb the thoughts of other peoples while yet remaining true to itself. The persistent misunderstanding which exists today, as it has for a thousand years, between the German and the French peoples does not exist between them and the Slavs. The craving to give itself up and be carried away is innate in their sympathetic, readily assimilative, receptive nature." As though corroborating the Russians, "great capacity for assimilation and adaptation", one of Dostoevsky's heroes (Versilov in *A Raw Youth*) sees in this feminine feature an advantage in so far as it enhances their universal sympathy and understanding, while yet fully preserving thereby their own national type. "A Frenchman," he says, "can serve not only his France, but humanity, only on condition that he remains French to the utmost possible degree, and it's the same for the Englishman and the German. Only to the Russian, even in our day, has been vouchsafed the capacity to become most of all Russian only when he is most European. That is the essential difference between us Russians and all the rest, and in that respect the position in Russia is as nowhere else. I am in France a Frenchman, with a German I am a German, with the ancient Greek I am a Greek, and by that very fact I am most typically Russian, for I am bringing out our leading idea."*

These definitions of the Russian character – by Russians – can be completed by some further remarks. If an Englishman, for example, makes one think of a secluded island (full of carefully camouflaged pitfalls and stumbling-blocks), a Russian finds his symbolic simile more easily in the broad and open steppe where everything can happen all of a sudden without any transition and on a large scale. It was the steppe which nourished as it were a Russian's nomadic propensity and turned him into a restless wanderer with no profound attachment to any particular place, however attached he may have remained to his "Mother Russia" as a whole. It is partly for this reason that even nowadays he seems to be less tied to a settled bourgeois existence than, let us say, a Frenchman, an Englishman, or a German. Nor does he mind

* Quoted from *A Raw Youth*, translated by Constance Garnett (Heinemann).

squandering his earthly possessions with the same reckless *largesse* which is typical of his excessive hospitality. Even his idea of freedom differs from the Western conceptions of political and civic liberties in so far at least as in his psychological make-up there still lurks a hidden corner where the lure of the anarchic "letting oneself go" persists and where the very endlessness of the steppe absolves him as it were from any sense of measure whether in good or evil. And as for external laws and regulations, they often have to be imposed upon him, or even tyranically enforced in order to be obeyed at all. A Russian hates impersonal or imposed drudgery of any kind, but he can be an enthusiastic worker when putting a "meaning" and the whole of his personality into what he has to do. In human contacts, too, he prefers the dictates of spontaneous personal sympathy to any obligatory and stereotyped formalities, even though his childlike (and at times childish) lack of ceremony does not exclude a fair amount of familiarity which may become unpleasant when combined with all sorts of intimate avowals and questions. But generally speaking, one is not wide of the mark by saying that it is precisely on account of some of his so-called "feminine" characteristics that a Russian secretly admires certain disciplined and sober "masculine" elements of the West. He is drawn towards them even when pretending to hate things European.

Whereas the climate of Russia was likely to foster quite a few extremes in the character and the mentality of her inhabitants, the infinite expanse of the Russian landscape has been responsible for their peculiar perception of space and time which may not tally with the one typical of the crowded West. When travelling from the Caucasus to the north, I once asked at a railway junction how long it would take from there to St. Petersburg. "Only three days," was the answer, but with the stress on *only*, no matter whether this referred to space or to time. Endowed with his traditional lack of hurry, a Russian knows that he can afford to wait when wait he must. The monotony of the landscape, on the other hand, has infected him also with "moodiness" and that nostalgic melancholy which can be felt in the Russian folksongs,

in the music of Tchaikovsky, and even in Russian *belles lettres*, notably in some of her poets. This curious melancholy, called *toská*, yet finds its frequent release in excesses of all kinds: in alchohol (which in a Russian is a psychological rather than physical need), in "Dionysian" dancing, in sensuous orgies, or even in religious ecstasies indulged in by some of the Russian sects.

2

In their steady expansion from the Kievan territory towards East and North-East the Russians never exterminated local populations. They infiltrated and absorbed them instead. In this way they acquired a number of Finnish, Turano–Mongolian, Tartar and other Eastern ingredients which may have imbued their Slav blood and mentality with several discordant elements not easily balanced. Or to quote Nicholas Berdyayev, "the Russians are a people in the highest degree polarised: they are a conglomeration of contradictions. One can be charmed by them, one can be disillusioned. The unexpected is always to be expected from them. They are as a people capable in the highest degree of inspiring both intense love and violent hatred. . . . The inconsistency and complexity of the Russian soul may be due to the fact that in Russia two streams of world history – East and West – jostle and influence one another. The Russian people is not purely European and it is not purely Asiatic. Russia is a complete section of the world – a colossal East–West. It unites two worlds, and within the Russian soul two principles are always engaged in strife – the Eastern and the Western. . . . In the Russian soul there is a sort of immensity, vagueness, a predilection for the infinity, such as is suggested by the great plain of Russia. For this reason the Russian people have found difficulty in achieving mastery over these vast expanses and in reducing them to orderly shape. There has been a vast elemental strength in the Russian people combined with a comparatively weak sense of form. The Russians have not been in any sense a people of culture, as the peoples of Western Europe have been, they have rather been a people of revelation and

inspiration. They have not been given to moderation and have readily gone to extremes."*

One cannot but agree with Berdyayev. Yet with all the actual or potential elements of chaos agitating the Russian character, a careful observer is bound to come to the conclusion that this is not the chaos of decay but of growth. For underneath it a tremendous vitality can be felt, the kind of vitality which only needs adequate channels in order to produce something momentous – even when these channels are full of wellnigh insurmountable obstacles. During the entire Tsarist period Russia had to contend with such obstacles in the shape of a regime which was not only despotic but corrupt to a degree. How difficult these conditions must have been at times can be gathered from the observations of numerous witnesses. One of these was Dr. E. Dillon – an Irish scholar who lived for years in Russia and eventually published, as far back as 1895, his *Russian Characteristics* (under the *nom de plume* of E. Lanin). In that book he summed up his general impressions as follows: "By nature the Russians are richly endowed; a keen, subtle understanding, remarkable quickness of apprehension; a sweet forgiving temper; a rude, persuasive eloquence, to which may be added an imitative faculty positively simian in range and intensity, constitute no mean outfit even for a people with the highest destinies in store. But these gifts, destined to bring forth abundant fruit under favourable circumstances, are turned into curses by political, social and religious conditions which make their free exercise and development impossible."

The corruption of the autocratic system was certainly more than likely to distort some of the best Russian features. But the population was in no two minds about it. In no European country was there a greater gap between the government and the governed than there was in Tsarist Russia. The authorities may have been feared but they were not respected: cheating them was almost tantamount to a moral virtue. And since the official Orthodox Church, too, was largely on the side of the government, its prestige (among the intellectuals at any rate) was bound to suffer.

* Quoted from N. Berdyayev's *The Russian Idea*, tr. by R. F. French (Bles).

The bulk of the left-wing intelligentsia was either agnostic, or else indifferent to religion; and as for the folk-masses, their Orthodoxy had a character of its own. It was not differentiated either from folklore or from superstition; but at its best it testified to the deep religious sense of the people, to their spirituality and even their eschatological expectations which often served as the only solace in the hardships they had to bear.

Moreover, sympathy, pity and compassion were also quite the usual feature of the Russian masses even when running parallel with cruelty, moral weakness and anarchy. The two strains, however contradictory, used to exist side by side, illustrating as it were Berdyayev's remark about the polarity of the Russian character. To quote Dr. Dillon once again, in Russia the "most damnable lie, the lie that blasts and kills, is sometimes uttered with apparent reluctance, with visible pity clothed in a voice trembling with compassion – a voice that seems to come from the heart, and go straight to the heart, pleading as it were for the wretched creature whom it dooms to ruin". On the other hand, a Russian who is painfully aware of his own wickedness and at the same time too weak or too self-divided to abstain from it may genuinely regret the misdeeds perpetrated by him. His moral aftermath may in fact become so strong indeed as to compel him not only to repent but to confess publicly and even exaggerate the evil nature of his guilt. Russian literature abounds in such confessions. And does not even Tolstoy accuse himself (in his personal *Confession*) of such crimes and indignities as no one would ever think of taking literally?

An exaggerated feeling of one's guilt and sinfulness is more than likely to save one from moral smugness, from the idiotic snobbery of "I am holier than thou". But it is also ready to infect one with disrespect for human beings whom one considers at least as unreliable, bad and guilty as oneself. It is enough to combine such a "knowing" attitude with the frustrated moral yearning and the undisciplined vitality of a basically good man in order to obtain the somewhat gushing broadness of a Mitya Karamazov – perhaps the most Russian type depicted in fiction. All things considered, the Russians represent a younger, more juvenile racial age and

consciousness than could be said of the Western nations. Still, their youth is not only an excuse, but also a promise – a promise of growth towards maturity even though in their case this process may differ from that in the West. There were in fact two important events which had set the Russians, at the very beginning of their history, more or less apart from Western Europe. One of these was their adherence to the Byzantine type of Christianity, and the other the Tartar invasion. Hence it may not be amiss to sum up, very briefly, at least the main phases of that evolution which was largely responsible for the ambivalent attitude of Russia towards Europe – an attitude of estrangement on the one hand, and of her attraction to the West on the other.

When the Grand Duke Vladimir of Kiev imposed (as late as the end of the tenth century) the Byzantine type of Christianity upon his subjects, he may have done this mainly for political reasons. The consequences, however, were far reaching not only politically but also spiritually and psychologically. For in contrast to the active, legalistic and hierarchic Roman Catholicism, Byzantine Christianity was contemplative, passive, more mystical than rationalistic. In some of its features it was also rather democratic and jealously suspicious of the Christian West. Nevertheless, the early rulers of Kievan Russia regarded themselves and their subjects as part of Europe and did not cut themselves off from her. They also intermarried with her royal families. One daughter of Vladimir's immediate successor, Yaroslav the Wise, was married to the king of France, another to the king of Hungary, and a third to the king of Norway. But after the schism in 1054 a gradual estrangement between Kievan Russia and the Roman Catholic West became unavoidable. The most formidable barrier between the two was erected however by the Tartar domination which lasted, roughly, from 1240 until 1480.

The Tartar period of Russian history, with its scant respect for human personality and its servile worship of might *qua* might, was bound to leave some unpleasant traces in the Russian character. On the other hand, it was during the Tartar yoke that the Orthodox Church, with her spiritual leadership and her numerous

monasteries, provided the only comfort for the afflicted people who were convinced that such an ordeal had been imposed upon Russia by God as a penalty for her sins. The strange Russian notion of a people's collective guilt before God – implying a strong group-consciousness – probably goes back to those times. And so does the Russian acceptance of suffering as something that has to be endured in order to expiate one's personal as well as collective transgressions. And the greater the suffering the sooner one is likely to placate God's anger. No wonder Dostoevsky wrote in his *Diary of an Author* that the "need of suffering in its extremest form is the basic need of the Russian people".

Meanwhile the centre of the Russian political life had been transferred from Kiev in the steppe to Moscow which was situated in the safer and better protected forest region. And since the main concern of the Tartars was tribute, the Moscow Grand Dukes, cunning and adroit as they were, succeeded in obtaining the right to collect taxes from other Russian principalities under the Tartars. This enhanced the prestige of Moscow as the rallying point for the whole of Russia, especially after Dmitry Donskoy had inflicted the first major defeat upon the Tartar army on the Kulikovo Field in 1380. Exactly a hundred years later the Grand Duke Ivan III (1462–1505) (who was married to the Byzantine Princess Sophia Paleologue) refused to pay any further tribute to the Golden Horde, and this was the end of the Tartar domination. His grandson Ivan IV (1533–1584), better known as Ivan the Terrible, conquered – with the help of foreign technicians – the Tartar capital Kazan itself. He then extended the Russian territory right down to Astrakhan on the Caspian Sea and added to his realm also most of Siberia.

The two hundred and forty odd years of the Tartar domination widened the gap between Muscovy and the West until the two were facing each other almost like two different worlds. For that was the period during which Western Europe had been passing through the Renaissance, with its gospel of individual freedom and its gradual secularisation of culture. Nor did Russia take part in the Reformation, in the birth of European science and technique, or

in the struggle of philosophic thought to make itself independent of theology. This does not mean that there was no intercourse whatever. Novgorod on the Volkhov river and Pskov had been in constant trading relations with Sweden as well as with the German Hansa. A considerable portion of the former Russian territory (notably the Ukraine, together with Kiev) went to Poland and Lithuania both of which were united in 1386. This brought its population into a closer contact with the West. And once Muscovy had thrown off the Tartar yoke, her own contacts with Western Europe were on the increase. Such contacts had become quite lively already under Ivan III, who had invited to Moscow a number of Italian architects (Aristotele Fioraventi of Bologna, Pietro Solari, and others) to begin with. It was with their help that he was able to build the walls of the Kremlin as well as the fine Kremlin churches, the Coronation church (*Uspensky Sobor*) included. There was also an influx of foreign engineers, technicians, traders, artisans and even soldiers who found Muscovy a profitable region for their services. This influx was welcomed by Ivan IV under whose rule trade with the West began to flourish.* The so-called German [i.e. Foreign] Quarter (*Nemetskaya Sloboda*) not far from the Kremlin was now growing to a respectable settlement in which all sorts of foreigners – Dutch, Germans, Scots, English, Swedes and even French – lived according to their own European standards so different from those of the illiterate and primitive Russian population. The very gap between the two was bound, however, to make the Russians keenly aware of their own backwardness, of their inferiority with regard to Europe. Such awareness was yet combined with secret resentment – a mood which required at least some compensation, and this was found in the assumption of Muscovite supremacy in matters of religion.

It should be borne in mind that after the fall of Constantinople in 1453 to the Turks the Muscovite rulers began to regard them-

---

* It was under Ivan IV or Ivan the Terrible that the English exploration of the North-East Passage resulted in Chancelour's visit to Moscow where he obtained special privileges for trade with England.

selves as successors to Byzantium. Under Vasily III (1505–1533) Moscow was actually proclaimed the "third Rome" and the only focus of true Christianity. But Moscow in this capacity meant nothing less than Byzantine Caesaropapism, suspicious of things and ideas that came from the "heretical" West. The centre of gravity immediately after the liberation from the Tartar yoke was, of course, upon the "gathering of Russian lands" – a process which reached the peak of ruthlessness under Ivan the Terrible. But even so after his death in 1584 Russia was plunged into a series of crises. His successor Boris Godunov promulgated the fateful law by virtue of which the peasants were reduced to actual serfdom; they were tied almost like slaves to big landowners in order to provide reliable labour for the "serving nobility". There followed the "troubled period" with the false Dimitry, the Polish invasions and the kind of chaos which threatened the very existence of Russia. Yet this crisis, too, like so many others, was weathered by the people, and with the election of the first Romanov to the throne (1613), things began to look brighter.

From that time on the rapprochement between Russia and the West was stepped up. In the middle of the seventeenth century – in 1654, to be precise – most of the Ukraine, with her Orthodox Cossacks, turned against Poland and joined Russia. Kiev, the capital of the Ukraine, thus became a mediator between Muscovy and the West. A number of Kievan monks were invited to Moscow where they taught in the newly founded Theological College – the first great-Russian institution aiming at higher learning. In the second half of the seventeenth century the "German" Quarter in Moscow suddenly became rather important in so far as the prospective Tsar Peter I spent much of his boyhood in that part of the town, where he acquired his notions of the European ways of life.

4

It is wrong to say that Peter the Great was the first to "open Russia's window on Europe". He only brought to a climax what

his predecessors had been doing since the liberation from the Tartars; but he did it on a colossal scale and with all that demonic vitality of his which refused to acknowledge any obstruction or limit. It was under him that thousands of European specialists and technicians were invited to come to Russia in order to help him in his task. He put an end to the "Moscow period" by inaugurating the "Petersburg period" of Russian history when laying the foundations of St. Petersburg as the new capital in 1702. But whereas from now on St. Petersburg was to be the bureaucratic Westernised capital of the Russian Empire, Moscow still remained the capital of the Russian people. Hence the difference and a certain antagonism between these two cities. At the same time Peter made a belated attempt to secularise Russian culture by separating it, as far as possible, from the Church in the days when Europe was already getting immersed in the thoroughly rationalistic eighteenth century. He abolished the Russian Patriarchate by turning the Orthodox Church herself into a department (the so-called Most Holy Synod) of the civil service.

Realising that in the process of her growth Russia needed a strong army and navy in the European style, he reorganised the entire administrative system according to the Western, or rather German, pattern. A number of important posts in the army, as well as in the navy which he had built up practically out of nothing, were allotted by him to foreigners. He was also responsible for the birth of the Russian Academy of Sciences, founded on the advice of the German philosophers Leibniz and Christian Wolff. Opened in 1725, it consisted in its early stages almost exclusively of foreign (mainly German) savants, since their Russian equivalents were not yet available. He knew that in order to breathe such an immense country as Russia would have to extend her boundaries to the Baltic on the one hand, and to the Black Sea on the other. Hence his campaigns against the Swedes in the north and against the Turks in the south. His conquest of the Baltic coast enabled him to get hold of its feudal German barons, who, from now on, kept supplying the country with experts, administrators, military commanders, and higher bureaucrats in

general. And these were far from being useless after the battle of Poltava (in 1709), when Russia had been turned into an undisputed great Power playing an increasingly important part in the affairs of Europe.

Utilitarian to the core, this tireless reformer paid attention above all to the technical and scientific achievements of Western Europe. It was these that he wanted to introduce to his own country in the first place. But as for the borrowed European manners and habits, they became obligatory for the nobility only. The peasants and the entire serfdom system remained intact. Education, too, was imposed only upon the children of the aristocracy and gentry. The gulf between the semi-Europeanised landowners and the illiterate peasantry thus became bigger than ever, for to the former social gap between the two castes there was now added an ever widening cultural gap as well. So much so that a large portion of the Russian nobility began to ape the Western ways of life and even to use in their families the French language in preference to their own. Many of them exaggerated their newly acquired Westernism: partly from a deep-seated feeling of inferiority with regard to Europe, and partly from a strong wish to dissociate, as far as possible, both Russia and themselves from the Asiatic East, since Muscovy before Peter the Great had been generally looked upon as part of Asia. The peasants, however, continued to stick to their own traditions and to the religious atmosphere of the pre-Petrine "Holy Russia". Certain communities, those of the "Old Believers"* for instance, saw in Peter's reforms nothing less than the work of the Antichrist. Some of them went so far indeed in their fanaticism that they preferred to burn themselves alive collectively rather than comply with the Tsar's interference with their rites and beliefs.

After a few minor setbacks during the reign of Peter's immediate successors the process of Europeanisation assumed a new

---

* The most stubborn and conservative members of the Orthodox Church who, in the seventeenth century, had refused to accept the reforms introduced by the Patriarch Nikon. This split was a great blow to the official Russian Church.

drive under Catherine II. This clever as well as highly energetic woman of German birth was proclaimed Empress of Russia by the aristocratic officers who, in a palace revolution (1762), "liquidated" her semi-imbecile husband Peter III. Like Peter the Great she too was helped by legions of foreign experts. It was under her rule that large territories of Poland (partitioned in 1772, 1793 and 1795) were allotted to Russia. Full of imperialistic ambitions, she conquered from Turkey the Crimea (in 1783) and a large stretch of the Black Sea coast. She also kept an eye on the Balkans where Russia was soon to pose as "protector of Christians" living under the Turkish yoke. As lewd as the age in which she lived and ruled, the "great Catherine" had at her disposal a host of able-bodied courtiers who competed with each other for due rewards. The nobles (to whom she was obliged for the throne) were now freed from their compulsory service to the State. As for her more enlightened propensities, she founded hundreds of schools and corresponded with advanced minds of the period, Voltaire and Diderot included. She even appointed, nominally at least, Diderot as her librarian. Nor was it surprising that she modelled her *Nakaz*, or Code of Laws (1766), on Montesquieu's *Esprit des lois* and on Beccaria's ideas, most of which remained but theory. In order to help agriculture she invited thousands of German peasants to settle in Russia. She also favoured the growth of freemasonry. The illuminati and the humanitarian freemasons under Catherine II included such men as the enterprising pamphleteer, editor and publisher Nikolai Novikov and the first virulent critic of serfdom – Alexander Radishchev. There were of course plenty of voices criticising both Russia and Europe. Prince M. M. Shcherbatov's pamphlet, *About the Deterioration of Manners in Russia*★ was a biting attack on post-Petrine Russia as he saw her. The dramatist Denis Fonvizin, on the other hand, turned (in his letters) most scathingly against Western Europe, or rather against France before the Revolution. "In nothing in this world have I ever been so mistaken as in my opinion about France," he wrote after a long stay in that country. "I am heartily glad to have seen her

★ First published in 1858 by Alexander Herzen in London.

personally, and that no one can any more delude me with tales about her."

The excesses of the French Revolution were, however, too much for Catherine II. Frightened of "dangerous thoughts" in practice, she shed her liberal skin almost overnight. Radishchev, the author of that indictment of the serfdom system, *A Journey from Petersburg to Moscow* (1790), was at first sentenced to death and then sent to Siberia, while Novikov was imprisoned in the notorious dungeons of Schluesselburg on the lake of Ladoga. Things became worse if anything after Catherine's death in 1796. Her crazy son Paul seemed to identify power with irresponsibility and self-will. The masonic lodges were disbanded. The only thing he really cared for were military parades and displays. But when this tyrant, too, like his father, had been "liquidated" (1800) in another palace revolt, there appeared signs of better times to come.

The man responsible for such new hopes was Catherine's grandson Alexander I, who is supposed to have been involved, at least indirectly, in the murder of his unbearable father. He started his reign in a spirit which augured well for Russia. From the outset he surrounded himself with liberal-minded men and promulgated several useful reforms. The masonic lodges were reopened and became quite a fashion in the first quarter of the nineteenth century. He also founded five new universities, not to mention other educational institutions. At the same time he took great interest in European affairs, since his armies were actively engaged in opposing and checking Napoleon's ambitions. The hopes and prospects rose particularly high after Napoleon's unsuccessful invasion of Russia in 1812. Eventually Alexander I became something of a top star in European politics. It was unfortunate, though, that Russian victories, as well as the adulation he had enjoyed in Paris and then in Vienna (during the "dancing" Congress), made the Tsar forget his ideas about transforming Russia into a progressive monarchy on liberal lines. The Holy Alliance, of which he was one of the main pillars, turned out to be but a most unholy medium for re-establishing the *status quo*. To make things worse he began to regard himself as the instrument of

divine Providence destined to save Europe from the "hydra of the Revolution". A prey to pseudo-mystical moods, which had been fostered in him also by that high-class adventuress, Mme Kruedener, he would not think of honouring any of his former liberal intentions. In the end he left the internal affairs of the State in the hands of the sadistic martinet Arakcheyev whose very name spelt fear and disaster.

5

The Tsar had not taken into account, however, the moods of the young officers who had fought Napoleon both in Russia and abroad. For no sooner had they come into contact with Europe than they were able to compare the Western conditions and ways of life with those in Russia. The comparison spoke for itself. Feeling ashamed of the backwardness of their own country, they awaited the more eagerly the reforms promised by Alexander I. And when these had been given up for good, the dissatisfaction of the young idealists was vented in secret societies at a time when such societies were springing up also in Italy, Germany, France – in fact all over Europe. The earliest founded in Russia (1817) bore the high-falutin title of the "Society of Salvation" or of the "True and Faithful Sons of the Fatherland". There followed the "Northern Society", with its southern branch in the Ukraine. Its members were young aristocrats who wanted to see a reborn and constitutional Russia. Some of them dreamt of a republic or even of a federation of all the Slavs led by Russia. Finally, on December 14th (O.S.) 1825, the ringleaders of the "Northern Society" organized an open revolt in St. Petersburg. Staged by liberal-minded officers, the revolt was directed against the new Tsar Nicholas I in favour of his elder brother Constantine.* Badly organised as it was, and devoid of any support by the masses, it was bound to collapse as a mere gentlemen's affair. It is said that the rebels' slogan, "for Constantine and Constitution" (*Konstantin i Konstitutsiya*), was interpreted by the fighting ranks as "for

* In 1820 Constantine had renounced his right to the throne.

Constantine and Constantine's wife". Five of these "Decembrists" (as they were called from now on) were hanged, one of them being the spirited civic poet Ryleyev and the other the democratic author of *The Russian Right* (*Russkaya Pravda*), Pavel Pestel, who is often referred to as a socialist before socialism. Some hundred and twenty of these aristocratic rebels were sent to the Siberian mines, and several of them were voluntarily followed by their wives. Such was the beginning of the new Tsar's "leaden regime" in all its realistic and symbolic significance.

Oppression above was matched by oppression below where the serfs were at the mercy of their brutal masters. It is enough to mention that between 1828 and 1854 there were, according to statistics, five hundred and forty-seven minor peasant-revolts against the serf-owners. Yet, paradoxically, it was during the thirty years of Nicholas' rule (and largely in opposition to it) that the literary and cultural life in Russia assumed a prodigious elan. The early years of that regime coincided with the "golden age" of Russian poetry and the maturity of Pushkin's genius. In the 1830s again we see the rise of Gogol – one of the founders of the Russian novel and Russian prose. The activities of the critic Belinsky began in the 1830s and continued until his premature death in 1848. The early masterpieces of the Russian school of music, founded by Glinka, were also products of those years. Even the Russian philosophic and social thought began to develop in the 1830s and assumed some quite notable aspects during the next few decades. Moreover, the failure of the "Decembrist" rising marked the end of the gentry-period in Russian culture, since – until then – literary and other cultural activities had been mainly in the hands of the nobles. After a brief interval, during which the focus of Russian culture was the University of Moscow, the intelligentsia period was ushered in, and it included members of the gentry and of educated "commoners" on a broader social basis. What they shared, no matter how different their social backgrounds, was their opposition to the autocratic regime, their unwritten code of integrity and their idealism to which they were ready to sacrifice all their personal interests and comforts. Belinsky himself, an

early leader of the intelligentsia, was a "commoner". And he, too, like so many others (K. Aksakov, Kireyevsky, Bakunin, Granovsky, etc.), came out of the circle which gathered around Nikolai Stankevich (1813–46) and was connected with Moscow University during the 1830s. Some of the greatest representatives of Russian literature – Lermontov, Gogol, Herzen, Turgenev, Dostoevsky, Goncharov, Tolstoy – made their debut while the tyrannical reign of Nicholas I was still at its height. Also the controversy between the Westerners and the Slavophiles, with the problem of Russia and Europe in the centre, arose during that very regime. And since the genesis of this controversy was more philosophic (or historiosophic) than political, it might be expedient to approach it first of all from this angle.

Philosophy and Politics

I

Russia's feeling of inferiority with regard to Europe was considerably lessened after 1812. In fact, after Napoleon's downfall her political and military prestige was at its peak. Those were the days of patriotic exultation, of glorifying things Russian and even Russia's past. Already in 1811 the poet and writer Nikolai M. Karamzin (a one-time admirer of Rousseau) addressed to the Tsar a special *Memorandum about Ancient and New Russia*, full of nostalgia for the Russian past duly idealised and tinged with a reactionary flavour. It was directed against Europe and even against Peter the Great.* This itself implied the idea that Russia might have a peculiar historical destiny of her own. Such an idea was actually gaining ground until – years later – it reached its climax in the ideology of the Slavophiles, beginning with Ivan Kireyevsky and Sergey Khomyakov. And a prelude to it were the patriotic dreams and ambitions of the young Russian intellectuals during the first quarter of the century.

One of the early stimuli in this direction came however from abroad – from the German philosophic writer Johann Gottfried Herder (1744–1803). A Prussian by birth, Herder spent some five years (1764–69) as teacher and preacher in Riga. It was here that he acquired a closer knowledge of Russia not only from books, but also from personal contacts and observations. As an enthusiast for enlightenment he became an ardent admirer of Peter the Great and

---

* The *arrière-pensée* of that Memorandum was probably a wish to undermine and discredit the Tsar's liberal-minded adviser Speransky – in which Karamzin seemed to have largely succeeded. Yet the same Karamzin had founded in 1802 the important periodical, *Vestnik Evropy* (*The European Messenger*), which he himself edited during 1802 and 1803.

28

Catherine II – the two rulers responsible for practically all that could be called Enlightenment in the Russia of that period. He conceived a great sympathy for Russians, as well as for the Slav race as a whole, in the days when the history of Russia, too, was being energetically explored by German scholars. In his bulky *Ideas about the Philosophy of Mankind's History (Ideen zur Philosophie der Geschichte der Menschheit,* 4 vols., 1784–1791) Herder made an attempt to formulate a philosophy of history based on the idea of Providence which presumably assigns to each nation a historical task of its own and thus guides the human race, even though it may conceal from man's mind the ultimate goal of it all. A romantic (or rather pre-romantic) of the German "Storm and Stress" movement, and a humanitarian of the Enlightenment period, Herder gave in this work a very favourable appraisal of the "peaceful" agricultural Slavs for the very reason that he identified Enlightenment itself with *Humanitaet* (humaneness, humanitarianism). In his opinion it was unfortunate for the Slavs that "their love of quiet and domestic industry was incompatible with any permanent military establishment, though they were not defective in valour in the heat of resistance: unfortunate, that their situation brought them so near to the Germans on the one side, and on the other left them exposed to the attacks of the Tartars from the east, from whom, particularly from the Mongols, they had much to suffer, and much they patiently bore".*

Herder thus became an inspiring figure not only for many a patriot in Russia, but also for the early leaders of the Slav *risorgimento* in Austria and elsewhere. He was known to Karamzin whose voluminous *History of the Russian State* (in twelve vols., 1816–1827), although devoid of serious scientific value, was yet a source of national pride among its readers. Fostered by the recent historical events, that pride was alive not only among the officers who had passed through the Napoleonic campaigns, but also among their younger contemporaries: the Russian youths born about 1800–1805, who had no war records to their credit and were

---

* Quoted from the English translation of the above work (*Outline of a Philosophy of History of Man* in two vols., 1803).

yet imbued with great patriotic enthusiasm during the 1820s and 1830s. Theirs was a kind of romantic ferment full of ideas and ideals, but again with the Western, i.e. German philosophic thought in the background. The general mood had been partly prepared by the Russian freemasons, among whom the influence of German mystics and quasi mystics (beginning with Boehme) was considerable. Anyhow, gone were the days when Voltaire and the encyclopaedists had been idolised by advanced minds in Russia. They were now replaced by such romantic philosophers as Schelling, Fichte and Hegel – all of them Germans. Schelling and (somewhat later) Hegel were the two names to swear by. It may be worth noting that Kant, with his severe logical mind, was not so much read by those young Russians among whom both Schelling and Hegel were perhaps even more discussed than in Germany herself. This does not mean that German idealistic philosophy was taken over entirely passively. Its enthusiastic adherents in Russia were usually anxious to penetrate through those two thinkers to what might have had a vital bearing upon the spiritual, mental and even political life of Russia herself.

Such a process was understandable at a time when in Russian literature, too, there was a tendency not to follow passively the Western influences, but to assimilate them in order to work out one's own national and personal originality. The whole of the eighteenth century had been a more or less imitative period on the part of Russian poets and writers. Yet during the second and third decades of the nineteenth century the genius of Pushkin marked out that turning point at which the creatively assimilated influences of the West became transfigured into something thoroughly Russian and at the same time European, or rather universal. Is it then surprising that the year 1820 (when Pushkin's delightful comic epic *Ruslan and Ludmila* appeared) was the beginning of the golden age of Russian poetry? Joined by a pleiade of other poets, Pushkin raised the standard of poetic production to a height which was as dazzling as it was exhilarating. That phase, short though it was, ceded ground to an equally flourishing period of prose whose formal aspects had been taken

from the West only to be filled with truly Russian contents and spirit. As for the philosophic thought in Russia, her assimilation of Western (in this case German) philosophy produced no spectacular results at first. It was yet marked by an enthusiastic quest for Russian values – a quest mingled with all sorts of religious, historiosophic, political and ethnic elements which make it, for this very reason, even more interesting to follow.

2

The impact of Schelling and his *Naturphilosophie* was an example. Friedrich Wilhelm J. Schelling (1775–1854) regarded Nature as a self-evolving spiritual organism. According to him the universe is a unity and expresses the Absolute which is working through Nature and history in order to reach its self-knowledge in and through the human mind. All Nature is slumbering intelligence which awakens in man's mind and spirit. In contrast to Kant's affirmation that our reason alone cannot penetrate to the ultimate secrets or the noumenal "things in themselves", Schelling believed that human mind – being part of these – is able to fathom the laws which are identical with the process going on in the universe. As for mankind's historical evolution, Schelling saw in it a contest between Freedom and Necessity, Freedom being a matter of conscious, and Necessity a matter of unconscious factors. Yet he conceived at the bottom of it all God's divine power which can manifest itself upon three consecutive levels: as blind fatum at the most primitive level; then as a system of mechanical laws; and finally as Providence. In God Necessity and Freedom coincide. The world has fallen off from God, but it has to return to Him. The gradual realisation of this need is given us through the process of history.

Schelling's philosophy (with some inherent elements of Plato, Spinoza and Leibniz) was the first German doctrine to become popular in both Russian capitals. Professor Vellansky, who was lecturing at St. Petersburg, had been a personal pupil of Schelling. Another important Schellingist in St. Petersburg was Professor

Galich. In Moscow again two Professors, Pavlov and Davydov, had both been influenced by Schelling whose teaching swayed the minds of the Russian youths until – in the 1830s and even more so during the 1840s – it was gradually superseded by that of Hegel. Moreover, in 1823 a group of Moscow youths founded the Society of Wisdom Lovers (*Lyubomudry*) whose chairman was Prince V.P. Odoyevsky (1803–1860), with the talented young poet Dmitry Venevitinov (1805–1827) as its secretary. Their short-lived periodical *Mnemosyna* even championed the idea that Russia should become the leading State in the realm of politics and morals, with a national philosophy, national literature and culture as its aim. Among the members of Wisdom Lovers were such budding Slavophiles as I. K. Kireyevsky, A. I. Koshelyov, as well as the subsequent historian and zealous fellow-traveller of Slavophilism, Mikhail Pogodin. Prince Odoyevsky himself anticipated the Slavophiles by writing a large collection of sketchy philosophic conversations under the title of *Russian Nights*. They appeared in book form as late as 1844, but a number of them were printed earlier and reflected the preoccupations of the young romantic Moscow intellectuals during the 1820s and 1830s. Intensely patriotic, these youths were yet full of enthusiasm for Schelling in the first place. To quote from Odoyevsky's *Russian Nights*, Schelling was to the romantic youths of the 1820s "what Christopher Columbus had been to the fifteenth century: he mapped out a new direction for the activity of man". It should be stressed, though, that their heated philosophic discussions were often but a kind of substitute for constructive practical activities, whether in politics or otherwise, from which they were debarred.

In their discussions and search for truth the Wisdom Lovers showed already then a certain antagonistic attitude towards Western Europe and her "feudalism of bankers and system of lies". It was not instinctive hatred of Europe that dictated to them such an attitude, but rather their awareness of the fact that Western life as a whole was getting more and more immersed in materialism, in spiritual and social fragmentation. Hence it was natural that they should have looked for something potentially different and

more constructive in their own country. Having absorbed those Western elements which she was in need of Russia should (in their opinion) preserve and build up all that was best in her own national character. For in doing this she might eventually help Europe herself to get out of the morass of a philistine existence. The poet Venevitinov wrote that formerly it was Europe who had influenced Russia, but now the process should be reversed: Russia ought to influence "old senile Europe and infuse new life into her". And Odoyevsky put it clearly enough when declaring that "the West senses the advent of the Slav spirit and is frightened of it in the same way as our forebears had been frightened of the West". On the other hand, he advocated a friendly collaboration with Europe. For only in such a collaboration might Russia be able to repay Western Europe for all she had borrowed from her since the days of Peter the Great.

The characters debating in *Russian Nights* may revel in the idea that the nineteenth century would belong to Russia, but Odoyevsky himself – patriotic though he was – remained outside any narrow nationalist tendencies. He was on the lookout for such universal cultural values as would be able to help both Russia and the West. This is why Professor P. N. Sakulin (the principal biographer of Odoyevsky) considered *Russian Nights* an original poem of philosophic seeking and a work "unique in the whole of Russian literature" in the same way as *Woe from Wit** and Pushkin's *Eugene Onyegin* are unique.

3

In 1833 to all these philosophic-patriotic tendencies a less acceptable political note was added in the shape of official patriotism. This was done by the Minister of Education Count Uvarov who proclaimed Autocracy, Orthodoxy and Nationalism† the guiding trinity for every true Russian. The nascent progressive

---

* A famous comedy by Griboyedov.

† The word *narodnost* which he used corresponds to the German word *Volkstum*, but what he really meant by it was nationalism.

intelligentsia would, however, have nothing to do with the slogans promulgated by the powers that be, and least of all with a slogan parading the word *autocracy*. Inspired by the Decembrist martyrs, the Western sympathizers were consistently in favour of the liberal and democratic institutions after the European pattern. And as for the patriotic-minded Slavophiles, they were, at that early stage, equally in opposition to the reactionary regime of Nicholas I. But since neither could do without some philosophic ideology, most of the Slavophiles remained loyal to Schelling, whereas the Westerners clung to Hegel – both of them duly modified, of course.

Quite an important part in these developments was played by the philosophy of history, imported above all from Germany. Herder himself had adhered to a philosophy of history according to which the various nations are vehicles of the plans devised by divine Providence. His romantic attitude towards the *Volksgeist* (folk-spirit) even made him collect and publish folk-songs of all nations* in a thoroughly supra-national spirit. For according to him the actual aim of history is and should be *Humanitaet*, i.e. humanitarianism or human solidarity in the best sense of this word. Progress itself can only be achieved in its name. "All our history is a school in which we ought to reach the beautiful crown of *Humanitaet* and human dignity." Then came Schelling's interpretation of history as a process of self-revelation on the part of the Universal Spirit.

Schelling's conception of the universe as an embodiment of the Absolute was taken up also by Hegel, but with a difference. According to him the Whole contains and determines all the parts constituting reality. And if so, then all that is real is also reasonable, since it proceeds from the Absolute, from the rational Universal Spirit. In short, whatever exists is right and reasonable – a doctrine which was bound to lead to a number of misunderstandings. Furthermore, Hegel's dialectical method of thesis, antithesis and synthesis, going on as a continuous process and

* He published them in two volumes under the title of *Stimmen der Voelker* (*Voices of Nations*) in 1778–79.

repeated each time upon a higher level of the historical spiral, was largely responsible for our modern idea of evolution. His *Philosophy of History*, on the other hand, caused considerable havoc among some of his Russian readers.

Hegel delivered his course of lectures on the philosophy of history at Berlin University during the winter term of 1830–31. What he was anxious to convey through those lectures was nothing less than the meaning of history. According to him history belongs to the realm of Universal or Absolute Spirit. In the same way as the seed bears in itself the whole of the tree, including the taste and the form of its fruits, the very first manifestations of Spirit contain (potentially) the whole of History. In the course of his further disquisitions Hegel came to the conclusion that the essential element of Universal Spirit is embodied in the State – "well constructed and internally powerful, when the private interest of its citizens is one with the common interest of the State; when the one finds its gratification and realisation in the other". In the lengthy introduction to that work he, moreover, asserted that the Germanic nations, influenced by Christianity, were "the first to attain the consciousness that man, as man, is free and that it is the freedom of Spirit which constitutes its essence". Surprisingly enough, the philosopher then discovered such freedom in the Prussian State as organised by its royal martinets. Frederick II in particular is mentioned as the ruler who inaugurated that epoch in which "practical *political interest* attains universality and receives an absolute sanction. Frederick II merits special notice as having comprehended the general object of the State and as having been the first sovereign who kept the general interest of the State steadily in view, ceasing to pay any respect to particular interests when they stood in the way of the common weal."

Hegel's implications were thus made clear enough. Since the police State of Prussia happened to be the embodiment of Absolute Spirit, each of its citizens should meekly submit to its regulations without even daring to question their reactionary aims or methods. But in theory at least Hegel insisted that, while preserving its own unity, the State at the same time protects the free expression of

every individual. In contrast to the despotic Asiatic East, the German-Christian nation alone knows – in Hegel's opinion – freedom as a prerogative of all. Here History becomes the "exhibition of the divine absolute development in its highest forms – that gradation by which it attains its truth and consciousness of itself". It manifests itself in three stages: as art, religion, and philosophy. But selective as it is, it finds its abode at each historical period in one nation only, especially singled out for such a high purpose. Having previously favoured some other nations or races, the Absolute Spirit chose at last the German nation, or rather the Prussian State, for its abode. Part V of Hegel's book, under the heading "The German World", actually begins as follows: "The German Spirit is the Spirit of the new world. Its aim is the realization of absolute Truth as the unlimited self-determination of Freedom – that Freedom which has its own form itself as its purport."*

One may be puzzled by the meaning of all this. Yet the manner in which Hegel made Prussia monopolise the Absolute Spirit itself could not but strike the non-German readers as unfair or even downright arrogant. The Russians and the other Slavs, for instance, were dismissed by Hegel with the curt verdict: "Lastly Poland, Russia, and the Slavonic Kingdoms (sic). They come only late into the series of historical States, and form and perpetuate the connection with Asia." The question which remained unanswered was what have all these "non-historical (*geschichtslose*) nations" done to be thus snubbed and bypassed by the Absolute Spirit for the greater glory of Prussia? This was bound to make many a thoughtful Russian inquire into the meaning and destiny of Russia's history in spite of Hegel. Besides, even one of Hegel's German followers and critics, Bruno Bauer, was soon to predict in his book *Russland und Germanentum* (*Russia and the German World*, 1853) the unavoidable end of Hegel's Christian-Germanic era and

---

* Quotations are taken from *Lectures on the Philosophy of History* (Bohn's Philosophical Library). In his critical attack of Hegel's philosophy (1839), Feuerbach called Hegel's "Absolute Spirit" simply *Unsinn des Absoluten* (Nonsense of the Absolute.)

the gradual rise of a new historical age initiated by Russia whose political might was in the ascendant. Bauer pointed out that already Catherine II had exercised a dictatorship over Europe which "in its power, influence and world-historical significance had by far outstripped the dictatorship of Charles V of Spain and Louis XIV of France". He went so far indeed as to anticipate Oswald Spengler and prophesy the downfall of Western civilisation – a catastrophe which, in Bauer's opinion, the Germans could survive only if they actively collaborated with Russia. And a few years before him the French traveller Custine, who was very critical of Russia and the Russians, envisaged in his book, *La Russie en 1839*, a more enlightened Russia which might rise in the end and assert herself against a somewhat exhausted Europe. He was even ready to see in the Russians of the future *des maîtres eclairés, plus eclairés que nous*, who would be able to learn from the mistakes and failures of the West.

4

The problem of Russia and the West thus became a dilemma which began to agitate the Russian intelligentsia as a whole. And since practical political activities were strictly confined to hidebound Tsarist bureaucracy, the intellectuals were all the more inclined to indulge in theories, i.e. in philosophic-political discussions of the Westerners and the Slavophiles, the main difference between them being in their basic approach to the problem itself. One of the explorers of that period* even goes so far as to maintain that the "conflict between the Westerners and the Slavophiles is a perennial Russian conflict, a continuous civil war which far transcends in historical and cultural importance the particular dispute in the middle of the nineteenth century and in which every Russian is to some extent divided against himself. Indeed it may be argued that Russia herself is an embodiment of that tension in which she and the West find themselves face to face in the very depth of European mankind."

* E. Lampert in his book, *Studies in Rebellion* (Methuen).

The "ideological" split on this ground took place among the Russian intellectuals in the second half of the 1840s, although it had been fermenting during the previous two decades among Wisdom Lovers and the Moscow young men belonging to the Stankevich circle. Stankevich himself was an admirer of German metaphysics, especially of Fichte and Hegel, and the integrity of his magnetic personality was so great that he succeeded in grouping together some of the finest youths of the period. Parallel with that circle there was the circle of Alexander Herzen and his friend the poet Ogaryov. Its members were interested mainly in social and political problems. Here Hegel's philosophy prevailed over that of Schelling. In both circles the problem of Russia and Europe was paramount and led to an endless controversy. Later on, it was via Feuerbach that some of those youths joined left-wing Hegelianism and adopted that critical attitude towards Russian reality which served as the principal fuel for the revolutionary moods during the second half of the nineteenth century. The critic Belinsky himself made the transition (under the influence of Herzen) from Hegel's "all reality is reasonable" to the radical left wing of Hegelianism, once he had experienced the reality of Russian autocracy upon his own back. Like so many other Russian thinkers, he became concerned with living life rather than with abstract theories. To change the world meant to him much more than to explain it, and he regarded the concrete human personality as more important than all philosophic systems *qua* systems.

An equally active idealist of this kind was Alexander Herzen. The youths gathering around him were interested in Hegel, in the Utopian French socialists, as well as in the writings of George Sand (who was extremely popular in Russia during the 1830s and 1840s). The gatherings of those intellectuals continued also after their university studies were over. Herzen himself, who was destined to be another leader of the intelligentsia, had been exiled for quite a while from Moscow in 1834, but on his return he stepped up his activities among his friends, in spite of the vigilant eye of the police. This is what he wrote about them many years later: "Such a circle of talented, cultured, many-sided, and

pure-hearted people I have met nowhere since, neither in the highest ranks of the political nor on the summits of the literary and aristocratic world. Our circle met frequently, sometimes at the house of one, sometimes of another, most often at mine. Together with jests, supper and wine, there was the most active, the most rapid exchange of ideas, of news, and knowledge. There was nothing of significance in any sphere of knowledge, in any literature, in any art, which did not come under the notice of some of us, and was not at once communicated to us all."*

Such were the young idealists, devoted to the common good and ready to defy the regime of Nicholas I in the days when the gap between the Slavophiles and the sympathizers with the West was not yet final in spite of their different approach to the problem itself. But even from the middle of the 1830s on those differences were bound to grow. They soon became further complicated by the intrusion of new factors, racial, political and cultural, from beyond the Russian border. One of these was the Slav problem regarding the racially and linguistically related Slav populations in the Balkans, as well as in Austria where the Slavs formed the majority of the population. The ethnic, political and cultural aspects of this problem were of vital concern to most Slavophiles. Its political side was bound to be tackled, eventually, also by the Russian government as part and parcel of imperialistic ambitions. On the other hand, it raised the dilemma of the relations between the Russians and the non-Russian Slavs during many a crisis affecting not only the fate of the Balkans but of the whole of central and south-eastern Europe.

* Herzen also gives an amusing example of how some of those youths emulated in their writings the involved and obscure German philosophic jargon: "The concretion of abstract ideas in the sphere of plastics presents that phase of the self-seeking spirit in which, defining itself for itself, it passes from the potentiality of natural immanence into the harmonious sphere of pictorial consciousness and beauty."

Russia, Austria and Slavdom

I

When, after the French Revolution and the Napoleonic wars, the national problem and the idea of Nation-States became paramount in Europe, most of the non-Russian Slavs were in a politically precarious position. Apart from tiny Montenegro, guarding its independence among the inaccessible Balkan mountains, there was only Serbia who – after more than four hundred years of slavery – rebelled (at the beginning of the nineteenth century) against her Turkish tyrants and thus actively asserted her will to live as a free nation. The rest of the Balkan Slavs continued to smart under the lawless Turkish rule. In Austria again the Slavs had to fight hard against Vienna's centralism on the one hand, and her tendency to impose the German language upon the whole of Austria on the other. The real purpose of this practice, which had been started by Maria Theresa and her son Joseph II, was to simplify the administration by using the same official language in such a multi-lingual empire as Austria. Yet when the Germanising character of it all became evident, the non-German nations, especially the Slavs, began to resist and to defend their own national rights. The early stages of this resistance were confined, of course, to the intellectuals – the masses were still too illiterate to take any real interest in it. The conscious awareness of their national identity came to them later – as a result of general education and a higher standard of living.

The notion of a close linguistic affinity and the racial kinship of the Slavs was not something new. The old-Russian chronicler Nestor was aware of it as far back as the twelfth century. One of the leaders of the Slovene Reformation and a pupil of Melanchton,

Adam Bohorich, published in 1584 his Slovene Grammar (in Latin) in which he expressly stated that anyone knowing Slovene could easily understand the other Slav languages. And the author of the quaint *Rerum Moscoviticarum Commentarii* (*Notes upon Muscovy*, 1549), Baron Sigismund von Herberstein – a native of Carniola, who had been sent as ambassador to Moscow by the Emperors Maximilian and Ferdinand I – says in the preface to his book that having the advantage of knowing the Slavonic [Slovene] "which is identical with the Russian and Muscovitic I have written these things and handed them down to posterity".* One could mention a number of other prominent men, from the Polish humanist and poet Jan Kochanowski (1530–1584) to the writers of old Dubrovnik (Ragusa) in whom this feeling of Slav consanguinity was very much alive. A particularly curious phenomenon in this respect was, however, the seventeenth century Croat priest Yury Križanić (1617–1683). In 1640 he was sent by the *Congregatio de Propaganda Fide* to Smolensk (then occupied by the Poles) in order to spread Catholicism. This was a short stay, but in 1659 he went to Moscow on his own with the idea of starting a peculiar Pan-Slav propaganda. According to him Russia should expel the Turks from the Balkans and become the leader of all the Slavs. He had no good word for the Germans whom he seemed to know quite well; yet he was far from ignoring the faults of the Russians or the Poles, and was most candid about them. He also championed the reunion of the Orthodox and Catholic Churches. For some obscure reason he was however soon exiled to Tobolsk in Siberia where he remained for sixteen years. It was there that he wrote most of his works in a curious mixture of Croat, Russian and Church-Slavonic. Later he was allowed to leave Russia and is supposed to have died while with the Polish army which defeated the Turks beleaguering Vienna in 1683.

* Another quotation from his book: "Their language agreeth much with the tongue of ye Bohemians, Croatians and Sclavons, so that the Sclavon doth plainly understande the Moscovite, although the Moscovian tongue be a more hard phrase of speech." (*Notes upon Russia II*, The Hakluyt Society, 1852).

In the second half of the eighteenth century, and especially during the romantic movement, the idea of all the Slavs being one nation speaking several dialects caused considerable enthusiasm among the Slav erudites, and also a certain amount of confusion. Held by the founder of the Slav philology, the Czech savant Joseph Dobrovský (1753–1829), this idea was endorsed even by such a solid German historian as August Ludwig Schloezer who had come to Russia from Goettingen in 1761. One of its most enthusiastic pioneers was however the Slovak Protestant pastor Jan Kollar (1793–1852) – an ardent admirer of Herder.* Kollar's patriotic Czech epic, *The Daughter of Slava* (*Slávy dcera*, 1824 and 1832) was written entirely in this strain. It should be pointed out, though, that he himself had been inspired by the romantic character of German nationalism which flourished after Napoleon's downfall. While devoid of any definite political programme, Kollar insisted on a close cultural rapprochement between the Slav nations. In his sentimental-romantic idealisation of Slavdom he even went so far as to expect – somewhat vaguely – a regeneration of mankind through the Slav spirit.

Following up the same general-Slav trend, several leaders of the Czech and Slovak national revival in the Habsburg Empire felt entitled to pay almost as much attention to the other Slav nations as they were paying to their own. Kollar's important German pamphlet on the need of cultural and literary contacts between the Slavs, *About the Reciprocity between the Various Branches and Dialects of the Slav Nation*, appeared in 1837. But even before that quite a few of his Czech and Slovak compatriots had been active in this sense. As early as 1817 Vaclav Hanka's *Serbian Songs* was published. The poet F. L. Čelakovský issued, in 1829, an excellent paraphrase of the Russian historical folk-songs under the title, *An Echo of Russian Songs*, which became a Czech classic. The same poet collected proverbs and sayings of the various Slav nations,

* It may be of some interest that when the Slovene scholar B. Kopitar published (1808) at Vienna his Slovene Grammar (in German), he called it a *Grammar of the Slav Language* as spoken in Carniola, Carinthia and Styria.

not to mention his three volumes of Slav folk-poetry (1822, 1825, 1827). In 1826 the Slovak scholar Pavel Šafařik published (in German) his *History of the Slav Language and Literature*. About ten years later his *Slav Antiquities* was printed and remained a standard work on the subject until the beginning of this century, when Professor Lubor Niederle's comprehensive and up to date explorings made their appearance. In Russia the slavist Bodyansky's treatise *About the Poetry of the Slav Peoples* appeared in 1837. Among the Poles it was the romantic poet Brodzinski in particular who admired the Slav folk-songs some of which he translated from Czech, Slovak, Serbian and Ukrainian.

In those years the numerous epic folk-songs of the Serbs, collected by Vuk S. Karadjić (1787–1864), aroused much interest all over Europe and played a certain part even in the controversy about the genesis of the Homeric epics. The two volumes of Serbian folk-poetry, turned into German by Miss Talvj* and published in 1825–26, were favourably commented on by Goethe himself who also translated some Serbian folk-ballads. In England it was Sir John Bowring (1792–1872) whose translations from Russian, Polish, Czech and Serbian did a great deal to popularise the poetry of those nations. In France, on the other hand, Prosper Mérimée (1803–70) deliberately mystified his readers with *La Guzla* – a pretended collection of "Illyrian" folk-songs which, although a fake, was at first accepted as genuine and was partly translated even by Pushkin (under the title, *Songs of the Western Slavs*).

2

All this must have undoubtedly flattered the Slav nations, especially those who had been so far unable to affirm themselves

---

* A pseudonym of Therese Albertine Louise von Jakob. Later she married the American professor Edward Robinson and, in 1850, published (in English) her enthusiastic *Historical View of the Languages and Literature of the Slavic Nations*.

culturally in the world at large. The Balkan Slavs, who still lived under Turkey, were however worse off in this respect than those living in Austria. Both suffered, of course, from political oppression. The awareness of this alone was enough to foster the idea of a close affinity not only with each other, but also with Russia. The Orthodox Slavs under the Turkish rule pinned their hopes to the great Orthodox colossus of Russia whom they expected to liberate them. The Austrian Slavs again, or rather quite a few of their intellectuals, were impressed by the size of the same colossus to the extent of indulging now and then in vague romantic dreams of a future Slav millennium under the leadership of Russia. The prestige of Russia may have stood high indeed after 1812; but there were a number of factors which were likely to make one think. The most obvious of these was the despotic and tyrannical Russian system itself – a system that could hardly appeal to the Austrian Slavs whose struggle for their own national freedom went hand in hand with the liberal-democratic ideas championed by the French Revolution and endorsed also by the romantic movement. They knew, moreover, that any weakening of Austria would encourage Tsarist imperialism to make use of such a line of least resistance in order to penetrate into that part of Europe. The democratic-minded Slav intellectuals could not envisage such a prospect with equanimity, however much some of them sympathised with the Russian nation (of which, incidentally, they knew – in those days – very little).

Another obstacle was the Russo-Polish problem. Although pure Slavs, the Poles were staunch Roman Catholics and regarded themselves as the farthest outpost of Western civilisation and a bulwark against the Byzantine-Orthodox "barbarity" of Muscovy. They also had a fairly strong humanist and Renaissance tradition from which the Russians had been debarred. Furthermore, it was mainly with the connivance of Catherine II of Russia and Frederick II of Prussia that the first division of Poland (in 1772) took place to be followed by two other divisions and the "finis Polaniae" in 1795. This historical crime against a whole nation, which became split between Russia, Prussia and Austria,

burned in the heart of every Pole. So much so as to make many of them refuse even the idea of Slav solidarity as long as the latter had anything to do with Russia and the Russians. It was not unlike the one-time Irish attitude towards the English. This was particularly the case after the two unsuccessful Polish rebellions against Russian domination: in 1831 and 1863. Even that father of modern anarchism, Michael Bakunin, who was wholeheartedly on the side of the Poles, wrote in a letter to his equally Polonophile friend Alexander Herzen: "The very best of Poles is our enemy in so far as we are Russians." And one of the Russian Slavophiles (Samarin), who was a sincere friend of the Poles, regarded these nevertheless as a "sharp wedge" thrust by the West into the Slav world in order to undermine it. As though in defiance of Russian Slavophilism, the Polish émigrés (after 1831) devised their own "politico-mystical" doctrine according to which "Poland crucified between the two thieves – Germany and Russia" – would be resurrected as a Saviour of nations in the spirit of true Christianity. Preached by the mathematician Hoehne-Wronsky (1778–1853) and, independently of him, by Towianski (1799–1878), this Messianic doctrine counted among its adepts even the greatest Polish poet Adam Mickiewicz (1798–1855). Nor did the brilliant romantic poet, Juliusz Slowacki (1809–49), escape its influence. Mickiewicz believed in Slavdom as a contrast to the materialistic West. But while being anti-Western in this respect, he was also anti-Russian. In fact, he cherished the idea of a union of Western Slavs led by Poland and hostile to Russia. Because of the propaganda he was making on behalf of his "Messianic" convictions he forfeited (in 1840) his professorship of Slav literatures at the Collège de France. And significantly enough, he died in Constantinople while recruiting Polish volunteers to fight Russia during the Crimean Campaign.

Like the Russian Slavophile movement, this Polish "Messianism" had a pseudo-mystical and religious flavour. But for this very reason it found no strong echo among the Austrian Slavs, the Poles in Galicia (which had been annexed by Austria during the first division of Poland) excluded. Among the Czechs and the

Slovaks the national revival had little to do with religion, how-ever much some of their leaders may have admired the ethical ideals of the old Hussite movement. What they were fighting for were the political rights and freedoms of their nation. The same was the case with the Austrian Yugoslavs: the Slovenes, the Croats, and the Serbs in the Vojvodina (the Banat and Bačka region in Southern Hungary). During the early stages of their national revival these nations showed frequent sentimental enthusiasm for a kind of idealized Russia. And this was hardly surprising, since their own rulers, the Habsburgs, were not only German, but also consistently anti-liberal in their incurable conser-vatism. For instead of trying to understand and accept the new forces in history, the Habsburgs either ignored or else fought these forces with might and main.* But actually Russia was in this respect even worse – under the appalling burden of autocracy and serfdom. An unbiased observer was therefore bound to come to the conclusion that Austria, with all her faults and drawbacks, was a lesser evil. And since the Slavs were by far in the majority in the Habsburg Monarchy, they sensibly cherished the hope that their common efforts might, in due course, make her change her structure and become a democratic-federal State which would be her only salvation. Such was the deeper reason of that Austro-Slavism which found its ideologist in the Czech historian and political leader Francis Palacký (1798–1876) and also in the spirited pamphleteer Karel Havliček (1821–56). The possibility of Russia's expansion at the expense of Austria was Palacký's principal nightmare. Being the finest type of a liberal Western European, he saw in such a threat an "unspeakable evil" which might stifle all free aspirations of the nations concerned. As for Havliček, he had some personal experience of Russia. He went there in 1842 and stayed for quite a time as private tutor first in the family of Professor Pogodin and then in that of Professor Shevyryov – an inveterate hater of Western Europe. But having seen more than he had bargained for, he became so disgusted with

* The only enlightened rule in this respect was that of Joseph II (1780–90), and even he had to withdraw most of his reforms.

the "leaden regime" of Nicholas I that he returned home a firm supporter of the federal Austro-Slav idea championed by Palacký.

3

This trend was not devoid of realism in those agitated years when a number of Austrian Pan-Germans were willing to sacrifice their own country to the dream of a greater Germany (*Grossdeutschland*). In the Hungarian part again the chauvinistic Magyar feudals were anxious to make Hungary independent of the Habsburgs in order to assimilate more easily the non-Magyar nations (the Slovaks, Rumanians, Ruthenians, Croats and the Vojvodina Serbs) living within her geographic boundaries. Many Slavs were thus logically induced to cling to the idea of Austria's survival, since this was a potential guarantee of their own national survival as well. A powerful Austria, based on a federal principle, would (in Palacký's opinion) not only serve as a safeguard against any aggressive designs of either Russia or Germany, but might also provide the world with a proof that several nations could exist and work in harmony within the boundaries of one and the same State. To bring this about, however, the Austrian Germans were to give up any attempts to foster their hegemony in the Austrian half proper, while the Magyars should do the same in the Hungarian half of the Monarchy. This was why already in January 1848 Palacký made the proposition that Austria should be reconstructed upon a sound federal basis.*

An idea such as this went far beyond mere politics in its narrow sense and touched upon the very *raison d'être* of Austria's historical existence. For centuries Austria's task had been to defend Western civilisation from being swamped by the Turks – a task in which, incidentally, the Croats and the Slovenes had to bear the brunt of the Moslem invasions. But once the Turkish danger was over, the

---

* He advocated the following eight federal units: German, Czecho-Slovak, Polish-Ukrainian (in Galicia), Magyar, Serbo-Croat, Slovene, Italian (in Lombardy, etc.) and Rumanian.

Habsburg Monarchy had to find a new task in order to justify her existence. The first step in this direction would have been, according to Palacký, Austria as a federal State in the very heart of Europe. In such a State all its diverse nations should enjoy equal rights and freedoms in the name of a supra-national Austrian patriotism which might thus preclude any separatist nationalisms. For there is a difference between the two. They may, of course, overlap but not necessarily so. In certain cases they may even be at cross-purposes and turn against each other. Whereas nationalism stands for the allegiance to one's ethnic or racial stock and language, patriotism implies above all the attachment to one's native country with its customs, traditions, as well as its peculiar historical pattern which may be shared by several nations living within the same geographic and political boundaries. Old Austria, for example, comprised some twelve nations, which were kept together by a common historical experience and also by their attachment to the same territory and the same ruling dynasty. Yet no sooner had the Germans and the Magyars begun to show their nationalistic ambitions in an aggressive manner than the non-German and non-Magyar ethnic units had to defend themselves as best they could. As a result all sorts of other nationalisms were being gradually let loose – each one more disruptive than the last. As a contrast Switzerland could be mentioned. Here a strong and balanced Swiss patriotism transcends any potential nationalistic tendencies on the part of the German, French, Italian and Romansh communities living peacefully together in one and the same State.

Unfortunately, neither the Austrian Germans nor the Magyars were anxious to turn the Habsburg Monarchy into such a League of Nations in practice, since this would have put an end to their assimilative ambitions and appetites. Austria thus became a very hotbed of nationalistic wrangles, threatening to undermine her from within. There was, however, one element which might have been turned into a reliable cementing force but for the invariable obstruction on the part of the Magyars – above all the Magyars. This element was Austro-Slavism, one of whose important

by-products during the 1830s and 1840s was the so-called Illyrian*
movement among the Croats and the Austrian Serbs. It was
initiated by the Croat leader Ludevit Gaj (1809–72), a practical
follower of Jan Kollar. The aim of this movement was to make the
Croats (whose old kingdom had become – through personal union
– an autonomous part of Hungary in 1102) replace their literary
language, based on the local Zagreb dialect, by the similar but
widely used speech of south-eastern Croats and of the Serbs
(whether in Austria or in Serbia). This kind of literary rapprochement between them served as an early step towards a later cultural
union of the Yugoslavs in general. Although the Croats, being
Catholics, were using the Latin script, while the Orthodox Serbs
continued (and still continue) to stick to their Cyrillic alphabet,
Gaj's Illyrism did a great deal to strengthen the national and
Yugoslav consciousness among the Croats. He himself was above
all an opportunist in chronic need of money which he took
wherever it came from – whether from Austria, Serbia or Russia.
He would not drop his Austro-Slavism, while at the same time he
flirted with Russia and in 1838 even sent a Memorandum to
Nicholas I in which he called him the leader of all the Slavs. It is
significant that according to the old Austrian slogan of "divide and
rule", the Chancellor Metternich himself had supported for a
while the Illyrian movement – as long as he saw in it a brake on the
rapidly growing Magyar appetites. And even after Metternich's
fall in 1848 the Court supported the Illyrian-minded Croat Ban
Jelačić in his resistance to the Magyars who were anxious not only
to secede from Austria but to destroy any traces of Croat autonomy as well.

4

This was, however, an ambiguous task in so far as in helping to
defeat the Magyar insurgents, Jelačić had to side with the loyal
Austrian forces opposed not only to the Magyars but also to the

* The name "Illyrian" was partly due to the mistaken idea that the ancient
Illyrians were the ancestors of contemporary Yugoslavs.

radical rebels during the explosive months of 1848 and early 1849. It was in fact on March 13, 1848, that the rioters, led by students, began a rising in Vienna which spread – in due course – also to some other cities, notably to Budapest and Prague. The Chancellor Metternich had to abdicate. A number of concessions, among them freedom of the press, had to be made. On April 25 even a liberal Constitution was announced, and in the second half of July the Parliament was opened. Yet because of further revolutionary outbursts in Vienna the Emperor and the Court fled (on May 17) first to Innsbruck and later, in October, to Olomouc (Olmuetz) where, on December 2, 1848, Francis Joseph – a youth of eighteen – was proclaimed Emperor, thus replacing his feebleminded uncle Ferdinand. At the same time the Parliament which, from November 22, 1848, had been sitting at Kroměříž (Kremsier) continued its work in the new liberal spirit of the movement. One of the reforms to its credit was the abolition of the last remnants of serfdom. It was also working on the project of a federal arrangement for Austria in order to reconcile her various nations. But the reactionary elements, too, were on the alert. On March 7, 1849, the troops of Prince Schwarzenberg dispersed the Parliament. The broad liberal Constitution was now replaced by a stunted would-be Constitution by virtue of which Army, Aristocracy and Church were installed as the joint guardians of law and order.

New complications arose when, on April 14, 1849, the Magyar Parliament, sitting at that time in Debreczen, deposed the Habsburgs and proclaimed Lajos Kossuth the governor of Hungary. Prince Windischgraetz and Ban Jelačić fought the Magyars, but without much success. In the end Tsar Nicholas I was begged by Francis Joseph to rescue – in the name of the Holy Alliance – both Austria and the Habsburgs. The Tsar's response was prompt. He sent to Hungary an army of 200,000 soldiers who defeated the Magyar insurgents at Világos (on August 13, 1849) and thus made Vienna triumph over Budapest. The regime of centralised absolutism which was to follow turned Austria for at least ten

years into a "prison of nations" which could not but exasperate all liberal-minded spirits.*

As the Magyars had been fighting only for their own freedom (which also meant to them freedom to assimilate the non-Magyar nations in Hungary), their debacle caused considerable relief among the Croat enthusiasts for Illyrism. It strengthened the notion of the kinship of all Yugoslavs, whether inside or outside Austria. Yet the Slovenes did not join the movement, however much a number of their intellectuals – above all in Carinthia and Styria – may have sympathised with it. As it happened, they knew full well that, in the fight for their national identity, they were likely to resist Germanisation much more efficiently under their own name, that is as Slovenes, than under a new and borrowed label. Besides, their great poet, Francè Prešeren (1800–49), who was a poet of European stature, had laid by then a solid foundation for a Slovene national literature.†

Throughout these two agitated years, when the very existence of Austria was at stake, the Austrian Slavs, with all their awakened national consciousness, remained loyal to the Habsburgs simply because they had no other plausible alternatives. Russia, weighed down by her autocracy, certainly was not one of them. Nor was the idea of a united "greater Germany", as planned by the liberal Pan-German *Vorparlament* (gathered at Frankfurt), for the very reason that it would involve the dissolution of the Habsburg Empire. If incorporated within Germany, the Austrian Slavs would be doomed to be assimilated sooner or later by their new German masters. If however the non-German nations were left out, the only country to benefit from it would be Russia. What such a situation might imply was clearly stated in the famous letter

* As an example of such exasperation the Slovak poet and patriot Ludovit Štur may be mentioned. His German pamphlet, *Slavdom and the World to Come* written in the early 1850s) even advocated a union of the Slav nations under the leadership of Russia – provided she would give up her reactionary regime. Nor was he averse to adopting Orthodoxy and recommending Russian as the literary language of all the Slavs.

† Yet one of the best poets of the Illyrian movement was Stanko Vraz – a Slovene from Styria.

Palacký sent – on April 11, 1848 – to the organizers of the Frank-furt *Vorparlament* after they had invited him to join them. As a liberal-minded leader of the Czechs he declined the invitation in a letter which expressed the very quintessence of his Austro-Slavism. Here are some of its vital passages.

"You know, gentlemen, what Power it is that holds the entire East of our Continent. You know that this Power, now grown to vast dimensions, increased and expanded of itself decade by decade in far greater measure than is possible for the countries of the West. You know that, secure of its own centre against practically every attack, it has become, and has for a long time been, a menace to its neighbours; and that, although it has unhindered access to the North, it is nevertheless, led by natural instinct, always seeking, and will continue to seek, to extend its borders southwards. You know, too, that every further step which it will take forward on this path threatens at an ever accelerated pace to give birth to, and to establish a universal monarchy, that is to say, an infinite and inexpressible evil, a misfortune without measure or bound, such as I, though heart and soul a Slav, would nevertheless profoundly regret from the standpoint of humanity even though that monarchy be proclaimed a Slavonic one.... I am not, I would declare loudly and publicly, an enemy of the Russians: on the contrary, I observe with pleasure and sympathy every step for-ward which that great nation makes within its natural borders along the path of civilisation; but with all my fervid love of my own nation I always pay greater respect to the good of humanity and learning than to the national good, and for this reason the bare possibility of a universal Russian monarchy has no more determined opponent and foe than myself – not because that monarchy would be Russian but because it would be universal."

Then he proceeded to state that the principal defence against such an expansion of a reactionary and despotic Russia was the group of nations along the Danube, i.e. the Austrian Empire which ought to remain effective in this historical task in the interests of humanity. "Assuredly, if the Austrian State had not existed for ages, it would have been a behest for us in the

interests of Europe and indeed of humanity to create it as soon as possible.

"Why is it, then, that we have seen this State, which by nature and history is predestined to be the bulwark and guardian of Europe against Asiatic elements of every possible type – why is it that we have seen it at a critical moment lacking help and almost devoid of counsel in the face of an advancing storm? It is because, in the unhappy blindness that has long afflicted her, Austria has failed to recognise the real juridical and moral basis of her existence, and has denied it: the fundamental rule, that is, that all the nations and all the religions under her sceptre should enjoy complete equality of rights and respect in common.... I am convinced that even now it is not too late for this fundamental role of justice, this *sacra ancora* for a vessel in danger of foundering, to be publicly and sincerely proclaimed in the Austrian Empire and energetically carried out in all sectors by common consent. Every moment, however, is precious; for God's sake do not let us delay another hour with this! Metternich did not fall merely because he was the greatest foe of liberty but also because he was the bitterest, the most determined enemy of the Slav races in Austria.... If Europe is to be saved, Vienna must not sink to the role of a provincial town. If there exist in Vienna people who ask to have your Frankfurt for their capital, we can only cry: Lord forgive them, for they know not what they ask." It was there and then that Palacký also underlined his own readiness to help any activity which might strengthen the independence of Austria, and well he knew why.

5

This letter was written at a time when Austria herself enjoyed a spell – however turbulent – of freedom which alas! was not to last long. But during the spell Palacký himself played a very conspicuous role in the all-Slav Congress which took place in Prague in the first half of June, 1848. In some respects this was a Slav answer to the Pan-German National Assembly at Frankfurt, but

the enthusiasm with which the atmosphere of this Slav Congress was permeated had nothing to do either with Russia or even with Russian Slavophilism. Organised by the leaders of the Czech and Slovak national revival, it was inspired by the advanced liberal ideas of the age, and these were hardly likely to appeal to the Russia of Nicholas I or even to religious-minded Slavophiles. The only Russian subject present was that arch-revolutionary Michael Bakunin. The Congress was presided over by Palacký, and among the 365 delegates there were quite a number of Poles – mainly from the Posen province in Germany. The note of any political Pan-Slav tendencies was superseded during those gatherings by that of federative Austro-Slavism, but in the name of liberty and justice for all other nations as well. This was clearly expressed in the Manifesto which the delegates addressed to the world at large.

"Taking our stand," it said, "on the conviction that the mighty current of thought of today demands new political formation and that the States must be reconstructed, if not within new bounds at least upon new foundations, we have proposed to the Austrian Emperor, under whose constitutional rule the majority of us live, that the imperial State be converted into a federation of nations, all enjoying equal rights. We see in such a federal union not only our own salvation but also liberty, enlightenment and humanity generally; and we are confident that civilised Europe would readily contribute to the realisation of that union. In any case we are determined to ensure for our nationality in Austria, by all the means available to us, a full recognition of the same rights in the State as the German and Magyar nations already enjoy, and in this we rely upon the powerful demand for all genuine rights which wells warmly in every truly free breast. . . . In the name of liberty, equality and fraternity of all nations.

Fr. Palacký
President of the Slav Congress."*

The fruits of it all were, however, rather meagre. The uplift prevailing at the gatherings was marred by the revolutionary out-

* Quoted from the *Slavonic and East European Review*, XXVII (p. 305), 1947–48.

burst and military savagery in the streets of Prague on June 12 – only two days before the Congress was due to end. Martial law, with the usual reprisals, formed an ugly anticlimax to the mood of the previous days.

In the meantime Russia herself, whose image kept intriguing many a promoter of the Slav revival in Austria and elsewhere, was (apart from the Polish rising in 1831) practically untouched by the revolutionary storms abroad. Yet the ideological ferment among the intellectuals, with its dichotomy between Westernism and Slavophilism, continued. Even the official circles showed a certain interest in Slavdom, or at least in Orthodox Slavdom, in so far as the latter could foster Russia's political influence and expansion – a trend which had actually started even before Catherine II. As far back as 1712 distant Montenegro had obtained the assurance of protection from Peter the Great. Later, in the early years of the nineteenth century, V. N. Karazin even suggested – during the Serbian rebellion against the Turks in 1804–to Tsar Alexander I the idea of a Slav Empire with one of the Tsar's brothers at its head. Nor was the idea of Slav solidarity foreign to Russian freemasons either. Thus in 1818 a Masonic Lodge of Slav solidarity was founded at Kiev with a mixed membership of Poles and Russians. Among the Decembrists, too, there was a Society of United Slavs (as a branch of the "Southern Society") which was connected with the Poles and dreamed of a free and liberal union of all the Slavs. Several years later, at the end of 1846, there was established, in Kiev once more, a secret Brotherhood of St. Cyril and Methodius aiming at a spiritual and political union of the Slavs. The main initiative for it came from the Ukrainian historian N. I. Kostomarov; but one of the leading spirits of that Brotherhood was the great Ukrainian poet Taras Shevchenko (1814–61) who had to pay rather dearly for his Slav dreams once the Brotherhood had been detected by the Tsarist police.

After the Polish rising in 1831 the hostility of the Poles, and especially of the Polish émigrés abroad made, however, any real collaboration between them and the Russians difficult, if not impossible. Count Adam Czartoryski, a one-time Minister of

Foreign Affairs under Alexander I, championed (among the émigrés) a Slav federation, but anti-Russian and under the leadership of the Poles. Another prominent émigré, the Polish historian F. Duchinski (1817–93), even denied that the Russians were Slavs at all. According to him they were Turanians or Finno-Mongols speaking a Slav language and with only a sprinkling of Slav blood in their veins. This antagonism went on while the Russian intelligentsia was getting increasingly split up between the Westernising and the Slavophile factions. And the man who was responsible for some of the most provocative aspects of their controversy was the first Russian philosopher of history – Peter Chaadayev.

Some Early Antagonists
(Chaadayev, Gogol, Belinsky and Herzen)

I

In the ferment of ideas and ideologies during the "leaden regime" of Nicholas I (1824–55) it was Peter Chaadayev who made one of the daring challenges to everything cherished by Russia and her traditions. His assessment of Russia as compared with Europe was certainly frank in the extreme. Having thus secured for himself quite a prominent place in the early history of the Russian intelligentsia, he deserves more than a passing mention with regard to both his personality and his work.

Born in 1793 into a highly aristocratic Moscow family, Chaadayev belonged to the generation of Decembrist rebels. He was given a brilliant education and during Napoleon's invasion of Russia fought the French army at Borodino and later at Leipzig. In 1814 he stayed with his regiment in Paris. When back in St. Petersburg (1817), he was already in a rather critical mood which became the more bitter because of his genuine patriotism. He was on friendly terms with Pushkin, as well as with several Decembrists, but he never became a member of their circle. Pushkin dedicated to him three poems one of which ends with the challenging prediction that the ruins of autocracy will be adorned with the names of such dissatisfied young men as Chaadayev and Pushkin himself.

After some misunderstanding with the Tsar during the meeting of the Holy Alliance in Troppau (1820), whither he had been sent as a courier, Chaadayev gave up his commission. In the summer of 1823 he went abroad, once again, and stayed in Western Europe for nearly three years. He visited Germany, Switzerland, France,

England and Italy, all of which made him only more deeply realise the backwardness of his own country. On his return journey he passed through Venice, Vienna and Dresden. While at Karlsbad he met the philosopher Schelling with whom he remained in correspondence. Once back in Moscow, he was severely questioned by the police about his former association with the Decembrists. But he succeeded in clearing himself and, with the leisure now available, gave all his time to studies of problems connected with history and the philosophy of history. Puzzled by Russia's past as compared with that of Western Europe, he made his own conclusions which were likely to disturb not only the champions of a "Russian" culture, but the liberal and radical sympathisers with the West as well. He evidently planned a more comprehensive work on the philosophy of history several ideas of which have been left by him in a fragmentary form. But some time between 1829 and 1831 he wrote in French a series of *Philosophic Letters* addressed to a private person – a lady.* The first of these letters was rendered into Russian and appeared, in 1836, as a truly sensational piece in the *Telescope* – a periodical whose editor Nadezhdin, a one-time enthusiast for a national Russian civilisation, had himself become (by the middle of the 1830s) somewhat sceptical about it.

We are here concerned mainly with the first *Philosophic Letter*, since this was the only one published in Russia and in Russian at the time. And whatever its actual value, it still looks equivocal enough to make one understand the violent reactions to it both on the left and on the right. Although a Westerner by his outlook, Chaadayev yet repudiated the secularised aspects of Western civilisation and proclaimed the religious element the only true guiding force in history and in life, whether public or private. Influenced by Schelling on the one hand, and by Joseph de Maistre, de Bonald and Lamennais on the other, Chaadayev believed in the workings of divine Providence in history with the object of leading man and mankind to moral perfection according to the will of

* First published in the French original (only four of them) in *Oeuvres choisies de Pierre Chaadayev*, edited by P. Gagarin. Paris-Leipzig, 1862.

God. Yet in Chaadayev's opinion God's will does not imply determinism. On the contrary, he insisted on man's inner freedom and on his moral responsibility for the facts of history. Anxious to see the whole of life transfigured by religion, Chaadayev became a Christian by conviction. Only he discovered the true religious spirit not in Russian Orthodoxy (beloved by the Slavophiles) but in the Catholic West, especially as represented by its period of medieval Universalism. He saw in Western Europe before the schism and the Reformation one large family of Christian nations inspired by the same religious and moral ideals. Outwardly Chaadayev's romantic Catholicism was not devoid of a certain flavour of the Holy Alliance. On the other hand, in some of its aspects it was (as in Lamennais) quite revolutionary. His philosophic thought conformed to that pre-Kantian plane by virtue of which he considered intuitive religious truths superior to those of mere intellect in matters concerning the ultimate secrets of existence. And, like Lamennais, he demanded that all moral and social obligations of Christianity should be accepted voluntarily, without compulsion.

2

Having found true spiritual wholeness in the Catholic West, Chaadayev interpreted the entire history of Russia as the reverse of such wholeness. In the third of his *Philosophic Letters* he even postulated that Russia, being devoid of a cultural past of her own, should endeavour to become, as far as possible, one with the West, which she was already partly doing. "If the few habitudes of mind, of traditions and memories we possess; if the antecedents of our past do not tie us to any nation on earth; if in fact we do not belong to any system of the moral universe, we yet veer by our social surface towards the Western world. This tie, which is very weak indeed, does not unite us as closely with Europe as one might imagine, nor does it make us experience with all our being the grand movement which is there in process; on the other hand, it makes our future destinies depend on those of European society.

And so the more we try to be amalagmated with it the better for us."

But all this sounds mild when compared with the indictments Chaadayev hurled at Russia in his printed first *Philosophic Letter*. Devoid of any illusions, he attacked her defects without beating about the bush. Russia as he saw her was a nondescript and stagnant part of the world, neither East nor West. As for her history, she was devoid of any organic process, let alone a specific historical task or mission of her own. And the Russians themselves seemed to him to exist only as a warning to other nations. "We [Russians] are among those nations which do not fit into the structure of humanity but are here only in order to serve as a kind of lesson to the world." Russia might find her salvation if she joined the Catholic West from which she had been severed not only by her history, her habits and ways of life, but also by her lack of any true culture of her own. She lived outside history as it were and grew old without maturing. Wounded in his own pride as a Russian, Chaadayev deliberately exaggerated all those defects which he wanted his country to get rid of. Hence the ring of intense bitterness vibrating in one sentence after the other.

"In our homes we live as though in bivouacs: we are strangers in our own families; in our cities we are like nomads – worse than the tribes wandering in our steppes, because those tribes are more attached to their steppes than we are to our towns. . . . At the dawn of our history there was savage barbarism, then crude superstition, after which there came the brutal and humiliating Tartar domination whose traces have not quite disappeared from our lives even now. Such is the painful history of our early period. We have never known an age of endless activity and the poetic play of moral forces. Our social life in that period was but a dark, flavourless existence, devoid of strength and energy. Our memory does not harbour any enchanting reminiscences, and our tradition knows of no edifying examples. If you look back at the centuries of our history and at the enormous territory we occupy on this planet, you will not find a single memory which would make you

stop, or a moment which would speak of our past in a powerful, lively and colourful manner. One has to hammer into our heads things which with other nations are a matter of instinct and habit. Our memories do not go farther back than yesterday, and we remain as it were strangers to ourselves." And so on, and so forth.

Exaggerations such as these were at least partly due to the author's frustrated feeling of pride with regard to his country – a disposition which often used to make even the most intelligent of Russians decry everything Russian. The tyranny imposed by Nicholas I certainly could not but breed additional pessimism in a man of Chaadayev's stamp.

3

The effect produced by the *Philosophic Letter* was that of a bomb-shell. And the first casualty was the author himself. The *Telescope* was suppressed for good. Its editor Nadezhdin was exiled to the provinces, while the censor who had passed such an "unpatriotic" article was severely rebuked and sacked. Chaadayev was saved from a much harder ordeal only by being proclaimed officially mad. He was handed over to the tender mercies of a psychiatrist whose duty it was to look after his mental health for about a year. In spite of all these measures the impression made by the *Letter* could not be undone. The members of the intelligentsia realised full well that the vital questions formulated in such ruthless terms concerned them all. Was Russia really nothing more than "an illegitimate child of history" as Chaadayev would have it? Even those liberal-minded or radical Westerners who were willing to agree with his views were repelled by Chaadayev's partiality for religion, especially for Roman Catholicism. Those, however, who sided with the Slavophile trend forgave him neither his denigra-tion of Russia nor his sympathies with the Catholic Church at the expense of Orthodoxy. In fact, it did not take long before some of them submitted both Catholicism and the West to a criticism as merciless as the one Chaadayev had piled upon Russia.

His *Philosophic Letter* thus helped to widen the rift between the

two trends whose essential differences became definitely formulated during the next few years. Until then their ideological gap did not interfere even with personal relations between the opposing parties. Chaadayev himself, although a Westerner, was on friendly terms with such Slavophiles as Khomyakov, Kireyevsky, Samarin and Konstantin Aksakov, all of whom may have had frequent discussions with him. It should, however, be stressed again that the early Slavophiles, for all their patriarchal traditionalism, were not reactionaries. Some of them were as much persecuted by the Tsarist police as any progressive Westerners. On the other hand, the very fact that they stood for Orthodoxy (however much idealised), for "Russianness" and monarchism, made some rapprochement with the official patriots possible. There even were active links between the two, such as the historian Professor M. Pogodin and his periodical *Moskvityanin* (*The Muscovite*), founded in 1841.

For various reasons Chaadayev's *Philosophic Letter* can be regarded as a kind of landmark in the evolution of the Russian intelligentsia precisely because the breach between the two factions was not yet complete at the time. And it was during the subsequent widening of this breach that the intelligentsia became stirred by another bombshell entirely different from that of Chaadayev's: namely by Gogol's *Selected Passages from Correspondence with My Friends*. This book appeared at the beginning of 1847 and reflected not so much the ideological muddle of the period as of Gogol himself. Essentially an indignant and disappointed romantic in his outlook, Gogol felt as much of a stranger as Chaadayev did among the realities of Russian life. He gave vent to his indignation in his satirical comedy, *The Inspector General*, and even more in his novel, *Dead Souls*. It was only during his prolonged stay in Rome (which he loved more than any other place in Europe) that he found life bearable at all. But once back in Russia, the spectre of aimlessness, frustration and boredom hung over him like a curse. Unable to come to terms with life, he took refuge in the somewhat primitive religious meditations imbued with that spirit of Orthodoxy which had been grafted upon him

during his childhood and boyhood by his not exactly bright
mother. He now regarded his great literary talent as a special gift
bestowed by God who had chosen him as the spiritual guide
Russia was so much in need of. This conviction began to grow
stronger in him after Pushkin's tragic death in 1837 and reached
its peak after the success of the first volume of his *Dead Souls* (in
1842). The unfinished second volume of that novel was already
full of didactic tendencies and exhortations – an unmistakable sign
that Gogol's creative genius was getting exhausted. Aware of this,
he now intensified his "religious" moods and tried to impose his
influence upon the public as a didactic moral teacher pure and
simple. This was why he decided to issue his *Selected Passages from
Correspondence with My Friends* – a work as irritating as Chaadayev's *Philosophic Letter*, but in the narrow Orthodox sense. Moreover, his flirtations with the official Church and official Russia had
such a reactionary lining as was bound to cause consternation
among the Westerners and the Slavophiles alike. What the
Westerners thought of it was fully expressed in the famous letter
Belinksy sent to Gogol from Salzbrunn in the summer of 1847.
Here are a few passages taken from it at random and yet eloquent
enough to show what the anger of a Russian Westerner at his best
was like.

"You do not realise," he raged at Gogol, "that Russia's salvation
lies not in mysticism and pietism, but in the progress of civilisation
and in the growth of that human dignity which for centuries has
been dragged in mud and dung. . . . One can bear the feeling of
wounded pride, but it is impossible to bear the feeling of outraged
truth, of outraged humanity. It is impossible to be silent when,
under the cloak of religion and the protection of the knout, lies
and immorality are preached as truth and virtue. . . . I can well
understand why you base your doctrine on the Orthodox Church:
she has always been a supporter of the knout and a flatterer of
despotism; but why should you mix Christ with all this? What
have you found in common between Him and any Church,
especially the Orthodox Church? He was the first to announce to
men the doctrine of freedom, equality and brotherhood, and it

was with His own martyrdom that He sealed the sincerity of His teaching, which remained a salvation for man only until it was organised into a Church and based on dogmas. And the Church itself became hierarchic, that is a defender of inequality, a flatterer of power, an enemy of brotherhood among men – which she still is in our days."

The contrast between Chaadayev and Gogol is thus made obvious. Yet both of them were anxious to reunite culture with religion: Chaadayev from the Western-Catholic, and Gogol from the Russian-Orthodox angle. And since Belinsky himself was on the side of secularised civilisation, he could not agree with either, and least of all with Gogol. It is significant, though, that Gogol, who was terribly hurt by Belinsky's letter, tried to write an answer in which the following sentences might be singled out: "You say that the salvation of Russia consists in European civilisation, but what an immense and limitless word this is! Had you at least defined what one ought to understand by the name of European civilisation. We find in it all sorts of phalansteres, red ones and others – and all of them are ready to tear up each other, and all of them are full of such destructive, such subversive principles that each thinking mind trembles in Europe and keeps asking: Where is our civilisation?"

Chaadayev and Gogol thus represent two widely divergent attitudes towards the West as well as towards Russia. The quasi-religious outlet championed by Gogol was, for all its nearness to Slavophilism, reactionary enough to repel not only those Westerners who otherwise admired his literary work, but also the Slavophiles themselves. No wonder it was Belinsky's type of Westernism that prevailed among the Russian intelligentsia. This means that the Churches of whatever denomination hardly came in at all except as a matter deserving sharp criticism. Yet while discarding any official religion, the best members of the Westernising intelligentsia preserved much of their religious temperament, as well as their high ethical standard, to the full. A number of them, whether positivists, agnostics or atheists by their convictions, were also men willing to sacrifice their very lives to the cause of

freedom, justice and human brotherhood they believed in. Even those extremists among them who preached and practised destruction were anxious to destroy only in order to build up upon the ruins a new life or what they understood by it.

It is true that many radical sympathisers with the West believed in European science, theories and ideas rather uncritically. The fervour with which they adopted them was itself sufficient to alarm those members of the Slavophile camp who were sceptical of European civilisation and alarmed at the impact some of its fruits often had upon the less trained Russian minds. True enough, the secularising process, so ruthlessly enforced by Peter the Great, had been confined only to the upper classes. What would happen, though, if and when it should reach also the primitive peasantry, was a problem which kept disturbing many a thinking person. Joseph de Maistre (1754–1821) who had spent, as ambassador of Sardinia, a number of years in St. Petersburg, was sure that a process of this kind among the *moujiks* might mean nothing less than a passage from superstition to atheism and anarchy. The Slavophiles, looking back to the past, still clung to their faith in the virtues preserved by the Russian peasant masses through all the vicissitudes of history. The sympathisers with the West, on the other hand, believed that Western enlightenment was necessary to the whole of Russia, so long as it was rightly directed and rightly handled. All this made the two factions the more aware of their ideological differences. But before tackling these it may not be irrelevant to mention some of Chaadayev's own changes and mutations.

4

About a year after the appearance of his *Philosophic Letter* the harrowed author began writing – in French – his *Apologie d'un fou (The Apology of a Madman)* which remained in manuscript and unfinished. To those who blamed him for his lack of patriotism he answered here curtly that "love for one's fatherland is a good thing, but there is something higher than this – love of truth". It

was in the name of truth that he defended his Western sympathies against those opponents of his who refused to cast off their anti-Western blinkers. "Peter the Great found a sheet of paper and wrote on it: Russia and the West. . . . But now the West is no longer recognised, the work of Peter the Great is repudiated, one wishes to return to the desert. . . . And full of fervent zeal the most recent representatives of our patriotism keep proclaiming us the favourite children of the East. . . . You see that a real revolution is now taking place in our midst – a passionate reaction against enlightenment and Western ideas, against that enlightenment and those ideas which have made us what we are."

He still criticised Russia, but this time he treated the problem of Russia and Europe no longer in terms of black and white. His native country now seemed to him an enigma which he tried to unravel as best he could. He went so far as to admit that, no matter how insignificant Russia's past, there yet might be a great future in store for her, or even the task of settling the most serious questions that preoccupy the human race. There is, moreover, a well-nigh Slavophile flavour in the letter addressed to the Governor of Moscow in terms such as these: "I think we [Russians] come so late after the other nations in order to do things better than they have done. . . . I am deeply convinced that we are called upon to solve the major part of the ideas which have arisen in societies of the old order."

One may be inclined to think that Chaadayev, vexed and tired as he was of being in the position of an official madman, wanted to perform a kind of ideological Canossa* and thus make up for his harsh judgements on his own country. Yet such a view is open to doubt. His ambivalent attitude towards Russia must have been there considerably earlier, since in 1835 (that is a year before the publication of his *Philosophic Letter*) he wrote to his friend Alexander Turgenev in a spirit entirely different from the one expressed in that ill-fated document. "Do not laugh, you know my

* Th. G. Masaryk, in his *Spirit of Russia* (*Europe and Russia* in the original), seems to suspect in him a certain amount of opportunism when quoting Chaadayev's supposed remark: *On tient à sa peau* (One guards one's skin).

intimate conviction," he confessed to his friend. "The day will come when we shall place ourselves in the middle of intellectual Europe, and shall be stronger by our intelligence than we are today by our material power. Such will be the result of our long solitude; all great things have come from the desert. . . ." This he said not in antagonism to the West, but rather in the hope that Russia would rise to the status of a partner of the West in the historical tasks facing humanity as a whole. In this sense he tried to interpret even the policy of Alexander I who, in the last period of his reign, had seemed to be more concerned with Europe than with Russia herself. Or as Chaadayev put it in that letter: "Providence has made us too great for being egoists: she has placed us outside the interests of any single nation and has put on our shoulders the interests of mankind."

This attitude might be looked upon as a weapon directed against Chaadayev's own national inferiority complex. No wonder that the same man, from whom in 1836 Russia had heard some of the fiercest indictments ever addressed to her, should have written, ten years later, to the poet Prince Vyazemsky: "Our ways are not the same as those along which other people move; in time we shall certainly attain to all those blessings towards which the human race is striving; perhaps even, led by our faith [the Orthodox faith, this time!], we shall be the first to see the goal which God has set to humanity. The meaning of the part played by us in the world is still so profoundly hidden in the mysteries of Providence that it would be senseless to exalt ourselves before our elder brothers. They are not better than we are, but they have more experience."

His former notions of Russia's inferiority with regard to the West turned into one of possible equality between Russia and Europe, while his personal sympathies still remained with the West. What he really seemed to wish for was sincere cultural collaboration if not an eventual fusion between the two. In this respect, at any rate, he expressed the hopes of some of the best Russians of that or any subsequent period, even though doubts with regard to Europe were already on the increase not only

among the Slavophiles but also among some of those one-time Westerners who had come into a closer contact with European realities after 1848. A remarkable *volte-face* of this kind was that undergone by Alexander Herzen – one of the most brilliant Russian intellectuals of the post-Decembrist period.

5

Alexander Ivanovich Herzen (1812–70) was the illegitimate son of a wealthy landowner (Yakovlev) whose large estate he inherited and thus became a man of independent means. Deeply moved by the Decembrist tragedy, he decided even as a boy to fight autocracy and serfdom to the bitter end. While at Moscow University he became an admirer of Fourier and Saint-Simon whose socialist ideas landed him in two exiles during his short-lived attempts at civil service. Eventually he came to the conclusion that a successful struggle against Russia's evil was possible only from abroad where the truth about his own country could not be interfered with by Russian police and censorship. For this reason he left, in 1847, for Paris.

Yet this voluntary exile of his was soon fraught with a number of disappointments. What happened was that he witnessed the abortive revolutions of 1848 in which the reactionary elements gained a victory all over Europe. As a sympathiser with the working classes Herzen was the more repelled by the bourgeoisie triumphant, the more he saw how deeply rooted its mentality was in greed and envy. And since this mentality seemed to be prevailing in the West, he began to fear that in Europe even the socialist movement itself would in the end degenerate into a kind of bourgeois philistinism for all, no matter how much blood had been or might still be shed in this cause.

"What will come of this blood?" he asked in his book *From the Other Shore* – a matchless post-mortem of 1848 – and answered despondently: "Whatever comes of it it is enough that in this orgy of madness, revenge, strife, retribution, the world will perish, the world in which the new man cannot breathe or live, which

holds back the coming of the future." In the Introduction to the Russian edition of the same book* this former enthusiast for Western progress passed the following judgement upon Europe after the storm: "I see the inevitable doom of old Europe and feel no pity for anything that now exists." Moreover, in his long letter to Jules Michelet about the Russian people and socialism he expressed his own mood in these terms: "Men grow worried, disturbed. They ask themselves, is it still possible for Europe, that hoary Proteus, that decaying organism, to find within itself the strength to care about its own recovery? And having asked the question, they dread the answer. They tremble with suspense."†

Unlike Chaadayev or the Slavophiles, Herzen – a positivist by his outlook – was unable as well as unwilling to expect to find an outlet in religion. Even had he been swayed in that direction, his intellectual honesty would have averted him from adopting such a refuge. So the only alternative at his disposal was provided by his innate sympathy for the Russian people, the Russian peasant masses in whose traditional *mir* or village commune he discovered the possibility of a Russian type of agrarian socialism. In this respect he anticipated the Russian populist or *narodniki* movement of the 1860s and 1870s. Such was his new faith. As he himself exclaimed in his *Letters from France and Italy*: "It all ended for me by a spiritual return to my homeland. My faith in Russia was my salvation when I was on the very brink of ruin."

He even made one step further. Since the Russian people belonged to the Slav race, Herzen extended his sympathies to all the Slavs, beginning with the Poles. As though in the wake of some Decembrists (Pestel, Muravyov) he even thought of a free federal union of the Slavs, but with a difference. He pointed out to Michelet that "the idea of a union based on the principle of freedom must not be confused with imperial Panslavism, as it has been expounded in the past by the misguided or corrupted men". Yet in contrast to Palacký he maintained even at that stage that

---

* The introduction was written on March 1, 1849. The book itself was first published in a German translation, *Vom anderen Ufer*.

† Quoted from the English translation published by Weidenfeldt.

"without Russia the Slav world has no future: without Russia it will wither away, it will miscarry, it will be swallowed up by the German element, it will become Austria, it will fail to be itself. But I cannot believe that this in fact is to be its mission, its fate. . . . Once the Slav world has become unified, and knit together into an association of free autonomous peoples, it will at last be able to enter on its true historical existence."*

Unable to endure Paris any longer, Herzen left (in 1852) for London where he soon founded a free Russian press and began publishing two radical Russian periodicals: *The Polar Star* and the weekly *Bell* (*Kólokol*). The latter in particular was being regularly smuggled into Russia, and its merciless exposure of all the evils and misdeeds of the Tsarist bureaucracy was more than welcomed by the radical intelligentsia. His sympathies with Poland during the Polish rising in 1863 impaired, however, the popularity of *The Bell* among its Russian readers. Eventually Herzen left London for Geneva where he continued to publish it for a while in French, but this time without much success. He died in 1870 in Paris and was buried at Nice.

* ibid.

Kireyevsky and the Rise of Slavophilism

I

However critically one may view at present the Slavophile movement, one can by no means deny the part played by it in the
evolution of the Russian consciousness. Nor should one underrate
its explorings of the problem of culture as well as of Russia's
position with regard to Europe and the Western world. According
to the leftish historian and politician P. Milyukov, the Slavophile
current consisted of three important ingredients. Protest against
borrowings from Western civilisation was one of them. Insistence on the national originality (*samobytnost*) of Russia was the
second. And a Pan-Slav tendency, which implied sympathies with
the non-Russian Slavs, most of whom were under foreign domination, was the third. But even these three elements do not exhaust
the nature of Slavophilism. The movement itself was complex and
varied enough to include a number of facets: historiosophical,
religious, political, cultural, ethnic, racial, and even archaeological.
Consciously or subconsciously it was rooted, to some extent, in
Russia's innate feeling of inferiority with regard to Europe. And
so it was quite tempting to argue – in the way of compensation –
that the European West was "decadent", played out, and that
Russia, whatever her defects, was in the ascendant, with a glorious
historical and cultural task awaiting her in the future. The Slavophiles viewed the movement mainly in this sense, and their compensatory cultural and religious-philosophic perspectives had, of
course, a great deal in common with the romantic wave characteristic of the first half of the nineteenth century. Idealisation of
the Russian past, a quasi-Rousseauesque cult of the people, a
strong emphasis upon the individual character of the Russian
nation *qua* nation – all this was part and parcel of that romantic

nationalism which was fostered by such early Slavophiles as Ivan Kireyevsky and Alexey Khomyakov.

The very background responsible for the development of these two pioneers of the Slavophile movement was enough to make them work out practically all the tenets upon which it rested. Kireyevsky's earliest stimulus was that of Moscow, where he was born in 1806 and where he started (in the 1820s) his career as one of the exclusive "archive dandies" in the Collegium for Foreign Affairs. Here he was associated with the poet Dmitry Venevitinov and became a member of the "Wisdom Lovers" at a time when among the intellectuals of both Russian capitals Schelling's influence was paramount.

Even the atmosphere of Kireyevsky's ancestral estate of Dolbino in the Tula province was not devoid of cultural stimuli. His mother was a relation of the sentimental-romantic poet Vasily Zhukovsky who lived for a while at Dolbino and took great interest in Ivan and his younger brother Peter – the subsequent collector of the Russian *byliny*. Having lost her husband when her sons were still in their teens, their mother married a certain Yelagin – a man of wide interests and even something of a philosopher who proved to be an ideal stepfather to the two boys. As if prompted by the Moscow atmosphere of the 1820s, Kireyevsky decided to dedicate himself to a literary and philosophic career. Like Prince Odoyevsky he thought that it was about time to evolve a philosophy corresponding to the Russian mind and character, and above all to Russia's needs. He was also among the first to point out – in his excellent *Survey of Russian Literature for 1829* – the thoroughly national genius embodied in Pushkin's poetry. And even at that early period he contended that Russia, backward as she was, ought to absorb and assimilate what she needed of European civilisation, but in such a way as not to lose her own identity. Nor was he a stranger to the idea of a possible fusion of Russian and European cultural elements which could thus produce a new civilisation benefiting humanity as a whole.

While planning his literary future, he gave up his government post and in 1830 left for abroad with the intention of getting first-

hand knowledge of Western Europe. He remained outside Russia for some eight months, and this only in Germany where he did not seem very happy. In one of his letters he complained that there "does not exist on our planet a nation which is worse, more soulless, more stupid and boring than the Germans". In spite of such sweeping statements he was glad to attend in Berlin Hegel's lectures on the philosophy of history. He was introduced to Hegel personally, as well as to some of his followers. During his visit to Munich he also made personal acquaintance with Schelling; but on hearing of an outbreak of cholera in Moscow he hurried back to Russia in order to share the danger with the other members of the family. On his return to Moscow he began taking part in the discussions going on in a number of aristocratic salons. He, moreover, realised one of his literary ambitions by starting, in 1832, a periodical of his own which he called, surprisingly enough, *The European* (*Evropeyets*).

2

The very title of the periodical suggests that the young editor considered Russia to be part of Europe and wanted to treat her as such. This does not mean that he regarded her as a cultural satellite of Europe. He looked upon Russian culture as a specific ingredient of human culture in general. At the same time the romantic idea of a cultural synthesis, in this case the synthesis between East and West, between Russia and Europe, kept cropping up in his writings time and again. The idea itself was "in the air". Even such an official patriot as Professor Pogodin was able to write in one of his essays (on Peter the Great) about the one-sidedness and incompleteness of either Western or Russian culture taken separately. "They ought to unite, complete each other, and form a new and thoroughly West-Eastern, European-Russian culture."

This tendency remained a kind of *leitmotif* among the best of the Slavophiles, however severe their attitude towards Europe may often have been. Such severity was yet hardly apparent in the

young Kireyevsky when he started his periodical. Anxious to launch in it as many vital ideas as the censors and conditions would allow, he secured as his actual or potential contributors some of the best literary men of the day, including such poets as Baratynsky, Yazykov and Zhukovsky. Even Pushkin appeared on his list. In short, the periodical gave a fair promise to become a brilliant organ of the younger generation. With this hope Kireyevsky himself wrote for it a few critical articles and a somewhat provocative essay under the title, *The Nineteenth Century*. The essay contained several well observed characteristics of the century which was then in its third decade. It also expressed the author's admiration for the organic wholeness of Western culture – an attitude which he shared with Chaadayev.* Like Chaadayev he approved of the reforms of Peter the Great and wished for a close rapprochement between Europe and Russia. While regarding the French Revolution as a dividing line between the eighteenth and the nineteenth centuries, he emphasised the changes made by Europe since then. In art the former artificiality was being replaced by the beauty of truth, in religion one saw more tolerance, in human relations more simplicity, and in philosophy the tendency to reconcile realism with new idealism. In short, whatever the difficulties, Europe – practical as she was – still had a culture and even believed in it. Written on the whole in an objective and quiet manner, the essay yet failed to please the Tsar and the guardians of law and order. They sensed in it all sorts of subversive ideas "between the lines". Into such ordinary words as civilisation, enlightenment and free activity they read nothing less than liberty, constitution and even revolution. After the second issue the periodical was suspended by the police. The censor lost his job, and Kireyevsky himself was from now on regarded as suspect. He also forfeited in advance the chair of philosophy at Moscow University which he was anxious to obtain. Worst of all, he was forbidden to print his writings in any periodicals whatever.

Frustrated in this manner, he wrote little during the next eleven

* Kireyevsky knew Chaadayev personally and even may have read in MS. Chaadayev's *Philosophic Letter* long before it was printed.

years. And when he resumed writing once more, he showed the change he had undergone during all that period of silent meditation. There had of course been some outward influences. His brother Peter – an indefatigable admirer and collector of things Russian – was one of them. The enthusiastic co-founder of Slavophilism, Alexey Khomyakov, was the other. And finally, after his marriage in 1834, Kireyevsky often retired to his estate of Dolbino which was not far from the Optina monastery,* famous on account of its Elders or *Startsy*. As he was paying frequent visits to the monastery, his conversations with some of the monks fostered his own religious instinct which gradually took the direction of what he came to regard as the very spirit of a Christian culture. One of the peculiar activities of that monastery consisted in studying and commenting upon the writings of the Fathers of the Eastern Church. Kireyevsky himself was drawn into it and soon found in their writings "more wisdom than in entire German philosophy". According to him, theirs was the wisdom of genuine inner experience – as distinct from the intricate logical spinning in the West, however clever. More than once Kireyevsky expressed his regret that those writings were practically unknown in Europe. It was during the years of frustration and police supervision that he tried to work out the type of a "Russian" philosophy he had in mind. Under the religious stimuli he had meanwhile undergone he now definitely turned against the abstract rationalistic systems as such. What he wanted was a philosophy which might be capable not only of influencing our opinions but of transforming our consciousness and through it the whole of our existence.

In the 1840s Kireyevsky was aroused to more active efforts by the controversy between the Russian champions of Schelling and those of Hegel. He himself was on the side of Schelling whom he hoped to adapt to his own views and propensities now that the Westerners and the Slavophiles were getting increasingly differentiated or even mutually hostile. In 1845 he became, through Khomyakov's mediation, editor of Pogodin's periodical *The*

* The monastery described in Dostoevsky's novel, *The Brothers Karamazov*.

Muscovite which was hardly friendly to Europe.* Kireyevsky's Slavophile views were already settled when he took on the editorship. He and some of his sympathisers even thought that *The Muscovite* might be turned into a genuine Slavophile organ, but such hopes came to nothing. Kireyevsky himself edited only three issues, after which he gave up the job: partly because he had no official permission to edit the periodical. A few years later (in 1852) he contributed to Ivan Aksakov's *Moscow Miscellany* (*Moskovsky Sbornik*) his essay, *About the Enlightenment in Europe and the Enlightenment in Russia.* The Russian word for enlightenment – *prosveschenie* – stands here simply for culture, and it was in this sense that Kireyevsky used it. The tendency of the essay was as Russian as it could be. In spite of that the police found it subversive enough to clamp down, because of it, this publication as well.

When, soon after, the Crimean War broke out, the problem of Europe and Russia became of vital importance, since the two great European powers sided with Turkey against Russia. Fortunately, the defeat of Russia and the death of Nicholas I (on March 2, 1855) proved to be a blessing in disguise. Kireyevsky himself acknowledged in a letter to Pogodin (31, XI, 1855) that "we could have rotted away and got stifled without this shake-up of our very bones. Russia is in pain, but her trials are the pangs of birth. He does not know Russia and comprehend her in the depth of his heart who fails to see and to feel that something great and unique in the world is now being born by her." The accession to the throne of Alexander II inaugurated a new and better era. In April 1856 the Slavophiles were even allowed to start their own periodical, *The Russian Discourse* (*Russkaya Beseda*) under the general editorship of Alexander Koshelyov. The Slavophile spirit in this periodical (which existed for four years) showed however no hostility to what was considered good in Europe and her civilisation. At home it advocated the abolition of serfdom as the first condition for any improvements after the humiliating Crimean

---

* In the very first number of that periodical (which began to appear in 1841) Professor Shevyryov – a notorious official patriot – referred to Western Europe as a "reeking corpse".

defeat. It was for this journal that Kireyevsky wrote his last essay, *On the Need and the Possibilities of New Principles in Philosophy*, which he evidently intended to expand into a larger work written in the spirit of a "Russian" philosophy. But even before the essay was printed, he died of cholera on June 11, 1856.

3

Kireyevsky, like Chaadayev, was not a prolific writer. Still, in whatever he wrote he showed the mind of a thinker who refused to divorce philosophy from religion. The religious outlook on which the Slavophiles insisted, was really a battle they waged in order to save religion as an essential part of culture at a time when in Western Europe religion as such was on the defensive. The liberal ideas bequeathed by the French Revolution, the cult of science, and the entire background of the practical middle classes could not but undermine the spirit of that religiosity which had once animated the European West. In Russia things were different at least in so far as the uneducated lower classes and the peasantry had remained untouched by any sceptical or "nihilist" ideas. This itself was regarded by the Slavophiles as an advantage in their fight against the encroachments of Western atheism and the inner devastation caused by it. And since all of them had been steeped in the Russo-Byzantine faith, they were naturally anxious to discover in its deeper recesses the very core of that Christian spirit which they were determined to defend to the bitter end.

This does not mean that the early phase of this struggle was either fierce or fanatical. In the case of Kireyevsky, for instance, it was at first benevolently compromising as one can conclude from his suppressed periodical *The European*. In his own leading article, *The Nineteenth Century*, he adhered to Guizot's theory of our civilisation being the result of Greco-Roman, Christian and barbaric ingredients cemented into a unity by what it had inherited from ancient Rome. Of these Russia had not known the first one, and this explains many a defect in Russian life. Critical though he was of his own country, he yet implied the opinion that Europe

77

was getting exhausted while Russia was full of vitality. Instead of antagonising Europe, he argued, Russia should build up her own culture not in a spirit of enmity but in the name of a creative collaboration between the Western values and those which were peculiarly her own. In this way she should contribute what was best in her also to Europe and to mankind at large.

The idea of such a cultural collaboration between Russia and the West continued to preoccupy the Slavophiles even when they were anxious to stress the qualitative differences between the two. Thus in his essay, *About the Enlightenment in Europe and the Enlightenment in Russia* (written in the form of a long letter to the Slavophile-minded Count E. E. Komarovsky), Kireyevsky himself treated the two types of "enlightenment" as more or less antithetic. In one of his previous writings he had divided the enlightenment into two categories, one of them being part of man's spirit and inner make-up, while the other represented the purely external knowledge and the cold formal development of one's intellect. In a period of decay – so he says – one is always inclined to identify the second with complete truth and knowledge. This theme is here expanded and further developed in its application to the problem of Russia and Europe. Science and technique may have reached their climax in the West but, as Kireyevsky argued, cold intellectual analysis has already destroyed in Western Europe that essential meaning of life which alone might give the right direction to our existence and all our doings. Yet at the height of its power man's intellect came to the awareness of its own limitations by reaching the conclusion that vital higher truths are beyond the competence of mere abstract reasoning. After the superficial rationalistic optimism of the eighteenth century Western man saw the futility of such reasoning and became increasingly sceptical of his own intellect as far as the solution of the ultimate riddles of existence was concerned. Hence he either clung to the convictions and notions of life which had prevailed before that era, or else he grew indifferent to everything that was outside his materialistic gains and sensual appetites. Life in the West fell a prey to general "fragmentation" and cold individualism. Eventually one could

not help seeing the inadequacy of what Europe could offer to Russia.

But despite such a critical mood, Kireyevsky was still in a conciliatory frame of mind. "Both our love for European culture and our love for our own culture unite in their final point in one single love, in one single effort towards a living and therefore pan-human Christian culture." Such was his formula at the time. Instead of trying to get rid of all European influences in Russia, he only wanted to combine them with, and counterbalance them by, the best elements of that pre-Petrine Russia which had had no close contacts with the secularising humanistic process of European civilisation. While discussing this problem, Kireyevsky pointed out three specifically "Russian" features which seemed to him highly important: the spirit of the Orthodox Church; the essence of the true Russian enlightenment as something different from that of the West; and the peculiar formation of the Russian State. The problem of Russia and Europe, of East and West, which emerged from all that, was from now on in the centre of Kireyevsky's speculations. These assumed a strong religious flavour which had, however, nothing in common with Chaadayev's Catholic leanings and sympathies.

Aware of the fact that in Western Europe the Catholic Church had adopted (and adapted) Aristotle, while the Eastern Church preferred the wisdom of Plato, Kireyevsky became an inveterate admirer of the contemplative spirit of the East. Whereas in the Western Church the legal tradition of ancient Rome still persisted, the Byzantine Church laid stress not so much upon external legality as upon man's conscience and his innate sense of justice – a feature which Kireyevsky regarded as typical of the old Russian enlightenment. And as for the Russian State, it had arisen (so he says) peacefully, out of the social and religious consciousness of the people. How far this is historically true is a different matter. Furthermore, in the West there had existed all along a fierce struggle between the Church and worldly power on the one hand, and between religion and man's intellect on the other. Russia, however, having remained outside the influence of Rome,

Renaissance and Reformation, was able to escape all that. She had also avoided those excesses of abstract reasoning which, according to Kireyevsky, had weakened the creative power of Western Europe and were largely responsible for an enormous technical civilisation at the expense of inner culture. At the same time Western individualism, let loose, degenerated into egoistic self-indulgence at its worst. It became an agent of division and isolation so typical of modern man. Far from being against true individualism, Kireyevsky was convinced that the latter can be achieved only through man's self-realisation or self-fulfilment upon a spiritual or religious plane. Apart from such a plane man was bound to grow increasingly uprooted and "fragmented", what has actually happened in the West.

The edifice of European "enlightenment" was thus undermined by the factors which had either been latent in it or else were produced by it. At the same time abstract rationalism kept obscuring those living truths which transcend mere logic. Wisdom and life became divorced, and in the end philosophy turned against life itself. The father of modern philosophy, Descartes, confessed to being aware of his own existence not spontaneously but through logical syllogisms: *cogito ergo sum*. The sceptical philosophy of Hume and, eventually, Kant's conclusions with regard to the incompetence of man's "pure reason" (in so far as the ultimate truths of our being are concerned) did the rest. Kant himself pointed to the need of overcoming this blind-alley by some other means of cognition. Hegel brought the logical method to its climax, while Schelling demonstrated the onesidedness of Hegel's pan-logism and devised his own theory of the self-evolving "World-Soul" reaching in man's consciousness its own awareness. But Kireyevsky found Schelling, too, insufficient. So he continued his own peculiar quest which brought him even closer to the spirit of the Eastern Church at her most ideal. It was in the light of this spirit that he began to evaluate (whether rightly or wrongly) the "enlightenment" of Russia before Peter the Great in his last essay, *On the Need and Possibility of New Principles in Philosophy*.

4

As has already been pointed out, this essay reads like a draft for a larger work – planned, though never written. But even as it is, it illustrates Kireyevsky's final attitude towards the problems involved. It also marks his final attempt to pass from Western intellectualism to that supra-rational intuition which he thought he had found embodied in the Russo-Byzantine Christian consciousness. In his criticism of the philosophic thought of Bacon and Descartes he once again tried to show the inadequacy of a mere abstract intellectual approach. "For if a man rejects all authority except that of his own abstract thought, he can hardly go beyond that outlook according to which the existence of the world itself seems but transparent dialectics of his own reason." The truth behind the appearances can only be reached through the wholeness or totality of man's spirit, which means the immediate contact of one's consciousness with the mysterious universal Will. Kireyevsky thought that Pascal might have created such a new and essentially religious type of philosophy, had he lived long enough to complete his work. What prevailed instead was the influence of the English philosophic thought, followed by Voltaire, rationalism and scepticism. But when reason detaches itself in this manner from the entire sphere of the spirit and begins to function on its own, it severs the cognitive process from the deeper reality of things. This was why Kireyevsky came to consider German philosophic idealism, with its abstract intellectual spinning, basically wrong. At the same time he disapproved of those Western minds who tried to save religion by separating it from both intellect and philosophy, since such separation was bound to harm religion itself.

Preoccupied with the universal message of Christianity as bequeathed by the spirit of the Eastern Church, Kireyevsky pointed out that not only in Catholicism, but in the Protestant religion, too, the boundary line between intellect and religious consciousness has been disturbed and distorted. Moreover, since in Protestantism there was no general agreement about the essential

religious truths, every one of its adherents considered it appropriate to interpret them in his own way. This fostered the rise of rationalist philosophy. In the West intellect and religion were bound to become hostile to each other despite the repeated single efforts to reconcile them. Instead of serving life Western philosophy thus lost its touch with living life and became a destructive agent. Cut off from the inner essence of things, Western man fell a prey to the external physical or material world to such an extent as to lose all interest in religious and spiritual values. In Kireyevsky's opinion Russia alone, or rather the people of Russia, had been spared such a fate. In spite of the reforms of Peter the Great, the Russian masses preserved their religion and the unity imparted by it as the most vital factor in man's existence. Such was the people's Russia as distinct from the Russia of the Westernised upper classes.

Convinced that man is able to penetrate to the heart of reality only through the whole of his being, Kireyevsky insisted that logical or purely rational thinking should be subordinated to that intuitive supra-rational plane on which such elements as reason, will, faith and feeling could find their unifying focus and be guided by it. Here at any rate man's heart and intellect might be harmonised, provided his moral will, too, were directed towards it. He sincerely thought he had found the inner wholeness of this kind in the Orthodoxy of the Russian people. Hence he could not help rejecting the "fragmented" ways of the Russian upper classes and the intelligentsia who had no roots in the people's religion and therefore knew nothing of the inner wholeness imparted by it. According to Kireyevsky, it is only on the plane of such complete wholeness that the highest supra-rational Truth might co-ordinate the lower truths in its service. Left to themselves, these truths become split up, isolated, and hostile to any unity, hostile to man and life.

5

In his further explorations Kireyevsky contrasted the religious consciousness of the Russian people with the cold erudition of the

Russian elite. One of his fears was that the type of erudition borrowed by the Russian intellectuals from the West and irreligious by its nature, might infect the people and ravage them spiritually – a process which would result in a victory of the materialistic European element with all the ensuing conflicts and confusions. The opposite possibility existed, however, in so far as the people might, perhaps, win the intellectuals over and make them assimilate the adopted European influences without forfeiting the religious spirit inherent in the Russian masses. Such a fusion might even produce a new kind of "enlightenment". Something similar happened when Christianity was paving its way from the pagan erudition to the wisdom recorded by the Fathers of the Eastern Church. For us it would be impossible to repeat the process in exactly the same manner as in those days. Our conditions are more complex, and so are the problems we are called upon to cope with. Yet by integrating the true religious vision and wisdom of old with our contemporary knowledge, we could obtain a type of philosophy which, instead of remaining on the bookshelves, might permeate and change the whole of our existence.

While pointing out the difference between the two German words *Verstand* and *Vernunft*, Kireyevsky agreed with Schelling that Western philosophy had become a series of schematic intellectual propositions. And so he demanded a deeper, a more direct method of cognition. Convinced that the element of faith underlies all our knowledge, he insisted upon what he called the "believing reason" or the intuitive "reason of faith" which, according to him, is at the core of man's true being. He warned us, however, that such reason should not be confused with man's "natural reason". The latter is competent in dealing with external matters only, whereas the "believing reason" (as he interprets it) can serve as a link between man, God and the world. Once this link has been lost, man too is lost. He becomes a stranger in the universe, a stranger to others and to himself.

Kireyevsky looked upon the West as a world which had lost such a link. Hence the "fragmented" humanity of Europe with its

egoism and egotism run amok. In the despotic organisations of the East, where the individual human ego is of no account, the situation was equally bad as far as true human relations were concerned – bad from the other end. The task of Russia should be to provide a remedy for both by giving the world a genuine religious culture in which one's inner freedom and the fulness of existence of each single individual should go hand in hand with the universal sympathy and brotherhood of man. On this basis also a final reconciliation between Russia and Europe, between East and West could and should be achieved.

It was in the name of such a culture that Kireyevsky proceeded to work out the tenets of that religious-philosophic ideology which served as a basis for Slavophilism especially in its early stages. In the days when Hegel's philosophy was gaining ground in Russia at a rapidly increasing pace, Kireyevsky rejected Hegel, Hegel's *Philosophy of History* included. He rejected the latter above all on account of its determinism which seemed, to him at least, to exclude freedom and chance in history. At the same time he regarded as absurd the very thought that at each historical period only a certain "chosen" nation should lead the rest of mankind towards its appointed goal. On the contrary, such progress is achieved through the efforts and endeavours of all nations – each according to its own capacity. And if an important role in this new era be assigned to Russia at all, it is only on condition that she might correct the mistakes made by the West and thus show the way out of the impasse in which humanity has been landed by these mistakes. Hence the idea of a synthesis of Russia and Europe was not a futile one. It may have sounded plausible even according to Hegel's triade. If the antique civilisation was the *thesis* and the Western civilisation the *antithesis*, then the Russian (or Russian-Slav) civilisation would provide the *synthesis* to come. Such a synthesis would bring about also a solution of the problem of Russia and Europe in the name of a universal union of mankind. But of course, being a Slavophile, Kiryevsky wished that the leading role in this universalism should be assigned to Russia.

To conclude, the whole of Kireyevsky's philosophy remained

in the shape of a torso. In this he resembles Chaadayev. Yet it was he who gave the direction to the Slavophile movement, although he himself had not avoided some of those pitfalls which resulted from his idealisation of the Russian past, as well as from not making sufficient distinction between what might be called essential Christianity and that official Russian Church which had received such hard blows in Belinsky's letter to Gogol. Still, the integrity of Kireyevsky's thought and aspirations was beyond doubt. This was why even such a radical anti-religious and anti-philosophic Westerner as the "nihilist" Pisarev referred to him as an honest Russian Don Quixote. "Slavophilism," he wrote in 1861, "is not an epidemic which has come to us from heaven knows where; this is a psychological phenomenon, due to unsatisfied dreams. Kireyevsky was anxious to live a reasonable existence, to enjoy all that man's soul aspires to, to love, to believe. But real life failed to provide him with all this. On the other hand, he animated it, idealised it and coloured it according to his own wishes. In this manner he became a Knight of the Doleful Countenance, resembling the unforgettable Don Quixote who was sighing for the incomparable Dulcinea de Toboso."

CHAPTER SIX

Khomyakov and Others

I

In spite of the sketchy nature of his work, Ivan Kireyevsky had launched those tenets of Slavophilism which were expanded by other members of the movement, notably by Alexey Khomyakov – the most active early ideologist of the Slavophile faction. In him, too, one can study that peculiar mixture of religiosity, romanticism and Schelling which swept the Slavophile current at the time. He struggled for the religious principle in life all the more valiantly because he could not help being painfully aware that among the educated classes of Russia religion had lost or else was rapidly losing its importance. His basic principles did not essentially differ from those of Kireyevsky. His conception of the "wholeness of existence" was practically the same. And so was his stress on the role of the supra-logical (or supra-rational) element in life for the sake of which he fought the unswerving logical reasoning of Hegel and his followers. Realising that after Hegel any further quest in that direction was futile, he became a religious philosopher *par excellence* in the days when in Denmark, too, Soeren Kierkegaard fought a similar, though much more individual, battle. Like Kireyevsky, Khomyakov rejected also Hegel's philosophy of history, proclaiming it a "systematic ghost in which severe logical consistency and assumed determinism only serve as a mask behind which there hides the limitless wilfulness of the learned systematiser himself". And like Kireyevsky again he clung to the same Orthodox ideal in whose spiritual and moral freedom he thought he had found the essence of Christianity. It was largely on this ground that he contrasted the religious spirit of Russia and Europe with the subsequent emphasis on the importance of the Slav world in general. In the circle of such Slavo-

philes as Kireyevsky, the brothers Aksakov, Yury Samarin and Alexander Koshelyov, Khomyakov stands out as a truly dynamic, versatile and colourful personality of the movement. In his writings the struggle for a cultural way of life based on religion reached its climax. And the intensity of that struggle made him increasingly anti-European – in so far as the scientific and positivist West seemed to be less and less in favour of a religious ideal. Like Kierkegaard in Scandinavia, Khomyakov gave the whole of his life to his cause. And some of the weapons with which he fought for it were ingenious enough to deserve a closer scrutiny.

Not unlike the rest of the Slavophiles, Alexey Stepanovich Khomyakov came of a well-to-do patriarchal gentry family. His parents owned estates in the provinces of Tula, Ryazan and Smolensk, as well as a house in Moscow where Alexey was born on May 1, 1804. He became much attached to that city whose picturesque and warm "Russianness" seemed to him (as well as to other Slavophiles) the very opposite of the cold, bureaucratic and Westernised St. Petersburg. It was at Moscow University that he graduated. As a boy of seventeen he had tried to run away from home in order to join the Greeks in their fight for freedom, but was stopped at the last moment. After his service in the army, he left – in 1825 – for Paris where he remained for about eighteen months. His impressions of Western Europe were already then somewhat ambiguous. What left, however, a pleasant memory in him was the hospitality he had enjoyed among the Austrian Slavs on his return journey to Moscow. In 1828, when Russia declared war on Turkey, Khomyakov promptly rejoined the army. During that campaign he came into contact with another Slav nation while fighting the Turks in Bulgaria whose sturdy peasantry he liked and admired.

Khomyakov's proper ambience was and remained Moscow. He spent much of his time on his estates, yet he was always glad to be back in the old Russian capital. Here he was a welcome guest in a number of salons which were anxious to be *au courant* of up-to-date trends and ideas. As a formidable controversialist he was admired not only by his followers but also by his opponents.

Besides, whatever he did, bore the stamp of a man endowed with that irrepressible energy which needed several outlets and directions. Khomyakov was many-sided enough to include in his writings philosophy, history, theology, a number of poems, two tragedies, not to mention his essays, articles and polemics written in a clear, beautiful prose. In addition he was an inventor, a painter, a homeopath, a student of Sanscrit, a passionate hunter, and a successful agriculturist – especially after his marriage (in 1836) to the poet Yazykov's sister, Ekaterina Mikhailovna, with whom he was exceedingly happy until her death in 1852. He was interested in all current problems, and most particularly in the abolition of serfdom which he regarded as the greatest social and moral evil of his country. Thus in a letter he wrote in 1848 to Countess Bludov he frankly called the serf-owners (himself included) enemies of Russia: "We are her enemies because we are the lords of our enslaved compatriots, because we debase the people and at the same time deprive ourselves of true civilisation."

2

Khomyakov's many activities received an even wider scope after his journey to England which he undertook in 1847 together with his wife and two children. He liked England. He admired her stability, her traditionalism, and even her tories struck him as a necessary factor in the pattern of British life. "Of all countries I have visited in my short journey," he wrote (in English) on September 8, 1847, to his friend William Palmer,* "England is the only one which I shall think about with a deep feeling of sympathy. . . . I know very well that England lacks perhaps as much as Germany itself, the blessing of religious unity; but delusive as it is, still its appearance is more consoling than its manifest absence." A contrast was provided by what he said in the same letter about Berlin where it was written: "Here in Berlin it would

---

* A fellow of the Magdalen College and member of the Oxford Movement. His correspondence with Khomyakov is a reliable approach to the latter's ideas. Subsequently, Palmer became a Roman Catholic.

be difficult to find a single point of faith, or even of feeling, which could be considered as a link of true spiritual communion in the Christian meaning of the word. Even the desire for harmony seems to be extinguished, and predominance of individualism, that spiritual solitude among the ever-busy crowd, sends to the heart a feeling of dreariness and desolation."* A pleasanter atmosphere during his return journey awaited Khomyakov in Prague where the All-Slav Congress of 1848 was soon to take place. In the old Czech capital Khomyakov felt more at home. He saw a great deal of Vaclav Hanka – an incorrigible Russophile and a Czech counterpart of James Macpherson.† No wonder Prague figures in Khomyakov's verses as well.

The strain which the disastrous Crimean War had put on the Slavophiles, and indeed on the entire intelligentsia whatever their ideological complexion, can hardly be exaggerated. Yet, as has already been pointed out, the political "thaw" which followed upon the death of Nicholas I and the end of the campaign, allowed also the Slavophiles to breathe more freely. Konstantin Aksakov even sent to the Emperor Alexander II a Memorandum about the situation in Russia worded in terms of unusual frankness. Also the forthcoming emancipation of the serfs was now taken for granted. Needless to say, Khomyakov became a frequent contributor to the Slavophile *Russkaya Beseda* (*The Russian Discourse*) and wrote on a variety of topics. At the same time he continued to take part in the lively discussions as a debater who always had the courage of his own opinions, especially when these failed to coincide with the accepted trends of thought. Alexander Herzen, who happened to be on good personal terms with Khomyakov, suspected in him a certain amount of Eastern cunning, however much he admired his many gifts as well as his debating skill.

* Quoted from *Russia and the English Church* by W. J. Birkbeck.

† In his patriotic zeal Hanka had become one of the forgers of "ancient" Czech manuscripts whose main purpose was to show to the world that his own nation, too, could boast of fine medieval poetry. The controversy about the authenticity of those manuscripts went on for several decades before their falsification was definitely proved. An English version of the poems appeared in 1853. Their translator was Count Kolowrat.

Pogodin, on the other hand, who was not a bad judge of men, said (many years later) that in Khomyakov's arguments, writings and conversations "there was much that was paradoxical, his propositions were sometimes inaccurate, and even his conclusions, perhaps, contradictory; but his sallies were so original, so unexpected and fresh in their character, and were delivered with such kindliness, good nature and skill, that they were always suggestive and pleasant to listen to".

In 1859 Khomyakov was elected president of the Society of Friends of Russian Literature. It was he who in February of the same year greeted Leo Tolstoy as a new member of the Society. And, strange to say, in that welcoming speech Tolstoy was rebuked on account of his art-for-art's sake method in some of his early writings. In the following year Khomyakov was spending the summer on his estate at Ivanovskoe in the Ryazan province. One night, while completing a long letter to Samarin, he had a sudden attack of cholera – contracted from the stricken peasants whom he was trying to cure. The neighbouring squire (Muromtsev) came at once to help him, but all efforts were in vain. On September 23, 1860, Khomyakov was carried off by the same disease of which (some four years earlier) Kireyevsky, too, had died.

3

A short cut to Khomyakov's thought might be provided by his own philosophy of history,* as well as by his numerous letters, especially those addressed to his English friend William Palmer. It was towards the end of the 1830s that he began jotting down his ideas about mankind's history. He continued to do so to the end of his life without finishing or even properly systematising the planned work which, for some obscure reason, he called *Semiramida* (Semiramis). At the basis of his erratic historical speculations he put the idea of the struggle between Freedom and Necessity

* There are several studies of Khomyakov available in English, notably by N. Berdyayev, N. Zernov, B. L. Brazol, and more recently by Peter Christoff.

passing throughout the entire human development. In this he followed Schelling and Hegel who identified Spirit with freedom, and Matter (which is subject to the law of gravity) with the opposite of freedom. Hence he divided the nations into those which have realised in their existence the "Iranian" principle of freedom on the one hand, and those which have succumbed to the "Kushite"* principle of necessity on the other. While using this exotic terminology of his own, Khomyakov saw in the struggle between the two principles the drama of history.

Among the early "Kushite" states Khomyakov mentions Ethiopia, Babylon, Egypt, Syria, Chaldea and Southern India. All these were, in his opinion, devoid of that inner freedom which, later on, was more or less embodied in the "Iranian" white race. According to him, each nation or race adheres to one of these two trends, or else is subject to a mixture of both. And since he, too, regarded religion as the most important force in the evolution of any individual, community, nation, or culture, he evaluated everything from this particular angle. According to him a true social body is a free community cemented from within by the religious power of spirit and love. Only such a community is a social organism as distinct from a mere social mechanism. But once its spiritual force is spent, gradual decay or disintegration sets in, no matter how much one tries to disguise it by external bustle and activities. Starting with these premises, Khomyakov came to the conclusion that the highest spiritual force keeping individuals and communities together was the spirit of the Christian Church which he identified, of course, with the Russian-Orthodox Church as he saw (or wanted to see) her. It was in his own interpretation of Russian Orthodoxy that he thought he had found the embodiment of that spiritual unity in freedom and freedom in unity in the name of which he rejected the entire character of Catholicism, for example. Khomyakov, like Kireyevsky, saw in Catholicism above all compulsory external law inherited from

* Kush is the name of an ancient region with a fairly high African civilisation along the middle Nile between Egypt and Sudan. Herodotus refers to Kushites as Ethiopians.

ancient Rome and taking the upper hand over one's free conscience and love, an attitude which had been stressed also by another Slavophile – Yury Samarin. Here freedom had become a victim sacrificed to the imperial unity under the Popes. Yet under that unity there was also a great deal of rationalism which was later adopted and strengthened by the various Protestant denominations to such an extent as to reverse the Catholic attitude and to champion freedom at the expense of unity. This led not only to countless sects but also to that kind of personal quest for truth which culminated in the philosophy of Kant and Hegel. Still, the one-sided rationalistic intellect which had severed philosophy from religion, that is from the true realm of spirit, was bound to inflict upon Europe her materialism and, together with it, that worship of prosperity which became so prominent a feature in a number of Protestant countries. In some respects Khomyakov anticipated such critics of Protestantism as Overbeck and Lagarde, while yet preserving his blinkers with regard to Russian Orthodoxy. At the same time he was convinced that the atrophy of religious consciousness was responsible also for the restive and revolutionary disposition typical of Western man. References to the decay of Europe – once a "land of holy wonders" – can be found also in Khomyakov's poetry.

The conclusion was obvious. Convinced that, in contrast to the West, the true Christian spirit continued to live in the ideal Russo-Byzantine Church and in the religious consciousness of the Russian people, Khomyakov was only too ready to provide some tangible proof to this effect. And he thought he had found it in the Russian *mir* or *obshchina* – the agricultural village commune in which the land was owned not individually but by the entire village and was redistributed periodically between individual households according to their needs. Another valuable Russian institution was the *artel*: a co-operative association of artisans who agreed to work together in their respective professions according to a high code of honour and efficiency. Like several other Slavophiles, Khomyakov considered the *mir* not so much an economic as primarily a moral factor which he admired rather uncritically

and without reserve. Most of all was he impressed by the fact that in vital matters the unanimous consensus of all the members of the *mir* was required. This proceeding he found basically different from the majority principle adopted by the legalistic West. And since he saw in it the voice of conscience, of the "inner truth", felt as it were by all the members alike, he was naturally anxious to connect it with his own idea of the Church. A link between the two was his ingeniously worked out concept of the *sobornost* – typical of a community integrated from within through the power of love and spiritual freedom. According to Nicholas Berdyayev, who was one of Khomyakov's partial modern followers, the untranslatable word *sobornost* "signifies a quality of life which affirms the reality of freedom by widening the scope of freedom and by revealing its transcendent, universal dimension. The recognition of the absolute priority of freedom does not, therefore, denote, as some would like to make out, individualistic self-assertion. Freedom of the spirit has in fact nothing in common with such individualism: to be free is not to be insulated, it is not to shut oneself up, but on the contrary, to break through in a creative act to the fulness and the universality of existence."* In another work (*The Beginning and the End*) the same author says that "*sobornost* is not a collective reality which stands higher than man and issues orders to him. It is the highest spiritual qualitative power in men; it is entering into the communion of the living and the dead. The *sobornost* can have no rational juridical expression. Each must take upon himself the responsibility for all."

In his own explanation of this communal spirit Khomyakov turned the *sobornost* even into a peculiar way of cognition. He was convinced that mere analytical intellect, clinging to an impoverished egoistic soul, can know only the formal relations between things, since the noumenal essence of things, Kant's *das Ding an sich* (thing in itself) is hidden from man's logic and reason. Hence he rejected Western philosophy in so far as it had mistaken the logical reason for the totality of man's spirit, and logical concepts

---

* Quoted from Berdyayev's *Dream and Reality* (Bles). In the above passage the word individualism is obviously substituted for egoism and narrow egotism.

for the only basis of knowledge. He actually insisted on what Kireyevsky had defined as the intuitive "believing reason" which he himself was inclined to combine with the unanimous consensus of all, as exemplified by the *sobornost*. He went so far indeed as to assert that a fundamental truth, inaccessible to single individuals, might be revealed – evidently through a kind of *participation mystique* – to the consciousness of an entire collective body united on the plane of that *sobornost* which he regarded as part and parcel of the ideal (or rather idealised) Orthodox Church. Referring to Catholicism as tyranny, and to Protestantism as unprincipled revolt, he had to ask the question as to where, then, unity could be found without tyranny, and freedom without revolt. Quite oblivious of the record of official Orthodoxy, he asserted that there is only one true Church. And this Church is called Orthodox, Eastern, or Graeco-Russian. In short, *ex oriente lux*.*

This meant that Russia was presumably the only country in which an organic unity between religion and life, between culture and religion, was still preserved. So much for Khomyakov's desperate battle for religion. He thought that in spite of Europe's stupendous quantitative achievements Russia was qualitatively superior to her, since the *direction* in which she was going was the right one. Hence it was not for Europe to lead Russia, but the other way round. Russia's traditional feeling of inferiority with regard to Europe was thus turned by Slavophilism into one of superiority. The very salvation of the West now depended as it were on Russia. In short, the materialistic Europe was doomed to perdition unless Russia revealed and imparted to her the essential Christian spirit, the spirit of universal sympathy and love. Such was in fact Russia's historical mission as cherished by the early Slavophiles. Khomyakov was of course fully aware of the faults and vices of his own country. He enumerated these in his poem *To*

---

* Khomyakov's three theological (and intensely polemical) pamphlets published in French in 1853, 1855 and 1858 under the title *Quelques mots par un Chrétien orthodoxe sur les communions occidentales* are beyond the scope of this brief chapter. Suffice it to say that in spite of his polemics with other Christian denominations, he too sincerely wished for a reunion of the Churches.

Russia, for example, without any reticence.* Yet hoping that his nation might be great enough to redeem them, he also wished that Russia and the Slav East in general should become "not the East of Xerxes, but of Christ", i.e. animated by a supra-national universal idea of brotherhood. Like Dostoevsky after him, he saw in this the Russian question *sub specie aeternitatis*. "The Russian question in all its aspects is undoubtedly the only true universal question of our time," he wrote to Samarin on June 23, 1845. And Dostoevsky himself was echoing Khomyakov when writing in the 1870s: "The future Russian Idea is not yet born, but the entire earth awaits it in pain and suffering. . . . I make no attempt to compare Russia with the Western nations in the matter of economic and scientific renown. I only say that the Russian people are perhaps among all nations the most capable of upholding the ideal of universal union of mankind, of brotherly love, of the calm conception which forgives contrasts. This is not an economic, but a moral trait."

Is it then surprising that Khomyakov, while strongly resenting the low opinion the Western nations had about Russia, was doing all he could to show that his country was not so black as it looked, or as it was painted? He, too, was anxious to prove – hardly very convincingly – that even the Russian State had evolved not through conquest and violence (like the States in Western Europe), but out of the spirit of the *mir* and the innate moral character of the people. And however active Western Europe may have been in the past, he thought that her leading role in history was now as good as finished. Russia was destined to take over the leadership, whether Europe liked it or not. But it transpired that Europe neither relished such a prospect nor did she seem very anxious to change her attitude towards Russia. The only Europeans among whom Russia had few or no detractors were the non-Russian Slavs, however much they disapproved of the Tsarist tyranny. Apart from such hereditary enemies of things Russian as the Poles, these Slavs, conscious of being of the same race, continued to look

* This poem found a strange echo in one of A. Blok's poems beginning with the words, "To sin shamelessly", written in 1914.

upon Russia and the Russians as their potential allies, protectors and, perhaps, also liberators. Moreover, a large portion of them – the Serbs, the Bulgarians and Macedonians in the Balkans – were of the Orthodox faith; which was a further reason why the Slavophiles should be interested in them and keep in contact with them. One of the most enthusiastic promoters of such contacts was undoubtedly Khomyakov.

4

During his two visits to Austria Khomyakov had enjoyed such a friendly reception among the Czechs as he could never forget. While in Prague in 1847 he even wrote in Hanka's album a brief prayer "for Russia and all the Slavs" which could serve as a motto for Slavophile activities in general. A great deal for the rapprochements of this kind was done also by the lecturers and professors of the Slav studies at Russian universities. In 1835 chairs of Slav languages and literatures were established at the Universities of St. Petersburg, Moscow, Kazan, and Kharkov. And quite a number of Russian scholars were sent to the Slav countries for the sake of their studies. In 1836 Professor Sreznevsky made, while stopping in Ljubljana, personal acquaintance with the Slovene poet Preseren who dedicated to him a few lines written in the spirit of Slav brotherhood. Some ten years later Professor Hilferding undertook an extensive journey among the Southern Slavs and wrote a lively account of his impressions of Bosnia and Hercegovina. A frequent visitor to the Slav countries was Professor Pogodin. Several minor representatives of the Slavophile movement (V. A. Panov, P. V. Chizhov, A. N. Popov, D. A. Valuyev) also made repeated journeys among the Western and Southern Slavs, and the records of their impressions helped to inform the Russian readers about those kindred nations and the countries they lived in. Later, in 1860, Ivan Aksakov, too, travelled among the Slavs.

It should be pointed out, though, that among the problems waiting to be solved the Russo-Polish problem was still looming

forward as the thorniest of them all. And as the years went on it seemed to be less and less susceptible of a solution. Another thing which must have unpleasantly surprised Khomyakov was the fact that the great Slav Congress at Prague had proceeded in the spirit of Western liberal principles and without the participation of a single Slavophile even as an observer, although among the delegates there were a number of Serbs. Was this a danger signal to the effect that even the Orthodox Southern Slavs might be tempted to look for their cultural orientation no longer in Russia but in the West? Such a fear was expressed by Khomyakov in the letter he wrote to his friend Popov on March 17, 1848, that is only two months and a half before the Congress. While referring to the possibility of Austria's dissolution and the liberation of the dis-contented Austrian Slavs, Khomyakov proceeded: "But shall we be able to benefit from it? It is sad, but I must acknowledge that there will be as many fears as hopes. The majority of the Slavs (Bohemia and Poland) have been spoilt by the German-Latin element to the marrow of their bones. The others, less spoilt (the Slovaks, the Slovenes etc.) will have leanings towards us, but the first joy, the first drunkenness with freedom, will probably draw them towards the countries from which the actual movement (of freedom) has come, that is towards the West. The races which have remained least contaminated (the Serbs) will probably succumb to the temptation of the political organization as well as of the material civilisation by which we, too, have been carried away since Peter the Great. These are probable or certain dangers which threaten us: this is what we have to fight against."

Apprehensions of this kind may explain why Khomyakov sent, some twelve years after the Prague Congress, a didactic-rhetorical *Message from Moscow*, addressed to the Serbian nation and signed by ten other Slavophiles as well. The whole of that *Message* was a warning to the Serbs that they should be on their guard against the West and look for their guidance in Russia rather than in Western Europe. At any rate, they were Slavs, but Slavdom alone was no longer enough. They should not be "led astray by the Western lie". They should not give up their Orthodoxy and their own

patriarchal Christian virtues by aping and imitating the European West as the bulk of the Russian intelligentsia were doing. "May God save you from an ordeal of this kind."

Khomyakov's anti-Westernism was yet a matter of *odi et amo*, of hatred and love combined. What he repudiated in the West was the complete secularisation of its culture; but his hope that Russia might ultimately "save" Western Europe from its materialistic blind-alley was itself a proof that he, too, wished to see a united humanity, a united East-West. In this respect he was unlike some of the later Slavophiles, such as Danilevsky and Leontyev, both of whom rejected – each for reasons of his own – any affiliation with the West. But before tackling their deviations, a cursory mention of the brothers Aksakov is necessary. And also of their fellow-fighter, Yury Samarin.

5

The two Aksakovs, Konstantin (1817–60) and Ivan (1823–86) were sons of the author Sergey Aksakov whose classical *Family Chronicle* unfolds before the reader an unforgettable panorama of life on a remote patriarchal estate where even serfdom had a certain idyllic flavour, provided the squire was not a brute but a human being. Both brothers were brought up in the atmosphere of Moscow and in their youth belonged to the Stankevich circle. The elder brother, Konstantin, owed his philosophic development more to Hegel than to Schelling, but he had been strongly influenced by Khomyakov as well. Like Khomyakov, he was keenly interested in history and wrote poetry, plays, and articles on philology. He also translated from Goethe and Schiller. As critic again he made a mark with his early essay about Gogol's *Dead Souls*.

At the age of twenty-one he left for abroad. The five months he spent in Europe gave him a fair idea of how and where Western life differed from that of Russia. This only enhanced that Slavophile outlook of his with which he viewed his own country's past and present. Imbued with the spirit of Orthodox religion at its

best, he disapproved first of all of the legalistic pattern of Western existence. This he contrasted by that specifically "Russian" attitude which, according to him, too, was based upon conscience rather than upon any external laws. A proof to this effect he thought he had found in the Russian word *pravda* which means truth and justice in one. During the Crimean Campaign the two brothers were among the staunchest supporters of the Slav cause in the Balkans. In this they were joined by Yury Samarin who was also a champion of the liberation of the serfs. (In 1857 he became a member of the special commission set up to work out the best method of how to abolish the serfdom system.) A great blow to the Slav cause in Russia was Konstantin Aksakov's death at the age of forty-three.

As though eager to make up for it, his brother Ivan intensified his own Slavophile activities and became the most enterprising political journalist of the entire group. Since he was also truly eloquent, his articles were read all over Russia. Yet his editorial ventures had their ups and downs during the whole of his life. A few years after the Crimean War Ivan Aksakov began to edit, with Samarin's help, the newspaper *Den* (*The Day*), but as the latter failed to please the authorities it was clamped down in 1865. Nor was his *Moskva* (*Moscow*), which appeared in 1867, of long duration. The last phase of his life coincided with his work for the newpaper *Rus* (*The Russian Land*) which he edited, with less trouble, from 1880 until 1885. It was during those years, too, that he wrote his major literary work – a biography of his father-in-law, the poet Tyutchev.

Aksakov's spirited Slav propaganda was at its height during the Russo-Turkish War in 1877–78. He became such an outspoken champion of the liberation of the Balkan Slavs from the Turkish yoke that some Bulgarians were even inclined to propose him as a candidate for the Bulgarian throne. Because of the vigour with which he attacked the inefficiency of the Russian diplomats at the Berlin Congress in 1878 he was exiled for several months from Moscow. But this did not diminish the verve with which he defended his views during the subsequent years when militant

Slavophilism was already a matter of the past. Its last effective public flash was Dostoevsky's Pushkin Speech in Moscow on June 8, 1880, after which there came a gradual state of decay. But it is only fair to say that even during its previous agitated period the liberal and radical-minded intellectuals, while wrangling with the Slavophiles, took on the whole little real interest in the non-Russian Slavs.* Among the notable exceptions in this respect was however the father of modern anarchism, Michael Bakunin. The role which Bakunin played as a link between Russia and Slavdom is one of the most colourful episodes in the history of the Russian left-wing intelligentsia. This alone is enough to mark out his career as something out of the ordinary.

* Yet the first author of an authoritative book on Slav literatures was the literary historian A. N. Pypin – a Russian liberal. Together with the Pole W. D. Spasowicz he published, in 1865, the *Survey of History of Slav Literatures* whose enlarged second edition (in two vols.) appeared in 1879–81.

CHAPTER SEVEN

Bakunin

I

Michael Bakunin is known to the world as a great rebel. His admirers are, however, less familiar with the fact that before he embarked upon his gospel of anarchism, he had been one of the most impetuous champions of Slavdom, but with a difference. For in contrast to the quietist and religious-minded early Slavophiles Bakunin's exploits on behalf of the Slav idea were dictated by his innate revolutionary instinct and his demonic passion for destruction. He himself acknowledged that in his character there was a love of the "fantastic, unusual, unheard of adventures", and that he was simply unable to put up with any normal surroundings. Such a disposition on his part was further complicated by his well-nigh elemental and undisciplined vitality in which there was yet a secret flaw. Medically speaking, he was sexually impotent. As though offended in his manly pride because of this, he found something of a compensation first of all in exercising his own personal power over those people he was associating with. He wanted to be not so much their companion as their leader. "He is anxious to dominate, not to love," Belinsky wrote (in a letter) about him. Bakunin's second and as it were complementary urge was his will to protest against and to destroy what he disagreed with. Unable to stand anybody's tyranny except his own, he fomented trouble wherever he saw oppression of any kind. As a result he took part in ever so many revolts, spent several years in prisons, and then in Siberia whence he escaped in order to continue his stormy existence and to become an international legend while still alive.

Born in 1814 into a gentry family in the province of Tver (now Kalinin), Michael Bakunin spent his early years on the family estate of Premukhino, somewhere half-way between Moscow and

St. Petersburg. There were numerous children in the family, all of them watched over by their mother whose bossy character may have sown in the little Michael the first seeds of resistance and rebellion. At the age of fourteen the boy was sent to the artillery school at St. Petersburg, but he was far from enjoying the army drill and discipline. No sooner had he been promoted to the rank of ensign than he left the army and decided to study – preferably philosophy. Disregarding his parents' disappointment, he went (in 1834) to Moscow where he joined the Stankevich circle. Because of his eloquence and forceful personality he excelled in discussions even with such people as Belinsky and Herzen. And when, in 1837, the consumptive Stankevich left for abroad, Bakunin actually managed to impose himself upon the circle as his provisional substitute.

Unable to do anything in a lukewarm way, he embraced at that time the philosophy of Hegel dogmatically and to the exclusion of everything else. Under the influence of Hegel's confusing dictum that "all that is real is reasonable", he was inclined to regard (for a while) even the Russian reality under Nicholas I as reasonable. His introduction to Hegel's *Grammar School Speeches*, which he translated into Russian,* was written in this spirit. A fervent idealist, he admired in those days both Hegel and Fichte and, like so many other Russian youths of that generation, revelled in Schiller's poetry. With this he combined a temperament which was both expansive and impetuous enough to make him look larger than life. It was the magic of his personality rather than his convictions that overwhelmed many a follower of his who otherwise might have been repelled by his inconsistency, his careless manners, and his lack of scruples in money matters. But whatever his defects, underneath them all there smouldered the flame of a rebel and a fighter, waiting for his chance. He did not have to wait long. It should be remembered that in those days Berlin was a kind of Mecca for young Russians who were anxious to complete their education. Bakunin, too, left in 1840 for Germany. As he had little or no financial help from home, he went to Berlin on

* It was printed in *The Moscow Observer* (*Moskovsky nablyudatel*) in 1838.

borrowed money (borrowed mainly from Herzen). From now on he depended on cash supplied as a rule by his friends and acquaintances – a procedure in which he became a virtuoso and remained so for the rest of his life.

Bakunin spent in Berlin some eighteen months. But this was enough to make him thoroughly disappointed with German professors. Hence he shifted his interest from philosophy to radical politics, and with such abandon too, as to outstrip all his democratic-minded acquaintances. Incidentally, it was in the Prussian capital that he met the young writer Ivan Turgenev who was to give a rather pathetic portrait of Bakunin in the character of Rudin – the hero of the novel published under the same title in 1855.* From Berlin he went to Dresden. Here he was introduced to the left Hegelian Arnold Ruge to whose *Deutsche Jahrbuecher* (*German Yearbooks*) he contributed one of his brilliant early essays, *Reaction in Germany*, which ends with the typical Bakunian sentence: "The passion of destruction is a creative passion." In Dresden he was befriended, among others, by the revolutionary German poet Georg Herwegh (1817–75) who was destined to play a rather distasteful role in Herzen's life. It was in Herwegh's company that Bakunin went to Berne where he met the Swiss communist Wilhelm Weitling, the author of the *Gospel of a Poor Sinner*. But he did not remain in Switzerland very long and left, together with the radical-minded pianist Adolf Reichel, for Brussels – a town which, in those days, was full of Polish refugees including the historian Jachym Lelewel.

Bakunin's inner change was by then complete. Any Hegelian conciliation with reality was now a matter of the past as far as he was concerned. And so were all kinds of abstract philosophic musings for their own sake. What mattered to him henceforth

---

* Bakunin is portrayed in this novel somewhat one-sidedly, without the real dynamic drive which was his outstanding feature. Turgenev depicts him as a great talker (and sponger) who knows how to infect other people, and especially women, with his ideas, but when it comes to deeds he proves to be a coward who fails to achieve anything positive. He is contrasted by Pokorsky – a portrait of Stankevich.

was active life on the plane of politics which meant above all a
fight for freedom in the reactionary era of the Holy Alliance.
Unable ever to stop halfway, he embraced this fight with the kind
of zeal which demanded utter dedication on his part. As a Russian
and a Slav he naturally directed his fight against the oppression of
the Slavs, wherever they had to bear their yoke.

2

Having been initiated by Lelewel into all the intricacies of the
Polish problem, Bakunin took the tragedy of Poland to his heart
and became one of the most loyal supporters of her cause. But
such a step on his part could not be looked upon with favour by
the Russian authorities, whether at home or abroad. He was
officially summoned to return to Russia. As the Russia of Nicholas
I was the last country he now had any wish to see again, he was
deprived of his title of nobility and was, moreover, threatened
with penal servitude in the event he should ever return later on.
Undaunted by this he repaired (together with Reichel) in 1844
from Brussels to Paris. Here he was introduced to a number of
prominent figures such as Pierre Leroux, Michelet, Quinet,
Lamennais and George Sand. While in the French capital he met
also Proudhon and the Polish poet Adam Mickiewicz whose
"politico-mystical" gospel he regarded as an unconscious hoax,
however much he himself sympathised with the Polish struggle
for independence. At a banquet commemorating the Warsaw
rising of 1831 Bakunin delivered such a fiery speech against all
tyranny that the Russian *chargé d'affaires* Kiselyov found it necessary
to discredit him by spreading the deliberate lie that this irrepressible Polonophile was really a spy and *agent provocateur* in the pay
of the Tsarist police. Such a rumour did him considerable harm at
first. Even Karl Marx seemed to have believed it for a while.

Undaunted by dirty tricks of this kind, Bakunin increased his
activities as well as his hectic movements. When the February
Revolution in 1848 broke out he was in Brussels, but he immediately hurried to Paris where he is supposed to have helped the

workers manning the barricades. From Paris he left for Germany which seemed to him a suitable ground for any subversive action. He hoped (wrongly enough) for a revolution among the Poles in Posen which might infect Eastern Europe, Russia, and even the Slav parts of Austria. On his way to Berlin he stopped at Frankfurt where members of the liberal *Vorparlament* were gathered, but he could not summon any enthusiasm for their plans and doings. Further disappointments awaited him in Berlin. For no sooner had he arrived there than he was arrested and escorted by the police to Leipzig, whence he went to Breslau. As it happened, Breslau was teeming with Polish refugees who were indefatigable in their propaganda against the Russian regime. But more important things were going on in Austria, and these were too tempting to be resisted. On May 15, 1848 a renewed rising took place in Vienna. Bakunin made all the arrangements for joining it and arrived in Austria just in time to attend the Slav Congress which opened in Prague on June 2.

Here Bakunin came into contact with all the non-Russian Slavs (except the Bulgarians who were absent), and his ambition to combine the Slav cause with that of radical democracy may not have looked futile. He did not rate the political acumen of the assembled Slav representatives very high, but he was impressed by their freshness and their natural intelligence which he put far above that of the Germans. He himself acknowledged that in Prague his Slav heart had awakened to the extent of making him at first forget "all the democratic sympathies connecting me with Western Europe". As the only Russian attending the Congress,* he was heartily welcomed by its president Palacký whom he is supposed to have helped in editing the subsequent Appeal addressed to European nations in the name of justice and freedom. Otherwise Palacký's Austro-Slavism was far from being Bakunin's cup of tea. According to his own later account he had attacked there and then both Austria and Russia as the two greatest enemies of freedom.

* Miloradov, a priest of the dissenting Old Believers, who was also present, was not a native of Russia but of Austrian Bukovina.

"I know that many of you hope," he harangued the Austrian Slavs, "for the support of the Austrian dynasty. She now promises you everything, she now flatters you because she needs you: but will she keep her promises and will she be in a position to fulfil them once her undermined power is restored by your help? . . . You will see, the Austrian dynasty will not only forget your services but will also take revenge upon you for her own shameful weakness which in the past has made her humble herself before you and flatter your seditious demands. . . . Slav unity, Slav freedom, Slav regeneration are possible only through a complete destruction of the Austrian Empire." He was equally frank with those naïve Russophiles (Hanka, Jungmann) who still expected their national salvation to come from a union with Russia. "If you joined the Emperor Nicholas, you would thereby enter the grave of any national life and any freedom. True enough, without Russia the Slav unity would not be complete and there would be no Slav Power; yet it would be madness on the part of the Slavs to expect salvation and help from present-day Russia. What, then, is the alternative for you? Do unite, to begin with, outside Russia without excluding her but waiting and hoping for her speedy liberation; she will be carried away by your example, and you will be liberators of the Russian people who, on their part, will become a powerful shield for you."*

When, on June 12 the Prague students and workers had improvised a sudden rebellion, Bakunin was soon in the thick of the fray. The troops of Prince Windischgraetz were, however, prompt enough to quash the rising. Bakunin had to flee for dear life and hide in Germany. As the tiny State of Anhalt had something resembling a constitution, he settled for a while at Koethen whence he launched, in December 1848, his personal *Appeal to the Slavs*.† Its spirit was anti-Palacký (that is anti-Austrian) and contained a call to revolution addressed to all the Slavs. "Our libera-

---

* This passage is taken from the *Confession* which Bakunin wrote at the request of Nicholas I in the Peter and Paul dungeon in 1851.

† He wrote it in French, but a German translation, *Aurfuf an die Slawen*, was printed in Leipzig at the beginning of 1849.

tion is in the revolution! Surrender to it fully and completely! Without it there is no Slavdom."

Where he was wrong, though, was his belief that a general revolution in Russia was imminent. Nor was he clairvoyant either when expecting Austria to crack and disintegrate amidst her growing difficulties; yet his appeal was sincere and stirring enough. "Who is for Austria is against freedom.... You ought to know that as a Russian I can see the liberation of my compatriots only in the union with all the Slav peoples united in one free and federated family. You ought to know that the attainment of this great and holy task has become the aim of my life."

The abortive risings in Prague, Paris, Frankfurt and Vienna did not damp Bakunin's faith in a Slav revolution. He was still pinning his hopes on the dissatisfied Russian peasants and seemed to be ready to welcome even an alliance between the Slavs, the rebellious Magyars and the radical-minded section of the Germans. While expecting the Poles to mediate between the Slavs and the Magyars, he was quite willing to serve as a link between the Germans and the Slavs. The rising itself was to start in Bohemia, with Prague as its centre; the more so because he was now in contact with some revolutionary Czech patriots. When in May, 1849, an insurrection took place in Dresden, Bakunin promptly joined it with the idea that a revolution in Saxony might infect Bohemia. What was happening at Dresden, though, proved to be a rather amateurish affair and this was a new frustration for him. It was among the Dresden rebels that Bakunin met also the young Richard Wagner who was however prudent enough to escape to Switzerland as soon as he saw that the rebellion in Saxony was a flop. More foolhardy than Wagner, Bakunin stayed on, was captured, jailed and sentenced to death. Then he was handed over to Austria where another death-sentence was waiting for him. Finally, this incorrigible rebel was delivered (at the beginning of 1851) to the Russian authorities who were to dispose of him as they deemed fit.

3

Brought in chains to St. Petersburg, Bakunin was tucked away in the dungeons of the notorious Peter-and-Paul fortress. Nicholas I realised only too well what a dangerous revolutionary he now had in his claws. As he decided to make use of this opportunity for displaying his own histrionic nature, he sent to the dungeon his aide-de-camp, Count Orlov, with the suggestion that, in order to alleviate his own fate, the prisoner should submit to the Tsar personally a written account of his dreadful past in the same contrite spirit as if he were talking to his father confessor. Behind such a step there was, of course, the Tsar's cunning manœuvre to make Bakunin betray all those Russian and Russian-Polish rebels who were engaged in seditious activities abroad. Bakunin did not give away a single name. On the other hand, beguiled by the Tsar's hypocritical magnanimity, he concocted a *Confession* which is one of the strangest and hardly credible psychological documents.*

It took Bakunin more than two months to put down all he wanted to say. So his *Confession* swelled to the size of a pamphlet each page of which is more surprising than the last. First of all one is taken aback by the tone of a repentant (or would-be repentant) sinner regretting his past misdeeds. ("It only remains for me to thank God that He had stopped me in time on the road to all the crimes.") Abject servility, calculating flattery, even "piety", unexpected frankness, as well as arrogant criticism of the police-ridden Russian regime – all this is mixed up in that unique deposition. Bakunin speaks with particular bitterness about Austria, while yet stressing his own Russian and Slav patriotism. At the same time he warns the Tsar against any kind of compulsory Russification practised upon the Poles by the official nationalists and imperialists. Supposing Russia did conquer the non-Russian Slavs with the object of turning them into Russians, what would happen? "She would be hated by all those Slavs as much as she is

* It was found in the government's secret archives after the revolution of 1917 and was first published in 1926.

now hated by the Poles; instead of being a liberator she would only become an oppressor of the family of the Slavs at the cost of her own welfare and freedom; finally, she would end by hating herself as a result of being hated by all, and in her victories by force she would find nothing except torment and slavery. If she killed the Slavs she would kill herself as well. Should such be the end of the scarcely beginning Slav life and Slav history?"

The way in which Bakunin explains what he means by his idea of a Slav Union, based on the ruins of Russian autocracy, staggers one precisely because one is not quite sure whether the whole of it is a piece of crazy daring on his part or else of a complete indifference to his own fate. "In a word, Sire," he continues, "I was convinced that Russia, in order to save her honour and her future, should raise a revolution, depose your *Imperial Power** destroy the monarchic system and, having freed herself from her internal slavery, should stand at the head of the Slav movement: she should turn her weapons against the Emperor of Austria, against the king of Prussia, the Sultan of Turkey, and if necessary also against Germany and against the Magyars, in short against the entire world for the sake of a final liberation of the Slav peoples from the foreign yoke. Half of Prussian Silesia, the larger part of West and East Prussia, briefly all the provinces in which Slav, Polish, is spoken, ought to be taken away from Germany. My imagination went even further: I thought, I hoped, that the Magyar nation, compelled by circumstances, by her isolated position between the Slav peoples, as well as by her oriental rather than Western character – that all the Moldavians and Rumanians, and finally even Greece, would join the Slav Union and that in this manner a free Eastern Empire would be built up which might regenerate the world – as a contrast to, though not as an enemy of, the West, with Constantinople as its capital."

As though to flatter the Tsar's vanity Bakunin made, after this Slavophile outburst, a hint that Nicholas himself might eventually become a historical leader of a Pan-Slav federation.† But parallel

* Italics are his.

† It is known that Nicholas I did not care for the Slav problem as such.

with this the "penitent" sinner did not mind cringing before his imperial majesty and beating his breast. "I am conscious to the very depths of my soul that I am a criminal, most of all against you, Sire, a criminal against Russia, and that my transgressions condemn me to the cruellest of executions."* But a contrite, or would-be contrite, passage of this kind was not without due effect. For in the margin of the MS. the Tsar jotted down the remark: "Repentant head is not chopped off by the sword, may God forgive him." Still, there the matter rested. Bakunin remained in the same dungeon for another three years, after which he was transferred to the equally harsh prison of Schluesselburg. It was only in 1857, that is two years after Nicholas's death, that his imprisonment was commuted to perpetual exile in Siberia.

In Siberia Bakunin settled at Tomsk where he was at least relatively free. Moreover, the Governor-General of Eastern Siberia, Nikolai Muruvyyov-Amursky, happened to be his maternal uncle. Thanks to him his wayward nephew was soon transferred from Tomsk to the bigger town of Irkutsk and even obtained some employment. But while still at Tomsk, he had married a seventeen-year old Polish girl, Tonia Kwiatkowska, although he must have know full well that because of his physical disability the marriage would never be consummated. What he hoped for was that eventually he would be allowed to return, together with her, to European Russia. From Irkutsk he kept sending to Alexander II one petition after the other, but in vain. So the only alternative left to him was to escape, which he did (without his wife) in 1861.

4

Imprisonment and Siberia had claimed more than ten years of Bakunin's life. But once free, he decided to make good use of whatever chance he had. Having fled first to Japan and then to America, he wrote from St. Francisco to both Herzen and

* Passages such as this sound like a curious anticipation of "confessions" squeezed out of Stalin's opponents during the 1930s by his secret police.

Ogaryov that he was coming to London in order to work in Herzen's *Kolokol* (*The Bell*) for the cause which he still regarded as his life-task. "I will work for you in the Polish-Slav question which was my *idée fixe* in 1846 and my practical speciality in 1848 and 1849. Destruction, complete destruction of the Austrian Empire will be my last word. . . . And behind it there appears a glorious free Slav federation – the only outlet for Russia, the Ukraine, Poland, and all the Slav nations in general."

At the end of 1861 he was already in London. But it soon transpired that such a firebrand as Bakunin would hardly be able to get on in the long run with the balanced and cautious Alexander Herzen who cared for the fate of the Russian people in the first place, although he may have had a soft spot for the other Slavs as well. Still, the non-Russian Slavs were more remote to him than to Bakunin who was now willing to put up even with a Tsar of the Romanov dynasty, provided the latter would become a genuine people's Tsar and a leader of all the Slavs towards the craved for Pan-Slav federation. In his pamphlet, *The People's Cause, or Pugachov, Romanov or Pestel* (1862), he stated bluntly that "our attitude towards the Romanov is clear: we are neither his friends nor enemies; we are friends of the people's Russia and of the Slav action. If the Tsar is at its head – we are with him. And whenever he goes against it, we shall be his enemies."* His idea of a Slav federation was reiterated in the same year also in his new appeal, *To the Russian, Polish and all the Slav Countries*, but in less glowing terms than in 1848–49.

It was obvious that Bakunin's revolutionary exploits, death sentences, prisons, Siberia, and his dramatic escape should have found a strong echo in the press. In the radical circles of Europe he actually became something of a myth which persisted also later on when he had left his Slav phase behind him and adopted, with the same urge, his ideal of anarchism. The dividing line between the two periods was the Polish rising of 1863.

* This sudden flexibility on the part of Bakunin might have been due to reforms achieved by Alexander II at a time when Herzen, too, was inclined to believe in the possibility of a revolution from above.

When that unfortunate rebellion broke out, both Herzen and Bakunin were wholeheartedly on the side of the Poles. Herzen gave them as much support as he could in his weekly, but even this was taken amiss by its Russian readers and led to a gradual boycott of the *Kolokol*. Bakunin, on the other hand, was all astir and expected the Polish revolt to be a step towards a general rising in Russia, with the hoped for Slav Union in the prospect. A patriotic Polish millionaire even hired an English boat on which he tried to smuggle – via Sweden – a number of volunteers into Poland. These were joined by Bakunin, but it all came to a tragicomic end in the Swedish port of Malmö, where they remained stuck. Meanwhile the predicament of the Polish rebels was going from bad to worse. Devoid of the peasants' support, the rising was above all one of the landed gentry (*szlachta*) and the politically immature intellectuals whose ideal was a Poland restored within her historical boundaries before 1772. This would have included a large portion of the Ukraine and Belo-Russia with millions of non-Polish inhabitants. Those Poles who had engineered the rebellion in the hope that foreign powers would intervene and help them were, of course, bitterly disappointed. And so was Bakunin, but for reasons of his own: he came to the conclusion that the rebellious Poles, like the Magyars in 1849, were fighting for the cause of aggressive nationalism and wanted freedom only for themselves, since they were claiming ever so many of their former subjects of non-Polish nationality. From now on he began to shed his Pan-Slav enthusiasm and eventually gave a final shape to that doctrine of international anarchism which is still closely connected with his name.

5

After the collapse of the Polish rebellion Bakunin was unexpectedly joined by his young Polish wife Tonia who came from distant Siberia in order to share – for better or for worse – his hectic existence. As Bakunin's relations with Herzen were now deteriorating, he and Tonia spent the next three years mostly in Italy, first in Florence and then in Naples, where the gospel of his

short-lived International Brotherhood found quite a few sympathisers. In September 1867 he attended the Congress of the League
of Peace and Freedom in Geneva and distinguished himself as one
of its fiery speakers.* A year later he became a member of the
First International headed by Marx and Engels with its centre in
London. But he was also a member of the Executive Committee
of the League of Peace and Freedom, and evidently wanted to
combine the two movements. Yet Marx would not hear of it, for
he considered the League itself but a radical bourgeois institution.
Still, Bakunin came to Marx's International only after having
founded (in 1868) his own Social-Democratic Alliance. Backed by
the latter, he attended – in 1869 – the Basle Congress of the First
International as one of its members. But Marx started a campaign
against him and during the Congress at Hague in 1872 succeeded
in throwing him out of the party as an undesirable.

This happened after the collapse of the Paris Commune (1871)
in which Bakunin had played a conspicuous role, while Marx and
Engels kept aloof. Marx even predicted its failure, but this made
no difference to Bakunin. Impetuous as always, he urged the
workers to man the barricades and even took part in the fighting,
Marx or no Marx. Besides, the continuous enmity between these
two men was perhaps not so much a conflict between different
ideologies as between different temperaments. The only feature
the two had in common was that they both wanted to lead and
not to be led. But while Marx, with his German education, had a
sober methodical mind, favouring authority and organisation,
Bakunin – a typical Slav – was an ebullient and somewhat irresponsible romantic idealist who could not suffer either authorities
or organisations. If Marx was persuasive by his disciplined pur-
posefulness and logic, Bakunin fascinated the audiences by the

---

* Some debates of that Congress were heard by Dostoevsky who wrote
rather scathingly about them to his Moscow niece Sonya Ivanova. He is
supposed to have conceived the idea for his novel *The Possessed* during these
debates. Incidentally, it was at this Congress that Bakunin met also the well
known Serbian socialist (of the "populist" variety) and writer Svetozar Marko-
vic who was a champion of an independent federal union of all Southern Slavs.

spontaneous driving force of his character. No wonder Marx found a man of Bakunin's type unbearable. Be this as it may, four years after the expulsion of Bakunin from its ranks, the First International itself came to an end. Bakunin on the other hand founded, as a contrast to Marx's collectivist International, his own Anarchist International – based on the principle of individualism and aiming at stateless associations of free communities on a world-wide scale.

In October 1869 he had settled in Italian Switzerland, at Locarno. He lived there with his wife Tonia whom he treated with good-natured tolerance even after she had presented him with children, fathered by one of his best Italian friends and followers (Gambuzzi). Nor did he mind when, after a visit to Siberia, during 1872–73, Tonia returned to Locarno in the company of her father and sister all of whom were now living at Bakunin's expense, despite the fact that both his finances and his health were rapidly deteriorating. His revolutionary activity was not much of a success either. His participation in the September rising at Lyons in 1870 (during the Franco-Prussian War) had been a complete fiasco. The last straw was, however, his abortive attempt to organise a rebellion at Bologna in 1874. Its failure seemed to indicate to him that, after the debacle of the Paris Commune, there was not much revolutionary ardour left in the masses.

A sadder but hardly a much wiser man, he bore all his disappointments with considerable patience. To his physical ailments the increasing financial troubles were added – due to his irresponsible borrowing and handling of money. His only solace was that his own anarchist doctrine was finding a number of followers at least in the Latin countries. In 1872 he even founded at Zürich a Slav Section of his Anarchist International. In Russia his name was associated with the extreme Left during the 1860s and 1870s. His last years at Locarno, painful though they must have been, were not devoid of friends and visitors. Among these there were always some Russians, Poles and Serbs, since he never lost or wanted to lose his former Slav sympathies. He died in Berne on July 1, 1876.

CHAPTER EIGHT

Populists and Slavophiles

I

The anti-European bent in the Russian consciousness was not confined to the Slavophiles alone. It soon emerged also in a large section of the radical-minded Russian intellectuals known as populists or *narodniki*.* Disappointed in Europe they, too, began to pin their hopes for a better future on the Russian peasant masses: not for any religious reasons like the Slavophiles but for social reasons pure and simple. In some respects populism might even strike one as a kind of secularised Slavophilism – with due reservations, of course. Both the Slavophiles and the populists cherished a sincere love for the Russian people, to begin with. Both factions were also convinced that Russia had a historical destiny of her own. They shared their enthusiasm for such time-honoured institutions as the village commune and the artisans' guild (the *artel*). In the *mir* or *obschchina* they both saw an establishment of great ethical and social significance, but from different angles. To the Slavophiles it was a symbol of the patriarchal-idyllic "brotherly" unity (in a religious sense) among the people. The populists, on the other hand, saw in the *mir* above all a promise of that agrarian socialism which would – presumably – be based on the collectivised agricultural land and peasantry, and not on the industrial proletariat as the Marxian socialists would have it. While the Slavophiles persisted in looking back to the pre-Petrine past, the populists kept turning their thoughts and eyes towards the future. But they were not so firmly rooted in the soil and people as the Slavophiles. A considerable portion of the populists were uprooted "superfluous individuals" – with a passionate but often futile desire to be in a closer organic contact with the people. An

* From the Russian word *narod* (the people).

isolated middle-class intellectual in Western Europe found his obvious outlet in nineteenth-century nationalism. But a radical Russian intellectual could not contemplate such an issue, since Western nationalism itself was a bourgeois movement, while in Russia it had been sponsored by the reactionary Tsarist government. Whereas the Slavophile sympathies with the people were due to patriarchal-religious reasons, the populists were drawn towards it mainly for social or else social-revolutionary reasons. The two parties were opponents also in so far as they looked for their ideals in opposite directions, although their affection for the toiling peasant masses may have been equally sincere.

"Yes, we were opponents but very strange ones," Alexander Herzen wrote years later when referring to the two trends. "We had one love, although it differed. They [the Slavophiles] and we succumbed from our earliest years to one powerful irrational feeling – the feeling of a limitless all-embracing love for the Russian people. And we, like Janus, like the two-headed eagle, looked in different directions while at the same time we had one and the same heart. . . . They looked for living Russia in the annals, like Mary Magdalen looking for Christ in the tomb. . . . To them the Russian people was above all Orthodox, i.e. closest to the heavenly city; to us it was above all a social entity, i.e. closest to the earthly city."

Neither the populists nor the Slavophiles had any love for the capitalist trend of Western civilisation. They both hoped that Russia, with her peculiar historical and economic development, might be able to avoid the evils of capitalism. Herzen himself, an intellectual of the same generation as Belinsky, was among the first Westernising radicals to turn against the West and to lay the early foundations of that populist movement whose purpose was the "earthly city" in the most humane and humanitarian meaning of the word. Disgusted with the triumph of the French bourgeoisie in 1848, he himself stated in *My Past and Thoughts*: "I had lost my faith in words and portents, in canonised humanity and in the only all-saving church of Western civilisation."

But once Herzen's illusions about that civilisation were gone, it was natural that his hopes should have shifted to the less "civilised" Russian people. At the same time the dilemma of Russia and Europe was taken up by him also in order to warn Russia about Europe. It was in the *mir* or *obshchina* as a peculiar Russian institution that he discovered the kernel of an agrarian type of socialism resting mainly upon the common ownership of land. This was why he thought that Russia, with her collective mentality, would be able to bypass the bourgeois-capitalist era and all the social, moral as well as economic ravages implied by it. In this love for the *mir* and their aversion to the capitalist West both the Slavophiles and the populists found an important point of contact. Herzen himself said that the Slavophiles had been the first to see in the oppressed Russian people great possibilities of an independent evolution of its own. The populist interpretation of such possibilities differed from that of the Slavophiles; yet he referred to both when he wrote: "Is it a surprise that there were persons who understood that the people which had the *obshchina* and the *artel*, as well as an independent attitude towards the ownership of land, was nearer to an economic, i.e. social, revolution than the Roman, feudal, bourgeois Europe?"

2

Both the populists and the Slavophiles were afraid above all of wholesale commercialisation and one-sided technical advance without an adequate moral progress on the part of their nation. They saw in such a cash-and-credit attitude towards life something basically wrong and dehumanising. But whereas the Slavophiles gleaned their enthusiasm from the Russian people's religious consciousness, the populists derived it from their own humanitarian and utilitarian theories which also contained a certain amount of Rousseauism. Prompted by the mentality of the "repentant noblemen", as well as by that of the uprooted "superfluous individual", many of them found in populism a shelter

from their own isolated egos. The majority of the gentry-populists showed, however, not only a tendency to bridge the gap between themselves and the people, but also a strong impulse to atone for the misdeeds committed by their serf-owning ancestors against the enslaved peasant masses. The feeling of that guilt (a feeling which goes at least as far back as Radischev), strengthened by the wish to overcome their own uprootedness, became so powerful indeed among the populist intellectuals during the 1870s that it created a kind of moral epidemic which made hundreds, or even thousands, of aristocratic youths and girls give up their social privileges in order to "go to the people" and work together with them, preparing them for a revolution and for better times to come. But the distrust of the people with regard to anything coming from the "gentlemen" was so great that those naïve idealists were often denounced to the police by the very peasants and workers whom they were anxious to help.* What the peasants wanted was not propaganda, but more land.

This did not lessen, however, the sincerity and the good will implicit in the populist movement. Stimulated at first by Herzen, Bakunin and Lavrov, it reached its peak under the guidance of Nikolai Mikhailovsky. Mikhailovsky was familiar with the teaching of Auguste Comte, Stuart Mill and Herbert Spencer, yet remained a thoroughly Russian intellectual of the best kind. The same applies to Chernyshevsky whose influence had been at its height in the 1860s – after the publication (in 1863) of his tendentious novel, *What Is To Be Done*. Mikhailovsky himself was a determinist but not a fatalist. His social ideal (to quote his own words) was to see "as full and many-sided division of work as possible, and the smallest possible division among human beings". He, too, was convinced that the *obshchina* and the *artel* were a good foundation upon which to build up the kind of socialism which would save Russia from a capitalist era after the Western pattern. He appreciated many a tenet in the Marxian theory as well, while yet keeping to his own views and to his uncompromising moral sense.

* Turgenev's novel *Virgin Soil* describes the tragic futility of those populist efforts.

In Berdyayev's opinion the philosophy of Mikhailovsky was "very poor, but his sociology and his socialism were built on ethical foundations and on a belief in human personality. . . . His subjective method in sociology – which meant that social science should be studied not disinterestedly, like natural science, but in terms of human progress in which man's individuality was the supreme and only value, not to be sacrificed to society – contained for me an indisputable truth".* Mikhailovsky was particularly in love with the Russian word *pravda* (combining the idea of truth and justice in one) as had been before him also the Slavophile Konstantin Aksakov.

Another feature which the Slavophiles and the populists had in common was the fact that both of them ascribed to Russia a historical mission, however much they differed with regard to the nature of that mission. Whereas the Slavophiles saw in the Russian people the bearer of the true Christian spirit which they ought to reveal to the rest of Europe or even of mankind, the populists expected the Russian peasants to promulgate true socialism and eventually bring about the realisation of the "earthly city" in terms of an agrarian millennium. The *obshchina* was to serve as one of the moral and social bases for either of these two missions. There were, however, two snags (and quite substantial ones) in all this. Both the populists and the Slavophiles overlooked the simple truth that an institution such as the *obshchina* or *mir* was a primitive archaic relic and by no means exclusively Russian. Its equivalent had existed also in some other countries until it was replaced by more advanced economic patterns. One of the reasons why it continued to linger on in Russia was the fiscal advantage the government derived from it. Since the *obshchina* as a whole was responsible for the tax of each of its individual members, the collection of taxes was thus made easier than by any cumbersome bureaucratic method. On the other hand, the *obshchina* exercised too great a pressure upon the individual who in it was of little value.

* Quoted from Berdyayev's *Dream and Reality* (Bles).

Like the Slavophiles, the populists derived a number of their ideological tenets from German philosophy, to which the influence of Comte and of the English utilitarians should be added. But while the Slavophiles continued to stick to Schelling, many of the socialist *narodniki* adhered to the left-wing Hegelians. Some of them adopted also the terrorist methods as something legitimate in their struggle for justice. As it happened, their argument was logical enough. Since all that exists develops only through dialectical opposition, terrorism itself seemed to them a useful and often necessary weapon in the service of opposition. One group of the populists – the "People's Freedom" (*Narodnaya volya*)* – was even responsible for the assassination of Alexander II on March 13, 1881. This was a great disaster in so far as it introduced a new reactionary era and precluded some further liberal reforms which might have saved Russia from her subsequent revolutions. But that deed already marked the decay of the populist movement itself.

As for Slavophilism, it reaped its last successes during the Russo-Turkish War in 1877–78, after which its decline was as imminent as that of the populist current whose heyday was over by the end of the 1870s. The assassination of Alexander II was followed by an ideological standstill, but the idea of an agrarian type of socialism survived in the Social-Revolutionary Party (actually founded in 1892 and renewed in 1901). The champions of this party were above all those younger idealists who had remained loyal to the teaching of the *narodniki* and continued to profess their radical ideas at a time when some of the latter-day Slavophiles were already veering towards all sorts of reactionary "isms".

What made the situation as a whole even more complex was the unavoidable industrialisation of Russia – a process whose pace became accelerated from 1890 onwards. From now on it was obvious that, far from being spared the bourgeois-capitalist phase, Russia, too, would have to put up with it and with all the

* The Russian word *volya* means both will and freedom.

drawbacks implied. No wonder that so many Russian intellectuals of that period looked upon the despondent Chekhov as their favourite author. Others found shelter in Tolstoy's moral perfectionism which advocated abstention from all organised political activities. Several former populists switched over to the Marxian type of socialism, which was beginning to gain ground in Russia. One of these was George Plekhanov. Having emigrated to Switzerland, Plekhanov formed there (in 1883) the first nucleus of the Russian Marxian movement. It did not take long before Marxian propaganda was rife in St. Petersburg, as well as in some other industrial centres of Russia.* The Russian Social-Democratic Party of Labour was founded in 1898, and its Bolshevist left wing in 1903. The Marxians were convinced that – owing to its inner contradictions – the capitalist system was bound to be eventually replaced by their type of socialism which was based on the proletariat as the leader of the revolution to come. In the abortive upheaval of 1905 the Social-Revolutionary Party was still able to play a considerable role. In the cataclysm of 1917, however, this party was definitely ousted by its Marxian-Leninist rival.

Whatever the historical fate of the Slavophile and the populist doctrines, their direct or indirect impact upon Russian literature, too, was considerable. Even some of the best Russian authors have been affected, one way or the other, by those two trends. The Slavophiles had at least one great poet among their sympathisers, namely Tyutchev. (Khomyakov, an enthusiastic Slavophile also in, his verses, was an occasional good poet rather than a great one.) Among the poets who stood close to the Slavophiles were also Yazykov (Khomyakov's brother-in-law), and two of Dostoevsky's friends: Apollon Grigoryev and Apollon Maikov. The populists, on the other hand, are entitled to call Nekrasov their poetic champion, since he was at his best when singing about the peasants, the village life, and the "people's woe". The difference

* Marx's *Das Kapital I* had been translated into Russia in 1872, that is earlier than into any other European language. But the man who had tried to translate it even before that was – strange to say – Marx's great opponent Michael Bakunin.

between Tyutchev and Nekrasov is fairly indicative of the moods and dispositions characteristic of the two camps. Whereas Nekrasov was irreligious and as "realistic" in his poetry as he could be, Tyutchev remained a Slavophile to the end. He also adopted (under the influence of Schelling's *Naturphilosophie* a kind of metaphysical pantheism, and some of his best poems render the awe of a man who is haunted by the chaos lurking behind the apparent external order of the universe. Tyutchev's nature lyrics are particularly strong, and so are his love poems, especially those of his last tragic love at the decline of his life.*

As for the prose-writers of that period, Nikolai Leskov (1831–95), the author of such fine narratives as *The Sealed Angel*, *The Enchanted Traveller*, and *The Cathedral Folk* (not to mention his numerous legends), can be regarded as a literary link between the *narodniki* and the Slavophiles, but his own political convictions were anti-radical. The populists themselves had a group of writers of whom three at least should be mentioned: N. N. Zlatovratsky (1845–1911), Gleb Uspensky (1840–1902) and Vladimir Korolenko (1851–1921). Zlatovratsky gained considerable popularity in the 1870s as a tendentious author of populist narratives. He was an inveterate believer in the people and the *obshchina* which he idealised to the uttermost. Of a bigger calibre was Gleb Uspensky whose sketches and the peasant novel *Power of the Soil* are full of incisive realism, compassion and humour. Disappointed in his populist hopes and ideals, he committed suicide. That humane fighter for justice Vladimir Korolenko, on the other hand, lived long enough to witness the most fateful revolution in modern history. Of no small significance is also the fact that even the two greatest representatives of Russian literature, Dostoevsky and

* It may not be irrelevant to mention that in 1848 Tyutchev wrote for the *Revue des Deux Mondes* his intensely anti-radical treatise *Russie et la Revolution* in which he branded the revolutionary West as anti-Christian. Russia is represented as the opposite of the rebellious West and, firm like a rock, breaking up all the waves of the revolution. He gave vent to a similar idea also in one of his allegorical poems. His second French treatise, *La Papauté et la Question Romaine*, printed in the same periodical in 1850, is highly anti-Catholic in the Slavophile sense. He, like Pogodin, favoured political Pan-Slavism.

Tolstoy, have both been affected by Slavophilism and populism respectively. While such a balanced Westerner as Ivan Turgenev had always tried to be objective and *au dessus de la mêlée*, Dostoevsky had very strong Slavophile affiliations. Tolstoy, on the other hand, had a number of points in common with the populists. Certain tenets of these two movements have thus penetrated, through their writings, into world literature.

4

During his ordeals in Siberia Dostoevsky had made the change from a one-time revolutionary to a convert championing the Messianic myth of Russia and even Russian autocracy. His subsequent Slavophile enthusiasm was anticipated by his earlier interest in the Slav question. Thus on January 16, 1856, he wrote from Siberia to his Petersburg friend, the poet Apollon Maikov: "I completely share your patriotic feeling concerning the *moral* liberation of the Slavs. This is the part to be played by Russia, great and noble Russia, our sacred mother. . . ." Twelve years later he stressed more explicitly in a letter to the same friend (on March 1, 1868) from abroad, where he was travelling with his second wife, Anna Grigoryevna, that the whole world was waiting for regeneration through the Russian Idea, inseparable in his opinion from Orthodoxy on the one hand, and from Russia's political and military might on the other. For which purpose "it is necessary that the Great Russian people should extend their right and supremacy over the entire Slav world as a final and indisputable fact. . . ." And on October 7, 1868, he modified his imperialistic idea in another letter to Maikov: "We should not run after the Slavs, not too much. What is necessary is that they themselves should come to us."

Soon after his return from Siberia (in 1859) Dostoevsky and his brother Michael started publishing the periodical *Vremya* (*Time*) and, when this had been forbidden, it was replaced by the *Epokha* (*The Epoch*). Backed up by the poet and critic Apollon Grigoryev, as well as by the philosopher Nikolai Strakhov, Dostoevsky

championed in both periodicals the need of organic rootedness in the Russian soil and people. It was a brand of democratic Slavophilism by means of which he hoped to provide a bridge of reconciliation between the Westerners and the Slavophiles. But since such organic integration with the people also implied the acceptance of the people's religious turn of mind, all sorts of sceptical or agnostic intellectuals, especially those of the uprooted "superfluous" variety, found it quite impossible to make a change of this kind. Dostoevsky himself had to fight not only his erstwhile rebellious temper, but also his own scepticism which kept tormenting him to the end of his life. What he took from the Slavophiles was their peculiar Orthodoxy, their patriotism, and the belief that the Russian people were particularly able to sympathise with other nations and thus promote that universalism in which he saw the only salvation of mankind. Apart from this the Slavophile worship of the past left him fairly indifferent. Nor did he condemn Peter's reforms, although he himself said that the Orthodox Church (to which he clung) was in a "state of paralysis since Peter the Great".

As far as Western Europe was concerned, he had reasons of his own for not being well disposed towards her. He was a man of forty-one when (in 1862) he made his first trip to Europe – an experience which he recorded with biting humour in his *Winter Notes of Summer Impressions* (1863). It was above all France under Napoleon III that came in for a shower of his venomous comments. And as for Victorian London (where he met Alexander Herzen), he described its appalling night life – in the chapter *Baal* with a truly Dostoevskian verve. He travelled in Europe again in 1865 when, in a fit of gambling mania, he lost all his money. Finally, in 1867 he and Anna Grigoryevna left Russia in order to wander for some four years abroad, undergoing a series of almost incredible ordeals, due to penury and to his continuous losses at roulette. Judging by some of his letters of that period, Dostoevsky conceived such a dislike of things European as was not easy to cure.

In addition he was distrustful of Europe's "advanced ideas". He

could not find words hard enough to condemn the radical-minded Russian intellectuals peddling those ideas among the youths of their own country almost as a substitute for religion. This was particularly the case in the 1860s when the younger generation used to whip up the prevailing revolutionary moods even by the spell of materialistic philosophies such as those of Buechner and Moleschott. No wonder that Dostoevsky turned his novel *The Possessed* into a most indignant diatribe against the militant "nihilists" of the period. Through the horrors of that novel one can even follow up the author's conviction that the destructive revolutionaries of the 1860s were direct descendants of the harmless and benign Westernising liberals of the 1840s. One of such Westerners in the same novel (Stepan Trofimovich) was in fact so horrified by the savage anarchism as a result of the "new" ideas coming from the West that – shortly before his death – he embraced the people's Orthodox faith just as any Slavophile would have wished him to. Preoccupied with the deeper psychological and metaphysical problems of the Revolution, Dostoevsky gave in *The Possessed* not only one of the most anti-revolutionary novels ever written, but also a gruesome warning to those Russians who were enamoured with Western civilisation. A further powerful warning was given by him in Ivan Karamazov's *Legend of the Grand Inquisitor:* an anticipation of the worst kind of totalitarianism as a horrid alternative by which to keep a dehumanised humanity from anarchy and chaos.

Behind Dostoevsky's Slavophile sympathies there was a great deal of Russian nationalism and patriotism. Even the idea of a united humanity was dear to him mainly in so far as such unity was likely to be achieved by Russia. Certain pages of his *Diary of an Author for 1876–77* even breathe the spirit of Russian imperialism. Yet he was convinced that the Russian people was fit by its very inner make-up eventually to integrate mankind. And this itself was Slavophilism at its most ambitious. In the Manifesto of his periodical *Vremya* he announced the following programme: "We foresee, and we see it with a sense of reverence, that the character of our future activity must be international in the highest

degree; that the Russian Idea is, perhaps, to become the synthesis of all those ideas which Europe is developing with pertinacity and such courage within its separate nationalities that, perhaps, everything that is hostile will find its reconciliation and further development in the Russian national spirit."

What he calls here international should really be called universal. Convinced that a true unity of this kind could take place not upon a mere secular but upon a spiritual-religious basis, Dostoevsky began to preach those Christian ideals which the Slavophiles believed to have found in the religious consciousness of the Russian people. It was this attitude that made him overcome his anti-Western feeling and write during the Russo-Turkish War in 1877: "Our Russian problem has developed into a world-wide universal one, with an extraordinary predestined significance." By calling the uprooted Russian intellectuals back to the soil and the people he was thinking of a reconciliation not only between the Westerners and the Slavophiles but also between Europe and Russia, between East and West, in the name of that pan-human unity which was cherished by the finest Russian intellectuals during the last century. In his novel, *A Raw Youth*, his mouthpiece Versilov says that "among us Russians has been created by the ages a type of the highest culture, never seen before and existing nowhere else in the world – the type of world-wide sympathy for all". By virtue of which he concludes, or forces himself to conclude that "to the Russian, Europe is as precious as Russia: every stone in her is cherished and dear. Europe is as much our fatherland as Russia."* That synthesis of Russia and Europe, which was a romantic dream of the Slavophiles, thus found in Dostoevsky a formula, whatever he may have secretly thought of the European West.

It should be pointed out, though, once again that such pan-human unity was dear to Dostoevsky and the Slavophiles mainly in so far as the historical task of achieving it should be allotted to Russia. Dostoevsky himself believed (or was doing his best to

* Quoted from Dostoevsky's Works translated by Constance Garnett (Heinemann).

believe) that this was the real mission of Russia and the "god-bearing" Russian people. Such an attitude was further endorsed by him in his Pushkin Speech at Moscow on June 8, 1880. "To a true Russian," he said, "Europe and the destiny of all the mighty Aryan* family are as dear as Russia herself; because our destiny is universality won not by the sword, but by the strength of brotherhood and our fraternal aspirations to reunite mankind. And in the course of time, I believe, that we shall, without exception, understand that to be a Russian does mean to aspire finally to reconcile the contradictions of Europe, to show the aim of our European yearnings in our Russian soul, omni-human and all-uniting, to include within our soul by brotherly love all our brethren, and at last it may be, to pronounce the final word of the great general harmony, of the general communion of all nations in accordance with the law and gospel of Christ."†

5

Whereas Dostoevsky was acclaimed by the Slavophiles as one of their own, Tolstoy stood nearer to the radical *narodniki* even though he rejected all politics, let alone all terrorist acts as weapons in the political struggle. In his so-called Christian anarchism he accepted only the law of his own conscience and dismissed everything else as irrelevant. The Slav problem simply did not exist for him. When, in 1876, the Russian press and opinion were full of enthusiasm for the liberation of the Balkan Slavs, Tolstoy wrote in *Anna Karenina* about the fuss concerning "our Slav brethren" in such an ironical tone that the editor Katkov refused to print the respective chapters of the novel in his *Russky Vestnik* (*Russian Messenger*).‡

* And why only Aryan? J. L.
† op. cit.
‡ Towards the end of his life Tolstoy seemed to show more interest in the Slavs. He was on friendly terms with Thomas Masaryk who was able, probably better than anyone else, to explain to him certain tenets of the Slav problem. In his last flight from Yasnaya Polyana Tolstoy even contemplated going to Bulgaria.

Among the features which Tolstoy shared with the *narodniki* were his love for the Russian people *qua* people, his uncompromising attitude towards the land question, his moral earnestness, and also his rationalism. In contrast to Dostoevsky's hatred of revolutionaries, Tolstoy depicted them (in *Resurrection*) in a favourable light, since he himself was in full sympathy with their protest against tyranny and injustice, however much he may have disliked the methods of their struggle. He was, moreover, an admirer of Alexander Herzen. "The main point in which I am close to him," he once acknowledged to Gorky, "is his love for the Russian people." And as for his own attitude towards the *obshchina*, he expressed it as early as 1865 in terms which might have been used by any radical populist. "The world task of Russia," he said, "is to provide a social structure devoid of the individual ownership of land." He anticipated some other populist ideas also in his periodical *Yasnaya Polyana*, published by him during 1862. On several occasions he expressed his belief that the Russian people would show to the world not only how to solve the problem of land-ownership, but also how to live happily as a united humanity without any capitalist exploitation and slavery. There was, however, one feature in which Tolstoy was anxious to outstrip even the populists themselves: his tendency to *identify* himself and to merge with the peasant masses as completely as the conditions he lived in would allow him. In his later years he dressed like a peasant and worked in the fields, sowing, mowing and ploughing like any tiller of the soil. Also his scathing attitude towards the upper classes and their culture was typical in this respect, albeit it had first originated in his enthusiasm for Rousseau. Furthermore, the aristocrat Pierre Bezoukhov (in *War and Peace*) and the squire Levin (in *Anna Karenina*) were both saved from their inner impasse by the wisdom of simple illiterate *moujiks*.

This does not mean that Tolstoy was not aware of the disturbing negative characteristics among the peasants. In his early work, *The Morning of a Landowner*, he depicted (with consummate realism) their sloth, their distrust and dogged indolence. And his drama, *The Power of Darkness*, which he wrote in his advanced years, is a

sufficient proof of how much he felt the moral decay of the village. Yet such decay was attributed by him primarily to the disintegrating influence which modern capitalism was having upon the peasantry – an opinion that might have been endorsed by any populist as well.

Both the populist and the Slavophile currents had to lose much of their ground once it became clear that the *obshchina*, together with many another patriarchal tradition, was being undermined by the somewhat belated yet rapid progress of capitalism in Russia. The financial policy of Count Witte was responsible for the penetration of foreign capital into the country on an alarming scale. Numerous factories called for cheap labour, and the growing industrial proletariat began to organise itself upon an ideological and a class basis. So much so that in the revolutionary year of 1905 it was already able to threaten the very foundations of autocracy. But no sooner had that rehearsal for a bigger revolution been suppressed than the Prime Minister Stolypin did all he could (on November 22, 1906) to cause the dissolution of the village communes in favour of private ownership of land among the peasants. Whatever his intentions, such a step was bound to increase not only the economic antagonism among the villagers, but also the power of the "energetic" *kulak*-type mercilessly exploiting them. Yet while the country as a whole was still in the throes of its social and political ferment, the First World War broke out and eventually landed Russia in her cataclysm of 1917 which made a clean sweep of her past and opened up an entirely new era of global importance.

6

It is of no small interest that during that period of bloodshed and chaos the Revolution itself found in the verses of Alexander Blok a poetic affirmation of the universal, as well as apocalyptic, significance of the happenings that were taking place. In his powerful poem, *The Twelve*, Blok depicted twelve bolshevist soldiers patrolling at night the streets of St. Petersburg during the worst ordeals inflicted upon that city by the revolutionary turmoil.

There is suffering, there are crimes and chaos, while the snowy blizzard rages all around. Yet the soldiers march on and on, fully conscious that – in spite of all – their cause is the cause of justice and human fellowship to come. This is why they suddenly find themselves led by an unexpected radiant phantom "gently walking on the snow". It is the figure of Jesus Christ – the symbol of brotherhood and love. Also that other leader of the symbolist movement, Andrey Bely, hailed the revolution in the Messianic spirit of a renewal of man and life.

In the contrast between the revolutionary poetry of Vladimir Mayakovsky and that of Sergey Esenin one can see, however, the clash between the two strains still contending for the new age. Whereas Mayakovsky in his grotesque *Mystery-Booffe* proclaimed a coming millennium engineered by proletarians, the one-time village lad Esenin dreamed of a utopian golden age of the peasants – quite in the spirit of populism at its most idyllic. And when the events proved that the Revolution had brought in not a new agrarian but a new industrial age, Esenin reacted by that sadness of the "last poet of the village" which ended in his suicide in 1925.

> The little thatched hut I was born in
>   Lies bare to the sky,
> And in these crooked alleys of Moscow
>   I am fated to die.*

Such is the beginning and the end of a poem characteristic of his last period. Nor was Blok himself saved from disappointments and frustrations. These were due partly to the excesses of the civil war (let loose by the Revolution) and partly to the policy of Russia's former allies who had failed, or else had refused, to see the world-historical impact of what was taking place. Hoping against hope that the era of universal brotherhood, of which both the Slavophiles and the populists had been dreaming, would yet come to stay, Blok addressed, in his poem *The Scythians*, the distrustful and reluctant Western nations with these lines:

* Translated by R. M. Hewitt.

Yes, you have long since ceased to love
As our cold blood can love; the taste
You have forgotten of a love
That burns like fire and like fire lays waste.

Yes, Russia is a Sphinx. Exulting, grieving,
And sweating blood, she cannot sate
Her eyes that gaze and gaze and gaze
At you with stone-lipped love for you and hate.

He admonished the Western world to abandon its murderous religion of the golden calf and replace it by that of humanity united in a universal fellowship of man.

Comrades, while it is not too late
Sheathe the sword! May brotherhood be blessed.

As though foreboding that a call such as this might fall on deaf ears as far as the Western hemisphere was concerned, Blok saw the only alternative to unity in a new conflict ahead – perhaps a final conflict between the West and the whole of the revengeful Asian East rising against the "white devils". And he made no bones as to where a misunderstood and abandoned Russia would stand in such a conflict:

We will not move when the ferocious Hun
Despoils the corpse and leaves it bare,
Burns towns, herds cattle in the church
And smell of white flesh roasting fills the air.*

This was where the problem was left by the poetic voice of Alexander Blok who soon after died. And this is where the problem of East and West still stands, full of potential shocks and surprises looming large upon the horizon.

* Translated by Babette Deutsch and Avrahm Yarmolinsky (M. Lawrence).

CHAPTER NINE

Pan-Slavism and Pan-Russism

I

Whatever the virtues and defects of the Slavophiles, their apprehension that, culturally at least, a thoroughly Westernised Russia might become a kind of second-rate or third-rate Europe was not without some foundation. At a time when the whole of Western life was getting increasingly materialistic and as it were emptied of its deeper contents, the Slavophiles could not help keeping their eyes fixed on those "Russian" values which they regarded as being still able to counter the negative spirit of the age and all that it stood for. Their criticism of the West was often to the point; but what they offered instead was hardly convincing enough to make one follow them without a number of questions. The Slavophile frame of mind harboured, moreover, certain pitfalls of a psychological and moral nature which cannot be overlooked either. One of Tyutchev's best known poems, for instance, depicted Christ walking in the garb of a slave all over Russia and blessing her. . . . This kind of pseudo-Christian humility was one of the dangers threatening Slavophilism. The second danger was of the opposite kind: one of national pride exalting Russia over the West which she wanted to "save", provided it still could be saved at all. Of course, there remained a third issue: that Russia should mind her own business and leave the rest of the world to its own fate, while yet drawing from its predicaments as much advantage for herself as possible.

The first two of these issues were latent in the Slavophile teaching from the outset. And as for the third, its temptations came to the fore at a later stage, when Slavophilism and nationalist imperialism began to converge and flirt with one another. This trend stood, tacitly at any rate, for the expansion of Russia's might

in any direction that offered the line of least resistance. Those Orthodox Slavs in the Balkans who until 1878 were ruled by the Turks, for example, could always be used as a pretext for Russia's interventions, since she happened to be their avowed "Christian protector". It was here, too, that the aims of the later Slavophiles, official patriots, and rabid imperialists coincided. The Slavs under Turkey, and to some extent even those in Austria, began to be looked upon as a convenient material waiting to be "liberated" by Russia and thus strengthen her imperial power as such. In short, Pan-Slavism tended to become Pan-Russism pure and simple. Even the historian M. Pogodin, with all his enthusiasm and vitality, was unable to draw a clear line between his imperialist-Russian and his Slav proclivities. And the same was largely true of Dostoevsky, not to mention a number of other latter-day Slavophiles or would-be Slavophiles. General Rostislav Fadeyev (1824–83) went so far indeed as to openly advocate, in his one-time sensational pamphlet, *An Opinion on the Eastern Question* (1869), an invincible Pan-Slav empire headed by Russia, with Constantinople as its capital, and extending from the Adriatic right up to the Pacific. His formula sounded: "Formerly the East meant Turkey and Islam: now it means Slavdom and Orthodoxy." He championed a Slav federation in the sense that each Slav nation should have its own government for internal affairs, but under a great ruler, or "big brother," guiding and protecting their common interests. By Pan-Slav he thus actually meant Pan-Russian.*

Another Russian General and militant Slavophile, N. I. Dragomirov (1830–1909), fully agreed with the plan that Russia should unite all the Slavs in order to form a great world empire – the very idea of which was Palacký's nightmare. Still, one should not forget another aspect lurking behind the voices of Fadeyev and Dragomirov: the threatening military might of Bismarck's Germany. Aware of the Teutonic danger looming forward,

---

* A concomitant of all this was the idea that Russian should become the general literary language of all the Slavs, as the Russian scholar Vladimir I. Lamansky (1833–1914) would have it.

Fadeyev in particular saw the best way of countering the rise of Pan-Germanism by the rise of Pan-Slavism. In his opinion Russia needed the non-Russian Slavs for her own national safety, although official Russia still refused to face this problem frankly and openly even at a time when such men as Louis Napoleon, Bismarck, Cavour and a legion of lesser politicians were busy exploiting the nationalist trends for the benefit of their own countries. She preferred to camouflage her imperialistic designs by the more popular device (especially in the Balkans) of Orthodoxy which never failed to appeal to the masses.

In Austria the hopes and aspirations of her peoples were curbed by the triumph of reaction in 1848–49. Neither the Slav Congress in Prague nor the separatist rebellion of the Magyars (crushed by the Russian army) had any immediate liberating consequences. As soon as Francis Joseph felt safe on his throne, the Habsburg Monarchy became once more a "prison of nations" and remained so for some ten years, all the time jealously guarded by Bach and his "Hussars". But when the Bach regime too came to an end, Austria had to cope with further difficulties not the least of which was the national problem as it was being raised time and again by the Slavs. In the Tsarist Empire, on the other hand, the Slavophiles were joined by a few thinkers in whose theories the problem of Russia, Slavdom and the West assumed certain new and rather striking aspects.

2

One of these thinkers was Nikolai Danilevsky (1822–95) whose provocative study, *Russia and Europe*, appeared in the same year as General Fadeyev's pamphlet. The sub-title of his work was: *An Enquiry into the Cultural and Political Relations between the Slavs and the German-Latin World.* A Slavophile by his sympathies and a botanist, or rather a biologist, by profession (an opponent of Charles Darwin), Danilevsky was anxious to put forward the "biological" reasons why Russia and the Slavs in general should ultimately triumph over the West. Dismissing the idea of a united

humanity as a naïve Utopia, he believed in the existence of definite cultural-historical types, independent of each other and subject to the biological process of youth, manhood, old age and death. He analysed ten such types, beginning with the Egyptian and ending with the Germano-Latin type. According to him the European type of evolution had already left its blossoming period far behind and was now in its unavoidable stage of decay.* Russia as a champion of the Slavs (minus the Poles) was, however, still young enough to have a great future.

Danilevsky, with his anti-European bias, was convinced that Russia or Slavdom as a whole would create a cultural type representing a synthesis of religious, political, cultural and social-economic factors. Hence the Slavs were destined to play a leading part in history, as had been prophesied already by Herder. After the forthcoming liquidation of Turkey and Austria, the Magyars, the Rumanians and the Greeks, too, although not belonging to the Slav race, would be hitched as "satellites" to the Pan-Slav federation, with Constantinople as its capital. Russia would, of course, be the leader.

In 1876 there appeared another highly controversial essay, *Byzantinism and Slavdom*, by Konstantin Leontyev (1831–91), and about ten years later his hardly less provocative *The East, Russia and Slavdom*. Leontyev was keenly interested in the Slav problem, but he treated it from an angle which did not coincide with the usual Slavophile approach. What he shared with the Slavophiles was his sympathy with the Greek-Orthodox religion, but even here he took a line which was as puzzling as was his entire personality. As a patriot he was in love with Russia's might, while at the same time distrusting the anarchic instincts of the Russians. The only remedy he saw was severe authoritarianism, however unpopular such an attitude was likely to make him among the

---

* The similarity between Danilevsky's theory and that of Oswald Spengler's *The Downfall of the West* (*Der Untergang des Abendlandes*) has often been pointed out. Yet the idea itself had first been put forward in 1857 by the German historian Heinrich Rückert in his *Lehrbuch der Weltgeschichte*. Some hints at it can be found even in Herder's *Ideas to the Philosophy of Mankind's History*.

ranks of the intelligentsia. But Leontyev was the last person to care for the reactions on the part of his readers. His capricious and erratic mind asserted itself with relish against anything conventional or generally accepted. His very career was unconventional enough. He had started his series of professions as a physician (in the Crimean War), after which he entered the Russian consular service in Turkey and the Balkans. At the same time he became a many-sided author and journalist, then a censor, a literary critic, and finally a monk. By a strange freak of fate he combined an uncompromising aesthetic outlook with a great admiration for the rigid Byzantine pattern of existence. Although a voluptuary by nature, he championed the Byzantine ideal of asceticism, perhaps as a safeguard against his own sensual propensities. Moreover, when in the 1860s and 1870s Russia was in the grip of utilitarian ideas and ideals, Leontyev came forward with his aristocratic-aesthetic trend at the risk of being ostracised, as he actually was, by the whole of the progressive intelligentsia.

The most salient feature in Leontyev was, however, his well-nigh pathological spite of the bourgeois style of life. It was in the East that he was able to gratify his aesthetic and social sense; for what he had found there was not only colourful, but (in those days) still devoid of the philistine and commercial ways of Europe which he loathed. He looked with scorn above all upon Western bourgeois democracy which he identified with mediocrity, vulgarity and drabness. Beauty, and preferably tragic beauty, he regarded as the most desirable and necessary ingredient of life, even if this should entail inequality, suffering and injustice. As for human beings, beautiful and dignified forms of existence should be shaped out of them, whatever the cost. The State itself ought to be not a democratic institution, but an edifice of unlimited power, majesty and beauty – endorsed by religion even when compelled to be ruthless and "beyond good and evil" in its methods. In short, Leontyev was a kind of Nietzsche with the makings of a Byzantine monk. After his various careers he actually entered the Optina monastery and then the Trinity monastery (now Zagorsk,

in the vicinity of Moscow), where he became a monk shortly before his death at the age of sixty.

As far as Leontyev's basic ideas are concerned, he shared some of them with Danilevsky, notably the one about the three stages of culture: youth, manhood and decay. These were marked by him as (1) the period of primary simplicity; (2) the flowering period of positive or creative complexity and differentiation; and (3) the period of secondary simplicity, or simplification, with its inherent process of confusion, disintegration and death. He also approved of Danilevsky's view concerning the future of the cultural and politico-historical significance of Russia; but he took it in its Euro-Asiastic rather than Slav sense. Even his hatred of Western Europe was due not to any Slavophile propensities, but to his contempt for the European middle-classes and their philistine existence. Socialism itself meant to him only an extension of that very mentality – bourgeois philistinism and comfort for all. Far from admiring the democratic reforms of Alexander II, he was afraid that Russia herself might gradually fall a prey to liberal bourgeoisie and thus be landed in the same decay and confusion of all values as was the case with the whole of the Western world. This he feared in the days when also the Russian intelligentsia, reinforced by the recruits from the newly enriched commercial layer, was assuming a more and more bourgeois style of life reminiscent of the West. Nor could he ever overcome his distrust of the common people. Even his love of Russia was confined mainly to the Russian State whose growing might be admired in the first place. Yet he remained a stranger to any nationalism proper, whether Russian or Slav. He thought that the policy of the Byzantine spirit should prevail over the policy of Slav flesh. While in Turkey, he was more in sympathy with the Greeks and Turks than with the Balkan Slavs whom he found much too democratic for his taste.

Leontyev's reactionary imperialism, as well as his political will to power, was certainly devoid of any general Slav complexion. He did not believe in a common Slav denominator either, since the non-Russian Slavs seemed to him culturally different

from the Russians. Any democratic Pan-Slavism struck him as dangerous to Russia: by incorporating the other Slavs within her orbit she herself might become contaminated with their liberal and egalitarian spirit which would spell her ruin. Constantinople itself should be envisaged not as the prospective capital of a Pan-Slav Empire (as Fadeyev and Danilevsky would have it), but as the very heart of a self-contained Russia keeping to a hierarchic and severely disciplined Byzantine pattern of existence. Despite such wishes, Leontyev was yet able to predict (in the 1880s) the cataclysm that was to shatter the present-day world. He foreboded the victory of the "anti-Christian" principle, while some other representatives of the Slavophile current were already indulging in all sorts of reactionary affiliations. The trend itself was assuming such a colouring that a deservedly sharp criticism was bound to come. And come it did.

3

The man best qualified for such a task was the philosopher Vladimir Solovyov (1853–1900) who, at an early stage, had himself been under the influence of both Kireyevsky and Khomyakov. He found his inspiration in their religious-philosophic thought, with Christian universalism as his ideal. Like Dostoevsky (who happened to be his friend) and the best of the Slavophiles, Solovyov aimed at an integration of culture and religion as the only salvation from the blind-alley of our age. Aware of the dichotomy in the Russian consciousness, he wanted to overcome it not by pitting Russia against Europe, but by the kind of synthesis Dostoevsky had hinted at in his Pushkin Speech, albeit without Dostoevsky's partiality for Russia. In the very difference between the two Solovyov saw a world-historical process to which both East and West were necessary as two complementary units. This was one of the reasons why he dealt so harshly with some of the later Slavophiles, beginning with Danilevsky. In an essay (bearing the same title as Danilevsky's book *Russia and Europe*) he denounced – in 1888 – Danilevsky's theory of autonomous cultural

types as being false even historically. Was not the Roman Empire a collection of ever so many minor cultures merging in one *universal* culture? Outside that universal culture there were only a few sterile cultural types, or just savages. In some of his further statements he contended that Russia herself owed all her significant achievements in literature and elsewhere mainly to her partnership with Europe. Nor were there any pure and exclusive cultural types left either in Europe or anywhere else in the world. Another mistake made by Danilevsky was to lump the Russians and the non-Russian Slavs together even while excluding the Poles. Can there be a greater difference than the one which exists between the Russians and the Westernised Catholic Czechs? Why, even the culture of the Serbs and the Bulgarians is different from that of the Russians despite the fact that they all share the same Orthodox religion. True enough, the best of the Slavophiles did not stop at the Slavs. They saw in them their allies in that mission of Russia which – in their opinion – should lead to the eventual universal fellowship of nations. Yet Solovyov made a sharp distinction between a mission which aims at national self-realisation in the service of humanity, and the one whose task is mere national self-assertion at the expense of humanity.

He dealt with the various aspects of this dilemma in his book *The National Problem in Russia*, the second edition of which (1888) was provided with a suggestive preface. While agreeing with certain tenets of the early Slavophiles, especially with their insistence that politics should not be divorced from moral values, he criticised, and devastatingly so, those representatives of the Slavophile movement who saw or wanted to see, in the mission of Russia the privilege of a "chosen people". Their claim that Russia should hold the central position in world history was regarded by him as presumptuous and dangerous. He himself harboured no hatred of the West. Nor did he revel in Orthodoxy as a special attribute of the Russian people. On the contrary, he pointed out, with great acumen, all the weaknesses of the official Orthodox Church, notably her servility towards the State. Having no sympathies with pre-Petrine Russia either, he said quite frankly

that by transferring their ideal into the Russian past the Slavophiles had turned it into a false ideal.

4

The severest criticism of the later Slavophiles can be found, however, in Solovyov's polemical essay *Ideals and Idols* (1891) – a kind of post mortem of the Slavophile movement which, in his opinion, was already in a process of disintegration. Some of its elements had been absorbed by populism, others by reactionary obscurantism, even by anti-Semitism. But if so, he concluded, then the Slavophile current was no longer an organic phenomenon; it had, in fact, ceased to exist. As a religious thinker again Solovyov did not share the Slavophile (and for that matter Dostoevsky's) prejudice against Catholicism. He was on friendly terms with that great champion of Southern Slav unity, the Croat Bishop Strossmayer and even stayed, for a time, as his guest at Djakovo in Slavonia. Knowing only too well the weakness of any single Christian denomination standing by itself, Solovyov hoped for a renewal of the Christian spirit from a reunion of the Churches. It was with this in view that he wrote his French treatise *La Russie et l'église universelle* (1889). He championed such a reunion also in his quaintly apocalyptic work, *Three Conversations*, which reflected his not very optimistic mood as to the future of humanity.

While the Slavophile movement was already in decline, Solovyov continued to dream of the world-historical process as one undivided whole, accompanied by a synthesis of the philosophic, scientific, and Christian-religious thought. He was anxious to "bring all elements of human existence – individual and social – into the right relation with the ultimate principle of life, and through it and in it also to a harmonious relation with each other". But such had been the real aim of Kireyevsky and Khomyakov as well. And so instead of entirely discarding, Solovyov only corrected the Slavophile idea of a Russian mission. He, too, thought that because of some of its inherent characteristics, the

Russian people was an eminently suitable unifying factor in human history. In this respect he echoed as it were Dostoevsky who, for all his contradictions and imperialistic leanings, wrote (in 1877) in his *Journal of an Author*: "The fact is that in Russia, despite all discordance, people still agree and concur in the ultimate general idea of the universal fellowship of men. This fact is undeniable and, in itself, is surprising because this feeling, in the form of so vivid and fundamental an urge, exists in no other people."

But whereas Dostoevsky's wish was that the task of uniting the whole of humanity should be allotted to the Russians (and exclusively to the Russians), Solovyov regarded this as a common task of all nations, although Russia might perhaps be particularly helpful in it. He moreover wished that Russia should eventually put even her political might to the service of such a purpose. Small wonder that he became a valuable link between what was really constructive in the Slavophile ideology and the revived religious-philosophic thought among the Russian intellectuals at the beginning of this century: a valiant attempt to save religion or what was still left of it. And, strangely enough, this time the wave of religious revival came from a group of former Marxists (Berdyayev, Bulgakov, S. Frank, Peter Struve, etc.) as well as from quite a few modernist writers. This final battle for a spiritual and religious basis of life was inaugurated in 1909 by the collection of essays under the title of *Vekhi* (*Signposts*) which made a stir in the ranks of the liberal-minded intelligentsia, since the one-time radicals themselves now proclaimed *urbi et orbi* that Socialism alone was not enough. It was largely due to Solovyov that several of them changed their former attitudes and turned to the religious values so dear to the Slavophiles and to Dostoevsky. Solovyov had a certain impact even upon the symbolist current of Russian poetry, since he was not only a philosopher but a talented poet as well. The two leaders of the specifically Russian school of symbolism, Alexander Blok and Andrey Bely, were both indebted (each in his own way) to Solovyov the thinker, the visionary and the poet. That school reached its height during the first decade of the twentieth

century, when the Slav problem, too, suddenly assumed a new lease of life in Russia and among the non-Russian Slavs as well. Such transformation was due, however, to a number of international happenings the final result of which was a new and different Europe, in fact a new and different world. A brief historical retrospect may, perhaps, clarify some of the issues involved.

CHAPTER TEN

Towards the Last Act

I

The Balkan peninsula has the distinction, or rather the misfortune, of being a most vital and therefore most coveted territory in South-Eastern Europe. The majority of its inhabitants (apart from Greeks and Albanians) are Orthodox Slavs of whom – at the time of the Berlin Congress in 1878 – only Serbia and Montenegro were free from the Turkish rule. As Russia and Austria were Turkey's immediate neighbours, they both aspired to those Balkan countries the eventual possession of which might have served their interests. What Austria aimed at was to penetrate as far as the port of Salonika which was essential for her trade and economic expansion. But in order to get there she would have had to pave her way through Serbia, Bosnia-Hercegovina and a large portion of Macedonia right down to the Aegean Sea. Russia, on the other hand, needed certain regions in the Balkans above all as a hinterland which would ensure for her a free passage from the Black Sea through the craved for Bosphorus and the Dardanelles into the Mediterranean.

Yet a powerful Russian fleet in the Mediterranean might have hampered not only benefits derived from Salonika, but also the trade route between Great Britain and the Asiatic East, especially India.* Hence it was quite logical that during the Crimean Campaign Austria should have given her diplomatic and political

---

* At the very height of the Crimean War between Russia, Great Britain and France in 1855 Lord Clarendon sent the following dispatch to the Queen's representatives abroad: "This present war has been undertaken in order to provide securities against those ambitious designs of Russia, which menace the safety of Turkey and the future of Europe; and in short, to prevent, so far as Turkey is concerned, the accomplishment of the wishes and the views of Peter, of Catherine, of Alexander and of Nicholas."

support to Russia's enemies, albeit only a few years earlier her very existence had been saved by the army which Tsar Nicholas I had sent to Hungary. Whenever Russia wanted to get some advantage by fomenting trouble in the Balkans, she could always do it under the pretext of being a "protector" of the Orthodox religion in those parts of the Turkish Empire. The position of Austria, with her expansionist aims, was however more complex in this respect because it was interwoven with the intricacies of the Slav problem which had a direct bearing upon her doings not only in the Balkans, but also at home.

It should be remembered that after her defeat in the Crimea Russia entered upon an era of solid reforms, whereas in Austria the notorious Bach regime continued until 1859 when her reverses in Italy and the loss of Lombardy compelled her also to introduce certain reforms. But as soon as her absolutist decade was over, the problem of federation versus centralism was bound to crop up again. It was here that the interests of the Austrian Slavs clashed with those of the Germans and the Magyars who knew only too well that a federal Austria would be to their disadvantage since it would deprive them of lording over those ethnic groups which they hoped to assimilate in the course of time. Knowing the appetites of his German and Magyar compatriots only too well, Francis Palacký warned Vienna, in 1865, once again that the only alternative to a prospective dissolution of the Habsburg Monarchy was a federal system. He did this in his pamphlet, *The Idea of the Austrian State*, in which he demanded that in her own interests such a federal Austria should become "a Mother to all her nations, and a Stepmother to none". A year later the Habsburg Monarchy lost also Venetia, while in the conflict with Prussia, who wanted to replace her as the leader of the German Confederation (as created by the Vienna Congress in 1815), she was beaten in the battle of Sadova. Defeated, she was moreover excluded from the Confederation itself. This might have served as an incentive for putting her own house in order on a federal basis; but nothing of the sort happened. On the contrary, Vienna preferred to come to terms with the arrogant Magyar feudals instead and to adopt the dualist

system of Austria-Hungary: a step by which she signed the death-warrant of the Habsburg Empire. In the Austrian part proper or Cisleithania the Slavs remained at the mercy of the Germans, whereas in the Hungarian half or Transleithania all the non-Magyar nations (including quite a large number of Germans) were delivered to the chauvinistic appetites of their Magyar bosses.*

From now on Francis Joseph was the Emperor of Austria and the King of Hungary. The latter was, however, independent in every respect except in matters of foreign policy, defence and finances – these she still had to share with Vienna. It should be said, though, in fairness that Francis Joseph himself may have had a sincere wish, in the interests of the dynasty, to turn his monarchy into a working multi-racial or rather multi-lingual state which would be above any nationalistic jealousies. But as the idea of such a solution invariably met with opposition on the part of the Austrian Germans and was fanatically rejected by the Magyars (the two politically dominant nations in the Habsburg Empire)†any thought of it had to be abandoned. It was in fact dead and buried only to be resuscitated much later 'and at a historical moment which had already become too muddled and too critical even for such a solution.

2

As soon as the dual system of Austria-Hungary was introduced, it caused a great deal of rancour among the Austrian Slavs, especially among the Czechs whose Austro-Slav sympathies were thus damped down, while their faith in the future of the Habsburg

* In 1868 the Croats succeeded in making an agreement with Hungary which secured for them a kind of autonomy within the frame of the Hungarian territory. Yet the Croat province of Dalmatia, which until 1797 had been under Venice, remained in the Austrian half, while Rijeka (Fiume) was grabbed from the Croats by the Magyars and became a free port under Hungarian control.

† Vienna had made certain concessions also to the Poles in Galicia, at whose mercy was however the large Ukrainian population of that province. In this way the Polish politicians were bribed in order to side with Vienna even against the Slav interests when required.

Monarchy was getting increasingly shaky. Anxious to make use of the moment and to enhance the lingering pro-Russian sympathies among the dissatisfied Austrian Slavs, the Russian Slavophiles and their fellow-travellers organised (under official patronage) a new Slav Congress which took place at Moscow in the summer of 1867: on the occasion of the all-Slav ethnographic exhibition in that city. But there were only eighty-four non-Russian delegates present, and no Poles at all. Tyutchev welcomed the Slav guests with some appropriate verses, yet this time there were no signs of the intense liberal spirit which had prevailed in Prague nineteen years earlier. The emphasis was mainly on Russism and Orthodoxy. In fact, the Russian hosts consisted of a strange medley of Slavophiles, official patriots, bureaucrats and imperialists, Professor Pogodin and Mikhail Katkov (the Editor of the *Russian Messenger*) being among their prominent members. The rather strong Czech group, led by Palacký and his son-in-law, Dr. F. R. Rieger, may have gone to Moscow in defiance of Vienna; but once there, they could hardly find a common language with the Russians, least of all when the Polish problem – only four years after the disastrous Polish rebellion of 1863 – was discussed. Otherwise it is more than possible that even in the eyes of Palacký the Russia of Alexander II, with the abolition of serfdom, the introduction of *zemstvos* (local self-administration) and other reforms, was not what she had been under Nicholas I and no longer represented an immediate threat to freedom. Such a threat was now more likely to come from the "Germanising fury" of Prussia and her growing imperialism. Many Slav patriots even seemed to hope that Germany's greedy appetites might be checked by a strong Russia, in which case Slavdom as a whole would benefit after all.

Under Austria-Hungary Vienna's policy towards the Slav nations remained, in spite of some improvements, basically the same as before. It was not much altered even after the Franco-Prussian War in 1870, when the triumph of German militarism began casting its shadow over Europe which was soon stirred, however, by events in the Balkans once more. It all started with the rebellion of the Christian population in Hercegovina against

their Turkish oppressors in 1875. As a consequence Serbia and Montenegro declared, in 1876, war on Turkey – a step to which neither Austria-Hungary nor Russia could be indifferent. The Russian press and public were suddenly carried away by a surge of Slav (and Orthodox) sympathies. The Tsarist General Chernyayev joined the Serbs as commander-in-chief of their army fighting the Turks. There was no lack of other Russian volunteers either. A war between Russia and Turkey became unavoidable, and it broke out in 1877.

The situation was fraught with dangers in so far as the Balkans and Near East were – as ever – the arena of several competing imperialisms. Great Britain certainly could not afford to contemplate the possibility of the Bosphorus and the Dardanelles falling into Russian hands. The rivalry between Austria-Hungary and Russia was also acute, while Germany kept waiting and watching how things could be turned to her own advantage in the end. Yet among the Germans themselves there were some sober warnings. Among the numerous topical pamphlets pouring out of the press at the time there was one by a certain Constantin Frantz under the title *A German Answer to the Eastern Problem* (1877). Here its author explored the chances of a peaceful or even friendly co-existence between the Germans and the non-Russian Slavs in a supranational Middle Europe devoid of any chauvinistic *Nationalitaetsschwaermerei*. Such a union ought to "raise the respective populations above the level of narrow nationalist politics and thereby pave the way towards a new European development which was possible only through the collaboration of the various European nations. It is above all the Germans and the Slavs who should unite for such a purpose. The initiative for it ought to come, however, from Germany." The author, moreover, advised Germany to develop a supra-national mentality for the very reason that she was surrounded by so many non-Germans. He was particularly keen on a rapprochement between the Germans and the non-Russian Slavs, since this might preclude a further Russian expansion in Europe, because the Slav nations "are in no way inclined to disappear in Russism (*Russentum*). The Poles, the Czechs, the

Croats as well as the Serbs want to preserve their own individuality."

As a matter of fact, the Slavs in Austria-Hungary welcomed with enthusiasm the Russian victories in the Balkans. The more so because they knew that the Dual Monarchy was not in a position to interfere. Its Foreign Minister Count Andrassy had actually promised (in 1875) to his Russian counterpart Gorchakov that in case of a Russo-Turkish war Austria-Hungary would remain neutral – an attitude which he later regretted. The Slavophiles were of course filled with exultation by every Russian success against the Turks. Harangued by Dostoevsky and Ivan Aksakov, they revived their dreams of the Orthodox cross upon the dome of St. Sophia, although Dostoevsky was now voicing a "Russian" and not a general-Slav Constantinople. A number of political conjectures and possibilities were in the air. Turkey, the "sick man of the Bosphorus", was on the point of dying and being ejected into Asia Minor. But when the Russian army was at the gates of Constantinople, the politician Disraeli won (again with Vienna's support and approval) a victory over the strategist Skobelev. The peace treaty of San Stefano, signed on March 3, 1878, was followed by the Berlin Congress, initiated by Disraeli and presided by Bismarck. The Congress, which took place in June and July, 1878, was marked by a series of diplomatic defeats for Russia and Slavdom, since Disraeli distrusted Russia on account of her Near- and Middle-East policy, while Bismarck's former conciliatory attitude towards the Tsarist Empire was no longer reliable either: the "Iron Chancellor's" political calculations were already veering towards a close alliance with Austria-Hungary.*

In any case, the Congress did everything it could to prevent the formation of a strong Slav State in the Balkans. What happened instead was that Turkey, far from being expelled from Europe, was allowed to retain Thrace, the whole of Macedonia, Albania

---

* This alliance was actually concluded in October 1879. Three years later it was joined by Italy in order to form the Triple Alliance – a political move which gradually drove Russia to a rapprochement with France (1894) and later – from 1907 on – also with England, thus paving the way for World War I.

and certain regions which once had belonged to old Serbia. Montenegro and Serbia (whose independence was now fully recognised), obtained but tiny additions to their territories. In order to make a collaboration between the two impossible, they were separated by a wedge in the Sandjak district, still belonging to Turkey but occupied – after the Congress – by the Austrian army. The main object of such a division was to prevent Serbia from reaching the Adriatic and thus emancipating herself from the economic pressure on the part of Austria-Hungary which now secured for herself a firm foot-hold in the Balkans by occupying Bosnia and Hercegovina. These two large territories, speaking pure Serbo-Croat, were handed over by the Berlin Congress to Austrian administration, although nominally they remained under Turkish suzerainty. Most irritating was however the fact that the two provinces were treated from now on by Austria-Hungary as her own colonial region, with all sorts of colonial methods used and misused. Even the Turkish feudal system was not changed. Bulgaria, on the other hand, liberated by the Russians, was divided at Berlin into two separate principalities – Bulgaria and Eastern Rumalia, whose reunion took place, under rather tense conditions, only in 1885.

The mistake made by Russia was that she began to treat Bulgaria as if the latter were a territory conquered for Russia's benefit. Such a policy could not but arouse anti-Russian feelings among the Bulgarians themselves who were already split into two rival parties: the liberals and the conservatives. The first Bulgarian ruler, Prince Alexander of Battenberg, one of the Tsar's nephews, had thus plenty of difficulties to cope with until – in 1886 – he was compelled to abdicate. Serbia, on the other hand, resented not only her own paltry war gains, but also Russia's partiality for Bulgaria – a situation which was promptly exploited by Vienna. The Serbian King Milan even became her tool in the Balkans, although the sympathies of the Serbian people were traditionally on the Russian side. When, in 1885, Bulgaria and Eastern Rumalia became united, the balance between the Balkan countries and nations was disturbed. Serbia was so enraged by it that she

declared war on her Bulgarian neighbour, but was soon defeated. It was now Vienna who negotiated a peace between the two on the basis of the *status quo*. After the abdication of Alexander of Battenberg the Bulgarian throne was offered to the "foxy" Ferdinand of Saxen-Coburg – a protégé of Austria and not exactly in love with St. Petersburg. As though disgusted with her diplomatic fiasco in the Balkans, Russia now directed her attention, and more successfully so, towards Asia and the Far East as she had done also after her defeat in the Crimea.

3

The Berlin treaty turned the territory of the Balkan Slavs into an ideal playground for the competing Great Powers. The Balkans became the proverbial powder-cellar of European politics. Austria's occupation of Bosnia and Hercegovina intensified the expansionist policy of the Habsburgs in that direction. Russia had at least temporarily to comply with what was going on, whatever her fears and disapproval. She was not able to keep even Bulgaria within the orbit of her exclusive influence, while the Serbian King Milan was not averse even to pawning his country to Austria-Hungary. Because of this he was in 1889 compelled to abdicate in favour of his son Alexander. But as Alexander abrogated the newly introduced constitutional reforms and was more than inclined to continue his father's pro-Austrian policy, he and his unpopular wife Draga were brutally murdered in 1903. The Serbian throne then passed to Peter I of the rival Karageorge dynasty. This meant a complete political reorientation in Belgrade: to Russia's advantage.

Even before that dramatic change had taken place the political situation among the Yugoslavs in Austria-Hungary was getting rather hectic. When, in 1879, Count Taaffe became "Imperial Minister" of Austria, he made serious efforts to reconcile the multiple nations, Germans and Slavs in particular, in the Cisleithanian half of the Monarchy. Yet his recognition of Czech as the official language (alongside with German) in Bohemia, Moravia

and Silesia aroused utter animosity among Austrian Germans. Count Kazimir Badeni – a Pole who succeeded Taaffe – made some further concessions to the Slavs, but the relative freedom now granted to the Austrian nations, was not conducive either to harmony or to true co-operation. On the contrary, the Germans resented the fact that any other language should have been put on a par with their own and they did not mind showing it. Many of them began turning their hopes again to Germany proper. As for the Magyars, they would not concede the most elementary rights to non-Magyars in Hungary and were encroaching even upon the Croat autonomy – curtailed as it was already.

It was here, however, that the trouble started. When in 1895 Francis Joseph paid a visit to Croatia, the students of Zagreb University publicly burned the Hungarian flag as a protest against the oppressive measures practised by Budapest. From that time on the anti-Magyar demonstrations were a regular feature of political life in Croatia. Several of those demonstrations were imbued with the spirit of Serbo-Croat solidarity, although the party of Croatian Rights, led by Ante Starčević, was opposed to any collaboration with the Serbs and kept dreaming of a "Greater Croatia" à tout prix. His ideal was a prospective union of Croatia, Slavonia, Dalmatia, Bosnia and Hercegovina in one Croat State within the Habsburg Empire. After Starčević's death in 1896, the leader of the party founded by him became the unscrupulous opportunist and intriguer Josip Frank.*

In the spring of 1897 Austria and Russia signed an agreement about the Balkans which reduced – at least temporarily – the danger of a conflict between the two rivals. At the same time the collaboration between the Croats and the Serbs in the dual Monarchy was not at a standstill either. Thus a group of the more responsible politicians formed, in 1906, the so-called Croat-Serb coalition at Rijeka (Fiume). As it happened, those were the days when a number of Austrian Yugoslavs were already looking upon

---

* Ante Pavelić the bloodstained Fascist *poglavnik* (chief) of "independent" Croatia, set up – during World War II – with the help of Hitler and Mussolini, was a political descendant of Josip Frank.

Serbia as a kind of potential Piedmont in their struggle for freedom. And again the ferment was rife above all among the students. Many young Slovenes, Croats and Serbs were doing their studies in Prague where their ideas were likely to assume a solid character under the influence of Professor Thomas G. Masaryk (1850-1937) and also of the neo-Slav current as represented by Dr. Kramař (1860-1937). Masaryk, like Palacký, held no illusions about the real nature of the Russian system and was, with all his Slav sympathies, a thorough humanist and humanitarian of the Western kind. In his opinion all Slav nations ought to be treated as equals in the name of true democracy and freedom. What mattered to him in politics were practical possibilities. The present and the future were more important to him than any historical past, however colourful. And the same was largely true of Dr. Kramař as well. In this respect their trend was a useful corrective to the somewhat exaggerated historicism bequeathed by Palacký.

Dr. Kramař's neo-Slav trend affected some liberal-minded intellectuals also among the Poles. After the unsuccessful Russian revolution in 1905-6 several Polish democrats became less intransigent and were willing to work together even with the democratic factions of Russia. Some representatives of neo-Slavism were also in favour of a rapprochement between Austria and Russia as though hoping thereby to alleviate the dangerous rivalries between the two in the Balkans. But there were the voices to the contrary on the part of German and Magyar nationalists. The Austrian Pan-Germans were not averse to seeing even the disappearance of Austria in a greater Germany, or else in a powerful *Mitteleuropa* bossed by the Teutons, while the Magyars were more than ever determined to assimilate in the shortest possible time the non-Magyar nations living in Hungary, no matter what the Germans were doing or intended to do. The Austrian government (but not that of Hungary) was compelled to enlarge the electoral rights in 1896, and eleven years later (1907) universal suffrage was introduced, but again only in Austria. Even the idea of federalism, of the "united states of great Austria"

under the Habsburgs, was being tentatively voiced, although neither the Austrian Pan-Germans nor the Magyar chauvinists would have anything to do with such a scheme. The fiercest opponents of any concessions were, of course, the Magyars. Some further troubles were bound to arise when Russia herself, after her defeat in the Far East by Japan, began to increase her vigilance in the Balkans and the Near East.

This happened at a time when King Peter was making quite successful efforts at bringing Serbia and Bulgaria closer together in the interests of both countries. A potential alliance of this kind was however contrary to the aims and designs of the Dual Monarchy. In addition, the Young Turks' revolt in 1908, having overthrown Abdul Hamid, promised to be the starting-point of a series of reforms. Its leaders were even likely to claim back sooner or later Bosnia and Hercegovina which, anyway, were not too happy under the Austrian administration. This however was not to the taste of Austria-Hungary whose Minister of Foreign Affairs, L. L. Aehrenthal, suddenly took advantage of Russia's military weakness and, in October 1908, annexed both Bosnia and Herce- govina. Russia, exhausted by her reverses in the Far East as well as by the revolution at home, had to keep quiet. Serbia, on the other hand, was profoundly shocked by the seizure of the two Serbian- speaking provinces which by right should be hers. This was a step by which the Dual Monarchy wanted to curb the national ambi- tions of Serbia and at the same time strengthen her own position in the Balkans for the sake of the Austrian (as well as German) *Drang nach Osten* – a prospect which could hardly please Great Britain.* The annexation itself stirred, however, the anti-Austrian feelings among the Bosnian students and intellectuals whose secret association, "Young Bosnia", soon became one of the disruptive elements in the Habsburg Empire; the more so because it was connected with such a society as "Unity or Death" (better known as the "Black Hand") formed in Serbia proper by Colonel D. Dimitrijević-Apis, though not working with the Serbian

* One more reason why in those years a gradual rapprochement between Great Britain and Russia was taking place.

government.* Incidentally, Apis was one of the men responsible for the murder of King Alexander and his wife Draga.

It should be stressed, however, that a number of Austrian Slavs, especially the Croats, welcomed the annexation of the two provinces for the obvious reason that it further increased the Slav population in Austria-Hungary and thus made their national struggle more efficient. Unfortunately, both Vienna and Budapest made the annexation a pretext for fostering the animosities between the Serbs and the Croats both of whom wanted to proclaim their exclusive rights on the annexed regions.† While trying to turn one section of the population against the other, Vienna now made use also of the "trialist" idea – at least theoretically. It was the heir apparent, Francis Ferdinand, who adopted the idea of possibly adding to the Dual Monarchy a third partner consisting of Yugoslav provinces pointing to the centre and the south of the Balkans, thus jeopardising the future of Serbia. There was, of course, no love lost between the Austrian heir apparent and the Slavs, but he played with the plan of trialism mainly in order to frighten the Magyars whom he hated on account of their separatist anti-Habsburg tendencies. Otherwise he was known as a champion of clericalism, a worshipper of military power and an opponent of anti-German tendencies in a predominantly Slav State.‡

4

In Russia the Austrian annexation of Bosnia-Hercegovina caused great commotion, not only among the military and governing

* Anti-Austrian "Youth" movements sprang up also among the Serbo-Croat and Slovene students in the Dual Monarchy. Those movements were in contact and worked together with the student associations in Serbia.

† Although speaking the same language, the population of Bosnia-Hercegovina is divided between three religions, Orthodox, Catholic and Mohammedan. But the Orthodox prevails.

‡ Even before the annexation of Bosnia-Hercegovina there were in the Habsburg Empire, according to statistics, 23½ million Slavs (45%), 12 million Germans (23%) and about 10 million Magyars (19%).

circles, but also among the intellectuals, especially among those in academic professions, who now began taking a livelier interest in the Slav problem. A number of well known Russian scholars, headed by the psychiatrist Professor Bekhterev (the founder and chairman of the Slav Scientists Association), were in close contact with their colleagues in other Slav countries, notably with the Czechs. In the summer of 1910 a new Slav Congress, backed by a strong Russian delegation, took place in Sophia. This time, too, the Poles were absent. And so were the Ukrainians. Still, the Congress proceeded mainly on the lines of the more practical neo-Slavism, although without any staggering results. Another organisation which served as a link between the Slavs was the *Sokol* (Falkon) movement. Having been sponsored by the Czechs as a Slav counterpart of the German *Turnvereine* in 1866, it gradually assumed a strong cultural, educational and political character. As such it spread among the other Slav nations, and the great *Sokol* Festival, which took place in Prague in 1912, was an imposing manifestation of their actual or potential solidarity.

Official Russia, nonplussed at first by Aehernthal's policy, was now anxious to follow with a more careful eye what was happening in the Balkans. Moreover, she sent there some able diplomats the most active of whom was N. H. Hartvig, stationed at Belgrade. It was largely due to their efforts that a coalition of Serbia, Bulgaria, Greece and Montenegro was formed with a view of expelling the Turks from Macedonia as well as from the other regions of the Balkans which were still under the Turkish rule. A Serbo-Bulgarian pact, signed to this effect in March 1912, was soon strengthened by Greece and Montenegro. In the summer of the same year the Bulgarian Prime-Minister demanded from Turkey that some sweeping reforms should be made in Macedonia, the bulk of whose population was of Slav stock.* As nothing of the sort was done, a war between Turkey and the four Balkan allies could not be avoided. Tiny Montenegro was the first to start it (on October 10, 1912), and the other three followed suit.

* The Macedonian language is something of a link between Serbian and Bulgarian, but is successfully developing a literature of its own.

The war proved to be disastrous for the Turks. They were driven as far back as Chataldja – the outer defences of Constantinople. The interest with which the whole of Russia accompanied those victories can be imagined. The Slav sympathies infected for a while all the strata of her population. In Austria-Hungary, too, each Serbian victory in particular was greeted by the Slavs with enthusiasm, but not so by the Germans and the Magyars, let alone the official circles. It was in fact Vienna again who spoiled (with Italy's support) the game also this time.

According to the agreement between the Balkan allies, Serbia was to obtain an outlet to the Adriatic (on the north-Albanian coast) in order to be able to build the projected trans-Balkan railway from Belgrade and thus make herself independent of any economic restrictions on the part of Austria-Hungary. But this did not suit the book of Vienna. Determined to prevent it Vienna now suddenly became an ardent defender of small nations and demanded – during the meeting of the Great Powers in London – that Albania should become a new "sovereign" State. On May 30, 1913, the Treaty of London was signed. According to it Turkey was to abandon the whole of the Balkans, with the exception of the narrow strip of land (the line of Midia – Enos) just outside the Turkish capital. Albania was proclaimed a "free" country, with Durazzo as its capital and with a German ruler (Prince Wied) on its throne. Serbia, thus separated from the Adriatic and exposed to the caprices of an Austrian tariff-war, knew only too well what this meant in terms of economics. So it was imperative for her to make a counter-move. The only compensation would have been a free use of the port of Salonika at the end of the Vardar valley in Macedonia which had been allotted to Bulgaria. But when the Serbs asked the Bulgarians to cede to them the zone needed (most of which had been freed by Serbian troops), they met with a categorical refusal. Even the arbitration offered by the Russian Tsar was ignored by the Bulgarians. Moreover, incited by the Austrian Minister of Foreign Affairs, Count Berchtold, and ordered by the "foxy" Ferdinand, the Bulgarians treacherously attacked (on July 1, 1913) the Serbian army in the

region of the river Bregalnitsa, where they suffered a disastrous defeat.

In the tragi-comic imbroglio that followed Bulgaria lost practically all her gains. She also had to surrender southern Dobrudja to the Rumanians who now "entered the war" without firing a shot. The bulk of Macedonia went to the Serbs, whereas her Western part, Salonika, and most of Thrace were taken by Greece. Even the defeated Turks were able to gather enough strength in order to reoccupy Adrianople and the surrounding districts. It goes without saying that the enthusiasm for the Slavs, which at the beginning of the campaign had reached something of a climax all over Russia, was followed by a cynical eclipse.

Yet the prestige of Serbia among the Yugoslavs in Austria-Hungary stood now higher than ever. This alone was enough to make Vienna as well as Budapest provocative and vindictive. The entire region bordering on Serbia was put on the alert. The situation was almost too tense for a peaceful solution. But in the Habsburg Monarchy the outlook was not rosy either. The Vienna parliament, with its eternal squabbles and antagonisms, was degenerating into a kind of parody while nationalistic and other demagogues only added to the general confusion. In Hungary again the oppression of non-Magyars was so unbearable that its results were often the exact reverse of what the Magyar chauvinists had expected.★

Serbia, on the other hand, was full of apprehensions and ready for anything to happen. Things came to a climax when, in defiance of the prevailing political pathology, the Archduke Francis Ferdinand decided to pay a visit to Sarajevo on June 28, 1914.†
The Archduke had apparently been warned about the risky nature of that visit, but in vain. It was a Bosnian Serb who fired the fatal shots at him and his morganatic wife – the Duchess of

★ What that oppression was like can be gathered from a series of articles by the Norwegian author Bjoernstjerne Bjoernson who, after extensive travels in Hungary, described his impressions in *Le Courier Européen* (1906).

† June 28 is the national day of Serbia as well as a day of mourning since it commemorates the loss of her freedom in the battle with the Turks in 1389.

Hohenberg – and thus gave a pretext for unleashing World War I.

5

The truth about all the facts and factors behind the Sarajevo tragedy is still somewhat obscure.* The main plotters, such as Gavrilo Princip and his helpers, were immature "Young Bosnia" members dreaming of an independent Yugoslav State with its centre in Serbia. Behind them was the "Black Hand" society whose leader Colonel Apis provided the plotters with arms and sent them over the Bosnian border to Sarajevo where they waited for the Archduke's arrival. The Serbian government, so it seems, had nothing to do with the affair. But quite a few details connected with it all remain a matter of guesses – one more uncertain than the last. What became only too certain, though, were the horrors of the war or wars that followed.

The paradox of it was that neither Austria nor Russia nor even Germany contemplated war at precisely that moment. Kaiser Wilhelm II (who had paid a visit to Vienna in October 1913) and his military advisers were of course sure that a ruthless *Blitzkrieg* would make a victorious Germany replace Great Britain as the principal Great Power on land and sea. Austria-Hungary and her Chief of Staff, Conrad von Hoetzendorf, were anxious to solve once and for all the problem of Serbia and the Balkans in favour of the Habsburgs, although militarily they were probably not yet quite ready. Russia was not ready either but she was the first to mobilise her army: mainly in order to warn Vienna and prevent her from attacking Serbia. The tension between Austria and Serbia could have been solved peacefully, had only Serbia accepted the Austrian ultimatum on July 23. Belgrade was at first inclined to do so, but on second thoughts it snubbed Vienna, after which the latter, fully relying on Germany, was bound to attack. Austria-Hungary declared war on Serbia on July 28, 1914. Two

* All the known facts connected with it can be found in V. Dedijer's book: *Sarajevo, 1914.*

days later Germany was at war with Russia, and on August 2 with France. On August 4, however, Great Britain stepped in on the side of France and Russia; and so the "lamps went out" all over Europe.

Austria-Hungary, who had been the first to start the Armageddon, was also the first to be confronted by a number of insoluble dilemmas. Francis Joseph himself was eighty-four at the time: a tragic father-figure whose son Rudolf had committed suicide, while the Empress Elizabeth had been stabbed to death at Geneva by an Italian anarchist. But otherwise the Habsburg dynasty (supported by Court circles, the prosperous middle classes and the Church) was already losing its glamour in the eyes of the working classes and the younger intellectuals of the non-German populations. In the clash of imperialisms during the First World War many educated young Slavs saw no reason why on earth they should fight for a dynasty and a State which hardly ever paid any attention to their rightful claims. On the very eve of the war the leader of the Young-Czech party, Dr. Karel Kramař, felt so sure of Austria's impending doom that he worked out the plan for a Pan-Slav federation with Russia in the lead. But official Russia, even while engaged in the fiercest struggle with the Habsburgs and the Hohenzollerns, still had no solution of the Slav problem except the vague formula that this was (among other things) a war between the Slavs and the Teutons – a pronouncement uttered also by the German Chancellor Bethmann-Hollweg, but with a different and more ominous inflection. The most paradoxical position was however that of the Poles who, by a freak of historical fate, had to fight on three fronts: in the Austrian, German and Russian armies, without paying true allegiance to any of them.

As was to be expected, Austria gave a bad account of herself when, at the very outset, she was beaten by the Serbs and the Russians. In October 1915 she invaded, with the help of the Germans and the Bulgarians (Macedonia still being their *idée fixe*) the Serbian territory, while the Serbian army made its incredible retreat through the Albanian mountains right down to Salonika

and then to Corfu. From here it was sent, later on, to the Salonika front in order to reconquer the mother-country at a time when the Austrian Empire was about to fall to pieces. And what else could the ramshackle Monarchy have done, since its armies were already disintegrating? The Austrian Slav soldiers continued to surrender to the Russians in quite fantastic numbers. The Czech deserters even organised in Russia an imposing Czecho-Slovak Legion ready to fight the Central Powers. Many of the Austrian and Hungarian Yugoslavs, who had succeeded in fleeing over to the Russians, did the same, the heroic resistance of the Serbian army having been one of their main stimuli.

The first stage of World War I was marked by something like a renewed interest in the Slav idea even among the average Russians. Despite Rasputinism, and the distrust between the government and the *zemstvos*, there was a fair amount of Slav enthusiasm at the beginning. But corruption, economic muddle, military setbacks and lack of any faith in the government soon led to weariness and disappointment. Hence the revolution of 1917 became a welcome relief – at least in its early phase. The new authorities were however much too inexperienced to be a match for Lenin whose unexpected *coup d'état* victimised first of all those very intellectuals who had been responsible for the fall of the Tsarist government. The upheaval which had started in the name of freedom thus landed the country in the dictatorship of a single party at the expense of freedom. Luckily it was evident that in spite of Russia's defection the Central Powers could not win, once Austria began to look as if she was going to disintegrate exactly as Palacký had repeatedly predicted years before.

The death of Francis Joseph on November 21, 1916 spelled the end of his dynasty and his Empire. His nephew and successor, Emperor Charles, hoped that the Habsburg Monarchy still might be saved by secret negotiations and a private peace treaty with the enemies. These hopes proved to be futile. He had plenty of good will in a situation which looked more and more desperate both from a military and political point of view. When, on January 8, 1918 President Wilson's fourteen points had promised self-deter-

mination and independence to all oppressed ethnic groups, Emperor Charles seemed to be among those who accepted their implications without reserve. In October of the same year he made a final attempt at turning the Dual Monarchy into a federation of equals, but it was too late. The Habsburg Empire fell to pieces with a crash the consequences of which form an important part of contemporary history.

The Cataclysm and After

I

The end of the First World War meant nothing less than the end of a historical era. Europe's supremacy in world politics, world economics and perhaps even in world civilisation was to be, from now on, a matter of the past. The focus of history began shifting away from her in two opposite directions: Washington and Moscow. The surest symptom of a morally and politically bankrupt Continent was the sudden rise of Fascism and Nazism – both of them suicidal in their cynical aggressiveness and perversion of all values. On the other hand, the awakening racial consciousness among the coloured peoples of Asia and Africa was getting strong enough to foreshadow new troubles, including the prospective break up of the old colonial systems as well as the rise of post-colonial nationalisms. Nor did the remade map of Europe promise any real stability. Even the Slav States which arose on the ruins of Austria-Hungary were much too unsettled and preoccupied (each with its own particular problems) to bother about any partnership or genuine collaboration with others. They were not on ideal terms with the Soviet Union either, since Czecho-Slovakia and royal Yugoslavia were among the chief recipients of Russian refugees, most of whom were intellectuals anxious to work with might and main against everything the Soviets stood for.

Quite apart from this, Poland and Czecho-Slovakia had, at the very beginning of their independence, a violent quarrel over the coal-mining district of Teshin. Yugoslavia (or the Kingdom of Serbs, Croats and Slovenes, as she was called in those days) looked with suspicion on all her neighbours, while her neighbours paid her back in the same coin. Austria, now reduced to her German-ethnic size, was like a body whose legs and arms had been chopped

off. Hungary, equally chastised, kept licking her own wounds in the hope that some further international muddle might enable her to regain at least some of her lost non-Magyar territories. Nor was Bulgaria in a better position as a former ally of the defeated Central Powers. There existed, moreover, plenty of inner friction within each of the newly created Slav States: between the Czechs and the Slovaks in Czecho-Slovakia; between the Poles and the Ukrainians in Poland; between the Serbs and the Croats, as well as between the Serbs and the Macedonians, in Yugoslavia. Animosities which thus arose were greater than expected and served as an eloquent illustration of the old paradox of nationalism: once an oppressed nation has conquered her freedom, she is usually tempted to look around for smaller ethnic groups which she herself might assimilate in turn. Among the more spectacular results of the First World War was undoubtedly the resurrection of Poland. Yet having recovered their own liberty, the Poles were far from eager to grant the same national freedom to the large Ukrainian minority (about five millions of them) living within the boundaries of new Poland. Even in Masaryk's Czecho-Slovakia – the most solid and democratic of these States – the Czechs could not help nibbling at their national minorities. And as for Yugoslavia, King Alexander and his clique were only too willing to transform the entire country into a centralised "greater Serbia", whereas the Croat chauvinists refused to give up their dream of a "greater Croatia"* whatever the cost. Wrangles of this kind constituted a factor disruptive enough to weaken the new States from within. Then there were in all of them the subversive activities of the communist parties which showed a great deal of tenacity and organising power, especially when driven underground.

In order to counter, as far as possible, all sorts of inner and outward dangers, Yugoslavia and Czecho-Slovakia formed, in 1920, the so-called Little Entente which was soon joined by Rumania. Still, the process of consolidation seemed to be slow. In 1928 the

---

* Even Stepan Radić, the leader of the Croat Peasant Party, hardly differed in this respect from the nationalists of the Starčević brand.

Croat politician S. Radić was assassinated in the Belgrade Parliament by a Montenegrin fanatic. A few months later the internal situation in Yugoslavia became so precarious that King Alexander abolished the Constitution and became, to all intents and purposes, a dictator. Masaryk, the President of Czecho-Slovakia, was perhaps the only statesman the mention of whose name did not provoke ironical smiles; but he was an old man, and there was no personality of his calibre to replace him. In 1934 Yugoslavia, Greece, Turkey and Rumania concluded a Balkan Entente but, on October 9 of the same year, King Alexander was murdered at Marseilles by a Macedonian who had been specially trained for that kind of business in Horthy's Hungary. The situation looked the more sinister because Mussolini's Fascists in Italy and Hitler's Nazis in Germany would not even think of disguising their plans and their gangster methods. Particularly disturbing were the old animosities between Poland and Russia which, after the armed conflict between the two in 1920, only grew worse than ever. Disunity and insecurity on the one hand, and the growing threat of the Nazi-Fascist Powers on the other, became the main ingredients of the political climate during the 1930s.

In spite of this, a historical miracle happened: in less than one generation since the cataclysm of 1914–18 the Slav Idea, this time with Soviet Russia at the head of it, was resuscitated on an entirely new basis and with such staggering results as would have exceeded one's most fantastic hopes and expectations. The two men primarily responsible for this were the Teuton Adolf Hitler and the Georgian Stalin, neither of whom had any Slav blood in his veins.

2

When, in the autumn of 1917, the bolsheviks took power into their hands, they gave the Revolution a thoroughly international trend and character. What they aimed at was a world revolution on Marxian lines. As for Russian nationalism, it was rather discredited on account of its former association with autocracy and officialdom. And so was the official Orthodox Church, the perse-

cution of which by the new authorities turned into a persecution of religion (the "opium of the people") in general. Soviet Russia became – overnight as it were – more secularised than any other country in the world. Those thinkers who had anything to do with religion (Berdyayev, Bulgakov, Professor Lossky, S. Frank, P. Struve, etc.) joined the tide of emigration during the exodus of intellectuals in 1922 or otherwise. As a result a prodigious amount of interesting religious-philosophic and other writings in Russian appeared abroad. Among the exiles were also such authors as Bunin, Shmelyov, Boris Zaitsev, Alexey Remizov and Mark Aldanov none of whom could see eye-to-eye with the Soviets. There was an influx of Russian refugees in Bulgaria, Yugoslavia and Czecho-Slovakia. In Prague there even functioned for their benefit a Russian as well as a Ukrainian University and a Slav Institute all of which were kept busy during the years of freedom.

Among the strongest centres of the Russian *diaspora* were, however, Paris and Berlin (until Hitler's accession to power). The younger Russian émigrés in particular were now in a position to observe and personally evaluate all that Western civilisation could offer them. Their conclusions were not necessarily enthusiastic. Thus during the 1920s there arose among them even the so-called Euro-Asiatic movement (*evraziystvo*) which repudiated, partly under the impact of Oswald Spengler, the "decayed" Western civilisation and largely also Western Slavdom. One of the leaders of this current, Prince N. S. Trubetskoy, took the cue from Leontyev and defined the Euro-Asian trend of the movement as follows: "Ethnographically the Russian people are no exclusive representative of Slavdom. The Russians form, together with the Ugrofinns and the Volga-Tartars, a special culture-zone which contains elements of both the Slav and the Tartar East, while it is yet difficult to say which of these two may be stronger and more durable." In his opinion it was important for the Russians to be aware not so much of their Slav as of their Turanian or Turano-Arian character.

Those were the days when Stalin's formula, "Socialism in one country" prevailed, while in Europe herself the nationalist

hooliganism of Mussolini and Hitler began to rage out of all proportion, since both history and human irresponsibility seemed to be playing into their hands. When, in 1933, Hitler assumed power in Germany, it was not difficult to guess what this meant for the future of Europe, and especially for Soviet Russia. Goebbels defined the Nazi aims as the German way of thinking poured into a new form, the form of the Third Reich. . . . "We do not want a bourgeois State, we do not want a proletarian State. We want a German State." But he might as well have added, "a German State at the expense of Europe, and most of all at the expense of Russia". For it was no secret that the fertile Ukrainian plains were one of the main objectives those fanatics of the Third Reich had in mind. The extermination of such economic and commercial rivals as the Jews would be followed by the equally methodical and "scientific" extermination (or else resettlement) of the Slavs wherever more *Lebensraum* for Germans was deemed necessary, after which the turn of other European nations would come. All in good time. In his mad drive for power Hitler had, however, forgotten three things: first, that Stalin could be as cynical and ruthless as Hitler himself, while yet remaining master of his own nerves; second, that Soviet Russia was getting rapidly industrialised and on a large scale, too, in order to match the menace (if need be) even of such an over-industrialised country as Germany; and third, that she was capable of as much patriotism as any other nation when put to a supreme test.

Aware of what was at stake, the Soviet Union was one of the first countries willing to form a common front against Hitler. In her desire for a closer link with the West she became, in 1934, a member of the League of Nations, which was soon enlivened by Litvinov as the most active champion of "indivisible peace" and collective security. In May 1935 Russia concluded a Franco-Soviet pact of mutual assistance. This was followed by her pact with Czecho-Slovakia, according to which the latter was to be defended by both Soviet Russia and France in case of Hitler's attack. During the growing menace of Nazism Soviet Russia herself was being gradually swept by a patriotic wave – quite in

contrast to her former international *profession de foi*. The great deeds and figures of Russian history and culture were glorified once again: not so much in the name of an exclusive Russian nationalism (which might have provoked nationalist resentment of the many non-Russian populations living within the Soviet Union) as for the sake of a supra-national Soviet patriotism. Even religion was allowed to co-exist, after a fashion, with the communist creed. The intense anti-religious propaganda, formerly encouraged by the regime, was losing its impetus.

Events taking place in Europe became particularly nauseating after the Spanish civil war (1936) which had its prelude in the Nazi's bombing of Guernica, and ended with the triumph of Franco and his reactionary supporters, within and outside Spain. At the same time Soviet Russia was darkened by a series of "purges" some of which (notably the one followed by the execution of the able Russian strategist Tukhachevsky) would seem to have been hatched in Germany. Things were going, however, from bad to worse when in the summer of 1937, Baldwin was succeeded by Chamberlain as British Prime Minister. Equipped with his protective umbrella, he became an apostle of appeasement, behind which there lurked however the wish that Hitler might eventually attack the Soviet Union and leave the respectable West alone. The naïveté with which Chamberlain peddled around the formula of "peace in our time" was appalling enough to arouse the worst suspicions of the Soviets. When in 1938 Stalin was anxious to conclude an alliance against Hitler, he received little encouragement either from Great Britain or France both of whom were as distrustful of Moscow as Moscow was of them. To crown it all, at Munich, Chamberlain handed over to Hitler (on September 29, 1938) the last stronghold of democracy: Czecho-Slovakia, "That country which we know so little about," to use Chamberlain's own classical phrase.* In the middle of March,

---

* The smug hypocrisy of his attitude came out in a boosting film in which Chamberlain was sanctimoniously glorified as "that valiant knight in shining armour, looking for the Holy Grail". The film was laughed out of existence as soon as it appeared.

1939, that is less than six months later, Hitler occupied Prague. But even after such a shock Chamberlain refused to conclude an agreement with the U.S.S.R. On March 31, 1939, he made a unilateral pact with Poland (and Rumania), to whom he gave a guarantee, instead. Exasperated as he was, Stalin still hoped to come to terms with Britain and France. In the summer of the same year, they both sent a Military Mission to Moscow – not by plane, despite the urgency of the moment, but by boat. During the negotiations, which dragged on and on, the Russians demanded (on August 15) that in case of a conflict with Germany the Soviet troops should be allowed a free passage through Poland, but the Poles repudiated such a clause. When final deadlock was reached, Molotov signed the non-aggression pact with Ribbentrop while the British-French Mission was still in Moscow. Hitler was thus free to do what he wanted in the West. A few weeks later Europe was ablaze.

3

German successes during the early stages of the war were a direct result of the previous shortsighted policy on the part of Great Britain and France. As Sir Winston Churchill remarks,* had the allies resisted Hitler's Rhineland occupation in 1936, "a mere operation of police would have sufficed; or since Munich, when Germany, occupied with Czecho-Slovakia, could spare but thirteen divisions for the Western front; or even since September, 1939, when, while the Polish resistance lasted, there were but forty-two German divisions in the West". Fortunately, the final issue of Hitler's *Blitz* campaign began to look problematic already after the Battle of Britain in which his Luftwaffe was crippled. Even the fall of France in 1940, and the collaboration of the Vichy government, hardly made much difference once the U.S. army had joined the allies. At last Hitler decided – pact or no pact – to attack the Soviet Union, evidently expecting his opponents to be more amenable now that he had opened a crusade against Com-

* *The Second World War.* "The Gathering Storm" (Cassell).

munism. Such a snare, however, could not beguile a man of Churchill's stamp. He knew only too well with whom he was dealing. Hitler on the other hand may have cherished the hope that a quick German victory against the Russians would not only secure the much coveted *Lebensraum* for the Germans but would put at his disposal also the enormous natural resources of Russia, all of which might bolster up the morale of the German people on the one hand and further discourage his Western opponents on the other. But such calculations, too, proved to be futile.

When in the summer of 1941 Hitler invaded Soviet territory, all the non-Russian Slavs were already under his mailed jackboot. A German victory over them seemed complete. Yet the common calamity, accompanied by the fear of systematic extermination, was bound to bring the Slavs morally and politically together. The strongest unifying factor in this respect was Hitler's own brutality – unparalleled since the time of Genghis Khan. His methodical and cold sadism was itself enough to turn against him even those who, for reasons of their own, were at first willing to welcome him. Like the Yugoslavs, whose guerrilla detachments were one of Hitler's headaches, the Russians, too, promptly organised partisan cadres which began to harass the enemy from within and from the rear. Moreover, immediate steps were taken by the Russians themselves to get into contact with other Slav victims of Nazism. Appalled by atrocities which for a civilised European nation had seemed unthinkable, they combined moral indignation with a strong anti-German feeling. In August of the same year a Slav or Pan-Slav Committee was formed in Moscow. Its members issued a Manifesto to all the Slav nations in which the following sentences are emphatic: "Here we are uniting as equals with equals. We have one task and purpose: the defeat of Hitler's armies and the destruction of Hitlerism. We have one all-embracing wish: that the Slav nations, just as any other nations, may be able to develop in peace and freedom within the boundaries of their own States. We resolutely and firmly reject the idea of Pan-Slavism as a reactionary idea hostile to the high ideals of the

equal rights of nations and of national development of all States."*

The committee was headed by such prominent men as the novelist Alexey Tolstoy, the composer Shostakovich, the poet Tikhonov and the writer Fadeyev. It acted not only as an informative body, but also as a symbol of Slav unity cemented by the resistance to a common foe. In 1942, i.e. during the height of the campaign, they started publishing a monthly, *The Slavs* (*Slavyane*), as their organ of information. Meanwhile the senseless Nazi atrocities convinced even the Poles that the Russians were a lesser evil than the Germans. And once the German armies had been driven as far back as Berlin, the nightmare of Nazism seemed to be over. Another good tiding was the rumour of Hitler's suicide, while most of his henchmen were either on the run, or else under lock and key to be tried and in due time adequately punished. Final victory in the Slav-German struggle was on the side of the Slavs. Nor was it irrelevant that after the second World War the prosperous German colonies in Russia and in the Balkans were broken up. A similar fate was in store for the Sudeten Germans in Czecho-Slovakia, once the allied victory was complete. The previously wide-spread area of the German language was thus shrunk to the size of the Reich and German-Austria. Yet even when the fighting had ceased, the general rapprochement between the Slavs continued and even tinged the policy of the Soviet Union. In 1945 Stalin himself said during one of his conversations with Djilas: "If the Slavs keep united and maintain solidarity, no one in the future will be able to move a finger. Not even a finger."† Stalin knew very well indeed that henceforth the Poles, too, would have to rely upon Russia, whether they liked it or not. And the same was largely true of the Czechs – the most Western-orientated Slav nation which yet now looked with rancour upon the West because of Chamberlain's betrayal of their country at Munich. In the first half of December, 1946, a new Slav Congress was held in Belgrade (under the sign of Communism) – mainly

* Quoted from *Panslavism* by V. Clementis.

† Milovan Djilas, *My Conversations with Stalin*, 1964.

in order to affirm the Slav solidarity headed by Moscow. A few months later the Cominform was established – also in Belgrade. Finally, the Prague Communists seized power (1948) in Czecho-Slovakia. Poland, too, within her ethnic boundaries, was in the hands of the Polish Communist Party and controlled by Moscow, although Stalin's shabby treatment of Warsaw during the most critical fighting between the Poles and the Germans in that city was hardly likely to lessen the traditional Polish distrust of anything coming from Moscow. Still, it was for the first time in history that all the Slavs now found themselves united – under the watchful eye of the Russian colossus as their "big brother". There was a continuity of Slav territories from the Pacific right down to the Adriatic. Also Bakunin's and Danilevsky's conjecture that the Magyars and Rumanians might be incorporated in such a Pan-Slav *bloc* came true. Even Albania was compelled to join it at first. But for the armed intervention of British and U.S. forces Greece, too, might have been included in the same *bloc*. The wildest dreams of former Pan-Slavists were thus turned into a historical reality by Stalin, a Georgian by birth. But the man primarily responsible for all this was the crazy Pan-German Hitler. Such are the vagaries and paradoxes of history.

Stalin's equation of the Slav rapprochement with Communist solidarity may have been one of his assets in the subsequent competition between the Soviet Union and its former allies. For when the war was over, the antagonism between the Soviets and the West flared up once more. Needless to say, the Soviet dictator's methods during the "cold war" were much too un-European to be put up with meekly even by some Western Communists. The earliest reaction to it all came from Tito's Yugoslavia. Disgusted with Stalin's totalitarian ways, she turned against Moscow in June 1948 – less than three years after the end of the war. The historical significance of Tito's defection was obvious. This was the first blow which shook the monolithic structure of Communism, dominated by Stalin's iron grip. And the fact that Tito's "heresy" had remained – despite all the threats – unpunished, gave a certain amount of courage to other satellites, such as Poland and

Hungary, to think more independently and without waiting to be told by Moscow in advance what was right and what was wrong.

It is, of course, no idle question whether anyone less ruthless than Stalin could have pulled the Soviet Union through Hitler's invasion during the most critical months in Russia's history. That cruel gatherer of the Russian lands, Ivan the Terrible, thus found a hardly less cruel counterpart in Stalin the Terrible who now became the gatherer of the Communist lands in both Europe and Asia. Yet after his death in 1953, the process of de-Stalinisation became imminent. Beria, the notorious chief of Stalin's secret police, was executed; and the police itself, having ceased to be a state within the state, came under Party control. In the struggle for power between Malenkov, Molotov and Khrushchov the victory was won by Khrushchov. As the First Secretary of the Party and the actual ruler of the Soviet Union he made some momentous changes, however clownish his behaviour may have been at times. During the twentieth Party Congress in February 1956 he, more-over, debunked Stalin and the personality cult in such unflattering terms as were bound to astonish the world. In the Soviet Union itself the first symptoms of the "thaw" which came after that, were welcomed by all. The terror of the labour camps, as well as of the political witch hunt, seemed to be lessening or even disappearing. And as for the world at large, Khrushchov modified the militant character of Communism by starting a policy of co-existence instead of Stalin's cold war with the West. In the same year Khrushchov and Bulganin came – cap in hand – to Belgrade in order to close the political and ideological gap between the two countries. But Yugoslavia was still much too diffident to turn that visit into a Soviet success. The relations seemed to improve to some extent after Brezhnev's visit to Yugoslavia in September 1962. In December of the same year Tito returned the visit by going to Moscow where he had a warm welcome; yet he did not commit himself to any drastic promises. Sticking to her own type of socialism, Yugoslavia gave unmistakable proofs that she was willing to be only an independent partner but not an obedient satellite and servant of the Soviet Union.

4

There were two disturbing events, though, which took place during the de-Stalinisation period as initiated by Khrushchov. The Hungarian revolt in 1956 was one of them, and the defection of China the other. The revolt in Hungary was crushed in no time, but instead of the usual reprisals Moscow now preferred to adopt the more tolerant policy of gradual concessions. Such a method was not without effect upon some other satellites, especially Poland and Rumania, both of whom were anxious to affirm the principle of partnership at the expense of blind subservience. A more complex problem was, however, Pekin's quarrel with Moscow. The obvious purpose of China was, of course, to transfer – under some pretext or other – the focus of Communism, or at least of Asian Communism, from Moscow to Pekin. But whatever the ulterior motives of the Chinese rulers, their defiance of the Soviet Union made a further and much greater gap in the one-time monolithic character of the movement.

It is beyond the scope of this book to deal with the intricate facets, whether political, ideological or psychological, of the tension between the Soviets and China – a tension which began in all seriousness after the Moscow Conference in 1957.* As is known, the Chinese delegates persisted in their dogma that a Communist millennium could only be achieved by another world war which – according to Marx – is bound to come and crush capitalism for ever. But Khrushchov would have none of this. Using his common-sense, he argued that, Marx or no Marx, a war with the capitalist countries in a nuclear age would be an act of folly, probably resulting in the destruction of mankind itself. He adopted the "revisionist" policy of co-existence with the West as the only *modus vivendi*, since, anyhow, co-existence is preferable to non-existence. In 1959 he even paid a visit to the U.S.A. – an unforgivable sin in the eyes of Pekin. No wonder that at the Bucarest Conference in June 1960 and at another Moscow

* A helpful account of the situation is given by Edward Crankshaw in his book, *The New Cold War Moscow v. Pekin* (A Penguin Special, 1965).

Conference in the autumn of the same year the split between Moscow and Pekin became irreparable.

The struggle itself has, of course, several aspects. Behind it lies the basic difference between the dogmatic and the pragmatic types of Socialism, to begin with. Whereas the former sticks to fixed formulae from which one is not allowed to deviate, the latter is more like a flexible way of life, which adapts itself – as far as necessary – to any historical and economic conditions *in order to adapt them to itself*. The Chinese mentality evidently favours the dogmatic type, whereas the Russians after Stalin seem to prefer its pragmatic double. (The latter has already proved to be a good working proposition in Yugoslavia.) In the first case man is claimed to exist for the sake of the Sabbath, but in the second case the Sabbath is here for the sake of man even if this should require a series of necessary "revisionisms".

Another reason for Chinese behaviour may have been due to their realisation that, whatever their socialist system, they will need, sooner or later, more territory for their huge and still rapidly expanding population. As such an aim could be achieved mainly at the expense of the Soviet Far East and Outer Mongolia (protected by the Soviets), unconditional friendship with Moscow cannot be in China's interests. This may have been one of the reasons why the Soviets refused to share their nuclear secrets with Pekin. Viewed from such an angle, an armed conflict between the U.S.A. and the Soviet Union, for instance, would certainly be more than welcomed by China who might find some plausible pretext for grabbing the coveted parts of Siberia. Be this as it may, China's defection made a final fissure in the Communist *bloc*. But by open hostility to Moscow she only encouraged a gradual rapprochement between the Soviet Union and the entire Western world. The improved relations between Washington and Moscow (under Khrushchov) were one of the major results of China's wayward policy. And these relations may be in favour of peace, whatever further somersaults may be made by the deified Mao and his pious worshippers.

Edward Crankshaw explained this aspect of the situation in his

pamphlet, *The Great Schism*,* where he pointed out that the "Soviet government has adapted itself to a changing world, a world in which a major war cannot be seriously considered either as an instrument of policy or a consummation to be desired. Soviet thinking was, if anything, slightly ahead of American thinking on this matter until very recently. It means the acceptance of the two systems dwelling side by side into an indefinite future, but not necessarily for ever. It means that Khrushchov hopes, and perhaps believes, that some sort of Communism will inherit the earth, no longer through violence, but because it will itself be better adapted than capitalism for survival in the modern world."

So far so good. It even looked as if in such a process the non-Russian Slavs might be able to play a useful part as mediators. For although the majority of them belong to the Western culture zone, they can yet understand (being Slavs) the workings of the Russian mind and character considerably better than any other Europeans, let alone Americans. They might even have formed a certain balance between East and West, had the Khrushchov line (with its "thaw") been allowed to continue. Such hopes were however gone as soon as in the jealous struggle for power Khrushchov was cunningly ousted and replaced by party bosses intent on reintroducing, through the back door, a new brand of Stalinism at the moment when a *détente* between East and West was practically in the air. It should be remembered that, with all his unconventional ways, Khrushchov had some constructive ideas of his own and often meant what he said, which is quite rare in a politician. His successors, on the other hand, seem to be dogmatic bureaucrats whose shortsightedness reached its climax during the invasion of Czecho-Slovakia in the summer of 1968 by an army of some 600,000 troops – a blunder which caused consternation all over the world.

5

A more insane action, however sophisticated its pretexts, could

* Reprinted from *The Observer*, 1960.

hardly have been imagined. For one thing, the new rulers of the Soviet Union succeeded by their cynical Nazi methods in turning even such staunch friends of Russia as the Czechs and Slovaks into implacable enemies of everything Russian. And this attitude was supported by the unanimous reaction of world opinion. The Soviet invaders thus "liquidated," as it were overnight, also the problem of Slav unification – at least in so far as Russia was concerned. What had happened was the very thing of which the Czech historian Palacký had been mortally afraid some hundred years ago: Russia had penetrated into the heart of Central Europe, and this at a time when she knew there was no great power willing or strong enough to oppose such a step. Whether a policy of this aggressively expansionist kind was or is likely to be approved by the Russian people, is of course a different matter; the more so because the traditional gap between the government and the governed, which persisted throughout Russian history, seems to continue also in the Soviet Union. On the other hand, such a step has done considerable damage also to the idea of a united Europe, as well as a united humanity – an idea which, however painfully and slowly, has yet been gaining ground in the very teeth of our political and economic chaos.

Present-day complications actually postulate a new consciousness working towards an integrated mankind and an integrated world, since the question of "to be or not to be" in our nuclear age concerns the human race as a whole. Yet even while mobilising our best will in this direction, one cannot help contending with two obstacles in particular, one of them being of a psychological and the other of a technical nature. Psychologically speaking, we all feel the spiritual and moral aftermath of the second World War which has revealed to us a "naked" mankind raving and raging in its subhuman fury. With millions of victims gassed at Auschwitz and countless other death factories our faith in humanity has been undermined to its very core. Yet without such a faith one is bound to fall a prey to nihilism or else to the philistine indifference with regard to anything that goes beyond one's personal gain and appetites – a state of mind which is even worse than nihilism. The

second factor concerns, however, our tremendous scientific and technical achievements which have come to us on such an overwhelming scale before we are morally ripe for them. These achievements, most of which have been perfected and commercially exploited with an eye on their destructive military potential, have now reached such a pitch as to enable some crazy power-maniac to destroy the human race by the "mere pressing of a button". Mankind stands for the first time in its history before the paradoxical possibility of being annihilated by the very progress of its own science. The awareness of all this is hardly conducive to any rosy hopes or vistas for the future. But for this very reason one cannot dismiss the notion that the only outlet still left to both the individual and society is a new humanism working on a global scale and animated by the idea that humanity itself, whatever its languages and colour, should become indivisible if it is to survive at all.

This is all the more important in an age when the abolition of distance between the various parts of the world has already reduced our planet to such a ridiculously small size as to make the old Machiavellian power-politics look frankly suicidal. But while nations and races are thus necessarily getting more and more interdependent, their politicians, generals and financial speculators persist in old atavistic ambitions, jealousies, hatreds and intrigues, for which the word *criminal* is much too mild. Hence the universal restlessness of the younger generations whose members know what they are fighting against without being sure of what they could and should be fighting for.

In the growing *malaise* of the present-day world one yet *has* to go on hoping and looking for a path leading to that kind of human solidarity, freedom and justice which would preclude any further attempts at disguised totalitarianisms whether from the right or from the left. A first successful action in this direction might perhaps be undertaken (even as a matter of mere self-preservation) by those countries or nations which are neither big nor rich enough to ape any super-powers and have yet preserved enough common sense to be able to form such constructive and

morally binding federations as would have to be reckoned with. Needless to say, the non-Russian Slavs are in this category. The more so because they realise only too well what a nuclear Armageddon would be like should it ever be let loose. And this applies to quite a number of other small and middle nations whether they be "satellites" or not. Hence also their instinctive clamour for the abolition of the atom bomb lest the atom bomb abolish us all.

Yet, human nature being what it is, there is no guarantee that even a definite universal decision of the sort would be reliable in the long run. That acute judge of the *Zeitgeist*, the philosopher Karl Jaspers, contends that should the scare of the nuclear bomb at last compel man to make this world a better place to live in, "the danger of mankind perishing by human action will always be with us – it will never vanish again. It will have to be met constantly and surmounted afresh. . . . The moment he relaxes in the illusion of final success, the extreme menace will once more be real, and he will finally lose his mere existence, after all. . . . Man either grows in freedom, maintains the tension of this growth, or he forfeits the right to live."*

In short, humanity will survive only if it deserves to survive. Our scientific and technological advance may even accelerate our doom unless we summon in time all our will and moral courage working towards a united humanity. An effort of this kind should rely, however, not on governments and politicians, but on the masses of simple people whose true life-values have not yet been erased by the atrocities and commercialised imbecilities of the present-day world. Whatever the mistakes and blunders of their governments, the Russian masses would undoubtedly be only too willing to endorse any movement towards universal solidarity since such an impulse, whatever its specific reasons, seems to be innate in their national character. And here they might be joined, once again, by the other Slavs who, after the terrible experiences during the last war, know that in our atomic age a gradual integration of mankind is – ultimately – the only alternative

* *The Future of Mankind* by Karl Jaspers. (The University of Chicago Press.)

to its possible or even probable extinction. Integration of mankind has now become a historical imperative concerning us all.
And if we are no longer able to summon enough faith and
will for such a task, then all the worse for us and for the world
we live in.

Bibliography

Aksakov, I. S., *Sočinenija* (6 vols.), 1887–8.

Aksakov, K. S., *Polnoe sobranie sočinenij* (3 vols.), 1861–80.

Bartz, Karl, *Peter der Grosse*, 1941.

Baumfeld, A., *Towianski i Towianizm*, 1908.

Bazon, Pierre, Abbé, *A. S. Khomiakov*, 1940.

Berdyayev, Nicholas, *Khomjakov* (in Russian), 1912.

Berdyayev, Nicholas, *Leontjev* (in Russian), 1912.

Berdyayev, Nicholas, *The Origin of Russian Communism*, 1937.

Berdyayev, Nicholas, *The Russian Idea*, 1947.

Billington, H. N., *Mikhailovsky and Russian Populism*, 1958.

Birkbeck, J., *Russia and the English Church*, 1895.

Borgese, J. A., *Russland-Wesen und Werden*, 1950.

Brazol, B. L., *Khomyakov*, 1954.

Brodskij, N. L., *Rannie slavjanofily*, 1910.

Browning, O., *Peter the Great*, 1898.

Brückner, Alexander, *Die Europaeisierung Russlands*, 1888.

Čaadayev, P. J., *Sočinenija* (2 vols.), 1913.

Carew-Hunt, R. N., *Theory and Practice of Communism*, 1962.

Carr, E. G., *The Romantic Exiles*, 1933.

Carr, E. G., *Michael Bakunin*, 1937.

Carr, E. G., *German-Soviet Relations*, 1951.

Carr, E. G., *The Russian Revolution* (3 vols.), 1950–53.

Chancelour, Richard, *The Book of the Great and Mighty Emperor of Russia and Duke of Moscovia*, 1598.

Christoff, Peter, *A. S. Khomyakov*, 1961.

Crankshaw, Edward, *The Fall of the House of Habsburg*, 1963.

Custine, A. L., *La Russie en 1839* (4 vols.), 1846.

Danilevsky, N. J., *Rossija i Evropa*, 1869.

Dedijer, Vladimir, *Sarajevo 1914*, 1966.

Denis, E., *La Bohême depuis la Montagne Blanche*, 1903.

Deutscher, I., *Stalin, a Political Biography*, 1949.

Dorn, N., *Kirejevskij* (in Russian), 1938.

Dostoevsky, F. M., *The Diary of a Writer* (2 vols.), 1949.

Eisenmann, Louis, *Le Compromis austro-hongrois de 1867*, 1904.

Fedotov, G., *The Russian Religious Mind*, 1946.

Fischel, Alfred, *Der Panslavismus bis zum Weltkrieg*, 1919.

Flechtheimer, Ossip, *Weltkommunismus im Wandel*, 1965.

Florinsky, Michael, *The End of the Russian Empire*, 1931.

Florovsky, A. V., *The Czechs and Eastern Slavs* (2 vols.), 1935, 1947.

Florovsky, Georgiy, *Dostoevsky i Evropa*, 1922.

Friedjung, Heinrich, *Oesterreich von 1848 bis 1860* (2 vols.), 1912.

Lo Gatto, Ettore, *Gli artisti italiani in Russia*, 1943.

Lo Gatto, Ettore, *Storia della Russia*, 1946.

Gerhard, Dietrich, *England und der Aufstieg Russlands*, 1933.

Gershenzon, M. O., *Čaadajev*, 1908. *Istorija mo odoj Rossii*, 1908.

Gorer, G. and Rickman, J., *The People of Great Russia*, 1949.

Graham, Stephen, *Ivan the Terrible*, 1933.

Gratieux, A. S., *Khomiakov et le Mouvement Slavophile* (2 vols.), 1939.

Gratieux, A. S., *Le mouvement slavophile à la veille de la Revolution*, 1953.

Grekov, B. D., *Dokumenty k istorii slavjanovedenija v Rossii 1850–1912*, 1948.

Hecker, J., *Religion under the Soviets*, 1927.

Helmreich, E. C., *The Diplomacy of the Balkan Wars*, 1939.

Hare, R., *Pioneers of Russian Social Thought*, 1954.

Hepner, Benoit, *Bakounnine et le Panslavisme Revolutionnaire*, 1950.

Herberstein, Sigmund, *Rerum Moscovitarum Commentarii*, 1549.

Herzen (Gertsen), Alexander *Polnoe sobranie sočinenij* (30 vols.), 1954.

Hildebrand, Walter, *Die Sovietunion, Macht und Krise*, 1955.

Ilyin, I. A., *Wesen und Eigenart der russischen Kultur*, 1942.

Ivanov-Razumnik, *Istorija russkoj obščestvennoj mysli* (2 vols.) 1908.

Kaufmann, A. A., *Russkaja obščina v processe eja razloženija i rosta*, 1908.

Khomyakov, A. S., *Polnoe sobranie sočinenij* (8 vols.), 1914.

A Father Before Christmas

Also by Neil Boyd

BLESS ME, FATHER

Writing as Peter de Rosa

Theology

JESUS WHO BECAME CHRIST
A BIBLE-PRAYERBOOK FOR TODAY
COME HOLY SPIRIT

Humour

PRAYERS FOR PAGANS AND HYPOCRITES

Fables

THE BEE AND THE ROSE
THE BEST OF ALL POSSIBLE WORLDS
CLOUDCUCKOO LAND

A Father Before Christmas

NEIL BOYD

BOOK CLUB ASSOCIATES LONDON

Printed in Great Britain by
Richard Clay (The Chaucer Press), Ltd.,
Bungay Suffolk

For
M and F and D
With Love

CONTENTS

A FATHER BEFORE CHRISTMAS

One

MY FIRST BAPTISM

'That uproarious wretch, that blighted black-eyed potato of a woman.' Fr Charles Duddleswell, my parish priest, was performing on the landing.

'What's up?' I said, poking my head round my study door.

'Me keys,' he snapped, his blue eyes frothing behind his steel-rimmed spectacles. 'Can I find me keys? Indeed I cannot. Mrs Pring has filched them from me dresser and neither she nor the blessèd St Anthony has any idea where she has deposited them.'

I took one look at him and said, 'You've tried your pockets, Father?'

'Is it an idiot you think I ...?' He was busy scratching the smooth outer skin of his cassock like an itchy monkey. 'In me pockets?' he asked now only half in scorn. 'Me pockets, you say?' His hand had settled around a bulky something in his bottom left pocket. He slowly brought the keys into the light of day. 'That accursèd daughter of Eve,' he muttered, 'has she not hidden 'em in the recesses of me very own pocket?' He suddenly yelled down the staircase. 'Mrs Pring!'

Unhurriedly our plump, white-haired Mrs Pring appeared at the foot of the stairs, clasping a broom like a crosier. 'You've found them, then,' she said, 'I'll get the choir to sing the *Te Deum* in thanksgiving.'

' 'Twas not meself that found them,' came thundering back at her, 'but Father Neil.'

'And *where* did he find them?'

'Does it at all matter, woman, where he found them, seeing as he found them?'

Mrs Pring suggested none too politely that they had never gone missing.

'Woman,' he cried, 'I will not have you coming at me with a full udder of incivility. Now, I am asking you, could Father Neil have found them if they were never lost? Father Neil,' he bellowed in my direction, 'would you be so kind as to inform this lady, who is astray of her wits, that you ...'

But I retreated into my study to let them sort out for themselves who was to blame for losing Fr Duddleswell's enormous bunch of keys in his cassock pocket.

I settled down again and opened my breviary but I was in no mood for praying. I preferred that October morning to reflect on my career thus far at St Jude's.

Four crowded months had passed since I first presented myself at the presbytery door, to be greeted by Mrs Pring and the uncertain sound of *Gilbert and Sullivan* coming from Fr Duddleswell's hand-cranked gramophone. I was at that time, I recalled with a smile, as green and helpless as a pea from the pod.

By now, I was used to hearing confessions and no longer feared I would forget the formula of absolution in the middle. Preaching, while not a pleasure, had ceased to be a torment. I enjoyed taking Holy Communion to the elderly and the bed-ridden and they were always genuinely pleased to see me.

It wasn't so bad visiting people in their homes once I was inside. There was always a moment just before I knocked or rang when the devil put it into my heart to wonder whether I should call again some other day. I was particularly

daunted by three old tenement buildings, known locally as Stonehenge, in the middle of my patch. They had no lights and no lifts. Most of the stone steps were chipped or broken and they smelled of carbolic or worse. Often there were no numbers on the doors. I had to take pot luck, whisper 'Come Holy Ghost', and hope to God I had come to the right place. It never mattered. Non-Catholics were invariably polite to 'the cloth' and keen to redirect me to where lapsed Catholics were hiding out. Sometimes I was sure they were zealous in helping me find my lost sheep out of spite, and I admit I was relieved whenever I received no answer. The Lord could not accuse me of not trying even if the results of my labours were negative.

Continuing the habit of years I exchanged letters with my mother every couple of weeks. The family were well. My salary was only £40 a year—Fr Duddleswell paid me for the first quarter in half-crowns—but this was supplemented by Mass stipends which, at five shillings a time and sometimes more, brought in another £2 a week. There were other sources of income too. At St Jude's there had recently been several weddings, a funeral and a dozen baptisms. Fr Duddleswell had officiated at all of them but he had shared out the proceeds, called stole-fees. He did not mention how he divided them but my portion was so generous I never doubted that he gave me half. Board and lodging were free so I was able for the first time in my life to send the occasional postal order to my younger brothers and sisters who were still at school. I missed them, especially on Bank Holidays when there was nothing for me to do and nowhere to go.

There were other gains besides my new-found affluence. I had my very own radio. Though it was an old three valve model and crackled as if it were permanently on short-wave,

it did enable me to listen to the news and find out what was happening in the world. In the seminary, I was not allowed a newspaper or magazine, except *The Catholic Herald*. I had read only half a dozen novels in my life. Their contents were far too trivial and worldly for one with his sights on eternal things.

My greatest gain at St Jude's was living alongside Fr Duddleswell and Mrs Pring. My parish priest, who claimed to be 'as old and whiskered as a bog mist', had taught me the value of discretion. 'Open wide your heart, Father Neil,' was his advice, 'but fasten down the shutters of your mind. Should you turn your head inside-out in front of the good people where is the use? 'Twill only worry and confuse them and have they not enough complications in their lives already, like?' As for Mrs Pring, she was a staunch ally who showed in a hundred quiet ways that she cared for me. Their altercations seldom involved me, and the intensity of them, I sensed, was an index of their mutual regard.

I was even developing a fondness for urban life. After years of being surrounded by rolling hills, trees, tractors and grazing cows, the town, particularly our district of Fairwater, had not initially appealed to me. It was by comparison noisy, dusty and congested. Greys predominated instead of greens. The wide sweep of the sky was foreshortened and broken up by T.V. aerials and chimney pots. But I was now able to find my way around. I knew the names of the streets and was beginning to recognize some of the faces of those who walked them. In spite of the coolness creeping into the October air, and the premature yellowing of the leaves on the city trees, I was content.

Ahead of me stretched the calmest months of the Church's year. No Lenten fast. No long Holy Week services. Only Advent as we prepared for the Coming of the Lord. Then

14

Christmas itself, the season of peace and goodwill.

There was a rap on my door.

'May the divil tear you from the hearse in front of all the funeral.' Fr Duddleswell was not addressing me; he was concluding his conversation with Mrs Pring over the disappearance of his keys.

Flushed with what he took for victory, he laughed: 'I have had quite enough of *her* babblement. That female would quarrel with her own two shins.'

He settled down to tell me how pleased he was to see me 'coming out like a flower', and to broaden the scope of my apostolate, he had arranged a christening for me on the following Sunday.

'Jimmy and Jeannie Dobbs are the parents, Father Neil. Good practising Catholics. Ditto the godparents. Nothing could be easier. And by the by, Father Neil, one important consideration.'

'Yes, Father?'

'Do not be so foolish as to leave your keys unchaperoned in this house. There is a lady tolerated here who has a propensity to conceal 'em in places no reasonable creature would pretend to look.' His eye had a lost, far-away look. 'Have I not just purchased her another vacuum cleaner, and she plays a trick on me like that?' He shook his head in secret despair. 'Ah, but it conflaberates me marvellously to see her standing idly by, swallowing herself with a yawn.'

Soon after he had gone, conflaberated, I could hear him exclaiming, 'Will you stop acting the maggot, woman, and start fisting that broom around yon filthy floor.' And Mrs Pring's stout reply: 'I'll put your request on the long finger, Fr D.'

I took my commission as a sign of Fr Duddleswell's grow-

ing confidence in me. I opened up my Roman Ritual to remind myself of my duties.

'Nothing could be easier,' he had said, and on the face of it he was right. But my experience of christening was limited to pouring water over the head of a doll under the somnolent eye of the Professor of Moral Theology in my last year at the seminary.

Canon Flynn had taught us that baptism is not valid if anything is used but water for washing. I remembered his emphasis on that phrase. 'Not liquids made up of water,' he said, 'which people do not normally use for washing. Not tea, therefore, nor coffee, neither beer nor lemonade.'

I took it for granted that Fr Duddleswell did not allow such beverages in his font.

As Sunday afternoon approached, my chief concern was to pronounce the baptismal formula while actually pouring water over the head. Simultaneity of words and action was essential for validity. I kept wishing I'd had more time to practise on that doll.

One thing I was determined to do was to read the formula from the book. According to Canon Flynn, it was only too easy after a while to repeat in Latin the confessional form, *I absolve you* instead of the baptismal form, *I baptize you.*

After Sunday lunch, Fr Duddleswell said, 'Make sure you put all the details in the book; names of the child, parents and godparents. And enter them legibly, Father Neil, not like Dr Daley writing out a prescription for mumps.'

These seemed matters of small consequence in the light of other disasters I could think of.

In the event, the christening was a relaxed family affair. Paul John Dobbs, three weeks old, was blue-eyed and as bald as a new lamb of the Flock should be. I read the vital words 'I baptize you in the name of the Father and of the Son and

of the Holy Ghost' while pouring over him a liquid no Devil's Advocate would dare suggest was anything but Adam's ale. The baby did not cry at any stage of the ceremony, not even when I put the salt of wisdom on his tongue or poured autumnal water on his shiny head.

Afterwards, I filled in the baptism register, legibly, in capitals. As I closed the book, Mr Pickles, the godfather, coughed nervously and greased my palm with a pound note. I congratulated myself on the fact that everything had passed off better than I could have wished. And it was with a light heart that I accepted an invitation to the christening party at 1 Pimms Road, close by the railway junction.

The reception was as uncomplicated as the baptism itself. There was tea, cucumber sandwiches and trifle. The new Christian was lying asleep in his cradle next to the settee. When after half an hour he awoke, Mrs Dobbs, a sturdy north country girl and former teacher, picked him up. She dipped her fingers in a square shaped jar and started rubbing his head.

That was when my worries began.

I edged my way over to where Mrs Dobbs was sitting. 'What are you doing?' I asked as casually as I could.

'Rubbing his scalp, Father. A trick my mother taught me.'

'What with?'

'Vaseline. My mother swears it strengthens the roots.'

I did not want to know what Vaseline was supposed to do because of my fear at what it had already done. Vaseline was waterproof. What if the baptismal water had not touched the baby's head at all? Trembling, I said, 'Do you do that often, Mrs Dobbs?'

'Three times a day at least, Father.'

'This morning, too?'

She nodded, tickled by my interest in the number of times

17

she rubbed her child's head with Vaseline, I swigged my tea, blindly shook a circle of hands, and said goodbye.

'Please come again soon, won't you, Father,' said Mrs Dobbs. It was an invitation for which I had reason subsequently to be grateful.

I walked the sound proof Sunday afternoon streets wrestling with the overwhelming problem posed by that Vaseline. I was beginning to understand how Canon Flynn's national reputation as a moralist had been won. He had warned us repeatedly that many mothers saturate their babies' heads with creams, oils, lotions.

'Take care,' he had said, 'that the water flows over the child's scalp. Not merely the hair. Hair is composed of dead cells and is only doubtfully identifiable with the living child. See to it that there's no protective coating of cream on his head otherwise'—one of his rare jokes—'it might protect him from becoming a Christian.'

The sacrament of baptism, I reflected, is a sign of washing. Unless the water *flows* and *washes* the body, there is no sacramental sign and thus no cleansing of the soul. God has a right, I have to admit, to lay down certain requirements for salvation. 'His demands are not harsh but his ministers, especially after six years of preparation, have their part to play. What if I have sent away a pagan instead of a Christian from the font?

Madly, I switched from self-pity to self-loathing and back. My mother used to say that when a baby cries at a christening it is only the devil going out of him. An old wives' tale. Still, how I wished Paul had screamed blue murder at the font.

Surely God was not so arbitrary or cruel as to deprive a child of the grace of baptism simply because a fond mother

had spread a film of Vaseline on his head? Yet I had heard of a child being killed on a level-crossing while his mother was pushing him to church to be christened. No Catholic theologian, as far as I knew, had ever suggested that the poor little mite could get to Heaven. The consensus was that the child was borne to Limbo care of British Railways. Why, then, had the Church discarded the earliest and by far the safest method of baptism—by immersion?

'Mighty pleased I am to see you taking the air, Father Neil.'

It was Fr Duddleswell on a late afternoon stroll after his siesta. He was sporting the kind of floppy, broad-brimmed hat that artists wear. Would he be able to read the guilt written in capitals on my face?

'Hope I did not interrupt your meditation, like?'

I shook my head and agreed to walk with him to the Embankment. Soon, with our backs to the line of trees, we were leaning on the black wall overlooking the rust-coloured waters of the Thames. Beyond, on the south side, were wharves and cranes and tall chimneys spewing out grey smoke. I brought the conversation round to baptism by handing over the stole-fee for the christening. To accept any part of it would have been to add crookedness to incompetence.

'How did it go this afternoon, Father Neil?' Before I could answer, he said, 'And tell me, now, did you write all the details clearly in the register?'

I assured him of that. It set his mind at rest. How trivial the concerns and quiet the soul of the seasoned campaigner.

'Funny thing, Father,' I began.

'What is that?'

'Baptism. Making a Christian with a few words and less than half a pint of water.'

'*Unless a man be born again of water and the Holy Ghost,*' he replied, quoting Jesus' words to Nicodemus. 'John's Gospel, Chapter three, verse five. Our Blessed Lord's disciples must all have been baptized, saving His Holy Mother naturally who was conceived without original sin.'

I put it to him that other Christians are not as careful as Catholics in administering the sacrament.

'The eastern Orthodox are,' he insisted. 'But I agree with you, not the Protestants. To start with, I do not think three quarters of them believe in original sin. And—you will not credit this, mind—it has come to me ears that our Anglican friend the Rev. Percival Probble sometimes baptizes several babies at once. Sprinkles them. Not so much as a cat's lick. Well, you know how 'tis at the Asperges before High Mass. Not everyone is so fortunate as to get splashed in the eye with Holy Water. No matter. They are Christians already. Deprived of a few hundred days Indulgence they may be, but they can compensate for that by bowing their head at the Holy Name. But baptism, now, that is another kettle of fish altogether.' His eyes swept over the Thames as though it were the Styx. 'God alone knows how many innocent babes who die in infancy are deprived of the Beatific Vision because of the negligence of foreign clergymen.'

I was not deriving any comfort from the conversation. 'The river's high today,' I said.

Undeterred, he continued, 'If the water does not reach the body, where is the sacrament, Father Neil?'

I was too wounded to reply.

'D'you know,' he went on, 'I had not long ago a most untypical case.' He paused to let a noisy barge go by. 'There was this Spanish lass of seventeen summers came to me to get married. I told her: "Write your parish priest in Barcelona for your baptism and confirmation certificates me darlin."

He sent back word of her confirmation but said all baptismal registers had been burned in the Civil War. I spoke to Bishop O'Reilly about her and he said, "You will have to baptize her again conditionally to be on the safe side, like." Well, God save us, Father Neil, I confides to meself, has not our microdot of a Bishop this time surpassed himself in caution. After all, the Señorita had received Holy Communion every Sunday for a score of years, had she not? But what d'you suppose, Father Neil?' I tried without success to keep my mind a blank. 'Her mother owned up. Her daughter had been born just prior to the Red occupation. She was too terried to have her baptized before and too negligent after.'

'Baptism of desire,' I suggested, clutching at a theological wisp too thin to be called a straw.

He agreed. 'But think of the many graces and blessings she has been deprived of all her life. And what is more, her Confirmation and all the Holy Communions were *invalid* because she was not even a baptized Christian.'

Once more I tried to change the subject but failed.

'Give credit to the Bishop, Father Neil. Had we sailed ahead with the wedding without baptizing the Señorita, 'twould not have counted in the sight of God. Never would she have become a Señora and ...'

I could see him visualizing a great brood of illegitimate Spanish babies filing by under the sad gaze of God the Almighty.

In the days that followed, my mind was preoccupied with the spiritual state of Paul John Dobbs. Why are souls invisible so you can't see what is going on in them? If I *had* failed in my first Christening and if, God forbid, Paul died before the age of reason, he would be consigned to Limbo

together with that unfortunate baby who was mowed down by a train.

Limbo, the Church teaches, is a place of perfect natural felicity. But it's not the same as Heaven where Paul's Catholic parents had every right to expect to find him when they eventually arrived. It was no consolation to me to know that my mistake would only be detected 'on the other side'.

The nights were terrible. I could not sleep. At manic speed, I went over a song from *Iolanthe* which, until then, I'd not been aware I knew by heart.

> *When you're lying awake with a dismal headache*
> *And repose is tabooed by anxiety*
> *I conceive you may use any language you choose*
> *To indulge in without impropriety*
> *For your brain is on fire, the bedclothes conspire*
> *Of usual slumber to plunder you*
> *First your counterpane goes and uncovers your toes*
> *And your sheet slips demurely from under you ...*

All the verses. In four seconds flat. At the same time, I kept telling myself that Paul was a perfectly healthy little boy. He was sure to survive to the age of seven and qualify for the baptism of desire. No Limbo for him, only the straight choice set before every grown up soul of Heaven or Hell. On the debit side, I conceded he would be deprived of the Church's sacraments like Fr Duddleswell's Señorita. And there would be no intervention of the Bishop in his case to stop him becoming an unmarried husband and father.

Then came a night which I classified unhesitatingly as the worst of my life.

About one o'clock I took three sleeping tablets and drifted into a restless sleep. In my dream I saw Paul, handsome and upright in his late teens. Not being a Señorita, he was able to

enter a seminary. He was ordained a priest. It was invalid, of course. Due to my negligence he was still a pagan. I pictured him offering daily Mass, dispensing Communion, giving hundreds of absolutions—all of them invalid, too. I saw him anointing the dying. Many of these poor creatures, thinking quite reasonably that Paul was a genuine priest, had not sufficient contrition to merit final forgiveness of their sins. They ended up, surprised and aggrieved, in the wrong place where they cursed me heatedly for ever and ever.

The irony was that the only sacrament Paul was able to administer validly was the one which a film of Vaseline had deprived him of: baptism. Even laymen can baptize if they take proper care.

The depths were about to be plumbed. Paul, having been ordained, was consecrated bishop. Looking for all the world like Bishop O'Reilly, he handed on Holy Orders tirelessly, but his ordinations, unbeknown to anyone but God, did not 'take'. I saw in consequence hundreds of supposed priests dispensing hundreds of supposed sacraments year after year, century after century. In the diocese where Paul reigned there was a kind of huge, spiritual emptiness. No grace, no sacraments, no Christian hope. In that benighted place, the Catholic Church was no better off than the Church of England whose orders Leo XIII had solemnly declared in 1896 to be invalid.

I awoke in a sweat and with a fiercely pumping head, grateful that Paul had not gone on to become Pope. It was three o'clock. Certain that I would not sleep again that night, I stepped into my slippers and crept downstairs to the kitchen to make myself a cup of tea. While I was waiting for the kettle to boil I thought I heard a click. In normal circumstances I would have had no difficulty in identifying it but there was so much clamour inside my head I was not

bothering about a tiny noise outside.

I was sitting at table about to sip my tea when I heard a car racing in the direction of the presbytery. It screeched to a halt near the front door. From the hall came the sound of the bolts being hastily drawn and Fr Duddleswell's conspiratorial voice, 'In there.' Fast, heavy footfalls in the street, then in the hall. Next, the whole kitchen seemed suddenly to contract as it filled with uniformed men breathing heavily and mouthing obscenities to keep their spirits up.

As I sprang up my right arm was gripped in a vice and pinioned behind my back. My head jerked back in a reflex action and thwacked my assailant somewhere about the face. He cried out in agony and released me. My relief was short-lived. Someone in front of me put the knee in, and I passed out.

I came round possibly a few seconds later in Mrs Pring's upholstered rocking chair. My eyes were watering, I felt sick and I had difficulty in breathing.

Fr Duddleswell was pouring a cup of cold water over my bowed head and slapping my cheek. I was dimly aware that Mrs Pring, cold-creamed, curlered, and in her dressing gown, had joined a misty throng. She was assuring Fr Duddleswell that 'poor Father Neil has been baptized already without you drenching him in my kitchen'. She took over from him and placed smelling salts under my nose of such potency my head was all but lifted from my shoulders.

Gradually the haze began to clear. I made out two policemen. One was applying a cold compress to his colleague's eye. It was puffy and purple. I would have shown sympathy had I not been preoccupied with nausea, and shooting pains in my infernal regions.

I heard Fr Duddleswell rambling on about new Hoovers and neighbourhood thieves who did wicked things with

them, and Mrs Pring's obdurate tendency to mislay keys and to bolt the back door with a boiled carrot.

Mrs Pring soon set the room to rights and responded to Fr Duddleswell's request to 'wet the tay' for all. She offered me three steaming cups in her three right hands. 'You'll feel all the better, Father Neil, for pouring that down the red lane.'

P.C. Winkworth, who had nearly bisected me, slowly undid the button of his tunic and took out a notebook. As he came into focus, I saw his cap was off. His straw hair stood on end, topping a brown furrowed face and a small red nose. His head looked like a pineapple with a cherry stuck on. Nodding towards Mrs Pring, he said to Fr Duddleswell, 'Your Missis I take it, sir.'

Fr Duddleswell swelled indignantly as he drew in his breath. 'No, Constable, we only live together.' He made haste to explain that Mrs Pring was his housekeeper and that while she had a good pair of shoulders underneath her head they did not so much as share an opinion or a tube of toothpaste.

'I see, sir. And your name, please, sir.'

'Duddleswell. *Father* Duddleswell.'

'Is that prefix some sort of title, sir?'

My parish priest explained carefully his central role in the community.

'And this young man, I take it, sir,' the policeman said, indicating me, 'is an associate of yours?'

'I have not me spectacles on me nose, Officer, but his features bear an uncanny resemblance to me curate.'

'Am I to assume, sir,' the policeman plodded on, 'that you are not wanting to prefer charges?'

Fr Duddleswell looked at me sitting hunched up at the table clad in slippers and pyjamas. He was obviously at a loss

to know what he could charge me with except the misfortune of being his assistant. 'No,' he said generously. 'If Father Neil is prepared to forget the incident, so am I.'

'Well,' went on P.C. Winkworth, 'that makes it rather difficult for us, sir. You see, sir, Central Control logged your call. They ordered us to proceed here. They will also be able to ascertain from the state of P.C. Richards's eye that the young gentleman over there assaulted a police officer while resisting arrest.'

It took my accuser ten minutes to accept that he had no legitimate cause to arrest a curate for sipping tea in his own kitchen even if he was responding to the invitation of the parish priest.

Eventually the two coppers left. Mrs Pring thereupon started badgering Fr Duddleswell for not letting the curate make himself a cup of tea at night without dialling 999 and summoning the police. 'Be careful, woman,' he threatened, 'for you are busy planting me with a mustard seed of wrath.'

I slunk upstairs throbbing in more places than one. I was still miserable and yet, for no reason I could pin down, I found myself repeating the lines, *But the darkness has past, And it's daylight at last.* As soon as my head hit the pillow, I fell into a dreamless sleep.

I awoke next morning at the usual time with a clear head and buoyant spirits, troubled only by a bruise below. I set about marshalling the facts.

It was not for me to turn my cranium inside out in front of the faithful. I could not go along to Mr and Mrs Dobbs and apologize for failing to baptize their infant. They had seen me do it. I could hardly expect them to appreciate the finer points of theology. Nor could I offer to rebaptize their son. That would be worse than a doctor re-inoculating a

child because he had forgotten to put vaccine in the syringe the first time.

Poor Father Neil has been baptized already without you drenching him in my kitchen. Mrs Pring's words echoed in my mind. If *I* could be 're-baptized' in domestic surroundings, why not Paul John Dobbs? Fr Duddleswell had not scrupled to do that in the case of a little girl in Birmingham with far less justification than I now had. There was one important difference, of course. My baptism would be so private that even the parents themselves wouldn't know.

At breakfast, Fr Duddleswell tried to make light of 'last evening's entertainment'.

Mrs Pring brought him to a sharp halt with a special glower and went out.

'She will put a fat lip on her for a month of Sundays,' he complained. 'What can you expect of the unfair sex, Father Neil?' I smiled compliantly. 'Always remember when arguing with a woman that conclusive evidence does not prove a thing.' I promised to store away that pearl of wisdom. 'I was but doing me duty as I saw it, like. No hard feelings?'

'No,' I said, relieved that my problem was in principle resolved.

He squeezed my arm in gratitude. 'May you live as long as a proverb, Father Neil.'

On Thursday I went to Mrs Pring's kitchen for a morning cup of tea and to find out how long it takes a kettle of water to boil. I also picked a five inch shrimp paste jar with a screw-on lid out of the dustbin.

As soon as Fr Duddleswell left for the day, I crept into his study and borrowed the keys to the baptistery.

In church there was an annoying stream of parishioners praying before the Blessed Sacrament. It was nearly an hour before I could unlock the baptistery gates and the padlock on

the font without being seen. Begging the Lord's pardon, I filled my jar with oily water from the font. After lunch, I remained in my study until 2.30 praying that Mr Dobbs would be at work and Paul conveniently placed for christening.

'Please come in, Father,' said Mrs Dobbs. 'Surprised to see you so soon.'

I was not sure whether this was a welcome or a rebuke for returning before my shadow was dry on the wall.

Paul was sleeping soundly in his cradle but to my dismay there was a neighbour present. Mrs Ivy Burns, a surly looking creature, had not been invited to the christening. Her hair was tied up in a kerchief so it looked as if she was carrying a workman's lunch on her head. I got the impression she could jabber on all day.

To justify my visit I had bought Paul a christening gift. I handed Mrs Dobbs a paper bag with 'Woolworth' in red on the outside.

Mrs Dobbs opened it up and took out a fire-engine. 'Oh, you shouldn't have, Father.'

'Bit young for it, ain't he?' croaked Mrs Burns, who was puffing away at her hand-rolled cigarette.

'It's for when he grows up,' I said.

'Like a cup of tea, Father?' asked Mrs Dobbs kindly.

With Mrs Burns there, my plan had misfired and I was out of pocket for nothing. 'No thank you. I've just had two large cups of coffee.'

I am not by nature impolite but it occurred to me there was a way to get rid of the intruder. I must keep my mouth shut. Whenever I was addressed by either of the ladies I replied with a nod or a shake of the head while looking Ivy stolidly in the eyes. Something had to give. Mrs Burns surrendered and took her leave. I immediately came to life,

wished her a very warm goodbye and expressed the hope that our paths would cross again soon. Then I turned my attention to Paul's mother.

'Maybe I would, Mrs Dobbs.'

'*Would*, Father?'

'I would like a cup of tea, after all.'

'Good,' she said. If she was puzzled by my strange behaviour and sudden thirst she did not show it. 'I'll join you. I'll put the kettle on.'

I reckoned on having at least a minute while she was in the kitchen. As I stepped across to Paul's cradle I could hear Mrs Dobbs drawing water into the kettle. I had unscrewed the shrimp paste jar when Mrs Dobbs returned. I barely had time to thrust the jar into my left trouser pocket.

Mrs Dobbs, seeing me hovering and now cooing over her sleeping infant, came and stood beside me. In a whisper, she said, 'Our pride and joy, Father.'

'And rightly so,' I returned, as I felt cold water streaming down my leg.

'We've been married a year now.'

'Is he your first then?' I asked, not immediately taking in what she had said and shaking my leg uneasily.

I bent down slightly over Paul's reclining figure and from there could see my black herring-bone trousers turning all glossy at the crotch and down one leg. I hoped my woollen sock would soak up the water. I didn't want Mrs Dobbs to have to tell her husband that the curate, besides insulting Ivy Burns, had relieved himself on the dining room floor.

We stood there side by side gazing at Paul with widely differing emotions until a whistle from the kitchen signalled that the kettle was boiling.

'I'll make the tea, Father. Won't be long.'

'Take as long as you like, Mrs Dobbs.'

'Any biscuits?'

'Yes, lots, please.'

'I'll bring the tin so you can help yourself.'

My second and last chance. I took out the jar and was delighted to find it was still half full. Bending down, I whiffed the faint baby smell of ammonia. I rubbed a big patch of Paul's scalp with my handkerchief, then with unsteady hand poured what was left in the shrimp paste jar over it.

'*Paule, ego te baptizo . . .*' I managed to finish the formula but not before the new Christian gave irrefutable evidence that the devil had gone out of him. Never have I seen so much trouble on such a tiny face. So stupendous was the caterwauling he emitted that his mother, though weighed down with a large tea tray, came running in.

Caught in that downward position I had no choice. I barely had a moment to wipe Paul's forehead, tuck the shrimp paste jar under the quilt and take him in my arms. 'I'm sorry, Mrs Dobbs,' I said, 'I must have disturbed him, so I picked him up.'

Seeing my evident fondness for her pride and joy, she relaxed and gave a smile of approval. 'I'll put this tray down, Father, then I'll take him. He may be a bit wet and I don't want him to christen *you*.' She blushed and apologized for her 'slip of the tongue'.

I handed Paul, still bawling, to his mother. He was transformed instantly into a whimpering bundle in her arms.

In essence, my mission was accomplished, but two problems remained. First, though the water spilt on Paul's bedding could be explained, I felt I ought to remove the shrimp paste jar. Only I or Ivy Burns could have put it there, and I couldn't see her taking the rap for me.

Second, I was sure that sooner or later Mrs Dobbs was bound to notice the wet patch on my trousers, far too large

for a month-old baby in water-proof pants to have made.

I would solve both problems at once. 'Since you're holding the baby,' I said, 'why not let me pour?'

'That's very kind of you, Father.'

I filled a cup, made to pass it to her, and accidentally split the contents on my vitals. 'O my God!' I screamed, clutching myself immodestly in the spot where I was already wounded. Why hadn't I at least had the sense to put the milk in first?

My outburst roused Paul to fresh operatic heights. Mrs Dobbs, encircling him with one arm, proposed to fetch me a cloth from the kitchen.

In those precious seconds, through tears of pain, I retrieved the jar and returned it to my pocket.

Mrs Dobbs handed me a tea towel. I dabbed myself gently until the worst of the throbbing was over.

'Can I help in any way, Father?'

I said I didn't see how she could. She said she'd meant by calling a doctor or something.

'It's nothing, Mrs Dobbs, really. I'm maladroit, always doing careless things like this. I'm sure there won't even be a blister to speak of.'

After we had mopped up, we sat down and quietly drank our tea.

'Biscuit, Father?'

There was no need to explain my reluctance to prolong the visit, but before I left I gave Paul my blessing and a light-hearted pat on his head for luck.

Ah, I murmured when I was in the street, who would have thought it was such a costly business turning pagans into Christians?

Two

FEMME FATALE

I am no expert when it comes to jewelry but I couldn't help feeling that the rosary which the lady asked me to bless after Mass was strung with pearls. She thanked me in a quiet voice and handed me an envelope before threading her way through the emerging Sunday congregation. I watched her walk to a white Rolls Royce. As the chauffeur opened the door for her I spied two white, well groomed French poodles on the rear seat, yapping excitedly.

I returned to my study before opening the envelope. It was pink, embossed and scented. Inside was a £10 note.

Not knowing whether the reward for blessing a rosary was classed in the trade as a stole-fee, I put the matter to Fr Duddleswell. His immediate response was to rub his hands and say, 'Miss Davenport is back.'

Miss Davenport was the only child of a financier long dead. She had inherited everything, and *everything*, it appeared, was not a bad description of what she had inherited. The family business had continued to flourish because she took no interest in it. She was in the habit of passing each winter in a secluded Georgian house just over the border in the neighbouring parish of All Saints. If past experience was anything to go by, her patronage of St Jude's was likely to be generous.

'We will have less difficulty paying the schools' bills these next twelve month,' Fr Duddleswell forecast, 'provided we

play our cards right. And for our part we can help this lady, too. Miss Davenport is, shall we say, a trifle whimsical? Promise me solemnly, now, that you will humour her.'

Not knowing then the full nature of her eccentricities but liking the first of them I'd met with, I gave him the assurance he sought. As to the money in the envelope, he said, enigmatically, that all things considered I was entitled to it this time.

That meeting on the church steps with Miss Davenport was the first of many. In the next two weeks she appeared daily at Mass—always at my Mass, whether I was celebrating the 7.30 or the 8 o'clock. Afterwards, she came into the sacristy as I was unvesting to ask me to bless a medal or a picture of the Sacred Heart. Each time she handed me a pink scented envelope. Thoroughly embarrassed by now, I told her that the parish was very grateful for her support and I would place her offering in the Poor Box.

I breathed again when no monetary reward followed the blessing of what looked like a jewel-encrusted dog-collar. Mrs Pring, though, made a wry comment when the local wine merchant delivered a crate of half bottles of champagne to the presbytery door marked URGENT. FOR THE ATTENTION OF THE REVEREND FR BOYD.

I could only naturally conclude that Miss Davenport had taken a fancy to me. But how could I be sure? This might be one of the lady's whimsies which Fr Duddleswell had spoken about. When at Mass I turned round to face the congregation to say *Dominus vobiscum*, 'The Lord be with you,' my eyes were drawn to hers as if by a magnet. She seemed to glow with expectancy. She put me off so much I kept stumbling over the words of the Mass and losing my place in the Missal.

Until then, my sexual fantasies had taken the shape of

being hotly pursued by dark and languorous females. They usually wore grass skirts, were garlanded with flowers, and had bare bosoms bumping up and down like bunches of grapes. Miss Davenport was hardly the kind of Judy whom Bishop O'Reilly had warned us against when he ordained us. She was more an embarrassment than a temptation.

At a guess she was twenty-five years my senior. Fur-wrapped and affluent, but flat-chested and not exactly beautiful. Her eyebrows, pencilled thin and blue, gave a haloed appearance to piercing brown eyes. There were lines on her forehead and down her neck, and her hair done up in a bun was streaked with grey. My conclusion was that it was silly and unfair to consider Miss Davenport some kind of *femme fatale* when perhaps she looked on me as a son.

True to my word, I handed over the envelopes to Fr Duddleswell who saw nothing incongruous in the scale of the offerings. His view was that if the good lady insisted on throwing her money around like snuff at a wake it was imperative the right people should be there to gather it up. I was fast becoming a financial asset to St Jude's if nothing else.

One morning the telephone rang while Fr Duddleswell was giving me instructions for the day. He answered it, gagged the mouthpiece, and whispered, ''Tis Miss Davenport for yourself, Father Neil.'

She sounded distressed. Her pet canary was unwell. I asked her if she had called in the vet. Yes, a specialist from Harley Street was with him at this moment, but what he really needed was a priest. I had so far spoken in ambiguous terms to spare Fr Duddleswell the bizarreness of the lady's conversation, but there was no way I could avoid asking, 'You did say your *canary*, Miss Davenport?'

Fr Duddleswell was not in the slightest put out at hearing

who was in need of my ministrations. 'Tut, tut,' he said softly, 'poor little creature.'

I advised Miss Davenport that if a Harley Street specialist was with him, her pet was in very capable hands. Fr Duddleswell signalled me to gag the receiver again before tapping my chest with his breviary and saying hoarsely, 'Is it a cooking apple you have in there, you great Gazebo of a man?'

I gathered I was expected to accede to Miss Davenport's request. I momentarily rebelled and played one more card. 'I'd be delighted to help, Miss Davenport'—Fr Duddleswell smirked—'but, you see, you live in All Saints parish, and really you ought to ask Monsignor Clarke to ...'

Fr Duddleswell's shaky fist was promptly over the mouth-piece. 'Jesus, Mary and Joseph,' he grinded out, 'tell the bloody lady you will bloody well be there in bloody double quick time.'

I only hoped he had a sound-proofed hand. I relayed the message to Miss Davenport in milder terms and replaced the receiver.

All the time I was changing from cassock to jacket, walking down the stairs, putting on my bicycle clips and wheeling out my bike, Fr Duddleswell was hovering over me, giving me a sermon on dropping once and for all this petty, trade union, demarcation-line mentality that was ruining the country and, instead, blessing the bloody canary and any other bloody thing necessary, as Jesus Himself would have done. I had never known him spit out so much blood.

I promised I would not disappoint the rich Miss Davenport and sped off as fast as two wheels would carry me.

The detached, white-pillared house was in a leafy square. It overlooked a small, fenced-in private park sparkling with well watered grass on a bright October morning. I rested and padlocked my bicycle against the black wrought-iron

railings, next to a sign which read LE CASINO.

A French maid wished me '*Bonjour, mon père*,' and ushered me into the lounge where 'Madame is anxiously attending you.'

I was born an impressionist. I feel things but I do not always see them too clearly. I took in a Siamese cat sensually rubbing its side against heavy damask curtains. It was wearing the bejewelled collar I had blessed a few days before. I caught the distant barking of Miss Davenport's French poodles. I sensed I was in the presence of incongruous opulence. It reminded me of the set of a Molière play we had once put on at school.

Miss Davenport rose from her Chesterfield where she had been reclining as she contemplated with damp eyes the canary in its gilded cage. With ringed hand she set me beside her on the cool leather and took my hand. It was some time before she would give it back.

The symptom of the canary's sickness was that it refused every incitement to sing. 'I have had him as a bosom companion,' she murmured, 'for quite six months, Fr Boyd, and never has he denied me this pleasure before.'

'When did it ... he ...'

'Timmy is his name,' she said, clasping my hand more tightly as though the name somehow bound us closer together.

'When did Timmy sing last, Miss Davenport?'

'Yesterday evening.' She looked around her. 'Did you not bring your vestments, Fr Boyd?' She explained that she was expecting me to pray for Timmy's recovery and give him my sacerdotal blessing.

Fortunately, I had taken Holy Communion to a sick person that morning before Mass and I still had a small stole, a bottle of Holy Water and my Ritual in my pocket. Miss

Davenport thanked me for coming prepared and withdrew her hand reluctantly.

I put on my stole, white side up, and thumbed rapidly through the Ritual in search of a suitable benediction. The closest parallel I could find was the blessing of an aeroplane.

I raised my right hand over the little bird sitting sullenly on his perch and prepared to read the Latin formula.

'What is his name, Father?'

I was puzzled. 'You just told me his name was Timmy, Miss Davenport. I'm not baptizing him ...'

'No, he is baptized already, Father Boyd. I meant, what is Timmy's name in Latin so that I can recognize it when you utter it.'

'*Timotheus.*' I was thankful the canary had a simple Christian name and also that Miss Davenport's ignorance of Latin guaranteed she'd not realize my prayer had been written with a weightier sky-traveller in mind. At random moments during the prayer, I slowed down to say '*Timotheus*' at which Miss Davenport, who was kneeling reverently, bowed her head. At the end she said 'Amen.' Still no cheep from Timmy himself.

To complete the ceremony, I picked up the Holy Water sprinkler. It was simply a medicine bottle. The cork had been pierced to allow a few beads of water to escape when it was shaken over the sick. I aimed it at Timmy and began '*Benedicat te, Timotheus, omnipotens Deus ...*' As I jerked the bottle, the cork flew out and a stream of water went in Timmy's eye. Before the blessing was finished, the canary was in full voice.

Miss Davenport was ecstatic at so sudden a cure. She sat down at her bureau twittering something about not needing to call in that ineffectual 'médecin' from Harley Street and writing out a cheque. She sealed it in a pink envelope and

gave it to me. WITH BOUNDLESS GRATITUDE, I read. 'Do you love cats, too, Father Boyd?' was her final question.

'We dislike the same things,' I replied diplomatically.

Outside the house, I was so incensed at being forced to make a fool of myself I tore up the envelope and stuffed the pieces in my back pocket. I cycled around town for half an hour, furious with Fr Duddleswell for casting me into the thin arms of a potty old girl merely to make a few extra bob for the coffers of St Jude's. When I had cooled down, I returned to the presbytery.

Fr Duddleswell met me at the back door. 'Miss Davenport rang,' he said, 'to make sure you returned ...'

I wheeled my bike into the yard and, without a word, walked past him up to my study. The atmosphere between us was strained until the next day when he visited my room to make peace.

'D'you know your trouble in all this, Father Neil?' I played the silent innocent. He lifted his spectacles on to his forehead and licked his lips noisily. 'You are a snob.'

I stiffened at the unexpected rebuke.

He raised his 'sermon fingers' at me, the first two on his right hand, and continued. 'Now be truthful with me, Father Neil. Had an old age pensioner called you to her flat in Stonehenge to bless her canary that had fallen ill with laryngitis, would you have obliged?' I nodded. He removed his fingers from before my nose. 'The rich are no different from the poor, Father Neil, except they have a lot more money, you follow?'

I apologized for sulking. Miss Davenport's distress at her canary's ailment was genuine enough. I should have sympathized more.

Fr Duddleswell coughed and said he would be obliged if I

would give him my signature. From his breast pocket he took out a cheque.

'Mrs Pring found the pieces in your waste-paper basket when she was cleaning this morning, Father Neil. I have taken the liberty of pasting it together, like.'

After I had signed THE REV. BOYD on the back, my resolution cracked. I turned it over to discover I had nearly thrown away twenty-five pounds.

When two days later, Miss Davenport begged me to bury her Siamese cat, Sleeky, who had been knocked over by a car I went prepared and in a more charitable frame of mind. I took my black bag with me and on the journey, with each revolution of the pedal, I told myself that Miss Davenport was only a poor little old lady with a pile of money.

Sleekius was interred with almost military honours and his mistress's many tears. I promised her I would say a Requiem Mass for the deceased on condition I did not have to announce the intention publicly from the pulpit.

Back at St Jude's, Fr Duddleswell summed it up by saying that after my success with Timmy it was best for my reputation as a healer that Sleeky had been 'killed beyond repair'.

Apart from magnetizing my eyes at every *Dominus vobiscum*, Miss Davenport did not trouble me again for another week. Then she phoned one Friday morning at around 11.30. Fr Duddleswell had been in my study for ninety minutes talking trivialities until I wondered if he would ever leave.

Miss Davenport asked if I could be at LE CASINO at eight. I was free, but I consulted my diary, trying to conjure up an excuse to stay at home. Fr Duddleswell's grimaces left me in no doubt that it was my duty to humour the good lady. Having heard me say yes, he left before I had replaced the receiver.

At the evening meal, Fr Duddleswell seemed miles away. He was reminiscing about obscure tribulations he had had to endure when he was a curate. Mrs Pring had cooked sausages and mash. In a moment of total vacancy, Fr Duddleswell served me a *single* sausage; hardly enough for one about to face the rigours of officiating at Miss Davenport's imediately afterwards. I asked for three more, buried them in a mound of mash and helped it down with a bottle of champagne. After that, plum pudding and custard. With a final flurry, I grimly drained two cups of Mrs Pring's tar-black tea.

'You are off, then, Father Neil? To Miss Davenport's is it?' I nodded. 'The best of luck, lad,' he said without his usual smile.

'Won't be long,' I called as I rode off. How was I to know that at Miss Davenport's there awaited me something more simple and more terrible than anything I could have imagined?

At the front door of LE CASINO, the maid and the chauffeur, presumably her husband, were on the point of leaving. The maid curtseyed to Miss Davenport, kissed her hand and said, '*Encore,* Madame, my sincerest *condoléances.*' Which member of the menagerie was dead now?

I walked in to find Madame attired not in black but in full evening dress.

In the hall, Miss Davenport monopolized my hand. The dining room door was open. Inside I could see the table tastefully dressed and lit by candlelight.

'I'm awfully sorry, Miss Davenport,' I stammered, 'if you're expecting guests I can come back tomorrow.'

'Only you, Father.'

O my God, I thought, do I have to dine with Miss Daven-

port by candlelight without any witnesses present?

Only then did I grasp the significance of the hour: eight o'clock. Dinner! *Damn!*

'You do have an appetite, Father?' purred my regal-looking hostess.

'Usually, Miss Davenport.' I was beginning to distinguish dangerous details in the candlelight. Her low cut dress, the pearl necklace, her hair brushing her shoulders and crowned with a kind of shimmering tiara. Taking my arm as well as my hand she propelled me to where the meal was waiting. Soft intimate music was being played in the background.

I helped her sit down before making my way to the other end and slumping down myself. I was surrounded by more cutlery and glass than I had ever had to deal with. Staring up at me malevolently were six large oysters bedded in crushed ice.

'You like oysters, Fr Boyd?'

Never having been that close to them before I was non-committal. 'Is there anyone who doesn't, Miss Davenport?' I had no idea how to eat the blessed things, or were you supposed to drink them?

I took a long time unfolding the starched table-napkin while keeping a sharp look-out for which piece of silver she would select. A tiny fork. She squeezed a lemon over the oyster and made a little slicing movement with her fork. She picked up the shell and, as it were, tossed the contents down her throat.

My aim was never very good and I was worried that oysters would not be companionable towards the *hors d'oeuvre* I had eaten with Fr Duddleswell. After the first throw I found my mouth full of a viscous substance like the raw white of an egg. It nearly made me vomit. My hostess's eyes were not yet accustomed to the light or she might have

suspected something. I went on chewing surreptitiously behind my table-napkin till I managed to swallow.

In front of me was a Menu printed on parchment paper in silver lettering. It read:

> *Oysters*
>
> *Tournedos Béarnaise*
> *Potatoes Lyonnaise*
> *Tossed Green Salad with French Dressing*
>
> *Tarte aux Abricots Bourdaloue*
>
> *Cheese*
> *Fruit*
>
> *Coffee*

To drink there was *Château Haut-Brion* (1918) and *Haut-Peyraguey*, and finally *Cognac Courvoisier*.

'Would you care to pour for the next course, Father?' Miss Davenport pointed to the wines. I was glad to do anything that afforded me some respite from another oyster.

As I rose, it occurred to me that I did not know which wine was which or which to serve first. The white wine was on ice and the red on the side-board.

'Have you any preferences, Miss Davenport?'

'Yes, on these occasions, always *Château Haut-Brion* (1918).'

There was nothing for it. I chose the bottle resting on the ice. In the nick of time I read *Haut-Peyraguey* on the label. With considerable presence of mind, I half whispered, 'What a splendid wine to follow, Miss Davenport.'

'I am so pleased you know your *Sauternes*, Father,' she said.

43

I picked up the red and put my napkin under it as if it were a Stradivarius violin. Approaching my hostess I realized another distressing gap in my knowledge of etiquette. Into which glass should I pour the wine? Another hasty decision was forced on me, and with less fortunate results.

'That's the water glass, Father,' said Miss Davenport, touching my arm tenderly. She helped me by apologizing for the meagre light given by the candles.

Back at my place I looked down at the five-eyed monster on the platter in front of me. I noticed that the front of the Menu bore the initials *D.D.* and *N.B.*

'Fr Boyd,' said Miss Davenport as I was about to tackle another oyster, 'do you have a first name?'

I put down my fork. 'Yes, Miss Davenport.'

'May I be let in on your little secret?'

Since my initials were on the Menu and my full name was printed in capitals above my confessional, I did not mind revealing it.

'Neil? *Neil.*' She ran it over her tongue appreciatively like wine. 'Such an excellent vintage. It suits you. It *is* you. Now you have told me that your name is Neil, I could not conceive of you possessing any other name. I shall call my next Siamese Neil—if it is a boy, of course.' I acknowledged the compliment. 'May I, *dare* I, call you Neil?'

'I don't think Fr Duddleswell ...' I began as I directed another oyster towards my throat.

'Charles?' she said. I swallowed the oyster without difficulty. 'Ah, Charles would not begrudge me such an innocent pleasure.'

'Charles?' I managed to get out.

'I am Daisy.'

'I'm sure you are, Miss Davenport.'

'You see, dear Neil, I feel we have to be on Christian name

44

terms if I am to confess to you the story of my love.'

I stood up, seeing my first opportunity to escape that insupportable meal. 'Miss Davenport, you are a Catholic and I am a priest.'

'Daisy.'

Less forcefully I repeated my objection preceding it with 'Daisy.'

'It is *because* you are a priest, Neil, that I can tell you without inhibitions of my love for ...' I was about to stamp out when I heard the word 'Henri.'

'Henri. Monsieur le Comte. My first, my only love.'

I sat down as though I had been shot. It was only my ear Miss Davenport was wanting to grab, after all. It meant I would have to see the meal through to the bitter end. Miss Davenport was destined to be my *femme fatale* in a way the moralists had not envisaged when they advised, 'Never be alone with a woman, *Numquam solus cum sola.*'

As the meal progressed and the candle flame burned low I learned that Miss Davenport had met Monsieur le Comte in the Casino at Monte Carlo when she was seventeen. He was, *hélas*, a married man with a beautiful but boring wife, an ancient château on the Loire, and half a dozen children. It was a sad tale and it moved me deeply.

Miss Davenport, having despatched her *Tournedos Béarnaise* touched her mouth with her napkin. 'Rarely does it happen,' she whispered reverentially, 'that the perfect wine comes into being.' As she fingered the stem of her glass, the candlelight played upon the ruby contents and from them flashed a star with the brilliancy of Bethlehem's. 'Such marvellous blending of rain and sunlight is required, wind and soil, too, and perhaps the protecting curvature of some small hill. Celestial chemistry, Neil. Only such unique conditions can produce a *Château Haut-Brion* (1918) or a genius like

Bach—or a Monsieur le Comte.'

Count Henri must have been a veritable bouquet of a man, handsome, high principled, bronzed, most subtle in speech and elegant in dress. The culture of his palate was evidenced in our meal; it was his favourite. It was the meal he had chosen to eat with Daisy the evening they said good-bye.

My pity was equally divided between Miss Davenport's past sorrows and my present predicament. Even as she related her sad *histoire* she remained the perfect hostess, urging me to eat this and drink that. My bladder was filled to over-flowing.

I should have excused myself for a few moments and asked where the bathroom was. This, I felt quite reasonably, would have dampened her discourse. And afterwards, how could I return to my place as if nothing had happened, especially if the plumbing of the water closet was such that it left hiss-ings and pipe reverberations? Like a fool, I decided to sit it out.

My eyes started to water with the discomfort, and when the candlelight caught them in its glow Miss Davenport took it as a sign of sympathy and rapport.

'It was passionate but pure, Neil,' she was saying. 'Only one such as you committed to *la vie célibataire* could possibly comprehend my heartache and the subsequent solitude.'

I did not know what time it was but it must have turned 11 o'clock, curfew hour at the presbytery. What if Fr Dud-dleswell, not realizing I was out, had bolted the door?

The strain was now intolerable. 'Miss Davenport.' I changed to 'Daisy' of my own accord to show the evening had not been wasted on me. 'Daisy, I have a confession to make to you.'

'Tell me, Neil.' There was a touch of drama in her voice.

46

'I'm feeling ill, Daisy.'

'Where, Neil?'

I did not want to put too fine a point upon it. 'In my stomach. Frightfully, frightfully ill.'

'Not the food, I hope?' she asked in some distress.

'I wasn't too well before I came, Miss Davenport. If you don't mind ...'

'A cognac before you go. It is so good for an upset stomach, as Henri used to say.'

To speed things up, I gulped down a small cognac, grabbed my hat from the hall and took my leave. I had the presence of mind to kiss her hand. 'Daisy, adieu.'

She was deeply moved and, fortunately for me, closed the door behind me immediately. I unchained my bicycle but was unable to lift my leg high enough to sit on the saddle. To avoid permanent injury I began to wheel my bike home. Then a flash of inspiration ignited by desperate need, I hailed a passing taxi.

The taxi came to a halt and the driver put his capped head out of the window and asked in puzzled tones, 'Trouble, Rev.?'

'Deep trouble,' I said.

'Puncture?'

'Almost.'

'Want me to take the bike an' all?'

I had opened the back door and was already dragging my bicycle in after me. I thanked God for the sensible design of the London taxi.

'First time I've ever had a bike for a fare,' called the driver good-naturedly over his shoulder. 'Where to, Guv.?' I gave the address. 'Roman Catholic, then, are you, Father?'

'Yes.'

The driver relaxed his hand on the wheel and half turned

round. 'My old woman's a Catholic. Could you tell me something, Rev.?'

'I can't tell you a thing,' I said, clasping myself where it hurt, 'please get us home quick.'

He slammed the glass partition between us with an 'O-bleeding-kay, if that's the way you want it,' and sped off through the city traffic like a maniac. Whenever he went through the red lights I gave him a special benediction. I prayed frantically that Fr Duddleswell had not bolted the door, otherwise I might have to pee against a lamp post.

The taxi jerked to a stop outside the presbytery. The driver touched the clock and said, 'And an extra threepence for your bleeding bike.' I handed him a pound note and told him to keep the change. I was not prepared to wait for it. I hoped the liberality of the tip would soften his attitude to the leaders of his wife's religion.

The front door was already ajar and Fr Duddleswell stood there against the light in dressing gown and slippers. He must have heard the familiar ticking over sound of the taxi. I expected a reprimand for being out after hours, but nothing of the sort. He merely pointed. 'Quick, up the wooden hill with you, Father Neil. The bathroom is free.' I left my bicycle in his charge and heaved myself heavenwards.

Ah, such simple, unsung ecstasies. Such blessed relief. Never had life seemed so sweet, so very sweet.

Outside the bathroom Fr Duddleswell was waiting with a bottle of Milk of Magnesia and a dessert spoon. I went with him into my study. 'At your age, Father Neil, you have to be more careful that the Jordan does not burst its banks.'

'She rang, then,' I said, collapsing into a chair.

'Who, Miss Davenport?'

'Yes.'

'No.' I had swigged three spoonfuls of the medicine before

48

it sank in that Fr Duddleswell knew my plight in some detail without being told.

'Monsieur le Comte,' he said.

'You know about him?'

From his pocket he drew a dog-eared Menu, a replica of the one on the table that evening except it was initialled *D.D.* and *C.D.*

'Charles,' I exploded.

'We have all to go through it the once, Father Neil. I did meself and so did me two curates before you. Take your ease and I will tell you about it.'

He had known tonight was the night because of the date, October 13th, the anniversary of Daisy's final farewell to Henri. The incidents with the pets were part of the usual build up to the banquet.

When I suggested that we should not make fools of ourselves for money, Fr Duddleswell looked hurt.

' 'Tis true, Father Neil, that in a couple of days I will receive a cheque for £500 for the Schools' Fund as has happened a trinity of times before. But as God is me witness I did it all for Daisy.'

It was news to me that anyone else had been involved apart from myself.

He went on to explain that Miss Davenport had renounced her beloved rather than break up his marriage. She had acted in strict obedience to the Church's law on marriage and divorce. With her purchasing power she could have bought out any half-baked Frenchman. The meal I had just shared was, in his view, a kind of eucharistic memorial of the last supper when Daisy sacrificed herself for her faith.

'You believe her story?' I asked.

'To speak the truth, I have not the faintest idea whether it happened like that or she imagined it. What matters is

that 'tis real for her, you follow?—and the rich are especially worthy of a priest's consideration.' He slowly raised his head and dropped it. 'You see, lad, they cannot take refuge in the ultimate human illusion that money is the cure of every form of ill.'

I nodded, truly sorry for having misjudged both him and Daisy.

'One thing, Father,' I said in a more sober tone, 'you knew what was in store for me. Why did you let me eat that vast quantity of stodge beforehand?'

'Well, Father Neil, you had got so fractious over the mere blessing of a canary I thought you might opt out altogether, like. Besides, did I not try to let you off lightly by rationing you to a single sausage?' He stretched out his podgy hand in fellowship. 'No hard feelings, lad?'

But this time I could not forgive him. I was lurching back to the bathroom on a far more urgent errand.

Three

FR DUDDLESWELL IS DRUNK IN CHARGE

Mrs Pring was serving breakfast in a new bottle green dress and black patent leather shoes, a sure sign that today was her birthday.

I complimented her on her hair-do and presented her with a Parker pen. Fr Duddleswell's gifts were more exotic. The housekeeper's excitement mounted as she rummaged in the carrier bag he had placed on the window-ledge. A cameo brooch, a microlite table lamp for her bedside and, last, well wrapped up, a bottle of Gordon's gin.

'I don't know what to say,' she got out.

'If I had known it needed but a little gift to render you speechless, woman,' said Fr Duddleswell, 'I would have practised magnanimity towards you long ago.'

Instinctively I stood up and planted a kiss on Mrs Pring's plump cheek. That brought on the tears which Fr Duddleswell's remark was designed to check.

'Now, Mrs Pring,' he warned, 'I will not have you behaving here like a Jew in Babylon, else I will give you the full of me mouth, your twenty-first birthday or no.' I had never known him have such a blunt edge to his tongue. 'Now, wash that Ash Wednesday mug of yours, will you not? And be ready, mind, when your daughter comes to fetch you.'

At 9.30 a grey Morris Minor drew up at the back door. On hearing it, Fr Duddleswell bade me accompany him to the

kitchen. Half a dozen cards were displayed on the mantel-piece and Mrs Pring was adding another from her daughter.

'Helen,' cried Fr Duddleswell delightedly.

'Uncle Charlie,' returned Helen, and she raced towards him with outstretched arms.

When the embrace was over, Fr Duddleswell introduced me to his 'niece'. Helen Phipps was in her early thirties, pretty, petite and smartly dressed.

'Father Neil,' said Fr Duddleswell, drawing himself up to his full five feet seven, 'is not this the beautifulest colleen that ever set foot in St Jude's?' I did not say no. 'Take that pair of sparkling eyes, now, those rosy lips. And those teeth, what are they if not Solomon's flock of even-shorn white sheep? Is she not living proof, Father Neil, that God Almighty can make a silk purse out of a sow's ear?'

'He's scrag end of mutton himself,' said Mrs Pring, stifling her real emotions, 'and he pretends he's fillet steak.' A few more tears escaped and glossed her cheek.

'Did you not hear me tell you,' said Fr Duddleswell stamping his foot, 'I will not have you dripping hot and cold in me kitchen.'

'*My* kitchen,' shouted back Mrs Pring, quite recovered all of a sudden, and Fr Duddleswell, as his costliest birthday gift to her, conceded the point. ' 'Tis worth more than double,' he said, 'so she takes her knuckles out of her eyes.'

After a few more minutes' banter and detailed instructions from Mrs Pring on how to heat up the stew for supper, Fr Duddleswell produced a two pound box of chocolates for the three grandchildren. Then a sharp, 'Be off with the both of you, and say a prayer to St Christopher, mind.'

That day we lunched at the Clinton Hotel. Fr Duddleswell told me how Mrs Pring had been with him 'the worst part of

twenty years'. It had not hit me before that Helen, whom I had met for the first time that morning, must have been with her mother when Mrs Pring 'took up office'.

Every time my parish priest spoke of Helen his eyes shone. As the meal wore on he was quite voluble in her praises. It could be his two half pints of ale had something to do with it.

After coffee, he asked if I were ready for home. I had drunk my usual couple of glasses of wine. 'Certainly, Uncle Charlie,' I said. I thought my impertinence may have affected him because it was with difficulty that he rose to his feet.

Though drowsy, I noticed in the car that he kept blinking furiously, and once he leaned over the wheel to rub the windscreen with his sleeve as if it were misted up.

His erratic driving shook me out of my somnolence. I hung on to my seat with both hands and joined Mrs Pring and daughter in fervent prayers to St Christopher.

It was market day in the High Street. There Fr Duddleswell swerved and hit a greengrocer's stall. Fortunately, we had slowed to about five miles per hour, but the barrow collapsed instantly. Pyramids of apples, oranges, tomatoes and melons were tossed in all directions. Many burst and squelched under the tyres of buses and cars.

Fr Duddleswell braked in a daze, his face ashen and his knuckles white. As he clutched the wheel, he was shaking visibly.

A noisy crowd was gathering and the stall holder was cursing in colourful cockney as he tried to recover some of his fruit and veg.

Within thirty seconds a police car was on the scene and out stepped the two constables who had invaded Mrs Pring's kitchen on the night I couldn't sleep.

P.C. Winkworth and P.C. Richards, approaching slowly

from the front, recognized us immediately and exchanged a glance. Once more the senior of them started to take out his notebook.

He opened the door on Fr Duddleswell's side. 'Would you care to step outside for a moment, sir, and show me your driving licence?'

Fr Duddleswell heaved himself out and held on to the door to stop himself falling. 'I'm not feeling ...' he began.

P.C. Winkworth sniffed sardonically through his small red nose. 'Been wetting your whistle, have you, sir?'

I leaned over and called out, 'Only two halves of ale, Officer.'

P.C. Richards, still sporting a black eye, poked his arm through the window and grabbing my shoulder, said, 'When we want a statement from you, we'll ask for it, *sir*.'

The stall holder, senses restored, pushed to the front of the crowd. He saw for the first time that it was Fr Duddleswell who had done the damage. 'Are you okay, Father?' he asked with concern.

'I am in no way wounded, thank you, Michael,' said Fr Duddleswell, grateful no doubt that the stall holder was one of the good people of his parish.

He summed up Fr Duddleswell's predicament in a flash and, having no love for the Law, he apologized for pushing his barrow too far into the road. 'I might 'ave caused you two Fathers to be involved in a ruddy accident.'

The two coppers took the hint, but P.C. Winkworth declared doggedly that they would have to run the older clergyman in on suspicion of being drunk while driving.

Since I couldn't drive, P.C. Richards radioed Control for a breakdown van to tow our car to the police compound. Then we were driven to the Station.

There again fortune smiled on us. The Sergeant on duty

was Patrick O'Hara. He touched his forelock in salute as we approached his desk attended by his two junior colleagues.

The reception area, with its pale blue walls, was as inhospitable as a public lavatory. 'I have not been to gaol,' muttered Fr Duddleswell, 'since me last game of Monopoly.'

'Drunk in charge,' asserted Black Eye.

'Is that so, now?' said Sergeant O'Hara, peering over an enormous nose. 'And which of the two reverend gentlemen would you be accusing of this heinous crime?'

'The short fat one,' growled P.C. Winkworth, aware of forces at work here beyond his comprehension.

The Sergeant persuaded the two constables to leave the matter with him for a few minutes while they bought themselves a well-earned cup of tea. After they had gone, with some reluctance, Sergeant O'Hara made no bones about it: when there was a conflict between the Law and the Gospel, it was his duty as a policeman to uphold the Gospel.

'There is not a word of truth to it, Paddy,' whispered Fr Duddleswell in a confessional tone of voice. 'I came over queer, I am telling you, but not even a girl-child could become inebriated on one pint of diluted ale. Must have been something I ate.'

Sergeant O'Hara broke the news to Fr Duddleswell that it was his sad duty to summon one of the doctors on their list. 'What would you say, Father, to being examined by a Dr Daley?'

In ten minutes, Dr Daley arrived in bulk. Beads of perspiration stood out on a pink head bald but for a narrow circlet of white hair. His eyes were more bloodshot than usual. A cigarette was wedged in the corner of his mouth. The smell of whisky preceded him as he advanced, humming for our benefit, 'When constabulary duty's to be done, to be done.'

Having listened with scant interest to the charge in the presence of the two constables, he asked the Sergeant to be allowed to examine the accused in the politeness of a cell.

The three of us sat round a table on which Dr Daley placed his black bag. 'Now, Charles,' he said, 'I hear it rumoured you have been drowning the shamrock, like.'

'A few sips of ale only, Donal. Barely enough to wet me tonsils.'

'I cannot smell any alcohol on your breath, Charles, that's for sure,' said Dr Daley, suppressing a burp.

'Donal,' said Fr Duddleswell, 'in all the years we have been acquainted, have you ever known me be guilty of foolishness?'

'Indeed I have not. I have confessed to you the same many a time,' said Dr Daley choking, 'and I have another assignation with you next Saturday night and all, when my hope is you will pity me as now I pity you.' He sighed audibly and tapped his waistcoated tummy. 'It shames me that when I'm in my cups, my brogue betrayeth me and I betray the Green.' Another heave of his broad chest. 'Sweet Jesus, but it is hard, Charles, mighty hard to mortify the meat.' He slowly shook his head. 'I have this thirst on me, you see, like a fire. It is stoked by quenching.'

He went mawkishly on about his shame at allowing himself to become over the years 'as round as a pickled onion and more entirely tonsured by time, Charles, than even yourself.'

At length, he emerged from his reverie to assure Fr Duddleswell he would vouch for the innocence of one who had never raised his hand at any man, saving in holy benediction. It was blasphemous to contemplate his reverence being brought before a hanging magistrate and having his licence endorsed or taken away.

Dr Daley opened his bag. A bottle clinked as he took out his stethoscope. Good, I thought, as he put it round his neck, at last the medical examination is about to begin. I was wrong. It had just ended. The doctor was walking briskly towards the door. He paused with his hand on the knob to ask, 'And why, Charles, do you think these constables are endeavouring to smirch your excellent good name?'

Fr Duddleswell staggered to his feet. He explained that they had burst into our house one night without a warrant screaming obscenities and Father Neil had bravely blacked the eye of one before the other kneed him in the unmentionables.

Dr Daley nodded sagely. 'That clears that up, then.' He flung the door open, pushed Fr Duddleswell ahead of him and proclaimed in the manner of Pontius Pilate, 'Look at this man. I can find nothing to charge him with.'

'But,' protested Black Eye, 'you haven't made him walk the gang-plank yet.'

'Nor have I, Constable,' said Dr Daley. 'Nor have I.' He gestured to a thin white line parallel to the wall and indicated to Fr Duddleswell that he should walk carefully.

'Father Neil,' whispered Fr Duddleswell in my ear, 'I never had much of a talent for treading the straight and narrow.'

I patted him on the back for luck and he followed the white line steadily enough until the end when he lurched to his right.

'There, what did we say?' called out Constable Winkworth, 'he's drunk.'

'He is as shober, shir,' said Dr Daley, 'as you or I. Watch me.' He gave a dramatic slow motion imitation of a tightrope walker that would have earned him half a dozen deaths.

Sergeant O'Hara was completely convinced. 'Well, lads,'

he said kindly to the constables, 'it seems as if we'll have to drop charges.'

Outside, Dr Daley expressed himself satisfied that justice had been seen to be done. He told Fr Duddleswell he was probably suffering from a bilious attack. Nothing that a good dose of salts wouldn't care. 'If not,' he said, 'pay me a visit at my surgery.'

He volunteered to give us a lift home but we preferred to walk and go on living. I phoned George Walker, a trusted parishioner, asking him to pick up Fr Duddleswell's car from the police compound and took 'the drunk' home in a taxi.

At the presbytery, Fr Duddleswell leaned on me as he went upstairs to his bedroom. When I left him, I heard him bumping into things. After that, silence.

He did not appear at tea, and as supper approached he banged on my wall. I found him propped up in bed. 'Everything keeps spinning round, Father Neil, like a catherine wheel,' he said, 'till the world turns white as the skirt of a poached egg.'

I ate the stew alone and waited anxiously for Mrs Pring's return. At 10 o'clock, she came in with Helen. She sensed that something was wrong and rushed upstairs leaving me to chat awhile across the kitchen table with Helen.

It was easy to talk to Helen. She told me that when she was in her early teens her mother couldn't make ends meet on a war widow's pension. Jobs were hard to come by during and after the Depression. Fr Duddleswell had given her mother employment and both of them a roof over their heads. 'I never knew my father,' she said simply, 'so Uncle Charlie was a kind of father to me.'

Helen had lived in presbyteries until she married Bill, a solicitor. 'He had to give a good account of himself to Uncle

Charlie, I can tell you,' she laughed. 'Uncle Charlie even pressurized him into becoming a Catholic. He didn't want any mixed marriage for "our Helen", he used to say, and for once Mum agreed with him.'

I felt sufficiently at ease to ask Helen why her mother and Fr Duddleswell were always at one another's throats. 'That's his way of showing her affection without competing with my father,' Helen replied. 'Once he said to me, "Helen, I only ridicule your mother so she realizes that in my eyes she is not beneath contempt." It slipped out really, Father, but I think he was trying to say that if he was merely polite to her as most priests are to their housekeepers he would not be respecting her as she deserved.'

It sounded to me more like an enigma than an explanation but just then Mrs Pring returned. 'A real puzzle,' she said. 'He has no temperature and he's not vomiting, and yet he feels terribly sick and dizzy. It's either biliousness or food poisoning.'

At the Clinton Hotel, he had eaten pork fillet whereas I had chosen lamb cutlets. The pork might have been off but that was unlikely in view of the Hotel's high standard of catering and the speed with which Fr Duddleswell had succumbed after lunch. Only time would tell what was really wrong with him.

For the next few days, I was Fr Duddleswell's constant companion. I assisted him at Mass. I made sure he didn't drop the chalice and I distributed Holy Communion for him.

' 'Tis a strange thing, Father Neil,' he said. 'Me head turns round faster when I am lying down than when I am standing up.' He was sleeping well enough provided he was propped up in bed, and his appetite was normal.

Mrs Pring decided that Fr D wasn't larking about this

time and insisted that Dr Daley give him a thorough examination. This was arranged for 8 p.m.

The doctor, smelling of peppermint, tapped and listened with his 'cruel Siberian stethoscope on a tropical chest', he shone a torch into his patient's eyes and ears. Afterwards, he delivered his diagnosis in one word: 'Labyrinthitis.'

'It sounds,' said Fr Duddleswell, 'as though I have a horned Minotaur prowling up and down inside me head.'

Dr Daley explained that it was not his head that was the trouble. Labyrinthitis is a virus infection of the inner ear which interferes with the balance mechanism. 'That's what I think anyhow,' he concluded.

'Do you not know for sure, Donal?'

'Dogma is your own business, Charles. I'm but a poor relation in the guessing game.'

In answer to how long it would last the doctor said, 'Ah, it is not so easy to heal the sick as to forgive sins. It usually clears up in about ten days. In the meanwhile, stay on the perpendicular as much as possible. Don't drink or drive until you get the all-clear, and get yourself a walking stick. It'll lengthen the odds on you falling over arsy-varsy.'

'I beg your pardon,' I said, not sure if I had heard correctly.

'I said I do not want our beloved P.P. pirouetting in the street like a drunken ballerina and falling bang on his bum.' My ears were in perfect working order.

The doctor prescribed tablets and promised to arrange for X-rays at the Sussex, one of the finest teaching hospitals in London, to verify his findings.

Three days later, Fr Duddleswell and I took a taxi to the Sussex. First, he was examined by Mr Taylor, a specialist who wore a kind of miner's lamp in the centre of his forehead. Fr Duddleswell complained that he was as non-committal as a

canon lawyer. After that, a nurse escorted us to a room where another white coated gentleman made Fr Duddleswell lie on a bed and directed warm water from a nozzle into his ear.

Fr Duddleswell immediately noticed that pasted on the ceiling was 'a lewd photograph'. True enough, smiling down on us from on high was a picture of a young woman in a low cut dress. Fr Duddleswell interrupted proceedings to demand an explanation for the strange location of such filth in a National Health Hospital.

The doctor said that injecting water into his ear would cause his head to spin and the picture would revolve wildly. His job was to time with a stop-watch how long it takes the patient to recover normal vision.

'Never,' returned Fr Duddleswell, 'while that hussy *in impuris naturalibus* is leering down at me.' He closed his eyes firmly until they sent for a workman with a ladder to replace the pin-up with a picture of a Beefeater on duty outside the Tower of London.

Fr Duddleswell could only manage water in one ear. When the Beefeater finally came back into focus, he felt violently sick. 'Me stomach's bid goodbye to its cage,' he said, looking not white but green about the gills.

When he had recovered, I supported him downstairs to the X-ray room. 'Take your clothes off, please, sir,' said a West Indian nurse.

'I have not the slightest intention of peeling meself like a spud beneath the public gaze,' retorted Fr Duddleswell, waving his stick at her. ' 'Tis an X-ray I am here for, not a Turkish bath.'

According to the nurse, he only had to take off his spectacles, his upper garments as far as his vest and to step out of his shoes.

Mumbling something about Soho and striptease, and

being seen in 'the altogether' and not feeling like a human being at all without his clerical collar, he complied.

A doctor appeared and pointed to a kind of operating table. 'Help your old dad up there,' he said to me. 'Oh, and by the way, get rid of that lucky charm he's wearing round his neck.' Fr Duddleswell kissed his miraculous medal passionately and handed it to me for safe custody.

Once on the horizontal, he was strapped down to prevent him moving his head while being X-rayed. Just before the pictures were taken he summoned me to him and said out of the corner of his mouth, 'Tell me truly, Father Neil, d'you reckon I will make a tolerable Frankenstein?'

As he was putting his clothes back on I realized something else was wrong with him. Not only was he unsteady on his feet, he was wriggling violently from side to side like a snake sloughing off its skin.

'What's the matter, Father?'

' 'Tis the ultimate tragedy, Father Neil,' he confided. 'Me bloody collar stud has slipped down me back.'

I encouraged him to keep wriggling and the stud was bound to reappear at the bottom of a trouser leg. After three minutes of contortions it was clear I'd been too optimistic.

'I am afraid,' he said through clenched teeth, 'that the cursèd thing is stranded inside me Long Johns.'

I looked at him in surprise. The weather was still far too mild to justify him taking to his winter woollies.

'I was not aiming under any circumstances, you follow Father Neil? to parade up and down this hospital like Adam before the Fall.'

There was nothing for it but to locate the stud and work it downwards. I fingered it as far as his left calf, after which it would not budge. I asked the coloured nurse if she could lend me a pair of surgical scissors. The only pair she had

were the size of garden shears. I snipped a hole in the Long Johns and Fr Duddleswell was happy again. 'Me curate has just removed a worrying little abscess, nurse,' he explained.

As we were leaving, the nurse took me aside and advised me to go straight home and put the 'poor old chap' to bed with a hot water bottle and a couple of aspirins.

'Father Neil,' the poor old chap said to me the next morning, '*you* will have to do it.' When I asked *what*, he replied that his imitation of Boris Karloff had gone far enough. Because he distrusted the shakiness of his hand he was now sporting a five-day growth and ' 'tis against diocesan regulations to show a chin as tufted as a billy goat's.'

I offered to shave him with my electric razor but he professed abhorrence of such new fangled gadgetry. He would much rather use sand-paper.

He drew me to the bathroom and opened up the cabinet where he stored his shaving gear. Out came a long, black handled cut-throat razor, lethal looking.

'I can't, Father,' I stammered, 'I'm maladroit, you know that.'

' 'Tis a scrubbish, mean man, so y'are, Father Neil.' I acknowledged it. 'A soft, wet potato.' No description, I said, ever suited me better.

Mrs Pring overheard us and volunteered for the job. The equipment was set up in her kitchen. A Toby jug for the soap mix was on the table and the leather strap hung from a hook on the door. 'Keep stropping that razor, lad,' Fr Duddleswell urged, 'unless 'tis sharp, 'twill cut me to ribbons.'

Mrs Pring sat him down on a straight backed dining room chair and draped a towel round his neck so that he looked like a criminal in the stocks. 'I'll never have a better op-

portunity,' she giggled. She removed his spectacles and asked him if he wished to be blindfolded. 'Any last requests, Fr D? Burial? Cremation?' Then she lathered him to his eyes.

I handed her the razor. She rubbed the edge lightly against her left index finger. 'Into Thy hands, O Lord,' he prayed. She made a scything movement in the air and expressed satisfaction that now Father Neil had given her the tools, she would finish the job.

'He was led,' intoned Fr Duddleswell, 'like a lamb to the slaughter.'

'And,' took up Mrs Pring, 'he opened not his mouth.'

'Neither *will* I, woman, provided you do not wave that thing around like a crazy Samurai.'

'Close it,' she warned, pointing the razor at his frothing mouth, and he obliged by closing his eyes, too.

For two minutes not a sound from Fr Duddleswell, only the crunch and scrape of the razor on his beard. 'Not so much of your lip, please, Samson,' rejoiced Mrs Pring, as she wiped the razor clean on a piece of tissue paper.

He only yelled once when she very slightly grazed his chin. 'Oh,' cried Mrs Pring, 'he's haemorrhaging. Father Neil, go fast and fetch Dr Daley to patch up his pimple.'

Her last great moment came as she was finishing off his upper lip. '*Alo-ong came a blackbird*,' she sang, '*and*'—zip—'*pe-ecked off his nose.*'

Fr Duddleswell rose unsteadily and walked off without a word. 'One thing, Father Neil,' Mrs Pring said to me with a wink which had more worry than humour in it, 'there's proof that you *can* get blood out of a stone.'

Mrs Pring did not take her day off that week. It showed how anxious she was about him. She gave me an envelope containing a ten shilling note 'for a Mass for Fr D' and she con-

fessed to saying not just the rosary, but the trimmings as well for his recovery.

That evening I heard Fr Duddleswell groaning in his bedroom and went to see what was wrong. 'You will never believe this, lad,' he said, 'but now I have the bloody toothache. Am I not stricken enough without fresh pains in me kneaders and grinders?'

Mrs Pring's hearing was very acute. She was at his side in an instant.

He turned a swollen cheek to me. 'Am I all the while to have that bold woman on sentry duty at me door, Father Neil, staring at me with both ears?'

Mrs Pring declared she would call the dentist first thing in the morning and fix an appointment.

'If I am to die, Mrs Pring,' he said, upright against the pillow, 'what is the purpose of me suffering first in the dentist's chair?'

'Oh, Father,' I blurted out, 'surely you don't want to die with a toothache'—at which they both laughed heartily.

Mrs Pring had her way and at 11 o'clock next morning Fr Duddleswell was in the torturer's chair.

'Well, what is the verdict, Tom?' he said to the tall, thin, slightly cross-eyed dentist who had examined him. 'Are you about to shove your road digging equipment down me throat, then?'

Tom Read lowered his white mask, bit the inside of his lip and shook his head. 'It'll have to come out, Father.'

'Never! 'Tis me best ivory by far, the last of me wisdom teeth.'

'I'll give you an injection for it, Father.'

'May be so, Tom,' said Fr Duddleswell, eyeing the long syringe on the glass table top, 'but what will you give me for the injection?'

As the young lady assistant prepared the instruments, Fr Duddleswell recounted briefly the course of his distintegration. Vertigo, being shaved by a woman, having to walk on his curate's arm, or with the aid of a walking stick, and now the last worthwhile tooth in his head about to bite the dust.

I closed my eyes at the point where Fr Duddleswell seemed to be swallowing the dentist's fist.

On our return, Mrs Pring immediately noticed the blood on Fr Duddleswell's lips. ''Tis nothing,' he said with merciful speed. 'I have only parted company till resurrection day with one of me teeth.'

Mrs Pring's rejoinder was instantaneous. 'That's one less for your Reverence to gnash in the Fire.'

He sat down and screwed his tongue into the blood filled cavity before turning to me. 'Father Neil, here am I, down on me luck like Job on his dunghill, and there is herself taunting me like Eliphaz the Temanite.'

Mrs Pring offered him sixpence for the tooth. 'If the mice don't want it,' she said, 'I can always leave it to the diocese as a first-class relic.'

Fr Duddleswell did not appear to mind the fact that his most valuable pair of scissors no longer matched. I think it was because he was so relieved the vertigo was disappearing. When he reclined in Tom Read's chair he had expected his head to start whirling faster than a dentist's drill. Instead, he felt no ill effects. 'What is left of me,' he prophesied, 'is on the mend.'

On the morning we returned to the Sussex Hospital to learn the results of his X-ray, Fr Duddleswell was in buoyant mood. He was sure he would be given a clean bill of health.

A stunning Korean nurse ushered us into a cubicle where we were asked to wait for Mr Taylor.

'Did you see that nurse, Father Neil?' he whistled. 'She is wearing black stockings in mourningful anticipation of me decease. Some of them have such sweet faces on 'em they would turn me head any day of the week.'

He went on to joke about the kind of funeral he looked forward to. A hearse drawn by six black horses. A solemn sung Requiem with the Bishop preaching a panegyric packed with the most beauteous mendacities. Trembling hands lowering him gently into the narrow house. The clergy chanting *In Paradisum*, tongue-in-cheek, and after, while their tears rolled down their cheeks into their whisky glasses, taking bets on who would be the next to go. And, of course, leading the procession in a black hair net, old Mrs Pring.

That was when we became aware of Mr Taylor's voice drifting in from an inner room. He was talking on the phone in a somewhat tired voice like a judge. At that distance, I could only pick up snatches of his conversation but I distinctly made out, 'Nice old chap ... Good job there's not the complication of wife and kids ... No doubt about it ... X-rays ... Tumour on the brain ... Yep, quite inoperable ... Should see Christmas through with a bit of luck ... No pain, no ... Shall I tell him or will you? ... Thanks, Doctor ... I'll see you get all the ...'

All this time Fr Duddleswell's grip was tightening on my arm. There flashed through my mind the memory of an old lady I had once met in hospital when I was a student. She was dying and she kept describing how her head was in a whirl and she felt as if she was falling, falling from great height.

The specialist entered and peered over the top of his half-moon spectacles. 'The Reverend Charles Duddleswell?' He

was obviously surprised to see us sitting there.

'Yes,' I said.

As the specialist picked up the X-ray photographs, Fr Duddleswell sighed heavily, 'I heard your prognosis.'

'Prognosis?'

Fr Duddleswell said he didn't particularly want to leave the discussing of such sorrowful topics to his old friend Dr Daley. Mr Taylor sat there stunned for a moment trying to fathom out the situation.

He burst out with a laugh. 'I was gassing with a colleague on the phone and it wasn't about you, Mr Duddleswell. The worst you've got is a flea in the ear, so to speak.' He went on to explain that virus was a word used by the medical profession to cover up its almost total ignorance of the causes of many maladies. We were not interested.

A couple of minutes later, we shook hands with the doctor and went out, doing our best to support each other.

'Father Neil,' Fr Duddleswell said, while we waited for the taxi, 'that gentleman did not seem to realize that in the space of sixty seconds he had condemned me to death and reprieved me. Did you not hear him laugh?' And after a few moments of reflection, ' 'Tis strange how sadness and hilarity grow from the same stem like roses and thorns.'

Mrs Pring was waiting on the doorstep to check up on the efficacy of her Mass stipend. Her first sight of us could hardly have increased her hopes. We were both looking white and shaken as we stepped out of the taxi.

To Mrs Pring's enquiry, Fr Duddleswell replied with his usual delayed humour, ' 'Tis bad news, I am afraid.' Before he could conclude with, 'I am going to live,' I was stooping down to pick the housekeeper off the floor. Fortunately, she had fallen without banging her head.

I carried her to Fr Duddleswell's study, settled her in a

chair and ran to the kitchen for a glass of water. When I got back, she was already regaining consciousness. She was saying, 'Oh my head. Everything's spinning round and round.'

Fr Duddleswell said he knew how she felt.

'I'll look after you, Father dear,' she kept repeating, 'I'll look after you.'

Fr Duddleswell tried to break it gently to her that she might have a long and arduous job ahead.

'You *are* going to die, Father D?' she asked suspiciously, and she would not be fobbed off with another sip of water which was all he offered her for an answer.

I took the glass from him and stooped over Mrs Pring to make her drink but she was so outraged at his deception that she knocked me sideways. As I lifted my head, I cracked it on the stone mantelpiece right in the tender spot which had blacked the policeman's eye. There was an explosion of white light inside my skull and I sank down slowly on the carpet. When I opened my eyes, there were the three of us in a circle, clasping our heads.

Fr Duddleswell held out his hands to us guiltily. '*Ring-a ring of roses?*'

Mrs Pring pushed his hand aside. 'You are a fraud,' she cried. 'Do you hear me, Father D?'

'Mrs P,' he said, breathing heavily through his nose, 'I could hear you in me deafest ear.'

'A fraud. A fraud.'

'Be careful, woman,' he said menacingly, 'or I will raise these hands to you with the fingers hid.'

I had made my exit and bathed my bump in the bathroom a long while before the argument downstairs had ceased.

Four

THE NOVEMBER BLUES

The sermon began: ' 'Twas fifteen hundred long years ago when Edwin King of the Anglo Saxons was betwixt and between whether to receive the Christian missionaries into his kingdom.'

The sermon was being delivered in my room. 'At a banquet, one of the King's nobles arose and said, "Sire, this life compared with the life to come reminds me of one of the winter feasts which you partake of with your generals and ministers of state." '

The sermon was being given to me alone. By Mrs Pring. ' "Imagine, me dear people," says the nobleman to his King, "the snowy cold without, the blazing hearth within. Driven by the storm, a tiny threadbare sparrow enters at one door and flies in a flurry of delight around the great hall before making his way out the other." '

At this point, Mrs Pring's congregation doubled. Fr Duddleswell entered silent as a bird, and stood beside her. ' "No chill does that wee sparrow feel while he is with us, Sire. But short is his hour of warmth and contentment here. Then out flies he again into the raging tempest and the dreaded dark." '

Here Mrs Pring raised her sermon fingers solemnly. ' "Brief is man's life, Sire, as is the sparrow's." '

In chorus with the preacher, Fr Duddleswell declaimed, ' "We are as ignorant of the state which preceded our life as

71

of that which follows it." '

As Mrs Pring tailed off in surprise, Fr Duddleswell continued quietly, ' "Therefore do I feel, Sire, that if this new faith can give us more certainty than we now have, it deserves to be believed." '

After a strange lull, Fr Duddleswell said, ' 'Tis a mighty fine sermon you preach, woman.' There was not a trace of sarcasm in his voice.

Mrs Pring had forewarned me that as Mary's month of October was passing Fr Duddleswell was due for his usual fit of the November blues. November is the month of prayer for the souls in Purgatory. The purple vestments, she maintained, darkened his soul like black frost on the window pane.

' 'Twill be no ordinary November for me,' he said out of her hearing. His recent experience at the hospital had, he swore, completely refashioned him. He had examined his conscience in so far as it would stand still long enough and learned a few home truths about himself.

'Just being told you are going to die, Father Neil, is sufficient to kill you. And did I accept it? Indeed, I did not. No act of contrition. No *In manus tuas, Domine. E contra*, me faith flew into fragments and there stood I, knock-kneed and thrilled with fear. I could only picture meself stretched out like a sardine and carried on four black shoulders.' He plucked three times at his breast like the strings of a double bass and sighed. 'I always knew I was mortal, like, but not till that black day, that *dies irae*, did it so much as occur to me that I was going to die.'

I sensed that as this was an oration it would be foolish of me to interrupt.

'There is worse to come, Father Neil. When the specialist told me someone else is doomed to die instead of me, I re-

72

joiced like a heretic when the faggots went out. And though this unknown had no kith and kin to assist him through his last days I did not think even to ask for his name and address.' When I said nothing, he added, 'Not that they would have given them to me, mind.'

He slowly rose and crossed to the fire. There he sank down on his haunches and picked up a lump of coal and said:

> 'I sat on me hunkers
> I looked through me peepers
> I saw the dead buryin' the livin' '

After which he dropped the coal on to the hungry flame. 'In my case, Father Neil,' he said, rising, 'growing old is like driving backwards down a long, dark tunnel. You think you are seeing further when you are only seeing less.'

I stammered something about not judging oneself too harshly and leaning on the forgiveness of Christ, but he had not quite finished. He had decided that his life was sodden with deviousness and uncharity. He apologized for his past misdeeds and assured me from his heart that he was about to turn over a new leaf.

As October drew to its close, many other old leaves started to turn as they tumbled in golden showers to the ground. The weather was chilly and when I cycled on my early morning rounds to distribute Communion to the sick there was a mist sometimes high on the tower blocks and in the cul-de-sacs. Mrs Pring bustled about lighting fires before breakfast 'to warm and content my two wee sparrows.'

Fr Duddleswell kept his word. Whenever Mrs Pring tried to rile him, she found him lock-jawed. There he sat in a daunting silence. He gritted and bared his teeth in a pass-

able imitation of a grinning skeleton.

'Ah, Father Neil,' said Mrs Pring, 'at least he died a happy death. Has his Reverence yet reached that driving-back-wards-down-a-long-black-tunnel bit?'

He saved his remark for when she had left the room. 'Women have the advantage over us, you see, Father Neil. They have an inexhaustible fund of ignorance to draw on.' He meant this not as an insult but as a plain statement of fact.

I was the uncharitable one. I had cut back Mrs Rollings' instructions to once a fortnight so that my wounds would have a chance to heal.

That Wednesday she came clutching a copy of *The Watchtower* which a Jehovah's Witness had put through her letter-box. My heart soared for a moment at the possibility of her embracing an alien faith and then crash-landed when she said she simply wanted me to answer all their accusations against the Catholics.

The magazine had gone to town on Indulgences. I explained to my only convert—forced on me by Fr Duddles-well—that after forgiveness there remains the punishment due to sins. An Indulgence is a remission of the punishment which a holy soul in Purgatory would otherwise have to suffer.

Where did this remission come from? From the infinite treasury of Christ's merits and those of his saints. Yes, Mrs Rollings, that's why the Pope grants so many Indulgences and, yes, Mrs Rollings, only Catholics out of all mankind are eligible for them. And the days in question, Mrs Rollings, refer to the days which the early Christians spent in harsh penitential exercises and which have been commuted in recent times to prayers and good works.

'So all these lies are true, then,' she said. I asked her to

instance some of their calumnies so I might judge for myself.

'*The Watchtower* says,' she answered, 'that for a single Mass in San Francisco there was once an Indulgence attached of 32,310 years 10 days and 6 hours.' I blinked in disbelief at the sheer crudity of the fabricated figures.

'Is that more or less than a plenary Indulgence, Father?' I confessed I had no idea.

She proceeded to read for my benefit how Spaniards at five-pence a person used to pay £200,000 a year to qualify for Indulgences and how the first plenary was given by the Pope to pious Crusaders for slaughtering the Turks.

I asked caustically if the author of the scurrilous article quoted any sources. 'Yes, Father,' she said, and mentioned *A History Of The Church* by a famous Jesuit historian.

I let her ramble on, hoping she would not notice my own Papal Indulgence resplendent in its frame on the wall above her head. It entitled me to a plenary Indulgence at the moment of death provided I was in a state of grace, prayed for the Pope's intention and uttered the holy name of Jesus. Dying is bound to be a busy time.

'By wearing a scapular of the Immaculate Conception,' Mrs Rollings continued, 'a Catholic can obtain 433 plenary Indulgences and lots of partial ones.'

I could not let that pass. 'Authorities, please,' I demanded. She stumbled over the name, 'Alphonsus ... and something that looks like "liquorice".'

'Liguori?' I said and spelt it.

'That's right, Father.'

St Alphonsus is a doctor of the Church but I did not tell her that. I made a resolution not to intervene again.

'The Pope in a Jubilee year grants not merely a plenary but a *most* plenary Indulgence.' She paused and lifted her eyes from the page. 'Why should Catholics need more than a

plenary, Father?' I shook my head. 'And if,' she reasoned, 'you can earn, say, a million days of Indulgences every twenty-four hours just by saying prayers, that's not very fair on the early Christians, is it?' I felt it was not for a curate to settle issues of that magnitude. 'After all, Father, the early Christians had to scourge themselves for months on end for their pardon, and Christians today only have to recite the rosary.'

I only dimly heard her after that. Her theme was the folly of Catholics believing that souls, which are spiritual, can burn in Purgatory, and the pluck of Martin Luther, and Pope Leo X rebuilding St Peter's in Rome on the proceeds of the sale of Indulgences.

Did I have to be condemned to death and reprieved like Fr Duddleswell before I could learn to love everyone?

At supper, I chanced to say I had been talking to Mrs Rollings about Indulgences. Fr Duddleswell congratulated me on preparing for November and asked if I had told her the story of Sixtus IV's visit to the Franciscan nuns at Foligno in 1476.

'No, Father Neil? Well, now, perhaps you did not realize yourself how the Pope gave the good sisters a plenary Indulgence for the coming Feast of the Virgin. But the Holy Ghost moved him to give them something special.' I was expecting the Pope to grant the nuns a most plenary Indulgence. 'Pope Sixtus said, "Sisters, I give you full immunity from your guilt *and* your punishment every time you go to confession."'

'Fantastic,' I said.

Fr Duddleswell smiled. 'The Cardinals present had the same reaction, Father Neil. "*Every* time, Holy Father?" they gasped. His Holiness put his old hand to his heart and said, "Yes, I give these lovely sisters everything I have, like." And

76

what then, Father Neil? The Cardinals all went down on their knees pleading, "Us as well, Holy Father, us as well." "All right," said His Holiness, "you as well." ' Fr Duddleswell's eyes were glistening. 'Such a tender tale,' he said. 'I love it, indeed I do.'

I repeated one or two of the details Mrs Rollings had read from *The Watchtower*. Before I could quote the references Fr Duddleswell had drawn in a deep breath and exhaled it to dismiss the Church's accusers in a single satisfying word: 'Bigots!'

Halloween and the Feast of All Saints did nothing to lift his spirits. No more joyful songs from his gramophone. Even at Mass on All Saints Day he preached about another sparrow that rubbed its beak upon a mountain top. Every thousand years another bird of the same family followed suit. 'And when eventually, me dear people, that mighty heap was levelled to the ground, the first moment of eternity had scarcely begun.'

On November 2nd, the Feast of All Souls, he revived. Up at the crack of dawn, he popped in and out of church, praying for the departed. He celebrated each of his three Requiem Masses on the trot with lugubrious glee, pausing only to point out to his congregations that if they recited six *Paters*, *Aves* and *Glorias* and prayed for the Holy Father's intention 'a holy soul will obtain a plenary Indulgence and be freed forthwith from the pangs of Purgatory.'

My Masses followed, and after breakfast we spent the morning freeing the dead, *toties quoties*, a soul a visit, so to speak. One gulp of fresh air at the church door was sufficient to mark off one visit from another. Owing to the speed with which Fr Duddleswell prayed, by my reckoning he helped two dozen more holy souls than I to freedom. Perhaps mine,

77

I consoled myself, had been the greater sinners.

We were visiting with the Blessed Sacrament again after lunch when we spotted a shifty looking character in a brown mackintosh reading the notices pinned to the church door.

'Take a close look at Pinky Weston,' Fr Duddleswell whispered.

In the presbytery, he told me I had just seen my first Rapper. Someone who raps on doors to find out if the tenants have anything of value they are prepared to part with. Rappers are often ignoramuses which is why they mostly work in cahoots with antique dealers.

'I see,' I said, though it was only through a glass darkly.

Rappers, he told me, peep through windows hoping to find a bargain. They team up with window cleaners, interior decorators, meter readers, with anyone in fact who will give them a nod and a wink when they come across something that looks like an antique. It might be furniture, silver, pottery or glass.

Pinky Weston had a special reason for reading the notices at the back of our church. A Requiem Mass alerts him to look up the deceased's address in the Electoral Register. He visits the house before the corpse is cold, hoping a destitute widow will part with an item of value for a pittance if only to pay for the funeral.

Fr Duddleswell reported the rumour that when Pinky's offer on, say, a piece of pottery is refused, he sometimes fingers it and cracks it.

My surprise provoked Fr Duddleswell to say, 'He cracks it expertly, apologizes for the little "accident", and out of the kindness of his heart repeats his original offer. Most times the owner says he can have it now and good riddance. Pinky takes it to his dealer who fixes it so you cannot see the join. Well, what d'you say to that, Father Neil?'

'It's wrong, Father.'

'God's holy Mother, lad, 'tis bloody facinorous, so 'tis.'

'Very wrong,' I said heatedly.

I expected to be sent back into church to release a few more holy souls but the sight of Pinky Weston had turned his attention to other matters. He invited me, instead, to accompany him by underground train to the antique market in Portobello Road.

Above the roar and rattle of the train he told me how their family house in Bath, and later the one in Portobello Road, had been of great beauty. 'Full of it,' he repeated with a yell. 'Can you *hear* me? *Can you* ...'

I nodded.

I enjoyed the chatter and bustle of the cosmopolitan crowd in Portobello Road. Pigeons, like dun-coloured Holy Ghosts, pecked away at scraps on the pavement. Chestnuts were being roasted on braziers. With Bonfire Night only three days off, children stood beside stuffed scarecrows piping out, 'Penny for the Guy.' We sifted through bric-à-brac on the stalls and flattened our noses against shop windows.

He taught me about Hepplewhite armchairs, when the Sheraton period was, and once he called out, 'Look, Father Neil, a genuine Queen Anne chest of drawers dating from 1705.' I, who couldn't tell whether a woman was twenty-five or thirty-five, was terribly impressed.

We were passing a shop pasted with notices UNDER NEW MANAGEMENT when a middle-aged couple emerged. The lady wore a bright, flowered dress and butterfly-winged glasses. She tossed her blue-rinsed head derisively at the remains of a chair in the window and called to her husband who had a camera round his neck, 'Chuck, what a goddam load of junk.'

'Ten pounds for that *thing*,' said Chuck, tugging on his camera strap.

'What's that in dollars, honey?'

'A helluva lot,' grunted Chuck. 'Back home in New York, the garbage collectors would charge to take it away.'

Fr Duddleswell seized my arm and dragged me after him. Twenty yards further on, he released me and said, 'Did you hear that, Father Neil?'

'Americans,' I began, 'coming over here and ...'

'Shut your mouth. I mean, Father Neil, listen to what I am telling you. That "thing" is a bloody Chippendale.' I was about to say the chair was without a seat when I remembered that the Venus de Milo didn't have any arms and nobody seemed to mind.

'Now, hear me, Father Neil, this is what we are about to do.'

Five minutes later, we were inside the shop admiring a statue, two and a half feet high, of the Madonna and Child.

'Would you suppose,' said Fr Duddleswell in his preaching voice, 'that Mrs Pring would like to have this?'

Before I could reply, a young assistant in jeans had pushed his hair out of his eyes to enquire if he could be of help.

After some sales patter about the statue's age, its haunting beauty, the beechwood of which it was carved, its Flemish origin, he said that for us the price was £250.

Fr Duddleswell blinked, removed his spectacles and breathed on them carefully like the risen Jesus on the Apostles. He said, as he rubbed away the mist, that he thought the young gentleman had told him the statue was very old. A brand new one would surely be cheaper.

'How much did you want to spend on this lady, Guv?' the assistant sniffed.

'About five pounds,' answered Fr Duddleswell, 'maybe six.'

'What's wrong with a fountain pen?' said the assistant before retiring to an inner room where he doubtless elaborated his suggestion to a young woman in slacks who was manicuring her nails.

We moved towards the door. Fr Duddleswell half opened it and called to the young man, 'Could I perhaps have that old chair in the window for a fiver?'

The assistant, without looking up, said, 'Ninety quid.' I was thinking the Americans had got it wrong when the lad added, 'But since it's opening day you can have it for nine.'

Fr Duddleswell opened the door wider before asking me if Mrs Pring would care for that. 'Could be,' I said.

'You would not take six, I suppose?' asked Fr Duddleswell.

The young man wrenched his eyes away from his girl. 'Seven pounds ten,' he said, 'and that's my final offer.'

Grudgingly, Fr Duddleswell re-entered the shop. 'Take a cheque?'

'Cash.' And the deal was closed. 'Sorry I can't wrap it,' was the assistant's last audible irony.

Fr Duddleswell was in raptures. At breakneck speed, he sucked me in his wake until we reached DUDDLESWELL'S, formerly his father's business. Fred Dobie, the proprietor, greeted us with a smile. 'Going that way?' he asked, pointing to the railway bridge where secondhand stuff was for sale. Then, 'Good God, Fr Duddleswell, a Chippy.'

Fr Duddleswell told him how he had acquired it and, after some hard bargaining, handed over the chair in exchange for fifty pounds. Cash.

'Now,' said Fr Duddleswell to me, 'I will buy you a cup of tay.'

In the café I insisted on paying for the teas and two doughnuts. He noticed that the chap at the counter had charged

me tuppence too much and refused on principle to waive the excess fare.

I ate and drank in silence while he tried to convince me that he had not diddled the vendor; talent in recognizing *objets d'art* is what the antique trade is all about. Portobello Road would close tomorrow if people did business in any other way. The chair did not even have a seat to it. Fred Dobie was likely congratulating himself this very minute on putting one over on *him*.

My silence was more telling than any counter-argument. Gradually, he was reduced to disconnected phrases like, 'Turning over a new leaf', 'no deviousness and no uncharity', 'poor young things just starting out in the trade', and 'on November 2nd when I should have been releasing holy souls'.

His tea was untouched when he jumped up and marched out of the café. I followed him back to the shop. He told the startled young man what was what, wrote him out a cheque for £20 'to more or less split the difference', assuring him that his signature was genuine, and left.

The young man came running after him with the statue of the Madonna and Child. 'I'm grateful, truly grateful,' he said. 'Please take this as a gift for your lady friend.'

I was staggered at such generosity. 'Virtue is rewarded.' I crowed, when the young man was back inside his shop chatting up his girl.

'Do not be such a bloody fool, Father Neil,' he snarled. 'Nobody here gives you a handful of water for nothing.'

'A fake, Father?'

He nodded. 'At least 'twill never suffer from woodworm.'

'Plaster?'

Another nod. 'Woolworth's could not sell it for sixpence. Still, I reckon Mrs Pring will prefer it to a Chippendale that

is as open as a navvy's toilet.' He handed the statue to me as if it was more than his reputation was worth to be seen in its company.

In Pembroke Road, seeing a single leaf floating down from a sycamore tree, he recited something about angel hosts that fall '*Thick as autumnal leaves that strow the brooks/In Vallombrosa.*'

His continuing purpose of amendment impressed me. If only it had not brought upon him another fit of the November blues.

On the way home it was all *Ecclesiastes* and *Omar Khayyám*. '*Vanity of vanities*' followed by '*Alas that Spring should vanish with the Rose*'. The only interlude was when we stopped at a Games Shop in the High Street. Fr Duddleswell ordered five pounds worth of assorted fireworks to be delivered to the orphanage for Guy Fawkes Day, November 5th.

At the presbytery door we were met by Mrs Pring. 'I'm glad you're back, Fr D. Someone just phoned to say Jack Dodson is sinking.'

Fr Duddleswell snatched the statue from me, placed it in her arms and rushed to collect the holy oils. Mrs Pring called out over the Virgin's crowned head that he should wear his overcoat against the cold, but he was already on his way. 'Take care of the confessions for me, Father Neil, in case I should be late.'

I did duty for him in the confessional and ate supper alone. My worries grew when curfew hour arrived and still no sign of him. At 11.15, Mrs Pring put a thermos flask in his study and retired for the night.

At nearly midnight, Fr Duddleswell came in panting furiously. He charged past me as I stood at the foot of the stairs

saying, 'Tell you about it later.' I could hear him unbolting the church door.

In two minutes the bolts clanged to, and he reappeared. In his study he frantically unscrewed the top of the thermos flask and poured himself a cup of Ovaltine. He had taken one sip when the clock on his shelf chimed 'the Mephistophelean hour'. He put his drink down disappointedly. He could drink no more if he was to celebrate Mass the next morning.

I was concerned about him. He had not eaten or drunk a thing since lunch and not even a drop of water would pass his lips until after his second Sunday Mass at 10 o'clock.

I apologized for having ruined his tea. ' 'Tis of no consequence, Father Neil,' he said gallantly. 'This afternoon, you saved me from further deviousness and uncharity. I am much obliged to you.'

I asked about Mr Dodson. 'He passed over at 10.30.' My parish priest looked tired and sad. ' *"The Leaves of Life keep falling one by one."*' He rubbed his eyes beneath his spectacles. 'I stayed to console the widow, like, on this her longest day. Ah, for her to be single-bedded after all these years. 'Tis enough to make an onion weep. No man at night to snug her and melt her with his breath.' Then a thought cheered him up a bit. 'Went off in style, though, did old Jack. It happened well to him. The last rites. He had it all, including the Papal Blessing. A very healthy death. Most likely he went straight home to God on angels' wings.'

Since Mr Dodson had obtained a plenary Indulgence from the Pope, why had Fr Duddleswell rushed into the church before All Souls' Day was over to get him another?

He read me. ' 'Twas to make sure, like.'

On Monday morning at 10.00, we set off together to comfort

the widow Dodson. On our walk, Fr Duddleswell expounded his views on Purgatory, the Catholics' half-way house to Heaven.

'The trouble with Protestant theologians, Father Neil, is they have no imagination. 'Tis their mistaken opinion that the bereaved like to think of their loved ones being taken immediately to Paradise.'

My reaction must have put me among the Protestants. 'When you lose someone you love,' he explained, 'you experience the overpowering need to comfort them. 'Tis hard indeed to picture the dead as blissfully content while you are still shattered and torn by the losing of them. There must be attunement betwixt living and dead, you follow? The Church's teaching on Purgatory takes account of this.' His view was that when the sorrows of the bereaved ease off and they leave *their* Purgatory then they are ready to feel that their dead have entered the joys of Heaven.

'What about the plenary Indulgence for the dead?' I asked.

'The faithful believe it and they do not believe it,' he said, which made the faithful seem as devious as himself.

The Dodsons lived in a prefab, that single story, factory-built house, lowered into position almost in one piece.

Mrs Dodson, white-haired and almost worn away to nothing by time, was touched by our visit. 'Come in, Fathers,' she said, 'while I make ye a cup of tea.'

Fr Duddleswell took her right forearm, pressed it tightly and simply said, 'Mary.'

Mrs Dodson put the kettle on the hob. While waiting for it to boil, she reminisced. Fifty-three years they had been together. God was good to let them see in the Gold.

'You'll never believe it, Fathers,' she confided, 'but when we wed, we couldn't afford a ring. So I went to the haber-

dasher's and bought myself a brass curtain hook. One farthing it cost.'

That hook had lasted fifty years when they bought each other a fourteen carat gold ring. 'His was engraved FOR MY DARLING JACK and mine has FOR MY DARLING MARY. I could have kept his, Fathers,' she said, wiping away a tear, 'but I thought it'd be nice if he wore it to Heaven.'

'A wise fellow, your Jack, Mary,' Fr Duddleswell put in hastily, 'arranging to go on the most propitious day of the year, All Souls, when Purgatory is cleaned out.'

'God's help is nearer than the door,' she said. As she made the tea she explained that out of their savings she was paying for a splendid funeral. 'He didn't want to go owing nobody nothing, Fathers.' The money even ran to a solid oak coffin.

'That's nice,' I said for something to say.

We sat sipping our tea until Fr Duddleswell picked up a large, pitted silver pot from the sideboard. 'How interesting,' he said with a curious nostalgic smile, 'how *very* interesting. Mary, did you know ...?'

The doorbell interrupted him. Probably a neighbour calling to offer sympathy. When Mrs Dodson opened the door, we heard a simpering voice say, 'Mrs Dodson?'

'Yes.'

'I was a close friend of your husband.'

The caller's name was Philip Weston. 'But friends of mine like your James call me Pinky.'

Father Duddleswell confided to me, 'That sharper must have the periscopic eyes of a toad.'

Mrs Dodson had to admit that her Jack had never mentioned him but she thanked him for the courtesy of his call.

'I used to have the odd drink with Jack in the local.'

Mrs Dodson said it must have been a long time ago because he had been bed-ridden for the last ten years. Pinky Weston conceded it was a long time ago. 'But you don't forget easy an old crony like Jack Dodson.'

Mrs Dodson was unwilling to let Pinky in until Fr Duddleswell called out, ' 'Tis all right, Mary, we are just about to take our leave.'

Pinky Weston's flat white face looked as if it were permanently pressed against a windowpane. Fr Duddleswell took no notice of him. Still with the pot in his hand, he said, 'As I was telling you, Mary, I am very intrigued by this pot.'

'My granma gave it me years ago,' said Mary. '*Her* granny, I believe, gave it to *her*.'

Fr Duddleswell smiled broadly. 'That accounts for it, then. My own father, God rest him, had one like this. Elizabethan silver.' When Mary expressed surprise at it being real silver, he said that the coating was worn off and perhaps she didn't realize that antiques are often worth considerably less when they are re-silvered.

Patrick Duddleswell Senior had sold his for £95. 'Mark you, Mary, 'twould be worth every penny of £200 were it up for sale today.' He pointed to indentations on the lid. 'There, it looks as if a fork has pressed down on the metal. Tiger marks.'

It seemed to me that Fr Duddleswell had cleverly warned Mary not to part with a family treasure. Pinky Weston must also have known that if he swindled the old widow he would have to answer for it to the Church.

At the door, Fr Duddleswell said, 'Keep in mind the old saying, Mary: "The three most beautiful things in the world are a ship under sail, a tree in bloom and a holy man on his death-bed." ' Mrs Dodson half-smiled and half-cried. 'Oh,

and by the way, Mary, which undertaker have you settled on?'

'Bottesford's,' she said.

I apologized for making no contribution to the visit. 'You are wrong,' he returned. 'You said but little but you said it well. Times there are, Father Neil, when words spoil meanings. 'Tis pitiful but when the deer of their woods has departed, what can you do but grasp them with kindness?'

He fell into a reverie, only coming out of it from time to time to utter the name Bottesford. He clicked his fingers and a few minutes later we were on the doorstep of Bottesford's Funeral Parlour.

I had not seen the proprietor since he ran out of the church some weeks earlier. He was fat—Fr Duddleswell said his hand was too kind to his mouth—and he wore an atrocious ginger wig that did not blend at all well with the greying hair beneath. He had a nose that reminded me of Charles Laughton's Quasimodo in *The Hunchback of Notre Dame*. And his nostrils pointed skywards like a double-barrelled gun.

He was in the backroom. We disturbed him while he was planing the lid of a coffin which rested on a carpenter's bench.

' 'Tis a sad day for the Dismal Trade when there is no funeral, Bottesford,' said Fr Duddleswell.

The undertaker went on shuffling his plane back and forth. 'People don't die to please me,' he snapped.

Fr Duddleswell asked to be taken to the Chapel of Rest in order to pray over Mr Dodson. Mr Bottesford's attitude changed at once from defiance to anxiety. He insisted he would have to go first and prepare the Chapel. It would only

take a few minutes and in the meantime he invited us to take a seat.

When he went out, Fr Duddleswell seemed intent on taking something else. There was a large cabinet in the room full of small drawers. Fr Duddleswell opened up one after another until he came across the thing he was looking for. Whatever it was, he put it smartly in his pocket.

He made a gesture towards the coffin nearing completion. 'Look at the quality of that wood, Father Neil. Orange boxes banged together, nothing more. 'Twould not keep a corpse dry in an April shower. Not only does he fake his hair by putting a bird's nest upon his head, he also fakes coffins. What can you expect, Father Neil, of a man who makes a living out of death?'

Mr Bottesford returned puffing and blowing. He led us out and across a small grey courtyard into his Chapel of Rest. It wasn't much more than a large garden shed. Black drapes from the war years kept out the light. In the centre was a catafalque on which rested a superb oak coffin lit up at each corner by candles of yellow-ochre. No orange box in this case, I thought.

Fr Duddleswell suggested we all kneel for the *De Profundis*. '*Out of the depths have I cried to Thee, O Lord,*' he began, '*Lord, hear my voice,*' and Mr Bottesford and I joined forces with '*Let Thine ear be attentive to the voice of my supplication.*'

When the prayer was over, Fr Duddleswell approached the catafalque. 'I congratulate you, Bottesford,' he whispered, 'a most beautiful coffin.'

'Casket,' Mr Bottesford corrected him with the term favoured by the trade.

Without warning, Fr Duddleswell hammered on the coffin lid with his fist. The effect in that confined space and waver-

ing light was shattering. Mr Bottesford and I almost embraced each other in fright. Fr Duddleswell repeated his onslaught on the coffin from various angles. His recent preoccupation with death must have unhinged the old boy.

'Bottesford,' he said threateningly, ''tis as hollow as is your heart. Where is he, tell me, now, this instant.' Had the undertaker sold the body for the purposes of necromancy or scientific research? Mr Bottesford pointed to an object in shadow by the wall. 'Bring a candle, Bottesford.'

The undertaker pulled one of the huge candles out of its socket and carried it with quivering hand to where Fr Duddleswell was standing. 'Take it off,' he ordered, pointing to a tarpaulin covering something of indistinct shape.

I turned away almost expecting to see under it Jack Dodson's corpse. It was only a second coffin. It had on it a brass plate with Jack's name, his dates of birth and death, and R.I.P.

'An orange box,' said Fr Duddleswell disgustedly, 'masquerading as a coffin.' Even by candlelight I could see that the coffin was neatly covered by a kind of wallpaper of oak design. Tear-filled eyes at a funeral might not notice it.

I was sickened by the undertaker's deceit, but worse was to come. Fr Duddleswell said imperiously, 'Take it off, Bottesford. The lid, unscrew it, Bottesford.' No doubting his meaning this time.

'I can't,' he said hoarsely.

'There is no need for an exhumation order, Bottesford. He is not buried yet.'

Mr Bottesford's nerves were completely out of control. He bowed his head and the crackling candle flame shot up and singed his hair. Sparks flew and there was the odour of acrid fumes. He dropped the candle, tugged his wig off and stamped on it.

Fr Duddleswell said, ' 'Tis but a foretaste of the cremation that the Lord has in store for you, Bottesford, if you do not alter the evil of your doings.'

I couldn't help feeling sorry for him as he stood there in the macabre light, bald and trembling. But Fr Duddleswell was still not content. ' 'Tis not there is it, Bottesford?'

'He's in there all right, Father, I swear it. Please don't make me unscrew the lid.'

'You know well enough, man, I said not *he* but *it* is not in there.'

'I don't know what the hell you're spouting about,' yelled Mr Bottesford, his spirit returning as he stooped to pick up his wig.

Fr Duddleswell put his hand in his pocket and pulled out a small object that gleamed in the candlelight. 'The ring, Bottesford,' he said, almost touching the undertaker's nose with it.

'You pinched it,' whimpered Mr Bottesford, lifting his head like a dog.

'No, Bottesford, you are the miscreant who pinched it. Black you are without and black within. Father Neil is me witness that I found this ring inscribed TO ME DARLING JACK in a drawer of your workroom. 'Twas not, I take it, the corpse that placed it there.'

He made Bottesford promise on his 'Catholic's honour' that the body would be transferred to the oak coffin—'casket', muttered Mr Bottesford, his professionalism coming through—and the ring replaced on the finger.

We returned to the workshop. 'Does the name Pinky Weston mean anything to you, Bottesford?'

It was evident to Fr Duddleswell that only the undertaker could have tipped off the Rapper because no notice of Jack Dodson's death had been posted on the church door. He

warned Bottesford that if Pinky Weston had swindled old
Mary, he would get the bill. A final admonition: 'Mend your
devious ways, Bottesford, else I will see to it you no more
box or heap the cold sod on parishioners of mine.'

On the way home, I expressed disgust at Bottesford's
goings-on. Fr Duddleswell, firm in his charitable resolve, did
not entirely agree. ''Tis true that grave-digger would con-
diddle the chocolate out of a child's mouth.' All the same,
Bottesford performed the least loved of the corporal works
of mercy, bedding down the dead.

'A man's profession is bound to set its mark on him, Father
Neil, if you're still with me. 'Tis no laughing matter tailor-
ing wooden suits and attending a hundred funerals a year.
For that he needs a heart that cannot feel and a nose that
cannot smell.'

I reminded him of his words about Mr Bottesford making
a living out of death. 'And do not we with our Requiems,
lad? After all, Bottesford is not Adam. He did not invent
death. Indeed, by raising the cost of dying, he might even be
said to discourage it.'

Even when I mentioned the ring, Fr Duddleswell inclined
to forgiveness. ''Tis easy to get hot under the round collar,
Father Neil, but casting prejudice aside, to rob a cold ruin is
not nearly so bad as robbing the living.'

I was thoroughly irritated by his willingness to excuse the
undertaker. 'He robbed the living, too,' I said. 'He over-
charged Mrs Dodson for the coffin.'

'Casket,' he corrected me with a wink.

'And nearly lost her that lovely silver pot.'

Overcharging Mary, he agreed, was a different matter. No
recently bereaved person likes haggling over the price of a
funeral. It seems mean and a slur on the memory of the
departed. 'But then, Father Neil,' he said smiling, 'if I do not

judge him too harshly for that even, d'you not think I owe him something?'

We were at tea when the doorbell rang. Mrs Pring announced that it was Mrs Dodson. In a flash, Fr Duddleswell was on his feet to invite her in. He paid no heed to her protests. 'Fetch Mary a cup, will you not, Mrs Pring? And, Mary dear, pity your poor feet and sit yourself down.'

Mary's story was that Mr Weston had prevailed on her to part with her Elizabethan pot for £75 in crisp new fivers.

'That's daylight robbery,' I cried.

Fr Duddleswell told me to hear Mary out and not get so uppity for God Almighty's sake.

Mary looked crestfallen at my remark. 'It's not as if my Jack had strong attachments to that pot, Fathers.' She went on to praise Mr Weston's honesty. He had accidentally twisted one of the handles and didn't reduce his offer for all that.

Fr Duddleswell flashed at me a warning to itch where I could scratch. 'Anyone in your position obviously has need of the money, Mary.'

Mrs Dodson explained that Jack's illness took up so much of their savings 'and we're—I'm—only an old age pensioner.' When the soil had settled on the grave she would now be able to afford a nice headstone.

Mary brightened up when Fr Duddleswell congratulated her on acting so wisely. All things considered, it was not a bad price. The pot *was* damaged. Pinky had to pass it on to a dealer who would want his rake-off, and selling to dealers is not always easy. Fashions change. Pinky took a risk in that there might not be a ready market for that kind of pot at this time.

'And now, Mary,' Fr Duddleswell concluded, 'tomorrow

we will lay your darling man to rest. No more thistles where he lies, Mary, and prayers of yours will provide him with pillows of roses for his head. Ah,' he sighed, ' 'tis nice to contemplate that when yourself gets to Heaven 'twill be a country where you are well acquainted.'

He took twenty-five pounds out of his wallet saying, ' 'Tis your lucky day, Mary. Only Saturday last I rid meself of a perfectly useless chair and would you believe it, now? this is what I was paid for it.' He thrust the money into Mary's hand before she could say no. ' 'Tis not for you, Mary, mind, 'tis for Jack. Towards his headstone, you follow?'

He led the widow to the door as if she were a queen. 'Make sure, Mary, you order him a *beautiful* stone.'

When he came back half singing, *'As leaves of the trees, such is the life of man,'* I tackled him with, 'Father, don't try and excuse Mr Weston's rotten trick this time.'

'Me soul detests it, Father Neil,' he replied earnestly. 'Would that I could poke me digit in his eye.'

'Imagine cheating a dear old lady out of so much money.'

'Abso-bloody-lutely, Father Neil, except that the pot was but a common or garden tea caddy worth less than half a dollar.'

Five

HELL AND HIGH WATER

'It's a lonesome wash that there's not a man's shirt in,' said Mrs Pring. My bedroom door was open and I could see her putting my clean linen in a drawer. I nodded, knowing that she was referring to the widow Dodson who had just gone home.

I offered her the opportunity for a chat. 'Going to stoke up my fire, Mrs P?'

A couple of minutes later she was piling on the coals in my study. 'At first when you're widowed,' she puffed, as she knelt at the fireplace, 'you can't believe it's true, or if it's true it can't be happening to you. It must be either a dream or someone in the War Office got the name and number wrong. Grief draws slowly like the morning fire.'

She talked unemotionally about losing her husband. It was a long time ago. A whirlwind war time courtship. Love at first sight and she never wanted another.

One thing bothered her: she could not honestly remember the colour of his eyes. 'I know they were a sort of greeny brown, Father Neil, but I can't picture them, you see?' I pursed my lips and nodded.

'We were only married a couple of months,' she went on, brushing the grate. 'My Ted was much younger than you, of course.' I was glad she did not see my reaction to that. 'I wrote to him straight away, soon as I knew, telling him that a little someone was on the way. But the letter came back

95

with a batch of others, and with his effects. The only one unopened, it was. He was already gone, you ...' She was still for a moment. 'Two months after, the war was over. All the killing stopped.' She paused again. 'Thank God.' I wanted to touch her on the shoulder but I was too shy. 'It meant my Helen was half orphaned before she saw the light of a candle.' She wiped her eyes on her sleeve because her hands had coal dust on them. As she got up, she said, 'I think people round here like talking to you, Father Neil.' I blushed at the compliment. 'You're a listening man.'

The change of topic was abrupt. 'At least *his* attack of the sullens'—she pointed below—'is over and he's back to abnormality.'

I sat her down and told her how Fr Duddleswell had tricked Pinky Weston. I expected her to show some disapproval but as usual when we were alone she was not too hard on him.

'He's as slippery as an eel's tail,' she said, 'but he never lied to the Rapper, did he, now? He only let him lie to himself.' She blew a stray hair out of her eyes. 'Ah, if only he was half as wicked as he thinks he is he'd be such a nice man. And much more fun to live with.'

Through the floorboards, confirming Mrs Pring's view that Fr Duddleswell's November blues were over, came strains of '*The flowers that bloom in the Spring, tra la.*' Perhaps it was this song that caused Mrs Pring's *lapsus linguae*. She said, 'He may be an old sour puss outside but never mind him, inside he's full of the springs of joy.' The song ceased suddenly when the telephone rang and Fr Duddleswell took the call.

Mrs Pring was keen to know if I felt really settled in St Jude's. In my reply I carefully avoided the word 'settled'. I said life was full of interest.

'Don't take too much notice of Fr D,' she advised. As his steps sounded on the stairs, she stood up. 'As you've probably guessed by now, his great weakness is the strength of his convictions.'

There was a thump on the door. 'Are you alone, Father Neil?' When I called out that only Mrs Pring was with me he made as if to retrace his steps saying, 'That giddy woman is too many for me altogether.'

Mrs Pring opened the door and signalled to him that she was on the point of leaving. She was not offensive to him, may be to reward him for his good work on behalf of widows.

His own uncharity and deviousness had returned full blast. 'I cannot understand why you associate with her, Father Neil,' he barked. 'In every other particular you are a commendable curate. D'you not know that herself would build a nest in your ear and twitter-twitter all the day long?'

'She was talking about her husband,' I said.

That quietened him down. ' 'Tis always the young,' he said, biting his lip, 'who die in old men's wars.' He settled into an armchair clutching a large tome. 'As to the purpose of me visit.'

First came a reminder of the next day's Clergy Conference on Life After Death. Interdenominational, it was to be held at St Luke's under the chairmanship of the Anglican incumbent, the Rev. Percival Probble. In addition to the three Anglican ministers, two Methodists and a Jewish Rabbi had agreed to take part. The true Church was to be represented by the two of us and Canon Mahoney, D.D. The Canon was Bishop O'Reilly's personal theologian. He had been deputed to keep us on the path of orthodoxy and answer all non-Catholic objections.

Fr Duddleswell handed me his tome. *The Mysteries of*

Christianity by Matthias Scheeben, priced $7.50. 'Hot from the States,' he said. The author was the greatest nineteenth century German theologian. 'I want you to mug up the passages on life after death, you follow? in case the Canon and meself are unable to cope, like.' He was being funny, I think. 'If the Protestants suggest we pray for reunion, we will do no such thing, you hear me? We are far too divided to pray with them for *that*.'

The phone call had been from Mother Stephen, Superior of the Convent. She had invited herself and Sister Perpetua, our sacristan, to the presbytery in thirty minutes time. No reason had been given for the visit but Fr Duddleswell needed no telling. It was the same every year. Mother Stephen wanted to cancel the Fireworks Display at the last moment. The pretext was usually the likelihood of damage to the Convent's lawn or trees, or complaints from neighbours about the noise, or the good sisters having to keep the children in order when they should be reciting the divine office in chapel according to the rules of their holy Founder. 'Be ready to buttress me should I begin to flag,' he concluded.

On the dot of five, *Laudetur Jesus Christus* from Mother Stephen and *Semper laudetur*, 'May Christ be always praised' from Fr Duddleswell. The Superior dismissed the offer of tea with a twitch of her bony hand.

'Fr Duddleswell, I have not come to ask you to cancel the Fireworks Display tomorrow evening.' So the old man was mistaken. 'No, Father, I have been obliged to cancel it myself already.'

Fr Duddleswell enquired the reason. He was unruffled as if he were used to setbacks of this sort.

'Two-fold, Father.' For first-fold, Mother Stephen had recently read a book on the Gunpowder Plot written by a

convert to Catholicism. His thesis was that Guy Fawkes Day was a Protestant ruse to blacken Holy Mother Church. Guy Fawkes's attempt to blow up the Houses of Parliament in 1605 had been made a pretext to persecute Roman Catholics ever since.

'I should imagine, Mother,' said Fr Duddleswell, 'that had he succeeded, the whole country would have been beholden to him.' The joke was lost on the black shroud seated opposite him.

Fr Duddleswell stated politely that the Bishop had appointed *him* defender of the faith in this area and he was perfectly satisfied with the theological propriety of burning a straw man on a bonfire. In fact, it was irrefutable proof of Catholicism, a proof not immediately evident to Mother Stephen or to me. Protestants ridicule Catholics, he said, for making use of images in their religion, and here are the Protestants availing themselves of Catholic methods of festivalizing. Before Mother Stephen could object he instanced the burning of heretics at *autos da fé*, apart from Catholic belief in the retributive fires of Hell and Purgatory.

It convinced me that Guy Fawkes Day was a sound Catholic investment. Fr Duddleswell looked across at me as if to say, one down and one to go.

Mother Stephen was already fumbling in the folds of her habit for her second argument. 'This leaflet, Father,' she said, 'has been sent us by the Council. The police have co-operated with the fire brigade and the local hospitals to provide statistics of accidents to minors during last Guy Fawkes night.' She read out figures. Five children under ten had burned their hands and sixteen under six had burned their legs, and so on. It was pretty grisly.

Fr Duddleswell pretended to see no significance in the figures whatsoever.

'Fr Duddleswell, I have taken the liberty of going through the parcel of lethals you despatched to our Convent. Crackers, rockets, smellies, smokies, catherine wheels—a whole arsenal of destruction.'

Fr Duddleswell forced her to grind to a halt as he unfolded a leaflet taken from his inside pocket. He pressed out the creases noisily. 'Police statistics, Mother, on the local children killed on the road in the last year, together with the number of accidents on the pedestrian crossings themselves.' He smiled pityingly. 'You are not proposing, Mother, that children should be forbidden to cross the roads?'

The Superior accused him of flippancy. Crossing the roads was a necessity, whereas she was about to prove that a Fireworks Display was not. He was already promising that he and I would set off the fireworks. 'The only persons, Mother, in any danger are meself and me curate.' He seemed confident that Mother Stephen would agree to the Display on such generous terms.

'Fr Duddleswell, you may set yourself alight or indulge in any other solitary pleasure on our Convent lawn that brings you satisfaction. Our children will not be there to see it.'

She was rising to her feet when Mrs Pring banged on the door and entered without an invitation. Fr Duddleswell was annoyed at being interrupted at this delicate stage in the negotiations.

Mrs Pring, clasping a copy of *The Universe*, was not in the least perturbed. 'Father, I only wanted to ask you something about the Display tomorrow evening.' His face fell to below zero. 'Are you using the Holy Father's blessing?'

Fr Duddleswell thawed instantly and met her enquiry with a quizzical smile.

'Last New Year's Eve,' she explained, 'the Pope blessed the fireworks and the children of Rome. A lovely prayer, as you

remember, Father. Will you be using this'—she pointed to
where the prayer was printed in capitals in the newspaper—
'or the one in the Ritual?'

Fr Duddleswell assured her that of course he would be
using the Holy Father's own blessing written specially for
such occasions.

Mrs Pring departed to be followed soon by Mother
Stephen. She had been faced with a straight choice: to obey
God or Caesar. Sister Perpetua bowed out her defeated
Superior before winking at us.

'Sister Perpetua,' croaked Mother Stephen without turning round, 'would you kindly regulate the movements of
your eyelids in the manner of which our holy Foundress
would have approved.'

Mrs Pring expressed delight that the poor little orphans
would not be deprived of a rare chance to enjoy themselves
and Fr Duddleswell took the opportunity to relate his
favourite tale about statistics.

In the west of Ireland, 'in the dark days', a local deputation approached the English Chief Secretary, then visiting,
with statistics proving that they needed finance for the railway so they could send their produce to market. Next day,
another deputation arrived with another sheaf of statistics
proving conclusively that they needed food subsidies because
not so much as a sprig of parsley would grow on their land.
Fr Duddleswell laughed merrily before putting on a very
posh English accent. ' "Now, my good man," said the Chief
Secretary to the leader of the second deputation, "yesterday's
statistics prove the exact opposite of yours. How do you
account for it?" "So be it, your Honour," says the leader of
the second deputation, "but y'see, yesterday's statistics was
compiled for an entirely different purpose." '

The rest of that evening I spent with Scheeben, reading about death, judgement, Heaven and Hell.

After breakfast, Fr Duddleswell drove off to an unknown destination. He was back well in time to transport Canon Mahoney and me to the Vicarage.

In a committee room, we drank coffee before grouping around the table. The three Anglicans wore cassocks with capes which we always held to be an affectation. Of the two Methodists, Sobb was bearded and Tinsey was clean shaven. At the end of the table opposite Mr Probble sat Rabbi Epstein. He wore a broad-brimmed black hat on the back of his head, a bushy beard and spectacles that covered the rest of his face. He was still in a frayed black satin overcoat and, for some undisclosed reason, he had another draped across his knees. He came from somewhere east of Dover.

The Rev. d'Arcy, the Senior Anglican curate, read a thirty-minute position paper on 'Life after Death in the Old and New Testaments'. It contained frequent references to *zoè aiònios* which at first I thought was a girl's name until it dawned on me that it was Greek for 'eternal life'. Mr d'Arcy had read Greats at Oxford and his classical learning put most of what he said beyond my reach.

The first comment was made by Rabbi Epstein. Very politely he objected to the use of the *Old* Testament. 'You must remimber well,' he said in his broken English, 'that for us it only is the Jewish Bibble. *You* call him old because you think your Bibble is newer. For us, the Jewish Bibble is always newest.'

The Rev. d'Arcy apologized profusely for his careless use of terms in the present company.

'Thank you,' said the Rabbi—his 'th' was pronounced like a 'z' in the Slavonic fashion. 'Now where Heaven is? I ask

myself.' Nobody round the table was anxious to help him answer his question. 'Where God is, there Heaven is.' He tapped his outstretched fingers together as if applauding himself. 'Heaven has not a place,' he went on in a semi-mystical vein. 'God is, as we say in Talmud "*ha-Geburah*, The Might". He is the place where the world is. That is what we Jews think.'

Canon Mahoney scratched his bald head and exchanged a glance with Fr Duddleswell indicating that it is not easy looking for the invisible wee folk in the pitch dark.

'We Jews,' went on the Rabbi, his eyes so radiant it looked as if two lighted cigarettes had been sunk in the sockets, 'we Jews believe passionately in *gehenna*, the pit of the fire.' Fr Duddleswell nodded approval. 'Also *Gan Eden*, the Garden of the Bliss and the Delight.' The Canon and Fr Duddleswell both saw signs of hope in that. 'In the pit of the fire,' continued Rabbi Epstein, 'the naughty boys go.' I could see my two colleagues beginning to wonder what differences remained between ourselves and our Jewish brethren when the Rabbi said, 'What more certain could be than that Jesus in the Garden of Delight is? He was a good Jew. But,' he swung his head like a pendulum, 'some of his followers, aaaah.' That 'ah' went down his throat like the last of the bathwater, in a noisy vortex, down the drain. Well, this was a curate's egg. The rest was all bad. 'The *very* naughty boys sometimes spend a whole year in the pit of the fire before they enter the Paradise.'

Everyone at the table disapproved of that, and the Rabbi, not wishing to proselytize, said nothing after that except, 'We Jews believe there are no ghettoes in Heaven and no pogroms in Hell.'

The fat Rev. Pinkerton, puffing on his cigarette without ever removing it from his mouth, delivered his opinion on

Hell. The fire was a symbol, like the worm that never dies and the teeth that gnash on endlessly, like Christ's command to pluck out your eye rather than let it look on wickedness.

Canon Mahoney, sucking his dead pipe, launched the counter-attack, ably supported by Fr Duddleswell. The Church has taught for nigh on two thousand years the reality of the fires of Hell and the eternity of the roasting prepared for those who die unrepentant. In this the Church was simply reinforcing the teaching of our Blessed Lord who five times in the course of the Sermon on the Mount stressed the everlasting pains of the damned.

The Rev. Pinkerton stubbed out one cigarette and lit another before commenting caustically on the arbitrariness of the Catholic God. Why should He cut off one man's life immediately after mortal sin and another's immediately after he had repented of mortal sin?

Canon Mahoney handled that with ease. God in His divine foreknowledge sees how both of them *would* behave whatever opportunities for repentance He offered them.

I was very glad the Canon was in my team. But, objected Fatty, did we really think God was so cruel as to punish eternally an evil deed done in time? Fr Duddleswell drily asked the Rev. Pinkerton if *he* expected to be rewarded eternally for some good deed he might do in time.

'Okay,' wheezed Fatty, blowing out and filling the room with a pillar of cloud, 'tell me how parents can possibly be happy knowing that their children are burning for ever in Hell?'

'It is the very sweetness of divine justice,' replied Canon Mahoney, 'that will obliterate the pain, as will the vision of the beatific God.'

Mr Probble was becoming increasingly agitated as the temperature of the discussion rose. He was smiling and mur-

muring words about keeping the ecumenical spirit alive and abiding by the Great Commandment to love one another.

Mr Tinsy, an alto, demanded to know if, in Catholic dogma, children were eligible for Hell. Fr Duddleswell replied that naturally they were, provided they had reached the age of reason.

'Which is?' peeped Mr Tinsy.

'Seven or thereabouts,' answered Fr Duddleswell. Catching sight of Fatty almost swallowing his cigarette in a rage, he explained that Catholics respect the dignity of choice even among God's little ones.

Mr Tinsy remarked that 'sevens' were not even old enough to play with fireworks.

The bearded Mr Sobb asked how fire could burn bodies *and* souls, and burn them for ever without consuming them.

It was just the question I was hoping for. 'May I?' I began.

'Certainly not,' snapped Fr Duddleswell, turning to Canon Mahoney for the official answer to that conundrum.

'Let the lad say his piece, Charlie,' the Canon said kindly.

I opened my Scheeben at page 693 and read in a trembling voice:

'Hell fire differs from natural fire in this respect, that its flame is not the result of a natural, chemical process, but is sustained by divine power and therefore does not dissolve the body which it envelops, but precerves it forever in the comdition of burning agony.'

I don't know if that answered the Methodists' objections, it certainly silenced them. It even seemed to precipitate the end of the Conference. There was only small talk after that.

We Catholic clergy repaired to the Clinton Hotel. The consensus was that there was no value in such conferences and the Canon would report this to the Bishop. Jews were as incomprehensible as a woman's tantrums. The Protestants,

especially 'that fat twerp', were so stubborn in their unbelief that there was little chance of converting them.

'You'd as soon convert a cock into a hen,' suggested Fr Duddleswell.

Canon Mahoney peered moodily into his empty wine glass, proffered it to me to replenish and sighed, 'They went into a skid 400 years ago at the Reformation, Charlie, and they've been facing the wrong way ever since.'

It was a matter of amazement to us that men of the cloth could doubt the everlasting flames when they were written large and clear in the Holy Book.

The Canon savoured the wine on his tongue and smoothed out a crease on his head. 'No reverence have they, Charlie, for the Undebatables.'

' 'Tis the ultimate proof, Seamus,' said Fr Duddleswell, downing his last drop of heavy wet, 'that only the Catholic Church has the authority to keep the harsh truths of the faith alive in their pristine purity.'

Mrs Pring accompanied us in the car to the Orphanage. It was a clear, crisp, windless evening lit by moon and stars.

The Convent lawn, between bare trees, formed a kind of amphitheatre. My shoes were crunching acorns as we approached a huge bonfire built in a clearing with a Guy on top not easily distinguishable against the sky. Mother Stephen, for all her hesitations, had done us proud.

A few feet from the bonfire was a crate of empty milk bottles for the rockets and there were large flat stones for the crackers and the Roman candles.

A bell had been rung on our arrival and the children were parading in noisy expectation behind a rope at the opposite end of the lawn.

Fr Duddleswell crossed to greet them and they cheered. A

group of them came up to me holding their right hands aloft and telling me their ages, $5\frac{1}{2}$, $6\frac{3}{4}$ and so on. A minute fellow in a dwarf's cap and Wellington boots trod on my toe to attract attention and crooked his finger to make me bend down. 'A secret, Father. You won't split?' I promised. 'I'm two and four quarters,' he whispered.

I patted him on the head. 'Congratulations.' He crooked his finger again. 'Yes, son?'

'Can I have sixpence?' he said.

As soon as the nuns were present I shone a torch on to Fr Duddleswell's paper to enable him to read the Holy Father's blessing. Two sisters brought forward the fireworks which had been stored in a tin tub. These, too, he blessed. While the children sang two verses of *Faith of our Fathers*, he and I carried the tub towards the bonfire.

Fr Duddleswell wanted to begin spectacularly with a rocket. He put one in a bottle, lit the blue paper and we retreated to a safe distance away. The rocket rose about two feet in the air and nose-dived into the fire. Groans and ironic applause from the children. Mother Stephen's voice could be heard above the din asking for more respect for 'our parish priest'.

He tried again. After using five or six matches, our parish priest could not so much as set the fuse alight. He bade me shine the torch on the fireworks. They were standing in at least eight inches of water. Sabotage.

Mother Stephen crunched her way solicitously across the grass. 'Having trouble, Fr Duddleswell?'

'A temporary inconvenience, Mother, nothing more.' He motioned to me to join him. We returned to the car, to groans and catcalls from the Lord's little darlings.

Fr Duddleswell opened the car boot. There was a box of fireworks even bigger than the first. 'Never underestimate the

opposition, Father Neil. As innocent as doves we must be but as wise as serpents, besides.'

The children adored the display. 'Oohs' and 'ahs' and spontaneous applause from them with the sisters dancing around as excitedly as anyone. Fr Duddleswell and I stuffed our pockets with 'lethals' and ran here and there letting off rockets and jumping-crackers and the catherine wheels which we had pinned to the trunks of trees.

Mother Superior reappeared out of the gloom with two sisters who were carrying an enormous iron grid on which were laid vast quantities of potatoes already half baked. 'With the compliments of the Convent, Fathers,' she said.

We put the jacketed potatoes at the base of the bonfire and Fr Duddleswell waved to the children, held up a lighted match and applied it to the tinder. It flared up at once, illuminating the Guy who, I had to confess, looked very much like our parish priest. Black sacking did for a cassock. Its head was a kind of white soccer ball with spectacles inked on, and a few strands of a yellow mop were plastered over the top for hair.

Mother Stephen, who had remained in the vicinity, said above the crackle and splutter of the fire, 'The only authentic replica of *you*, Fr Duddleswell, at present in existence.' Fr Duddleswell went closer to the fire to examine the insult. 'I do agree with you, Father,' his underestimated adversary went on. 'There is something terribly Catholic about burning somebody in effigy.'

Fr Duddleswell had approached too close to the blaze. The heat must have ignited the fireworks on his person for he suffered the same fate as Mr Bottesford. Smoke and sparks flew out of his right cassock pocket and loud rumblings were heard.

Mother Stephen and I had the same thought. I snatched

the first box of fireworks out of the tub and we each took a handle and threw the contents over Fr Duddleswell. The fire on him was extinguished with a swish. He jumped up and down, damp, frightened and miserable. The children roared more delightedly than ever as he gave a good imitation of the *Danse Macabre*, etched as he was against the red flames.

'Was I not branded like a steer, now, Father Neil?'

In spite of the early hour, Fr Duddleswell was in pyjamas and dressing-gown in front of the fire. Mrs Pring had brought us both a cup of cocoa. ' 'Tis a good job me foundations are firm, like.' The same foundations were turned to the fire in the grate but not as close as before. 'Next year, I have no doubts, I will appear in Mother Stephen's statistics with the under fives and under tens. Imagine, now, "One under sixty with a burnt bum." '

I told him to have no regrets. Mother Stephen was so impressed with his performance she might demand a repeat next year.

'Ah, me one consolation in me hour of need was having a curate to stand by me come Hell or high water.'

As I sipped my cocoa, it burned my lip. 'Father,' I said, referring back to the morning, 'do you really think God will allow a son or daughter of His to burn in Hell for ever and ever?'

'In some cases,' contributed Mrs Pring, indicating her boss, 'the Almighty has no other choice.'

'But, Father, do you really believe that Scheeben stuff I read out at the Conference?' Fr Duddleswell puffed and blew and touched his scorched thigh. I persisted: 'People, ordinary people like you and me and Mrs Pring?'

Fr Duddleswell looked at me witheringly. 'Father Neil.' A pause, a deep sigh and a new beginning. 'Father Neil, Holy

Mother Church bids us believe docilely in the reality of the eternal fires of Hell. Yet who but a raving lunatic would claim there is anybody there?'

Six

ONE SINNER WHO WILL NOT REPENT

In early September, Fr Duddleswell had shown me how to make the rounds of St Jude's Junior School. It began in the playground before morning lessons. He crouched down to play marbles with a group of children. He cheated outrageously, kicking the marble in the right direction if his hand had 'not dealt kindly' with him. He always won. Afterwards, he sold the losers their marbles back at a reduced rate and gave the proceeds to more needy children—'like Robin Hood, you follow?'

In each class it was the boy or girl who could answer three Catechism questions in the shortest time without hesitations who received a silver threepenny piece. The winner had to go to the front of the class and fix it on his upturned nose. Failure to keep it there until he was back at his place meant Fr Duddleswell confiscated it on the spot.

He was convinced of the value of *The Penny Catechism*. It had served the Church well since Victorian times. It contained in a brief and eloquent form the main tenets of the Catholic faith. The child may not grasp all its subtleties at once, but in the years ahead, with maturity, would come recognition and guidance. Remembrance was guaranteed by the sheer music of the words.

'*God made me to know Him,*' he recited for my benefit, '*to love Him and to serve Him in this world, and to be happy*

with Him for ever in the next.' He dared me to suggest that Shakespeare himself ever penned more memorable lines than those.

I started with the best of intentions one Monday morning armed with two hundred assorted marbles from Fr Duddleswell's collection in a canvas bag. Unfortunately, I was no great shakes at marbles and worse still at cheating. I made little contact with the children because I lost every one of my marbles in the first twenty minutes.

In Class Five, the nines to tens, the form teacher was a charming, fair-haired Mrs Hughes. Her class knew their religion so well I could hardly make up my mind which of them could repeat the catechism fastest. Eventually I decided that a dark-haired girl in the back row had pipped the rest at the post. I signalled to her to come to the front for her reward. Mrs Hughes whispered to me, 'That's Esther, Father.'

'Esther,' I said, giving her a silver threepenny piece in her grubby little hand, 'I hope you will always know your faith as well as you do today. And may it stand you in good stead throughout your life.'

There was a stunned silence in the class. I thought the other children did not agree with my verdict or were jealous.

When Esther had returned to her place nodding to right and left—with her tongue out, I suspected—Mrs Hughes whispered again, 'Esther is Jewish, Father.'

Out of the corner of my mouth, I whispered back, 'Are there any other non-Catholics, Mrs Hughes?'

'Only one, Father.'

'Would you point to whoever it is?'

Mrs Hughes gently stabbed herself with her finger. 'I'm a Methodist,' she said.

During that Christmas term I grew to like Mrs Hughes' class best of all. They were disciplined and yet alive and full

of fun. The top class became so surly and disagreeable they refused to answer any of my questions even for sixpence. Not wanting to see them caned for a lack of interest in the religion of love, I was reduced to asking Mr Bullimore, the form teacher, to get them to write out their questions and put them in a box to which I alone had the key. I promised the children anonymity. Some of the questions were obscene, some merely abusive. Most were illiterate.

One contribution read: 'If it's a *free* cuntry why do I have to go to school eh? *and* drink milk. call *that* a free cuntry eh?' Another provided me with a piece of unwanted domestic information: 'In our hous we call dad Mosis cos he gives us 10 comandments evry day befour brekfirst.' Another was a plain affirmation: 'I don't like going to school bicause there's nothing to do when you get there except learn lots of things I don't wanner know. Another thing if they put old Bully on the telly I would switch him off before he came on.'

Interestingly enough, only the obscene ones were signed. No doubt with someone else's name.

On the morning after Fr Duddleswell had been 'burnt in more than effigy', I entered Mrs Hughes' class hoping for a taste of sanity. The children were their usual enthusiastic selves. Before I could finish any of my November questions on death, judgement, Hell and Heaven, they were bouncing their bottoms on their benches with vibrating arms outstretched and calling 'Please, Father, please, Father.'

When I had adjudged Philip in the front row to be the winner, I asked them a few more unscripted questions. 'I don't suppose any boy or girl has ever been to a funeral?'

Philip, of course, had been to everything. 'Please, Father. I went to a terrific funeral once.'

'Really, Philip?'

'Yes, Father. I saw these four dead men carrying a big box.'

Johnny, a Jamaican lad, said in a loud drawl, 'Souls don't get buried, do they, Father?'

'No, Johnny,' I assured him, 'souls go straight home to God. We only bury bodies.'

Johnny looked shattered at that. 'What do they do with the heads, then?'

Up leapt Robert, his hand in the air. 'Last year our granny came and died with us, Father.' Before I could offer him my condolences, he added joyfully, 'But we made sure she was dead before they planted her.'

Lucy Mary had more melancholy tidings. 'When Suzy my rabbit died and went to Heaven, Father,' she murmured, 'she left her carrot behind.'

Even this news did not dampen the youngsters' spirits for long. Mark said, 'Please, Father, our grandma died and went to Heaven and everyone's pleased but not grandma.'

Frank, a fat boy in long trousers, turned the tables on me by asking, 'My gran said when she gets to Heaven she'll pray for us. What makes her so sure, Father?' I said I could not answer that because I didn't know his gran.

'You must know her, Father,' Frank insisted, 'she wears glasses and brown shoes.'

'Mrs Phipps, Father,' said Sean breathlessly, 'Mrs Phipps who lives next door is dead but Dad say there's nothing else wrong with her.'

I was about to tell him that many people die only of death but satisfied myself by assuring Sean his Dad would not have said what he did if it wasn't true.

Sean had an afterthought. 'She's moved now, Father.'

To stem the tide a bit, I asked them what happens to people when they die. 'In your own words, please, children.'

That was inviting trouble.

Patricia, who looked like a little barn owl, spoke up for the rest of the class. 'If their soul's white they go to Heaven, if it's black they go to Hell and if it's got measles they go to Purgatory till it clears up.'

I glanced at Mrs Hughes to enquire whether she was trying to undermine Catholic teaching on life after death. She shrugged her shoulders disclaiming any responsibility for these heterodox opinions.

That was when I glimpsed Jimmy Baxter sitting at his desk to my right with tears running down his cheeks. It struck me that Jimmy, one of the brightest in the class, had not contributed anything that morning.

Ken piped up from the back row next to Esther. 'When my grandpa went to Heaven, Father, he was very, very old so I don't s'ppose he'll last there long, will he?' I was too distracted by Jimmy's tears to reply to that, or to correct Judy who called out, 'Stupid! In Heaven everybody's made of stainless steel, aren't they, Father?'

'Please, Father,' shouted Dean, the terror of the class, 'when you go to Hell can you take your dog with you?'

'Certainly not,' I said, still looking at Jimmy Baxter out of the corner of my eye.

'Mine likes it in front of the fire, Father.'

Mrs Hughes called things to a halt by telling the children to get on with their sums. It gave me the chance to ask her what was the matter with Jimmy. She referred me to the Headmistress.

Miss Bumple, of uncertain age, had been teaching long before systematic training had been devised for teachers. She was an amiable eccentric. Somewhere in her long campaign, she had been decorated with a cauliflower ear, the only one

I had ever seen on a woman. She still wore an earring in it. Her mother had had her ears pierced when she was a baby and it wasn't like Miss Bumple 'to waste the holes'.

Her eyebrows were white but her short cut hair was dyed an unnatural black. Fr Duddleswell had briefed me on her vocabulary which consisted basically of permutations of the one word 'egregious'. 'Egregious' for Miss Bumple meant 'normal'. 'Highly egregious' meant 'entertaining'. 'Exceedingly egregious' meant 'very funny'. 'Excessively egregious' meant 'intolerable', 'beyond the joke'.

For all her strangeness, Miss Bumple, according to Fr Duddleswell, was entirely trustworthy. Whatever you said to her in confidence went in one of her ears and was corked by the other.

On this November 6th, the Head, dressed in her usual tweeds, was in her jumble sale of an office surrounded by cups and trophies that looked gold until closer inspection revealed them to be of tarnished silver.

Taking a big pull on her cheroot, she rose to greet me. 'Fr Boyd,' she exhaled all over me with gusto, '*delighted.*' When she spoke she tightened her cheek muscles and pursed her lips as if she were about to blow a trumpet. Her voice, with an East London edge to it, was both musical and compelling. She grabbed my hand and almost wrenched my arm out of its socket.

I told her I was worried about Jimmy Baxter. 'Dearie me,' she said, 'that is not exceedingly egregious.' Jimmy's grandfather, Mr Bingley, had been poorly for some time and now was proper poorly. Jimmy was very attached to him. Since his dad had died, Jimmy had been brought up by his grandfather.

When I offered to help, Miss Bumple surprised me by her insistence that I was no use in this instance. Jimmy was

simply frightened that because his grandfather did not believe in God and never went to Church he would go to Hell
when he died.

'If, Fr Boyd, you tell children there is a Hell and that unrepentant sinners go there,' trumpeted Miss Bumple, 'they
are bound to draw their own conclusions. Mr Bingley, you
see, is a lapsed Catholic. This makes the matter'—she loosed
a huge current of smoke—'excessively egregious'.

I returned to the presbytery in an unhappy frame of mind.
Mrs Pring informed me that 'the Rooster' was in the garage.
I found him lying on an old rug underneath his car. When
I hailed him, he slid out and eyed me from the ground. He
had on a Churchillian boiler-suit, his face and hands were
covered in oil.

Bingley, J.J., he told me, had once been a model Catholic.
His misfortune was at the age of twenty-five to marry a girl
who turned out to be a whore. She had walked out on him
after only three months in favour of a Russian sailor. After
ten years, J.J. had divorced her and married again outside
the Church. His second wife was a Catholic, too. It was the
great sorrow of her life that she was barred from the sacraments. J.J. took a more truculent line. He repudiated the
harshness of the Church's teaching, renounced his faith in
God and joined the ranks of the Friday meat-eaters. He even
became a paid-up member of the Communist Party.
Maureen, his wife, had insisted all the same in bringing up
the two girls as Catholics. The elder of the two, Janice, was
Jimmy's mother.

I remembered that Mr Bingley was a widower. 'Hadn't
that made a difference?'

'Only for the worse, Father Neil. I anointed Maureen
and buried her meself. J.J. would not attend her funeral. It
made him even more bitter to learn that now his woman was

taken from him he was free to return to the Church. He would *not*. If his wife was deprived of the sacraments throughout their marriage, so would he be till his dying day. And I believe he is unshaken in his resolve. He is one sinner who will not repent.'

When he saw my eagerness to help he let me go to the hospital with the warning not to be disappointed if I did not succeed. 'J.J. is as loggerheaded a fellow as you are ever likely to meet.'

Jimmy's mother was by her father's bed at the end of a long ward. From a distance I could see them chatting. Mrs Baxter was tucking in the bedclothes and patting the pillow. When she caught sight of me, I thought I saw both pleasure and apprehension on her face.

I introduced myself. Mr Bingley was high up in the bed with his long white hair trailing on the pillow. His skin was taut over his face as though it were covered with a white stocking. And he stared right through me.

It was an unnerving experience. Nothing I said made any impression on him. Not a smile or the blink of an eyelid. As far as he was concerned I did not exist.

I spoke to Mrs Baxter. 'Would you leave us for a few moments, please?' Mrs Baxter immediately rose up and went. I explained very simply to the old man why I had come. Not for his sake but for Jimmy's. I told him about my visit to the school and Jimmy's tears.

He could have been carved out of granite. After a couple of minutes, I gave up, murmured 'God bless you' and joined Mrs Baxter in the corridor. She was crying. She knew her father hadn't long left. Jimmy, she said, would never get over it if her father died without confessing his sins so he could go to Heaven with grandma.

With nurses passing to and fro nearby, I explained as best

I could that only God knows what goes on in a man's heart. Someone could receive the sacraments and still be a bad man. Another could refuse the sacraments and still be humble and acceptable to God like the publican in Jesus' lovely parable.

It consoled her a little. 'But how can I explain that to a nine-year-old, Father?' she asked. 'Jimmy keeps saying grandpa commits a mortal sin every Sunday and Holy day by not attending Mass and I say it's not a new mortal sin each time, Jimmy.' She looked up at me to enquire whether or not she was propounding heresy. 'It's not a lot of mortal sins, is it, Father?' I didn't reply. 'Isn't it just one? A big one, perhaps? But just one?' She pleaded with me for a merciful reply.

'Once is enough,' I said hedging. I followed it with the only answer that would fit the situation, slightly modified from *The Confessions Of St Augustine*. 'It's impossible for Mr Bingley to perish when his little grandson is crying for him.'

Mrs Baxter said, 'Father, even if God is good to my father and he goes to Heaven, you won't be able to bury him with mum, will you?' I was not sure what Fr Duddleswell would say to that. 'It hurts, Father, the thought that dad won't be buried by a priest and they'll be separated in death after all their years together here.'

'Why don't you put that to your father, Mrs Baxter?'

'I have. He says my mum is only dust and ashes now and there'll be no separation because after death there's nothing.'

Fortunately, the ward sister was in her office. She confided to me that Mr Bingley was not expected to last more than a day or two. He could go any time. The drugs were very effective in taking away the pain and occasional whiffs of oxygen

perked him up but there wasn't any long term hope.

I reported on my visit to Fr Duddleswell. He was surprised to learn that the end was near. He slipped out of his boiler suit and went to clean up. After that, I expected him to race off to the hospital but he made no move. He went into the church to pray. After a quick lunch, he did not take his siesta but returned to the church and stayed there until tea time on his knees. After tea, he proclaimed that at last he was spiritually ready 'to have a go at J.J.'.

Jimmy was with his mother at Mr Bingley's bedside. We were hesitant about breaking up a family group that would soon be dissolved by a sterner hand. I could not help admiring the old fellow for the strength of his convictions.

Fr Duddleswell went into the ward and soon Jimmy and his mother kissed Mr Bingley and came to join me. From afar, we saw Fr Duddleswell earnestly talking to Mr Bingley who treated him as he had earlier treated me. I could feel mother and child next to me grow tense with disappointment at the total absence of response.

Then Fr Duddleswell bent over and whispered something in Mr Bingley's ear. From then on, it was like watching someone on the receiving end of one of Jesus' instant miracles. The patient immediately sat up and spoke. Fr Duddleswell listened intently and bent over him again, at which Mr Bingley became quite voluble. We couldn't make out what was being said but he and Fr Duddleswell were deep in conversation. Fr Duddleswell brought it to an end by raising his hand high above the patient's head and bringing it down so sharply that had it landed it might have despatched him aloft straight away. We relaxed. It was only the first part of a huge blessing.

The Baxters' tears turned into tears of joy. Fr Duddleswell returned like a conquering hero. Jimmy spoke in secret

to his mother and she gave him a silver threepenny piece which Jimmy fixed on Fr Duddleswell's nose. He couldn't keep it there and when it fell to the floor Jimmy pocketed it.

'Well, now,' said Fr Duddleswell warmly, 'you can both be content, like. I have done everything for him in me power. You can safely leave the rest to the Almighty.'

Mrs Baxter wanted to know if her father could now be buried in her mother's grave. Fr Duddleswell told her to ask Jimmy, and Jimmy said of course he could because he was a Catholic again.

On the way home, Fr Duddleswell said buoyantly, *'Nil desperandum*, Father Neil, Never give up, like.'

His long vigil before the Blessed Sacrament had paid off. I confessed I thought there was no chance of the old chap repenting. I had never seen anyone so hardened against the grace of God.

Fr Duddleswell recalled a phrase from a curious French writer Charles Péguy, a Catholic who could not bring himself to believe in Hell. ' "The appalling strangeness of the mercy of God," Father Neil. An apt description of the case in question, would you not say?'

I said I presumed he would return later and clean up, so to speak, by giving Mr Bingley Extreme Unction, Viaticum and the Papal Blessing.

'To be perfectly honest with you, Father Neil, 'twas not entirely as it seemed.' What had caused Mr Bingley to sit up was Fr Duddleswell whispering in his ear, 'J.J., you have been a bloody fool all your life and you will be a bloody fool to the bitter end.'

I was astonished. God's mercy *must* be appallingly strange if abuse can bring a lost sheep back to the fold when kindness fails. 'What did he actually say to that, Father?'

'He cast dreadful aspersions on the honour of me mother,

Father Neil. Then 'twas'—my parish priest was blushing—'then 'twas I bent down again and ... I bit his ear, God forgive me.'

'But at what point did he *repent*, Father?'

'Did not St Peter, the Prince of the Apostles himself sever Malchus' ear completely with a sword in the Garden?'

I repeated my question.

'Did I ever say to you he repented, now? Did he not swear at me and I at him? And did he not threaten to do unspeakable things to me if I did not sling my hook? That was when I nearly brought me fist crashing down on his head. Only the appalling strangeness of God's mercy sweetened me fury and transformed me blow into a benediction.'

'That was all?'

'Almost, Father Neil. His last solemn words uttered in me hearing were "Sod off." And that, me dear boy, is a euphemism, like.'

Fr Duddleswell and I were chatting about finance in his study next morning at ten when Mrs Pring ushered in Mrs Baxter. Her eyes were shining with joy and grief.

'He passed over in the night, Fathers.'

We signed ourselves. Fr Duddleswell said, 'May he rest in peace,' and squeezed her arm.

Mrs Baxter expressed relief and gratitude that at least her father had made his peace with God. She had already telephoned the undertaker and Jimmy had rushed off to school to tell Mrs Hughes the good news.

As she was leaving, Mrs Baxter said, 'It's a real case of between the stirrup and the ground, isn't it, Fathers?'

Fr Duddleswell kissed her hand. 'God's mercy, Janice, is fathomless.' She slipped him a five pound note for a Requiem Mass. 'Heaven be in your road,' he said.

Afterwards, he held the fiver up. 'Father Neil, it pays to be kind to the dying, does it not?'

I was more concerned to know how a professed atheist and card-carrying Communist was eligible for a Catholic burial.

He winked at me like a schoolboy. 'Father Neil, did I not tell you before that to please a child I would, in full regalia, bury a hedgehog or a tin mouse. I have no quarrel with the dead.'

When I tried reasoning theologically, he stopped me. 'That Rabbi at the Conference had something, Father Neil. No ghettoes in Heaven, no pogroms in Hell. Somehow I feel that in the Hereafter we shall all of us be model Catholics.'

He walked over to the crucifix on the wall and gazed up at it as though he were St Francis expecting the Crucified to talk to him. 'Tell me truly, now, Father Neil, was I right or wrong?'

I'm not God. I couldn't settle the matter of his conscience for him.

'The way I look at it, Father Neil, is this. Old J.J. made his daughter and grandson sad enough while he was alive without adding to their misery after he is dead.' Reflecting on Jimmy's tears I savoured the truth of that. 'J.J.,' went on Fr Duddleswell, 'was a kind enough man, kinder than was life to him, you follow? Deep in his heart, at a level neither you nor I could hope to reach, he was ever a Catholic and the dear Lord grasped him there with kindness.'

I said plainly that I agreed with him.

He flared up in anger at that. 'You have no business agreeing with me, you young whipper-snapper. I came to me un-canonical views only after years of blood, sweat, toil and tears. You are not entitled to such views until you have suffered likewise. *Agree* with me, indeed!'

I waited till he had simmered down. He picked up the five pound note again. 'D'you know what, Father Neil? Whatever malignities he uttered against me mother, I am going to send J.J. the most expensive wreath in the shop. Whether he likes it or not.' He smiled his dolphin smile. 'After all, 'tis not every day I lay to rest a corpse with me teeth marks on his ear.'

Seven

MY FIRST MIRACLE

Fr Duddleswell, having convinced himself that I was now settled at St Jude's and was keen to do hospital work, announced his intention of appointing me official chaplain at the Kenworthy General. I had stepped in for him on his days off but it was a sign of his growing confidence in me that I was to have full responsibility for 400 beds.

' 'Twill be an entertaining experience for you,' he promised. 'You will be surprised how the wickedest folk will be calling out for you immediately God horizontalizes them.'

His advice was very practical. I had to register in the Chaplain's Office the chief details about the Catholics, especially whether the patient was married or not. 'Mind you, Father Neil, I counsel you not to put that question to the women in maternity.' In his experience, it was often less embarrassing to ask them for the name and address of their next of kin.

He repeated the prohibition on lighting candles when baptizing an infant in an oxygen tent, otherwise a premature death would follow hard on a premature birth. 'The poor mother, you see, might not take too kindly to the speed with which her baby went to God. Another thing,' he said with a twinkle in his eye, 'do not bite too many ears, like.'

His main concern was my relationship to the Matron, Miss Norah Bottomly. 'An extremely funny woman, Father Neil.'

'A great sense of humour?'

'None at all. Nevertheless she is in every sense the biggest thing in the K.G. Like the mercy of God itself, pressed down and running over. Not that she has much in there,' he said, tapping his temple. 'There is less to her than meets the eye, that's for sure. Finally, let me warn you, Father Neil, that Matron is a model of rectitude, the sort that puts a premium on wrongitude.'

Matron was in her high ceilinged office on the ground floor. Not a pen or piece of paper or stick of furniture was out of place, MISS NORAH BOTTOMLY—that was the name on the door —looked as though she had been laundered and starched inside her dark blue uniform.

Her hand was as smooth and hard as a statue's. 'Be seated, please, Fr Boyd.'

Matron's sentences mostly began with 'We in the Kenworthy General' or 'Our policy is.' It was like being addressed personally by a Papal Encyclical. Every nook and cranny of the Hospital was, as it were, a valley in Wales. In a most chilling voice, Matron said, 'You will find a warm welcome in every ward, Fr Boyd.'

Perched on the edge of my chair, I kept nodding at appropriate moments with 'Thank you, Matron. Thank you. Thank you very much.'

Every word and gesture of this formidable lady was intended to impress on me that, in whatever Church I had been ordained, in the Kenworthy General she was High Priestess.

'In conclusion, Fr Boyd, may I be permitted to say this? For as long as you remain strictly within the province of caring for souls, there will be between us nothing but the most unbounded harmony, co-operation and good will. Now you may go.'

I scooped myself up and bowed and scraped my way to the door.

From the first I enjoyed my work at the K.G. As Fr Duddles-well had forecast, Catholics who had lapsed from the Church for twenty years and more were keen to see me. This may have been due to the strangeness and boredom of hospital life, or the sense of being nearer to God the nearer they were to surgery.

Twice a week, I chatted with the patients individually, heard their confessions behind curtains that could not be relied on to keep out the draught and, in the early mornings, took them Holy Communion.

In Prince Albert Ward, a man's ward on the third floor, I came across Nurse Owen. I had met her before on my occasional visits and I had seen more of her at the Bathing Beauty Contest in the summer. I was pleased that she was a Catholic. I instantly felt there was a very spiritual and loving atmosphere in Prince Albert Ward.

Lying in the second bed on the left was an African. I asked Nurse Owen if he was a Catholic because from childhood I had heard stories of white missionaries baptizing black people from morning till night until their arms ached.

Mr Bwani was not 'one of us' but a Muslim from the Gold Coast. Something drew me to Mr Bwani, may be my pity for him being a Muslim. I knew little about Islam beyond its ambivalent attitude towards the flesh. It forbade the eating of pork not only on Fridays as in Catholicism but through-out life, while it permitted polygamy. I was pleased if puzzled that Muslims are reputed to have a tender devotion to the Virgin Mary.

I stuck my right hand in my jacket pocket and blessed Mr Bwani from afar, praying for his welfare, bodily and

spiritual. I don't know if it helped him any but I was aware of two big eyes peeping over the sheets like a bunker and following me along the line of beds. My impression was that he needed me.

On my second visit I was introduced to the Sister in charge of Prince Albert Ward. Sister Dunne was as spectacularly thin as Matron was robust. Even the staff called her Old Barbed Wire.

I also spoke to Dr Spinks. He had nodded to me before, this time he was keen to deepen our acquaintance. Winking at me, he drew me into Sister's office and closed the door. 'It's okay,' he said, 'Old Barbed Wire won't be on duty for another hour. Spinks is the name, Jeremy Spinks. Senior House Officer.' He rubbed his right hand down his white coat as if to rid himself of microbes before seizing mine. I took an instant dislike to him.

'I'm Fr Boyd.' I was already beginning to feel exposed without my title. 'Fr Duddleswell's assistant.'

Dr Spinks, in his late twenties, tough looking, tanned and with a close-cropped head, went into an eulogy on Fr Duddleswell. Talk about a super bloke. Talk about his reputation with the locals who still remember him fire-watching every night of the Blitz. Talk about the guts of the guy, risking his life time after time to rescue families trapped in blazing buildings.

I had to admit this was the first I had heard of it.

Dr Spinks was sitting on Sister's desk, his legs dangling below his white coat. For some reason he was trying to intimidate me and doing rather well. He suddenly turned on me. To get straight to the point, there was something I could do to help. 'Fr Boyd, we have an African patient on our hands.'

'Mr Bwani?'

'Come on board, Father,' he said urgently. 'I need your help to cure him.'

I felt a wild surge of apprehension. 'I'd like to, Doctor, but I know very little about medicine. You see, we barely touched on it in our moral theology when I was a student.'

Dr Spinks swivelled off the desk and stood over me. 'It's a problem of the mind.'

I really hate people who glue you with their eyes. 'I'm not very good at psychology either,' I rushed to say 'especially black people's psychology.' I thought I had better come clean. 'To be frank, I've never actually spoken to a black man.'

Dr Spinks tried soothing me. It wasn't exactly formal psychology I was needed for. A bit of horse-sense would be enough.

'What's the matter with him, Doctor?'

'He's dying.'

'Poor man,' I gasped. 'What of?'

'Nothing.'

I stood up to make him understand I thought he was having me on. He pressed me down, gently but firmly, until my pants touched the chair. 'It's no leg pull, please believe me, Fr Boyd. Mr Bwani is not a dedicated Muslim. He is riddled with superstition. And he's dying because he is utterly convinced that he's going to die.'

Mr Bwani was a member of a Gold Coast community which had settled in Colborne, West London. They had brought their own witch-doctor with them. This medicine man was hired to put spells on his compatriots. If a chap wanted a house or a bicycle or someone else's wife, he called him in, paid a fee and the witch-doctor went to work.

When I had heard Dr Spinks out, I expressed myself sceptical of such superstitions but he was adamant. When in the

Navy, he told me, he had come across someone in sick bay who was stoned out of his mind because a witch-doctor had put a spell on him. 'In fact,' he said, 'two perfectly healthy patients of mine who'd been cursed actually ended up in Davy Jones's locker.' I had no idea of the effect of fear on people brought up in the bush.

'Now, Mr Bwani, Father. He's convinced that this witch-doctor has poisoned his blood. It's beginning to boil. When it has boiled long enough, he's going to die.' I continued sitting there listening to this nonsense because Dr Spinks gave me no choice. 'Unfortunately, Fr Boyd, when Bwani was admitted, the nurse took his blood pressure. Normal routine, you understand. But it was the worst thing she could have done in the circumstances. He felt the blood build up in his arm and, as he put it, he heard it bubbling.'

The Doctor moved away, confident no one could be a sceptic after that. 'Since then,' he said, 'Bwani hasn't stirred from his bed. He won't talk or touch his grub and he can't sleep. He's lost nearly twenty pounds in two weeks.'

'I'd like to help,' I said, preparing to make a quick getaway.

'Good,' he said. 'I knew you wouldn't let him down.'

I did not like his hectoring tone. 'I'll say the rosary for him.'

'That's not enough.'

I promise to offer Mass for Mr Bwani, privately, of course, because he was an infidel.

Dr Spinks impressed on me that I was required to help Bwani back to health, not pray for his conversion or cast devils out of him with the sign of the cross. But now that I was on my feet, I was less daunted. 'I'm sorry, Doctor,' I said, mindful of Matron's warning. 'I'm here to save souls not lives. That's *your* job.'

Dr Spinks went red in the face. Talk about a Good Samaritan. Talk about that good guy Duddleswell rushing into burning buildings. 'Think he felt guilty,' he threw at me, 'because he wasn't a fireman?' Talk about this crazy religion lark that stops you saving someone's life when only you can do it.

I challenged him to prove that only I was able to help Mr Bwani.

'Father,' he said, 'you must have seen those eyes following you up and down the ward. He looks on you as a white witch-doctor.'

I repudiated such a ridiculous title.

'I didn't say you *are* one,' he explained, 'only that he thinks you are. As far as he's concerned, you're the only one who might be powerful enough to break the spell he's under.' The whole matter, I felt, was now moving along humanistic lines. 'Father,' he said, 'I don't doubt that prayer works wonders in the long run but we're short of time. Bwani could be in the morgue in a couple of weeks.' His manner became menacing. 'You and I have got to use medicine.'

'No,' I said with alarm.

'Unorthodox medicine.'

'Doctor, I don't like unorthodox *anything*.'

In a final burst of exasperation, he asked, 'Father, are you going to help me or aren't you?'

I refused to be brow-beaten. 'May be,' I said.

Seeing he was making no headway, he invited me to the staff canteen. We bought ourselves coffee and joined Nurse Owen who was sitting alone drinking tea. If this was part of a prearranged plan I had no objections. After all, she was a Catholic.

Nurse Owen confirmed Dr Spinks' story. She felt personally responsible because she was the one who had taken Mr

Bwani's blood pressure when the trouble began. 'I could think of no more fitting role for a priest, Father,' she said, her eyelids fluttering attractively. 'Jesus was a priest, wasn't he? and He went all over Palestine healing the sick.'

Jesus Himself might have had second thoughts with someone like Miss Bottomly around. 'That's true,' I agreed.

Dr Spinks saw the opportunity to open out his plan. In every ward, next to the Sister's office, there was an amenity room usually reserved for the more serious cases. Bwani could be placed in there for observation. All I had to do was don my brightest Mass vestments and utter incantations over him. When I requested further elaboration, he mentioned incense, burnt feathers, chickens' blood and foreign-sounding formulas. It had to look authentic. He couldn't guarantee this would work but certainly nothing else would.

I had had a belly-full. I thanked him for the coffee and took my leave. I made one promise: I would mention the matter to Fr Duddleswell. That was safe enough. I already knew his enlightened views on superstitious and ungodly practices.

Fr Duddleswell heard me out with intense amusement. I was relieved to hear him deride Dr Spinks' proposals. I said, 'If Mr Bwani's going to die, Father, we'll have to accept it as God's will.'

'God's will, Father Neil?' he smiled. 'God's *will*? Let me tell you this, lad. If the will of God were done on earth as 'tis in Heaven 'twould lead to an impossible state of affairs.'

He was opposed to the Doctor's plan because he did not approve of voodoo and black magic, yet might there not be another less objectionable path to the same end? He left me in Limbo for twenty-four hours while he pondered. Then:

'Father Neil, is there any reason why you should not heal

this coloured gentleman with a perfectly straightforward miracle?'

I thought Fr Duddleswell's plan scarcely less bizarre than the Doctor's. Someone seeming to be seriously injured is to be planted in the amenity room alongside Mr Bwani. The nurse calls me in to cure him—not too difficult, seeing there is nothing wrong with him in the first place. Mr Bwani is so impressed, he is prepared to consider a cure in his own case.

I had a terrible vision of Miss Bottomly discovering my misdeeds. 'But, Father, remember the Matron,' I said apprehensively, 'I assume ...'

He cut across me. 'Father Neil, you would be well advised to leave assumptions to the Blessed Virgin. Let me do the worrying, will you not? Was I not already several years a priest when you were still smoking your dummy?'

Certain aspects of his plan still puzzled me. 'What kind of serious injury did you have in mind?' I asked.

'Why not a compound fracture—say, a leg broken in a couple of places? The leg will look very fine when 'tis splinted and wrapped.'

I protested with my usual vigour. I was not going to lie by claiming a man's leg was broken if it wasn't.

Fr Duddleswell put on his offended air. 'I was suggesting no more, Father Neil, than that you should say the patient's leg bends congenitally in two places.' And seeing me still puzzled, 'At the knee and ankle, you follow?' I followed though I had no wish to. 'You simply enter the room, sprinkle your patient who has a ... bent leg with holy water ...'

'*Holy* water, Father?'

'Secular water, if you prefer, straight from the pump, and *Miracolo!* much to Mr Bwani's astonishment, his partner in misfortune takes up his bed and walks.'

'Who does, Father?'

'Your patient.'

'But who *is* my patient?'

'Father Neil, this is your miracle, is it not? You can surely find some discreet parishioner to assist you in this charitable enterprise? A quick change into pyjamas and he will soon be restored to health, you can guarantee that.'

Fr Duddleswell asked for a few days grace to 'cogitate me plan further, like'. In the meantime, I was to set about finding a candidate for a Lourdes-like miracle.

It was becoming clear to me that things were going to have to get worse before they got even worse.

'Hello, Archie. Glad to find you at home.'

' 'Ello, Father.' Archie, my ex-crook friend, was pleased to see me. 'Come up the apples and pears.' As we ascended the stairs past the fat landlady who had let me in, Archie said, 'Got another job for me, then, 'ave yer, Father?'

I told him there was no one better qualified for what I had in mind.

Archie shared a dingy, second-floor flat with the retired accountant Peregrine Worsley. Peregrine was seated comfortably, his shirt sleeves rolled up, reading *The Sporting Times*. He carefully folded his paper, removed his bi-focals and rose to greet me. 'Delighted, sir, to make your acquaintance.' I reminded him that we had met only a few weeks before when, for reasons of his own, he had told me of Archie's criminal record. He said, 'Ah, yes, sir, but I meant informally, out of hours, for a *tête à tête*.'

Now I knew Peregrine himself was not the irreproachable citizen I had once taken him for. I liked him a lot.

'A pint of pig's ear, Father?' asked Archie.

'Not for me, thank you.' I explained at length the purpose of my visit.

'What a set up,' whistled Peregrine at the end of it.

'Cripes, what a con man you'd 'ave made, Father,' said Archie. I did not turn down the undeserved compliment. ' 'Course,' went on Archie, 'I wouldn't dream of lyin'.'

I said I honestly hadn't meant it to be a lie but that if he felt it was a problem ...

Archie cut in, 'No, 'taint no problem, Father. I did break one of me clothes pegs uncommon severe, not four years past.'

I was relieved that the way seemed clear for us to deceive Mr Bwani without any hint of a lie.

Archie had been making a dash from prison. He was just over a twenty-foot wall when the rope snapped 'and so did me bleedin' leg'.

After begging my pardon, he went on, 'I was laid up for six weeks with one leg in the air like a blinkin' can-can dancer.' Archie paused reflectively. 'Funny thin', Father. That's the only ever time I got remission for good conduct.'

Much to Archie's disgust, Peregrine wanted to talk terms. 'As to "the actual", young sir, how much remuneration will we be entitled to, should we manage to pull off this daring escapade?' I suggested a fiver. 'For each of us?' asked Peregrine. I nodded. 'Done,' concluded Peregrine, bringing down his paper on his knee like an auctioneer's hammer.

Archie coughed apologetically. 'Manners,' he said, putting his hand to his mouth. 'Am I s'pposed to wear pyjamas for this job, Father?'

'Only for a few minutes, Archie. I promise you there'll be no embarrassment.'

' 'Taint that I mind taking off me round the 'ouses in pub-

lic, Father. But, straight up, I've not 'ad a pair of pyjamas since I was a kid in Borstal.'

Fr Duddleswell was developing his plan in ways that boded ill for my future. He came home one day bearing a number of boxes and jars with strange symbols on, and a book which he had borrowed from the Municipal Library. I was unfortunate enough to notice that it was entitled *Elementary Chemistry*.

He went immediately to his bedroom and locked himself in. For three days, he spent all his spare time there. From the cracks in the door emerged thick vapours, evil odours, the sound of bubbling and the occasional bang.

Before supper on Wednesday, Mrs Pring warned me that Fr D was sporting his antlers. He had obviously done something 'tragic to his few head whiskers'. He must have been trying to invent a lotion either to make them grow or to dye the grey hairs.

Fr Duddleswell came down to eat in his biretta. The hair below it was a bright green. Neither Mrs Pring nor I made any reference to it during a subdued meal. When it was over, he monopolized the bathroom till bedtime.

Next morning, he announced that he had made all the necessary arrangements with Dr Spinks on the telephone. Thursday, being Old Barbed Wire's day off, was D-Day. He communicated 'the further refinements of me plan' and it would have been ungenerous of me not to admit that they were brilliant. But I had lived with him long enough by this time to know that he always had more up his sleeve than his elbow. When I showed reluctance to go through with it without being party to all the facts, he reprimanded me sharply. 'Deep is the rumble of a bull in a strange pen', he said inconsequentially.

'Right, Father', I said, 'you win. I'll do it next week.'

'Next week, lad?' he said with scorn. 'Next *week*? You will be doing it the day before tomorrow.'

We walked under a dappled sky to the Kenworthy General. I was carrying a new pair of pyjamas in a paper bag. In the lobby we teamed up with Dr Spinks who had already introduced himself to Peregrine and Archie.

On the stroke of ten we sneaked into Sister Dunne's office. Nurse Owen, having seen to it that the walking patients were in the day-room, was in the amenity room fussing over Mr Bwani.

Archie, without a blink, changed into my best pyjamas. They were several sizes too big for him but he was like a boy scout donning his first uniform. 'Can I keep 'em after, Father?'

'Sure, Archie,' I whispered, hinting that he should keep his voice down.

Dr Spinks asked Archie to sit on a chair and he started to cut off the left leg of the pyjamas with scissors.

'Nark it, Doc,' moaned Archie, a pearl in each eye. ''Ave you got to do that?'

'Sorry, chum. When the bandages are removed, I want Mr Bwani to see *these*.' He traced with his finger where Archie's leg showed signs of a nasty accident. Archie acquiesced, then settled down on a trolley from the operating theatre while the Doctor splinted and bandaged his leg. 'Pity I can't put it in plaster,' he grinned, 'but this is the best I can do in the time.'

'It's only a game, Doc,' said Archie.

Dr Spinks was saying that on the contrary it was a matter of life and death when he saw that Archie was eyeing his colleague. Peregrine, standing aloof with his hat on and

leaning on his rolled umbrella, began to phip-phip like a sparrow. He took off his bowler with a flourish and advanced with a wallet in his hand. 'Archie's quite right, Doctor. A child's prank.' Dr Spinks thrust the wallet into his back pocket without a word and went on bandaging.

'Father Neil,' muttered Fr Duddleswell, 'I commend you for your talent in casting such an *admirable* pair.'

At 10.15, Nurse Owen appeared and took charge of the trolley on which Archie was lying flat out. Peregrine, once more his serene self, put his bowler hat under his arm, adjusted his spectacles and prepared to accompany the bier. He touched Nurse Owen's shoulder, 'No tears, please, my dear.'

Fr Duddleswell said, 'You stay here, Father Neil, you are not required yet.'

Through the partition I could hear Peregrine and Archie talking in exaggerated tones as though rehearsing for a Christmas concert in Wormwood Scrubs. They were determined to earn their money.

'Does it hurt, Mr Lee?' I could just make out Nurse Owen's gentle voice.

'Doctor,' exclaimed Peregrine, 'has his leg been *broken*?' It was melodramatic but Mr Bwani, cowering under his blanket, might appreciate it.

Dr Spinks replied that a leg broken in two places, as was Mr Lee's, normally takes months to heal. With that, Doctor and Nurse joined me in Sister's office from where we heard Peregrine bidding adieu.

Archie said, 'I'm goin' to call in a real doctor.'

'A specialist, you mean?'

'A *real* doctor,' repeated Archie.

'Well, so long, old chappie,' drawled Peregrine. 'See you in a few months time if not before.'

He came into the office and whispered in my ear that in

his considered opinion his faultless performance entitled him to a tenner. When I refused, he went off in a huff. A few seconds later, a hand appeared round the door and stayed there palm upwards until I had put a fiver in it. It closed, turned over and waved goodbye with a wag of the index finger.

I heard Archie ask, 'Been in 'ere long, then, 'ave yer, mate? No audible response from Mr Bwani. Suddenly Archie burst out, 'Goo-er, me bleedin' leg. Just like that tea-leaf of a doctor to tie the bandages too tight. I'm losing all the circulation in me blood. "'Ell, said the Duchess."' Then more calmly: 'What's yer name, mate?'

Mr Bwani, perhaps out of compassion for the state of Archie's blood, must have mentioned his name. 'Bwani,' cried Archie. 'You're not Irish, I s'ppose. A joke, mate, no offence. Dunno about you but ever since I was a kid I've 'ad the mockers on me, grasp me meaning?'

'Yessir.'

'Nurse,' shouted Archie, 'I want my priest, do you 'ear?' Then more softly: 'Bwani boy, I've got a priest that'll shift me out of 'ere quicker'n you can say Man Friday. No 'arm meant, mate.'

'Yessir? Really, sir?' Mr Bwani was becoming garrulous.

When Archie went on to say I work miracles every morning before breakfast, it distressed me that, after a promising start, he should resort to telling lies.

'Yeah,' went on Archie. 'In church 'e conversations with Gawd and brings 'Im down to earth on a little stone. You b'lieve that, Bwani boy?' Archie was keeping strictly within the bounds of truth, after all.

'Nurse,' bawled Archie again, 'get me Fr Boyd.'

I took a deep breath and prepared to play the star role. Fr Duddleswell restrained me. 'No hurry,' he said. 'Give them

another thirty minutes together. We do not want to break up a beautiful friendship, like.'

The interval was filled with Archie's virtual monologue in praise of his priest, punctuated by screams for the same to be sent to him at once. Finally, Nurse Owen led me in.

'Thank Gawd you've come, Father,' cried Archie.

Mr Bwani, his face glum as a pickled walnut, was half raised up on his pillow. That seemed a good omen but, on orders from Fr Duddleswell, I took no notice of him. 'What's up, Archie?' I asked.

'Me leg's been broke, Father, and me life's got the mulli-grubs. You are Gawd's man, Father, so please 'elp me.'

I bade Archie put his trust in me, drew out my Roman Ritual and started reciting Latin prayers. I went through the baptismal ceremony and the blessing of a pregnant woman, followed by the thanksgiving for a safe delivery.

'Nurse,' I said, 'hand me the water.' I sprinkled Archie with it. Some spattered Mr Bwani who promptly dived under the sheet. I was relieved to see him reappear immediately. At all costs, he must not miss the next bit of the show.

'Nurse,' I ordered, 'remove this man's bandages. He is healed.'

I saw amazement in Mr Bwani's eyes. He lifted himself up to get a clearer view of Archie's hairy leg.

'Me smeller and snitch,' said Archie touching his nose, 'tells me I'm as good as new. Just the odd scar where the fractures was.'

'Stand up, Archie Lee,' I commanded.

He stood up, shakily because the bandages really had in-terfered with his circulation. It added conviction. 'I can walk again, Father,' Archie proclaimed ecstatically. He knelt down to kiss my feet. ' 'Ow can I ever thank yer enough, Father?'

I acted the real cad. 'By keeping the commandments, Archie, and by attending Mass on Sundays and Holy days. Will you promise me that, Archie?'

'Tell you what, Father,' said Archie, taken aback. 'I'll give it a lot of thought.'

The three of us left the amenity room. I judged it best not to speak to Mr Bwani. The first move would have to come from him.

Archie got dressed and I paid him his fiver. As he was leaving, he said, 'We're a smashing team, Father. Any time you wanner work another miracle, send for Archie.'

I gave him my word and watched him amble off with his precious pair of one-legged pyjamas tucked under his arm.

Nurse Owen returned to the amenity room to remake Archie's bed. I distinctly heard Mr Bwani say, 'Nurse, I want to see heem.'

'Who, Mr Bwani?'

'The prist. May I see heem? Pliz, Nurse.'

Fr Duddleswell rubbed his hands. ' 'Tis taking,' he said, 'but do not be too anxious to perform your miracles, Father Neil. Let us go home to lunch, and at 3 o'clock this afternoon he should be nice and ripe for a cure.'

'Hand Fr Boyd the syringe, Nurse.' Dr Spinks was about to rehearse in detail Fr Duddleswell's methods of healing Mr Bwani. 'You'll need first to draw out a drop of blood.'

I saw the vengeful gleam in his eye. 'Whose?' I asked.

'Before you take a blood sample from Bwani, Fr Boyd, you'll have to take one of your own.'

'Can't *you* do it, Doctor?'

'Afraid not, chum. It's vital that you draw out some of your own blood in Bwani's presence.'

'Father Neil,' put in Fr Duddleswell, 'will you please stop

moaning like a seal. Cannot you see that you have to obtain Mr Bwani's total confidence? You are the witch-doctor, not Dr Spinks nor anyone else. So take a sample and I will tell you what to do with it.' When I recoiled, he asked cruelly, 'Did not Jesus shed his blood for you?'

'No, Father,' I corrected him, 'other people shed it for him.'

Fr Duddleswell was in no mood for splitting hairs. 'Get on with it, now,' he threatened.

Nurse Owen tied a piece of rubber tubing round my upper arm; she rubbed the crook of my arm with a small disinfecting pad and said, 'Choose the biggest vein, Father.'

I asked if I could sit down. Nurse Owen brought me a chair and patted my shoulder. It gave me the strength I needed. I dug the needle in. She put a glass to my lips and I drank a few drops before raising the top of the syringe with my thumb and drawing up a fraction of blood. It was like being asked to operate on myself.

'A bit more', urged the prodigal Dr Spinks, 'you've lots to spare.' I drew out another half an inch and he was satisfied.

I extracted the needle. Nurse Owen swabbed the tiny puncture and wiped my brow with a cool, damp cloth. 'You're so brave, Father,' she said, and it seemed then all worthwhile.

Dr Spinks poured the remains of my glass into the saucer and added my blood to it, tinting the water. 'Right,' he said, 'action stations.'

I accompanied the Nurse to the amenity room. 'Now, Mr Bwani, I believe you wanted to see me.'

He indicated that he would like to whisper in my ear. He said, 'Mr Prist, sir, my witch-doctor curse me and I go dying.'

I nodded gravely. 'I believe you, Mr Bwani.'

His face lit up with joy at having found at last a healer

who did not ridicule his plight as so much jungle nonsense.
'Mr Prist, I want you pliz to uncurse me. My blood, she boil.
Terrible hot already, Mr Prist, sir.'

'Powerful curse, Mr Bwani. Power-*ful*.'

'Yessir, yes-*sir*.'

The tray which Nurse Owen was carrying held a medicine
glass, two saucers and a syringe. I gingerly fingered the
syringe and took another sample of my blood from the
identical hole. I emptied the contents on to the liquid in the
first saucer and turned it red. 'Now, Mr Bwani,' I said, 'it's
your turn.'

He eagerly stretched out his arm. He did not flinch as I
dug the needle in but at the sight of his own blood rising in
the syringe he shuddered violently.

I pressed out the contents on to the liquid in the second
saucer. Even I was staggered at the way it started to froth and
bubble and smoke. Hydrogen peroxide is potent and evil-
smelling stuff.

Mr Bwani's eyes popped, his mouth gaped like a frog's
and he fell back stiffly on his pillow. I thought he was dead
and wondered how Matron would react to the news. Nurse
Owen, unperturbed, raised Mr Bwani up and tried to coax
him back to consciousness.

'Mr Bwani,' I said, slapping his face. At the fifth attempt,
he heard me. 'Mr Bwani, heap plenty trouble here.'

'Plenny trouble,' he managed to gasp.

'Powerful medicine of black witch-doctor. Power-*ful*.' He
attempted to voice his agreement but no words came. 'Me
much more power-*ful*,' I said, continuing to give as good an
imitation of a Red Indian chief as I could. 'Me put bigger
spell still. You want?'

He wanted all right. Out came the Ritual and more Latin.
I sprinkled him with water and made an impressive sign of

the cross over him. Then I handed him the strong sedative in the medicine glass. As he relapsed into sleep I kept up the prayers, adding more promises to complete his recovery as soon as he came round. 'When you awake, Mr Bwani, no more hot blood. You be cured. No more curse.' My voice helped hypnotize him. 'Sleep, sleep, Mr Bwani.' He slept and snored mightily.

Dr Spinks had prepared about twenty ice-packs. We put them in the bed around Mr Bwani. Within twenty minutes his face whitened and his teeth started chattering. I was worried that he might get pneumonia or frostbite. The Doctor said this would help convince him that his blood had stopped boiling.

As he began to come to, we took away the ice-packs and brought in another tray. When everyone else had withdrawn, I patted Mr Bwani on the cheek. 'Awake, Mr Bwani, awake. Blood no boil no more.'

He kept repeating something like 'Bloody cold'. When I had interpreted it I said, 'Yes, Mr Bwani, blood cold, very cold.'

Soon he was restored to teeth-chattering consciousness. Once again, the trick with the syringe, his arm only. This time, his blood tinted the water without causing the slightest tremor on its surface.

Mr Bwani beamed. 'Curse fineeshed, Mr Prist. You are my father, my brother, my mother, my seester!'

Within a few days, Mr Bwani had put on weight and was completely well. Since he was to be discharged the following Thursday I was able to visit him undisturbed by Old Barbed Wire. I made him a present of a syringe and told him that should the witch-doctor curse him again he need not worry. My blessing was permanent like an injection against polio.

He would be able to prove it easily. 'Take saucer of water and put in drop of blood. Not too much, leave some in arm, savvy?'

Mr Bwani proclaimed, 'You are my father, my brother, my mother, my seester.'

These and many other relatives and friends, all gaily clad, were waiting for him in the vestibule. As soon as they saw him they broke into song. Mr Bwani made me anxious by telling the crowd that his recovery was due entirely to the white witch-doctor, at which they broke into loud applause.

When they left, I was about to go home myself when the fat Anglican curate from St Luke's, Mr Pinkerton, passed me puffing on a cigarette. 'There's a missive for you from Norah in the Chaplain's Office,' he said. 'I'll pray for you, old boy.'

This was the first note I had received from Matron. It was headed: REF: PRINCE ALBERT WARD and contained a brief injunction to appear before her that very day at 12 o'clock.

The next hour was spent in anguish and recriminations. The Bwani affair was bound to leak out, I was a fool not to realize that. Was it a criminal offence, I wondered, to practise medicine without qualifying as a doctor? Would Bishop O'Reilly haul me up and ask me to justify my extraordinary methods of evangelization?

I did not regret what I had done because I had saved a man's life. I regretted terribly what I had done for less elevated motives. One thing I was clear about: I would not implicate Nurse Owen in any way.

When I met Matron, she did not look any more severe than I had remembered her to be. 'It's about what happened in Prince Albert Ward, Fr Boyd.'

'I think I can explain, Matron,' I blurted out, not knowing what on earth I would say once I started.

'There is nothing to *explain*, Fr Boyd. This letter says it

all.' She put on her pince-nez and addressed me over them as though I were a refractory audience. 'It is from a retired Chartered Accountant.'

Hell, I thought. So Peregrine has split on me just because I wouldn't pay him an extra five quid. Iscariot!

Matron read the letter. It stated in three or four tortuous sentences that Fr Boyd had proved himself a marvellous chaplain when his friend Archibald Lee had been a patient in Prince Albert Ward. He had not only helped Archibald spiritually but also financially when he was down on his luck. He begged Matron to thank Fr Boyd personally for his ministrations.

'Really, Matron,' I stammered with relief, 'there is no need ...'

'Indeed there is not, Fr Boyd,' whence she proceeded to lecture me in a booming voice on the fact that she had sternly warned me in our first encounter to restrict myself to the religious sphere.

I have never seen a bittern but she looked like one.

'What you do with your money outside these walls, Fr Boyd, is entirely your concern. But here in the Kenworthy General we leave financial matters to the Lady Almoner.' She stressed that this was the last instance of indiscipline she would tolerate in her Junior House Chaplain. I was dismissed.

It was Purgatory but I had been expecting Hell.

At the presbytery, Fr Duddleswell asked if I had seen the black man safely off the premises. I said yes.

'Ah,' he complained, 'when medical science was powerless you prevented him dying by utilizing all the resources of the faith and doubtless you did not receive so much as a Mass stipend.'

I confirmed that the miracle was free on the National

Health. I did not say I was worse off to the tune of ten pounds and a new pair of pyjamas. He was himself a witness to the fact that I had shed blood for the cause.

Fr Duddleswell screwed up his eyes. 'Did he ask to become a Catholic, like?'

'No.' I said.

'Imagine that, now, Father Neil. You pull him back from the edge of the grave and he remains an infidel.' For a few moments he pondered the inexpressible sadness of a priest's life. 'Bloody heavens, Father Neil,' he exploded at last, 'what will you have to do to make your own first convert – raise the dead?'

Eight

A THIEF IN THE PARISH

'As a seamstress, Father Neil, she is without equal.' Fr Duddleswell was pointing proudly to the patch on his cassock around a previously charred right pocket.

'Magnificent,' I said, surprised at this rare paean of praise for Mrs Pring.

' 'Tis true, indeed. Once she puts reins on a needle, she is off at a gallop.' He stroked the patch as if it were a piece of mosaic he was pressing into place. 'Scarce of resources in the brain-box she may be, but she could mend spiders' webs and sow a feather back on a bird.'

Mrs Pring, the evening before, had taken a more detached view of her accomplishments. 'This is the last time, the very last. I'll not patch his patches no more, not no more.'

I doubted Fr Duddleswell had invited me into his study to admire Mrs Pring's handiwork, and I was right. 'Father Neil,' he said, 'there is a shortage of you as there is a glut of me.' I blinked, then stared. 'You are beginning to look, lad, as if you were me cheese ration for the week.' I sighed voicelessly. It encouraged him to say more emphatically, 'We cannot have you and me doing a Laurel and Hardy on the parish, you follow? No two ways about it,' he went on in a biblical vein, 'you must increase and I must decrease. The lady housekeeper suggests to me that, alas, poor brother, you need Bovril. In brief, you may be heading for a breakdown.'

So that was what he was wriggling towards. I insisted I had

never felt better in my life.

'Breakdowns in people, as in motor cars, Father Neil, can be very sudden, like. And when an Englishman goes to pieces, 'tis my experience he does so with panache, like a sliced loaf.'

Mrs Pring had reported to him that in a few days' time it was my parents' twenty-fifth wedding anniversary. The day after that was my twenty-fourth birthday. 'I don't know Father Neil, but that you need a holiday. So go home, now, and spend a couple of days in helping your dear ones celebrate.'

Celebrations were not the outstanding feature of our home. We lived happily in Hertfordshire, in the town of Clover Hill, thirty miles north of London. My father was a greengrocer. To the locals, BOYDS was the 'corner shop', which a tall, thin, cloth-capped gentleman, slightly deaf and with a grey brush moustache kept open at all hours.

He had not ever altered in my memory, my father. His habit was to sit sideways at table, invariably with his cap on. He preferred eating with a spoon. He even managed bacon and eggs with a spoon.

He was gruff and of few words. He sometimes shouted at his six children, of whom I was the eldest, but he never laid a finger on us either in anger, or affection. I admired him. More than that, I loved that silent, stubborn man.

Old corduroy trousers under a brown overall. In winter, a sack round his middle and khaki woollen mittens from which protruded raw fingers with nails permanently broken and packed with dirt from shovelling potatoes.

My father never had an assistant in his shop, which was really the converted front room of our house. He couldn't afford an assistant, he said, not with eight mouths to feed. At five o'clock most mornings, rain or shine, he would be off to

market or a nearby farm in his old Austin van. Often at night he would be working in the dark 'out the back', shelling peas. He had a talent for buying up sackfuls of peas with sticky pods which no one else wanted, shelling the peas into a bucket and selling them by the pint. The thumb of his right hand, I recall, was nearly always swollen.

We were not exactly the potato-less poor, but economies were his speciality, a kind of art form. He never smoked or drank or drove the van except on business. He never went to the cinema or read a book, and he only turned on the radio for the news, a habit he picked up during the war. Our holidays were walks to a lovely wooded park three miles away on Dad's half-days, where we picnicked when the weather was fine. Our clothes were second hand and hand-ons. It was a case of first up, best dressed. Dad made us use the paper wrapped round oranges for toilet paper.

On Friday nights, Dad took out his orders on a black three-wheeled carrier bike. For an hour or two, one of the children was made to mind the shop and see that no customers duped him into letting them have food on tick when Dad had blacklisted them for not paying their bills.

My father never tried to teach us anything, though he had learned a lot since he finished his schooling at thirteen. If a fuse blew or a tyre punctured or a window was smashed, it was he who mended it – and in secret. He had the unassailable pride of the uneducated man. His children might attend the grammar school and the convent – intellectuals, he called us – but in his house he did all the 'fixing'. He was the boss.

In fact, he was nothing of the sort. It was my mother who made all the major decisions about our schooling and our religion, and about my being sent away to the junior seminary. An inexhaustible fund of affection, she was what our seminary professors called one of the simple faithful. Her

151

faith was as unquestioning as a child's. It was her faith that saw me through the difficult times in the major seminary, especially the first two years. That was when I studied philosophy which was as intelligible to me as Chinese.

My mother was fond of calling to mind her own childhood. Her father was often without work and her mother had to stand at a wash-tub in a laundry from eight in the morning till eight at night for a shilling a day. 'Yet,' my mother said, 'we were happier in those days. Mind you, I wouldn't want them to return.' That was a paradox I could never resolve, for we were happy, too, though we had little enough of the things of the world.

I used to spend my Christmas and summer vacations at home. I was specially close to the youngest of the family, my two sisters, Meg and Jenny. After I was ordained, Mum wanted brother Bob, my junior by two years and a trainee accountant, to give up his attic bedroom to me. She said I needed a quiet room at the top where I could be alone to pray and to say my Office. I preferred to share with Bob, and at nights we talked into the early hours about the past, present and future.

Mum would now ask me to say Grace before and after meals. One look from her made the boss take off his cap, revealing a rare display of white hairs.

The silver wedding anniversary fell on a Sunday. I presided at a solemn sung Mass in the parish church at 11 o'clock. My parents had a special prie-dieu and chair on the sanctuary. Both were in new clothes, bought off the peg. Mother had a trim red hat. Father wore a three-piece suit *and* a new pair of mittens.

When I turned round after the Gospel to read a blessing over them, it was those mittens that made me choke. Not mother's love for us, their joint protection of us, but those

mittens and everything they stood for: the lack of opportunity in his life, the long, unbroken, indistinguishable
hours, his endurance of ice and cold and grime and dirt without a murmur for us. I blew my nose hard and got a grip on
myself. I managed to hold out. Just.

Although I was tired when I returned to St Jude's after
our celebration, I was full of joy and gratitude at belonging
to such a close knit family.

The parish was in a state of chaos.

'It all began yesterday with the washed Chinese carpet.'
Fr Duddleswell pointed grimly to the bare boards in front of
the Lady Altar. Lord Mitchin, our richest parishioner, had
donated it together with a Persian rug on the sanctuary
which had also been stolen. 'Worth £300 the pair, I'd say,
Father Neil. I do not know what we are going to do.'

He had called in the police but they were not interested in
petty theft. They could not be expected, in any case, to put
a round-the-clock watch on every church in the district.

Fr Duddleswell complained that he was not getting the
protection he was entitled to as a ratepayer. The first suggestion from the police was that he should lock up the church,
outside of services.

'But, Father Neil, we do not want a one-day-a-week church,
do we, now? The good people of the parish would not be
able to pray in front of the Blessed Sacrament. Think of the
Indulgences they would lose.'

The police next proposed that we should take out anything that was movable: carpets, statues, candlesticks, vases,
the lot. 'They have no appreciation of the fact that we are
Catholics, Father Neil. Can our folk be expected to pray
without the customary aids to devotion? Indeed they cannot.' He refused to turn his beautiful church into a bare

Protestant meeting hall. 'Who do these bobbies think they are, Father Neil, Henry VIII?'

It appeared the police had no idea who the thief was. It could be a tramp, a gang of kids, a regular criminal. 'In other words, they have about as many clues to our thief's identity,' he said, 'as to that of Jack the Ripper. We can but pray that the thief, whoever he is, turns his attentions elsewhere.'

But the anonymous thief retained his preference for St Jude's. Next day, he struck again. He walked off with a pair of silver candlesticks from the Sacred Heart Altar.

'Where is it going to end?' moaned Fr Duddleswell, when after lunch we witnessed the results of the latest depredations.

He knelt down before the life size statue of the Sacred Heart, saying, 'Let us say a prayer for the criminal, Father Neil.' And he proceeded to gabble, 'Hail Mary, full of grace ... pray for us sinners ... at the hour of our death, Amen.' All this before my knees could touch the floor.

I made a token sign of the cross to show willing. 'What's next, Father?' I asked.

'Doubtless, soon he will be breaking into the boxes.'

This prophecy, too, was fulfilled. That very evening. There were a number of boxes at the back of the church to receive the offerings of the faithful. Boxes for the Poor, the Holy Souls, Catholic Newspapers, Candles, Peter's Pence and Catholic Truth Society pamphlets. The thief showed the catholicity of his tastes. 'He has prized the lid off every one,' roared Fr Duddleswell, boiling with indignation.

I examined the locks and lids and suggested that the thief had used a screw driver.

Fr Duddleswell said, 'We are dealing with a blasphemer, are we not, Father Neil? Not only does he rob the poor and the Holy Father himself, he even breaks open boxes con-

taining money meant for the Holy Souls. And that is a problem on its own.'

I asked him what he meant.

'If the thief stole five shillings from the Holy Souls' Box,' he explained, 'that is the price of a Mass stipend and we ought to say a Mass for the donors' intentions.'

I agreed. It would be terrible if a Holy Soul remained one minute longer in the cleansing fires of purgatory than was strictly necessary because the Mass he was entitled to had not been celebrated. 'I'll offer a Requiem tomorrow, Father.'

'Ah, there, your heart is in the right place, Father Neil. I would offer the same meself but for the fact that I have already promised Janet Murphy to say Mass in the morning for her cat. She is having an operation. A hysterectomy. And she will be lonely, you follow?'

Finding this information highly ambiguous, I said I quite understood he couldn't disappoint Mrs Murphy or her cat.

A locksmith was called in. For £3 he mended the boxes and put a heavy padlock on each. 'That's the best I can do, sirs,' he said, already hinting that his best might not be good enough.

And so it proved. The thief's screw driver managed once more to prize open the boxes without touching the padlocks. This time he had also broken the lock on the baptistery and stolen the casket with the small silver phials of holy oils used for baptisms and anointing the dying.

Fr Duddleswell was crestfallen. It would cost him another £3 to replace the oil stocks and then he'd have to go to the Cathedral to beg for a refill. 'Pray to the Holy Mother,' he counselled me, 'that no one decides to die on us, Father Neil, before a fresh supply of holy oil arrives.'

If that were to happen, I could see myself offering another free Mass for the repose of a brand new Holy Soul.

'God help us, Father Neil, but this thief is a thorn in me eye. He is spoiling me sweet repose and putting the whole of the parish through the mincer.' He decided to draw up a rota of watchers to keep an eye on things, 'as we did during the war, like'.

We were to ask for volunteers on Sunday but in the meantime we would have to take turns ourselves.

'Just you and me?' I asked, wondering whether I could survive vigils of several hours at a stretch. And Sunday was five days away.

'Mrs Pring will be only too glad to help, that's for sure,' he said. 'She has a nose sharper than a briar and more eyes than a fisherman's net. Besides', he added loudly, 'she would far sooner park her bum on a bench than lick this house with a broom.'

Out in the hall, Mrs Pring started up a kind of boating chant. 'Hewing and drawing, cooking and frying, rubbing and scrubbing, washing and drying.'

Fr Duddleswell muttered, 'The voice of the turtle is heard in our land. By the law of averages she was bound sooner or later to blunder into poesie.'

After Mrs Pring had sung her song a few times, she moaned, 'I'm just a beast of burden, I am. A beast of burden.'

'Well, Father Neil,' Fr Duddleswell confided to me, 'she is not Balaam's ass that spoke but once, that's for sure.'

No sooner was Fr Duddleswell's scheme put into operation than I realized its futility. For security reasons, he kept the door leading from the sacristy to the church permanently locked and barred. Whenever a watcher started to open it from the sacristy side, a thief would have half a minute to make his getaway. Another thing, the watcher had to sit or kneel in the benches in front of the boxes so that any prospective thief would see immediately if anyone was on guard.

It was very embarrassing having to turn round whenever a worshipper dropped into church. The faithful resent being spied on by the clergy at their devotions.

Once I tried sitting in the dark of my confessional. Mrs Betty Ryder, President of the Legion of Mary, spied me. She came in and poured out her very fluid soul. After a forty-minute drenching, I chose to sit a couple of rows from the back relying on my ears to warn me if anything out of the ordinary happened.

On Wednesday I ate a big lunch and Fr Duddleswell left me to keep watch while he took his siesta. I must have dozed off because when he came to relieve me at 3.30, red eyed from sleep, not only had the Poor Box been broken into but all the candles had been pinched.

'He must be an indigent eskimo,' observed Fr Duddleswell, when he had made an inventory of our losses, 'but what the mischief came over you, lad?'

I apologized profusely. The thief had been in my grasp and I had let him go.

Fr Duddleswell scratched his forehead and acknowledged the improbability of the thief being so stupid as to return that day. He was wrong. The rest of the boxes were emptied before supper.

'Father Neil, when the bait is worth more than the fish, 'tis time to stop fishing.' After that, he refused to have the boxes mended any more.

I determined to make amends for my unplanned siesta. After supper, I called on Archie Lee, who, as ever, was delighted to see me. From a clothes line by the fireplace hung my pair of pyjamas.

'Sorry Peregrine's out, Father. 'E's gone to Bedford to see 'is old auntie. She's been taken ill.' Anxious not to be caught

out in a lie, he told me this was a code for Perry being at the Races. Perry's gambling was the reason he was always skint. He kept back one fiver to wrap round pieces of newspaper and stuffed the lot in his wallet to make himself look plush. 'Sometimes,' complained Archie, 'Perry goes to the gee-gees and leaves me working in a shop all bleedin' day.'

I told Archie I had come to see *him*.

'Another 'orspital job, Father?' said Archie eagerly, rolling up his pyjamas and hiding them under his pillow.

I explained what had been going on in church and said I wanted his help in finding out who the culprit was.

He smiled. 'No trouble there, Father.'

'Not you and Peregrine?' Archie was shocked at the suggestion after he had proved his honesty in so many ways.

'But,' I said after an apology, 'I thought you said you *knew*.'

'Right,' said Archie. 'I'm surprised the fuzz don't. Most like they do but they aint lettin' on.' He explained that every thief is a sort of craftsman with his own little trade marks. 'The marks in this case,' he said, 'is clear as 'is autograph. 'Cept the bloke in question can't write.'

'Will you tell *me* who he is?'

'I might,' said Archie cannily, 'and then I might not.'

'I can't raise much cash this time, Archie. That hospital job cleaned me out.'

'It aint the bread, Father, I just don't wanner grass on one of me old mates. It don't do to shop one of yer own kind.'

I said I fully understood his sense of honour.

'Right, *right*,' reflected Archie, who approved of that way of putting it. 'Also, this bloke is one of us.'

'A con man?'

'You've been and gawn an' done it again,' Archie said reproachfully. 'I mean 'e's an 'oly Roman, like you an' me.'

'That makes it worse.'

'That makes it better—for 'im, I mean,' said Archie. ' 'E knows 'is way round the church, where all the goodies is, when the boxes is fattest with the lolly an' that type of thin'.'

When I assured him we didn't want to have the thief arrested, Archie relaxed. I knew that when Fr Duddleswell heard the thief was a Catholic, he would want to save him for himself, redeem him, reform him.

' 'E'll never manage that, Father.'

'Well, at least *stop* him.'

'Even that'll take some doing,' said Archie. 'This gaffer's been pilfering from churches since 'e were six.' It had started when he went to Sunday school. The boxes were crammed after the morning Masses and the habit developed from there. 'Went from strength to strength, see?' I nodded. ' 'E don't mean no 'arm by it. Knows no different. 'Ow else would 'e eat, tell me that?'

'Either he goes out of business or we do,' I said.

'Bad as that, is it?'

'If I promise we won't "shop" him, Archie, or disclose who put us on to him, will you tell me who he is ... for old time's sake?' I was so excited at the prospect of finding the culprit I was not above a bit of blackmail. Archie hesitated. 'I give you my word that he'll come to no harm, Archie, and we'll do our best to see he gets a chance in life. Like you,' I added.

'Ah,' sighed Archie. 'If only 'e'd go straight like me and Perry, 'E's never 'ad our chance, 'as 'e? And 'e's about as bright in the 'ead as a star by day.'

'This might be his last opportunity, then.'

'It's Bud Norton,' burst out Archie.

'Where does he live?'

' 'E don't live nowhere. Or, rather, 'e lives everywhere, but not somewhere.'

'No fixed abode.'

'That's what I just said, didn't I? You'd as easy find a wisp of smoke from yesterday's fire.'

I was thinking we would have to catch Bud Norton in the act, after all, when Archie asked if Bud had taken more than money.

'Yes, the silver stocks containing the holy oils.'

'Wicked,' said Archie. 'You'll 'ave to get on 'im before 'e breaks open yer tabernacle. Anythin' else?' I told him the rest. Archie frowned and said, 'Wanner know where to get 'em?'

I could hardly believe my luck. 'You mean you know where Bud Norton keeps his stolen goods?'

' 'E don't keep 'em. 'E passes 'em on to a bloke name of Pedlow in Larkin Street.' Larkin Street was off the King's Road in Chelsea. 'Pedlow buys up everythin' from Bud for a bleedin' song. Real bent, 'e is, and as genuine as a sea breeze off a winkle stall.'

'I'll keep mum, Archie,' I said, touching the side of my nose, 'you can trust Fr Boyd. Oh, *yes*.'

Next morning after breakfast, while Mrs Pring was keeping watch, I took a bus to the King's Road. Larkin Street had a narrow entrance and was deep in shadow. The only shop in the street was PEDLOW AND SON, FURNITURE DEALERS, EST. 1881.

In the very front row of the window display were our two candlesticks. A notice on them said, PRICELESS SILVERWARE, £35 THE PAIR. I couldn't see the carpets.

Now I'd arrived at the shop, my nerve failed me. There was no sign of an assistant. What if he turned out to be a typical example of the criminal classes and brutally assaulted me?

I plucked up courage, prayed to the Holy Ghost and went in. An old-fashioned bell fixed on top of the door tinkled and I was assailed by the odour of old furniture, mildew and cold stale air.

A white-faced man, about five feet two inches tall, shuffled in from a back room in carpet slippers. He hadn't a hair on his head. A pair of rimless spectacles gave the appearance of a short-sighted egg. He wore, in striking contrast to his face, a black corduroy jacket set off by a drooping black cravat.

Seeing my clerical collar, he broke into a smile. 'James Pedlow, at your service, sir.'

'I've come for the candlesticks in the window.'

'You have admirable taste I *can* see, sir, and an eagle's eye for a bargain, *if* I might say so.' He had a habit of accenting unexpected words. 'Where else *in* London,' he continued, 'could you pick up a pair of antique silver candlesticks *like* that for only £35?'

'I haven't come to buy them, only to claim them,' I said.

'I beg *your* pardon, sir,' said Mr Pedlow, taking one sharp shuffle backwards.

I told him I had come to claim them because they were stolen from our church. His demeanour instantly altered. 'What's your *little* game, then, eh?'

'Game?'

'What are you, a cop?'

'Do I look like one?'

He lifted his spectacles on to his forehead and ran his eye up all six feet and more of me. 'As a *matter* of fact, you do. *Are* you in plain clothes or something?'

Fingering my clerical collar, I replied that I was in my normal uniform.

'You must *be* a con man, then,' he said.

What twisted minds these crooks have, I thought. 'I hap-

pen to be a Roman Catholic priest, Mr Pedlow. No,' I added, to forestall a further question, 'this is not a front.'

When he demanded to see identification I realized that I hadn't any except for my name inscribed on my miraculous medal. I didn't think that would do.

'Have you a visiting card?'

'I have only just been appointed to St Jude's and I've not had one printed yet.'

'A driving licence perhaps?'

'I ride a bicycle.'

'A cheque book?'

'I haven't got a bank account.'

This must have been the crushing proof that I was a Catholic priest. He cracked. Like Humpty Dumpty, he was never the same again. 'Well, sir,' he said, bracing himself, 'that's *as* may be. But that gives you no entitlement to claim my candlesticks as your own. I purchased them in good faith *on* the open market.'

I felt my star was in the ascendant. 'You did no such thing,' I affirmed, 'you received them from Bud Norton.'

He cowered in my shadow like a naughty schoolboy. 'That's the first time in twenty years Bud's grassed on me.'

'He didn't,' I said. 'I got a tip-off.' Those Hollywood gangster movies were proving useful.

'An enemy has done this,' he said, sounding quite biblical to my ears.

'It doesn't matter who did it, it's done,' I cried, 'and I demand my candlesticks back, otherwise I'll prosecute you for theft.'

'Theft!' exclaimed Mr Pedlow, riled by the word. 'Theft! I have never stolen anything *in* my life.'

'To receive or retain what you know belongs to another is as much theft as if you had taken it yourself. Whoever steals

through another is himself a thief.' Moral theology had its uses, too.

Mr Pedlow appeared to think I was quoting from a law book. 'How *can* you prove they belong to you?' he asked more respectfully.

Time for my trump card. 'Here,' I said, pulling out a picture from my inside pocket, 'is a photo of those candlesticks in the place Bud Norton stole them from: the Sacred Heart Altar.'

He didn't even bother to look. 'They're yours,' he said miserably.

My triumph could not have been more complete if I had pulled a gun on him. 'Do you want me to call the cops?' I thundered, revelling in my role of bully-boy.

'What's up?' he said timorously. 'Didn't you hear *me* say they're yours?'

'The carpets. I want them back, too.'

'Which ones, sir?'

'Chinese and Persian.'

'Come with me, sir,' he said with a gesture of defeat.

I followed him into the back room and searched a tall pile of carpets till I found the two belonging to St Jude's. 'Finally,' I said greedily, 'where are the candles?'

'I don't stock candles.'

That jogged my memory. 'Forget the candles.' I could afford to be generous. 'Where are the stocks with the holy oils?'

He knew exactly what I meant. He crossed to a cupboard and drew out the casket with the three silver phials. As if despairing of mankind, I asked, 'What possible use could anyone have found for these?'

'They would *have* made such nice snuff boxes,' he whimpered.

I struggled with the stolen goods up to the King's Road where I stopped a taxi. As luck would have it, out of the hundreds of cabbies in London, it had to be the one who had taken me and my bike home in less happy circumstances. He took one look at my haul of furniture and said, 'Don't tell me. St Jude's.'

When Fr Duddleswell saw his precious possessions, he raised his eyes to heaven, saying, '*Magnificat anima mea Dominum.*' Then in a more earthly tone: 'So you tracked him down, Father Neil?'

'It's useful having one or two contacts in the underworld, Father.' I proceeded to tell him the whole story, adding a spice of drama here and there, but leaving out the thief's name. 'That,' I said, 'is a professional secret.'

'You cannot even tell me his initials?' I shook my head.

He didn't press the point. Once he knew the thief was an R.C. he felt a special responsibility towards him. Besides, to take him to court would only bring Holy Mother Church into disrepute.

'Shall I take the carpets and candlesticks into the church, Father?' I asked. It seemed clear to me that if the thief were to see them there, he would know we were on to him and leave us in peace.

Fr Duddleswell didn't agree. On past evidence, the thief was quite capable of stealing them and offering them again to the Chelsea fence. He had devised his own method of stopping the thief's tricks. 'Come with me, Father Neil, and I will show you something that escaped me notice before.'

In the church, Mrs Pring was keeping solitary vigil. He put her on guard outside so that the burglar would not be tempted to enter and went up ahead of me into the organ loft.

'Well, Father Neil, we never thought to keep a look-out up here, did we?'

The loft overhangs the back of the church. 'But this is no use,' I said, peering over the wooden balustrade. 'We've no view of the boxes from here.' This was why we had discounted the place as a watchtower in the first place.

Fr Duddleswell drew my attention to the back of the loft. 'Look down there.' In the floorboards was a crack half an inch thick. 'Here,' he said, 'we can see without being seen.'

I made the point that by the time we clattered down the spiral stairs the thief would be further away than the Houses of Parliament.

'Ah, to be sure. But since he is a Catholic, Father Neil, we are not aiming to nab him. Only reform him. And,' he said mysteriously, 'we will accomplish that without laying a finger on his person, without so much as letting him set eyes on us.'

He outlined his plan. In our parish lived Paul J. Bentley, a radio actor in the B.B.C.'s drama company. The idea was to get him to put a message on tape. When the thief appeared, we would play this message very loudly from our hiding place in the loft.

Within twenty-four hours, the recording was in our hands. In Fr Duddleswell's study it sounded stupendous. A B.B.C. engineer had added a sinister echo effect.

Fr Duddleswell was to have the tape recorder all warmed up, and when Bud Norton came in, I was to give a signal. He only needed to release the pause button and Bud would get the message.

Next morning at eleven, after we had been watching for an hour, an elderly, balding gentleman in a black overcoat appeared. He sank to his knees in silent prayer for fully five

minutes. I had seen enough of life lately not to be taken in by pious attitudes. When he rose, looked around him furtively to see no one was looking and crossed to the Poor Box, I gave Fr Duddleswell the agreed signal. The recorder gave out a full blast:

'THIEVES WHO ARE UNREPENTANT WILL PERISH ... PERISH ... PERISH ...'

The natural echo of the building intensified the ghostly echo on the tape. It chilled me to the marrow. Fr Duddleswell pressed the pause button down and we kept quite still, scarcely daring to breathe.

Below there was no sound. Puzzled by the silence, I peeped through the crack in the floorboards to find that the thief had returned to his place and was once more lost in contemplation. His conversion must have been as sudden as St Paul's. I beckoned Fr Duddleswell to me. He tiptoed across and put his eye to the crack.

'Holy Jesus,' he whispered, putting a shaky finger to his lips. ' 'Tis Lord Mitchin himself. Deaf as a trumpet. He cannot be wearing his hearing-aid today.'

'Lucky for us,' I whispered back.

'*Deo* bloody *gratias*,' he said, signing himself.

When after a quarter of an hour, Lord Mitchin left, Fr Duddleswell wound the tape back. I asked him if we should go on with it.

'How else, Father Neil, are we to recover one of Christ's lost sheep, tell me that, now?'

I went back to my post and Fr Duddleswell bent down, his finger poised to release the button. There was a clatter of feet. This time, when I looked through the chink in the floor, there was this shabby, shifty looking character. Bud Norton for sure. An army greatcoat reached to his ankles. Beneath it was a pair of shoes without toecaps and with string for

laces. On his hands he wore a pair of khaki mittens.

Bud made no pretence of praying. He simply stood there, his face raised and his body arched like a squirrel's, listening. I saw his grimy bald head, his grizzled face, his red-rimmed watery eyes. My heart, in a mad gallop, went out to him. It was the mittens that did it.

Until this moment, Bud Norton had been a shadow among shadows, a thief, a nuisance, a name stirred half jokingly into conversations. Now here he was, a common, shameless, pitiable vagrant who walked the streets in toeless shoes by day and slept where he could at nights. 'As bright in the 'ead as a star by day,' as Archie in his mercy put it, and as much soft flesh and warm blood as Fr Duddleswell or I.

Bud went over to the Poor Box. A rusty screwdriver was in his hand. Out of the corner of my eye, I saw Fr Duddleswell getting tense as he waited for my signal. It was cowardly of me but I gave it.

The ugly sound from the tape-recorder reverberated round the church. Bud stood there paralysed.

'Once more?' Fr Duddleswell mouthed in my direction.

I nodded and the next message must have gone right to the heart of poor, old Bud Norton.

'THOU SHALT NOT STEAL ... STEAL ... STEAL ...'

I saw Bud start and shiver, and I heard him say in a hoarse whisper, 'Godalmighty!' Then something which, together with his mittens, broke me up. He genuflected. The next moment, he was gone.

In the organ loft, we both stayed motionless for a while. I closed my eyes, only opening them when I felt Fr Duddleswell's hand on my shoulder.

'Get up, lad,' he said gently. 'I feel the same as you. 'Tis a dangerous game, playing God, to be sure, even to put a stop to a man's thieving.' He stood up. 'I only barked so I would

not have to bite. But I should have devised another scheme.'

Fr Duddleswell was at last able to have the locks on the boxes fixed permanently. Together we combed the district looking for Bud for three days till late in the evening. We called in at the local Doss House and the Salvation Army Hostel. One old dosser, reeking of methylated spirits, claimed to have seen Bud three days before but not since. 'Imagine,' said Fr Duddleswell, 'no one has so much as heard a taste of him.'

It was cold and wintering early. The Lord had started to shake his salt-cellar over the nights and mornings. I was wobbly on my feet as if I was heading for a bout of 'flu and Fr Duddleswell confessed to feeling as wretched as a Christmas without snow.

We were forced to conclude that Bud had moved away. In a last desperate effort at atonement I persuaded Fr Duddleswell to come with me to Archie Lee's. Archie was on his own, eating lunch. He pointed to his poached eggs on toast. 'Adam and Eve on a raft,' he said, laughing.

When I put Archie in the picture, he asked what day it was. I said it was Saturday. No, he wanted to know the day of the month. November 30th.

'And what's the hour?' asked Archie.

In exasperation, I said, '12.45.'

'Then,' said Archie glumly, 'I can't 'elp yer, 'cept to tell you 'e could be an 'undred miles away by now.' The only predictable thing about Bud Norton was that he only stayed one month in any district. On the last day of the month, before midday, he was off. 'By tonight,' said Archie, ' 'e could be in Land's End or John o' Groats.'

That was that. Fr Duddleswell shook Archie's hand papering the palm with a pound note and we walked slowly home to St Jude's.

Before we went into the presbytery, Fr Duddleswell suggested we pray for Bud in front of the Blessed Sacrament. Neither of us could have guessed when the whole miserable business began how overjoyed we would be to find that for the last time the boxes had been rifled.

Nine

SEX BOWS ITS LOVELY HEAD

During the night I could hear awful howls and screams. In a daze, I kept asking myself if it was the wind, or had a huge dog been let loose in the alley? It occurred to me that I might be responsible for the noise but that was impossible, I was in no pain.

I was a tall tree which a lumberjack felled with a single stroke of the axe and lifted up in one hand and felled again. Each time I hit the ground my body shook and threatened to disintegrate.

I was dreaming and in my dream I was by the sea and the racket I had heard was the wind and waves pounding the shore and there was salt spray on my face and lips and I slipped on the rocks and fell into black waters and was drowning.

The room was an orange split down the middle. Red, molten light was shaken on to my eyeballs. Fr Duddleswell, a total stranger in his dressing gown. Mrs Pring in spectral curlers and hairnet. The pugnacious smell of whisky, and Dr Daley with a halo like a blister round his entire head was wheezing something about pneumonia and hospital.

I desperately wanted to help whoever was ill but I could not shake myself awake. I was still drowning, slowly but surely. The river-bed of my throat was as narrow and clogged as a capillary tube.

Now I was on my back in a hammock. There were fireflies

in the night sky and a long white liquid road stretched up to the moon.

'A hundred and two, Father.'

Was I as old as that? Nurse Owen had not aged and here was I all of a sudden one hundred and two.

'It's going down, Father,' Nurse Owen said. And so was I, coughing my dry cough, and going down, down, down, into the waters.

Dr Daley, half drunk, was still a good diagnostician. I had pneumonia. I came round in the amenity room where I had cured but failed to convert Mr Bwani.

For a few days I had terrible pains in the chest and a fever. Nurse Owen sweetened every aspect of my discomfort. Ever by my side, she soothed my brow, took my temperature and held my wrist to try to catch up with my racing pulse. I fervently wished Archie had not walked off with my best pair of pyjamas.

When I could breathe more deeply again, there followed days of bewildering happiness. Nurse Owen was giving me more of her time, I was convinced, than I was entitled to as a mere patient. The amenity room made it possible for us to talk in a quiet, natural way. About our work, mainly.

On her day off, when I did not see her, the hours limped along like wounded grasshoppers. Feeling sorry for myself, I reflected that I had passed my life in entirely male dominated surroundings since I was fourteen. That was when I entered the junior seminary. My mother and sisters apart, women had only walked on the horizon of my world. I had never taken a girl to the cinema, or been to a dance. I went to my last party at the age of twelve.

I had no female friends of any sort. Yes, I was chaplain to the Legion of Mary. Most members were pop-eyed, middle-

aged ladies who talked world without end about 'true Marian devotion'.

I was welcomed as a polite, anonymous stranger at many a hearth. But to no one could I allow myself the luxury of saying who I was. To them I was Melchizedek: no father or mother or brothers or sisters or antecedents. Worse, no present feelings and no future hopes.

'Give me, good Lord,' I prayed each night with Lacordaire, 'a heart of flesh for charity and a heart of steel for chastity.' Outside the amenity room, I felt my life was becoming steelier and lonelier every day.

When Fr Duddleswell and Mrs Pring visited me, bearing gifts like the Magi, I kept saying I was very keen to return to work. Mrs Pring arranged the chrysanthemums while Fr Duddleswell opened up the Get Well cards in between swallowing my grapes. 'By the time you leave here, Father Neil,' he said, his mouth full of purple mush, 'provided they do not starve your plate, like, your shadow should be considerably fatter.'

How could I tell this quaint, benign couple that in the centre of my being I never wanted to quit the Kenworthy General?

Fr Duddleswell suggested I be transferred to the private hospital run by nuns where the sick clergy of the diocese were usually treated. I would not hear of him being put to any inconvenience. Nor did I want to convalesce in a rest home by the sea, also run by the good sisters.

After that, no further attempts were made to evict me from Paradise.

Once or twice I asked myself if that strange flutter in the region of my stomach when Nurse Owen held my hand was the stirrings of love. I put it out of my mind. Fr Duddleswell was bringing me Holy Communion every morning at

first light and I was keen to be worthy of the Lord's coming.

Such bliss could not last. The dark day came when the doctor signed my discharge. I was free to go home. It was more like a sentence of perpetual banishment.

Half an hour before Fr Duddleswell came to collect me, Nurse Owen appeared and shyly thanked me for being a model patient.

'I'm very grateful, Nurse,' I said 'for *everything*.' She shrugged and smiled as if to say it was all in the course of duty. 'Anyway, Nurse, I'll see you around the ward before long.' However long would be too long.

She left to attend to a fat Greek boy nomel Nicos who had developed a fever after having his appendix out. Happy. happy Nicos.

For a few days, Fr Duddleswell 'adamantinely' refused to let me loose on the parish. During my enforced confinement I tried to sort out my ambiguous relationship with Nurse Owen. Was her shyness really coyness, or was it respect for the priesthood? What did I feel for her? Did she feel anything for me? With such questioning, the mornings no longer came before my head hit the pillow at night. Hours pretended they were months. I was afraid to go into the kitchen at night for tea in case the police should invade the place.

Nothing had been resolved by the time I resumed my chaplaincy work. All I knew was I wanted to talk to Nurse Owen privately from time to time. I would ask her if she was of the same mind.

I walked up the staircase to Prince Albert Ward with a thumping head. Fortunately, she was alone in Sister's office writing up her reports.

'Hello, Nurse.' I smiled nervously.

She beamed back at me. 'Fr Boyd, how nice to see you up and about.'

I judged her welcome to be more than friendly. She was aglow. If I did not say quickly what I had prepared I would never say it.

'Nurse Owen.'

'Yes, Father?'

'Nurse, I feel really indebted to you for all you have done for me.' She cast her lovely brown eyes downwards, without a word. 'I was wondering, Nurse, if I might ask you a personal question.'

The Holy Ghost must have been on my side at that moment. I saw she was wearing a diamond ring. I pointed to it stricken, but smiling bravely.

'Yes, Jeremy ... that is, Dr Spinks, has asked me to marry him. We became engaged last Saturday.' She began twirling the thing round her finger in front of me. 'I shouldn't be wearing it really while I'm on duty, Father, but it is still such a novelty.'

'Congratulations,' I said, commiserating with myself. With all the lucidity of mind keen pain can bring I added, 'As I was saying, Nurse, I want to give you a box of chocolates and I'd like to know the sort you like best.'

'Oh, Black Magic are my favourites.'

'You are sure you didn't mind me asking?' I added confusedly.

'Not in the least.'

'Fine, well, Nurse, if you'll allow me, I'll bring you ... and Dr Spinks ... a pound box of Black Magic next time I pass this way.'

I left Kenworthy General without attending to a single patient.

* * *

I was hurt. I was humiliated. I was angry. At first I wondered why she had gone out of her way to be so nice to me. What made *her* think she could be nice to me? Soon I realized I was being stupid. Why should Nurse Owen single me out for an uncharacteristic attack of nastiness?

Guilt waxed in me as anger waned. I started to blame myself. I knew that if I wasn't careful I'd blame myself too much and accuse myself of impure thoughts and desires. If that happened, I would find myself in the altogether murkier realm of mortal sin which, as I had told Mrs Rollings, required confession – number and species. It was wiser to forget the whole affair.

But my conscience gave me no peace. What if I was no longer in a state of grace and making things worse by celebrating Mass and administering the sacraments when I needed absolution myself?

I had to get it off my chest. I did not want to trouble my normal confessor at the Cathedral who knew me for my laziness, exaggerations and impatience. I chose to pop along instead to a nearby Jesuit House of Studies and confess to a priest who did not know me from Adam.

One morning at ten o'clock, I plucked up courage and rang the bell. A Brother with a club foot opened the door. 'Come for confession, Father?' Was guilt written so large on my face that a total stranger could read it at once? 'No one here at the moment, save Fr Strood. An American, Father. But I dare say if you're in a hurry.' I said I was. 'Second Floor, Room 12, then. There's no phone in his room so you'll just have to go on up.'

I knocked on Room 12 and was greeted by a loud, drawling, 'Come in, please.' The voice was Jimmy Cagney in a friendly mood.

I opened the door only to recoil in horror. There in the

middle of the room was a crew-cut, middle-aged gentleman clad only in the briefest of blue underpants. He was holding a towel but not for protection.

'I'm sorry to disturb you,' I said.

'What makes you think you're disturbing *me*? I was about to freshen up, that's all.' Sensing my embarrassment, he added, 'I *am* wearing my fig leaf.'

'I was looking for a priest,' I stammered, 'for confession.'

'That's okay, Father, you've found one. Only too glad to oblige.' He promptly collapsed on to a chair, put the towel round his neck like a stole and motioned to me to kneel beside him. 'Ready?' he said. 'Shoot.'

I told him it was four days since my last confession. 'Great, Father,' he smiled, 'glad to know you frequent the sacrament. Now, what's on your mind?'

I explained as best I could my feelings towards the Nurse who had looked after me, first of tenderness and lately of bitterness.

'Gee,' he said, tugging on the ends of his towel and then scratching his hairy chest. 'I've been hospitalized three times in seven years and I've fallen in love with my nurse *every* time, can you imagine? *Different* ones at that. I guess I'm just *promiscuous*.' He paused as if contemplating the pretty faces of all the nurses whose hands he had been through. 'Plan to see her again, Father?'

I answered that I was bound to see her on my rounds but she had become engaged to a doctor. 'That's probably what made me so sore,' I admitted.

'I *read* you, Father. Anything else?' I hadn't prepared anything else. 'Okay, Father, tell the good Lord you're sorry for all the sins of your past life. For your penance, I want you to pray that your nurse friend will be very happy.' Through two or three camel-like yawns, he gave me absolution.

As I stood up, he grabbed me by the hand and squeezed it till it hurt. 'Frank Strood from Jersey City,' he said, grinning from ear to ear. 'And you, do you have a name, too?' I wasn't used to shaking hands with underpanted Jesuits but I told him who I was. 'Great to meet you, Neil. See you again, I hope.'

'Thank you, Father,' I said, retreating to the door. I was afraid that if I didn't get out in a hurry he might want to confess his promiscuities to me. 'You've been extremely helpful, Father.'

He waved the towel after me like a handkerchief. 'Think nothing of it. Bye, now, Neil. Bye.'

'Here are the chocolates, Nurse. Sorry I didn't remember them before.' Lies. I had thought of nothing but her and her chocolates for days.

She thanked me, adding out of politeness, 'I'd forgotten all about them, Father.'

With a bitterness that surprised me, I thought, 'I bet you did.'

To prove to her and myself that I had no designs on her I had bought her a half pound box of Cadbury's Milk Tray. She seemed pleased all the same as she clutched them to her breast.

'Father,' she said, 'I was wondering if you could possibly help me' – oh, yes – 'help *us*' – oh, no. 'Jeremy and I are planning to marry next spring.' Remembering the confessor's admonition I wished her every happiness.

She had been told that Jeremy had to have three or four instructions before marriage.

'He's not a Catholic, then, I take it, Nurse?'

'Jeremy's not anything.' It staggered me that a beautiful, devout, apparently intelligent Catholic should contemplate

giving herself away to a self-confessed pagan. 'It helps, doesn't it, Father,' she asked eagerly, 'him not believing in anything?'

'I suppose so,' I replied. 'It means he won't object to the children being Catholics.'

Her rose-like face rushed into full bloom at the mention of children. I explained that non-Catholics had to sign in advance a promise that all children born of the union will be baptized and brought up in the Catholic faith. This seemed to upset her.

'Look, Nurse, he's not likely to raise any objections, is he? You made the point yourself he hasn't any faith.'

'No, Father, but he does have very strong convictions.'

Blind prejudice, I thought, and nothing more. I said, 'Presumably, he'll want you to follow your conscience?'

'What about *his* conscience? What if he wants ... any children born of the union ... to decide for themselves when they're old enough?'

'Awkward,' I said unsympathetically.

Nurse Owen looked irresistible as she clutched her small box of chocolates to her heaving bosom. 'That's why I was looking to you for help, Father. Could you have a meal with us?'

This was rubbing salt in the wound. 'When's best for you, Nurse?' She mentioned Friday evening at 8. My diary was blank on that day but a streak of perversity made me say, 'Sorry I can't make that evening. The Friday after is all right.'

She was so grateful and so quintessentially nice that if I'd had the talent I would have kicked my own backside. By eating at her place I would at least be spared having to share the bill. I was beginning to think that curates don't get paid nearly enough for all they have to suffer.

'Flat 6A, Flood Court,' she said. 'I share with a secretary. She goes out Friday evenings, so we can have a quiet meal, just the three of us.'

The prospect of instructing Dr Spinks on the rights and duties of marriage made me nervous. He had seen sex in the raw, I had only met it in Brown's four volumes of *Moral Theology*. There all the spicy bits had been put into Latin, presumably so that inquisitive lay folk could not read it. Unfortunately, I was never very good at Latin.

Apart from Brown, there were only two ways we seminarists had been formally instructed on sex.

One was when Canon Flynn, our Professor, called us up two by two to his dais in the lecture room. This was in our fifth year. Spread out on his desk was a battered old tome with two sectional drawings, suitably distanced, of the '*Respective Anatomies*'. The text was in French, the parts were listed in Latin. To cap it all, sectional drawings, even of cars and aeroplanes, never meant anything to me.

The Canon darted here and there with his long pencil, taking care not to touch the page. He hurriedly gave the names and functions of various arcane organs which Brown had referred to in a lump as *membra minus honesta*.

'Any questions?'

There were never any questions. The chief point of seminary training was that you should know all the answers and none of the questions. It was all over in forty-five seconds.

In our sixth and final year, any gaps in our knowledge of sex and procreation were to be filled by Father Head, a Scottish priest who had been a surgeon before his ordination.

He turned out to be the leanest, most highly strung individual I have ever seen. He stood at the blackboard, from

which were hung enormous charts, red-faced and quivering, and proceeded to describe the act of intercourse as if it were a torrid, North African tank battle between Rommel and Montgomery.

I remember Jimmy Farrelly, the wag of the year, declaring afterwards, 'Jesus! I still can't figure out who won.'

I was in dire need of help when I went to Fr Duddleswell's study. He was engrossed in a tabloid newspaper which he bought regularly for Mrs Pring. He looked up at me and tutted: 'Father Neil, newspapers these days. 'Tis all bosoms and etceteras. Cast your eye over this.'

The picture in the centre spread was of a pretty girl in a nothing dress. The caption was *Thigh Priestess*. He was at a loss to know why the media chose to advertise those parts of the human person so devoid of interest that previous generations had refrained from showing them at all.

'Seen one, seen 'em all,' he said. 'Like elbows. D'you not think, Father Neil, that sex is a bit like the aroma of coffee. It promises far more than it can possibly deliver.'

I decided to take his word for it and nodded agreement.

He asked, 'Be honest, now, can you imagine any sane individual getting titillation from the likes of *this*?'

'No, Father,' I gulped, amazed at what age does to a man. I told him I had a mixed marriage arranged for the new year and wanted to know how to go about it.

He went across to his filing cabinet for the forms. The most important was the dispensation form for disparity of cult. The non-Catholic had to sign promising never to interfere with the faith of the Catholic partner and to allow the children to be brought up in the true faith.

I told him the bride was a nurse and the groom a non-Catholic doctor from the K.G. 'Well, Father Neil,' he said, 'be sure to put him right about birth-control, divorce, abor-

tion and things of that sort.' I was particularly to stress the Church's teaching on contraception. Sex is not a child's plaything. It is a most marvellous mechanism for the manufacture of children. In this, he continued to inform me, men as far apart as Gandhi and Bernard Shaw were in agreement with the Church. Birth-control usually meant no birth and no control.

I asked whether the dispensation was granted easily. 'No trouble these days,' he replied, 'provided there is a reason for the marriage. Is the girl pregnant, for instance?'

'I shouldn't think so,' I said, biting my lip to hide my indignation.

'Better check, Father Neil. Pregnancy is by far the most acceptable of the canonical reasons. Then there is *firmum propositum nubendi*, a firm determination to marry.'

I acknowledged grudgingly that she had that. 'What I mean is,' he explained, 'would she marry in the Register Office if the Church refused her a dispensation?' I said I guessed not because she's a pious Catholic. 'If we are not careful,' he winked mischievously, 'she will prove to be too pious and we will find *no* canonical pretext for marrying her off. Is she *super-adulta*, now?'

'What is over-age, Father?'

'Twenty-four. Any girl above that is reckoned to have distinctly reduced chances of marrying. That is why the Church allows a dispensation, especially if she has a face like an old boot into the bargain.'

Seeing I was stunned at what constituted advanced years in a woman, he explained that the law was made with Latin ladies, fed on a diet of spaghetti Bolognese, in mind. 'They are mostly blown like autumn roses before our own women are in bud, you follow? But if canon law works to our advantage in this instance, why complain?'

I said that the girl in question couldn't be more than twenty-two and was not really ugly, so I supposed, almost joyfully, that was the end of it.

'Nothing of the sort, Father Neil,' he came back, dashing my last hope. 'The matter is exceedingly simple. Do not forward the application for a dispensation till the last minute and plead *omnia parata*. You tell the Chancellor of the diocese that everything is ready for the wedding and it would cause a ripe shemozzle if at this late hour 'twere to be called off.'

I put it to him that canon lawyers would find a loophole to let Satan have a holiday from Hell.

'Father Neil, the Church has all the loving deviousness of a mother, if you are still with me.' I had to make sure the forms were filled in but not dated. If I reminded him to countersign them four days before the wedding, he would pass them on to the Chancellor himself. 'And warn that young medic, mind, I want no hanky-panky over birth-control.'

With polished shoes and brushed suit I rat-tatted on the door of Flat 6A. Nurse Owen, her long red hair cascading on to her shoulders, answered my knock clad in a long cherry-coloured dress. I admired the propriety of its high neckline.

Spinks was a mess in sandals, jeans and open-necked shirt. The only bosom on show was his.

'Jerry it is,' he said in a friendly tone. Since he already knew my name I shook his hand in silence. 'Glad Sarah could persuade you to come.'

Sarah. Sarah Owen. What a lovely name.

'Our paths have hardly crossed,' Dr Spinks went on, 'since you cured that chap from the Gold Coast.'

He actually had a small bald patch on top, the size of a

florin. What was Sarah up to, hitching herself to a prematurely balding pagan? The Church really shouldn't be so liberal with her dispensations.

'Talk to Father, Jeremy,' urged Sarah, 'while I put the finishing touches to the meal.'

When she went to the kitchen, Dr Spinks said, 'Beer?'

'No thanks.'

'Sherry?' I shook my head. 'You *will* have a glass of wine with your meal?'

'Please.'

He looked relieved that I had some weaknesses. 'Tricky business, Fr Boyd, putting down the anchor.'

It was in his favour that he had addressed me correctly. 'I'm sure,' I said.

A black hole yawned in the conversation. Then he asked me if I would like a disc put on. I tried to shake myself out of my boorish mood and failed. 'Not particularly.'

Sarah must have had her ear pinned to the door. She returned and thrust a plate in front of me. 'Have a crisp, Father. And here's the cheese dip.' One glance at Dr Spinks told him, no discs tonight.

'Marriage is a sacrament, isn't it, Father?' she said. 'Jeremy is ever so keen to know what that means, aren't you Jeremy?'

I was happy to be on home ground. I replied that it is a sacrament provided both partners are baptized.

'You *have* been baptized, haven't you, Jeremy?'

Dr Spinks said 'yes, love' but he had repudiated all that when he was twelve. I insisted that if he had been baptized, he was in some marginal sense a Christian, and if he married another Christian it would be a sacrament.

'Whether I like it or not?'

'Yes,' I said aloud, and inwardly, whether you damn well like it or not. He asked what follows from that. 'To begin

with,' I answered, 'when the marriage has been consummated, there's no possibility of a divorce.'

'Consummated?' He spoke it plainly as a four syllable word. 'Just once?' I nodded. 'Bloody hell,' he laughed, winking at Sarah, 'only once *after* we're married and it's till death us do part.'

Sarah turned the colour of her dress and retreated into the kitchen. Was he such a swine as to cast aspersions on his fiancée's honour?

Through avocado pear, plaice and chips, and apple pie it was sex and marriage. Dr Spinks was against everything the Church stood for on moral issues. He argued the reasonableness of abortion if the prognosis is that the baby's likely to be born deformed or the mother's life is in danger. Likewise in cases of rape.

I did not care to pursue this topic over fish and chips but I made my position clear. God infuses the soul at conception and so the child in the womb has all the rights of a human being.

For him, talk about murdering embryos was mere rhetoric. The Church's teaching on birth-control was plain daft. 'I've been researching into women's periods,' he announced to Sarah's discomfort. 'I've had the nurses at the K.G. and half the girls from the Teachers' Training College keeping charts and thermometer checks.'

Sarah stood up to remove the dirty dishes. 'Cheese and biscuits to follow.'

'I even asked Norah if she'd care to take part,' Dr Spinks went on. 'Just to flatter her, of course.'

The conclusion of his survey was that women are about as reliable as the English weather. My experience of Sarah had taught me that already.

'Did you know, Father,' he confided in a boozy stage

whisper, 'Sarah is one of my menstrual girls?' He roared with laughter and overturned his glass of Beaujolais. 'Her cycles are so irregular, I call her Penny-Farthing. One is thirty-three days, the next is eighteen.' My right hand was volunteering to punch his nose.

He started dabbing up the wine with his table napkin. 'Just my luck to be marrying the most inconsistent girl in the whole bloody troupe. Her only safe period will be from fifty-five to ninety.' He chuckled at his own joke. 'I tell you this in strictest confidence. If, as your Church seems to want, I'm limited to every inconceivable opportunity, I might as well become one of the *castrati* in the heavenly choir.' He dug me in the ribs. 'Like you, old pal.'

I should not have come. There was always the risk of this detestable chumminess.

'Safe period,' Dr Spinks mocked. 'I heard your Church was against sex before marriage but denying it to a randy fellow *after* marriage is bloody ridiculous. Encourages infidelity.' Then without respite, 'And why should a celibate presume to instruct me on sex? It's as lunatic as allowing only orphans to be Marriage Counsellors.'

I was about to push his face in when the key turned in the lock. Sarah rushed in from the kitchen crying, 'Oh, no!'

A young woman was at the head of eight of nine dishevelled youngsters. All were loaded down with tins, bottles and French loaves.

'Debbie,' said Sarah, wringing her hands, 'you told me you were at Jane's for the evening.'

'We were, Sarah darling, but her parents returned un-expectedly from Sunderland. Puritans the pair of them. They even lock up the beds while they're away.'

Sarah introduced me to her flatmate. 'Debbie Shackles, Fr Boyd.'

'He's cute,' said Debbie, pursing her lips in a lewd fashion. 'Shake.'

A tousle-haired lad, looking like a pearly king in a black leather jacket sewn with silver buttons, caught sight of me. 'Sarah,' he rejoiced, 'you didn't tell us you were having a fancy-dress.'

Someone put on a jazz record and several started to bob and weave. Johnny, the lad who imagined I was all dressed up, pointed to where a girl had parked herself on the floor and was gazing blankly like a guru into space. 'Rebecca Sacks, Reverend. She's high.'

'I'm Roman Catholic,' I said.

'Care for a puff?' Johnny asked, after exhaling meticulously.

'No thanks, I don't smoke.'

'Sticking to cigarettes, eh?'

I went across to Rebecca and tried to shake her hand. It felt broken. 'Fr Boyd,' I said.

'Tweet-tweet.' She flapped her arms pathetically.

'My!' yelled Johnny from across the room. 'You've really made a hit with Becky, man. Stay with it and she's a regular communicant.'

Sarah took my arm and steered me towards the door. 'Father,' she said, 'I'm terribly sorry about this.'

'Don't apologize,' I shouted above the din.

As she let me out, Sarah was saying, 'You will come again, won't you, Father? If you talk to Jeremy long enough, he's bound to come round to our way of thinking.'

I was still licking my wounds next morning when the phone rang. A raucous voice: 'Jack Hately, here. My wife needs to be anointed. Come quick, Father.'

The phone went dead before I could ask the caller for his

address. I rushed down to Fr Duddleswell's study. He wasn't there. I raced to the kitchen to ask Mrs Pring if she could identify the caller.

Calmly, without raising her eyes from her ironing, she said, 'The Hatelys? Yes. They're on Fr D's side of the parish.' Mrs Hately had been seriously ill for years and Fr Duddleswell anointed her every month to be on the safe side.

'I'd better go along all the same, Mrs P.'

'Wouldn't if I were you. Fr D'll be back within the hour and he'll go himself.'

'You're *not* me,' I retorted, 'and I'm going.'

'Suit yourself,' said Mrs Pring with a toss of her head. '3 Springfield Road.'

I cycled there at speed. Effects of bombing were still to be seen in the battered buildings and vacant housing lots.

Number 3 was now the end house. Hardly a house. It was a basement, its outer wall buttressed by wooden beams sunk in the ground.

I knocked three or four times, louder and louder, until a woman's voice cried out, 'Jack, a visitor, a *visitor!*' and an old chap beyond the biblical span hobbled to the door. He had a loud, hollow voice. 'Is Fr Duddles away? You'll have to do, then.'

Behind him, propped up on a large, brass bed was his wife, her yellow-white hair splayed across a discoloured pillow. Desolation. Water dripping into a pitted zinc basin, shelves in disarray, greasy gas cooker, an ancient iron bath-tub, the pervasive smell of an old person's untended sick room.

'You the new curate?' Mrs Hately enquired hoarsely. 'I can see all the girls falling for you.' She was a flirt. 'You're easy on the eye. Much nicer'n my Jack.' I looked at Jack and marvelled at the minuteness of the compliment. 'I keep telling Jack, I do so admire men with thick wavy hair.'

Her bald-headed Jack nodded and smiled inanely. Only a deaf man could have absorbed so many insults without protest.

I asked Mrs Hately about her health. 'Haven't been well for centuries,' she replied.

'There, there,' boomed Jack in what was meant to be a soothing tone.

'First my arthritis, Father, and now'—indicating the faulty organ—'my heart.'

'There, there, me darlin'.'

I took out the holy oils. 'Fr Duddles,' she said, 'anointed me last week.'

'There, there,' sounded the drum.

'Oh, shut up, Jack, won't you?' she yelled at him. He smiled until he saw her grimacing. 'The anointing don't help me none,' she croaked. 'I'm a condemned building. Jack's done it. He'll be the death of me.' Jack smiled slyly and toothlessly from the far side of the room. 'The Church is taking my Jack away from me.'

What did she mean? What possible use would the Church find for dear old Jack?

'He's just longing for me to drain away and die, Father. So's he can return to the bosom of Holy Mother Church.'

Jack or Mrs Hately or both must have been married before. That made their present marriage invalid in the Church's eyes. If Mrs Hately died, Jack would be free to return to the sacraments.

I jumped to Jack's defence but she was not listening. 'Been together more'n forty years,' she moaned, 'and now he wants rid of me. The cold, damp sod for me, the warm bosom of Holy Mother Church for him.' She had evidently played this part before.

Jack stepped across to me and exploded in my ear. 'Care

for a nice cup of tea, Father?' My gesture of acceptance could not have been demonstrative enough. 'P'raps another time, then,' he said.

The scene was so dismal, so Dickensian, I couldn't wait to get out. 'You're not in any pain, Mrs Hately?' I said, preparing to leave.

'Never in anything else.' After a gesture of disgust in Jack's direction, she turned her face to the black and peeling wall.

'There, there,' cried Jack. He sat quite still, the tears pouring down his cheeks. 'There, there, me love, me precious.' Her back was iced against him. 'I'm never going to leave you, me dearest, never.'

I moved nearer to his wife to give her my blessing. There was no thawing of the little iceberg in the bed, so I blessed her from behind. With a large, scaly fist, Jack signed himself.

When I left the room that was a house, he was still crying and a deaf old woman was resolutely turned towards the wall.

'Mrs Pring informs me that you went to the Hatelys, Father Neil.' I was at my desk preparing Sunday's sermon. Fr Duddleswell said, 'You were not to know, lad.'

'That they are living in sin?'

He looked startled and wanted to know what I meant. I said I had worked it out that there must have been a previous marriage and divorce, as in the case of Mr Bingley.

'Nothing of the sort,' sighed Fr Duddleswell, sinking into a chair. 'Steel yourself, lad, while I tell you the whole unsavoury tale.' I was in no mood for the facts of life. 'You see,' he said, secretively, 'not to put too fine a point on it, Jack Hately is a priest.'

It was my turn to look startled.

'Now do not take it too hard, Father Neil. These things

happen, if you're still with me.' He outlined the story.

Jack Hately, now eighty-three, left the priesthood in his late thirties and married Betty, 'his partner,' in the Register Office. There had been two children. The first appeared 'far too soon' after they married. Both had emigrated to Australia.

Jack had been faithful to Betty according to his lights. He had worked hard as a postman and was not long retired when a land mine during the war sliced off the top two stories of his house. They had lived in the basement ever since.

Old Jack never went to church. He probably couldn't see the point because he and Betty were excommunicated and he was bitter as well. When an Indian Bishop came to St Jude's to appeal for money, Fr Duddleswell took him to see the Hatelys. He couldn't converse with Jack who was already deafer than a pillar-box, but as he was leaving, the Bishop knelt down. Jack gathered he was asking *him* for his blessing. 'Well, strike a light, Father Neil. Old Jack had not seen the inside of a church for more than forty years and here was a coffee-coloured Bishop kneeling at his feet, begging his blessing.'

Jack started going to Mass again. He couldn't receive Holy Communion, of course. Mrs Hately could because she was in danger of death and Catholics are entitled to lots of things in danger of death. Then eighteen months ago Jack came to the presbytery to say he wanted to apply to Rome to have his excommunication lifted. This explained Mrs Hately's fear that the Church was going to take Jack away from her. She was doubly upset at the moment because Fr Duddleswell had received word from Bishop's House that Rome had at last replied to Jack's appeal.

'Tomorrow,' said Fr Duddleswell, 'I am off to see the Vicar General to hear what Rome has decreed.'

As soon as he returned from Bishop's House next day at 11.30, he called for a cup of coffee, 'the strongest the handle will take, Mrs Pring, if you please.'

After that, he took a large white envelope from his brief-case and drew out of it a Latin document footed by a big red seal. The gist of it was that the excommunication could be lifted provided Jack and Betty swore solemnly to live hence-forward as brother and sister.

Fr Duddleswell slapped the document like a naughty child.

'According to this, Father Neil, should there be one sexual lapse on Jack's part, he will re-incur all past censures and we will have to start the long judicial process all over again.'

'That's inhuman,' I gasped.

'But very wise, very *worldly* wise, would you not say, Father Neil? Mother Church realizes only too well that the flesh is weak.'

I protested. 'Father, Jack's eighty-three. His flesh is far too feeble to be weak.' But I had to admit that at his age and with his wife a permanent invalid, their living together as brother and sister was not too harsh an imposition.

Fr Duddleswell guessed that what would upset Betty Hately most was a condition laid down by the Vicar General. To ensure that Rome's terms were carried out to the letter, he personally decreed that Jack and Betty had to sleep in separate rooms. 'When I told him, Father Neil, that they only have one room, he insisted that at least Jack and Betty should have separate beds.'

'Poor old sods,' I said.

Fr Duddleswell did not reprimand me but he said quietly

and firmly as if to silence insubordination, 'Jack is a priest, you follow, Father Neil? He may die soon and the V.G. wishes him to die in his own bed not in hers.'

I did not accompany Fr Duddleswell when he briefed the Hatelys on Rome's decision. He came back, not too dispirited, to report that the old lady had sung her usual lament and started once more to outstare the wall. She had cheered up, though, when she learned that Jack was not about to leave home, after all.

'Now, Father Neil, there is the little matter of a pair of single beds.'

At Franklin's Store, Fr Duddleswell went into a huddle with the manager of the bedding department. It was a slack period and the manager agreed to two divan beds being delivered immediately.

We were at 3 Springfield Road half an hour later when the van arrived. The delivery men screwed on the legs and, to my surprise, joined the divans together to make one double bed.

Fr Duddleswell winked at me. 'Father Neil,' he joked, 'in me seminary days we used to say: beware of bulls and canon lawyers. They have minds like razors, you see, as sharp and as narrow. Better to let 'em have their own way, don't y'think?'

Jack Hately was delighted to have the best of both worlds: to sleep next to his wife and yet have a bed of his own. He lay down on it, sat on it, and bumped up and down on it.

As we were leaving, Fr Duddleswell slipped Jack a fiver which he pocketed out of sight of his arthritic mate. Then we drove off.

On the homeward journey, I said I thought it would be more merciful of the Church to dispense priests like Jack from the vow of celibacy if they wish to marry.

To my surprise, Fr Duddleswell was vehemently opposed to the idea. 'Merciful?' he exclaimed. 'Merciful? To whom, Father Neil? Tell me that, now. Is not the Church's first concern for the majority of priests who do not give up their Latin to run off with women? And are not those who stay confirmed in their vow by the Church's firmness in never granting dispensations?' He whistled through clenched teeth. 'Priests who are tempted to wed in the Register Office are mightily dissuaded by the knowledge that they will never be able to marry in the sight of God or offer a woman the blessing of a Christian home.'

It seemed to me that Jack must have felt as lonely as a sparrow on a roof top when he teamed up with Betty. 'What about special cases?' I asked.

'Father Neil, believe you me, *all* cases are special. The strength of our Church lies in the fact that her rules are bent for nobody. She will no more allow a divorced barmaid to remarry than King Henry VIII. She will no more dispense a priest one year in the ministry than one who is middle-aged with a dozen illegitimate children to his discredit. Everybody, priest and layman alike, knows exactly where he stands.'

He went on to give me a sharp lesson on the value of celibacy. In the seminary, we had learned that priests do not marry so that, freed from domestic ties, they can look after their people day and night. Fr Duddleswell had an altogether broader vision.

For him, a priest is 'no tin cock on a church steeple'. The whole system of Catholicism, its ethic, its creed and its discipline, rests on priestly celibacy. It is celibacy that gives the priest moral authority to teach unpalatable truths. He may be out of touch in many things but none of his congregation ever doubts that he has freely made an enormous sacrifice

for their sake. He has the *right* to hand on the tough Catholic teaching on birth-control, abortion, divorce and homo-sexuality because he is a sign of Jesus lonely and crucified in their midst. 'In the priest, Father Neil, sex bows its lovely head to something lovelier: self-sacrifice.'

I had had recent experience of what he meant.

'Furthermore, Father Neil', he said peering through the windscreen as if he were gazing at some impossibly hideous futuristic vision, 'should the Church ever relax her discipline on celibacy, the whole pack of cards will come tumbling down. Even bishops will be found making exceptions in special cases to birth-control and divorce. The good sisters, seeing the laxity of the clergy, will themselves leave their convents like flocks of migrating birds. And in the end, we will have Catholics advocating euthanasia for babies born handicapped and for old people who are incurably ill or a burden on the community.' He was silent for a few moments before adding, 'Merciful, he says. *Merciful.*'

We had reached the garage gates. I prepared to jump out and open up for him but he touched my arm. 'One more thing to further your education, lad.' I looked at him won-dering what next. 'The Vicar General said that Bishop O'Reilly wants me to persuade Betty to retire to an old folks' home. She will be well looked after there and he will foot all the bills.'

'And old Jack?' I said, shocked at the prospect for one so near the grave.

He leaned his forearms on the wheel. 'The Bishop would like him to go into the Dogs' House.' This was the clergy's name for the Monastery of St Michael's, a kind of reforma-tory for naughty priests. 'The Bishop's idea, Father Neil, is that Jack should end his days there. After a few months, Rome might be prevailed on to let the Prodigal say Mass

again. That way, he could die with dignity.'

However impressive the principle of celibacy, this was too much for my stomach. 'Father,' I burst out angrily, 'Mrs Hately's old and infirm and in constant pain. *I* think Jack has a duty to stay with her as long as she lives.'

'Whatever the Bishop says?'

I didn't hesitate. 'Yes, whatever the Bishop says.'

Fr Duddleswell looked at me with wrath all over his face. 'Young man,' he snapped, 'have you no regard for the wishes of your Superior and father in God? Get out with you and open that gate.' I rose but before I could slam the door on him, he leaned over and said, 'I tell you this, Father Neil. If old Jack should ever leave his Missis after all these years, I will knock his bloody block off.'

Ten

THE SEASON OF GOOD WILL

Fr Duddleswell told me at breakfast of his decision to invite the Rev. Percival Probble, the Anglican Vicar, and 'his good lady' to tea.

'He is convinced, you see, that at the summer swimming gala he saved me from a watery grave.' I could not deny it. 'I have no wish to disabuse him and so injure his self-esteem.'

Mrs Pring put the dishes down with a clatter which showed what she thought of serving a clergyman's wife at our table.

Fr Duddleswell was looking for support. 'What do *you* think, lad?' Honesty compelled me to say that Mrs Pring's opinion should be taken into consideration. What I meant was that she was, in a sense, our good lady and she never ate with us.

'Well, then,' said Fr Duddleswell, 'that makes a slender majority of one to two in me favour.' He obviously did not count votes, he weighed them. When Mrs Pring walked off in a huff, he said, 'That will muffle her clapper for a while.'

The prospect of tea with a married cleric reminded him of the time he had been on a pilgrimage to Rome before the war. In his Hotel just off the Veneto was an Anglican bishop who was well and truly '*conjugally*' *matrimonified*. 'Now, Father Neil, the waiters in the restaurant were so flabbergasted that the Bishop, *il Vescovo*, should have a family that they called his wife *la Vescova* and the kiddies *i Vescovini*.'

He was shaking with mirth.

'Did they?'

My dry response dampened his ebullience. 'I suppose, Father Neil, you would have to know Italian to appreciate the finer points of the joke.' I kept silent to tease him further. 'It seemed strange to them, you follow? that a man in a Roman collar should have a wife and *bambini*.'

'Why strange?'

He said lamely, 'They were not used to it.'

'Is something "strange", Father, simply because an Italian waiter in an Italian restaurant in Italian Italy is not used to it?' He must have thought a little divil had got into me that morning. 'Didn't you tell them, Father, that St Peter who emigrated to Italy had a mother-in-law and so presumably a good lady of his own?'

He was in rapid retreat. 'I did not think of it, like.'

'More's the pity,' I said, sucking in the air like soup. 'Those Italian waiters would have been very droll on the topic, I'm sure. Imagine, now, the first *Papa* having a *Papava* and, who knows, even a few *Papavini*?'

He slid off the end of the conversation by rising to his feet and saying his Grace-after-meals in a single movement. 'I've fixed tay for tomorrow at four. Sharp. And, remember, Father Neil,' he bawled, ' 'tis the season of good will to all.' He slammed the door behind him.

Mrs Probble over tea reinforced every argument I had ever heard in favour of celibacy. Obese and topped by a plumed hat of Royal Ascot dimensions, she was one long verbalized stream of consciousness.

When the Vicar managed to edge in a word and attributed Christ's prayer, 'That they may be one' to Luke instead of John, Mrs Probble squawked at him, 'Husband, I *told* you to leave the theology to me.'

She was intrigued to know how we made so much money each year on our Bazaar. She herself toiled like a Trojan to make a success of St Luke's Garden Fête with the most meagre results. 'How *do* you manage it, Fr Duddleswell?' She pronounced it Duddle-swell.

My parish priest explained to 'Mrs Prob-bull' that we Catholic priests have more numerous female helpers than Solomon himself. Their womanly hearts are so touched by our masculine ineptitude that they rally round us without needing to ask.

Mrs Probble seemed to contemplate for an instant the possibility that she was a liability to her husband and not the huge asset she had always presumed. 'Is that how you explain it?' she said.

'Now, it can hardly be sex-appeal, can it, Mrs Prob-bull?'

'Evidently not,' replied the Vicar's good lady haughtily. If she replied less haughtily than she might have done, it was because she had a favour to ask for her husband. On the last Sunday before Christmas, St Luke's was to have a visitation from the Anglican Bishop of the diocese. A social gathering had been organized to greet him in St Luke's Church Hall. Fr Duddleswell must know that Anglicans, for all their deeply held Christian beliefs, were not so good at attending as Roman Catholics. And what Mrs Probble wanted to ask, as did the Rev. Mr Probble, of course, was this: Would Fr Duddleswell, in the spirit of the season, bring some of his own flock to swell the numbers?

As the request unfolded, I could see Fr Duddleswell's good will being stretched to its limits. He disliked intensely the ascription of episcopacy to a 'doubtfully baptized Anglican layman'. He also loathed the idea of any remotely religious association with those 'Church of England cuckoos who threw us out of our nest.'

The Rev. Mr Probble, sensitive to Fr Duddleswell's religious scruples, assured him that they were cancelling Evensong. It was to be a simple fraternal with beer laid on for those who wanted it. Fr Duddleswell's Benediction of the Blessed Sacrament was at 5.30, which would enable him to bring as many of St Jude's congregation to St Luke's at six o'clock as had a mind to come.

Fr Duddleswell listened in silence as the Vicar explained that to have three Anglican clergy present, and only the usual twenty to thirty of their parishioners, would not create a very fortunate impression on Bishop Pontin—another wince from my parish priest.

It was Mrs Probble who let the cat out of the bag. 'It will so help Percival's preferment, you see, Fr Duddleswell.' She pronounced his name this time with meticulous accuracy.

The Rev. Mr Probble was man enough to admit that he had his eye on a Cathedral canonry, 'but far be it from me, Father, to ask you to violate your Catholic conscience.' It was a good pay-off line.

Fr Duddleswell eyed me to see if I was voting with him but I stayed disenfranchised. 'You promise me, Vicar, no Evensong?'

The Vicar gave his word and made things easier by pointing out that our co-religionist Councillor, Albert Appleby the Mayor, had graciously accepted his invitation to meet the Bishop.

When the Vicar and his wife had left, Fr Duddleswell tried to make light of his defeat. 'I am not one to renege on me debts,' he said, 'when there is no matter of principle involved.' Then changing the subject with a rueful laugh: 'Such is the "felicity of unbounded domesticity".'

His laughter became less forced when I replied, 'The

Vicar, now, he is a regular Duke of Plaza-Toro and no mistake.'

Preparations for Christmas began in earnest. Paper chains and bells were hung in the hall and the dining room. Dangling from the ceiling above Fr Duddleswell's chair, in hope forlorn, was a sprig of mistletoe. The large plaster figures for the crib were taken down from the organ loft and given their annual dusting.

Mrs Pring was stirring silver threepenny pieces into the Christmas cake-mix, as thick as cement, in an enormous bowl. I heard Fr Duddleswell tell her that he would provide the turkey.

The carols on the radio attuned our minds to the peace and good will of the festive season. I had even arranged for Mrs Rollings to be received into the Church on Christmas Eve. She was not ready for it and never would be, but at least, with Christmas over, I could begin the new year without the prospect of instructing her every couple of weeks.

The mood started to change on Fr Duddleswell's last day off before Christmas. In the afternoon, Mrs Pring went to Siddenhall to visit her daughter. Being at a loose end, I donned an old polo-necked pullover and gumboots and pottered around in the garden. The weather had turned mild and I put in a spot of digging with the garden fork. I was well stationed to hear the telephone and the front door bell.

It was the side door bell that rang about 3.15 just as dusk was coming on. Standing there were two sturdy, clean-cut young men in dark suits. At first, I thought they were policemen in plain clothes. One of them put his foot in the door while the other thrust a huge open book in front of my nose. It was too black to see but I smelled it was a Bible. Having only a garden tool in my hand I was at a disadvantage.

'May we come in, Brother?' said Brother Frank, the Bible-bearer, in an American accent, pushing past me. I did not like being addressed below my rank but what could I do?

They carried me with them into Mrs Pring's kitchen and deposited me in a chair at the table. Brother Frank and Brother Hank sat down opposite me and told me that they represented the Church of Christ Shepherd.

Was I a Christian? A Catholic, gee. Well, they wanted to tell me there and then that in their eyes nobody was beyond the mercy of God.

They had a beautiful message for me personally, from Jesus, if only my eyes were not blind and my ears not deaf.

There followed a long but speedy history of 'the fastest growing religious movement in the history of this planet.' I would be relieved to know that their beautiful Founder, the divine Father Shepherd from Scranton, Pennsylvania, had no hang-ups about sex, indeed he positively encouraged the exercise of 'all these beautiful faculties', and they could prove his assertions from this beautiful and holy Book.

Now to the nitty-gritty. In the Church of Christ Shepherd, every member had to freely contribute the biblical tithe of his salary. 'So how much do *you* earn, Brother?' asked Brother Hank, advancing keenly.

I was so surprised at being allowed to speak I couldn't get the words out. After further encouragement, I said, 'Forty pounds a year.'

'Are you on welfare, Brother?' said Brother Frank.

'No, I'm a Roman Catholic priest.'

'Jesus Christ!' they exclaimed in chorus. I instinctively bowed my head, followed them as they raced to the door and bolted it after them. They couldn't have made a quicker exit had I admitted to being a leper.

In the morning, Mrs Pring took me aside. 'Any visitors

yesterday, Father Neil?'

I said that two religious cranks had tried to convert me. 'Why?'

'Because,' she whispered, 'the clock on my mantelpiece went missing.'

I apologized and promised I would buy her another for Christmas. She wouldn't hear of it. It had never worked and was purely ornamental. If she raked around in the garden, she said, she would probably find it there. At least, they hadn't stolen the new Hoover.

I thanked her for not splitting on me to Fr D. In my heart, I could not be sure the young men had taken the clock. I hadn't seen them take it and they seemed sincere. What made me furious was their vicious method of evangelization. They muscled in, took over your castle and brought out the worst in you. I was glad Catholics did not brow-beat people like that.

Later, above the cooing of pigeons, I heard Fr Duddleswell talking to Billy Buzzle the Bookie across the garden fence. 'Seeing 'tis the season of good will,' Father Duddleswell had tossed Pontius, Billy's black Labrador, an enormous bone. Billy was maintaining that two of our flock had knocked on his door the afternoon before and tried to convert him. Fr Duddleswell replied that none of his parishioners was stupid enough to attempt any such impossible thing.

'They had Irish brogues and they wanted to sell me a Bible,' said Billy. This was proof for Fr Duddleswell that they were none of his. Orangemen at worst. Catholics rely on the teaching authority of the Church and do not go in for Bible-hawking.

'Anyway, Fr O'Duddleswell,' said Billy, 'they didn't succeed. I persuaded them instead to put £5 at 10 to 1 on

Twinkletoes in the 3.00 at Plumpton. It came in last.'

He asked Fr Duddleswell if he would care for a little wager himself. It was already snowing in Scotland, Yorkshire and North Wales. Billy would bet £5 even money that it would snow in Fairwater in the next three days. Fr Duddleswell said that, whatever the forecast, his rheumatics told him the opposite. The final terms agreed were these: If it snowed within three days, Fr Duddleswell would fork out £5. If it didn't Billy would give Fr Duddleswell a ten foot Christmas tree for the church, and a fifteen pound turkey.

A large round thrush alighted on the fence in time to see the two men, in the spirit of the season, shake hands on it.

My mood darkened further when Mrs Rollings came for her final instruction prior to her reception. I had run through the ceremony with her including the mechanics of confession when she burst out, 'I don't know how to say this, Father.' She found a way to tell me that, while she accepted without argument the Catholic doctrine on Hell, Indulgences, Papal Infallibility, the Real Presence of Christ in the Blessed Sacrament and the Virgin Birth, she could not agree with the teaching on birth-control.

If she had broken the news to me three months before I would have rejoiced. I had not wanted her in the first place, but to lose her after all that agony was hurtful and humiliating. On reflection, was it naïve of me not to realize that something might be wrong with her marriage when she had twins of eight and no more children?

I had to be true to my convictions. There could be no compromise on a matter of principle and I had no intention of brow-beating her in the manner of those phoney evangelists.

We shook hands on the doorstep and said our last goodbye. I would not have believed it possible but there were

tears in her eyes as she left and not a few pangs in my heart, too.

I told Fr Duddleswell the bad news at the first opportunity. He treated it as a huge joke. As far as he was concerned there was no question of me losing my first scalp. He paid tribute to my long-suffering.

I wanted to know how he could take it so lightly.

'Well, you see, Father Neil, in ethical matters I am far more concerned that she practises what the Church preaches than gives it her full-hearted consent. I have already assured the Bishop that she will be a model Catholic, at least in that respect.'

I said it was a mystery to me how he expected Mrs Rollings to practise what she did not believe in.

'To tell the truth,' he said, ' 'twould be needless expense on her part to contravene the Church's law and 'twould require the operation of the Angel Gabriel for her to conceive again.' He explained that 'the necessary equipment' had been taken from her after the twins were born.

He immediately got on the phone to the baker. 'Wilf,' he said, 'get your woman over here on Christmas Eve at 8 a.m. sharp. Fr Boyd will do the drowning himself.'

Fr Duddleswell's rheumatics proved an accurate barometer. A tall Christmas tree was duly delivered to the church and a turkey to the presbytery with a terse note attached to its neck: TO THE LUCK OF THE IRISH. Fr Duddleswell pinched his arm and prophesied that God would not whiten the world before Christmas Day itself.

On the evening of Sunday December 22nd, Fr Duddleswell conducted a short Benediction with the three standard hymns, *O Salutaris, Tantum Ergo* and *Adoremus*. The hundred or so present were reinforced by members of the Legion

of Mary, the Saint Vincent de Paul Society and the Union of Catholic Mothers, as well as various unattached parishioners who had heard rumours of free Anglican beer.

By 5.45, Fr Duddleswell and I led our well-muffled army through the streets of Fairwater singing carols. A thoughtful Irishman, Paddy Feeney, took a collection from the passers-by on our way. There must have been two-hundred of us.

In ten minutes we were in the warm climate of St Luke's Church Hall. The Anglican clergy and their wives and about twenty parishioners were waiting to greet us. On the stroke of six, the Mayor arrived and, soon, Bishop Pontin, modestly dressed by Catholic standards in a black suit with a clerical collar above a purple stock.

The Rev. Mr Probble introduced Fr Duddleswell and me to the Bishop, adding barely coherent comments on the excellence of inter-Church relationships in Fairwater.

The Bishop, speaking Oxford English, thanked Fr Duddleswell for bringing along one or two of his parishioners.

'Or three or four, sir,' replied Fr Duddleswell.

After thirty minutes of eating and drinking in small groups, the Vicar clapped his hands at a signal from Mrs Probble to announce that the fraternal would have to close until the Carol Concert in the church was over.

Fr Duddleswell, who had no idea it was going to begin, was furious at the deception practised upon him by his opposite number. The Mayor, forewarned no doubt, took him by the shoulder. 'Don't be upset, Farver,' he whispered. 'It's Mrs Probble's doing. No 'arm. I'm attending it myself.'

'Well may you, Bert, but I have no official position to maintain, d'you hear? To enter that mausoleum would be tantamount to *communicatio in sacris*. 'Twould be to desecrate all within me that is holy.' He gritted his teeth. 'I am

withdrawing meself, me curate and me entire flock.'

'Farver, Farver,' pleaded Mr Appleby, 'you can't do that in the season of good will.' He argued that if angels could sing hymns for Jewish shepherds, there was nothing to stop Catholics singing a few carols for the conversion of Protestants. 'Besides, Farver,' he said, 'I am officially deputing you to act in this civil function. You can give out the food parcels to the old-age pensioners.' A bus load of them were at that very moment stepping down and trooping into the church.

That seemed to pacify Fr Duddleswell's conscience. Before the Vicar invited him to accompany the Bishop to the vestry, I saw Mayor Appleby slip Fr Duddleswell his own small mother of pearl rosary.

We were into the third carol before Fr Duddleswell appeared. In spite of the disguise, there was no doubting the fact that it *was* indeed he, dressed as Father Christmas. At least he wasn't required to sing with us—and the beard hid his blushes.

He told me afterwards that his being cheated in earnest was all made worthwhile by the Bishop remarking to the Rev. and Mrs Probble in his hearing.

'Percy, my dear fellow, I do congratulate you on having so many devout Irishmen in your congregation.'

Just before 8 o'clock next morning, Mrs Rollings appeared white-faced in the sacristy as I was preparing to vest. She was clutching a Catholic Truth Society pamphlet in which was printed the ceremony for the reception of a convert. She was worried that in the part about abjuring heresies she would have to denounce totally her former religious upbringing and all its errors.

'I can't say it, Father,' she sniffled.

I tried an entirely different approach. 'All right, Mrs Roll-

ings,' I said ironically, 'if you can't say it, try whispering it.'

Instead of slapping my face, she brightened up immediately. 'It won't be so bad like that, will it, Father?' and she returned to the front bench to join her family.

Everything went well until her confession. I led her down the church to the confessional. Before I could stop her she had gone into my side and closed the door. It took some time to sort it out and get her kneeling on the prie-dieu in her proper place. She was muttering something about the 'number and species of all my mortal sins'.

Fr Duddleswell's opinion was that there are basically two types of female penitents. Those that suffer verbally from either diarrhoea or constipation. 'The latter sort,' he had said, 'need a liberal laxative of kindness.'

Mrs Rollings was of the latter sort when it came to confessing her sins and I was running out of kindness. The confession took fully twenty minutes. I did not know if she had got everything off her chest. If it was still a bit grimy, I consoled myself with the thought that it was her responsibility not mine.

When it came to the conditional baptism, I longed for the return of the ancient practice of three-fold total immersion. After all, I had a strong right arm.

Of course, I was sorry for my wicked thoughts afterwards and deeply humbled when I saw the joy on the faces of the Rollings family. The nominal head of it took me aside when Mass was over. 'Fr Boyd, since my wife started her instructions, she is a different person.'

'So am I, Mr Rollings,' I said.

All dismal reflections were banished by the approach of Christmas and the birth of Christ. Ever since I was a child, the highlight for me has been Midnight Mass.

The church looked gorgeous with its flowers and potted plants, the lights and decorations on the Christmas tree and the crib with the Babe in the manger.

Some strong men in the parish had been deputed to bring a couple of hundred extra stacking chairs from Tipton Hall and to keep out the drunks. Fr Duddleswell and I, clad in cassock and biretta, began by greeting the parishioners as they trooped in smilingly.

The Rollings family was there and old Jack Hately and Mrs Dodson and Dr Daley and Lord Mitchin and Mr Appleby with his wife. To my great joy, Archie and Peregrine arrived early and sat in the front row. It hurt me that Fr Duddleswell should tell me to make sure 'that fine pair keep their hands out of the till'.

Mr Bottesford, the undertaker, sneaked in and sat at the back like a publican. Mother Stephen led a representation from the Convent. Even Billy Buzzle put in a brief appearance to cast his eye over his Christmas tree. 'Tell you what, Fr O'Duddleswell,' he said, 'I'd willingly swop my takings for yours tonight.' There was bound to be a congregation of five hundred.

We spent the last quarter of an hour before Mass hearing confessions. When I opened my box to go to the sacristy, who should I see but Nurse Owen with Spinks, the abortionist, in tow? Herod come to worship the Lord, I thought. I could have sworn that his bald patch was now as big as a half crown.

Fr Duddleswell was to sing the Mass and preach while I assisted him. Already the church was bursting at the seams. In the loft, the choir was in full voice. *Adeste fideles* and then *Silent Night, Holy Night*. 'Ah, 'tis enough,' I said, as I helped Fr Duddleswell struggle into his white vestments, 'to turn your taps on.'

His sermon, full of theatrical gestures, was superb. It was received in utter silence. For his text he chose St Paul's words: *Christ, though rich, became poor to enrich us with his poverty.*

He began by calling attention to the Christmas tree, 'donated by a devout parishioner'. That tree was the most Christian of all our symbols. Did not the first Adam eat from a tree in disobedience to God? And did not the second Adam, Jesus, eat the bitter fruit of another tree out of obedience to God His Father? Legend has it that the cross of Calvary was planted in the very spot where once grew the tree of the knowledge of good and evil.

Was not the Christmas tree itself the signal proof of God's power to bring life out of death? Here it was, green wood in the deadness of the year. Like a Child born of a Virgin Mother. Like resurrection following upon Calvary's death when our Lord and Saviour Jesus Christ flew on His wooden bird to God the Father.

God, according to Fr Duddleswell, is deviousness carried to infinity. He quoted Crashaw's lines on the birth of Christ:

> *Welcome all wonders in one sight!*
> *Eternity shut in a span,*
> *Summer in winter, day in night,*
> *Heaven in earth and God in man.*

Jesus forsook his eternity to enter time. He gave up His infinite riches to become poor for us and to enrich us with His poverty. He forsook the bosom of His Father for birth in a cave. None of this could have happened had not God humbled Himself to become as a child in order to enter the Kingdom of Man. God planned it so that Mary the Virgin would be her Maker's maker and her Father's mother.

And what is the meaning of all this?

'That we, me dear people, should ourselves forsake guile to merit the blessing God gives to the weak and foolish of the world. That we should forsake our love of earthly riches for the sake of the spiritual blessings brought to us in abundance by the poor little Babe of Bethlehem.'

Throughout the recitation of the Creed that followed the sermon, the congregation were rustling through pockets and purses to forsake some of their money. The Christmas offering, the most generous of the year, is by tradition the personal gift of Catholics to their priests. As the collection was being harvested, glimpsing out of the corner of my eye, I could only marvel at the sight of the notes mounting in a dozen plates borne by the parish jury of twelve just men. I was already contemplating buying Meg and Jenny a bicycle each.

So eloquent was the sermon, so beautiful the singing, that for the first time I could remember there was no mass exodus of parishioners as soon as the celebrant gave the last blessing.

Fr Duddleswell and I put on our birettas prior to leaving the sanctuary. He handed me the precious tabernacle key saying, 'Put this in the safe, Father Neil, and then join me in the porch.'

Within a minute, I had locked the key away and, having removed my cotta, joined him at the church door to wish the congregation a happy Christmas as they threaded between us.

When we were left alone, Fr Duddleswell locked the front door and we retired to the sacristy where he unvested.

'Ah, Father Neil,' he said, 'the old saying is true: the Christmas midnight Mass equals twenty-one Masses.'

He was the first to notice that there was something dis-

turbing about the collection plates. They contained only silver and the usual assortment of brass with Irish pennies predominating. The notes, the cheques, and the envelopes specially designed to hold the offering of a whole family had disappeared.

My heart experienced a great pang when I saw what the loss of the money meant to him. He seemed so unexpectedly vulnerable.

'There must have been nigh on £300 in notes,' he gulped. 'Have you any idea where the divil it can be, Father Neil?'

Half jokingly I said, 'Search me, Father,' and turned my cassock pockets inside out to reveal nothing but a bunch of keys. As an afterthought, I asked, 'This is serious, isn't it, Father? You're not having me on?'

He did not hear me. He was muttering something about cash being the only thing not covered by the insurance. He opened the door leading to the house and asked Mrs Pring if she had taken the big money into the presbytery for protection. I heard Mrs Pring deny stridently that in all these years she had laid one finger on his filthy lucre.

I helped him search the vestment drawers and cupboards. We looked into the confessionals and he even rummaged in the straw of the crib. Not a smell of it.

'Father Neil,' he sighed in desperation. 'I want you to dial 999 and get the police here immediately.'

When I returned a couple of minutes later, the lights in the church were ablaze. I saw him turf the baby Jesus out of his crib in case the thief had temporarily hidden the loot there.

We unbolted the front door and stood there waiting for the police. 'Did they give you any indication when they would arrive, Father Neil?'

I said no. The police prided themselves on answering any

emergency call in any part of London within three minutes but, of course, this *was* Christmas Eve.

Fr Duddleswell's glasses were steaming and he was thumping his arms diagonally against his shoulders to stop himself from shivering.

Outside the church, the scene was one of perfect peace. In the windows of houses across the road the lights of Christmas trees were winking off and on. Smoke from chimneys was ascending like incense to heaven. In that mild winter, a few rose bushes, caught in the shaft of light from the church, could be seen still bearing flowers.

As we waited, he went crazily through the suspects. Archie and Peregrine he accused first. I defended them stoutly. Peregrine was capable of anything but surely Fr Duddleswell remembered how Archie had made him give the doctor back his wallet.

He turned his ire on Billy Buzzle. In revenge for losing his bet. Billy could have climbed the fence, got in through our back door and slipped into the sacristy after the collection. Even Fr Duddleswell discounted this theory. Billy Buzzle, he admitted, was far too crooked to stoop to straightforward theft.

Bottesford, now, what about Bottesford? He certainly had a score to settle. Another ludicrous suggestion. He was a rich man and found it far less hazardous robbing the dead than the living.

Still no sign of the infernal police. He sent me to look in the confessionals again. I reported that I'd had no luck.

'Father,' I said, 'isn't it more likely that the thief is someone without any criminal record who found all that money lying around too great a temptation?'

'One thing, lad,' he said ... 'Oh, where are these bloody police? When they arrive there will be no Silent bloody

Night, Holy bloody Night around here. And they will probably send that brute who biffed you under the counter.' He
was now able to pick up the thread of the thought. 'One
thing, I promise you, lad. *You* will not go short. I will make
it up to you.'

'Please, Father, no,' I replied staunchly. 'If Jesus became
poor for ...'

He interrupted me. 'You cannot sole your shoes on £40 a
year without your fair share of the Christmas offering, you
follow? Neither can I, come to that. Oh, where in heaven's
bloody name are the police?'

Mrs Pring addressed us over our shoulders. 'Isn't it about
time you two men came in from the cold?'

Fr Duddleswell pulled his biretta more firmly down on his
head. 'This is man's work, woman, and we are awaiting the
police.'

Mrs Pring said, 'They're not coming.'

'They are delayed, woman, but they will be here any hour
now.' Mrs Pring was adamant that they were not coming. He
turned to me. 'Father Neil, did you not phone them?'

I carefully removed my biretta and smartly turned it up-
side down so as not to lose any of the precious collection of
notes, cheques and envelopes.

He sat down on the cold step, rubbed his eyes inside his
glasses, puffed, and rubbed his eyes again. Then he sprang
up as if to box my ears.

I took one step backwards. 'Now, remember, Father
Charles, 'tis the season of good will.'

Mrs Pring roared with laughter. He silenced her by giving
her a mistletoe peck on the forehead and wishing her a
merry Christmas.

'Lock up, Fathers,' she said in a snuffly voice. 'I've boiled

the kettle and there's an Abishag waiting for each of you in your beds.'

We stayed there together for a few moments longer looking out on to the quiet scene. In the light of the street lamps, we saw the first snow of the winter fall. A large flake settled on my eyelash till I blinked it away.

'Ah, Father Neil,' said Fr Duddleswell serenely, 'are they not the only pure white doves this sordid city sees?' I nodded, half asleep now. Suddenly he turned on me. 'I have something else I have been meaning to say to you.' I didn't think he would let me off that lightly.

He stretched up his arms and embraced me. 'Merry Christmas to you, Neil.'

'Merry Christmas, Father,' I said.

2

De klas was stil. Doodstil. De stem van Bjorn klonk nog na. Hij liet het blad met de tekst zakken en grinnikte onhoorbaar.

'Leg eens uit, Bjorn.'

'Wat, mevrouw?'

De lerares kneep haar ogen tot spleetjes. Waarom had zij opnieuw de indruk dat hij en zij alleen in de klas waren? Waarom leek het alsof Bjorn en zij in het licht stonden en de anderen schaduwen waren?

'Wat, mevrouw?'

'Je opdracht was een profiel van Theseus schrijven. De anderen hebben dat gedaan, schematisch, met trefwoorden. Jij maakt een verhaal. Toegegeven, het heeft kracht en als je het hoort lezen, grijpt het je aan. Misschien een beetje gezocht dramatisch af en toe, wat overladen. Maar dat doet er nu niet toe. Waarom een verhaal? Dat wil ik weten.'

De rest van de klas, vier jongens en drie meisjes, zweeg. Bjorn streek een lok bruin haar van zijn voorhoofd en knikte drie keer.

'Omdat ik vond dat het zo moest. Ik heb het werk van Geert en Frank gezien. Het maakte niets duidelijk over die figuur. Wat heb je nu aan woorden als doorzetter, durver, onbetrouwbaar figuur. Die Theseus leeft niet. Wat betekenen die woorden als je de figuur Theseus op de planken wilt brengen?'

'Stik jij,' siste Geert, 'het is genoeg dat je ons te kakken zet, je hoeft ons niet ook nog in de stront te trappen.'

'Geert?'

'Ik vond dat we ons aan de opdracht moesten houden. En ik heb de termen "schematisch" en "trefwoorden" gehoord.'

'Dat vind ik juist niet!' ging Bjorn verder. 'Elke opdracht moet je interpreteren tot ze zin heeft. Anders ben je nutteloos bezig. Wie een personage echt op toneel wil zetten, moet dat personage zijn en niet alleen tics of gebaren overnemen op basis van een profielschets. Hoe doe je dat, een durver uitbeelden? Door met je spierballen te gaan rollen? Nee, ik wil Theseus zíjn. En dat heb ik met die tekst bereikt. Voor mezelf. Het gaat om details. Hij gaat niet, hij marcheert. Zijn pad loopt eigenzinnig rechtdoor, hij wil niet wijken voor hindernissen. Zijn herinneringen blijven hem achtervolgen, ze zijn sterker dan hijzelf, al beseft hij dat herinneringen waardeloos zijn. Hij heeft van alles opgegeven en wil daar niet mee leven. Maar vooral, hij heeft een excuus voor alles wat hij gedaan heeft, wat hij doet, wat hij zal doen! Vooral met vrouwen die van hem houden.'

De klas stond paf. Elke kauwde op haar lip. Ze kon haar ogen niet van Bjorn afhouden. De vonken sloegen van hem af als hij zo praatte. Hij maakte haar bang, maar trok haar tegelijk onweerstaanbaar aan.

'Wat je gedaan hebt, Bjorn, is eigenlijk meer het werk van een dramaturg. Je interpreteert, heel persoonlijk, zonder rekening te houden met je mogelijke tegenspelers. Theater maken is een groepsgebeuren. Bovendien, krijg je de rol van Theseus wel? Stel dat dat niet zo is.'

Bjorn keek de lerares staalhard aan. Niet jij! zeiden zijn ogen. Jij snapt het toch wel?

Ze was opeens in de war, maar nog niet bereid om te ontwapenen.

'Stel dat het niet zo is,' herhaalde ze. 'Dan zullen jouw reacties op wat Theseus zegt, bepaald worden door wat je vooraf had gedacht. Laat dat aan de dramaturg en de regisseur over. Maar verder, prima werk, Bjorn.'

Bjorn knikte. De spanning verdween uit zijn schouders.

'O ja, nog een vraagje. Waarom beschrijf je Theseus aan het eind van zijn leven, in zijn vrijwillige ballingschap op Skyros? Daarover gaat het stuk niet.'

'Ik heb verder gekeken dan de strijd tegen de Minotaurus, mevrouw. Een man als Theseus eindigt altijd eenzaam.'

'Uitslover,' zuchtte Frank.

'Frank, laat hem. Hij mag toch?'

Andrea, de sombere, donkere schoonheid, nam het ook al voor Bjorn op. Natuurlijk, dacht de lerares, zij koos altijd de kant van de sterkste. Of was er meer aan de hand en hadden die drie vrouwtjes in wording ook gevoeld wat zij voelde.

'Ga door, Bjorn.'

'Door wat hij heeft gedacht en gedaan, is hij dit soort man geworden. Ik vind dat de elementen die hem hebben gevormd al aanwezig moeten zijn in het personage dat je neerzet.'

De lerares knikte.

'Goed, dat was het voor vandaag. Morgen lezen we de eerste scènes hier. Zorg dat je de tekst hebt doorgenomen.'

'Je kunt hem misschien al uit het hoofd leren, Bjorn!' lachte Willem.

'Of alleen de tekst van Theseus?' viel Frank hem bij.

'Dat was het, heb ik gezegd!' De lerares sloot haar tekstboek met een klap. Hommeles, dat voelde ze zo. Maar dat belette niet dat Bjorn ontzettend veel talent had, dat hij je met zijn stem, met de gebaren van zijn hand en met zijn geraffineerde mimiek kon raken. Ook haar.

Zet hem op Skyros en ook zijn paadje tussen de zee en het huis zou koppig rechtdoor lopen, over rotsen en kloven. Hij slofte niet naar buiten, hij marcheerde. Ze hoorde zijn hakken tikken op de stenen vloer. Hij droeg schoenen, geen Nikes of Reeboks zoals de anderen.

Toen Bjorn op zijn kamer was, liet hij zich op zijn bed vallen en lachte hard. Hij pakte zijn tekstboek, *De goden grijnzen,* van Ganymedes Theofilos, een jonge Griek die met zijn tragedies in klassieke stijl op dit ogenblik triomfen oogstte in de hele wereld.

EERSTE BEDRIJF

Geen doek. Twee volksmensen die de rol van het koor op zich zullen nemen, komen op. De ene, Heros, verhaalt in de loop van het stuk de heldhaftige geschiedenis van Theseus. De tweede, Hubris, zal zijn daden telkens interpreteren vanuit het grote motief dat Theseus' leven heeft beheerst, de grenzeloze eerzucht die uiteindelijk zijn ondergang zal betekenen.

HEROS: Dit is het einde van de wereld! Als zelfs de helden schaamteloos worden vermoord door kleine tirannen als Lycomedes van Skyros, moeten de goden huilend het hoofd afwenden. O, Theseus...

HUBRIS: Theseus? Vermoord? Die hooghartige, zelfzuchtige vadermoordenaar dood? En jij denkt dat de goden daarbij één traan zullen plengen? De goden zitten nu te grijnslachen, ze wrijven zich in de handen en betreuren dat zij niet kunnen baden in zijn bloed, dat zij zijn ingewanden niet kunnen roosteren op het hemelvuur!

HEROS: O, Theseus, hoe kunnen kleine mensen, mieren die in spleten leven, begrijpen wat een berg is! Waarom is het noodlot de held te sterk? Waarom blijft geen reus overeind als mieren de grond onder zijn voeten met hun gewriemel doorwroeten?

HUBRIS: Praat toch geen onzin. Zijn je ogen nog altijd niet geopend? Heb jij je vereerde Theseus ooit echt gekend? Heb jij dan niet gezien hoe de eerzucht hem oogkleppen voorbond, zodat hij als een renpaard vooruitstormde, steigerend en schoppend onder de zweep van zijn harteloze, nietsontziende overmoed? Ik heb hem gekend! Ik was een van zijn vrienden. Tenminste, dat dacht ik. Nu weet ik beter. De eerzuchtige heeft geen vrienden. Wie hij ontmoet, wordt een stapsteen, een sport in de ladder naar zijn eigen roem. Het begon al toen hij terugkeerde uit Troezen...

Bjorn kwam langzaam overeind en toen hij stond, draaide hij snel op zijn hakken om naar de wasbak. Hij hield zijn hoofd luisterend schuin. Zijn hand maakte een gebaar alsof hij een deur openduwde. Hij zag de scène voor zich. Het publiek kuchte zachtjes toen het donker werd. Stoelen kraakten, voeten schuifelden. De schouwburg leefde.

Hij las verder.

Het licht dooft op het tweetal.
De troonzaal van Aegeus, koning van Athene. Aegeus zit in een
stoel met een hoge rug en houdt een lange staf in de hand. De ziener
Oratos staat naast zijn troon. Buiten klinkt het rumoer van mensen,
het zwelt langzaam aan, vrouwenstemmen klagen luidruchtig. Ae-
geus verbergt zijn hoofd in zijn handen.

AEGEUS: Houdt dit dan nooit op? Nauwelijks zijn de wonden geheeld of de harteloze tijd brengt er nieuwe toe.

ORATOS: Dat is het perfide aan de wraak van Minos. Een zwaardhouw die je hand afhakt, een bliksem die je treft, veroorzaakt een flits van verblindende pijn, maar dan krijg je de kans om te herstellen. Dit is sluipend gif, de angst die even wegdoezelt en dan weer wakker schrikt bij het schuiven van de seizoenen. Het tellen van de manen die groeien en verschrompelen...

AEGEUS: Zwijg, Oratos, als dat alles is wat je kunt zeggen! Moeten we die dodelijke grillen van Minos dan blijven inwilligen?

ORATOS: Vraagt de rots of ze zich door het opkomende stormtij moet laten overspoelen? Vraagt de rietstengel of hij moet buigen voor de wervelwind?

AEGEUS: Is het bloed van Androgeus nog altijd niet weggespoeld door het bloed van onze kinderen? Telkens opnieuw zie ik de zoon van Minos vallen, genadeloos getroffen door mijn speer, vastgespijkerd aan de rode aarde. Ik heb het niet gewild! Waarom was hij zo gehaast om te zien waar mijn speer zou neerkomen? Waarom strekte hij al zegevierend de armen in de lucht? Welke god tilde de speer in de handen van een windvlaag opnieuw op en joeg ze voort tot ze trillend in zijn hart geplant was?

ORATOS: Koning, waarom stel je de vraag niet anders? Kon je ontkomen aan dit lot? Het begon allemaal veel vroeger. Welke god deed bij jou de gedachte ontstaan dat het goed zou zijn als mensen zich met elkaar konden meten in het lopen, het worstelen, het speerwerpen of het slingeren van de discus? Of welke god maakte als eerste bij de mens het verlangen wakker om een ander in kracht of snelheid te overtreffen?

AEGEUS: Als de goden inderdaad een plan hebben met ons, waarom tekenen ze dan ook niet de gevolgen van onze daden voor ons uit? Denk je dat ik ooit spelen zou hebben ingericht waaraan de zonen van vorsten en hooggeplaatsten op aarde zouden meedoen als ik had geweten dat daarvoor zoveel bloed zou vloeien? Waarom spreken wij van het blinde noodlot, terwijl het onze ogen zijn die niet over de grens van de dagen kunnen kijken?

Het gejoel wordt nog sterker. Er wordt één woord gescandeerd, al is niet te verstaan welk woord. Het gehuil wordt gejuich.

ORATOS: Koning, jou treft geen verwijt. Minos heeft de dood van zijn zoon gewoon aangegrepen om zijn macht over de zee en over Attica uit te breiden. Het gaf hem een wettelijk lijkend voorwendsel om jou te onderwerpen. Wat een spel, een wedkamp had moeten zijn, werd een oorlogsverklaring. En de buit die hij meesleept na zijn overwinning is jong, ongeschonden leven.

AEGEUS: Ik zal me verzetten, ik maak er een eind aan, ik zal...

ORATOS: Je zult niks. Je weet dat woorden afketsen op wapens. De schepen van Minos spuwen in tien tellen meer gewapende krijgers uit op onze stranden dan wij er in vijftien jaar op de been kunnen brengen. Soms is het nodig jonge levens te offeren om het leven van jong en oud te sparen!

AEGEUS: Waarom...

Er klinkt nu woedend geschreeuw en het geluid van een worsteling voor de deur van de troonzaal.

Wat moet dat? Wachters! Wachters!

ORATOS: Het noodlot klopt alweer aan. De goden grijnzen!

Twee wachters worden naar binnen geduwd door een jongeman. Ze proberen zich te verzetten, maar hij maait ze onderuit.

Bjorn zwaaide zijn rechterbeen uit en duwde een denkbeeldige deur open. Hij was niet meer in zijn kamer. Hij snoof de geur op van make-up en talkpoeder, van baardlijm. Hij voelde de tocht die uit de zaal kwam toen hij op de scène stapte.

THESEUS: Als ik mijn vader wil bezoeken, zal geen mens me dat beletten.

AEGEUS: Vader? Mijn zoon? Theseus!

THESEUS: Jawel, vader! Het paleis van mijn grootvader werd me te eng. En zoals ik het zie, is hier wat aan de hand. Waarom staan de Atheners buiten te jammeren als oude wijven? Wat betekenen die gesloten gezichten, die schichtige blikken, dat steelse wegsluipen?

AEGEUS: *Omhelst Theseus.*

Theseus, ben jij het echt? Ik heb je weggestuurd naar Pittheus van Troezen als een kind en je komt terug als een man. Gaat de tijd echt zo snel?

THESEUS: Snel? De tijd? De tijd kruipt als een landschildpad. Wanneer gebeurt er wat? Wanneer komt de aarde eindelijk in beweging? Dat zijn de vragen die ik me voortdurend stel.

ORATOS: Het ongeduld van de jeugd die haar dagen wil vullen tot aan de rand. Welkom, prins Theseus.

THESEUS: Dank je. Wie is hij, vader?

AEGEUS: Oratos, mijn raadgever. Hij lijkt het vermogen te hebben in de boezem van de tijd te kijken, geheimen te ontsluieren waar onze ogen blind blijven.

THESEUS: Mooi zo. Oratos, ontsluier dan het geheim. Wat is er aan de hand in Athene? Waarom kreunt heel Attica?

AEGEUS: Ik ben blij dat je hier bent, Theseus. Soms voel ik het gewicht van de jaren op me wegen.

ORATOS: Alleen de jaren brengen de zegen van de wijsheid, koning! De jeugd is als een wild paard dat steigert en bokt en de flanken schurkt tegen de omheining van de tijd. En om een land te besturen is wijsheid belangrijker dan ongeduld.

THESEUS: Ach wat, alweer oudewijvenpraat. Wat is hier aan de hand? Ik hoor vreemde dingen over een schatting, over een monster dat de kinderen van dit land en van deze stad zou verslinden, over een koning die te zwak is om zijn volk te beschermen? Vertellen ze dat over jou, vader?

AEGEUS: Ze zullen het wel over mij hebben, maar ik weet dat de pijn, het verdriet hun geesten verduistert.

THESEUS: Lulkoek! Een koning mag dat niet laten zeggen. Het gewone volk moet opkijken naar zijn vorst...

ORATOS: Prins Theseus, zou je niet eerst het verhaal van onze rampspoed willen horen? Jouw woorden lijken wel angels.

THESEUS: *Grijpt Oratos beet.*

Ik heb van jou geen lessen te ontvangen. Maar goed, vertel op, vader.

AEGEUS: Theseus, ik wil geen geweld hier. Dit paleis is een huis, een woning en wie er mijn gast is, heeft recht op een voorname behandeling. Het verhaal is trouwens gauw verteld. Ik wilde de onderlinge naijver tussen de Grieken en hun buren in goede banen leiden. Ze mochten elkaar ongewapend bekampen in wedstrijden. Zo zouden we eerlijk uitmaken wie het snelst liep, wie het verst kon springen, wie de speer of de discus verder kon slingeren dan de anderen. We zouden ongewapend worstelen. Het leek te werken. Alle steden sloten vrede en stuurden hun beste mannen. Ook Minos, de koning van Kreta, stuurde iemand. Zijn eigen zoon. In het speerwerpen stonden wij tegenover elkaar. Androgeus gooide eerst. Erg ver. Ik nam mijn aanloop en slingerde mijn speer weg. De wind droeg ze verder dan ik kon hopen. Helaas. Androgeus stond in de baan van mijn worp. Mijn speer heeft hem gedood. Minos was razend van pijn. Hij luisterde niet naar mijn woorden, maar wilde alleen wraak. Hij stuurde meteen een vloot hierheen, nam de stad in en dreigde ze te verwoesten. Uiteindelijk nam hij genoegen met een vreemde losprijs. Wij zouden om de zeven jaar zeven jongens en zeven meisjes overleveren...

THESEUS: Atheners die slaaf worden? Vader! Dat is schandelijk.

AEGEUS: Het is zelfs erger. De meisjes en de jongens worden in het paleis van Minos opgesloten in een doolhof. Daar huist een afschuwelijk monster dat alleen mensenvlees eet. Onze kinderen dienen als voedsel voor dat monster. O, waarom hebben de goden ons zo getroffen?

THESEUS: Wat heeft dat met de goden te maken? Dit heeft te maken met macht, met de wil om te heersen, zich niet te onderwerpen aan de grillen van een tiran. Dit heeft te maken met dapperheid, met de plicht van een koning!

ORATOS: Prins Theseus, op het gevaar af opnieuw je woede te wekken, je praat zonder na te denken. Als je vader weigert de jonge losprijs te betalen, wordt deze stad verwoest. De overmacht van Minos is te groot en zolang de Minotaurus in zijn paleis huist, is hij oppermachtig. De Minotaurus, het monster, is half stier, half mens, geboren uit de liefde van een vrouw en de woede van een god. Minos van Kreta koestert het monster als teken van onderwerping aan die god. En dus mag hij op de bescherming van de god rekenen.

'Mag ik naar binnen komen?'
Bjorn leek wakker te schrikken uit een droom.

'De deur staat open.'

Elke ging naar binnen. Bjorn stond voor de wastafel met het tekstboek van *De goden grijnzen* in zijn handen. Hij knipperde met zijn ogen.

'Hou jij nooit op met werken?'

'Zelden. Ik heb geen tijd te verliezen.'

Hij bladerde in zijn tekstboek. Boven zijn bed had hij een vel papier opgehangen met de woorden *London, here I come!!!* Met drie uitroeptekens. Londen... Onvoorstelbaar toch, dat hij dacht dat hij een kans maakte.

'Is met vrienden praten tijdverlies?'

'Vrienden? Waar zijn die dan?' snauwde Bjorn.

'Ik dacht dat wij vrienden waren. Ik ben geen concurrente, wees gerust.'

Bjorn liet het tekstboek zakken.

'De anderen ook niet.'

'Dat klinkt ontzettend pretentieus.'

'Maar het is zo. Wat doen ze hier? Ze konden net zo goed gekozen hebben voor zeilen of skeeleren. Het maakt ze geen moer uit waarmee ze hun zielige dagen vullen.'

Elke zweeg en schudde haar hoofd. Ze waren nu al dagen samen, maar Bjorn leek met niemand van de cursisten echt contact te willen hebben. Af en toe deed hij wel mee aan de ontspanning, maar meestal was hij het gezelschap van de anderen gauw beu. Weer een van zijn buien?

'Nee, geen bui, maar als je wat wilt bereiken, zie je alleen dat doel en de weg ernaartoe.' Hij liet zich op zijn bed vallen, het tekstboek klapte dicht.

'Je woorden lijken zo uit je tekstboek te komen. Komaan, Bjorn, laten we gaan wandelen of tafeltennissen. Toe nou.'

Ze sjorde aan zijn arm en probeerde hem overeind te trekken.

Onwillig stond de jongen op.

'Je moet af en toe... Ach, laat maar zitten, zoals jij zelf altijd zegt,' zuchtte Elke. 'Geloof je nu echt dat je Londen haalt?'

'Was ik anders hierheen gekomen? Heeft een kat een snor?'

De jongen reikte naar de tafel naast zijn bed, gooide wat boeken opzij en zwaaide met een folder.

'Herinner je je dit?'

Elke knikte en schudde toen haar hoofd.

'Kun je dan niet begrijpen dat iemand dit doet omdat zij of hij het leuk vindt? Gewoon omdat het leuk is en je in je vakantie wat anders wilt doen?'

Bjorn gooide zijn handen in de lucht.

'Leuk vinden! Leuk vinden! Dat is alles wat je hoort vandaag.'

Elke legde haar handen op zijn schouders.

'Bjorn, weet je nog... vorige week? Dat vond je ook leuk.'

Het meisje legde haar hoofd op zijn borst en keek omhoog.

'Goed, je lacht weer.'

Bjorn glimlachte inderdaad en drukte toen een vlinderlichte kus op haar voorhoofd.

'Maar dat verandert hieraan niets!'

Hij waaierde met de folder.

INSTITUTE FOR YOUNG ACTORS - SUMMERSCHOOL
VEROVER LONDEN! TRIOMFEER IN DE GROTE THEATERS!

Acteerstudio

Eén maand lang werken we met professionele regisseurs. De slotweek wordt besteed aan de voorbereiding van het stuk *De goden grijnzen*. Dit stuk van Ganymedes Theofilos werd door het London Youth Theater gekozen als slotproductie voor het komende seizoen. Kandidaten voor de cast worden gezocht in alle landen van de Europese Unie waar het Institute for Young Actors haar Summerschools inricht. Een prachtkans dus voor talentvolle jongeren die op het toneel hun dromen willen waarmaken.

Hij praatte opeens weer veel heftiger.

'Ja, ik wil naar Londen. En ja, ik denk dat ik een kans maak. En nog eens ja, ik zal alles doen om die kans te grijpen! Alles.'

Elke knikte. Als hij zo tekeerging, werd ze een beetje bang van hem. Ze herkende nog nauwelijks de jongen die drie weken geleden schuchter en vooral onhandig was komen vragen of ze met hem wat dialogen wilde inoefenen. Een heerlijke herinnering anders.

'Ik ben Bjorn.'

'Ik heet Elke. Wil je ook wat?'

Ze stak haar blikje frisdrank naar hem uit. Hij glimlachte dankbaar, pakte het blikje en likte de condensatiedruppels eraf. Toen gaf hij het blikje terug.

'Wat doe je in 's hemelsnaam?'

'Dat zag je toch?'

'Maar waarom? Ik bedoelde dat je best een slok mocht nemen.'

'Weet ik, maar ik wil eerst de buitenkant proeven.'

Hij lachte wat schuw.

'Ik ben niet iemand die gauw, weet je, ik ben nogal bang om... ach, laat maar zitten.'

Ze zaten naast elkaar op een bank in het park. Op de achtergrond stond het gerestaureerde kasteel waar de theatercursus werd georganiseerd. Twee klassen, beginners en gevorderden. Tot haar verbazing was Elke na een eerste test bij de groep van de gevorderden ingedeeld. Best leuk trouwens.

Bjorn was haar meteen opgevallen, al bij de eerste lessen de vorige dag. Maar echt gepraat had ze niet met hem. Met niemand trouwens. De studenten van de Acteerstudio leken katten die om elkaar heen snuffelden.

'Weet je dat je mooie ogen hebt?' vroeg ze.

Hij draaide zich naar haar toe.

'Gewoonlijk zegt een jongen dat tegen een meisje.'

'Tegenwoordig niet meer. Ik vind je trouwens helemaal knap.'

'Draag je meestal een bril? Ik zie eruit als een vogelverschrikker. Te lang, te mager. Maar ik ga nu als een wildeman fitnessen, om spieren te krijgen.'

Hij lachte.

'Waarom?'

'Ken jij dat stuk van die Griek waarmee we gaan werken? Nee? Het gaat over een held. Ik kan moeilijk die held spelen met een lijf waar aan alle kanten ribben en knoken uitsteken. Of wel?'

Ze lachte.

'Ik vind anders dat jij er ook leuk uitziet. Mooie haren,' zei hij.
'You must be joking!'
'Yes. Ik maakte een grapje.'
Nu lachten ze allebei.
'Maar de kleur van honing en oker is heel speciaal.'
'Dank je. Jouw haren, charmante prins, zijn zwartblauw als de nacht.'
Hij boog zijn hoofd.
'Ik heb je bezig gezien en gehoord. Ik vind dat je heel goed acteert. Je hebt ook een mooie, volle stem. Meestal vind ik meisjes mekkeren. Jij niet. Rook je?'
Ze schudde haar hoofd, wist niet meteen wat te antwoorden. Zijn complimentjes waren wel heel direct. Ze klonken bijna arrogant. Waar haalde hij het om haar meteen te gaan beoordelen?
'Wil je met me dialogen inoefenen?'
Weg arrogantie. Vragend, smekend.
'Waarom?'
'Omdat je net zo goed bent als ik.'
Meende hij dat nou?
'Wel?'
Er klonk ongeduld in zijn stem.
'Goed. Wanneer?'
'Vanavond. Na het eten.'
'Maar dan is er ontspanning!'
Hij snoof.
'Je hoeft het niet zomaar te doen. Je krijgt wat van me.'
Hij haalde een vel papier te voorschijn.
'Voor jou geschreven. Gisteren, meteen nadat ik je "De wolken" van Martinus Nijhoff had horen voordragen. Je deed het heerlijk.'
Hij wachtte even, dacht na en sprak toen met een hese, bijna mistige stem de derde strofe van 'De wolken' uit.

Toen kwam de tijd dat 'k niet naar boven keek,
Ofschoon de hemel vol van wolken hing,
Ik greep niet naar de vlucht van 't vreemde ding
Dat met zijn schaduw langs mijn leven streek.

'Ik hoop dat je mijn gedicht ook eens voor me voordraagt.'
Bjorn gaf haar het gedicht. Ze las en haar ogen werden vochtig.

Oase

Het zwerven door de jaren
etste nog geen lijnen op mijn huid.
Maar ik was een struikrover van uren
en telde dag aan dag de buit.

De oase van jouw eenzaamheid
lag ongeweten
aan de rand van mijn woestijn.
Diep in je ogen traanden sterren,
gestorven zilver, harde pijn.

De tocht naar die oase
lijkt de overjaarse wijzen
een onderneming van een dwaze.
Maar ik zal die grijze,
nu al afgestorven slaven laten zien
hoe trots de jonge hengsten
over frisse groene weiden draven.

Ik heb mijn zekerheid, mijn eigenzinnig willen
van de verliefde eeuwigheid geërfd.
Ik zal je ziel, je lichaam kneden
tot waar je warme adem
hijgend in mijn haren sterft.

There is more...

De raadselachtige laatste woorden hadden haar niet meer losgela-
ten, maar elke poging om achteraf met Bjorn over het gedicht te praten, waren op een zucht of een bot zwijgen afgeketst. Het leek wel
alsof hij intussen spijt had van wat hij had geschreven.
   'Krijg jij die vreselijke tekst van dat stuk gezegd?' vroeg Elke, en ze

merkte toen pas dat ze bij dezelfde bank stonden, de bank waar hij haar het gedicht had gegeven.

'Ik heb er geen probleem mee. Je verwacht toch niet dat een Atheense koning en zijn zoon praten als Jan Lul bij een voetbalwedstrijd?'

Hij was opeens weer heel intens.

'Ik voel de tekst. Theofilos voelde hem ook toen hij hem schreef. Ik weet het wel, dat plechtige, dat hoogdravende valt sommigen zwaar. Maar als je verder leest, waar de jongelui gewoon met elkaar zitten te kletsen, heeft hij een heel andere taal gebruikt. Dat is knap. Ook voor acteurs. Het geeft ze de gelegenheid te laten zien dat ze meer dan één stem aankunnen.'

'Als jij zou mogen kiezen, welke rol zou je dan spelen?'

'Meen je dat nou?'

Ze knikte. Waarom zou ze het trouwens niet menen?

'Er is toch maar één rol die mij zou liggen?'

'Je bedoelt... O, je bent onmogelijk, jij! Je staat gewoon niet langer met je voeten op de grond. Ben je al aan het fitnessen?'

Ze probeerde hem te raken.

'Drie keer per dag. Me veertig keer opdrukken.'

3

Bea Vandenberghe keek uit haar raam. De avond sloop het kasteel-
park in. De rietkraag langs de vijver kreeg een sluier van mist. Eén
jongen liep nog door het park. Natuurlijk. Bjorn. Als altijd met dat
tekstboek. Ze zuchtte en draaide zich om. Haar gezicht viel in de
spiegel. Een hoog voorhoofd onder vol, asblond haar, blauwe ogen
met rimpeltjes in de hoeken, een rechte neus, dunne, expressieve
lippen, een lange nek...
Ze lachte kort. Wat ze zag, was een vrouw van bijna veertig. Een
vrouw die had gedacht dat ze alles had gehoord, gezien en gevoeld.
En nu?
Sinds ze Bjorn had ontmoet...

'Mevrouw?'
'Mevrouw is er niet. Zeg maar Bea. Wat kan ik voor je doen?'
De jongen had schuchter op de deur van haar kamer geklopt. Het
was stil, en avond. Alleen de echo van gelach weerklonk nu en dan
in de gangen van het kasteel. Jonge stemmen.
'Mag ik wat vragen?'
Bea knikte, een beetje op haar hoede wel. Ze was die morgen de
repetitiezaal binnengegaan om met de cursisten het Griekse stuk
voor te bereiden. Nog voor de middag hadden ze een eerste sessie
gehad, een soort kennismaking waarbij de jongelui hadden voorge-
lezen of gedeclameerd. Ze had Bjorn meteen opgemerkt. Hij had
haar aangekeken alsof zij de eerste vrouw was die hij zag. Ze had
zijn ogen voelen branden, inbeelding natuurlijk, maar ze hadden
gebrand op haar gezicht, haar borsten, haar dijen. Nu was hij weer
anders. Alsof iemand binnen in hem het licht had uitgedraaid.
Zoals hij daar in de deuropening stond, zag hij er vooral verloren
en hulpeloos uit.
'Mevrouw,' hield hij vol, achter de afsluiting van zijn schuchter-
heid, 'u zei vanmiddag iets over stemzetting. Wat bedoelde u?'
Ze groef in haar geheugen. O ja, ze had hem gezegd dat hij meer
ontspannen moest praten, meer vooraan in zijn mond om vermoeidheid te vermijden als hij een grote rol te spelen kreeg.

25

'Wel,' zei ze, 'als je lang moet praten in een grote ruimte, en dat is een theater toch, moet je ervoor zorgen dat je stem draagt. Omdat je vaak elke dag moet spelen, soms twee keer per dag, lijdt je stem eronder als je er te veel van vergt. Dat doe je als je achteraan in je keel praat. Kom, ik zal het je laten voelen.'

Ze had niet kunnen vermoeden wat er toen gebeurde. Het was een heel gewone aanraking geweest, met twee vingers van haar rechterhand had ze over zijn adamsappel gestreeld, zijn kin opgeheven.

Maar de jongen had haar aangekeken alsof ze zijn minnares was. Zijn hand was naar haar lichaam gegaan en was toen in de lucht blijven hangen. Ze had niet meer geweten wat ze moest zeggen en had zich omgedraaid. Ondersteboven.

Ze had nog een hele tijd onzichtbaar gebeefd.

Bjorn keek onwillekeurig op. Bea stond voor haar raam. Haar ellebogen leunen op de vensterbank, het licht achter haar tekende haar scherp.

Ze was mooi, vond Bjorn. Diep doorleefd mooi. En zij was het die de rollen zou verdelen morgen. Hij durfde gewoon niet te twijfelen. Hoe zou het lopen? Waarop zou ze letten?

Bea wist zich intussen geen raad met haar houding. Moest ze nu opeens weggaan van voor het raam, doen alsof ze betrapt was? Wat had ze toch? Zo'n knul van zestien, misschien zeventien keek haar aan, bewoog zijn hand naar haar toe en ze werd als boter. Hij was knap, dat wel. Niet mooi als die piepschuimen jongetjes die je in popbandjes zag rondhuppelen, maar knap op een heel persoonlijke manier. Een man met de huid en de gestalte van een jongen.

Bea! Je kon zijn moeder zijn! Je bent misschien nog wat overspannen na dat gedoe met Paul. Je hebt behoefte aan armen om je heen. Maar niet die van Bjorn! Hij is een jongetje dat om aandacht vraagt, meer niet.

Bjorn keek weer naar zijn tekstboek. Hij voelde dat ze hem in de gaten hield. Waarom? Hij wist het niet. Hij had best gemerkt dat er wat aan de hand was geweest de vorige avond, maar waarom? Nu ja, als ze... Hij schudde zijn hoofd, hij wilde er niet op doorgaan. Hij boog zijn hoofd en las hardop de replieken van Theseus. De andere mompelde hij.

THESEUS: Geklets van bange sukkels die gewoon een verontschuldiging zoeken voor hun angst. Als de Minotaurus, als dat monster de oorzaak is van onze ellende, moeten we de Minotaurus opruimen. Zo eenvoudig ligt het.

AEGEUS: Theseus, je doet me pijn. Denk je nou echt dat wij dat niet al honderd keer hebben overwogen? Niemand kan de Minotaurus doden, alleen al omdat niemand ooit het paleis van Minos kan binnendringen.

Theseus lacht onbedaarlijk.

Theseus, dit is niet het ogenblik...

THESEUS: Zie je nou wel? Jullie zijn zo bang dat je niet verder kijkt dan je neus lang is. Niemand kan het paleis van Minos binnen? Veertien Atheners zullen er over enkele dagen in komen. De meisjes en jongens die Minos als losprijs heeft geëist! Wel? Wat zeggen jullie daarvan? Veertien Atheners voor één monster?

ORATOS: Prins Theseus, ik...

THESEUS: Alweer wat op aan te merken? Oratos, ik begin te denken dat je me niet kunt luchten omdat ik jouw mooie praatjes doorprik als zeepbellen, omdat je bang bent dat ik jouw plaats naast mijn vader zou kunnen innemen.

ORATOS: Prins, jouw mening is jouw mening. Ik wil alleen maar zeggen dat de veertien kinderen weerloos zijn, ongewapend, zonder hoop om te ontsnappen. Want het monster huist in een eindeloze doolhof...

Oratos klapt in zijn handen. Een van de wachters maakt de deur open.

THESEUS: Wil je me laten arresteren?

ORATOS: Integendeel. Wachter, vraag bouwmeester Daedalus om hierheen te komen. Nu meteen.

De wachter verdwijnt. Het blijft stil. De drie kijken elkaar onderzoekend aan, alsof ze elkaars krachten willen inschatten.

AEGEUS: Oratos, wat moet je met Daedalus? Eigenlijk vind ik dat de woorden van mijn zoon het overwegen waard zijn.

THESEUS: Natuurlijk, vader! Er is geen enkel probleem waar je geen oplossing voor kunt bedenken. Oratos draait de zaken om! Voor hem is er geen oplossing waarvoor hij niet meteen een probleem kan vinden.

ORATOS: Zoals je wilt, prins.

De deur gaat open. Daedalus komt naar binnen, loopt naar de troon en buigt.

DAEDALUS: Koning? Wat kan ik...

THESEUS: Hou op met die onderdanige onzin. Ben jij de bouwmeester van dat paleis van Minos? Ik heb van je gehoord, maar ik dacht dat je er indrukwekkender zou uitzien.

ORATOS: Daedalus, ik wil dat je deze jongeman vertelt dat Minos onbereikbaar is voor...

THESEUS: Je legt hem jouw woorden in de mond! Kan hij niet voor zichzelf denken?

DAEDALUS: Ik begrijp niet wat er aan de hand is.

AEGEUS: Heel eenvoudig. Je weet dat de schepen van Kreta hier vandaag aankomen om de levende losprijs te komen ophalen. Mijn zoon, Theseus, wil dat we wat ondernemen...

THESEUS: Ik wil zelf wat ondernemen. Ik wil met die schepen meegaan, de Minotaurus doden en een eind maken aan dit gejammer!

DAEDALUS: Ik vrees dat ik je moet teleurstellen, prins. Ik heb inderdaad het paleis gebouwd. Mijn opdracht was het plan zo ingewikkeld te maken dat niemand, zelfs de koning niet, alle kamers en gangen kent. In de ingewanden van dat labyrint huist de Minotaurus. Ik heb het monster nooit gezien, wist niet eens dat het bouwsel voor hem bedoeld was. Evenmin wist ik dat de koning het ook op mijn leven gemunt had.

THESEUS: Op jouw leven? Je hebt een paleis voor hem gebouwd!

DAEDALUS: Minos is een tiran. Net als alle tirannen is hij doodsbang. Je ruikt de angst die uit alle poriën van zijn lijf zweet. Hij wilde dat paleis vol doolwegen en verborgen kamers om, als dat nodig zou zijn, te kunnen schuilen voor zijn tegenstanders. Toen het bouwsel klaar was, verplichtte hij me persoonlijk de laatste hand te leggen aan de binnenste kamers. Ik werkte er een paar dagen samen met mijn zoon. Minos liet de plannen stelen door een van zijn trawanten. En wij, de bouwers? We konden de uitgang niet meer terugvinden. Net wat Minos wilde. Zo zou ik nooit iemand over het labyrint kunnen vertellen.

ORATOS: Prins?

THESEUS: En toch sta je hier?

DAEDALUS: Jawel. Ik heb jarenlang nagedacht over een manier om uit het paleis weg te komen. Tenslotte heb ik vleugels gemaakt van was en veren en ben ik samen met mijn zoon weggewiekt...
THESEUS: Zie je wel? Desnoods vlieg ik er zelf ook heen.
AEGEUS: Theseus, je moet ook de rest van het verhaal horen. Je overmoed maakt me bang. Ikarus, de zoon van deze man, was een jongen als jij. Toen hij door de hemel kliefde, wilde hij de zon van dichtbij zien. Hij schroeide zijn vleugels en stortte in zee!
THESEUS: Waarom zou ik de zon van dichtbij willen zien? De aarde is mijn wereld, de aarde. Vader, alles wat ik heb gehoord, sterkt me alleen in mijn overtuiging. Het moet ophouden.
ORATOS: Prins, denk na. Koningen en prinsen hoeven geen helden te zijn!

Bjorn sloot even zijn tekstboek en hield zijn wijsvinger tussen de pagina's. Theseus. Hoe dacht hij er zelf over? Moesten prinsen en koningen beter zijn dan andere mensen? Of moest je de zaak omkeren, moesten de betere mensen prins of koning zijn? Hij dacht het laatste. Niet wie je vader was, mocht bepalen wat je werd, wel wat je zelf was. Daarom zou hij meer dan ooit proberen Theseus te zijn. Het moest en desnoods liep hij iedereen die hem in de weg stond onderuit.
Hij klapte het tekstboek weer open.

THESEUS: Daar denk ik dan anders over! Koningen en prinsen moeten hun leven wagen, alles zetten op één worp met de dobbelstenen. Groots en meeslepend moet dat leven zijn. Alleen dan krijgen ze van hun onderdanen genoeg geloof en respect om eisen te kunnen stellen. Oratos, als ik koning zou zijn, zou jij...
ORATOS: Ik weet het, prins Theseus. We zijn water en vuur. Maar bedenk dat vuur water laat borrelen en koken, terwijl water datzelfde vuur kan blussen. Voor altijd.
THESEUS: Is dat een bedreiging?
Hij springt op Oratos toe.
AEGEUS: Genoeg! Beheers je, Theseus! Laat me nu alleen, ik wil nadenken.

THESEUS: Vader, dat hoeft niet langer. Je weet dat ik vastbesloten ben...

ORATOS: Wie zei ook weer dat de goden hem die ze willen vernietigen met overmoed slaan?

Daedalus en hij gaan naar buiten. Aegeus volgt hen langzaam. Theseus kijkt de mannen na. Het licht dooft langzaam. Eén lichtstraal op Theseus. Hij loopt naar de troon, gaat erop zitten en lacht.

Bea zag Bjorn naar een bank lopen. Hij ging zitten en gooide zijn arm achteloos over de leuning. Zijn houding had iets koninklijks. Ook toen hij achteroverleunde en hardop leek te lachen. Ze duwde zich overeind en liep achteruit haar kamer in. Ze dacht te veel aan Bjorn, akelig veel te veel.

4

'Acteren is anders leven, als iemand anders leven. Dat maakt het zo moeilijk, maar tegelijk zo boeiend. Bjorn?'

'Mag ik eerst nog wat anders vragen, mevrouw?'

Bea knikte.

'Menen ze dat nu, dat voor de cast van dit stuk in alle landen van de Europese Unie naar kandidaten wordt gezocht?'

'Ik denk inderdaad dat ze dat menen. Ja. Dit is het eerste Europese project dat Artscene is gedoopt. Vroeger had je Erasmusprojecten en zo, maar daarbij ging het altijd om wetenschap, filosofie en dergelijke. In het nieuwe Europa wil men ook de cultuur internationaliseren.'

'Maar hoe kennen ze ons? Want als wij dit stuk instuderen, betekent dat...'

'Juist, normaal gesproken, zijn jullie de kandidaten voor dit land.'

'Normaal gesproken?'

Bea zuchtte.

'Luister, Bjorn, ik heb dezelfde vragen als jij, want ook dramaturgen, regisseurs, decorontwerpers, kostuumontwerpers en belichtingsmensen zullen uit verschillende Europese landen komen. Tenminste, dat is de bedoeling. Aan het eind van deze week maak ik een rapport over jullie, maakt iemand anders een rapport over mij en wat ik met jullie heb gedaan. Dat alles moet dan in Londen worden beoordeeld. Vergelijk het met een Europees kampioenschap van een sport. Wij spelen nu de voorronde. Duidelijk?'

Bjorn knikte, maar stak meteen zijn hand op.

'Dan moeten we eigenlijk een keer alle rollen kunnen spelen?'

'Hé zeg!' schreeuwde Frank. 'Ik heb geen zin om jou te zoenen. Dat laat ik aan Andrea over.'

'Je zou niet eens de kans krijgen, stinkerd!'

Andrea. Als ze het goed begreep, was er wat tussen Andrea en Bjorn. Bea voelde een prik van jaloersheid.

'Vooruit, jullie!'

Bea klapte in haar handen, meer om haar eigen emoties weg te jagen dan om de voelbare spanning te breken.

'Nee, Bjorn, dat hoeft echt niet. Ik denk dat ik ervaring genoeg heb om uit te maken voor welke rol iemand helemaal ongeschikt is.'

'Jij mag zo de Minotaurus spelen,' pestte Frank weer.

'Afgelopen! Frank en Celine spelen de twee figuren die Theofilos als koor laat optreden. Elke is Althea, Andrea wordt Agos... Ja, Andrea, ik weet dat Agos een jongen is die een meisjesrol speelt. Juist daarom. Speel jij nou maar een jongen die een meisje speelt.'

Een kleine wraakneming voor iets wat misschien niets voorstelde. Bea keek op het lijstje met namen. Weer voelde ze dat onbekende gloeien, nu op haar voorhoofd. De blik van Bjorn brandde letterlijk. En nee, ze zou niet toegeven!

'Willem, jij speelt Parmenides...'

Verrek, nee, dan bleef er in dat tweede bedrijf alleen nog Theseus over. En ze wist best wat Bjorn wilde. Nee!

'Nee, Willem, speel jij Theseus... Parmenides is voor jou.'

Toen ze Bjorn aankeek, leek het alsof hij haar een klap gaf met zijn ogen. Ze probeerde onbewogen terug te kijken.

'Komaan. Daar. Ik hoef nog geen geweldige acteerprestaties te zien. Ik wil die tekst wel voelen leven. Aan de slag. Ik luister.'

TWEEDE BEDRIJF

Het decor uiterst links suggereert het ruim van een schip. Er liggen wat vaten, visnetten, een tweede anker. De wind en het geruis van golven als achtergrondgeluid. Rechts enkele zuilen op een verhoging, die het paleis van Minos moeten voorstellen. De scheiding tussen de twee hoogteniveaus wordt geaccentueerd door de belichting.

HEROS: Vond je het dan niet bewonderenswaardig? Theseus, prins Theseus, de opvolger van zijn vader, kon leven in weelde...

HUBRIS: Je snapt het nog altijd niet. Sommige mensen geven geen moer om weelde. Ze willen maar één ding: roem, eerbetuigingen, macht over hun medemensen.

HEROS: Daar noem je drie dingen.

HUBRIS: Ik noem één en hetzelfde ding. Roem is erkenning door wie minder is of tenminste denkt minder te zijn. Eerbetuigingen krijg je van wie je als zijn meerdere erkent. En dan kun je heersen. Het woord van een eerzuchtige is een scepter...

Heros: Hoe komt het toch dat je geen goed woord kunt zeggen over prins Theseus? Vind je het soms goed dat hij nu in dat verre land vermoord is? Je lijkt er zelfs tevreden mee.

Hubris: Ja, dat ben ik! Ik grijnslach met de goden mee. Theseus heeft zijn leven verloren nadat hij het leven van zovele anderen op het spel heeft gezet zonder te weten of hij ooit kon winnen. Waarom zou ik dan een goed woord voor hem over hebben?

Heros: De helden hebben rechten waarvan de gewone sterveling niet eens kan dromen.

Hubris: Helden zijn stervelingen voor wie het leven van anderen geen waarde heeft. Ze hebben geen extra rechten, ze zijn blind! Helden zijn stervelingen die te dom of te hoogmoedig zijn om bang te worden. Maar wij waren bang, wij waren de prijs die Theseus bereid was te betalen voor zijn roem, voor zijn waanzin!

Heros: Ik geloof je niet. Voerde het schip geen zwarte zeilen toen het uitvoer, zwart, de kleur van de rouw? Had Theseus geen witte zeilen meegenomen, die hij zou hijsen als het schip terugkwam naar Athene? Terugkomen betekende toch dat hij jullie zou hebben gered en Athene zou hebben bevrijd?

Hubris: Laat ik je dan vertellen wat er gebeurd is. Theseus wilde inderdaad terugkomen. Inderdaad. Maar daarvoor moest hij wel eerst vertrekken. De koning, Oratos, Daedalus, iedereen probeerde Theseus van zijn plan af te brengen. Toen al wist ik dat het niet zou lukken. Ik had hem gezien toen hij op de troon was gaan zitten. Hij kon op dat moment niet vermoeden dat er ogen waren die hem volgden. Hij zat op de troon, schurkte zijn billen tegen de kussens en lachte! Ik wist dat hij van dat ogenblik af maar aan één ding zou denken...

Licht op het ruim. De jongelui tuimelen de scène op alsof iemand ze brutaal duwt. Theseus worstelt het langst.

Theseus: Laat me los, schoft! Ik sla je desnoods de hersens in!

Agos: Dat heb je nou! Waarom kon je boven je mond niet houden, Theseus?

Parmenides: Ja, waarom moest je zo nodig herrie schoppen? Nu zitten we hier in dit stinkende ruim in plaats van voor het laatst te genieten van de zon, de wind en de zee.

Theseus: Hoor me die liefjes nou toch eens aan!

33

AGOS: En pest me niet met die meisjeskleren. Jij hebt ze me doen aantrekken! Het is jouw ellendige, krankzinnige idee!

THESEUS: Je was het er toch mee eens? Kan ik het helpen dat je kin rond is als die van een meisje, dat je huid blank is als het schuim op de golven, dat je haren over je schouders stromen als de zoete geuren van de nacht?

Hij lacht hard.

PARMENIDES: Ik vind het helemaal niet prettig. Ik heb die meisjeskleren aangetrokken toen je het vroeg omdat ik je geloofde, toen je zei dat we zo meer kans maakten...

THESEUS: En is dat niet zo? In plaats van zeven jongens en zeven meisjes krijgt de Minotaurus negen jonge mannen en slechts vijf meisjes tegenover zich. Bovendien heb ik niet zonder reden herrie geschopt. We moesten hier beneden, in het ruim van het schip, komen en dat kon niet ongemerkt.

ALTHEA: Theseus, ik wist wel dat je een plan had! Ik wist wel dat je ons niet zomaar zou laten opsluiten. O, Theseus!

Ze loopt naar hem toe en probeert hem te omarmen.

PARMENIDES: Geef het op, Althea! Je bent voor hem niet meer dan een meisje! Gewoon een meisje!

ALTHEA: Parmenides! Wat weet jij van wat zich in ons hart afspeelt?

THESEUS: Genoeg, jullie. Ik had nog wat te vertellen.

AGOS: Vertel het haar, Theseus! Vertel haar wat je ons hebt gezegd. Vertel haar van je plan! Zeg haar nu dat ze met de meisjes op de Minotaurus moet afstormen, dat ze moeten proberen hem bezig te houden terwijl wij hem overvallen! Bezighouden? Ze moeten zich als eersten laten verslinden! Zeg haar dat je hebt geflikflooid tot ze gek genoeg was om voor jou door het vuur te gaan, zo krankzinnig verliefd dat ze de tanden en klauwen van de Minotaurus wil tarten tot jij de kans krijgt hem te overmeesteren!

THESEUS: Ik zei genoeg, Agos! Bek toe, Parmenides! In iedere oorlog hou je rekening met verliezen, maar die hoeven er niet noodzakelijk te zijn. Als we dit plan willen laten slagen, Althea, moet iedereen zijn rol vervullen. Gevoelens kunnen we nu best missen.

ALTHEA: Is dat alles waar je aan denkt, Theseus? Wat moet ik dan met al die blikken, al die kleine gebaren, die woorden van je?

THESEUS: Woorden? Meeuwen op de wind van de tijd. Wie weet

wanneer die ooit neerstrijken... Maar neerstrijken doen ze, Althea, zo gaat het altijd. Geloof me nou maar.

PARMENIDES: En daarmee, meisje, heb je het gehad! Wat moest je hier beneden, Theseus?

Stilte. Iedereen keek naar Bea, die in kleermakerszit op de grond zat en nog even zweeg. 'Goed,' zei ze toen. 'Heel goed!' Een nauwelijks waarneembaar geluid. Opluchting, verbazing. 'Tenminste, als jullie bij het gezelschap Vreugde Verheft in Sullegem willen spelen. Daar zullen ze jullie met graagte zien komen. Maar dit was voor een Acteerstudio!'

De stilte kreeg ijspegels aan de rand.

'Jullie hebben geschreeuwd en gelachen met kartonnen gezichten, gebaren gemaakt... Maar hebben jullie er ook wat bij gevoeld? Bjorn?'

Alweer hij. Alweer dat treiterige gebaar, die hand in de lucht.

'Mevrouw...'

'Noem me bij mijn voornaam.'

'Bea, is dat niet wat ik gisteren ook al zei toen we het over mijn tekst hadden? Kun je geloofwaardig spelen wat je niet voelt, wat je niet bent?'

God in de hemel, dat jongetje daagde haar uit! Wat hij bedoelde was: 'Laat mij Theseus spelen en je zult het wel zien!' Ook goed, ze zou hem lik op stuk geven. En toch, ze voelde weer die vreemde verwarring die warme rillingen door haar lichaam joeg. Ze moest antwoorden, ze moest hem overtuigen, niet hem overtroeven.

'Nee, je kunt niet spelen wat je niet voelt. Maar je kunt leren voelen wat je speelt. Je moet niet je personage zíjn om het op de planken te zetten, je moet het personage zijn dat je op de planken zet. Snap je me?'

Ze bladerde in het tekstboek.

'Ik heb één zin gehoord die eerlijk klonk. Toen Althea Parmenides vroeg of hij kon weten wat er zich in haar hart afspeelde. De rest was opgeklopt schuim. Als je blaast, is het weg. Opnieuw. Welke gevoelens moet ik horen knetteren in deze tekst?'

'Haat, medelijden, angst, frustratie, verliefdheid, ontgoocheling...'

De woorden buitelden over elkaar.

'Doe dat dan. Je blijft roerloos staan en de klank van je woorden, de intonatie, het ritme van wat je zegt, is het enige wat die boodschap doet overkomen. Vooruit!'

'Bjorn?'

Elke bleef staan in de deuropening. Buiten gloeide de zonsondergang boven de boomtoppen van het park. Wat moest dat? Bjorn rukte woedend de tekst 'London, here I come!!!' van de muur, frommelde het papier tot een bal en gooide het door de kamer. Toen propte hij de rest van zijn kleren in een weekendtas en keilde het tekstboek van *De goden grijnzen* in een hoek.

'Bjorn, wat doe je?'

Elke liep de kamer in en raakt heel voorzichtig zijn rug aan. Bjorn draaide zich om en hief zijn hand. Zijn ogen stonden alsof hij haar wilde verscheuren.

'Bjorn?'

'Ik ga weg!'

'Je bent gek!'

Bjorn knikte.

'Klopt. Anders was ik niet hierheen gekomen.'

'Maar waarom wil je weg?'

'Omdat dit zinloos is. Ik krijg gewoon geen kans. Niemand heeft me ooit een kans gegeven, ook nu niet! En zeg niet dat ik overdrijf. Ik zag aan je gezicht dat je dat wilde zeggen. Zeg niet dat ik overdrijf. Je weet geen moer van me af.'

Elke slikte.

'Kun je erover praten?'

'Met jou? Wil je soms dat ik hier blijf?'

'Ja.'

Het klonk rustig. Bjorn bleef staan.

'Waarom?'

'Daarom.'

'Je weet best dat "daarom" geen antwoord is.'

Elke merkte aan kleine dingen dat hij minder gespannen was.

'Je weet dat ik op je gesteld ben? Misschien zelfs een tikkeltje verliefd?'

36

Zijn ogen vluchtten weg van de hare.

'Bjorn?'

Hij liep naar de deur en schopte die dicht. Hij leunde ertegenaan.

'Je hebt gehoord wat Bea zei? De enige zin die klonk, was wat ik tegen jou zei.'

'Ze heeft nog wel meer gezegd achteraf. En jij zei het niêt tegen mij. Althea vroeg Parmenides of hij wist wat er in haar hart gebeurde.'

'Is dat niet een beetje hetzelfde?'

'Nee, want ik ben Parmenides niet, ik ben...'

Hij zweeg.

'Nu moet ik jou vragen waarom.'

'Daarom. Bea, ik bedoel, Elke, ik heb geen zin om je mijn hele leven te vertellen. En wees gerust. Ik heb geen ongelukkige jeugd gehad, mijn ouders zijn niet gescheiden, ik ben niet misbruikt, ben nooit ziekelijk of zo geweest. Ik heb alleen geen kansen gehad.'

'Dat blijf jij maar zeggen terwijl ik hier sta. Ik ben een kans.'

Elke schrok van zichzelf. Bood ze zich zomaar aan, verdomme.

'Echt?'

Het klonk cynisch, zijn blik bleef hard. Hij duwde zich af van de deur, zette twee, drie stappen en opende zijn armen.

Elke haalde een schoen onder zich vandaan toen ze op het bed lag en Bjorn met zijn lippen haar ogen dichtstreelde. Toen greep hij haar beet, ruw, wanhopig.

'Wat bedoelde je toen je zei dat je nooit kansen had gekregen?'

Bjorn lag naast Elke, haar hand in zijn hand. Kalm nu.

'Mijn leven was uiterlijk volmaakt. Nee, Elke, dit wil je niet horen.'

'Hoe weet je dat?'

Ze drukte nog een zoen op zijn oor.

'Het is allemaal zo persoonlijk.'

'Wat daarstraks gebeurde, was ook nogal persoonlijk.'

Bjorn kwam overeind.

'Er is niets gebeurd.'

'Als je bedoelt dat het niet gebeurde, heb je gelijk. Ik hoop alleen dat je niet denkt dat ik gewoonlijk met jongens op bed ga liggen en ze streel, me laat strelen...'

'Je wilde het toch zelf ook. Doe nou niet alsof het een geschenk van jou voor mij was.'

Elke vond geen woorden. Wat een onmogelijke schoft was die kerel.

'Sorry. Ik ben in de war. Ik kan me... ik ben bang.'

Het meisje zweeg.

'Het heeft te maken met mijn grootvader.'

Bjorn ging weer liggen. Zijn vingers vonden haar hand.

'Hij is geweldig. Groot, imposant, vreselijk verstandig, autoritair. Altijd bezig. Ik was heel vaak bij hem. We woonden in een groot huis met veel licht, een tuin om in te verdwalen. Hij had zijn deel van het huis. Slaapkamer, zitkamer, studeerkamer... Een huis in het huis eigenlijk. Het rook er naar boeken en muziek. Heb je nooit ondervonden dat je muziek kunt ruiken? Ik wel. Gregoriaans ruik ik meteen. Wierook en graniet. Mozart is appelen en talkpoeder. Beethoven is wol, natte bomen in een park. Techno is verbrand rubber. Get Ready heeft de geur van luiers. Vuile.'

Elke lachte hardop.

'Je bent gek!'

'Misschien.'

'Maar wat heeft dat met kansen te maken? Als ik je hoor, had je het thuis inderdaad prima.'

'Zie je wel, dat jij het ook niet snapt. Soms weet ik het zelf niet echt meer. Het heeft alles met mijn grootvader te maken. Hij had me beloofd om me wegwijs te maken, ik zou zijn leerling zijn, hij mijn goeroe, mijn wijze man...'

Bjorn mompelde als in halfslaap. Elke bewoog niet.

Dit was herinnering, teruggaan in de tijd, alleen. Zij was er niet bij betrokken.

'Maar hij hield zijn woord niet. Ik was dertien toen hij wegging. Dertien, snap je? Hij was lang in het ziekenhuis geweest, maar wilde terug naar huis, naar zijn boeken, naar zijn muziek. Zo had hij het gezegd. Niet naar zijn familie. Boeken en muziek. Daarin is de eeuwigheid opgeslagen, zei hij altijd. Niemand kent het begin en niemand het eind van wat daarin zit. Eeuwigheid.'

Bjorn zweeg. Minutenlang.

'Dus hij kwam naar huis. Hij wist dat hij daar zou sterven, maar weigerde dat te aanvaarden. Ik mocht niet lang bij hem zitten. Mijn ouders wilden me beschermen. Maar die nacht wist ik dat ik moest gaan. Ik sloop naar zijn slaapkamer. Hij zat overeind in bed, met kussens in zijn rug. Hij wilde niet gaan liggen, was razend omdat hij ziek was, omdat hij alles de baas had gekund, maar niet die ene ziekte. Het enige wat goed is, is het volmaakte. De enige mens die het waard is om te leven is de beste mens. Als je in wat je doet niet de beste kunt zijn, laat het dan. Dat waren de woorden die hij altijd weer herhaalde, altijd opnieuw, elke dag.

De lamp was aan. Hij probeerde te werken. Naast hem op het bed lagen boeken opengeslagen. Hij had een schrijfblok voor zich liggen, grijs gerecycleerd papier. Hij schreef altijd met potloden, gele met een gummetje.

Ik zei dat hij probeerde te werken, maar het ging niet meer. Hij had zijn ogen gesloten, maar zijn vingers dwaalden af en toe over het bed, pakten een boek vast, lieten het weer los. Toen hoorde ik één woord. Lees. Hij siste het bijna en tikte op een boek. Een blauwe band met gouden letters. Het Tibetaanse Dodenboek.

Kruis, hijgde hij. Ik pakte het boek op en op pagina drieënvijftig was een beverig kruis getrokken bij de laatste alinea. Ik las, bij het licht dat grijzig door de ramen kwam. Het was bijna morgen.'

De jongen leek in een soort trance. Hij lag roerloos, was zich niet bewust van wat er om hem heen gebeurde.

'Als een mens op sterven ligt, is het uitermate belangrijk dat hij zich zijn goede daden voor de geest haalt, dat hij weet dat zijn leven zinvol is geweest en dat hij daarom de dood gerust in het gezicht kan kijken. Daarom vermijden wij gehuil en gejammer, blijven de verwanten ver van de stervende, want hun pijn en verdriet zouden ze niet onderdrukken en dat zou de stervende kunnen hinderen in zijn overgang naar de andere wereld.'

Elke schoof dichter tegen Bjorn aan en legde haar vingers op zijn mond.

'Stil maar,' zei ze.

'Zeg de stervende wat hij goed heeft gedaan. De stervende hoort de woorden nog, kan zich zijn goede daden herinneren en schrijdt zonder angst over de drempel. Als de stervende met geconcentreerde aandacht voor het goede de tussentoestand betreedt, krijgt hij inzicht in het oerlicht en blijft hij rustig. Hij weet aanvankelijk niet dat hij dood is. Hij ziet zichzelf nog als levend en verbaast zich erover

dat de anderen zich opeens anders gedragen. De dode is een geest-wezen geworden dat weliswaar alles om zich heen waarneemt, maar dat door de gewone mens niet gezien of gehoord kan worden.'
'Bjorn, alsjeblieft. Stil, ik ben hier.'
Elke schudde Bjorn bij de schouder, maar de verdoving bleef.
'Toen kwam de zon op. Een witte streep, niet echt wit, gelig, op de vloer. Ze werd groter, kroop naar het bed. Toen hoorde ik het. Een gescharrel bij het raam. Een merel. Hij zat zwart op de vensterbank en keek naar me met zijn ronde oog, zwart en geel. Zijn bek stond half open, alsof hij sprak. Hij tikte met zijn bek tegen het glas en sloeg met zijn vleugels, alsof hij erin wilde. Toen zat hij doodstil. Achter mij was het ook stil. Mijn grootvader was gestorven. Toen ik me naar het raam omdraaide, zag ik de vogel wegvliegen. Hij neemt de ziel van mijn grootvader met zich mee, dacht ik. Ik weet niet hoe mijn grootvader het had gedaan, maar met zijn laatste krachten had hij iets geschreven, hanenpotige letters: *Je kunt pas tevreden zijn als je de beste bent geweest.*'
Bjorn leek opeens te ontwaken. Hij sprong op van het bed, liep naar de wastafel en begon zijn tanden te poetsen.
'Bjorn?'
Gemompel. Spoelen.
'Hoe komt het dat je die teksten uit het hoofd kent?'
'Ik onthou goed en deze hebben een speciale betekenis. Wil je de tekst van zijn doodsprentje horen?'
Hij wachtte niet eens, maar reciteerde ingehouden.

Opa is gestorven.
Zomaar weggegaan, zeggen de grote mensen.
Dat kan niet.
Hij streelde me over mijn hoofd,
gaf me iets van zijn vroeger door, ·
kneep even in mijn wang,
beloofde me iets van zijn morgen
en wuifde bij de hoek.
En nu is opa weggegaan, zeggen de grote mensen?
Gedoofd in zijn slaap.
Hij is gelukkig nu.

Alleen ik weet dat opa ook gisteren gelukkig was.
Hij streelde me.

Stilte.

'Bjorn, wat mooi!' zei Elke tenslotte.

'Mooi? Het is onzin. Ze hebben het in mijn plaats gemaakt, net alsof ik het geschreven had. En dat is niet zo! Ik noemde hem nooit 'opa'. Opa is iets voor oude mannetjes die sprookjes voorlezen bij het haardvuur. Hij was mijn groot-vader. *Groot,* snap je? Groot en vader! Hij vertelde me geen sprookjes, hij wilde me leren leven. Geen dwerg, maar een reus!'

Elke wist het niet meer, ze schudde haar hoofd.

'Wat heeft dat allemaal te maken met kansen krijgen?'

'Snap je dat niet? Heb je me dan niet gehoord? Heb je niet gehoord wat hij van me wilde? Snap jij het ook niet?'

Elke schoof van het bed, schikte haar kleren en schudde opnieuw haar hoofd.

'Ik heb het je net nog gezegd. De woorden uit het Dodenboek. De woorden die mijn grootvader me wilde laten onthouden. Zijn laatste les, zijn testament voor de rest van mijn leven. Als een mens op sterven ligt, is het uitermate belangrijk dat hij zich zijn goede daden voor de geest haalt, dat hij weet dat zijn leven zinvol is geweest en dat hij daarom de dood gerust in het gezicht kan kijken.'

'Bjorn, je ligt niet op sterven. Je bent jong.'

'Dat was mijn vriend ook toen een dronken chauffeur hem aan flarden reed. En ik heb vandaag, vanmiddag een merel gezien. Hij zat op mijn vensterbank. Zijn bek tikte op het glas. Net alsof hij naar binnen wilde, net als die nacht met mijn grootvader.'

Elke rilde. Dit ging fout. Hierop wilde ze niet doorgaan. Ze zocht een uitweg, maakte een schijnbeweging.

'Ik snap nog altijd niet wat je met die kansen bedoelt.'

'Als je in wat je doet niet de beste kunt zijn, laat het dan! Bea moet mij de kans geven de beste te zijn en dat doet ze niet. Dus laat ik het! Nu gesnapt? Ik ga weg.'

Elke zuchtte, liep naar de deur, pakte de sleutel en liep naar buiten. Voor Bjorn wat dan ook kon doen, hoorde hij het slot klikken.

5

In de gang leunde Elke tegen de muur. Ze hoorde Bjorn aan de deur rukken, vloeken, schoppen en schreeuwen dat ze hem eruit moest laten. Na een minuut werd het stil.

Waarom bemoeide ze zich ermee? Misschien was ze inderdaad een tikkeltje verliefd op hem. Nee, het was meer beschermend medelijden. Iets wat ze ook had met zwerfhonden. Ze moest en zou ze strelen, ook al wist ze dat ze achteraf vol vlooien zou zitten.

Ze ademde diep in en liep weg. De nachtverlichting tekende schaduwen in de gang. Ze zou met Bea gaan praten. Bea... Opeens viel het haar in dat Bjorn haar een keer Bea had genoemd, alsof hij met haar praatte en daarbij aan Bea dacht. Elke bleef staan. Misschien gebruikte hij haar op een heel geraffineerde manier. Nee, ze mocht zich geen dingen inbeelden, moest realiteit en toneeltekst uit elkaar houden. Hoewel. Misschien was Bjorn inderdaad meer Theseus dan zij kon vermoeden. Woorden die Andrea als het personage Agos had uitgesproken, dreunden opeens in haar hoofd.

Zeg haar nu dat ze met de meisjes op de Minotaurus moet afstormen, dat ze moeten proberen hem bezig te houden terwijl wij hem overvallen! Bezighouden? Ze moeten zich als eersten laten verslinden! Zeg haar dat je hebt geflikflooid tot ze gek genoeg was om voor jou door het vuur te gaan, zo krankzinnig verliefd dat ze de tanden en klauwen van de Minotaurus wil tarten tot jij de kans krijgt hem te overmeesteren!

Nee, dat was te ver gezocht. Bjorn kon onmogelijk weten dat zij nu naar Bea zou gaan en Bea was niet de Minotaurus. En Bjorn had niet met haar geflikflooid. Het gedicht was zijn stap geweest. Wat een uur geleden in zijn kamer was gebeurd, had zij gewild en uitgelokt. Bjorn was alleen vreselijk onzeker, wilde tegelijk aantrekken en afstoten, was bang om zichzelf te verliezen als hij zich aan iemand overleverde.

Elke lachte onhoorbaar.

Je praat als een figuur uit een stationsromannetje, vloekte ze tegen zichzelf. En je gedraagt je ook zo. Tenslotte is die jongen niets meer dan een jongen die je toevallig kent omdat hij dezelfde toneelcursus volgt. Wel dan?

Bea ijsbeerde door haar kamer. Ze probeerde de rolverdeling voor de volgende dag op papier te krijgen. Wat moest ze met Bjorn? Als ze objectief was, moest ze toegeven dat hij de enige was met talent, met verschroeiend talent zelfs. Elke en Andrea waren begaafd. De ene had charme, de andere die donkere schoonheid waarbij je als toeschouwer minieme fouten in dictie en interpretatie vergeet. De rest van de groep, Celine en de jongens, waren net goed genoeg voor een soap op een commerciële zender, meer niet. Dus kon ze Bjorn maar beter zijn zin geven en hem Theseus laten spelen. Alleen nog Theseus. En stel dat hij het haalde, dat hij naar Londen mocht voor een test. Dan was het háár Theseus die daar op de planken stond. En de hemel wist dat ze een succes best kon gebruiken sinds haar breuk met Paul. Vroeger had ze nooit beseft dat ze eigenlijk meedreef op zijn bekendheid. Ze was voor de theaterwereld meer 'de vrouw van Paul Derieux' dan Bea Vandenberghe geweest. Nu wist ze het duidelijk, want de deuren die vroeger wijd open waren gegaan, bleven nu dicht of werden hooguit op een kier gezet.

'I got you under my skin,' zong iemand op de radio. Bea sloot haar ogen. Wat stond ze zichzelf daar voor te liegen! Het was niet alleen haar carrière, niet alleen het succes. Het zat dieper, in haar vrouwzijn. Bjorn had haar op een of andere manier betoverd. Hij maakte verlangens bij haar los die haar beletten nuchter te denken. Waanzin was het! Hij een jongen van zestien, zeventien, zij bijna veertig...

Iemand klopte op haar deur. Vragend. Nee, niet hij, niet op dit ogenblik. Of toch, alsjeblieft, laat hij het zijn... later.

Nog een klopje. Bea beet op haar bovenlip, sloot haar ogen en probeerde het jagen van haar hart onder controle te krijgen.

'Elke?'

'Bjorn wil ermee kappen. Hij wil weg.'

Geen inleiding, maar recht voor de raap. En beschuldigend. Jouw schuld, Bea.

'Wil hij weg? Waarom dan? Toch niet omdat...'

Elke knikte.

'Hij is gek! Wat is dit nu allemaal? Hij krijgt echt wel de kans...'

'Kun jij niet met hem praten, Bea?'

'Elke, kom nou! Je wilt toch niet dat ik een van mijn leerlingen ga smeken om mee te doen? Ik denk er niet aan.'

Het meisje boog haar hoofd.

'Het is zo belangrijk voor hem. Het heeft met zijn grootvader te maken. En hij is echt goed!'

'Ik kan het gewoon niet maken. Wat zouden de anderen ervan denken?'

'De anderen? Waarom zouden die wat denken? Die zitten er niet echt mee. De cursus was voor hen, denk ik, vooral een leuke vakantiebezigheid. Ze hadden net zo goed kunnen gaan zeilen of skeeleren.'

'En voor Bjorn is het anders?'

'Ja.'

Bea zuchtte.

'Ik ben bang,' zuchtte Elke. 'Hij praat maar over doodgaan en zo.'

Het meisje zag er nu zielig uit. Ze had haar armen om zichzelf heen geslagen. Het was alsof iemand haar onverwacht in de maag had gestompt.

Bea pakte haar arm.

'Stil maar,' zei ze. 'Stil maar.'

'Alsjeblieft,' zei Elke.

Bea haalde diep adem. Nee, ze zou het niet doen. Het leek wel een samenzwering tussen haar gevoelens en deze dramatische schreeuw om hulp.

'Elke, dit gaat te ver. Ik kan dit niet doen. Hij wil alleen aandacht trekken, daar draait het allemaal om.'

Bea tilde het gezicht van het meisje op en streek een sliert haar van haar voorhoofd.

'Je moet opletten dat je hier niet te erg bij betrokken raakt.'

Kun je net zo goed tegen jezelf zeggen, dacht ze intussen.

'Bjorn meent het,' zei Elke. 'Als het fout gaat, heb jij het op je geweten.'

'Wat?'

'Ik bedoel, als hij iets stoms doet.'

'Je denkt er niet aan dat hij dit echt doet om aandacht te krijgen, van jou, van mij, van iedereen?'

Elke keek haar triest en boos aan.

'Je weet niet wat voor een ellende je hebt aangericht,' zei ze.

Bea keek haar ongelovig aan.

'O, God!' snauwde ze toen. 'Hij heeft je laten geloven dat hij het slachtoffer is, terwijl hij alleen maar een arrogant strebertje is, een jongetje dat niet gewend is dat hij niet krijgt wat hij wil.' Je maakt hem af omdat je bang bent voor je eigen gevoelens, dacht ze.

'Bjorn heeft me niets wijsgemaakt. Jij bent de leugenaar!' krijste Elke opeens.

'Wat wil je daarmee zeggen?'

'Jij denkt dat je het allemaal weet, je beweert dat jij de enige bent die hem doorziet! En dat is een leugen!'

'Elke, je doet hysterisch!'

'Hysterisch? Ik mag toch wel woedend zijn als iemand mijn vriend kapotmaakt? Waarom geef je hem zijn zin niet? Het draait er toch op uit dat hij Theseus wordt, niet?'

Het bleef stil. Twee paar ogen staarden, maar zagen alleen wat ze wilden zien.

Bea was de eerste die bewoog. Ze draaide zich om, pakte het schrijfblok van haar werktafel en liet dat aan Elke zien.

'Kijk,' zei ze, 'dit had ik voor morgen opgeschreven.'

Haar vinger tikte op de naam van Bjorn. Er stond 'Theseus' achter.

Elke zei niets, maar stak de sleutel van Bjorns kamer in de hoogte, drukte die toen in de hand van Bea, mompelde 'alsjeblieft' en rende weg.

'Verdomme, verdomme!' Bea bleef maar naar de sleutel staren. Dit leek wel een theaterstuk. Ze wilde niet wat ze wilde...

En die kleine Elke had haar de sleutel gegeven. Verrekt symbolisch... Zij kreeg de mogelijkheid om Bjorn te bevrijden. Waaruit? Waarvan?

Hoe dan ook moest ze nu met die sleutel naar zijn kamer.

Lekker excuus, dacht ze, en ze liep de gang op.

'Bjorn?'

Geen antwoord.

'Bjorn? Mag ik naar binnen komen?'

Het bleef stil. Bea voelde angst opkomen. Ze stak de sleutel in het slot en duwde de deur open. Een tochtvlaag hield haar even tegen.

Bjorn stond op de vensterbank en worstelde met de vergrendeling van het raam. De ramen op de tuin konden op twee manieren open. Alleen het bovenste gedeelte, dat normaal naar buiten opensloeg, of het hele raam, als je de onderste klink omdraaide. Bjorn sloeg ongeduldig met zijn vuist op het metaal. De twee vleugels van het raam klapten open.

'Bjorn, wat doe je?'

Hij keek om en Bea schrok van de leegte in zijn ogen.

'Hij is teruggekomen om me te halen. Ik vlieg met hem mee,' fluisterde hij en leunde naar buiten.

'Bjorn, alsjeblieft, wat is dit voor gekheid?'

'Gekheid? En dat vraag jij? Jij maakt alles stuk! Ik wil een arend zijn en jij laat me scharrelen als een kip.'

Het klonk onecht.

Bea zette een stap dichterbij en rekende uit hoe hoog het gebouw was. Tweede verdieping.

'Bjorn, gaat het echt om die rol van Theseus?'

'Ook, maar het gaat om veel meer.'

'Kunnen we er niet over praten?'

Hij waaierde met zijn armen. Bea zette nog twee stappen. Bijna kon ze hem aanraken.

'Wat helpt praten?'

Hij draaide zich opnieuw een beetje om en glimlachte verzaligd, alsof hij zich opeens met de hele wereld had verzoend. Maar dat maakte Bea juist bang. Hij ging op zijn tenen staan, hief zijn armen...

Bea had zijn sweater te pakken en rukte hem terug.

Ze vielen op de grond. Bjorn kronkelde en sloot haar in zijn armen. Bea voelde zich vloeibaar worden. Zijn lichaam vormde zich naar het hare, ze versmolten.

'Bjorn?'

Hij drukte zijn hoofd nog harder tegen haar borst, alsof hij zich schaamde.

'Bjorn, dit... Laat me los, alsjeblieft.'

Hij schudde zijn hoofd, snikte.

'Bjorn, dit is niet goed. Dit is niet goed.'

Ze bewoog haar hoofd en zoende hem, net onder zijn oor, heel even. Hij verstijfde.

'Hé, doe tenminste die deur dicht als je wilt stoeien! Bea?'

Bjorn duwde zich op zijn handen half overeind. Frank stond in de deuropening. In de ogen van Bjorn zag Bea moordlustige haat. Ze was opeens doodsbang. Frank trok de deur dicht en verdween.

Bea was nog altijd verbijsterd. Ze had net Bruno Storms, de projectleider, de man die voor het Nederlandse taalgebied de Summerschool van het Institute for Young Actors organiseerde, aan de lijn gekregen. Het hele verhaal was er met horten en stoten uit gekomen. 'Je moet dit op een of andere manier oplossen!' 'Dat weet ik ook wel,' had ze gesnauwd. 'Alleen had ik graag een paar ideeën van je gekregen.' 'Ik zou gaan praten met die jongen die het heeft gezien. Vanavond nog, voor hij de kans krijgt om een ongelukkig toeval met zijn fantasie te kleuren. Probeer hem ervan te overtuigen dat hij zich vergist. Leg hem voorzichtig uit dat Bjorn een probleem heeft. Laat hem de tekst lezen die je me hebt gefaxt. Heeft die Bjorn dat echt zelf bedacht?' 'Hij heeft het inderdaad neergeschreven, maar hij heeft het van zijn grootvader. Dat is, was, Gerard Pieter Vanderhaeghen.' 'De filosoof? Die kerel die ons allemaal wilde vormen tot we supermensen zouden zijn? Ik wist niet dat die dood was.' 'Ik ook niet. Maar dat doet er nu even niet toe. Bjorns grootvader heeft zijn kleinzoon dingen aangepraat die onleefbaar zijn voor een jongen van zijn leeftijd. Voor de meeste mensen trouwens.' 'Ik snap het. Kun je die Bjorn niet gewoon naar huis sturen?' 'Bruno, hij is de gedroomde Theseus! Bovendien, hij redt het misschien niet als ik hem wandelen stuur. Die jongen staat op instorten, Bruno!'

Blijf jezelf maar voor de gek houden, had Bea gedacht. Je wilt hem gewoon in je buurt houden.

'Nu, bekijk het maar. Probeer in elk geval met die andere jongen te praten. O ja, je krijgt morgen versterking. Pim Brauns is van een trap gedonderd. Beenbreuk en hersenschudding. De Nederlanders komen naar jou toe. De assistent van Pim zal er ook zijn.'

Bea had vol ongeloof voor zich uit gestaard.

'Bedoel je,' had ze gezegd, 'dat er nog meer jongelui hierheen komen?'

'Ja. Je hebt hoe dan ook meer personages nodig.'
'Die zijn onbelangrijk. Ik wilde ze uit de debutantenklas halen.'
'Het kan niet anders. En wees blij dat de Nederlanders er helemaal niet moeilijk over doen dat ze met jou moeten werken. Dat is ook goed voor jouw reputatie. Ik kom wel eens langs.'
'Maar logeren ze hier ook?'
'Ja, natuurlijk. Daar moet ik morgen nog even doorheen fietsen, maar er is plaats genoeg. Probeer het op een akkoordje te gooien met die assistent, zodat jullie de repetitieruimte onder elkaar kunnen verdelen. Tot dan!'

Bea knikte nog eens. Toen pakte ze de tekst die Bjorn haar had gegeven weer op. Zijn handschrift rende met krachtige sprongen over het papier.

Aan wie dit leest

Ik zit op mijn kamer. De avondzon werpt een schitterend licht op de muur. Oranje, oker, vermengd met het doffe groen van het komende najaar. De wind gooit ze door elkaar. Het is bijna onwerkelijk. Het ergste is dat dit allemaal over heel korte tijd voorbij is. Elke seconde verandert het, maar veranderen betekent hier hoe dan ook het einde.

Is het ook zo met mij? Ik zit aan tafel met mijn handen op het houten blad. Naast me staan schoenen. Ik probeer mezelf gerust te stellen, probeer van boven af aan mezelf te denken, aan mijn buitenkant. Aan mijn haar, mijn neus, mijn borst, mijn benen, aan alles wat de mensen van me zien.

Ik voel dat mensen aan me denken, dat er over me wordt gepraat. Het voelt onvriendelijk aan. Ik ben daarom ergens aan de rand van de werkelijkheid, waar de angst voor wat met me kan gebeuren vermengd raakt met de feiten.

Ik ben voor anderen een illusie. Niemand snapt het.

Maakt het voor de hele wereld wat uit of ik faal? Sommige mensen falen zelfs zonder dat ze het zelf merken. Is het echt zo belangrijk of ik slaag of faal? Als ik erover nadenk, zou ik moeten zeggen dat het niet zo is, ook al voel ik het anders aan.

Mijn grootvader zei het me vaak genoeg: 'Gewone mensen moeten

evenveel recht op falen als op slagen krijgen. Maar jij niet. Jij, mijn jongen, hebt maar één opdracht: slagen. En dat moet je ook bewust doen. Je kunt niet aan het eind van je leven komen en dan pas vragen gaan stellen. Ja, ook al doet het pijn. Wie niet weet dat hij faalt, kent ook niet de pijn ervan en heeft heel onvolledig geleefd. Je moet dus heel vroeg weten hoe het met je staat. En daaruit de motivatie putten om door te gaan.'
Ik weet dat ik heb gefaald. Ik heb eruit geleerd, ben beter geworden. En daaruit heb ik motivatie geput. Ik ben veranderd, net op tijd. Ik kan slagen. Maar nu hebben anderen mijn leven overgenomen. Ik kan niet meer beslissen. Al mijn energie gaat op aan het verwerken van die ontgoocheling. Waarom zou ik doorgaan? Ik krijg de kans niet om de beste te zijn. Mijn grootvader zei daarover: 'Als je iets doet, moet je daarin de beste zijn. Lukt dat niet, dan moet je ermee kappen.' Vandaar.

Bjorn Vanderhaeghen

En dát moest ze volgens Bruno Storms aan Frank laten lezen? Dan zou die begrijpen wat er aan de hand was? Kom nou.

Iemand roffelde op haar deur.

'Bea! Ze vechten! Kom gauw!' De paniekerige stem van Celine.

Ze rukte haar deur open.

'Daar, in de andere gang!'

Bea rende.

Voor de deur van Bjorns kamer worstelden twee gestalten in het vage schijnsel van de nachtverlichting. Frank had Bjorn blijkbaar bij de nek. Frank was veel kleiner dan Bjorn, maar ook steviger gebouwd. Het was een vreemd gezicht. Bjorn duwde zich met zijn linkervoet af tegen de muur en probeerde zich om te draaien, maar Frank pakte zijn pols beet en duwde hem naar voren. De jongen was heel even verrast, struikelde vooruit en staarde in het donkere trapgat.

'Frank!' gilde Bea. 'Niet doen! Frank!'

Frank rukte Bjorn achteruit.

'Frank,' fluisterde Bea en haar stem klonk opeens schor. 'Wat bezielt jou?'

'Wat mij bezielt? Ik maakte een grapje en hij wou me vermoorden!'

'Een grapje?' kraste Bjorn. 'Noem je dat een grapje?'

Intussen stonden alle studenten van de Summerschool op de gang. Bea stuurde ze weg en de ene deur na de andere klapte onwillig dicht.

'Waar ging het over?'

'Ach,' schokschouderde Frank. 'Niks!'

'Hij zei me dat ik me in jouw gunst neukte! Dat ik de rol zou krijgen omdat ik jou plat had gekregen!'

Bea kneep haar ogen half dicht.

'Is dat zo?'

Stilte.

'Hij heeft me niet geneukt, Frank. Het was helemaal niet wat jij denkt!'

De jongen snoof en grinnikte toen.

'Dat zeggen ze in films ook altijd.'

'Frank! Wat denk je wel? Ik kan zijn moeder zijn!'

Het klonk zwakjes. Bea bloosde meteen.

'En als hij een rol krijgt, heeft hij die verdiend, net als jij, net als iedereen!'

Gesnuif en gegrinnik.

'Ik kan echt wel mijn eigen boontjes doppen, lul!' snauwde Bjorn.

'Ik eis dat je je verontschuldigt!'

Bea stelde opeens vast dat Bjorn haar handig tot zijn bondgenote had gemaakt, gewoon door een stap opzij te zetten en naast haar te komen staan, tegenover Frank.

'Sorry, mevrouw.'

'Noem me bij mijn voornaam.'

'Mag dat nog... van hem?'

Bjorn gaf Frank een klap. Bea frommelde het blad papier, dat ze nog altijd in haar hand hield, tot een bal.

6

'Zijn ze er al?'

'Ja, Bruno, net aangekomen. Ze zijn naar hun kamer gegaan. We beginnen over een kwartier.'

'Leuke groep, niet?'

'Dat kan ik voorlopig niet beoordelen, maar ze lijken wel mee te vallen,' zuchtte Bea.

'O ja, een van die meisjes is de dochter van Sir Denis McGregor. Nee, je hoeft niet te denken dat ze daarom de selectie heeft gehaald. Ze haalde ze trouwens in Nederland. Haar moeder is Nederlandse en ze spreekt de twee talen feilloos. Ze is echt goed. Gael McGregor, onthou die naam. Ik zie je nog wel.'

Niets bleef haar bespaard, dacht Bea. Al dan niet geveinsde zelfmoordgedachten, een gevecht, een slapeloze nacht vol verwarde overwegingen en opstandige, scherpe gevoelens, een door ambitie bezeten jongeman en nu ook nog de dochter van de voorzitter van het Institute for Young Actors.

Ze liep naar het repetitielokaal.

Frank zat er al. Hij las een magazine, niet zijn tekstboek.

'Frank? Kunnen we praten nu we weer kalm zijn?'

Hij haalde zijn schouders op.

'Ik hoef dit eigenlijk niet te doen, Frank, maar je hebt wat gisteren gebeurd is helemaal fout geïnterpreteerd. En alsjeblieft, begin niet weer te snuiven en te grinniken. O, shit, wat is dit moeilijk.'

Frank zweeg.

'Bjorn heeft een vreselijke ervaring achter de rug met de dood van zijn grootvader. Die was filosoof. Heel bekend, maar misschien de koudste, meest harteloze man die ooit een pen vasthield. Hij was helemaal gericht op wat hij noemde 'de beste zijn'. Wie niet in dat concept past, zou vanzelf moeten verdwijnen. Ach, ik kan het niet in enkele woorden uitdrukken. Ik heb boeken van hem gelezen en hij deed me denken aan...'

Bea sprak het niet uit.

'Het lijkt wel op wat de nazi's predikten.'

Bea knikte. Ze voelde zich nog altijd idioot omdat ze zich als een pubermeisje stond te verdedigen tegen een jongen van zestien.

'Maar moet je hem daarom knuffelen?'

'Hij wilde, althans, ik dacht dat hij dat wilde, uit het raam springen. Ik pakte hem beet en we vielen. Toen klemde hij zich aan me vast. Dat is alles.'

Frank zuchtte.

'Je dacht toch niet dat ik met hem over de vloer zou liggen rollen en zou vergeten de deur te sluiten?' Ze probeerde het luchtig te doen klinken, maar besefte meteen dat ze zich had versproken. Dus, kon hij denken, als de deur dicht was, zou je het wel doen.

'Zoals ik zei, Frank, kunnen we dit vergeten, alsjeblieft? Ik wil niet dat deze cursus een puinhoop wordt. Zeker niet met die nieuwe groep erbij.'

Gestommel bij de deur. De Nederlanders kwamen eraan. In groep. Wat later kwamen ook de anderen. Ze gingen aan de andere kant van de repetitieruimte zitten.

De Nederlandse begeleider, een man die eruitzag als een verdwaalde tuinman, stond op.

'Bedankt dat we met jullie mee mogen doen en nu al sorry voor de aanpassing. Mijn naam is Bram Hillenius. Ik was de assistent van Pim Brauns, die van de trap is gedonderd. De meisjes heten Gael, Brenda, Senta en Felicia. De jongens Arthur, Mirko en Poppy.'

Als ze hun naam hoorden, wuifden de meisjes en jongens even met hun hand. Alleen Poppy sprong op, maakte een theatrale buiging en grijnsde zijn hagelwitte tanden bloot. Ze schitterden gewoon in zijn donkere gezicht.

'Ik hoef al niet meer te vertellen wie de grapjas van ons gezelschap is?' zei Bram nog en ging weer zitten. Uit de zakken van zijn overall diepte hij een pakje shag op en begon een sigaret te draaien. Jouw beurt, Bea, betekende dat.

Bea stelde haar groep voor.

'Wij zouden vandaag beginnen met de lezing van de scène waarin Theseus zijn plan ontvouwt en ze aan land gaan op Kreta. Wij hebben voorlopig nog niemand op een rol vastgepind. Al wordt voor mij wel een en ander duidelijk.'

Bea probeerde haar stem neutraal te laten klinken, maar ze voelde hoe de spieren van haar schouders zich spanden. Uit haar ooghoek kon ze zien hoe Frank naar Bjorn keek. Die had zijn handen gevouwen. Zijn knokkels waren wit.

'Ik ken jullie helemaal niet, dus ik stel voor dat wij die tekst lezen en herlezen en dat ik dan kan zien...'

'Prima,' zei Bram. 'Ik zou nog één ding willen zeggen, Bea. We werken nu wel samen omdat we in die korte tijd geen andere regisseur konden vinden in Nederland. Maar het is duidelijk dat uit deze groep de eventuele Nederlandse kandidaten komen voor Londen. Dus stel ik voor dat zij de rol blijven spelen die ze toebedeeld kregen. Omdat we maar met z'n zevenen zijn, hebben sommigen een kleine dubbelrol ingeoefend, maar in hoofdzaak spelen zij één personage.'

Bea knikte. Geen probleem.

'Gael is Ariadne, Brenda is Althea, Senta is Heros en Felicia speelt Parmenides.'

'Omdat ze toch geen tieten heeft en praat als een vent!'

Mirko lachte het hardst om wat hij als een geslaagde grap beschouwde.

Felicia, een rank maar gespierd meisje, stak de middelvinger van haar rechterhand op, maar antwoordde niet. Het bleef even ongezellig stil.

'Mirko is, zoals je had vermoed, de monsterlijke Minotaurus...'

'Die jullie allemaal zal verslinden...' gromde Mirko en hij rolde met zijn ogen.

'Arthur speelt Minos.'

Bea zag de spanning op het gezicht van Bjorn. Zijn wenkbrauwen leken naar elkaar toe te groeien, hij kneep zijn ogen half dicht en zijn tongpunt kwam te voorschijn. Was er dan geen Theseus in de groep?

'En Poppy is een geweldige Theseus.'

Bjorn schudde onmerkbaar zijn hoofd. Ongelovig keek hij naar de zwarte jongen, die deze keer niet reageerde.

'Zoals gezegd, neemt wie niet echt in een scène thuishoort de kleinere rollen voor zijn of haar rekening. Dat geldt vooral voor Senta en Mirko. Zullen we dan maar?'

Ze hadden dezelfde tekstboeken, zag Bjorn. Dezelfde letter, maar bij hen was de omslag oranje.

Theseus loopt naar een van de vaten, graait erin en haalt drie zwaarden te voorschijn.

THESEUS: Hierom! Zwaarden! We zullen die Minotaurus een les leren die hij nooit meer vergeet... Als hij achteraf nog in staat is ze te onthouden.

PARMENIDES: Zwaarden? Hoe heb je die hier gekregen? Ze hebben ons... nou ja...

THESEUS: Juist, ze hebben ons gefouilleerd! Ik zie nog jouw lieve snoetje toen die geile soldaat naar je tietjes tastte. En het zijne toen hij ze niet vond! Ik heb een hoofd gekregen om te denken. Dus heb ik die dingen aan boord gebracht in de nacht voordat we moesten inschepen.

AGOS: Hoe kom je erbij? Hoe...

THESEUS: Dat, mijn lieve vriend, is het verschil tussen jullie en mijzelf.

ALTHEA: Je wordt stilletjes aan onuitstaanbaar, Theseus! Luister! Er gebeurt wat!

'Mooi zo,' knikte Bea. 'Ik ben erg tevreden met wat jullie doen. Er is weinig verschil in aanpak. En individueel mogen jullie de personages een ander accent geven. Als het fundamenteel maar klopt. Ik ga me daarmee niet bezig houden, akkoord? Ik zal bij jullie vooral letten op details, het samenspel beter helpen maken, een eenheid proberen te creëren. Als jullie of enkelen van jullie Londen halen, begint alles toch weer van voor af aan. We hebben uit Londen een aantal basisideeën gekregen voor de regie, meer niet. Ik heb het tegen mijn jongelui ook al gezegd, ik bedoel tegen het groepje dat eerder hier was dan jullie: wat wij doen, is eigenlijk niet meer dan de voorronde van een groot tornooi.'

'O, wat zijn die Belgen stil! O, wat zijn die Belgen stil!' zong Mirko het bekende voetbaldeuntje. Nu lachte iedereen. Behalve Bjorn. Die staarde als gebiologeerd naar Poppy. De jongen merkte het. Hij draaide zich naar Bjorn om.

'Hé, maatje, heb ik soms kleren van je aan?'

Bjorn rukte zijn mondhoeken omhoog tot een glimlach.

'Ach, ik zat te dromen,' zei hij.

'Goed, volgende scène. Een belangrijke scène, een wending in het stuk. Hier komen we stilletjes aan tot de kern van de zaak. Arthur is Theros, Mirko is Minos, Frank doet nog eens Parmenides, Elke blijft Althea. Let op, Elke, je moet echt opletten voor overdrijvingen. Je gevoelens mogen je niet meeslepen. Probeer echt te voelen wat je overkomt en dat heel intens te zeggen. Andrea, je krijgt nog eens een jongensrol...'

'En ik heb wél tieten!' riep Andrea naar Mirko. Gelach.

'Eén punt voor jou,' kaatste Mirko terug. 'Ik kom straks kijken of je me niks voorliegt.'

'Komaan, jongens, ernst! Bjorn, jij speelt Theseus...'

'Wie had dat nou gedacht?' mompelde Frank half hardop.

'En Ariadne... Gael, is het niet?'

Het meisje knikte. Ze droeg een crêmekleurige jurk van een soepele stof die elke beweging van haar lichaam onderstreepte.

'Jij, Gael, hebt misschien de moeilijkste opdracht. Als je het mij vraagt, is jouw personage in dit stuk het minst sterk getekend. En toch moet je van nu af aan echt mee de handeling dragen. Wat de auteur er niet heeft in gestopt, moet dus van jou komen.'

'Geen probleem!' Weer Mirko. 'Ze is super!'

'Dat zien we dan wel. Aan het werk.'

Bjorn stond op en legde heel ostentatief zijn tekstboek op een vensterbank.

Er klinkt gejuich. De jongelui wankelen alsof het schip een onverwachte beweging maakt. Nog meer gejuich. Geschetter van trompetten, getoeter van hoorns.

THESEUS: Het schip legt aan. Ik wist niet dat dat zo gauw zou gebeuren. Gelukkig hebben wij de zwaarden.

ALTHEA: Theseus? Hou je van me?

THESEUS: Ja, natuurlijk hou ik van je! Ik hou van de hele wereld!

PARMENIDES: Maar vooral van jezelf, niet, Theseus?

THESEUS: En wat is daar verkeerd aan in mijn geval, Parmenides? Ik hou dan van de man die Athene van het meest vernederende, het meest vreselijke zal bevrijden. Dat kun jij voorlopig niet zeggen.

PARMENIDES: Ik...
ALTHEA: Hou op! Niet nu! We moeten de anderen redden.
STEM: Naar boven jullie! En geen geintjes of ik sla je kop eraf! Dan
heeft de Minotaurus het nog makkelijker.
*Het viertal loopt naar de rechterkant van de scène. Licht op Minos,
Theros, zijn raadgever, twee wachters en Ariadne, zijn dochter.*

'Ogenblikje. Geert, Willem. Spelen jullie nu even die wachters. Je hoeft
niet te praten, maar het is wel belangrijk voor de opstelling. Goed? Be-
dankt, jongens. Ja, daar, aan beide kanten van dat groepje. Mirko, pro-
beer er koninklijk uit te zien. Gael, jij staat er wat onverschillig bij.'
'Mevrouw?'
De stem van dat meisje leek vloeibaar goud.
'Zeg maar Bea, ja?'
'Waarom onverschillig?'
Bea keek op haar tekstboek.
'Laten we zeggen gemaakt onverschillig. Wat zou jij doen?'
'Gemaakt hooghartig, wat cynisch. Dan kan het contrast met wat
ze later zegt, dat ze het erg vindt en zo, nog sterker worden.'
Iedereen keek naar Gael. Opeens was ze uit de schaduw gekomen,
stond ze in het volle licht. Ze had een natuurlijke autoriteit. Was ze
mooi? Misschien. Het was niet eens belangrijk. Ze straalde iets uit dat
ervoor zorgde dat je niet op haar uiterlijk lette. Bea merkte het meteen.
Dit was Ariadne. In dat nog onvolwassen lichaam, in die wat te lange
armen, in die iets te grote oren die ze nog niet verborg onder haar kap-
sel, zaten alle passies van een vrouw opgestapeld. Indrukwekkend.
'We zitten daarmee niet zo ver van elkaar af, wel?'
'Nee, Bea. Oké, ik ben klaar.'
In de 'oké' klonk iets Engels door. Okay. Dus toch?
Bea gaf een teken, ze speelden door.

MINOS: Wat moet dat? Waarom zijn jullie niet samen met de andere gevangenen van boord gekomen?
THESEUS: Omdat uw zeelui, koning, ons dat hebben belet. Ze hebben ons in dat stinkende ruim opgesloten.

56

THEROS: Zwijg, hond uit Athene, je praat tegen de koning.

THESEUS: Hond? Ik? Kijk naar jezelf. Ik hoef niet te kwispelen zoals jij, man! Ik hoef niemands handen te likken. Ik ben Theseus, ik ben een prins en in mijn lijf stroomt koninklijk bloed. En jij? Blaf eens, dat ik me je stem herinner...

THEROS: Dat is te veel. Ik...

MINOS: Wind je niet op, Theros... Jij mag dan blaffen, hij zal janken. Wachters! Of heb je nog een wens, Athener?

THESEUS: Jawel. Omdat we in dat stinkende ruim opgesloten hebben gezeten, wilde ik nog een uur van de open lucht genieten.

MINOS: Jammer dat je het niet verder zult vertellen, ik ben namelijk niet de onmens voor wie men me houdt. Toegestaan. Tot zonsopgang kun je op deze binnenplaats blijven. Tot kijk, al zal ook dat een vrome wens blijven. En groet hoe dan ook de Minotaurus van me.

Minos en Theros af. Ariadne aarzelt duidelijk, maar volgt dan toch. Theseus loopt even rond en gaat dan tegen een zuil zitten.

Bea stond op en klapte in haar handen.

'Mooi zo. Bjorn?'

De jongen stond op.

'Wat je zegt, de manier waarop, je ritme, alles is prima. Maar een acteur praat ook met zijn lichaam. Jouw lichaamstaal laat je woorden klinken als een leugen. Ik moet ook zien wat je zegt, snap je? Dat lukt niet zo best. Je schouders lijken van hout. Je speelt als een standbeeld. Vorstelijk en zo, dat wel, maar niet erg natuurlijk. Probeer losser te bewegen.'

Bjorn knikte, al voelde hij het bloed door zijn hoofd razen. Dit hoefde toch niet terwijl alle anderen erbij waren! Waarom deed ze dat? Ze zette hem voor schut, verdomme, net nu die vreemden erbij waren. Hij slikte zijn keel vrij en ging weer zitten, nonchalant. Bea herkende meteen de houding die hij in het park had aangenomen toen hij dacht dat niemand hem kon zien.

'Doorgaan!' zei ze.

ALTHEA: *Komt dichterbij, kijkt behoedzaam om en om. Maar de twee anderen zijn verderop bij elkaar gaan zitten.*

Theseus? Het wordt avond nu. Is dit niet het ogenblik waarop de meeuwen neerstrijken? Misschien is het een van onze laatste uren samen. Misschien...

THESEUS: Heb je dat meisje gezien dat bij de koning stond? Slank als een droom, mooi als de nevel bij dageraad...

ALTHEA: Theseus! Je praat tegen mij over een ander meisje! Theseus!

THESEUS: Ik vraag me af wie ze is. Zou ze de dochter van Minos zijn? En als ze zijn dochter is...

ALTHEA: *Barst in snikken uit.*

Je bent een schoft, Theseus! Tel ik dan niet meer mee? Moet ik dan denken dat alles wat je me hebt gezegd, dat al die lieve gebaren niets anders waren dan theater?

THESEUS: Laat me denken, Althea. Morgen kan alles voorbij zijn...

ALTHEA: Precies! Daarom wil ik deze laatste uren met jou... Theseus?

THESEUS: *Komt overeind en staart in de verte. Licht langzaam op Ariadne, die daar staat en aarzelend wacht.*

Stil! Daar komt ze. Althea, vertrouw me. Misschien kan zij helpen. Maak dat je wegkomt, ga naar de anderen, wacht daar.

Althea kijkt hem ongelovig aan, kijkt naar Ariadne, naar Theseus, maakt een woedend gebaar en loopt weg.

AGOS: Arme Althea, ze heeft haar hoop op de verkeerde gesteld.

PARMENIDES: Theseus? Dat had ze toch kunnen raden. Ach, ik ben er zelf ook ingetuind. De eerste dagen, toen hij net terug was, toen hij met ons kwam praten, dacht ik dat hij inderdaad een goede vriend kon worden.

ALTHEA: Hij heeft me hierheen gestuurd.

AGOS: Je kon wat opgewekter zijn! Ben je niet tevreden nu je ons gezelschap kunt houden?

Wil zijn arm om haar heen leggen. Althea slaat die weg.

ALTHEA: Handen thuis, Agos. Je vergeet blijkbaar dat je nu een meisje bent. En bovendien, je hoeft niet te denken dat je zomaar de plaats van Theseus kunt innemen.

De volgende scènes worden naast elkaar gespeeld. De regie moet duidelijk maken dat de beide groepjes elkaar niet kunnen horen.

'Pauze!' riep Bea.

De jongelui leken te ontwaken. Er was een intense spanning voelbaar.

Gael stond wat verderop te wachten. Bram Hillenius raapte het tekstboek op dat ze naast zich had neergelegd en gooide het zonder kijken op een stoel. Een blad papier gleed eruit en dwarrelde naar de grond.

'Het loopt lekker,' zei Bram. 'Heel lekker! Jullie zijn goed, hoor! Hartstikke goed.'

De bromstem van de man klonk eerlijk.

'Ik stel voor, Bea, als jij dat goed vindt, dat we straks nog een paar scènes doen en dat we dan gaan mixen. Mijn meisjes en jongens kennen het best hun tekst, denk ik, behalve jij dan... Bert of Bart?'

'Bjorn.'

'Juist, sorry, behalve jij dan, Bjorn. Als we het hele stuk hebben doorgenomen, moet ook voor jullie duidelijk zijn wat je het liefste wilt doen en wat je kunt. We hoeven er ook niet omheen te draaien. Niet iedereen is Theseus of de Minotaurus of Althea. Dan splitsen we de hele groep in twee kleinere groepen waarin telkens een zinvolle doublure zit. En dan gooien we die groepjes elke keer door elkaar. Snappen jullie wat ik bedoel?'

De jongelui knikten.

'Vind ik prima,' zei Bea. 'Dan neem ik telkens een groep voor een aantal scènes, zet die stukken in elkaar en jij, Bram, gaat door met oefenen op basis van wat we hebben neergezet. Intussen ga ik weer met de andere groep aan de slag.'

De stem van Bea klonk opgelucht.

'Goed, tijd voor koffie,' zei Bram Hillenius. 'Over een halfuurtje gaan we door. Niet later. Mirko, blijf in de buurt. De tuin mag, maar je komt het hek niet uit.'

De groep brokkelde uit elkaar. Mirko liep naar Andrea toe.

'Wij hadden nog wat te bespreken, niet?' Ze lachten allebei.

Gael keek rond, zocht iets. Bjorn pakte het tekstboek van de stoel en wuifde ermee.

'Is dit wat je zoekt?'

'O ja, bedankt.'

Ze glimlachte en draaide zich meteen weer om.

'Senta! Wacht. Zullen we die kamer van ons meteen aan kant doen? Ik heb mijn spullen zomaar neergegooid.'

Frank stond bij Brenda en Willem legde Felicia uit hoe ze bij de telefoon kon komen. Elke wachtte bij de deur. Ze zuchtte. Bjorn had alleen oog voor die Gael. Ze zag het Nederlandse meisje naar de deur lopen. Tegen het licht van het raam werd de omtrek van haar lichaam onder de stof van de lange jurk zichtbaar.

'Bjorn! Kom je?'

Het klonk scheller dan ze had bedoeld.

'Ja, ik zie je bij de koffieautomaat.'

Zijn wuifgebaar, zo van 'jaja, niet zeuren, ik kom wel', maakte haar wit van woede.

'Stik, rotsukkel!'

Elke draaide zich om en liep naar buiten. Toen bleef ze staan. Nee, ze zou niet zomaar verdwijnen, ze liet zich niet wegwuiven.

Bjorn raapte het vel papier op dat uit het tekstboek van Gael was gevallen en vouwde het open. Een brief.

Hij aarzelde.

'Bjorn?'

Elke weer. Bjorn vouwde de brief dicht en stopte hem in de zak van zijn jeansbroek.

'Ja, ik kom!'

7

Geluid van vorken en lepels op borden. Gelach dat af en toe naar het hoge plafond klaterde. De twee groepjes waren in elkaar opgegaan. Bea tikte tegen haar glas.

'Mag ik even?'

Het geroezemoes stierf weg.

'Normaal werken we 's avonds niet echt door. Maar gezien de situatie... Het inpassen van de tweede groep vraagt tijd. Daarom dit voorstel. We werken nog twee uur en dan heeft iedereen de kans gehad om zijn rol te spelen. Behalve Mirko, als Minotaurus.'

'Hoeft niet. Hij is monsterlijk van zichzelf!' riep Andrea, die naast de Nederlandse jongen aan tafel zat.

'Klopt!' vulde Mirko zelf aan. 'En zij heeft me al beloofd dat ik haar toch mag opvreten, straks, privé!'

Bea knikte ongeduldig.

'Morgen beginnen we een halfuurtje later, want iedereen moet zo stilaan zijn tekst gaan instuderen. Akkoord?'

Niemand protesteerde.

'Dan zie ik jullie zo dadelijk in de repetitiezaal. En bedankt voor het begrip.'

THESEUS: Goeienavond. Heb ik jou niet eerder gezien?

ARIADNE: Ik mag dan op een eiland wonen en jij mag dan uit Athene komen, maar een trucje als dit is wel heel slap. Ja, natuurlijk, heb je mij al gezien. Niet lang geleden.

THESEUS: Jij bent niet op je mondje gevallen. Hoe heet je? Wie ben je?

ARIADNE: Nee. Ariadne. Mezelf.

THESEUS: Wat zég je?

ARIADNE: Drie vragen, drie antwoorden... Nee, ik ben niet op mijn mondje gevallen, ik heet Ariadne en ik ben gewoon mezelf!

Ze lachen allebei.

PARMENIDES: Moet je hem zien! Hij is nu al vergeten waar hij is! Hij staat te smoezen met de dochter van Minos!

ALTHEA: Ken je haar dan?

AGOS: Denk toch na.

THESEUS: Laat me eens nadenken... Je stond naast de koning toen wij aankwamen, je ziet eruit als de dochter van de koning, je mag vrij rondlopen zonder dat een wachtpost je wat vraagt... Jij moet prinses zijn.

Hij doet een knieval, pakt de zoom van haar kleed en kust die.

ARIADNE: Goed! Heel goed! En wie ben jij? Je maakte wel een scène, met Theros. Je lijkt niet te weten hoe gevaarlijk hij is. Iedereen is doodsbang voor hem.

THESEUS: Niet iedereen. Ik bijvoorbeeld niet. Bovendien, wat kan het me schelen dat hij gevaarlijk is? Over enkele uren moeten we daar naar binnen. En als de verhalen kloppen, zal de Minotaurus korte metten met ons maken. Weet jij waar de andere kinderen zijn, de kinderen die eerder dan wij van boord zijn gehaald?

ARIADNE: Onbekende, ik... Ze zijn... Mijn vader...

THESEUS: Dus toch? Nu al? De Minotaurus?

ALTHEA: Hoe is het mogelijk! Wij staan op het punt te sterven! De andere jonge Atheners zijn intussen de prooi geworden van dat monster en hij vindt de tijd om haar het hof te maken?

AGOS: Kalm, Althea. Misschien is hij wel wat van plan...

PARMENIDES: Precies, ik kan niet geloven dat Theseus iets zomaar doet. Hij heeft altijd wel een plannetje in zijn hoofd. Stil, ze kijken in onze richting.

ARIADNE: Je drie vriendinnen zitten er wat triest bij?

THESEUS: Ze zijn bang, ongelukkig. Het lot heeft hen uitgekozen om te sterven. Hoe zou jij het vinden om uit het leven te moeten verdwijnen nog voor je de beker van de dagen aan je lippen hebt gezet? Hoe zou jij je voelen als je met je bloed moest betalen voor iets waar je niet eens weet van had?

ARIADNE: Wind je niet op! Ik vind het even erg als jij! Ik probeer mijn vader te overtuigen...

THESEUS: Erg? Vind je het erg? Meen je dat?

ARIADNE: Natuurlijk! Denk je dat ik het prettig vind dat iedereen mijn vader een bloeddorstige tiran noemt? Dat iedereen voor hem kruipt, siddert en rilt? En waarom? Omdat mijn broer ooit is gedood. Het was een ongeval, niet?

THESEUS: Het was een ongeval. Ariadne?
ARIADNE: Theseus?
THESEUS: Nee, ik durf je niet te vragen...
ALTHEA: Kijk hem, hij draait haar rond zijn vinger net zoals hij het met mij heeft gedaan. Waarschijnlijk zegt hij nu: 'Ik durf je niet te vragen om me te helpen!'
AGOS: Hoe zou zij kunnen helpen?
PARMENIDES: Misschien weet zij een uitweg uit die doolhof...
ARIADNE: Wat durf je niet te vragen?
THESEUS: Als je het dan toch zo vreselijk vindt, wil je ons dan helpen? Ken jij de weg in het labyrint? Weet je hoe je eruit komt?

Stilte. De spanning brak. Poppy draaide zich naar de rest van de groep en boog. Ze begonnen spontaan in hun handen te klappen. Toen pakte hij de hand van Gael beet en samen maakten ze nog een buiging, alsof ze in een heuse schouwburg voor een groot publiek hadden gespeeld.

Bjorn beet op zijn onderlip.

'Tjee, hij is goed, niet?' vroeg Elke.

Bjorn knikte.

'Jammer dat hij zwart is.'

'Wat? Wat zei je?'

'Niks.'

Het applaus stierf uit, verstikt onder het gelach dat nu losbrak. Andrea was naar de twee acteurs gelopen en viel voor Poppy op haar knieën. Ze stak hem een denkbeeldige ruiker bloemen toe. Opnieuw applaus. Bea moest er een eind aan maken.

'De laatste scène van dit bedrijf. Bjorn, jij neemt de plaats van Poppy in. Felicia, doe jij nou maar eens Althea. Willem en Geert Parmenides en Agos. Opschieten. Ja, daar, Willem.'

Bjorn liep naar Gael. Ze hadden meteen contact, merkte Bea, en ze voelde zich weer wat onwennig. De jongen legde zijn hand op de arm van het meisje, herhaalde de vraag waarmee Poppy geëindigd was. Waar haalde die knul het! Het was gewoon op en top professioneel zoals hij die overgang verwerkte. En meteen had hij zijn tegenspeelster in zijn greep. Letterlijk en figuurlijk.

THESEUS: Als je het dan toch zo vreselijk vindt, wil je ons dan helpen? Ken jij de weg in het labyrint? Weet je hoe je eruit komt?

ARIADNE: Nee! Niemand kent die. Je gaat er naar binnen, je ziet gangen en zalen en elke hoek lijkt je verder te lokken, verder weg van de uitgang. Het is een bijzonder vernuftig, een dodelijk vernuftig bouwsel. En dan is er de Minotaurus...

THESEUS: Weet je wie hij is?

ARIADNE: *Doet heel onrustig, kijkt om zich heen, neemt Theseus bij de hand.*

Er wordt zoveel gefluisterd! Het is het grote, woeste geheim van mijn vader. Mijn slavin heeft me onlangs gezegd dat de Minotaurus een kind is van mijn moeder, een kind dat bij haar is verwekt door een witte stier die aan Poseidon gewijd was. Mijn moeder is op het dier verliefd geworden... De vrucht van hun liefde is door mijn vader opgesloten en is daarom zo woest dat...

THESEUS: Zo? Dan is er toch iets menselijks aan dat monster. Ik kan het lot wel vervloeken! Net nu ik in mijn hart voel... Ach, ik mag jou daar niet mee lastigvallen.

ARIADNE: Waarmee?

ALTHEA: Hij is in de aanval gegaan. Hij zal haar hart belegeren, het bestormen met zijn mooie woorden.

AGOS: Dan wil hij wat van haar! Hij zal haar zover krijgen dat ze helpt!

PARMENIDES: En opeens is hij weer de held, niet, Agos?

ALTHEA: Ja, nu vind je weer goed wat hij doet, niet?

AGOS: Ik wil maar één ding, Althea, hier wegkomen! En als Theseus daarvoor de dochter van de koning moet versieren...

ARIADNE: Zeg het me! Ik kan het niet hebben dat je zo zielig troosteloos voor je uit zit te kijken.

THESEUS: *Probeert te glimlachen, pakt dan haar hand.*

Ik wist dat ik zou sterven toen ik in Athene inscheepte. Ik was bereid mijn leven te offeren om dat van een andere jongen te redden, dat van een jongen die de enige steun was van zijn oude moeder. Ik heb zijn plaats ingenomen. Ik ben blij én doodbedroefd...

ARIADNE: Ga door, Theseus. Ga door.

THESEUS: Ik ben blij dat ik jou daardoor heb ontmoet, maar ik huil omdat ik afscheid moet nemen van je, afscheid nog voor ik je echt heb gekend. Je bent voor mij de dageraad bij avond, de regenboog in een winterstorm, de bloem die op een dorre stengel is opengebloeid! Ik weet dat het wanhopig klinkt, Ariadne, maar ik hou van je!

ARIADNE: Theseus! Ook in mijn hart, in mijn lichaam is er wat gebeurd toen ik je zag. Ik heb niet zoveel mooie woorden, maar ik weet dat ik ook van je hou! Ik zal je helpen! Je moet de Minotaurus verslaan, je moet terugkomen en me meenemen naar jouw land. Wacht hier.

Springt op en holt weg.

ALTHEA: Hahaha, deze keer heeft Theseus zijn slag niet thuis gehaald! Ze loopt van hem weg.

PARMENIDES: Wacht, hij komt hierheen.

THESEUS: Een onverwachte bondgenote. Zij is Ariadne, de dochter van Minos. Ze zal ons helpen.

ALTHEA: Helpen? Zij? Bedoel je dat ze met ons het labyrint in loopt? Gaat ze met haar kleed staan wapperen om de Minotaurus te lokken en zoengeluidjes maken om hem gek te krijgen? Daarvoor hoefde je haar niet te versieren, Theseus!

THESEUS: Als ik je niet beter kende, zou ik denken dat je jaloers bent, Althea.

ALTHEA: En ik ken jou goed genoeg om te weten dat je echt een schoft bent, Theseus. Waarom gun je mij de laatste uren van dit leven niet? Waarom heb je mij tot je vrouw gemaakt en schop je me nu in een hoek? Waarom? Waarom moest je een speeltje van me maken?

THESEUS: Althea! Ik wil alleen dat we hier wegkomen. Als ik daarvoor Ariadne kan gebruiken, zal ik dat doen.

Licht uit, doek.

Bjorn bleef staan, een beetje dramatisch, met gebogen hoofd. Het was nog altijd stil toen hij naar zijn plaats liep.

Toen klapte toch iemand in de handen. En nog iemand. Het applaus brak door. Bjorn glimlachte flauwtjes en knikte als dank. Hij keek om naar Gael. Die glimlachte breed en applaudisseerde nog harder.

Het was stil in het kasteel. Iedereen was in zijn kamer of wandelde nog wat in het park.

Bjorn had net zijn tanden gepoetst en wilde een trainingspak aantrekken toen hij zich de brief herinnerde die hij in de zak van zijn jeansbroek had gestopt. Hij vouwde het blad open en fronste zijn voorhoofd. Het logo van het Institute for Young Actors.

Dear Gael

Engels. Een sterk, mooi handschrift. Woorden die netjes in het gelid liepen. Zwarte inkt.

Je snapt wel dat ik heel erg met gemengde gevoelens reageerde toen ik je enthousiaste brief kreeg. Het is haar gelukt! Dat was mijn eerste reactie en ik sprong in gedachten boven op mijn stoel om te juichen. Het is haar bovendien in Nederland gelukt! Nog maar eens gejuich. Dus, schatje, gefeliciteerd. Je oude vader heeft ongelijk gehad en jij hebt meer van je koppige, begaafde moeder dan ik kon vermoeden.

Maar ik zou oneerlijk zijn als ik je niet vertelde dat ik het moeilijk blijf vinden. Ja, ik weet het wel, je hebt aan die schiftingsproeven deelgenomen onder de naam van je moeder en eigenlijk heb ik niet zoveel met de hele zaak te maken. Maar geloof je nou echt dat niet her en der iemand zal denken dat je er gekomen bent omdat je nu eenmaal de dochter bent van de voorzitter van het Institute?

Bjorn liet de brief zakken. Had hij wel dat goed gelezen? Zijn ogen vlogen weer over de tekst. Gael was de dochter van Sir Denis McGregor, de voorzitter van het Institute for Young Actors! En dat Institute moest de definitieve keuze maken voor de rol van Theseus!

Liefje, ik weet dat dit je niet op andere gedachten zal brengen en ik ben hoe dan ook blij dat ik zo'n talentvolle dochter heb. Maar als je ooit gekozen wordt voor de eindronde, zal ik een stap terug zetten en zeker niet bij de besprekingen aanwezig zijn. Je moeder is boos geworden toen ik haar dat via de telefoon vertelde, maar ik hoop dat jij het snapt. Bovendien zal alles toch beslist moeten worden op basis van de lokale rapporten die we krijgen. Ik heb gehoord dat je hebt leren surfen

op het Internet? Nou, dat komt dan mooi uit. Kun je me boodschap-
pen sturen met e-mail. Op het kaartje dat ik hierbij stop, vind je alle
gegevens. Ik wil het voorlopig niet weten, maar ik hoop dat je een
mooie rol krijgt. Als vader zou ik in de wolken zijn als je in de cast van
het stuk zou zitten. Daar heb ik zelfs wat slapeloze nachten voor over.
Een stevige knuffel van je oude vader.

De handtekening liep over de helft van de bladzijde.

'Bjorn?'

De jongen knipperde even met zijn ogen. Toen vouwde hij de brief langzaam dicht en schoof hem onder zijn tekstboek. Hij draaide zich om en glimlachte naar Elke, maar zijn ogen bleven koud.

'Hoi!'

'Bjorn, wat is er nou weer?'

Hij haalde zijn schouders op.

'Doe niet alsof je niet snapt wat ik bedoel. Je hebt niet eens meer naar me gekeken. Je bent meteen naar je kamer gegaan.'

'Ik moet die tekst instuderen.'

'Je kent die tekst van achteren naar voren. Wat is er? Heb ik iets ge-daan, gezegd, gevraagd...?'

'Nee, maar ik weet niet waarom ik speciaal met jou zou moeten blijven praten? Waarom vraag je me dat?'

Elke tikte met haar vinger tegen haar voorhoofd.

'Ik geloof dat er hier en daar iets niet meer in orde is in je hoofd.'

'Wat wil je daarmee zeggen?'

'Gisteren bijvoorbeeld. Wat moest dat? En vandaag. Die opmerking over Poppy? Je bent zo geobsedeerd door deze hele toestand, dat je...'

'Ik ben niet geobsedeerd!'

'Hoe noem je het dan? Je grootvadersyndroom?'

Bjorn keek haar woedend aan terwijl hij voorover boog. Hij leek een roofdier dat klaarstond om te springen en te doden.

'Zeg dat nooit meer!'

'Goed, maar leg dan eens uit wat dit allemaal te betekenen heeft. Ik dacht dat we vrienden waren, heel wat meer dan vrienden zelfs, na gisteren...'

'Ik denk niet aan wat voorbij is. Snap je dat nou niet? En wat gisteren gebeurd is, was iets wat we allebei wilden, wat we allebei lekker vonden.'

'Meer niet?'

Bjorn schudde zijn hoofd.

'Ik vind je zielig, Bjorn. Zielig! En voor mij was het echt wel meer. Toen ik je kuste, toen ik je streelde, toen ik je voelde reageren, toen je... Ach, laat zitten. Waarom? Dat zou ik willen weten. Tegenover wie wil je wat bewijzen? Wat wil je bewijzen?'

Bjorn haalde zijn schouders op en draaide zich naar het raam.

'Dat snap je toch niet.'

Elke klapte in haar handen.

'Dat is het snuggerste antwoord dat je kon bedenken. Voor de zoveelste keer laat je iemand merken dat er twee soorten wezens bestaan, de stommelingen en Bjorn Vanderhaeghen. De zwartjes en de witte ridder! Val dood, Bjorn. En veel geluk met je nieuwe liefje.'

Elke gooide de deur achter zich dicht. Keihard.

8

'Ja?'

Bea zette haar bril af en draaide zich half om in haar stoel. De deur ging open.

'Sorry,' zei Bjorn, 'maar ik wil je wat vragen.'

'Kom erin. Een snoepje? Bram heeft een doos Haagse Hopjes voor me meegebracht en ik zit al de hele avond te sabbelen. Slecht voor de lijn uiteraard.'

Bjorn grinnikte.

'Je mag nog een hele vrachtwagen snoep hebben voor er wat met je lijn...'

Bea maakte een gebaar dat hem deed zwijgen. Ze stond op.

'Kom toch binnen. Wat kan ik voor je doen?'

De jongen zette een stapje dichterbij en sloot toen de deur.

'Ik moet de hele tijd aan gisteren denken,' zuchtte hij.

Bea rilde. Gisteren?

'Het was zo...'

'Bjorn, luister. Ik weet ook wel dat...'

'Nu maken we allebei onze zin niet af.'

Bea probeerde te lachen. Opeens leken haar zintuigen gescherpt. De New Age-muziek op de radio, het gedimde licht in de kamer, de kring van helder licht op haar werktafel, het geruis van hun ademhaling, de geur van shampoo of aftershave.

Bjorn keek haar aan. Zijn ogen boorden zich opnieuw in haar, haar huid gloeide en haar mond was droog. Wat deden haar handen vreemd. Ze strekten zich naar hem uit. Bjorn. Haar handen streken neer op zijn harde schouders en drukten. Hij ging zitten op het vloerkleedje voor haar bed. Ze zag zijn handen bewegen, naar haar borsten toe. Hij boog vooover, klaar om haar te kussen. Zijn ogen bleven hard.

'Ik hou van je!' fluisterde hij.

'Je bent gek,' ademde Bea. 'Ik kan je moeder zijn.'

'Dat ben je niet. Ik kan je minnaar zijn.'

Het klonk zo ingestudeerd, zo uit een tweederangs soap gehaald, dat Bea schrok en ontwaakte uit een droom. De verwarring was voorbij. Alles viel weer op zijn plaats.

Ze stond op, stak haar hand uit en trok hem overeind.

'Dit was een leuk stukje acteren,' zei ze en meteen wist ze dat hij boos zou worden.

'Maar ik meende het! Waarom speel je met me? Waarom doe je dit? En waarom moest je me voor schut zetten toen we repeteerden?' Bij elke vraag ging zijn stem schriller klinken.

'Bjorn, zo is het genoeg. Sorry, ik was één ogenblik in verwarring. Ik denk dat de spanning me heeft uitgeput. Sorry, ik had beter moeten weten. Je bent nog maar een jongen. Laten we het vergeten.'

'Dat kan ik niet en dat kun jij ook niet. En praat niet over uitputting. Je voelde wat je voelde.'

Onvoorstelbaar, dacht Bea. Dat jongetje spelt me de les!

'Maar als het dat is wat je wilt... Vergeten? Goed, we praten er niet meer over. Dat is al iets.'

'Zou je echt met me naar bed zijn gegaan? Nee, schrik maar niet, ik wil dit uitpraten.'

'Waarom niet?' zei Bjorn.

'Waarom wel? Omdat ik dan aan je overgeleverd zou zijn? Omdat je dacht dat ik jou dan anders zou zien? Omdat ik een betere beoordeling over je zou schrijven? Zou je het echt zo ver drijven? Nee, laat me uitspreken. En geef me een eerlijk antwoord. Ik merk het meteen als je liegt.'

'Ik heb je al gezegd dat je mijn moeder niet bent.'

Bjorn was nu lijkbleek en rilde over zijn hele lichaam.

'O? Omdat je moeder het merkt als je liegt?'

'Dat heeft er niets mee te maken.'

'Wijk dan zelf niet af van het onderwerp. Waarom kwam je vanavond?'

'Omdat ik de rol van Theseus wil.'

Het grote woord was gevallen. Bea knikte. Waarom was ze nou toch teleurgesteld? Ze had het toch kunnen weten! Zij was bijna veertig en verward omdat ze in de steek was gelaten. Die jonge, ambitieuze aap had aangevoeld dat ze kwetsbaar was. Verdomme nog aan toe! Maar nu hij het recht voor de raap zei, was ze ontgoocheld.

'Je zou er echt alles voor doen, niet? Ja ja, ik ken het verhaal van je grootvader intussen wel. Maar er is meer, niet? En je schijnt toch niet alles te snappen, Bjorn. Ook als jij hier de rol van Theseus zou krijgen, komen er uit veertien andere landen ook jongelui die die rol spelen. Het is een Europees project, weet je nog?'

'Ja, dat weet ik nog. Maar waarom kan die Poppy dan de rol krijgen?'

'Hij is een Nederlander.'

'Hij is zwart! Hij behoort tot een ander ras. Hij...'

Hij leek opeens te begrijpen dat hij te veel had gezegd.

'Wat heeft dat ermee te maken?'

'Het zou toch gek zijn? Een zwarte Theseus, een neger die een blanke Griekse koningszoon moet spelen?'

Bea ging weer zitten.

'Dit gebeurt niet. Ik zit niet naar die onzin van je te luisteren. Wat ben jij eigenlijk voor een kereltje? Eerst probeer je je omhoog te neuken, en dan blijk je bovendien een racist te zijn. Wat nog meer? Eruit.'

'Bea, dat bedoelde ik niet.'

De stem van de jongen klonk wanhopig.

'Ben je soms bang dat ik je uit de cursus trap? Nee, dat zal ik niet doen. Ik zal zelfs proberen je alleen te beoordelen als acteur. Maar kom niet meer met je trieste verhalen aan. Ik heb je door, jongetje. En als het wat voor je betekent... Wacht eventjes.'

Ze rommelde in de stapel papier op haar werktafel.

'Hier, ken je dit nog?'

Bjorn herkende het verhaal dat hij bij het begin van de tekststudie had geschreven.

'Toen al had ik je moeten begrijpen. Je bent inderdaad een soort Theseus!'

Bea draaide de dichtbeschreven pagina's om. Ze las hardop.

'Omdat elke vrouw die me liefheeft door de goden wordt gestraft. En omdat ik hun wapen ben.'

Phoebe kon geen woord uitbrengen.

'Soms doet het pijn.'

Zo praatte een man niet eens met zijn eigen vrouw op Skyros. En haar meester, een koning, liet zijn slavin in het diepst van zijn hart kijken? Was hij dan zo eenzaam? Ze voelde tranen achter haar ogen zitten.

'Je bent jong, Phoebe, jong en mooi. Ik zou je graag beminnen. Dat is me nu opeens duidelijk geworden. Maar zodra ik je aanraak, al was het maar met een woord van liefde, zullen de goden je straffen met hun woede, met hun haat. Je zou de grote leegte zien waarin de angst draaikolken vormt en de afgunst verterende vlammen laat oplaaien.'

'Dit, Bjorn, is een geval voor psychiaters. Maar één ding wil ik je zeggen. Het zijn niet de vrouwen die je bemint die door de goden worden gestraft. Jij wordt gestraft omdat je niet snapt dat iemand van je kan houden, omdat jij niet in staat bent van iemand te houden zonder bijbedoelingen, omdat jij zelf altijd weer in die draaikolk van angst en in de hel van de afgunst zult zitten. Tenzij je anders wordt. Nu. Het is dinsdagavond, tweeëntwintig uur dertien. Slaap lekker. Trek de deur achter je dicht.'

9

Bjorn leunde tegen de muur naast de deur. Hij had het koud. Hij probeerde zijn keel vrij te slikken. De vrouwen die hij liefhad, werden het wapen van de goden. Het wapen dat zich tegen hem keerde. Dat was wat Bea had gezegd. Maar het klopte niet. Ze wist het niet. Ze begreep niets van hem. Hij was Theseus, hij had een opdracht te vervullen, hij moest...

Er liep iemand door de zijgang die naar de vleugel leidde waar de Nederlanders logeerden. Een beetje onzeker, zoekend naar evenwicht.

Poppy? Zijn zwarte huid contrasteerde met het wit van zijn boxershort. De jongen wankelde en moest tegen de muur leunen. Had hij gedronken?

Bjorn duwde zich van de muur af en liep verder de gang in. Poppy wankelde opnieuw. Hij probeerde de deur van de badkamer open te krijgen. Dat lukte pas na de derde keer en hij struikelde naar binnen.

'Straalbezopen!' fluisterde Bjorn tegen zichzelf. 'Daar ga je dan, zwarte Theseus!'

Hij rende geluidloos naar de zijgang en gluurde om de hoek.

De zwarte jongen was niet langer te zien. Bjorn probeerde rustig te ademen, na te denken. Een kans als deze kon hij niet laten liggen. Bea op de hoogte brengen en Bram erbij halen, dat was wat hij moest doen. Dan konden ze allebei zien...

Poppy kreunde daarbinnen. Het klonk akelig.

Bjorn duwde de deur wat verder open. Poppy stond bij een van de wastafels en graaide naar een glas. In zijn linkerhand rammelde een flesje pillen.

Ook dat nog. Niet alleen dronken, ook onder de pillen. Bjorn schudde zijn hoofd en grinnikte. Zelfs dat zachte geluid leek als een donderslag te klinken in de oren van Poppy.

Hij draaide zich om, zijn ogen wijd open en zijn mond opengesperd. Maar hij zag niets, wist Bjorn. Zijn armen en benen begonnen opeens te schokken. Hij kreunde. Zijn ogen draaiden weg, alleen het wit was nog te zien. Hij kreunde weer. Toen kreeg hij schuim op de mond en plaste hij zijn boxershort nat.

Bjorn verstijfde. Dit was niet goed, helemaal niet.

Poppy gleed naar de vloer, zijn vingers verkrampten. Het flesje rolde tot voor de voeten van Bjorn. Instinctief raapte hij het op. Tegretol.

'Wat gebeurt hier?'

Brenda duwde Bjorn opzij.

'Idioot! Zie je niet dat die jongen een toeval krijgt! Ga iemand halen. Gauw! Gotverse stommeling! Gauw dan!'

Ze trok haar sweatshirt uit en vouwde het tot een kussen. Toen stopte ze een washandje tussen de tanden van Poppy, die nog harder met zijn hoofd sloeg.

Bjorn wist niet waarheen. Bea? Hij rende en beukte op haar deur.

'Bea! Poppy is...'

Bea liep hem al voorbij.

Bjorn had nog altijd het flesje in zijn handen. Hij stopte het in zijn zak.

'Maak je geen zorgen. Poppy komt het wel te boven. Hij heeft een aanval van epilepsie gehad. Jullie weten zeker dat niemand hem wat te drinken gegeven heeft? Alcohol, bedoel ik.'

Bram Hillenius zag er hondsmoe uit die morgen. Niemand reageerde.

'Goed, hij had moeten vertellen dat hij af en toe problemen heeft. Maar ja, je zegt niet graag dat je ziek bent. Als hij zijn pillen neemt, is er meestal weinig aan de hand.'

'Waarom deed hij het dan niet? Ik schrok me rot gisteren, toen ik hem daar zag liggen.'

'Dat kan hij alleen vertellen. Ik heb met de dokter gepraat en die legde me uit dat geneesmiddelen om epilepsie te onderdrukken ook de hersenactiviteit verminderen. Poppy wilde blijkbaar met een absoluut helder hoofd zijn rol instuderen. Dat en de druk zijn fataal geweest.'

'Komt hij gauw terug?' vroeg Bjorn.

Gael keek in zijn richting. Ze glimlachte vaag.

'Het probleem is dat de dokters niet weten welke medicatie hij voorgeschreven kreeg. Poppy zelf kan het voorlopig niet vertellen, zijn ouders lijken op reis te zijn en de artsen die hem vroeger behandelden, zijn niet te bereiken. Het is erg gevaarlijk om andere geneesmiddelen dan die die de zieke gewend is voor te schrijven. Dus behandelen ze hem voorlopig met kalmeermiddelen, maar... Ach, dit is zo jammer!'

De hele groep knikte. Bjorn tastte naar het flesje pillen zijn zak.

'Ik vrees dus dat we niet langer op Poppy kunnen rekenen. Arthur, wil jij zijn rol proberen te spelen?'

De jongen schudde zijn hoofd.

'Nee, dank je, ik heb genoeg gezwoegd op dat rolletje van Theros. Ik heb geen studiehoofd.'

'Ik sluit me aan bij de vorige spreker!'

Mirko grijnsde.

'Laat Bjorn maar. Hij is goed. Niet zo goed als Poppy, maar toch beregoed.'

De stemming sloeg om. Ze konden weer lachen.

Bea volgde het gesprek en probeerde te raden wat er zich nu in het hoofd van Bjorn afspeelde.

'Mij goed, jongens. Bea, zullen we het nog maar eens omgooien?'

'Hoe bedoel je?'

'Nou, van enige concurrentie is hier eigenlijk geen sprake meer. Ik stel voor dat je uit de twee groepen telkens één figuur kiest, dat we een Vlaams-Nederlandse cast uitwerken en dan echt gaan repeteren. Wie wil absoluut Londen halen? En wie vindt het welletjes als we aan het eind van de week een redelijke voorstelling op de planken kunnen zetten voor ouders en vrienden?'

De jongelui keken elkaar aan.

'Londen?' vroeg Bram.

Bjorn beet op zijn tanden tot zijn hele gezicht pijn deed. Toen ging er een hand omhoog. Senta.

'Ja, ik wil echt graag. Het liefst in de rol van Hubris.'

Bram en Bea knikten. Bea schreef het op.

'Althea.' Meer zei Elke niet. 'Of Hubris.'

'Mag er geen tweede Althea zijn? Mag het niet of dachten jullie...'

Bram schudde zijn hoofd.

'Het is niet wat wij willen of niet willen. Jij beslist, Andrea.'

'Doen, meid!' schreeuwde Mirko. 'Ik wil ook gaan. Als Minotaurus. En je weet, je bent mijn favoriete hap.'

Gelach.

Bea zuchtte. Waarom was zij lang niet zo veerkrachtig als die jongelui? Waarom bleef zij inwendig zeuren om wat ze 'haar verlies' noemde. Zij maakten een kuiltje van grapjes en begroeven een verloren vriend meteen. Over tot de orde van de dag. Was dat de beruchte oppervlakkigheid van de jeugd?

'Bea?'

'Sorry, ik was er eventjes niet bij met mijn gedachten. Ja?'

'Bjorn wil Theseus doen en Gael Ariadne.'

Bea noteerde.

'Goed, bedankt voor de eerlijkheid. En dan gaan we nu keihard aan het werk. Derde bedrijf? Iedereen tekstvast?'

Gelach en gemompel.

'Een eerste keer nog met de tekstboeken? Liever zo? Doen we. En verder, concentratie, inlevingsvermogen, overtuigingskracht. Goed?'

Bea stelde de groep op.

'Het zou makkelijker zijn met een echt decor, maar tegen zondag zorgen we wel voor enkele stukken, zodat je weet hoe je moet lopen. Daar gaan we.'

DERDE BEDRIJF

Heros en Hubris komen op, druk pratend. Ze blijven in het midden van de scène staan. Heros gelooft nog altijd fanatiek in Theseus. Hubris wordt steeds scherper.

HEROS: Ik geloof je niet. Er moet wat gebeurd zijn. Waarom zou iedereen het fout zien en jij alleen niet? Waarom?

HUBRIS: Wat is dat voor vreemde redenering? Is het dan zo dat het gelijk of ongelijk afhangt van het aantal? Kan het ook niet zo zijn dat ik inderdaad scherper zie, altijd scherper heb gezien? Ik heb je al gezegd dat ik Theseus heb gekend, dat ik heb gehoord, gevoeld, gezien wat voor iemand hij was. Jij en al die anderen blijven doof, omdat je niet wilt horen.

HEROS: Zo? En waarom dan wel? Waarom zouden wij de waarheid afwijzen? Welk belang...

HUBRIS: Mag ik de vraag omdraaien? Welk belang zou ik kunnen hebben bij het feit dat iedereen Theseus zou gaan zien zoals hij werkelijk was, een ondraaglijk eerzuchtige schoft? Waarom? Zeker nu hij niet meer leeft?

HEROS: Misschien vind jij het wel prettig om te ontheiligen? Misschien ben je wel jaloers, kun je het niet hebben dat Theseus op handen wordt gedragen?

HUBRIS: Op handen gedragen? Waarom hebben zijn Atheners hem dan verbannen? Of ga je nu zeggen dat zijn figuur, zijn plannen te groot waren voor deze stad?

HEROS: Die verbanning is en blijft een vergissing. Alles had goed kunnen komen, met de hulp van de goden...

HUBRIS: De goden? Theseus had dus de hulp van de goden nodig om aan de macht te blijven? Juist zij hebben de val van Theseus gewild. De goden hebben eindelijk ingegrepen. Ze konden niet langer aanzien dat hij, Theseus, hun gunsten beantwoordde met zijn steeds afschuwelijkere misdaden. De grijns van de goden kun je aflezen van de hemel. Misschien zijn zelfs de goden ooit misleid door jouw Theseus? Hij kon iedereen betoveren met zijn woorden, waarom dan ook niet de goden?

HEROS: Orfeus wordt geëerd omdat hij met zijn stem de dieren kon laten luisteren, waarom zou je dan Theseus verafschuwen?

HUBRIS: Je wilt het niet begrijpen, niet? Ik verafschuw Theseus omdat hij iedereen gebruikte, blind, alsof we niet meer waren dan... Ach, wat helpt het allemaal? Ik zal jou toch niet overtuigen. Jou niet en niemand. Helden worden niet geboren, ze worden gecreëerd door mensen die nood hebben aan idolen, die in hun kleinheid willen opkijken naar iets onbereikbaars, zelfs als dat slecht is. Als het maar onbereikbaar, ongrijpbaar is, wordt het groots.

HEROS: Ik vind je afschuwelijk hoogmoedig. Iedereen...

HUBRIS: De macht van het getal geeft wel macht, maar maakt leugen niet tot waarheid. Theseus mag dan een bijzonder handige schoft zijn geweest, hij blijft een schoft en ik spuw op zijn herinnering. Hij heeft ons destijds gewoon geofferd...

Bea sprong op. Senta en Willem bleven staan.

'Dit was heel goed, Senta. Heel gemeen, uit de grond van je hart. Willem, je geeft te weinig terug. Je moet dwepen met Theseus, evenveel als Senta hem haat.'

Willem schudde zijn hoofd.

'Dat is moeilijk. Ik vind die Theseus niet zo geweldig. Ik voel het niet echt. En zij overdondert me gewoon. Ze haat hem echt.'

Senta lachte en gooide haar blonde haar achteruit.

'Hij is ook een klotekereltje, niet?'

Bea stond achter haar en keek naar de kleine groep die klaarstond voor de volgende scène. Ze hoopte dat Bjorn hoorde wat Senta zei. Hij glimlachte wat hooghartig. Nee, misschien interpreteerde ze zijn blik wel. Zij wist trouwens meer dan de jongelui. Ze moest objectief blijven. Elke. Die had Bjorn een tik gegeven met haar elleboog. Juist. Zij had hem intussen ook door. Dan had ze het toch goed gezien toen ze dacht dat die twee wat met elkaar hadden.

Elke zette een stap opzij en ruimde de plaats voor Andrea. Er was wat. Elke liet zich meestal niet op de kop zitten. Andrea mocht spelen.

Bea zuchtte. Het werd alsmaar ingewikkelder.

'De volgende scène is weer erg belangrijk,' zei ze. 'Dus doorgaan. Vooral Althea en Theseus. Vooruit!'

Licht uit op Hubris en Heros. Het viertal Agos, Althea, Parmenides en Theseus komen op terwijl Heros en Hubris weggaan. Schemerlicht achteraan op de scène.

PARMENIDES: De morgen komt, de morgen van onze laatste dag.

THESEUS: Of de morgen van de vrijheid voor Athene? Waarom zo triest? Waarom zouden we vanavond niet als vrije jonge mannen inschepen? Waarom zouden wij al over enkele dagen niet de haven van Athene binnenzeilen onder het uitzinnige gejuich van onze medeburgers? Waarom zouden we intussen niet de Minotaurus hebben gedood? Waarom niet?

ALTHEA: Theseus heeft gelijk, waarom niet? Wat is er opeens met jullie? Is het de duisternis van de nacht, is het de vermoeidheid, het gebrek aan slaap dat jullie opeens zo somber maakt?

AGOS: Goed zo, Althea! Niet opgeven, meisje. Misschien wordt Theseus wel ooit koning. Zie jij jezelf al terwijl je naast hem zit en genadig knikt naar wie je om een gunst komt vragen? Heb je opeens weer zijn kant gekozen?

THESEUS: Agos! Wat hebben jullie toch? We wisten toch precies wat hier zou gebeuren? We hebben toch alles netjes...

AGOS: Jij hebt alles netjes in elkaar laten passen, jij weet blijkbaar precies waar je naartoe wilt en hoe je het moet doen!

PARMENIDES: Nu ben je inderdaad onredelijk, Agos. Ik ben ook bang, ik begin ook te twijfelen, maar we hebben inderdaad beslist om Theseus te volgen en als wij het van de Minotaurus winnen, zullen wij met hem delen in de roem.

THESEUS: En jullie beschuldigen mij ervan dat ik dit onderneem uit eerzucht? Kijk toch naar jezelf!

AGOS: Nee, Theseus, dat is al te makkelijk. Vertel jij eens wat je ziet als je naar me kijkt?

THESEUS: Een leuk kind, hoog op de benen, met een frisse snoet, al zitten er wat rimpels in je voorhoofd, hier, boven je neuswortel. Maar verder leuk, echt...

PARMENIDES: *Houdt Agos die Theseus wil aanvliegen tegen.* Stop, Agos! En jij, Theseus, je moet hem, niet ons opjutten. Agos! Laat dat zwaard...

ALTHEA: Doe niet gek, Agos! Als er een wachtpost komt en ziet dat je een zwaard hebt, verknoei je onze kansen helemaal!

AGOS: Sukkels, blinde sukkels! Zie je niet wat voor een spelletje hij speelt? O, ik weet het niet meer, ik weet niet meer wat ik moet denken, hopen of geloven. Hebben de goden ons nu al verlaten? Ik begrijp dit allemaal niet.

THESEUS: Rustig, Agos, het is de spanning. Ik weet zeker dat je zo dadelijk zult vechten als een leeuw, dat de Minotaurus zal bloeden uit honderden wonden.

PARMENIDES: Ja, we moeten hier samen doorheen!

ALTHEA: Juist, en we moeten Theseus vertrouwen. Heeft hij niet de stier van Marathon verslagen en Procrustes gedood? Kan de Minotaurus vreselijker zijn?

AGOS: Ik ken de heldendaden van jouw Theseus wel, Althea! Jouw Theseus is...

Bram klapte in zijn handen en zuchtte. Bea keek op van haar tekstboek.

'Jullie zeggen het allemaal zo netjes. Ik voel geen passie. Althea, vertel me eens hoe je je tijdens die scène voelt.'

Andrea beet op haar lip en keek naar de vloer.

'Ik ben onzeker. Eigenlijk ben ik bang dat Theseus iets heeft met Ariadne, maar nu we weer samen zijn, wil ik hem steunen.'

'Doe dan wat je zegt. Je loopt erbij als een zwijmelende trut, niet als iemand die voor haar vent wil vechten!'

Andrea steigerde. Zwijmelende trut! Hé, zeg! Maar Bram lette al niet meer op haar.

'En jij, Parmenides, je bent geen haar beter. Jullie hebben allebei een rol waaruit de verwarring moet blijken die een figuur als Theseus altijd weer veroorzaakt... Bjorn, je doet het goed, dat aantrekken en afstoten. Maar ik hoorde graag wat meer variatie in je stemgebruik. De ene keer moet je spotten, de andere keer overtuigen, een volgende keer schelden. Niet alleen de woorden die je zegt, ook de klank van je stem moet dat uitdrukken. Bea, sorry dat ik er even tussen kwam.'

'Je hebt volkomen gelijk, Bram,' glimlachte Bea.

Laat Bjorn niet merken dat ik met mezelf overhoop lig, dat ik meer met hem bezig ben dan met de rest. Ze voelde alweer die blikken van hem.

'Ook in de volgende scène moeten er heel wat verschillende emoties opborrelen en de tekst daarbij is vrij summier. Bjorn?'

'Ik heb het moeilijk met die brutale overgang. Daarstraks stond ik de anderen nog op te peppen en praatte ik over honderden wonden, en nu opeens moet ik bang en zenuwachtig overkomen omdat Ariadne er niet is.'

'Omdat je Ariadne nodig hebt! En omdat je eigenlijk niet zo'n held bent als je zelf graag gelooft.'

'Juist,' ging Brenda hierop door. 'Ventjes als jij zijn niets zonder ons, vrouwen.'

'Ik weet anders een oplossing, hoor!' zei Frank met een geaffecteerd stemmetje terwijl hij heupwiegend naar Brenda liep, verbaasd stilstond en zich toen naar Arthur omdraaide met een lokkende glimlach.

'Juist!' zuchtte Bea. 'Daar gaat het niet om. Bjorn, misschien had die overgang in de tekst wat duidelijker uitgewerkt kunnen zijn, maar probeer de breuk te overbruggen met stevig acteerwerk. Je krijgt de kans zodra die wachter opkomt.'

'Mag ik geen zinnetje of drie inlassen?' vroeg Bjorn.

'Nee!'

Bjorn ging hoofdschuddend bij de anderen staan.

WACHTER: *Op van links. Gewapend met speer en schild.*
Wat hoor ik? Iedereen al klaar voor de nieuwe dag? Wil je nog genieten van de laatste keer dat je de zon ziet opgaan boven zee? Meekomen! Het is tijd. De Minotaurus wacht op jullie.

THESEUS: *Kijkt verbaasd zenuwachtig rond.*
Is het nu al tijd? De morgen is nog grauw. Geef ons een uur meer, laat de zon nog één keer mijn voorhoofd zoenen.
Tegen Parmenides.
Waar is Ariadne? Ze zou me helpen!

WACHTER: Geen ogenblik langer, jongetje. Minos heeft gesproken.

PARMENIDES: Wij smeken je!

THESEUS: Ik smeek je!

THEROS: *Op van rechts, triomfantelijk.*
Oho, ik ben dus net op tijd om de trotse Theseus te zien smeken? Je zingt dus duidelijk anders dan gisteren?

THESEUS: Daar heb je Minos' schoothondje ook nog.

THEROS: Ik laat me door jou niet meer boos maken, jongetje! Ik wil genieten van je gejank als dat uit de ingewanden van het labyrint opstijgt. De Minotaurus wacht, is hongerig naar je bloed, ventje.

THESEUS: *Steekt zijn hand in zijn tuniek en wil zijn wapen grijpen. Althea springt naar hem toe.*
Ventje? Ik? Ik ben de zoon van de koning van Athene, de toekomstige koning van de Atheners! Ik zal je de smaak van je eigen bloed...

ALTHEA: Theseus! Denk aan wat ik tegen Agos heb gezegd. Slik je trots in.

THEROS: Hahahaha! De toekomstige koning! Hahahaha! Willen de Atheners een zak afgekloven botten op de troon? Ik zal de Minotaurus vragen dat hij je ribben niet splijt, je armen en benen niet met zijn tanden versplintert om het merg uit elk bot te zuigen!

Bea stond op en krabde aan haar rechterwenkbrauw.

'Theros, jij overdrijft nu weer een beetje. Je moet dat cynisme, die triomfantelijke wraakgevoelens wat meer ingehouden overbrengen. En sta niet zo met je handen te wapperen. Doe uit de hoogte. Heeft iemand een stok of bezem die als staf kan dienen?'

'Wil je op je bezem het raam uit vliegen?' lachte Mirko. 'Sorry, Bea, niet kwaad bedoeld. Grapje.'

'Als ik een clown nodig heb in een volgend stuk, zal ik aan je denken, Mirko. Nu rem je de boel af. Nog een keer. Elke in de plaats van Andrea. Arthur, jij Parmenides. En je moet de confrontatie aandurven. Spelen maar. En we gaan meteen door naar de scène waar Ariadne toch nog net op tijd opduikt.'

De groep stelde zich weer op. Andrea ging naast Bea zitten en draaide een lok om haar wijsvinger.

'Is er wat, Bea?'

'Nee, waarom?'

'Je handen trillen zo.'

'Een beetje moe en dan die toestand met Poppy. Stil maar, ik moet opletten.'

De scène zat goed. Elke zette de figuur van Althea veel geloofwaardiger neer en de anderen speelden daarop in. Naadloos liep de ene scène in de andere over. Gael verscheen, beheerst opgewonden, en speelde haar verrassing prima. Een geboren Ariadne. En dan die sierlijke, soepele bewegingen die door haar lange kleed werden vertolkt als een symfonie van jonge vrouwelijkheid. Bea voelde opnieuw een prik van jaloersheid.

ARIADNE: *Op met een kluwen draad in haar handen.*
Theros? Wat moet jij hier? Wat een pret hebben jullie! Mag ik meegenieten?

THEROS: Dat knulletje blijft maar zaniken dat hij koning van Athene wordt. Ik heb hem net beloofd dat ik zijn gebeente naar Athene zal sturen om het in een zak op de troon te zetten.

ARIADNE: Schitterend! Bijzonder grappig. Theros, wil je geloven dat ik ook zoiets had bedacht? Ik heb de hele nacht die hooghartige smoel van hem gezien...

ALTHEA: Hé daar...Wat...

ARIADNE: Zwijgen, wicht, of ik laat je geselen voor je naar binnen gaat!

PARMENIDES: Wat is dit allemaal? Vannacht...

THESEUS: *Pakt hem beet en slingert hem achteruit.*
Zwijg, Parmenides.
Fluisterend.
Ze is iets van plan, ze wil ons op een of andere manier helpen.
Laat mij begaan.
Tegen Ariadne.
Als je wat te zeggen hebt, moet je dat tegen mij doen. Wat is er met mijn smoel? Heb je je eigen rattensnuit al eens bekeken?

De spanning was nu om te snijden. Theseus en Ariadne, je kon de vonken horen knetteren tussen die twee. Dit ging verder dan toneel, dit was leven, dit was... Bea vond geen woorden voor wat ze zag. Hun gezichten drukten het hele gamma van emoties uit. Gael slaagde erin de blik van tederheid, gemengd met onrust, te laten doven terwijl een gespeelde woede opgloeide. Zeldzaam, een close-up op het toneel. Geweldig, dat kind.

ARIADNE: *Stormt naar Theseus en geeft hem een draai om zijn oren.*
Wat durf jij tegen me zeggen? Voer voor de Minotaurus, dat ben je! En ik zal inderdaad je gebeente in een zak naar Athene sturen!

THESEUS: Dat dacht je! Hoe zul je mijn gebeente terugvinden tussen de knekelberg die in dat labyrint rondslingert? Hé, hoe wil je dat doen?

ARIADNE: Je wilt slim zijn? Je wilt me te slim af zijn? Je blijft jezelf bijzonder knap vinden, niet?

THESEUS: Ken uzelf! Wel, dat doe ik.

ARIADNE: Hier!
Steekt het kluwen garen op.
Het ene eind bind ik om je pols, het andere maak ik hierbuiten vast. Als de Minotaurus je heeft verslonden, zal ik je vinden. Wachter, breng die anderen weg!

83

WACHTER: Zoals u beveelt, prinses, maar uw vader...

ARIADNE: O, hij komt echt wel aan de beurt. Laat eerst de anderen maar verslinden. Het maakt het Theros en mij makkelijker hem later terug te vinden.

THESEUS: Nee, ik wil samen met mijn vrienden...

Het licht dooft. De figuren bevriezen. Hubris en Heros op. Ze lopen over de scène en verdwijnen opnieuw.

HEROS: Zie je wel? Je begrijpt alles helemaal verkeerd. Theseus wilde alleen maar zijn stad bevrijden van de brutale wreedheid van Minos en zijn trawanten. Dat hij daarbij probeerde hulp te krijgen van Ariadne...

HUBRIS: Je had zijn gezicht moeten zien. Ik heb nooit beweerd dat Theseus dom was. Integendeel. Hij was sluw als een vos, even genadeloos als een bergleeuw. Hij snapte meteen wat Ariadne van plan was. Ze speelde een spelletje, maakte dat zelfs Theros haar plannetje goedkeurde, zorgde op die manier voor rugdekking en had het genoegen om Theseus nog eventjes bij zich te houden.

HEROS: Geen genade voor Theseus, hé? Je wilt niets, maar dan ook niets van hem heel laten, niet?

HUBRIS: Nee! En ik weet ook waarom!

Allebei af. De scène tussen Theseus en Ariadne gaat gewoon verder.

ARIADNE: Wil je niet nog eventjes bij me blijven? Wil je soms met haar mee, met dat akelige wicht...

ALTHEA: Ik? Jij, sloerie, intrigante, smerige...

THEROS: Genoeg! Geen beledigingen aan het adres van de prinses. Wachter, afvoeren!

WACHTER: Vooruit jullie!

Theseus wil meegaan, maar wordt teruggegooid.

Nee, niet jij, schoffie!

ARIADNE: Theseus, hier bij mij! Ik zal je merken met de draad van Ariadne...

De anderen worden afgevoerd.

Theros! Pak hem, duw hem op de knieën en sleep hem hierheen! Ik zal hem leren zijn hersens te gebruiken en zijn mond dicht te houden!

Theros brengt Theseus bij haar. De prins maakt opeens een erg neerslachtige indruk.

THESEUS: De overmacht is te groot. Maar, prinses, je juicht misschien vroeger dan je eigenlijk zou moeten doen. Als ik levend uit dit avontuur kom, sleep ik je mee naar Athene! Dan zal ik naar je kijken als ik op de troon zit!

ARIADNE: Daarop reken ik zelfs, Theseus! Ik wacht hier zelfs op jou! Je weet maar nooit dat je de Minotaurus de baas blijft. Hahahahaha! En dat je dan nog de weg terugvindt. Hahaha... ik besterf het bijna van het lachen. Theros, is hij niet grappig?

THEROS: Bijzonder grappig, prinses.

THESEUS: Onderschat mij niet, prinses. Ik heb de reus Procrustes...

THEROS: Woorden, Theseus. Ik wens je het beste. Steek je hand uit.

THESEUS: Het zij zo.

Ariadne bindt de draad om de pols van Theseus. Hij kijkt haar lang aan, draait zich om en verdwijnt terwijl de draad zich afrolt. Theros buigt voor de prinses, wenkt de wachter en gaat op zijn beurt weg.

ARIADNE: *Wacht tot het toneel leeg is.*

Geluk, Theseus. Ik weet niet wat je wacht, maar ik hoop dat mijn liefde je vuisten dubbele kracht zal geven. Je ogen hebben me verteld dat je me hebt begrepen. Ik wou dat ik met je mee kon gaan, dat ik kon zien hoe je nu door de duistere krochten sluipt. *Ze komt vooraan links op de scène staan. Achterin tegen een lichte achtergrond speelt zich het schimmenspel af dat de tocht van Agos, Althea en Parmenides suggereert. Tegen het einde van Ariadnes monoloog verschijnt ook de schaduw van Theseus en vinden de vier elkaar terug. De normale verlichting gaat weer aan en de vier acteren in een decor van zwarte doeken de ontmoeting met de Minotaurus.*

ARIADNE: Ik heb je gezien, je gestalte gedronken met mijn ogen. Je hand heeft niet alleen mijn hand beroerd, maar ook mijn hart geraakt. Ik was prinses, ik werd opeens slavin, een veertje op de wind van mijn verlangen naar jou. En nu loop jij het labyrint in, elke stap brengt je verder weg van mij en dichter bij je lotsbestemming. Ik ben bang, Theseus. Misschien hoor jij nu al het geschuifel van de voeten van je vrienden, hun angstige geschreeuw in het donker, hun kreet om hulp, het gebrul van de Minotaurus, die hun jonge geur heeft opgesnoven? Hun stappen worden aarzelend, ze tasten elke vloertegel af met voorzichtige tenen, luisterend. De angst wordt levend. Ze zijn verloren zonder jou, net zo verloren als ik nu ben, Theseus! O, Theseus! Misschien springt dat monster nu uit het diepste duister op jou? Misschien plant het nu zijn klauwen in jouw schouders, ontbloot het zijn tanden, bijt het? Néé!

Ze slaat haar handen voor haar gezicht en stort neer. Licht op de vier.

10

'Je was geweldig, Gael.'

Het meisje stond bij de vijver in het park en keek naar een water-lelie. Naast haar spiegelbeeld verscheen dat van Bjorn.

'Vond je?'

Ze keek niet op, zag een koperkleurige vis lucht happen en weer naar de diepe donkerte verdwijnen.

'Vond je het zelf niet?'

Ze haalde haar schouders op.

'Kom nou, niet naar nog meer complimentjes vissen.'

'Het is zo moeilijk dat evenwicht te vinden tussen passie en beheersing.'

'Wat een uitspraak! En wat een prachtige samenvatting voor het hele leven.'

Nu keek ze wel op. Stond hij haar echt voor de gek te houden?

Bjorn voelde de spanning en glimlachte meteen verontschuldigend.

'Hou me niet voor de gek, wil je?'

'Dat wil ik helemaal niet. Zeker jou niet. Ik denk, let op mijn woorden, ik denk dat jij de ideale Ariadne bent. Maar wie ben ik?'

Gael lachte. Het was goed dat te horen. Bjorn meende het. Ze had tot dusver moeilijk hoogte van hem kunnen krijgen, maar nu viel hij haar mee.

'Waarom zeg je dat?'

Bjorn blies met bolle wangen.

'Het zal wel lullig klinken, maar hoe weet ik nou waarom ik dat zeg? Omdat ik het meen, omdat ik het zo voel. Als toneelspelen ook een kunst is, dan is de beoordeling toch heel persoonlijk, heel subjectief?'

Gael knikte.

'Ik vond jou trouwens ook heel goed. Er sprong iets over tussen ons, vond je niet?'

Nu was hij opeens op zijn hoede. Ze wilde hem blijkbaar uit zijn tent lokken.

'Ja,' zei hij, 'ja. Ik ben blij dat je het ook gemerkt hebt. Ik wist er niet meteen raad mee.'

'Waarmee? O, je bedoelt...' Ze lachte. 'Dat is nou precies wat mijn moeder me altijd vertelt. Ze is een erg goede actrice geweest. Nu doceert ze alleen nog maar. Ze zou dolgraag opnieuw op de planken staan. Als iemand haar een kans geeft, wacht ze geen ogenblik.'

'Wat zegt ze altijd?'

'Dat je af en toe vonken voelt overspringen en dat het dan zaak is te weten waar dat gebeurt, in je leven of in je rol.'

Bjorn boog zijn hoofd, stak zijn handen in zijn zakken en zuchtte hoorbaar.

'Hé, wat heb je opeens?'

'Met mijn hoofd zeg ik dat het niet kan. We kennen elkaar nog maar net, maar hier voel ik... Sorry, Gael, ik stel me aan.'

'En wat als ik je nou eens zei dat het met mij net zo is?'

Hij rukte zijn hoofd omhoog.

'Echt?'

'Wat ik bedoel, is dat ik het niet weet, maar dat ik het hoop en er bang voor ben.'

'Mag ik je dan dit geven?'

Ze nam het dichtgevouwen vel papier van hem aan en wilde het openmaken.

'Nee, niet nu. Wil je wachten? En me later zeggen wat je ervan vindt? Alsjeblieft?'

Het klonk smekend, bijna zielig. Gael knikte. Bjorn draaide zich om en holde bijna weg. Het papier brandde tussen haar vingers. Langzaam vouwde ze het open en las.

Oase

Het zwerven door de jaren
etste nog geen lijnen op mijn huid.
Maar ik was een struikrover van uren
en telde dag aan dag de buit.

Uit het raam van haar kamer zag Elke Bjorn rennen. Eigenlijk was het meer een wild, ongeremd springen. Wat was er met hem aan de hand? Ach, ze kon hem maar beter vergeten. Het werd toch niets. Hij was een harteloze streber. Ze pakte haar tekstboek om de rest van dat derde bedrijf in te studeren.

Gael zat verweesd op een bank toen Senta bij haar kwam zitten.

'Gaat het, meid?'

'Ik weet het eigenlijk niet. Zou Bjorn kunnen weten wie ik ben?'

'Hoe bedoel je dat nou weer? Luister, we zijn nou al hoeveel jaren wat ze noemen boezemvriendinnen...'

'Jij meer boezem, ik meer vriendin,' zei Gael en ze lachten nog maar eens om het grapje dat ze al zo lang vertelden, elke keer weer.

'Juist. Boezemvriendinnen dus, maar ik durf niet te beweren dat ik weet wie je bent. Wat bedoel je met die vraag? Weet Bjorn dat je Gael McGregor bent en dus de dochter van? Of vraag je me of ik denk dat hij de echte, lieve, sterke, zachte dwingeland Gael kent? Op de eerste vraag zou ik antwoorden dat dat weinig waarschijnlijk is, op de tweede antwoord ik "onmogelijk".'

Gael gaf haar een vriendschappelijke stomp.

'Ik vind hem wel lief,' zuchtte ze toen.

'En?'

'Hij mij ook, maar ik vertrouw het niet echt. Hij Theseus, ik Ariadne...'

'O, je denkt aan de afloop van het stuk. Nou, je kent mijn spreuk. Wie niet waagt, blijft maagd! Beter een blauwtje lopen dan een groentje blijven. Hij is een leuke knul. Dus, waarom niet?'

'Lees dit eens.'

Senta las en floot toen zachtjes.

'Van hem?'

Gael knikte.

'Bofkont! En met een beetje geluk zijn jullie nog samen in Londen ook.'

'Jij gaat toch ook?'

'Wat je wilt en wat gebeurt, is niet altijd hetzelfde. Nee, ik denk niet dat ik een kans maak.'

Senta sprong op.

'Maar daarom niet getreurd. Sorry dat ik je prille geluk moet verstoren, maar het is tijd voor de volgende repetitie.'

Uit het raam van haar kamer zag Elke Senta en Gael naar het kasteel toe komen. Ze liepen arm in arm en hadden duidelijk iets te bespreken. Senta gaf Gael een vel papier. Achter de twee meisjes sloop

Bjorn terug naar de vijver. Wat deed die gek nou? Hij haalde iets uit zijn zak, bekeek het en gooide het toen met een wijde boog het water in. De zon vonkte eventjes op bruin glas.

Ze moest naar de repetitiezaal. Maar er was wat aan de gang, dat stond vast.

'Oké, Elke? Jij de tweede keer. Andrea, jouw beurt. En Mirko, afgelopen met de grapjes over hapjes. Laat maar eens zien wat je kunt.'

De jongen boog galant.

'O ja, we hebben een telefoontje gekregen van het ziekenhuis. Poppy maakt het beter. Hij herinnert zich nu half dat hij zijn kamer uit is gekomen om in de badkamer een glas water te halen. Hij voelde de aanval komen en wilde een pil nemen. Heeft iemand het flesje toevallig ergens gevonden?'

Bram keek rond. Niemand bewoog.

'Brenda, jij was bij hem?'

Het meisje schudde haar hoofd.

'Hij was er ook.'

Bjorn knikte.

'Niks gezien.'

Elke verjoeg het beeld dat zich aan haar opdrong. Bjorn die iets in het water gooide. Bruin glas. Misschien een stuk steen. Maar waarom zou hij dat uit zijn zak hebben gehaald?

'Waarom nemen ze geen nieuw flesje? Hij is toch in een ziekenhuis?'

'Gek genoeg weet Poppy nog altijd niet hoe het geneesmiddel heet. Selectieve amnesie, geheugenverlies. Daarom willen ze het flesje terugvinden. Maar goed, jullie hebben de groeten van Poppy en de rest zien we wel.'

De repetitie begon.

'Dus de drie zijn in het labyrint en Theseus heeft van Ariadne een draad om de pols gekregen. Even concentreren op de emoties bij de verschillende personages. Stilte. Als je voelt dat het kan, ga je je gang maar.'

Bea ging zitten en keek naar Bjorn. Zijn schouders zaten weer muurvast. Hij moest leren zich te ontspannen.

AGOS: Stil! Hoor ik daar niet het geschuifel van voeten?

ALTHEA: Nee. Ik hoor niets.

PARMENIDES: Als het de Minotaurus is, moeten we vechten. Je zwaard, Agos. Nu!

THESEUS: Hé, ik ben het, Theseus.

ALTHEA: Theseus? Jij? Wat is er gebeurd? Wat is dit?

THESEUS: Een draad die prinses Ariadne om mijn pols heeft gebonden. Als we hebben afgerekend met de Minotaurus, kunnen we op die manier de uitgang terugvinden. Zij heeft het uiteinde buiten vastgemaakt. We hoeven alleen maar de draad te volgen.

ALTHEA: Ariadne! Altijd weer Ariadne.

PARMENIDES: Althea, het is een schitterend plan. Het lost ons grootste probleem op.

AGOS: Je bent wel erg gauw tevreden, Parmenides. Ik dacht dat de Minotaurus ons grootste probleem was.

THESEUS: Helemaal niet. Die moeten we echt wel de baas kunnen. Daarvoor hebben we onze zwaarden. Nee, Parmenides heeft gelijk. Als we met hem klaar zijn, begint het pas. Weer wegkomen. Hebben jullie wat gehoord of gezien van de andere kinderen die samen met ons hierheen zijn gekomen?

ALTHEA: En wat heb jij Ariadne moeten beloven in ruil voor die draad? Dat je met haar huwt? Dat ze jouw koningin wordt? Heb je haar net zo gek gepraat als je het met mij hebt gedaan?

PARMENIDES: Hou op, Althea. We kunnen ons leven niet op het spel zetten omdat jij jaloers bent op Ariadne.

'Ja, Elke?'

'Bea, dit rammelt toch?' Elke zuchtte.

'Wat bedoel je?

'Kan het echt dat een meisje in zo'n situatie nog jaloers is?'

'Dat kan ik jou beter vragen. En ik weet niet of je als acteur een stuk moet gaan herschrijven. Je moet vertrouwen hebben in de auteur. Mij is het niet opgevallen. Ik denk dat jaloersheid heel sterk is, het is misschien de sterkste vorm van overlevingsdrift. En daarover gaat het hier toch? Misschien denkt Althea dat gewoon overleven voor haar geen zin heeft als ze het zonder Theseus moet doen?'

Elke knikte. Bjorn grijnsde naar haar en ze stak haar tong uit. Rotzak!

Frank had het gemerkt en haalde zijn schouders op. Laat hem toch, betekende dat. Hij knipoogde.

'Frank?'

'Niets, Bea. Nee, niets.'

'Dan komen we nu bij de Minotaurus terecht. Maar denk erom, het publiek weet nergens van, verwacht iets heel anders. Omgekeerde spanning dus, het gevolg van verrassing. Je moet dat echt goed spelen. Klaar?'

STEM: Hé daar, jullie. Kan het wat zachter? Het is nog zo ijselijk vroeg. Ik wil slapen.

THESEUS: Wie spreekt daar?

Hij en de anderen trekken hun zwaard.

STEM: Moet ik jullie nu al brengen?

ALTHEA: Brengen? Wie is hij?

PARMENIDES: Wie ben je? Kom te voorschijn!

AGOS: Ja, kom te voorschijn! Laat zien wie je bent!

STEM: O, mijn hoofd. Ik ben nog moe... Ik...

Van achter de coulissen komt een in voddige kleren gehulde gestalte te voorschijn, slenterend, walgelijk vies, hinkend.

ALTHEA: Wat is dat? Bah, die geur van dood en verrotting!

AGOS: Walgelijk! Wie ben je? Wat doe je hier?

MINOTAURUS: Ik? Ik woon hier! Dit is mijn onderaardse, onontwarbare koninkrijk! Duisternis! Ik beweeg als een vleermuis van zuil naar zuil, sleep me voort van zaal naar zaal in de hoop ooit licht te zien...

THESEUS: Jij woont hier? Hier? Dan ben jij...

ALTHEA: ... de Minotaurus?

MINOTAURUS: Ik heb gehoord dat ze me zo noemen, ja, dat is de naam die al die kinderen gebruiken. Eigenlijk heet ik anders, maar het is zo lang geleden dat iemand die naam nog heeft gebruikt... Hoe was het ook weer?

AGOS: Hij moet gek zijn. Dit kan niet. Dit menselijke wrak zou de Minotaurus zijn?

PARMENIDES: *Springt op de Minotaurus en zet zijn zwaard tegen de keel van het 'monster'.*
Vertel op! De Minotaurus moet een vreselijk monster zijn, geboren uit de liefde van een vrouw en een stier!
MINOTAURUS: Hihihihi! Vertellen ze dat daarboven nog altijd? Geloven ze dat nog altijd? Stier en vrouw? Hihihi! Minos heeft dat verhaaltje verzonnen.
THESEUS: Wat is dit voor waanzin? Waar is dat bloeddorstige monster dat kinderen verslindt?
MINOTAURUS: Dat monster ben ik! Jawel, maar ik heb nog nooit een kind gedood. Opgegeten wel. De brokken die hij me toewerpt.

'Mooi zo! Mirko, je bent bijna perfect, maar ga nou niet cabotineren.'
'In vredesnaam, Bea, wat wil je nou zeggen?'
'Je mag je niet aanstellen, niet overdrijven. Dat hinken en met je voet slepen samen is net iets te veel. En je stem mag dan wat krasserig worden, je moet verstaanbaar blijven. Dus iets minder is goed genoeg.'
Mirko knikte en wijzigde zijn houding lichtjes.
'Nee, je hebt te vaak naar *De klokkenluider van de Notre-Dame* gekeken. Niet nabootsen, zelf je gestalte vinden. Ja, dat is beter.'
Gael en Bjorn hadden intussen oogcontact. Het meisje leek te gloeien.
'Doorgaan.'

AGOS: Ofwel droom ik, ofwel word ik gek?
THESEUS: *Grijpt de Minotaurus beet.*
Genoeg gezwetst. Wat betekent dit? Je wilt toch niet zeggen dat Minos ons, Atheners, heeft opgesloten in een blinde, panische angst voor jou? Je gaat me toch niet vertellen dat de beste van de jongens en meisjes uit Athene hierheen zijn gekomen voor een hersenschim?
MINOTAURUS: Doe me geen pijn. Ik ben zwak en word iedere dag of nacht zwakker... Ik zal je het verhaal van de Minotaurus vertellen als je dat wilt. Het maakt niet uit. Hoewel. Hoe komen jullie aan die zwaarden?

PARMENIDES: Vertel of je weet meteen wat we met die zwaarden doen!

ALTHEA: Ik vind hem vies en zielig!

THESEUS: Zwijg! Laat hem praten!

MINOTAURUS: Geloof je me als ik zeg dat ik het prettig vind om met jullie te praten? Meestal zijn de sukkels die hier verdwalen half-dood van angst en luisteren ze niet eens meer als ik wat zeg. Dan lopen ze als schapen achter me aan naar de plek waar ik ze heen brengen moet.

AGOS: Ik moet dromen... Al die verhalen! En dat gebrul!

MINOTAURUS: Indrukwekkend, niet? O, je moet precies weten waar je moet staan en dan rommelt een kuchje als de donder uit de in-gewanden van dit labyrint, duizenden keren versterkt en weer-kaatst door de echo. Hihihi, ik ben blij dat een keer te horen.

THESEUS: Mijn geduld is op. Wat is hier aan de hand?

MINOTAURUS: Ken je Minos? Weet je hoe trots hij is? Kun je je inbeel-den hoe iemand als Minos zou reageren als zijn vrouw verliefd wordt op een andere man, als ze een kind ter wereld brengt dat niet het zijne is? Minos? Hij die zichzelf ziet als de machtigste ko-ning van deze aarde? Bedrogen door zijn echtgenote en zijn beste vriend, zijn raadsman? Die raadsman die hem op veldtocht stuur-de en toen zelf de nachten stoeiend doorbracht in het bed van de afwezige?

PARMENIDES: Was die witte stier van Poseidon de vriend van Minos?

MINOTAURUS: Witte stier van Poseidon? Die is goed! Nee hoor, ik ben een kind van menselijk vlees en bloed. Maar dat was voor Minos niet te harden! Dat kon niet! Toen hij mijn bestaan niet kon loochenen, moest ik het kind van een god worden en maak-te hij in zijn verhalen een afschuwelijk monster van me.

THESEUS: Wacht eens even. Je vertelt me dus dat jij een buitenech-telijk kind bent van de koningin en van de raadsheer van Minos?

MINOTAURUS: Juist! Dat ben ik.

THESEUS: En na je geboorte heeft Minos het gerucht verspreid van die verhouding van zijn vrouw met de stier van Poseidon en jou hier opgesloten, zogenaamd omdat je een monster bent?

MINOTAURUS: Dat heb je meteen goed begrepen. En ik ben een monster. Ik eet mensenvlees, de resten van de offers...

Iedereen kende het stuk en wist welk woord tegen het volgende aan zou ketsen. En toch keken ze ademloos naar de confrontatie tussen het zielige bedrog en de ontgoochelde eerzucht. Bjorn gaf zich helemaal. Indrukwekkend, vond Bea. En dat met het enorme talent van Gael tegenover zich. Ze was opeens heel tevreden dat ze er nu zo over kon denken. Bjorn en Mirko sleepten de anderen mee. Elke bloeide open als een bloem in de morgen.

ALTHEA: Nee! Viezerd! Kijk niet zo naar me! Ik...
MINOTAURUS: Zelfs niet een hapje? Hihihihi, een klein hapje?
AGOS: Dit kan niet! Alles verzonnen? Dit kan gewoon niet!
THESEUS: Maar wie doodt dan die kinderen? En waarom?
MINOTAURUS: Wraak! Krankzinnige wraak, mijn beste! Zal ik je brengen?
THESEUS: Brengen? Wat bedoel je?
MINOTAURUS: Je naar de offerplaats brengen, natuurlijk! Kom mee. Ik brul, dan komt hij meteen.
THESEUS: Hou even je mond, wil je? Parmenides, Agos... We moeten nadenken. Zijn we hierheen gekomen om dit te bevechten? Dit onmenselijke wrak? Is dat de vreselijke Minotaurus? Moeten we door het doden van dit kreng roem en eer oogsten?
AGOS: Nou, ik wil best leven zonder roem en eer als ik het er levend afbreng.
PARMENIDES: Ik ook, laten we gaan. We hebben het raadsel ontsluierd! De Minotaurus sterft vanzelf als wij vertellen hoe de vork in de steel zit. Spot, het lachen van het volk, is voor een tiran een dodelijker wapen dan een zwaard of een dolk. Wij moeten buiten alles vertellen. En met de draad van Ariadne komen we buiten.
ALTHEA: We sluipen gewoon naar de haven... Of nee, we komen te voorschijn als overwinnaars, we zeggen dat de Minotaurus gedood is! We schepen in...
THESEUS: Wie overwint zonder gevaar, triomfeert zonder glorie.

'Stop even. Bjorn, hier moet je vertragen. Je gaat te snel. Hier komt voor het publiek de echte Theseus op de proppen. Voor het eerst.

Denk aan de tegenstelling tussen Hubris en Heros. Het publiek is verward, weet nog niet wat het moet denken, heeft nog niet gekozen. Dat moet nu gebeuren. Ook hier weer is niet de tekst het belangrijkste. Jij moet het nu doen. Komaan, geconcentreerd. Het moet lukken. Dan zijn we klaar voor vandaag.'

Bea balde een vuist. Bjorn knikte.

MINOTAURUS: Gaan jullie mee? Zal ik nu brullen? Kom mee. Het hoort zo! Willen jullie niet weten wie de echte moordenaar is?

ALTHEA: Nee! Verdwijn, onding! En jij, Theseus, je stem klinkt alsof je het jammer vindt dat er geen gevaar is voor ons!

MINOTAURUS: O, o, o! Dat heb ik niet gezegd. Het gevaar is hier overal in de buurt. Jullie komen er nooit meer uit, hihihihi, jullie zullen rondlopen, rondkruipen, rondkreunen en tenslotte ergens blijven liggen.

THESEUS: Dat gebeurt niet! Laat me denken! Laat me alsjeblieft denken.

ALTHEA: Wat valt er te denken! Je volgt de draad die Ariadne je heeft gegeven en we lopen naar buiten. Theseus, ik wil hier weg.

Ze pakt zijn arm en wil hem meetrekken, maar Theseus duwt haar ruw van zich af. De Minotaurus schuifelt ongemerkt weg.

THESEUS: Laat me met rust! Ik wil denken! Ik moet een oplossing vinden.

ALTHEA: Waarvoor dan?

AGOS: Ik snap je ook niet, Theseus!

PARMENIDES: Ja, je moet...

THESEUS: Ik moet niets! Ik wil hier niet weg zonder dat ik zeker weet dat de hele wereld hoort dat de Minotaurus is gestorven door mijn hand! Ik wil de geschiedenis ingaan als de overwinnaar van de Minotaurus, de bevrijder van mijn volk! Hé! Waar is hij? Waar is dat onding?

Op dat ogenblik klinkt een luid gebrul, vervormd door de echo, waarin een aandachtig toehoorder de naam Minos kan herkennen.

THESEUS: Snel! Hij mag niet wegkomen! Ga mee! Snel!

PARMENIDES: Nee! Ik wil hier weg. We kennen de waarheid, we hoeven hier niet langer te blijven.

THESEUS: De waarheid? Is dat wat je kwam zoeken? Ik heb niets aan die waarheid! Meekomen!

PARMENIDES: Nee! Ik...

Theseus slaat hem met een zwaardhouw neer.

THESEUS: Verrader! Dat is je verdiende loon. Meekomen jullie, of...

STEM: Goed zo, Theseus! Heel goed! Hoewel, ik had gehoopt op een echt gevecht deze keer. Ik was dat tamme doden, dat slachtofferen van weerloze angsthazen een beetje beu.

THESEUS: Die stem? Dat is...

MINOS: Inderdaad. De echte Minotaurus ben ik.

Minos verschijnt. Hij houdt een schaal en een offermes in de handen.

11

'Bjorn?'

'Elke, ik moet werken. En ik dacht dat we alles hadden gezegd.'

Het meisje stond met haar armen gekruist tegen de deurpost.

'Nee, Bjorn, alles is niet gezegd. Waarom doe je dit allemaal?'

'Wat?'

'Je snapt best wat ik bedoel.'

'Nee, dat snap ik niet.'

Elke probeerde kalm te blijven.

'Je kruipt meer en meer in de huid van Theseus. Jij zou stilaan ook iemand doodslaan als die in je weg liep, niet?'

'Komaan, Elke, laat zitten, wil je? Waar haal je zoiets? Ik heb je al uitgelegd dat je moet proberen de beste in iets te zijn.'

'Bjorn, dat is je grootvader die spreekt. Waarom heb je het nooit over je ouders? Bestaan die wel?'

'Natuurlijk bestaan die.'

'Dat weet ik. Ik heb naar je thuis gebeld.'

Elke wachtte af. Bjorn bevroor.

'Wát heb je gedaan?'

Zijn stem klonk ijzig en hees.

'Ik heb naar je thuis gebeld. Met een smoes. Ik heb gezegd dat ik een vriendinnetje was.'

'Je bent gek. Waar haalde je het telefoonnummer?'

'Er bestaat zoiets als een telefoongids. En Vanderhaeghens zijn er niet zoveel. Ik wist dat je uit Deerlijk kwam. Dus.'

Bjorn zweeg.

'Waarom?'

'Ik weet het niet.'

'Dat is geen antwoord.'

'Toch wel, Bjorn. Ik ben verliefd geworden op jou. En verliefde mensen doen dingen waarvan ze niet weten waarom ze die doen. Dat gevoel ken jij niet, denk ik.'

Nu draaide Bjorn zich helemaal om.

'Of moet ik zeggen dat je er bang voor bent na wat er met je vader is gebeurd?'

'Elke!'

Het klonk dreigend, maar het meisje gaf geen krimp.

'We hebben ontzettend lang gepraat, je moeder en ik.'

'Je bent gek.'

'Je moeder zit vreselijk met je in. Toen ik haar zei dat je de laatste tijd wat vreemd doet, zuchtte ze dat ze hoopte dat je hier je zelfvertrouwen zou terugvinden.'

'Ik heb zelfvertrouwen te koop!'

Elke schudde haar hoofd.

'Niks van! Je bent het onlangs kwijtgeraakt. Je vader is ervandoor met een andere vrouw, een meisje eigenlijk, een van zijn studentes. En jij denkt dat het gebeurd is omdat je gezakt was op school. Jij denkt dat hij is weggelopen omdat hij zich schaamde, omdat hij de verwijten van zijn eigen vader niet meer wilde horen. Jouw grootvader verweet hem dat jij mislukt was.'

'Je bent gek. Mijn moeder is gek. En jij gelooft haar.'

Elke lachte kort.

'Nee, Bjorn, bekijk het nu eens eerlijk. Je bent op zoek naar een nieuw zelf.'

'Grote woorden uit zo'n pruimenmondje.'

'Oké, begin maar weer te schelden. Dan hoef je niet naar jezelf te kijken, dan zie je het niet.'

'Wat zie ik niet?' Bjorn sloeg woedend op tafel en sprong op.

'Dat je een zielig jongetje bent dat loopt te fluiten in het donker.'

'Ik ben niet zielig! Ik haal Londen! En in Londen zal ik de beste zijn. Ik word beroemd...'

'Nu komen we er. En als je gezicht in alle kranten staat, als je geïnterviewd wordt op het scherm, komt je vader beslist terug. Want dan ziet hij in dat jij niet mislukt bent, dat je alleen verkeerd bezig was. En dan kun jij je grootvader vertellen dat je de beste bent, dat je een zwarte jongen hebt uitgeschakeld om de beste te zijn, dat hij daarom je vader moet vergeven.'

Bjorn stond ongelovig met zijn hoofd te schudden.

'Geef het toe. Geef het jezelf tenminste toe. Ik vraag me af hoe je ermee kunt leven dat je desnoods letterlijk over lijken wilt lopen om te worden wie je nooit zult zijn!'

'Weg!' hijgde de jongen. 'Ga weg! Je bent gek! Gek!'

'Zorg maar dat je geen toeval krijgt. Want ik kan je geen pillen geven. Dat flesje ligt in de vijver. Dat vind je nooit meer terug!' Elke bitste die laatste zinnen, de doodsteek van de stier in de arena. Ze sloeg de deur dicht. Bjorn zakte neer op bed, met zijn hoofd tussen zijn handen. Wat moest hij doen? Hij stond in het midden van een vrouwelijke driehoek. Hij kon proberen met Elke te praten, proberen haar opnieuw te betoveren. Maar dan liep het fout met Gael. En zij was voorlopig belangrijker. Bea had beloofd alles te vergeten en objectief te zijn. Dat zat dus goed. Elke wist niet zeker dat hij het flesje pillen had weggegooid. Ze raadde er gewoon naar. Misschien had ze gezien dat hij iets in de vijver gooide, maar niemand zou die gaan leegpompen om het flesje te zoeken. Daar kwam hij wel onderuit. Bovendien had het niets met Londen te maken. Niemand zou eraan gedacht hebben om een zwarte Theseus te kiezen. Meer zelfs, hij had Poppy eigenlijk een dienst bewezen, een ontgoocheling bespaard. Hij moest dus alles inzetten op de kaart Gael. Hij knikte.

Buiten kleurde de avondhemel roze.

'Senta?'

Gael pakte haar vriendin bij de arm.

'Ja, snoes, wat kan ik voor je doen?'

'Naar me luisteren. Vanavond is er ontspanning meteen na het eten. Bjorn verdwijnt dan altijd naar zijn kamer. Jij moet hem tegenhouden.'

'Ik? Wil je hem soms in mijn armen schuiven? Je weet niet wat voor risico's je neemt.'

Gael lachte.

'Ik kan het niet zelf doen. Het zou opvallen. Ik vrees dat hij er dan meteen vandoor gaat. Maar jij kunt hem wat vragen over het stuk. En dan kom ik zogenaamd toevallig langslopen, hoor jullie praten, stap in het gesprek...'

'En ik kras op. Begrepen, sluwe jonkvrouw. Je hebt het dus echt te pakken?'

Gael knikte.

'Ik vrees het ergste.'

'Dan vrees ik ook het ergste voor jou. Goed, ik zal hem lijmen en dan mag jij hem opvreten. Kom hier, geef me een zoen. Ik ben blij voor je.'

Het avondeten was voorbij. Bjorn had stil voor zich uit zitten kijken en had lang op elke hap gekauwd.

'Hoi, Bjorn.'

Hij schrok op uit zijn gedachten.

'Ik wou je wat vragen,' zei Senta. 'Ik vind dat je dit stuk prima begrijpt. Ik heb het hier en daar moeilijk.'

Bjorn knikte, duidelijk gestreeld door de aandacht van Senta. 'Vraag maar. Als ik je kan helpen.'

'Lopen we de tuin in? Ik heb mijn tekstboek bij me.'

'Ik kan het stuk intussen zowat dromen.'

'Alle rollen?'

'Zo goed als. Ik wil best. Kom.'

Opscheppertje, dacht Senta. Iedereen moet weten hoe knap je bent, niet? Maar goed. Mij een zorg. Als Gael je wil, dan is dat prima voor mij. Ze draaide zich wervelend om.

In de tuin sloeg ze haar tekstboek open.

'Lees jij Heros, dan doe ik Hubris. Ik hou van die rol.'

VIERDE BEDRIJF

Heros en Hubris komen op van rechts. De spanning tussen de twee is nu om te snijden. Agressieve gebaren.

HEROS: Hoe weet je dat allemaal? Ben je er zeker van dat diegene...

HUBRIS: Zie je wel? Jouw goddelijke Theseus splijt zelfs de vriendschap en het vertrouwen dat we jaren hebben gekoesterd. Je zou me geen vragen stellen over mijn verleden.

HEROS: Wat heb je dan te verbergen? En wat heeft Theseus met dit alles te maken? Ik vraag me af...

HUBRIS: De goden...

HEROS: Ik heb mijn vertrouwen in de goden nu wel verloren! Waarom moet iemand als Theseus door het blinde, moordzuchtige lot worden achtervolgd? Waarom? Dat is de vraag die ik me aldoor stel!

HUBRIS: Het lot? Nee, wat Theseus is overkomen, is gewoon wat hij zelf heeft gezocht. Hij heeft met zijn daden, met zijn woorden, met zijn gedachten het staal gesmeed dat hem heeft getroffen. Dit moest gebeuren. Waarom geloof je me niet?
HEROS: Waarom spreek je dan niet vrijuit? Vertel dan wat je weet en hoe je het weet! Vertel me dan eindelijk waarom je Theseus zo bent blijven haten!
HUBRIS: Kun jij me vertellen waarom je hem zo bewondert? Kun jij mij duidelijk maken waarom je het beeld dat je van hem hebt overeind houdt? Deze hele stad heeft hem uitgespuwd, ze hebben hem doorzien, konden niet langer dulden dat hij mensen eigenzinnig naar de vernietiging voerde!
HEROS: Dat zeg jij! Heb je de rouwstoet niet gezien die na het bericht van zijn dood...
HUBRIS: Rouwstoet? Angststoet, gevormd door mensen die gunsten van hem hebben gekregen. Dat is Theseus' politiek geweest, mensen met beloften en kleine gunsten aan zich binden zolang het hem paste, zolang hij ze kon gebruiken voor zijn eigen doelstellingen. En dan... uitspuwen, als de pit van een olijf, weggooien, als de broodkruimels na de maaltijd. Net als toen. Niemand mocht overblijven om de echte waarheid te vertellen. En toch... hij kon niet vermoeden dat iemand zijn vreselijke daad zou overleven. Maar als hij me had gevonden...

Senta ademde hoorbaar uit.
'Sterk toch, niet?'
Bjorn knikte en glimlachte.
'Wat snap je nou niet?'
'Wel, op school had de juf het altijd over die held Theseus. Altijd is natuurlijk overdreven. Ik bedoel alleen maar dat we dat verhaal over Theseus zo anders hebben geleerd. Waarom?'
'Ik denk dat elke schrijver het recht heeft een verhaal te vertellen zoals hij het ziet. Theseus kan een held zijn geweest. Theseus kan held zijn geweest én koning hebben willen worden. Theseus kan een arrogante streber zijn geweest. Wie weet het echt? Wie weet wat zich in dat labyrint heeft afgespeeld?'

Senta dacht na. Waar bleef Gael in 's hemelsnaam?

'Zoals jij nou Heros hebt gelezen. Je lijkt goed te keuren wat Theseus doet?'

'Heros keurt het goed. Niet ik. Ik weet al te veel. Heros nog niet. Die heeft nog altijd zijn blinddoek voor. En zelfs als hij zou weten hoe de vork in de steel zit, zou hij Theseus blijven vereren. Het is zoals met voetbalgekken die, wat er ook gebeurt, achter hun club blijven staan. Ze willen zich desnoods in elkaar laten timmeren voor hun club. Superdom, maar menselijk.'

'Hoi!'

Gael stond voor de bank en keek neer op het tweetal.

'Hé, Gael! We hadden het net over Theseus.'

'Je doet niet veel anders.'

'Af en toe een gedicht schrijven,' kaatste Bjorn terug. 'Kom erbij zitten.'

Senta geloofde haar ogen niet. Haar vriendin, de superintelligente, begaafde, koele Gael, het meisje met het Britse flegma, zwijmelde zowat. Voor Bjorn? Nee, ze zag het niet zitten voor zichzelf. Knap? Ja, maar dat waren er zoveel. Gael voelde duidelijk niet de ijskoude, harde schelp waarin die knul zat. Ze zou er zich pijn aan doen, misschien wel littekens overhouden aan deze tijd. Dat zou ze haar vertellen, maar nu nog niet.

'Bedankt, Bjorn. Ik heb nog wat te doen voor morgen.'

'Ik loop wel met je mee,' zei Gael.

Senta zag uit een ooghoek de vinger op de arm van Gael, waarmee Bjorn haar vriendin tegenhield. Operatie in-de-armen-schuiven geslaagd. Dank je wel, Senta, en dan mag je nu van je eigen prins gaan dromen in je eenzame bedje.

'Tot straks!'

'Leuk meisje,' zei Bjorn. 'Kenden jullie elkaar al voor je hierheen kwam?'

Gael knikte.

'Ik heb je gezegd dat mijn moeder docente is aan een toneelschool. Daar heb ik haar voor het eerst gezien. Ik zat toen zo in de put. Mijn ouders hadden net besloten uit elkaar te gaan. Ze zouden niet scheiden, maar ook niet langer samenleven. Ze waren eigenlijk stilletjes uit elkaar gegroeid, elk hun weg gegaan. Mam nam mij mee naar Nederland omdat ze haar daar een baan hadden aangeboden. Ik voelde me als een jonge boom die met wortel en al was uitgerukt en ergens anders in de grond gestopt. Senta kreeg me al bij de tweede keer dat we elkaar zagen aan het lachen. Dus we werden vrienden.'

Bjorn knikte dat hij het begreep.

'Wat zei je nu? Dat je moeder je meenam naar Nederland? Woonde je daar vroeger dan niet?'

'Nee, ik kom uit Engeland, uit Londen om precies te zijn. Mijn vader...'

Ze zweeg.

'Is hij Engelsman?'

'Brit. Ja. Mijn moeder is Nederlandse. Als actrice is ze ooit in Londen terechtgekomen en toen leerden ze elkaar kennen en ze kregen een kind. Dat kind was ik. Ze beweerden altijd dat ik het beste van beide werelden in me had.'

'Zie je je vader nog vaak?'

Gael fronste haar voorhoofd. Waarom klonk er zoveel pijn door in een schijnbaar eenvoudige vraag?

'Waarom?'

'Ik mis mijn vader enorm. Mijn ouders zijn ook uit elkaar. Hij is weggegaan. Ik krijg geen contact meer met hem. Hij heeft er geen behoefte aan en mijn moeder laat het me ook niet toe. Nu ja, ik hoef jou niet te vervelen met mijn ellende. We hadden het over jou.'

'Wat erg voor je,' fluisterde Gael.

'En daarom is dit, deze toneelstage en Londen, zo belangrijk voor me. Ik ben blij dat ik er met jou over kan praten. Jij kunt goed luisteren.'

Hij legde zijn slanke maar krachtige hand op haar handen. Er ging een reeks stroomstootjes door haar heen.

'Hoe is het met jouw vader?'

'We zien elkaar af en toe als ik met vakantie ga naar Engeland. En dan hebben we nu natuurlijk e-mail.'

'Wat hebben jullie?'

'E-mail, elektronische post. We sturen elkaar brieven met de computer. Overal waar we zijn, kunnen we elkaar meteen bereiken via Internet. Ik heb een laptop op mijn kamer hier.'

Bjorn floot.

'Maar het leukste van alles vind ik een met de hand geschreven brief. Gek, niet? Zo'n brief geeft me het gevoel dat mijn vader echt met me bezig is geweest. E-mail is onpersoonlijker, iets wat je tussendoor doet. Nu ja, ik ben al blij als ik wat van hem hoor.'

'Wat doet je vader?'

Gael aarzelde. Nee, zo ver kon ze nog niet gaan. Ze was bang dat hij het fout zou begrijpen, ze wilde niet 'de dochter van' zijn.

'O, iets voor een instituut. Bjorn?'

Hij keek naar haar.

'Dat gedicht. Het is zo mooi. Waarom denk je dat ik eenzaam ben?'

'Is het niet zo?'

Gael haalde diep adem.

'Ik besefte het niet voor ik het las. Ik wist het niet. Maar nu...'

'Het hoeft niet zo te zijn. Mijn gedicht was een aanbod.'

Het klonk bijna zakelijk.

'Denk je dat ik een kans maak om naar Londen te gaan?' vroeg Bjorn zonder overgang.

'Waarom vraag je dat aan mij?'

'Omdat jij gaat.'

Gael gooide haar hoofd achteruit en lachte.

'Waarom denk je dat? En wat heeft dat ermee te maken?'

'Je bent gewoon super. Niemand van de groep wil of kan Ariadne zijn. Ik wil graag met jou naar Londen.'

Het klonk zo ontroerend naïef dat Gael er warm van werd.

'Het lukt wel,' fluisterde ze.

Elke probeerde kalm te worden, maar het lukte niet. Zoals ze Bjorn daar zag zitten met Gael. En dan legde dat wicht ook nog haar arm om Bjorns schouders en drukte een zoen op zijn wang!

Ze graaide een vel papier van haar tafel en beende haar kamer uit.

Toen ze voor de bank bleef staan, keek Bjorn haar woedend aan. Zijn ogen werden streepjes toen hij het vel papier in haar hand zag.

'Hier,' snauwde ze, 'misschien kun je het nog gebruiken.'

Gael zag nog net het woord 'Oase' voor Bjorn het papier tot een prop samenkneep.

'Rotzak!' zei Elke.

12

'Bjorn, waarom was ze zo kwaad?'

'Ach, ze heeft zich van alles ingebeeld. Ik heb in het begin met haar een paar scènes gedaan. Zij Althea, ik Theseus. Maar toen begon ze de realiteit en het theater met elkaar te verwarren. Ze begreep en wilde meer dan ik bedoelde.'

'Maar ze had dat gedicht!'

Bjorn knikte.

'Ik had het zitten schrijven. De avond toen jullie aangekomen zijn. Ik was... Het klinkt puberachtig, maar ik was meteen weg van je. Ik kende je niet, maar ik beeldde me een hoop dingen in. Ze kwam wat vragen en zag het gedicht. Ze dacht dat het voor haar was. En ik zei dat ze het mee kon nemen. Stom natuurlijk, maar ik weet echt niet hoe ik met meisjes om moet gaan. Ik voel me altijd weer idioot. Behalve met jou.'

Gael bleef op een veilige emotionele afstand, opeens achterdochtig. Er was wat met Bjorn, iets wat ze niet vatte.

'Ik schaam me eigenlijk,' zuchtte hij. 'Wat moet je van me denken? Dat ik van de ene naar de andere fladder?'

Gael glimlachte, nog altijd op haar hoede.

'Je kunt je toch vergissen? Ik vind Elke een leuk kind, meer niet. Ze is ook goed in haar rol. Alleen, ze snapte niet dat ik toneel speelde, dat ik toen niet was wie ik echt ben.'

'Maak je maar niet druk, Bjorn.'

'Dat doe ik wel!'

Hij had een koppige frons op zijn gezicht, zijn stem klonk dof.

'Waarom dan?'

'Gael, ik wil niet dat jij me fout inschat.'

'Waarom zou ik dat doen? We hebben toch nog niets met elkaar?'

Bjorn moest moeite doen om het niet uit te schreeuwen. Ze had de deur wel wat dichtgeduwd, maar de kier was zo breed gebleven dat hij moeiteloos weer naar binnen kon. We hebben toch *nog* niets met elkaar, had ze gezegd!

'Als je me niet gelooft, wordt het ook nooit wat. Sorry, Gael, dat ik mijn hart zomaar voor je voeten gooi. Ga er alsjeblieft niet op staan dansen.'

Hij drukte een zoen op haar voorhoofd, draaide zich om en liep naar het kasteel.

Gael stond roerloos te kijken. Pas toen merkte ze dat het al helemaal donker was en dat er achter de meeste ramen licht brandde. Ze bleef staan tot er nóg een raam verlicht was. Zijn kamer.

Bea leunde achterover in haar stoel.

'Ja, misschien heb je gelijk,' zei ze en nam een slokje van de whisky die Bram had meegebracht.

'Ik heb net hetzelfde probleem met Gael. Ik vind dat zij de enige en echte Ariadne is. Ze heeft dat beetje wild opstandige, intelligent rebelse, dat eeuwig onberekenbaar vrouwelijke dat die figuur vraagt. Ze heeft bovendien fysiek alles mee, niet mooi maar aantrekkelijk, geen kind meer en nog geen vrouw, alles wat haar geloofwaardig maakt. Ze heeft ook een stem en présence.'

'Wat is dan het probleem?' vroeg Bea.

'Dat ik dat niet allemaal kan zeggen zonder dat iemand denkt dat ik haar vader te vriend wil houden. Snap je? Als ik dit allemaal schrijf, denken ze daar dat ik haar naar voren schuif om haar vader een plezier te doen. Dan jaag ik die lui tegen haar in het harnas. Doe ik het niet, dan valt ze misschien uit de boot.'

Bea zweeg bijna een minuut lang.

'Bij Bjorn ligt het toch anders.'

'Natuurlijk ligt het anders, maar uiteindelijk is het ook bij hem zo dat je hem of de hemel in prijst, of de hel in stuurt.'

'Waarom? Ik hoef hem niet aan te prijzen, ik hoef hem niet te verkopen!'

'Je kunt ook niet liegen,' zei Bram. 'Je persoonlijke emoties hebben er niets mee te maken.'

'Hoho! Wat bedoel je daarmee?'

'Kom nou, Bea, ik ben niet blind. Je bent er waarschijnlijk overheen, maar je viel voor hem. Nee, correctie, je struikelde voor hem. En dat is verdomme geen wonder. Want Bjorn hééft het nou eenmaal! Talent dat bovendien in het juiste lichaam schuilt en gedragen wordt door een nietsontziende wilskracht is zo zeldzaam. Hij doet me denken aan de grote methodeacteurs. Je weet wel, Robert de Niro en zo. Wist je dat die man zijn lichaam liet verloederen om in *Ra-*

ging Bull Jake te kunnen spelen? Hij vrat zich in geen tijd dik! Wel, dat extreme heeft Bjorn ook. En Mirko. Op een andere manier, maar even extreem.'

'Overdrijf je nou niet een beetje?'

'Over die nietsontziende wilskracht? Nee. Hij zal niemand ontzien, geloof me. Het zit me zelfs niet lekker. Brenda zegt dat hij over Poppy gebogen stond toen ze die avond de badkamer binnenging. Ze heeft hem niets zien oprapen, dat niet. Maar het is ook niet onmogelijk. Hij zou alles doen om een concurrent uit te schakelen... Dat moet je ook rapporteren.'

Bea draaide de whisky in haar glas, zag de amberkleurige drank het licht opvangen.

'Hoe?'

'Niet zo direct natuurlijk, maar ze moeten weten wie ze voor zich krijgen. We zijn op een punt gekomen dat er knopen moeten worden doorgehakt. Eén, er is geen andere Theseus dan deze. Twee, als deze jongen daar niet meteen wordt opgevangen, komt er herrie. Er is namelijk veel kans dat er in die groep kandidaten nog een hoop kerels zitten als hij. Ze spelen wat ze zijn of worden wat ze spelen. Daarom zijn ze jong, daarom is theater hun vorm van zoeken naar zichzelf.'

Bea knikte. Ze worstelde met zichzelf.

'Ik heb nog twee dagen,' zei ze. 'We zien wel.'

'Juist, we zien wel. Slaap lekker.'

Bram dronk zijn glas leeg, zette het op de werktafel van Bea en drukte een vriendschappelijke zoen boven op haar hoofd. Ze pakte zijn hand.

'Zit je in de knoop?' vroeg Bram.

'Heel erg,' zei ze. 'Paul heeft me in de steek gelaten. Iedereen laat iedereen aldoor weer in de steek. Waarom?'

'Omdat we mensen zijn,' zei Bram. 'En vooral omdat ze ons dat de laatste tijd altijd weer zeggen. We zijn maar mensen. Vroeger moest je een heilige zijn. Dan liet je niemand in de steek. Tenminste niet zo dat iemand het kon merken.'

Hij ging weg. De deur gleed zachtjes dicht.

Bea keek naar de notities die voor haar lagen. Nog twee dagen. Dan zou ze haar computer openklappen, haar vingers zouden woorden op het scherm ratelen, een druk op een knop en in Londen zou iemand een lichtje zien knipperen dat een boodschap aankondigde. En dan zou over het lot van Bjorn, Gael, Senta, Elke, Mirko en Andrea worden beslist. Alleen op basis van haar woorden.

'De voorlaatste dag hard werken. Zondagavond spelen, morgen drie keer doorlopen.'

Bea hief haar hand toen het rumoer nog toenam.

'Watjes!' schreeuwde Bram. 'Dacht je dat je hier op je luie kont kon zitten en toch acteur kon worden?'

Nog meer gejoel.

'Vanmiddag zetten we een aantal decorstukken. Nog vragen?'

'Is de rolverdeling nu definitief?'

Mirko klonk voor één keer ernstig.

'Zij die zich kandidaat hebben gesteld voor Londen spelen hun rol. Dat betekent niet dat ze al, hoe moet ik het noemen, geslaagd zijn. We beoordelen pas zondag. Maandag gaat alles met e-mail naar Londen. Alle landen sturen hun rapporten op dezelfde dag door. We maken ook video-opnamen voor Londen. En dan verwacht ik een beslissing binnen de week, nog voor het nieuwe schooljaar begint dus.'

Het werd stil. Dit klonk opeens heel serieus, heel definitief.

'Wie niet naar Londen wil, speelt de rollen die overblijven. We kunnen voor elk bedrijf wisselen als dat zo uitkomt. Is er nog iemand die zich heeft bedacht?'

Bea keek het lokaal rond. Eén hand.

'Frank?'

'Ik wil ook proberen Theseus te spelen.'

Het werd doodstil. Iedereen voelde dat er wat kon gebeuren.

'Waarom?' vroeg Bram.

'Zolang Poppy kandidaat was, wist ik dat ik het niet kon halen. Hij was zo goed. Maar nu?'

'Frank,' zei Bram, 'weet je dat je een klootzak bent?'

De anderen zaten stil. Wat zij min of meer hadden gedacht, klonk hardop uit de mond van Bram.

'Omdat je zit te zeiken, daarom. Je weet precies waarom je het doet, niet? Je weet het verdomme heel goed. En laat ik je zeggen, jongetje, ik kan je natuurlijk niet tegenhouden, maar vraag je maar eens af wat je aan het doen bent. Je wilt Bjorn een hak zetten omdat je een hekel aan hem hebt.'

'Hij is de pretentieuze klootzak, om jouw woorden te gebruiken, Bram!'

'Dat kan best, maar dat maakt van jou nog geen Theseus. Jij doet het om hem dwars te zitten en het kan je geen klap schelen dat je zo de laatste drie dagen hier verziekt. Nou?'

'Goed. Dan maar niet.'

'Prima. Mag ik je nou nog wat zeggen? Als ik jou was, ging ik mijn kans als Parmenides. En dat meen ik.'

'Noteer me dan maar,' zei Frank en knipoogde naar Elke. 'Alleen, ik ben wel al dood.'

Opnieuw knipoogde hij naar Elke. Die bloosde toen ze merkte dat Bjorn star naar haar keek.

Af. Doek op. Minos en het viertal staan nog zoals aan het eind van het derde bedrijf.

THESEUS: Jij? Dat kan niet!

MINOS: Wat bedoel je, dat kan niet? Dat kan ik niet geloven? Dat had ik nooit gedacht?

AGOS: Minos? Laten we vluchten, Theseus.

ALTHEA: Ja, laten we vluchten!

MINOS: Onmogelijk! Niemand komt uit het labyrint! Bovendien, mijn Minotaurus moet nog te eten hebben, vandaag. Kom, Theseus, meet je kracht met mij! Kijk om je heen, overal liggen de afgekloven botten van je jonge stadsgenoten. Ik heb ze met dit mes, met deze handen over de scheiding tussen leven en dood geholpen en ik heb gelachen bij hun kreten van angst, bij hun gekreun, bij de doodsreutel uit hun mond als ik hun keel afsneed en het warme Atheense bloed over mijn vingers gulpte. Ik heb in hun zachte vlees geknepen terwijl ik hun ledematen afrukte en ze mijn Minotaurus, mijn levenslange nachtmerrie, toewierp. Ik heb genoten van mijn wraak, had binnenpretjes bij de goedgelovigheid van je vader...

THESEUS: Schoft!

Valt aan met zijn zwaard. Minos pareert de stoot.

110

'Arthur! We hernemen die laatste repliek van Minos. Arthur, je bent een psychopaat. Misschien is die Minos wel gek geworden na het verlies van zijn zoon. Heb je *Silence of the Lambs* gezien? Of nee, beter nog, *Cape Fear*, met Robert de Niro. Dat effect moet je krijgen. Dat genieten van de weerzin die je zelf voelt voor je eigen daden. Snap je? Gemaakt vrolijk omdat je niet kunt of wilt lijden onder je eigen dwangmatige gedrag.'

Bram zweeg en keek Arthur aan. Bea voelde zich opeens klein en onzeker. De man die zo de gevoelens van een figuur kon ontleden, was assistent. Betekende zijn uitval dat hij vond dat ze haar werk niet goed deed?

'We hebben dit gisteravond zitten bespreken, Bea en ik. Ze zou je zo ook onderbroken hebben, maar ik was te ongeduldig. Sorry, Bea, had ik niet mogen doen.'

Bea maakte een gebaar van laat maar zitten. Ze was Bram opeens dankbaar. Hij had haar reputatie gered.

'Ja, ik wilde hier onderbreken. Hebben jullie die houten zwaarden niet gezien? Ik had er zelf aan moeten denken. Ja, op de vensterbank.'

De twee jongens kregen elk een zwaard. Ze zwaaiden er eerst wat onwennig mee, maar toen gingen ze door.

THESEUS: Schoft!
Valt aan met zijn zwaard. Minos pareert de stoot.
MINOS: Eindelijk, een tegenstander die een koning waardig is. Zie je de ironie van het lot niet, Theseus? Mijn zoon die viel door de hand van jouw vader terwijl ik hier nu jouw leven tussen mijn vingers hou?
THESEUS: Dat had je gedacht. Ik heb mijn eigen leven nog altijd stevig in handen! Jij sterft, Minos, niet ik!
MINOS: O? En waarom?
Nieuwe aanval van Theseus.
THESEUS: Omdat ik leef van de toekomst, omdat ik een droom in me draag en jij alleen nog teert op het verleden. Het verleden dat nooit meer morgen wordt! Het verleden dat je kent, dat je je herinnert. Een verleden kun je niet dromen, Minos!

111

ALTHEA: Theseus! Kijk uit!

De Minotaurus waagt een schuchtere aanval. Theseus ontwijkt, slaat toe en het monster krijst.

THESEUS: Wat staan jullie daar als bevroren? Agos! Val aan!

AGOS: Hou ermee op, Theseus. Dit leidt nergens toe. Je kent het geheim en dat is de dood van de Minotaurus. Minos, de koningkindermoordenaar. Laten we ons een weg naar buiten vechten en de wereld vertellen wat we weten. Dan rekent die wereld wel met deze schoft af. Zijn onderdanen zullen bevrijd zijn van hun angst en hun walging over hem uitspuwen. Zijn vijanden zullen in woede ontsteken, niet alleen om wat hij heeft gedaan, maar omdat ze zich hebben laten belazeren. Ze zullen zich op hem storten als de roofdieren die ze in hun hart zijn. Ze zullen hem verscheuren en zijn resten verspreiden over dit hele vervloekte eiland!

THESEUS: Agos, je snapt er niets van! Ik wil niet dat de wereld mijn taak overneemt!

ALTHEA: Jouw taak? Theseus! Wij hebben onze taak volbracht. We hebben een eind gemaakt aan de angst en de pijn van onze stad. Wat spreek je over taak?

THESEUS: Althea, hou jij je mond, jij hebt helemaal geen verstand van dit alles!

Bea sprong op.

'Wat scheelt jou zo opeens, Elke? Je staat erbij als een zure oude vrijster! Theseus is de jongen van wie je nog altijd houdt, ook al heb je je twijfels. Herinner je je opmerking van gisteren. We waren het erover eens dat ze jaloers is, dat die jaloersheid haar erg bezighoudt, maar jaloers zijn betekent altijd dat je op iemand gesteld bent. Pas als hij je zegt dat je je mond moet houden omdat je de dingen niet snapt... Elke?'

Het meisje draaide zich om en rende naar buiten.

'Wat is er nou weer aan de hand?' gromde Bram, die achter haar aan ging.

'Doorgaan. Andrea, neem over. Niet op letten. Dat is normaal, de spanning naar het einde toe.'

Andrea keek Bjorn hoofdschuddend aan. Het maakte hem onrustig. Het leek erop dat Elke had gekletst.

'Komaan, opschieten. Vanmiddag wil ik de eerste doorloop doen. Met dat decor. We hebben echt geen tijd te verliezen.'

Bjorn haalde diep adem. Hij moest geconcentreerd blijven. Alles was onder controle. Niemand zou het verhaal van Elke geloven. Hij kon zeggen dat ze zich wilde wreken omdat hij haar dromen niet waarmaakte. Iedereen wist...

Gael wuifde naar hem met drie vingers van haar rechterhand. Hij glimlachte, maar het deed pijn.

'En let ook op voor die gevechtsscènes. Niet overdrijven, jullie zijn geen stuntmannen.'

MINOS: Het lijkt wel alsof je erg alleen komt te staan, prins Theseus. Zullen we het op een akkoordje gooien?

THESEUS: Jij doet niets meer, Minos! Hier eindigt het voor jou. Of dacht je dat ik je de kans zou geven om nog meer verhaaltjes te verzinnen?

MINOS: Ik wil best rondvertellen dat je de Minotaurus hebt gedood. Ik wil zelfs heel veel misbaar laten maken, grote rouwfeesten laten houden... Dit mag wat mij betreft verdwijnen!

Wijst naar de Minotaurus.

THESEUS: Daarstraks vertelde je dat je eindelijk een waardige tegenstander had gevonden en nu wil je het met mij op een akkoordje gooien? Wat is je bedoeling, Minos?

Onverwachte aanval van de koning. Theseus wordt geraakt, struikelt achteruit en valt.

MINOS: Jouw aandacht afleiden, jongetje! Nu heb ik je!

Springt naar Theseus. Die rolt weg en komt overeind.

THESEUS: Nog niet! Je hebt me gewaarschuwd, nu laat ik me niet meer afleiden. En ik weet ook dat ik je niet kan vertrouwen. Toen je me voorstelde om rond te vertellen dat ik de Minotaurus had gedood, vroeg je eigenlijk dat ik je zou vertrouwen. Hoe kan ik zeker weten dat je niet meteen je verhaal verandert en iets nieuws verzint?

MINOS: Dat kun je alleen zeker weten als je me doodt.

Springt onverwachts op Agos toe, slaat het zwaard uit zijn handen en zet het mes op zijn keel.
Laat je wapen vallen, Theseus, of ik maak je vriend af. De rollen zijn nog maar eens omgekeerd.

THESEUS: Je mag voor mijn part met hem doen wat je wilt. Dat maakt niets uit. We zijn hierheen gekomen met de gedachte dat we het misschien niet zouden overleven.

AGOS: Theseus! Geef het op. Je praat over mijn dood!

ALTHEA: Je veroordeelt hem koelbloedig en het maakt je geen klap uit!

THESEUS: Ik heb je gezegd dat je moet zwijgen, Althea! Minos neemt me werk uit handen.

MINOS: Wat bedoel je? Ben je je verstand kwijt, prins Theseus?

THESEUS: Nee, hij moest hoe dan ook sterven. Ik wil geen getuigen van deze mislukking. Ik wil mijn heldhaftige verhaal zelf verzinnen, bij gebrek aan een eervolle waarheid, en het vertellen zonder bang te hoeven zijn dat iemand...

ALTHEA: Bedoel je dat wij... Is dat alles wat je hier kwam zoeken? Wierook voor jezelf?

THESEUS: Het spijt me, Althea, ik moet het belang van Athene hoger stellen dan dat van enkele vrienden.

AGOS: Ik wist het al langer, ik voelde het, maar vond de woorden niet. Wij waren voer voor de Minotaurus... En jij wilt koning zijn?

ALTHEA: Ik geloof niet wat je zegt, Theseus. Nee!

Theseus zet een stap naar Minos. Die heft zijn mes. Althea krijgt de arm van Theseus te pakken, maar hij slaat haar gewoon neer. Hij zet nog een stap. Minos schudt zijn hoofd, haalt uit en doodt Agos.

MINOS: Hoe zinloos! Ik weet niet wat het ergste is, moorden uit wraak of uit eerzucht.

THESEUS: Nu blijven wij tweeën over, wij alleen. En ik heb geen behoefte aan jouw oordeel over wat ik doe, niet het oordeel van iemand die zijn wraak met stromen onschuldig bloed heeft gevoed.

MINOS: Je vergeet hem daar!

Wijst op de Minotaurus.

THESEUS: Die heb je zopas zelf ter dood veroordeeld. Wij rekenen eerst af.

MINOS: We hebben afgerekend. Als je wint, wat ik betwijfel, kom je hier nooit meer uit. Niemand behalve ik kent de weg.

THESEUS: Wat een grap, je lijkt opeens om me bekommerd. Maar dat hoeft niet. O ja, ik wil dat je rustig sterft. Ik heb een feilloze manier gevonden om uit dit labyrint weg te komen. Jouw dochter!

MINOS: Mijn dochter? Wat bedoel je? Wat heeft Ariadne met dit alles te maken?

THESEUS: Ze houdt van me, beweert ze. Ze heeft me een kluwen draad meegegeven en die hoef ik maar te volgen... Minos... je uur is gekomen!

Valt brutaal aan, zwaaiend met zijn zwaard, Minos wijkt, de Minotaurus licht de koning de voet. Minos struikelt, verliest zijn mes. Theseus plant zijn zwaard op de keel van de koning.

Voorbij, Minos. Voorbij! Je hebt nauwelijks enkele ogenblikken meer te leven. Je dochter heeft je de rug toe gekeerd en nu zorgt het monster dat je hebt geschapen, je eigen Minotaurus, ervoor dat je in minder dan een oogwenk het onderspit delft.

MINOTAURUS: Ja, goed van me, niet, hihihihi! Ik heb eigenlijk lang gewacht...

MINOS: Je hebt je eigen doodvonnis getekend, Minotaurus. Je leven was dat van een zielige vleermuis, maar je leefde tenminste nog. Nu loopt het ook voor jou af. Vaarwel, tot in de onderwereld.

Probeert Theseus af te schudden, maar die steekt toe.

THESEUS: *Staat op, kijkt naar het dode lichaam van Minos.*

Vreemd toch. Het ene ogenblik heerst een man over de halve wereld, het volgende glijdt een handlang koud staal zijn lichaam in en blijft van hem niet meer over dan een stuk vlees.

MINOTAURUS: Vreemd dat jij daaraan denkt! Jij wilt toch net als hij heersen, je wil opleggen? Jij wilt toch net als hij...

THESEUS: Zwijg! Geniet van je laatste ogenblikken.

MINOTAURUS: Wat bedoel je? Ga je mij ook doden? Ik heb je geholpen!

THESEUS: Geholpen? Je hebt de strijd misschien ingekort, maar me geholpen? De afloop stond vast. Minos kon het niet van me winnen. Bovendien, ik kan je niet laten leven. Ook jij, vooral jij zou ooit de waarheid aan het licht kunnen brengen.

MINOTAURUS: Ik kom hier nooit uit weg!

THESEUS: Dat weet je niet. Er zijn wel meer mensen ontsnapt uit dit bouwsel. Daedalus, Ikarus, straks ik... Waarom zou jij niet ooit een uitweg vinden. Die bestaat, weet je? Minos kende hem...

MINOTAURUS: Ik heb al zo lang gezocht! Kijk naar me, ik ben zielig. Nu er geen offers meer komen, zal ik sterven van de honger. Mijn laatste voedselvoorraad ligt daar...

THESEUS: Zwijg, smerig mensdier! Je praat over het stoffelijk overschot van mijn vrienden!

MINOTAURUS: Je vrienden? Je hebt ze vermoord!

THESEUS: Ik heb ze gemaakt tot wat ze nooit uit zichzelf hadden kunnen worden. In mijn woorden daarbuiten zullen ze groter zijn dan hun eigen diepste droombeeld, ze worden helden, de helden die de Minotaurus hebben overwonnen. Ik zal hun herinnering koesteren...

MINOTAURUS: Ik geloof mijn oren niet! Zo'n schoft als jij bestaat niet.

THESEUS: Let op je woorden!

MINOTAURUS: Woorden? Woorden? Altijd woorden! Je had het daarstraks over jouw woorden die je vrienden groter zullen maken. Jouw woorden hebben mij moediger gemaakt omdat ik woedend ben. Jouw woorden hebben mij eindelijk het gevoel gegeven, ook al is het maar voor even, dat ik heb geleefd! Ik haat je, ik veracht je, ik...

Theseus steekt toe.

THESEUS: Nu blijft alleen nog de leegte om me heen, maar die was nodig. Alles is met de grond gelijk gemaakt. Ik kan eindelijk beginnen bouwen.

Gaat nu naar het publiek voor een monoloog.

Bjorn aarzelde. Het was ijzig stil in de repetitieruimte. Bea zat met een elleboog op haar knie en hield haar kin vast. Haar ogen stonden leeg.

'Zou je dat nog eens kunnen doen?' zuchtte ze toen. 'Of nee, wacht. We doen straks alleen deze scène nog eens, met decor. Ik wil dan alle bewegingen gemeten uitgevoerd zien. Voor de belichting.'

Bjorn stond te wachten. Nu kwam een van zijn lievelingsscènes, zijn monoloog, zijn getuigenis.

'We houden hier even op. Pauze. O ja, willen jullie eens in je spullen snuffelen? Ik veronderstel dat iedereen nog schone kleren heeft voor de opvoering van zondag?'

'Spelen we in onze gewone kleren?' vroeg Andrea en je kon horen dat ze ontgoocheld was.

'Dacht je dat we speciaal kostuums gingen maken?'

'Nee, maar die jongens die meisjes moeten spelen...'

'We lenen wel wat,' grapte Frank. 'En als dessert krijgen we vast nog sinaasappelen.'

Niemand lachte.

'Zal ik dan? Die monoloog?'

'Ik heb het volste vertrouwen in je, Bjorn. Die monoloog doe je prima. Hoeft niet. Ik weet het zo wel.'

Bjorn knikte, draaide zich om en liep naar buiten. In zijn hoofd echode elk woord van de ijzersterke tekst. Hij kreeg zijn kans nog wel om een publiek plat te spelen.

THESEUS: Hoor ik een stem? Hoor ik zelfs maar een gedachte? Is er iemand die afkeurt wat ik doe? Of wat ik heb gedaan? Is het dan niet zo dat een koning leeft volgens andere regels dan de gewone sterveling? Moet een koning niet denken in grote dromen? Moet een koning niet de adem van de tijd en de toekomst durven voelen in zijn daden, in plaats van te aarzelen en stil te staan bij het lot van een enkeling?

O, ieder van u denkt dat ik handel uit zelfzucht, dat ik eerzuchtig ben! Denk dan gauw wat anders. Zelfzucht eist iets anders dan de zware lasten van het koningschap, de dagelijkse beslommeringen om het lot van de mensheid. Eerzucht vraagt wat anders dan urenlang luisteren naar het klagerige gepiep van ondankbaren!

Ik heb van de goden een taak gekregen en ik moet kunnen beslissen hoe ik die opdracht vervul. Als daarbij mensen moeten worden geofferd, zelfs al zijn het vrienden, mag ik niet aarzelen! En ik zeg u meteen, ik heb nog niet het gevoel dat er één druppel nutteloos bloed is vergoten, dat er één wonde is geslagen die niet nodig was.

Wat? Wat hoor ik? Begrijpt iemand niet hoe ik zo wreed, zo laaghartig kan zijn? Wreed? Laaghartig? Ik? Is het wreed een leven te aanvaarden dat de andere had aangeboden voor het grote doel? Dacht iemand dat zij hadden gehoopt te overleven? Is het laaghartig het monster te doden dat al deze ellende heeft aangericht? Was dat niet de bedoeling van bij het begin? Het doel, Athene bevrijden, is hetzelfde gebleven. Het middel, de Minotaurus doden, is hetzelfde gebleven. De persoon die het moest doen, die het wilde doen, is dezelfde... Moeten dan niet nu de vruchten worden geplukt van wat is gezaaid? Denkt iemand dat ik minder resultaten zal bereiken bij het regeren van mijn volk als ik terugkeer als een held? Is het niet zo dat het beeld dat ze van mij hebben nog groeit als ik, en ik alleen, de slachting overleef? Moet dit niet het grote geheim blijven tussen de goden en mij? Wel dan? Wie heeft nog wat te zeggen? Niemand? Goed, dan nu afrekenen met... Ariadne.

13

Gael stapte uit de douche. Achter haar klaterde het water in een onstuitbare straal omlaag. Haar moeder zou weer boos zijn, als ze het zag. Water verspilde je niet. De kleine badkamer had zich met stoom gevuld. De wolken die ze om haar lichaam had zien opstijgen, waren nu gestold op de spiegel. Een laag mist van waaruit haar gezicht haar vaag aanstaarde. Een druppel rolde uit haar oog omlaag. Gael rilde. Een voorteken, misschien.

Met de handdoek wreef ze de spiegel schoon. Haar spiegelbeeld keek nu scherp terug. Ze legde haar handen onder haar kleine borsten en duwde ze wat omhoog en naar elkaar toe. De minuscule tepels waren roze. Vreemd dat ze anders naar zichzelf keek sinds ze verslingerd was op Bjorn. Vroeger had ze altijd smalend gedaan over wat ze het 'narcisme' van haar moeder noemde, haar overdreven zorg voor haar figuur en haar uiterlijk. Mama wilde geen gram zwaarder wegen dan vijftig kilogram terwijl ze meer dan een meter zeventig groot was. Twee keer per dag speurde ze in een manshoge spiegel haar lichaam af. Ze trainde, met halters en toestellen, en haar spieren waren lang en glad onder haar gezonde huid.

Mama, lieve mama... Opeens trof de gedachte Gael als een pijl. Had ze door naar haar lichaam te kijken ontdekt dat haar moeder er misschien een minnaar op nahield? Zij zelf had aan Bjorn gedacht en zich afgevraagd of hij haar mooi vond of alleen maar aantrekkelijk omdat ze Ariadne was. Dat was misschien net zo met haar moeder. Natuurlijk waren er mannen in haar buurt. Maar dat hoefde nog niet te betekenen dat ze een minnaar had. Of toch? Die collega die alleen in superlatieven over haar sprak? Het wond Gael meer op dan ze voor mogelijk had gehouden. Ze sloot even haar ogen en zag in haar verbeelding het lichaam van haar moeder, omstrengeld, half bedekt door een mannenlichaam zonder gezicht. Een beeld van zichzelf en Bjorn schoof als in een film over het andere heen. Gael kreunde zachtjes. Het beeld verdween.

Ze luisterde. Had iemand op haar deur geklopt? Ze wikkelde een badlaken om zich heen en liep naar de deur. Op de vloer buiten lag een bundeltje papier. Ze raapte het op en herkende het handschrift van Bjorn. Wat nu?

Haar ogen vlogen over de tekst. Een verhaal. Zachtjes sloot ze de deur en leunde ertegenaan.

Aan het eind van de tekst had iemand met brutale markeerstifthalen dingen aangestreept.

Ze zette nog twee stappen en zag de krachtige vorm van zijn lichaam. Ze gleed naast haar meester op het bed en streelde zijn gespannen schouders met vlinderlichte vingers.

'Denk je nog aan haar?' ademde ze. 'Kun je haar niet vergeten?'

Theseus antwoordde niet, zijn ademhaling werd dieper, zijn spieren ontspanden zich. Hij draaide zich weer om, sloeg zijn arm om haar heen, maar de aanraking drong niet door tot in de diepste grotten van zijn slaap.

Phoebe bleef stil liggen. Bang en genietend, schichtig verlangend, meer dan ooit tegelijk meisje en vrouw. En opeens was ze ook slavin met de dromen van een koningin. Ook zij sliep in.

Het zonlicht kroop over de vloer naar de slaapbank.

'Phoebe! Wat moet dat? Wat...'

Slaapdronken schoot het meisje overeind. Theseus bekeek haar. Ze voelde zijn blik over haar jonge lichaam dwalen, helemaal anders dan de vorige dagen.

'Je droomde,' zei ze. 'Ik heb je schouders gestreeld en toen sliep je rustig.'

Opeens genoot ze van de verwarring die ze zo duidelijk uit zijn houding kon opmaken.

'Maar je bent een meisje! Een jonge vrouw.'

Nu lachte ze hardop.

'Ik ben ook een slavin.'

'Ga weg! Ga weg en trek kleren aan. Ik hou niet van dit soort spelletjes.'

Phoebe viel met een klap op de aarde terug. De goden hadden haar van haar verstand beroofd. Ze sprong overeind. Haar slanke, gladde lichaam bleef als vanzelf staan bij de deuropening.

'Wil je me niet omdat je nog aan die andere denkt?'

120

'Welke andere? Praat geen onzin. Je bent mijn vrouw niet, waarom zou ik dan met je slapen?'

Phoebe lachte kort.

'Op Skyros slaapt elke meester wel eens met zijn slavinnen. Of met jonge slaven.'

Theseus gromde.

'Ik heb je gezegd dat je je kleren moet aantrekken.'

Phoebe verdween. Theseus zag haar gaan en slikte. Slavin, had het meisje gezegd. Vreemd. Zo had hij lang niet meer aan haar gedacht. Ze waren ongemerkt in een andere verhouding gestapt. Hij werd zich opeens bewust van zijn onuitgesproken tederheid voor haar, van het onbewuste verlangen dat nu, onverwachts, opdook.

Wat later zat hij voor het huis. Phoebe bracht brood en schapenkaas en olijven. In een beker had ze sterk verdunde wijn geschonken.

'Phoebe?'

Het meisje bleef staan, maar keek niet om.

'Waarom heb je dat gedaan?'

Hij praatte met haar als met een vrije vrouw. Nu ze erover nadacht, had hij dat al vrij vlug gedaan nadat ze bij hem was gekomen. Zij was hem meester blijven noemen, maar dat woord had niet zijn eigenlijke inhoud gehad. Hij schreeuwde niet tegen haar, sloeg haar niet, gooide haar het huis niet uit. Het was meer een naam geweest dan een woord dat de relatie tussen hen duidelijk maakte, een naam die ze gebruikte omdat ze zijn echte naam niet kende. Maar nu was het opeens weer vreemd.

'Ik wilde je rustig zien slapen,' zei ze. 'Je woelde. Je schreeuwde een naam in je slaap. Ariadne. Ik voelde dat je eenzaam en droevig was.'

Theseus kneep zijn ogen half dicht. Waakzaam.

'Is het waar, meester? Was je koning in Athene? Was Ariadne de koningin?'

Theseus nam een hap van het platte brood, kauwde, slikte.

'Vergeet wat je hebt gehoord, Phoebe... En je moet weten dat ik nooit meer een vrouw wil beminnen.'

'Maar waarom?'

Ze schrok van haar eigen vrijpostigheid, van de oncontroleerbare gretigheid in haar vraag.

'Omdat elke vrouw die me liefheeft door de goden wordt gestraft. En
omdat ik hun wapen ben.'
Phoebe kon geen woord uitbrengen.
'Soms doet het pijn.'
Zo praatte een man niet eens met zijn eigen vrouw op Skyros. En haar
meester, een koning, liet zijn slavin in het diepst van zijn hart kijken?
Was hij dan zo eenzaam? Ze voelde tranen achter haar ogen zitten.
'Je bent jong, Phoebe, jong en mooi. Ik zou je graag beminnen. Dat
is me nu opeens duidelijk geworden. Maar zodra ik je aanraak, al was
het maar met een woord van liefde, zullen de goden je straffen met
hun woede, met hun haat. Je zou de grote leegte zien waarin de angst
draaikolken vormt en de afgunst verterende vlammen laat oplaaien.'
Theseus boog zijn hoofd en sloeg zijn handen voor zijn gezicht. Er
gleden tranen over de rug van zijn handen, kleine beken pijn die hun
weg zochten in een dooraderd, verweerd landschap.
Phoebe stak haar hand uit, maar voelde alleen kilte.

Een haastige hand had er onderaan iets bij gekrabbeld: 'Dit schreef
hij voor jij hier was. Je bent gewaarschuwd. Ik wil niet dat jou wat
overkomt, dat jij pijn hebt.'

Geen naam, geen handtekening, een verward handschrift. Opzettelijk?

'Ik heb dus een geheime bewonderaar,' zuchtte ze. 'Of er loopt een
jaloers wicht rond. Waarschijnlijk het laatste. Dit heeft hij geschreven. Het is dus niet Bjorn die me dit geeft.'

Ze droogde zich af en harkte door haar haren met haar vingers.
Toen kleedde ze zich aan en liep de kamer uit. Misschien deed ze
wel iets heel stoms, maar ze wilde het weten.

Ze klopte aan bij Bjorn. Er scheen nog licht onder de deur en ze
hoorde muziek. Barokmuziek.

'Gael?'

Eerlijke verbazing. Eén ding stond dus vast, hij had niet zelf de
tekst voor haar deur neergelegd.

'Mag ik erin?'

Bjorn keek rechts en links de gang in.

'Vind je dit een goed idee?'

'Is damesbezoek verboden?'

Bjorn grijnsde ongemakkelijk. Hij droeg een slobberig joggingpak. 'Nee,' zei hij, 'maar dat bedoelde ik ook niet.'

Bea zat half rechtop op bed, met twee kussens in haar rug. Ze hoopte maar dat Gael de boodschap goed inschatte. Ze wilde niet dat het meisje gekwetst raakte. Ze had de blikken gezien, de kleine gebaren van Gael, de duidelijke schittering in haar ogen en het zacht blozende gloeien van haar huid. Bea schudde haar hoofd. Nee, het zou niet helpen. De magnetische uitstraling van Bjorn was te groot. Zij, Elke en nu Gael. Bjorn had het misschien toch bij het rechte eind gehad met zijn analyse van Theseus. Hij was het wapen van de goden dat tegen elke vrouw werd gericht die hij beminde. Hoewel, beminnen. Houden van of nemen van. Dat was de vraag.

Bjorn zat tegen het hoofdeinde van het bed, een beetje onderuitgezakt. Hij steunde op zijn onderarmen en zijn handen kropen heen en weer over het dekbed. Hij had blosjes van opwinding op zijn knappe gezicht.

'Wat ben je mooi,' zei hij, zo hees en zo zacht dat Gael hoopte dat ze zich niet vergiste.

Ze zat tussen zijn enkels, met haar armen om haar opgetrokken knieën. Ze voelde zijn voeten onder haar billen. Haar slapen klopten.

Ze glimlachte, wat verlegen, verlangend.

'Wat zei je?'

'Ik vind je mooi. Dat zei ik.'

Het bleef zo stil dat ze ergens een deur hoorde opengaan.

'Vind je dat echt?'

Ze glimlachte nu breeduit, maar een van haar mondhoeken trilde. Ze probeerde het zenuwtrekje te verbergen.

Bjorn pakte haar hand.

'Huil je?'

'Nee, nee. Het is niets. Bjorn, heb jij een verhaal geschreven over Theseus?'

'Hoe weet je dat?'

Zijn ogen stonden opeens waakzaam.

'Iemand heeft de tekst voor mijn deur gelegd. Iemand wil me wat vertellen. Er staan dingen in aangestreept.'

Ze stak hem het bundeltje papier toe. Bjorn legde het gewoon weg.

'Wat dan? Dat over Theseus, die voor zijn vrouwen het wapen van de goden wordt?

Ze knikte.

Zijn hersenen draaiden op volle toeren. Bea. Niemand anders had de tekst. Hij kon zich niet voorstellen dat ze die had doorgegeven.

'Ik weet niet wat het betekent.'

'Waarschijnlijk een grapje van Elke. Je weet hoe ze is. Ik vond dat ze zich vreselijk aanstelde toen ze huilend wegliep omdat iemand haar een opmerking maakte.'

Gael knikte.

'Denk je dat het alleen daarom was?'

'Ik weet het niet. Die tekst gaat over Theseus, niet over mij.'

Het bleef weer stil en het leek alsof het warmer werd in de kamer.

'Gael, ik heb al jaren het gevoel dat ik me ooit in een meisje zal verliezen. Mijn leven was een glazen kom met een deksel erop. Ik droeg de kom, kon die niet loslaten. Alleen als ik de kom kon laten vallen, zou het gebeuren. Ik denk dat de scherven daar nu ergens liggen.'

Gael knikte.

'Praat jij altijd zo?'

'Mijn grootvader heeft me geleerd met woorden om te gaan. En ik zei je toch dat ik al jaren met dat gevoel rondloop. Ik heb er de juiste woorden voor gevonden. Ja.'

Ze keek Bjorn gespannen aan. Zijn wangen en zijn voorhoofd glansden. Ze stak haar handen uit en streelde hem. Toen vouwde ze haar handen achter zijn hoofd en trok hem zachtjes naar zich toe. Hij ademde zwaar. Haar mond raakte zijn voorhoofd. Ze proefde zweet. De nauwelijks zichtbare haartjes boven zijn lippen deden haar lippen tintelen.

Ze keek in zijn donkere ogen en had de indruk dat ze zichzelf kon zien in de pupillen. Ze zag een erg verliefd gezicht.

'Je bent ook mooi en heel lief,' fluisterde ze.

Net toen ze haar mond op de zijne wilde drukken, kraakten er voetstappen die stilhielden voor de deur. Ze trok haar handen terug, draaide haar benen van het bed en stond op. Ze keek naar Bjorn en probeerde te glimlachen. Zijn gezicht was bijna uitdrukkingsloos, alleen de spierbewegingen onder zijn oren verraadden hoe gespannen hij was.

Iemand klopte aan.

'Ja?'

De deur ging open.

'Sorry,' zei Frank.

'Je stoort niet,' loog Bjorn.

'Ik wou zeggen dat ik een idioot ben geweest. Sorry, Bjorn. Het was echt stom.'

'Ach,' zei Bjorn. 'Dan zien we het morgen wel, Gael?'

'Ja,' zei ze. 'Het wordt spannend. Ik denk dat ik nu in bed duik en morgenvroeg ga joggen om de spanning eruit te lopen. Goeienacht, jongens.'

14

Bjorn rende door het park. Zijn T-shirt kleefde op zijn rug. De spanning eruit lopen, had Gael gezegd. Het lukte niet. Hij bleef maar hollen, zijn adem jaagde, zijn hart sprong zowat uit zijn lijf, maar de spanning bleef. En waar was Gael? Had ze zich verslapen? Hij bleef staan, wat voorovergebogen. Hijgend.

'Bjorn?'

Gael. Dan toch. Ze droeg een soepel vallend trainingspak en loopschoenen die duidelijk vaak waren gebruikt.

'Hé, heb jij een marathon gelopen?'

Bjorn wiste het zweet van zijn voorhoofd.

'Ik dacht dat jij er ook zou zijn.'

'Ik ben er. Hou je ermee op?'

'Ik loop nog een rondje met je mee.'

Ze jogde, Bjorn volgde vrij moeiteloos. Alleen, Gael bleef maar lopen, hetzelfde tempo, met lange, soepele passen. Een kwartier later moest Bjorn afhaken.

'Morgen wacht ik op je, tot straks.'

'Ik dacht dat jij met Ariadne zou afrekenen,' plaagde Gael.

'Er is een groot verschil tussen het toneel en het leven. En daag me niet uit. Ik heb er al een halfuur opzitten. Morgen loop ik je in de vernieling.'

Ze lachten allebei schuw.

'Bjorn!'

De jongen sloot zijn ogen. Elke.

'Ik zocht je.'

'Waarom?'

'Omdat ik met je moet praten.'

'Dan laat ik jullie. Tot straks.'

Gael draaide zich om.

'Gael!'

Ze luisterde niet, wilde niet bevestigd horen wat ze vreesde. Nee, Bjorn had het haar uitgelegd. Hij kon het niet helpen dat een meisje op hem verliefd werd, elk gebaar fout begreep en zich dingen ging inbeelden. Toneel en leven hadden met elkaar te maken, maar waren totaal verschillend. Ook licht en schaduw hadden met elkaar te maken.

'Wat ben je nu eigenlijk van plan?' vroeg Elke.

'Wat wil je van me? Laat me nou eindelijk eens met rust! Ik weet niet wat ik met jou te maken heb,' snauwde Bjorn haar toe.

Elke had opeens tranen in haar ogen. 'Waarom, Bjorn? We waren toch...'

'Wij waren niets. Jij was. Ik was. Maar wij? Nee. En laat me nu alsjeblieft gaan. Ik wil douchen.'

'Wat zegt Gael van deze toestand?'

'Welke toestand? Denk jij nou echt dat we geen interessantere dingen hebben om over te praten? Jij bent geen onderwerp van gesprek.'

Het klonk zo beledigend dat Elke uithaalde. De klap klonk hard. Bjorn kikte niet.

'Je hebt mij gebruikt, je hebt Bea gebruikt, en nu gebruik je haar!'

'Dat weet jij niet en zelfs als dat zo was, heb je er niets mee te maken.'

Bjorn draaide zich om en liep terug naar het kasteel.

Het was aan iedereen te merken. De spanning steeg met het uur. Kleine incidentjes werden drama's. Bea probeerde alles in de hand te houden, maar dat lukte niet.

'Maak je geen zorgen,' zei Bram terwijl ze tijdens een pauze koffie dronken. 'Je werkt voor het eerst met jonge mensen op dit niveau, niet?'

Bea knikte.

'Het is altijd zo. Je moet het er gewoon bij nemen. De jongens zijn altijd haantjes, de meisjes geen volgzame kippetjes... Komaan, we gaan weer aan de slag, dat vijfde bedrijf moet er in een uurtje op zitten. En dan beginnen we aan de doorlopen. Ik wil vanavond ook nog die video-opname maken. Dan is het licht mooier en we kunnen die muur als achtergrond gebruiken. Wat denk je?'

Bea knikte en zuchtte tegelijk. Ja, die video-opname. Die was ze bijna vergeten.

De jongelui zaten her en der verspreid teksten te repeteren.

VIJFDE BEDRIJF

Hubris en Heros op. Rood licht op de achtergrond.
HUBRIS: De avond komt met de kleur van bloed. Een zoveelste teken van de goden op de dag waarop de wandaden van Theseus
zijn gewroken.
HEROS: Gewroken. Ik geloof je, maar ik blijf met de vraag zitten hoe
je dit alles weet, waarom niemand dat ooit heeft gehoord, waarom je niet eerder hebt gesproken?
HUBRIS: Vraag je waarom de wind waait? Waarom zou ik hebben
gesproken? Wat zou er gebeurd zijn? Ik zou zijn opgepakt zodra
ik mijn mond opendeed. De kliek rond Theseus zou me hebben
gedood zonder me de kans te geven te beleven wat ik altijd heb
gedroomd, dat waarvoor ik heb gebeden! En mijn enige, mijn
laatste reden om te leven was deze dag zien opgaan, de dag
waarop Theseus met gelijke munt zou worden betaald. Ik kan
nu rustig verdwijnen, mijn ogen met een glimlach sluiten en
gaan slapen.
HEROS: Theseus is jarenlang vereerd door zijn Atheners...
HUBRIS: Dat hebben we al gehad, niet? Heb jij ooit in het hart van
mensen gelezen? Betekent het feit dat ze juichen echt dat ze blij
zijn? Kun je er zeker van zijn dat ze iemand bewonderen omdat
ze met palmtakken en kleurige kleren zwaaien of dat ze van
hem houden omdat ze voor hem knielen en zijn handen kussen? Theseus had de macht in Athene, speelde in op het triomfantelijke gevoel van de mensen die volgens hem het voorrecht
hadden in een grote stad te wonen. Mieren die in spleten wonen,
hebben geen kijk op de ware afmetingen van een berg.
HEROS: En toch treurden ze met hem toen zijn vader Aegeus zo tragisch stierf.
HUBRIS: Dat heb ik destijds gehoord, ja! Theseus heeft de tranen
van de Atheners als zilvergeld opgestreken en ze later met rente
terugbetaald. Treuren om zijn vader? Het zou wat...
Af. Licht op rechts, waar de uitgang van het labyrint moet liggen.
ARIADNE: *Komt op en gaat naar de draad kijken.*
Hoe lang nog? Mijn hart huppelt als een verschrikt hert in en uit
het struikgewas van mijn angst. Ik heb al uren geleden het ge-

brul van de Minotaurus gehoord. Daarna niets meer... Theseus!
Theseus!
THEROS: *Haastig op.*
Prinses! Wat doet u hier?
ARIADNE: Wachten op Theseus. Ja, loop maar naar mijn vader en
vertel het hem. Ik ben verliefd op Theseus, hopeloos verliefd.
THEROS: Prinses Ariadne, u heeft waarschijnlijk het hoofd verloren!
ARIADNE: Mijn hoofd? Jawel, en mijn hart en ik wil alles verliezen
als Theseus maar terugkomt.
THEROS: Prinses! Toen Theseus vertrok naar zijn uiteindelijke lots-
bestemming, heb je hem beschimpt en zelfs geslagen!
ARIADNE: Verdwijn, Theros! Dit begrijp jij niet.
THEROS: Hoeft ook niet, prinses Ariadne, ik moet er alleen voor
zorgen dat u zich waardig gedraagt. Ik zal uw vader, de koning,
inderdaad waarschuwen. Bovendien, u droomt. Niemand heeft
het ooit van de Minotaurus gewonnen en zelfs al zou dat kunnen, dan nog komt niemand uit het labyrint terug. Wie daar
naar binnen gaat, is verloren en moet alle hoop laten varen.
ARIADNE: Niet als hij weet hoe hij de weg terug kan vinden. Zie je
deze draad, Theros? Deze draad heeft twee uiteinden. Het andere heb ik om de pols van Theseus gebonden, weet je wel? Zogenaamd omdat we zijn gebeente terug zouden kunnen vinden. In
werkelijkheid om hem de kans te geven terug te komen. Meer
dan een wapen gaf deze draad hem uitzicht op die terugkeer. Je
bent er met open ogen in gelopen, Theros!
THEROS: *Rukt de draad uit haar handen.*
Prinses, dit is verraad!
ARIADNE: Nee, Theros, liefde!

'Goed zo! Perfect! Bijzonder goed, Geert. Ik zou je bijna willen ver-
plichten toch maar kandidaat te worden voor Londen. Je zet een bijzonder geloofwaardige Theros neer.'
'Nee, Bea, bedankt, maar dat lukt je toch niet.'
'En als ik het je zou vragen?' Senta kronkelde zich om Geert en
keek diep in zijn ogen.
'Vraag je het?'

De anderen lachten.

'Gael, jij gaat er nog op vooruit. Alleen, je lijkt te zeker van die terugkeer. Probeer je verlangen te mengen met twijfel. Geef het publiek de kans te twijfelen aan de afloop. Tenslotte is dit een Griekse tragedie. En nu de terugkeer van Theseus.'

THEROS: En toch zal het niet lukken. Deze draad...
Theseus verschijnt. Theros deinst terug. Ariadne loopt naar de jongeman toe.
ARIADNE: Theseus!
THESEUS: Wat is er met deze draad?
ARIADNE: Theseus! Let niet op hem. Neem me in je armen! Hou me vast. Theseus! Je bent teruggekomen!
THESEUS: Mijn werk is nog niet af.
Theros vlucht.
ARIADNE: Theseus, snel! Hij zal de wacht waarschuwen. We moeten vertrekken. Ik ben net nog in de haven geweest. Je schip ligt klaar om uit te zeilen. De wind staat gunstig, de bemanning heeft de handen aan de riemen, de stuurman staat op de achterplecht...
THESEUS: Goed om horen. Vaarwel, Ariadne.
ARIADNE: Wat bedoel je? Vaarwel? Theseus?
THESEUS: *Duwt haar van zich af.*
Vaarwel betekent dat ik je het beste toewens. Een heel eenvoudig woord dat zelfs jij zou moeten snappen.
ARIADNE: Ik ken de betekenis van 'vaarwel', maar ik begrijp niet wat je ermee bedoelt, waarom je het woord nu gebruikt.

'Nee, Gael, nee! Voor een keer zit je er helemaal naast. Ik weet het, er is weer een probleem met die tekst. In drie replieken moet je van uiterste opluchting en vreugde naar de diepste twijfel. En tussendoor moet je nog een praktische mededeling doen over dat schip. Hoe los je zoiets op? In elk geval niet door sneller te gaan praten.'

'Kan de stilte die volgt op de vlucht van Theros niet langer?' zei Brenda. 'Dan kan Ariadne met gebaren en mimiek die verandering duidelijk maken.'

130

'Dat zou kunnen, maar dan loop je het gevaar dat het mimetheater wordt. En dat kan hier niet.'

'Tekst invoegen,' zei Mirko.

'Nee! Daarover hebben we het al gehad. Ariadne ziet Theros vluchten, pakt Theseus beet en zegt *we*. De opgewonden opluchting en de opwinding van de vlucht die ze plannen, liggen erg dicht bij elkaar. Die twee zinnetjes waarin het woord "vaarwel" valt, vormen het scharniermoment. Probeer maar.'

De derde keer was Bea tevreden. Bram noteerde iets.

THESEUS: Ik vertrek. Jij blijft hier!

ARIADNE: Je laat me hier achter? Mij? Theseus, je houdt van me!

THESEUS: Ik? Houden van de dochter van een genadeloze moordenaar, van een man die niet kon leven als hij niet het bloed van weerloze slachtoffers over zijn handen voelde stromen?

ARIADNE: Ik? Ik ben de dochter van koning Minos! Ik ben een prinses. Mijn bloed is even nobel als het jouwe.

THESEUS: Nee, Ariadne, nee! De echte Minotaurus, het echte monster in het labyrint was jouw vader! Je zult de enige zijn die dit ooit weet, je zult dit onvoorstelbare geheim moeten dragen.

ARIADNE: Theseus, herinner je je dan niets meer van de nacht...

THESEUS: Ik moest je aan mijn kant krijgen, Ariadne. Jij was de enige die me kon helpen. Je hebt mijn leven gered, ik schenk jou het jouwe. Normaal gesproken zou ik de dochter van een moordenaar hebben gedood, zou jouw leven een minieme vergelding zijn geweest voor de tientallen levens die Athene heeft moeten betalen voor de onhandigheid, de fout van één man. Daarmee zijn onze rekeningen vereffend.

ARIADNE: Nee, Theseus! Dat kun je niet doen. Mijn hart brandt van liefde voor jou! Ik wil niet leven zonder dat jij dat leven met me wilt delen!

THESEUS: Dat is jouw zaak. Ik heb je het leven geschonken en met je geschenk doe je wat je wilt.

ARIADNE: Ik begrijp het nog altijd niet! Vertel me dan tenminste alles!

THESEUS: Dat wil ik wel doen, in het kort. De vreselijke Minotaurus was niets meer dan een zielige bastaard van je moeder. Je vader heeft hem in het labyrint opgesloten, waar hij zich voedde met de resten van de slachtoffers die je vader hem toewierp. Want jouw vader, Minos, doodde het jonge, levende losgeld dat wij betaalden, gewoon om zijn trieste wraak met Atheens bloed te blussen. En daaraan heb ik een eind gemaakt, Ariadne.

ARIADNE: Hoe vreselijk ook, waarom moet ik daarvoor boeten?

THESEUS: Dacht je nu werkelijk dat ik jou met me mee zou kunnen nemen? In elk gebaar van jou zou ik de gebaren van je vader herkennen, in elk woord van jou zijn stem. En dan zou ik met jou in Athene moeten verschijnen?

ARIADNE: Dus je laat mij boeten voor de wandaden van mijn vader?

THESEUS: Doen we dat niet allemaal? Zou ik hier zijn geweest als mijn vader zijn speer een meter meer naar rechts of naar links had geworpen? Zou je broer gestorven zijn als jouw vader hem destijds niet naar Athene had gestuurd? Wij, kinderen, zijn de pijlen die ouders afschieten op een doel, soms met een heldere blik, soms blindelings. Een pijl verandert niet van bestemming. Wij hebben elkaar ontmoet, gekruist tijdens onze vlucht. Dat is alles.

Theseus draait zich om, schrikt en wil weglopen. Ariadne probeert hem nog tegen te houden, maar hij gooit haar ruw van zich af.

Bea keek boos om. Dit was toch echt niet het moment om te storen. Bjorn mocht zichzelf zijn in deze scène, zijn ware ik mocht bovenkomen, meer nog dan in zijn monoloog. Hij was overweldigend goed.

'Ja?'

De receptioniste van het kasteel gaf haar een briefje.

'Gael! Telefoon voor jou. Heel dringend.'

De stilte was pijnlijk.

'Wie?'

Gael holde achter de receptioniste aan. Iedereen wachtte. Bjorn werd weer Bjorn en wist zich helemaal geen raad meer met zijn handen.

Het duurde lang voor Gael de zaal weer binnenkwam. Ze glimlachte, maar haar ogen vertelden een ander verhaal.

'We kunnen doorgaan,' zei ze. 'Geen probleem. Niet echt.'

Ze ging opnieuw naast Bjorn staan.

'Krijg ik die laatste zinnen nog eens van je? Vanaf die zin over de kinderen.'

Bjorn knikte, haalde adem en probeerde zich te concentreren.

THESEUS: Wij, kinderen, zijn de pijlen die ouders afschieten op een doel, soms met een heldere blik, soms blindelings. Een pijl verandert niet van bestemming. Wij hebben elkaar ontmoet, gekruist tijdens onze vlucht. Dat is alles.
Theseus draait zich om, schrikt en wil weglopen. Ariadne probeert hem nog tegen te houden, maar hij gooit haar ruw van zich af.
ARIADNE: Theseus! Ik vervloek je! Jouw beurt komt nog!
THESEUS: Vergeet dat maar, de goden lachen me toe! Ik ga naar Athene om er koning te worden. En jouw wacht zal me niet tegenhouden.
Hij verdwijnt. Ariadne in het midden van de scène.
ARIADNE: Hier sta ik dan! Weggegooid, vernederd, vrouw. Ik haat je, Theseus, ik veracht je, man!
Licht uit.

Het was middagpauze. Bjorn kreeg nauwelijks een hap door zijn keel. Voortdurend dwaalden zijn ogen naar Gael, die aan de tafel van de Nederlandse groep was gaan zitten, zoals ze dat altijd deed. Ze keek af en toe ook naar hem en probeerde hem duidelijk te maken dat hij zich geen zorgen hoefde te maken.

Maar ze deed het wel op een afstand, alsof ze helemaal niet wilde dat iemand wist dat Bjorn en zij wat met elkaar hadden.

Elke praatte uitbundig.

'Zou het niet geweldig zijn om samen in Londen te zijn? Hoe zal het daar gaan? Moeten we zelf een kamer vinden? Bjorn, zoeken we dan samen een flatje? Dat komt goedkoper uit.'

De anderen namen deel aan de woordenvloed. Bjorn niet.

'We beginnen opnieuw om één uur. Ja, vroeger dan anders, maar het moet.'

Bea luisterde niet naar het protest. Ze pakte een appel van de schaal en liep naar buiten. Bij de tafel van de Nederlanders bleef ze even staan en ze wenkte Gael.

Bjorn voelde zijn hart weer hameren, net als bij het lopen die morgen.

Bea wachtte tot Gael buiten was.

'Gael, misschien vind je dat ik me met dingen bemoei die me niet aangaan, maar ik wil je toch wat vragen.'

Gael kauwde op haar onderlip.

'Wat is er met Bjorn aan de hand?'

Gael keek alsof Bea opeens drie neuzen had gekregen.

'Met Bjorn?'

Bea knikte.

'Ik weet het niet. Wat zou er met hem aan de hand moeten zijn?'

'Maak jij je geen zorgen om hem?'

Gael stootte een kort lachje uit.

'Wat bedoel je, Bea? Zorgen? Ik?'

Bea keek haar aan. De stilte was verstikkend. Toen ging Bea opnieuw in de aanval.

'Wat is er sinds eergisteren tussen jullie gebeurd?'

Gael keek strak naar de deur achter Bea, met een blik die moeiteloos te herkennen was.

'Wat wil je daar nou weer mee zeggen? Bea, ik snap helemaal niets van dit gesprek.'

De stem van Gael klonk zo zachtjes dat het moeilijk was haar te horen.

'Ik bedoel dat het niet bepaald een goed idee is om emotioneel betrokken te raken bij mensen met wie je op het toneel moet staan. Theater is een schijnwereld.'

'Precies daarom ben ik er niet bang voor. Theseus gooit Ariadne als een afgedankt speeltje in de hoek, maar dat betekent niet...'

'Zo denk jij erover. Maar Bjorn? Ik denk dat hij het leven vanuit een andere hoek bekijkt.'

'Bea, waarom voeren wij dit gesprek eigenlijk? Wil je me waarschuwen? Heb jij die tekst soms voor mijn deur gelegd?'

Bea rukte haar hoofd omhoog en keek in de grijsblauwe ogen van het meisje.

'Ja! En weet je waarom? Bjorn is gevaarlijk. Hij gebruikt je, en als jij niets meer voor hem kunt of wilt doen, is het uit. En dat doet pijn. Dat wil ik je besparen. Dus ja, ik waarschuw je.'

Gael voelde haar hart in haar keel kloppen. Ze voelde dat ze bloosde. Bea pakte haar hand vast.

'Ik heb de hele tijd het gevoel dat er wat veranderd is tussen jullie. Ik wil alleen maar zeggen dat dit niet de echte wereld is. Toen ik je voor het eerst zag, was ik onder de indruk. Ik wil niet dat iemand als jij stuk wordt gemaakt door iemand als Bjorn. Nu ben je zestien en is het leuk om zo betoverd te worden. Als het je later overkomt, als het blijft duren en je tovenaar je de hele tijd blijkt te misbruiken, doet het pijn. Heel erg pijn. En iemand als Bjorn doet dat.'

Het klonk zo giftig. Iemand als Bjorn. Gael schudde haar hoofd. Niemand kon weten hoe hij echt was. Niemand. Zij wel. Het gedicht, de avond van gisteren, de stilte, de geuren in zijn kamer, de glanzende warmte van zijn huid, zijn adem.

Inderdaad, het zou jammer zijn als dit stukging. Maar iemand als Bjorn zou het niet stukmaken.

'Gael, ik ben bang dat dit toneelstuk ons leven voor een deel in bezit neemt. Ik voel het, we gaan naar een tragisch hoogtepunt. En dat is typisch Grieks.'

Bea zweeg, want ze merkte dat haar woorden niet meer tot het meisje doordrongen.

'Bea,' zei Gael, 'ik vind het fijn dat je je zorgen maakt om mij. Maar ik kan me echt wel behelpen. Mijn vader... Ik ben nog altijd "de dochter van". Ik heb dus al een familienaam. Nu wil ik voor mezelf een voornaam. Mijn moeder is een lieve egoïste. Ze belde vanmorgen dat ze morgen niet naar de opvoering komt. Ze krijgt de zoveelste kans van haar leven. Althans, dat beweerde ze. In Stockholm spelen ze Macbeth en hun Lady Macbeth heeft een stemprobleem. Of ze niet kan invallen? Natuurlijk doet ze dat. Want ook zij is nog aan het vechten. Ook zij is in de eerste plaats "de vrouw van". Dat heb je met mensen als mijn vader. Dus ze gaat. En ze snapt niet eens dat ze haar vragen omdat ze "de vrouw van" is en dus ergens in een adressenboekje terecht is gekomen. Met Bjorn en mij is het anders. Hij houdt van mij. Hij weet niet eens wie ik ben.'

Bea knikte, maar ze geloofde er geen snars van. De Bjorn die niet wist wie Gael was, was niet de Bjorn die zij kende. Helemaal niet.

15

'Ja, tante. Ik wacht even.'

Bjorn huppelde zowat van de ene voet op de andere. Ook al was zijn plan krankzinnig, het was meer dan de moeite waard.

'Hoi, Sil. Ik ben het, Bjorn.'

'Yeah!'

Bjorn kon zich precies voorstellen hoe zijn nichtje Silvia er nu bij stond. Een veel te wijde jeans, een veel te groot sweatshirt, haar petje achterstevoren met de klep in de nek, een brilletje met blauwe, ronde glazen.

'Je hebt me ooit verteld dat je zowat elke computer kunt kraken.'

'Niet zowat elke computer.'

'Wat bedoel je?'

'Ik kan *alle* computers kraken.'

'Ben je er maandag?'

'Ik ben er altijd. Yow, man!'

De verbinding was verbroken. Bjorn keek naar het toestel. Hij moest nu nog één ding opknappen. Hij liep de statige trap op. De kamer van Gael lag op de tweede verdieping en keek uit op de grote vijver.

Hij klopte.

'Gael? Gael?'

Hij legde zijn oor tegen de deur en hoorde vaag onduidelijke geluiden.

'Wie is daar?'

'Bjorn.'

De deur ging langzaam open. Gael had een badlaken om.

'Geef me twee minuten. Ik trek wat aan.'

'Mag ik niet kijken?'

'Nee.'

De deur ging dicht. Bjorn staarde nadenkend voor zich uit. Gael had hem meteen op zijn nummer gezet. Hij hoopte maar dat Bea daarmee niets te maken had.

De deur ging weer open. Gael droeg haar trainingspak.

'Kom erin.'

De oude warmte was er nog. Bjorn legde zijn hand achter in haar nek en voelde de natte haarslierten. Hij drukte een zoen op haar neus.

'Hoe doe je het?' vroeg hij.

'Wat?'

'Met haren als een verzopen kat nog altijd zo mooi zijn?'

'Laat maar zitten. Ik weet hoe ik er nu uitzie.'

'Wat was dat met dat telefoontje?'

Bjorn ging op het bed zitten, Gael vond een plekje op de vensterbank. Buiten hoorden ze stemmen. Gelach en gejoel. De Nederlanders voetbalden tegen de Vlamingen op het grasveldje voor het bordes. Felicia had gescoord.

'Een telefoontje van mijn moeder. Ze zou komen kijken en me achteraf meenemen. Maar dat kan nu niet meer, want ze gaat Lady Macbeth spelen in Stockholm. Dus moet ik maar zien hoe ik thuiskom en waar ik de volgende dagen blijf.'

Bjorn glimlachte breed.

'Is het in deze verwarde tijden nog mogelijk om een eenzame en eerzame jonkvrouw onderdak te bieden?'

Gael keek hem aan.

'Mijn moeder komt wél kijken,' ging Bjorn door. 'Je kunt met ons meerijden. We hebben een prima logeerkamer en ik zou het zalig vinden als je nog enkele dagen langer mijn dagen en nachten vulde.'

'Zeg je nou echt dat je wilt dat ik bij jou thuis kom logeren?'

'Dat is de eenvoudige versie van wat ik zo sierlijk wist uit te drukken.'

'Je bent gek.'

'Op jou!'

Bjorn merkte dat er een bres was gekomen in de dijk van haar gevoelens.

'Je moet alleen je vader op de hoogte brengen dat je niet thuis zult zijn. Je moeder zal hem toch wel hebben verteld van Stockholm?'

Gael knikte.

'En dat doe je met die tovercomputer van je. Hoe zei je dat ook weer? Een druk op de knop en mijn brieven zijn bij hem?'

'En jouw moeder? Wat vindt die ervan?'

'Geen probleem. Ze kijkt er al naar uit. Eindelijk een intelligent wezen om mee te kletsen. Laat je niet door haar inpakken. Ze is walgelijk lief.'

Gael aarzelde. Zonder dat ze het goed besefte, had ze aan een oplossing als deze gedacht. Romantisch, natuurlijk. Ze was bang voor de kloof van eenzaamheid tussen de warmte van de cursusweken en de kilte van het verlaten huis waar ze terecht zou komen.

'Meen je dat nou?'

'Ja,' zei Bjorn.

'Bjorn?'

Gael duwde zich overeind.

'Gisteren waren we heel dicht bij elkaar. De stemming in jouw kamer was zalig. Misschien zou ik met je hebben gevrijd als ze niet hadden aangeklopt. Ik weet het niet. Ik zou misschien wat stuurloos op mijn gevoelens gedobberd hebben, en als jij dan het bootje had gestuurd, was het misschien gebeurd. Maar nu weet ik het niet meer.'

Ze kwam vlak bij hem staan en streelde zijn haren.

'Ik heb nog nooit met een jongen...'

'Jij zou mijn eerste meisje zijn geweest.'

Ze keken elkaar aan. Hun blikken leken aan elkaar vastgeklonken. Ze kusten.

'Ik vind je...'

'Ik jou ook.'

'We moeten gaan. We zijn nou al te laat. Zo meteen komt iemand de kamer binnen.'

Gael sprong zenuwachtig op en trok haar T-shirt naar beneden.

'Eruit, ik moet me omkleden.'

'Mag ik nog altijd niet kijken? Ik weet intussen wel meer.'

'Vergeet het, schoft, ik ben een keurig meisje.'

'Houden zo,' lachte Bjorn. 'Ik zie je beneden.'

Toen eerst Bjorn en wat later Gael met blosjes op de wangen naar binnen kwam, knikte Bea gelaten. Woorden waren nog nooit in staat geweest om gevoelens aan de ketting te houden. Ook nu niet. Gael was voor hem gevallen, net als zij, net als Elke. De steen die hij op hun pad had gegooid om hen te doen struikelen, was telkens een andere geweest, maar gevallen waren ze.

'Om één uur, had ik gezegd! We houden niet van wachten.' Ze snauwde het.

'Drie minuten!' zei Bjorn.

'Kom drie minuten te laat op en het publiek is weg.'

'Begin nou maar,' gromde Bram, die niet begreep waarom Bea zo overdreef.

Theseus links, samen met een figurant, de stuurman. Een mast met zeil suggereert een schip. Rechts staan Aegeus en twee andere figuren, Oratos en Daedalus. Door afwisselende belichting schakelt men van de ene naar de andere over naargelang de dialoog vordert. Pas als Aegeus het schip ziet aankomen, worden beide groepjes samen belicht.

THESEUS: Vol zeil! Koers naar Athene, we varen naar de triomf!

STUURMAN: Vol zeil! Koers naar Athene!

AEGEUS: De zee blijft leeg...

ORATOS: Niet zo somber, koning, we tellen de dagen sinds het vertrek van Theseus nog altijd op één hand.

DAEDALUS: Misschien heeft Minos het offer uitgesteld...

AEGEUS: Dank je voor de troostende woorden. De tijd lijkt wel kleverig hars, elk uur sleept zich voort voor een angstig wachtend hart.

THESEUS: Ik vraag me af of iemand al naar me uitkijkt, of iemand gelooft dat ik dit aankon. Waarom is die zee zo breed? Ik brand van ongeduld om het gejuich van mijn stadsgenoten te horen, om de kroon te voelen wegen op mijn haren.

STUURMAN: Is u niet een beetje te ongeduldig, prins Theseus? Uw vader, koning Aegeus, is niet zo oud en nog sterk. Als de goden het willen...

THESEUS: Stuurman, ik voel hoe een stormwind van ongeduld me voortdrijft. Het is de tijd die de goden hebben voorzien. Athene moet ontwaken uit zijn dommelige, onderworpen bestaan. De stad, haar volk en haar koning moeten schitteren als een kroon op het hoofd van deze aarde! Dát is de wil van de goden. Aegeus heeft zijn tijd gehad... Je zult zien, de goden regelen de loop van zijn verdere leven, en die van het mijne.

ORATOS: Koning, de avond komt, uw ogen zijn vermoeid, de wind jaagt tranen te voorschijn...

AEGEUS: De wind, Oratos? Waarom blijft de zee leeg? Daar! Is dat niet het zeil van een schip? Daar!

DAEDALUS: Een golftop? Het opspattende schuim? Het silhouet van een rots? Koning, uw verlangen vervormt alles...

AEGEUS: Nee! Ik zie wat ik zie! Kijk! Het zeil wordt groter! Daar!

STUURMAN: Land in zicht! Land ver vooruit! Theseus, is de tijd niet gekomen om een wit zeil te hijsen om onze triomfantelijke terugkeer te vieren? Dat was toch afgesproken?

THESEUS: Triomfantelijk? Al mijn vrienden dood, de bloem van Athenes jeugd vermoord! En dat noem jij een triomfantelijke terugkeer?

AEGEUS: Welke kleur van zeil voert het schip? Kijk dan toch! Kijk!

DAEDALUS: De kleur van de zee en de golven kleurt alles vaag en de ondergaande zon verdoezelt...

AEGEUS: Hou me niet voor de gek! Welke kleur?

ORATOS: Ik kan de kleur niet onderscheiden, maar over minder dan een uur...

STUURMAN: Ik schat nog zowat één uur voor we de stad en de burcht zullen zien. Prins Theseus, ik dacht... in alle nederigheid natuurlijk, ik dacht dat het witte zeil moest worden gehesen als u levend terugkeerde!

THESEUS: Kan ik dan triomferen en blij aan land gaan als in alle andere families tranen vloeien om de dood van die kinderen? Ze zouden mij mijn vreugde nooit vergeven. En terecht!

'Zeg eens, wat zat er in het eten vanmiddag? Dit lijkt nergens naar! Het is gewoon niet te geloven. Iedereen staat daar te praten, te declameren. Jullie worden geacht levende mensen te zijn, geen personages van piepschuim of bordkarton.'

Het groepje jongens keek naar de vloer.

'We hebben dit nooit eerder gedaan, Bram,' zei Willem.

'Kun je dan nooit iets meteen de eerste keer goed doen?'

Bjorn keek Bram woedend aan.

'We kwamen hier om wat te leren. Als we het allemaal al konden, hoefde dat niet.'

'Zeg eens,' barstte Bram uit. Hij zweeg toen Bea haar hand op zijn arm legde.

'Geen herrie. We doen het opnieuw. Denk aan wie of wat je was bij het begin van het stuk. Goed? Spelen maar.'

De tweede poging was beter, de accenten lagen goed, de gebaren waren minder theatraal, de woorden kwamen natuurlijker.

Bea gaf ze meteen het teken om door te gaan.

STUURMAN: Uw vader zal wanhopig zijn als hij het zwarte zeil ziet op dit schip.

THESEUS: Een groot koning kan met zijn gevoelens geen rekening houden als het gaat om de vreugde en de pijn van zijn volk!

ORATOS: Koning, wacht met de beslissing...

AEGEUS: Als het zeil zwart is, wil ik niet langer leven! Ik kan niet nog eens de schande van een vernedering dragen. Alle Atheense ogen volgen elke van mijn bewegingen. Het geklaag, gejammer en gemor over de onmogelijke vrede met Minos klinken steeds luider.

DAEDALUS: Koning, u heeft niet geaarzeld om ook uw zoon mee te laten gaan.

AEGEUS: Dat was niet het belangrijkste, wel de hoop dat iemand uit mijn geslacht de vloek zou opheffen die ik over de stad en haar mensen heb gebracht toen ik die speer slingerde en hoogmoedig wilde dat ze verder neerkwam dan die van Minos' zoon! Alsof ik zo zou hebben bewezen dat de mannen van Athene... Het zeil...

ORATOS: Ja, koning... Het zeil... is zwart.

Aegeus verdwijnt. Er klinkt een schreeuw. De twee raadsheren buigen het hoofd.

THESEUS: Athene! Eindelijk! Wat is dat? Iemand stort zich van de rots!

Hij steekt zijn handen in de lucht en lacht.

Stuurman, kijk, de stralen van de ondergaande zon kronen mijn hoofd met rood goud.

STUURMAN: Bloedrood goud!

Licht uit.

HUBRIS: Dat is het verhaal. De stuurman heb ik later ontmoet, een wrak was die man geworden, een wrak door drank en pijn en wroeging. Hij had begrepen dat Theseus dat zwarte zeil wetens en willens had gehesen om zijn vader te doden en zo de troon voor zichzelf vrij te maken, net als die keer toen hij zijn billen schurkte in de kussens.

HEROS: Vreselijk. En het ergste is dat ik je nu geloof. Theseus is voor de tweede keer gestorven en zijn tweede dood is nog vreselijker dan de eerste omdat hij zo oneervol is. Nu moet je me zeggen wie je bent, hoe je dit alles met zoveel zekerheid weet.

HUBRIS: Als dat je geest rust kan geven. Ik ben Parmenides. Ik was met Theseus in het labyrint. Hij heeft me wel neergeslagen, maar niet gedood. Doodsbang ben ik blijven liggen. Ik deed alsof ik bewusteloos, dood was. Theseus heeft niet eens meer naar me omgekeken. Trots is altijd blind. Toen hij weg was, heb ik mijn vrienden en zelfs mijn vijanden de laatste eer bewezen. Ik heb de draad naar het leven gevolgd, heb Ariadne ontmoet, gek van verdriet en wraakzucht. Daarna heb ik de stuurman ontmoet en heb gewacht tot de goden eindelijk... eindelijk rechtvaardig zouden zijn, gewacht tot hun glimlach een grimlach zou worden. Goeienavond, Heros, mijn werk is gedaan, mijn wachttijd is om. Ik ga een beker wijn drinken!

Er kwam spontaan applaus van de hele groep. De acteurs bogen en maakten grapjes om te verbergen hoe leuk ze dat vonden.

'Jammer dat ik de feestvreugde moet temperen,' zei Bea. 'Ga iets drinken en dan beginnen we meteen met de eerste doorloop. Een kwartiertje. Een kwartier!'

Bjorn wist dat ze het tegen hem had.

'Moeten we onze kleren van zondag al aan?' vroeg Felicia.

'Morgen is tijd genoeg. Jij morst toch altijd aan tafel.'

'Jij, Mirko, moet je mond houden. Jij kwijlt de hele tijd.'

'Omdat ik Andrea zie!'

Het ruwe complimentje lokte nauwelijks gelach uit.

Bjorn haalde een blik cola uit de automaat en rende naar het secretariaat om zijn moeder op te bellen en haar te vertellen dat er bezoek kwam. Belangrijk bezoek.

'Ja, een meisje. Een schat, mam. Morgenavond. Ja, ze rijdt mee naar huis na de voorstelling. Een Hollandse, ja. Verliefd? Mam, zo gaat het vandaag niet meer. Je kunt gewoon vriendinnetjes hebben.

Nee, mam, de logeerkamer. Tot morgen. Ik voel me geweldig. Echt. Moe? Een beetje, maar de spanning zorgt ervoor dat we dat niet voelen. Vanavond maken we video-opnamen, voor Londen. Ja. Daag.'

'Laat me nou maar eens zien wat je met dat toverdoosje kunt.'
Gael had het deksel van haar laptop opgeklapt. Het scherm schemerde groen.
'Internet is gewoon een wereldwijd telefoonsysteem met zo'n veertig miljoen gebruikers. Alleen bestaat er geen telefoonboek, geen maatschappij die je inlichtingen kan geven. Dus als je iets wilt weten, moet je het zelf zoeken.'
Bjorn knikte.
'Dit is een modem, een toestelletje dat de digitale signalen van deze computer omzet in geluiden. Die gaan dan met een telefoonlijn naar hun bestemming en worden daar weer omgezet in lettertjes en cijfertjes. Tenminste, als daar een computer staat te luisteren. O ja, je moet ook toegang hebben tot dat Internet, inbeltoegang. Die krijg je van een firma, een Internetprovider.'
'En dat zit allemaal in dat knappe kopje van je.'
'Slijmerd.'
Ze lachten allebei.
'Die provider heeft me software bezorgd en de telefoonnummers die mijn modem moet kiezen om met Internet in verbinding te komen. En ik heb ook een account gekregen. Tjonge, ik voelde me apetrots. People on Line, ook wel POL genoemd, liet me weten dat ik gamacgre@pol.priv was. Dat is dus mijn adres op Internet. Knap spannend.'
Bjorn knikte opnieuw.
'Wat is die gamacgre? Jouw naam? Het klinkt als een hoestbui.'
'Gael McGregor.'
'En jouw vader?'
'Die heeft een andere account. Ik communiceer met de computer van zijn werk. Daar is het enquiries@ifya.drama.dir.uk. Wacht even, ik ga inloggen.'
Ze pakte een draagbare telefoon. Ook dat nog? Bjorn zat er lichtjes verbijsterd bij. Hij leek wel een Neanderthaler naast haar.
Ze luisterde even. Toen bewogen haar vingers bliksemsnel over het klavier van de laptop.

143

'Mag ik je adres?' vroeg ze achteloos.

'Mijn adres?'

'Ja, je adres en je telefoonnummer. Als ik dan toch bij jou intrek, wil ik dat mijn vader weet waar hij me kan vinden.'

Terwijl zij haar boodschap intikte, krabbelde Bjorn achter haar rug op een stukje papier 'enquiries@ifya.drama.dir.uk' en stopte dat in zijn zak.

'Zo, papa weet dat zijn dochtertje in goede handen is. Nee, ik bedoelde dat niet letterlijk!'

Bjorn kreeg een tikje op zijn vingers. Ze lachten weer, vrolijk als kinderen.

16

'Lekker geslapen?'

Gael nam een slokje vers geperst sinaasappelsap.

'Heerlijk, mevrouw. Ik weet nog altijd niet hoe ik je moet bedanken. Ik mag er niet aan denken dat ik nu in een stille, eenzame flat zou zitten. Alles trilt nog in me.'

Gael sloeg haar armen om zich heen.

'Het was een schitterende opvoering,' knikte Bjorns moeder. 'Ik wist niet dat mijn zoon dat kon. En jij was ook uitmuntend.'

'Ja, hij is geweldig,' zuchtte Gael.

De hele vorige dag, avond en nacht, de opvoering, het donderende applaus, het opgewonden afscheid, de beloftes om elkaar terug te zien, het kwam allemaal in flitsen terug. En toch had ze diep en droomloos geslapen en voelde ze zich fris als het spreekwoordelijke hoentje.

Bjorn niet. Toen hij de kamer binnenkwam, zag hij er afgepeigerd uit en bovendien zenuwachtig en humeurig.

'Nachtmerries!' zei hij nog voor iemand wat had kunnen vragen. 'Ik kreeg een brief waarin stond dat ik naar Londen moest zonder jou.'

Gael gaf hem een klapje op zijn schouder.

'Of je liegt, of je ware natuur komt boven. Jij wilt echt naar Londen en wat er met mij gebeurt, kan je niet schelen.'

Bjorn ging opeens wat meer rechtop zitten. Zijn moeder was naar de keuken om koffie te halen.

'Weet je dat we heel snel kunnen weten of we samen gaan of niet?'

Gael schrok van de spanning die in zijn stem doorklonk.

'Is het waar dat jouw vader directeur is van het Institute for Young Actors?'

'Hoe kom je daar nou bij?'

'Is het waar, Gael?'

'Ik wil eerst horen hoe je dat weet.'

'Elke gooide het me gisteren naar mijn hoofd. Ze beweerde dat ik met jou aanpapte omdat ik op een goed blaadje wilde staan bij jouw vader. Ze zei dat jij vanzelf geselecteerd zou zijn, dat je niet eens naar de cursus had hoeven komen.'

'Dat is nonsens.'

Bjorn knikte.

'Waarom heb je me dat niet gezegd, Gael?'

'Zou het wat hebben uitgemaakt? Ik kan mijn vader en moeder niet kiezen. Dat kun jij ook niet.'

Bjorn knikte en kauwde afwezig.

'Je vrienden kun je wel kiezen.'

'Bjorn, hou nou eens op met in raadsels te praten.'

'Ik ben gewoon bang. Misschien denken ze echt dat ik met jou...'

'Je wist het niet!'

Bjorn knikte.

'Ik zou willen weten of Bea bijvoorbeeld er zo over denkt.'

'Bel haar dan.'

Bjorn schudde zijn hoofd. 'Er is een andere manier.'

'Hoe dan?'

'Ach, misschien is het gekheid, maar ik zou graag haar rapport lezen. Ze heeft toch zelf gezegd dat ze de rapporten vandaag met e-mail naar Londen stuurt? Die gaan naar het Institute for Young Actors. Naar jouw vader.'

Gael keek hem nu met open mond aan.

'Bedoel je nu dat ik mijn vader moet vragen om me te vertellen wat er in jouw en mijn beoordeling staat?'

'Waarom niet?'

Gael schudde haar hoofd.

'Theseus, dan kan ik mijn vader, Minos, net zo goed vragen om zelf de draad te spinnen die jou uit het labyrint moet leiden.'

Bjorn lachte.

'Nu breng je me op een heel stoute gedachte.'

'Vergeet het maar. Mijn vader zou dat nooit doen. Hij was er zelfs helemaal niet voor te vinden dat ik wilde proberen bij de cast te komen. Dus zou hij me zeker niet...'

'Ik zei dat ik een stoute gedachte had. Jij hebt me toch verteld dat het Internet zoiets is als een telefoonsysteem waarbinnen je zelf je weg kunt vinden? Waarom proberen we dan niet in de computer van het instituut te komen en zelf te lezen...'

'Vergeet het! Als dat ooit uitlekt, krijgt mijn vader de schuld.'

'Maar waarom?'

'Omdat niemand gelooft dat hij er niets mee te maken zou hebben. Mijn vader zou razend op me zijn. Als hij aan één ding een hekel heeft, is het aan gesjoemel.'

Gael nam een slok lauwe koffie en keek weer naar Bjorn. Ze voelde zich akelig bij zijn gespannen zwijgen.

'Ik bedoel, waarom zou iemand aan jou denken?'

'Omdat ik zijn adres heb.'

'Dat kunnen andere mensen ook hebben. En zelfs als ze aan jou denken, wat dan nog?'

'Vraag je me om tegen mijn vader te kiezen? Wil je dat ik iets doe dat hem in gevaar zou brengen?'

'Nee, Ariadne, je hoeft niet tegen je vader te kiezen. Ik vraag je om voor mij te kiezen. Dat is heel wat anders.'

'En dan, Bjorn? Dat verslag zal zijn wat het is.'

'Ik wil het alleen maar weten.'

Gael aarzelde.

'En het kan heel spannend zijn, vind je niet?' hakte Bjorn op haar in. 'Theseus en de draad van Ariadne op Internet.'

'Bjorn, ik krijg dat niet voor elkaar. Daarvoor heb je een computerkraker nodig. En niet zomaar een beginneling. Het Institute zal wel zorgen dat alles netjes beveiligd is.'

'Betekent wat je nu zegt dat je mee wilt doen als ik een computerkraker vind?'

'Doe niet zo gek, Bjorn, laten we erover zwijgen.'

Bjorn sprong op, liep om de tafel heen en pakte het gezicht van Gael tussen zijn handen.

'Het is zowat leven of dood voor me. Ik was niet van plan het ooit tegen iemand te vertellen, maar jij mag het weten. Ik ben een jongetje dat loopt te fluiten in het donker.'

Gael sloot haar ogen toen zijn lippen haar voorhoofd raakten.

'Ik zal je het hele verhaal vertellen als je wilt. Maar beslis.'

Toen Bjorns moeder terugkwam, was er niemand meer in de kamer.

Gael luisterde verbijsterd. Het hele verhaal over Bjorns grootvader, zijn verwijten aan het adres van Bjorns vader, de nieuwe kans om te bewijzen dat hij echt wat kon, de mogelijke terugkeer van zijn vader.

Bjorn vertelde het met zoveel passie dat ze er koud van werd.

'Bjorn,' zei ze, 'ik wist niet dat het zo belangrijk voor je was allemaal. En als het fout gaat?'

'Dan ben ik niemand meer.'

Het klonk vals, maar Gael reageerde niet.

'Bjorn, ik vind het allemaal zo onwaarschijnlijk. Wat kun je winnen als je dat rapport leest? En wat als iemand ontdekt dat je in die computer bent ingebroken?'

'We praten als twee blinden over kleuren, Gael. Proberen we het? Mijn nichtje Silvia is een van die computer whizzkids. Ze kan gewoon alles met computers. Als ik het haar vraag, helpt ze. Maar ik wil niets doen zonder dat jij het goedvindt. Toe nou, Gael, alsjeblieft. Als er ook maar iets fout dreigt te gaan, houden we er meteen mee op.'

Gael pakte wanhopig zijn hand beet en drukte die tegen haar lippen.

'Oké, Bjorn, maar beloof je echt dat het in orde komt? Je snapt toch ook dat ik niet wil dat mijn vader erbij betrokken raakt, dat iemand alleen maar zou kunnen denken dat hij er iets mee te maken heeft.'

'Dat beloof ik je. Ik bel Silvia meteen.'

Silvia was er al na een halfuur. Gael fronste haar voorhoofd. Nichtje? De persoon die naar binnen kwam met een rugzak en een laptop in een beschermtas, zag er helemaal niet uit als een meisje.

'Yow!' zei ze en tikte tegen het petje dat met de klep in de nek op haar blonde kop stond.

'Sil, dit is Gael.'

'Neuk je haar?' vroeg Sil. Ze bekeek Gael brutaal door haar ronde blauwe brilletje en lachte hinnikend.

Bjorn gaf Sil een duw tegen haar schouder.

'Niet op letten, Gael. Sil wil maar één ding: in het *Guiness Book of Records* komen als het meest onbeschofte, het meest brutale en het meest vuilbekkende wicht van vijftien. Mijn tante is de waanzin nabij.'

'Je bent achterop, eikel. Je tante is intussen knettermaf. Ze heeft minder hersens dan een kip tieten. Wat wil je van me? Ik doe alles.'

Sil banjerde naar de woonkamer. De veel te wijde jeansbroek slobberde om haar dunne benen en de pijpen waren bij haar hakken gerafeld.

'Wat krijgen we nou?' vroeg Gael toen ze de schelle stem in de woonkamer hoorde zeggen dat een bak koffie er wel in zou gaan. 'De wanhoop van mijn tante. Ze is best een leuk kind, maar ze heeft een probleem. Ze is doodsbang dat iemand haar zou verlinken. Het is een obsessie. Ze vindt dat ze geen enkel risico loopt als ze niemand in haar buurt laat komen. Dus bekt ze iedereen af, verschanst ze zich in de loopgraven van haar brutale uitvallen. Haar manier van overleven. Ze maakt veel lawaai, maar heeft een goed hart en bijt niet.'

Sil zat omgekeerd op een stoel. Met haar armen over de rugleuning slurpte ze opzettelijk hard van de koffie en boerde.

'Sil,' zei Bjorn, 'Gael gelooft het al. Je bent onmogelijk. Doe geen moeite meer.'

'Oké! Let's play ball!' zei Sil. 'Ik heb geen tijd te verliezen en vanaf nu loopt de klok, jongetje. Uurtarief? Twee whoppers en een coke.'

Ze pakte haar tassen en keek rond. Bjorns moeder zat hoofdschuddend in een stoel en had medelijden met haar zus.

'Ik heb een telefoonaansluiting op mijn kamer.'

'Juist. En jij, dame, heb je een en ander bij je? Want ik stel voor dat jullie gaan rollebollen en mij laten werken.'

Ze liepen de brede trap op naar de eerste verdieping. De kamer van Bjorn was ruim en keek uit op een tuin waarin alles netjes in de rij stond. Gael zag boekenrekken, een lange werktafel, één poster aan de muur. Sir Laurence Olivier als Henry v. Naast het bed, op een nachtkastje, zat een oude speelgoedbeer te loensen.

'Ik word niet goed. Moet ik hier werken?'

Sil sloeg haar handen voor haar borst.

'Hoezo?'

'Ik ben de vorstin van de chaos, jongetje! Oh, shit, fuck, prick and dick! Hoe kun je hierin leven? Nou goed, ik ben hier maar even.'

Ze gooide de rugzak op het bed, drukte met haar handpalm op de matras en knikte goedkeurend.

'Moet lekker wippen.'

'Wat heb je nodig om een computer te kraken?' vroeg Bjorn. Hij was vastbesloten niet in te gaan op haar uitdagende uitlatingen.

'Een hamer en vijf harde klappen,' zei Sil gemaakt ernstig.

Bjorn reageerde gespannen. Voor hem was het speelkwartier voorbij.

'Doe niet zo kloterig.'

'Oké, big boy. Ik heb mijn eigen laptop. Ik wil een 14,4 externe modem. Hihi, heb ik ook bij me, lekker high speed. Dan heb ik mijn kraakspullen. Kleine, machtige schijfjes. Je snapt het niet, maar dat zijn een lijst met out-dials, een kopie van de C-programmeertaal voor alle soorten UNIX, een complete lijst van Internetlocaties en nog wat softwarefuncties. Gesnopen? Nee, natuurlijk niet, holbewoner.'

Gael en Bjorn zaten wat suf naast elkaar op het bed terwijl Sil met draden en stekkers, met schijfjes en notitieboekjes aan de slag ging.

'En vertel me nu eens wat je wilt. Duidelijk graag.'

'Mag ik nog wat vragen?'

Sil knikte naar Gael.

'Waar heb je dit allemaal geleerd? En hoe kom je aan die spullen?'

'Wie is zij? Een onderzoeksrechter? Politie?'

Sil stootte weer haar hinnikende lachje uit.

'Oké, meid. Toen ik twaalf was, kreeg ik van een buurman een oude Apple-computer. Daarvoor moest ik het wel goedvinden dat die vent af en toe mijn billetjes streelde. Niets meer, maar het was knap vervelend. Ik begon met dat ding te stoeien, dag en nacht, en mijn Apple werd een appeltje voor de dorst, de honger en alle andere kwalen. In drie jaar tijd was ik een volleerd kraker en kenden ze op Internet mijn gebruikersnaam van Alaska tot Zanzibar. Notiz! Ik begon buurman Viezevinger meteen een poot uit te draaien. Ik bespaar je de details, maar ik kraakte zijn bankrekening en hevelde een beetje van het geld dat daarop stond over naar mijn eigen rekening. En daarmee kocht ik wat meer apparatuur.'

'Dat is toch diefstal?'

'Betaling voor bewezen diensten, zul je bedoelen. Hoeveel zou jij rekenen om iemand aan je billen te laten frunniken tot hij klaarkomt?'

Gael sprong op.

'Bjorn, ik hou ermee op.'

'Hihihiha! Je gelooft het! Niet doen, nooit geloven wat ik zeg. Nee, ik heb alles wat je hier ziet eerlijk verdiend. Stomweg door een programma te schrijven voor een begrafenisondernemer. Zo weet die precies hoeveel lijken hij mag verwachten volgend jaar, hoeveel kisten en zerken hij moet bestellen, wie hij een rekening stuurt en wanneer hij een herinneringsbrief moet schrijven.'

Sil sprong op van de stoel, kwam naar Gael toe en drukte een zoen op haar voorhoofd.

'Je bent lief. Laat je door hem niet kisten. Wat willen jullie?'

Bjorn vertelde het haar.

'Oké, mee naar cyberspace! Krijg ik dat e-mailadres van je?'

Sil drukte enkele toetsen. Het scherm van de laptop lichtte op.

Gael slikte.

'Bjorn?'

'Alsjeblieft, Gael?'

'Enquiries@ifya.drama.dir.uk.'

'Yeah, World on Line. Lekker!'

De vingers van Sil ratelden over de toetsen.

'Ik veronderstel dat jullie niet willen dat iemand weet waar deze inbreker vandaan komt?'

Bjorn knikte meteen.

'Dan gaan we via Scannet, een remailer in Stockholm.'

'Wat is dit allemaal, Sil? Ik volg niet.'

'Zo'n remailer is een computer die de identiteit verbergt van de mensen die er berichten naartoe stuurt. Ik stuur nu een bericht naar die ifya en de remailer zorgt ervoor dat mijn naam, Notiz, omgezet wordt in een code. Dat bericht gaat door alsof het afkomstig zou zijn van Scannet.'

Het scherm liep vol met lettertjes en die losten zich op in de geheimzinnige boodschap:

telnet ring2ice. scannet. priv.
try phone 0024162345

Geen tien seconden later was het

connected ring2ice. scannet.priv.
escape = '^)'
compaqos UNIX
login:

Sil tikte Notiz in.

Scannet reageerde bijna meteen met *password*.

Sil draaide zich om.

'Je kent waarschijnlijk het wachtwoord van je vader niet?'

'Bedoel je dat je nu al in de computer van het Instituut bent?'

'Een fluitje van een cent. De beveiliging van de buitenste schil stelt niks voor. Bekijk het als een ui. De buitenste schil hebben we er nu afgepeld, maar het begint pas. Ik weet niet hoeveel lagen er nog komen. Ken je dat wachtwoord?'

Gael schudde haar hoofd.

'Dan heb ik nog wat. Ik heb Crack van Internet gedownloaded.'

Bjorn kreunde. Kon Sil echt geen Nederlands meer praten?

'Wees blij dat ik met zo'n voorhistoriër als jij wil praten. Crack is een lijst met computerwachtwoorden. Als ik dit programma laat lopen, begint het de computer waar we nu naar binnen willen te bestoken met wachtwoorden, zo'n tienduizend, die bliksemsnel worden afgevuurd. Als de computer er eentje herkent, zijn we binnen. Het probleem zou kunnen zijn dat ze maar een beperkt aantal pogingen toelaten, drie bijvoorbeeld, en dat we niet meteen het juiste wachtwoord hebben. Als dat het geval is, gooien ze er ons gewoon uit en heeft het geen zin om nog langs deze weg te proberen.'

Ze drukte op de entertoets.

'Yes!' schreeuwde ze. 'We zijn binnen. Een van de wachtwoorden heeft gewerkt.'

'En nu?'

'Nu kruip ik via SysAdmin, het e-mailsysteem van het Instituut, naar binnen en ik kan lezen en schrijven wat ik maar wil. Ik kan ook de rekeningen controleren als je dat wilt?'

'Nee, laat dat. Bestaat er zoiets als een lijst van berichten die binnenkomen en buitengaan?'

Sil rammelde op het toetsenbord. Over het scherm rolde een lijst met data, korte boodschappen, tijdsaanduidingen, namen.

'En wat zoeken jullie?'

'Iets wat uit België gekomen is vandaag.'

'De hoeveelste zijn we? O ja, negentiende.'

Geen boodschappen op het scherm.

'Misschien is Bea laat?' zei Bjorn ontgoocheld. 'Kunnen we wachten?'

'Wat mij betreft wel. Maar hoe langer je ingelogd blijft, hoe meer risico je loopt. Hun systeembeheerder zou een back-fingerprogramma hebben kunnen lopen. Dat vertelt hem dat iemand met de computer correspondeert en wie die iemand is.'

'Ik dacht dat jij met je remailer...'

'Ik zeg niet dat hij meteen hier op dit nummer uitkomt, maar hij zal zich heel gauw afvragen wie of wat Scannet is. En dan sluit hij Scannet buiten... Hé, wacht!'

Op het scherm verscheen nu een oproep uit België, bestemd voor Sir Denis McGregor.

In Londen zag de systeembeheerder opeens een klein rechthoekje knipperen in de rechterbovenhoek van zijn scherm. Wat moest dat? Iemand was het systeem binnengedrongen met een oud wachtwoord dat iemand niet had veranderd. Hij had al wel twintig nota's naar alle medewerkers gestuurd om het te veranderen. Die computeridioten beseften gewoon niet waarmee ze bezig waren. Hell, nu was het genoeg. Voortaan zou hij alles centraal regelen.

17

Bjorn keek naar de tekst op het scherm. De heks! De schofterige heks!

'Downloaden en afsluiten?' vroeg Sil.

Gael legde haar hand op de schouder van het meisje.

De computer zoemde en spuwde een zwart schijfje uit, het scherm werd dof. Bjorn bewoog niet.

'En dit, lieve mensen, was ons eerste misdrijf samen.'

Sil stak haar hand uit naar de stekker.

'Wacht,' zei Bjorn.

'Wat nu weer?'

'Kun je die tekst veranderen? Kun je dat ook?'

'Als ik een tekst kan lezen en ik ken de editor, het tekstverwerkingsprogramma, kan dat even makkelijk als eieren klutsen. Waarom?'

Gael verstijfde.

'Bjorn, dat kun je niet doen! Dat is bedrog!'

'Wat Bea daar heeft geschreven, is bedrog. Wraak! Ze wil me kelderen omdat ze... omdat ze...'

Gael pakte hem nu bij de schouder.

'Je wilt me toch niet vertellen dat zij ook woest is omdat je haar hebt afgewezen?'

Bjorn draaide zich naar haar om. Zijn gezicht was lijkbleek, zijn ogen schramden haar hart.

'Jij weet niet wat ik allemaal heb doorgemaakt! Dat weet jij niet. Sil, verander die tekst.'

'Oké, sir!'

De computer zoemde aan.

'Nee,' zei Gael. 'Nee!'

'Hou me niet tegen, Gael, alsjeblieft. Maak dit niet stuk voor we ervan geproefd hebben!'

Het klonk ronduit smekend.

'Maar waarom? Wie vertelt jou dat iemand daar rekening houdt met die ene opmerking. De rest van het rapport is schitterend!'

Bjorn sloeg met zijn vuist op tafel.

'Oeps!' zei Sil, die alweer op haar toetsenbord ratelde.

'Waarom schrijft ze dat dan? *Conclusie: bijzonder getalenteerd, maar onmogelijk te sturen en niet in staat om te functioneren in een groep.* Uiterst egocentrisch en genadeloos ambitieus. Snapt ze niet dat ze mijn hele carrière naar de bliksem helpt?'

'Je kunt nog altijd computermisdadiger worden. Hihihiha!' hinnikte Sil. 'Ik kruip weer naar binnen, jongens! Daar zijn we!'

De tekst van het rapport over Bjorn stond weer op het scherm.

'Ik wist niet dat jij zo knap was, neefje. Ik ben bijna trots op je. En dat laatste stuk? Perfect om in het leven te slagen, zou mijn papa de bankier zeggen. Wat verander ik?'

'Mag ik?' vroeg Bjorn. 'Gewoon tikken?'

Sil schoof van de stoel en liet hem zitten. Bjorn stuurde de cursor over de tekst.

Conclusie: bijzonder getalenteerd, niet eenvoudig te sturen door zijn sterke persoonlijkheid, maar perfect in staat om te functioneren in een groep. Uiterst intelligent, begiftigd met een groot inlevingsvermogen en gezond ambitieus.

Sil giechelde terwijl ze over Bjorns schouder meekeek.

'Als je wat doet, moet je het meteen goed doen. Wil jij ook je rapport zien, Gael?'

Gael schudde haar hoofd.

'Ik vind dit niet eerlijk.'

'Wat Bea gedaan heeft, is niet eerlijk. Wat weet zij daar nou van? Ben ik de jongen die zij beschrijft? Ben ik dat?'

Gael durfde niet meer te antwoorden.

In Londen fronste de systeembeheerder zijn voorhoofd. Wat gebeurde er nu weer?

Sil was opnieuw voor het scherm gaan zitten en tikte.

In Londen verscheen op het scherm: 'A little bitch like me bit een big bully like you. Notiz!'

De systeembeheerder krabde in zijn haar. Wie probeerde hem nu weer een hak te zetten via de e-mailbestanden? Hij liet de lijst over zijn scherm rollen en fronste zijn voorhoofd toen hij van dat bericht uit België, bestemd voor Sir Denis, een alias, een tweede versie vond. Hij opende de files. Geen verschil? Vreemd. Waarom had iemand dezelfde tekst twee keer doorgestuurd? Computeranalfabeten twijfel-den altijd. Maar dat loste het opduiken van het knipperende waarschuwingsvierkantje niet op. En die scheldwoorden. Wie was Notiz? Hé, het verdween. Nou, als het maar met die e-mailbestanden was dat iemand ging stoeien, kon er niet veel gebeuren.

'En ziedaar het bewijs,' declameerde Sil, 'dat we voortaan niet alleen over de hele wereld kunnen worden gehoord, dat we overal informatie kunnen opvragen, maar dat Internet ook de mogelijkheid geeft om leugens wereldwijd te verspreiden, geheimen over vriend en vijand te achterhalen, mensen te maken en te breken. Het is de nieuwe jungle, waar terroristen en piraten, criminelen en gekken zonder sporen na te laten ronddolen, hun slag slaan en verdwijnen. Welkom in cyberhell.'

Gael wist nog altijd niet hoe ze moest reageren.

'See you folks.'

In een oogwenk had Sil haar computer, haar modem en haar schijfjes ingepakt.

'Sil?'

'Yow!'

'Bedankt. Als ik ooit wat voor je kan doen?'

Sil grijnsde en stak haar middelvinger op.

'Zeg eens, wat betekent Notiz? Hoe kom je aan die naam?'

Een nieuwe grijns. Sil trok haar windjak uit.

'Je spreekt het fout uit. Zeg het eens op zijn Duits.'

Bjorn zei 'notits'.

'Snap je het nog niet?'

Bjorn schudde zijn hoofd. Sil rukte het ruitjeshemd dat ze onder haar jak had gedragen open.

'No tits, geen tieten!' zei ze en streelde over haar volkomen platte jongensborst.

'Dus, misschien kun je ooit wat voor me doen. Transplant... Gek, wat sta je naar me te kijken? Ik zal het mijn moeder vertellen, viezerd.'

Lachend wervelde ze de deur uit.

De telefoon rinkelde.

'Met Bjorn?'

Een secretaressestem vroeg naar miss Gael McGregor voor Sir Denis. Bjorn wenkte Gael en gaf haar de hoorn.

'Dad?'

Ze ratelde in bijzonder snel Engels. Het enthousiasme droop eraf.

'When?'

Ze luisterde.

'This week? The situation is very clear? I hope so. Yes, you can call me here. I'll let you know when. Kisses, dad. Yes, miss you.'

Ze hing op en draaide zich om.

'Bjorn, ik vind het niet goed wat we hebben gedaan.'

'Jij hebt niets gedaan, liefje, ik heb het gedaan.'

'Ik heb je dat adres gegeven.'

'Dat zou Sil in geen tijd hebben gevonden. Ze zei toch zelf dat ze een lijst had met alle locaties?'

Gael probeerde hem te geloven. Ze vocht tegen de twijfel die op haar inbeukte als een woeste branding en die haar dreigde te verzwelgen. Bjorn opende zijn armen en ze vluchtte er wanhopig in, op zoek naar een houvast. Ze gleden samen op het bed, ze voelde opnieuw hoe hard en gespierd zijn lichaam was. Er gleed een traan uit haar ogen. Bjorn likte die weg. Gael had het gevoel dat ze een aanloop nam voor een sprong in een onbekende diepte.

Toen zijn hand haar borst streelde, ademde ze verrast diep in, ze zweefde eventjes, leek een vrije val te maken, het werd donker. Ze voelde zijn hart kloppen, zijn adem warmde haar schouder. Ze voelde zijn gewicht op haar en wist dat het fout was, maar weigerde het te geloven. Na het zweven zou de landing hard zijn, en pijnlijk.

18

Bjorn schoot overeind in zijn bed en luisterde. Hij vergiste zich niet, het was geen geluid dat uit zijn droom afkomstig was. Iemand stond als gek op de bel te drukken beneden.

Hij rende naar beneden en struikelde toen hij een joggingbroek wilde aantrekken net voor hij de deur openmaakte.

'Ja, een ogenblik!' schreeuwde hij tegen het rinkelen in. Het werd stil. Bjorn draaide het nachtslot terug en opende de deur.

'Sil?'

Sil stond inderdaad voor hem op de stoep.

'Wat moet jij hier midden in de nacht?'

'Is het nacht?'

'Sil, doe niet stom. Wat is er?'

'Alles! Ik ben een superoen, een cyberdrol, een Internetgehandicapte.'

'Wat heb ik daarmee te maken?'

Sil zweeg en beet op haar bovenlip.

'Zul je razend op me zijn?'

'Sil, ik weet niet eens waarover je het hebt!'

'Ik ben stom geweest. Ik heb je die tekst laten veranderen en heb die dan doorgestuurd.'

'Ja, en? Dat wilde ik toch?'

'Ik heb de eerste tekst, die van dat eerste rapport, niet gewist. Ik was zo opgewonden dat ik er niet meer aan gedacht heb.'

Bjorn snapte nog altijd niet helemaal wat Sil probeerde te vertellen.

'En dus hebben ze daar nu twee teksten. Snap je dat dan niet?'

De waarheid sijpelde langzaam, heel langzaam door.

'Wil je nu zeggen dat ze in Londen kunnen ontdekken dat iemand met die tekst heeft geknoeid?'

Sil knikte.

'Ik kon niet in slaap komen en ben gaan surfen. Ik ben weer naar binnen geglipt in die site en zag op die lijst jouw tekst en een alias, een tweede versie. Maar wat erger is, beide boodschappen waren al geprint. Dus ja, ze weten nu dat er wat aan de hand is met die tekst.'

Bjorn bleef zijn nichtje ongelovig aankijken.

'Ik weet niet wat ze nu zullen doen. Sorry hoor, vergeet die whoppers en die coke maar. Je hoeft me niet te betalen.'

Sil trok zelf de deur dicht. Bjorn stond alleen in de gang.

Het was niet eens negen uur toen er alweer werd aangebeld.

'Ja, mevrouw. Wat een verrassing! Bjorn zal blij zijn... Is er wat?'

Die raadselachtige woorden deden Bjorn opspringen. Wie was dat?

'Bjorn? Die mevrouw van de cursus is er voor jou.'

De deur van de woonkamer draaide open. Bea kwam naar binnen.

'Gael?'

'Hoi, Bea. Bjorns moeder was zo lief me uit te nodigen. Ik wilde niet alleen in die... Bea, is er wat?'

'Heeft Bjorn je dat niet verteld?'

Bjorns moeder, Gael, Bjorn zelf. Drie roerloze figuren.

'Mam? Wil jij koffie zetten? Of heb je liever thee, Bea?'

Bjorn slaagde erin zijn stem normaal te laten klinken.

'Ik... ja, koffie is prima.'

'Ga toch zitten,' zei Bjorns moeder, die wel voelde dat er wat was, maar er niets van begreep. Ze ging de kamer uit.

'Jij weet waarom ik hier ben?'

Bjorn schudde zijn hoofd.

Bea zuchtte en wreef over haar voorhoofd.

'Weet jij het, Gael?'

Bea merkte best dat Bjorn zijn hand op die van Gael legde.

'Bjorn, waarom? Waarom heb je dit nou gedaan? Heb je ooit gedacht dat je dit kon doen zonder dat iemand het merkte?'

'Het is fout gegaan door dat stomme nichtje van me! Ik had beter moeten weten. Alleen wat je zelf doet, is goed gedaan. Het had best kunnen lukken.'

Gael sloeg haar handen voor haar gezicht.

'Gael, heb jij hem geholpen?'

De stem van Bea droop van ongeloof.

'Laat haar met rust. Ik heb het gedaan,' zei Bjorn. 'En ik vond dat ik het recht had. Wat jij geschreven had, klopte niet. Het was pure wraak, het was laster, je wilde me kraken! En dat hoef ik niet te pikken.'

Bea draaide langzaam haar hoofd naar hem toe.

'Ik geloof dat je dat nog meent ook?'

'Natuurlijk. Is het soms niet zo?'

'Bjorn, je weet niet wat je zegt! Ik heb eerlijk geschreven wat ik meende, zonder mijn gevoelens te laten meespreken. Maar dat jij dat verslag hebt vervalst! Je had het recht niet! Wat je gedaan hebt, is hetzelfde als een brief openmaken die niet voor jou bestemd was.'

'Bea, het is ook mijn schuld. Ik heb hem het adres gegeven.'

'Gael, je hebt er niets mee te maken. Ik zou het adres ook anders gevonden hebben. Of Sil zou het van Internet hebben geplukt. Nee, je was er toevallig bij. Meer niet. Je hoeft je eigen kansen niet voor me op te offeren.'

Bjorn probeerde het meisje te laten zwijgen, wat niet lukte.

'Ik heb je geholpen. Ik bedoelde er niets kwaads mee. Ik... het was zo belangrijk voor je. Ik wilde het voor jou doen.'

'Het verhaal van je grootvader en je vader, met weer een nieuw sausje opgediend?' Bea spuwde de zin uit.

Bjorn rilde.

'Dat vind ik nog het ergste van alles. Waarom heb je mij, waarom heb je Elke verteld dat je grootvader is gestorven? Waarom? Heeft hij jou dat ook verteld, Gael? Je bent een, een... ik heb er geen woorden voor! Je laat mensen sterven als dat je beter uitkomt voor je verhalen. Je grootvader is helemaal niet dood, Bjorn! Ik heb hem aan de telefoon gehad.'

Bjorn wist zich geen raad meer. Als een roofdier viel hij aan.

'Dat snap jij niet, natuurlijk. Jij hebt het allemaal zo netjes op een rijtje, niet? Jij hebt je weg gemaakt en nu mag je iedereen naar de vernieling sturen. Je mag mij afmaken!'

'Dit heeft geen zin, Bjorn. Weet je waaraan je me doet denken? Aan een kikker in een waterput. Die ziet alleen de wanden van de put en de lucht boven hem. Hij probeert aldoor in die lucht te springen en weet niet eens dat naast en rond de waterput een hele wereld liggen.'

De telefoon rinkelde.

'Vanderhaeghen. Yes? Gael? Yes.'

Gael was al bij het eerste Engelse woord opgesprongen. Haar hand ging langzaam naar de hoorn die Bjorn haar aanreikte.

'Dad?'

Gael kromp in elkaar terwijl ze luisterde.

'Yes, dad! But I...'

Ze liet de hoorn zakken. Er liepen tranen over haar gezicht.

'Wat?'

Bjorn stond nog altijd naast Gael.

'Ik moet naar huis. Mijn vader is razend.'

'Begrijp jij het tenminste, Gael?' Bea sprak zacht maar indringend. Het meisje knikte.

'En jij, Bjorn, zult misschien denken dat de vrouwen in je leven het wapen zijn geworden dat jou heeft verslagen. Fout, je bent je eigen dodelijke wapen geweest.'

'Jij en de anderen hebben me nooit kunnen luchten. Jullie hadden al vooraf een beeld van me. Jullie waren bang...'

Bea stak haar hand op en keek Bjorn triest glimlachend aan.

'Ik wil je één ding vertellen. Met de woorden van Anton Tsjechov, de grote Russische toneelauteur. Die woorden zijn mijn bijbel geweest sinds ik begon met theater.'

'Ik heb geen zaken met jouw bijbel!'

'En toch zul je luisteren. *Ik bekijk etiketjes en namen als vooroordelen. Mijn heiligste der heiligen is het menselijk lichaam, zijn gezondheid, zijn intelligentie, talent, inspiratie, liefde en de meest absolute afwezigheid van geweld en leugen. Het maakt me niets uit welke vorm die twee hebben aangenomen. Ze mogen niet bestaan.*'

Bjorn zat alleen op zijn kamer.

'Bjorn? Kun je me eens uitleggen wat er eigenlijk gebeurd is? Wat moest die mevrouw nu van je? Ik snap het niet. Alles was toch goed?'

'Mama, niets was goed. Die mevrouw heeft het allemaal naar de kloten geholpen! Ze kon me niet luchten. Ze was verliefd op me en toen ik niet met haar naar bed wilde, heeft ze gelogen. Ze heeft dingen geschreven die niet waar zijn. En dat heb ik willen rechtzetten. En dat heeft ze me weer kwalijk genomen.'

'Maar waarom moest Gael meteen weg? Waarom huilde ze toen ze vertrok? Je had haar tenminste naar het station kunnen brengen.'

Bjorn zweeg.

'Kun je het me niet zeggen?'

'Nee, mama, ik wil er niet over praten.'

In letters van vuur verscheen een stuk tekst in zijn herinnering.

THESEUS: Dat wil ik wel doen, in het kort. De vreselijke Minotaurus was niets meer dan een zielige bastaard van je moeder. Je vader heeft hem in het labyrint opgesloten, waar hij zich voedde met de resten van de slachtoffers die je vader hem toewierp. Want jouw vader, Minos, doodde het jonge, levende losgeld dat wij betaalden, gewoon om zijn trieste wraak met Atheens bloed te blussen. En daaraan heb ik een eind gemaakt, Ariadne.

ARIADNE: Hoe vreselijk ook, waarom moet ik daarvoor boeten?

THESEUS: Dacht je nu werkelijk dat ik jou met me mee zou kunnen nemen? In elk gebaar van jou zou ik de gebaren van je vader herkennen, in elk woord van jou zijn stem. En dan zou ik met jou in Athene moeten verschijnen?

ARIADNE: Dus je laat mij boeten voor de wandaden van mijn vader?

'Jullie konden het toch goed met elkaar vinden?'

'Toen kende ik haar niet.'

Hij staarde naar de poster van Sir Laurence Olivier.

'Ze zat mee in het complot. Je weet dat ze een telefoontje heeft gekregen? Dat was haar vader. En die is de directeur van dat instituut in Londen.'

'Ja? En? Is dat soms een misdaad?'

Bjorn zag dat zijn moeder boos werd.

'Ze moest ons allemaal bespieden. Dat heeft ze net bekend. En toen heeft ze me in de val gelokt. Ze liet me geloven dat ik de rol van Theseus kon krijgen. Ze was gewoon een valse spionne die mij moest uitdagen. En ik ben erin gelopen.'

'Had je het met haar niet kunnen uitpraten?'

'Heb jij het ooit met papa kunnen uitpraten? Weet je wat je zei toen hij je bekend had dat hij wat had met dat wicht waarmee hij nu ligt te stoeien? Weet je dat nog?'

'Ik heb toen zoveel gezegd. Ik was vreselijk gekwetst.'

'En ik dan?'

De jongen sprong op en rukte de poster van de muur.

'Bjorn!'

'Toen zei jij dat je hem nooit meer zou kussen. Elk gebaar van hem zou jou doen terugdenken aan wat hij met haar deed, elk woord zou klinken alsof hij het tegen haar zei. En dan zou jij willen dat ik het wel kon vergeten?'

'Dus jij laat dat meisje boeten voor iets wat haar vader heeft gedaan? Bjorn, ik kan moeilijk geloven...'

'Dan doe je dat maar niet.'

Hij stormde de kamer uit. De voordeur knalde dicht. Hij voelde zich net als Theseus op zijn eiland. Een volmaakte eenzame.

19

'Ik wil je zien. Vanmiddag.'
De stem denderde nog in zijn hersenen terwijl Bjorn naar zijn grootvader fietste. Elke pedaalslag was een marteling, elke straat leek te hellen en een woeste tegenwind leek op hem in te beuken. Opa zat in zijn werkkamer. Hij stond niet op. Bjorn durfde hem niet aan te kijken.

Hij zag hoe opa de afstandsbediening op de videorecorder richtte. Het televisiescherm lichtte op.

'Het eerste Europese theaterproject voor jonge acteurs uit alle landen van de Europese Unie staat in de steigers. Zoals eerder gemeld, wordt het stuk *De goden grijnzen* van de jonge Griekse auteur Ganymedes Theofilos opgevoerd om de voltooiing van de Europese eenmaking te vieren. De auteur heeft de Theseuslegende opnieuw verteld. Het is een symbolische, sterk persoonlijke interpretatie geworden waarmee hij duidelijk wil maken dat de Europeanen hun persoonlijke ambitie moeten opbergen, omdat persoonlijke ambitie altijd leidt tot drama's.'

'Wat een onzin!' snauwde opa naar de reporter, die voor de gevel van het Londense theater in een gele microfoon stond te praten.

'In Londen werd vandaag de definitieve rolverdeling bekendgemaakt. Zoals de kijkers waarschijnlijk weten, werden in alle landen van de Europese Unie studieweken georganiseerd waaraan jonge, niet-professionele acteurs konden deelnemen. Uit die groepen zijn dan de acteurs geselecteerd die in aanmerking komen voor de internationale cast. Ook in ons land werd zo'n cursus georganiseerd. Insiders vertelden ons dat er in de Vlaams-Nederlandse groep diverse kandidaten zaten, zelfs voor de hoofdrol van Theseus. Jammer genoeg probeerde een van de grootste kanshebbers, volgens mensen die de video's hebben gezien zelfs dé kanshebber, te sjoemelen. Daarom werd de jongeman uitgesloten. Een mooie carrière is afgebroken nog voor ze begonnen is. De rolverdeling is als volgt.'

De stem van de omroeper verdween, het scherm sneeuwde.

'En?'

Bjorn staarde naar het tapijt.